With Fire and Sword

. Novogrod

POLISH-LITHUANIAN COMMONWEALTH
· 16th-17th Centuries ·

Dvina R.

·Vitebsk

GRAND DUCHY OF LITHUANIA

Dnieper R. Smolensk

Berezina R.

BYELORUSIA

·Mozyr
·Brahin

·rov

Tchernobyl
Tchernihov

UKRAINE

·Kiev

·antinov

Bielo Tzerkiev

Pereyaslaw
·Lubnie

Zolotonosha
Tcherkasy

·Mahnovka

·Korsun

PODOLIA

·Uman

Tchehryn

·Bratslaw

·Mohylov

Beh R.

WILD LANDS

Dniester R.

VALACHIA

MOSCOW

GREAT RUSSIA (MUSCOVY)

Kaluga·

·Orzel

BELGOROD TARTARS

Vorskla R. ·Belgorod

·Karkov

Dnieper R.

·Kudak

·Sietch

ZAPOROHJE

CRIMEAN TARTARS

BLACK SEA

BY W. S. KUNICZAK

Novels:
Valedictory
The March
The Thousand Hour Day

Translations:
Quo Vadis (Henryk Sienkiewicz)
"The Trilogy" (Henryk Sienkiewicz)
I *With Fire and Sword*
II *The Deluge*
III *Fire in the Steppe*

History:
My Name is Million

Entertainments:
The Sempinski Affair

With Fire and Sword

Henryk Sienkiewicz

In Modern Translation by
W. S. Kuniczak

Foreword by
James A. Michener

COLLIER BOOKS
MACMILLAN PUBLISHING COMPANY
NEW YORK

Maxwell Macmillan Canada
Toronto

Maxwell Macmillan International
New York   Oxford   Singapore   Sydney

This work and all its hopes are dedicated
to all men and women of Polish Heritage scattered
throughout the world.

"Sursum Corda"

Copyright © 1991 by W. S. Kuniczak

Collier Books
Macmillan Publishing Company
866 Third Avenue
New York, NY 10022

Maxwell Macmillan Canada, Inc.
1200 Eglinton Avenue East
Suite 200
Don Mills, Ontario M3C 3N1

Macmillan Publishing Company is part of the
Maxwell Communication Group of Companies.

Library of Congress Cataloging-in-Publication Data
Sienkiewicz, Henryk, 1846–1916.
    [Ogniem i mieczem. English]
    With fire and sword/Henryk Sienkiewicz;
in modern translation by W.S. Kuniczak; foreword by
James A. Michener.—1st Collier Books ed.
        p.   cm.
    ISBN 0-02-082044-5
    1. Cossacks—Poland—Fiction.   2. Cossacks—Ukraine—
Fiction.   3. Poland—History—John II Casimir, 1648–1668—
Fiction.   I. Kuniczak, W. S., 1930–   . II. Title.
[PG7158.S40413   1993]   93-6524   CIP
891.8'536—dc20

Macmillan books are available at special discounts for bulk
purchases for sales promotions, premiums, fund-raising,
or educational use. For details, contact: Special Sales
Director, Macmillan Publishing Company, 866 Third Avenue,
New York, NY 10022.

First Collier Books Edition 1993

10   9   8   7   6   5   4   3   2   1

Printed in the United States of America

Map by Eugenia Gore

Henryk Sienkiewicz

When I was a boy of eight my mother used to gather us children about her after supper and read to us from the great books of the time, a commendable custom which enabled me later to become a writer of my own books. The first she read was Charles Dickens' *Oliver Twist,* a fantastically appropriate book under the circumstances. This was followed by *Great Expectations* and *David Copperfield,* by which time the love of exciting narration was ingrained in me, as were the rhythms of the English language. Then, after a reading of Charles Reade's *The Cloister and the Hearth,* she was provided, by our local minister, with a copy of a novel then in great vogue among religious people in the United States and Europe. It was the extremely popular *Quo Vadis?* by a Polish writer named Henryk Sienkiewicz.

The translation we had contained a helpful note: *The author's name is pronounced Sin-KAY-vitch* and those syllables became a mnemonic for me. I whispered them to myself again and again, gratified that I knew how to pronounce them while others didn't. I liked the story of *Quo Vadis?* and imagined myself as an early Christian hiding in the catacombs and withstanding the persecutions of Rome. Later, when I understood such things, I was delighted to learn that my old friend Sienkiewicz had won the Nobel Prize for Literature, because this confirmed my belief that he was good.

What I did not know then, or until much later, was that he won his prize not for *Quo Vadis?* but for three powerful interrelated novels which have since become known as "The Trilogy," and which depicted certain crucial events in Polish and European history. The first and most widely read, *With Fire and Sword* (1884), dealt with the terrible Hmyelnitzki Rebellion of Ukrainian Cossacks, and bloody Tartar wars in the first half of the 17th Century, which drained the stamina and military power of the Poles and gave the barbaric Muscovites the time they needed to turn themselves into the Russian Empire. The second, *The Deluge* (1886), was a masterful account of the Swedish, Prussian and Hungarian invasions just a few years later which generated the expansion of the Prussian state. The trilogy ended with a more complex novel, *Pan Wolodyjowski* (1887–88)—entitled in this translation *Fire in the Steppe*—which focused on the Poles' heroic stand against the Turks toward the end of the 17th Century.

Whereas *Quo Vadis?*, not written until 1896, would be immediately translated into most of the literary languages and win world-wide fame for its author and itself, the much more powerful and important "Trilogy" would be largely ignored outside Poland. I had never heard of it until 1956 when, because of the Hungarian Revolution of that year, I started serious research into Polish history. An explanation for my ignorance existed: there was no satisfactory English translation of these three great books. Indeed, the only one available when I started my research was an abominable affair adapted not from Polish but from a cheap Russian redaction, fleshed out with passages lifted not from the books themselves but from the newspaper serials in which they first appeared. The result of this inattention was that even readers like me, who were hungry to study things Polish, were cut off from one of the great masterpieces of European literature, and my loss was deplorable.

The Sienkiewicz "Trilogy" stands with that handful of novels which not only depict but also help to determine the soul and character of the nation they describe. Alessandro Manzoni's *I Promessi Sposi* (The Promised Bride, 1825–27) played such an important role in helping to create the Italian nation that when he died his funeral cortege was enormous, with princes and politicians walking behind his coffin, but the abiding memorials to his contribution to Italy were his novel and the soaring Requiem which Giuseppe Verdi composed in his honor.

In Scandinavia the far-ranging novels of two gifted women writers, the Swedish Selma Lagerlof and the Norwegian Sigrid Undset, both Nobel Prize winners, played a somewhat similar role in identifying national values and characteristics, but with fewer dramatic results than those of Manzoni and with a more restricted historical coverage than that of Sienkiewicz.

France, the United States, South America and China have all failed to produce national novels that define their civilizations.

Spain comes close with Miguel Cervantes' *Don Quixote,* while Lady Murasaki's *Tale of the Genji* speaks to the heart of Japan, but depicts only a somewhat effete royal stratum of the nation's life. Shakespeare's historical plays perform a noble function for England, but Sienkiewicz and Manzoni remain the soaring prototypes of the national epic and we should honor them.

In Sienkiewicz's case, the message and the values proved so enduring, having withstood the test of time for more than 100 years, that he has just as much to say to English readers today as he did to the Poles of the 1880's. A gifted Polish writer and patriot has told me: "I know of no other books in the literatures of the world that have had such a powerful and lasting effect on any one People, and it is high time that intelligent readers in America have a translation adapted to their language and needs."

Such publication in the United States is especially appropriate because one of the books that brought Sienkiewicz to public attention was his collected *Letters from America* (1876–78), whose brilliant imagery of our western prairies, the Mississippi River, and life in the American West, gave him the descriptions of the Dnieper and the Ukrainian Steppe which he adapted so creatively in the early pages of *With Fire and Sword.* He loved our country and learned much from it.

When, in the late 1970's, I committed myself to a serious study of Polish life in preparation for a comprehensive novel that I planned to write, I immersed myself in the ancient chronicles describing the furious assaults on Poland (or the Polish Lithuanian Commonwealth as it was at that time) by the hordes from Central Asia, then the roaring accounts of Swedish and German invasions, and later the doleful stories about the three separate partitions of the nation among Russia, Germany and Austria.

But as I worked, interested Polish friends kept reminding me that what I really ought to read was Henryk Sienkiewicz's "Trilogy." All I could find, however, when I tried to read it, were creaking translations that masked the glory and the fire of the original. As a boy I had loved and learned from *Quo Vadis?* but as a man I could learn little from "The Trilogy."

Then a Polish scholar whom I respected told me: "If you want to understand the role that the Shrine at Czestochowa played in the formation of Poland you simply must read *The Deluge.*" So, with whatever translation was available, I picked my way slowly through that powerful story and then doubled back to *With Fire and Sword*. The third book of the trilogy made for less eager reading since I was not focusing on the ground covered in that novel, nor was I satisfied with the awkward translation to which I was restricted.

I am therefore pleased as a reader to learn that a skilled Polish-born American novelist like W. S. Kuniczak who has proved with his own novels that he knows how to captivate readers, has interrupted his own writing for more than six years to put into attractive English the more than 1,850,000 words of the Sienkiewicz masterpiece. Such willingness to put aside one's own work to pay tribute to one's national hero represents a degree of dedication that few writers would have.

It has been a worthy task. Sienkiewicz's trilogy is the portrait of a nation. Its credentials have been forged in the affections of millions of Poles. It kept national hopes alive during those mournful years when the three occupying powers—Russia, Germany and Austria—would not allow the nation itself to exist. "The Trilogy" also provided courage when Nazi Germany tried to extinguish all things Polish and later when Communist Russia laid such a heavy hand on the nation.

The "Trilogy" is a sacred book. Sienkiewicz wrote *Quo Vadis?* for the entire world and the world took it to its heart. He wrote "The Trilogy" for the people of Poland and they absorbed it into their souls. Now it is time for this national epic to be made available in distinguished prose and handsome physical presentation to all in the world who can read English.

James A. Michener
Professor Emeritus

Introduction

More than 100 years ago, on May 2, 1883, a Warsaw newspaper started a serialization of a new novel, *Ogniem i Mieczem* or *With Fire and Sword,* and a great new literary reputation was made overnight. The author was Henryk Sienkiewicz, the 36-year-old editor of *Slowo,* the newspaper that published his novel. He was known to the reading public mostly through short stories and some interesting reportage from his journey across America in 1876–78, but the young writer was by no means Poland's leading author.

Then came *With Fire and Sword* and Sienkiewicz became an on-the-spot celebrity while his novel and the two sequels that combined in time to form his famous "Trilogy" became instant classics. Such was the readers' interest and enthusiasm for the work, and such was its immediate literary reputation, that both the work and author acquired almost mythological dimensions. In a phenomenon that approached the Bible, Sienkiewicz's "Trilogy" became a national bestseller which would stay at the top of the charts in Poland for 100 years, maintaining its status despite changing times, styles and literary fashions. Even in the most ruthless era of communist domination in the late 1940's and the 1950's, when Poland existed in an atmosphere of censorship and strict cultural controls, every new edition of the "Trilogy" was sold out the day it appeared.

Since then it has seen print in more than 30 languages and a variety of forms that included children's comic-strips. Generations of Polish readers think of it as among the greatest novels in their literary history while Polish film directors use its scope and setting for successful historical adventure dramas of unusual color. In short, the continuous success of these three interrelated novels testifies to their vitality and importance which ignore national and cultural boundaries, spans the gaps in time between literary eras, and demands that these works be known in any time and language no matter how far removed from Sienkiewicz's Poland they might be.

They appeared on the Polish literary scene in an era much like our own today, marked by a sober and pragmatic approach to reality, and requiring authors to present a candid and clear-sighted view of the social and political problems of their times. Readers, as critics insisted, demanded novels that depicted their own time and age, reflecting on their own lives in society, and helping them to understand the world around them in a clear and uncomplicated manner. The name of the game was Realism, proclaimed in *fin-de-siecle* 19th Century Europe by such famous novelists as Flaubert in France, Turgenev in Russia, and an expatriate American, Henry James, in England. The time of Tolstoy and Joseph Conrad was still some years distant.

But once aroused, the readers' appetite for "real" people in their novels' pages—vibrant and exciting men and women who were believable in their attitudes and motives—could be projected into times past as well. Sir Walter Scott had already signaled historical realism in his chivalric novels, making his medieval settings seem as tangible as the contemporary images of Paris and London. The great historical adventures of Alexandre Dumas' *Three Musketeers* and *Count of Monte Cristo* had enthralled vast international audiences since the 1840s with their fast-paced, colorful action-drama set against a rich and accurately rendered historical background. The precedent for bringing history to new life through the techniques of the contemporary novel already existed, but in Poland, despite many attempts in that field, the historical novel before Sienkiewicz had never been a spectacular success. He changed that once and for all.

Sienkiewicz had spent two happy and exciting years in the United States, traveling down the great rivers and across the continent in the time of wagon trains, stage coaches and Indian campaigns, hunting, fishing and camping in the Sierras, and absorbing both the beauty and the dangers of the vast open spaces at their unspoiled best. His *Letters from America,* which established his reputation as a perceptive and incisive reporter, ring with authenticity and that love of nature that permeates the early chapters of *With Fire and Sword* where the narrative descriptions of the Ukrainian Steppe glow with remembered American imagery. There is something both moving and appealing in the image of this young Polish writer wandering through the prairies, breathing the vastness of America and the variety of its many peoples, while George Armstrong Custer made his last stand at the Little Big Horn and the great Indian nations of the Plains receded into history.

It's easy to see these American impressions in the early pages of *With Fire and Sword* where Sienkiewicz, who had never set foot in the legendary "Wildlands" which bordered the 17th Century Polish-Lithuanian Commonwealth that he writes about, transposes his vision of the prairies, the endless landscapes, and the sea of grass *"where a man might ride unseen, for days, like a diver drifting through an ocean"* onto the rich and turbulent canvas of his imagined Ukrainian Steppe. Even a bateau journey down the Mississippi finds its counterpart in a voyage down the Dnieper River by Sienkiewicz's young hero, Yan Skshetuski, whose awe-struck sense of wonder is heightened by the sight of *"huge reptiles"*—clearly remembered from America—slipping into the vast stream out of the muddy sandbars. Not much imagination is required a few moments later, when Skshetuski and his small detachment are overwhelmed by Tartars on an island where they stop to rest, to hear the volleys of Custer's doomed troopers in the desperate musketry of Skshetuski's dragoons.

In a few short stories that Sienkiewicz wrote after his return to Poland in 1879, including *The Lighthouse Keeper,* he drew on his American experience to explore the Polish ethos of patriotism and remembrance, looking into the past for clues about the future, and celebrating a fierce love of freedom. That issue of personal liberty, in both its worthy and unworthy aspects, became the main theme of *With Fire and Sword.* It must be remembered that the savage era in which the work is set represents the sunset years of the Polish-Lithuanian Commonwealth, the rise of Russia and Prussia as modern empires, and the loss of national existence for the Poles who wouldn't have a country of their own for more than a century.

The Polish-Ukrainian borderlands, or *kresy* as they were known in Poland, have had a long and often fabulous history marked with love and hatred, passionate unity and violent disagreements, and moments of near-idyllic coexistence that were invariably ruptured by treachery, selfishness and greed. Deeply steeped in folklore, age-old legends of departed glories and traditions of unbridled freedom, the *kresy* had created whole populations of colorful and turbulent heroes whose lives abounded in conflicts and emotions that simply begged for the pen of a skilled literary artist. And while the Ukrainian Cossacks found their spokesman in Nicolai Gogol, whose *Taras Bulba* romanticized their history, Polish readers had to wait 30 years longer for Sienkiewicz and his epic of their Golden Age. It should be noted here that the strangely glowing and poetic spirit of those vast, open and untrammeled lands, combining lyric beauty with the fierceness of a prairie fire, found its ultimate expression in the English masterpieces of Joseph Conrad who had been born in a *kresy* manor house as Jozef Korzeniowski in the 1830s.

All the ingredients needed for a literary masterwork—realism and an underlying romantic tradition, the author's sensitivity to nature and his love of freedom along with a deep-seated longing for human understanding, brotherhood and justice—came together in Sienkiewicz's novel thanks largely to his remarkable talents as a storyteller.

In his case, however, these elements were to serve a deeper social and historic purpose, coinciding with a popular need for literature that would help a nation in distress retain its identity. Ruthlessly divided in the 1790s between the neighboring empires of Russia, Prussia and Austria, the Polish nation fought back in bloody uprisings that left their fields and forests littered with their dead and dotted their landscapes with ruins and gibbets. Arrests, mass deportations to Siberia, curtailment of civil rights to such a drastic point that the Polish language was banned in schools and offices, and tragic persecution on all social levels, had left the Poles with no means of national existence other than dimly recalled memories of disaster. The realistic novels of Polish writers were so heavily censored by the Tsarist Russian authorities in Warsaw that the best of them, *The Doll* by Boleslaw Prus, couldn't even mention Poland's Russian masters, although this brutish and malevolent presence was felt in all its pages. Sienkiewicz himself, writing a horrifying expose of the "Russification" of Polish schoolchildren in 1879, found it expedient to relocate his story to the Prussian-held territories of Poznan in order to maintain his uneasy standing with the Russian censors in his part of Poland. Thus only by stepping deeper into history could he recall and resurrect the waning spirit of his prostrate nation and give his People a badly needed reassurance that "Poland Is Not Yet Lost," as the Napoleonic-era song, soon to become their national anthem, continued to remind.

Setting out to *"uplift the hearts of my countrymen,"* as he put it, and in the process creating a work of such profound universal values that William Faulkner found in it a beacon for his own literary career, Sienkiewicz chose one of the bloodiest and most dramatic periods of Poland's long history: a local uprising of disgruntled Cossacks against Polish landlords that changed into a full-scale civil war in the 1640s. Against this violent background, full of swords and fire, which shook the foundations of the Polish-Lithuanian Commonwealth that had ruled those regions for 100 years, he projected an adventure story full of love and murder, friendship and betrayal, cold-blooded treason and passionate devotion, sacrifice and cynicism and cowardice and courage; painting, in short, a portrait of humanity at its best and at its most absurd, with all its pathos and humor and frailties and follies. *With Fire and Sword* is a novel that invades the reader and takes command of all his emotions so that the only question he or she can ask as they turn the pages is a breathless and impatient: "What's next?"

And then, just as the headlong rush of images and events proves almost overwhelming, giving the reader little time to stop and ponder the deeper meanings that flow beneath the story, there come those moments of profound reflection that mean as much to today's English-speaking readers as they did to the troubled Poles of Sienkiewicz's era. The reader stops to ask whether there might be more to life than pure enjoyment and the spirit of adventure. He begins to grasp and understand the power of a cause that can be more important to private men and women than their own personal welfare and unrestrained individual liberties.

"How can he do this?" the reader asks, in wonder, watching Yan Skshetuski as he suppresses his most fervent longings so that he might devote himself wholly to his country. "What kind of man could be that selfless in a public cause or that oblivious of his own well-being?"

And the age-old Polish answer comes at once from Skshetuski's own comrades and companions—the heroes as well as the rollicking buffoons—that life is only worth living and enjoying if each of us has something for which he would be willing to give up his life no matter how much he loves the idea of living. It seems that just as individuals have to interrupt their materialistic concerns now and then, and take time-out to ponder their lives' real meaning, so do great nations and organized societies. But these are matters that readers discover for themselves while exploring the rich environment that Sienkiewicz created for our fascination.

The first readers of *With Fire and Sword* were quick to spot all these themes and currents even as they devoured the pages in pure enjoyment of an action story. Stanislaw Tarnowski, the leading Polish critic and literary historian of his time, speculated in 1897 that *"Sometime in the future, our memoirs and perhaps even literary histories will recall that when With Fire and Sword made its first appearance, there was hardly a conversation that didn't start and end with that topic . . . that the protagonists of the novel were thought and talked about as if they were real . . . that young children, writing home from school, would first report on their own health and that of their siblings, and then relate the latest thing said by Zagloba or Skshetuski . . . and that while young ladies either wrote or wanted to write to the author, begging him—for God's sake!—to save Skshetuski in the next installment, their mothers and grandmothers offered tearful prayers that their own sons might rise to the greatness of Skshetuski's soul."*

A typically unsatisfactory aspect of Jeremiah Curtin's first translation into English, made more than 100 years ago, lies in his strange decision to provide his version of *With Fire and Sword* with a labored and lengthy Russian "apologia" in which he argues against Sienkiewicz's vision of the *kresy* borderlands and the relationships between the various nationalities who lived there. That kind of editorial intervention forms a wholly unwarranted intrusion into a work as universally oriented as this one, with heroes and villains richly apportioned to each side, and no one, in either the literature or the history, presented without some redeeming features.

Today it's safe to view this work as a timeless historical novel of equal meaning to anyone who reads it. The novel's unmistakably Polish character is all the more appealing for Americans who have always cherished traditions of freedom, independence, courage and adventure. We hope that in this first modern translation from Polish, made from my father's revised 1948 edition and adapted for today's English-speaking readers, this treasured Polish author will speak to everyone as clearly and as beautifully as he has for 100 years to countless millions of his countrymen all over the world.

Jerzy R. Krzyzanowski, PhD.
The Ohio State University

Part One

". . . to uplift the hearts."
—Sienkiewicz

Chapter One

THE YEAR 1647 abounded with omens. Strange signs and portents of terrible disasters appeared on earth and in the skies. A plague of locusts spilled out of the Wild Lands in the Spring: a sure sign of Tartar incursions, possibly even a great war. In early Summer the sun disappeared under an eclipse. Soon afterwards a comet trailed fire through the sky. In Warsaw, people saw tombs and fiery crosses in the clouds, and so gave alms and fasted, reading in these signs a terrible calamity that would fall on the land and ravage all mankind. When Winter came it was so mild that the oldest people couldn't remember anything to match it. No ice gripped the rivers of the south; swollen with rain and melting snows they burst from their courses and flooded the Steppe. Rain streamed down in torrents of silver. The open Steppes became one vast, quaking swamp; and in the Bratzlav Territory at the eastern boundary, and all across the unpopulated Wild Lands, the noon sun burned with such intense Summer brightness that a green blanket of new grasses sprung up in December. Beehives hummed in the border settlements and herds of cattle bellowed the restless calls of Spring.

With all these signs and warnings, and with the natural order of the seasons so unnaturally reversed, all eyes in the eastern territories turned fearfully to the Wild Lands since peril of every kind could come from those untamed spaces quicker than from any other quarter. But nothing unusual seemed to be happening there in that extraordinary year. There were no battles, wars, raids, or killings other than those that were as common to that savage landscape as the immense seas of blowing, head-high grass where only eagles, hawks and vultures, and the fleeting grey wolves running in the night, could serve as witnesses and possible accusers.

Such were these Wild Lands: a continent of grass stamped with savage beauty. Billowing pastures where a mounted man could vanish like a diver in a lake. Violent chasms torn out of the earth, gaunt breastworks of crumbling clay and limestone that opened without warning under a horse's hooves. A wilderness of forest, fallen timbers, sudden glittering lakes and rivers exploding into cataracts.

The last traces of human settlement ended at Tchehryn on the Dnieper River and in the Uman territory along the unpopulated borders. Beyond them lay the rolling emptiness of the Steppe that flowed like an uncharted, multicolored ocean all the way to the Black Sea, the Caspian and the Sea of Azov. Cossack life swarmed like turbulent wild bees in the distant *Nijh* and along the streams and pastures hidden in the coils of the Dnieper beyond the cataracts, but nothing human lived in the Wild Lands themselves. It was a land as vast as all of Western Europe, subject in name to the dominion of the Crown of Poland but, in effect, belonging only to those who lived by claw, fleet foot, and arrows shot out of ambush in the night. The Tartars grazed their horseherds there by treaty permission; and Cossack horsethieves turned these pastures into battlefields where the sounds of slaughter, the screams of dying men, the drumming of hooves galloping out of ambush, the clash of steel, and the hiss of the Tartar arrow and the whirling lariat seemed to hang forever on the wind, carried from unknown beginnings into an endless future like the Steppe itself.

No one knew how many battles were fought there in the years gone by, nor how many men left their bones scattered in the Steppe for the wolves and vultures. Armed travelers who heard the whirring of great wings, or saw the black swarms of carrion birds wheeling in the sky, knew at once that corpses or bleached bones lay somewhere ahead and looked to their weapons. Men hunted each other in this menacing green sea with no more feeling than they'd have in running down a hare; everyone there was both the hunter and the prey. This was the immemorial home of outlaws hiding from the law and the hangman's rope. Armed shepherds—as savage as their untamed flocks and herds—guarded lean sheep, fierce stallions and wild cattle. Bandits sought loot. Cossacks trailed Tartars and Tartars hunted

Cossacks. It was common practice for entire *vatahas* of light cavalry to guard the immense horseherds while raiding marauders came a thousand strong; and all of them, no matter whom they served, were men for whom words like gentleness and mercy had never held a meaning.

The Steppes were wholly desolate and unpeopled yet filled with living menace. Silent and still yet seething with hidden violence, peaceful in their immensity yet infinitely dangerous, these boundless spaces were a masterless, untamed country created for ruthless men who acknowledged no one as their overlord.

At times great wars would fill these territories, and then the sea of grass seemed to become a real ocean in which lesser tides of crimson Cossack caps flowed between horizons. The grey Tartar *tchambuls* spread there in crescent waves, and the winged regiments of Polish horsemen rode in their leopard and wolf-skin cloaks draped over glittering armor, and then a forest of spears and lances and horsetail standards and a blazing rainbow of many-colored banners rose above the Steppe. At night the neighing of the warriors' horses and the howl of wolves echoed in grim prophecy through this wilderness, and the booming of the kettledrums and the blare of copper horns and bugles flowed all the way to the misty Lakes of Ovidov and to the shores of the Turkish Sultan's seas. At such times the desolate Black Trail and the Kutchmansky Track became human rivers engulfing everything before them, and terror flew on birds' wings before this flood of animals and riders.

★ ★ ★

But that Winter no birds came cawing to the southern lands with their raucous warnings. The immemorial routes of Tartar invasions were quiet and still. The Steppes crouched waiting, still as death in their shrouds of mist. And on this day, the day of a particularly breathless silence, the red light of late afternoon lit up a gaunt and skeletal land. Nothing moved on the tall banks of the Omelnitchek in the southernmost reaches of the darkening Steppe. The day was ending. The sun showed only the top half of its scarlet shield above the horizon and each passing moment sheathed the landscape in a deeper shadow.

On the high left bank of the river, gleaming in the reds and yellows of the sinking sun, lay the heaped and tumbled rubble of a walled *stannitza*, one of those lonely outposts that guarded these borders. It was built years ago, perhaps as long as a generation earlier, but whole decades of raids, assaults and tidal waves of war had swept over it since then; the hot winds of the Steppe eroded the fortress into bleached timbers and crumbling white stone, rounding it out as smoothly as a burial mound; and now a long, symmetrical shadow fell from this height of land and sunk in the broad waters of the Omelnitchek which turned towards the Dniester River at this point.

The sun set rapidly, as if anxious to get out of sight. Light fled from the Steppe and seeped out of the sky where mournful flights of cranes were beating their way heavily to the sea. Night came, and with it came the Hour of the Spirits.

The soldiers of the Steppe *stannitzas* told stories about murdered men who rose from their graves and stalked through the Wild Lands after the sun went down, and muttered prayers for lost souls when the tallow candles burned down in the guardhouse to show the midnight hour. They spoke of ghostly riders who'd block the path of travelers and beg for the sign of the cross that might give them rest, and of vampires and werewolves leaping from their lairs. It took an experienced ear to tell the difference between the ordinary baying of the wolves and the howl of vampires. Sometimes entire regiments of tormented souls were seen to drift across the moonlit Steppe so that sentries sounded the alarm and the garrisons stood to arms. But such ghostly armies were seen only before a great war. Lone shades were met more often. They brought no good fortune, to be sure, but they didn't necessarily forecast a disaster since living men, as secretive about their business as the restless spirits, were just as likely to appear and vanish in that spectral country as genuine apparitions.

And so, that night, there was nothing strange about the dark rider whose shadow rose among the ruins as soon as night settled on the Omelnitchek.

Moonlight poured over him and on the ghostly ruin and streaked the shadowed wilderness with silver. Below the silent mounted man, among the nodding thistles of the undergrowth, other black forms appeared and vanished as the clouds boiled up between them and the moon. They crept towards the crest of the mound, their movements as forbidding as the Steppe itself. The Dniester winds were hissing through the thistles, making their burred heads bob and nod as if in premonition. But then the creeping shadows went to ground and lay as still as the old scorched timbers rotting in the rubble and only the solitary rider stood in the dead white light on the crest of the mound.

Some sound alerted him.

He spurred his horse to the sharp edge of the crest and peered carefully into the darkened Steppe. The wind died down at that moment; its soft whispers ceased.

And suddenly the shrill reedy scream of a Tartar whistle cut through the deep silence, the creeping shadows leaped up with a savage howl and the lone rider vanished, swept off his horse by a whirling rope. But now fresh hoofbeats drummed out of the shadows, and fierce voices bellowed: "*Allah! Allah! Jezu! Chryste! Kill!*" and red muzzle blasts flicked out of the night like scarlet tongues licking at the darkness. There was a quick, sharp clash of iron and shrill cries of terror, and a new swarm of riders burst out of the Steppe as if a sudden storm had boiled out of the wilderness.

Then there was only the moaning of the wounded. And then there was silence.

★　★　★

The horsemen who had sprung so suddenly out of nowhere assembled on the mound with nothing much to say after the sharp, swift fight. Some of them jumped down to the ground and peered with casual indifference at the dark, huddled shape of the ambushed man, and then a hard, clear voice, young but ringing with authority, swept them into motion.

"Strike some lights! Jump to it!"

At once there came the dry rasping sound of iron striking against flint, and red sparks spilled upward, and a sudden flame leaped up among the bundles of pitch-soaked firewood that travelers always carried with them in the Wild Lands, and soon the firelight revealed clusters of tall, burly men who drove sharpened stakes into the ground and fastened burning torches in their iron sockets, and then the bright cheerful glow of a campfire began to sweep over the mound and dance among the ruins.

The men were soldiers, dressed in crimson coats with hooded wolfskin cloaks fastened about their shoulders. They peered at the prone, silent figure on the ground out of fierce, bearded faces, and made room for their leader who leaped lightly off his horse.

"Well, sergeant? Is he alive or dead?"

"Still alive, Your Honor, still breathing. But he's short on air. The rope's choked it all out of him."

"What's he look like to you?"

"He's not a Tartar, sir. Quality, I'd say."

"So much the better." The young officer peered sharply at the man whom he and his troopers had rescued from the ambush and nodded with quiet satisfaction. "Looks almost like a Hetman, doesn't he."

"And his horse, lieutenant. That's a real beauty. The Tartar Khan wouldn't have anything better in his stables."

The sergeant pointed to an Arab thoroughbred held by two soldiers in the circle of light. The horse had pressed his ears flat against his finely chiseled head and stared nervously at his fallen master, and the young lieutenant grinned with appreciation at the trembling stallion.

"He's a beauty, alright."

"That'll be ours, sir, won't it?" A note of worry entered the old sergeant's voice. "That will be for us?"

The officer turned hard eyes on the bearded sergeant. "What's the matter with you? You'd take a Christian's horse away from him in the Steppe?"

"Well, Excellency, it's a battle trophy, right?"

Anxious not to irritate his officer, the sergeant was persistent none the less.

"What they call spoils of war . . . ?"

But a harsh, half-strangled cough came from the fallen man just then and they turned towards him.

"Feed him some liquor, sergeant," the lieutenant ordered. "And loosen his belt."

"Aye, sir. Are we to bivouac here, then?"

"Might as well. See to the horses and get the cook-fires going."

The soldiers jumped up at once and started setting up the bivouac. Some got to work on the fallen man, rubbing his arms and loosening his clothing. Others sprang into the deadwood tangle of the riverbank, among the hidden caves and gullies at the foot of the mound, to hack at dry logs and to gather firewood. Still others brought up bearskins and camel robes and spread them out for sleeping.

Meanwhile the young lieutenant turned his back on the gasping man who'd been half-choked by the Tartar lariat. He loosened his broad embroidered sash and took out his weapons and threw himself down on the traveling robe that his men spread for him near the fire. The flames lit up his tall, broadshouldered frame and the young, dusky face burned almost black by the hot southern winds that swept through the Steppes for most of the year, and his thick black beard and mustache glinted in the firelight. Seen in that sharp, crackling light, it was a harsh, adventurous face, fierce as a Steppe hawk's and proud as the Devil. But there was laughter in the eyes and a lean carefree youthfulness to the powerful body, and there was an untroubled cheerful confidence about him that went a long way to erase the hint of savagery.

He stretched out on the robes while the soldiers worked. Two servant lads set about preparing the supper. Whole sides of mutton were spitted across the coals and, next to them, a flock of birds and dozens of field hares; wild pigs and deer that the horsemen had shot during the day were swiftly ripped out of their skins and feathers and thrown over the fire.

The flames leaped and danced, throwing wide circles of light into the wilderness, and then the gasping, half-choked man began to revive. His bloodshot eyes sprung open and swept carefully across the grim, bearded faces that hovered over him. The sergeant propped him up and helped him to his feet. Another soldier slipped a slim, long-handled war club into his fist and he leaned on it heavily as if on a cane. His face was crimson and suffused with blood and the swollen veins bulged on his neck and forehead as thick as the plaited rawhide with which he'd been bound.

"Water," he croaked, and the soldiers handed him a gourd of raw spirits.

He drank long and deep. The fiery liquid spilled down the broken corners of his mouth, ran past his mustache that trailed downward in the limp Steppe fashion adopted from the Tartars, and glittered with reflected firelight in his long black beard. But when he tossed the leather flask aside his voice was clear and strong.

"In whose hands am I?"

The young officer got up. "You're in the hands of those who rescued you," he said.

"So it wasn't you who roped me like an ox?"

The lieutenant's proud young face darkened in quick anger. "We're soldiers," he snapped. "Our business is done with sabers, not with ropes. You were pulled down by some bush marauders dressed up as Tartars."

Then he shrugged and pointed to the row of corpses stretched along the slope.

"They're all down there, laid out like dressed mutton. Take a look if you're interested."

The stranger glanced quickly at the corpses, sighed and turned away.

"Well, in that case," he said softly. "Let me rest a little."

Two soldiers spread a quilted horse blanket on the bare ground and the rescued man lowered himself on it gingerly and turned towards the shadows. He sat withdrawn deep into his own thoughts and the young lieutenant studied him with interest. The stranger's face and bearing caught him by surprise, as did his poise and the rich cut and quality of his clothes. He was a man somewhere on the threshold of a hard-lived and vigorous middle age, not especially tall but with unusually wide shoulders, a heavily proportioned body, and sharp, watchful features that seemed harsh and ruthless in his weathered face. His head was large, with a broad bulging forehead. His black eyes slanted like a Tartar's under heavy brows. A long black mustache swept past his narrow lips and hung straight down in a stringy line combed out at the ends.

It was a face that seemed at once compelling and repellent, stamped with ferocity, daring and authority; it combined the pride and dignity of a Hetman with a Tartar's cunning, the young soldier thought.

The rescued man sat quite still, hunched over his own thoughts, and then he rose, and the young lieutenant prepared himself for the expected ritual of thanks. None came. Instead, the stranger walked abruptly down the slope and began to pace back and forth among the corpses, staring intently into each dead face.

"Lout," the lieutenant muttered.

Meanwhile, the stranger was studying the dead. Each frozen

face, with teeth bared in terror and the eyes turned upward, drew his whole attention. He nodded thoughtfully like a man for whom there could be no more mysteries about anything and who'd resolved the last of his doubts. Then he turned slowly and climbed back to the crest of the mound-shaped hillock, and walked to the fire, his hands groping for his sash by instinct as if he wished to thrust a hand into it.

The young lieutenant shot him a disdainful glance out of the corners of his eyes and then stared hard into his wide, dark face.

"A man might think you were looking for old friends among those cut-throats," he said scornfully, and a cold, arrogant note slipped into his voice. "Or maybe saying prayers for their souls?"

The stranger's chilly smile was much like his own.

"You're wrong about that, young sir," the man said and nodded his large head slowly up and down. "Yet . . . not entirely. No. I was, indeed, looking for an old acquaintance. Those people,"—and his bitter gesture dismissed his slaughtered captors as if they were offal—"belong to a certain gentleman, a neighbor of mine. They aren't just common bandits."

"Ah . . . I see that you don't drink out of the same well with this neighbor of yours," the young man snorted, quoting a local saying, while a quick, cruel smile flitted across the stranger's narrow mouth.

"And there you're also wrong," he said abruptly and grunted with amusement at something that only he would understand.

Then, as if he'd suddenly recollected more important business, his voice became both courteous and cajoling.

"But forgive me, young man, for not thanking you properly right away. You've saved me from sure death and, I'd guess, not a pleasant one. Your courage, sir, made up for my carelessness in riding out too far ahead of my people. I hope my gratitude can match your brave spirit."

Smiling, he thrust his right hand towards the young man who, however, was in no hurry to accept it.

"I'd like to know first who I'm dealing with," the young officer said, still piqued by the other's earlier lack of manners. "Nameless thanks are not much use to me."

The stranger laughed.

"You're right. I should have started with my name. I'm Zenobius Abdank, a landholder in the Kiev Territory, and a colonel in the Cossack regiment of Prince Dominic Zaslavski."

"And I'm Yan Skshetuski, lieutenant in the armored regiment of Prince Yeremi Vishnovyetzki."

"You serve under a famous soldier," the Cossack colonel said and nodded with appreciation. "Let me shake your hand to show that I'm grateful."

This time the young lieutenant didn't hesitate. While normally the soldiers who served in the elite regiments of heavy cavalry, the armored *Husaria* who charged into battle with long, curved frames of eagle wings fastened to their shoulders, looked down their noses at light-cavalrymen, Cossacks and Dragoons, and at contingents of Lithuanian Light Horse and hired foreign soldiers, he and the man he'd rescued were meeting in the Steppe where such distinctions didn't make a difference. Moreover he was dealing with a colonel whose rank was verified at once. The soldiers who ran up with Abdank's sash and saber also brought his regimental commander's *bulava*—a miniature mace with a short ivory handle and a carved round head of glazed horn stained to the color of dark cherry-wine and polished like a mirror. Such symbols of rank were widely used by colonels of Cossacks. And there was something else about the rescued man that testified to his authority and status: his rich clothes and haughty bearing, along with his well-formed speech and somewhat careless manner, suggested that here was a man accustomed to high thresholds, a noble used to dealing with the great, and not some rag-tag provincial boor like much of the rank and file gentry.

Satisfied about his guest's credentials, Pan Yan invited him to share his soldiers' meal. The smell of roasting meats and the hiss of juices dripping on the coals drifted from the cook-fires, along with the crackle of burned hide and the snap of marrow bursting from the bones, and rich red lights gleamed cheerfully on the edges of the copper bowls, and when the serving lads ran up with a full goatskin of Moldavian wine, everyone's tongue moved a little easier.

"To a safe homecoming," Pan Yan raised a toast.

"Home?" The rescued man looked up with quick curiosity. "So you've been away somewhere? Where did you go?"

"A long way. To the Crimea."

"Carrying ransom, were you?"

"Not this time. I went to see the Khan."

"The Khan, eh? Well now, you keep exalted company, I see. And what did you go to see the Khan about?"

"I carried letters from Prince Yeremi."

"Ah! An envoy, were you?" Abdank leaned forward eagerly. "And what did the Prince have to say to the Tartar Khan?"

But at this point the young lieutenant looked at his accidental dinner guest out of narrowed eyes.

"Look, colonel," he snapped out coldly. "If you want to go peering into the dead eyes of cut-throats who roped you like an ox, that's your business and you're welcome to it. But what the Prince wrote to the Khan is neither your business nor mine."

Abdank sank back on his robes, his eyes sly and watchful, then barked with quick laughter. "Oh, I was just surprised that His Highness picked such a young man for an ambassador. But I see you're only young in years."

"How's that?"

"Young in years but old in experience. Mature in judgment, is what I want to say."

Still young enough for flattery, the lieutenant smiled with satisfaction and lifted his hand proudly to his mustache. But he thought that he'd do well to do some questioning of his own; he wanted to know more about this mysterious Pan Zenobius whose imposing features and drawing room courtesies didn't quite fit the image of a noose thrown around his neck out of ambush on a dark Steppe night.

"And you sir," he asked. "What are you doing all alone on the Omelnitchek?"

"I didn't come alone," Abdank cocked his head as if to listen to every word he uttered and guard his tongue against a careless slip. "I've a few men with me. But I left them a couple of furlongs back of me, a piece of carelessness I'm not likely to repeat. I'm on my way to Kudak with letters from the Hetman to old Pan Grodjitzki who commands the fortress."

"So why didn't you go by water?" the young lieutenant questioned. It was all sounding a bit mysterious to him. "It's faster and safer this time of the year."

"Such were my orders," Abdank said and shrugged.

"Strange orders, colonel, since it was out here on dry land that you ran into trouble. You'd have been safe enough on the Dnieper boats."

"Ah, the Steppe is quiet and peaceful nowadays, there isn't

much danger." Abdank shrugged again and glanced away, dismissing the subject. "I know my way around here well enough.
And anyway, what happened to me is a private matter, a bit of
ordinary human jealousy, envy and ill-will. Those can reach out
for you anywhere."

"Who hates you so much, then?"

"It's a long story." The powerful, ringing voice was suddenly
dark with hatred. "I have a neighbor . . . an evil, unforgiving
man who burned my properties, robbed me of my possessions,
killed a son of mine and, as you've just seen, hounds me even
here."

"Why don't you stop him, then?" The young man's careless
voice hardened with contempt. "Don't you wear a saber?"

Abdank's huge, swollen face flamed with sudden bitterness
and a gloomy light burned darkly in his eyes.

"Oh yes. I have a saber," he ground out a curse. "And, so God
help me from now on, that's what I'll use to get some justice
against my enemies."

★   ★   ★

The young lieutenant wanted to say something more; he
opened his mouth and raised a finger to underscore a point that
he wished to make, when suddenly the Steppe began to echo
with the hurried pounding of many horses' hooves. There was a
swift, urgent splashing among the tall, sodden grasses wet with
heavy dew, and then a sentry ran up to report new riders coming
out of the wilderness towards the encampment on the mound.

"That will be my lot," Abdank looked up quickly. "I left
them behind the Tasmina, not expecting any treachery. We were
to meet here."

A moment later a troop of horsemen surrounded the hillock.
The firelight played on the bowed heads of the horses whose
flared nostrils were snorting with fatigue. The animals had been
ridden hard and over some distance. The horsemen leaned
forward in their saddles, shielding their eyes with their hands,
and peered into the light.

"Hey people! Hey there! Who are you?" Abdank shouted to
them.

"God's children," soft sing-song voices called out from the
darkness in Ruthenian.

"They're mine." The Cossack colonel nodded. "Come on then! Come on up here!"

The Cossacks leaped out of their saddles and came swiftly uphill towards the fire.

"Ay, how we hurried, Little Father. How we hurried. How is it with you, *Batko?*"

"There was an ambush. Hvedko, the traitor, knew the place and waited with some others. They got a noose around me."

"The son of a bitch!" Fierce curses crackled out in the chilly air. "The plague on him, then! But who's that little Polack over there beside you?" They used the Ruthenian word which carried at least as much respect as derision. "What's the '*Lah*' doing here?"

The Steppe rovers stared like hungry wolves at Pan Yan and his troopers, their wolfish faces black and red in the light of the fire.

"They're all good men, good soldiers," Abdank reassured them. "By their help and God's mercy I'm alive and well."

"God's mercy, then!" the Cossacks called out. "God's will be done!"

They crowded forward then, and massed around the fire, rubbing their chilled hands and stamping booted feet on the ground to warm them. The night was clear but cold. An acrid stench of sweat, tallow grease and tired animals came from the men and horses who clustered on the mound, and Pan Yan stared curiously at the tall, heavy-shouldered riders and their small Steppe mustangs that had all but disappeared behind the billows of their own harshly steaming breath. Men and animals alike looked in that leaping firelight as if they'd been painted with alternating black and crimson stripes.

There were about forty men who came crowding up the hill to stare quietly at the Cossack colonel: rough, hard-eyed men armed to the teeth and wrapped in hides and furs. They didn't look at all like the enlisted Cossacks who served for pay in the Crown regiments of the Commonwealth commanders or in the private armies of the powerful Polish and Ruthenian magnates of the borderlands. There was a wild, untamed and challenging air about each of them, like that of wolves sniffing at fresh prey, and Pan Yan stared at them in surprise.

None of this, he thought, was quite what it seemed. There

were too many questions that remained unanswered. Why
would the Hetman assign such a powerful escort for a messenger to a friendly fortress? And if the Grand Hetman had,
indeed, sent this Abdank to Kudak he'd have given him an
escort of his household troops and not—as was clear at once to
Skshetuski's young but war-wise and experienced eyes—from
among freebooting Zaporohjan Cossacks who seldom enlisted
with the Colors anyway, having their own army.

And why order him to go by land from Tchehryn? Between
that river town and the old fortress on the lower Dnieper—the
last great bastion of the Commonwealth before the hostile,
southern wilderness and the permanent Cossack war camp of
the *Sietch*—lay a dozen tributary rivers, lakes and cataracts, all
of them at full flood in that unnaturally mild Winter and all to
be forded; it was a long and arduous journey full of dangers
each step of the way, and it began to seem to Pan Yan as if his
mysterious guest wanted to slip past Kudak unobserved rather
than go there.

But it was the man himself who poised the greatest question.
His Cossacks, who normally treated their various officers with
the coarse disrespect they showed to everybody else, stared at
him with such unnatural deference, and treated him with such
docile humility, as if he were indeed that powerful royal general—or '*Hetman*' as Crown commanders were known in those
days—whom he resembled with his authority and bearing.
Even now, Pan Yan noted with surprise, they were peering at
him with the dumb, worshipful loyalty and obedience of wolfhounds crouched at their master's heel.

This, he decided, had to be some great and famous warlord of
the Steppes, a legendary knight of immense renown, and that
was all the more astonishing for the young lieutenant because
he'd never heard of him anywhere before. He knew the Ukraine
on both banks of the Dnieper; he knew it because he was a part
of it, sensitive to all the pulses that beat in its soil and familiar
with all its legends and its turbulent traditions, but he had never
heard a single campfire whisper of this or any other Abdank.

There was, moreover, a strange and rare quality in the man's
stormy face, a poorly hidden sense of power pulsing like a
flame, along with all the tell-tale signs of an iron will and an
inner strength beyond anything that an ordinary man might
find in himself. Just such a natural aura of authority lay about

Prince Yeremi Vishnovyetzki, the almost royal despot of the eastern lands, but what that magnate carried in his person as an inborn talent, due to his birth and station and office and position, seemed quite astounding in a man whose name meant nothing and who rode alone at night in the Steppe.

Pan Yan thought hard and long.

It occurred to him that this could be some powerful '*banita*,' a high-born outlaw hounded by the courts, who may have taken refuge in the Wild Lands. There were many such. Or he could be the chief of some particularly fearsome band of Steppe marauders, but that was the least believable possibility. The way he spoke, dressed, moved and acted showed qualities impossible for a bandit, no matter how renowned.

Not knowing what to think, the young officer kept a watchful eye on his unusual guest and on his unnaturally meek followers as well, and in the meantime Abdank called for his horse and prepared to leave.

"Well, my young friend," he said. "It's time for me to be on my way. Once more, let me thank you for your help. God willing, someday I'll pay you back in kind."

"I rescued a stranger in the Steppe," the young man said simply. "I didn't do anything out of the ordinary to deserve your thanks."

"Don't be too modest," Abdank cautioned. "You may have done far more than you know. And now accept this ring."

He held out his hand again towards the young soldier but Pan Yan aimed another scornful look at him and at the large jewel glinting in his fingers and took a step backwards. Abdank smiled. He nodded as if he'd expected nothing else. Then his voice softened. It became paternal. And then once more he held out the ring.

"Look at it carefully." His voice was strangely sad. "It's not worth a fortune. But it has other virtues. As a young man captured by the Tartars, I got it from a pilgrim to the Holy Land. Dust from the tomb of Christ is locked behind this stone. No one would need to feel ashamed to take such a gift even if it came from the hands of a criminal. You're still young. You're a soldier. And if even an old man can never tell what might be waiting for him from one hour to the next, what about you with all those years ahead of you? And with your occupation? This ring may help you, my young friend, when Judgment Day comes to these Wild Lands again. And I am telling you that such a day is coming."

Then he was silent, nodding into his own distant thoughts, and the stillness seemed so endless and profound in that telling moment, that even the darkened Steppe seemed to hold its breath like something that was both alive and crouched in expectation. And then the wind picked up again, and all the horses neighed, and the flames shot up wildly among the hissing coals, while from the far canyons shrouded by the darkness came the mournful baying of the grey Steppe wolves.

"Yes. Judgment Day is coming," Abdank went on heavily as if speaking only to himself. "And when it comes . . . God help everything that lives."

Pan Yan took the ring and held it as if mesmerized, hearing this strange man's even stranger words long after the silence fell again. He watched, still wondering about him, as Abdank walked slowly to his dappled stallion, as he mounted, and then as he sat and stared far into the black Steppe where a soft rain had begun to fall.

"Ride!" the dark, glowering man shouted suddenly to his followers. And to Pan Yan he said: "Keep well. We live in such times that a man can't trust even his own brother."

"What do you mean by that?"

"I didn't tell you who I really am."

"So your name's not Abdank, then?"

"That's my clan calling and the name given to my coat of arms. You don't know whom you rescued."

"So what's your family name?"

"Bohdan Zenobius Hmyelnitzki."

Then the man spurred his horse down the slope, rode off the hillock and vanished in the darkness. His Cossacks formed up behind him and followed like a pack of hounds. Night swallowed them. The wind brought back stray snatches of the plaintive Steppe song that trailed behind them for a time. And then their voices dwindled and died away in the harsh swift air that swirled up suddenly from the gullies below the mound.

Chapter Two

NEXT MORNING Skshetuski led his troop into Tchehryn. They rode directly to Prince Yeremi's house, one of several small palaces that this great magnate kept in towns close to his own possessions, weary after their long, hard journey from the sea. At any other time they would have come by water, riding the river barges from the Isthmus of Perekop to Tchehryn, but that Winter no galley could make its way upriver through the flooded rapids of the lower Dnieper.

Skshetuski rested for part of the morning, then went to call on Pan Zachvilihovski, a former Commonwealth commissioner for the Ukraine and a famous soldier in his youth. Zachvilihovski did not serve the Prince but was his trusted confidant and friend. Pan Yan wanted to see if there were any new orders for him from the Prince at Lubnie, but the master of all the lands beyond the Dnieper had sent no new instructions. If the negotiations with the Tartar Khan had gone well, Skshetuski was to make his way to Lubnie by easy stages so as to spare unnecessary hardships to his men and horses. As for the Khan, what the prince demanded was punishment for certain Tartar *murjahs* who'd sent raiding *tchambuls* into the prince's Transdnieper territories, and whom he'd crushed and scattered anyway. The Khan had proved amiably inclined. He promised to send a special embassy to Lubnie in April, to give his *murjahs* painful proof of his displeasure with them and, anxious to placate the powerful border magnate, sent him a priceless robe of black and silver sables and a stallion of extraordinary beauty. Pan Yan had much to do with the success of that difficult assignment, which was proof in itself of Prince Yeremi's confidence in him, and was quite ready to cool his heels in Tchehryn for a while. But Pan Zachvilihovski felt far less confident about the times ahead. The old man knew all too well what terrifying forces were gathering in his beloved Ukraine. His grief and foreboding were difficult to bear.

They made their way to Dopul's, the tavern kept by an old Valachian in the angle of the town square known as the Bell Corners, where the local gentry gathered on market day. They got there early but the place was already packed with Tchehryn officials, freehold tenants of the powerful Konyetzpolskis whose territory this was, independent squires, minor Crown and local officeholders, a few manor bailiffs and a scattering of high-ranking Cossacks, who sat on benches drawn up to long oak tables that were stained almost black with the wine spilled on them through the years and rubbed as smooth as glass by innumerable elbows. All of them were talking about the greatest scandal to shake Tchehryn in years: the escape of Hmyelnitzki.

Pan Yan was immediately curious to hear more about it. "Who is this Hmyelnitzki?"

"Bohdan Hmyelnitzki holds the office of military secretary to the Zaporohjan Cossacks," the old man explained once they found seats for themselves in a quiet corner. "He owns a manor in Subotov and,"—he added in a lowered, cautious tone—"he's a distant kinsman of mine as well."

"So he's a nobleman?"

"As much as you and I."

"A soldier, is he?"

"It doesn't pay to say this out loud these days, but that man has a Hetman's head on his shoulders. Few of our leaders in the Commonwealth have his military skill and battle experience. The Cossacks trail after him like a pack of dogs."

"That's a dangerous influence for one man," Pan Skshetuski said and the old commissioner shrugged sadly and heaved a heavy sigh.

"They'd rather listen to him than to their own elected *atamans*. He has enormous talents and a first-rate mind. But he's also a ruthless, unforgiving man, proud as sin and restless as the wind, and when hatred grabs him by the hair he can be terrifying."

"Why did he have to run from Tchehryn?"

The old man shrugged again.

"Ah . . . the usual story. He and the local Sheriff hereabouts, *Starosta* Tchaplinski, have been poisoning each other's lives for years. It's not the first time this kind of thing has happened, nor the last, and there's nothing startling about it if you know our gentry. The story is that he had an eye for Tchaplinski's wife—a worthless, easy woman, any way you take her—but that didn't raise too many eyebrows either because he and she played about a bit before she married Tchaplinski. But the real trouble goes deeper than that. There's a lot more behind it than most people see."

"Such as what?"

"It's a serious business. What happened is that over in Tcherkassy, a day's ride from here, there lives an old retired Cossack colonel named Barabas, a good and faithful son of the Commonwealth, who had some letters from the King in which—as people tell it—the old King urged the Cossacks to stand up to the gentry and demand their rights. You can imagine what effect such urging would have among the Zaporohjans. It'd be enough to hurl another bloody rebellion on our heads."

"That it would," Skshetuski murmured, nodding.

"Well, Barabas is a good, decent and peace-loving man and he knows his Cossacks. He kept quiet about those letters and hid them away, but he didn't reckon with Hmyelnitzki! That man invited him here to Tchehryn for a night of drinking, got him soused as a boar and sent some men to Tcherkassy to steal the letters from the old man's house! God only knows what he intends to do with those inflammatory papers. And God only knows where he's vanished to."

"What a fox!" Pan Yan murmured and shook his head in wonder. "What a fool he made out of me last night."

"What? You met him, then?"

"Met him? I cut him off a rope's end in the Steppe."

"For God's sake!" The old man seized his head with both hands and his eyes bulged out. "What are you saying? That just can't be true!"

"It can and it is," the young man said quietly. "He told me he was a colonel under Prince Dominic Zaslavski, going to Kudak with letters from the Hetman. I didn't believe that part because he was traveling overland instead of taking boats. But I certainly fell for the rest of it."

"That man has the cunning of Ulysses," the old man muttered. "But where did this happen?"

"On the Omelnitchek, across the Dnieper on the Tartar side. It looks like he was heading for the *Sietch*."

"Yes, he'd want to slip past Kudak so that's the way he'd go. Ah, now everything is clear! Did he have many men with him?"

"About forty. But they came too late. If it hadn't been for my own men, your *Starosta's* hangmen would've had him dangling."

"Wait now," the old man interrupted. "Wait a minute. What's this about the *Starosta*? What's that about his men?"

"That's what Hmyelnitzki called the men who ambushed him."

"But how would Tchaplinski know where to look for him when everyone else in town is still scratching his head?"

"I couldn't say. Hmyelnitzki said something about somebody named Hvedko, does that ring any bells? Besides, he could've been lying about all his troubles with Tchaplinski to make his own cause sound a little stronger, couldn't he?"

"That I don't believe. But do you know that there are arrest warrants issued against that man by the Grand Hetman himself? He's to be caught and held for trial at all cost! My God, man, you could be charged as an accessory!"

★   ★   ★

But before the young lieutenant could think of an answer, the outer doors crashed open and a florid, violent-looking man strode into the tavern.

He slammed the door behind him, opened it and slammed it again to draw everyone's attention to himself, yelled out a greeting to the drinking gentry, and some reluctant voices rose in reply here and there. This was Tchaplinski, the Tchehryn *Starosta*, a servant and confidant of the Konyetzpolskis. Aged about forty at this time, he was a quarrelsome little man with large, protruding eyes that looked like ripe black plums ready to pop out of his choleric face. He had no friends in the town and many enemies because he was a crude, foul-tempered, grasping braggart and a petty tyrant whose persecutions of less influential people had few if any limits. But since the long reach of the Konyetzpolskis was even more to be feared than Tchaplinski's temper, some people thought it wise to be polite to him.

Pan Zachvilihovski called out to him and waved him over to their table. "Well," he asked, troubled but also wanting to needle the strutting little despot. "Is there anything new about Hmyelnitzki?"

"He hangs, dear brothers!" The *Starosta* laughed. "He hangs as surely as my name's Tchaplinski! And if he's not already feeding the crows somewhere he'll be doing it soon enough! Just let me get my hands on him now that the Hetman has issued his warrants!"

So saying, the protege of the Konyetzpolskis pounded the table with his fist. Some wine spilled out of the pewter goblets and splashed on the oak boards.

"Don't spill the wine," Pan Yan asked him calmly.

But Pan Zachvilihovski wasn't done with the crowing noble. "How do you know you'll catch him? Nobody knows where he's vanished to."

"Nobody, eh?" Pleased with himself, the self-important noble shouted, struck a pose, and glared about the room where everyone was listening. "I know, as my name's Tchaplinski! And how do I know? Well, you've heard of Hvedko, haven't you? Hvedko serves Hmyelnitzki but he serves me too! He'll be Hmyelnitzki's Judas! He knows everything that man's up to and he left Tchehryn ahead of Hmyelnitzki, knowing where to set a trap for that piece of carrion! Ha! What the devil! We'll have him dangling in no time!"

So saying, Tchaplinski brayed again and struck the table once more with his fist, spilling some more wine.

"Don't spill the wine," Pan Yan said evenly.

Tchaplinski's amber face flushed an angry crimson. He swung his bulging eyes at the young officer, ready to pick a quarrel, but the sight of the Vishnovyetzki uniform calmed him down a little. While the House of the Konyetzpolskis was none too friendly with the prince at Lubnie at this time, that fortress city lay too close to Tchehryn for anyone to risk offending him. Moreover, everyone in the Ukraine knew how carefully Prince Yeremi picked his men; it would be worth anybody's while to think twice before starting up a ruckus with an officer of the Vishnovyetzkis.

"So you think Hvedko will bring Hmyelnitzki to you?" the old man went on.

"He will, I tell you! He will! As my name's Tchaplinski!"

"And I tell you he won't. Hmyelnitzki is free. He got out of your trap and he's riding for the *Sietch* at this very moment! That's something the Grand Hetman ought to know at once because there's no fooling with that dreadful man, as you should remember."

"What? What? But how could that happen?"

"Did you ever hear about counting chickens before they are hatched?" Worried as he was about Hmyelnitzki's successful escape to the Zaporohjans, the old commissioner couldn't help seizing on one more chance to deflate Tchaplinski. "To put it bluntly, my dear *Starosta*, your would-be victim has sharper wits than you, a harder hand, and his luck's a lot better too, even though he doesn't bellow as loud as you do. And if you don't believe me, ask this officer who saw Hmyelnitzki safe and sound in the Steppe last night."

Tchaplinski seized his head in both hands, just as the old man had done only moments earlier. "That just can't be!" he howled. "It can't be!"

"Moreover," the old commissioner continued without mercy, "it was this young man who pulled him out of the clutches of your hired ruffians, slaughtered them like sheep, and sent him on his way. He didn't know about the Hetman's warrants since he'd been away on an embassy to the Khan. When he saw a lone man ambushed by a gang of cut-throats he did what any one of us would have done, so he can't be blamed. I tell you this only as a warning in case Hmyelnitzki pays you a little visit with his Zaporohjans. I've a feeling you wouldn't like it much."

But this was too much for the enraged *Starosta*. He threw all caution to the winds and leaped to his feet as if the tail of his coat had suddenly caught fire. His face ballooned. His mouth gaped and closed and opened again but no words emerged. Rage shook him, his face turned purple, and his bulging eyes looked as if they were about to fly out of his head. Up on his feet and swaying like a drunken man, he glared at Skshetuski, unable to spit out more than broken, disconnected phrases.

"What! Despite the warrants . . .! Despite the Hetman's orders . . .!"

The young lieutenant sat as quietly as if none of this splutter-

ing and shouting had anything to do with him. He rested his
elbows on the table, his chin on his fists, peering up at the
raging man with that deceptive calmness with which a hawk
studies a hopping sparrow. But when Tchaplinski went on
screaming and howling in his fury, Pan Yan finally stirred and
uttered a heavy sigh.

"Will you stop all this noise?" he asked reasonably. "You've
clamped yourself to me like a tick to a dog's tail. Let it be, go
away, and stop all that shouting."

But the enraged little braggart was now beyond all ability to
reason. "I'll . . . have you thrown in gaol!" he howled. "Like a
common felon! I'll . . . have you up on charges . . . in the
stocks! What! Despite the warrants . . .! I'll have my Cossacks
drag you by the heels!"

His yelling drowned out all other conversations in the room,
and the drinking gentry craned their necks across each other's
shoulders, anxious not to miss a word of what was going on.
There was nothing new about Tchaplinski's shouting; everyone
was accustomed to his brawls and bluster. But this time he was
challenging old Zachvilihovski of whom he'd always been secretly afraid and he had picked a quarrel with an officer of the
Vishnovyetzkis.

"Will you shut down all this bellowing and leave us in peace?"
Zachvilihovski asked. "This young man is my guest."

"I'll . . . you . . . to gaol . . .!" Tchaplinski choked and
spluttered. "On a chain . . .!"

But now Skshetuski had about as much as he could take of
the yells and insults.

He sighed again.

He rose to his feet.

He didn't draw his heavy military saber but reached down
and grasped it halfway down the scabbard and jerked it up so
that the iron hilt and cross-piece lay right under the *Starosta's*
nose.

"Take a whiff of that," he said dangerously.

"Murder! Assassin! Cut him down!" Tchaplinski howled and
clutched at his own saber, but before he could haul the weapon
out of its ornamental sheath, the young lieutenant twisted him
around, grasped him by the neck and the seat of his breeches,
lifted him overhead and carried him to the door while he gasped
and leaped about like a netted carp.

"Room for the buck, gentlemen," the young man called out. "Make room for the buck! Watch out for his horns!"

He hit the door open with Tchaplinski's body and tossed him out into the street. Then he walked back to the corner table where he'd started from and sat down quietly beside Zachvilihovski.

A long, hushed stillness settled on the room. The drinking gentry put down their mugs and cups and stared in disbelief first at each other, then at Pan Yan, and then at the broken door that hung askew on one of its hinges. Then eyes began to bulge all around the room, and mouths fell open in astonishment. No one seemed able to believe what they had just seen. No one had ever treated Tchaplinski in that fashion. And then their broad, silk sashes started to jump and quiver, and the flushed faces reddened even deeper and the great bellies shook, and they began to laugh. The laughter grew and spread and became a helpless, uncontrollable roar that boomed against the ceiling, and cries of "*Long live the Vishnovyetzki men!*" echoed through the tavern. Only a small group of Tchaplinski's cronies kept quiet at their tables and peered at the lieutenant with cold, gloomy eyes.

★ ★ ★

Old Pan Zachvilihovski laughed and laughed until tears were flowing down his weathered face.

"Ah, that Tchaplinski . . ."

"A mongrel dog!" a hoarse new voice bellowed from the crowd and a fat, bald knight came up to their table. One of his eyes was glazed over with the white film of blindness, and naked bone shined like yellow ivory through a round hole, the size of an imperial thaler, that gaped in his forehead.

"A yowling whelp, I say! Allow me, sir," he went on, bowing to Skshetuski. "My compliments to you. I am Yan Zagloba! My family crest is known as '*In-the-forehead*,' which anyone can tell by looking at this proof of martyrdom I wear. A bandit's bullet did that to me while I was on a pilgrimage to the Holy Land to make amends for the sins of my hot-blooded youth."

"Come now, Zagloba," chided Zachvilihovski. "You've told me that you had that hole knocked out with a beer mug in Radom."

"A bandit's bullet, as I live! That Radom business was something altogether different."

"Well," the old man said, laughing. "You may have had a stray thought about a pilgrimage but it's certain you never went on one."

"True, true." The fat noble nodded and went on as naturally and smoothly as if no one had challenged the truth of his story. "But that was only because I'd already earned my martyrdom among the Turks where the Sultan allowed himself certain gross indignities against me. Call me a prince of mongrels if I'm lying! To your good health, lieutenant!"

Meanwhile a crowd of others had followed Zagloba to Skshetuski's table, to shake his hand and clink their copper mugs against his. Tchaplinski was so universally detested that, as the gentry said, it was a joy to see him brought down so low. It was, perhaps a sign of those stormy and impatient times, hard to imagine in a later telling, that all the turbulent gentry of the region sided with Hmyelnitzki in his quarrels with the Tchehryn *Starosta*. Besides, everyone knew that the King in Warsaw thought well of him and valued his advice. As for his wrangling and feuding with the detested Sheriff, no one attached any more importance to it than they would to any of the thousands of similar petty hatreds, jealousies, brawls and squabbles that were as common in all the eastern territories as thistles in the fields.

And so the laughing gentry marched to Pan Yan's table with their cups and goblets and the wine flowed by the cask and flagon. The laughter boomed in the hot, crowded room as sweating, beaded foreheads gleamed and began to steam, and no one could foresee in all this blustering, buffoonery and shouting, and in the carefree clatter of the drinking cups, the terrible years that were on their way, already gathering like a storm cloud in the Wild Lands.

Pan Zagloba, who was always ready to outdrink and outshout the entire Commonwealth if he wasn't paying for his own refreshment, proved to be the thirstiest and the loudest of them all.

"Gentlemen!" he bellowed until the windows rang. "I've sent a summons to the Sultan! I'm taking him to court for his crimes against me while I was in his hands at Galata!"

"What's that? A summons?"

"As I live and breathe!"

"More lies! You'll fray your mouth with them!"

"What? You don't believe me?" Pleased to be the center of

attention, the fat knight turned to Latin which the gentry used as the language of law and erudition. "Listen then: '*Quator articuli judicii castrensis: stuprum, incendium, latrocinium et vis armata aedibus illata.*' And isn't what the Sultan did to me a clear case of *vis armata*? I'll sue his last minaret out of him!"

This brought another howl of laughter from everyone around.

"Oh . . . that's enough, enough!" the reeling nobles cried through their helpless tears.

"And I'll win the case!" Pan Zagloba bellowed. "And he'll be posted an outlaw, stripped of his name and substance! And then we'll go to war with him with a clear conscience!"

"To your good health!" the gentry cried and drank.

Heads, hands and broad shoulders quivered. Bellies shook with laughter. Tears went on flowing down the fierce, mustached faces, and still more wine splashed into brass and copper, and the clash and rattle of the drinking cups sounded like a battle.

★ ★ ★

Skshetuski laughed no less than the others, especially since his own eyes were starting to slip out of focus, while the fat noble harangued them, boasted, threatened invisible enemies and appealed for justice: much like a gobbling woodcock enchanted by the sound of his own voice. But then a new figure appeared at Zagloba's side, a gentle hand tugged at his sleeve, and a soft, sing-song Lithuanian voice asked for an introduction to the young lieutenant.

"Certainly! This is Pan Povsinoga," the fat knight boomed out, making a joke out of the other's name since '*Povsinoga*' meant a lazy lay-about, unworthy of notice.

"Podbipyenta," corrected the other.

"It makes no difference! His armorial bearings are known as '*Skirtlifter!*'"

"Cowlsnatcher," the newcomer corrected.

"It makes no difference! He comes from some place called Psyekishki, which in a more civilized language, like our own, means '*Guts of a Dog!*'"

"Myshykishki," corrected the other while everyone howled at Zagloba's exploitation of this play on words since, in translation, the odd Lithuanian name of the new arrival's hometown properties made reference to the intestinal track of mice.

"And that's even less of a difference, if you need one!" Zagloba rolled his eyes in mock disgust. "I don't know which set of animal guts I'd less like to live in. In the first place it's hard to stay put for any length of time in either one of them and, in the second place, the exits aren't exactly scenic. But I've been drinking this man's wine for a solid week and I can testify that his purse is as heavy as that monstrous sword he's got stuck behind his belt, and the sword is as heavy, and possibly as dull, as his wits! Anyway, if I've ever had my drinking bills paid by a greater freak I'll let you all call me as big a fool as the man who's been taking care of my thirst."

"That's gratitude for you!" roared the laughing gentry.

But the Lithuanian took no offense. He only closed his eyes, shook his head and smiled his helpless smile. "Ah, what a terrible man this is," he murmured. "It's a shame to listen . . ."

But Pan Yan stared in open wonder at this new arrival who, indeed, deserved to be called something of a freak. So tall that his head brushed against the ceiling, he was cadaverously thin, and his gaunt body made him seem even taller than he was. Huge shoulders and a thickly corded neck suggested great strength but, for the rest, he seemed to consist of little more than leathery skin stretched over meatless bones. His sunken belly had fallen so deep under his bulging ribcage that he looked like the corpse of a man who had been starved to death and left to dry out under a desert sun. Tight-sleeved, form-fitting clothes and a pair of thigh-high Swedish boots added to the impression of height and emaciation, but if he ever suffered any hunger pangs it was clearly by choice rather than necessity. A wide, well-stuffed elkskin belt dangled on his hips for lack of firmer anchorage further up his body and an enormous sword protruded from behind this costly leatherwork. Broad as a man's hand, the blade was so long that its iron grip was partly hidden in the giant's armpit. Not in two hundred years had such a weapon been in common use; it was one of those huge two-handed swords, almost two yards long, which the Teutonic Knights had brought into Prussia, a murderous tool made infamous in history by the armored monks of the Germanic Order.

But if the frightful weapon caused alarm, its owner's gentle face calmed even the most nervous dispositions. Caved in and hollow-eyed around its high cheekbones, it was festooned with great drooping eyebrows and a foot-long moustache, as soft and pale as cotton before spinning, that dangled all the way down to his chest. Comical in its trusting, childlike innocence, it was the face of a man who couldn't hurt a fly; the downswept bushy eyebrows and the dangling moustache gave him a mournful air but in that face this seemed no more than a caricature of sadness. At first glance he seemed to be a man who went through life like a dry leaf propelled by every wind, and driven by events which always surprised him, but Pan Yan liked him at once none the less. There was such transparent honesty in that unusual face, such infinite patience, kindness and good humor, that they'd melt the stone heart of a caryatid, the young lieutenant thought.

"And are you really with Prince Yeremi, sir?" this gentle apparition asked in its lilting accent.

"Yes I am."

The Lithuanian pressed his palms together and raised his eyes to the ceiling as if he were praying. "Ah, what a warrior! What a knight! What a great commander!"

Proud of his master, Pan Yan was pleased to hear him praised in public. "Our Commonwealth could use many like him."

"That it could! But tell me . . . do you think someone like me could enlist with him? Do you think there's a chance of that?"

"I think he'd be glad to have you," Pan Skshetuski said.

But here Zagloba butted in again.

"He'd be delighted! That would give him two roasting-spits for his kitchen. He'd turn you into one and that mile of iron you've got in your armpit into another! Or he might make an executioner out of you, or use you for a gibbet on which to hang horsethieves, or he could lay you out like a yardstick to cut cloth for blankets! '*Tfui!*' What the devil! Aren't you ashamed, as both a Christian and a human being, to be as long as a serpent or a heathen's spear?"

But the tall knight didn't take offense. He merely stuck his fingers in his ears and smiled his patient smile.

"Ah, it's a shame to listen . . ."

Skshetuski laughed, then asked the Lithuanian to introduce himself again. "You did it once, I know, but Pan Zagloba harassed you so much that I couldn't make out a word of it."

"I'm Podbipyenta," said the gentle knight.

"*Povsinoga!*" Zagloba shouted as before.

"From Myshykishki . . ."

"The village of 'Dog's Guts'! His calling is *Skirtlifter*!"

"Cowlsnatcher," corrected the tall knight.

"All heathen names. One's worse than the other."

"And how long have you been traveling?" Skshetuski was intrigued by everything connected with the gentle giant.

"Ah, I've been in Tchehryn for two Sundays now. Pan Zachvilihovski told me you'd be passing through. And so I waited, hoping I could ask you to speak for me to Prince Yeremi . . . and maybe go to Lubnie."

Dim light ran along the blade of the Lithuanian's sword which made the gaunt giant's shank look as if it were sheathed in steel and Skshetuski stared at it with interest.

"A dreadful looking weapon" he said. "Why do you carry such a thing?"

"It's an old battle trophy. It's been in my family for two hundred years," the giant said softly. "I wear it to honor an ancestor and, if God wills it, to fulfill a vow."

"Looks heavy. It must be for two hands?"

"Could be for two. Could be for one . . ."

"Could I try it, then?"

The Lithuanian drew the huge blade and handed it over but Pan Yan's hand dropped at once under its great weight. He put all his strength into the effort to lift the massive weapon, and felt the blood mounting to his head and the veins swelling on his neck as he heaved and strained. The sword rose slowly, an inch at a time. He managed at last to raise it overhead and hold it with one hand, but that was all; to cut, thrust or parry, or to wheel it about his shoulders, was out of the question. Redfaced and gasping, he asked if any other man among the watching gentry could strike a clean blow.

"We've tried! We've all tried!" several voices called. "Only the old commissioner can get it off the ground but even he can't do anything with it."

"A monstrous weapon," Skshetuski agreed and returned the sword to the Lithuanian who caught it up as lightly as if it were a reed, cut, parried, thrust and twirled it like a fencing foil until the air whirred in the silent room and a cold wind fanned the faces of the watching men.

"The devil take you," cried the young lieutenant. "You're as good as wearing the Prince's uniform right now!"

"God grant it," the Lithuanian sighed. "At least my sword won't rust in his service."

"But your wits will," Zagloba put in quickly. "Since you can't make them fly like that piece of iron."

★　★　★

Then Pan Zachvilihovski rose and took his leave of the celebrating gentry. Both he and Skshetuski were halfway to the door when it creaked open, and a bowed old man, gnarled as an ancient tree stump and white as a dove, came into the tavern and raised both his arms towards Zachvilihovski with a childlike smile.

"I've looked for you everywhere," he murmured. "Could we talk somewhere?"

"Of course," Zachvilihovski said. "Come with us to my rooms. There's so much smoke and hot air in here that you can't see your hand in front of your face."

Introduced, the old man proved to be Barabas, the old commander of the Tcherkassy Cossacks, whom age had hollowed out like one of those great white forest oaks that stand and wait for the next wind to come and throw them to the ground. In times past great storms had broken over them, Pan Yan thought, watching the proud old man, but their days were done.

Out in the street, Barabas asked at once if there was any news about Hmyelnitzki but for some time Zachvilihovski couldn't answer him. They were engulfed by crowds. The whole town seemed filled to overflowing as they pushed their way through the jostling mass. Moreover, the huge cattle herds driven to the camps of the Grand Hetman's army at Korsun were passing through Tchehryn that day, so that the narrow streets were jammed with savage herdsmen and drovers who looked even wilder than the beasts they herded, while less alarming people took shelter behind shuttered windows and barred doors.

When they reached some clear space, Zachvilihovski nodded to Barabas. "He's gone to the *Sietch*. This officer met him in the Steppe last night."

"Ah, so he didn't take the Dnieper boats," the old Cossack groaned in a despairing tone. "I sent word to Kudak to warn them about him . . . .. But if he's in the Steppe, then that's all for nothing . . ." And the old Cossack colonel grasped his head and muttered in a breaking voice: "*Chryste*, have mercy. Have mercy . . ."

"Is it those letters that worry you so much?"

"You know what they are! You know what will happen if they're read out to the Zaporohjans! God help us if the King doesn't call us all together this year and lead us against the Turks."

"Then you expect rebellion?"

"Expect it?" The old man's reddened eyes were sunk deep in grief. "I already see it. Hmyelnitzki can do more than all the other rebels even dreamed about."

"But who'll follow him?"

"Who? All of the Zaporohjans . . . the *Nijh* and the *Sietch* . . . the runaway peasants, serfs . . . the enlisted Cossacks, those wild restless masses that fret on the land . . . And,"—he pointed a trembling hand at the vast, dark crowds that choked the street around them—"and all of this too!"

It seemed at first as if the old Cossack was talking about the bellowing mass of lean, grey cattle which filled the town square and its thoroughfares from one side to the other. They were wild, red-eyed beasts: scarred and murderous, with long, swinging horns. Running beside them was a howling mob of half-wild *tchabany*, the Steppe herdsmen who spent their whole lives in the wilderness. They were nightmare figures in tangled sheepskins torn open to the waist, more wolflike than the animals themselves. Men without need for faith or consciousness of law, Pan Yan thought. Wild creatures that lived without any human instincts other than primitive survival. Their naked chests, indifferent to the seasons, were scorched black by Steppe winds, stained by the smoke of a thousand campfires, and glistening with tallow grease that they smeared all over themselves to keep off the horseflies. Each of them carried either a horn-bow and a Tartar arrow-case slung across his back, a butcher knife and firelock, a Turkish scimitar, a rusty saber, a scythe with the great curved blade set with its point upward like a spear, or a long pole with the gaping jawbone of a horse nailed to its top. Among them moved the slant-eyed Cossacks of the Lower *Nijh*, no less menacing and much better armed, who were hauling their bales of smoked fish and game and slabs of cured mutton to the Hetman's army.

It was market day and Tchehryn had filled up with harsh,

bearded figures which brought barrels of wild honey from the
forest clearings; lone settlers who lived hidden from the world
in the ghostly canyons and ravines beyond the Tchertomelik—
that dark, rocky stream that people called '*The Devil's
Gristmill*'—and strange snarling creatures who could no longer
speak a recognizable language and who had long lost any sim-
ilarity to other human beings.

There were pitchmakers from beyond the dark borders of
civilization; and silent, bearlike creatures bent under loads of
wild bees' wax, tallow and coarse grey salt; and dour peasants
driving remount horses. Then came long sullen waves of enlisted Cossacks trooping to the army; Belgorod Tartars with
flickering, hungry eyes and teeth that gleamed like the fangs of
wolves at the sight of trade-goods that the Tchehryn merchants
hastily locked away; and every other kind of rootless rabble,
accustomed to bloodshed and quite indifferent to the thought of
dying, who were ready to become marauders, pillagers, murderers and looters at the first sign of war. They were, Pan Yan
thought, like a gathering of vultures waiting for spilled blood.

"*Uh-ha!*" they howled and hooted. "*Uh-ha!*"

Vodka splashed out of open barrels in which dancing Cossacks dipped their steaming heads and other nightmare shapes
reeled about in alcoholic frenzy. Huge bonfires burned in the
streets and in the town square where whole carcasses roasted on
the spits, and flaming casks of pitch cast a lurid glow on the
shuttered windows. The scarlet shadows of reflected fires that
leaped about along the tiled rooftops made it seem as if the town
was already burning. Nothing seemed human in that savage
mass, wild as a storm at sea. Its sound was crazed laughter, the
bellowing of slaughtered animals, and wild howls and brays
that would have been more natural if they'd come from wolves.
In all that frightful chaos, shrill Tartar whistles piped a hellish
music while blind men, the wandering soothsayers of the
Ukraine, kept time for mournful Cossack ditties with their
lyres, fiddles and rattles made out of hollow bones.

★   ★   ★

One glance at this scene was enough to tell that a single
inflammatory spark thrown on this powder keg would turn the
Ukraine into a funeral pyre and let loose a holocaust of murder
such as the country had never seen before.

And behind these mobs stood the armed, regimented brotherhoods of freebooting Cossacks who lived along the *Nijh*, and
all of the Zaporohjan *Sietch* which had been beaten down only
recently into an uneasy, muttering submission. The terrible
Cossack risings were crushed one after another but the embers
of revolt were always ready to flare up again. Hating restraint
and the landed gentry which, more than any punishment for
their bloody risings, stripped them of their ancient Cossack
privileges, the armed freebooters of the Steppe needed only a
single, charismatic leader who could articulate and express their
longings and whom they could follow.

What did these people want? Young as he was, Skshetuski
understood why the Cossacks dreamed of the gentry's privileges, guaranteed to everyone who had the right to bear arms,
and to own property in exchange for military service, by the
Articles of the Union which had turned the Polish Kingdom
and the Grand Duchy of Lithuania into a united Republic of the
Gentry.

But the eastern gentry of the Commonwealth, the native
Ruthenians right along with the Poles and the Lithuanians,
looked at the Cossacks as little more than truculent, jumped-up
serfs, useful in war but peasants none the less, while the real
landless peasantry of the Ukraine were no less bitter and impatient than the rebellious Cossacks. Elsewhere in the world, they
might have been docile and resigned to their hopeless lives; here
all they had to do was glance beyond the Tchertomelik to see no
masters, no indentured labor, and to smell heaps of loot. They'd
beat their scythes into spears and their hoes into battleaxes at the
first sign of the gentry's weakness.

Knowing all this, and feeling it around him all the more
because he loved his Ukraine like a devoted son, the old commissioner didn't have much to say as Pan Yan and Barabas
followed him to his home. Dark thoughts tormented him, and
Pan Yan knew better than to interrupt them. As an old *Rusin* of
the Eastern Lands, as much a Ruthenian as almost everybody
else in those territories including Prince Yeremi, the old commissioner remembered the bloody times of Nalevayko, Loboda
and Kremski who had roused the Cossacks and then died,
impaled, among the slaughtered thousands they had led. He
knew the horror of the Ukraine in a fratricidal war. He also
knew that where the others failed, being little more than mur-

derous, infuriated serfs driven beyond endurance, Hmyelnitzki
could succeed. That gloomy, restless genius of the Steppes was
worth a hundred Nalevaykos and Lobodas, especially if he came
to these seething masses with royal letters that urged them to
resist the gentry.

★ ★ ★

The two old soldiers and Pan Yan walked in worried silence
to Zachvilihovski's simple quarters at the edge of town. But
once there, with a demijohn of aged mead on the table, the old
commissioner's natural optimism returned.

"Well," he said. "It could all blow over, there's still a little
time. If, as it's rumored, the King will go to war with the Sultan
in the Spring, then all this anger could turn against the Turks.
Whatever happens here it won't be tomorrow, so let's see what
we can do about it. Old friend,"—and here he nodded gently at
the Cossack colonel—"why don't you go to the *Sietch* and try to
dampen all those fires for a while? The Cossacks respect you.
You could do something to counteract Hmyelnitzki's influence
among them."

But the snowy-haired old man only shook his head. His voice
was bleak and dark with resignation.

"Influence? Respect? I'll just say this much: at the first rumor
that Hmyelnitzki had gone to the *Sietch* half my Tcherkassy
men deserted me last night. What can I say to the Cossacks any
more? I'm an old man. My times are long over. It makes more
sense for me to think about the grave than about horsetail
standards and *bulavas.*"

Zachvilihovski nodded. He wouldn't press the old man who,
he knew, could no longer control anyone. But, he thought
bitterly, it was with just such men that the Warsaw statesmen
tried to rule the Cossacks whom, in turn, they used as a check
against their own ungovernable gentry.

"Well," he said. "I'll go to Korsun. I'll tell the Grand Hetman
what is happening here and beg him to move a few regular
regiments a little closer to us. I don't know if it'll do much
good, our proud Pan Mikolai Pototzki doesn't take kindly to
anyone's advice, but it's worth a try. You, colonel, do your best
to restrain our own local Cossacks. And you, lieutenant, warn
Prince Yeremi to keep his eyes on the *Sietch.* Oh yes, I know, the
Sietch is empty at this time of the year and the '*Sitchovtzy*' have

scattered after fish and game. A lot of water will go down the Dnieper before they gather together again from their winter quarters in the villages. But the Prince's name has a terrifying sound in the Zaporohje. When they find out that he's watching them they might quieten down."

"I can leave for Lubnie anytime," Skshetuski said.

"Good. The sooner the better." Then, without looking at old Barabas, the commissioner said: "And you, colonel, send a fast word to Pan Konyetzpolski and Prince Dominic . . ."

But the old Cossack was nodding in his sleep with his head dangling on his chest and his hands cradled on his belly. After a while he began to snore.

"Look now," Zachvilihovski murmured. "It's such hands as these that are supposed to hold back an ocean of fire. Our statesmen in Warsaw trusted Hmyelnitzki too."

"Why would they need to?" the young soldier asked. "The Cossacks make good fighting men but we have plenty of our own."

"You were at Dopul's with me," Zachvilihovski said in explanation. "You know about our gentry, what they're like. We are both the glory and despair of the Commonwealth, my friend. All those bickerings and quarrels, those endless petty diets and convocations, parliaments and squabbles . . . Yes, we elect our monarchs. They rule through the Diet. We make royal absolutism impossible in this land but we also make it impossible to govern the country. Think of our 'golden freedoms' and *liberum veto* with which any one of eight hundred thousand men like Tchaplinski, Zagloba and even Hmyelnitzki can kill any measure proposed in the Diet just by saying '*No!*' Strong rule in Warsaw is seen by such people as a greater threat to their rights and privileges than any rebellion. And the royal ministers see the Cossacks as a counter force with which to balance the power of the gentry."

Thoughtful and silent for a moment, he roused himself as if from a dream and went on: "Who is right and who's wrong? And is this the time to ask about such things? Each of us must make his own decisions according to his conscience and yours will do as well for you as anything I might say."

Shaken, Pan Yan agreed. Barabas snored on. Through his half-open lips came a groaning whisper: "*Spasi, Chryste . . .* mercy . . . Have mercy, Christ . . . have mercy . . .*"

* * *

Night came soon after and it was time for the young man to leave. He needed sleep. He was depressed and worried. The sky above Tchehryn glowed scarlet from the open fires as if the whole town was in flames and dying after pillage; an omen or a vision of the future, Pan Yan thought, call it what you will. The sounds of savage celebrations sharpened as the night grew darker. The *tchaban* mobs howled their mournful ditties, drunk Zaporohjans leaped among the barrels, tearing the night apart with wild pistol shots and ragged musket fire and hurling their caps into the lurid sky, and sprawled-out bodies—some drunk and some dead—littered the cobblestones.

Skshetuski felt exhausted and unwell. Not even his normally cheerful and lighthearted spirits could come to his aid; even the natural ebullience of his youth was useless against the dark and threatening thoughts that settled on him like a flock of ravens. He forced his way through the mobs by using his sheathed saber like a cudgel and thought: '*That's what it'll look like. That's how it'll sound. This is the face and voice of the rebellion.*"

He thought that he could see menacing glances, full of savage hatred, caught out of the corners of his eyes. He thought he heard half-stifled, muttered curses as he passed the crowds, and in his ears rang the hopeless, helpless "*Spasi, Chryste . . . spasi*" of the aged Barabas.

He went on, trying to clear terrifying images from his mind while the Cossacks howled, danced and immersed themselves from head to heel in the liquor barrels. The rattle of musketry and the roar of the *tchaban* mobs followed him to his cot. He lay a long time without sleep, quite sure that what he heard flooding through his windows was the voice of the inevitable future.

Chapter Three

SKSHETUSKI AND HIS MEN rode out towards Lubnie before the week ended. They crossed the Dnieper and took the broad, Steppe highway that ran from Tchehryn to Prince Yeremi's chief city and then continued on to Khorol, Zhuki and the other towns of Vishnovyetzki's vast Transdnieper country. Another such road ran northwest from Lubnie all the way to Kiev.

It was only within recent years that this rich countryside, now as productive as it once was deadly, had started to change. The smoke of village chimneys, the gilded cupolas of churches, and the white walls of steeples, monasteries, manors and small towns, broke through the black paling of the forests on the borders of an arid wilderness where, only yesterday it seemed, smoke stood for rape and murder and a gleam of whiteness could only mean bleached bones dragged about by wolves.

Settlement took uneasy, cautious root in these enormous spaces rich in fish and game and swarming with birds. It took time to fill the woods with clearings, and for the clearings to fill up with people. But now four hundred water wheels and countless windmills ground maize and corn flour where only Tartar arrows used to fly. Forty thousand tenants worked to tame this black, blood-soaked soil safe behind the iron backs of Prince Yeremi's soldiers.

The Prince's country began just beyond Tchehryn and stretched as far as Konotop and Romne, a territory broader than the British Isles; it was a land of forests, lakes and fields that stretched from one invisible horizon to the other. Uncounted herds of mustangs, tamed horses and cattle grazed in what had been a wilderness as terrible as the nearby Steppe. Great bears, bearded aurochs, bison, boar, antelope and deer still roamed the woods freely but the roving Cossack watched his step in those territories, and the Tartar '*beys*' sniffed the winds a long time along the Orel and the Vorskla Rivers before they dared to send their *tchambuls* raiding to the west. The nameless, rootless raiders and marauders who were so much more terrifying than any animal or Tartar, were either dead on sharpened stakes and gibbets or rotting in the deep, stone dungeons under Lubnie Castle, or they'd been turned into the country's best and fiercest protectors and defenders, brought to heel like a pack of wolf-hounds and chained by iron military discipline under the Prince's standards.

Skshetuski rode cheerfully enough in this familiar country which still held some menace here and there but was no longer deadly. In places the land was somnolent, untouched by plow and axe and dreaming in the undisturbed seclusion of a thousand years. Elsewhere it crouched in the shadows of ancient burial mounds and hillocks which the winds had piled over the ruins of long-forgotten towns which hadn't even left a legend behind them, but the young officer had happier matters on his mind. He had done well in the Crimea and a warm welcome waited for him from the Prince in Lubnie, but he anticipated yet another welcome from the bright eyes of Anusia Krasienska, one of the young ladies-in-waiting of Princess Grizelda.

It didn't worry Pan Yan that Anusia, who flirted mercilessly with every officer at the Prince's court, would send warm smiles to Pan Byhovietz of the Prince's Light Tartar Regiment, to glum Pan Vurtzel of the Cannoneers, to little Pan Volodyovski of the Red Dragoons and even to old Pan Baranovski of Skshetuski's own armored *Husaria*. That was her way and it was innocent enough since Princess Grizelda kept her women under a discipline as strict as that of her husband's soldiers. What mattered to that cunning little creature was that every man at the court of Lubnie claimed to be mortally in love with her, and sighed, and rolled his eyes at her, and sang ballads under her window and fought harmless duels. Pan Yan himself had crossed swords with little Pan Michal Volodyovski over her, which neither damaged their great friendship nor improved either young man's chances with Anusia. Still, Pan Yan had been away a long time, and there she would be, eager to reclaim her hold on his heart which had never been too serious in the first place. It was a good homecoming to look forward to.

The young lieutenant grinned and sang songs, wheeling his horse in the high Steppe road beside the mournful, plodding Courland mare of Pan Longinus Podbipyenta who had joined him in Tchehryn with his own troop of armed grooms and lackeys. Now the Lithuanian giant rode with his drooping mustache and dangling Teuton sword beside Pan Yan's spirited Tartar gelding. Behind them rolled the carts and carriages of Lord Rozvan Ursu, ambassador to the Court of Lubnie from the Valachian Hospodar, who had attached himself to Skshetuski's caravan for safety. This gentleman was now snoring in one of his wagons and the two knights rode alone.

"How many men does the Prince have under arms?" the gentle Lithuanian was anxious to know.

"About eight thousand, not counting the Cossack companies in the border forts and guarding the herds. But Zachvilihovski told me in Tchehryn that new levies have started."

"Ah! Then perhaps there'll be a new campaign under His Highness soon?"

"So they say. There's to be a great war against the Turks in Spring. The King and all the power of the Commonwealth are to march this time. I know this much, the annual gifts to the Crimean Khan have been held back this year and the Tartars are shaking in their boots. It's common knowledge among them that when the King and the Hetmans move against the Turks, the Prince is to storm the Crimea and wipe them off the face of the earth. It's certain that no one else would be able to do it."

Pan Longinus raised both his arms and eyes piously to the sky.

"Oh, do you really think so? Oh God, make it true!"

Pan Yan laughed. "Are you that bloodthirsty?"

"Good friend, it's not my thirst that bothers me and it's not blood I'm after. But there's a certain vow I have to fulfill."

"A vow?" Skshetuski broke in, laughing. "You certainly are a knight in the classic manner."

"Classic or not," the tall knight said sadly, "only a certain deed can free me from that promise."

And again the gaunt giant heaved a heavy sigh and his mustache quivered, and his long drooping brows bunched together in such a show of weighty desperation that they looked as if they were about to slide down on his nose.

"Tell me about this vow," Pan Yan urged, curious about the man as well as his story.

"I'll keep no secrets from you," Pan Longinus said. "As you know, my crest and clan are both named '*Cowlsnatcher*,' and that's because at the battle of Grunwald, where King Vladyslav Yagiello broke the Teutonic Order two hundred years ago, an ancestor of mine, Stoveyko Podbipyenta, killed three German knights with one blow of his sword. They rode at him side by side, you see, and he swung his sword . . . and . . . ah . . . beheaded them."

"I see that your ancestor had a hand as heavy as yours," Pan Yan prompted. "But what about the vow?"

"It's all a part of it," the sad giant sighed. "The King gave my ancestor his knighthood and a crest: three goats' heads on a silver field, since each of the beheaded Germans had such a goat painted on his shield. That crest, together with this sword of mine, has been passed down from one generation to another in my family. Each generation has tried to add to the family's good name and to the reputation of our sword."

"Hmm. Very commendable," Pan Yan said. "But where does the vow come in?"

"Well, you see, I've tried to outdo all the others," the sad giant confessed. "I am, you see, the last of my clan, and I vowed to the Holy Mother in the church at Troki to live in innocence, never to touch a woman or to marry, until she allowed me to match ancestor Stoveyko and let me take three heads at one blow. Merciful God, what didn't I do! I've lived like a monk although I have a naturally warm and eager nature. I sought out wars! I fought! But with no luck at all."

"No three heads?" The young lieutenant grinned.

"Never!" cried the giant. "The Blessed Lady never let it happen. Two at a time, yes, often enough . . . but never those three! Either I couldn't make the right approach or the enemy didn't ride close enough together . . ."

"Well, it's hard to ask them to line up properly and hold still," Pan Yan said and grinned. "I mean in the heat of a battle and all that."

"God sees my troubles!" Pan Longinus went on mournfully

while Skshetuski averted his face to conceal his laughter. "There is strength to spare in my bones, there's enough ardor to start a dozen families, there's property and reasonable wealth . . . everything that might appeal to a warmhearted woman! But *adolescencia* is drifting away, my fortieth year is coming, the heart longs for something warmer than a saddle and the three heads are as elusive as ever. That's the kind of Cowlsnatcher I turned out to be; a butt for jokes and laughter, as Pan Zagloba says."

The Lithuanian sighed again, this time with such a depth of feeling, that his great mare shuddered and heaved an immense sigh of her own as if in sympathy with her master.

"Well," Pan Yan said. "All I can tell you is that if you don't find your opportunity under Prince Yeremi, you won't find it at all."

"I know it," Pan Longinus said. "That's why I'm coming with you, to beg the Prince to take me into his service and give me my chance."

★ ★ ★

They rode in silence after that—Pan Yan biting the ends of his mustache to keep himself from laughing, the mournful giant heaving thunderous sighs—when a great beating of wings tore through the air above them.

In that warm Winter the birds hadn't flown across the seas. The rivers didn't freeze so that each stretch of water, spilled wide by the rains and whatever snow there had been to melt, was as thick with bird life as if it were Spring. The two knights had ridden up to the glittering sheet of the Kahamlik and a great flock of cranes soared upward before them, wings beating and long beaks held high.

"They fly as if something was after them," Skshetuski remarked and the Lithuanian pointed to a small white bird that slanted through the sun-streaked air under the rising cranes. "A falcon! He won't let them settle. The ambassador has falcons. He must have loosed that one."

Rozvan Ursu galloped up just then on an Anatolian gelding with his falconer behind him.

"Come hunting, gentlemen!" he called out.

They spurred their horses forward. The falconer leaned back in his saddle, eyes fixed on the falcon, encouraging the bird with

shrill cries. The falcon shot under the cranes to force them away
from the protecting reeds and undergrowth of the riverbank,
then climbed high over them and hung suspended like a glittering white star. The cranes huddled closer so that their great
wings seemed to brush each other. They raised their beaks,
screaming at measured intervals, and waited for the small raptor
to dive down on them, but the white bird circled on stiff wings,
wafted up and down by the air currents, while under him a
hundred sharp beaks rose like a hedge of spears.

And then the falcon's wings whirred and he darted away from
the river and the cranes with the speed of a bolt shot out of a
crossbow and fell like a bright stone beyond the dark tree
crowns where the road took a turn.

Pan Yan spurred his horse and leaped after him, and the
others followed wildly down the road among the reaching
branches, and rounded the bend, and there the young lieutenant
hauled back on the reins. In the middle of the highway lay an
overturned *kolaska* with a broken axle, and two Cossack lads
held a pair of horses at the side of the road, and beyond them
stood two women in hooded fur robes. One, with fox furs
draped on her rawboned frame, and with a coarse, imperious
face and thick, manlike features, was shouting at the Cossacks.
The other stood silent. She was looking up at the young soldier
from under a soft hood trimmed with otter— half frightened
and half surprised—while the falcon sat in quiet contentment on
her shoulder, smoothing down his ruffled feathers with his
beak.

Pan Yan pulled up his horse in mid-stride and the animal slid
forward on all four hooves in a cloud of dust. It stood trembling, and the young soldier sat without a word, his hand at his
cap, as if turned to stone. The small, gentle face that lifted
towards him from under the girl's hood held him mesmerized,
as if he'd been immobilized by a spell.

He thought that he was looking at a painting, not a living
woman, because he had never seen a face as beautiful as this one:
framed in black braided hair, dark-eyed and delicate, with lips
parted in wonder and startled as a doe.

And so he sat, confused like a schoolboy, his hastily bared
head as useless as an empty barrel. He knew that he should say
something—a greeting of some kind. Or he could ask to have
the falcon back. But no words came. He was about to blurt out

something anyway when Rozvan Ursu and Pan Podbipyenta arrived in their own showers of gravel and dust.

The girl raised her hand to her shoulder and the falcon stepped on it readily enough and then Skshetuski came to life and leaped down from his saddle. He was before her in two strides, and bowing to the ground, and then the bird reached out with one spurred, cruel set of talons and caught the young man's hand and drew it to the girl's.

'An omen,' Pan Yan thought with a sense of astonishment and wonder.

He felt as if a regiment of ants had started marching up and down his spine when his hand touched the girl's. The falcon held his fingers tightly on those of the young woman, its small head tilted and uttering shrill cries, and it was only when the falconer ran up with an iron hoop and hooded the bird that the talons opened and Pan Yan's empty fist fell back to his side.

He shook his head to clear it but that didn't help. He'd have stood like that indefinitely, he supposed, but then the older woman spoke—loud and commanding, more like a dragoon than a gentlewoman—and shattered the spell.

"Whoever you are," she said harshly. "And wherever you've come from, give us a hand here. You see what's happened to us. I've sent the coachman home for help but night will come before my sons can get a fresh wagon sent to us and this is a cursed place. There are old graves around here. Burial mounds. It's sure death to be alone here after dark."

Startled by her coarse voice and unwieldy phrases, Pan Yan bowed none the less. "You can count on us, my lady. I don't have wagons but his lordship the ambassador does. I'm sure he'll put one at your service."

Rozvan Ursu took off his sable cap and stepped up at once with a courtly compliment and moments later his falconer was galloping back towards the wagons which they'd left far behind them in the chase.

Pan Yan remained transfixed.

He couldn't take his eyes off the young woman in the otter hood who seemed more like a figure lifted straight out of Greek mythology than a girl who might live in one of those crude fortress manors of the Ruthenian gentry which always re-minded the young soldier of armories and barracks on the eve of siege. His temples pounded and his chest seemed ready to explode. He stared at her, aware of a need and hunger he had never known, while she shot one shy, quick glance at him, met his eyes head-on, and looked away, disturbed.

Meanwhile the old woman went on thanking them for their providential help and invited them, with effusive roughness, to break their journey at her home. She was, she said with a touch of pride, the widow of *Knaz* Kurtzevitch-Bulyhov, one of those warrior princes of old Ruthenia, not to be compared, to be sure, with the magnate princes like the Vishnovyetzkis but, for all that, noble enough in that rough-hewn country. The girl, she said, was not her daughter but the orphan of her husband's brother. She and her sons held the manor of Rozloghi, known as '*Rozloghi-of-the-Wolves*' because of the huge packs of timber wolves that ran through their land. Her sons were at home, back from a raid in the Tartar lands on the lower Dnieper. She and the girl had been to Tcherkassy on a visit.

"On our way back . . . well, you see what happened," she went on, coarse and loud, and yet with a sly watchful undertone as if each word was carefully calculated to give the impression of rough simplicity. "We'd have had to spend the night in this evil place if God hadn't sent you."

Her husband's name, revered by soldiers throughout the Ukraine, astonished Pan Yan who found it difficult to reconcile it with her coarse-grained manner. But when he asked if she was the widow of Prince Vasil Kurtzevitch, she snapped at him like a she-wolf.

"No! I was the wife of Constantine, his brother." And she flicked her hand carelessly at the silent girl. "That's Vasil's daughter, Helen."

"We honor *Knaz* Vasil's memory in Lubnie," Pan Yan said at once. "He was a great soldier."

But if this speech was calculated to please the old woman it fell short of the mark. Her face flushed with anger and her small eyes narrowed with suspicion.

"I don't know what people talk about in Lubnie," she said flintily. "And I don't know what kind of a soldier he was. As to his infamy later on, that's known well enough!"

Skshetuski closed his mouth, even more astonished by her cruelty. The silent girl stood with cast-down eyes, so pale that her skin had the transparency of alabaster, and he saw the bright gleam of tears breaking out under the long fringe of her black eyelashes.

"*Knaz* Vasil was the victim of a terrible injustice," he said quietly. "Condemned on perjured evidence to loss of life and honor, he had to save himself by flight. When his innocence was proved beyond doubt many years later, he was restored to his own good name which nobody who knew him ever questioned anyway. And if this restoration came too late to make amends for all his suffering that adds to his credit."

The old *Knahina's* eyes bored into him like a pair of lances and her mouth trembled with a bitter answer, but there was so much quiet strength and dignity in the young soldier's face, and his voice rang with such sincerity, that she bit back whatever she wanted to say.

Instead, she turned angrily on the girl. "That's not for you to hear," she snapped out. "Go and look after the bundles in the wagon."

"And I'll walk with you," Pan Yan said.

★　★　★

It didn't seem at first that they'd be able to say anything to each other even when they were well out of the others' hearing. Skshetuski kept quiet, wondering what was going on. He was badly shaken by the old woman's vehemence and by the girl's tears. There was something about the old *Knahina* and her brutal treatment of this girl that he simply didn't understand. The girl was also silent. They reached the overturned carriage and stood beside it with the open door like a fence between them before the girl's eyes locked on his and a smile of great warmth, and as bright as the sun, lighted up her face, and he was totally astonished when she asked what she could do to thank him.

"For what?"

"You took my father's part," she said with so much joy and wonder in her voice, and with such wealth of feeling, that he felt as if he were about to soar into the sky like the falcon that had drawn her hand into his. "You stood up for him against those who should be the kindest to his memory but who malign him worse than anyone."

"I'd gladly jump through fire for you," he heard himself

saying. "Gladly . . . with all my heart!" But his attention was
focused entirely on her voice. She seemed to be speaking to him
across a great distance but he didn't mind. He thought that he
was hearing gentle flutes and lyres, as if the sound of music in
her voice mattered more to him just then than what she was
saying.

But she looked startled.

"If simple thanks aren't enough," she voiced an anxious fear,
"I've nothing else with which to show I'm grateful."

"Not enough?" Pan Yan could hardly believe his ears.
"They're worth much more to me than I can ever earn. But let
me really earn them! Let me serve you! Then such words as
'thanks' may make some sense between us."

The young woman stared at him intently for a silent moment
and then blood rushed into her cheeks and she turned away.

"You'd find only misfortune in such service," she murmured,
staring at the ground.

But the young soldier leaned forward across the open carriage
door and said in a voice that was both firm and gentle: "I'll find
what I'll find. That's for God to say. But even if it is to be some
kind of misfortune, I'm ready to go down on my knees and to
beg you for it."

Her eyes searched his and continued searching, wide but no
longer fearful, but when she spoke it was to voice a doubt.

"It can't be . . . that having only just met me . . . you'd be so
anxious for this service . . ."

But Pan Yan knew that he had never felt more certain of
anything in his life.

"I knew from the moment I set eyes on you that nothing else
could ever mean anything to me," he said and knew that he was
telling her exactly what he felt. "Whatever I've wanted out of
life ceased to be important. It just doesn't matter anymore. I
knew right then that I was no longer a free man, but if that's
God's will, so be it. I didn't ask for any kind of love, didn't look
for it; but here it is, like a Tartar arrow shot out of an ambush,
and that's all there's to it. I tell you, though, if someone told me
yesterday that that's how it happens I wouldn't have believed
him."

The doubt in her voice had been replaced by wonder. "But if
you, yourself wouldn't have believed it yesterday, then . . ."

"You can't believe it today, is that what you mean? Let time prove it to you. As to whether I mean what I say, just look at me!" The young lieutenant felt as if his passion for her and commitment to her were written across his forehead with letters of fire. "Surely you can see it?"

The girl's long lashes rose again and she looked into the open, honest eyes of the fierce Steppe soldier, and she saw so much love in them, and such a wealth of undisguised devotion, that her cheeks flushed as scarlet as a poppy but she no longer turned her face away. And so they stood for a long time, saying nothing, and looking at each other like two lost, wandering strangers meeting in the Steppe who know that they've met a kindred soul at last and that the rest of their journey would be no longer lonely.

Then the sharp, angry cry of the old *Knahina* shook Helen out of this quiet enchantment. The envoy's carts and wagons had arrived. Helen and the old woman climbed into Lord Rozvan's comfortable carriage. The men mounted horses and the convoy started out again.

$$\star \quad \star \quad \star$$

The day ended slowly. The wide-spilled waters of the Kahamlik caught the red rays of the disappearing sun, and the white clouds, now edged in gold and scarlet, settled to rest in the darkening corners of the sky.

Skshetuski rode next to the window on Helen's side of the coach but he said nothing to her. He couldn't speak to her in front of the others the way he'd spoken when they were alone and any other words would have been a sham. The cavalcade moved rapidly enough in the quiet, evening light, with only the creak of the wheels, the snorting of the horses, and an occasional rattle of a scabbard against stirrup irons breaking into the stillness of the falling night. Lord Rozvan Ursu's mounted archers at the rear of the column took up a soft, melodious song of the Valachian plains but it soon died away. Pan Longinus intoned the evening prayer and they all joined in until the light sunk and dwindled behind the trees and the river.

They entered a deep forest. But no sooner had the dark crowns of giant oaks closed over them, blotting out the starlight, when the pounding of hurrying hooves echoed ahead of them and five riders, followed by a light Cossack wagon drawn by four horses, galloped into view.

"Is that you, lads?" the old *Knahina* boomed out like a sentry and the riders pulled their mounts to a hard stop around the coach.

"It's us, mother!"

"God bless you then! But I don't need your help thanks to these good knights here. These,"—she went on in clumsy introduction—"are my sons. Symeon, Yur, Andrei and that's Mikolai . . . and who's the fifth one there? Ey, if my old eyes can still see at night, is that Bohun? Eh?"

But at the sound of this name, the girl pressed herself deep into the cushions of the envoy's coach.

"Greetings to you, *Knahina*. And to you, Princess Helen," the fifth rider said and the old woman looked at him with undisguised affection.

"Bohun, you Steppe hawk! Here from your regiment, are you? Welcome as always! Here lads," she ordered harshly, "I've asked these good men to spend the night with us in Rozloghi, and now you ask them too. Welcome them, I tell you!"

The four young princes bared their heads at once as if they were peasants and began to bow repeatedly in the Cossack manner.

"We humbly beg you into our poor home," they boomed in rough chorus.

"Well, let's go on then!" the old woman ordered as the convoy moved forward once again, and then turned to Rozvan Ursu who rode by her window and went on in a bitter, whining voice: "It's been a long time since we've known fat comforts. There are still rich Kurtzevitch manors in Volhynia and in Lithuania and there they keep retainers and live like great lords. But they forget about their poor relations, which God will note when they stand before Him. Ey, it's a lean Cossack life with us, my gentlemen, as you'll see. But we'll do our poor, humble best to make you feel welcome under our roof. My five sons and I hold just the one pitiful village and a few small pastures, and then there's this girl on our hands to add to our troubles."

She went on complaining about her poverty and Pan Yan's astonishment continued to grow. He'd heard in Lubnie that Rozloghi was a rich estate; *Knaz* Vasil had worked hard to wrest his lands and forests from the wilderness. All of this lower country belonged to Helen's father to whom it had been granted by the Vishnovyetzkis. But Pan Yan couldn't think of an inoffensive way to ask how it had passed to Constantine's widow.

"So you have five sons, dear lady?" the envoy inquired.

"I had five. Like lions, they were, every one of them. But the oldest, Vasil, had his eyes put out when the Tartars took him and his mind cracked from the suffering. Now when the other lads leave home I'm left alone with him and this girl who's more hindrance than help to anyone."

There was so much scorn, anger and ill-will in her grating voice that Pan Yan felt a fury of his own stirring in his chest and a curse trembled at the tip of his tongue. But before he could spit it out he caught sight of Helen's face, pale and wet with tears in the moon's cold light.

"What is it?" he asked quietly. "Why are you crying?"

But she didn't answer.

"I can't stand your tears," he went on and dipped his head towards Helen's window; then, seeing that the *Knahina* was preoccupied in talk with Rozvan Ursu, he began to plead with Helen to tell him what to do to make her less unhappy.

But suddenly he felt a horse and rider crowding into him, pressing so close that the two horses brushed against each other, and when he jerked back and looked around he saw two eyes, luminous with moonlight, staring at him in challenge.

'*What the devil!*' he thought, more surprised than angry, and peered through the darkness into the face of the crowding rider which was little more than a blurred shadow in the night around them. The gleaming eyes, however, bright as the eyes of wolves, fixed themselves to his own face like leeches.

"What do you want?" he snapped but the silent rider only pressed him harder. "If it's lonely for you in the dark, fellow, strike a light! And if the road's too narrow, get off it!"

"And you fly away from that window, little bird," the other rider's voice drawled softly in Ruthenian.

Blood surged at once into Skshetuski's face, rage jerked him by the hair and he kicked the Cossack's horse hard under the ribs. The animal groaned and leaped aside and then stood shivering at the roadside while its rider struggled to keep it from falling, and it seemed for one quick, moonlit moment that he'd hurl himself like a lynx at the young soldier's throat. Then the *Knahina* shouted in her sharp, commanding voice: "Bohun! *Scho s'toboyu?*"

The dark horseman wheeled his mount at once and crossed the road to the *Knahina's* window in a single bound where she went on chiding him hoarsely in Ruthenian.

"*Scho s'toboyu*? What's the matter with you? You're not in your Pereyaslav now, nor in the Crimea! You're in Rozloghi, so watch yourself, you hear? Now ride ahead and lead the way through the canyon. Go now, you devil, ride!"

The Cossack spurred his horse without a word and vanished in the darkness where the forest fell away at the mouth of a deep gorge littered with fallen trees and boulders.

"A madman," she muttered.

It was clear to Skshetuski that the young Cossack wanted to pick a quarrel with him which, in those times, meant bloodshed, and he wondered why since they'd never met anywhere before. Helen, he thought, could be a part of this, and when he looked at her he knew that he was right. She had become as pale as if she were ill and her eyes were wide with terror and filled with revulsion.

"Is this some hired Cossack servant of your sons?" he asked the old woman, to show his contempt for his challenger as well as the challenge, and then watched as she threw herself against the backrest of the carriage seat, slack-mouthed with amazement.

"What are you saying?" she cried out. "That's Bohun! A man as famous as the Ukraine is wide! He's like a brother to my sons and a sixth son to me. It can't be that you haven't heard of him!"

It went without saying that Pan Yan knew all about this famous Steppe darling of the minstrels whose exploits made him a legend of recklessness and courage on both sides of the Dnieper. No one knew who he really was, or where he had come from, but he lived like a man created for danger. He gloried in war, according to the ballads that were sung about him from one end of the Ukraine to the other. As wild as the Steppe winds, he'd listen by the hour to the wandering blind folk-singers before showering them with gold, but no one knew what he wanted out of life, what drove him or where he was going, even though his name rang louder among the people than those of any other famous Steppe commander; and all his warriors, who were just as dedicated to loot and Cossack glory as he was himself, would follow him to Hell if that's where he led them.

Pan Yan thought carefully about all this, remembering the challenge in the gleaming eyes, and felt his heart beat faster in anticipation. It wasn't Bohun's way to let such matters drop, and not his own either. He'd have gladly spurred his horse after the young colonel of Pereyaslav Cossacks but nothing could have made him leave Helen's side that night. And then the winding, narrow valley floor rose into the forest, and the forest parted, and the yellow lights of the Rozloghi village appeared in the distance.

The night had cooled.

The convoy rolled out of the forest into a broad clearing and Pan Yan took his eyes off Helen's face long enough to see the dark looming mass of the Kurtzevitch manor. It was more a fortress than a home, as he knew it would be, and he wondered about Helen's life in such a primitive, coarse setting, and he swore to himself that he would take her out of it as soon as he could.

The carts, coaches, wagons and horses clattered across a wooden bridge dropped over a broad defensive ditch, past a tall palisade of sharpened stakes and a loopholed earthwall, and then between a pair of massive gates hewn out of whole oaks. Then they were in the *maydan*—a treeless, grassless space trodden down like a military drill ground—and moving past two creaking wells and a row of stables, past wooden barracks for Cossack men-at-arms and sheds for manor servants, past the forge, the wash-house and the storehouse, and then along a row of barns and granaries where a tame captive bear watched them from a cartwheel nailed to the top of an upright tree trunk.

The main house was a low, sprawling, single-storey structure built out of massive timbers locked into each other, whose windows were only a little wider than a musketeer's loophole.

The guests entered the house through a narrow door and stood, looking about with curiosity, around a great hall where entire pine trees burned in two giant fireplaces. Their crimson light lit up rows of armor, spears, breastplates, Turkish *yataghans* and daggers glittering with jewels, Polish and Tartar sabers, helmets, shirts-of-mail, bundles of ermine pelts and deep piles of wolf and otter robes. Rows of hooded hawks, falcons and giant Berkut eagles used for hunting wolves slept along each wall on their iron hoops.

Beyond this hall was an even larger chamber where they stood bemused while yet another fireplace cast its light into the brilliant prisms of Venetian crystal, cut glass, sterling goblets and crested gold plate heaped and scattered along a plain trestle table, pewter and copper candelabra, brass-studded chests, carved oriental boxes thrown carelessly on mounds of Persian carpets, silk pillows piled on rough-hewn deal benches, and priceless damasks, cloth-of-gold and woven tapestries nailed to bare planks. It was a curious blend of primitive savagery and barbaric splendor.

Looking at it, Skshetuski was reminded of the dark young Cossack who had challenged him. '*A whirlwind,*' he thought, '*ready for anything*' . . .

But then, he thought, so was he himself.

★ ★ ★

But if Pan Yan wondered about Bohun that night so did the *Knahina*. She was a shrewd old woman, cunning as a she-wolf when it came to looking after her young and getting what she wanted, and the sudden blaze of anger that had flared up between the two young men didn't escape her notice. She had good reasons to be careful of them both; each could be either an ally or a threat to her calculations, and each, in his special way, was important to her.

And so no sooner had the convoy rolled into the *maydan* than she summoned the young Cossack to her.

"Listen to me," she said. "I don't have much time. I saw you sharpening your teeth at that young officer."

"Ay, *maty*," the young Cossack said softly and bent to kiss the old woman's hand.

"Where do you know him from? What's he done to you?"

"The world is wide, *maty*," the young Cossack murmured. "He has his roads, I have mine. I've never seen him anywhere before, never heard of him . . ."

"Then what's the matter with you?"

"Don't let him come near the girl, *matushka*," the young Cossack said. His voice was low and gentle but the unspoken threat hung clearly on his words. "Don't let him look at her like a hungry hawk or I'll strike a light for him with a saber that'll shine for him all the way to Hell."

"What?" The old *Knahina* threw herself into a tall-backed chair. "You'll do what, you wild Cossack hothead? Do you want us dead? That's *Yarema's* man, and an officer at that! They sent him with letters to the Khan so he counts for something with the Prince in Lubnie. Let just one hair fall off his head under this roof and d'you know the next thing that'll happen?

The Prince will turn his eyes on us, avenge his death, scatter us to the four winds and take Helen back into his own house! What will you do then, you miserable soul? Make war on *Yarema*? Will you storm his Lubnie? Try it, why don't you, if you want a taste of the stake!"

"Ey, the heart aches for her, *maty*," the young Cossack sighed. "The soul's crying for her."

"Oh you doomed Cossack spirit!" the old woman cried. "So a young noble looks at a girl, so what? Let him look! He'll be gone tomorrow and there'll be no harm done. Step in his way and you'll bury us in rubble and ashes and lose Helen as surely as if she was dead."

The Cossack bit his lips and gnawed his mustache ends and groaned and tugged at his thick black hair with both hands, but he knew that the *Knahina* was right, and there was nothing he could do about it if he was to get from her what he had been promised.

"Alright, *maty*," he said. "They'll be gone tomorrow. I'll hold myself on short reins till then. But don't let the girl come out to them tonight."

"Not have her come out? So they'll think she's imprisoned here? So *Yarema* can remember that she's his ward and that his father gave Rozloghi to Vasil, not to us? She'll come out because I say she will! That's the way I want it! You don't give the orders in this house, my lad!"

"Ay, don't be angry, *Knahina*."

The Cossack knelt and pressed his hot, dark forehead to the old woman's hand.

"I'll be as sweet to them as Turkish sugarbread if that's how it's got to be. I won't grind a tooth . . . won't touch a knife even if anger burns out all my feelings. Ah, let the soul burn! Let it burn! I'll do as you want."

"That's the way to speak, my young falcon. Bite down on your grief. Swallow your suffering. Take up your lyre, play a little, ease your soul a bit. And remember what we promised you."

"A Cossack's word is more than smoke, *maty*," Bohun said and sighed. "I'll hold out."

"You'll hold out, falcon. All the pains end when the illness passes. And now come with me to the guests."

They left the old woman's room together and entered the rich chamber where the guests were waiting.

Chapter Four

THE OLD *KNAHINA'S* GUESTS waited in the great hall, as amazed by the careless profusion of treasures heaped everywhere around them as if they had stumbled upon a prince's ransom piled in rooms no better than a stable. Pan Yan was less surprised. He was used to the rough, homespun ways of the borderland's old Ruthenian gentry, but the Valachian envoy and the Lithuanian giant stared about as if unable to believe their eyes.

Skshetuski's sharp glance focused at once on Bohun, searching for a challenge, but the Steppe raider's face beamed with such open friendliness that the most experienced eye would have been deceived. The young lieutenant was especially curious about this Cossack hero because his exploits had become a byword in the Ukraine, and so he watched him carefully, assessing what he saw.

And what he saw was a slim, young, dark-complexioned man with finely chiseled features, a high forehead and thick black hair combed down in jagged wisps above curving eyebrows. His strong white teeth gleamed with every smile. He had dressed himself with special care in brocades and velvets which, next to the *Knahina's* sons in their coarse sheepskin jackets and untanned leather boots, made him look like a high-born magnate among stable hands. But all his finery, including the rich cloth-of-silver undercoat and the crimson *kontush* of the Pereyaslav Cossacks, paled beside the dazzling Turkish dagger thrust into his sash; the golden sheath and handle of this costly weapon were so thickly studded with precious stones that they seemed to scatter sparks of multicolored fire.

Then, having listened politely to Pan Longinus' story about

ancestor Stoveyko, the Cossack hero turned to Skshetuski with
a pleasant smile.

"You've been to the Khan, I hear?"

"Yes," said Pan Yan, his voice dry.

"I've been among the Tartars myself a few times." The Cossack's voice was soft with remembered moments of violence
and danger. "Maybe I never got as far as the Khan's palace," he
grinned like a wolf, "but even that might happen if the news we
hear turns out to be true."

"And what news is that?"

"What people say about a war in Spring. All the Ukraine is
talking about it . . . Ey,"—and the young Cossack laughed with
savage pleasure—"if we don't get to dance a little in the Khan's
seraglio, what with the Great Prince leading us, we'll never get
to do it!"

"We'll do it!" the old *Knahina's* sons growled out in rough
chorus.

Pan Yan smiled. There was such admiration for Prince Yeremi
in the Cossack's words that it quite won him over and his own
voice lost its guarded chill.

"I see that even your great fame isn't enough for you," he
said.

The Cossack shrugged.

"Small wars, small glory," he said. "Knighthoods aren't
earned in longboats raiding down the Dnieper."

Pan Yan was about to answer but at that moment the inner
doors of the chamber were flung wide and Helen entered leading the blinded Vasil, the oldest of the *Knahina's* sons. He came
in gently as a child, so pale and thin and with such intense
suffering stamped into his tortured face that he seemed more
like a Byzantine icon than a living man. Two raw, red holes
gaped where his eyes had been, his long white hair drifted to his
shoulders, and in his hands he carried a brass crucifix with
which he blessed the four corners of the room.

"In the name of the Father, the Spirit, and the Holy Virgin,"
he cried out. "Welcome to you if you're the apostles. Welcome if
you bring the good news of His second coming."

"Don't pay any attention to him," the old *Knahina* muttered
but the gaunt, martyred figure turned its red sockets on each
guest in turn.

"As it was written . . . '*Those who shed their blood for the true faith shall be saved,'"* he chanted. "'*Those who seek only to enrich themselves shall be doomed!*' Pray for God's mercy, brothers! Woe to us! Woe to me! We made war for booty and profit! Save us, oh Father! Be merciful, oh God! And you, travelers, what news do you bring us? Are you the apostles come to announce His return among us?"

He held his head twisted to one side as if listening to voices that only he could hear and Pan Yan was the first to break the spell of horror that settled like a dark pall on the gathering.

"It's a long way for us to such exalted station," he said gently. "We are simple soldiers. But we're ready to die for the Faith whenever God wills it."

"Then you'll be saved!" the blind man cried out. "But the hour of salvation is not yet at hand . . . Woe to you brothers, woe to all of us . . .!"

His ending words rang out with such despair that the visitors didn't know where to turn their eyes. In the meantime Helen helped the blind prince to a bench, struck a chord on the lute she had brought and began to sing. The blind man listened with his head thrown back and his empty sockets glaring at the ceiling. His face began to lose its stricken look of terror. At last his head slumped forward and hung on his chest. He sat without moving, half asleep and half in a trance, lost in the dark corridors of his ruined mind, and Helen went on singing gently and with pity. She seemed so beautiful and fragile beside the gaunt wreckage of the mad blind prince—her eyes half-closed, the lute in her arms— that Pan Yan couldn't take his eyes off her. He felt his heart expanding in his chest, letting himself become quite lost in her beauty, and then the old *Knahina's* sharp voice cut into his thoughts.

"That's enough! He'll sleep now. Let's go in to dinner."

Rozvan Ursu offered her his arm with a courtly bow and Pan Yan moved swiftly to Helen with his own hand extended and when he felt her fingers resting on his arm everything inside him trembled as if ten hearts were pounding in his chest.

"You sing so beautifully," he murmured, "that even the angels must be envious. I think I'd gladly have my own eyes put out if I could hear such singing every day. But what am I saying? If I was blind I'd be unable to see you! And that would be real suffering."

Her smile was sad. It was as if she wanted to believe him but didn't think she should.

"You'll ride away tomorrow and in a week you'll forget us all . . ."

"I won't forget!"

He caught sight of Bohun's face as if through a mist. The sharp, swarthy features had turned as white and twisted as a winding-sheet but Skshetuski didn't give a thought to what that might mean.

"I've fallen so completely in love with you," he said "that I don't even want to know any other feeling."

She started to say something; her lips parted, blood mounted to her face, her breast moved. But no words came just then and Pan Yan went on in a teasing manner: "Ah, it's more likely that you'll forget about *me* with that splendid Cossack near you."

"Never!" Her whisper was full of loathing and a desperate terror. "But you . . . take care, guard yourself! That's a terrible man."

He laughed again. He felt as if he'd been lifted above the company, free and soaring in a sunlit air where nothing could touch him.

"Ah, what does some Cossack matter to me!" he said carelessly. "I'd dare anything for you even if he held the whole of the *Sietch* in the palm of his hand. There's just no life for me without you anymore."

"And none for me without you," the girl said softly but in the young soldier's ears the words sounded like a choir of angels. He felt then as if kettledrums were thundering in his chest, his eyes filled with new and sharper colors, and every sound grew magnified out of all proportion.

His feet were moving, he knew, as they walked to the table but he couldn't feel the hard oak planks under them; all he could think about was that Helen was sitting close to him. Her shoulder brushed and rested occasionally against his. He saw the rapid rise and fall of her breast, stared into her eyes—covered with lashes or, when she looked up at him, shining brighter than any Steppe stars he had ever seen—and watched a great joy flowing across her face.

Should he have been surprised? This was, after all, the daughter of a passionate People living in violent times; in her veins ran the hot blood of warriors who had mastered this untamed land across generations and who moved through life as if they carried fire in their souls. It would take only one warm ray of a man's love, he knew, to touch off the flames banked in her own heart, and so she shined beside him, and glowed with animation, and her face filled with courage and happiness and wonder.

Looking at her Pan Yan thought that at any moment he'd leap right out of his own skin. He drank by the quart but the mead had no effect on him. He had eyes for no one except Helen in that room. He didn't see the desperate, tortured mask of Bohun's bloodless face nor the trembling fingers that clawed at the Turkish dagger in the Cossack's sash. He didn't hear Pan Podbipyenta's third rendition of the Stoveyko story nor the young princes' accounts of their expeditions "after the Sultan's goods."

He hardly even noticed when the dinner ended and sleepy Cossack lads were turned out of their bedding to dance and to sing.

The four young princes threw themselves into a savage Zaporohjan dance, and the old *Knahina*, hands cocked on her hips, tapped her feet and trod the floorboards in place like a village girl; and Pan Yan caught Helen by the waist and whirled her around the room; and when her flying braids twisted themselves around his neck, and he felt her moving against him as if they were one he bent down and kissed her.

★   ★   ★

Night was already greying when the young soldier, alone with Pan Longinus in the room where they were to sleep, pressed his hot face against the window pane, too stirred and excited to think about sleeping.

"It'll be a different man who'll go with you to Lubnie tomorrow," he said finally.

Pan Longinus stared. "Why? Are you staying here?"

"No, but the best part of me will stay. What travels with you will be just a shell without a heart or soul."

"Ah, then you've fallen in love with the princess?"

"I have. And now I feel like a powder barrel that's been set on fire. I think I'm going to burst with all that joy inside me! I'm telling you all this because I think that you, with your own longings and hungers for affection, will know what I mean."

At once, as if on signal, Pan Longinus began to sigh and

groan to show that he was terribly familiar with all the pains of loving and then asked, in mournful expectation: "And did you also vow to live in innocence?"

"I did not!" Pan Yan grinned broadly and hugged the Lithuanian's shoulders. "If everyone made such a vow, my friend, the *genus humanum* wouldn't last much longer!"

The quiet knocking of a servant interrupted them and an old Tartar came into the room with a sharp, watchful gleam in his slanted eyes and a secretive smile on his wrinkled face. Moving past Skshetuski he murmured: "I've word for you from the Lady, master."

"You do! Quick with it then!" the young soldier shouted.

The Tartar drew a length of ribbon from his sleeve.

"The Lady sends you this token, master. She said to tell you she loves you with all her heart."

The young man grasped the ribbon with both hands as if it were an icon or a treasure and kissed it and pressed it to his chest while Pan Longinus sighed and raised his eyes mournfully to the ceiling.

The Tartar watched them both with a secret smile.

"Ha, so she said she loves me?" Pan Yan cried. "Is that what she said?"

"That she loves you, master. With all her heart."

"Is that what she said? Here's a gold-piece for you! So she said she loves me?"

"Yes, master."

"Here's another gold-piece! God bless her. Tell her . . . no, wait! I'll write to her myself. Bring me some ink and paper and sharpen some pens."

"What was that, master?"

"Quills, paper, ink!"

"There's no such thing in this house," the Tartar shrugged and said. "We had some under *Knaz* Vasil, and then later on when they had a monk from Kiev down here to try to teach the young princes how to write. But that was long ago."

Pan Yan snapped his fingers with impatience.

"What's to write anyway?" The Tartar grinned and squatted by the fire and blew on the coals. "The Lady's gone to bed. If anybody wants to tell her something he can do it tomorrow."

"You think so? You're a good man. Here's another gold-piece. How long have you been with her?"

"Ho, ho! It's been forty years since *Knaz* Vasil took me in the Steppe. I've served him from that time until he disappeared. Now I serve her."

"She must have been just a little girl when he rode away."

"A child. He came that night, pursued, and swore his brother on the cross to be a father to her, and then he said to me: *'Tchehly, never leave her side. Guard her like your own soul.'*"

"And you've done that for her?"

"I've done it."

"You've watched over her?"

"I've watched."

"And what do you see? How is it for her here?"

"Bad, master. It was good while *Knaz* Constantine was alive. But now it is bad. The old woman is no kin to her. They think badly of the Lady because they want to give her to Bohun who is a mad dog."

"Nothing will come of that!" the young soldier cried fiercely.

"That's what they want to do, though," the old Tartar said. "They want Bohun to carry her away into the Steppe and leave Rozloghi to them. Because this is her land, through *Knaz* Vasil, not theirs. And once she's gone nobody'll ever ask how they came by it."

"And Bohun doesn't want Rozloghi for himself?"

"He's a wild Steppe dog, what would he want with land? Besides, people say he's got more gold hidden in the bends of the Dnieper than there's sand in the *maydan* here. He just wants the Lady. And she fears him and can't stand to look at him from the time he killed a man right in front of her. Blood fell between them and hate grew. Allah willed it."

Hours later, long after the old Tartar left and Pan Longinus had fallen asleep, the young soldier paced the room in deep thought.

He stared at the moon, counted the pale Winter stars and wondered what to do; he made one plan after another and discarded each of them in turn. Now that he understood the *Knahina's* motives everything that had astonished him before became starkly clear. He could see why she had allowed her sons to grow up like wild Cossack mustangs—ignorant, illiterate and as primitive as peasants—more at home in the *Sietch* among the *Nijhovtsy* than in the company of civilized people. Lubnie lay near; she could have sent them to learn in the Prince's court or chancellery or under his standards, but she didn't dare. Because what would happen if the Prince suddenly remembered who was the real owner of their lands and which of the Bulyhov princes had got Rozloghi from his father Michal?

And what if the Prince asked for an accounting of their stewardship? What if he looked into the care given to the orphaned Helen?

There'd be nothing left for the savage widow and her hulking sons except empty pockets, the four winds blowing them about the world and the open Steppe as their only home; it was better for them to have everyone forget that they and Rozloghi had ever existed. And now the grown and beautiful Helen had become a threat because if any of the local gentry asked for her in marriage he'd ask for her property as well . . . Ah, but if the brilliant, young Cossack *vatashka* took her off into the vast, wild Steppe . . .

Pan Yan clenched his fists and clutched his saber at the thought. He knew that he could wreck the old *Knahina's* plans with one word at Lubnie but that wouldn't bring him closer to marrying Helen. He needed the old woman's consent as the law required and he knew that there was only one sure way to get it.

★   ★   ★

The roosters had already crowed before Skshetuski threw himself down on the sleeping robes. Exhausted, he slept hard, without dreaming, and when he got up he felt drawn but rested and at ease. He dressed rapidly. The Valachian envoy's wagons were already rumbling through the *maydan* and his own soldiers were mounted and waiting at the gate as he went in search of the old woman and her sons. His thoughts were orderly and calm when he confronted them in the hall of arms and he told them bluntly, without wasting words, that he wanted Helen.

"You . . . what?"

The old *Knahina* stared at him out of narrowed eyes. The young Bulyhovs stood peering at each other with their mouths ajar and he thought with contempt that the effect would have been the same if he had thrown a burning powder keg among them. They glared at him out of bulging eyes and shot quick, uncertain glances at their mother, and Pan Yan looked at them commandingly and sternly until the old woman finally found some words.

"How is that? You come . . . about Helen?"

"Yes."

A deep silence followed.

He could read the old woman's every thought in that telling moment, and he grew colder and more determined, knowing how she'd answer, and what he'd say in his own turn and how it would end. It was, he thought, as if he were a field commander standing on a height and watching all his troops deployed in the field before him, and the enemy's regiments massing to advance, and knowing exactly where the attack would come and how he would meet it and how and where he'd strike every counter blow.

But at last the *Knahina* got over the shock, although her voice was as dry as dust when she gave him the expected answer.

"Forgive us, sir," she hissed with mock civility. "You do us . . . a great honor. But Helen has been promised to another man."

He didn't voice either his loathing or contempt. If anything, his tone grew softer as if to match the old woman's carefully chosen phrases but both the threat and the mockery were clear in every word.

"Ah . . . but as a loving guardian, gracious lady, please consider whether this other man can make the princess happy, and whether she loves him. And also if his origins and position are high enough for the honor you are doing him."

"That's for me to judge," the *Knahina* snapped out, suddenly alert and aware that the young soldier knew more than he was supposed to. "We know him. We don't know anything about you!"

"But I know you, thieves and traitors," Skshetuski said softly. "You want to sell your own blood-kin to a peasant just so he'll let you live in your stolen house!"

"Traitor yourself!" the old woman shrilled, crouching like a she-wolf and ready to spring. "Viper! Dog! Is that how you pay for our hospitality?"

The four young princes began to growl and mutter, and to rub their hands nervously along their flanks, and they threw quick glances at the arms and armor hanging on the walls, but Pan Yan stood as still and unconcerned about them as if they weren't there.

"You've forced yourselves onto an orphan's lands," he snapped in his turn, launching his cold phrases as if they were charging companies of soldiers. "You hold another man's home without right or title. You plot destruction to a ward of the Prince. But he'll know all about you in just one more day. What will you do then, you flesh-peddling thieves?"

The old woman screamed, spittle foaming at the corners of her mouth, and seized a boar spear and aimed it at Skshetuski while the four young men who had been staring at their mother's swollen and contorted face ran to the walls for weapons.

"So you'll go to the Prince, will you?" the old woman howled as her sons clutched at the knives, javelins and sabers on the walls and spread around Skshetuski like grey wolves, panting and licking their dry lips. "And what makes you think you'll leave here alive?"

The young soldier didn't even bother to meet their furious eyes. He crossed his arms on his chest and stared in calm disdain into the distant corners of the hall.

"I am Prince Yeremi's envoy and this is his country," he said scornfully. "Let me lose one drop of blood among you and in three days there won't be even any ashes here for the wind to scatter! And you? You'll rot to death in the cells in Lubnie. So don't grind your teeth at me, you petty little people, because they're not sharp enough to bite with."

"So we'll die!" the old woman howled. "But you'll die before us!"

"Then go ahead." And the young soldier spread his arms wide to expose his chest. "What are you waiting for? Strike."

The four Bulyhovs glared and panted and growled in their throats and clutched at their weapons but neither they nor their ferocious mother could move against him, as he knew they wouldn't. It was as if the Prince's terrifying name had weighed them down with chains.

"That's better," Pan Yan said. "Now listen to me. I know what you expect from Bohun. I'll grant you the same. I don't need this land and this house any more than he does, I've my own lands and incomes. It's Helen I want, not her property. Give her to me and you can keep Rozloghi."

"Don't give us presents that aren't yours to give," the old woman snarled while her sons watched her bloodshot eyes in search of a signal.

"I wouldn't give you the mud off my boots," Pan Yan said coldly, looking at the quivering old woman as if she were a roadside stone worth no more than a passing glance. "All that you'll get from me is a promise about your own future and it's up to you to decide what that's going to be. Either try to account to the Prince for your care of Helen and her properties, and then go begging wherever the Devil takes you, or give me the girl and keep what you've stolen. Those are your only choices."

A long silence followed. The dim-lit, stale air seemed thick with fear and hatred. And then the boar spear slipped slowly from the woman's hands and clattered to the floor with a dull ringing sound.

"What's it to be then?" Pan Yan said again. "Choose. And be quick about it."

"It's . . . fortunate . . . that Bohun had to go back to his regiment last night," the old woman muttered after another pause. "This . . . wouldn't have ended without bloodshed if he was here among us."

Skshetuski shrugged, looked away.

"I don't wear a saber just to make my belt sag on my hip," he said.

"But consider, sir," the old woman murmured, casting about for a way out of her dilemma. "Is it right for you to come into our home and force us like this, eh? You come for the girl like a Turk . . . like a Tartar . . ."

"Or a Cossack? A peasant who wants her against her will?"

"Ah, that's not fair, not fair, that's not how it is," a whining note crept into the *Knahina's* bitter voice. "Bohun may not know who his parents were but he's a famous and powerful man in his own right. He's as much a knight as a lot of others, with or without a title and a coat-of-arms . . .! And it's not as if we were throwing the girl into a stranger's hands; we've known him since he was a boy! Ah, but it'll be all the same for him whether you take the girl or stab him with a knife . . ."

Skshetuski nodded calmly and looked through the narrow, heavily timbered window into the *maydan* where the Valachian envoy's wagons were passing through the gates. His own men were waiting.

"It's time for me to go," he said. "What's the choice you're making?"

The old *Knahina* stared at him for a moment longer then

turned to her sons. Her voice was bitter with humiliation and defeat.

"Well? What do you say? Speak up! Shall we accept this cavalier's . . . courteous application?"

The young Bulyhovs looked at each other with dull eyes and nudged each other sharply with their elbows but none of them wanted to be the first to speak.

Then Symeon muttered: "You tell us, *maty*. If you say to kill him, we'll kill him. If you say to give him the girl, we'll give her."

"Either way it's bad."

"So you tell us, *maty*."

The old *Knahina* thought a moment longer.

If there had been a way to kill Skshetuski so that no word of it would reach the Prince at Lubnie she wouldn't hesitate for a moment, he knew very well. She'd murder him herself if she thought that she could get away with it, but there was no such way. Outside in the crisp morning air his troopers sat on their snorting horses like iron statues wrapped in hooded wolfskins, and the Valachian envoy's archers trooped about their wagons, and only two days' ride away the terrible Prince was waiting for his ambassador's return. The old woman's eyes were bitter but resigned and the gleam of murder had begun to dim and dissipate in them.

"You've got our backs against the wall," she muttered. "Ay . . . you're a hard man! But so's Bohun. A Devil when he's crossed. Who'll protect us from him, eh? Who? You? The Prince may hang him later but he'll destroy us first! So what are we to do?"

"That's your problem," Skshetuski said coldly. "You take care of it. All I want to hear from you is the choice you're making. So what's it to be?"

"All right," the woman said at last. "This is how we'll do it. We'll keep this a secret from Bohun. He'll be back here soon but we'll send him back to Pereyaslav in a day or two. Then we'll bring the girl to the Prince in Lubnie. You, meanwhile, ask the Prince to send us a garrison to Rozloghi, will you? Bohun,"— she went on with a flash of fear—"will go off his head when he hears what happened. You can't take Helen with you right away because he has half his regiment an hour's ride away and he'd take her from you on the road. So go your way now, keep it all a secret, and wait for us at Lubnie."

"So you'll have time to think of some safe way to play the Judas with me?"

"If only we could!" the old woman cried out in helpless fury. "But we can't! You know it! Give us your word that you won't breathe about this to a soul!"

"You have it. And the girl?"

"She's yours. Ah, though it'll be hard on Bohun . . ."

Skshetuski laughed harshly and looked at the young Bulyhovs with open contempt.

"Look at yourselves," he said. "Four grown men, big as forest oaks. Afraid of one Cossack and having to resort to treachery! And even now, even as you're trading Helen for Rozloghi, it never occurred to you to ask her if she'd have me!"

"Then we'll ask her now," the old woman hissed, quivering with anger.

* * *

She nodded at her sons and Symeon went out to bring Helen to them, and when she came into that dark and gloomy chamber it seemed to Pan Yan as if the sour air started to taste clean again and that a bright new light had entered the room. Her gentle face glowed like a sun among the angry stares and the recent threats and the memory of insults that hung like storm clouds among discarded weapons.

"This is your husband if you want him," the *Knahina* muttered pointing at Skshetuski.

Helen's face lost all color.

She made a small sound that was half a cry and half a sob, raised both her hands to her eyes as if unable to believe what she saw and heard, and then stretched both her arms toward the young soldier.

"Is that true?" she asked.

He nodded, too full of emotion to trust his own voice. And even though the darkly glowering faces of the old woman and the young Bulyhovs hung in that martial hall like leaden weights heavy with premonition, he felt light and hopeful and untroubled about anything the future could bring.

He left soon after.

The image of Helen's brightly glowing face, so full of wonder, love and overwhelming happiness, floated before his eyes all the way to Lubnie.

Chapter Five

THE DAYS THAT FOLLOWED tormented the young soldier. The Prince was away when Pan Yan led his convoy through the city gates and weeks would pass before he returned and, in the meantime, Skshetuski couldn't free himself from anxiety. He went up on the city walls each morning to see if he could spot the old *knahina's* wagons coming down the highway, and dark, oppressive dreams crowded about his pillow every night as he thought of Bohun.

His friends gave him a tumultuous welcome, coming each evening to his quarters to drink and to talk but he listened to them with half an ear at best. He grew drawn and thin; his normally cheerful face hollowed-out with worry. His promise to the old *knahina* to wait, do nothing and keep it all a secret made him powerless; he couldn't even confide in anyone until the Prince returned. Yet all he could think about was Helen left in the grasping hands of her untrustworthy kinsmen and about the violent young Cossack at her heels.

The late Winter turned into an early Spring and with it came torrential rains that turned the broad fields bordering the rivers into a vast swamp. Roads sank, bridges washed away, fords became roaring cataracts that swept men and horses like dry straw into the boiling rapids. No one could travel until the sun had dried out the Steppe and, in the meantime, Helen was alone in a den of wolves.

He thought that the Bulyhovs would probably keep their promise—he'd left them little choice—but they lived in the shadow of Bohun who could force them to give up the girl any time he wished.

At this thought Pan Yan shook as if in a fever, clawing at his

69

impatience like a captive bear. He wasn't used to letting events tell him what to do; it was much more his way to bend fate to his liking, riding his luck like a mustang broken to his will, and forcing life to give him what he wanted. And so he fled each day to the banks of the Slonitza River where he'd wander about with a bird gun in his hand, startling flocks of water birds and herds of deer and antelope, and sometimes even riding down a thundering herd of bison, but not even hunting could offer him distraction. Mostly he sat in thought on some mound or ruin or walked about the ancient battlefield where Hetman Zolkievski slaughtered Nalevayko's Cossacks in their last rebellion. All traces of that battle had long disappeared both from men's memories and the battlefield itself; only occasionally did the sodden earth throw up yellow bones on what had been the Zaporohjans' earthworks behind the broad stream. But Pan Yan's fear for Helen's safety tormented him no less among the thick grey mists that hung above the riverside desolation, and in the empty silence and the stunted groves of that haunted wilderness, than in the noise, gaiety, intrigue and glitter of the court.

And yet this court was the heart of his chosen life where a stranger would always believe that he had stumbled into an armed camp on the eve of battle rather than the residence of a splendid magnate and the administrative center of a Steppe empire. There were ten soldiers for every courtier, clerk, merchant and official in the Prince's capital. There was more steel than gold-plate. The streets were crowded with the finest warriors in the Commonwealth. Regiments marched out every day to the border forts hidden in the tall grasses beyond the horizon, other regiments rode into the city, and the brassy calls of warhorns and trumpets cut through the air from morning to night. Whoever felt a longing for a taste of war came to the court of Lubnie. All the adventurous gentry of the Transdnieper and the Eastern Lands swarmed under Prince Yeremi's standards, and with them came the best of the Mazovians, Lithuanians, men from Malopolska, and the stern knights of Mazuria, Polish Prussia and the Baltic countries.

This was Skshetuski's element. He'd been in love with it from his earliest boyhood. But neither the martial bustle of the garrison, nor the stir of camp life, nor the noisy, raucous celebrations in the regimental messes, managed to distract him after his return; and not even Anusia's bright, impatient eyes—puzzled and piqued by the young soldier's sudden lack of interest—did anything to relieve his grey days and troubled nights.

★ ★ ★

If his friends noticed the change in him, they were careful to say as little as they could about it.

Pan Michal Volodyovski, the diminutive dragoon who was never happy unless he was unhappily in love, did try to help him by reporting that Anusia said kind things about him during his six-month absence but Pan Yan hardly heard a word he said.

The girl, however, had her own ideas about that. She was used to being adored and pursued more or less seriously by every man in Lubnie. She couldn't understand why Pan Yan failed to pay her the homage she'd come to expect from all the young soldiers. So she decided to find out what was wrong with him, set all sorts of innocent traps for him, and finally ambushed him one night as he was leaving the Prince's anterooms.

"Ah!" she cried, running full-tilt into him and then jumping back with a small exclamation of surprise. "How you've frightened me! Good evening, lieutenant!"

"Good evening," Pan Yan said and smiled, knowing that Anusia was only as frightened as she wished to be.

The girl stood as if confused and stricken by shyness, twisting the ends of her braids with one hand, the other clutching the embroidery bag which had been her excuse to leave Princess Grizelda's apartments at that hour.

"Am I such a monster that I'd terrify you?" Pan Yan asked.

"Ah . . . no. That's not it at all!" Then she shot a quick, sharp look into Pan Yan's face. "But . . . are you angry with me?"

"Angry?" Pan Yan feigned a vast astonishment. "And why should the beautiful Lady Anusia care if I'm angry?"

"Oh . . . I don't care! Why should I? Maybe you think that I'll be all upset and that I'll start crying right away? Pan Byhovietz is a lot more pleasant . . ."

"Well," Pan Yan smiled. "If that's the case I'd better yield the field. It's clear the best man has won."

"Best man has won? Well, but . . . well, if that's what you think! I won't try to change your mind for you!"

And Anusia immediately stepped in front of the young soldier so that he couldn't get away from her.

"So you've been visiting with the Khan?" she said after a moment.

"With the Khan," he agreed.

"And what did you bring back?"

"I've brought Pan Longinus Podbipyenta," Pan Yan smiled and said. "A very fine and gentle cavalier whom I'm sure you've noticed."

"A lot more gentle than you!" Anusia sniffed pretending vast indifference, then asked at once: "And why did Pan Longinus Podbipyenta come here?"

"So that you can try all your charms and irresistible little tricks on him." Fond of the girl, Pan Yan grinned. "But I'd suggest an all-out attack because I know a secret about him that makes him invincible to women."

"Oh . . . invincible!" Anusia shrugged as if she couldn't care less. "Why is he invincible?"

"Because he can't marry."

"Oh," she cried. "Marry! As if I cared if he could marry! But why can't he marry?"

Skshetuski leaned close to the girl's ear as if to whisper a secret and then said loudly: "Because he's pledged to chastity!"

Anusia squealed and fled.

Pan Yan went to his quarters, laughing for a change. He wanted to tell Pan Michal about Anusia's unsuccessful ambush but the little knight, who had declared himself in love with no less a person than the Princess Anne, the Prince's older daughter, had gone up on the castle walls to mourn his unattainable ideal along with the Lithuanian giant who had some sighing of his own to do.

That night, however, Anusia took a careful look at the Lithuanian. The Prince had returned and his banquet hall was particularly splendid, with many foreign guests and local dignitaries and gentry, as well as all the leading officers and courtiers glittering in their finest clothes and with their richest weapons. Pan Longinus had dressed with special care to show that he had the necessary private means to support himself in Skshetuski's elite armored regiment, and looked most impressive in a white velvet undercoat and a sky-blue satin *kontush* with split sleeves, which he flung back to display the white silk lining with its matching facings, and all of it was richly studded with gold knots, studs, jeweled ornaments and clasps. In place of his murderous Cowlsnatcher he carried a light curved saber in a gilded sheath.

Anusia's bright eyes shot questioning glances at the splendid giant, largely to provoke and irritate Skshetuski, but he wouldn't have even noticed anything if Pan Michal didn't mention it to him.

"May the Tartars take me for a captive if Anusia isn't making eyes at our new Lithuanian bean-pole!" he remarked, letting his pointed little mustache twitch up and down like an alarmed beetle.

"So tell him about it," Pan Yan said.

"I will." The little knight grinned widely. "They'll make a great pair."

"He'll be able to wear her like a button on his coat. That's about the proportion between them."

"Or as a medallion in his cap."

And Pan Michal trotted over to the Lithuanian who had been wandering mournfully about the great hall, careful to keep his eyes away from all temptations.

"Ay, my long friend," Pan Michal said to him, "you've only just joined us but I see that you work faster than all the rest of us together!"

"And how is that, dear brother?" Pan Longinus murmured anxiously. "How is that?"

"Well, you've snapped up the choicest little morsel at this court," Pan Michal grinned and said. "Fast work indeed! Tell me, how do you do it?"

"Sweet brother!" The Lithuanian giant looked stricken with terror. "What are you saying? What?"

"Well . . ." The little knight grinned wickedly and pointed to Anusia. "Just look over there. We're all desperately in love with that little devil but she's been burning holes in your coat all night."

"Holes? What holes?" Pan Longinus shuddered.

"With her eyes! Don't tell me you're such a lady-killer you haven't even noticed? But take care she doesn't burn you up as completely as she's roasted all the rest of us."

★ ★ ★

Pan Michal hopped back into the crowd and disappeared at once, leaving the puzzled Lithuanian to himself. He glanced at

Anusia, shuddered, blushed a beetroot crimson and fled to the farthest corner of the banquet hall. But wherever he turned he seemed to see those two bright eyes glowing like small coals behind Princess Grizelda's shoulder, glowing and burning into him with persistence and curiosity, and he began to struggle like a netted bear against a wish to look at her again.

"*Ave Satanas!* Get thee behind me, Satan," he muttered in utmost terror and felt his hair rising on his head. He made a desperate sign of the cross, prayed and summoned up stern visions of his ancestor Stoveyko, but this particular little Satan didn't disappear. On the contrary, when he stole a quick glance in the girl's direction he saw that her eyes were shining even more invitingly than before!

He clamped his own eyes shut and kept them tightly closed for the rest of the evening. But long before daybreak he was knocking on Skshetuski's door.

"Lieutenant! Dear friend," he cried rushing in. "How soon are we leaving? When is that war supposed to begin?"

"Ah, so your vow is itching?" Pan Yan grinned and shook his head in sympathy. "Hmm . . . that's serious business . . . But be patient at least until you enlist. I've a vacancy in my company and the Prince agreed to give it to you but you have to wait until the next quarter and that's not till April."

"I know, I know!" cried the desperate giant. "But didn't His Highness say anything about the war?"

"Nothing," Pan Yan said. "People say that the King won't stop thinking about it until the day he dies but the Diets are deadset against it."

"But they were saying in Tchehryn that there's a Cossack rebellion on the way?"

"That's true enough. But nothing's going to happen until Spring. It's only February, the weather can still change, and the Cossacks never move until they're sure that the ground won't freeze. They can't stand up to us in the open field but few people can match them in digging entrenchments."

"Ah!" the sad giant cried. "So we must wait even for the Cossacks?"

"So it seems," Pan Yan nodded and started to explain. "The Hetmans don't believe that the Cossacks will stir at all this year. Our Prince is less sure. We're moving a few regiments closer to the Dnieper but even Prince Yeremi thinks that it'll all blow over and that Hmyelnitzki will come to his senses."

"Oh dear! Do you think he will?"

"Well," Pan Yan reasoned. "What can he gain by throwing himself on the full power of the Commonwealth? How can he gather the might he'd need to even scratch the surface? He has to know what he is up against, he's a brilliant man. And this is his own country as much as it's ours, isn't it? The Commonwealth belongs to the Cossacks just like the rest of us. No man attacks his own mother willingly."

"Ay!" the Lithuanian cried. "So there may not be a war even against the Cossacks?"

"Ho!" Pan Yan laughed. "You *are* in a sudden hurry, aren't you! But are you sure that three Cossack heads will free you from your vow? They're our own people, after all. Teutonic Knights and Turks are one thing but this is our own flesh and blood you're talking about. We and the Cossacks are the same mother's children, so to speak."

The anxious giant seized his head in both his hands. "Oh great God!" he cried. "Is that so? What am I to do? Do you think the Prince's chaplain could resolve this for me?"

"Oh, he'll resolve it," Pan Yan soothed the desperate Lithuanian. "Father Muhovyetzki is a wise man, widely read and eloquent as few others. But I don't think he'll tell you anything that you'd want to hear. A civil war is a war among brothers, my poor friend."

"But what if some foreign power . . . say the Turks or Tartars . . . came to help the rebels?"

"Ah, then you'd have no problem. All I can advise for now is patience and endurance. Just settle down and wait and let everything take its natural course."

★ ★ ★

But that was one piece of advice that Pan Yan himself was quite unable to follow. He felt more troubled and isolated every day. The life of the court and the camp oppressed him equally and even his old friends began to irritate him with their puzzled glances.

The Prince returned to Lubnie but this was the season for budgets and accounts and economic planning, for settling quarrels and territorial disputes among the tenant gentry, and for road-building and construction and financial matters, so that even the turbulent life of the soldiers settled down to a dry garrison routine and Pan Yan found no chance to talk to the Prince about his private worries. With the roads impassable, he couldn't even send a messenger to Helen. Yet he was desperate to know what the Bulyhovs might have in their minds, and whether Bohun suspected anything, and where he was just then and what he was doing.

Then March came. The sun returned and the roads dried out enough for a determined rider to try his luck among the steaming marshes, and Pan Yan ordered his shrewd young body servant to pack his saddlebags.

"Listen, Zjendjan," he told him. "You'll go to Rozloghi."

"To Rozloghi, master." The lad, whom nothing seemed to worry or surprise, nodded as calmly as if he'd just been ordered to walk to the vintner's for a flagon of mead.

"You'll take a letter from me to the young lady there and get one from her, understand? Don't tell anyone who sent you. Pretend you're just riding through to Tchehryn. Keep your eyes open and your mouth shut tight. Watch everything, see how they're treating the princess, find out what you can about Bohun and come back as fast as you can."

"You can count on me, sir," Zjendjan said and stared with absolute assurance at his worried master.

"Hmm. Yes. I know."

The boy, Pan Yan knew, was quick-witted and resourceful enough to do everything that he had to do, and to do it well, but his own worry was beginning to undermine his faith in everyone around him.

"But are you sure you'll manage it alright? This is no joke, you know. You'll really have to keep all your wits about you."

Zjendjan grinned and nodded. His shrewd little eyes peered at Skshetuski out of a pink pudgy face that made him seem as innocent as a child, but it was an innocence of his own devising. Barely sixteen, he had been with Pan Yan for more than a year and the young lieutenant knew that he could trust him and depend on him in almost anything, particularly if there was some way for the cunning lad to turn a profit out of whatever he was told to do.

The boy set out that night, supplied with ink and goose quills and a few sheets of parchment so that Helen might have something with which to write her letter, and Pan Yan settled down to wait with whatever patience he could still command.

Ten days passed and each seemed like a week of anxiety and waiting. He grew so pale and drawn that Anusia started asking if he was unwell and the Prince sent his personal physician, a longnosed Italian named Carboni, to bolster him up with a foul-smelling potion. But Pan Yan needed a different kind of medicine. Each day convinced him that his misery came from a heart weighed down with a truly great love, the kind that ancient authors wrote their tragedies about. It was no trivial, passing infatuation, he was sure, but a powerful emotion that would blow him apart unless it was eased.

And then one morning as Pan Yan sat hunched over a mug of mulled wine, dull-eyed and weary after another sleepless night of tormenting visions, Zjendjan came trotting into his rooms—covered with mud and tired but grinning from ear to ear—and the young lieutenant leaped up and seized him in his arms.

"You have a letter?"

"Yes master!" The boy turned it over. "Here it is!"

Skshetuski clutched the pages and began to read as avidly as if his life depended on each word. He wasn't sure if there'd be a letter, not knowing whether Helen had been taught to write. Few women were given any kind of education in those days, especially if they lived in the lone, out-of-the-way manors of the borderlands, and she, moreover, lived among illiterates. But if her words lacked the polish of the court, the classical allusions and fanciful ornamentation common to those times, they carried a straightforward simplicity and honesty that rang as clear as crystal and wrenched Pan Yan's heart more than any intricate word-play could have done.

'You ask if I've forgotten you,' the Steppe princess had written. *'It's more likely that you've forgotten me because, as I hear it, there are lots of distractions at the court. But since you sent your lad all that long way to see me it must be that you care for me, as I do for you, and I don't know how to thank you for that loving sign. I don't know if it's proper for me to be writing so much about caring and loving. It's probably something a woman shouldn't do. But I do love you and surely it's better to tell the truth about it than to hide it or to lie about it*

in some clever way, especially when the heart is as full of it as mine.'

"May God forget me if I ever forget you, my sweet girl," the young soldier murmured and read on.

'I've questioned Zjendjan about your life at court,' Helen wrote, *'and when he told me about the many beautiful ladies there I thought my heart would break . . .'*

Here the lieutenant glared at his messenger.

"What did you tell her, you damned fool?"

"Only the good things, master," the boy assured him swiftly and Pan Yan went on reading.

' . . . Because how am I to outshine them? How could I compare? But when he told me that you don't even want to look at them I took heart at once.'

"Ha!" Pan Yan cried. "You did that bit right!"

"Yes, master!"

Zjendjan had no idea why he was being praised but he tried to look modest about his achievement. Pan Yan was reading the letter quietly to himself, and there was no way for the lad to know what he had *'done right,'* but he assumed a serious, knowing air and coughed once or twice in a manner meant to signify both intelligence and virtue.

' . . . I took heart at once,' Pan Yan continued reading. *'I pray every day that nothing ever comes between us. Life is hard to bear all alone, but thinking about you makes it easier for me, because only you matter to me or mean anything I could care about.'*

She went on to say that the *Knahina* planned to come to Lubnie as soon as the roads made travel possible. She had, indeed, advanced her calculations because the news from Tchehryn was worse every week. Each day brought fresh word of Cossack restlessness and of an ominous grumbling among the peasant masses. The old woman was only waiting for her sons to come home from the annual horse fair at Boguslav.

'You must be truly a magician,' Helen wrote, *'to have won her over like you did,'* and Pan Yan made a wry face at the thought of the magic he had used.

He read the letter over and over until he was sure that he'd be able to recite it like a prayer. Then he began to question the tired lad. But all had gone well. The quick-witted boy had been well received. The old woman put him through a close interrogation about the lieutenant and when she found out that he was highly thought of at the Prince's court, and that he had his own substantial properties and a brilliant future, she warmed up considerably.

"She asked me, master, if you were the kind of man who kept his promises," Zjendjan added with his most innocent expression.

"She did, did she? And what did you tell her?"

"I said: '*My lady, if my master promised me that little Valachian mare I rode here all the way from Lubnie, I'd be thinking of her as already mine.*'"

"You said that, did you?" Pan Yan laughed. "Well . . . since you've staked my reputation on that mare you had better keep her."

"Thank you, master," Zjendjan said and grinned.

"Hmm. So you told them straight out that I sent you?"

"Yes, I did. Because I saw that it would do no harm. And at once they all started treating me even better, especially the young lady who is so beautiful that there can't be another like her in the world. Reading your letter, master, she wept all over it."

Pan Yan felt as though he would choke. "Hmm . . . She wept, you say?"

"From happiness, master. Out of joy."

"Hmm . . . And what's Bohun up to? What did you find out?"

"Ah, that's another story. It didn't seem right to ask the young lady or the old woman either. But I had a word with old Tchehly, the Tartar, who may be a heathen but who's a loyal servant and loves the young lady like she was his own. He said that they all grumbled about you at first, master, but then they made their peace. Especially after they found out that all that talk about Bohun's treasures was just a lot of gossip."

"Gossip, you say? And how did they find out it was a lot of gossip?"

"Well, sir, it seems they had some debts to pay and asked Bohun to lend them the money and he told them he didn't have a groat! He'd thrown it all away as fast as he got it, you know sir, like a Cossack! '*I've some Turkish loot hidden here and there,*' he said, '*but the gold's all gone.*' So right away they started thinking a lot less of him."

"You did well, my lad," Pan Yan said, delighted, and hugged the grinning boy. "There's no doubt about that."

"Ah master . . ." Zjendjan raised his eyes piously to the ceiling. "If I'd done one thing well and another badly you'd be able to say: '*You've given me a horse but without a saddle.*' And what good is a horse without a saddle?"

Pan Yan burst out laughing.

"All right, then," he said and smiled at the amazing lad who always found a way to make a profit out of everything. "You'd better keep the saddle along with that mare."

"Thank you, master! Well, they sent Bohun off to Pereyaslav, as they said they would, and so I thought: Why not go there as well? I'll find out more, my master will be pleased, and I'll get a new suit of clothes that much sooner . . ."

"You'll get it with the new quarter," Pan Yan said and shook his head in wonder at the grinning boy.

"Thank you, master! Well, so I went to Pereyaslav but Bohun isn't there. He's gone across to the right bank of the Dnieper, to what they call the Ruthenian side, and what Cossacks didn't go with him deserted to the *Sietch*. People say there's no more than a handful of them left at the regimental barracks . . . Well, when I found out he'd gone I thought that our young lady would be safe from him, so I came back home."

"You've done well," Pan Yan said again, joyful and relieved. "Was it a hard journey?"

"No, master," Zjendjan said, eying Skshetuski's untouched morning meal. "It wasn't all that bad. Only . . . I got awfully hungry on the way back home."

"Then sit down and eat!"

Zjendjan sat down and helped himself at once and Pan Yan read Helen's letter again and again and pressed it to his lips. There was so much goodness and sincerity in her hurried pages, so much love and longing, decency and kindness, that he felt as if new life was pouring into him.

Hope filled him.

He felt strong and vibrant and alive again, and free of all his fears, and all his faith and confidence returned and he laughed with joy. He dressed with special care and went to the castle chapel to give thanks to God. On the way he passed the long-nosed, sallow-faced Physician Carboni who was amazed to see that his potions cured the young soldier after all.

Chapter Six

IF PAN YAN SEEMED to walk with seven-league strides after Zjendjan's mission, and if his young, cheerful face was alive with happiness, confident and untroubled, few others in the Ukraine and the Transdnieper country had much reason to be hopeful about anything that Spring.

Strange murmurs swept across the land like the hot winds that gather before a great storm. A troubled sense of danger and a fearful restlessness flew from village to village and from one lonely forest manor to another, spreading as swiftly as the powdery yellow thistle seeds that the Steppe winds scattered across the Wild Lands every Autumn.

In the towns, people whispered about a great war. No one knew who'd be fighting whom nor when the war would start but no one doubted that a war was coming. The country folk held back on their plowing although Spring had come with all its green, fresh-smelling promises of new life, and the evening skies filled with nightingales. But there were other portents. The moon climbed out of the forests in the evenings like a scarlet stain. Mysterious lights drifted through the skies. Soothsayers prophesied catastrophes or a royal death, and all this doubt and watchfulness and uncertainty were especially troubling along the eastern borders because this was a land accustomed to bloodshed. Fear was rare among these hardy people for whom violence sometimes seemed as natural as breathing.

But two signs which no one could ignore stood out like warnings carved in stone among all these prophecies and supernatural omens. First, an unheard of multitude of beggars, story-

tellers, wandering bards and minstrels appeared in every hamlet
of the land, and among them were many strangers whom no
one had seen before and who spoke darkly about Judgment Day
coming from the Steppe. The second sign, as clear in that
country as if Tartar fires were already glowing in the sky at
night, was that the *Nijhovtsy* had begun to drink.

They drank *na umor*—"to the death," as these bouts were
known—as if to create for themselves a foretaste of dying. They
drank up all their money, houses, tools and everything they
owned, and when they had nothing left with which to buy
vodka they drank on credit against future loot. Whenever that
happened the *starostas* fortified their castles, great lords called in
their companies from the Steppe and the border outposts, and
the manor gentry sent their wives and children to safety behind
city walls and looked to their powder kegs and sabers. This was
the one infallible sign of war in the Eastern Lands, surer than all
the Horsemen of the Apocalypse galloping through the skies,
and that Spring the Cossacks began drinking as never before.

The permanent camps and settlements of the Zaporohjan
Nijh—that is to say all the swampy grasslands, rivulets and
islands in and around the river of that name—were too narrow
to contain all its warlike people, nor could the Steppe sustain
them all the year round, and so each year the Cossacks scattered
throughout the Ukraine, and far west into the peaceful territories of Ruthenia where Tartar wars existed only in legends and
in Winter tales. Some of them enlisted in the sheriffs' companies
and in the private regiments of the great lords and princelings,
others peddled vodka on the highways or traded in furs, or
went to work as wheelwrights, blacksmiths, tanners, brewers,
candlemakers, fishermen and trappers. In every Ukrainian village there would be one hut built at an aloof distance from the
peasant dwellings; there lived the Zaporohjan, the *Nijhovyetz*,
the man from the *Sietch*. He lived there when he wanted to,
coming and going whenever he pleased, and he was always
welcome because he could do anything. He knew every trade.
He could build a house, sew a saddle, trap game, and apply
healing herbs. A Cossack in a village was worth his weight in
salt to the peasants there because he'd work harder than all of
them together but he was also a warrior and went his own way.
And it took only a shout at the crossroads, or a whispered
promise of bloodshed and loot, and all these hardworking set-

tlers flew in like hungry ravens from all around the land. Whoever wanted to settle a quarrel with a neighbor without waiting for a court decree, or whoever expected such rough justice coming his own way, had only to send out the word and he'd have a hundred armed men waiting for his orders. In peacetime the Cossacks might live quietly in the villages for a year or more, working like no others from sunrise to sunset, and then there'd come news of some famous ataman's campaign against the Tartars or the Polish *Lahy*, or of some Polish prince against the Turks or into Valachia, and all those peaceful wheel-wrights, blacksmiths, handymen and tanners would throw down their tools and begin to drink.

And that Spring they drank as if they'd never get another taste of their coarse, homebrewed '*gojhalka*,' and they did it not merely in one territory or in one prince's country but throughout the length and breadth of that enormous land from the Black Sea to the River San.

And then came tales of barn burnings, hamstrung cattle, and isolated manors blazing in the night, and peasants murdering a Jew here and there and refusing to obey the orders of their masters, and rumors about Hmyelnitzki, and the mass deser-tions of manor Cossacks to the *Sietch* spread so far and fast that the news seemed to fly on birds' wings even before it happened.

★ ★ ★

This gradually swelling murmur of the coming storm seeped through the walls of Lubnie as everywhere else. The Grand Hetman of the Crown wrote that he didn't think that anything much would happen but Pan Zachvilihovski begged Prince Yeremi not to ignore all these tell-tale warnings.

'*A sea of fire is coming our way out of the Wild Lands,*' he wrote to the Prince. '*Hmyelnitzki has gone to the Crimea to get help from the Khan, and friends in the Sietch tell me that the Chief Ataman is calling in all the Cossack regiments, both horse and foot, without telling anyone why he's doing it, and that's why I think that they're getting ready to throw themselves on us. And if the Tartars come to join the Cossacks, which is something they had never done before, then God help us all!*'

The Prince respected Zachvilihovski's knowledge of the Cos-sacks even more than the opinions of the Hetmans, and so new levies started throughout his whole country, and messengers rode out of Lubnie to summon distant troops. But, more than anything, he wanted accurate information about the *Sietch* which, suddenly, became a land of silence as if the walls of grass around it had turned into stone. And so one day in early March he summoned young Pan Byhovietz and ordered him to get ready to travel down the Dnieper.

"You'll go as my envoy to the Chief Ataman," he told him. "I'll give you some letters. But that's only an excuse for you to be there. I want you to keep your eyes and ears open, find out what they're up to, how many regiments they've called in and if more are coming. Above all, find out all you can about Hmyelnitzki. I want to know where he is, what he's doing, what he plans to do, and if it's true that he's gone to the Crimea to get Tartar help. Is that clear so far?"

"Yes, my lord," said the overjoyed Byhovietz.

"You'll go through Tchehryn. Pan Zachvilihovski will give you letters to some kinsmen he has in the *Sietch*. Be careful how you deliver them. Your head and theirs will depend on secrecy. From Tchehryn you'll go by ship to Kudak. Pan Grodjitzki will give you guides to take you farther on and see you safely past the cataracts. And once you're in the *Sietch*: watch, listen and come back if you can."

"If I can, my lord?"

"That's what I said. This isn't an ordinary embassy and these aren't normal times."

"Should I take men, my lord?"

"Take forty troopers. You'll leave before nightfall."

Byhovietz strode out of the Prince's apartments as if the long stone halls were carpeted with clouds, for such was the love of these soldiers for their leader that they saw the most desperately dangerous missions as marks of his favor.

But in the antechambers he ran into Skshetuski.

"Why all these happy grins?" Pan Yan asked. "Has Anusia finally succumbed to your sighs and groaning?"

"If only she would. No, it's not that. The Prince has given me a job of work. I'm leaving tonight!"

"Oh? Where to?"

"To Tchehryn and farther."

"To Tchehryn? Then come with me for a moment. I've something to ask you."

Pan Yan took his friend to his quarters and began to plead to have the dangerous mission reassigned to him.

"What do you want?" he begged. "Horses? Money? My gratitude? They're yours if I can go in your place. Just give the word and you can have anything I have."

And then he struck on the one argument sure to sway his brother officer. "Think about Anusia!"

"Anusia!" the lovesick young man groaned.

"Yes. Anusia. Think about how long you'll be away. Months. Maybe longer. And think of Anusia here flirting with everything in breeches. I know how you feel about her. I know she thinks about you a lot more warmly than she does about the rest of us. But can you think of one man around here who won't be trying to jump into your shoes once you're out of sight?"

Byhovietz groaned and Pan Yan pressed on.

"Oh they'll be trying. Believe me. Everybody will be after her when you're gone."

"Don't I know it!"

"And . . . you know Anusia!"

Byhovietz shuddered. Indeed, he knew Anusia. But would the Prince consent to change his orders?

"Would he hold it against me if you took my place?" the wretched young man asked.

"Leave that to me!" Pan Yan cried and set off at a run for the Prince's chambers.

He asked for an immediate audience, his heart pounding like a hammer in his chest, because this great magnate who ruled his vast dominion with the unswerving will of an anointed monarch hated to have his orders challenged in any way. But Prince Yeremi's face reflected only kindness when the pages ushered Skshetuski into his private study.

A stranger seeing Prince Yeremi for the first time would find it hard to reconcile his slight, youthful body and almost girlish features with the towering legend that he had become. Barely into his thirties, the Prince had inherited the long, soft black hair and pale skin of his Valachian mother and these gave him a gentle, delicate air that might have seemed effeminate to someone who didn't know the man. But Skshetuski knew better than to trust appearances, these or any other. Those small-boned features already bore the iron stamp of war and the hard campaigning that had won the man his awesome reputation. The luminous black eyes housed sleeping thunderheads, he knew, and God help him who drew those hidden lightnings on himself! Not even the most experienced diplomats and courtiers could bear to look into those eyes for long; they contained such a natural sense of majesty and power that all heads bowed before him without a second thought. This was a man who knew his own greatness and the full power of his vast resources and he had no mercy for anyone who questioned his authority. If an imperial crown were suddenly thrust upon his head, Pan Yan thought, he'd be neither surprised by it nor crushed by its weight.

But now, seeing Skshetuski, the Prince smiled at him and beckoned him forward.

"And what brings you here?"

Skshetuski dropped to one knee and bowed his head.

"My lord," he said. "I came to beg Your Highness to let me have Byhovietz's mission to the *Sietch*. He might, perhaps, step aside for me because he's my friend, but he'd let himself be torn apart by wild horses before he risked Your Highness' displeasure. As for me, it's more than my life's worth to go there at this time."

"God love you!" the Prince exclaimed with pleasure. "I'd rather send you than anybody else on something as difficult as this. But I thought you might've had enough traveling for a while."

"I'd go in that direction any day!" Pan Yan burst out and the Prince turned his great, piercing eyes on him as if to search the deepest crevice of his soul.

"And what do you have out there?"

Skshetuski flushed as crimson as a schoolboy. He'd risen back to his feet after his respectful genuflection, and stood before the Prince like a criminal who had been caught redhanded, feeling the fire of those probing eyes; and now he threw himself down on both his knees and confessed his happiness and worry: how he had met the daughter of *Knaz* Vasil, how he came to love her, and how he wished to bring her to Lubnie on his way back from the *Sietch* so that she might be safe from Cossack unrest and Bohun's ominous persistence.

He told it all except for the machinations of the old *Knahina*;

his promise bound him to protect her secret. And he begged the Prince so desperately to be allowed to make the dangerous journey among the Zaporohjans that finally Prince Yeremi nodded and smiled his consent.

"I'd have let you go for her anyway," he said and smiled kindly. "And I'd have given you whatever you needed to get her here safely. But since you've thought it out so cleverly for yourself, combining your love-life with my service, how can I refuse you?"

He clapped his hands and a page came running and then ran again to fetch Pan Byhovietz while Pan Yan grasped the Prince's hand and kissed it like a father's.

"Save that for warmer hands," Vishnovyetzki laughed. "You are one of my best. I value your devotion. And I'm really pleased that you've fallen in love with Vasil's daughter. He was a great favorite of my father's and his tragedy makes his memory all the dearer to me. Did you know that he wrote me once, long ago, from exile?"

"I did hear something about that, my lord," Pan Yan said.

"Yes." The Prince nodded thoughtfully. "That was when everyone turned against him, thinking him a traitor. I never believed that."

"Few people did as I recall it, Highness," Pan Yan said.

"And even fewer would've acted as honorably as he did in the circumstances," Vishnovyetzki said and a brief cloud of a distasteful, bitter memory passed across his eyes. "He could've laughed at all the tribunals under the sun and sat as safe as a fox in a burrow under our protection. Greater men than he do it all the time. But he was a truly noble man, he couldn't live with suspicion darkening his good name so he disappeared. There was some talk later on that he joined up with the Emperor's people and died in the German wars. Anyway, he'd written to me begging me to protect his daughter. I'd long meant to look into that but since her guardians never came to see me and I heard no complaints about them I thought they were good people and let matters rest. But now that you've reminded me about her I'll look after her as if she were one of my own daughters."

Then Byhovietz came and the Prince spoke as gently and as firmly to him as if he were his son, which was one of the many reasons why this powerful prince, whose heavy hand crushed anyone who went against his will, was loved and served so loyally by all his fierce young soldiers.

"My friend," he said. "I've said what I've said and I don't change my orders. If you still want to go to the *Sietch* you're welcome to do so. But I'd take it as a favor if you'd let Skshetuski go in your place. Will you do that for me? He has good reasons for wanting to go and I'll think of some other way to repay your generosity."

"My lord," Byhovietz said, overwhelmed. "You can command me to do anything . . . instead you ask! That's too much honor for me. What more could I need?"

"So be it." The Prince nodded. "Thank your friend," he told Skshetuski. "Then go and get ready."

Pan Yan did, indeed, thank Byhovietz warmly then hurried to his quarters to pack for the journey. In less than an hour he came to the Prince—armed, booted, cloaked and with a mounted troop waiting in the courtyard—for his last orders and the Prince's letters.

Long before nightfall he was on the Steppe with Zjendjan and forty troopers of the Prince's Cossack Regiment clattering behind him.

Riding among the billowing crests of this sea of grass, Pan Yan felt that he was, indeed, crossing a great ocean: endless and empty and so wide that even his impatience and imagination couldn't span the distances between the horizons. Only the domed Steppe sky could bridge them and carry his thoughts to their destination; it spread above him in a bright blue canopy where hawks hung motionless like little black crosses.

* * *

Night came soon after, followed by another day. Then came another and another and each one was the same as the one before. Great drops of dew formed diamond clusters at dawn in the undergrowth and a quick breeze moved above the pastures and dried the pools of rain and melting snow that glittered everywhere like small lakes.

The sun rose quickly on those fresh March mornings in the open Steppe. It kissed the earth and moved on like a careless lover, still there and smiling down but already passing out of sight, and the earth woke rich and heavy with spring grass. The

Steppe was stirring everywhere with newly planted life; the pulse of beating wings, the hum of the insects, and the tolling cry of wild geese overhead made these vast green spaces sound like a lyre stroked by a melancholy hand.

Then came another morning, their last before the dark woodlands of Rozloghi appeared on the horizon, and the weary riders blessed the rising sun. It would dry and harden the sodden earth that pulled their horses belly-deep into the mud. The men and horses were equally exhausted; there had been little rest in their three nights and days. An hour here and there on firmer high ground and on the occasional burial mounds that rose like islands above the liquid soil. Brief moments, too short to light cooking fires or unsaddle horses.

Skshetuski drove his Cossacks and himself to within the trembling limits of endurance as if he possessed some secret strength that no ordinary man could know anything about, and now, with the new day upon them, they were looking at him with superstitious awe. They hurried after him through the rising mist and, at midmorning, they passed through a dense wood that spilled across the trail, and then they saw the windmills beating the stilled air, and the smoke of chimneys, and they grinned at each other with sharp, joyful shouts at their journey's end.

Pan Yan's heart pounded like a blacksmith's hammer because these were Bulyhov lands. Another mile or two and he'd be riding into Rozloghi, past the huddle of rough-hewn peasant huts and wild cherry orchards that seemed more precious to him than all the riches of the Prince's court. He could see the crouched thatched roofs in his mind's eye long before they actually appeared before him, and he kicked his horse forward with his heels. The animal leaped onto the dried, hard-trodden surface of the village street, and Zjendjan spurred his own new mare behind him, and the Cossacks struck their horses' flanks with their short-handled whips—the rawhide, metal-tipped *nahaykas* which were their badge of distinction and superiority to ordinary peasants—and then the whole troop was thundering through the village, laughing and shouting now that they were within a short gallop of hot food and rest.

Mud flew from under the horses' hooves and the startled peasants ran out of their cabins; they gaped at the riders and made their quick triple signs of the cross along their chests and shoulders wondering what this was all about. Tartars or Devils? It was all one to them and none of it promised anything that might ease the bitter hardship of their lives.

And then the iron-shod hooves were drumming on the wooden bridge across the manor ditch, and splinters flew like sparks, and then Pan Yan pulled back on the reins and his panting horse slid to a halt under the overhang of the shuttered gates.

"Inside there! Open up! Look alive in there!"

The shouts, the barking of the countless village dogs, and the hammering of the troopers' heavy saber hilts on the thick oak gates brought frightened manor servants running to the walls.

"Who's there?"

"Open up!"

"The masters aren't home," cried uncertain voices.

"Open up at once, you damned pagan souls!" Pan Yan roared. "We're from the Prince at Lubnie!"

Some of the manor servants recognized him then. "Ah, it's you, Your Worship! At once, at once!"

The gates swung open and they clattered in.

★   ★   ★

The old *Knahina* came out on the porch and peered at them uncertainly, shielding her eyes against the sun behind them, and Pan Yan rode up to her and jumped off his horse.

"Do you remember me, my lady?"

"Ah." There was little warmth in her harsh, suspicious voice. Whatever she remembered seemed to be something she'd rather have forgotten. "Ah, it's you, lieutenant . . . I thought it was a Tartar raid, the way you thundered in here . . ."

Then she shrugged, resigned and made the necessary hospitable motions.

"But come in, come in."

In the great hall, glittering as before with weapons and rustling with the uneasy whisper of birds' wings and the rasp of taloned feet shifting on their perches, the old woman stared at Pan Yan with dull hostility.

She waited. He knew what she expected and his own brief laughter sounded harsh and cruel in his ears.

"Don't be surprised to see me," he said coldly. "I've kept my word. I'm only passing through on the Prince's business. But

His Highness told me himself to stop here on my way and give you his greetings."

"Did he, now," she muttered, dark with gloom. "I'm . . . grateful for his kindness. And how soon does he think to drive us off this land?"

"He doesn't think it at all," Pan Yan said and laughed. "He doesn't know that that's what you deserve. And I stand by my word. You'll stay in Rozloghi and maybe get something from me as well. I have enough elsewhere."

The *Knahina* stared at him for another long and silent moment before a pale smile stole across her face.

"Ah," she murmured softly, and he laughed again.

"But where's Princess Helen?" he demanded. "Is she well?"

"Well? Well?"

The old woman's smile broadened now that she felt a little more secure and at ease.

"Why shouldn't she be well? She's even plumping out with all that loving . . . Ha! But I know you didn't ride all the way here to see me. I'll go and send her to you."

She went out at once but there was no need to summon Helen there. Old Tchehly had seen Skshetuski riding through the gates and told her who had come. She ran in—out of breath, her breast rising, flushed like a cherry-apple and quite unable to speak. Only her wide dark eyes, filled with happiness and laughter, expressed what she felt. They shined with such transparent joy that Pan Yan felt as if his heart was turning cartwheels in his chest.

He caught her by her arms, drew her to him and pressed her against him, and kissed her mouth and hands, feeling as if he were about to melt like the snow outside, and she closed her eyes and then opened them again as if to make sure that he was really there.

"Ah, but I didn't expect you," she whispered. "Didn't think you'd come . . ."

"And I thought I'd dry up without you!" he cried out. "At last the Prince himself took mercy on me and sent me here to you."

"So the Prince knows?"

"I've told him everything. And he was glad, remembering *Knaz* Vasil. Ay, my sweet girl, you must have fed me some love potion when I was here last because I can't see anything except you in all the world!"

"It's God's mercy, such blindness," she murmured, then went on, pressing her hands against him. "But . . . don't you think that's an awful lot of kissing?"

"How am I to stop?" Pan Yan laughed and hugged her. "I've never tasted anything this sweet. Do you remember how the falcon brought our hands together?"

"I remember . . ."

"It was an omen, nothing less," Pan Yan said and believed every word of it. "I was so lonely for you in Lubnie that I thought I'd go mad. I'd go up along the Slonitza and I'd see you there, so real that I'd think it was truly you. But every time I'd call out and stretch out my arms for you, you'd be gone, vanished like a dream. Well, you won't get away from me again, sweet girl, because there's nothing that can come between us now."

"If something should," she murmured. "It won't be my doing."

"Tell me again you love me!" he cried out.

Helen closed her eyes. She smiled. Her voice was soft but firm and full of quiet pride.

"As I've never loved anyone in this world," she said.

"And in any other?"

"And in any other," she agreed, still smiling.

"I'd rather hear that from you than to have the King cover me with titles!" he cried out. "God only knows how I've earned such luck. I couldn't have done anything to deserve you."

She looked at him for a quiet moment and said: "You were kind to me."

"Kind? How could anyone be anything but kind to a girl like you?"

"It's been done before," she said quietly and sadly and then she smiled up at him and her voice rang out, clear and pure as crystal. "But you were good to me, and you stood up for me and made me feel loved and wanted and defended, and you spoke to me in words I never heard before. I don't know if what you're getting in return is all that wonderful but I will give you all my heart and my every thought and I'll do my best to see that you are never sorry for the things you said."

Skshetuski seized her hands again and pressed them to his face.

"You'll be more than any wife to me," he said. "You'll be my friend and guide and trusted companion who'll own everything I have and share equally in every moment of our lives together. Ay, but you're so beautiful I think I'll go blind!"

Helen's white teeth gleamed in a sudden smile.

"Hmm. Lady Anusia must be a hundred times more beautiful," she murmured.

"Anusia!" he cried, laughing. "Anusia? What Anusia? Ah, she is to you exactly what a copper kettle would be to the moon!"

"Hmm," she teased him. "Hmm. Master Zjendjan told me something different."

"Master Zjendjan will have a thick ear as soon as I catch him!" he shouted and laughed. "Ah, my sweet, what's that girl mean to me? What has she ever meant? Let other bees buzz around that flower. And . . . God knows, there's enough of them even for Anusia!"

★   ★   ★

The morning passed so swiftly that they hardly noticed when old Tchehly, the Tartar, came in to pay his respects to Pan Yan whom he already regarded as his future master.

"Well, old man," Pan Yan told him gently. "I'll take you too, along with the lady. You can serve her faithfully till you die."

"There's not long to wait for that, master," the old man said with his wolfish grin, bowing to the ground in the oriental manner. "But while I live, I'll serve her. *Allah ukbar!* It's all Allah's will."

"I'll be back from the *Sietch* in a month," Skshetuski told Helen. "Then we'll go to Lubnie where Father Muhovyetzki will be waiting for us. I'd send you there today, only the roads are still so terrible it's hard to get through on horseback far less in a coach and wagons."

"The *Sietch*?" Helen looked at him, suddenly afraid. "Is that where you're going?"

"The Prince sends me with letters, it's not much." He shrugged to dismiss her fears. "An ambassador is safe even among savages and they're all Christians there."

"How soon are you going?"

Her voice was steady. She was, after all, the daughter of one soldier and soon to become the wife of another, but she could not conceal the dismay in her eyes.

"Tonight. I must be in Tchehryn tomorrow." He tried to

sound matter-of-fact as if nothing unusual was likely to happen to him among the Zaporohjans. "Ah, but don't look so sad. The quicker I go, the quicker I'll be back. Besides, my time's not my own, you know how that is. It's the Prince's service."

She nodded, smiled, seemingly content. But some of the sunlight appeared to have left the day.

★　★　★

They ate a light meal later in the morning. The old *Knahina* looked at them with broad, indulgent smiles and made sly, coarse jokes but Pan Yan and Helen might have been alone for all that it mattered. They were quiet and happy. It was clear to them both that the old woman had finally dismissed Bohun from her calculations and now, thanks to Skshetuski's generosity, knew herself quite safe. She'd keep Rozloghi for her sons and herself *cum lasis, boris, granicebus et coloniis*, as such land-grants were defined in the gentry's Latin, as if those lands had always been hers under the law.

Pan Yan asked only when the young princes would come home because the fortress-manor would be safer with those warriors there.

"Any day now," the old woman told him. "Ah, they were angry with you! So angry at first. But later on, after they thought about the way you stood up to us, they were glad to have you for a future kinsman. It's hard to find a real man in these soft, spoiled times . . . Ah, nothing is like it used to be."

Then, with the sun edging into afternoon, Pan Yan and Helen went outside and she led him to the cherry orchard beyond the manor walls, where the bees droned among banks of early flowers heavy with the sweet smell of a renewing year. The orchard ran from the edge of the moat to a grove of oaks where a cuckoo's cry was hammering at the warm, still air.

"What do you think she's saying?" Helen wished to know.

The cuckoo, according to old Ruthenian legends, was the traditional messenger of the ancient Gods.

"She's wishing us good luck," Skshetuski said at once. "She's prophesying happy years for us. But perhaps we'd better ask her how many we'll have."

And facing the dark grove he called out: "*Zazulu, zazulu,* whom the old Gods loved! How many years will we live together, this lady and I?"

The bird counted off more than fifty years.

"God grant it!"

"The *zazula* always tells the truth," Helen observed quietly.

"Does she, now." Pan Yan grinned with a sly, sideways glance at the happy girl. "Hmm. Well. Then we'd better ask her something else. Ey, *zazulu*, and how many boys are we going to make?"

The bird obediently counted an even dozen and Pan Yan doubled up with laughter.

"I'll be a *starosta* with a troop like that! But you heard the cuckoo, didn't you? Eh?"

"No . . . I wasn't listening," Helen said, scarlet as a poppy. "I don't even know what you asked her."

"Then maybe I should ask again?"

"Oh, you don't have to . . ."

And that's how the day ended for them both, without fear or doubt of any kind. It was a warm and peaceful passage through the hours that seemed to go on forever, without limits, like the wide Steppe sky; and then they watched the red sun dip slowly into the woods which spread darkly on the near horizon.

But the hours followed their own remorseless courses and, in due time, Pan Yan had to be on his way. Pan Zachvilihovski was waiting impatiently in Tchehryn to hear from Prince Yeremi and Skshetuski's mission was too urgent for any long delays. He left Rozloghi shortly after dark, and his troubled sense of danger and uneasiness about what the future might bring to him and Helen returned with the night.

Chapter Seven

IN TCHEHRYN, Pan Zachvilihovski waited for the Prince's emissary in a real fever of impatience. The news that seeped out of the *Sietch* left no more room for doubt. The threatening storm was no longer a fearful supposition; war with the Zaporohjans was as certain as if death and pillage were already ravaging the land. Hmyelnitzki was getting ready to drown his enemies in blood and he would devastate his whole country right along beside them.

The Grand Hetman who paid scant attention to the warning signs now moved his cavalry to Tcherkassy. His vanguard reached Tchehryn, more as a means of hindering the Cossack desertions than in any hope of holding down that seething territory and, in the meantime, the gentry massed in fortified manors and walled towns. There was talk of a general call to arms, or '*Universal Levy*,' and so the gentry watched anxiously for the fiery crosses that would blaze on hilltops and summon them, '*armed and with armed retainers*,' to make their immemorial payment for years of privilege, for their lands and titles and their coats-of-arms, and for their right to wear a saber and elect a King. Not even Hmyelnitzki could have known the terrible extent of the coming storm nor what it would mean in the long run to his nation's history but, in the meantime, the Ukraine split itself in two. One half flowed like a vast pack of hungry wolves into the *Sietch*; the other gathered around the horsetail standards of the Hetmans.

Some men still hoped. Hmyelnitzki wrote impassioned letters to the Grand Hetman of the Crown, and to the commissioners and the royal ministers in Warsaw, full of complaint and sorrow about Cossack rights and pledges of his loyalty and love for King Vladyslav and the Commonwealth. Perhaps he really did believe that the time for negotiations hadn't passed beyond recall and that the conflagration he had lighted could still be controlled. Or perhaps, as some men warned, he merely played for time.

But Zachvilihovski and old Barabas had few illusions about anything. They knew the Cossacks. They understood the unforgiving hatreds that simmered in the hearts of the serfs and peasants. They didn't need to calculate the rapacious greed of all those savage, landless men who gathered in the Wild Lands. And they knew Hmyelnitzki.

The old Cossack colonel received a letter from him, full of threats and malice, which he passed with trembling hands to Pan Yan and Zachvilihovski.

"Look how he jeers at me," he said. "And yet it was I who taught him war and soldiering. He was like my son."

"He says that he is coming with the Zaporohjan Army to claim Cossack rights," the commissioner observed. "That means Civil War. And there's no conflict as terrible as that."

"I see I've got to hurry," Pan Yan said. "Can you give me letters of introduction to someone in the *Sietch*? There must be some loyal and reasonable men left there."

"Loyal? Reasonable?" Zachvilihovski laughed bitterly. "Is a firestorm loyal? Can you reason with a flood?" Then he sighed, shrugged, and went on: "Do you already have something for the Chief Ataman?"

"From the Prince himself."

"Well . . . Alright then, I'll write to one of the Leaders of the Circle, as they call their council. And Colonel Barabas has a kinsman there. They'll tell you what they can. But isn't it too late for that kind of mission? If the Prince wants to know what they're saying in the *Sietch*, there's one quick answer: they are talking war! And if he wants advice, there's only one sound course: gather as many men as possible and join up with the Hetmans."

"Then send that advice to the Prince. I must go anyway, I've no choice about it. Those are the Prince's orders."

"But don't you understand what you're getting into? Even

here the mobs are in such frenzy that they'd be at our throats right now if it weren't for the Hetman's vanguard. What must it be like over there? You'd be safer in a dragon's mouth."

"Ah sir," Skshetuski said simply. "Jonah was in a whale's belly, not just in his mouth, but with God's help he got out in one piece."

"Well, go then, go," Zachvilihovski said and a note of helpless resignation slipped into his voice. "You can get as far as Kudak, anyway, and see how things look to you from there. Pan Grodjitzki is an experienced soldier and he's spent half his life in that eagle's nest. He can advise you best. As for me, I'll go and join the Prince. If I'm to drag my old bones over battlefields again I'd rather do it under him than anybody else. Meanwhile I'll find you some good men and ships to get you to Kudak."

★ ★ ★

Skshetuski walked back to his quarters in the Prince's house feeling excitement and a curious sense of pleased anticipation. He harbored few illusions about the dangers waiting in the *Sietch*. But the long journey would take him down the whole length of the Dnieper, past the legendary cataracts and the *Nijh*, and that was a land known to few people of his generation.

Most men spent their whole lives in the Ukraine without being able to say that they had seen the *Sietch* unless they joined the Cossack brotherhoods and that didn't happen often anymore. The Polish and Ruthenian gentry no longer flowed in their adventurous thousands to live among the fierce brethren of the Zaporohje. Those that did were rare; too much blood had been spilled by both sides, the ill-will ran too deep, and the chasm between the Commonwealth and the *Sietch* had grown too wide for sharing anything, far less lives and friendship. Now if anyone went beyond the Wild Lands it was in flight from justice, or as an outlaw stripped of property and name, or to escape the consequences of such terrible misdeeds that they were beyond penance or atonement, so that an aura of mystery and curious speculation surrounded the freebooting republic along the Lower Dnieper. The young soldier knew that he'd be possibly the last of his kind to see what everyone else would know only by hearsay: the *Sietch*, the permanent war camp of the Zaporohjans whose name meant '*those who live beyond the cataracts*' and carried its own fierce air of daring and adventure. It was an unknown legendary country that was said to be splendid and full of wonders on the one hand and dreadful on the other.

He sat beside the open window of his room, letting his young imagination drift through those misty regions, when two men caught his eye in the square below. He thought he knew them. He looked with greater care and then he was sure: the men, walking arm-in-arm like loving brothers, were Pan Zagloba and Bohun. He watched them make their way to the Bell Corner and disappear in the tavern doorway and all his fears for Helen were suddenly resurrected.

"Zjendjan!" he cried.

The lad ran into the room.

"Go to Dopul's Tavern," Pan Yan ordered. "You'll find a fat noble with a big hole showing in his forehead. Tell him that someone has important business with him and bring him here to me. But if he asks who sent you, don't tell him. Understood?"

But Zjendjan was already running down the stairs. In moments, Pan Yan saw him in the square, dodging and weaving through the jostling crowds, and then he dived like a hunted hare into the darkened doorway. It didn't take long before he came out again with the fat knight beside him.

They crossed the square and he lost sight of them as they reached the gate under his window. But then he heard them stumbling along the cobbles in the courtyard and climbing the stairs; and then Pan Zagloba came into the room, peering about suspiciously with his one good eye.

"Good day to you, sir," Pan Yan said.

"Good day, good day, though it's a thirsty one," the fat knight observed. "And who may you be, my good friend? Ah . . . ah! I remember!"

"You remember me?"

"Do I remember?" Reassured, the fat knight grinned from ear to ear. "Let the Turks melt me down for tallow and burn me as harem candles if I don't remember! You opened Dopul's door with Tchaplinski's head a few months ago! That was particularly to my taste since I once freed myself from captivity in Istanbul in a similar manner, hang me if I didn't. Ah, and how is our Lithuanian hop-pole, these days? Our famous *Skirtlifter*, together with his virginity and his sword?"

"Pan Podbipyenta is well. He sends you his regards."

"Does he, now. Well, well. That is a monstrously rich knight but dull as a hammer. If he ever collects three heads like his own they'll add up to no more than a head and a half because he'll have beheaded three halfwits. Ah but . . . pfui . . .! What heat! And it's only March . . . My tongue is so stiff I can hardly talk."

Pan Yan smiled. "I've some good mead here. Perhaps a small cup . . .?"

"A fool refuses when a wise man offers," the fat knight said at once. "It just so happens that the local leech has prescribed mead for my *melancolia*. But how is a man to keep from being melancholy these days, hmm? Terrible times are coming . . . Terrible . . . *Dies irae et calamitatis*. Tchaplinski's tongue is hanging out in terror. He doesn't come to Dopul's anymore because that's where the ranking Cossacks do their drinking and I have to face them there alone. Ah . . .! What a mead! From the Prince's cellars?"

"His best. And are there many ranking Cossacks in Tchehryn these days?"

"Ha! Which of them isn't here! There's Fedor Yakubovitch, old Filon Djedjala and Danyeli Netchay . . . and with them Bohun, their little prince, the heart of their hearts, who's become my bosom friend since the day I drank him under the table and promised to adopt him. All of them sit here in Tchehryn sniffing the wind and wondering which way to jump. And if they don't all gallop off to Hmyelnitzki it'll be my doing!"

And the babbling fat knight held out his empty cup which Skshetuski refilled immediately.

"And how is that?"

"Hmm? How's what? Oh, yes, because while drinking with them I urge them to do their patriotic duty and warm their sentiments for the Commonwealth. And if the King doesn't make me at least a *starosta* for that public service then there's no justice left, we've lost all our virtues, and a man would do better to take cows to pasture than risk his head *pro publico bono*."

"You might do better with a saber than a demijohn," Skshetuski said quietly. "The way things are going with the Cossacks you're wasting your money."

Zagloba stared, astonished.

"My money? What do you take me for, good friend? Isn't it bad enough that I've got to swallow my dignity by drinking with peasants without paying for it too? Ah, but this is a rare mead . . . !"

Skshetuski laughed and refilled the fat knight's cup again which he drained at one gulp with every sign of pleasure.

"And this . . . ah . . . Bohun," Pan Yan said. "What's he doing here?"

"That one? He's got his ears pointed to the *Sietch* like the rest of them. Ah, he's their darling, their precious little jewel! They dance around him like trained apes because they know the Pereyaslav Regiment will follow him, not old Colonel Loboda. And who knows which way the rest of Kshetchovski's division will go? Hmm?"

"God grant they'll remain loyal," Pan Yan sighed. "But about this Bohun . . ."

"Hmm . . .?" Pan Zagloba helped himself to more mead, drank it thirstily, sighed with satisfaction and mopped his sweating forehead. "A fine mead, my dear sir, an excellent *Troyniak*. Phew, but it's hot!"

"Drink a little more."

"I will, I will! About Bohun . . . well, he's theirs, body and soul, but now he's hesitating. Because he told me when he was drunk one day that he's in love with some gentlewoman and wants to marry her so he can't go about with peasants anymore. Why, he even wants me to adopt him and admit him to my coat-of-arms! Ah but that's a fine mead . . . !"

"Drink a little more."

"Certainly! You don't find this kind of mead in a tap-room barrel . . ."

"And did Bohun tell you the name of this gentlewoman that he wants to marry?"

"Name . . .?" Pan Zagloba snorted with contempt. "My dear sir, what do I care about her name? All I know is that when I've fixed a set of antlers to Bohun's head she'll be known as a doe."

Skshetuski fought back a sudden urge to bring his fist down on Zagloba's head but the fat knight didn't seem to notice anything but the mead.

"Yes, yes," he went on. "I had some fine times with women in my youth! If only I could tell you how I came to be martyred in Galata! D'you see that hole in my forehead, hmm? Let me just say that it was put there by the eunuchs in the seraglio of a certain pasha."

"But didn't you once say it was a robber's bullet?"

"Did I? Then I said it well! Because every Turk is a robber, as God is my witness!"

★ ★ ★

Pan Zachvilihovski came into the room just then and the fat knight blinked, averted his face and buried his nose in his cup. It was clear that the two men didn't like each other.

"Well, lieutenant, your galleys are ready," the commissioner said. "Your mariners are all good men, you can depend on them. You can be on your way as soon as you wish. And here are your letters."

"Good," said Pan Yan, rising. "Then I'll tell my men to ride to the river."

"And where are you going?" Pan Zagloba asked.

"To Kudak."

"You'll find it hot there."

But Skshetuski didn't hear the warning, if that's what it was. He left the room and went down into the cobbled courtyard where his redcoated Cossack troopers waited beside their horses.

"Mount up," he ordered. "Ride to the landing, take the horses and supplies aboard and wait for me there!"

The Cossacks leaped into their saddles, wheeled their mounts and trotted through the gates, and Pan Yan went back into the house where the old commissioner was staring at the fat noble with distaste.

"I've heard that you've become the court jester of the Cossack colonels," he said scornfully as Skshetuski came near the door. "What's happened to your sense of shame?"

"It's all *pro publico bono*, my dear commissioner," the fat knight was mumbling. "*Pro publico bono.*"

"You've sharp wits and a quick tongue, Zagloba, that I'll grant you. Sharper, it seems, than your sense of decency and honor, but you're not fooling me! You're out to win a few friends for yourself in case they should come out on top!"

Pan Zagloba blinked rapidly with his one good eye and turned the other on the angry old man.

"Ah . . . is that what you think?"

"What else is there to think?"

"Hmm. Well, even if that was so," Pan Zagloba muttered. "Even if having been . . . ah . . . martyred by the Turks I don't want a repeat performance from the Cossacks . . . why should that surprise anyone? The best *borstch* can be spoiled by too many mushrooms. As to my shame, as you call it, I'm not asking anyone to share it, am I? I'll drink that cup of gall alone. True merit will come floating to the top in its own good time like oil on wine."

Skshetuski thought it time to step into the room.

"My men are on their way," he said. "It's time for me to follow."

Zachvilihovski sighed and filled the cups with the last of the mead. "Let's drink to your safe journey, then," he said.

"And a safe return," Pan Zagloba added.

$$\star \quad \star \quad \star$$

They went outside. The sun set quickly as they made their way to the boat landing along the Tasmina, Pan Yan and the old commissioner walking arm-in-arm and Pan Zagloba trailing behind with deep sighs and uneasy glances. A cold wind blew from the Dnieper when they reached the galleys.

"Well . . . a good journey," Zachvilihovski said. He pressed the young soldier's hand for a long moment. "Be careful, my young friend."

"I'll be careful."

"*Vive valeque,*" Pan Zagloba cried. "And if the water carries you as far as Istanbul give my regards to the Sultan! Tell him from me . . ."

And then he hesitated and his voice lost its booming confidence; perhaps it was the sudden chill that came off the water that subdued his bluster.

"Ah, to the devil with him. Hmm. That was a very fine mead . . . Brrr, but it's gotten cold."

Skshetuski stepped aboard.

"Go with God!" they called up after him.

"Stay with God," he said.

The long oars creaked and splashed into the water and the decked galleys moved into the river. The beacon fires burning along the shore grew smaller and smaller and Skshetuski

watched them a long time as they dwindled and fell away
behind him and he felt as if something precious had ebbed from
his life. And then the galleys rowed out of the narrow mouth of
the Tasmina into the wide, grey Dnieper and a sudden wind
blew out of the Steppes.

Cold, Pan Yan shuddered. He drew his cloak about him and
settled down on the pile of robes that the soldiers spread for him
on the galley's deck. The boatmen started a plaintive river song.
He thought about Helen waiting in Rozloghi, not yet safe in
Lubnie. And about Bohun who was staying near her while he
sailed away. Doubts, fears and premonitions settled about him
like cawing carrion birds. He struggled against them until he
was exhausted. Their forms changed and shifted in his imagination; they seemed to become part of the shrill Steppe wind, the
beat of the oars and the boatmen's voices.

Then he slept.

★   ★   ★

He woke refreshed and in better spirits although the night's
dark thoughts still stirred in the corners of his mind and haunted
him with their hints of danger.

The new day came in a blaze of many colors; the morning
was beautiful and clear. The huge river lay about the ships like a
gigantic mirror that the soft shore winds soon covered with a
latticework of wrinkles. The riverbanks lay hidden under a pale
mist that turned the river and the land into one endless and
unbroken plain so that it seemed as if the water lay motionless
between the horizons.

Zjendjan woke, rubbed his eyes and stared. "God's Mercy!
Master, are we on the sea?"

"It's a great river," Pan Yan said, "but it's not the sea. When
the mist lifts you'll see the land around us."

The ships moved swiftly. They passed other vessels— tall-
backed Dnieper galleys with banks of long oars, round-bot-
tomed barges, and the narrow black Cossack skiffs and longboats made of stiff, oiled leather stretched over wooden frames.
Some of these craft shot downriver to the sea; others worked
their difficult way upstream in the swollen water with creaking
oars and cracking sails and the rhythmic chants of the towmen
walking on the shore. They carried cargoes of fish, salt, tallow,
wax and dried fruit to the distant river towns and hurried back

to Kudak and the *Sietch* with wheat, gunpowder, tools and whatever else men might need to survive below the cataracts.

South of the tributary '*River of the Bees*' the land grew empty on both sides of the Dnieper; nothing moved there, there was no sign that man had ever put his foot ashore. The land was as it must have been in the beginning: unchanged, untouched, and unaware that humankind existed. But the river itself was an enormous highway. It was the only link between the *Sietch* and the rest of the world and in that time of year the traffic was heavy. The swollen waters were so high and swift that even galleys could risk running through the cataracts that could be threaded only by canoes at any other time. Only the sixth cataract, known as *Nyenasytetz* or "Old Insatiable," remained impassable. Nothing entered its murderous white water and came out alive at any time of year.

Pan Yan looked about eagerly while his two galleys rowed rapidly downstream.

The mists rose and blew away. The fog crept into the reeds along the hidden bays and dry riverside ravines where it was always dark and where not even wolves would shelter in Winter. The riverbanks loomed out of the mist. The low horizons narrowed. Flights of cranes, pelicans, cormorants and the giant wild ducks and geese that never left this land to fly across the sea, rose in shrill multicolored clouds from the hidden shore. The overgrown inlets and lagoons belled with such cawing, honking and warbling that it seemed as if a birds' parliament had opened its raucous session in the reeds.

Below the mouth of the tributary Kamentchug, the shoreline dipped and the horizons broadened.

"Look master!" Zjendjan cried. "Snow! Is it snow?"

Skshetuski stared in disbelief at the land around him. From one vast horizon to the other, beyond the reach of eyesight, both sides of the river gleamed with such brilliant whiteness that it hurt his eyes. Snow seemed impossible in that blazing sunlight.

"Hey! Sergeant!" he called out. "What is that?"

"Cherries, my lord," the old Cossack answered and they all looked again.

The endless whiteness was, indeed, a single forest of gnarled cherry trees whose wild fruit, as sweet as honey and larger than crab-apples, fed the birds and animals of this enchanted land.

Now, blooming with white flowers, it sent such a strong fragrance over the river that it made breathing difficult. Wild almonds grew among the cherries. The ground was an unbroken carpet of fallen white and yellow petals. The sound of millions of bees and insects rang there as loud as bells.

"Wonders! Wonders, master!" Zjendjan cried. "But why doesn't anybody live here? It's a paradise! Look at how many animals there are, sir!"

Snow hares, still in their winter coats, and huge grey jackrabbits moved like a turbulent undercurrent in that sea of whiteness while herds of longhorned antelope and deer watched the passing galleys with unfrightened eyes.

The ships sailed on.

The day passed.

The shoreline rose and fell, displaying broad panoramas of forest and Steppe, cliffs and mounds, and grasses tall and thick beyond belief. This was such beautiful country, so full of fruit and game and buoyant vegetation that Pan Yan asked himself as Zjendjan had done: why didn't anyone live there? But of course he knew. This land was rich as none other in the world but few were as dangerous. It would take the iron hand of some new Yeremi Vishnovyetzki to tame it, harness it and defend it from Tartars and marauders. Until such hands reached out and grasped this country, and flushed the human wolves out of the ravines and sent them to the gibbet and the sharpened stake, and carved roads and highways in the wilderness and built the castles and studded them with cannon, no man could plant his corn here and live to watch it grow. And so these riches waited, untouched and unused in an unpeopled land as vast as all the rest of Europe west of the Vistula.

Everything here grew taller, flew quicker and farther, stretched over greater distances and bloomed in brighter colors than anywhere else. The soil along the riverbanks was thick and black and glistening with rich oils; oats spilled carelessly from a horse's feedbag, or a cherry-pit spat out here in passing, sprouted a foot-long green stalk overnight, Pan Yan knew. It was a magic land, a wild world waiting for a master.

Hours passed. The galleys seemed to fly downstream as if they'd grown wings, propelled by the measured beating of the boatmen's oars. The wind was sharp and fresh and filled the square sails. The ships' prows seemed to leap across the foaming water. At times the river narrowed and the flat, calm water boiled among towering escarpments of onyx and crimson fire-stone, then wound in rapid coils between islands so thick with vegetation that nothing showed behind the curtains of dark leaves. And then the waters spilled into unsuspected bays, hidden lagoons and inlets dense with nodding reeds; they flooded the low riverside ravines and gouged dark caves out of the rocky banks. Such caves and bays were Cossack hideouts, Pan Yan knew, but now they were empty. The only living creatures that rose out of the tangled roots and reeds in the mouths of tributary streams and from the floating islands within the lagoons were the water birds.

All this was green and blue where the horizons lifted to the sky, and there were the scarlet splashes of strange blooms and the bright golden stalks of sunflowers swaying in the wind, and the air seemed to quiver in the white glare of the sun.

Then the sun dipped and the colors deepened, and the fresh breeze spilled out of the sails and died away in the still backwaters of the floating islands, and insects—some as thick as a man's thumb—rose out of the reeds and swooped down on the men and animals on the galleys' decks. And then the journey became a living nightmare of screaming horses and frantic men who cursed at the oars. The insects, never seen on the dry Steppes to the north, settled on them in clouds: mosquitoes big as bees, flying leeches, and fierce batlike flies that swarmed in the rotted undergrowth of the mangrove swamps. They struck like arrows and their bites tore away living flesh and left broad streams of blood running down the skin.

★　★　★

Skshetuski ordered his ships rowed into mid-river where the tormenting insects came in fewer numbers. The wind picked up again, the galleys moved into swifter water and ran downstream in a darkening world. The sun hung still for a long moment over the horizon as if in regret that the day was ending. Then it fell from the sky and the day was over. A cold wet darkness rolled out of the south, and they saw the pinpoint lights of fishermen's fires further down the river, and other lights gleamed suddenly and mysteriously in the distant Steppe and Pan Yan stared at them in astonishment.

"What lights are those, sergeant?"

"Ahead? That's Romanovka Island, lord. There's fishermen there."

"Always?"

"Always, lord."

"And the other fires? In the Steppe?"

The scarred old Cossack sergeant turned his narrow eyes to the glittering little lights farther to the east.

"I don't know, lord. Tartars, not Tartars . . . maybe devils. People don't go there much, not if they want to come back."

But it was time to tie up for the night. The oarsmen were tired; they looked up at Skshetuski with imploring eyes. He studied the black bulk of the Romanovka looming out of the moon-streaked darkness of the river and ordered his helmsman to bring the ship about. At once the wheel spun, the galley edged to the tall banks of the island, and the boatmen threw their anchors overboard and ran to fasten their mooring lines ashore. The second ship came about behind them.

"We'll sleep here, sergeant. Post guards. Stand-to an hour before dawn."

The sergeant touched his forelock and backed away. Soon the troopers disembarked their horses and led them ashore. But the men and animals had hardly settled for the night when quiet, dark forms rose out of the reeds and strange, half-human shapes with bloated, swollen faces began to sidle-up to the cooking fires.

"Who are you people?" Skshetuski called out.

"Men of the river," came the mumbled answer.

"What d'you want?"

"To talk. To see . . ."

"Then come up to the fires where we can see you!"

They came out of the darkness: coarse, ungainly creatures bent by a lifetime of crouching over their nets, with faces mutilated by the bites of insects. They were smeared from head to foot with tallow and strange yellow greases that lay in thick, shining folds in their hair and gleamed on necks and faces, reflecting the moonlight. These were the fisher folk of the Romanovka who caught and smoked and salted the bass and sturgeon of the Dnieper, and the huge carp and eels and giant pike that bred in the lagoons, and shipped them upriver to Kiev and Tchehryn and Tcherkassy and to Pereyaslav. Standing around the soldiers' bivouac fires they peered about and mut-

tered to each other. Their slitted eyes were alight with curiosity
and dark with speculation.

"Who are you people?" they said. "Where you going?"

"We're travelers," Pan Yan said and asked about the fires in
the Steppe.

"Men going to the *Sietch*," the fishermen shrugged and said.
"The Steppe's full of fires, we see them every night."

"The *Sietch*, eh? And why should people go to the *Sietch* this
time of the year?"

"People say there's going to be a war."

"Against whom?"

"The *Lahy*, they say."

There were no Zaporohjans among them, Skshetuski could
see and asked what happened to the Cossacks who normally
fished here.

"Their ataman called them. They go to the war."

That night Pan Yan slept badly, tormented by insects, but his
thoughts were even more troubling and persistent. He wondered if it weren't too late for his mission, after all; it would be
certain death to go on if the Zaporohjans had already started on
their march and if the war had begun in earnest. No one
expected the storm to break this soon but the young soldier had
little choice about what to do; he had his orders and the Prince's
letters. War or no war, he'd go as far downriver as he could;
there'd be more reason now than ever before to know just how
strong the Zaporohjans were.

The clouds of insects dispersed shortly before dawn when the
night was coldest and Pan Yan rose and watched his soldiers
stand to arms.

This was the Steppe's deadliest hour when the winged raptors
first began to stir, and the night-prowling animals slunk to their
caves and lairs, and the Tartar raider crept through the tall
grasses with his arrow notched, his short horn-bow ready, and
the curved, cruel *yataghan* clamped between his teeth.

But there was no attack that morning.

No alarm.

The ships were swiftly loaded and pushed into the stream and
the quick current and the morning breeze caught them in mid-
river and carried them south. They were abreast of the Tarenski
Rog, the broadest and the most spectacular of the majestic
bends, when the sun burst redly out of the darkened Steppe and

the new day began. They sailed past Dry Mountain and the Horse's Spur where huge reptiles crawled out of the swamps, and then the land grew gaunt and savage, and the waters quickened, and a low muttering came out of the south carried on the wind. It was like summer thunder booming in the sky beyond the horizon, Pan Yan thought, or like muffled war drums beaten underground. The young lieutenant had never heard anything quite like it and asked what it was.

The Cossack sergeant cocked his head and listened and a cold, distant light appeared in his narrowed eyes.

"The cataracts, lord . . ."

"So soon? So near?"

"Near?" The Cossack's slitted eyes communicated nothing. "They're not near, master."

"When will we reach them, then?"

"Maybe tomorrow," the old Cossack said. "Maybe the day after."

"They're that far away? And so loud already?"

And then the great black towers of Kudak broke through the horizon.

★　★　★

A whole day would go by before Skshetuski's ships could sail into the calm waters within the shadow of the fortress walls and, in the meantime, the landscape seemed to die a little more with each passing hour. It became bleak and grim and forbidding as if all the beauty and splendor of the country ended at this last bastion of the Commonwealth. The soil seemed scorched by fire and littered with split granite. The fortress rose out of the water on a great, sheer cliff, and the river was so narrow at this point that an arrow shot from the lofty walls could reach either bank. No vessel of any kind could go up or down the river without passing under the guns of Kudak. The fortress lay like a great crouching watchdog across this southern threshold of the Commonwealth, baring its rows of cannon at the *Sietch*.

They reached the fortress after sundown and spent the night outside. Pan Grodjitzki, the grim one-eyed commandant of Kudak, ordered his gates barred at sunset and kept them locked until his garrison stood to arms at dawn to greet the new day with leveled muskets and burning fuses poised above their cannon. No one could leave or approach the castle once the gates were closed.

If the King himself came to the fortress after sundown, Pan Yan knew, he'd have to sleep outside the walls, so he found shelter in the little village that had sprouted in the shadow of the castle's guns. It was no more than a cluster of adobe huts, no better than burrows, so cramped and narrow that men crawled into them on their hands and knees. But why should anyone build anything better at the foot of Kudak? As the dour villagers explained it, the castle's gunners blew the huts to dust each time that Tartars appeared on the horizon.

Once more sleep proved impossible. The young soldier's nightmares seemed so real that he leaped to his feet time and again with saber in hand. His premonitions of disaster and visions of Helen trapped or struggling in Bohun's hands grew sharper and more vivid every hour.

He was up long before dawn to pace back and forth at the foot of the cliff under the castle walls. His spirits lifted a little as he looked at those massive ramparts, thick as the towers of Lubnie, and at the long black necks of cannon stretched in silent rows out of the crenelated gun ports. Surely, he told himself, no one would be able to scale those cliffs and ramparts in the face of muskets; no cannon could batter down those gigantic bastions. The Cossack storm would spend itself among these precipices as so many others had done through the years.

★ ★ ★

At last the night ebbed, a streak of light appeared on the horizon and he heard the drums beating the call to arms on the castle walls, and when he sent word that Prince Yeremi's envoy was waiting in the village, Pan Grodjitzki came out in person to greet him and lead him inside.

Pan Yan looked curiously at this grim old soldier, the '*Cyclops of Kudak*' as he was known throughout the Ukraine, thinking that here was a man as hard and forbidding as the granite fortress he'd commanded for more than twenty years. He was then in his middle fifties, a gnarled silent man who exercised the power of life and death over everything that lived in that forgotten corner of the world, and who saw no civilized face anywhere near him for years at a time. His own face had been ravaged by disease and pitted with the scars left by Tartar arrows and he peered with his one cold eye out of those rocklike features with as little feeling as if he had become one with his stony unforgiving world.

They ate a simple breakfast in a cold stone chamber but the fortress commandant seemed restless and impatient to be out on his walls and scanning the horizons.

"So you're going to the *Sietch*," he growled finally.

"That's right," the young man said quickly. "The *Sietch*. D'you have any news from there, commandant?"

"War," the grim man muttered.

"Ah . . . so it's certain now?"

The one-eyed man shrugged and threw him a cold, gloomy glance.

"The Chief Ataman has pulled in all the Cossacks from every river, island, hovel and pasture . . . anywhere they'd gone for the Winter. Deserters from the Ukraine are coming in by the hundreds every day. They've gathered more than thirty thousand men already, and when they get into the Ukraine, when the Castle Cossacks and the peasants join them, they'll have a hundred thousand in a week."

"And Hmyelnitzki?"

"He'll be back with the Tartars any day. Maybe he's back already. You're wasting your time going to the *Sietch*."

"I've my orders, sir," Skshetuski said simply.

"You want to count those mad dogs for yourself?" The fierce old commandant laughed without amusement. "Stay right here then, they'll all be along in a day or two. There's no way for them to go around Kudak and you can bet your soul they won't leave it standing behind them once they've gone."

"But surely you can hold them off?"

Grodjitzki turned his gloomy, bitter eye on the young lieutenant.

"Hold them?" His voice betrayed no feeling; it was almost as if he didn't care. "No. I won't hold them."

"Why not?" Pan Yan couldn't hide his shock and disappointment. "This fortress is one of the strongest in the Commonwealth!"

But the commandant shrugged again and turned his face away.

"I've no gunpowder," he said quietly. "I've sent . . . oh, maybe twenty boats . . . asking for a little. Maybe my messengers got taken on the way. Maybe the Hetmans are short themselves. Who knows? Anyway, nothing came. I've enough on hand to last a couple of weeks but that's it. Ah, let me tell you, if I had full magazines I'd blow this place skyhigh before I let a Cossack set his foot in here. But, as it is . . ."

"So what will you do?"

"What do you think I'll do? They told me to crouch down here like a dog, I'm here. They said to watch and listen, I'm watching and listening. They said to growl and to show my teeth and that's what I'm doing. And when it comes to dying I'll know how to do that too."

"But can't you make your own powder?"

"For two months now the Zaporohjans have been seizing all the sulfur that comes upriver from the sea. But it doesn't make much of a difference one way or another. A soldier lives on borrowed time any way you see it."

"And what if you went north yourself to get what you need?"

"Young man, I can't leave Kudak, and I won't," Grodjitzki said harshly. "I've spent my life here. This is where I belong and it's as good a place as any to finish with living. As for you, young fellow, don't imagine that you're on your way to banquets and receptions! Or that your status as an envoy will count for anything with the Zaporohjans; they murder their own atamans whenever they feel like it! As long as I've been sitting on this rock I can't remember one of their commanders who died a natural death. You'll die there too, you can be sure of that, and that's all there's to it."

Infected by the other's gloom Skshetuski sat in silence, his head down, and the dour commandant threw him another grim assessing glance.

"I see your spirits are flagging a bit, young fellow," he drawled as he rose. "You'd better go back where you've come from, I expect. You might live a lot longer behind the walls in Lubnie."

But Skshetuski's voice flashed out like bared steel to match the old commander's icy bitterness.

"Think of a better story to frighten me with, commandant," he snapped angrily. "I've heard all these horror tales a dozen times over. They're starting to bore me. But if that's the advice you're ready to give me, maybe it's the advice you'd take in my place, eh? And if that's so then maybe powder isn't the only thing you lack to defend this fortress."

He sat back, breathing deeply, and watched a pale smile pass across Pan Grodjitzki's scarred and pitted face.

"Hmm. So the dog can bite," the old Steppe watchdog muttered in Ruthenian. "Forgive me, young friend. I see you know how to represent your Prince . . . and all of us, when it comes to that. Alright, then. I'll give you some longboats. You'd never get your galleys past the *Nyenasytetz*."

"That's what I've come for, sir," Pan Yan said at once and the one-eyed commandant nodded and offered some advice.

"When you get to the Sixth Cataract portage the boats overland. The water is high this year but it's never high enough in that place. And once you're on low waters again watch yourself, you hear? Ambush is easy there. Just keep in mind that cold steel and hot lead are the best arguments with those people down there— if you can call them people! All they've ever respected is a fist."

"When can I have the boats, then?"

"At sunrise." The old commander led the way outside. "Now come with me and I'll show you Kudak. You might be the last outsider who'll ever get to see it."

★   ★   ★

The day spent on the ramparts and parapets of the fortress did nothing to raise the young lieutenant's spirits. It was, indeed, a castle that might defy almost any siege, and Tartar captives worked around the clock in its galleries and bastions to raise the great walls by a foot each year, but knowing what he did about it Pan Yan looked at it with the grief he'd feel for some unconquerable knight who was dying of a secret internal disease. Without gunpowder the fortress was as good as taken; its garrison and commandant were as good as dead. Skshetuski knew that neither he nor any other man would ever see those border veterans again; they'd been condemned to death. But was his own fate to be any different? Death seemed a certainty in the *Sietch*.

He didn't think he'd be afraid to face it; he was a soldier and he'd faced death often. But life had never seemed as sweet to him before, it never promised him as much as it did now with Helen, and the persistent thought that he'd never see her again, and never know her love, became a real torment. He could imagine her caught up in the horrors of a peasant rising and the hair rose on his head in fear for her safety. Moreover, he realized that she would wait for him in Rozloghi because he'd told her to, and that the war would trap her and engulf her there! The Steppe was dry enough by now for Helen and the old *Knahina* to make their promised journey to the Prince in Lubnie, but it was Skshetuski himself who told them to wait until he returned from the *Sietch*!

Whatever happened to him didn't make much difference. He had to do his duty. But he could see Rozloghi in flames when he closed his eyes, he sensed Helen's terror as she was dragged away by a howling mob, he heard her crying out to him and saw her outstretched arms, and so he paced the stone floor and tore at his beard and twisted his hands not knowing what to do.

Zjendjan, who'd spread his bedding across the threshold of his master's room, watched him with worried eyes. He got up, saw to the torches that were burning in their iron rings, and began to move about without a real purpose other than to draw attention to himself and distract Pan Yan.

"Master . . . hey, master!" he spoke up at last but Skshetuski stared at him with glassy eyes as if he wasn't there. "Hey master?"

"Zjendjan," Pan Yan murmured, shaking himself free of his oppressive thoughts. "Are you afraid of dying?"

"What? Who? Dying?" The lad looked dumbstruck and scared out of his wits. "What are you saying, master?"

"There's no coming back from the *Sietch*, you know," Pan Yan told him quietly.

"No coming back? Then why are you going?"

"That's my business, lad. But *you* going there is another matter. You're nimble and quickwitted enough for most things, but you're not much more than a child and your wits won't get you out of that place alive. So go back to Tchehryn and then on to Lubnie."

Zjendjan stared at him with his mouth wide open and then began to scratch his tussled head. "What's the matter, master? You want me to leave you?"

"That's right. Go back to Lubnie when I go on tomorrow. Otherwise it's a sure death for you."

"Death?" The boy's plump, pink face became pale and solemn. "Sure I'm scared of her. Who wouldn't be? That's why God made her ugly, so we'd have something to be scared of.

And sure I know it's God who says when it's my time to die or it's a sin. But since you're going to your death of your own will, master, the sin will be yours as the master, not mine as the servant. So why should I leave you?"

"Because I want you to," Pan Yan told him gently.

"Well sir, hmm . . . well, master,"—and now the boy's face turned scarlet with feeling and his voice was trembling—"I know I'm supposed to do what you tell me . . . I mean you're the master and I'm just the servant . . . But I'm not going to leave you anyway! How can I? I'm not a peasant! My people may be poor as church mice, and so we have to go into service to make the ends meet, but we're gentry too and we know what's what! So how can I run out on my master when he needs me most?"

Moved, Skshetuski sighed. "I knew you were a good lad. So I'll just tell you this much. If you don't go back to Lubnie because you want to, you'll go by my order."

But Zjendjan raised both his fists, pushed them into his eyes like an angry child, and began to howl as if Skshetuski had taken a switch to him. "If you was to kill me, master, I won't go! What d'you take me for, sir? Some kind of a Judas?"

And he wept so bitterly that Pan Yan had to smile.

"Listen," Skshetuski said. "You won't be any help to me down there and you know I won't ask anybody to cut my throat for nothing. But you can do something for me that'll mean a lot more to me than keeping myself alive, understand?"

"What's more important than that, master?"

"Your going to Rozloghi."

Zjendjan stopped weeping. "To Rozloghi, master?"

"Yes. You'll tell the old *knahina* to take our princess to Lubnie at once, straight away, or they'll be swept up by the rebellion! And you'll make sure she does it! It's an important thing I'm asking you to do for me, my lad, something I'd ask of a trusted friend rather than a servant."

But the boy was still unconvinced. "Anybody can take a letter, master. Send somebody else!"

"Ah lad, lad," Skshetuski said gently. "Whom else can I trust to do this as well as I'd do it myself? Can't you understand what you'll be doing for me? Beg them to leave at once, on horseback, without packing if they have to! You'll save my life twice over because I can't live thinking about what might happen there!"

"Well," the boy mumbled. "If that's how it is . . . Well, then I have to go. But I don't want to, master!"

And the boy's plump, reddened face crumpled in a new flood of tears.

Skshetuski raised the lad off the floor where he had thrown himself at his master's feet. "Stop that bawling now and go back to sleep. And don't show any tears in Rozloghi."

"But aren't I going to see you again, master?"

"You will if God wills it. Now go to bed, you've a long trip tomorrow."

Sniffing and smearing smudged tears across his face the boy went back to his bedding and Pan Yan spent the rest of the night writing letters which Zjendjan was to deliver to Helen and to the Prince in Lubnie.

He tried to pray but peace of mind continued to elude him until the red dawn filled his narrow windows and the trumpeters called the garrison to arms on the walls and towers. He found some solace in the knowledge that he had done his best for Helen and the faithful lad, and made his own peace with what had to happen, and soon afterwards Pan Grodjitzki stepped into the room and told him that his boats were ready.

"So am I," Pan Yan said.

Chapter Eight

DAWN FOUND THEM on the river: a long line of boats running with the current. These were the kind of shallow-drafted boats which, in a later time and on another continent, would be known as *bateaux*, much bigger than the darting Cossack skiffs. They were sturdy enough to carry the horses as well as Pan Yan's troopers and the Kudak boatmen but not as large and heavy as the river galleys which they left behind at the fortress.

The *bateaux* took them safely down the river. They skimmed the boiling waters of the first two cataracts—known as the Surski and the Lohanny—then passed across the hungry rocks of the Voronovski Rapids on the crest of a ten-foot tidal wave that pushed up the river from the sea. The boatkeels grated and the gunnels ground against the jagged black cliffs of the Ksyonjhentsy Gorge, which was also known as the *Cataract of the Prince*, but they got through safely; and in the white water of the Streltzy they ran into submerged rocks and lost some of their rigging; but the auxiliary rudders which Pan Grodjitzki had his people mount in the prows of the boats helped to steer them past the deadly whirlpools.

At last they saw the thick white mists of the *Nyenasytetz* and heard the booming roar of its furious waters, and then, Skshetuski knew, it was time to run the boats ashore and drag them overland.

"To shore!" he ordered.

One by one, the boats turned and ran into the mud and gravel of the reedy bank, and the men and animals waded to dry land.

Pan Yan expected that the portage would take at least a day and possibly the night as well; from what he'd heard that was how long it took to go around the mile-long gorge of '*Old Insatiable.*' But the riverbanks were littered with round, smooth logs and sturdy poles left over from other portages and the work went swiftly. The troopers hitched their horses to the boats and dragged them from the water onto waiting rollers. Then the boatmen and Skshetuski's soldiers put their backs into the ropes and levers.

The young lieutenant walked alone to the top of the gorge. The land was barren here: rocky and glistening with wide-flung spray; the air was cold and filled with a damp penetrating chill. Nothing moved here. There was no sign of life as far as he could see up and down the river. Even the thick white mist appeared as something leprous and unclean and the dark cliff underfoot seemed to shake and tremble to the roaring of the furious water in the gorge.

He looked down and recoiled, sure that he was staring into the open jaws of Hell.

Across the width of the river ran seven stone barriers torn by the maddened water into jagged black teeth, huge fangs dripping with white foam, and narrow gaps ripped out of their walls. The river smashed against them with all of its weight and the stones hurled back the angry water, churned it into foam and sent it twisting and howling into giant whirlpools. The water bit into the black basalt cliffs, struck them with white-tipped ten-foot waves, and its deafening sound seemed like the roaring of a hundred cannon. And there was something else, another sound hidden in this roaring, as if tortured souls were screaming out and groaning and as if wolves were howling. It was easy to believe then that this raging gorge was just what the Steppe people said it was: the throat of the Devil.

The boatmen had seen this phenomenon before and they turned their eyes away and crossed themselves and urged the young lieutenant not to come too close to the edge of the precipice.

"Whoever looks too long into those waters, master, will go mad," said the steersman of Skshetuski's boat, who also acted as chief of the boatmen. "He'll see things that'll make him jump in there."

"I can believe it," Pan Yan said.

"And sometimes long black arms reach out of there and grab a man and drag him into Hell. That's when you hear frightful laughter booming in the gorge and anyone who hears it is sure to die next day. Even the Zaporohjans don't dare to drag their canoes past this place at night."

Pan Yan shrugged but he was curious none the less.

"Isn't it true that no one can join the *Nijhovtsy* until he's fought his way alone in a skiff through the cataracts?"

"Oh yes, it's true," the boatman muttered. "Yes. But nobody tries it in the *Nyenasytetz*. The minstrels say Bohun alone has done it. But nobody believes it."

★ ★ ★

The portage took most of the day.

The sun had long slid into the shadows of the afternoon when Pan Yan went aboard his boat again and the *bateaux* entered the calm waters that spilled out of the broad mouth of the tributary Nijh. The *Sietch* was near then. But Skshetuski didn't want to risk his boats at night in the treacherous labyrinth of the Tchertomelik which wound among its swampy islands all the way to the Zaporohjans' permanent walled encampment. He ordered his helmsman to steer for Hortytza Island which lay like a leafy, rocky fortress in the mouth of this final waterway. He hoped to find people there, maybe Zaporohjans, who'd take word of his coming to their stronghold. He wanted the savage brotherhood to know that he was an envoy coming from the Prince.

But the Hortytza was abandoned. Nothing stirred in its thick, tangled undergrowth; there was no sign of men, no trace of recent campfires. Even the boatmen were astonished and stared at each other with uneasy eyes; since the earliest days of the *Sietch* the Zaporohjans always posted armed companies on this island to watch for Tartars and stop anyone who came among them uninvited.

Skshetuski stared into the gathering darkness just as ill-at-ease and troubled as his men. If there'd been any need of a final sign to assure him that his mission would end in disaster, and that he'd come too late to find anything but death, he knew that he could read it clearly in the empty silence of Hortytza Island.

Ashore, he called two sections of his men together and led them inland but they found no one there. The island was too large to search completely before darkness fell but instinct told him that they were not alone there. Back at the boats, he ordered them dragged ashore. The boatmen lighted fires to ward off the clouds of insects that rose from the reeds. Then some of the men settled down to sleep. Others watched the darkness. But soon exhaustion overcame them all.

Most of the night passed quietly.

The soldiers and the boatmen slept around the fires and only the sentries stirred and peered sharply into the shifting shadows among the shrubs and rushes. From time to time they cast uneasy glances at the bowed, silent form of their young commander who sat in the circle of harsh yellow light cast by the largest fire. He was lost in his own dark thoughts. He couldn't sleep that night any more than he'd slept on any other night since the journey started. A cold, inner fever seemed to shake him as he tossed fresh chips of wood on the coals with a mindless gesture. Sometimes he thought that he could hear muffled footsteps coming out of the black emptiness of the island; sometimes he seemed to hear strange cries and hisses. The call of a night bird. The bleating of a goat.

And then, as the darkness on the near horizon became edged with grey, the senior of the watching troopers came up to him softly, trying to make no noise.

"What is it?" he asked.

"They are coming, master . . ."

The whisper was urgent.

"Who? Where from?"

"Maybe *Nijhovtsy*, sir. There's about forty of 'em . . ."

"Good. That's not many. Wake the men! Get the fires going!"

The troopers leaped to their feet and the fires blazed and all the sentries ran into the circle and formed up shoulder to shoulder, their backs to the boats. They waited quietly, listening to the wind that whistled through the reeds. No other sound came to them from the island. And then the other sound was there: the creak and rustle of a mass of men working their way towards them through the undergrowth.

It ceased suddenly. Then a thick, angry voice called out of the darkness.

"Who's that on the shore?"

"And who are you?" Skshetuski's sergeant shouted.

"Answer you devil's son or you'll get a bullet!"

"His Excellency the Ambassador of His Highness, the Prince Yeremi Vishnovyetzki, coming to see the Chief Ataman!" the sergeant cried out.

The murmuring voices died out in the darkness.

"Come up here, one of you!" the sergeant called. "Nobody harms an envoy, and that's a fact, but envoys don't harm anybody either!"

There were some growls and whispers in the darkness, and then a harsh muttering, and then the heavy footsteps crackled out again and soon forty or fifty dark figures loomed at the edge of light cast by the campfires. Their dark skins, dwarfed ungainly bodies and sheepskin coats worn with the wool outside, showed that most of them were Tartars. Skshetuski thought at once that Hmyelnitzki must have returned from the Crimea if there were Tartars on the Hortytza.

The headman of the troop, a huge Zaporohjan with a horribly twisted and disfigured face, lurched into the light and staggered to a halt.

"Which is the envoy?" he shouted, swaying on his feet. A thick stench of sour spirits spread from him like a reeking cloud. Drunk, he repeated: "Who's the envoy, then?"

"I am," Pan Yan said, stepping forward.

"You?"

"Show some respect, you drunken pig!" the old sergeant shouted. "You say '*Your Excellency*' and '*My Lord*' to an envoy! Don't you know that, you peasant?"

"To hell with you, you devil's sons!" the drunken giant bellowed. "Death take you, all you excellencies, lords, envoys, gentlemen . . .! An' what you want with the Ataman anyway?"

"That's not for you to know," Pan Yan snapped out. "But it'll be your neck unless you take me to him!"

The huge man staggered back as if he'd been struck. He looked as if he wanted to hurl himself at the young lieutenant and tear him apart with his bare hands. But then another Zaporohjan seized him by the collar, hurled him back into the crowd, and stepped out himself.

"We're from the Ataman!" he said. "He put us here to see that nobody from the *Lahy* comes too close, you get it? An' if they do, he said, we're to tie 'em up and bring 'em in. An' that's just what we'll do with you!"

"You won't put a rope on me," Skshetuski said quietly.

"We rope everybody!"

"Ay!" the drunken giant roared and staggered out into the

light again. "We'll take you to the Ataman if we got to drag you by the beard! Like this!"

And he reached out for Skshetuski's chin. But in that moment he moaned and fell as if struck by lightning. Pan Yan had crushed his skull with his battle hammer.

"*Koli! Koli!*" howled the maddened voices and the dark mob fell on the Prince's soldiers like a wall of trees torn out of the woods behind them.

The soldiers met them head on.

Muskets roared.

And then wild yells, curses, calls for help and furious howls that didn't have a meaning joined the clash of iron, the groans of the wounded, and the harsh cough of dying men trampled underfoot. The tightly packed mass of struggling men surged across the fires and soon there wasn't room to swing a saber or the butt of a musket, and so they stabbed with knives and tore at each other with their bare hands. Maddened by the sudden reek of blood they bit each other and tore out each other's beards and hair, and cracked bones and limbs, and gouged out the eyes and ripped ears and noses. The rolling bodies soon crushed and scattered the fires and they fought blindly in the darkness, feeling for the shape of a helmet or the coarse texture of wool and fur to distinguish enemies from a friend.

Dead men fell as thickly as bundled cornstalks at harvest time, and soon the Tartars and the Zaporohjans fell back with howls of terror, but new cries, signaling fresh attackers, came out of the darkness deeper on the island.

"To the boats!" Skshetuski ordered.

The soldiers ran to obey but the boats had been dragged too far ashore. They were firmly embedded in the mud, there was no way to launch them, and a fresh mass of Tartars and Zaporohjans poured from among the trees.

"Fire!" Pan Yan cried.

The musket volley hurled the charging mass back into the trees, leaving a dozen bodies trembling on the beach, and the crew worked like madmen to get the heavy *bateaux* back into the water. But the wet night air had softened the soil and the mud sucked the keels too far down to budge.

"We won't make it, master," the sergeant reported.

"We'll fight where we are, then," Skshetuski said calmly.

But now the enemy started killing from a distance, shooting out of the shadows of the trees, and soon the splash of lead balls spattering the water and the soft hiss of arrows became one with the moaning of the wounded. The cold night air filled with the high-pitched yelping of the Tartars, and the harsh Cossack cry of "*Koli! Koli* . . .! Kill . . .!" And, throughout, the calm voice of Skshetuski repeated at measured intervals: "Fire!"

Dawn came at last and threw its pale light on the battlefield. It seeped into the darkness around the trees where a great mob of Cossacks and Tartars stood with smoke-streaked faces pressed to their wooden gun butts or leaning back to draw the strings of their powerful, horn-plated bows. Wreathed in black smoke that hung in tendrils like a shredded curtain, the light revealed the boats held fast in the mud and the dark wall of smoke that flashed with red and yellow. The crash of musketry was as regular as the slow beat of a steady heart. Between this flashing cloud along the water's edge and the human mass seething among the trees lay the still, scattered bodies of the dead.

Pan Yan stood in plain sight on the deck of the nearest boat. His thoughts were as clear and steady as the bright volleys from his soldiers' muskets. This was where he would die, he knew, and he accepted his own death as naturally and calmly as any Steppe soldier. This was a soldier's destiny, a part of his calling, and so he looked with no more than a passing interest at the arrows that spattered the hardwood planks of the deck around him. He hardly noticed when one of the arrows pierced his sable cap and carried it away.

"Fire!" he ordered firmly and, again, a bright yellow flame split the black smoke curtain.

"We won't hold them, Excellency," the old sergeant whispered. "There's too many of them."

"Very good."

"Must be two . . . three hundred," the sergeant said, peering into the trees.

"Very good," the young lieutenant said.

"So . . . what shall we do, sir?"

But Skshetuski didn't answer him at once. Death, he knew, was very near then and he waited for it as calmly as if it were an everyday occurrence. He merely wanted his last moment to come as naturally as a meeting between old acquaintances. He didn't want to die—he was too young for that—but he had brushed against death so often that he was quite untroubled by the thought of dying. When death came for him, he knew, it would find him ready.

"Sir?" the old sergeant asked again. "What are we to do, then?"

"We'll die," he said simply.

"We'll die here, *bat'ku!*" his Cossack troopers cried out with a proud, fierce joy.

"Fire!" Skshetuski said.

Smoke wreathed the beached longboats once again. But from the far ends of the island came new mobs armed with scythes and handguns and then the attackers split into two uneven groups; one went on shooting, throwing a hailstorm of lead and arrows at the boats; the other, much larger, seethed impatiently among the shrubs and trees waiting for the moment to charge with steel in hand. Four long canoes crept out from the reeds to take Skshetuski's men from the flanks and rear.

★ ★ ★

Then it was full daylight. The sun hung redly overhead and all the shadows vanished. The wind died down and the smoke lay in long flat streamers about the battlefield. Pan Yan turned twenty of his men to face the canoes that rushed towards them along the still water, and the musket fire that held the Tartars back among the trees slackened and grew weak. That seemed to be what they had waited for. Their keening yelps rose to a wild new pitch and they began to edge into the open.

The sergeant came again to stand beside Pan Yan.

"They'll be coming now, sir." He pointed towards the trees where some three hundred savage, bowlegged men in sheepskins and untanned leather coats, leaped and howled feverishly with foam on their mouths. "See, sir? The Tartars are putting their knives in their teeth."

The milling Tartars were, indeed, preparing to attack. They were biting down on the blades of their curved *yataghans* and drew their crooked sabers. A mass of Zaporohjans ran to join them with scythes set on end.

"Very good," Pan Yan said. "Fire!"

He looked towards the open water where the canoes had come within range of his boats and formed a crescent about them. Their sides erupted with sudden flame and fire and his boats filled at once with the sound of moaning. Lead balls spattered so thickly on his decks that they brought to mind the rattle of a hailstorm in Winter. In moments, even as he watched, half his soldiers died. The rest staggered, wounded, and crawled to their weapons. They were fighting with that careless, grim contempt for death that belongs to men who know that their lives are over but who want to have their deaths remembered as something worthwhile. Their faces were black with gunsmoke and raw with powder burns; their eyes were blurring and the strength was ebbing from their arms. Just like Pan Yan himself, they peered through the acrid smoke, blinded with their own blood, while their nostrils filled with the stench of burning flesh that came from their own hands clasped about their redhot musket barrels.

"Fire!" Pan Yan said.

But now their volley seemed no louder than the scattered tapping of spent musket balls that landed around them, and then a great howl soared among the trees—a massed booming roar as if all the devils had sprung out of hell—and the Tartars charged.

In moments, they scattered the smoke with the rush of their own densely packed bodies and covered the longboats like a flock of vultures settling on cadavers. The thick mob howled and pushed and trampled everything, including its own fallen, and ripped and tore at everything in sight. Some of Skshetuski's soldiers were still on their feet, flaying about with sabers and clubbed muskets, but most of them were dead.

He fought with silent fury. His eyes were full of his own blood. Blood covered his face. His whole head was bloody. An arrow buried itself in his shoulder as far as the feathers. He stood huge and silent, head and shoulders lifted above the mob, as grim as a giant in the smoke, and as terrible as death. His saber flashed like lightning and each stroke brought screams of pain and the dry rattling cough of a dying man. The old Cossack sergeant and another soldier guarded his flanks and back. The massed Tartars and Zaporohjans crowded towards them, fell and died, recoiled with cries of fear and superstitious awe and came on again, pushed by the mob behind them.

"Take them alive! Alive! To the Ataman with them!" howled the savage voices. "Give up there! Surrender!"

But Pan Yan could no longer surrender to anyone on earth even if he wished to. His face was drained of color under its thick red coating of fresh blood. He swayed, saw nothing, and then he fell headlong on the deck.

"Get up, *bat'ku!*" the old sergeant shouted in a desperate voice and then he too was down and the dark Tartar mass covered the boats completely.

Part Two

Part Two

Chapter Nine

LATER THAT DAY two men sat drinking in the house of the *Kantarey* of the *Sietch*—a dimly lit, low-ceilinged mud and wattle hut—in the middle of the Hassan Pasha, the traders' quarter outside the palisade. One was the old *Kantarey* himself, the Cossack official charged with watch over the weights and measures in the trading sheds of the Kramny Bazaar; the other was his kinsman, Anton Tatartchuk, the ataman or elected leader of the Tchehryn Cossacks, whose massive trunk and scowling face made a violent contrast with the old man's frailty and mildness. They sat hunched over on two rough, deal benches and dipped their leather cups in a wooden tub of liquor set on the plank table between them.

They kept their voices low.

"So it's to be today, eh?" the old man muttered.

"Any moment now." The younger man's voice betrayed anxiety and fear. "They're only waiting for the Chief Ataman and for Tuhay-bey."

"And where did they go?"

"I don't know about the Ataman. But Tuhay-bey's taken Hmyelnitzki down to Bazavluk to inspect his Tartars. They're due back anytime and everything else is ready in the *maydan*. By tonight it'll all be over one way or another."

"Hmm . . ." Fylyp Zakhar, the *Kantarey*, was a cautious man. "It mightn't go so well."

"Not well?" Thick beads of sweat were shining on Tatartchuk's face. "Why shouldn't it go well?"

"Well . . . there were those letters."

"Is it true there was one for me?"

"I saw one." The gnarled old man spat between his boots and reached for more liquor. "I took the letters to the Ataman himself. There was one for him, one for you and one for young Barabas, the old colonel's nephew. Everybody in the *maydan* knows about them now."

"Ah . . . And who sent them? D'you know?"

"*Knaz* Yarema wrote to the Ataman. His seal's on the paper. But the others . . . who knows? Maybe the Devil sent them."

"*Sohroni Bih!*" the younger Cossack muttered.

"If they don't come right out and call you a friend of the Poles you ought to be alright."

"God help me!" Tatartchuk cursed again.

"You feel something, eh?"

"Me?" The smell of fear came clearly through the raw reek of *gojhalka*. "Why should I? What's there to feel?"

The old man looked away.

"Well . . ." His careful voice had become evasive. "Maybe the Chief Ataman will steal those letters and get rid of 'em . . . His own head's at stake."

"Ey, d'you think he will?" Hope glimmered briefly in Tatartchuk's voice. "That could happen, couldn't it!"

"It could. He's a careful man. But if you feel something bad you ought to run for it."

"Run? Where's to run? How? The Ataman has men watching every trail. The Tartars lie along the Bazavluk like a pack of wolves. A fish wouldn't slip past them . . . a bird wouldn't be able to fly over . . .!"

"Then hide."

"Where, for God's sake?"

The old man shrugged. He drank. "Wherever you can."

"They'll find me." Sweat poured down Tatartchuk's contorted face and dripped on the table. "Unless you hide me, little father! Hey, aren't you my kinsman? Hide me in the bazaar, somewhere, eh? Maybe in one of the barrels?"

"Hide you?" The old man spat again. "So I should die with you? I wouldn't hide my own brother and neither would you."

"Then I'm lost!"

The old man shrugged. "So get drunk if you're afraid of dying, you won't feel it then."

"But maybe there's nothing in that letter, eh?"

"Maybe. Maybe not."

Tatartchuk grasped his head with both his hands and his slanted eyes leaped from one object to another searching for some refuge.

"Ey, it's bad . . . bad!" The hoarse, cruel voice was thick with self-pity. "I'm a good Cossack, no friend of the *Lahy*, but who knows what that Pole they've caught on Hortytza will say at the meeting?"

"He won't say anything," the old *Kantarey* muttered. "That's a *Lah* like pure gold, that one. You know how they are, some of them. Like fire and iron."

"You think so, eh? You've seen him, little father?"

"I did. Fixed his wounds with tallow. Gave him good vodka to ease his pain a little. Ah, he's a hard one! They say he butchered more Tartars on Hortytza than pigs on a feast day. Don't you worry none about him, he'll keep his mouth shut."

They drank in silence after that. Tatartchuk gnawed his knuckles, grim with apprehension, but the old man let nothing show on his wrinkled face except that great age which his own shrewdness, ruthlessness and cunning allowed him to reach among the Zaporohjans who murdered each other with as little thought as if they were exterminating vermin. No help would come from him, Tatartchuk knew, and he expected neither help nor mercy from anyone else. And then they heard the deep, rolling thunder of the ceremonial drum beaten in the *maydan* and the younger Cossack hissed and leaped to his feet as if he'd been touched with a branding iron. "You hear that?"

The old man nodded.

"They're beating for the Council. *Sohroni Bih!* You, Fylyp, you won't tell them what we talked about, will you?"

The old man shrugged. Tatartchuk seized the wooden tub with both hands, lifted it to his mouth and leaned far back, head and body tilting, and gulped the raw spirits as if his salvation depended on oblivion. He drank *na umor*, all hope cast aside. And then the old man said that it was time to go.

Outside, the booming of the giant kettledrum seemed to rise out of the earth itself. It filled the dusty air and penetrated into every chest, and every heart picked up its threatening beat. It lay as heavy as a cloud above the huge encampment and spread along the Steppe and its many rivers and there seemed no way to get away from it.

Tatartchuk and his kinsman stepped out of the hut.

★ ★ ★

The Hassan Pasha quarter lay outside the earthworks, huddled under the great earth wall, beyond the shallow moat, and well away from the stockade made of rough-trimmed, pointed logs and stakes, with the black mouths of cannon gaping off the ramparts and from the tall stone tower that guarded the approaches to the bridge and gate. Zakhar's house lay in the middle of the quarter, among the huts and dugouts of lesser bazaar officials, surrounded by a broad, cleared space and sixty massive sheds. These—like the huts and houses—were no more than lairs in this womanless society: crude structures of rough-hewn, untrimmed oak roofed with reeds and branches.

Thirty-eight of these sheds belonged to the thirty-eight *Kujhenye* of the Zaporohjans—an old Ruthenian term for a council fire—which served the same purpose in the *Sietch* as clans and tribes did among other nations. The rest of the sheds were reserved for outsiders: Tartar and Valachian traders whose lust for profits might exceed their regard for safety. Few of these guest-sheds were ever in use; not many merchants were foolhardy enough to bring their caravans right into the *Sietch* where trading was often a prelude to robbery and murder, with which wise bazaar officials like the old *Kantarey* never interfered.

But the sheds and trading booths of the *Kujhenye* were always packed with people, and so were the thirty-eight drinking sheds behind them. There, among rotting heaps of refuse, dung, straw, piles of lumber and smashed liquor barrels, lay mounds of smoked fish, lance-shafts, church ornaments, brass copper crosses stripped from the onion cupolas of looted cathedrals, sheets of lead and copper torn off mansion roofs, broken knives and sabers with plain or jeweled hilts, and mountains of saddles. Some of these were little more than quilted leather pads, others seemed to drip with precious stones like an icy rainbow. This was the marketplace for loot taken in Valachia, from the rich lords of the Moldavian plain, out of the villas of Crimean Tartars, off the pirated galleys of the Turkish sultan, and from the Muslim pleasure palaces of the Anatolian coast.

Among these heaps of treasure and piles of garbage staggered a crowd of drunken, half-naked men black with mud and wood-smoke, with dung and straw drying on their backs, and with open wounds and running sores gaping on their bodies. But on this day the Hassan Pasha quarter was busier than usual. Thousands had gathered there, and when the shutters went up on the drinking sheds the vast mob flowed like a muddy river into the main encampment where the council drum thundered its fearsome summons.

Tatartchuk walked among these roaring thousands as if he was on his way to his execution. Men pushed and jostled him but he hardly noticed. Whatever hopes he had before the great drum started pounding in the square evaporated as soon as the planks of the drawbridge rattled under him.

Where could he go?

How could he hide?

The multitude swept him through the gates and into the *maydan* and he shot desperate glances everywhere around as if he'd never seen that familiar place before. Here was the heart of the Zaporohjan *Sietch*. Thousands of boots had trampled that red clay arena into a wide flat field surrounded by the thirty-eight longhouses that served as the barracks, arsenals, registries, treasuries and stables of the regular *Kujhenye* of the Zaporohjan Cossacks. There each *Kujhen* stored its powder, vodka, banners, lances, ammunition and its horsetail standards. Each barrack was exactly like every other, differing only in its name. One corner of the *maydan* was taken up by the Council House where the *Kujhen* atamans met to argue and to make decisions. The rest of the savage brotherhood, now drunk beyond belief, held its deliberations under the open sky, where the mob howled, fought and reeled about in its murderous thousands, and sent its staggering delegates to the Council House to find out what was going on inside, or to demand more vodka, or to claim a victim, or simply to exert its will and terrorize its leaders.

The sun was well down in the west by the time Zakhar and Tatartchuk pushed their way into the Council House. Pitch barrels flamed in the *maydan* behind them and cast a lurid glow into the darkening sky. Each *Kujhen* had set up tubs of liquor in front of its barrack where the savage brethren began their meeting among screams and curses, brutish laughter, pistol shots, and the thud of clubs with which the *Esauls*, or *Kujhen* lieutenants, attempted to keep order.

"Help me, Fylyp," Tatartchuk murmured to his kinsman but

the old man was already gone, vanished beyond the waiting doorway.

★ ★ ★

In the dim-lit council room, illuminated only by the red flames of an open hearth, Tatartchuk's fellow atamans stood about in uneasy groups, whispering to each other. A small plank table for the military scribe was their only furniture; the rest of them would sit on the skins and furs heaped against the walls on the bare floor but they were in no hurry to take their places and begin the meeting. They kept their eyes on the Chief Ataman who paced the hall, tugging at his beard, and then exploded into savage curses when they saw Tatartchuk.

He looked at them and shuddered, reading his fate in their bloodshot eyes and in the uproar that came from the *maydan*. Oh, he had friends among them . . . good friends, good brothers who'd fought beside him in a dozen wars . . . and they'd be friends again if everything went well. But what if it didn't? Only the vacant idiot stare and foolish grin of the young Barabas met his anxious eyes, and so he sighed and moved closer to him and felt more alone then ever when he stood beside him.

"Aren't you worried?" he whispered.

But young Barabas, known affectionately in the brotherhood as the Idiot Ataman, only grinned at him. He was a young man of great strength and beauty to which he owed his command of a *Kujhen* but he was feeble-minded, a child locked in the powerful body of a murderous warrior, and he'd have no idea that anything was wrong. His Cossacks followed him because he snapped horseshoes with his bare hands, and made them laugh, and because he didn't understand the meaning of fear. Other than that, he was a byword for stupidity.

"Worried?" He grinned his empty smile. "Why should I be worried?"

"The letters."

"A plague take your letters!" The huge young ataman's laughter sounded like the neighing of a horse. "I didn't write them, did I?"

"Laugh, laugh," Tatartchuk muttered. "Go ahead and laugh. You won't be laughing when they tie a millstone round your neck and drop you in the water."

But the Idiot Ataman only neighed again.

"What millstone? What water? Why should they do that?"

★ ★ ★

Before Tatartchuk could reply a sudden roar of welcome burst outside the windows, the doors banged open, and Bohdan Hmyelnitzki followed Tuhay-bey into the council hall. He carried the gilded *bulava* of the Hetman of the Zaporohjans but the shouts of welcome had been for the Tartar. Only a few months earlier this homicidal *murjah* had been the Cossacks' most hated enemy, but now they hurled their bright caps into the sky at the sight of him, and even Hmyelnitzki humbled his vast pride and walked a step behind him.

What else could he do? No royal warrant lifted him to power. He became the Zaporohjans' Hetman by the will of the mob when he came back from the Crimea with the Tartar Khan's promise of armed help against the Commonwealth. It was then that the mob lifted him on its shoulders, broke into the military treasury, and brought him the baton and the seal and the horse-tail standard. But what the mob created it could destroy as easily and Hmyelnitzki knew it. His whole standing with the brotherhood depended on the Tartars who, in turn, backed him just as long as he could feed their greed for captives, whom they sold in tens of thousands throughout Asia Minor or held for private ransom. So now he walked a step behind his terrible ally, and stifled his pride, while Tuhay-bey stared at the assembled Cossacks with contempt.

At last the Tartar threw himself on the thickest and deepest pile of furs and the atamans found places for themselves wherever they could.

Strange shadows seemed to pass across Hmyelnitzki's face as he prepared to speak. Pride and ambition struggled there against bitterness and anger.

And was there doubt?

Were there second thoughts?

Did this humiliated Hetman of the Zaporohjans feel that he still had time to put out the fires he'd lighted? Tuhay-bey's Tartar corps camped on the plains of Bazavluk numbered fewer than six thousand warriors and there were five times that many Cossacks in the *Sietch* alone. But would they follow him if he declared for the Commonwealth? Or would they turn against him? And what would happen to his dreams of vengeance if his enraged Zaporohjans hurled him, bound like a dog, at the Tartar's feet?

The silence in the council hall continued but the roar of the tens of thousands of excited voices came booming from the mobs outside and Hmyelnitzki listened for a moment longer. His eyes were dark with thought but when he rose to speak it was as if there'd never been one moment of uncertainty in his life.

He spoke with the slow, clumsy formality with which simple people decorate their speeches, and which the crude, unlettered atamans would recognize as something familiar, as he reminded them of "*the benevolence and friendship and wisdom of the Great Khan, lord of many peoples,*" and of "*our father, the good King Vladyslav who loves his Cossack children,*" and of "*the will and wishes of the brave Zaporohjan Army*" with whose combined permissions they, "*the innocent and abused,*" were about to set out to right all their wrongs.

Plaintive and sorrowful in one moment, and then threatening and accusing in the next, he reminded the listening atamans of "*all the sufferings that we've endured with patience, like good, honest Christians,*" and of "*the traitor gentry, and all the commissioners and sheriffs and bailiffs and their Jews,*" who had robbed them of their privileges.

"I've wept over this injustice," he cried out. "As you've wept. As the brave Zaporohjan Army wept. And that's why you gave me this *bulava* so that I can go and ask in the name of all our Zaporohjan brothers for just payment for all our miseries! But,"—and his voice softened, breaking as if in grief—"I'm sad to think that there might be some among us here who have secret dealings with the traitor *Lahy* . . . who get letters from them . . . and who'd tell them about our preparations."

The listening men started murmuring furiously among themselves, and bared their teeth, and shook fists, and glared at each other, while the animal howls outside grew stronger and louder.

Tatartchuk shuddered. But there was nothing in the letters that the scribe read out that sounded like treason. In one, the Prince asked the Chief Ataman to explain why the Cossacks were assembling in the *Sietch* and warned against war on a Christian country. The same warning came from Pan Grodjitzki. In the two other letters Pan Zachvilihovski and old Barabas asked Tatartchuk and the Idiot Ataman to take the Prince's envoy under their protection and help him with his mission. Weak with relief, Tatartchuk breathed again.

"Well, my good brothers," Hmyelnitzki asked softly when the scribe finished and put away the papers. "What about those letters brought here by an envoy of our enemy, Vishnovyetzki, who didn't come here as any envoy but as a spy to plot with traitors and betray us all?"

The atamans sat silent. Not even the most violent among them wanted to be the first to speak, as he knew they wouldn't. Like all crude, brutish, cunning and suspicious people, they were afraid of sounding foolish among their own kind, and so they sat like mutes, glaring at each other, and Hmyelnitzki let them stir uneasily for some moments longer as his dark, brooding eyes swept over each of them in turn.

Then he got up and walked over to the Chief Ataman and bent over him and kissed him on both cheeks.

"The Chief Ataman is our brother," he cried out. "A true friend. I trust him as I'd trust my soul! And anybody who thinks any different must have some evil reason to make us doubt our best man just as we're starting out on a terrible war! Our brother, the Ataman, is no traitor!"

"The Ataman's no traitor!" roared the *Kujhen* leaders.

"That's true, brothers," the old Ataman said, trembling with relief. "That's how it is, as God is my witness. I serve the Hetman. He tells me to call in all our people, I called them. Now let the Hetman lead them. As for that *Lah* envoy, since they sent him to me that makes him mine to do with what I want. So I give him to you! You punish the traitor!"

"That's right!" Hmyelnitzki cried and fixed his brooding eyes on Tatartchuk and the grinning young giant beside him. "You punish the traitors! But if our brother, the Ataman, isn't the traitor here then who is? Who has *Lah* friends? To whom do they send letters? Who is to help a *Lah* spy with his dirty work? Whom do we have to punish like that false *Lah* envoy will have to be punished? Who's the real traitor?"

Tatartchuk groaned. Sweat dripped into his eyes and his body quivered with anger and fear. He felt all the blood drain out of his face as the other atamans leaped to their feet and shook their fists at him and shouted and cursed him.

"Tatartchuk!" yelled one voice.

"Barabas!" howled another.

"Who?" The young idiot stared about, astonished, and suddenly burst into a loud peal of mindless, ringing laughter, like a child who is surprised and pleased to be the center of attention. "Me?"

He neighed and hooted and the atamans grinned and started laughing, and soon the room was booming with their laughter, but the wild howling of the mob outside suddenly struck the windows with fresh force and restored a suffocating silence.

Tatartchuk sighed. He rose. He turned to Hmyelnitzki.

"What did I do to you, Hetman, that you want my death?" he shouted. "What am I guilty of? So old Zachvilihovski writes me a letter . . . so what's wrong with that? *Knaz* Yarema wrote to the Chief Ataman, didn't he? And did I get that letter? Did I hide it from you? No! And if I did get it, what would I do with it? I don't know about writing and reading any more than any honest Cossack! I'd take it to the scribe here, to read it to me like he read it to you, so you'd all know what was in it anyway! So where's all this plotting you're talking about?

"Hey, brothers!" he called out, turning to the others. "Tatartchuk's no *Lah*! He's a Cossack, brothers! Didn't he go with you, good brothers, to Valachia? Didn't he ride with you to Smolensk? Didn't he fight beside you, good brothers, live with you, drink with you, hungered when you hungered . . .? And if the Hetman wants his death let him tell you why! What did I do to him?"

"Tatartchuk's no traitor!" some man cried.

"He's a good man, a good Cossack brother," cried several others.

★ ★ ★

Tatartchuk smiled. He could hardly believe that he had saved himself. But then Hmyelnitzki got slowly to his feet and started shaking his large, heavy head sadly from side to side as if quite crushed by sorrow. His voice was so low and mournful when he began to speak that all the atamans leaned forward and cupped their ears to hear him, and Tatartchuk was suddenly sick with the knowledge that nothing could help him after all. It came to him that he'd spoken at an earlier council against giving Hmyelnitzki the powers of a Hetman.

"Yes, you, Tatartchuk," Hmyelnitzki said sadly. "You are no *Lah*, we know that. You're our Cossack brother. And that's why I don't want your death, because you're a Cossack. Would I be as sad as I am now if it was a Pole who was the traitor here? Would I be weeping for him as I weep for you? No! I'd be happy if a Pole was the traitor so he could be punished! But if a Cossack is a traitor, if it's my brother who's got to be punished, then I must be sad! And if you've been to Valachia and Smolensk with your good Cossack brothers, if you've fought beside them, and got drunk with them, and hungered when they hungered, then your treason is all the worse *because* you're our brother!

"Look you," he cried out suddenly. "What does your *Lah* friend write to you? That you're to help a spy with his mission! And what could that be if not to murder me, your Hetman, and to murder our good friend Tuhay-bey, and to betray the whole Army of the Zaporohjans? And you, Barabas, you get a letter from your father's brother, the old traitor who wanted to keep our privileges from us! Isn't that true? Tell me if it isn't because I'm ready to swear on my soul that every word is true!"

"True! True! *Pravdu kahje*! It's all true!" shouted several voices.

"And if it's true," Hmyelnitzki went on slowly, "then you'd better go down on your knees, Tatartchuk, and beg these good atamans, your judges and brothers, to show you some mercy, and I'll beg with you because you're a Cossack, not a Pole, and because you're our brother, and because your treason is so great that nothing else can save you!"

Tatartchuk groaned. He knew that he was doomed. A whimper broke out of his cruel lips and he swayed suddenly on his feet. He cursed the day when he opposed Hmyelnitzki and argued against letting the Tartars loose in the Ukraine. Too late, he remembered that the terrible new Hetman of the Zaporohjans didn't know the meaning of forgiveness. As for the death of young Barabas, the reasons were as clear as his own destruction. His murder was Hmyelnitzki's vengeance on the Tcherkassy colonel who'd never turn against the Commonwealth, and who loved the feeble-minded youth as if he were his son.

★   ★   ★

But doomed or not, Tatartchuk didn't want to die the kind of death that waited for him outside in the *maydan*. He was a fearless warrior; he'd have laughed at a dozen sabers shining in his eyes, he'd have shown utter scorn and indifference to arrows and bullets, but knowing what the mob would do to him struck him cold with terror.

"In Christ's name!" he howled and threw himself down on his knees before his fellow atamans. "Brothers! Don't kill the innocent! I never even set eyes on that Pole, never talked to him! How would I know what he'd want from me? Ask him yourselves! I swear on Christ and his Mother, and on Saint Mikolai and the Archangel Michael that you'll be murdering an innocent soul!"

"Bring in the Pole!" the old *Kantarey* shouted. "Put him to the question!"

They were all on their feet. Everyone was shouting. "Bring in the Pole! Get him in here! Get some answers from him!" A crowd of them pushed into the next room to drag in the Polish prisoner. Others shook their fists at Barabas and Tatartchuk; and Hladko, the ataman of the Mirovsky *Kujhen,* glanced over at Hmyelnitzki and caught the icy look in the Hetman's eye.

"Death to them both!" he shouted.

The swarm of rank-and-file Cossacks who'd pushed into the room as representatives of the mob outside, lurched for the condemned men, arms grasping and hands reaching, and the terrible Ataman Tcharnota, feared for his cruelty even among these people, kicked open the door and ran into the *maydan*.

"Tatartchuk's a traitor!" he screamed out. "Barabas's a traitor! Death to them!"

"Death!" roared twenty thousand voices.

And then the huge, frenzied mass surged like an enormous wave and poured into the Council House, pushing and falling and trampling everything in its path, and a hundred hands reached out for the victims.

Tatartchuk let himself be seized without resisting. He uttered only one short high-pitched scream and sagged into the arms of his executioners. But young Barabas fought like a wounded bear. His empty mind finally grasped the fact that he was to be murdered and fury, terror and despair turned him into a howling animal. He threw himself about like a netted boar, bit his tormentors, clawed at them and tore himself out of their hands, but they caught him, threw him down, and tore him to pieces. His clothes were ripped off, his long top-knot was pulled out of his head, he choked on his own broken teeth and the bones of his smashed and splintered face. His killers dragged him and Tatartchuk outside and threw them to the mob, and there a thousand hands reached for them, fought over them, tore out their eyes and limbs and turned them into offal. Someone tossed a burning torch into a vodka barrel and a blue, ghostly light bathed the maddened crowd where, once in a while, the two shapeless corpses flew into the air and tumbled back under the trampling boots. A brilliant full moon hung overhead like an impassive witness.

★   ★   ★

As far as Hmyelnitzki was concerned the main business of the council was over as soon as Tatartchuk and Barabas were dragged to their deaths. All opposition to his power was now gone. He'd taken his vengeance. But the *Kujhen* leaders were howling for the death of the Polish envoy who had been pushed into the room among them, so he shrugged, not caring what happened to the captured noble, and settled down on the fur robes beside Tuhay-bey.

Someone called for more light and Hladko tossed fresh brushwood on the fire and the harsh new flames illuminated the prisoner's shadowed face. He stood before the grinning atamans as if he'd come to judge them, calm and unafraid, so that even the Zaporohjan Hetman felt a touch of interest. He glanced up, jerked erect, and smothered a quick curse. He recognized Skshetuski.

Beside him, Tuhay-bey pursed his thick lips and spat out a mouthful of sunflower seeds. "I know that *Lah*," he muttered. "He's been to the Khan."

"Death to him!" Hladko shouted.

"Death!" bellowed Tcharnota.

But it didn't take the Zaporohjan Hetman more than a moment to get over his surprise. He turned his cold glance on the atamans and they became immediately as quiet as if they'd lost their voices.

The old Chief Ataman, however, missed the sudden stillness in his Hetman's face. "Why d'you come here?" he shouted at Skshetuski.

"To see you, Ataman," the young man said quietly.

"Me? What for? Who sent you?"

"You know who sent me. I'm the Prince's envoy."

"You're no envoy! You've come to plot with traitors! And that makes you a traitor! And so you'll get what we give to traitors!"

"You're wrong," Skshetuski said. He turned to Hmyelnitzki. "And so are you, you self-styled Hetman of the Zaporohjans. If I brought letters of introduction that's what any envoy does going to strange places. I didn't come to plot against you but to turn you from your own treason against your mother country. And to save you from your own destruction.

"Think!" he cried out, as if he were the judge and they the accused. "Who is it that you're challenging? Against whom did you call-in the Tartars? It's the Commonwealth! You're the traitors here! And if you don't humble yourselves and come to your senses and go back to your duty and obedience you'll be crushed to dust! Haven't you had enough rebellions to teach you a lesson? Have you forgotten what happened to Pavluk and to Nalevayko? Don't think for a minute that anything different can happen to you!"

"You lie, dog!" the Chief Ataman shouted. "But neither your lies nor your plots are going to save you! We'll deal with you like we've dealt with the other traitors!"

A hoarse, angry roar of approval came from the atamans and the maddened delegates of the brotherhood, who jumped to their feet and howled for a new victim, but Pan Yan ignored them.

"Do what you like," he said. "I'm not afraid of dying. But the Prince will know well enough how to pay you for my death. So it's you who ought to be afraid!"

★   ★   ★

Reminded of the terrible Yeremi Vishnovyetzki, who never showed mercy to any kind of rebel, the Atamans stared dumbly at the floor. But Tuhay-bey looked up at the prisoner with a sudden interest.

"That's a fire-eater, that one," he grunted in Ruthenian. "*Serdyty Lah!*"

"But too proud, too unbending. He'll pay for it with his head."

The Tartar shrugged.

Outside, the murdering of Barabas and Tatartchuk had come to an end, and now clenched fists, boots and the butts of handguns were hammering on the door, and a new delegation from the brotherhood burst into the room. They were all drunk, reeling and steaming with fresh blood. Sweat streamed in yellow furrows down their mired faces.

"The Brotherhood bows to you, Atamans and Elders, and asks for the Pole!" they gasped, hoarse and out of breath. "So that the good brothers can play a little with him, like they played with Barabas and Tatartchuk!"

"Give them the Pole!" Tcharnota shouted.

"No! Wait! Don't give him! He's an envoy!" shouted other voices.

"Kill him! Death to him! *Na pohybel* with him!"

And then all eyes turned on Hmyelnitzki to see which way he'd want things to go.

"The Brotherhood asks!" the delegation shouted and started shaking fists and weapons at the atamans. "But if you don't give him to us we'll take him without asking! And maybe you along with him, if he's not enough!"

One man alone could save Skshetuski from the mob and Hmyelnitzki turned to him at once.

"He's yours," he whispered in Tuhay-bey's ear. "Will you give him up?"

"How is he mine?" The Tartar turned his cold, slitted eyes on the Zaporohjan. His cruel jaws moved slowly under his thin mustache.

"The Tartars took him on Hortytza so he belongs to you," Hmyelnitzki hissed quickly. "That's a rich noble. He can pay good ransom. And *Knaz* Yarema will pay for him too."

The Tartar blinked, stretched as if awakening, and got to his feet. His flat, bony face changed so suddenly into a mask of rage that it seemed as if a stranger stood among the Cossacks. His eyes glowed with murder. His thick lips curled away from yellow, wolflike teeth. And then he leaped in fury on the delegation.

"Out, dogs! Sons of goats! Unbelievers! Unclean animals!" He reached out, seized two giant Zaporohjans by their beards and smashed their skulls together. "Out, drunken swine! Pig eaters! Cattle! Sons of dogs and reptiles! You want my prisoner? My ransom?"

The terrified Cossacks howled and scattered, trampling each

other in their hurry to get away from their formidable ally and escape outside. He caught one by the neck and hurled him to the floor and stamped on him and kicked him. He tore the beard out of another's chin.

"Down on your faces, you sons of pigs and slaves!" he roared while spittle foamed at the corners of his mouth. "On your knees! Or I'll turn you all into the *yassyr* I came for! I'll fill the markets with you! I'll grind your whole *Sietch* to dust and carpet the whole Steppe with your rotting bodies!"

The drunken delegation burst out through the door and ran into the *maydan*, clutching bruised heads and howling that there'd be no games played with the *Lah* that day because he was a prisoner of Tuhay-bey and Tuhay-bey was angry.

"He's beaten us, innocents!" they wailed. "He's pulled out our beards! He's angry . . . ay! He's angry . . .!"

And the word *angry, angry* traveled through the mob, and "*Tuhay-bey is angry*" spread in a worried cry from one man to another, and then some shrill, moaning voice picked up the phrase and found a tune for it and a new Steppe song soared among the fires.

> "*Hey, hey, Tuhay-bey,*
> *God forsake your mother!*
> *Hey, hey, Tuhay-bey,*
> *Don't be angry, brother . . .*"

A thousand mournful voices picked it up, lifted it and sent it flying into the echoing ravines of the Tchertomelik and into the Steppe.

★　★　★

But suddenly the song died away, the crowd lurched and began to scatter with fresh howls of rage, while a dozen riders burst through the Hassan Gate without caring whom they knocked down and trampled under their horses' hooves.

"Make way! Letters for the Hetman!"

The Cossack leaders in the Council House were getting ready to go to their quarters when the messengers ran into the room.

"A letter for the Hetman!" an old Cossack shouted.

"Where from?"

"We're from Tchehryn. We've ridden for days."

"So where's the letter?"

"Here!"

Hmyelnitzki took the letter from the Cossack's hand, broke the seal and began to read, and then the flame of a sudden, overpowering joy blazed across his face.

"The Grand Hetman is sending his son against us!" he cried out. "It's war!"

A strange, soft whisper drifted through the room and hung in the still air as forty silent men released their pent-up breath, but Pan Yan couldn't tell whether this hushed sound represented fear or relief.

Hmyelnitzki, however, seemed to swell in stature. His face was glowing as he stepped into the center of the room. His head was high. His eyes sought out each man and struck him like a thunderbolt, sobering everyone at once. His joyful voice was resonant, confident and clear.

"Atamans, to your troops!" he cried. "Fire the tower cannon! Close the bazaar and smash all the barrels! We're marching before dawn."

From that moment on and for the rest of history there'd be no more councils in the *Sietch*, no meetings of atamans and elders, and no deputations. Hmyelnitzki was taking all power into his own hands.

That was the Zaporohjan way. Between wars, even if there was a Hetman in the camp, the mob could force its will on him and the other leaders, holding their lives at no greater value than those of anybody else. But once the signal cannon was fired on the gate of the Hassan Pasha, the Brotherhood became an army, the *kujhenye* turned into regiments and divisions, their atamans became generals and colonels with powers of life and death over everyone under their command, and the Hetman was their supreme ruler, answerable to no one.

Chapter Ten

IT WAS ALREADY long into the night, with dawn not far away, when Hmyelnitzki, Tuhay-bey and Pan Yan came to the house of the old Chief Ataman where they were to sleep. They were no sooner seated in the hut when the Cossack Hetman turned to his savage ally.

"How much d'you want in ransom for that man?"

The Tartar appraised Skshetuski. "You said he's got money?"

"Would I lie to you?"

"You'd lie to God," the Tartar growled and spat with contempt.

"The Pole can pay."

The Tartar nodded. "I believe you. If I didn't, he wouldn't be here. And he's an envoy of that devil, Yarema. Yarema loves his people. *Bishmillah*! One will pay and the other will pay. Together . . ."

He thought long and hard while the others waited.

"Two thousand thalers," he said finally.

"I'll give you two thousand for him out of my own pocket," Hmyelnitzki said at once.

"You?" The Tartar's yellow teeth glinted in a smile. "You'll give three thousand."

"Why should I give three when it's two for anybody else?"

"Because you want him. He's important to you. And if he's important you'll pay three."

"He saved my life," Hmyelnitzki muttered without thinking.

"Allah! That's worth another thousand."

But Pan Yan had enough of this haggling over his life or

death. "Tuhay-bey," he said. "I can't promise you anything out of the Prince's treasury but I can pay you three thousand on my own account. I don't want to owe either my life or my freedom to this man."

"What makes you think I'd give you either one?" Hmyelnitzki snapped at him then turned to the Tartar. "Listen Tuhay-bey, the war's just beginning. You'll send for ransom to the Prince but a lot of water will go down the Dnieper before you see your money. I can put gold in your hand tomorrow."

"You'll give four thousand?"

"If that's what you want. He's mine then?"

The Tartar nodded. He yawned. "Where do I sleep?"

The old Chief Ataman pointed to a bundle of furs heaped in a careless pile on the floor. It was a jumble of worn wolf and bear skins, costly ermine pelts, coarse sheepskins and raw, untanned horsehides crawling with lice and vermin but the Tartar threw himself on this crude bedding without another word. In moments he'd begun to snore.

Hmyelnitzki started pacing slowly through the narrow room. Thoughts quite as dark as Skshetuski's seemed to oppress the Hetman so that he halted from time to time and rubbed his forehead with the back of his hand as if to wipe away a tormenting vision.

"It's late . . . late," he muttered. "But I won't get to sleep tonight. Give me a keg, Ataman."

"Wine or spirits, Hetman?"

"Liquor. I need to stop thinking."

"Not long now 'til sunup, Hetman," the old man sighed and said.

"I know it, old friend. Why don't you get some rest? Drink a cup with me and then go to sleep."

The old Ataman filled the cups, sighed again and offered a toast. "Ah . . . to our Cossack glory, then? And another for our luck to hold true?"

"To our good luck," said Hmyelnitzki and drained the metal cup.

The old man wiped his mouth with his coat sleeve and buried himself in furs in the far corner of the room where his wheezing snores soon intermingled with the harsh horselike snorting of the sleeping Tartar. Hmyelnitzki sat in deep thought for some time. Then a dark tremor passed across his face and he shook himself awake like a sleeping dog.

"You're free," he told Skshetuski.

"I'm grateful," Pan Yan said. "Although I'd rather owe my freedom to anyone but you."

"Then keep your thanks. You saved my skin, I saved yours. We're even. I can't let you go right away in any event unless you give your word that you'll keep your mouth shut about what you've seen here. You know too much for now."

"I see you deal in short-lived freedoms," Skshetuski said coldly. "If I kept your secrets from the Prince it would be just as if I'd gone over to your side."

Hmyelnitzki shrugged. "My neck's at stake here. Everything depends on keeping all of you asleep a little longer. If the Grand Hetman knew what you know about us he'd come down on me with everything he's got. And that'd be the end. I've got to keep him thinking this is just another of those Cossack brushfires he can put out by waving his cap. Don't you think I know what I'm up against? Both the Hetmans. Your terrible prince. And the Zaslavskis and the Konyetzpolskis and all those other king-lets of the Ukraine who keep their boot heels on the Cossacks' necks . . . I've worked too hard to keep you all divided to let you come to your senses now."

"You're taking on a terrible power, Hetman."

But Hmyelnitzki seemed to be speaking to himself as much as to Skshetuski.

"Later, when all of the Ukraine is mine . . . after I've gathered up all of your own Cossacks . . . and your serfs and peasants, and all those great nameless masses of people without land or hope that your kind calls the *tchernya* . . . yes, once all these thousands stand behind me like the Zaporohjans and the Khan, then it won't matter. Then you can tell them anything you want. I'll be strong enough to face anybody. But now I need time. Time and luck. I've got to play the fox as much as the lion. Oh yes, I know the dangers that I'm facing. I see all the problems. But I can trust in God's justice, too. He knows what's in my heart. He will not desert me."

Eyes closed as if to shut out an oppressive vision, the Cossack Hetman rubbed his face again. Then he began to circle the room silently in great strides.

"Don't blaspheme," Skshetuski told him coldly. "Don't call

on God to help you burn down your own country just because your pride's been hurt. Haven't you started a civil war, the worst horror that can happen to a nation? Aren't you guilty of murder among brothers? Aren't you letting loose the Tartar barbarians against your own Christian countrymen? No matter if you win or lose you'll spill a sea of blood. You'll ravage the country like a plague of locusts and drown it in tears. You'll send your own people into Tartar slavery by the tens of thousands. You'll tear the Commonwealth apart. You'll raise your hand against your King, defile God's altars, loot His churches. And for what? Just because Tchaplinski stole a woman from you and spat in your face while drunk? Is nothing holier to you than your private vengeance? Listen, I'm in your hands and you can kill me anytime you like but I'll tell you this much: call on Hell to help you, not on God. Because that's where you'll find your real master."

Hmyelnitzki's face darkened with a rush of blood as Skshetuski spoke and his whole body started to shake and quiver. He tore a jewel-studded dagger from his belt and death glinted redly in his bloodshot eyes. But then the Zaporohjan Hetman forced himself back under control. Perhaps it was because he hadn't drunk enough and still had some of his wits about him. Or perhaps he caught a glimpse in his mind's eye of the firestorm he had conjured up, and saw the blood-red flames, the carnage and the pillage, and heard the wailing of the captive thousands, and suddenly remembered who he was and who his allies were.

"Hell . . . treason . . . private vengeance," he was muttering then and once more his eyes seemed to fix on his interior visions. "I'd kill anyone else who'd say that to me. How do you know it's only my own wrongs I want to avenge?" he asked bitterly. "Where would I get the men—those thousands who already stand behind me and those tens of thousands who will run to me as soon as I've set foot among them—if it was just a matter of settling my own scores? Look at the Ukraine! The earth so rich, the soil so ripe, the air so free! Hey, it's a land for laughter and for song, a paradise made for God himself! But who is sure of his tomorrows there? Who doesn't see his faith and his freedoms threatened every day? Who doesn't groan under your tyranny? Only the magnates and their handful of boot-licking gentry! It's *they* who have all the titles and rank and positions! *They* hold all the lands, *they've* all the people to work their huge holdings! *They* are the happy ones! And the rest of the nation weeps on its knees with arms raised to Heaven, begging God to end their misery with death because not even their own King's love can help them!"

Low now, as if he had forgotten that he was not alone, the thick, booming voice had dropped to a whisper.

"And it's not just the common people that groan in oppression," he went on as if to himself. "How many of the gentry have run like me for refuge to the *Sietch*? I don't want war with the King and the Commonwealth . . . He is our father and she is our mother! The King is a just and merciful man but those kinglets are another matter! There's no way for a man to live with them and their rents and their tithes and taxes . . . It's *their* tyranny that supports the Jews who squeeze blood out of this land like water from a cheese!"

Skshetuski stirred in protest as if about to speak and the great gloomy eyes turned on him again.

"Doesn't all that cry to the skies for vengeance?" the Zaporohjan Hetman asked fiercely. "Where's the gratitude for all the blood shed by the Cossacks in so many wars? Where are their rewards? The King gave them the privileges of the gentry but the kinglets stole them. Our wounds are still red from your Hetmans' sabers. Our tears are still wet for all the good men who've been slaughtered, beheaded or impaled just because we asked to have our services remembered. And now . . . look! Do you see that red fire in the sky? That's not a sunrise. No. That's not a burning comet. That's God's anger! That's His avenging whip! And if I'm to be the one who wields it here on earth . . . that's His will!"

And so he stood for long moments with his fists clenched towards the sky, red with the dawn's new light like a torch ablaze with God's awful anger, and then he groaned and shuddered and sunk to the bench as if unable to bear the weight of either his vision or his burden.

Neither he nor Skshetuski said anything for a long time after that. They sat in deep silence, each turned bitterly to his own thoughts and accusations. The young lieutenant stared at the stained, scarred table as if some answer to his grief and shame could be found on its soiled surface. He wanted to say something . . . anything . . . that might disprove the truth of what he'd just heard. But what was there to say? Hmyelnitzki's terrible indictment had the weight of granite.

★ ★ ★

When Pan Yan spoke again his voice was low and sad.

"It's . . . not all like that. But even if it was . . . even if all of us were evil, vicious men . . . if each of us mocked the law and made himself a tyrant . . . who are you to appoint yourself our judge and executioner? I won't defend oppressors. I won't try to justify their abuse of power and contempt for the law. But what kind of pride drives you to name yourself the instrument of justice? You denounce the magnates . . . the kinglets, as you call them . . . because they scoff at statutes and disobey the King. But what's the difference between their lawlessness and yours? You see the tyranny of the princes and the gentry's power but this you don't see: that if it wasn't for their blood, their sabers, their private regiments and castles and cannon, there'd be no hope at all for this beautiful, rich land. Who but they keep the Turks and Tartars out of the Ukraine and the Commonwealth? Whose breast was the rock on which all the Turkish conquests shattered for a hundred years? Who else defended you and yours and all the Christian world? Who settled the wilderness? Who built the towns and cities? Who brought us God and churches?"

His voice grew harder and sharper as he spoke while Hmyelnitzki fixed his gloomy eyes on the vodka barrel and worked his empty fists on the tabletop as if kneading air.

"And who are these tyrants, as you call them?" Skshetuski demanded. "Did they come from Germany or from among the Turks? Aren't they your own Ruthenian flesh and blood? They're *your* princes born of your own soil, and aren't we your own Ukrainian gentry? And if that's so then your sin goes beyond forgiveness because you're arming brothers against each other. In God's name, Hetman! Even if all of us were guilty let God judge us in the next life and the Diets in this one! But not you!"

Their eyes met and locked as each man struggled to control his passions.

"And can you really say that there's only innocence and righteousness on your side?" Pan Yan went on sadly. "Are you so free of sin that you can accuse others? I'll tell you what happened to the Cossack privileges. It's not just the princes who trampled on them, tore them up and threw them all away! It's you Zaporohjans!"

Careless about his own life since death was his most likely prospect anyway, the young man paid no attention to Hmyelnitzki's fury. One by one, he named the leaders of past rebellions who turned the Ukraine into a slaughterhouse and died on stakes and gibbets. He cited years of Cossack turmoil, countless raids and murders, burned towns and devastated regions, raped women, tortured children, looted monasteries and churches.

"Who lets the Tartars pass unmolested into the Commonwealth only to ambush them and rob them when they're returning with their loot? You! Who—and this defies belief!—sells their own people to the Tartar slavers? You! Whose name stands for murder, banditry and pillage so that no one in the Ukraine can feel free from fear? You and always you! You're worse than any Tartars because you are Christians! And now you want rewards?"

Sick to the depths of his soul because he couldn't deny the truth of all the Cossack claims and accusations, the young soldier struggled none the less to show how mutual hatred could spring up and grow through generations on both sides.

"You've been forgiven much more than whatever was taken away from you," he went on coldly while Hmyelnitzki stared at him in fury. "You've been a seeping wound that drains the life out of your mother country, a rotting limb that poisons the rest of her body. I can't think of any nation that would show such patience and forgiveness as you've had from the Commonwealth. Anywhere else you'd have been hunted down like mad dogs and ground into dust! But the Commonwealth wanted to cure the tumor you've become, not to burn it out, and how do you repay her?

"Look!"—and he pointed in disgust at the snoring Tartar — "Here's your friend and ally, peacefully sleeping under your protection. No, it's not some Ukrainian magnate but a Tartar *murjah* who's going to help you pillage your own country! Is he to sit in judgment on your brothers too? Will his rope feel better around your neck than those chains with which you say the lords and princes are weighing you down? Is that why you bend your back before him like a slave and hold his stirrup when he mounts his horse?"

Hmyelnitzki drained his cup, refilled it, drank again.

"When old Barabas and I went to the King," he muttered bitterly, "and when we wept before him, and showed him all our suffering, he asked if we didn't have sabers at our belts and if we were short of artillery and powder."

"If you stood before the King of Kings, he'd say: '*Did you forgive your enemies as I've forgiven mine?*'"

"I don't want war with the Commonwealth! She is my own mother!"

"But you are holding a knife to her throat."

"I go to free the Cossacks from your chains!"

"To put a Tartar rope around their necks . . ."

"Rome threatens our faith!"

"Will your ally save it?"

"Shut your mouth, you screech-owl!" Hmyelnitzki howled, enraged, and leaped to his feet. "Who made you my conscience?"

"You'll choke on your own country's blood," Pan Yan cried out fiercely. "You'll drown in its tears! The only thing that's waiting for you in the end is judgment and death!"

"Silence!" And Hmyelnitzki's knife glittered once more at Skshetuski's throat.

"Do it!" Skshetuski grated out. "Begin it with me!"

Shaking with fury Hmyelnitzki pressed the knife against Skshetuski's chest and held it there, muttering foul curses. His face twisted in a spasm of rage. It seemed to swell and lose its shape and features and then the man's whole body began to leap and quiver as he fought to regain control over his murderous seizure and stifle his overwhelming hatred. And then the knife fell out of his hand and he staggered backwards. He seized the keg and raised it to his mouth and gulped the raw liquor until the empty keg slipped out of his hands and clattered to the floor. He gasped then and fell against a wall. His eyes bulged, glazed over. He slid down the wall to a bench and collapsed on it as if all strength drained out of his body.

"Can't kill him," he muttered, his mouth loose and shaking. "Can't . . . It's late. Dawn's come. Too late to turn back. What's that you said about blood? And judgment? I've . . . drunk too much. Whose judgment? The Khan will help. Here's Tuhay-bey, sleeping. He's with me. Saint Michael the Conqueror is with me. Tomorrow we go. And if . . . and if . . . Ah, listen! I bought you from the Tartar, didn't I? You'll remember that? You'll tell them . . .? Too late to turn back."

His voice drifted and turned into a whisper. His head nodded slowly and sunk towards his chest. But suddenly he jerked erect and his wide-open eyes stared in utter terror into the dark shadows in the far corner of the room.

"Who's that?" he shouted. "Who's that standing there?"

" . . . Who's there?" the old Chief Ataman stirred and muttered in his sleep.

Hmyelnitzki's head fell forward.

His eyes closed.

"Whose judgment . . .?" he murmured and sleep pulled him down into its own darkness.

Pan Yan felt the last of his strength ebbing from his body. He lost a great deal of blood in the fight on Hortytza Island and now all his wounds broke open again. He swayed. His sight dimmed. His eyes clouded over. He thought that this could be the coming of his death. He began to pray.

★   ★   ★

Old Zakhar came for him soon afterwards and led him to the Zaporohjans' wagon train where days passed while he drifted between reality and hallucinations.

War, he thought then as later when the wagon train lurched across the Steppe. War . . . and here he was, tossing in fever on straw in a Cossack cart, ill and unarmed and hardly able to lift his head without Zakhar's help.

War. The Commonwealth in danger. In Lubnie the regiments are marching through the city gates. Bright helmets gleam, the banners snap and crackle in the wind, the war-horns are calling. Prince Yeremi stands in his silver armor with lightning in his eyes . . . And at this thought Pan Yan was wrenched by such deep sorrow and remorse and longing that he wished for death so that he'd be able to fly, at least as a spirit, to his friends in Lubnie.

Familiar faces drifted in his night.

. . . Little Volodyovski, the diminutive dragoon, leads his scarlet riders with his saber twirling like a toy. Ah, but that's a swordsman beyond compare; whoever crosses steel with him in anger does it only once.

Other names and faces. Pan Longinus lifts his huge Cowlsnatcher; Byhovietz smiles, calls out and passes out of memory; redheaded Vyershul, who commands the Prince's Tartar Light Horse, gallops by like a grinning poppy with his mounted archers. And then Skshetuski's own irresistible *Husaria*—three hundred iron men on gigantic horses, with eagle wings fixed to their armored shoulders in great curving frames—sweep by with bright pennons streaming from their lances . . .

In his fever, in his imagination, the young lieutenant watched Prince Yeremi pointing with his gold *bulava*; he heard the thunder as the charge began and the wind hissed and rattled through the curving wings and terrified the horses, and he could feel the shock of maddened animals crashing into the ranks of panicked enemies. On they'd come, irresistible, toppling men and horses as the lances splintered . . . and then the great long-swords and battle hammers would begin to whirl . . .

So real were these visions that he cried out with longing to be a part of them and tried to struggle up, groping for his weapons, and old Zakhar pushed him gently back into the straw and covered him with furs.

"Ey, what's the matter with you, lad? *Shtcho s'toboyu*, falcon? Lie back. You'll tear your wounds open."

And the familiar faces vanished.

The vast, sprawling Cossack wagon train—in part a mobile town and in part that fortress on wheels that the Zaporohjans knew how to defend so well—rolled through another night.

★　★　★

Ill though he was, he was too young to abandon hope. One night, as the wagons crept without lights past a gaunt, black mass that loomed against the lighter backdrop of the sky, he woke to hear the thunder of nearby cannon fire. The darkness flashed with red and yellow flames and cannon balls arched overhead and skipped across the Steppe, growling like angry dogs.

He knew where he was then but he had to ask. "Listen, Zakhar. Are we passing Kudak?"

"That we are, lad."

"And where are we heading?"

"Who knows?" The old Cossack smiled grimly in the darkness. "As long as God and the Hetman know it's all one to me. I just keep my eye on you and drive this here wagon. But people say there'll be a battle in the morning."

"Ah . . ." And his sense of excitement became so intense that Pan Yan almost ceased to breathe. "Then the Grand Hetman's army must be near?"

"They say his son is near."

"His son . . ." That, Pan Yan thought uneasily, would be young Stefan Pototzki, the Castellan of Krakow, a fine brave boy but without much experience. "The Grand Hetman wouldn't send him out against Hmyelnitzki without some old soldier to advise him."

"Who knows what the *Lahy* do? Or why? But our Hetman was real pleased when he heard about it. We were in camp, down by Komysha Voda, when he got the word."

"What word?"

"About the boy. Two men came in from the *Lah* camp. They told our Hetman the young master is coming overland with his *lytzari* horsemen and that there's others coming down the river in galleys. When old Hmyel heard about that he was so pleased he just about jumped out of his own hide."

"And how many men does the young castellan have with him? Did you hear?"

"I don't know how many he's got with him in the Steppe. But there's six thousand Pereyaslav Cossacks in the boats. Old Hmyel's eyes lit up like stars when he heard about them. He had us strike camp and move out at once, even though night was coming."

"Hmm. He did, did he?"

"Sure. Old Hmyel knows something. All our horsemen are far ahead already. They rode out fast, in light order, taking only what they could carry on horseback, and the Tartars with them. Didn't wait for us or the infantry."

"Hmm. And did you hear who commands those Pereyaslav Cossacks?"

"Kshetchovski, they say."

Pan Yan felt such relief that he laughed out loud despite his pain and fever.

"A famous soldier!" he murmured, weak with sudden joy. "I knew the Grand Hetman wouldn't send his young son against you without some wise old head and experienced hand to guide him. Kshetchovski! Now there's a man for you Cossacks to follow!"

"Maybe. Maybe not. It's all in God's hands," Zakhar shrugged and said.

★ ★ ★

The wagon train, or '*tabor*' as the Cossacks called it, rolled on like a huge quadrangular mass of horses, artillery and wagons while the bypassed fortress thundered in the night. Pan Yan thought that Hmyelnitzki would begin the war by besieging Kudak but the hasty march past the granite nest of the one-eyed Cyclops confirmed the nearness of the Hetman's army.

He had a moment of misgiving when he heard that it wasn't the Grand Hetman himself who was coming south to face the Zaporohjans. The Crown Contingent, as the Polish troops of the Commonwealth's standing army were known in that time, wasn't much larger than the force that Prince Yeremi maintained at his own expense, but it would be enough to destroy Hmyelnitzki. It was clear that the Hetmans didn't know how strong the Zaporohjans had become through the daily desertions from the Crown camp, from the border cities, and through the mutinies of the countless Cossack companies in the outposts of the wilderness. Skshetuski was even more alarmed when he heard that the punitive detachment was led by the young Castellan of Krakow. Stefan Pototzki was a brave and high-minded youth but he would be no match for the military genius of Bohdan Hmyelnitzki.

But the name of Kshetchovski reassured him. Few soldiers in the Commonwealth had the fame of this veteran commander of Pereyaslav Cossacks. The Grand Hetman must have thought long and hard before deciding to send his Cossack corps against the Zaporohjans but with Kshetchovski at their head there'd be no chance of treason. Besides, no one had such a following in the Ukraine. Kshetchovski walked in glory like a legendary hero, bards sang about his exploits even more than about the almost mythical adventures of Bohun. His name alone could be enough to shake the Zaporohjans' loyalty to Hmyelnitzki.

From what he knew about Bohun and Kshetchovski, the young lieutenant thought of them as the twin opposing facets of the borderlands, in whose combined characters lay the key to the Cossacks, to the Ukraine, and to the Commonwealth's role in these ancient lands where the western influences of Warsaw and Rome collided with the faith and spirit of Kievan Ruthenia.

But where Bohun was like a wild Steppe fire Kshetchovski

was like ice. Where Bohun cared about little except war and glory, Kshetchovski fought grimly to carve out a brilliant future for himself. He was ambitious as few others even in that land of driven, ruthless men, and the war would give him the opportunity he needed. The Grand Hetman, Pan Mikolai Pototzki, valued and trusted him. He'd been a protege of the powerful Pototzkis all his life; indeed, it was they who got him his first military command, his patent of nobility, and the rich lands he held for life in their country at the confluence of the Dniester and Ladava rivers.

True, Pan Yan knew, there'd been talk that he was cruelly disappointed when he did not become the *Starosta* of Litinsk, a high office that the Pototzkis worked to get for him, but he had time for that and much more besides. He was in his prime, barely fifty years old and rich in experience, and no one doubted that he'd blaze his own comet trail across the war-torn skies. And then his name would reach the ears of the King and he would hear those words so precious to the eastern gentry: '*He came before Us, and bowed down before Us, and We, conscious of his merit . . .*' And he would leave the King's audience chamber greater than when he entered it.

That was the immemorial Polish way in the Eastern Lands. The road to titles, riches and positions of influence and power began with that phrase, and vast tracts of unsettled wilderness passed in this manner into private hands, and ordinary men became great lords who could hope to see their sons among castellans and senators, and their grandchildren would lead their own armies to even greater fame and merit in the endless Wild Lands where principalities waited to be founded.

And so Skshetuski breathed his relief and prayed his thanks to God. The young Pototzki couldn't hope for a better mentor with whose experienced hands to strike down Hmyelnitzki.

"I could be free today!" Pan Yan murmured while tears of joy ran down his fevered face.

He lay—at rest now, and with his mind at peace—on his straw bedding in the creaking wagon, and listened to the fading thunder of the Kudak cannon.

The sound diminished as the miles increased between the fortress and the Zaporohjans, and soon—long before the sun burst redly out of that sea of grass—it was no more than a dull, bitter muttering below the horizon.

Chapter Eleven

THE DISTANT MUTTERING of Pan Grodjitzki's cannon drifted up the Dnieper; it echoed in the ravines and on the floating islands where the birds rose cawing in great flocks; it rang within the secret inlets and bayous of the river and across the Steppe where startled antelope fled into the scarlet morning. It sounded like the beat of muffled drums in the fleet of ships that sailed down the river.

The ships were Dnieper galleys, barges and *bateaux* which the Grand Hetman commandeered for the expedition, stripping the river of its shipping from Tchehryn all the way to Kiev. The swollen Dnieper swept them downstream as if they were cork, past the mouths of all the tributary streams and swamps and the rain-sodden Steppe, with long oars flashing and sails billowing and the tall decks bright with the steel of muskets and the brass of cannon. Aboard the ships were six thousand picked regulars of the scarlet-coated Pereyaslav Cossacks and one thousand hired German musketeers. It was a formidable force for that time and place, a powerful weapon forged for the hands of a determined leader, and Kshetchovski, who shared the command of this division with old Barabas, was fully conscious of it.

His Cossacks, he knew, were ready to leap into the cataracts at one word from him. As for the Germans, he thought them a commander's dream, men who seemed hammered out of stone and steel. Impervious to the shifting winds of feeling and the bonds of kinship that might affect allegiances in a civil war, they were a perfect instrument of destruction forged in the fires of the Thirty Years' War.

Watching their cold, unmoving ranks, he thought them a machine without love or hatred, and his own icily unsentimental mind responded with pleasure. His Cossacks loved him and would die for him, believing in the magic of his name; the Germans would die if they had to because of an order. It was this lack of feeling that raised the Germans' value in Kshetchovski's eyes. The man who wielded this disciplined weapon—so rare in the Commonwealth where unquestioning obedience was looked upon as fitting only for lackeys and peasants—could count his victories before he fought his battles.

And victories meant what?

'*Merit and glory,*' whispered his sense of duty.

'*Nothing . . . if shared with another,*' hissed the voice of egotism and ambition.

And so if there was anything to cast a cloud on his horizons on that brilliant morning it was the fact of his shared command with the old Barabas. Nothing else, he knew, could have caused him to pace his quarter-deck, head lowered in gloom, while his Cossacks watched and muttered and tried to keep out of his way. The day came up as if ordered for a wedding. It was cool and clear and promised good weather. The distant sound of cannon promised even more.

In truth, Kshetchovski knew that he didn't have to give a thought to Barabas. The old man had aged beyond recognition. He was so close to death that he showed little sign of life. The gentle swaying of the decks, the creak of ropes, and the measured beating of the oars put him to sleep early in the journey, and if he woke at all it was to eat, not to issue orders. But it was one thing for Kshetchovski to run the expedition and another to lay future claims to undivided merit, and his pride boiled at the thought of being saddled with shared leadership.

Besides, he thought, if old Barabas was no real rival there still remained young Stefan Pototzki, the Castellan of Krakow and his patron's son.

It was perhaps for that reason that he allowed his fleet to be swept downstream by the rushing river, away from young Pototzki's heavy cavalry which found the going hard on the rain-soaked Steppe, until so many miles separated him from the castellan's division that they couldn't be bridged.

He complained about the dragging pace and the inexperience of his young commander whenever there were any Germans near enough to hear him but he made no attempt to slow down his ships' rapid descent of the swollen river. Indeed, he ordered oarsmen to assist the currents so that he might be the first to confront Hmyelnitzki. And so on that morning, when the distant drumming of the Kudak cannon gave its faint alarm, Kshetchovski smiled grimly; he knew that he wouldn't need to share anything with the Grand Hetman's son.

★ ★ ★

Around him as he paced the deck, men stirred and looked at each other and tasted the fresh wind, and all eyes followed the course of the river which carried them towards the grumbling guns. The cannonade grew louder with each passing hour. It didn't wake old Barabas who shook and muttered in his octogenarian dreams. But Hans Flieck, commander of the Germans, had himself rowed in a skiff to Kshetchovski's galley.

"Guns, colonel," he observed as he came aboard. "What are your orders?"

Kshetchovski listened to the swelling thunder.

"Turn your boats inshore," he said.

"Are we to march on foot, then?"

"No. We'll wait here until tomorrow morning. And make sure there's no sign of your ships or men showing above the reeds."

But the veteran German colonel remembered other sieges and the experience of many other wars.

"Kudak is under siege," he said respectfully but with a touch of fire. "In my opinion we should march at once."

"I am not asking for opinions, *Oberst*," Kshetchovski said coldly. "I gave you an order. Halt your ships and wait."

The German stood undecided. He tugged angrily at his yellow beard, torn between disciplined obedience and hard-earned experience, but Kshetchovski knew that discipline would win over any other considerations in the end. Discipline was the German mercenary's stock in trade, that's what made it possible for Flieck and his kind to charge so much for their expensive service. On the other hand there were also rules of war and of knightly conduct and these were in conflict with Kshetchovski's orders.

But Kshetchovski knew what troubled the German. "The castellan may come up tomorrow with the cavalry," he said in a mild voice. "And not even Hmyelnitzki can take Kudak in one day."

"But what if the castellan doesn't come tomorrow?"

"Then we'll wait until he does. You don't know Kudak, Oberst Flieck. The Zaporohjans will crack their teeth on those walls and accomplish nothing. And in the meantime we'll find out a little more about them."

The German nodded, reassured, and soon the whole fleet moved to the right bank of the Dnieper, although there was no way to tell where the river ended and the shore began. The Steppe was widely flooded and for half a mile each way from the shoreline a forest of tall reeds dipped its furry heads. The ships slid under this rippling canopy, the masts were taken down and the oars lay still.

★ ★ ★

With the ships concealed and the soldiers silent, there was no sound of any kind on the empty river. Nothing showed in or above the reeds. The nodding rushes appeared undisturbed. The fleet seemed to have disappeared and seven thousand soldiers crouched on the decks and listened to the growling guns.

"Old Hmyel isn't joking," the Pereyaslav Cossacks whispered to each other. "But Pan Grodjitzki isn't joking either."

"Ay, it's got to be hot over there, brother."

"And it'll get hotter."

They were old soldiers, every one of them; they understood the language of cannon, and so did Kshetchovski.

He sat in the bows of his ship, deep in thought, and wondered how he could have misjudged Hmyelnitzki as badly as the cannonade suggested.

'How's that, then?' he thought. '*Having won over the Zaporohjans and beguiled the Khan, and amassed a force unheard of in the history of Cossack rebellions, this man is throwing it all away for nothing?*'

He knew Hmyelnitzki well.

He thought him a genius, the kind of rare man who needed only a vast historical arena to stage a drama that would lift him up to tower like a giant above all mankind. But now, instead of marching with all speed into the Ukraine to get a strong foothold in a populated country, to spread the rebellion, to swell his ranks with all the restless peasants and disaffected Cossacks, and to repel the Hetmans one by one before they were ready, this old, experienced soldier was storming a fortress that could hold him at bay for a year? And—having spent his best strength on those granite walls—will he wait under Grodjitzki's cannon until the Hetmans call in all their forces and trap him like they trapped Nalevayko on the Slonitza in the last uprising?

"He's lost," Kshetchovski muttered. "He's ruined. His own men will turn him over to the Hetmans' hangmen. One bloody assault on those walls and the Zaporohjans will lose their faith in him. The flame will die out of the rebellion and Hmyelnitzki won't mean any more than a broken saber . . . a barking dog without a tooth to bite with."

The man's a fool, he thought with contempt.

And so?

'*And so,*' he thought, '*tomorrow I'll put my men ashore. The next night I'll strike him where he least expects me. The Nijhovtsy will be dead-tired and demoralized after their attack on the fortress walls. I'll put them to the sword, every wild dog of them, and I'll toss Hmyelnitzki like a sack of oats under the Hetman's feet.*'

And then what?

Kshetchovski knew that young Pototzki would never manage to join him in time for the battle. No part in the battle meant no share in the victory. Who, then, would be the conqueror of the Zaporohjans and savior of the Ukraine?

Red sunlight glittered on the rippled water and the wind was hissing among the bowing reeds but for the smiling Pereyaslav colonel it was as if emeralds and rubies were shining at him from a golden baton while the horsetail standard of a Hetman snapped in the air above him.

"Hmyelnitzki will go under the axe," he muttered. "Too bad. But it's the fool's own fault. If he'd gone straight as an arrow into the Ukraine it could've been different. It's like a beehive there, they're thirsting for blood! A real powder keg waiting for a spark. The Commonwealth is powerful but she's weak out here. The King is old. His ministers are useless. One battle won by the Zaporohjans could have been enough . . ."

Instead the guns of Kudak kept growling and booming.

Kshetchovski bowed his head into his hands. He knew that after crushing the rebellion he'd be able to ask for anything he wanted. The rank and power of a Hetman of the Ukraine wouldn't be too much.

And yet, he thought, they didn't give him Litinsk.

"I wasn't good enough!" he hissed in quick fury.

The spasm of anger shook him, violent as a fever. It spread a twisted grimace on his brooding face. He clenched his fists and heard his powerful jaws grinding against each other. The world grew darker before his narrowed eyes and not only because the sun was slipping into evening. "*Litinsk!*" he snarled. Not even the backing of Mikolai Pototzki was enough to give him that office. He was a *Homo Novus*, his nobility was too new, and his successful rival was descended from a long line of Ruthenian princes.

'*Ah* . . .'— and his strong white teeth ground together in a savage fury—'*So it's not enough to be ennobled in this Commonwealth! A man must wait until his coat-of-arms is rusty like old iron! Crumbling! Bloodless with old age!*'

Hmyelnitzki could have changed all that. He could have broken the power of the magnates, humbled the jealous gentry. The King, as people said, wouldn't have been opposed . . .

Instead, the fool preferred to break his head against the walls of Kudak.

"So be it then."

He stared into the evening.

The day was almost ended and then night would come. Then there'd be one more day and then a night of battle. The Zaporohjans would be ground into the dust; Hmyelnitzki would be dead— beheaded or impaled alive or torn apart with horses or quartered like an ox—and he, Kshetchovski, would be wrapped in glory brighter than the sun.

His anger, bitterness, injured pride and disappointed hopes subsided as the hours passed. He grew calm. Nothing was lost, nothing was impossible, he thought. It didn't matter what the past refused him. The future was his.

"After tomorrow they won't be able to refuse me anything I want," he murmured. "Anything . . ."

' . . . *Castles and lands. Manors and distinctions. Miles of woods and forests.*'

His head fell forward. His eyes closed.

' . . . *Hetman of the Ukraine. Senator . . . Twenty thousand peasants working on my land.*'

"This time tomorrow it'll all begin," he murmured. Then he sighed, smiled and drifted into sleep.

★   ★   ★

When he awoke the stars were already pale and, in the east, the sky acquired the blue-grey transparency of water under ice. His men still slept. The ships lay silent in the reeds. There was no sound of any kind and it was this unnatural silence that had wakened him.

The damp, chilly river air was hushed before sunrise, with the light barely strong enough to seep through the mist and to streak the water with broad bands of silver. He knew that there was something not quite right about that still air. Its total lack of sound seemed suddenly ominous.

The Kudak cannon were no longer firing. Did that mean that the fortress had fallen? But no, that was impossible. The Zaporohjans couldn't have taken Kudak in òne wild assault. Its silence only meant that the first attack had been beaten off and now the wailing *Nijhovtsy* were crawling off to lick their wounds while grim, one-eyed Grodjitzki watched them through a sooty embrassure. They'd try again, of course. And when they ran howling into the Steppe again, shocked and decimated, they'd find a thousand German muskets blazing in their faces and six thousand Pereyaslav sabers falling on their necks.

So it wasn't Kudak's silence that made him uneasy. Something else was missing, some sound that had become so familiar on the river that it was noticed only in omission. The water made soft slapping sounds under the stern of his galley but, to Kshetchovski, this was like the diffident tapping of a sentry coming to report an unexplained new danger. He'd been a Steppe soldier long enough not to take anything for granted.

The light spread. Kshetchovski woke his men and soon all the others mustered on all the ships for the morning stand-to. He sent a canoe for Hans Flieck as soon as that was over.

"If the castellan doesn't come up by nightfall, *Herr Oberst*," he told him. "And if the attack on the fortress is resumed, we'll go there to help."

"My men are ready," Flieck said.

"Issue the powder, lead and cartridges."

"All have been issued."

"We'll go ashore tonight. We'll march through the Steppe. It's dry enough from here to Kudak. I know, I've been here before. And there's high ground between us and the Cossacks. We'll take them by surprise."

"*Gut! Sehr Gut*! But couldn't we move up closer in the ships?

It is a good four miles to the fortress, far for foot soldiers on strange ground at night."

"Mount your men behind mine."

"*Sehr Gut!*"

"And remember: silence. There's to be no talking, no sound of any kind. No one is to go ashore until we're all ready to disembark. Issue dry rations. I want no cooking fires. The smoke would give us away and spoil the surprise."

"In this fog it wouldn't show," the German observed. "But we'll do it as you want it, colonel."

"This is only the early morning mist. It'll lift as soon as the sun rises. Is everything clear?"

"*Jawohl!*"

Kshetchovski nodded. Flieck was rowed away. And soon canoes moved among the ships with paddles wrapped in cloth to reduce their splashing, and orders were passed from ship to ship in whispers, and the Cossacks fed their horses by hand to keep them from neighing, and everyone lay down on the decks to avoid an accidental sound.

Kshetchovski listened to the silence. He supposed that a man could ride past the hidden anchorage without ever knowing that seven thousand men and six thousand horses lay on a hundred ships no further than an arrow's flight away. He was pleased. The day was starting well. But he was still aware of his earlier restlessness and that unspecified suspicion that something wasn't right, and he wondered what it was that had been missing from the silent air and what was missing now.

And then he knew, and a cold sweat broke out on his temples, and he cursed himself for having missed the obvious. All his carefully constructed plans of the day before returned to mock him, as useless now as all his glittering dreams, and he knew that whatever happened on this day would have nothing to do with anything he'd hoped for.

There'd been no birds!

The vast sea of reeds and grass and tufted mounds of earth in which tens of thousands of wild geese, ducks, cranes and cormorants filled each morning's air with a cawing shrillness had been without a sound. All the birds were gone. And what had replaced them?

As if in answer to this bitter thought a chorus of countless voices rose out of the reeds and from the Steppe grass beyond.

"Pugu-Pugu!"

Kshetchovski knew that call and so did his Cossacks who stared at each other with wide eyes.

"Pugu-Pugu!"

The Pereyaslav men stirred uneasily and whispered among themselves, peering from ship to ship and into the reeds. They knew this greeting and recognition call of the Zaporohjans which sounded in part like the hooting of a hawk-owl, in part like the barking of a fox, and—for the most part—like the staccato drumming of a bird's beak on dry wood. It could mean almost anything and now the calls had become insistent.

"Pugu! Pugu!"

"Who's there?" Kshetchovski called at last.

"God's children!"

"And what do you want?"

"Bohdan Hmyelnitzki, Hetman of the Zaporohjans, sends word that his cannon are turned on the river."

"Tell him that mine are turned on the shore," Kshetchovski called back.

"Pugu! Pugu!"

"What else do you want?"

"Bohdan Hmyelnitzki, Hetman of the Zaporohjans, bows to his good friend and brother, Colonel Kshetchovski, and asks him for a talk."

"Let him send hostages."

"Ten *Kujhen* atamans?"

"Agreed!"

The mist began to lift from the reeds and grasses and a great cry of greeting swept across the Steppe which blazed with sudden color. Bright Cossack caps transformed the shore into a meadow flowering in blues, yellows, scarlets, crimsons and a dazzling white, and the Zaporohjans rose in tens of thousands from the hushed green stillness in which they had been hidden.

Kshetchovski looked and shrugged, his face wry. He'd been right, he thought, to worry about the silence; more than just a fleet of riverboats could be hidden in those reeds.

The mist began to vanish as the sun burned hotter and he could see far into the Steppe which seemed to sink under its own new lake of multicolored brightness. A shining river seemed to have spilled across the horizon. The Zaporohjan regiments flowed one after another behind the huge crimson banner of Archangel Michael, the patron of the brotherhood; and a hundred lesser flags and horsetail standards snapped and twisted above a moving forest of bare Cossack lances; and antlike streams of oxen hauled batteries of cannon that lurched and staggered in the Steppe like a herd of black, prehistoric beasts. And then the mile-wide rectangle of the Cossack *tabor* rolled over the skyline with its tall-sided, loopholed wagons and horse herds and cattle. The army of Bohdan Hmyelnitzki filled the vast spaces between the horizons until it seemed to have become the Steppe itself and the land looked as if dressed in festive brightness for a celebration.

And there was the singing of thirty-thousand voices, the booming roar of kettle-drums beaten with abandon, the bold flash of brass and copper trumpets, humming *teorbans*, the deep call of the great curved *krivulas* with which the Cossackry announced their invasions, and the shrill cry of Tartar pipes and flutes.

Banners dipped and waved.

Arms waved. Bright caps gleamed.

The Pereyaslav Cossacks answered with a shout.

It was more like a wedding celebration or the joyful meeting of old friends, Kshetchovski thought grimly, than a gathering of enemies preparing for battle. But he let nothing show on his icy face.

★   ★   ★

The Zaporohjan atamans came aboard the ships and Kshetchovski jumped into their boat, ignoring the bared heads and low respectful bowing of the oarsmen. They took him to Hmyelnitzki. The Zaporohjan Hetman doffed his own rich sable cap with its egret plume and jeweled clasps and badges and threw his arms open in a wide embrace.

"My friend," he began. "My good friend and brother!"

Kshetchovski kept silent. Cold and withdrawn, he merely nodded to acknowledge the greeting, and if he thought that once again he had misjudged Hmyelnitzki he showed none of it.

"I owe you so much," Hmyelnitzki went on warmly. "When the Grand Hetman issued his warrants against me you warned me, didn't you. I'd owe you all my gratitude just for that. But there's more, of course. You disobeyed him when he ordered you to go after me and let me escape."

"And now that you've got away you raised a rebellion," Kshetchovski said coldly.

"I go with the King's letters, which are the same as his permission, so to speak. Or with his blessing, if that's the way you want to look at it. And where am I going? To ask for simple justice for us all. For me and for you and for all the Cossack children of the Commonwealth! If that's rebellion, then I am a rebel. But I don't think our good King will hold it against me, and neither should you. We've been friends too long for such misunderstandings."

The Pereyaslav colonel looked long and hard into Hmyelnitzki's eyes.

"What about Kudak?" His meaning was clear.

"What about it? It stands where it's always stood. And it might stand there for quite a while longer."

"Are you besieging it?"

"What?" Hmyelnitzki burst into sudden laughter. "I'd have to be crazy! I went by that place without a pistol shot, even though the old Cyclops announced my coming with every gun he's got. I've no time for Kudak! Right now I'm driving my men and horses into the ground to get into the Ukraine, not to any Kudaks. And,"—he grinned broadly—"I was in a hurry to see you too, old friend!"

"I bet you were. And what d'you want from me?"

Hmyelnitzki smiled. He looked at the savage, grinning faces of his atamans. "Ride with me into the Steppe a little," he said and turned his horse into the tall grasses. "It's time for you and me to have a little talk."

Kshetchovski followed him without a word.

★ ★ ★

They were away an hour.

When they returned, Kshetchovski's face was bloodless. His skin was damp and grey and his pale mouth was twisted into a cruel parody of a triumphant smile. There was something about the haste with which he left Hmyelnitzki that suggested horror, as if he'd looked into the darkest pit of Hell and saw his own past and future reflected in its mirrors.

And it was with this twisted, ghastly mask stretched across his face that he went back aboard his galley where Barabas, Hans Flieck and other officers surrounded him at once.

"Well, what's the news? What's happening? What did he say to you?"

Kshetchovski stared at them with blind, unseeing eyes as if they weren't there.

"Unload the ships!" he ordered.

"What? What?"

"Disembark the men!" His voice seemed ghastly even to himself.

Then Barabas stirred. His weary parchment eyelids trembled upward and there was a sudden light in his tired old eyes.

"W-w-what's that?" he murmured.

"Disembark! We're . . . surrendering."

And then the broken, silver-haired old man whom Kshetchovski had dismissed as a 'living corpse'—too close to death to be worth considering as a rival—shuddered and blood surged into his yellow cheeks, and his stooped shoulders lifted and his bent back straightened as he rose from the upended kettledrum on which he was resting, and suddenly he was no longer that despised and ignored artifact from another era.

"Treason!" he roared in a voice like thunder.

"Treason," Flieck repeated and reached for his sword. But Kshetchovski's saber whistled through the air and the German fell while the Pereyaslav colonel turned and leaped overboard into a Zaporohjan skiff. "To the ships!" he cried and the swift boat fled like a swallow skimming over water.

"Children!" Kshetchovski rose and stood between the oarsmen and raised his cap on the end of his bloody saber. "We won't spill Cossack blood! Long live Bohdan Hmyelnitzki, our Hetman and brother!"

"Long live!" a hundred voices shouted in reply.

" 'Na pohybel Lahom!' Death to the Poles!"

"Death to them!" howled a thousand voices from the Pereyaslav galleys, and the ten thousand Zaporohjans massed along the shore added their roar of welcome to the shouts of joy that came from the river.

The news spread to the ships anchored farther off and then a madness seemed to seize the Pereyaslav Cossacks. Six thousand scarlet caps flew into the air and six thousand firelocks shattered whatever calmness remained to the morning and the galleys trembled under their dancing boots. The men wept and sang and howled and embraced each other and leaped in wild dances, and pushed and pulled each other and wrestled and tumbled into the water, and cheering Zaporohjans waded out to the ships through the reedy shallows to welcome their new brothers.

All that remained to seal their brotherhood was blood and even that was found. Old Barabas chose death over treason and half a company of his Tcherkassy men followed their commander. The ancient colonel who, only that morning, seemed husked and dry—a crumbling old man who was no longer quite alive and, at the same time, not quite dead—fought like a wakened lion. Summoned to lay down his arms, he answered with volleys. He stood as upright and erect as a youth, his voice was commanding, and his snow-white hair blew about him like a commander's plume.

His ship was hemmed in from all sides. The Zaporohjans and the Pereyaslav men struggled with each other to be the first aboard. The loyal Tcherkassy troop fought with the hopeless fury of despairing men and was quickly slaughtered. The deck ran with blood. Hacked corpses covered it so thickly from prow to stern that not a glimmer of the planking showed under the bodies, but the old man still roared and wheeled his great saber, and finally the attackers began to back off in superstitious awe. Neither Kshetchovski nor any of his men expected such resistance but Kshetchovski finally cut his way to the raging old man.

"Give in!" he shouted.

"Traitor!" Barabas roared and raised his sword and Kshetchovski leaped back into the crowd.

"Kill him!" he ordered but, for a moment, nobody obeyed him.

It seemed as if no one among these fierce warriors for whom contempt for death was a way of life wanted to be the first to strike the terrible old man. And so he roared and charged them and then his boots slipped in the blood, his feet slid out from under him, and he fell heavily to the deck. Fallen, he no longer awed or frightened anyone, or excited the Cossacks' admiration and respect, and twenty sabers plunged into his body.

"*Jezus Maria!*" he screamed in an old man's voice and then he was dead.

His dead body was hacked into pieces. His severed head flew from ship to ship, tossed like a ball by the laughing Cossacks. Then it fell into the water and the fight was over. Kshetchovski

sighed, relieved. There remained only the Germans to oppose
him, but this, he knew, wouldn't be as simple. The thousand
Germans could be counted on to take at least as many of his
Cossacks with them and he thought he'd rather lose the Cossacks than the Germans; it would mean much to him to be able
to deliver such a splendid regiment to Hmyelnitzki.

But, he thought, did he have to fight them? They were
mercenaries, weren't they? So couldn't they be bought? Treason, he thought with an icy smile, often depended on the
character of the commander. Hans Flieck would rather die than
change sides, and did so. Kshetchovski had killed him. But
Johann Werner, the musketeers' second in command, might
listen to reason. And reason always favored life over death and
profit before loss, didn't it? That at least seemed to be the way
things were done in that 'Civilized West' where the Germans
came from, and so Kshetchovski was full of optimism as he had
himself rowed to the Germans' ships.

They watched him coming—impervious, immovable and
magnificent—and he, in turn, counted them as if they were a
treasure. They stood shoulder to shoulder in deep, silent ranks
that made a bright, cold wall around the outer rim of their massed *bateaux*, so that they seemed like a soundless island in a sea
of Cossacks who howled and shook their weapons and hacked
the decks of their own circling ships with sabers in their impatience to attack.

What soldiers, he thought, and looked into their hard, disdainful faces. They stood at ease with the left foot forward as if
for musket drill. Each of them looked exactly like all of the
others with the left arm thrust out, the hand grasping the forked
rod on which the heavy muskets rested during firing. A polished weapon was cradled evenly on each man's right hip, broad
shoulders were thrust back, a thousand heads were held high
under yellow hats with the right rim pinned up under a short
plume, and the new sun seemed to add fresh luster to the
matched leather of their yellow coats. His power, Kshetchovski
knew, would rival Hmyelnitzki's if he could bring such a perfect
instrument of war to the Zaporohjans.

He looked for Werner, then found him in the first rank. The
German captain stood quietly and calmly with his sword-point
resting on the deck before him as if he was merely leaning on it

like a cane. Kshetchovski did not know him well. He thought him a cold, phlegmatic man, less of a knight-errant than his dead commander and surely more amenable to reason.

And, at first, it seemed as if the calm, attentive German would agree to come over to the Zaporohjans. The Commonwealth, as always, was late with its pay and Kshetchovski offered gold immediately. He'd make good whatever the Commonwealth owed the regiment and buy a year's service with full pay in advance. After a year the regiment would be free to march wherever it wanted, even into the camp of the Grand Hetman if that's what they had in mind.

"Those are my terms," he said.

"Most generous," said Werner.

"Then you agree?"

The German smiled briefly.

Around his ships lay the massed Cossack galleys. Six thousand savages and more were waiting to attack. He turned his slow, thoughtful eyes on his own soldiers and looked at them as if he'd never seen any of them before and wondered who they were, what moved them, what kind of men they were and what mattered to them.

Then he nodded. "We agree," he said.

"You won't regret it!" cried the overjoyed Kshetchovski.

"But there's one condition."

"You've got it in advance whatever it is!"

"Is that so?" The German nodded once more and again there was that small, enigmatic smile. "Ah, very good. Our term of service with the Commonwealth expires in June. We'll come to you then."

Kshetchovski felt the blood flooding into his head and a scarlet anger choked him for a moment. Foul curses burst out of him before he could stop them. But he hadn't come as far as he had in his climb to power without an icy self-control that might have rivaled the discipline of the Germans. He'd lived through years of slights and humiliations; he knew how to bite back anger and indignation and to hold his tongue, and now he found his own disdainful smile.

"A joke," he said. "Of course."

"Not at all."

"Then you must be mad."

"We're soldiers." Werner shrugged. "We keep our agreements. It's a simple matter of a soldier's honor. Our contract expires in June and that's all there's to it."

"That's a fine contract you've got,"—Kshetchovski's smile was now heavy with contempt—"they haven't paid you in a year."

"We'll be paid," The German said calmly. "Sooner or later we are always paid. But we weren't hired to worry about money. That's our employers' side of the bargain. Our job is to serve. We serve for money, true, but we are not traitors."

"How noble," hissed the turncoat colonel but he no longer smiled.

Werner shrugged. "Perhaps. It's also practical. Nobody would hire us if we couldn't be trusted anytime someone came up with a better price. Look at it this way, colonel, if you bought us today, how could you be sure we wouldn't sell you to the Poles tomorrow?"

"What is it that you want, then?" Kshetchovski asked with some exasperation.

"Allow us to leave."

"That'll never happen! You can be sure of that! I'll have you cut down to the last man, you fool!"

"But at what price, colonel?"

"Not one of you will leave here alive!"

"And half of you will die."

Each of them spoke the truth and each of them knew it and Kshetchovski cursed the stubborn Germans under his breath. He'd been a Steppe soldier for almost thirty years and he knew his Cossacks. He also knew the hard realities of luck, ruthless courage and the ability to go from victory to victory on which a leader's credit depended among them. There was no question of a German victory here. They were surrounded and outnumbered by more than twenty thousand of the fiercest warriors the world had ever seen. They'd die to a man. But Kshetchovski's reputation would suffer a blow that might take years to heal. The Cossacks followed their leaders blindly as long as they believed in them, but once a leader's aura of success was shattered, once failure tarnished his fame and robbed him of his followers' superstitious awe, then all respect and admiration ended. Once fallen, like old Barabas on his bloody deck, he was as good as dead.

And so Kshetchovski held back the signal for attack. "Think it over. I'll give you till sunset!" he shouted. "After that . . ." He passed the edge of his hand across his throat and hurried ashore.

★ ★ ★

The galleys of the Pereyaslav Cossacks drew a tighter ring around the silent Germans as the day passed into the afternoon. The Zaporohjans wheeled their cannon to the shore. Three thousand Tartar archers and Zaporohjan marksmen waded into the reeds and took up their positions as the sun marched steadily westward across the sky, taking its golden light off the river and the wide waters of the anchorage. Hour by hour the Cossack frenzy had grown in foaming madness. Inflamed by the butchery of Barabas and the Tcherkassy loyalists they howled for more blood. It didn't seem likely, not even to Kshetchovski, that the delicate threads of whatever passed for discipline among them would hold until dusk.

And then the sun was gone. A Cossack bugle called from beyond the reeds and Kshetchovski shouted: "It's time! What's your answer?"

Werner raised his sword.

"*Feuer!*" he said calmly.

The roar of a thousand muskets, fired as one, blew the last shreds of daylight from the sky and the splash of dead and wounded men tumbling into the water sounded like some terrible sort of avalanche. Then came a wail of rage, the furious drumbeat rattle of Cossack firelocks, the deep booming of the Zaporohjans' cannon, and a wall of fire blazed along the shore and in the reeds and on the tufted mud islands in the anchorage. It ran along the black sides of the Cossack galleys like a scarlet sash. It licked at the torn darkness with the long red tongues of guns bellowing on the shore. Lead and iron rained down on the Germans. A thick black cloud settled upon them and their splintering ships. It spread along the shore and boiled far into the Steppe, and it erupted on the Cossack galleys, and the night's darkness became studded with sudden constellations of red and yellow fires. There seemed to be only one great sound in that roaring darkness; a thick, dark sound made up of indistinguishable orders, shouts, cries of rage and pain, the hiss and clatter of the Tartar arrows raining on the decks, the bellowing of the cannon, the dry rattle of bandolets, firelocks and handguns, the crack of rending metal and splintering wood and the crash of the toppling masts. And throughout, as if to bring a sense of order to this savage chaos, the musketeers' volleys marked off the passing hours with the cold precision of a funeral drum.

Two hours after sunset, this measured beat weakened like a stricken heart. The flaming circle of the German volleys lost some of its brightness. In another hour there were long gaps of darkness in their belt of fire. The steady pulse of their volleys became ragged and uncertain, and then all the other sounds submerged it completely, and five thousand Tartars, Zaporohjans and Pereyaslav Cossacks threw themselves aboard the darkened German ships.

Hmyelnitzki, Tuhay-bey and the Pereyaslav colonel sat on their horses on the shore and watched as this dark, howling wave struck the ships and swept across the decks and drowned the small remaining islands of yellow-coated Germans. They breathed the acrid reek of blood and gunsmoke that drifted far beyond them into the open Steppe. They listened to the baying laughter of the murderers and to the dwindling cries of men who were being butchered. This was the first battle of the war and it was ending in a Zaporohjan victory.

Hmyelnitzki looked radiant. Kshetchovski was as pale as a corpse although he tried to smile.

"An omen!" he said.

"There'll be just the two of us in the Ukraine," Hmyelnitzki assured him. "Just you and me and only the King above us."

"If God grants the victories."

But Tuhay-bey bared his yellow teeth and flashed them at the two Cossack leaders like an angry mastiff. "I don't want such victories! Where's my *yassyr*? Where are all my captives?"

"You'll take them in the Ukraine," Hmyelnitzki assured him. "You'll fill all Asia with them!"

"I'll take you, if there's nothing else!"

Then the battle ended. Tuhay-bey turned his horse towards the camp and the others followed.

"And now for young Pototzki!" Hmyelnitzki cried out and the atamans cheered.

The sounds of the Cossack triumph beat for a long time against the dark night sky.

Chapter Twelve

PAN YAN LISTENED to the battle with raging impatience. His illness shook him like a dog worrying a bone. He bit his knuckles and clawed at his beard and struggled weakly to sit up on his straw bedding in old Zakhar's wagon.

"Soon! Soon!" he cried, waiting to be freed, and strained to hear the sounds of the fighting coming closer to the Zaporohjan camp. He listened for the brassy crowing of the Hetmans' trumpets, the roar of ten thousand voices shouting the Polish battlecry, and for the plaintive "*Spasi! Spasi!*" of the beaten, terror-stricken Cossacks.

He struggled feebly with old Zakhar who pushed him back into the straw and begged him to hold still, and his ears waited for the thunder of armored horsemen sweeping through the Steppe. He had no doubt, of course, that this was the long-awaited clash between Hmyelnitzki and both the Crown Hetmans. He knew that the young Castellan of Krakow led few troops, but he supposed them to be no more than the vanguard of the whole Crown Army. When it was time for battle, the young Pototzki would have fallen back, the Hetmans would have joined him, and now the whole great mass of iron men and horses was crushing the Zaporohjans for all time.

No other outcome was possible. On one side was the savage sea of Tartars and Cossacks—fierce, war-wise and hungry for the battle, to be sure, but for all that only an unbridled mob—and riding down on them were the disciplined regiments of the winged *husaria* who never lost a battle. Here, he thought with a blend of pride, joy, derision and disdain, was one upstart Cossack rebel and one Tartar chieftain; while there rode the Grand

179

Hetman of the Crown, the foremost soldier of the Commonwealth, and with him an iron corps of fifteen thousand warriors
who had kept all the power of the Turks at bay for a generation.

And so he waited, struggled and cursed. He yelled threats.
Old Zakhar finally had to make good his own threats of binding
him so that he wouldn't tear open all his wounds in his terrible
excitement. He couldn't wait to hear the panicked howls of
Hmyelnitzki's shattered fugitives searching for shelter in the
wagon train. Instead, all sound ceased.

It wasn't until a roar of triumph shook the Cossack camp that
Zakhar told him what happened on the Dnieper shore.

"Kshetchovski . . .?"

"God opened his heart."

"Say rather the Devil! His pride, greed, ambition, treachery!"

Zakhar shrugged. "What's treason for one man may be just a
way to stay alive for another. And you, lad, lie back now. Lie
still. If you die on me here old Hmyel will have my hide
stretched over a new drum."

But the young soldier couldn't be consoled. Kshetchovski's
treason and the massacre of the loyal Germans filled him with
foreboding. He knew what a large proportion of the Hetman's
army consisted of Cossacks. They filled the private regiments of
the magnates, the magistrates' gendarmerie in the Ukrainian
cities, the household troops of the great landowners and the law
enforcement companies of sheriffs and *starostas*. Prince Yeremi
himself had several Cossack regiments. What would happen if
all of them deserted to Hmyelnitzki?

The orgy of celebration in the Cossack camp was like a wind
that fanned his bitterness. How then, he asked himself: could
nothing be trusted? Was everything in jeopardy? Would the
entire Ukraine rise behind Hmyelnitzki as the Zaporohjan
leader prophesied only days ago? And how could the Ukraine
be saved and the Commonwealth protected from the combined
onslaught of Zaporohjans, Cossacks, Tartars and rebel peasant
mobs? All hope, he knew, lay with the two Crown Hetmans.
They had to be near! He couldn't believe that Pan Mikolai
Pototzki would so misread the signs! But there was no news of
the Hetmans in the Cossack camp. Or, if there was, old Zakhar
kept it from him.

Neither was there any news about Prince Yeremi.

The Grand Hetman had clearly made a terrible mistake.

Instead of crushing the rebellion under the guns of Kudak, before the firestorm that was now sweeping through the Steppe could carry one incendiary spark into the Ukraine, he split his forces, made treason possible, and gave first blood to the Zaporohjans. Hmyelnitzki's star shined even brighter than before. Six thousand more picked warriors rode behind his standards and a terrible new danger hung over the young Castellan of Krakow unless the Hetmans were marching on his heels. Weakened, inexperienced, cut off from help and stumbling in the flooded, unfamiliar Steppe, he'd be an easy victim.

The only bright star that the agonized young soldier could see in this threatening sky was his Prince Yeremi. But where was he now? Surely, Pan Yan thought, he must be on the move. Perhaps he had already joined his own army to that of the Hetmans. Everyone knew how bitterly the Grand Hetman envied the Prince's reputation but he'd hardly fail to accept his help in the face of the danger that threatened the Ukraine.

Well then, the young man thought as his spirits lifted: it was now up to the great prince and the Hetmans to dam the Cossack flood. The rebellion must come to its inevitable end on the threshold of the Ukraine, somewhere along the border of the Wild Lands where all other Cossack outbreaks were beaten down before. Yes, yes, he thought. That's how it'll be. The Cossack risings blazed up like dry Steppe grass fired by Summer lightning and died just as swiftly.

This thought sustained him through days of accumulating horrors so that he was able to trade stare for stare with the harsh Zaporohjan faces that peered down at him hungrily in his soiled straw, and the ropes seemed to slacken on his arms and body, and the hard, bouncing floor of the two-wheeled Cossack *telega* which was his moving prison seemed as soft as air.

★ ★ ★

And he did need something in which to believe during the days and nights when the tide of the rebellion poured across the Wild Lands.

Hmyelnitzki's army grew stronger every day. Cossacks in every kind of uniform poured into his ranks. The Light Horse and Dragoon regiments of the Crown and of the border magnates dwindled as their Ruthenian soldiers deserted to Hmyelnitzki, and along with them came an endless mass of runaway serfs and peasants and mobs of masterless men who crept out of the hidden creeks and canyons of the wilderness. They flowed into the swollen Zaporohjan columns like tributary streams into a mighty river. And this great river swallowed them and absorbed them and spilled ever wider. Conscious of its power, it burst from its courses and sent tidal waves against whatever little island dared to bar its progress, and flooded the Steppe.

This human torrent, Skshetuski knew, would leave its dreadful mark no matter how quickly it was stopped and dammed. And how could simple, ordinary people who were unaccustomed to hardship and danger survive it undamaged? How could the gentler, settled folk who didn't live the violent lives of soldiers weather it unscarred?

And what, he wondered anxiously, was happening to Helen in Rozloghi?

This thought tormented him more than any other. Its images were frightful. But here again the stern star of Prince Yeremi's reputation brightened the darkness of his premonitions. Because surely Helen was safe by now in Lubnie, in the Prince's country, and no spark of rebellion could ever touch anything within the reach of Yeremi Vishnovyetzki's hand. He could imagine her surrounded by friendly, caring faces, admired and protected, and worried only about him. And he was nearer to her every day! The Zaporohjans' march brought him closer with each traveled hour! Hmyelnitzki promised him his freedom but he knew that he would have it anyway once the rebellion smashed itself to pieces on the threshold of the Commonwealth. It would ebb and scatter and leave him free among its debris.

"Soon, soon," he murmured as the firestorm swept across the Steppe, whipped forward by Hmyelnitzki who hurried his weary animals and men without rest or mercy towards the corps led by the Grand Hetman's son.

*   *   *

There was no sure news about young Pototzki's strength. Cossack deserters from his camp said that he led about two thousand cavalry with about a dozen small artillery pieces and this confirmed Pan Yan's supposition that the young castellan was only a pathfinder for his father's army.

"How could you think any different?" the feverish young

soldier challenged the patient Zakhar. "D'you think the Hetman would condemn his own son to death? Your Hmyelnitzki's a bigger fool than I thought if that's what he believes."

"Pan Pototzki's a great soldier," old Zakhar agreed. "But old Hmyel's nobody's fool either, lad. He knows what he's doing."

"And even if the castellan is alone out there with nobody to help him it won't be easy for you," Skshetuski insisted. "His two thousand men and your thirty thousand . . . that's not a great difference. One *husaria* charge is often quite enough to crush ten times its own strength!"

Growing more cheerful about the outcome of the coming battle, Pan Yan refused to accept the possibility of another Commonwealth disaster even when Zakhar told him that the castellan's small army was, indeed, alone in the Steppe, without the Hetmans' regiments anywhere near him.

"So what?" he told the Cossack. "At Kirkholm, in the Swedish wars, Hetman Hodkevitch wiped eighteen thousand Swedes off the face of the earth with just three thousand of us. And at the battle of Klushyn, not long afterwards, one charge by three hundred *husaria* men smashed seven thousand prime Scots and English infantry."

"Aye, aye, that's how it used to be." Old Zakhar sighed and nodded and patted Skshetuski's arm as if to soothe him and to reassure him. "Aye, those were the days. The *Lah* and the Cossack were brothers then. Oh aye, I remember. We watered our horses side by side in the same rivers, slept under the same sky. But you *Lahy* are different now and the times are different."

"What's different about them?"

"Now there's blood between us."

"And whose fault is that?"

"Who's to say, lad? That's not for my head to worry about. Let Hmyel do the thinking. But you should've seen some of those other times. You should've heard how we young Cossacks cheered from the earthworks when your Pan Lantzkoronski's *lytzari* went for the Sultan's janissaries that time at Tzetzora! Hey, how we tossed our caps into the air and cried out to our Hetman, Sahaydatchny, '*Let us go with them, little father! Let us go! It's life and death for us with the Poles, our brothers!*' But now it's all different. So maybe what's going to happen will also be different."

And the two armies drew closer every hour even as the skies

became black with clouds and the rain poured steadily into the sodden Steppe, so that the whole world seemed to sag under the weight of the water, while the mud became a torment for the men and horses. Wagons bogged down. The cannon sunk into the quagmire so that only their iron necks protruded from the gurgling swamp. But Hmyelnitzki hurried his army forward as if their salvation depended on speed. Pan Yan saw him daily as he rode back and forth among the struggling regiments, his face ablaze and his hand urging the plodding ranks into greater effort, and soon all the Zaporohjans knew why they should be thanking God for their muddy hardships. Because if the Steppe turned into a real morass, the castellan's heavy cavalry would be unable to move! And without the crushing weight of their charge behind them, the huge iron knights would be no more dangerous than any other people.

"Just give me two more days of this," Hmyelnitzki cried to anyone who was near enough to hear him, pointing at the grey streams of water pouring from the sky. "And we'll fish them out of the mud like a sack of crayfish! You can see that God is on our side!"

And "*God is with us!*" cried the weary, struggling Zaporohjans, and they pushed forward towards the coming battle as eagerly as if they were going to a celebration.

And then, one morning, the Tartars of the vanguard galloped back with shouts. They'd seen the *Lahy*! The winged iron men, the terrible *lytzari*, were encamped along the edges of a broken field beside one of the Dnieper's tributary rivers whose sandy bottom and clay banks made its waters yellow. It was only then that Hmyelnitzki brought his army to a grateful halt and, for the first time since the rebellion started, the Cossacks faced the Poles beside a river known as Yellow Waters.

★　★　★

That night Pan Yan couldn't close his eyes in sleep even for a moment. He prayed and shook in a fever of anxiety. The rain fell in torrents. Lightning ripped and shredded the oily black darkness, lashing the Steppe as if in final warning before both God and Nature turned their backs on mankind and washed their hands of whatever happened on earth from then on.

The thunderstorms drifted away when daylight finally seeped into the sky but the rain went on. Thick black clouds twisted overhead as if a swamp were draining down into the

Steppe and, from midmorning on, the day became as dark as if it were twilight.

Both armies spent the day putting up their earthworks even though the rain undermined the walls and toppled the stockades. Batteries of cannon slid off the crumbling ramparts but the work went on amid prayers and curses, and the earthen walls rose slowly around the two camps. Chilled to the bone and without a dry piece of clothing on their bodies, the men suffered equally on both sides. Poles and Cossacks toiled with picks and shovels in the muddy soil from the first light of morning until an even colder darkness fell on them at nightfall.

When night returned the downpour swelled to such unparalleled violence that its roar drowned every other sound, and the lightning storm burst in the sky again and scrawled great fiery letters across the blackness that obscured the stars.

Once again Pan Yan couldn't think of sleeping. Indeed, he doubted that anyone slept in either camp; everyone was too cold and hungry and exhausted. The storm raged on and soon the water rushed in a torrent a foot deep between the *tabor* wagons, and then a freezing wind came up from the south.

His fever set his whole body on fire but deep inside he seemed to turn to ice. His wounds were burning. Dark dreams and nightmare visions fell on him out of the raging night and crowded so thickly in his staring eyes that he no longer knew whether anything was real.

He uttered mindless cries, incoherent even to himself. He shouted. He prayed. Each thought was a torment of anxiety, hope and foreboding. And then the night was over.

★   ★   ★

The new day came in the guise of a desolate morning spattered with grey water. The rain fell listlessly in thin streams as if strained through a sieve. A mournful trumpet cried a long, gloomy note from the Polish camp, and the drums growled out a dull, unurgent beat, and the Zaporohjan cannon roared out in reply.

Meanwhile, down in the Cossack camp, Pan Yan turned his fevered eyes on Zakhar who had a hangdog, troubled air and looked ill at ease.

"Listen, Zakhar," the young lieutenant whispered. "Take me up on the earthworks. I've got to see. I've got to."

"Ey lad, you'll just split open your wounds again . . ."

"Take me up!" Pan Yan threatened. "Or I'll tear off the bandages myself!"

Zakhar sighed and nodded. He too was curious to see the Polish army. He helped Pan Yan out of the *telega* and then half led and half carried him to the Cossack rampart. But they were no sooner on the earthwall, with the broad field and both the camps spread out before them in the dismal light, when Pan Yan swayed and seized his head in both his hands.

"In God's name!" he cried out. "That's no more than an outpost! Where's the Hetman's army?"

And indeed the Polish encampment looked like a dugout in comparison with the Zaporohjans' earthwalls which stretched for half a league east and west from where he was standing. The grey curtain of rain and the intervening distance dwarfed it even further. Skshetuski glanced at it once and closed his eyes in pain. Who could doubt that the Cossacks would triumph once again with such a pitiful force sent out against their thousands?

Ah, he thought, and felt his grief clutch at his heart with an icy fist: so he was not to be set free after all just yet. The hour of reckoning was not yet at hand. The day would throw more victims to the seething hordes and bring a new humiliation for the Commonwealth.

He felt hot tears gathering in his eyes and turned his head to hide them from Zakhar. But the old Cossack didn't look at him. He kept his eyes fixed on the rolling meadow that glistened between the two camps where the customary prelude to the battle was already started. There single horsemen and small groups of riders fought against each other in full view of both armies. They circled each other and maneuvered back and forth, spurred forward and withdrew, striking and whirling out of reach in much the same way that birds of prey fight in the Steppe sky. They crossed their miniature sabers, fired invisible pistols in soft, soundless puffs of smoke, threw their toy lances, whirled their string lariats and darted about like puppets in a children's show. Fresh groups of riders trotted out from behind the little Polish wall, dressed in the blue and yellow colors of the Pototzkis' household Cossack Light Horse, and a new cloud of Tartars poured out of the Zaporohjan earthworks.

All this had a certain playful innocence; it was impossible to believe that the darting little figures were men who were killing others and that other men were dying on that broad, green stage. Only the growing number of riderless horses galloping in the field showed that death was also a part of this performance.

But more and more Tartars poured into the field and soon the whole arena was thick with massed horsemen in black sheepskin jerkins who galloped while bent low over the necks of their shaggy ponies and who seemed to fly under a cloud of arrows. And then the Polish regiments began to come out from behind their wall and to form for battle. They were so near that Pan Yan could recognize their uniforms and banners and even some of the officers who took up their places at the right flank of the long front ranks.

His heart began to pound swiftly in his chest and his white face flushed and he began to call out the names of the regiments as they appeared in the sally-breaks between the Polish earthworks.

"Those are Balaban's dragoons! I saw them in Tcherkassy! And that's the Hetman's own Valachian Light Horse! All our own people serving there, of course, you wouldn't find a Valachian among them just as you wouldn't find any real Tartars in our Tartar Light Horse . . . Ah, and now the foot soldiers are coming off the walls!"

And then, with excitement lifting him out of his pain and illness: "The *Husaria* of Stefan Tcharnyetzki!"

The iron horsemen rode into the field in dressed ranks of six: huge men on heavy horses with the rain glistening on their armored chests and shoulders like a silver polish. Their feathered frames curved up from their shoulders like the great wings of eagles lifted for the kill. A forest of eighteen-foot wooden lances rose in a steel-tipped uniformity above them with green and black pennons fluttering and golden cords gleaming. They took their place in the center of the Polish line like a silent steel wall thrown up at the foot of their little earth-mound, and they stood there as calmly and unmoving as if for review, and at the sight of their steadiness and order and their perfectly dressed ranks, Pan Yan could neither hide nor hold back his tears of joy and relief.

How could he have doubted the outcome? It made no difference that the two armies drawn up in the field were so terribly uneven, or that the handful of Polish regiments looked like a foraging party beside the immense crescent of Cossacks and Tartars whose deep ranks disappeared from view beyond either flank. Pan Yan believed in victory. He knew that he'd be free before that grey day ended. His strength poured back into his body and his eyes were clear. He laughed out loud. He couldn't keep still.

"Ey, lad," old Zakhar muttered, smiling at him gently. "If your soul just had wings, eh?"

Pan Yan no longer bothered to hide his excitement.

★ ★ ★

And then the battle started.

The shrill cry of Tartar whistles, made out of reeds and hollowed marrow-bones, came from the shapeless mass that darkened each of the far-flung wings of Hmyelnitzki's army, a low keening drifted through the rain like the mournful baying of a giant wolfpack, and then two vast grey clouds broke away from those distant points in the Zaporohjan line where the recognizable shapes of animals and men became dim and blurred.

It was as if a dense forest of low shrubs had sprung to sudden life. The forest moved. A hundred long grey arms reached out of it into the open field between the two armies, and these arms thickened and turned into necks that pulled a thick, dark body, and then the heavy, threatening mass that flew so swiftly across the wet grass was no longer shapeless. It acquired form and features. The living forest turned into horsemen dressed in furs and sheepskins who bent so low behind their horses' necks that they seemed to become a part of the animals themselves. Their wooden arrow-cases slid through the air above them like the fins of sharks, and their ululating howl seemed to fill the Steppe. And then the grey air over them glittered with arrowheads, like a flying bridge thrown up between this galloping Tartar mass and the silent horsemen who waited at the foot of the Polish wall.

Black puffs of smoke bloomed on the wall like exotic flowers and the thin, dry coughing of light guns brought another sudden scream from the Tartar reed-flutes, and the vast horde split in two and wheeled as one man and galloped past the silent Polish ranks. It seemed to Pan Yan as if these were two stampeding mustang herds rather than hand-picked *tchambuls* of Crimean warriors. The riders were invisible behind the flying manes but the clouds of arrows went on soaring out of these dark masses until a sudden sound drew all attention to the Zaporohjans.

The great war drum of the *Sietch* began to thunder in the Cossack camp. It boomed with the deep hollow roar of the *Nyenasytetz* and twenty thousand voices raised one savage cry. It was a cry of fierce joy and challenge. It rang with such a certainty of triumph that it drowned the thunder of the drum and the roar of cannon on the Zaporohjan walls. And then the horses screamed and reared in their tens of thousands as their riders struck them with their spurs and beat them with the flat sides of sabers and the whole mass of animals and men flung itself headlong into the field. The earth seemed to groan and shudder under the sudden impact of eighty thousand hooves thrown into a gallop and the water surged up from the sodden soil as the great tide of horsemen swept forward in one giant wave with a glittering crest of sabers held high overhead.

The Zaporohjan gunners in the earthworks leaned far out across the parapets, their eyes wild.

"They'll drown the *Lahy*!" they screamed with excitement. "They'll tear them apart with their hooves!"

"Old Hmyel wants to crush them with one blow . . .!"

"He'll do it if they break! Will they break?"

"They'll break! They'll run! Who wouldn't?"

"Ah, it's a real sea, I tell you . . .!"

The surging mass of Zaporohjan horsemen did look like a tidal wave with the white foam of steel gleaming high above it. They were in full gallop from the start. In another moment their front ranks were a quarter of a mile away, their horses flying as if they'd grown wings and their sabers thrust out hungrily before them, but there were so many animals and men packed into this mass that their rear ranks were still within an arrow's flight from the Cossack ramparts.

"So what are the *Lahy* doing? Can you see? Are they running yet?"

"If they run we'll have them! And their camp!"

"Running?" Skshetuski shouted and laughed into the Zaporohjans' faces. "You'll see who'll be running! Oh, you'll see! These are the Hetman's men!"

The Cossacks stared at him as if he'd lost his mind and he began to look into the field with rising impatience. Why were Pototzki's horsemen standing still? Their long, steady lines seemed overstretched to his experienced eyes. He couldn't understand why they weren't moving. The green and black pennons hung limp in the rain from the wall of lances. Why weren't they charging down to meet and shatter that mass that rolled so irresistibly towards them? Half the effectiveness of the terrible *husaria* lay in the weight of armored men and horses smashing everything before them in a headlong charge.

The shining mirror of wet grass between the Zaporohjans and the still ranks before the Polish earthwall narrowed with each stride. Behind this galloping mass lay a morass of churned mud, growing wider.

And still they didn't move!

Skshetuski hissed and growled, trembling with impatience. "Now's the time," he muttered. "Will they never start?"

And then the brassy trumpets called out their arrogant command and the wall of lances dropped parallel to the ground beside the horses' ears. "*Husaria!*" Pan Yan shouted. "The *Husaria's* charging!" The long ranks of armored riders leaned forward in their saddles, and the trumpets brayed, and the heavy horses broke into full gallop with a sound like thunder, and it was then as if the earth had really groaned to heaven, unable to bear the weight of that iron wall thrown into sudden motion. Behind these gleaming ranks rode the colorful dragoons with sabers glinting overhead; the Pototzki Cossacks and Valachian Light Horse galloped on the flanks; and the whole battle line burst into instant movement like an arrow drawn far back and held long on the bowstring and suddenly released.

In moments they had covered the bright strip of meadow between the charging Zaporohjans and themselves and the two waves collided. There was a sound like a thousand hammers falling on an anvil, the splintering of a hundred trees, the ringing of ten thousand flails. Three thousand voices gave one terrible short cry as three *kujhenye* vanished underhoof and five hundred horses were hurled to the ground with riders tossed into the air like discarded dolls. There was one vast howl, one roar of shock and terror and one ringing crash.

The Zaporohjan Mirhorodsky Regiment and the two powerful *kujhenye* of Steblovsk vanished as if the hand of an angry God swept them off the Steppe. It seemed to Pan Yan—shouting and delirious among the dumbstruck Cossacks—as if a mythological beast had flown above the field and swallowed those three thousand men at one gulp along with standards, banners, spears and sabers . . . everything! First they were there, galloping and shouting, and then they were gone amid splintering lances. The screams of crushed men and the wild squeals of fallen, trampled horses brought cries of awe and fear among the Zaporohjans who watched from the earthworks.

"*Sohroni Bih!* God save us," they muttered, staring at each other.

But there was yet another terror raging on the battlefield. The speed of the charge sent the air rushing through the feathered frames fixed to the shoulders of the armored riders, and hissed and rattled there and maddened the horses, and drove them forward regardless of obstacles or danger. It also terrified the horses of the Zaporohjans so that they threw themselves back into their own ranks, flaying about with their hooves and throwing off their riders.

In moments the orderly center of the Zaporohjan army was a tumble of panicked animals and of desperate men who knew that to be thrown under those slashing hooves meant immediate death. The splendid *kujhenye* of Irkleyevsk, Kalnibolock, Minsk, Shkurynsk and Titorov shattered like dropped crystal. Whole companies of men and horses fell under the hooves. Other ranks flew apart and crashed into each other, pressed by the sudden rush of the Mirhorod survivors, and then they too broke and fled with hands clasped in the flying manes of horses and terror in their eyes.

And then the red-and-gold dragoons caught up with the hard-working men of the *husaria* and the dreadful harvest went on. The Vasurynski Regiment scattered and fled after a bitter but short-lived stand on the outer edge of the collapsing Zaporohjan center and a panicked mob rushed into the *tabor*.

Hmyelnitzki's battle line shuddered and convulsed like a great serpent struck a mortal blow. It bent back, twisted and pressed into itself under the weight of the armored horsemen who slashed and hammered it into a clotted jumble, and squeezed it and crushed it. Vast crowds of undirected, wild-eyed men on fear-crazed horses milled in disorder, unable to snatch a breath or take a bearing or shake off their terrible confusion or repair their ranks. And in their broken center lay that hard, steel wedge of seemingly inexhaustible men whose metaled arms rose and fell as if each blow were the first they'd struck in the battle, not the hundredth.

"They're devils, not *Lahy!*" Zakhar cried.

"Ah yes? Ah yes? And what did I tell you?"

And Pan Yan hammered on the Zaporohjan rampart with both fists. He was too ill to control himself or to know that there was anything that he should control. He didn't know if what he saw was really happening or if it was some wonderful dream of retribution that would come upon the Zaporohjans on another day. He wept and laughed and shouted commands as if he too were on the battlefield, leading his own winged riders to harvest a victory. Nothing could hold them back, he was sure. He saw and heard nothing except the dreadful spectacle under the Zaporohjan earthworks.

"Forward . . .!"

And then the delirious young man was swaying on top of the parapet with old Zakhar holding him by the coat-tails and pleading and cajoling.

Skshetuski broke free. Rain slashed into his face but he didn't feel it. He didn't hear the quickening rolls of thunder. He had the sudden strength of a berserk madman. Old Zakhar couldn't hold him and called for help but he and his prisoner were alone just then; the battle was rolling close to the Zaporohjan walls and the gunners were running to their cannon. The brass and iron tubes spewed plumes of smoke and fire under a fresh downpour that fell from the sky, and lightning split the clouds with its own cannonade, and the acrid smoke merely helped to thicken the day's sudden darkness.

The rain poured down in the familiar torrents of the night. It silenced the cannon. But the celestial bombardment resumed with even greater force. Broad, jagged belts of lightning bathed the battlefield in intermittent brilliance. The roar of thunder drowned all other sounds.

Out on the battlefield, the iron riders fell upon the Pashkov *kujhen*—the picked men of the Nijh and the Tchertomelik, the heart of the *Sietch*—who fought as fiercely as if the fate of the rebellion rested in their hands. They were the Zaporohjan Hetman's bodyguard; Hmyelnitzki himself rode among their ranks. They hurled themselves in dozens at the armored knights to drag them from their saddles into the mud among the horses' hooves. Struck down, they stabbed the horses' bellies with long knives. Dying, they sunk their teeth into the horses' unprotected legs. Four hundred of them fell in less time than it takes to say the evening prayer. And then a shout of horror welled out of the Zaporohjan ranks as the crimson banner of the Archangel Michael waved wildly and fell.

"It's over!" Pan Yan shouted.

"Over . . ." Zakhar repeated in a stricken voice. Wherever they looked they could see the Zaporohjan gunners running off the walls to hide among the wagons.

But in that moment another sheet of fire flashed across the sky and in its light they saw new riders swarming into the field. Deep, ordered ranks. Scarlet coats that the rain turned black as if in mourning.

"Kshetchovski!"

It was indeed the Pereyaslav colonel leading his Cossacks in a reckless charge. They saw him clearly in the bursts of fire that crisscrossed the sky. Hatless, exposed in the front rank of his charging horsemen, he sat stride a huge cream-colored stallion as if he wished to draw all attention to himself. He rode with a soundless cry on his parted lips and with both arms spread wide as if inviting every Polish saber to seek him out in those nameless thousands. Five thousand disciplined Crown regulars, the pick of the Grand Hetman's Cossack corps, followed him with the drilled precision of a single rider. The scattered, fleeing Zaporohjans recognized him and fell in behind him. Shocked regiments reformed. The crumbling battle line found new strength and its ranks drew tighter. Kshetchovski's corps collided with Balaban's red-and-gold dragoons, checked them and threw them back, and the dwindling battle blazed up anew in the center of the Zaporohjan line.

But it couldn't have gone on much longer anyway. The rain swamped the field. The Steppe became a lake. Wounded men and horses drowned in their hundreds where they lay. The sodden cannon, pistols, firelocks and muskets couldn't fire. Bowstrings grew wet and limp. The water poured into the faces of the fighting men and blinded them and sent their horses sliding into the mud. The crackling thunder and the hiss of rain drowned words of command and the sudden darkness concealed everything.

The silver trumpets of the Hetman and the long brass horns of the Zaporohjans called their exhausted riders back into their camps and old Zakhar led his joyful, laughing prisoner back to the shelter of the wagons.

Chapter Thirteen

THAT NIGHT, as the battered Cossacks streamed back into their camp, the Battle of Yellow Waters seemed won by the Poles. The Zaporohjans reeled, wailing among the wagons, or sat in the stunned silence of defeat in their makeshift shelters of horse-hides and reeds, or wandered about aimlessly under the open sky as if they were no more than shocked, dispirited shadows oblivious of the storm that howled through the night.

Hmyelnitzki burst into the camp among them like another storm cloud. Water streamed from his clothes. He was hatless, coatless. His eyes burned with fever and despair. Rage choked him. The Zaporohjans paid him no attention. Some camp servants put up a small tent of untanned camel hides, and tossed his bedding into it, and there he sat alone and unattended as if he'd already fulfilled his destiny of failure and oblivion.

His thoughts were terrifying. Now he could understand the full extent of what he had started; he pictured for himself the whole vast arena and the entire huge task with all its uncertainties and dangers. Here he was, beaten and repulsed, close to calamity in his first pitched battle! And against such a puny force that he couldn't even call it any kind of army! He knew how great were the Commonwealth's powers of resistance. He had no doubts about the inexhaustible endurance of her soldiers. He'd weighed all that in his calculations but he obviously miscounted.

How did that happen?

How could he, who convinced the cynical Tartar Khan to go to war with the Commonwealth and who assured the doubting *beys* and *murjahs* that he couldn't fail, be so terribly and irrevocably wrong?

And what will happen now?

What will he say when the atamans recover from their shock and start looking for a scapegoat? Oh they'll be along, no doubt about that, for an accounting of their dead and of their own damaged reputations. And what if the Zaporohjans repudiate him now? What if they come howling for his head the way they came for Tatartchuk and young Barabas? He could expect no help from the Tartars either; Tuhay-bey would be the first to throw him to the wolves.

And so he gnawed his lips and clawed at his mustache and grasped his head with both hands wanting to smash it against the nearest cannon.

And this, he thought, is only the beginning!

What will happen when he comes up against the battlewise, experienced Hetmans of the Crown with their armored thousands? What of the Commonwealth herself with all her warlike gentry flocking to the colors in hundreds of thousands and the riches she could devote to war? What of Vishnovyetzki and the other magnates with their private armies? They won't sleep forever! They'll open their eyes fast enough once the rebellion scorches their own borders. And then those armies—each one many times larger than the small force that battered him today—will come down on him like the wrath of God!

★ ★ ★

He sat with his head clasped in his hands, his eyes tightly closed, when the skins that screened the tent entrance were ripped aside and Tuhay-bey stumbled in. The Tartar's face was pale and contorted. His lips were quivering with rage. His *tchambuls* had been battered by Pototzki's Cossacks even worse than the center of Hmyelnitzki's line. Two horses were killed under him alone!

"Where's my loot?" he howled, half-mad and hoarse with fury. "Where's my *yassyr*? My captives? Where's Pototzki's head that you promised me?"

"There!" Hmyelnitzki leaped to his feet and pointed to the battlefield and the Poles' camp beyond it.

"Then go there!" The Tartar's mouth was flecked with foam. "Or I'll drag you by the neck all the way to Asia!"

"I'll go! I'll go today! And I'll take all the booty and the prisoners while you're down on your knees before the Khan explaining why you didn't want to fight!"

"Dog!" roared the Tartar. "Unclean animal! You're destroying the Army of the Khan!"

And so they faced each other with their heads thrust forward, teeth bared and snarling like mad dogs, and for a long moment history stood still, waiting at a crossroads, and the fate of the rebellion hung in desperate danger.

But fury passed. Rage dwindled. Hmyelnitzki was the first to come to his senses.

"Calm down, Tuhay-bey. The storm forced us to call off the battle just when Kshetchovski broke through the dragoons."

"And who kept the field?"

"Listen, I know the Poles, they'll fight with less heart tomorrow. The rain will do its work and the Steppe will turn into a swamp. The *husaria* won't be able to move, you'll see. We'll have them all tomorrow."

"I hear you," the Tartar hissed coldly but his fury ebbed. He stared about, looking for a pile of skins and furs to sit on, and Hmyelnitzki pointed to his own bedding.

"You heard me," he said calmly.

"And I'll remember!"

"Do so. I won't disappoint you. It'll all be as I said, believe me. They'll all be ours tomorrow."

Tuhay-bey threw himself down on Hmyelnitzki's furs and the Zaporohjan Hetman put on his warmest smile and spread his arms in his sunniest gesture. "Tuhay-bey," he chided, "my dear friend. The Great Khan sent you here to be my strong right arm! My brother and a terror to the Poles! Not to be my torment."

"You promised victories, not defeats!"

"Our first fight was a victory, wasn't it? Remember those Germans?"

"And how many of them can I sell?"

"Kshetchovski took a few dragoons today," Hmyelnitzki shrugged, conceding. "They're yours if you want them."

"What's the good of a handful like that? But alright, give them to me anyway, I'll have them impaled!"

"No," Hmyelnitzki murmured. "Don't do that. Free them. Let them go back to Pototzki."

"What for?"

"They're our own people," Hmyelnitzki said softly. "Ruthenians from the Ukraine. Send them back unharmed to pull the rest of Balaban's dragoons over to our side. It'll be like with Kshetchovski . . . do you understand?"

The Tartar was still muttering into his thin beard but now a grimace of grudging admiration passed across his face. He threw the Zaporohjan Hetman a quick, curious glance and looked at him with something like respect.

"Serpent . . ."

Hmyelnitzki shrugged. He smiled.

"Cunning is wisdom, isn't it? You've got to have that along with the courage. If we get the dragoons to come over to us at just the right moment not one man will get out of that *Lah* anthill alive! You follow my thinking?"

The Tartar nodded. His slitted eyes narrowed even further. "I want Pototzki. He's worth a fortune."

"So's Tcharnyetzki. You can have them both."

"Alright then." The Tartar licked his lips, mollified, then shivered in the damp chill. "Now get me some liquor. I'm cold."

"We're agreed then? I mean about tomorrow?"

Tuhay-bey nodded once more and reached for Hmyelnitzki's canteen of raw spirits and the Zaporohjan leader dropped down beside him on the pile of furs. The Tartar looked satisfied and content enough for the moment. He filled his mouth with sunflower seeds and chewed them and drank long and deep until an oily sweat broke out on his forehead. He'd be asleep soon, Hmyelnitzki knew. He kept his own eyes hidden from his frightening ally.

Thinking, he chewed the bitter seeds of his humiliation. He counted up all the cajolings, conciliations, pleadings and retreats that made up his days since the rebellion started. His pride boiled in him but he forced it down. He'd come too close to losing control of himself tonight. And what of the future, when he no longer needed Tuhay-bey's *tchambuls* but would have to keep him satisfied because, if he offended him, he'd turn the Khan against him and bring a quarter of a million Tartars on his Zaporohjans? Was he to take second place forever among his own people?

He held the quart tin to his lips until it was empty then reached for another. Outside, his men were drowning in the rain, and cold winds racked their exhausted bodies; they could be put to death if they touched liquor on the eve of battle. But no one questioned a Zaporohjan Hetman, any more than some Tartar shaman would ever challenge Tuhay-bey for breaking Allah's law against drinking spirits. He drank until the downpour seemed to be roaring in his skull. Tuhay-bey awoke, grunting, and he tossed him a fresh canteen and watched the Tartar guzzle the *gojhalka*. He knew that he'd be able to keep the savage *murjah* satisfied once his armies spread through the Ukraine. A hundred castles would turn into ruin, a thousand towns would burn and half a million people would walk the long trail to the Black Sea galleys, but Tuhay-bey would be his dog, his faithful wolfhound, to snarl at his bidding. Let him depopulate the country! Let him fill Asia Minor with the *yassyr* he'd take in the Ukraine just as long as the Tartars kept faith with Hmyelnitzki once he no longer needed them as allies.

★ ★ ★

They were still drinking, silent and withdrawn into their own thoughts, when Kshetchovski entered. The Pereyaslav colonel's swarthy face seemed as dark and stormy as the night outside but Hmyelnitzki greeted him with a glowing smile.

'*What he is seeing in his head must be even more terrible than what I see in mine,*' he thought with grim amusement. The turncoat colonel looked sick with doubt, fear and disappointment. All the distinctions, titles, rank, power and position he craved for so long would seem as insubstantial as a dream after the day's battle, and tomorrow might come a terrible awakening. The castles, riches and horsetail standards of his fantasies would all disappear, and the grim shadows of a gibbet and a hangman's noose would rise from that fog of doubt and second thoughts. Hmyelnitzki knew that if a thousand slaughtered Germans weren't piled like an accusing barrier between Kshetchovski and a new betrayal he'd be thinking right now about changing sides again.

But he let none of this awareness creep out on his face. He hid his suspicions along with his contempt and made his bright smile as open and sincere as if he was awash with trust and affection. His eyes seemed to shine with gratitude and friendship as he made room for the somber colonel on his muddied bedding.

"You're the day's hero," he said in a voice that quivered with emotion. "Drink, my dear friend. I'm really grateful to you."

Kshetchovski muttered something in his beard. He seized the flask and gulped it down as if he wanted to drown himself in the harsh, coarse liquor.

And so they sat, drinking and saying little and listening to the storm. Hmyelnitzki fell into another of his drunken rages sometime between midnight and first light, and rushed his regiments on foot across the churned meadow in an all-out assault on the Polish earthworks. But Kshetchovski seemed unable to get drunk no matter how many panikins of liquor he drained and tossed aside. Still sober, he pulled Hmyelnitzki off his horse, pushed him back into the tent and called off the attack.

Dawn came eventually. The new day, a Sunday, passed quietly in the Cossack camp. The violent storm abated but the rain went on falling hour after hour, turning the scarred and pitted battlefield into a sea of mud, and forming an impenetrable curtain that kept the enemy camps and armies hidden from each other. Hmyelnitzki slept. The Zaporohjans rested. But Tuhaybey sent the captured Balaban dragoons back to the castellan's encampment, and with them went certain letters for their Ruthenian troop leaders and sergeants, and for the *esauls* of Pototzki's Cossacks.

★　★　★

On Monday morning the battle flamed anew under a dull, red sun that glowed uncertainly through the twilight darkness. Skshetuski watched the battle as before from the Zaporohjan walls. His wounds had broken open. His fever burned in him with new intensity. Reality and imagination had become confused and he was less sure of what he was seeing. But he felt no doubt about the outcome of the day.

Today he'd be free and the Zaporohjans beaten. The iron horsemen showed what they could do; now they would finish what they had begun. Then, with the clouds dispersed and the storm blown back into the Steppe, he'd be able to think about his own happiness. It was all turning out as he thought it would: the Cossack avalanche was splintering on the first lances of the Commonwealth that charged into it. And so few lances at that! Such a little fragment of the might that lay behind it, unsummoned and untouched . . .! He trembled with pride and wept with open joy, too weak either to hide or hold back the tears. He felt as if all the vast resources of his country were coming to his aid and flooding his system with their own endless strength and irresistible power, and with this new awareness of who and what he was came pity for the Zaporohjans.

Guilty? Oh yes, they were guilty.

But they were also blinded and misled and all the more to be pitied because they'll be suffering such dreadful punishment so soon. They were like erring children, he thought with compassion, who let themselves be tossed into a firestorm by one ambitious man.

He was too ill to do more than lean against the shoulder of the kindly Zakhar on the Cossack wall. He smiled and whispered to himself but he was too weak for shouts, laughter or imagining that he was leading a *husaria* charge. Nor could he put up much of a struggle against the old Cossack's restraining hands.

★   ★   ★

He watched the start of the battle with calm, untroubled eyes and an expectant smile on his face, and saw the Crown regiments come out of their earthworks like they did on Saturday, and the dark mass of Tartars and Cossacks poured out against them as before. But this time no wall of steel met their charge with one of its own. The Steppe had turned into a morass. The heavy cavalry struggled in the mud like prehistoric beasts. Their horses sunk up to their bellies in the sodden plain across which the Tartar ponies seemed to skim like swallows.

And so the hopeful smile began to drift off Skshetuski's face. He started darting quick uneasy glances at the streaming sky and at the rolling waves of Zaporohjans who flung themselves against the narrow ribbon of Pototzki's soldiers. He peered in premonition at the growing mounds of dead men and horses under the walls of the little fort. The castellan's regiments fought with an icy fury, defending themselves behind a rampart of their fallen comrades with the same ferocity, but it seemed as if they'd lost their fire. No joy of battle carried them in headlong charges at ten times their numbers. They trampled no regiments before them as on the first day; they didn't break and scatter those powerful *kujhenye*, and drive them like cattle as they did before.

Feeling the first cold touch of anxiety among the singing, cheering Zaporohjans on the Cossack earthwall, Skshetuski watched the iron horsemen backed up against the palisade of the

Polish camp as if they weren't the same men who swept everything before them just two days ago. They fought and died in a
grim, sullen silence, as dangerous as boars beset by packs of
hungry hunting dogs, but with no sign of spirit. He listened in
vain for the rhythmic roar of their battle cries, the arrogant
trumpets and the maddening rattle of the wind in their eagle
feathers. They fought, he thought, as if aware of an inevitable
doom: joyless and embittered and driven only by discipline and
contempt for death.

Hours passed like that.

The rain turned into a lethargic drizzle that stopped by midmorning.

The shrinking lines of *husaria* in their silvered breastplates,
the blue and yellow coats of Pototzki's Cossacks, the red and
gold of Balaban's dragoons and the myriad rainbow hues of the
light cavalry dressed in the borrowed finery of Valachian nobles,
remained unbroken in front of the Polish fort. But the herd of
riderless horses that milled behind them grew thicker by the
minute, and the ground around them began to change color, as
the carpet of spilled and broken forms in brilliant uniforms
spread deeper and wider.

Skshetuski grew somber and depressed. He still refused to
doubt the final outcome; his feverish mind rebelled against such
thinking. But he began to bite his lips and twist his hands in
anxiety as he waited for the tide to turn once more in favor of
the castellan.

The sun crept out of its thin covering of clouds and moved
towards midday and then a fresh breeze blew across the meadow
and carried off the gunsmoke and the mists. It brought the
harsh battle cries and the clash of iron to the Zaporohjan earthworks but they were all either the joyful yells of Cossacks or the
shrill, triumphant warbling of the Tartars.

Hmyelnitzki brought fresh regiments from behind the earthworks with each passing hour and threw them into the attack
one after another. He led each *kujhen* in person, riding beside
the front rank of his cheering men until they were within a
spear's length of the castellan's formation, and then he pointed
with his saber to where he wanted each regiment to strike and
swerved aside as the crash of the colliding horses and the clang
of steel drowned his commanding voice.

He seemed to be everywhere at once as if he were magic and

able to multiply himself at will. His jeweled cap and crimson cloak flew like a battle flag along the whole length of the Zaporohjan crescent. Stray beams of sunlight gleamed like fire off his gold *bulava* and the Zaporohjans stared at him with wonder as if he were a God with lightning in his eyes and a voice of thunder.

Watching him from the wall as he reined his white Arabian stallion before some waiting *kujhen*, Skshetuski saw a thousand brightly colored caps flung into the air and heard the roar of a thousand voices, delirious with joy, echoing his irresistible enthusiasm.

"*Na Lahy!*" he shouted.

"*Na Pohybel!*" they roared in reply as if set on fire.

And then his saber whirled above his head like a flash of lightning, and the white stallion turned and stretched in full gallop like a milky arrow, and the wild horsemen charged behind him across the glistening field so that they seemed like the pent-up waters of a frozen lake suddenly set free by the heat of a new Spring sun.

They rode as if each moment that separated them from their bloody handiwork would earn them a hundred years of suffering in Hell, and as if eternal bliss would reward the first man who reached that struggling mass on the parapet of corpses.

They died in hundreds under the sabers of the iron soldiers who answered their fierce battle cries with grim, unsmiling silence. The steel arms rose and fell with the cold precision of men who fight only to take as many enemies with them as they can. But the exultant Zaporohjans came on as if to salvation. They raced each other to the flaming muskets, the whirling battle hammers and the stabbing lances. They climbed across the piled bodies of their dead and dying and fell in their own turn. Falling, they still shouted their triumphant cries and stabbed the air around them. Cut down, impaled on the spears, thrown back and crushed between the armored riders and the mob behind them, they fell back, regrouped and charged again without any orders. Dying, they'd catch a last glimpse of the creamy stallion and the glittering red rider with the silver sword who thundered across the field with new regiments behind him.

The Zaporohjans around Skshetuski cried and shouted in their own delirium and hacked the stockade madly with their sabers and stabbed the earthen ramparts with their knives.

"Hmyel! Hmyel!" they cried. "*Div*! A wonder!"

"*Div! Div*! It's a miracle! He has magic in him!"

"The *Lahy* are breaking!"

"Death to them! *Na Pohybel*!"

Enthusiasm flamed along the field wherever that crimson cloak and white stallion appeared and the Cossacks hurled themselves across the heaps of carcasses and corpses as joyfully as if his sword pointed the way to Paradise.

★ ★ ★

Midday came and went. The struggle continued. A terrible chill began to spread through Skshetuski's body as he watched. His own hopes were sinking in the mud under the growing mounds of the castellan's dead soldiers.

"No," he said, unaware that he spoke aloud. "This can't be happening. It's . . . impossible."

He strained to hear the trumpets of the Hetmans in the distant Steppe and searched the horizon for the forest of lances that should have been there. But all he saw was the savage slaughter that went on with ever growing fury. Still thinking that all this had to be a nightmare, part of the fevered chaos in his mind, he watched the castellan's long line start to bend and twist like a wrestler who is using the last of his strength to tear himself loose from a stranglehold. The light cavalry on the wings began to give ground. It was such an imperceptible shifting of position that only an experienced eye could spot what was happening when the horses leaped and staggered back under the shock of yet another charge. But when their riders turned them once more towards the enemy, they were no longer in the same place as before.

The armored center was still holding firm. The grim winged riders continued to stand, unmoved, behind the glittering wall of their swords and maces, but the far ends of the Polish line grew thin and began to waver. Men dressed in the bright regimental colors of the Commonwealth fell back in greater numbers and the rainbow caps of the Zaporohjans began to bloom among the dragoons and Pototzki's Cossacks.

"This just can't be," Skshetuski muttered anxiously to himself and waited for fresh Polish regiments to appear from behind the earthworks.

He told himself that the castellan had to be waiting for

Hmyelnitzki to use up the last of his reserves before throwing his own into a charge that would decide the battle. Or that the Hetmans, sure to appear at any moment now, were merely holding back until the Zaporohjans spent their strength. But there were no trumpets summoning these new armored thousands out of the misty Steppe. No sign of wings and lances in the open intervals set between the bastions, and no fresh troops rode out of the entrenchment.

The Polish line was shuddering along its whole length so that it brought to mind a ship that had run aground; and now, pounded too long by the breakers, it started to come apart. Long gaps began to show among the castellan's battered companies and the dark flood of Tartars and cheering Zaporohjans poured into them at once.

The Zaporohjan gunners on the Cossack earthwall seemed to go mad with joy.

"*Slava Bohu!* God be praised! A miracle! *Div! Div!*"

"They're done! They're going!"

"No, not yet! Not yet!"

"Any minute now!"

"Long life to Hmyel! Death to the *Lahy!*"

★   ★   ★

The rain died down as the sun climbed gently into a clear blue sky which spread above the drying Steppe like a brilliant lid. The straggling mists dissolved with the afternoon. Seen in that calm, white light, the battlefield became a glistening board of greens and browns set in a burnished frame of ponds and small lakes and swift, swollen streams that ran into the river where the sunlit sand and pale golden clay made the waters yellow. Beyond it lay the Steppe: empty and seemingly without end or sound or movement above the billowing waves of bright Spring grasses that flowed with the wind.

Skshetuski strained his aching eyes across this shining space but he saw no distant spearpoints to trap and reflect the light. No standards waved above the horizons. No drums were beating there and no trumpets brayed to announce the Hetmans. Only a vast black cloud of ravens, crows and vultures wheeled in their endless spirals above that peaceful silence, filling the air with their raucous cries.

And now, as Skshetuski watched, the outspread wings of the

castellan's small army curled back and folded on themselves, and a thick horde of Tartars swept around the earthworks so that no one would be able to escape. The battle had been fought with such remorseless fury that the plain before the Polish camp was heaped with barricades of dead men and horses and each of these successive ramparts rose higher than the one before. The final one was piling up so close to the earth-fort that the infantry on the wall began to add their rattling volleys to the battle sounds.

And still the terrible struggle went on, hour after hour. The sun marched steadily into the afternoon but its warm rays did nothing to relieve Skshetuski's icy chill. All of the mounted Cossack regiments were now in the field. The Zaporohjan camp and *tabor* were as empty as if they'd been abandoned. Whoever wasn't locked in that deadly struggle under the Polish wall stood on the Cossack ramparts; and now, unable to resist their own terrible excitement, even the watching gunners started to jump off the wall to run to the battle. He watched the staggering crowds of hacked, bloody and mutilated warriors who flowed back into the Cossack camp and fell among the wagons, but they came singing and with shouts of victory. They were drunk with glory and on fire with the joy of battle, and even as they lay choking in their own blood they whispered "*Na Pohybel Lahom* . . . Death to them . . . Long live Hmyel!"

Skshetuski had nothing more to say. His fevered eyes were dry; he'd spent all his tears. His face was as grey as if he was dying and he couldn't stand upright without Zakhar's help. Shamed, disappointed and frozen with despair, he stared at the battlefield with dulled and empty eyes, hardly able to comprehend the sight of the castellan's regiments retreating from the field. They were still fighting, still moving in good order, but they were falling back with a desperate hurry that even an inexperienced eye could read as defeat.

He heard the voices of twenty thousand Zaporohjan warriors soar into the sky in one exultant roar as the last of the castellan's rear guard vanished in the earthworks. Their infantry came up on the run and twelve cavalry *kujhenye* leaped out of their saddles to join them and the Tartars in a hand assault. Every gun in the Zaporohjan arsenal was firing into the smoking ruin of the Polish fort, and every trumpet, bugle, horn, fife and kettledrum in Hmyelnitzki's army broke out in such a cry of triumph that they drowned out the shouts and musketry and the soft, dry popping of the Polish field guns.

Skshetuski watched as the deep, dense ranks of the incomparable Zaporohjan infantry ran for the walls of the Polish camp and tightened their ring around it. Long tongues of powdery white smoke drifted towards them from the battered earthworks like the last icy breath of a dying giant. Cannon balls gouged broad furrows in their running mass, the Polish musket fire became as feverish as the coughing of a stricken man, and the crash and clatter of exploding shells became one uninterrupted roar. The thick human coils around the fort jerked and twisted like a wounded serpent but pressed ever tighter.

He listened to the Zaporohjans' rhythmic shouts and the deep, measured thudding of their boots as they crossed the field between the silent ramparts of the dead and the Polish earthwall. He saw them fill the last open ground under the battered mound where they boiled darkly like a seething cauldron and then the Zaporohjan cannon ceased to roar and bellow.

'Now they're safe,' he thought. *'Now the castellan's guns can't be depressed enough to do them any harm. Now they'll climb the wall . . .'*

He closed his eyes. His parched lips whispered prayers that he couldn't hear. His trembling hands flew about like birds and an icy tremor seized his entire body. His mind seemed paralyzed except for one question: What would he see on the Polish wall when his eyes sprung open? Would the familiar banners still be there?

He heard a new sound. It was as if a sudden cry of rage, fear, triumph and despair intruded on his willful blindness from behind the castellan's defenses.

"What is it?" he whispered to himself. "What has happened? Where?"

He forced his eyes to open and looked across the field.

"God in Heaven!" he cried out in despair.

The golden banner of the Crown and the familiar standards of the Commonwealth's regiments and commanders were gone from the earthwall. In their place waved the mulberry-colored banner of the Archangel Michael.

Chapter Fourteen

SKSHETUSKI DIDN'T HEAR how the castellan's camp was taken
until everything was over. He couldn't understand how it could
have fallen in the first assault until Zakhar told him what
Hmyelnitzki's cunning achieved the day before.

"Treason again, you say?"

"If that's what you call it."

"And it was Balaban's dragoons?"

"That's right, lad. Them and Pan Pototzki's Cossacks. They
hit the *Lahy* from inside the camp soon as our people started up
the walls."

But even with Kshetchovski's example fresh in memory Pan
Yan couldn't grasp how that could have happened. "I mean how
could it? These were regulars! And Pan Tcharnyetzki was there
to keep an eye on them!"

Zakhar shrugged and wagged his head in wonder.

"They say Hmyel turned them. Hey, that Hmyel, what a head
he's got! The *Lahy* went down like wheat stalks when the
dragoons took 'em from the rear. Whoever wasn't cut down
went into the ropes."

"No one escaped?"

"Some tried but the Tartars caught them. Hmyel didn't want
the word to get to the Hetmans."

"The Castellan?"

"Shot."

"Pan Tcharnyetzki . . .?

"Taken."

The young soldier sat as still as if he'd turned to stone. He
stared at Zakhar with unseeing eyes and it wasn't just because he

207

was still a prisoner. His shock and grief were for the Commonwealth; it was her new humiliation that filled him with shame.
Never before had Cossacks beaten Polish regulars in the field.
News of their victory would arm every peasant and each disgruntled soul in the entire country; no longer held to heel by
fear of retribution, the sullen mobs would turn at once into
bands of murderers and looters.

Now, he knew, nothing could save the Ukraine. Tales of this
Cossack triumph would fly with the wind and the dark, dour
peasant masses would rise up throughout the Eastern Lands.
Towns and villages and the gentry's manors would go up in
flames and the country would begin to drown in its own best
blood. In time, of course, the Commonwealth would overcome
them all; the Hetmans and the Prince would crush the rebellion.
But how many thousands would be butchered in the meantime?
How many years would it take for these wounds to heal? And
how many more defeats would there be before it all ended?
What other disasters? The cornerstone of his faith in the Commonwealth's invincibility was shaken loose, the edifice above it
seemed to tremble as if the earth was shaking under it, and a
dark web of cracks spread out across its surface.

And was it really possible for just one bitter man to do all that
so swiftly? Where, then, was this great inner strength and those
inexhaustible spiritual resources that guided and sustained
Skshetuski's nation for so many centuries?

No other power had been able to destroy it or to undermine
its long, triumphant tradition; the hordes of Asia . . . the Teutonic Knights . . . the Mongols, Tartars, Turks, Huns, Vandals,
Scythians, Avars and Hungarians—and all the other self-styled
Scourges of the Lord—came to these lands time and time again
with fire in their eyes and left the fields and forests littered with
their bones.

How was it, then? Could one Cossack rebel and one Tartar
murjah undo the work of centuries? It just didn't seem possible
to the stricken soldier that a mere uprising of disgruntled peasants could decide the life or death of such a mighty nation. But
neither did he ever think that he'd live to see the red Archangel
banner of the Zaporohjans waving above a camp of the Hetman's soldiers.

★   ★   ★

At nightfall, Skshetuski watched the prisoners driven into the Zaporohjan camp. Bedraggled, stripped and bloody, they staggered with cast-down eyes, dragged on Tartar ropes and hurried along with rawhide whips like cattle.

He watched the death of the young castellan. Shot with an arrow through the throat, he lived only a few hours in the Cossack camp. ("*Tell my father,*" the youth whispered as his eyes filmed over, "*tell him . . . I died . . . like a knight.*") Skshetuski knew that he'd remember that childlike face and those lifeless eyes as long as he lived.

He also knew that he'd remember the hard, granite face of Stefan Tcharnyetzki in whose arms young Pototzki died. Not one tear showed in those cold, grey eyes. Not a single flicker of emotion passed across the scarred and pitted features of that famous leader of armored cavalry even as he dipped his hand in his young friend's blood and vowed to wash away all the pain and ugliness of that death, and the humiliation of the Cossack triumph, in a sea of Tartar and Zaporohjan tears.

As for himself, he said, he had no tears to shed. His voice was harsh, unbending and beyond the possibility of defeat as he advised Skshetuski to rise above his grief, keep alive his hope and disdain despair.

"You think that everything is lost?" he demanded. "You feel shamed and helpless? You can't believe that this great human structure which sustains you and dresses you in pride can fail to overwhelm any enemy at will? You must be truly small in spirit to have so little faith! Listen, the Commonwealth has known many disasters. It's been struck such blows that no other nation could survive even a fraction of them. But where are those who struck them? Who remembers them? Even the wild winds no longer blow their ashes through the Steppe. But the Commonwealth endures! It's still here!"

Skshetuski bowed his head and the iron warrior went on in a softening voice.

"We aren't perfect. We sin and we are punished for our sins and that's as it should be. Before your time is up, young man, you'll see all the greed and empty pride and love of luxury that live among us side by side with all those qualities that made our nation walk in glory as bright as the sun through more than six centuries! And it's up to us who love this Commonwealth to add what we can. If each of us gives all his courage, all his faith, and all his capacities for endurance, and if he sacrifices every comfort and every private craving, taking nothing for himself but giving everything he can, then the balance between good and evil will be kept. The soul of our nation won't sicken and grow weak. To sink into despair because *your* pride's been shamed, and because *you* feel humiliated by some passing triumph of a mob, is just as bad as treason! Faith in God's justice and in the ultimate triumph of our People's spirit would serve your country better."

The young lieutenant listened and watched the gaunt, dark face, and counted the old wounds that crisscrossed those grim features with a latticework of scars, and read the message of the steel-grey eyes, and it seemed to him as if it wasn't a defeated captive who was speaking to him but a victorious Hetman at whose back streamed all the horsetail standards of a thousand years.

"Defeat," Tcharnyetzki said. "Yes, we've been defeated. But who are we, lad? Am I this dead boy's father? Was this the whole Army of the Crown? After Kshetchovski's treason we brought a mere eighteen-hundred men to this field. My God, boy, the Hetmans send more than that each day just to get hay for the army's horses! Their power is barely scratched! And your Prince Yeremi, does *he* count for nothing? True, this defeat will fuel the rebellion. The Ukraine will wallow in blood and so perhaps will all our eastern countries. But in the end the Hetmans and the Prince will grind Hmyelnitzki into dust. And the higher he rises in the meantime the longer we'll have peace after he is crushed."

Old Zakhar also tried to comfort the young man in his own simple way.

"Ey, lad, don't you carry on so bad. God gives what He wills. It's not young Pototzki who's waiting for us in the Ukraine. The work's only started and only God can tell how it'll all end. Hmyel will set you free 'cause he owes it to you an' you'll go back to your own kind no matter what happens. But I'll still be here, an old man alone in an empty wagon. The Steppe's no mother for old men. The world's a cold place for a man without a son to warm it. Hey, so we took some *Lah* loot here at Yellow Waters, but to take is one thing, to keep is another. And it won't go so easy for us with both the *Hetmany*, you can bet on that. And your Yarema, that's another hard one. If they ever get together against us . . . ey, it'll be hard."

★   ★   ★

And it seemed during the days that followed as if
Hmyelnitzki himself was haunted by this thought. The vision
of Prince Yeremi leading the combined armies of the Hetmans
as well as his own sent the Zaporohjan leader into fits of panic.
Facing such armies under such a leader was quite beyond his
means and so he drove his men day and night to reach the
Ukraine before the news of Yellow Waters could alert the Hetmans, and before Prince Yeremi could come from his own
country far across the Dnieper.

They moved at such speed that it began to seem as if neither
the Zaporohjan Hetman nor any of his men remembered what
it meant to sleep. They fed themselves and their horses on the
march out of the same grain bags and sharing water from the
same canteens. The Cossack flood poured across the Steppe at
such a frantic pace that it looked more like a desperate flight
towards some unknown refuge than the triumphant march of a
victorious army. It swept past ancient burial mounds and woods
and herds of startled antelope, wild mustangs and cattle,
watched at night by the unblinking green eyes of the wolves,
and swelling as it rolled. It stopped for nothing, pushed beyond
exhaustion or any thought of rest. It littered the Steppe around
river crossings with mired horses and overturned wagons. But
at each ford armed bands of peasants rose out of the reeds,
coming as often as not with the severed heads of their former
masters rotting on their pikes, and added their own numbers to
those of the army.

The news they brought from the Ukraine was little more than
rumor. It varied each day. Some said that Prince Yeremi was still
in his own country. Others told terrifying tales about the great
army he brought to the Hetmans. But all said that the Ukraine
was already in flames. The peasants not only fled in thousands
to join Hmyelnitzki but burned their villages, murdered all Jews
and gentry they caught anywhere, and armed themselves with
whatever came to hand. The Cossacks serving in the troops of
all the township and local officials were coming over everywhere to the side of the mobs.

This was what Hmyelnitzki had been counting on and he
drove his army all the harder.

★   ★   ★

And then, at last, the Ukraine lay before him.

Tchehryn threw its gates open to him, the Cossack garrison coming over to a man. And then as bells tolled joyfully as if to welcome a new age, and howls of triumph drowned the roar of guns fired in celebration, Hmyelnitzki took time to pause and draw a breath. He watched, content, as endless processions wound through the streets and in and out of churches while nights turned scarlet with the flames of pillage. He could taste his vengeance as the mobs tore down Tchaplinski's house brick by brick and razed it to the ground. He could sit back and count his successes while the maddened peasants searched the ruins for any Jews and gentry and dragged their victims to the market place for a public butchering.

The news that came to him was better than anything he dreamed of. Prince Yeremi was still beyond the Dnieper; his own vast country was seething with rebellion. He offered his services to the Crown commanders even before the war drum sounded in the *Sietch* but Pan Mikolai Pototzki declined this powerful reinforcement; acceptance would have placed the Prince among those who'd share in the expected victory. And so even as his young son rode off to Yellow Waters, the Grand Hetman wrote the Prince that this was no war for a warrior of Vishnovyetzki's stature. This was just another Cossack outburst; rawhide would be enough to lash the peasants back into the byres. '*Steel*,' wrote the proud Pototzki, '*is for nobler use.*'

And in the meantime the country around Tchehryn was a sea of flames. Whoever lived outside manor walls grasped an axe or scythe or pike or butcher knife and ran to join the Cossacks. Vast crowds flowed into the camp each day: impatient peasants sure that their time of freedom, loot and vengeance was at hand; the wild Steppe *tchabany* and the fierce forest dwellers dressed in animal skins, along with bandits and marauders and mutinied Cossack companies from throughout the country. And after them came the nameless hordes from beyond the Wild Lands who were drawn out of their distant lairs by the smoke of pillage. They came in thousands, then in tens of thousands. And with them rode all the Zaporohjans who hadn't managed to reach the *Sietch* before the war drum sounded.

Hmyelnitzki seized them like a windstorm and swept them north towards the two Crown Hetmans. He rode an ocean of rebellion, a scarlet tide of fire and blood, and he came on like an avalanche that crushed and consumed everything in its path. The country emptied with his passing; it turned into a landscape of ruins and corpses; and to all those terrified thousands who fled for their lives before him, he seemed less like a man than one of those legendary dragons whose footsteps pressed blood out of the soil and turned the rivers crimson.

The Hetmans fell back before him, suddenly aware of who he was and what he represented, and he pursued them like a forest fire. All his dissembling was now finished. He didn't have much time before all his enemies started to mass against him. He halted in Tcherkassy long enough to rest his weary horses, and sent Tuhay-bey and the fierce Krivoinos ahead to harass and slow down the retreating Hetmans. But they smelled loot and threw themselves on the Hetmans' wagons with their corps of fifty thousand Tartars, Zaporohjans and Cossack deserters without waiting for the rest of Hmyelnitzki's army, and the Hetmans crushed them. Repulsed and decimated, they scattered in panic and word of their disaster threatened the rebellion.

Hmyelnitzki rose at once with a hundred thousand men and drove his main army north towards Korsun. But the Crown army was no longer there. The Hetmans had begun to feel as if the earth was shaking under them and they hurried towards Boguslav where several thousand gentry gathered for protection. Sure now that the moment of decision was at hand, Hmyelnitzki left his wagons, herds, baggage and prisoners behind him and galloped in pursuit. His vanguard overtook the Hetmans' wagon train at Kruta Balka. The guns roared at once. The Army of the Crown and the rebel masses fell upon each other and Hmyelnitzki was, at last, in battle with the Hetmans.

★ ★ ★

Skshetuski didn't get to see that battle. He sat in the wrecked and looted hall of a Korsun mansion where Zakhar took him for safety from the mobs, and listened to the distant roar of cannon, and tried to read in those shifting sounds what might be happening on the battlefield. He pictured the swarms of Tartars sweeping from the wings and the light cavalry of the Hetmans coming out to meet them. He imagined the massed attack of the

Cossacks and the Zaporohjans spreading across the plain with the peasant mobs driven before them like a living shield.

('*And now,*' he thought, trembling with excitement, '*the husaria* is beginning its charge . . .')

Outside the windows the gutted body of the local noble who owned this house swung like a pendulum from the balcony and the mob was howling for the blood of the *Lah* inside. Zakhar had thrown a strong guard around the house—all the survivors of the Mirhorod *kujhen* shattered at Yellow Waters—but the mob was beyond anyone's control. It battered down every door and shutter behind which a fugitive might have taken refuge.

Thousands of drunken peasants reeled along the streets, covered with blood from head to foot and festooned with the entrails of their victims which they coiled around their bodies or tossed about on their pikes and pitchforks. From time to time a savage roar announced a newfound plaything—a pleading merchant, a howling noble or a shrieking Jew—and then a terrible butchery took place. The victims were skinned alive, boiling pitch was dripped into their eyes, their tongues were ripped out and their heads were tarred and set on fire. Pine stakes were hammered through their bellies. They were disemboweled. The butchers smeared themselves with blood and fought over scraps of flesh to save as mementos. They sawed off women's breasts and strung them around their necks or wore them as ornaments in their hair. They tore Jewish infants apart by the legs as if they were puppets and tossed them about to be speared in flight. Their howling laughter, Pan Yan thought, could have no comparable sound anywhere on earth.

But there were moments when the search of attics, cellars and heaps of rubble failed to yield a fresh sacrifice, and then the mobs stormed the houses where Cossacks and Tartars guarded those prisoners who were held for ransom. The guards beat them back with staves, pike-shafts, horn-bows and rawhide whips, and the Zaporohjans flogged the peasant mob with a special fury. The Cossacks took peasant help when they needed it but their hatred for the Ukrainian *hohols* far surpassed the gentry's contempt and disdain.

Skshetuski watched in silence as the *Mirhorodtsy* plied their savage whips. The rawhide cut as sharply as razors. It split scalps, sheered the flesh off the cheekbones, sliced off ears and noses. Blinded and disfigured, the peasants howled and fell back and begged for mercy and the Zaporohjans flogged them all the harder.

Old Zakhar, watching beside Skshetuski, spat at them with hatred. "Dogs," he muttered. "Listen to them howling. They'll howl a lot louder when the Tartars drive them down the trail to the sea. They don't know it yet, but Hmyel's already given them to Tuhay-bey for *yassyr*. There'll be so many of them on the block in Turkey that a slave will go for six horseshoe nails."

"But aren't they your own people?" Pan Yan asked.

"How can a dog be a brother to a hawk?" Zakhar asked in turn and shouted down to the sweating *Mirhorodtsy*: "Beat them harder! Lay it on thicker! Drive the scum away!"

And finally the mob's frenzy turned upon itself. The churning mob tore itself apart, hacking and trampling everything that stood in its way. It seemed more like a scene from Hell than anything that could happen among human beings, and the sun hurried from the sky as if unable to watch what lay below.

★　★　★

Night came at last but one whole side of the town square was on fire and the flames lit the scene as brightly as if the sun were still hanging overhead. Roofs burned through and fell into the ruins and sent thick showers of sparks into the clouds of smoke. Long tongues of flame licked around the cupola of a burning church. The roar of distant gunfire made the darkness tremble beyond the scarlet canopy that hung over the town and Zakhar cocked his head to listen to the cannonade.

"Hmm. The Hetmans aren't joking," he muttered. "That Pan Pototzki's a hard man. That's a real soldier. Those scurvy dogs down there are having themselves a good time right now. But if Hmyel gets beat there'll be somebody else having fun with them."

And then a new sound flooded through the broken windows— the panicked drumming of many hooves in a headlong gallop on the cobblestones—and a dark mass of horsemen rode into the crowd on wild-eyed animals spattered with mud and foam. The mob recoiled with loud wails of terror, trying to get away from the flaying hooves.

"*Spasaytes*! Have mercy!"

The riders' faces were black with burned gunpowder. Their coats were splashed with blood. Darkening rags were twisted

about their heads. Behind them stretched the road to Boguslav
and the swelling roar of the cannonade.

"People!" a thick, hoarse voice cried out of the galloping mass
which trampled everything before it. "Save yourselves! *Spasaytes*! The *Lahy* are coming!"

The crowd shuddered like an ocean struck by a hurricane.
Wild panic seized those faceless, howling thousands and the
great mass threw itself into headlong flight. But their own
wagons, rubble and the spilled contents of the looted buildings
blocked their way. The crowd fell back, twisted, surged this
way and that. Burning timbers rained down upon their heads
and burst among them in sheets of scarlet flame. Flames beat
them back but they pressed on, regardless, pushing hundreds of
their kind into the fiery barriers. They ran across their own
trampled dead or stood stock still in terror as if already waiting
their turn on the gibbet. They wept and shouted and prayed and
pleaded for mercy and died under the boots of their fleeing
brethren.

Skshetuski watched and listened and suddenly understood the
meaning of the scene. He felt the blood draining from his face in
his terrible excitement. His heart beat so swiftly that it seemed
as if it were about to leap out of his chest. It was all happening as
he'd known it would! As he believed in spite of every horror
that he witnessed since the rebellion started! Oh, he cried out to
himself, how could he have doubted this outcome for a moment?

"I knew it! There was no other way! Those are the Hetmans
there! That is the Commonwealth! And now comes the judgment! Now comes the punishment! Oh, dear God . . .!"

And he fell back into a chair, laughing and weeping in gratitude and joy.

But now the square below him filled with a fresh clatter of
hooves in flight from the battle and a dark mass of Tartars burst
into the mob.

"They run like the wind!" Zakhar cried.

And then another broken regiment crowded through the
streets, and then a second, and a third . . . Then came waves of
horsemen in numbers beyond counting who trampled and
sabered the dense, howling mob while their galloping horses
collided with each other and crashed to the ground. It was a

rout, Skshetuski thought with joy. It could be nothing else. Such panic could mean only an absolute disaster.

"The *Mirhorodtsy* won't hold out," Zakhar muttered grimly and ran out onto the balcony.

* * *

It seemed then to the feverish, overjoyed Skshetuski as if all the sounds and sights before him flowed into each other and turned into one. His eyes filled with smoke and the warped red glow hurled into the clouds by the burning city. He heard the crash of masonry spilling into the streets and saw the sheets of fire engulfing the mob. And locked inside that single unrelenting roar lay all the panicked shouts and the bellowing of cattle, the screams and neighing of the injured horses, the clatter of countless hooves on the cobblestones and the clash of iron.

"Great God," Skshetuski whispered as another panicked mass of horsemen rattled through the square. "Great merciful God. What a disaster it must be out there . . ."

The thunder of the distant cannon swelled to its own uninterrupted roar in the night; and then the voice of another rider who seemed mad with terror drifted across the square: "Run for it! Save yourselves! Hmyel's been killed! Kshetchovski's killed! Tuhay-bey is dead!"

That was the final stroke. Judgment Day came to the burning town and the mobs trapped among the flames. Beaten, sabered, trampled and robbed of all hope, the terrified crowd hurled itself headlong into the fires and began to burn.

Skshetuski knew that he must soon come to the end of his strength. He was exhausted and drained of all feeling. He could no longer react to anything around him. He knelt to offer his thanks to God, and to seek refuge from horror in prayer, but old Zakhar interrupted him, as hesitant and humble as if he was the young lieutenant's servant.

"Come out on the balcony, young master," he begged, his voice resigned and heavy. "Speak to the boys a little. Promise them mercy or they'll break and run. Those people down there . . . the *tchernya* . . . they've gone mad with fear. Nothing will stop them from breaking in here if our men run off. Then it'll be the end of you and me as well."

The young man rose and walked out onto the balcony, look-

ing down at the routed Cossacks, Tartars, *tchernya* and *tchabany*
running and galloping past in what seemed like thousands.
They were, he knew, only a fraction of Hmyelnitzki's army; his
main forces must be still resisting, to judge by the quickening
thunder of the cannonade. But there was no way for an experienced soldier to question the end result.

The Mirhorod men were milling about under the balcony in
fearful disorder, wondering if they too should try to save themselves in flight, and Skshetuski promised them their lives and
the Hetmans' mercy since they had served him so well with
their whips. The proud, fiercely independent Cossacks bent
their backs before him, and humble voices called out in that
plaintive, sing-song tone that always signified the hopelessness
of defeat and the numb resignation of serfs before their master.

"*Pomyluyte, pan'eh* . . .! Have mercy, your worship!"

"Nothing will happen to you," he told them again.

And, indeed, he was sure that he could save them from
impalement, which was the death that any rebel could expect in
that cruel era. He knew the Grand Hetman. He'd carried letters
to him from Prince Yeremi in the past and Pan Pototzki, the
proud Lord of Potok, had formed a liking for him. The war, the
young man thought, was over. The Zaporohjans were bowing
to the ground. They bared their heads so swiftly that it seemed
as if a sudden wind whipped off their caps and carried them
away and the young lieutenant looked with the pride of a victor
at their lowered heads and at the emptying square beyond them.
The storm was stopped and scattered on the nation's threshold.
Stefan Tcharnyetzki was right, Skshetuski murmured to himself in gratitude and wonder; the spirit of their Commonwealth
carried unlimited resources. It was invincible. It could never
fail.

He felt pride filling up his body like a resurrecting flame but it
was not the low, unworthy pride of anticipated vengeance that
comes from the humiliation of an enemy. It was a joyful pride in
his land and nation which always managed to rise above disasters in the same inevitable way that goodness triumphed over
evil. '*She conquered like a Queen,*' he thought of his victorious
Commonwealth. '*She'll forgive like a mother.*'

Meanwhile, the distant cannon fire turned into one constant,
uninterrupted sound. The burning town lay still, silent, empty
and deserted.

★ ★ ★

But the day for which Pan Yan had prayed wasn't yet at hand. Fresh hoofbeats clattered in the deserted streets and a single rider burst into the empty square with the suddenness of a thunderbolt. He was bareheaded. He had lost his coat. His horse had no saddle. His face was split open by a saber blow and blood trailed in the air behind him like a scarlet scarf. He pulled his horse to a skidding halt on the cobblestones and cried out between chaotic gasps for breath:

"Hmyel's winning! He's beating the *Lahy*! Beating the gentry and *lytzari* and *hetmany* and all . . .!"

Then he swayed and toppled headfirst to the ground while the Mirhorod men ran to lift him up.

A wave of fire seemed to sweep across Skshetuski's face and drained away into an icy pallor.

" . . . What did he say?"

But Zakhar didn't answer and suddenly Pan Yan was aware of a special stillness in the reddened air. The guns were quiet beyond the rim of light. Only the crackling sound of flames across the square and the occasional crash of a collapsing wall broke the spreading silence.

Then he heard fresh hoofbeats and new riders burst into the square shouting "Beaten! The *Lahy* are beaten!" and moments later a long column of Tartars passed slowly on their shaggy ponies with disarmed prisoners walking brokenly between them. A dull groan lifted from Skshetuski's chest as he recognized the uniforms of the Grand Hetman's *husaria*.

"No," he murmured in a voice as plaintive as a frightened child's. "No . . . this can't be happening. God, it can't be true!"

This had to be some separate, disconnected fragment of the battle; perhaps an earlier setback that would be put right again in a little while . . .! But out of all the streets that opened on the square, riding across the bloody litter of the *tchernya's* panic, flowed ranks of chanting Tartars and singing Zaporohjans and Skshetuski swayed as if about to fall. Their bared chests heaved with each rasping breath they took. Their faces were scorched and blackened with gunsmoke and lined with mortal weariness but the men were luminous with joy. Their heads were tilted back as if to savor an ecstatic memory and their eyes were half-closed as if in a dream.

That's how victorious soldiers come home after battle, Pan

Yan knew. He clutched the balustrade as Kshetchovski's Pereyaslav Cossacks rode into the square with thick bundles of flags, guidons and regimental standards clasped in their arms and then his shocked mind refused to serve him further.

'No,' he thought. '*Impossible.*' Not once in the Commonwealth's two hundred years had any enemy captured those insignia.

"It can't be," he said hoarsely. "It's impossible. No. The Commonwealth . . ."

But Zakhar ran out into the square with all the other Cossacks and he was alone. He watched, unable to believe his eyes, as the Cossacks hurled the banners of the Polish Army one by one into the dust. Not even the clatter of the flag-staffs convinced him that this was anything but a cruel nightmare.

But then he heard the rumbling of heavy wagon wheels and a long line of carts rolled into the square surrounded by Hmyelnitzki's Pashkov bodyguards. Two bowed and bareheaded men sat swaying gently in the straw of the leading wagon; they sat hunched over, nodding as if bemused or lost in some terrible nightmare of their own, while the wagon creaked and rattled on the cobblestones. Light from the burning church splashed them with its glow and streaked their pale faces with bright bars of scarlet.

Pan Yan looked at them, recognized them, and staggered back as if he'd been shot. His arms flayed wildly as if he were drowning. His mouth fell open. He gasped for air to breathe. His face acquired the stamped rigidity of death and his cry was one of mindless horror.

"The Hetmans . . .!"

And then he stumbled backwards and fell to the floor.

Some moments later three horsemen rode into the square at the head of their victorious army. They sat their horses proudly under the triple standard of the Commonwealth's principal commander while singing regiments and cohorts without number passed in a triumphant procession behind them.

The first was Hmyelnitzki, dressed in a blood-red coat and a crimson cloak, riding his milk-white stallion. He held a gold *bulava* at his hip like a royal scepter. Beside him rode Tuhay-bey and Kshetchovski. The Commonwealth lay in blood and dust under their horses' hooves.

Chapter Fifteen

IT SEEMED TO MANY PEOPLE in those days that the sky had fallen on them and their country. First came the news of Yellow Waters. Then, even less believable, came word of the catastrophe at Korsun in which the Army of the Crown was shattered and its Hetmans taken, and all of the Ukraine was caught up at once in a fiery holocaust that defied description or comparison with any other slaughter in the bloody history of mankind.

The shock was so sudden and profound that many couldn't bring themselves to believe the truth. Others simply lost their ability to reason. Whole populations wandered about in blind, uncomprehending stupor babbling about the Last Judgment and the Antichrist. All human bonds of family and of social order seemed to crack and wither along with the differences that demarcate between animals and men; it was as if Hell unleashed its evils so that, thereafter, mankind cast off decency and goodness and sought its constants in foulness and ill-will.

All the constraints of civilization were gone in a moment. Savagery, pillage and lawlessness took the place of labor, faith and conscience, and nature itself seemed to be reversed. The sun no longer lighted up the sky; a pall of smoke and ashes hung thickly above the whole country and turned the days into reddish twilight. At night, in place of moonlight and the stars, vast crimson conflagrations lit up the darkness between the horizons. Towns, villages, churches and country manors flamed like tinder among burning forests, and human beings lost the power of speech and either moaned or howled at each other like wild dogs. Life lost all value. Uncounted thousands died or vanished without a trace, and only one great figure rose out of this cataclysm and towered above it like a giant who cast his shadow over everything.

This was Hmyelnitzki.

Two hundred thousand warriors stood ready at his call. All Cossacks ran to join him and the grim mobs rose everywhere in bloody rebellion. The land was on fire from the Steppes to the Pripet River and the storm engulfed all of the eastern territories. The war burst out across Ruthenia, Podolia and Volhynia. It burned throughout the palatinates of Bratzlav, Kiev and Tchernihov and all the other former lands of the Lithuanian dukes grafted into the Polish Kingdom by the request of its Ruthenian princes. The power of the Cossack Hetman spread wider each day; never in its history could the Commonwealth command such forces as he ruled. Even the Holy Roman Empire couldn't match Hmyelnitzki.

The rebellion exceeded all his expectations and the Cossack Hetman himself found it difficult at first to grasp how far he had come. He still insisted on covering himself with loyalty to the Commonwealth, and in justifying all he did with restoration of Cossack rights and the curbing of the *magnateria*, but that was only because he still didn't understand that he was far beyond the need to explain anything, and as he grew in power so his sense of *right* became one with his sense of *self*. All the good and evil of the times—the people's craving for a life of dignity under law, along with the medieval cruelties and injustice—became one with his need for vengeance and his sense of grievance so that he was ready to curse the sun itself if it didn't shine when he wanted sunshine. All men and events were weighed in the scales of his own advantage so that he knew no limits in cruelty to an enemy but, at the same time, he showed a strange goodwill and a twisted sentimental faith that drove him to acts of boundless generosity towards anyone who rendered him any kind of service.

Only when drunk and blinded by his secret terrors did he become maniacal in excess. Then he raged and roared out those genocidal orders that he regretted later. And as his successes mounted so did the frequency of his drunken rages because each triumph increased his sense of unreality. It seemed to him at times that he was helpless before his own greatness. His boundless power terrified him quite as much as it terrified everybody else. He knew that the rebellion lifted him higher than he wished to go and the tidal wave carried him so swiftly on its crest that he lost all his former bearings. He may have hoped at the beginning that he could force the Commonwealth to negotiate concessions and to win some redress for his own private injuries but events swept him far beyond that point. Now there was only a struggle to the death, and who'd emerge victorious? Where would the tide of war cast him when it ebbed? And how long could he count on his own unbelievable good fortune?

★ ★ ★

He sought his answers from soothsayers and astrologers but all that he could see ahead was an impenetrable darkness, and then he felt the full weight of his doubts, and the hot touch of panic that clouded his reason, and a terrible despair would claw at his chest.

He had the breadth of vision to see farther and clearer than most men of his times. He knew that while the Commonwealth was racked by her internal conflicts, hardly aware of the might that lay at her command, she would be slow to gather her resources. But what if she suddenly found a man who could awake and harness all those dormant powers? And what if the present danger put an end to chaos, stifle the magnates' private jealousies and quarrels, call a halt to the interminable politicking of the lesser gentry and end the helplessness of the King? Then half a million men drawn only from the gentry could fall on the rebels and wipe them off the face of the earth no matter who helped them. The King spent a lifetime trying to gather up this power in a single hand; he even fed the flame of Cossack discontent to achieve that end. And would the Cossacks help to mobilize these forces only to be swept away themselves?

And so each fresh success increased Hmyelnitzki's fear because it brought closer the moment of the Commonwealth's awakening. Each heady triumph was lined with bitterness because he saw a future defeat in every new victory. Sometimes it seemed to him that he already heard the distant thunder of the storm gathering against him. All that this hurricane needed was a guiding hand. Even his unbelievable capture of the Hetmans had its darker side because it made room for a new man, one better fitted to inspire and unite the country, and no one—least of all Hmyelnitzki— doubted that Prince Yeremi Vishnovyetzki would be chosen as the new Grand Hetman.

And what would happen then?

Frightening rumors about this legendary ruler of the Trans-dnieper country were already seeping through the camp at Korsun where Hmyelnitzki halted to rest and reorganize his army. The Prince, it was said, was on the march in his own vast lands, crushing the rebellion wherever he appeared. No one could resist him. A forest of stakes and gibbets rose wherever he passed and impaled rebels were left to pray for death in the ashes of the villages that he left behind him. Stark terror flew before him to announce his coming. The cry "*Yarema's here!*" was enough to send the *tchernya* into headlong panic.

Alone in his quarters Hmyelnitzki wrestled with two choices. He could either hurl his whole might on Vishnovyetzki, or leave a strong part of it to fortify the Ukraine, reduce the castles that still resisted him, and lead the rest deep into the Common-wealth where he might force renewed negotiations and end the war without a need to face the terrifying prince. Despite the overwhelming numbers under his command he knew that he could lose a battle against Prince Yeremi; the peasant masses which formed the bulk of his unruly cohorts had already shown how they reacted to Vishnovyetzki's name. He needed time to transform his mobs into disciplined regiments that could stand up to the Transdnieper soldiers who were known to be the finest in the Commonwealth; and he could count only on the time that Vishnovyetzki needed to crush the rebellion in his own dominions before invading the Cossacks in the Ukraine.

But he had one more weapon that never failed him with Ruthenian princelings or the Polish gentry: to sow discord, feed personal ambitions and create confusion that caused indecision and delay. He could try his shrewd skills at diplomacy and his unmatched cunning on that Transdnieper magnate as he did so successfully with so many others.

In this regard, he suddenly remembered his prisoner, Skshetuski.

★ ★ ★

He had the young man brought to him in the mansion of the Korsun governor where he set up his quarters. Only Kshetchovski was present at this meeting which, as they both knew, could be critical at this state of the rebellion. Vish-novyetski had to be delayed. The streets outside were choked with panicked crowds as yet another rumor of Prince Yeremi's imminent arrival swept through the Cossack camp.

But Hmyelnitzki showed his prisoner nothing of what he thought.

"You did me a service once," he said coldly, then went on with the proud indifference of a magnate bestowing a favor. "I'm paying you in kind. I bought you from Tuhay-bey and promised you your freedom when the time was right. That time has now come."

Skshetuski said nothing in reply. No sign of joy appeared in his face. He stood unmoved before the Zaporohjan Hetman, staring straight ahead with unseeing eyes.

"Go back to your prince," Hmyelnitzki went on, distant and aloof like a sovereign ruler whose slightest whim disposed of the lives of thousands. "I'll give you a safeconduct that'll get you past all of my own people and an escort to keep you out of the hands of the mob. Well? Are you fit to travel?"

"He looks like a corpse," drawled the Pereyaslav colonel.

"Are you ill?"

Pan Yan knew that he looked very little like the strong, proud and confident young man whom Hmyelnitzki met on the banks of the Omelnitchek. His face had yellowed like a sheet of parchment on which everything that he experienced in captivity was etched in bitterness and pain. His long beard was tangled and unkempt. His wounds and illness sapped his strength, and the horrors he witnessed in the Cossack camps drained away all his natural optimism and humor, so that he seemed like his own gaunt shadow or like a sick man on the point of dying.

What was there left for him to see? Dragged in the wake of the Cossack triumph he watched everything that happened from the moment that the Zaporohjans rode out of the *Sietch*. He witnessed all the disasters and humiliations that overwhelmed his country. He saw the Hetmans in captivity, the pyramids of heads hacked off the shoulders of defeated soldiers, the gentry hanged on hooks driven between their ribs, the mutilated women and the raped and degraded girls. He saw acts of desperate courage along with all the cowardice and depravity that only terror makes possible among people and he felt it all as deeply as if he was responsible for every part of it.

And wasn't he? Didn't he cut Hmyelnitzki off a hangman's rope? And when he added his fear of what might be happening to Helen if, by some terrible mischance, she'd been unable to escape to Lubnie, he cursed God for keeping him alive.

He cursed, and then shocked by his blasphemy, pleaded for forgiveness. He was so completely ravaged by despair that even now the thought of being free lost its real meaning. '*As for this conqueror,*' he thought with bitter hatred, '*this triumphant Hetman who wants to show how magnanimous he can be,*' Pan Yan felt nothing beyond a dull loathing.

Hmyelnitzki watched him carefully and the young soldier saw the sharp impatience stirring in the man's pouched and piercing eyes as he kept his own stubborn silence.

"Well?" The irritation mounted in Hmyelnitzki's voice. "Make use of my generosity while you can! I know I'm letting loose an enemy! I know you'll fight against me!"

"If God gives me strength," Skshetuski said coldly.

He was staring at Hmyelnitzki with the bottomless contempt of one who could read the deepest and best-hidden secrets of the Cossack's soul, so that the dark, brooding eyes turned away from him and fixed their gaze on the floor between them.

"No matter . . ." A long moment passed before Hmyelnitzki spoke again. "I've come too far to worry about some petty little hater . . . You'll tell your prince what you've seen among us, I know that. Go ahead. It doesn't matter now. But tell him also to watch his step along the Dnieper, you hear? Or I might pay him a visit that he won't like at all!"

Skshetuski said nothing.

"I've always said this," Hmyelnitzki went on with a rising fury. "My war is not against the Commonwealth but against the kinglets! And Vishnovyetzki is the worst of them! He's my sworn enemy and an enemy of all the people in the Eastern Lands! A traitor to our faith, a cruel oppressor! I hear he's drowning the rebellion in blood in his country. Let him watch out or we'll spill some of his for him!"

Rage flooded thickly into the crimson face, foam speckled the Cossack leader's lips, and his bulging eyes filled with a rush of blood. They swelled and reddened and he began to hammer the arms of his chair with both fists. It was the first sign of that famous fury that the minstrels had begun to sing about: the madness he never remembered afterwards in which he lost all control, abandoned all restraints, and often fell unconscious at his victims' feet.

"I'll have Krivoinos tie him to his horse's tail!" he began to howl. "I'll use his head for a footstool when I mount my horse! I'll have him down on his face before me! I'll have him hold my stirrup like a groom!"

"Conquer him first," Skshetuski said calmly.

Kshetchovski, unemotional as ever, took a quick step forward. "Gently," he soothed, cold as ice. "Gently, Hetman. Where's your dignity? Why make yourself sick over one stiffnecked little noble? Let him go. Send him on his way. He's just goading you. You've promised him his freedom so he knows he's safe or he wouldn't dare to talk to you this way. Let him go, why don't you? It's either that or you'll be forced to break your word, and how would that look in a Hetman, eh?"

Hmyelnitzki made a massive effort to suppress his fury. His chest worked heavily as if he were drowning. But the rage had seized him firmly by the hair and it took time to force it down again.

"Let him go, then," he muttered thickly when speech was possible once more. "Give him a safeconduct and half a troop of Tartars so he'll know that I pay my debts. Measure for measure. Evil along with good. Tell the Tartars to take him all the way to Lubnie if they have to!"

Then, fixing his bloodshot eyes on the young soldier, he went on more calmly: "And you keep this in mind. We're even now. The account is settled. I've come to like you a bit. Yes, I've been patient with you. You wouldn't have got away with half the liberties you permit yourself if I didn't like you but that's all over now, understand? It won't save you the next time I get my hands on you."

★　★　★

He waived his arm in dismissal and Kshetchovski took Pan Yan out of the audience chamber and into the street where a cart and half a troop of Tartars were already waiting. The young man and the Cossack colonel knew each other slightly in the past and now Kshetchovski offered some advice.

"Listen, since the Hetman let you go with your neck and head still fixed to your shoulders, let me tell you something for old times' sake. Get away from here as far as you can. Go all the way to Warsaw, you might be safe there. But wherever you go make sure you don't set foot across the Dnieper again because none of you will leave that country alive. Your times are finished. We're going to drive out all the Vishnovyetzkis and Konyetzpolskis and Zaslavskis and the rest of you gentry, big and small, and everything you've had is going to be ours. Which, I'm thinking, must be the way God wants it or He wouldn't have let us get as far as we've got."

Skshetuski, deep in his own grim thoughts, hardly bothered to listen, but the Cossack colonel went on anyway.

"When I saw my former lord and benefactor with a Tartar rope around his neck, his excellency the Grand Hetman got on me right away for being a Judas and an ingrate. *'My Lord, how am I an ingrate?'* I asked him. *'Far from it!'* I told him. *'Why . . . once I'm the master on your lands I'll make you my bailiff. Only you've got to promise to keep your nose out of the bottle and not get drunk so often!'*

"Ey," he added, nodding. "Tuhay-bey's going to make a fortune out of those golden birds, that's why he guards them like a Sultan's treasure. We'd make them sing a far different song, believe me, if we could get our hands on them! But here's your wagon and the Tartars. So where d'you want to go?"

"To Tchehryn."

Kshetchovski shrugged.

"Well, it's your choice. Don't say I didn't warn you. The Tartars will take you right into Vishnovyetzki's camp if that's what you want. Try to keep your prince from having them impaled which is what he'd do if we gave you Cossacks. Not that we care one way or the other but our Hetman has his kinder moments. He even ordered your own horse given back to you so you'll speak well of us when you see Yarema. Tell him to come here and bow down to Hmyelnitzki before it's too late! Who knows, maybe we'll feel like showing him some mercy, eh? Well, be on your way!"

Skshetuski climbed into the wagon, the Tartars closed their ranks around it and the journey started.

★   ★   ★

They couldn't cross the city square. The Zaporohjans filled it from end to end, packed tightly around their cooking fires. Huge mobs of armed peasants wandered among the cauldrons, singing, eating, drinking and fighting with each other. They howled to the skies. Their songs, composed by the swarm of vagabond minstrels and soothsayers who descended on the Cossack camp in enormous numbers, were about their victories. Korsun and Yellow Waters. The end of the *Lah*. The start of a new Golden Age none of them could imagine. The town was scarred in the aftermath of unbridled pillage. All the doors and windows were ripped from their casements and the shattered remnants of countless household objects littered the streets in heaps of fouled straw, human waste and refuse, and the thick pools of grease that dripped from hundreds of slaughtered sheep and cattle spitted in the fires.

Skshetuski's Tartar escort pushed its way past the naked bodies of murdered women that lay everywhere among the cauldrons and the cooking fires. They rode around the mounds of heads hacked off the Grand Hetman's dead and wounded soldiers. Those grizzly trophies and the other objects of continuing mass rape had begun to rot but the mobs didn't seem to mind the stench of putrefaction. Murdered Jews whom the Cossacks hated with a passion bordering on madness hung from the eaves of every building, swaying on long ropes. The drunken mobs amused themselves by catching hold of the cadavers' feet and using them for swings.

One whole side of the square was black with burned and gutted buildings, the parish church among them. Smoke and the reek of burned meat filled the air there. Beyond that belt of ruins spread the huge enclosure of the Tartar *Kosh*—a name that had a particularly sinister connotation in Polish since it denoted a 'bushel' or a 'basket' as well as 'encampment.' Packed into that broad, open space were piles of loot and lowing herds of cattle and thousands of captives assembled for transport. Whoever hadn't managed to escape in time or hadn't fallen under peasant axes went into those pens. Among the captives lay the trussed-up soldiers taken in both the Cossack victories, petty town officials, gentry of all kinds, merchants and storekeepers. Women and children clung to each other, weeping and crying out in Polish and Ruthenian. Old people, unfit for the long overland drive into Tartar slavery, were murdered out of hand, but every other kind of man and woman was represented there, including masses of terrified peasants who looked no different at first sight from the wild drunken mobs of armed marauders who jeered at them outside the enclosures.

The Tartars had swept up entire villages on their march,

Skshetuski knew because he saw them do it. It wasn't rare for
men to seize scythes and axes and run to join the rebels while
the Tartars burned down their homes and drove their wives and
children into the slave enclosures. No one complained about it.
Nobody protested. The mobs renounced all their human ties
when they joined Hmyelnitzki. If Tartars took their women
they took other women to use and murder or sell to other
Tartars, so there was no shortage of strapping Ukrainian lasses
roped in threes and fours to the same wooden yokes as young
gentlewomen. Slavery and terror wiped out class distinctions.
Barely able to cover themselves with shreds of torn clothing,
exposed to the jeers and abuse of barbaric warriors who pushed
in howling masses through the throngs of captives, they were
whipped and pawed and thrown down on the ground and
clutched by creatures that hardly seemed human, and so they
lost their minds, memories and will. Some wept and moaned,
long past the point of screaming. Others, their eyes fixed
blindly on things that only they could see, found refuge in
madness and let themselves drift unresisting into whatever happened.

From time to time the shrill screaming of a butchered victim
cut through the constant hiss and crack of whips among the
male captives, the bellowing of terrified cattle, the neighing of
frightened horses, and the squeals of children. The *yassyr* was
still to be sorted out and readied for the long march across the
Steppe to the Black Sea galleys and then to the Crimea, and so
the carts, wagons, horses, cattle herds, sheep, camels, and captive men and women jostled and collided and trampled each
other among the mounds of looted vestments, clothing, bedding, ornaments, tapestries and piles of dented armor. Fresh
crowds of captives were driven in by Tartar convoys all day long
and new herds of cattle arrived without a pause. Flat-bottomed
barges, loaded high with loot, lay beached on the muddy banks
of the River Ros, while from the main Tartar camp came crowds
of warriors dressed in a nightmarish jumble of priests' vestments, ornate merchants' cloaks, embroidered Ukrainian jackets and in women's dresses to gape at these treasures and
calculate their shares.

Some of these visitors, drunk out of their minds on Tartar
kumys and Cossack *gojhalka*, started to fight and haggle over
their future spoils while the horseherders sprawled about, blow-

ing shrill music on reed pipes and whistles, and throwing dice made out of human knuckles. Hundreds of homeless dogs ran among them, fighting over whatever could be torn apart and devoured, and adding their savage snarls to this hellish noise.

★ ★ ★

Once past this pit of misery and terror Skshetuski hoped to breathe a freer air. But there were other horrors waiting along the highway. The main Tartar camp spread on the horizon like a grey sea of tents and horsehide *yurts* where thousands of men and animals were in constant motion. But closer to hand, in the fields that ran along the highway to Tchehryn, young warriors practiced their marksmanship on captives who were either too old or weak to survive the '*Trail of Tears*' to the Crimean markets. Several dozen bodies, holed like old sieves, were flung on the highway where some still twitched in their last convulsions, while those who still served for targets hung by their arms from the wayside trees.

"*Ukh! Ukh!* A good man!" The Tartar bowmen encouraged each other. "The bow's in good hands!"

Each well-placed arrow was greeted with hoots of laughter and shouts of approval.

Beyond this target range lay a broad plain on which beef, sheep and horses were being slaughtered as food for the army. The steaming ground had turned into scarlet mud. The butchers, bloodstained from head to foot, worked with their gutting knives among piles of offal while the hot mid-day sun burned down on them without relief. The reek of blood was overpowering. It took an hour for Skshetuski and his Tartar escort to make their way past these encampments and into open fields, but the massed sound of bellowing cattle, neighing horses and the hoarse murmur of thousands of voices floated behind them in the stifling air for many hours more. They rode past burned cottages, skeletal chimneys rising out of rubble, crushed fields of wheat and cherry orchards cut down for firewood, so that it seemed as if every tell-tale sign of a Tartar march was spread out for inspection. The bodies of dead animals and men, ballooning in the heat, lay scattered all along the highway mile after mile and the fields were dark with flocks of crows and ravens which lifted heavily into the sky as they plodded past. Hmyelnitzki's triumph was on full display and it was hard to understand why and against what enemy he had spilled these horrors since it was his own country that now lay in torment.

But the catalog of horrors seemed to have no end. In Mleyov they met new Tartar convoys driving a mass of captives. The town of Horodyshtze was burned to the ground; only the stone church steeple remained upright in the scorched, black rubble, along with one old oak in the market square. Terrible fruit hung from this tree: dozens of Jewish children, murdered three days earlier, swung softly from each branch. Other than that, the township was abandoned. Hundreds of local gentry had looked for refuge here from the pillaged towns of Konoplanka, Starosyel, Viezhovka, Balakley and Vodatchev but the inhabitants met them with axes and pitchforks and slaughtered them all, and now their bloating bodies were littering the rubble. The men who used to live there were gone to join Hmyelnitzki; their women fled into the woods in fear of retribution from Prince Yeremi's army.

From Horodyshtze, Pan Yan took the road for Smila, Zabotyn and Novosyeltze, stopping only long enough to rest his men and horses, and at noon on the second day of his dreadful journey he entered Tchehryn, which was the first Ukrainian town to throw its gates open to Hmyelnitzki and so escaped destruction. Only a few houses, Tchaplinski's among them, had been burned and looted, but terror lay as thick as smoke among the townspeople. Their eyes flicked constantly towards the Dnieper, and to the Vishnovyetzki lands beyond it, sure that Prince Yeremi would fall upon them any day and wreak a vengeance that would defy description.

He wanted news of Helen. Of the Prince. And of what was happening in the Prince's country. But not even the uneasy commander of the Cossack garrison could tell him anything. With all the longboats pulled over to the Tchehryn side no fugitives came from across the Dnieper so that no one knew what was happening there. Desperate to find out what became of Helen, Pan Yan ordered his Tartars to ford the broad river, abandoned his wagon for his horse, and drove his escort at breakneck speed for Rozloghi. Hope that she might be safe in Lubnie restored some of his strength.

★   ★   ★

They rode as if pursued in clouds of yellow dust through an unpeopled land, past settlements, villages and plantations in which nothing moved, and it was only when they neared the overgrown banks of the Kahamlik that the Tartars spotted some human shape hiding among the reeds. They leaped at once off their horses, dived into the brushwood and dragged out two trembling, naked men. One was so old and bowed that he seemed like an apparition out of ancient legends; the other was a youth barely in his teens. They trembled in such terror that the Tartars found it difficult to hold them.

"Where are you from?" Skshetuski demanded, then tried to calm their fear. "Come on now, speak up. Nothing will happen to you."

But terror had robbed them of their voices, if not of their wits.

"Are you from Rozloghi?"

"Us? Us?" the old man whined at last. "We're from no place, master. We beg on the roads. Me, I play the lyre. I'm blind. Him, he's dumb. He leads me . . ."

"But what's the last place you've come from? What village?"

The old man cocked his eyeless face into the wind, as if to sniff for danger, and it took him a long time to find a safe answer.

"Us, master? Ah . . . we've been all over. All over . . . 'Till some devil caught us right here in the reeds! He stripped us, poor innocents that we are! He took our coats, our boots! He even took my lyre . . ."

Driven out of patience, Skshetuski ordered him to speak or die but the old man took refuge in ignorance and a litany of his own complaints.

"We don' know nothin', master! I'm just an old naked beggar lookin' for some good folks to cover us, an' feed us. Ay, we're cold . . . We're hungry . . ."

"Speak up or I'll hang you!"

But the old man wailed that he knew nothing about anything, and went on complaining about the 'Devil' who jumped on him right here from the reeds, and then broke out into a stream of sing-song proverbs and Ruthenian sayings. It was clear that the cunning old man decided to play either a madman or a babbling fool.

Skshetuski tried once more. "Were you in Rozloghi?"

"I don' know nothing, master . . ."

"Hang him!" Skshetuski shouted at the Tartars.

"We was! We was! We was there!" the old man howled at
once, shrewd enough to know when matters had gone beyond a
joke.

"And what did you see there?"

"Me? Me? What does a blind man see? We was there . . . oh,
maybe four, maybe five days back . . . Then we was in Brovarki, at the fair. It was there we heard about the knights in that
other place . . ."

"What knights, fool?"

"I don' know, master! Knights, that's all, on horses."

"Poles? Cossacks? Who?"

"I don' know! *Lytzari*, like people was saying, that went to
Rozloghi. Some said it was *Lahy*, and others said Cossacks . . ."

"Ride!" Skshetuski shouted to his Tartars and kicked his horse
so savagely in both flanks that the animal groaned and leaped
into an instant gallop. The Tartars let their reins hang loose and
galloped after him.

They rode like the wind. The sun was already started on its
downward journey. The shadows were deepening. It was the
same kind of evening as when the young lieutenant rode along
that dark forest road beside the borrowed coach of the Valachian
envoy, with Helen and the old *knahina* a hand's reach away. The
Kahamlik seemed unchanged; it burned with the same gold and
purple fires and the day sunk into the same silence as it flowed
out of the afternoon into the chill of the night. The only
difference was that on the earlier journey Skshetuski was full of
confidence and happiness and hope. Now he was hurtling
through the darkening shadows like a condemned soul, swept
on by currents of fear and premonition.

Despair cried within him: '*That was Bohun! He's got her! You'll
never see her again!*'

And hope replied: '*She's saved! Those were the Prince's men!*'

The riders drove their horses until the animals began to
stagger with exhaustion. All daylight vanished. A pale moon
rolled out from behind the black canopy of the trees and began
its slow blind climb into a starless sky. The horses coughed and
groaned. They were streaked with sweat. Their breaths heaved

and rattled. The moon, Skshetuski thought, became even whiter as it rose; it seemed as desperately pale as the visions that leaped up in his imagination.

He rode as if demented among the trees, through the familiar ravine strewn with fallen timbers, and along the dried-out stream that twisted among the boulders. Soon now, he thought, they'd be in Rozloghi. Soon, all uncertainties and fears will be laid to rest . . .!

The wind was whistling in the young man's ears, his cap flew off and the hair rose up wildly on his head, and then the horse began to moan heavily under him as if about to fall. A moment more, he thought. One more leap forward and the ravine will end, the road will spill into the clearing before the moat and the fortified escarpment, the palisade and the Kurtzevitch manor . . .!

Now, he thought, as he urged his foundering horse out from behind the last of the trees and into the clearing and then a terrible cry escaped from Skshetuski. The manor, stables, out-buildings, barns, barracks and stockade—even the cherry or-chard!— had all disappeared. White moonlight lay as cold as death on the burned, black rubble, charred timbers, and the ashen aftermath of fire.

All was gone, destroyed. There was no sound in the still night air.

Skshetuski's horse collapsed before the moat and he stared at this scene of desolation as if unable to understand what had happened there. His arms rose and spread of their own volition but he couldn't speak. Slowly, as if the muscles of his neck were suddenly shrunk and withered, his head began to sway and roll from side to side. The Tartars were pulling up their panting horses all around him. He moved as in a dream, found the charred remnants of the bridge and crossed the ditch along a blackened beam. He looked around like a traveler who finds himself in a place he never saw before, searching for something that might seem familiar, and trying to orient himself under strange stars and among even stranger objects whose use he didn't know. He couldn't tell where he was nor when he had got there. He felt neither hot nor cold, all awareness left him. He found a stone to sit on in the yard, his arms lay still across his knees and his head hung down on his chest so that the wonder-ing Tartars started thinking that he was asleep. But the dreams or thoughts or images that passed before his eyes were fleeting and unclear. He saw Helen as she was when he'd seen her last, pale as the moon and lifting her arms to him in the cherry orchard where a cuckoo counted out their years together. Only her face seemed hidden in a veil of mist so that her features were obscured.

And suddenly he couldn't quite remember why he came to this unfamiliar place. Had he been there before? Ah yes. Yes. He thought he could remember. He'd come to take her from this dark environment but something went wrong and he couldn't do it. Yes. That's how it was. He wanted to take her away but he couldn't do it. So he had gone away. Yes. He'd gone somewhere. Where? He couldn't remember. And then the old town square of Tchehryn was passing before him. He saw Zachvilihovski. He recoiled from the vulgar, crudely cynical and impertinent mask of Zagloba's face with its sharp, knowing eye. That one good eye bored into him with particular insistence. It stared at him, as if transmitting signals through the mist, then vanished, and the cold gloomy eye of Pan Grodjitzki took its place. Then he saw Kudak, heard the cataracts, lived again through the bloody moment on Hortytza Island, the mission to the *Sietch*, and tasted the dark despair of his journey in the Cossack wagon. All the events of his captivity up to that time and place crowded in upon him but everything beyond that final lucid memory vanished in a vast, impenetrable darkness.

Where was he, anyway? What was happening to him? He had a vague notion that he was on his way to Rozloghi and Helen who was waiting for him as he'd asked her to, and that he stopped somewhere on his journey to rest in the rubble. He wanted to get up and go on, anxious to see Helen because it was terribly important to make sure she was safe, but he couldn't do it.

I'm tired, he thought. Ah . . . So terribly tired. He felt as if huge iron chains held him fastened to the ground like one of those mythological transgressors who had done something to offend the Gods, and he bowed down, no longer fully conscious, under their awesome weight.

The night went on deepening and darkening but Skshetuski didn't notice anything around him. He was as still and rigid as the blackened boulder on which he was sitting. The Tartars set up a bivouac. They started a small fire, roasted their rations of dried horsemeat, ate and went to sleep, but a strange new sound woke them in less than an hour and they rose to listen. Still muffled by the distance but growing ever louder, came the many jingling and clattering sounds that a large body of cavalry makes on a rapid march.

The Tartars leaped to their feet to throw new brushwood on their cooking fire and to hang a white sheet on a pole where it could be seen. The sharp click of hoofbeats, the snorting of horses and the rattle of sabers against stirrup irons neared them rapidly and soon the forest track darkened under a mass of mounted men who formed a tight ring around the escarpment. There were sharp murmurs of interrogation. The Tartars pointed to the hunched figure seated on the stone in the moonlit yard and, at once, a troop broke away from the larger body and rode up the slope. Their leader moved with caution, peering into the gloom, then suddenly straightened up, flung his arms wide open and shouted: "It's Skshetuski! As God lives, it's Skshetuski!"

The silent man gave no sign of life.

"Lieutenant! Don't you know me? I'm Byhovietz! Hey, what's the matter with you? Wake up, for God's sake! Hey everybody, come on up here! It's Skshetuski!"

But Skshetuski neither moved nor spoke.

★ ★ ★

Meanwhile the road, the woods and the fields beyond them filled with other horsemen. This was the Prince's army on the march. Byhovietz led the vanguard and now the rest came up. The news that Skshetuski had been found spread with the speed of lightning among the regiments and his friends ran from all sides to greet him. Little Pan Michal Volodyovski, the two Sleshinski brothers, Pan Dzik, Orpishevski, Migurski, Yakubovitch, Lens and the gaunt Longinus Podbipyenta raced a crowd of others into the scorched ruins. But Pan Yan was deaf to all their voices. He didn't feel their arms about his shoulders. They spoke to him, pulled at his hands and arms and tried to raise him to his feet and to hold him up. He stared at them with wide, indifferent eyes as if he'd never seen any of them before and didn't care about them one way or another, and this seemed all the more terrible to them because they were his best and closest friends. Then those among them who knew about his love for Helen, and by that time there were few who hadn't heard about it, looked around, recognized the place and saw the rubble, the scorched ruins and the soft grey ashes drifting among the trees, and understood what must have happened to him.

"He's lost his mind," one whispered. "His grief's made him sick."

"His pain's unhinged him," suggested another.

"Despair's turned him mad."

"Quick! Take him to the Prince. Maybe he'll get his wits together once he sees His Highness."

Pan Podbipyenta wrung and twisted his huge fists. The others stood in a stricken circle around the young lieutenant, whispering to each other and wondering what to do. Some of them wept like schoolboys, unashamed to show the depth of their pity and affection for him, smearing their tears across fiercely mustached faces. Others heaved hopeless sighs. Then Father Muhovyetzki, the Prince's confessor, stepped out of the circle and laid his hand on Skshetuski's head.

No one said anything. All the young officers went down on their knees as if expecting to see a miracle but there was nothing miraculous in what happened then. The priest kept his hand firmly on Skshetuski's head, lifted his eyes to the dark sky and began to pray.

"*'Pater noster, qu'es in coelis!'* Our Father . . . which art in Heaven . . . *'sanctificetur nomen Tuum, fiat voluntas Tua . . .'*"

He paused there and, after a moment, repeated in a harder, louder voice as if to stress the single fundamental tenet of their faith: "*'Fiat voluntas Tua . . .!* Thy Will be done . . .!"

And then Skshetuski stirred. A tremor passed across his whole body and he said in a voice of utter resignation: "On earth . . . as it is in Heaven . . ."

And then he fell to his knees, and bowed down to the ground with as much grief and pain as if some frozen barrier had broken within him, and slow hot tears started trickling down his face.

Part Three

Chapter Sixteen

ZJENDJAN CAME BACK to Tchehryn long before any of these events took place. The country was still at peace when he set out from Kudak, Hmyelnitzki was far from the borders of the Ukraine, and although the storm clouds were gathering everywhere along the great river there still were people in the bigger towns who thought that it might all blow over as it had before.

He left Kudak the day before Skshetuski set out for the *Sietch*, sailing up the Dnieper on a galley that Pan Grodjitzki sent north for munitions, but he found few reasons to be cheerful or pleased with himself even though he was a naturally curious, confident and lighthearted lad. He worried about his master. He reproached himself for having left him at a time that was clearly dangerous. The Steppes were still untroubled as he traveled up the great grey river but he knew he'd have to be a dimwit to miss the signs and portents. He thought it likely that he'd never see his master again, and took turns sniffling and grumbling at himself, but that didn't make him feel better about abandoning Skshetuski. True, he reasoned, he'd been *sent* away. He hadn't taken to his heels, or turned his back on the lieutenant by his own choice, but that was small comfort. At least, he thought, I'll do what my master wants. I'll get his letters delivered to the Lady and the old *Knahina*. Then I'll turn right around and go looking for him.

"That's it," he muttered to himself, his clear young forehead furrowing with decision. "That's just what I'll do."

But how he was going to set about it wasn't entirely clear.

The voyage up the swollen Dnieper was slow and exhausting at that time of year. Day after day the galley strained against the flood, and the oarsmen struggled without rest to make headway in the rushing waters, but eventually the white towers of Tchehryn showed on the horizon and soon afterwards the ship reached calmer waters. But they no sooner tied-up at the dock, and Zjendjan barely got the feel of firm ground under his boots again, when Cossack guards surrounded him with questions.

"Who are you? Where're you coming from? What's your business here?"

"Letters from Pan Grodjitzki for the Hetmans," he replied at once, thinking that this was only half a lie since Pan Grodjitzki's sailors were sure to have brought one.

"From Kudak, eh?" The Cossack sergeant seemed unsure what to do with the grinning boy whose confident air suggested that he belonged to somebody important. "Sure you're not from the *Sietch*?"

"From Kudak." The lad was impatient to be on his way. "What would I be doing coming from the *Sietch*?"

"The Devil knows these days." The Cossack sergeant shrugged. "Hmm. Well, you'd better go on up and see the colonel, then. He'll know what to do with you."

"What colonel's that?" Zjendjan asked cheerfully, bold as brass, and shrugged in his own turn. "And what do I want him for?"

"Old Colonel Loboda, our commander here. The Grand Hetman wants him to question anybody that looks like he's coming from the *Sietch*."

"Alright." Zjendjan grimaced but thought nothing of it. These Cossacks were regulars, part of the Hetman's army. He didn't think he had anything to fear now that he was back on this familiar ground. Tchehryn looked just as it did when he saw it last and such gloomy thoughts as those that troubled his master didn't belong among ordinary people in a peaceful town. "Take us to him, then."

The soldiers took him to a house near Dopul's tavern, the same noisy drinking place of the local gentry where he'd gone to fetch the fat, one-eyed knight on his master's orders, and he settled down in an anteroom to wait for the officer who was to question him. He waited a long time, fidgeting and yawning. He wasn't worried but he wanted to start for Rozloghi while it was still daylight; the idea of riding through those dark woods and that ghostly, boulder-strewn ravine at night and alone didn't appeal to him. He started fretting and grumbling about the delay when the doors of the inner chamber were flung open and the officer appeared. Zjendjan took one quick look at him, recognized Bohun, and felt as if his knees had suddenly turned to water.

"Colonel Loboda's away on business," the Cossack said. "I'm in charge here today. So what's this all about?"

Zjendjan's mouth fell open. He blinked rapidly but the unwelcome apparition didn't disappear. He tried to make himself as inconspicuous as possible while the boatswain of Pan Grodjitzki's galley handed Bohun a package of letters and explained that they were for the Hetman.

"From Kudak?" Bohun peered at the sealed package with curiosity. "And what does Pan Grodjitzki want from the Grand Hetman?"

"That I wouldn't know, colonel," the old sailor said.

"Hmm. Well . . ." The Cossack ataman turned the oilskin package in his hands, staring at the writing, and it was suddenly clear to Zjendjan that he couldn't read. "Well, it all seems in order . . ."

"Yes sir." The sailor bobbed his head and reached for the letters and Zjendjan released a long, cautious breath. "So can we go now, colonel?"

Bohun nodded and reached into his sash for the customary gold-piece with which Commonwealth garrison commanders rewarded a Grand Hetman's messenger when the street door rattled open and Pan Zagloba burst into the room.

"Hey, Bohun, listen!" the fat knight boomed and waved an earthenware demijohn over his bald head. "That traitor Dopul hid his best mead from us! Told me we'd drunk it all! Well, I had him take me down to his cellar for a look, and what do you think I saw? Hay and straw piled in a corner. '*And what's that over there?*' I asked him. '*Straw and hay,*' he says. '*Straw, is it?*' I said. I took a closer look and what did I find? The neck of a pretty jug sticking out of all that cattle fodder like a Tartar lurking in the grass! '*Oh you dog,*' I said, '*so that's your game, is it? You'd lie to the gentry?*' Well, I told him, there's a game that both of us could play. '*You eat the hay because you're as stupid as an ox, and I'll drink the mead because I'm a man!*' And that, to make it short, is just what happened. Ha! Anyway, I brought a jug along for a little sampling!"

And Pan Zagloba cocked one fist at the hip like a village dancer, raised the demijohn over his head with the other hand, and began to hop about and sing in a loud, hoarse voice.

"Hey Yasia, Hey Kasia, bring me a glass
And give me a kiss without any fuss . . .!"

Then he caught sight of Zjendjan in the back of the room and lowered the jug carefully to the table. "Ah, and who's this? Ha, as God's my witness! Aren't you Pan Skshetuski's lad?"

"Whose?" Bohun said quickly.

"Skshetuski," the fat old knight explained cheerfully. "A lieutenant of Prince Yeremi's. He's gone down to Kudak on some kind of mission. But before he left he treated me to a mead like I never tasted before or since! But what's happening with your master, lad? He's well, I hope? Hmm?"

Zjendjan wished the babbling old knight would drop dead or go to the Devil but, either way, it was now too late to hide his connection with Skshetuski. "The master's well," he muttered with an eye on Bohun. "And he . . . ah . . . told me to give you his regards, sir."

"Did he! Did he, now!" Pleased to be remembered, Pan Zagloba stroked his shaggy beard. "Well, that's good of him. That's a fine man, your master, lad. A fine cavalier. But what are you doing here in Tchehryn if he's still in Kudak?"

Zjendjan's face turned scarlet and he did his best to avoid Bohun's piercing stare. "The master . . .. well, you know how masters are, sir," he mumbled. "He had some private business to take care of in Lubnie. So since there wasn't much for me to do in Kudak that's where I am going."

"I know your master too," Bohun said quietly. "I met him in Rozloghi."

"Where, sir?" Zjendjan twisted his head to the side and cocked an ear as if he had trouble with his hearing.

"In Rozloghi."

"The Kurtzevitch property," Pan Zagloba added helpfully.

"Whose?"

"I see you've gone deaf all of a sudden," Bohun said in a cold, dry voice.

"Ah . . . no. No." Zjendjan blinked, yawned and stifled a quick, nervous shudder. "Not exactly, sir. Only I'm awful sleepy . . ."

"Is that so?" Bohun's tone was amiable enough but Zjendjan

felt as if there were hot irons glowing in the Cossack's eyes. "So you say your master's sending you to Lubnie?"

"Yes sir. That's what he's done, sir."

"Ah!" Pan Zagloba broke in to relieve the tension. "He probably has some little squirrel hidden away at court there, eh? And he's sending the boy to keep an eye on her. Let me tell you, friends . . . and I speak from experience, even though the foolishness of my hot-blooded youth may seem unlikely to someone who's known me only in my dignified maturity . . . there's nothing like a woman to make a man as fretful as a dog with fleas."

"Who knows sir!" Zjendjan broke out in a sweat, cursing the day he ever met Zagloba. "Maybe he has someone there, and maybe he doesn't!" Then he bowed hastily and turned towards the door. "Well, it's time for me to be going. God bless you both, kind sirs."

"And you too," Bohun murmured softly. "But wait a minute. What's the sudden hurry? And why didn't you tell me that you're Pan Skshetuski's servant?"

"Why? Why sir?" Zjendjan peered about desperately and edged towards the door. "Well . . . you didn't ask me, did you? No, you didn't. So I thought why should I waste time babbling about things nobody wants to hear? Wouldn't make much sense, would it? So that's why I didn't say anything about it. Well, I'll be going now sir, if it's the same to you."

"Wait, I said!" Bohun snapped. "And did your master give you any letters?"

"Eh? What was that? Letters? Well, maybe he did." Beads of sweat stood out on the boy's round face. "And maybe he didn't . . . It's for a master to write letters if he feels like writing and for a servant to deliver them. But only to those to whom they're addressed. So if it's all right with you gentlemen I'll just be on my way."

But Bohun's thick dark brows narrowed suddenly; he clapped his hands with a crack as loud as a pistol shot and half a dozen Cossacks rushed into the room.

"Search him!" he shouted and pointed at the boy.

"Help! Murder! Let me go!" the boy yelled and struggled in the grip of the Cossacks. "What is this? Let me go, I tell you! I'm from the gentry too! I know my rights! You'll hear from a tribunal about this, gentlemen!"

"Hey, Bohun, leave him be," Pan Zagloba urged, not at all pleased at the turn that events were taking. "The boy's right, you know. This could get quite serious."

But in the meantime one of Bohun's Cossacks found two letters inside Zjendjan's coat and handed them to his ataman. The grim young colonel dismissed his men at once; it was obvious, even to someone as frightened as the boy, that he didn't want them to know that he couldn't read.

"Who's he writing to?" Bohun asked Zagloba.

The fat knight weighed the letter in his hand for a thoughtful moment then closed his blind eye as if taking aim. He read out the name of the old *Knahina*.

"So, little bird," Bohun hissed at Zjendjan with an icy smile. "You never heard of Rozloghi, eh? And you're going to Lubnie?"

"I've heard what I've heard," Zjendjan muttered, stubborn to the end. "And I am going where I was told to go."

"Should I open this thing or what?" Zagloba stared at Bohun. "Breaking a noble's seal is no joke."

"The Grand Hetman ordered me to look at all papers," Bohun said. "Open it up and read it."

Zagloba broke the seal, unfolded the sheet and began to read: "'Dear Lady . . .' hmm . . . 'Know that I've come safely to Kudak from where, with God's help, I'll be leaving for the Sietch today.' Bohun, this is a private letter. It's none of your business."

"Read it," the Cossack hissed.

"Very well. 'But before leaving I must share some of my worries with you since they affect you all. I'm anxious about Bohun and what might happen to you in Rozloghi from him and his cut-throats . . .' hmm, I'd say he has a right to worry . . . 'And since it looks as if a great war might come upon us any day, and the mobs might rise up in rebellion, I beg you to waste no time but to leave at once, today if you can, even if the Steppe is not yet dry enough for comfortable travel, and place yourself and Helen under the protection of the Prince at Lubnie . . .' Bohun,"—the fat knight looked suddenly uneasy—"you're sure you want me to go on with this?"

"Read it, damn you!"

"Very well. 'I know that I won't come back in time to see you safely on your way . . .' hmm, yes, that seems likely . . . 'so I beg you to take no more chances with Bohun who won't be fooled for ever, but take the girl whom you've promised to me out of his reach at once. The

Prince is sure to garrison Rozloghi so that your property will also be protected . . .' and so on, and so on. Then he signs it. Phew!"

Here Pan Zagloba mopped his glistening forehead, fanned himself with the incriminating letter, and cocked his one good eye at Bohun who seemed stunned with shock.

"Well, Master Bohun." The fat knight grinned. "It looks like the lieutenant wants to fit you out with a pair of antlers and make a cuckold out of you even before a wedding. So you were both after the same girl, eh? Why didn't you tell me? But take comfort, these things happen every day. It even happened to me in my time, though you might find that hard to believe these days seeing as I'm the soul of propriety and decorum. Hey, let me tell you . . ."

But the tale died unfinished on Zagloba's lips as he took a better look at Bohun. The Cossack sat behind the table as still as a statue. All the blood drained out of his face which was contorted beyond recognition. His eyes were shut as tight as if he'd suffered a blow beyond enduring, and deep angry lines changed his livid features into a mask of hatred.

"Hey, what's wrong with you?" Zagloba said uneasily. "Are you sick or what?"

But the Cossack waved him impatiently into silence. "Read the other letter."

"That's . . . ah . . . to the Princess," Zagloba began.

"Read it," the Cossack grated out in a thick, hoarse voice.

"Well, all right." Pan Zagloba shrugged. He cleared his throat and shot another quick glance at the Cossack. "Here it is, then. *'My dearest, beloved Helen, my love and my Queen . . .'* Bohun, believe me, you don't want to hear this."

"Read it, damn you, read it!"

"Alright, then. *'Since I'm still not done with the Prince's business, I'm writing to your Aunt, urging her to take you to Lubnie at once, so that no harm may come to you from Bohun, and so that our love and future happiness won't be placed at risk . . .'*"

"Enough!" Bohun shouted and leaped to his feet.

Madness seemed to seize him. A short-handled iron mace flashed in his clenched fist, struck Zjendjan in the chest, and the boy moaned, clutched his heart and crashed to the floor. The fat knight bellowed in sudden terror of his own, snatched up the demijohn and jumped for shelter behind the clay stove in the corner of the room.

"In the name of the Father, the Son and the Spirit!" he howled from his refuge. "What's the matter with you? Calm yourself! Go pour some cold water on your head! Have you gone mad? Calm down! Do you hear me? Ah . . . what the devil . . .!"

"Blood!" Bohun roared.

"Have you lost your mind? Get hold of yourself, man! You want to smell blood, do you? You've got it right here, you mad dog! Look at that poor boy, he's done for, what more do you want? Has the Devil got into you, or what? Calm down, will you! And if you can't do that then go hang yourself, and the quicker the better!"

★ ★ ★

Cursing and yelling, Pan Zagloba edged around the table to where the boy lay fallen on the floor and started checking him for cracked ribs and mopping the blood that burst from his mouth. Bohun, meanwhile, was howling like a wolf, his fists in his hair, and then he leaped towards the door, kicked it open and ran into the hall outside.

"Ah go, go," the fat knight muttered, kneeling beside the boy. "Go smash your head against a stable wall, since that's just about all it's good for. Or better yet, go to the Devil and be done with it. Ha! Talk about mad dogs! I've seen a lot in my time but never anything like this, that's certain. Ah . . . hmm . . . that poor lad is still alive, still breathing, thank God. This mead ought to help him. If a fine liquor like this doesn't get him back on his feet then he lied about being a member of the gentry."

Muttering and talking to himself, Pan Zagloba pillowed Zjendjan's head on his knees and began to pour the mead slowly into the boy's mouth.

"Now we'll see what kind of blood you've got, laddie," he went on. "A Jew's blood mixed with a noble liquor turns bitter and boils, everybody knows that. Peasant blood, being thick and sour, sinks to the bottom and that's the end of it. But noble blood comes into its own and turns into a fine elixir that clears the wits and pumps courage into the body. Our good Lord Jesus knew what he was doing when he gave different kinds of drink to different kinds of people so that each might be consoled according to his nature."

Zjendjan groaned and stirred and the fat knight smiled and nodded with satisfaction. "Ah, you want some more, do you?

Good. Good. But wait a moment, will you? A physician has to cure himself as well as his patients." He raised the demijohn to his mouth, tilted his head back, and took a long and satisfying swig.

"Ah . . . hmm . . . yes. That's better. A noble liquor, like I said. And now that you've decided to come back from the dead, my poor little friend, I think I'd better get you hidden in some quiet corner before that Cossack madman comes back and tears you to pieces. Ha! That's dangerous company, I can see that now. So let him find his own road to Hell while I take another. His hand is a lot faster than his wits, that's certain."

So saying Pan Zagloba hoisted the boy in his arms as easily as if he were a child and carried him outside. A dozen Cossack troopers who were throwing dice in the cobbled courtyard rose respectfully when he nodded to them.

"Trying your luck, I see, eh?" he said and smiled kindly. "Good. Good. You never know when it'll turn on you. Why don't some of you put this poor, unlucky lad on some clean straw somewhere, hmm? And how about one of you running for a surgeon?"

The Cossacks jumped up to carry out his wishes as he knew they would. As Bohun's friend and constant boon companion, his standing among them borrowed much from the superstitious awe in which they held their legendary leader.

"Good lads," he said. "Christian charity earns you merit in Heaven and that makes the dice roll better for you too. But where is your colonel?"

"He called for his horse and went off to the regiment," the Cossack *esaul* told him. "Told us to saddle up and be ready to ride, sir. Which we are."

"Ah . . . so my horse is ready too?"

"That's so, your honor."

"Get him here, then." It was time to look for less dangerous company, the fat knight decided. "You say I'll find the colonel at the barracks?"

"Yes sir. But here he comes now."

"Hmm. Does he, now. Too bad."

Looking out through the dark tunnel of the courtyard gateway Pan Zagloba saw Bohun riding at a trot from the direction of the city square with a hundred Cossacks clattering behind him.

"Mount up!" Bohun shouted at the remaining soldiers. They ran for their horses and Zagloba strolled out beyond the gate and aimed a careful glance at the Cossack leader.

"You're going somewhere?"

"Yes."

"And where's the Devil taking you this time, if I may ask?"

"To a wedding."

"Hey, son, take care." Zagloba drew nearer and dropped his voice to a worried whisper. "Think about what you're doing. The Hetman told you to watch over the town and here you are, not only riding off yourself but taking your men with you. The mob can hardly wait to get at our throats. You're putting the whole town at risk and furthermore you're violating orders. The Hetman isn't going to like this, you know."

"To Hell with the town," Bohun snarled. "And with the Hetman too."

"Your own head's at stake, man."

"So to Hell with my head!"

Zagloba stepped back, wondering what to do. He realized that talking would do no good; the angry Cossack was in no mood to listen. Moreover the shrewd, old knight had a good idea where this sudden expedition was heading and he didn't want any part of it. But what choice was there? To go with Bohun looked like serious trouble and Pan Zagloba wasn't fond of risking his neck. To stay behind in Tchehryn promised nothing better; the restless, muttering *tchernya* was waiting only for news from the *Sietch* before they rose up to massacre the gentry; all that kept them quiet so far were Bohun and his soldiers. Pan Zagloba knew that he could take shelter with the Hetman's army but he had his own reasons for keeping his distance. Perhaps it was a matter of some injudicious bloodletting in the past. Or perhaps a little harmless juggling of accounts. Whatever it was he preferred not to draw official attention to himself, feeling that the foolish sins of hot-blooded youth shouldn't be allowed to intrude on the well-earned peace of maturity and wisdom.

He cursed the need to make a decision. He was fond of Tchehryn where no one ever asked any awkward questions and where he could drink and hobnob with the local gentry and the Cossack elders as much as he liked and for as long as their money lasted. True, the Cossacks started disappearing lately, and the gentry hardly dared to stick their noses beyond their own gateposts, but there was always Bohun with whom to drink, gamble and kick up his heels.

And now what? Should he stay or go? But was there really that much of a choice? When it came to waiting alone in Tchehryn for some peasant butcher to slit his throat, or riding into the unknown with the angry Cossack, he knew he'd go with Bohun any day.

"Maybe I'll manage to hold him back a little," Pan Zagloba muttered in his beard. "Temper his rashness, so to speak. Guide him with sound advice and keep him out of the worst kind of trouble he's likely to get into on his own. And keep myself out of trouble along with him, of course."

That way at least, he thought, he might avoid having his throat cut for a little longer.

"Alright, then," he said. "I'll go along with whatever you're getting yourself into, since it doesn't look as if you can think straight just now in any event. Maybe there'll be something useful I'll be able to do. Rein you back or something. Who knows? You and I fit each other like a hook and an eyelet, anyway, or like two sides of the same bad coin. So how can we be parted from each other, hmm? Still, I don't mind telling you, all this is something I never expected."

Bohun said nothing. Zagloba shrugged and went to get his horse and in half an hour two hundred Cossack troopers stood ready to march. Bohun rode out to the head of the column and Zagloba followed along behind him. Groups of impassive peasants watched the soldiers riding out of the town, muttering to each other and trying to guess if they'd be coming back or if this was the moment for which they were waiting: the time when the town was unprotected and theirs to loot and pillage.

Bohun rode in silence, locked within himself and as dark and gloomy as a winter night. The Cossacks didn't question where he might be leading them or why; they'd follow him anywhere, Pan Zagloba knew, even to Hell if need be.

★ ★ ★

They got themselves ferried across the Dnieper and rode out to the Prince's highway, jogging at a trot and sending thick yellow clouds of dust into the sky behind them. But the parched heat of the day soon streaked them and their horses with black bands of sweat. The long, ragged column spread out along the road like a tattered rope, and Bohun moved far ahead as if to gnaw on his anger by himself; and the fat knight who was bored, dripping sweat, and missing the sound of his own voice galloped up to join him.

The young Cossack's face looked calmer and that was a good sign. Zagloba breathed easier. Bohun was sad but at least the murderous rage that seized him when he heard the letters seemed to have subsided, and to dissipate in the blue-green distance that stretched farther behind them with each passing hour. He appeared to find a strange solace in the hot Steppe wind that scorched their hands and faces.

"What a furnace!" Zagloba complained. "Phew! It's hot enough out here to melt the tallow out of a Tartar's boots! Even this cotton shirt of mine is soaked to the last thread. Bohun? Hey, Bohun, listen for a minute."

The Cossack turned his dark, sad eyes on Zagloba as if he was waking from a troubled sleep.

"Watch yourself, son," Zagloba advised. "Take care that the *melancolia* doesn't eat you up. When bad humors leave the liver, which is their proper *locum*, and rise to the head, they can do damage to your wits. Phew! Hmm . . . I didn't know that you were such an ardent lover. Who'd have guessed it of you? You must have been born in May, the month of Aphrodite, which boils the blood and stirs up all the juices so that even something as dry and prickly as a thistle starts thinking about making little thistles, while men born in May are particularly susceptible to women. Are you listening, Bohun?"

The Cossack didn't say a word, as if he didn't hear, and Zagloba nodded and went on anyway, pleased to be talking whether anyone was listening.

"Nature is nature, as the ancients said. But success in matters of the heart usually goes to him who can control himself and does things patiently and slowly, as I could tell you from my own experience. Now's not the time for it, of course, and that kind of story is best told over a jug of wine, so I'll just tell you this much: give up your hard feelings. Maybe you've a right to an explanation, I'm not saying the girl's kin doesn't owe you that much, but is she the only girl in the entire world? Seems to me the last time I looked the place was full of them."

Bohun shook his head like a man in a dream. His voice was so low and so bereaved that he seemed to be replying to his own mournful thoughts as well as echoing Zagloba.

"One little bird . . . only one in the world . . ."

"Hmm? What? Well . . . even if that was so . . . Once she starts chirping for another man that's the end of you. Listen, son, the heart's a volunteer, it serves where it wants to, and that's all there's to it. Give some thought also to who and what she is because, as I hear, there's some fine blood in her veins. The Kurtzevitch line stems from real princes. Those are high thresholds, my lad."

"To Hell with your thresholds!" Bohun cried out then. "Devil take your bloodlines and your coats-of-arms! This,"—and he slapped the hilt of his saber—"is my pedigree. That's my law, my title, my matchmaker and priest too if I need one. Oh you damned lying dogs . . .!"

"Wait a minute," Zagloba stirred uneasily. "Wait a minute, will you? I haven't played any tricks on you, have I?"

But Bohun's furious stare was fixed once more on his inner turmoil. "So the Cossack was good enough for you when it came to fighting and sharing out the loot!" he cried out in fury. "He was good enough for raiding the Crimea! Then he was your brother, a son to your mother, and you promised him the girl and his happiness. And now what? Along comes a *Lah*, and what's the worth of all your promises? What happens to your Cossack brother? You cast him off, tear the heart out of him. The girl is for another and the Cossack can gnaw his own guts and chew on his fist! Ah, it's Hell . . . it's Hell, I tell you!"

Then there was silence in which Bohun's harsh breathing became as heavy and as difficult as if it was struggling out of a cave deep under a mountain. His pain and fury clawed at his untamed pride and inflamed his impulsive nature and Zagloba waited until he calmed down.

"What will you do then, you poor man?" the fat knight asked softly. "What will you do?"

"There's the Cossack way!"

"Hmm . . . I can see where that's likely to take you. But no matter. I'll tell you just one thing. This is Vishnovyetzki country, a stone's throw from Lubnie. Skshetuski wrote to the old woman to place herself under his protection, and that's not a man to trifle with, my lad."

"The Khan's also not a man to trifle with but I've trifled with him!"

"What?" Zagloba paused, astonished. "You'd take on the Prince?"

"Hmyelnitzki is going to take on the Hetmans, isn't he? So what's your Prince to me?"

Pan Zagloba was now sweating in earnest and the day's heat didn't have much to do with that. His reasonable, conciliatory manner wasn't getting him anywhere with Bohun and he was feeling worse and worse about his own prospects. '*How the Devil did I get myself mixed up with this madman?*' he chided himself. Things were turning out far from the way he liked them; there was a distinct smell of a hangman's noose about this situation, and he could see no way out of it for himself.

"*Tfui!*" He spat in disgust. "Ah, what the devil! This smells of rebellion. Nothing else. A clear case of *vis armata* and *raptus puellae*, or armed incursion and abduction followed by outlawry or *rebelia* . . . That's a one-way sleigh-ride with a hangman, a gibbet and a noose, my lad, a fine *troika* if you like the high road, but it won't take you far on the straight and level. The Kurtzevitches aren't going to let you take them either without a stiff price."

"So what?" The young Cossack's voice crackled with indifference. "Either they'll die or I will. Ey, I tell you, I'd have given my soul for them, those Kurtzevitch liars. They were my brothers, and that false old bitch was like my mother to me. I stared into her eyes like a dog! I'd do anything she wanted! Who do you think went to the Crimea to get Blind Vasil back for them? I did. I loved them and served them like a slave because I thought I'd earn the girl that way and they sold me out like a slave. They drove me out like a peasant that's done his work and deserves no thanks. So alright, I'll go. I don't belong among them anyway. But first I'll bow to them, down to the ground like a Cossack, and thank them for their bread and salt. And I'll pay them for it like a Cossack before I go my way."

"Where can you go, you lost soul, once you've picked a quarrel with the Prince? To Hmyelnitzki's camp?"

But Bohun was still speaking to the bitter images he saw in

his mind and these seemed to be more than just Helen's kinsmen.

"Aye, I'd have been your brother, your Cossack dog, your saber . . . you'd have owned my soul. I'd have taken my own men and called out others like them from all over the Ukraine and all the lands beyond it, and . . . hey! Hey! I'd take them against Hmyel and my own Zaporohjan brothers and scatter them like dust under your boots! And what would I want for that? Nothing! Just the girl! And the open Steppe. To live in peace somewhere, left alone and leaving everybody else alone to their business . . . But now . . . but now . . ."

"Now you've gone mad," Zagloba said quietly.

The Cossack said nothing. He slashed the flanks of his horse with his short rawhide whip and galloped ahead. Pan Zagloba was left alone to some glum and uncomfortable thinking of his own.

★ ★ ★

"Well here's a fine stew I've fixed for myself," he muttered in gloom. "But it looks like I'm in it up to my neck this time and the Devil's going to have a fine time chewing on my bones."

There was no doubt in his mind that Bohun meant to lead an armed raid on Rozloghi, avenge his betrayal and carry off the girl. That, as Zagloba knew, was a criminal matter but it wasn't necessarily as dangerous as it sounded; incursions and abductions weren't all that uncommon in the Ukraine and there was always a chance that the abductors might escape the hangman. True, things got far more complicated when the offending party wasn't a member of the gentry but where was the law to look for a Cossack? The Steppes were endless. A criminal could vanish in them as easily as a fox until some great war started up somewhere and all court verdicts went into abeyance. Then he could surface, redeem himself in battle, and even earn new merit and distinctions.

"And just because I'm along for the ride doesn't make me guilty," Pan Zagloba said.

But the trap into which the fat knight had fallen was tighter than that. Zagloba knew that if Bohun carried off the girl who was the fiance of the Prince's favorite, he'd be declaring war on Vishnovyetzki, which meant that if he wanted to survive that war he'd have to run to Hmyelnitzki and join the rebellion.

"And that," the fat knight muttered squirming on his saddle, "is yet another matter. Drinking and raising Hell with Bohun and the Cossacks is one thing, particularly if they're fool enough to pick up the tab, but murdering my own kind is something else again.

"*Tfui!*" he spat and went on muttering and cursing. "The Devil himself must've cooked up this weather! Hell couldn't be much hotter . . .! Well, I've had my fun twisting his tail and now he's taking his turn on my neck, and it looks like he's going to twist it right off. . . May lightning hit that Cossack! He's got a face as pretty as a woman's and a hand as murderous as a Tartar's. What a mess! Damn those Kurtzevitch double-dealers and damn all their women. How come they've had to show up in my life? What do I need them for? And what does that whole affair of theirs have to do with me? If that young Cossack devil feels the itch to get himself married let him get married and be damned to him! I'm not marrying anybody, am I? But I'm going to get it in the neck no matter who got this trouble started . . ."

He could see no safe way out of his dilemma no matter how he turned and twisted in his saddle, nor how loud he cursed, nor how desperately he mopped his sweating head.

"Phew, it's hot. And it's going to get a lot hotter for me, I can see. Vishnovyetzki will have a new drum stitched out of my skin if I go with Bohun. And if I leave Bohun, the mob will stuff my hide with straw and use it for a scarecrow, or he'll do it himself if the fancy strikes him! I can see where it's all going to lead me and it'll serve me right! That's what you get for hobnobbing with the lower orders. I've played the fool with a mad, Cossack hothead for a drinking partner and the time's come to pay my own tab for a change. Well, right now I'd rather be this dumb horse I'm sitting on because only a damn fool would want to be Zagloba."

With such dismal thoughts for company Pan Zagloba's good humor left him altogether. The sun burned down on him as if to give him a foretaste of a roasting spit. His horse began to groan and stagger under his slack weight. He was wet with sweat all the way down into his boots and he wished that he was anywhere but here.

"My God," he groaned. "What wouldn't I give right now to be sitting in the shade of a tavern arbor with a tankard of cold beer in my hand! Instead I'm frying in the sun, shaking all the wind out of my empty belly on this worthless nag and bouncing to God knows where in a Godforsaken wilderness . . . and with nothing but a gallows to look forward to."

Meanwhile the sun slid into the hottest quadrant of the afternoon and the galloping horses began to fail and falter. Bohun urged his riders to push on regardless but the exhausted animals themselves brought about a pause. The long, ragged column of galloping Cossacks slowed down on its own and the cavalcade staggered to a halt.

Then Bohun called his *esauls* and sergeants together and rode off with them into the Steppe to give them their orders.

Chapter Seventeen

THE PAUSE in the headlong gallop was barely enough to cool off the horses and to let the riders stretch their aching muscles. None of the Cossacks knew where they were going but they didn't care; they'd follow Bohun into hellfire, Pan Zagloba knew, and he urged his own animal towards the cluster of Bohun's lieutenants where he heard the last few words of his instructions to them.

" . . . a pistol shot. That'll be your signal."

"*Dobre, bat'ku,*" they murmured. "We know what to do."

Bohun turned suddenly to Zagloba. "You'll ride ahead with me?"

"I will?" Zagloba's gloomy prospects threw him into such a fit of hopelessness and futility, and landed him with such an irritating presentiment of disaster, that nothing mattered to him anymore.

"Well . . . why not? Since I've already sweated out one half of my soul in this mad ride of yours I might as well sweat out the other half. What else can I do? You and I are like a coat and lining, stitched together for good or for evil, so let the Devil take us both together! And the sooner he does it the better, I'm thinking, because Hell itself couldn't be much hotter than I feel right now."

"Let's ride, then."

"Let's break our necks, for all that I care. It's all one to me."

They set out at a gallop.

The Cossacks followed at a slower pace so that they soon fell behind and vanished in the dust cloud, and Bohun and Zagloba galloped on in silence. Each of them was preoccupied with his own thoughts. Zagloba tugged angrily at his mustache, shaking his head and muttering now and then, and peering sideways at the Cossack ataman on whose dark, wind-burned face a deep, regretful sadness and a savage fury appeared and reappeared like a light in a signal lantern. An odd thing, Pan Zagloba thought. Here was a hero straight out of a story book, as handsome as a painting on a chapel ceiling, and he couldn't bend one girl to his will . . .! True, he was just a Cossack, but he was also a famous soldier, a legend in the best romantic traditions of the Steppe, and it was only a matter of time before he got his patent of nobility. All he had to do was keep his nose out of the rebellion and a brilliant future was his for the asking. Skshetuski was a good catch for any girl but he was no match for the young Cossack either in looks or in dash and fire.

"Hey Bohun," the fat knight asked suddenly. "How well d'you know Skshetuski?"

"I know who he is," Bohun said abruptly.

"You won't have an easy time with him, I'll testify to that. I saw him break down a door one time with Tchaplinski's head. He's a tough nut to crack, my lad, make no mistake about it."

The Cossack made no answer. Both men retreated once more into their own thoughts, and only Pan Zagloba broke the silence for a time, muttering: '*Mmm . . . Yes . . . There's just no other way.*' The afternoon edged into evening as they galloped on, the sun dipped steadily towards Tchehryn behind them, and from the wide-open spaces to the east came a light cool breeze to drive the worst of the heat from the departing day.

Zagloba shivered then. He took his lynx-fur cap off his sweating head, passed a hand across his skimpy hair, sighed and said again: "That's how it has to be, then. There's no other way."

Bohun looked up at him, startled as if waking. "What did you say?"

"Nothing. Just that it'll be dark any minute now. How much farther is it?"

"Not far."

The sun began to set soon afterwards but they were already in a narrow, wooded defile with a few pale lights shining at the far end among the trees.

"That's Rozloghi," Bohun said suddenly.

"Yes?" Zagloba shuddered. "It's cold here all of a sudden, don't you think?"

"Hold up a minute," Bohun said and reined in his horse. Zagloba looked at him and shuddered again. The Cossack's eyes glowed in the sudden darkness like a pair of torches.

"What are we waiting for?"

But Bohun didn't answer. The two men sat quietly on their weary horses until the muted jingles, creaks of leather, and clicks and rattling of sabers drifted towards them from the ravine behind, and the long line of Bohun's soldiers appeared in single file beside them. Bohun once more whispered his orders to the *esauls*. Then he spurred ahead and Zagloba followed. A moment later their horses' hooves were clattering among the low, stooped cabins and outbuildings of the silent village where tallow candles flickered dimly behind a few windows. From the invisible orchards came the sweet scent of apples, flowers and blooming cherry-trees; the still, fragrant night lay about them in a deep, unsuspecting sleep. The manor was also silent; not even a dog was barking behind the palisade. A great full moon shined on the grey thatched roofs, turning them to silver.

Then the two riders halted in the shadow of the shuttered gateway.

"Who's there?" a watchman cried out.

"Don't you know me, Maksym?" Bohun called up softly.

"Ah, it's you, Your Honor! God be praised!"

"For ever and ever," Bohun replied quietly and Pan Zagloba found himself shuddering again.

The gate hinges groaned, the wooden bridge rumbled down across the broad ditch, and the two horsemen rode into the dark, flat space beyond the palisade.

"Hey, Maksym, listen," Bohun said as they passed the watchman. "Don't bar the gate, you hear? And don't pull up the bridge. I'm leaving right away."

"Ah, just a short visit then, Your Honor?" The watchman used the old-time phrase, dating back to the vanished ages when men borrowed fire from a neighbor's hearth to start up their own: "Like you've come for fire?"

"That's it. That's just what it is."

★　★　★

The young Kurtzevitch princes and the old *Knahina* were still at supper in the hall-of-arms that ran the full width of the manor house, stretching all the way from the entrance on the *maydan* side to the cherry orchard that began just beyond its windows. Only two of the old woman's four sons were at home that week: Symeon, who was down with a fever, and Mikolai, the youngest. Both of them leaped to their feet when Bohun and Zagloba walked into the room, while their mother's face showed a mixture of astonishment, irritation, and the fleeting shadow of a sudden fear.

"Bohun!" she cried with an uneasy smile. "What are you doing here?"

"I've come to see you again, *maty*," he said evenly. "Aren't you glad to see me?"

"Well, yes, of course I'm glad," the old woman said, still ill-at-ease and peering warily into Bohun's eyes. "I'm . . . just surprised, that's all, because I thought you were on duty in Tchehryn . . . Ah, but who's that with you?"

"That's Pan Zagloba. A noble, and a friend of mine."

"Well, make yourselves at home," the old woman said and nodded at the benches around the great oak table. "You're always welcome here, you know that."

"Ah my good lady," Zagloba intoned, eying the heaped platters, cups and flagons scattered about the table. "It's true that a guest coming as late as we, is about as welcome anywhere as a Tartar. But if a person wants to go to Heaven he or she must keep a hospitable home and welcome travelers at whatever hour. And feed the hungry. And, above all, make sure that the thirsty have plenty to drink!"

"So eat and drink," she said with gruff simplicity which, like her welcome, rang as false as a lead coin in Zagloba's ear. "There's enough here for any number. Only it's such a surprise to see you, that's all. We didn't expect you . . . But is there something special you want from us, Bohun?"

"Could be," he said quietly.

"So what is it?"

"Ah, we'll have time to talk about it later." The Cossack smiled at the fidgety old woman with such disarming candor that Pan Zagloba started wondering if he changed his mind. "Just let me rest a little, mother. Catch my breath. Get that good feeling a man gets when he's home again among his loving friends. We've come as fast as our animals could take us all the way from Tchehryn."

"You hurried, eh?" the *Knahina* said uneasily. "Must be a pressing matter . . ."

"Where else would I hurry if not here, *maty*?" the Cossack said softly. "This is my home, isn't it? You're my family, aren't you? And Princess Helen, how is she? In good health, I hope?"

"She's fine," the old woman said.

"It'll be good to see her one more time," Bohun murmured.

"She's asleep."

"Is she? That's too bad. Because I can't stay long tonight, you see."

"And where're you going?"

"To the war, mother! To the war!" There was something so ghastly in his sudden smile that Pan Zagloba knew the Cossack hadn't changed his mind about anything. "The Hetmans are likely to call me any time. Hey, it'll be a pity to fight our Zaporohjan brothers, don't you think, young princes? Weren't we all good brothers at one time, eh? Them and us? Didn't we go to war together and drink together and go together after the Sultan's goods? And now we've got to hate and kill each other. Isn't that a pity?"

The old *Knahina* threw him another wary glance, wondering perhaps if he was thinking of joining the rebellion and if he came to sniff out which way the winds were blowing in Rozloghi.

"So what do you have in mind to do?" she asked cautiously.

"Do, *maty*? What can a man do? It's hard to kill your kin, your own kind. But if you must, you must."

"That's the way we see it," Prince Symeon said.

"Hmyelnitzki's a traitor," young Mikolai added.

"And to Hell with all traitors," Bohun said. "Isn't that the way for a good man to think?"

"To the Devil with them," Zagloba threw in.

"*Na Pohybel!*" the two young princes shouted out in chorus.

They bent in silence over their food again and Zagloba nourished a fleeting hope that Bohun might have reconsidered his decision after all. But the young Cossack colonel began to speak again.

"Yes. Yes. That's how it is these days in the world. Today's loving friends are tomorrow's traitors. There's just nobody a man can trust anymore."

"Only honest people," the *Knahina* said quickly.

"Yes. Only honest people. Like you're honest people. That's why I trusted you and believed everything you ever said to me because you're honest people. Not liars and traitors."

There was something so strange and chilling in the Cossack's voice that a long silence followed, while the two young princes stared at each other with wide-open eyes. The old *Knahina* fixed her sharp, nervous gaze on him and Pan Zagloba started blinking at her even faster and harder than before.

"War's a hard-hearted mother," Bohun went on softly. "Not like you, *maty*. She's cruel to her children. That's why I've come here to see you all once more before I rode out. Who knows if I'll come back, eh? And you'd be sorry if I didn't, wouldn't you, because I'm like kin to you, am I right? I've been like a son and brother to you, haven't I?"

"As God's our witness!" The *Knahina* didn't let her eyes slip off Bohun's even for a moment. "We've known you since you were a boy."

"You're our brother," Symeon added and Mikolai nodded.

"Yes," Bohun went on softly as if to himself. "You're old-time princes here, you're all highborn gentry, but you opened your hearts to a nameless Cossack like he was your own. You didn't treat him with contempt like a common peasant. You gave him a family and a home and you promised him a girl of your own blood because you knew he couldn't live without her. You took pity on him."

"That's nothing," the *Knahina* said quickly. "It's not worth talking about. Forget it."

"No, *maty*," Bohun went on quietly, shaking his head slowly from side to side. "You're wrong there, mother. It is worth talking about and I won't forget it because you've been my friends and my benefactors and I want to prove myself worthy of your kindness. I've asked this gentleman here, this good friend of mine, to take me for his son so that I can be a noble too, so you wouldn't feel ashamed to give me your own flesh and blood like you promised me. To which Pan Zagloba has agreed, and so the two of us will go together to the Grand Hetman and ask him to speak for us in Warsaw like he's already done for Kshetchovski."

"May God also help you," the old woman murmured.

"Oh he will," Bohun said. "He will. He can look into people's hearts and tell good men from traitors, just like I've learned to tell honest people from cheats and betrayers. I know you're all good people here, not liars and deceivers, but before this war gets going good and proper I want to hear you tell me one more time that the girl is mine. That she's promised to me and not to another and that you'll keep your word. A noble's word isn't made of smoke. It doesn't blow away with every new wind. And you're more than just simple gentry here. You're old-time chiefs, you're princes. So your promise ought to be that much better, right?"

The Cossack's words fell slowly, one by one, with the chilling weight of stones dropped into a well, and his voice thickened and deepened with each phrase.

No one else said anything. Pan Zagloba kept his head down and his good eye fixed on the plate before him. The *Knahina* and her sons sat staring at each other like wolves in a trap who hear the trapper's footsteps nearing in the forest. And suddenly the great Berkut eagle that slumped on his hoop against the far wall uttered a shrill cry although the hour was still far from dawn, and all the other raptors in the hall awoke and started to beat their wings and to caw and scream. The fire died down in the hearth. The light dimmed and the chamber was full of threatening shadows.

"Mikolai, fix the fire," the *Knahina* said in an unsteady voice.

The young prince tossed an armful of fresh logs into the fireplace.

"Well?" Bohun said. "What about it, *maty*? Will you promise her to me again?"

"We'll have to ask her first," the *Knahina* muttered.

"I'll ask her later. She'll speak for herself. Now I'm asking you."

The old woman turned her wide, frightened eyes on her sons and they, in turn, watched her as if in a trance.

"Well then," she muttered slowly. "We promise."

"We promise," the young princes chorused.

The Cossack sighed. He turned to Zagloba.

"And now you ask them," he said so softly that the others leaned forward to hear him. "Go on, ask them for the girl. Maybe they'll promise her to you as well!"

"What is this!" the *Knahina* cried. "What's the matter with you? Are you drunk or what?"

But Bohun drew Skshetuski's letters from inside his coat and threw them on the table in front of Zagloba.

"Read them!" he ordered.

Pan Zagloba picked up the crumpled sheets, smoothed them out and began to read them aloud to the others. No one spoke while he read. No one broke the silence that settled like a judgment in the hall when the fat knight finished. Guilt crept out like a reptile on the *Knahina's* face. Her cold, pebble eyes, were now alight with fear. They fixed themselves to Bohun's pale face, while her two sons watched her for a signal, poised to leap at one word like a pair of mastiffs.

"Who's to have the girl, then?" Bohun snarled.

"Bohun . . .!" she cried, her terror in the open.

"Traitors!" he roared. "Deceivers! Liars whose word can't be trusted!"

"Arm yourselves, lads!" the woman screamed in fury and despair while the two young princes jumped to their feet and ran for the weapons hanging on the walls. "To arms, boys! Fight him! Kill . . .!"

"Wait! Wait . . .!" Pan Zagloba scrambled up from behind the table, mead spilling from the tankard in his hand, as he peered about for some corner in which he could hide. "Be calm, I beg you . . . just a moment there . . ."

But before he could think of anything that might mend matters, or at least postpone the disaster, Bohun drew a pistol from his belt and fired.

" . . . *Jezu*," Symeon groaned, dropped his saber and staggered in mid-step.

He lurched towards Bohun with one more weak, tottering pace, his outflung arms flapped in the air like the wings of a stricken bird, and he crashed facedown to the floor.

"Help! People! Here!" the old woman screamed, calling for her household, but her voice died, unheard, in the sudden rattle of musketry from the gate. Galloping hooves drummed in the *maydan* and the cherry orchard, and the outer rooms and corridors echoed with shouts, screams, yells, pistol shots and the clash of sabers. Almost at once all the doors and windows burst inward with a crash and several dozen Cossacks leaped into the chamber.

"*Na Pohybel!*" yelled the savage voices.

Out in the yard the gate-bell began to sound the tocsin. Dogs howled. The chained birds in the hall screamed and beat their wings. And then the shouts, curses, yells, pistol shots, and the dull thud and clatter of bodies falling to the floor, replaced the earlier sleepy silence of the manor house.

★   ★   ★

The fierce, uneven fight was over almost as soon as it began. *Knaz* Symeon died first. The old *Knahina* was choked to death by the Cossacks who jumped on her and pinned her to the floor as she clawed her way, howling like a she-wolf, to her murdered child. The powerful young Mikolai defended himself with a savage fury until Bohun shoved his men aside, leaped on him like a lynx, and sabered him down after a sharp duel. The Cossack yells and cheers mingled with the howling of the manor servants and then the looting started.

Bohun was like a man in a trance or like one whose worst nightmares had suddenly come to life. His men ran wild and he let them do whatever they wanted. He had been slashed twice across the head in his fight with Mikolai, and now he leaned against the door that led to Helen's rooms, barring the way and staring at the slaughter with despairing eyes. The floor was heaped with corpses and slippery with blood. The walls were stripped bare as his Cossacks dragged their loot outside. Even the hawks and falcons hung strangled from their perches. Smoke and the reek of gunpowder drifted through the hall and Bohun's panting breath sounded like a sob. His face was splashed with blood, most of it his own, and streaked black with gunsmoke, and his sad, uncomprehending eyes swept with a curious resignation across the bodies of the dead young princes and the old *Knahina*.

And suddenly the door behind him opened and the mad, blind Prince Vasil appeared with a crucifix held above his head. Beside him, eyes and mouth wide with terror and as white as the linen shift in which she was dressed, was Helen.

Bohun stepped back at once.

"In the name of the Father, the Son and the Holy Ghost," the blind man cried in a voice of such hopeless sorrow that it seemed as if a spirit of judgment and retribution stepped into the chamber. "In the name of the Holy Mother . . ."

The Cossacks stumbled back at once, crying out with superstitious horror, as the red eye-sockets of the apparition turned emptily towards them.

" . . . And you, do you come in God's name?" the martyred

man went on. "What news do you bring us? Are you the apostles? Because it's written: '*Blessed is he who walks along the roads spreading the Word of God . . .*' "

"*Hospody pomyluy,*" muttered the awed Cossacks, while Vasil turned slowly in front of them with the crucifix held before his face.

" . . . Woe to you, brothers, if you've come to make war for vengeance or profit . . . Pray for mercy for you will be damned! Woe to you . . . woe to all of us . . ."

"*Hospody pomyluy*! God save us!"

Awestruck Cossacks fell to their knees on the bloody floor and made desperate signs of the cross across their chests and shoulders while others stumbled from the room as if they'd seen a ghost.

"Stand fast . . .!" the white-faced Bohun cried out suddenly and swayed on his feet.

They turned to him at once.

"*Bat'ku*! You're wounded!"

"That's right," he whispered. "But it's not much . . . just lost some blood, that's all . . . Hey, lads, watch after this girl like she's your own life, you hear me? Surround the house. Don't let anybody leave . . ."

Then his lips turned the color of ashes. The whites of his eyes flickered upward in his bloodless face. He looked at Helen, uttered one short, pleading cry as if trying to explain something terribly important and, at the same time, beg her forgiveness and her understanding, and collapsed into the arms of the Cossacks who crowded around him. Zagloba was beside him almost instantly, emerging from whatever hiding place he'd found during the massacre, and taking charge at once.

"Find a bed for the ataman!" he ordered. "Carry him gently now. That's it. That's it. Get me some bread and cobwebs to stop the blood and then get out of here! Go find yourselves some women to play with outside. I'll take care of him here. He'll be as good as new tomorrow, you'll see, now get out! Get out! Come on now, get moving!"

★ ★ ★

Two Cossack *esauls* carried their unconscious young commander from the room and the rest pushed their way outside into the courtyard where the squeals and laughter of the manor women promised new amusement. Pan Zagloba looked swiftly around, found that no one was looking at him in that moment, stepped up to Helen and winked furiously at her with his one good eye.

"Don't be afraid," he whispered. "Trust me, I'm a friend of Skshetuski. Just put your Holy Man to bed and wait for me in your room, do you understand? I'll be along as soon as I can."

Then he followed the *esauls* who carried Bohun into an adjoining bedroom and laid him with great care on a trestle bed. When some other Cossacks came running with the bread and cobwebs, the fat knight kneaded these two traditional borderland remedies into a sticky poultice and started dressing the young Cossack's wounds with all the confidence and skill of a practiced surgeon.

"Hmm . . . Hmm . . ." he muttered, feeling Bohun's skull while the worried *esauls* peered across his shoulders. "Nothing's broken. Not much damage there. Don't worry about him. Tell the men that your ataman will be just fine tomorrow. True, he's cut up a bit, lost a lot of blood, but there's lots more inside. Tomorrow's his wedding day, even though we'll have to do without a priest, so see to it that the boys celebrate it properly! Find the cellars and break out the liquor, understand? Make sure that everybody gets plenty to drink to the ataman's good health. Now get out of here and let your colonel get a little rest."

The *esauls* bowed, relieved, and backed out of the chamber.

"And don't drink up the whole cellar!" Zagloba shouted after them. "Make sure there's something left for me!"

Then he sat down on the bed beside the helpless Bohun and nodded at him thoughtfully and gravely.

"Well," he said. "It looks like the Devil won't get you this time. Hmm. Hmm. Too bad. Yes. You'll survive. But you won't be able to stir hand or foot for two days, that's certain. Yes, yes, my lad, the saber didn't want to steal you from the hangman's noose because that's where you're heading, and that's why you and I are going to part company.

"That's right," he went on. "You've a good head for drinking, I'll grant you that much, but not for much else. So you thought that I was going to burn down manor houses with you, eh? No, no, little brother. I may have done a lot of questionable things but that's where I draw the line. Look for company among your own cut-throat kind because murdering young boys and strangling old women just isn't my trade. When they do finally have you dancing on a gibbet, the Devil will make a draw-string puppet out of you to amuse his children, but I've got better use for my throat then getting it shaved by a heads-man's axe."

Bohun groaned then, his face as white as the sheets on which he was lying, and Pan Zagloba jumped back in alarm but the Cossack was too weak to move.

"Ah, feel like moaning, do you?" the fat knight inquired. "Go ahead and moan. You'll moan a lot harder tomorrow, you damned pagan soul, when you look for that pretty little bird and find she's flown away. Hmm. Hmm. So you've acquired a taste for the finer things, have you? Can't say I blame you. That's a tasty little dish if I've ever seen one but she's not for you. Indeed, if I can't think of a way to get her to safety—and myself too, of course, that goes without saying—then I'll trade my head for a milk-churn and sell my wits to the Jews to use as glue for mending cracked pots at a country fair."

Too weak to lift an arm or even to move his head, Bohun was staring at him all the while with horror-stricken eyes in which a slow and terrible understanding appeared and grew, and then gave way to rage and a furious hatred. He made a huge effort to struggle up in his blood-soaked bedding. But Pan Zagloba pushed him down without any trouble and then trussed him up with his own belt and sash.

"Hold still," he muttered. "You might hurt yourself, thrash-ing around like that. Can't have that happen, can we. And just in case you strain yourself by shouting we'd better stick some-thing into your mouth as well. Why don't you bite down on your cap for a while? Hmm? Ah yes, that's better. That'll hold you quiet. I ought to cut your throat right now and be done with it but why should I deprive the hangman of the pleasure? Besides, murdering helpless people in their beds is a peasant pastime, which is something you'd know more about than I."

Coarse laughter and the shouts and squeals of drunken men and women came through the shuttered window from the yard outside, and the fat knight listened to them for a moment then nodded and smiled.

"Aha, so you've found the cellar, have you, my thirsty young cut-throats?" he asked, grinning at the ceiling. "Good. Good. Drink yourselves blind and go to sleep like good little children. I'll do your watching for you here . . . and outside as well."

So saying, Pan Zagloba strolled out of the house to see how well the Cossacks were obeying his order to help themselves to the contents of the manor cellars. They had bonfires burning all across the yard, and he could see open vats and barrels of mead, vodka, wine and raw spirits everywhere. The Cossacks crowded around them, dipping out the liquor with quart tins and buckets. Others, already drunk, were chasing the manor women up and down the *maydan* amid shrill bursts of laughter that sounded like the neighing of wild mares.

"That's it! That's it!" the fat knight urged them on from the manor porch. "Go to it! Don't spare the barrels, you can't take them with you! You live just once, lads, and only God knows how soon that's likely to be over!"

The dancing Cossacks laughed and leaped among the fires while others cheered Pan Zagloba and pounded on the barrels with tin drinking mugs.

"U-u-ha! U-u-ha!"

The shouts grew louder. Dogs barked. Horses neighed. Women screamed and giggled. Oxen bellowed, slaughtered in dozens for the feast, and far beyond the rim of the light cast by the blazing bonfires, stirred the dark, silent mass of the Rozloghi peasants who had run up from the village to see what was happening. They didn't come to defend their masters— they'd hate them too much for that, Pan Zagloba knew—but they stood in a thick, muttering crowd just outside the firelight, whispering and nudging each other towards the liquor barrels, and edging cautiously out of their sheltering darkness.

"U-u-ha!"

★   ★   ★

The celebration grew wilder as the hours passed and soon the Cossacks didn't bother to use panikins to draw the liquor from the broken barrels but plunged their heads into them up to the neck and drank the raw spirits straight from the source like horses watering in a stream. Many were already reeling about and tripping over each other. Others fought and squabbled over bits of loot, or lay in stupor among the cooking fires, or staggered about in pursuit of the women who either fled across the fires or let themselves be pulled about and doused in the barrels. Pan Zagloba nodded with satisfaction on the manor porch, then cast a glance at the clouded sky.

"Hmm. Good and dark," he muttered. "Once the moon's set not one of them will be able to tell his own mother from a brood mare."

Then he descended slowly off the porch and moved towards the barrels and the staggering Cossacks.

"That's it, boys!" he shouted. "Drink it up! Have yourselves a time! No use saving it for a rainy day, you might not live long enough to see one! A man's a tràitor if he doesn't get drunk tonight to the ataman's good health! U-ha! U-ha! Go to it!"

"U-u-ha!" howled the Cossacks.

Zagloba peered around and suddenly cried out: "But what's this? What's this? So you're all getting soused as boars in a mudhole and those poor lads on watch aren't getting even a sniff of the good stuff? Where's your heart, boys? Where's your Cossack love for each other, hmm? Relieve the posts at once! Jump to it, d'you hear?"

Two or three dozen Cossacks staggered off to obey the order and, in another moment, the relieved sentries hurried to the barrels eager to make up for lost time.

"That's it, lads!" Pan Zagloba urged them. "Drink up! Enjoy yourselves!"

"We thank you kindly, master," they replied in chorus, dipping their panikins and canteens in the liquor barrels. "We thank you!"

"Change the posts again in an hour," Zagloba told the grinning *esauls*. "Understand?"

"Aye, sir." The sergeants and lieutenants nodded and saluted. "We'll change them."

"And get drunk yourselves!"

None of the Cossacks questioned Zagloba's right to give orders in place of the wounded Bohun. This wasn't the first time he'd acted as deputy to their colonel. Besides, the troop officers and sergeants liked the easy-going fat knight because he didn't know the first thing about discipline, always let the men do whatever they wanted, and cheerfully accepted the responsibility for everything they did while under his orders.

Meanwhile, Pan Zagloba sauntered benignly among the Rozloghi peasants who swept their caps off their heads and bowed to the ground before him.

"Hey, peasant," he turned loudly to a gnarled old man. "Is it far to Lubnie?"

"Aye, master. It's far."

"Can a man get there by morning?"

"No, master."

"How about by midday?"

"Maybe. More like by afternoon."

"And how does one get there?"

"There's the highway, master."

"Ah . . .!" Zagloba shouted. "So there's a highway, is there? All the way to Lubnie?"

The old peasant shrugged. "*Knaz* Yarema said there was to be a highway so there is one. And since he wanted it to go to Lubnie that's where it goes."

Zagloba spoke especially loud so that some of the nearby Cossacks would hear and remember. Then he told them to let the peasants drink some liquor too.

"But first get me a little mead," he ordered. "I feel the morning chill creeping into my bones and God only knows when the next good barrel is likely to come my way."

One of the Cossacks carefully filled a two-quart copper mug with mead, placed it on his own crumpled cap, and brought it to the fat knight in both hands. Pan Zagloba sighed. He seized the brimming mug with reverence, raised the rim to his mouth and tilted his head back until the bottom of the panikin was pointing at the stars.

The Cossacks grinned and nudged each other.

"You see that? Didn't even take a breath . . ."

"*Serdysty Lah*. He's got a heart in him."

"Uh-ha! He drinks like a Cossack."

Meanwhile Zagloba's head continued to tilt backwards until the mug was empty and his face was crimson and shining with sweat.

"Ah . . ." he said. "Hmm. Yes."

Then he wiped his mustache carefully with both hands and sighed with satisfaction, having discovered once again that magical elixir he liked to talk about, the one which added fire to a noble's wits, gave strength to his body, and filled his heart with courage.

"Hmm . . . Not bad. Not bad at all," he murmured. "Quite well aged, in fact . . . It's a shame to waste such a good *Troyniak* on a peasant throat, my lads, so leave it to me. Raw spirits are more to your taste anyway, I am sure, and since that's why God made them it'd be a sin for you to complain. Ah . . . ah, but I'm beginning to feel much better about everything. Yes, it's a fine mead."

He motioned to the Cossacks to keep drinking and paced slowly through the entire courtyard, inspecting everything with the care of a good commander. He crossed the drawbridge to check on the outposts, found the sentries snoring, and nodded with contentment.

"Quite so," he mused. "Drunk as hogs, every one of them. I could truss one up and take him along for a body servant but I'd better not. He'd probably turn out to be a thief or a lazy lout. Or worse yet, he'd drink too much and fall asleep on duty. It's too bad, but that's the way people are turning out everywhere these days. There's just nobody to trust anywhere."

Then he paced slowly back to the silent manor, looked in on the roped, gagged and unconscious Bohun, and made his way quietly to Helen's rooms where he let himself in without a sound.

Chapter Eighteen

LATER THAT NIGHT two horsemen slipped quietly through the dark ravine, taking pains to make as little noise as possible. They picked their way carefully among the boulders and through the treacherous deadfall of uprooted trees that threatened to break their horses' legs at almost every step.

The night was black as pitch. There was no light at all. The moon had hidden long before in the heavy clouds. The cautious riders could see only two or three paces in front of them, and their nervous horses tripped and stumbled in the thickly matted undergrowth and the tangled roots that covered the dark floor of the wooded defile. But once the trees thinned out and the valley opened into the silvery emptiness of the Steppe, the larger of the two riders whispered hoarsely, "*Ride!*" and kicked his own mount into a gallop.

They flew like two Tartar arrows after that, skimming the flat, open country, and pursued only by the pounding echoes of their horses' hooves. Dark shapes loomed out of the night around them; thick clumps of oak clustered near the highway and grasped at them with gnarled, skeletal arms like something from a nightmare. It must have seemed to the two speeding riders that they were standing still, frozen in mid-step on motionless horses, and that the Steppe itself had come alive under them, drifting and falling away behind them in the darkness.

They spurred their weary horses on and on as the hours crept into the morning until their mounts began to press their ears flat along their heads and their heaving breaths thickened into a dry, rattling sound. It was clear, then, that neither the animals nor their headlong gallop could be kept going much longer without a break.

"No help for it," wheezed the larger of the two darkly silhouetted riders. "We have to give them a breather or they'll drop."

The far horizon began to turn pale and vast distances emerged from the shadows as the light seeped gradually into the ebbing night. The gigantic Steppe thistles, some of them towering as tall as the horsemen, loomed out of the departing darkness and began to nod coldly in the morning breeze. The round, black domes of ancient burial mounds and the sparse stands of gaunt, windswept trees rose out of the greying landscape. And as the harsh new light grew and brightened it revealed the faces of the fleeing riders.

"No help for it," Zagloba repeated. "The horses are dead tired. They came a long way yesterday and they can't run much farther. We'll lose them altogether if we keep pushing them like this."

Then he threw a glance at his slim companion.

"But let me look at you by daylight," he went on. "Ho ho, where did you get that smart little outfit? You make a very handsome little Cossack, my lady! As long as I've lived I've never had a groom like you but I'm afraid Skshetuski will take you away from me fast enough! Ay, ay, but what's this? For God's sake, my girl, roll up your hair, will you? Anybody with one good eye in his head would guess what you are no matter how you're dressed!"

Helen reached back with both hands for the cascade of long black hair that spilled out behind her like a flying cloak and started stuffing it under her Cossack cap.

"Where are we going?" she asked.

"Wherever our horses take us."

"Aren't we going to Lubnie?" Fear showed briefly in her pale face. Distrust reappeared in the quick, sharp glance she threw at Zagloba.

"No, we're not."

"But that's where you said last night . . ."

"I said a lot of things last night. To you and to anyone who'd listen and that included Bohun. Look, I've a brain of sorts in my skull, and the one thought that's always rattling around in there

is '*Never run to where they're going to chase you.*' Why not?
Because they might catch you. If Bohun's men are already after
us, which they might be if they've sobered up, they're heading
for Lubnie. Why? First because that's the obvious place we'd
run to, and second because that's what I wanted them to think.
So we'll go towards Tcherkassy, not Lubnie, and by the time it
dawns on them they're chasing shadows on the Lubnie highway
we'll have gained a couple of days' start. In the meantime we'll
get to Tcherkassy where the regiments of Pan Pivnitzki and Pan
Rudomin are quartered. And if that's not enough to roll in
Bohun's way, we've got the whole of the Hetmans' army in
Korsun, a stone's throw from there."

"I understand," Helen said and smiled with such open
warmth and admiration at the fat old knight that he wished he
was thirty years younger.

"I don't know who you are or how you came to be with
Bohun in Rozloghi," she went on, "but I think that God must
have sent you especially to protect me and to save my life. I'll be
grateful to you for that as long as I live."

"Your life was never threatened, my lady. Not by Bohun.
He'd die himself before he'd let any harm come to you, I'll give
him that much credit."

"He'd die if he touched me," Helen said so simply and with
such firm conviction, that Zagloba, who knew something of
the mettle of the border women, didn't doubt it for a moment.
"Or I would, because I'd kill myself before I let that murderer
come near me."

"Yes," he said. "I believe you'd do it. So maybe I did save
your life after all. And his own too, it seems, though he won't
thank me for it. Stealing you away is like ripping the heart right
out of his chest. He's obsessed with you."

"What did I do to deserve that?" Anger and bitterness competed in her voice with disgust and shame. "I've known him for
years and I've never felt anything for him except fear and
loathing. Why won't he leave me alone? Aren't there any other
women in the world?"

"Not for him, it seems."

"And now he's murdered my whole family because of me,"
she cried. "Dear God, when I think about that . . . ah, what can
I do? Where can I go to get away from him? Forgive my
complaining, but there has to be an end to this somewhere!"

A wave of crimson swept into the young woman's face, and tears of pain and anger shined in her eyes and then spilled out and flowed down her cheeks, squeezed out by helplessness and humiliation.

"I can't argue that a terrible misfortune fell on your family," Zagloba said quickly. "But in some measure the fault was their own. They shouldn't have promised you to the Cossack in the first place. Once he found out the truth he went off his head and that's all there's to it. But I'm sorry about your brothers, especially that young one. He was practically a baby but you could see he'd have grown into a fine knight."

Helen began to weep in earnest then, unable to hold back her bitter, angry tears.

"Hey, hey, my lady," Zagloba said kindly. "Your tears don't go with the clothes you're wearing. So dry them and just tell yourself that what happened couldn't be avoided. It was God's will, that's all. What's done is done and God will punish the murderer in his own good time. Come to think of it, some of that punishment has already touched him since he's lost all hope of ever changing your feelings about him."

Here the fat knight grew silent for a moment and peered about uneasily as if expecting ambush. "But I hate to think what'll happen if he ever gets his claws on me. Phew! He'll have my hide tanned and dressed thin enough to have dancing pumps sewn out of it. You don't know this, my girl, but I've already been martyred once in Galata, by the Turks, and I don't need another ticket to salvation.

"Yes, I admit," he went on, "it would be fine if we could go straight to the Prince in Lubnie. There's no doubt that's the quickest way to safety. But is it the best way? Bohun's groom woke last night when I was getting the horses, he could've got them going after us and they'd have caught up with us in an hour. And then what? Eh? That doesn't bear thinking about, believe me. That Bohun's a wild dog, let me tell you. I'd rather meet the Devil in person then come face to face with him again."

Calmed down a little and forcing her own anxiety and grief back under control, Helen responded to the fat knight's worried muttering with firmness and courage.

"God will save us from him."

"Let's pray he does. But Bohun's sealed his own fate now, and no mistake. He abandoned Tchehryn against the Hetman's orders, and that's worth a court-martial and a firing squad at a time like this, and now he's tangled with the Prince as well. I don't envy him. The only road open to him now is joining the rebellion and even that might be too late from what I heard in town. Zjendjan met the Hetmans' fleet under old Barabas and Kshetchovski going down the Dnieper, and young Pan Stefan Pototzki was leading the *husaria* overland a day or two behind them. That was at least ten days ago. They could've crushed the Cossacks already by this time. We were expecting to hear the news any minute in Tchehryn."

"So it was Zjendjan who brought those letters from Pan Yan in Kudak?" Helen asked.

"That's right. A shrewd, clever lad, if ever there was one. Reminds me a little of myself when I was a boy. It was plain bad luck that he ran into Bohun like he did."

Pan Zagloba's voice dropped a little then as he remembered another piece of bad luck that Zjendjan encountered. "Once Bohun heard those letters and knew what's been going on behind his back that was the end of any cleverness. He laid out the boy with one blow of a battle mace and went off to settle his accounts with your relatives as if all the devils from Hell were after him. Even I couldn't reason with him."

"The poor lad!" Helen cried. "More innocent blood spilled because of me . . ."

"Don't you fret about him, my lady," Zagloba said quickly, anxious to gloss over his own role in the affair. "He'll be alright. He'll live. And he's sharp enough to find a way out of his predicament once he's back on his feet."

"When did it all happen?"

"Yesterday morning, though right now it seems like another lifetime. Hey, for Bohun to kill or knock down a man is like tossing down a drink. One gulp and it's done and that's the end of all arguments about it. Ah but you should've heard him howling when he heard those letters! A madman, I tell you! All of Tchehryn must've been shaking with the noise he made."

★ ★ ★

They said nothing for a while after that. Daylight was bright all around them by this time and they could see all of the Steppe before them. The air was crisp and fresh. The horses, moving at a walk through the tall wet grass, snorted with contentment.

"Well, let's get on the highway and run them for a bit again," Zagloba suggested. "They've had their breather and we've no time to waste."

They kicked their animals into another gallop and ran along the road for about a mile when, suddenly, a small dark object appeared on the skyline before them and began to approach them at great speed.

"What's that, eh?" the fat knight peered uneasily into the bright new daylight although the sun was at their backs and the hurtling object came out of the west. "What can that be about? Ey, that's a man on horseback!"

A closer look revealed that the speeding object was, indeed, a horseman heading towards them from the direction of Tchehryn as if the air were on fire behind him. His head was bent low over his horse's neck and his face was hidden in the flying mane which he clutched with one hand while the other flogged the animal in the utmost panic.

"What kind of mad devil is that, then?" Pan Zagloba reined his horse to a halt at the roadside and Helen paused beside him. "And what's his damned hurry? Well, I'll just draw and cock a pistol in case we need to slow him down a little . . . Ah, but he'll kill his horse if he goes on like that much longer."

Then, because the panicked rider was now within thirty paces of Helen and himself, the fat knight pointed the huge horse-pistol and shouted: "Hey! Stop! Pull up, there, will you? Who the devil are you?"

The rider hauled back on his reins and at the same time sat up in his saddle. "Pan Zagloba!" he cried out. "Don't you remember me? I'm Plesnyevski, I work for the *Starosta* in Tchehryn!"

"Eh? What? What? Hey, is that you, Plesnyevski? I wouldn't have known you. But what are you doing all the way out here? And where are you going as if all Hell was galloping behind you?"

"Run for your life!" the new arrival shouted. "Turn around and follow me or you'll ride right into that Hell yourself! It's Judgment Day behind me!"

"What's that? What?" Pan Zagloba glared at him, alarmed and

bewildered. "What Hell? What Judgment Day? What's this all about?"

"Tchehryn's been taken by the Zaporohjans! The mobs are butchering the gentry! It's God's judgment on us all, I tell you!"

"In the Name of the Father . . .!" The fat knight's mouth fell open. "What's that you're saying? Are you drunk? Have you lost your wits?"

"Young Pototzki's dead!" the fugitive gasped out. He was out of breath and nearly out of his mind as well. "Pan Tchar-nyetzki's taken prisoner! The Tartars are riding with the Cos-sacks . . . Tuhay-bey . . . Hmyelnitzki . . .!"

"And old Colonel Barabas and Kshetchovski's corps? What happened to them?"

"The old man's been murdered. Kshetchovski's gone over to Hmyelnitzki. They're in Tchehryn right now . . . an enormous army. Krivoinos left with a huge force last night to attack the Hetmans. The whole country's on fire, the peasants are rising everywhere . . .! It's slaughter . . . murder . . . wherever you look! Run for your life while you can because God only knows how long we've got left!"

Zagloba's mouth hung open but he couldn't find a word to say. "Jesus and Mary!" he whispered finally, too frightened and confused for much more than that.

"My God, my God," Helen began to pray.

"Run for your life!" Plesnyevski cried again. "Get away while there's still some place left to run to!"

"Run . . . yes. Run. But where?" Zagloba stared about as shocked and bewildered as if a boulder had fallen from the sky and struck him on the head. "What's still safe? Where?"

"In Lubnie, where else? With the Prince! That's the only place I'd trust these days!"

"Is that where you're going?"

"That's right. To the Prince."

"Ah, may the Devil take all this!" Zagloba shouted in utter desperation as all his shrewdly calculated plans fell apart around him. "The road to Lubnie isn't quite as safe as you think it is! Not since this morning! And where are the Hetmans?"

"Near Korsun, falling back and gathering up whatever gentry managed to get away. But old 'Hooknose' Krivoinos is sure to have caught up with them already."

"To the devil with Krivoinos!" the fat knight bellowed in exasperation. "May he burst along with his nose—hooked, crooked or whatever! So that way's closed too?"

"Heading for Korsun right now is like crawling down the Devil's throat. It's pure hell out there! I'm running as fast as I can to Lubnie because I can't think of any other place where there's still some protection."

"Well, make sure you go around Rozloghi," Zagloba remembered to advise. "Because Bohun's there. He's joining the rebellion too."

"My God, he too! They were saying in Tchehryn that all the *tchernya* in the Transdnieper country is going to rise up any day as well . . ."

"Is that so?" Zagloba muttered, tugging at his mustache. "Yes, that's sure to happen. Well, you go your way and I'll find another because I've got to start thinking about my own skin."

"That's just what I'm doing!" Plesnyevski cried out and struck his horse with his whip again.

"Remember to bypass Rozloghi!" Zagloba shouted after him. "And if you see Bohun don't tell him you saw me!"

But Plesnyevski was already beyond the reach of his voice.

★ ★ ★

It was rare for Zagloba to be at a loss for a new idea, or to admit that any obstacle or problem might be too much for his sharp wits or his ready tongue, but at this moment he was almost ready to throw up his arms and sink into despair.

"Well," he said at last and started cursing himself as much as the situation in which he was trapped. "What now? Eh? I've squeezed out of some tight corners in my time but I've never been in a spot as unpromising as this one. Hmyelnitzki ahead of me and Bohun behind me . . . *tfui*! That's a choice? I wouldn't give one broken groat for any part of me right now, front *or* rear! I was a damn fool not to take you straight to Lubnie while we had the time. We might have made it too. But no, I had to outsmart a bunch of drunken peasants who are getting ready right now to use my neck for a whetting stone. That's what comes of trying to live by one's wits, you end up dancing in the air on the end of a rope. *Tfui*, I tell you! What the devil are we to do now? Where can we go? My brains aren't worth the price of boot-grease at this moment. I can't think of one quiet corner in this Commonwealth where a man could die in his own bed and in his own good time. Ah, Devil take all this!"

Helen was just as frightened and bewildered as Zagloba but she was the first to regain her senses. "My two stepbrothers, Yur and Fedor, are in Zolotonosha," she offered. "Couldn't we get help there?"

"Where? What?" The fat knight was ready to grasp at any straw. "What was that you said? Zolotonosha? That's even farther than Tcherkassy. But when we've nothing better and closer to hand we might as well go to Zolotonosha. Ah, Devil take it, what a mess."

"Don't give up now," Helen begged him.

"Give up? Who's giving up?"

With some kind of goal in mind and his quick wits responding to a fresh idea, Pan Zagloba brightened up considerably.

"Of course we'll have to leave the highway, that's the first thing to do. We'd be safer going cross country anyway no matter where we're heading. Hmm. Yes. This is all starting to look a lot better to me. We aren't likely to meet many people in the woods and in the open Steppe, not at this stage in the rebellion anyway, and those we can't avoid we can handle in some other way. How? We'll get across that bridge when we come to it. That's why God gave us heads in the first place, to think with and not just so we'd have something on which to wear a cap. But I'd give anything if we could just find ourselves some quiet spot somewhere where we might lie low until the Hetmans finish with Hmyelnitzki!"

"We may yet," Helen said. "Remember how well you've done for us so far. God didn't let you take me out of Bohun's hands just so we'd die for nothing somewhere else."

"You think so, eh?" Confronted by the girl's courage and determination, the fat knight had no choice but to play the man. "Ah, ah, my lady, wait . . . I feel my spirits rising. Ah, that's better. Perhaps things aren't as bad as they seem. What? It could be worse, eh? Someday when we've the time I'll tell you what happened to me in Galata, and then you'll see that my head isn't entirely useless. But right now we've got to get off this highway, that's for sure. So turn off, my lady . . . that's it! That's the way! By God, you ride like a real Cossack, it's a joy to see it.

And the grass is so tall out here in the Steppe that nobody will even know we're here!"

The lush Spring grass was soon towering so high over them that they vanished from sight altogether. But the farther they rode into the Steppe, and the deeper they sank into that dark green ocean of tangled vegetation, the harder it became for their horses to run without stumbling, so that at last they had to halt and dismount to let their animals get a little rest.

★ ★ ★

Zagloba unsaddled the horses and let them wander off to feed and roll themselves on the dark, damp soil where the sun never reached through the tall thick grasses. Then he unpacked the saddlebags where he had stowed provisions for the journey. At the sight of food and a panikin of something stronger than spring water, his good spirits returned immediately.

"Everyone needs refreshment for the flesh as well as the spirit," he began. "People as well as horses. Let them eat the grass and we'll have some of this bread and roast beef I took last night out of your aunt's larder. And a good thing I did. There's an old saying, *'On an empty belly your wits turn to jelly.'* And another says: *'For a brain that's fickle, try roast beef and pickles.'* Well, my brains were pretty fickle yesterday because it's clear that we'd have done better to go straight to Lubnie. But what's done is done and there's no point in worrying about it. And Zolotonosha might not be so bad anyway. They've a nice little fort there, I remember, though the tavern isn't worth a visit, and the Hetmans might have put a garrison in there to keep an eye on things. The Prince will also be on the march by now, to support the Hetmans."

"I don't think things are bad at all," Helen encouraged him. "God will look after us and good people will help us and we'll get out of it all alive, I am sure."

"But dear God," Pan Zagloba worried. "Have there ever been such dreadful times? A civil war is the worst kind there is. In a day or two there won't be a quiet hole for a mouse to hide in throughout the whole country, and if a mouse is going to have a hard time finding a hiding place, what about a knight of my girth and size? I tell you, I'd have done better to become a priest, to which I had a certain calling in my youth since I'm a naturally peaceful, modest and abstemious man. I could've been a cathedral dean by now since I've a fine singing voice and a flair for liturgy. But fate chose otherwise. In my younger days I was quite irresistible to women. All I had to do was toss one look at a girl and she'd think she was struck by lightning! Ha! If only I could shrug off twenty years, Pan Skshetuski would have something to worry about! Ah, but eat, my lady . . ."

So saying, the fat knight spread out the cold meat and bread on a saddle-blanket and pulled a short knife out of his boot to divide the rations.

Eating, he went on talking. "I must say, though, that you make a shapely little Cossack. No wonder all these good-looking young men are biting off each other's heads about you. Phew, but it's getting hot. It's going to be another furnace of a day, that's certain."

"How long have you and Pan Skshetuski been friends?" Helen wished to know.

"Not long. But we liked each other at first sight. I was with him when *Starosta* Tchaplinski got on his wrong side in Tchehryn, and he . . . granted that he'd drunk a bit in jolly company . . . caught that braying braggart by the neck and the seat of his pants and banged him so hard against the door that all of Tchaplinski's bones jumped out of their sockets!"

"He did that?" Helen laughed.

"Oh he's a fiery cavalier, and no mistake about it! Pan Zachvilihovski also told me that your fiance is a great knight and the Prince's favorite, which doesn't surprise me because our Prince Yeremi is known for the fine men he picks. And I could see for myself, having some experience in military matters, that he's a great soldier too. Phew, but it's getting hot."

The sun was, indeed, blazing like a bed of coals high above the Steppe and the day promised to be just as hot as the fat knight feared.

"I enjoy your company, my lady," he sighed, "but I wish we were already in Zolotonosha. I think we'd better lie low in the daytime and travel at night. We've a long way to go. I wonder, though, if you can stand such hardships."

"I'm in good health," the young woman said at once. "I can stand the journey. We could start out right now, if you're ready."

"Well, in that case I'll saddle up again." Pan Zagloba packed up what was left of their provisions and got to his feet. "I won't feel safe until we get to the Kahamlik and hide in those reeds. The Devil himself wouldn't be able to find us in there. We've got about a mile to get to the river and tomorrow we can see about getting ourselves across it."

He stretched, yawned, sighed and scratched his balding head reflectively.

"I've got to tell you, though, I'm getting awfully sleepy. My last night in Tchehryn wasn't exactly an uneventful one, all of yesterday I spent in the saddle shaking my bones behind that damned Cossack, and last night we were on the road from Rozloghi. Ooof, I'm so tired I don't even feel like talking anymore. So I think I'll doze off for a bit on this sorry nag as we ride along."

"Good," Helen said. "Do that. I'll watch as we're riding."

* * *

They were no sooner mounted and on their way again among the tall grasses when Pan Zagloba began to sway and pitch in his saddle like a ship at sea. The heat, his fatigue, and the soft hiss of the parting grass-stems pushed aside by the broad chests of the walking horses, lulled him so that he sighed and mumbled for a bit and closed his worn eyes. Finally the old knight broke out into wheezing snores and his head dropped down on his chest.

Helen let herself drift off into thought.

Despite all her courage, she was bewildered, worried and numbed at times by fear, and the images in her mind filled her with pain and horror. Last night's events and the miracle of her escape fell on her so swiftly, following each other with such intensity and speed, that she didn't have the time to piece them together and come to terms with what was happening to her. The raid on Rozloghi, the scenes of murder she had witnessed there, the horror and the certainty of death by her own hand, the unexpected rescue, and now the flight across the Steppe into the unknown, came suddenly together to strike her like a single terrifying storm.

And there was even more to find out about before she could have anything like peace of mind. Who was this man who rescued her? And why did he do it? She knew his name but that didn't tell her anything; it explained neither the man nor his motives. How did he happen to be in Rozloghi with Bohun?

Did they come together? If so, it meant he was one of Bohun's friends, perhaps a murderer himself. He certainly had the rag-tag look of doubtful reliability and few of those qualities that might justify her trust. But if that was the case, why was he risking the terrible Cossack's enmity and vengeance? He was quite right, she knew, in believing that Bohun would skin him alive if he ever caught up with the fugitives. So why did this strange old man take such a dreadful risk on her behalf?

She was confused. It was too much to grasp as quickly as she had to if she was to understand everything that was happening to her. Just yesterday . . . unless that was also something she had dreamed . . . she'd gone to sleep in safety, under her own roof, and feeling for the first time in years that her future held a promise of happiness and joy. Today her home was the open Steppe, the sky and a horse's back, and she was sharing it with a stranger who would have inspired her with distrust and revulsion barely two days earlier.

What kind of man was he, then? Kind, of that she was sure. Brave and resourceful in his own strange fashion. But could she place any trust in him?

Nothing seemed safe any longer, there wasn't anything of which she could be sure. God only knew what was waiting for her. All she knew for certain was that a blood-mad Cossack was pursuing her and ahead of her lay a sea of slaughter, civil war, rape, pillage, inhumanity and fire.

"God help me," she whispered and then a dear and precious image appeared in her mind. Skshetuski could be near. He was sure to be back from the *Sietch* if the war has already broken out. Perhaps he was riding somewhere in the same Steppe, under the same sky. He'll search for her and find her and she'll be able to forget all the horrors that haunted her like unhallowed ghosts, and lay to rest all the terrors of that dreadful night. Then a wonderful happiness will replace all her doubts and fears, and new joy will restore everything she lost.

The Steppe whispered to her, the grasses were rich with the fresh scents of Spring. The air was still and heavy but laden with fragrance. Helen's hopes grew stronger, fortified and lifted by her determination. Nothing, she thought, has been lost for-ever. She was alive and free and riding towards her future, wherever that might be. She would regain her ability to feel trust and love and joy beside Skshetuski. If nothing else, she was free of an unhappy past in which she was regarded less as a woman and a human being than as an object to be held hostage under her own roof, or traded off without her consent by people whom she wanted to love as a family but for whom she never had any real value. And in the meantime this strange and funny old man, that unexpected and unlikely rescuer, would help to keep her out of Bohun's hands.

She watched the ripe, nodding heads of many-colored flowers, and the tall, blooming thistles that bowed heavily towards her in hues of red and purple, and a deep, reassuring peace came to her from the rich, wide emptiness of the open Steppe. The memory of slaughter and the scenes of horror began to grow dim behind her falling eyelids.

She felt the sun. The warmth. The soft morning breeze.

Then she slept.

Chapter Nineteen

SHE WOKE TO THE BAYING of dogs and saw a huge old oak, some dilapidated sheds and a stone well in a broad, fenced-in clearing trodden into the grass straight ahead of her. Startled and worried because they wanted to avoid human settlements, she woke her companion.

" . . . What? What's this?" Zagloba opened both his eyes and focused the good one. "Where've we come to?"

"I don't know," she said.

He peered about. "Hmm. Wait a minute. This looks like a Cossack wintering hut . . . The kind used by drovers. Not the best kind of company for us at this moment."

"That's right," she agreed.

"The last thing we need right now, my girl, is to stumble on a gang of horseherders. Damn those dogs! What are they making so much noise about? Do you see anyone around?"

She peered ahead, saw some men and horses near the far fence, and pointed them out. "*Tchabany?*"

"Hmm. That's what they look like. Well, they've seen us too. There's nothing for it now but to ride on in and make the best of it otherwise they'll think we're afraid of them and come at us like wolves after a lame mare. Ha, that bit of sleep helped, I must say. You must've slept a little too, eh?"

"Yes," she said. "A little."

But Zagloba was already counting the men and the horses huddled together at the far end of the herders' clearing as if the men had urgent news to share.

"Four of them! Well, that's not too many. You notice how

288

they seem to have a lot to say to each other, hmm? Looks almost like a war council, eh? So, my lady, are you ready for them?"

"I'm ready," Helen said.

"Alright then," Zagloba said and began to shout: "Hey people! People! Come here, one of you!"

All four of the dark, unkempt figures rose at once and started towards them. These were, indeed, some of the masterless *tchaban* horseherders of the Steppe who watched over the huge herds of mustangs that ran free in Summer through the open grasslands, and Zagloba noted with relief that only one of them was armed with a matchlock firearm and a rusted saber. The other three carried the long, yellow pole-axes of their kind, fashioned out of the lower jaws of horses nailed to the tops of weathered wooden shafts.

"A murderous looking lot, aren't they," he muttered. "There's no safe refuge for us here, that's certain."

The four herdsmen were staring up and down at the riders with cold, suspicious eyes; no feeling other than dour hostility showed on their bearded, weatherbeaten faces.

"What d'you want?" one of them barked out.

"*Slava Bohu*," Pan Zagloba answered in Ruthenian. "God be praised."

But the herdsmen ignored the cheerful greeting. "What d'you want?" their leader snarled again.

"Hmm, so that's the way the wind blows here," Zagloba muttered to himself, then spoke out sharply: "How far to Surovata?"

"We don' know about no Surovata."

"Ah . . . what d'you call this place, then?"

"Hushla. What's it to you?"

"Hushla. Hmm." The fat knight nodded, as if satisfied. "Alright then. So it's Hushla. Bring us some water for the horses, will you?"

"We got no water." The *tchabany* started to close slowly around the two riders. "Where've you two come from?"

"From Krivoi Ruda," Pan Zagloba said, naming a settlement on the way to Lubnie.

"And where're you goin'?"

"To Tchehryn."

"To Tchehryn, eh?"

The *tchabany* were glancing sideways at each other and edging ever closer. Their leader, a broad-shouldered man with narrow black eyes slitted like a Tartar's, began to stare attentively at Zagloba.

"So how come you got off the highway if you're goin' to Tchehryn?"

"Because it's hot there," Zagloba said calmly.

The *tchaban* leader whose dark, twisted face was scorched and blackened by years of living under the open sky, put both his hands on the reins of Zagloba's horse. "Get down off there," he said.

"Why should I?"

"'Cause there's nothing for you in Tchehryn."

"Is that so?" Zagloba asked quietly. "And why not?"

"'Cause that's where the *Lahy* are gettin' their throats slit," the dark-faced man said and grinned and nodded at one of his companions. "He's just come from there. It's all over for you and your kind in Tchehryn."

"And you," Zagloba said coldly, looking down at the nearing herdsmen as if he were their master. "D'you know who's riding to Tchehryn behind us?"

The *tchaban* leader spat coldly on the ground. "What's that to us?" He shrugged.

"*Knaz* Yarema, that's who!" Zagloba roared out. "Does that interest you?"

The four horseherders whipped their caps off their heads so fast at the sound of that terrifying name that it seemed as if a sudden wind had blown across the Steppe and swept the shaggy fur caps into the wilderness. They stumbled back, bareheaded and bowing, their savage faces wreathed in placating smiles.

"And do you know what the *Lahy* do to those who slit throats and murder people?" Zagloba roared fiercely. "They hang them! They impale them! They cut off their heads! And do you know what a great army the Prince has riding with him? And that he's less than half a mile from here? Eh? Eh? What now? Eh? You've a little less to say to me now, eh? So there's no water for our horses, is that right? What's the matter, you damn rebel dogs, your well's gone dry in Spring? Ah . . . let me at you! I'll show you! I'll show you . . .!"

"*Ne serdytes, pa'neh!*" the savage herdsmen pleaded. "Don' be angry, master! The well's gone dry and that's the God's own truth!"

"How do you water your own livestock, then?" Zagloba demanded.

"If we need water we fetch it from the river."

"Dogs! Offal!" Pan Zagloba raged. "Ah, you sons of bitches!"

"It's the truth, master! The well's dry! But we'll run and get you water from the Kahamlik, if you want us to!"

"Forget it!" Pan Zagloba bellowed, intoxicated by his own performance. "Never mind that now! I'll go there myself! Where's that damn river from here anyway?"

The horseherders began to explain at once just how this two-man scouting party of Prince Yeremi's army might get to the river but the fat knight had another game to play.

"And how do I get back to the highway from this place?" he demanded. "This way again or along the bank?"

"Along the bank, master . . . The river bends to the road less'n a mile from here . . ."

"Good!" Zagloba said and turned to the silent Helen. "Jump to it, lad! Scout the way for me!"

She spurred her horse into a gallop and cleared the far fence and he turned his threatening eye on the horseherders again. "Listen, you dogs! When the army comes here, you tell them I've gone to the highway along the bank. You've got that?"

"Yes master," they cried out, bowing to the ground. "We've got it. Along the bank. We'll tell them . . ."

The fat knight twirled his mustache, threw the terrified *tchabany* another threatening glare, kneed his horse forward and trotted away.

★ ★ ★

In less than a quarter of an hour he caught up with Helen who was waiting for him near the riverbank.

"Well, I invented the Prince for them just in time," he said, winking his good eye. "Now they'll sit quiet as rabbits in the grass, waiting for the Vishnovyetzki army . . . Ah, but did you see how they started shaking when they heard Prince Yeremi's name?"

"I see, sir, that you're just as quick-witted as you said you were," Helen said.

"Eh? What? And didn't I tell you?"

She shook her head in wonder. Her smile showed pleased surprise. "Thank God for that. And thank God you're here."

"Sharp wits, eh? What?" Pan Zagloba grinned and stroked his beard in great satisfaction. "It's not for nothing that I've been compared to Ulysses in my time! If I didn't have a good head on my neck I'd have been feeding crows a long time ago. As for those savages back there, they've a right to believe that the Prince is coming because, sooner or later, he's sure to get here! I just wish he'd step on Bohun while he is about it; I'll make a barefoot pilgrimage to Tchenstohova if he'll just do that . . ."

They put their horses into a quick trot towards the hidden river and Pan Zagloba went on muttering and grumbling in a worried voice.

"Ah, but did you notice how bold these cut-throats are getting? That's a bad sign for us. It means that Hmyelnitzki's victories must be common knowledge in these parts and the peasants will be getting much harder to deal with. We'll have to keep to open country now because the villages will be dangerous. God grant the Prince comes quickly because we've got ourselves into such a fix that I can't remember another one like it."

Fear, once more, touched Helen, and along with it came anger that she had to be afraid at all. Thinking that she might draw some cheerier words out of her glum companion, she smiled at him in encouragement. "But I believe that you'll save us both no matter what happens."

"That goes without saying. The trouble is, where? That Zolotonosha doesn't promise to be a great deal safer than any other place."

"Well, I do know that my step-brothers are there," Helen said again.

"Maybe they are and maybe they aren't. They could've left for home. And if they're heading back towards Rozloghi we aren't likely to meet them in the Steppe. I'm counting more on some kind of garrison in the fort . . ."

Then they saw the thick, nodding reeds that marked the broad muddy banks of the river.

"Well, here's the Kahamlik at last," Pan Zagloba said. "At least we've some reeds to hide in. I'll find a ford and then we'll go upriver instead of downstream towards the highway like I said we'd do . . . True, that'll take us back towards Rozloghi but at least we'll have confused the trail."

"We'll come closer to Brovarki, too," Helen said. "And that's on the road to Zolotonosha."

"So much the better then."

They watered their horses. Then, having hidden Helen in the reeds, Zagloba rode off to find a crossing which he did quite easily; hundreds of muddy hoofprints marked the ford which the *tchabany* used to drive their herds to the high pastures beyond the Kahamlik. The river was broad but shallow at this point, and flowing less swiftly, and they could swim their horses to the other side with hardly any trouble. But the low, marshy land beyond the river was a morass of broad, grassy ponds, deep quagmires and tributary streams in which the horses sunk up to their bellies so that, at times, it seemed as if their journey would end then and there. They pushed on up the riverbank hour after hour, fording a dozen streams and struggling against the soft, treacherous soil underfoot, until long after a dense, dark night had fallen around them.

Then, finally, they reached a ridge of dry, high ground bristling with young oaks, and Zagloba called a halt. He thought that to go on through the marshland in such impenetrable darkness was too great a risk.

"It's so black out here you can't see the ears on your horse right in front of you," he grumbled. "The Devil made such darkness! We'll camp here for the rest of the night and push on in the morning. It'd be just too easy, riding blind like this, to stumble into some mudpit and get sucked down for good."

Too tired to speak, Helen only nodded.

The old knight unsaddled the horses, hobbled them lightly so that they wouldn't stray too far in the darkness, and put them out to graze lower down the slope. Then he gathered up a bed of dry leaves which he covered with his coat and their saddle blankets.

"Well, child, you might as well get some sleep," he suggested gently. "The dew and the night air will cool your anxieties and that's all to the good. I'll also go and get my head down on a saddle somewhere because I feel as if the marrow's turned to glue in my bones. We'll have to do without a fire, that goes without saying, but the nights are short this time of the year and you'll be warm enough. Sleep well and don't worry. We haven't

put much distance between us and Rozloghi but we've confused
the trail better than any fox. It'd take someone who's smart
enough to outwit the Devil to find us tonight. So good night to
you."

"Good night," Helen said.

She knelt to pray, raising her tired eyes to the starless sky, and
prayed for a long time. Zagloba hoisted his saddle on his back
and trudged off a short distance into the darkness further along
the bank where he'd spotted a dry patch of leaves for his own
rough bedding. Too tired to struggle with his own anxieties and
none too willing to look into the threatening and uncertain
future, he cast an approving and experienced eye on their temporary refuge none the less.

He'd chosen well, he thought.

The ground was dry and airy and free of the mosquitoes that
tormented them earlier in the marshland. A thick roof of leaves
provided shelter from the rain. And, if it came to that, the tall,
wooded ridge could be defended for as long as lead and powder
lasted.

★   ★   ★

It took the girl a long time to fall asleep that night. She was
tormented by her thoughts and, later, by her dreams, in which
everything that had happened to her became translated into a
terrifying present, so that she thought herself still frozen in
shock and disbelief in the blood-stained hall, fixed like a statue
carved from ice in the scene of the carnage.

The dead faces of her murdered family pressed upon her out
of the surrounding darkness. She was (she thought) locked with
their corpses in the great, dark hall and Bohun was only a step
away. She saw his desperate pallor, his black eyebrows drawn
together in pain and suffering and his luminous eyes fixed on
her intently, and such a sense of horror came upon her then that
it took all her willpower to keep herself from crying out aloud.
But what, she thought in terror, if a real pair of glowing eyes
gleamed suddenly in the darkness . . .?

Moonlight broke briefly out of the thick, rolling banks of
night-cloud and fell in a dead, white light on the stunted trees,
changing their shapes and form and making them seem ill-
omened and grotesque. She heard the nightbirds crying out,
and the Steppe animals calling to each other, and these sharp,

shrill sounds which might have been frightening at any other moment helped to restore her sense of time and place and brought her some calmness. The horses snorted and skipped stiff-legged in their hobbling ropes, chewing on the grass and growing quieter as they moved deeper into the darkness.

All these sounds soothed and steadied her and called back her courage and determination. They told her that her persistent visions were merely an illusion born out of fatigue. She was safe, after all. At the edge of the Steppe. Only a few days earlier, she thought, the idea of being lost and alone in the wilderness would have been frightening in itself but now it was exactly this recollection and awareness of where she found herself, along with the sight of the cold stars and the naked sky hanging above the dark and ghostly banks of the Kahamlik, that brought her some peace and made sleep possible.

She listened to the night sounds of the riverbank and to the soft rustling of the wind in the pale, dry branches of the moonlit trees. Her eyes closed. Her eyelids seemed too heavy for her to keep open any longer no matter how she tried. And then, despite her terrifying memories and dreams, she drifted out of consciousness and slept.

★ ★ ★

Dawn was already close when she became aware of other sounds, terrible and urgent. She struggled to awake. She was again wide-eyed with terror, trying to understand these harsh snarls and groans and then the one shrill scream of agonizing pain that brought her leaping to her feet and trembling in an icy sweat.

She didn't know where to run or what to do. The terrible sounds seemed to be coming from everywhere around her. She caught a glimpse of Zagloba, hatless and with his thin grey hair standing up in a wispy fringe around his gleaming pate, running past with a pistol in each hand. She heard his voice, diminished in the distance and the darkness, crying out: "U-ha! U-ha! Devils . . .! Sons of bitches . . .!" And then there came the flat crack of a pistol shot and silence returned. She thought that hours passed before she heard the fat knight stumbling and crashing through the undergrowth on the riverbank again, and then she heard his cursing.

"May the dogs tear out your guts!" the old man was shouting

in a voice that trembled with despair. "May you get flayed alive! May the Jews make coat-collars out of you and wear you on their hats!"

"What happened?" she called out.

"What happened?" Zagloba staggered, wheezing, out of the dark. "What happened? The wolves gutted our horses, that's what happened."

"*Jezus Maria!*" Helen cried. "Both of them?"

"Both. One is ripped open well enough for stuffing. The other's hurt so bad he won't walk half a mile. They strayed a bit . . . a miserable hundred yards . . . and look what happened! Oh, it's too much, I tell you."

"So what'll we do now?"

"What'll we do? We'll whittle a couple of wooden hob-byhorses for ourselves, that's what we'll do. How do I know what we're going to do? Of all the damned, miserable luck! I tell you, my girl, the Devil himself is out to get us, there's no doubt about it. I can't say that this surprises me a lot because they've got to be related to each other, he and Bohun, or at least they're sure to be close friends born and bred in Hell! But what, indeed, can we do? If I knew how to go about it I'd change into a horse so that you, at least, would have something to ride on. I'll be damned if I was ever in a worse mess than this!"

"Perhaps we can walk," she offered and, at this, Zagloba lost all control over his bitterness and despair.

"Walk! Walk she says! That's all right for you, light as a feather that you are, and with your handful of young years on your little shoulders! But what about me? It's not just hot air I'm carrying in my belly!"

She tried to think of something she could say that might restore the desperate old man's good humor but he was obviously beyond consolation.

"Walk, she says!" he bellowed. "Let dogs walk, they've got four legs to do it on and a tail to fan the air behind them. In this country even peasants get to ride on something. This is the limit, I'm telling you! This is the last straw!"

But one of Pan Zagloba's greatest virtues was that his sharp wits were seldom hobbled by what his mouth was saying and that his fertile mind produced ideas even faster than his glib tongue managed to spit out the words.

"Walk. Hmm. Walk? Certainly. We'll have to. We can't spend

the rest of our lives in this swamp. But how long will it take us to get to Zolotonosha on foot? It seemed dangerous and long enough on horseback, and now this? Ah, to the Devil with it all! Serves me right! I've played the fool and acted like a jackass so now I might as well turn into a mule and carry all our provisions on my back."

"I'll help," she said at once. "You won't have to carry everything by yourself."

Her anxiety about him had an immediate effect on Zagloba who regained his composure almost at once. He went on snorting and huffing like a winded horse for a while longer but he calmed down, brightened up a little, and began to reason.

"I'd have to be some kind of a Turk to let you do that," he said gently. "That slim little back wasn't made for bending under burdens. I've been far too temperate in eating and drinking and that's why I get out of breath so easily but I'll manage all the carrying. We'll take just the horse-blankets and the food which won't be that much anyway after we've had breakfast."

They sat down to eat. The new challenge seemed to bring fresh strength to the fat knight who immediately abandoned that lifelong moderation that he talked about and turned to their provisions with considerable enthusiasm. The thing to do, as he put it, was to increase the supply of air in the lungs by way of the belly and, at the same time, to decrease the load that they'd have to carry.

★   ★   ★

Then they set out on foot. Close to noon, they came to a river crossing, easily marked on both sides of the water by clusters of hoofprints and the ruts of wagon-wheels in the thick brown mud.

"Perhaps that's the way to Zolotonosha," Helen said.

"It could be. But who is there to ask? Fish may be good table company on a Friday night but I've never heard one of them tell me anything I wanted to hear."

But the old knight had no sooner spoken when they heard voices across the river and hid in the reeds.

"Who's there?" Helen whispered, and Zagloba peered cautiously through the undergrowth. "Can you see anything?"

"Hmm. Yes. I see them. It's a blind old beggar with a lyre on his back. A young lad's leading him. Aha . . . now they're taking off their boots. Looks like they're going to cross the river here."

After a moment the sound of splashing announced that the travelers were coming through the ford and Helen and Zagloba emerged from their hiding place.

"*Slava Bohu*," the fat knight said.

"For ever an' ever," the blind beggar whined in his song-song voice, twisting his head all around and cocking his ears. "Ah, ah, who's there, then? Eh? Who's there?"

"Godfearing souls," Zagloba intoned piously in his turn. "Here's a coin for you, old man."

"*Sh'tchob vam Svyatyi Mikolay dav zdorovla y sh'tchastya!*" the beggar sang out, grinning and bowing as he tested the small copper coin between his yellow teeth. "May the Holy Nicholas give you health and luck."

"And the same to you. But where are you coming from, old man?"

"From Brovarki, *pa'neh*"

"And this road, where does it go to?"

"To the *hutory*, master. To a village."

"Does it go to Zolotonosha?"

"It does if you take it, *pa'neh.*"

"Well we're not taking it but it does no harm to ask because the more a man asks the more he finds out. And when did you leave Brovarki?"

"Yesterday mornin' *pa'neh.*"

"And were you in Rozloghi?"

"We was. But people say there's been a big fight there. Knights came . . . *lytzari* came . . . and what they did there is too terrible to tell, people say."

"Ah. And who told you all this?"

"They said it in Brovarki, people did. One of the servants of the old *Knahina* got there on a horse. And what he told was terrible . . . ay, terrible . . ."

"And did you see him with your own eyes, old man?"

"Me? No, *pa'neh*. I don't see nobody. I'm blind. The lad's got good eyes and does the seeing for me but he's got no tongue. Nobody but me can make out his noises."

"Is that so," Zagloba said quietly. "Hmm. Is that so." A new idea began to flicker in his head, he fingered the sleeve of the blind man's homespun Ruthenian *sukmana*, and suddenly he seized the deaf-mute lad by the scruff of the neck and began to bellow: "Thieves! Vagabonds! I've got you now! So that's your story, is it? Blind beggars, are you? I'll show you blind beggars! You're spies and traitors inciting peasants to rebellion, that's what you are! Hey Maksym! Olesha! Fedor! Grab them and strip them and string them up or drown them, whichever you like! Kill the spies and rebels! Kill them!"

Howling as loudly as he could he lifted the terrified deaf-mute overhead and shook him like a sack of oats. His victim started uttering strangled, inarticulate cries. The blind old beggar howled in his own turn and fell to his knees, calling on all the saints and begging for mercy.

Helen stared, astonished.

"What are you doing?" she cried.

But Zagloba yelled and shouted all the louder, summoned his non-existent servants, threatened death and torture, and called upon all the powers of Heaven and Hell to witness what he was about to do to these 'spies and traitors.'

"Kill them! Impale them! Flay them! Boil them in oil!"

Helen began to back away, sure that the old knight had finally lost his mind.

"That's right! Make yourself scarce!" he shouted after her. "You shouldn't look at what's going to happen here because it'll offend your modesty and it won't be a pretty sight anyway. Run, I tell you! Run!"

"But what in God's name are you doing?"

"What am I doing? Hmm? You'll see if you're not careful." And to the old man he shouted: "Strip! Take off your clothes, you old goat! I'll have you cut up into fish bait if you're not standing here stark naked in one minute!"

Then throwing the babbling deaf-mute to the ground he started ripping off his clothes with both hands. The old beggar, sure that his last hour had come, threw down his lyre and his begging sack.

"Everything!" howled Zagloba. "Take off everything, or you're a dead dog!"

The beggar started tearing off his shirt.

Helen backed off in earnest, trying to make some sense out of this sudden change in her rescuer, while Zagloba's yells and curses followed her into the bushes where she stopped uncertain where to go. She sat down on a fallen tree trunk and waited until the yelling ended and the startled water birds resumed their trills and chatter in the reeds, and not long after that she heard the clump of heavy footsteps and the fat knight appeared carrying his loot: two pairs of boots, two homespun shirts and clean grey coats, the breeches, the blind beggar's satchel and the lyre.

" . . .Ooof!" He was out of breath with all his exertions and quite delighted with himself. "Did you hear that noise? No court bailiff ever yelled that much! It's made me quite hoarse but I got what I wanted. I've turned them into Turkish holy men, naked as a couple of fishes, and if the Sultan doesn't make me at least a pasha then he's a damn ingrate. And look at all this stuff, it's as good as new. They must do good business begging on the highways if they can afford to dress themselves this well. From now on I'm giving up my knightly profession and I'll take to robbing beggars on the roads. I can see that that's the way to fortune."

"But why did you rob and terrify those poor people like that?" Helen asked. "What good will it do you?"

"What good will it do us? You don't understand? Well, then wait a bit longer over here and I'll go and show you."

So saying, Pan Zagloba took half the clothing and the lyre and disappeared in a clump of bushes. A few moments later there was the plaintive sound of a Ruthenian ditty and from the bushes stepped a genuine Ukrainian *staretz*, one of those innumerable wandering singers and village story-tellers complete with one blind eye and a tangled grey beard, who were as common everywhere in that countryside as swallows in the Springtime. The old *staretz* came up to Helen, winked at her with his one good eye, and started singing in a powerful though hoarse bass voice while strumming on the lyre.

" '*Sokole yasnyi, brate mi ridnyi*
   Tih visoko litayesh, Tih shiroko vidayesh . . ."

She laughed then, and clapped her hands and shook her head again in astonishment. "If I didn't know who you were I wouldn't have guessed!"

"Hmm? What? A good masquerade, eh?" Pan Zagloba looked down at himself with a great deal of pleasure. "I had a look at myself in the river just now and if there ever was a better looking *staretz* in these parts I'll hang myself on the strap of my own begging sack. I won't run out of songs or stories either so I'll even earn our bread for us along the way!"

"So that's why you attacked those poor people," Helen said, still laughing. "To get a disguise!"

"Of course. Why else? We have to become invisible, my girl. Here in the Transdnieper the common people are fiercer and wilder than anywhere else. Only fear of the Prince keeps them all from murdering each other. And now that they've heard how the war is going nothing will keep them from joining the rebellion. How could I take you among such people without a disguise? You'd have been a lot better off in Bohun's hands."

"I'd rather be dead," Helen said.

"And I'd rather live," Zagloba said quietly. "Dying is something you do only once and there's no way to cancel the order if you change your mind. God must've sent us those two beggars. I scared them so badly they'll sit shaking in those reeds for two days at least. Meanwhile we'll assume their *personae* and get to Zolotonosha. If we find your brothers, all will be well and good. If we don't, we'll go on. Where? Maybe to the Hetmans. Maybe we'll find a safe burrow somewhere and wait for the Prince. Either way a *staretz* is holy to the peasants and safe from the Cossacks. All we have to watch for are the Tartars because they'd take you captive and turn me into a sieve after target practice. A young lad is worth his weight in gold to them."

"So I've got to disguise myself as well?"

"That's right. You're a sight too pretty for a peasant boy, just as I'm too handsome for a beggar, but that won't matter in a day or two. The sun and the wind will darken your skin and my belly will collapse with walking. You know, when the Valachians were burning out my eyes I thought that evil times had come on me but now I see that it was for the best. A *staretz* with two good eyes wouldn't be convincing, nor would he need a deaf-mute to lead him by the hand. Now go and change into your new clothing."

★ ★ ★

Zagloba walked away to give her privacy and Helen began her own transformation. She threw off the frogged Cossack *zhupan* coat she wore for her escape from Rozloghi, the soft riding boots and ballooning, Turkish-style trousers, bathed herself in the river, braided her long hair, and dressed in the grey homespun peasant coat and leggings, straw hat and bast boots that the fat knight had stripped off the terrified deaf-mute. Luckily the boy had been slight and slim so that his clothing fitted her quite well.

"My God," Zagloba said, returning. "If every blind beggar could count on a guide like you all of our young gentry would be out begging on the roads. In fact I know one *husaria* lieutenant who'd be sure to do it. But we've got to do something about your hair, my girl; I've seen some pretty boys on the block in Istanbul, but never one with hair so long he could sit on it."

"God grant that my looks don't get us into trouble," Helen said in a quiet, gentle voice but the old knight could see that she was pleased to have her beauty praised.

"A fine face and figure are never a bad thing," he pronounced at once. "And I'm a good example. Because when those Turks in Galata were burning out my eyes it was the wife of their pasha who got me away, drawn as she was to my amazing beauty."

"Turks?" Helen asked and grinned. "Didn't you tell me it was the Valachians who burned out your eyes?"

"Valachians, only they let themselves be turned into Turks, serving the Pasha of Galata."

"But they didn't really burn out any of your eyes, did they?" she teased him.

"What difference does that make? One of my eyes filmed over from the heat of the iron. But what are you going to do about those long braids of yours?"

"What can I do? We'll have to cut them off."

"Hmm. I can see that. But how?"

"With your saber."

"Sabers are good for cutting off a head, but hair? I wouldn't know *qua modo*, or how to go about it."

"I know how," she said and smiled sadly. "I'll just sit down here on the ground, throw my hair across this fallen tree trunk, and you'll cut it off. Only try not to cut off my head along with my hair, will you please?"

Then she did as she said she would and raised her deep, black eyes towards Zagloba.

"I'm ready," she said softly. "Cut."

"Hmm. Hmm," the fat knight muttered, ill-at-ease and feeling as if he were about to do something shameful and unclean. "I don't like this at all. A hangman may cut off the hair of a witch so that the Devil can't hide in it and interfere with the torturing. But you're not a witch and I'm not a hangman. And if Pan Skshetuski fails to crop my ears for this ugly act I'll be much surprised. Will you at least close your eyes? I feel quite unwell."

"They're closed," Helen said.

Sitting astride the tree trunk, Pan Zagloba rose slightly on his haunches like a rider standing in his stirrups for a saber stroke. Then he raised the curved, *karabela* saber, the flat steel blade hissed downward through the air, and the long twin streams of gleaming black hair slid to the ground behind the massive log.

"It's done," Zagloba grunted.

Helen rose swiftly and, at once, her newly-cut short hair spread in a dark circle about her pale face. She flushed and looked away and two tears flowed slowly down her reddening cheeks. Zagloba hid their sabers under the old tree trunk, feeling as sad and shamed by the need to cut off the girl's long braids as Helen did herself. Neither regret was due to vanity. The cutting of her braids signified a particular disgrace for a young woman in those days. As for the disarmed old knight, he couldn't have been less at ease if he were stark naked. The wearing of a saber was so much a symbol of the gentry that he felt as if he'd been suddenly reduced to the level of that peasantry whom he pretended to despise. The thick wooden cudgel of the blind old beggar was a poor substitute, he thought, for a noble's saber.

But Pan Zagloba, who kept his history and antecedents just as secret as his surface life was open for all to see, seldom allowed changes in his fortune to bother him for long. He tried a few broad strokes with the beggar's cudgel, inspected the sharp flints with which it was studded, and announced himself satisfied enough with that peasant weapon.

"It'll do for the dogs and wolves," he said. "Unless they come at us in a pack. I might even be able to crack a few human skulls with it. The worst thing about our new plebeian condition is that we'll have to walk. But worse things have happened to many people in this world and even worse is sure to happen in the days to come. So God be with us and let's begin our journey."

"I'm ready," Helen said.

Her eyes were dry and clear as she looked at him, even though her saddened face was still shining with tears, and he felt a sudden overwhelming fondness for this brave young woman and swore to himself to get her through whatever lay ahead at whatever cost.

They picked up their satchels, slung them across their backs, and began to walk.

Chapter Twenty

LATER THAT DAY two travelers appeared in the open country beyond the Kahamlik. One was a slim, dark-haired peasant lad of extraordinary beauty; the other was an old, one-eyed *staretz* who cursed and sweated with every step he took even though a mild fresh breeze blew across the grassland.

"Oo-oof," he wheezed and grunted. "That beggar back there told me we'd come across a deep ravine near here, then an old burial mound with three oaks growing out of it, and the road to Demyanovka was supposed to start just beyond that. Was he lying, or what? This is no way for civilized people to travel, let me tell you. If God meant the gentry to go about on foot he wouldn't have created horses."

The day turned hotter as the sun rose higher, and soon a scorching wind started to darken the boy's pale skin, and the old man who stumbled through the undergrowth behind him cursed even more bitterly than before. But then they reached a gaunt, ragged fold of land with a spring of pure crystal water seeping out of it, and just beyond it crouched the dark dome of an old burial mound under three young oaks, and the long yellow ribbon of a sandy track unwound behind it across the green Steppe.

"Well, so he wasn't lying," the old man grunted and mopped his sweating forehead. "It looks like even beggars tell the truth sometimes, especially when the point of a saber is tickling their necks. There's the road we want. But where are all those carters and drovers he told me about? Where's the ride we are supposed to be able to hitch here?"

That yellow ribbon shining in the Steppe was, indeed, a

rough country road bright with small, wild flowers that grew out of the scattered piles of manure left by driven cattle, but there was no sign of carts hauling pitch and produce, and no plodding oxen pulling at the traces. Only dry bones picked clean by the ravens, scattered by the wolves and bleached by the sun, gleamed here and there among the yellow blooms.

The travelers went on, resting from time to time in the shade of oak groves, and then the lad tried to sleep, worn to the point of collapse, while the old man watched. Sometimes they spent hours walking up and down the banks of swift streams in search of a crossing; at other times the broad-backed old man lifted the boy in his arms and carried him through the quick dark waters of a flooded defile, showing surprising strength for a man who begged for his bread. But by sunset they both reached their limits of endurance. The child—the disguised Helen—slid to the ground beside an oak in a roadside grove and confessed that she couldn't take another step.

"Ah, damn this wilderness anyway!" The old man's trembling voice betrayed anxiety as well as exhaustion. "No huts, not even a shed to creep into for the night. No living soul anywhere in sight. Night's coming, it'll be dark as pitch in an hour. And do you hear what I'm hearing, hmm?"

They cocked their ears to listen to the mournful cry that seemed to be coming out of the earth itself but which, in reality, rose from a nearby ravine hidden among the trees.

"Wolves," Pan Zagloba said. "Last night they ate our horses, damn their greedy guts. Tonight is our turn. True, I've a pistol hidden in my coat but the powder won't stretch to more than two shots and I don't fancy being served up as dessert at a lupine banquet. There, d'you hear it again?"

The mournful baying seemed to be coming closer.

"On your feet, child," the old man said, groaned and reached down towards the seated Helen. "There's no help for it, we've got to keep moving. I'll carry you if I have to. I must say that worrying about somebody else's skin is a new experience for me but I've become as fond of you as if you were my own flesh and blood. Maybe that's because I've no legitimate descendants of my own, never having married. As for whatever progeny I might have here and there, born outside the blanket so to speak, they are all pagans, I am sure, since I lived a long time among the Turks."

Grown suddenly reflective, Zagloba heaved a sigh. "I'm the last of my line," he confided. "The name of Zagloba will end with me. You may have to take care of me in my old age if I ever reach one but right now either start walking or climb on my shoulders."

"I'll try to walk," Helen said. "But I can't promise much."

"The main thing is never to give up," Zagloba went on. "No matter how bad things are they can be much worse. But wait a minute! Listen! D'you hear that? As I love God, that sounds like dogs barking! That's it, it's dogs this time, not wolves! This must be that Demyanovka the beggar was telling me about and since that's one of the Prince's villages there ought to be a steward or a bailiff there. We'll get some news. A nice mulled ale would help a little too. Glory be to God! That's dogs, alright, d'you hear?"

"Let's go, then," Helen said. She struggled up to her feet, stepped out from among the trees, and a moment later they saw the three small onion domes of the rough-trimmed, clapboard village church glowing in the sunset and closer to hand a smithy filled the sky with sparks flying from its chimney.

"Just remember that you're a deaf-mute," Zagloba reminded. "I know the local dialects around here just as well as I know my Latin, so let me do the talking until we know what's what. We aren't safe yet. No, not by a long shot. See those bonfires there?"

He jerked his head towards a shallow dip on the threshold of the village where several dozen dark forms stood around a half-dozen small bonfires, while the red firelight of the smithy flickered over them from the open doors and through the ventilation holes punched into the walls. The hammers in the smithy beat out in counterpoint to the gloomy ditties sung around the fires, to the harsh mutter of excited voices, and to the savage barking of the village dogs.

Pan Zagloba turned at once towards this gathering. He struck a few chords on his lyre and began to sing.

> *"Ey tam na horih . . . zhentchi zjhnut*
> *A popid horoyu, popid zelenoyu*
> *Kozaki idut . . ."*

"Well, here we go," he muttered. "Dear God, look kindly on your faithful servant. We'll see soon enough if we can get away with another masquerade."

★ ★ ★

He looked around as they neared the firelight in the gathering darkness, saw a crowd of peasants, and noted that most of them were drunk. All but a few grasped long wooden staves topped with the makeshift spearheads known throughout the borderlands as *spisy*, or with the sharp, curved blades of scythes reset with the edged point upward like long-bladed halberds. The blacksmiths were hammering out more such weapons for the rest of the men who waited outside the forge.

"Ey, look, a *staretz*!" glad voices cried out in the crowd.

"*Slava Bohu*!" Pan Zagloba said. "Praise God!"

"*Na viki vikiv*! For ever an' ever!"

"So tell me, children, is this Demyanovka?"

"It is. What of it?"

"Ah, well, people told me that good folks live here," the old wanderer said in the chanting, sing-song voice of the storyteller. "The kind who'll look after an old man, feed him and give him shelter and maybe a few copper *hroshi* too. God will bless you, and *Sviaty Mikolai* will bless you, praise their holy names . . . I'm an old man, come far, and my poor mute lad is so worn out he can hardly move. He can't talk, so at least he can't complain, and I'm almost blind. Oh yes, one eye still has some light in it, God and his kind saints saw to that, but the other's as dark as the grave. And so I go about the world, play songs and tell stories, and live like a bird on whatever falls from good people's hands."

"And where're you comin' from, old man?"

"Ah, from far . . . far away!"

"And what's the good news you've heard?" the village headman asked kindly, leaning on his spear.

"Well, there's this and that but I don't know if it's such good news. It might be good for some but evil for others . . . People say Hmyelnitzki beat the Hetman's son and his *lytzari*. But who knows, eh? Other people say that folks are rising up against their masters over across the river . . . All of the west bank is on fire, they say."

The crowd clustered at once around Zagloba who, having found a seat for himself and Helen on a rough wooden bench, wheezed and nodded his head sadly and struck mournful notes on his lyre now and then.

"Ah, so that's what you've heard, father? That people are rising?"

"So they say. Ey, it's a hard fate for us poor humble folk, God keep our unhappy peasant souls . . ."

"But don't they say how it'll all end?"

"Well . . . they say there's been writing found on an altar in Kiev . . . writing from Christ himself. And in it there's word about a cruel war and a lot of blood that's going to be spilled in the Ukraine."

"You say there's been a letter?"

"From Christ himself. About war and rivers turning into blood, and about living fire, and . . . ah, ah . . . but I can't say any more. My throat's so dry that words die in it like travelers lost in the Steppe in Summer . . ."

Half a dozen panikins of *gojhalka* were thrust out towards him at once. He seized one, drained it, smacked his lips and reached for another.

"So tell us, father," the peasant elder said. "What're we to do? You've been to different places, you know what is happening. We heard that a dark hour's comin' on the masters. So we got our scythes and *spisy* ready so we wouldn't be the last to rise up against them. But now we don't know. Should we start up by ourself right now or wait for word from Hmyel? Or what?"

"Start it now! Start it now!" a dozen voices shouted and Zagloba sat nodding for a while and then asked quietly: "And who's been telling you to rise up by yourselves?"

"Nobody!" The scythes and spears rattled in the callused hands with a threatening sound. "We want to, that's all! If the *Zaporoshtzy* beat the *pa'ny* then it's time to start!"

Then they waited for this wandering soothsayer and prophet to tell them that their hour of vengeance had come at last, and that now was the time to rise up and massacre their masters, but he sat deep in thought while the blacksmiths' hammers beat out their warlike rhythms.

"Whose people are you?" he spoke up finally.

"We're *Knaz* Yarema's."

"So who are you going to rise up against?" he asked and shook his head sadly while the silent peasants stared at each other with sudden hopelessness and fear. "Him?"

"*Ey, ne zderjhymo* . . ." gloomy voices murmured. "We won't manage much against him."

"That's right, children, that's right. *Ne zderjhyte* . . . I've been to Lubnie too, and I know. I've seen him. He walks about there

like a burning fire, so bright that even I could see him with my
one poor eye. And a terrible sight he is too! The trees shake in
the forests when he shouts, and the earth splits when he stamps
his foot! The King himself is scared of him . . . Ey, it's not you
who'll go looking for the likes of him, you poor peasant souls.
No, no, *he'll* come looking for *you* when he hears what you've
got in mind! And there's this other thing I know that you ought
to hear: when he sends out the call, every *lah* alive will come
running to him. And where there's a *lah* there's a saber, you
know that."

A glum silence settled once more on the crowd; the blind
soothsayer raised his eyes to the moon as if consulting visions,
struck another sad chord on his lyre, and went on:

"Ay, the *Knaz* is coming . . . coming . . . He is on his way.
And there's more spears and swords shining beside him, and
more bright flags waving at his back, than there's stars in the sky
or thistles in the Steppe. The wind flies before him, and it howls
and mourns, and d'you know what it's mourning?"

"No, father. Tell us."

"It mourns for you, children."

"*Spasi, Chryste*! Christ have mercy on us!"

"And Mother Death flies before him too, ringing with her
scythe, and d'you know why she's ringing, hmm?"

"No, father, no. What's she ringing for?"

"For your burial, children."

"*Hospody pomyluy*," murmured trembling voices and then
only the clanging of the blacksmiths' hammers broke the
gloomy silence.

"Who's the Prince's steward here?" the *staretz* asked at last.

"Pan Gdeshynski . . ."

"And where is he now?"

"He's run off."

"And why did he run off?"

"'Cause he heard how we was gettin' the scythes and the *spisy*
ready."

"All the worse for you, children," the *staretz* murmured sadly.
"And d'you know why it's so bad for you that the Prince's
steward has run off?"

"No. Why? You tell us, father."

"Because he'll tell *Knaz* Yarema about you and what you are
doing."

"God help us," the peasants murmured, staring at each other. "*Hospody pomyluy.*"

And again there was that dark and gloomy silence.

★ ★ ★

Pan Zagloba threw a quick, warning glance at Helen to make sure she remembered her role as the deaf-mute, feeble-minded boy but her exhaustion finally got the better of her and she fell asleep. She leaned against him, sleeping like a child among those hard, cruel words and even harsher faces, and a sudden rush of pity and affection for her spurred his determination to overcome all obstacles before them, and to survive no matter what it cost. And if this meant that he would have to urge the peasants to join the rebellion he was prepared to do even that. The gnarled peasant elder was already staring down at him with suspicious eyes and Pan Zagloba knew that he'd have to change his tune, stop his horror stories, and start telling these eager candidates for loot, rape and murder something they wanted to hear.

"How come you're screeching here like a hoot-owl about death and dying and *Knaz* Yarema and all that?" The village headman leaned on his scythe and glared at Zagloba. "You're not the only *staretz* we've had here. We've had word before. And we know the last hour's come for the *lahy* masters. There won't be none of 'em soon on either side of the river! *Nyi panov, nyi knaziov*, neither lords nor princes. And there won't be no rents, and no harvest tax, and no mill tithes, and no highway tolls, and none of them Jews either to squeeze the land dry! There'll be only free people and Cossacks living under God's sky. So *Knaz* Yarema's strong, is he? So what's that to us? Hmyel's as strong as Yarema, let them try each other."

"God give him the power," the *staretz* said quietly. "Ey, it's a hard life these days for us simple people, that's all that I meant. It used to be different."

"Sure it was!" the old peasant shouted. "And that's how it's goin' to be again! Whose is the land today? Whose cattle? Whose timber? Who's the master over God's free Steppe and owns all the horseherds? One man, Yarema, that's who!"

Zagloba sighed and nodded.

"In other times all of it belonged to God alone," the old peasant said. "And whoever came here first took it for himself and didn't owe nobody anything, and that's the way it's got to be again."

"God knows what's right," the *staretz* sighed and murmured while the peasants crowded close to listen. "He will judge and punish, and I'll just tell you one more thing that'll keep you walking this good earth alive. You know you won't hold out against Yarema here in his country, so if you want to rise up against the masters and spill some *lah* blood, get away from here! Don't do anything on your own under Yarema's eyes but run to Hmyel, as fast as you can. Today or tomorrow won't be too soon because Yarema's coming, as God is my witness. Hmyel's got his work cut out for him with the *hetmany* and then with Yarema, so run to him and help him or he won't hold out either. Go to Hmyel and you'll be helping him and saving yourselves too."

"*Pravdu kajhe!*" cried a dozen voices. "He's telling the truth!"

"*Muhdry dyid!*" others told each other. "Listen to him. That's a wise old man."

"Hey, father," others questioned. "So you saw *Knaz* Yarema on his way here, did you?"

"Maybe I did, maybe not. But I heard over in Brovarki that he's already started out from Lubnie. He's burning and killing everything that looks wrong to him. And wherever he finds one spear or one scythe set on end like yours he leaves nothing standing between the earth and the sky."

"*Hospody pomyluy!* So where's Hmyel? Where are we to look for him?"

"That's why I've come here, children, to tell you where to go," Zagloba said quietly. "First you'll go to Zolotonosha, and then you'll take the Trehtymirov track to the Dnieper and go across into the Ukraine at the Prohorovka ferry, and that's where Hmyel and the *Nijhovtsy* and the Tartars will be waiting for you. Go there and you'll keep yourselves alive. Stay here and *Knaz* Yarema won't let one of you walk and breathe God's air anywhere between Mother Earth and God's sky."

"And you, father, you'll go with us?"

"Maybe I will if you hitch a team to a wagon for me and stuff it well with straw. My old legs won't carry me much farther, children, and my lad's worn out too, as you see . . ."

"We'll hitch up a *telega* for you, father," the peasant elder said.

"Good, good. There's nothing better for traveling than a

straw-stuffed *telega*. And when we get to Zolotonosha, me and the boy will go on ahead to scout out the land and see if there's any *lah* soldiers there. And now give me some food and drink, will you? God will repay your kindness in saving Christian souls because I'm just about dead of thirst and hunger and so's my poor lad. We'll rest tonight and start out tomorrow. Terrible times are coming so we'd all better start praying for God's mercy and blessing. *Hospody pomyluy!* I've heard that ghosts are out in the Steppe in daylight these days, crying out for blood, and dead men are rising everywhere from their graves . . ."

Fear and uncertainty showed on many faces now that the hour of decision was fixed for the assembled rebels and some of them started glancing uneasily at each other.

Finally, one of them cried: "To Zolotonosha!"

"To Zolotonosha!" all the others shouted with such relief and fervor as if that was the one place on earth where they'd find safety for themselves along with everything they had ever wanted.

"To the Ukraine! To the Trehtymirov Country!"

"Death to the *pa'ny* and the *lahy!*"

They howled and shook their scythes, and none of them noticed the sadness on the worn, grey face of their silent *staretz*. "Death to them! Kill them all! *Na pohybel!*"

Suddenly a young Cossack leaped out of the circle, shook his spear and shouted: "*Bat'ki!* Hey, brothers! If we're off to Zolotonosha tomorrow, let's burn down the master's manor now!"

"Burn it down!" they roared out together. "Take what's in there!"

But the *staretz*, who sat with downcast eyes as if he couldn't face the storm stirring up around him, looked up at them and shook his head in warning.

"Ey, children, leave the manor alone. You'll set fire to it and the glow will light up the sky, and what'll happen then? What if the Prince is near? He'll see the fire in the sky and come here at once and then you'll roast in some of *his* fires . . . You'd do better right now to feed an old man and show him where he might get a little rest."

"*Pravdu kajhe,*" murmured several voices. "Yarema would fall on us like the plague if he saw the fires."

"Good words, good advice!" Some of the older peasants

shook their fists at the young Cossack who proposed the burning. "And you, Maksym, you're an idiot, see? Listen to the *staretz!*"

"Good words, indeed," the village headman said. "God must have sent you to us or we surely wouldn't get to Hmyel and help him against the masters. So come to my house for the night, father, it'd be an honor. There's some bread and mutton in the larder and a quart of honey in the cellar, and you're welcome to it. And then you and your lad can stretch out on fresh straw in the cattle barn."

"*Slava Bohu.*"

Zagloba rose and tugged gently at the sleeve of Helen's coat but she slept too deeply and too soundly to awake at once.

"See how the lad's worn-out, the poor soul," he said to the elder. "Even the hammering doesn't wake him . . ."

But to himself he whispered so softly that the peasant wasn't able to hear him: "What can it be like to be so innocent that you can sleep like a baby among these knives and spears . . .? God and all His angels must be looking out for you, my girl. And if I stick close to you . . . they might save me too."

He woke her and helped her to her feet and they followed the elder to the village which lay within an easy walk along the forest path, bright with stars and moonlight. The night was quiet and peaceful once they were beyond the sound of the beating hammers. The old peasant went ahead to show the way and Zagloba trailed behind him, his hand clasping Helen's.

"'*Lord God forgive our sins!*'" he intoned loudly in Ruthenian while he whispered to the tired girl beside him. "See the help this peasant disguise has been to us so far? '*Bless us, Holy Mother . . .!*' We'll eat and sleep tonight and tomorrow we'll ride to Zolotonosha in a wagon instead of wearing out our feet on the road. May the plague choke these peasants . . . '*Amin, amin, amin . . .!*' Bohun may track us down to this place because my tricks won't fool him for long. '*God's mercy upon us . . .!*' But it'll be too late. We'll cross the Dnieper at Prohorovka and that's a stone's throw from Korsun where the Hetmans are gathering their army. '*The Devil has no power over the innocent . . .!*' Here all Hell will break out any day. '*Amin, amin . . .!*' D'you hear how they're howling at the smithy, eh? '*Saints protect us all . . .!*' May the Black Death strangle all this vermin along with their mothers, may the Devil sing their lullabies and the hangman rock them all to sleep, may they die in torment."

"What's that you're saying there, father?" the peasant elder asked, glancing back.

"Nothing, nothing. Just praying for your health," Pan Zagloba said.

"And I pray for yours. Well, here we are. Here's my home. Come in and be welcome."

"*Slava Bohu.*"

"*Na viki vikiv.* Come and eat and rest."

"May God pay you well for all your intentions."

In the old peasant's hut Pan Zagloba helped himself to half a side of mutton and drank his fill of liquor. Then he and Helen covered themselves with straw in a dry, warm barn and slept until the sunrise.

★ ★ ★

The next day, at dawn, the peasants of Demyanovka set out for the war. Armed with spears and scythes, they rode the horses looted from the manor, while their *staretz* played the lyre for them and sang songs and told them strange tales. The old man and his deaf-mute lad lay comfortably in the straw in the two-wheeled *telega* through all the days of their journey back to the Ukraine. They rode through the seething streets of Ka-vrayetz and among the hushed huts and byres of Tchernopyl whose people were already gone beyond the Dnieper. They passed the village of Kropivna whose armed peasants ran to join their party. Everywhere around them the people of the fields and forests were arming themselves and flocking together or fashioning weapons out of farming tools; in every dip and defile outside every village the blacksmiths' forges glowed with scarlet fires and echoed day and night with their ringing hammers. Only the terrifying name of Yeremi Vishnovyetzki held the Transdnieper country from open rebellion.

But west of the Dnieper the storm raged in its full and open fury. News of the Hetmans' disaster at Korsun spread like a Steppe fire through all of Ruthenia and everyone who was able to escape his master ran to join Hmyelnitzki.

Chapter Twenty-one

BOHUN'S COSSACKS FOUND him gagged, bound and unconscious the morning after Zagloba's escape, but since his wounds weren't deep, and Pan Zagloba's bread-and-cobweb poultice had drawn out the fever, the young ataman struggled up on his feet by midday. It took him only moments to recall everything that happened and he went mad with rage. He bloodied his hands on his own slashed head, roared like a frenzied animal and lashed out at anyone who came within his reach, so that his worried men took care to keep away from him.

Still too weak to ride, he ordered a hammock stuffed with a featherbed and slung between two horses and rode in it in a wild pursuit along the Lubnie highway. Pale as a corpse and covered with blood and goosedown, he seemed like a vengeful ghost or a ravening vampire as he drove his faithful Cossacks in a crazed gallop across the Steppe, so that they were sure they were all going to their deaths.

They flew like that as far as the small market town of Vasilovka where a hundred men of the Prince's Hungarian infantry were in garrison. The maddened ataman threw himself headlong into their musket fire as if he were sick of life and anxious to die and slaughtered all of them except a handful whom he kept for questioning under torture.

Finding out from them that no one resembling the two fugitives passed through Vasilovka he seemed to go mad again, and howled and clawed his wounds. To go on meant death since every village and settlement between that point and Lubnie held Vishnovyetzki's soldiers who'd know about his attack on Vasilovka from the fleeing traders. He wanted to go on anyway, but his anxious troopers seized him and carried him back to Rozloghi where they found only burned corpses and smoldering ruins. The Kurtzevitchs' peasants looted the manor and burned it to the ground, along with all its other buildings and the blind Prince Vasil who was trapped inside, knowing that if Prince Yeremi ever wanted vengeance, they'd be able to blame this destruction on Bohun and his Cossacks. Such was the peasants' hatred for their Bulyhov masters that they cut down and burned every tree in the cherry orchard and murdered all the manor servants who didn't get away. To stay there, with the tell-tale smoke still hanging in the air, was just as dangerous for Bohun and his men as to go on to Lubnie.

But just beyond the scorched ruins of Rozloghi they caught the terrified Plesnyevski. Questioned, he couldn't give a satisfactory account of himself, so Bohun had him spreadeagled over a bed of coals where he sang out everything he knew about young Pototzki's defeat at Yellow Waters and also about Zagloba and his 'little Cossack' whom he met the day before on the Tchehryn highway. This at least pointed Bohun in the right direction. He had Plesnyevski hanged on the nearest tree and went off again, certain this time that he'd have his hands on the fat knight before the day was over. The horseherding *tchabany*, fooled by Zagloba's inspired deception, sent him towards the Kahamlik but all traces of the fugitives vanished at the crossing as if the broad, muddy stream had swallowed them up.

Another day and night passed in a fruitless search up and down the river and since the chase towards Vasilovka had also taken two full days, it seemed as if Zagloba managed to gain an insurmountable advantage in time and in distance. The feverish Bohun felt as if he had run up against a wall. He raged in a mindless and impotent fury and promised himself that it would take the fat noble at least a day to die when he finally got his hands on him but, in the meantime, he had no idea where to look for his hated enemy.

It seemed to the frenzied ataman that his overwhelming need to worship and possess the Kurtzevitch princess would never be more than a hopeless dream and that he'd never get to quench his thirst for vengeance on the fat knight who made a fool of him in front of his men. But in that desperate moment the *esaul* Anton, a hardbitten old Steppe wolf who'd spent his whole life tracking Tartars along the grassland trails, offered a suggestion.

"*Bat'ku,*" he said. "Look you now. First they were running to Tchehryn. Not where we thought they'd go. And they were smart to do that because they gained time. But when they found out from Plesnyevski about Hmyel and his Yellow Waters victory they had to double back. You've seen yourself how they left the highway and dodged across the river."

"Into the Steppe, you think?"

"I'd find them in the Steppe and that old fox knows it. So he's going to try something else we don't expect. I'll stake my head they've gone towards the Dnieper to get to the Hetmans, which means they're heading either for Tcherkassy or Zolotonosha. That's their two best ways. So let's split up and go after them both ways at once. But we've got to hurry, *bat'ku,* we've no time to waste, 'cause if they get across the Dnieper they'll either reach the Hetmans or the Tartars will sweep them up somewhere."

"Good man! You've got it," Bohun said relieved. "So you take half the men to Zolotonosha and I'll try Tcherkassy."

"Very good, *bat'ku.*"

"But watch yourself. That's a cunning old dog you're tracking."

"I'm a cunning old dog myself, *bat'ku,*" old Anton grinned and said.

"You get those two back to me alive and in one piece and you're made for life," Bohun told him. "I'll cover you with so much gold you'll buy yourself a kingdom!"

Then, as he wheeled with half of his two hundred troopers downriver towards Tcherkassy, old Anton gathered their remaining riders and started tracing Zagloba's muddied tracks towards the old carters' trail that led to Zolotonosha and beyond.

★   ★   ★

Night was already falling on Demyanovka when Anton's company clattered into the village street. At first sight the village looked abandoned. Not even dogs barked there. All the men were gone north towards the Dnieper to join up with Hmyelnitzki and only a few women were left behind in the rundown cabins. Seeing armed horsemen, and not knowing whose side they were on, the women buried themselves in straw in the barns and byres, and crawled into the rafters, and

Anton's men had to search every hut for hours before they came across an old, withered crone who was so near to death that she no longer feared anyone, not even the Tartars.

"Where's all the men, Mother?" Anton asked her when she crouched before him outside her tumbled cabin.

"How would I know?" she snapped back showing yellow teeth.

"We're Cossacks, Mother," the *esaul* assured her. "We're not from the *Lahy*, you've no need to be scared of us."

"To Hell with the *Lahy*," she muttered darkly.

"That's right, to Hell with 'em," Anton agreed quickly. "You're on our side, right?"

"And to Hell with you too," the old woman said.

Anton began to scratch his head, wondering how he was going to get anything useful out of this fierce old witch whom he could neither frighten nor cajole, when a door creaked open across the street behind him and a young, pretty woman stepped out of another of the thatched, white-painted mud and wattle huts.

"Ey, boys!" she cried out. "I hear you're not with the *Lahy*, is that right?"

"That's right!" Anton said.

"You've come from Hmyel?"

"We have."

"So why're you askin' about our men?"

"No reason. Just to know if they've already gone over the river, that's all."

"Aye, they've gone."

"*Slava Bohu*, then. But tell me, girl, did you see one of those cursed *Lahy* escaping this way? He might've had his daughter with him. You see anyone like that?"

"A noble? A *Lah*? Not that I saw. Not here."

"Nobody like that came through here, eh?"

"Nobody. Just an old *staretz* came. It was him that told the men to go to Hmyel, over by Zolotonosha, 'cause he said that *Knaz* Yarema was comin' over here."

"*Knaz* Yarema's coming? Where?"

"Here, where else? That's what the *staretz* said."

"And it was him that told the men to rise up against the *Lahy*?"

"That he did."

"Hmm . . . and was he alone?"

"He had a dumb boy with him."

"He did, eh? And what did he look like?"

"He looked like a *staretz*, what else would he look like? An old, old man, or that's what people said . . . He had this deaf an' dumb lad along with him but I didn't get to see either one of them. I just heard about them. He played the lyre, sang songs, told some stories . . . You know how they are, these wandering old men."

"Hmm . . . Yes, I know. And you're sure it was him that got the men on their way to join up with Hmyel?" Anton asked again.

"That's what people said."

"Hmm . . ." Thoughtful, Anton set his horse once more into motion. "Well, God keep you girl."

"And you too," she cried after him and his trotting Cossacks.

★ ★ ★

Riding out into the night again Anton had some puzzling questions to answer for himself. If that old wandering soothsayer was the disguised Zagloba why would he urge the peasants to run to Hmyelnitzki? And where would he get the costume and the deaf-mute guide? And what had he done with the horses he'd taken in Rozloghi? They'd have been the easiest part of the fugitives' trail to follow because cavalry horses were too valuable to escape any peasant's notice. But what confused the shrewd old Cossack *esaul* more than anything was the thought that a fleeing member of the Polish gentry would be stirring up the peasants against his own kind and warning them about Vishnovyetzki.

"No," he muttered, making up his mind. "That's just an old beggar, that's all. Has to be. Not much point now going on to Zolotonosha."

The idea that Prince Yeremi might be coming this way was something else the Cossack didn't want to think about just then. The terrible Prince was sure to have got word about the attack on his Vasilovka, and suddenly a newly trimmed gate-post that Anton was passing looked exactly like a freshly sharpened stake.

There didn't seem to be enough air to breathe at this moment for the old Steppe rover. The horizons narrowed, the space around him shrunk into a noose, and the sky itself looked ready to come down on him like a crushing weight. Furthermore, he had an uneasy feeling that Pan Zagloba might be just too cunning and too experienced in saving his own skin for anyone to track him down when he wished to cover up his traces.

But suddenly he pulled up his horse and slapped his own forehead. If this mysterious, wandering old beggar was leading the Demyanovka peasants to Hmyelnitzki, why did he urge them to go to Zolotonosha? Hmyel wasn't there! On the contrary, just beyond that town lay the small river settlement of Prohorovka and a ferryboat, and the main camp of the Hetmans' army began just beyond it! One way or another, a close look at that river crossing might be worth the trouble. If, once he reached the Dnieper, he found the Hetmans' soldiers on the other side, he'd bypass the crossing and go downriver to meet up with Bohun. Either way, he'd get some reliable news about Hmyelnitzki. He knew from Plesnyevski's tale that the Zaporohjans had taken Tchehryn and that Krivoinos had been sent ahead to harass the Hetmans while Hmyelnitzki and Tuhaybey were to follow shortly. As an experienced old soldier who knew how long it took troops to move across open country, Anton assumed that the main battle must have been fought already so it would pay to know who won and what to do about it. If, as he supposed, Hmyelnitzki was beaten, then the pursuing Crown soldiers would be spreading out through the whole Dnieper country to hunt down the rebels. In which case it was high time to look for a hideout.

"Ey," he muttered, hurrying his men along the drovers' trail, "it'd be a lot smarter for the ataman to start thinking about his own skin 'stead of chasing all over Hell after a girl, no matter how good she looks. We could get across the river near Tchehryn and then go down to the *Sietch* while there's still time to run . . . Here, with the Hetmans hunting him on one side of the river and *Knaz* Yarema on the other, it'll be hard for him to find a quiet bolt-hole."

★　★　★

Thinking about matters of that kind, he drove his Cossacks towards the River Sula which barred his way along the Prohorovka trail.

Luck seemed to change for him at the riverside settlement of

Mohylna where he found rafts and boatmen who worked day and night ferrying the peasants who were on the run to the Dnieper and Hmyelnitzki. The Transdnieper country didn't dare to stir under Vishnovyetzki's hand but the news of the Yellow Waters victory winged like a bird across the whole region and the peasantry was up and running to join the rebellion. Anton knew that Prince Yeremi was a fair master, much better than most, and his stewards, bailiffs and commissioners were too closely watched to squeeze the people harder than they dared, but many of these so-called peaceful farmers and woodcutters still remembered their own days as freebooting robbers, cut-throats and marauders, and the sudden hope of new unbridled freedoms drew them like a magnet. Mohylna, like Demyanovka, was empty of men other than the few left behind to work the rafts at the river crossing. In many villages even the women armed themselves and marched to join Hmyelnitzki. In Tchabanovka and Vysokye the entire population set out to the rebellion, having set fire to their homes so that they wouldn't be tempted to turn back.

Loading his men and horses on the rafts Anton questioned the Sula ferrymen for news of what might be happening beyond the Dnieper but all he got from them were the usual rumors. All of them knew that Hmyel was fighting the Hetmans somewhere but no one knew who won. Everyone kept a worried eye on the horizon, expecting Prince Yeremi's soldiers any minute. Fear multiplied his regiments into an army vast enough to be everywhere at once, and Anton noted quickly that everyone thought him and his men to be the Prince's vanguard.

But he managed to put the ferrymen at ease and soothe their suspicions.

"Did the Demyanovka people come this way already?" he asked, and they all nodded.

"Sure they did," the ferry foreman said. "We got them across maybe a day back. Maybe two."

"Did they have a *staretz* with them?"

"Sure did."

"And a deaf-mute boy?"

"Him too."

"What did the old man look like?"

"Not so old as you'd think for a *staretz*. Fat, too. He had big bulging eyes, like a fish. One of them was all whitened over like he was blind in it."

"That's him," Anton muttered, grim with sudden joy, and went on with his questions. "And what about that lad?"

"Oy! *Kajhe prosto cheruvym!* So pretty you'd think he was an angel. We never seen any boy like him before."

Anton grinned and nodded as he led his men ashore across the river. "Hey, hey, looks like we'll have a gift for the ataman," he muttered, pleased and already thinking about Bohun's legendary generosity whenever luck turned his way.

Then, turning to his troopers, he ordered:

"Now ride like the Devil!"

★ ★ ★

They flew like startled birds although the country was difficult thereabouts, cracked into gaping chasms and sudden ravines. They entered one of these deep natural corridors that led all the way to the border settlement of Kavrayetz and galloped several miles without a pause for rest. Anton, riding the best horse, was far in the lead. They were almost at the end of the canyon when, suddenly, the old *esaul* pulled back on his reins so hard that the horse's hooves screeched on the shale under him, sliding to a halt.

"*Ah shtcho tze?*" his Cossacks cried behind him. "What's the matter?"

The wide, gaping mouth of the ravine was dark with men and horses who rode in swiftly and formed up at once in tight military sixes. There may have been about three hundred of them. Anton glanced at them and his heart began to hammer in his chest even though he'd been a violent border warrior for two dozen years. He recognized the crimson uniforms of Vishnovyetzki's dragoons.

It was too late to turn and run. Fewer than two hundred paces lay between Anton's troop and the dragoons who advanced towards them at a trot, carbines cocked and ready, and the Cossack horses were too exhausted after their long gallop to last long in any attempt to escape. Anton sat helplessly and cursed his shaking hands while the Vishnovyetzki soldiers surrounded his clustered and uneasy Cossacks.

"Who are you?" their lieutenant challenged Anton fiercely.

"We're Bohun's men!" Anton told the truth since their scarlet uniforms betrayed them anyway. But recognizing the lieutenant, whom he'd seen in Pereyaslav now and then, he cried out with pretended joy: "Lieutenant Kushel! It's you! *Slava Bohu!*"

"Ah, it's you Anton, is it?" The young lieutenant eyed the old Cossack carefully up and down. "What are you up to out this way? And where's your ataman?"

"*Kajhe, pa'ne,*" the old *esaul* cast about for something that might be believed. "The Grand Hetman sent our ataman with letters to Lubnie, to ask the Prince to come and give him a hand, and us . . . we're out here to watch for deserters."

Anton lied as if inspired, trusting in the fact that the dragoons were coming from the direction of the Dnieper and so they'd be unlikely to know about the massacre in Rozloghi, the attack on Vasilovka or any other of Bohun's recent actions. But the Vishnovyetzki officer wasn't fooled that easily.

"Looks to me more like you're on your way to join up with the rebels," he said.

"Ey, *pa'ne* . . ." Anton tried to laugh. "If we was on our way to Hmyel we'd have gone across the Dnieper at Tchehryn."

"That's true," the dragoon lieutenant agreed after a moment. "Yes, that's what you'd have done. But your ataman won't find the Prince in Lubnie."

"Oh? Where's His Highness, then?"

"He was in Pryluki. If he's gone back to Lubnie he wouldn't have set out much before last night."

"Ah, that's too bad," Anton pretended to be troubled by this lucky news. If the Prince was out in his provinces then word of Bohun's actions might not have reached him yet. "Looks like our ataman will miss him, then . . . But you, your worship, if it's all right to ask, are you coming from Zolotonosha?"

"No. We were in garrison in Kalenka. Now there's an order for all the regiments to concentrate in Lubnie so the whole army can march out together. And where are you bound for?"

"Prohorovka, *pa'ne*. Because that's where those damn peasant dogs are crossing the river."

"Have many of them gone?"

"Oy, *bahato, bahato!* Many, sir, many! People say there's thousands of 'em at the Prohorovka ferry waiting to get across."

"Well, teach them a lesson, then. And Godspeed to you."

"And you too, Your Honor!" Anton cried. "Thank you, sir. Thank you! Ride with God!"

The dragoons parted their tight, crimson ranks and Anton's troop passed peacefully between them to the canyon's mouth. Once they were out of sight in the open Steppe, the Cossacks halted and waited in silence, and Anton listened carefully until the last echoes of the dragoon regiment vanished in the ravine behind them.

Then he turned to his grinning men.

"Know this, you numbskulls," he told them, shaking with relief but trying to cover up his own recent terror with a snarling gruffness. "You owe me your lives! And remember that if it wasn't for me you'd be twitching on the stakes in Lubnie before this day was over. And now ride 'til you drop!"

They spurred their horses into instant gallop and rode like the wind.

"Good, good," the old *esaul* muttered grimly under his thick mustache as the miles passed swiftly under his horse's hooves. He could hardly believe in his own good luck. "One," he counted off the first and foremost of his lucky breaks, "is that we saved our hides. And the next is that Zagloba missed those dragoons in Zolotonosha. 'Cause if he'd run into them he'd be safe like a dog back in his own kennel. If he's still waiting to cross at Prohorovka then he's ours."

★ ★ ★

Meanwhile Pan Zagloba was nearer than Anton supposed, cursing his own luck for failing him in a number of terrifying ways. First, having missed Kushel's regiment, he remained a hunted fugitive in ever greater danger. And then, in the midst of far more desperate historical events, he found himself trapped with no way out right in the heart of the flaming, triumphant rebellion.

News of the Hetmans' disaster at Korsun struck him like a thunderbolt as soon as he and Helen arrived in Prohorovka. They heard all kinds of rumors about a great battle in all the wintering huts and settlements they passed on their way from Zolotonosha— there'd even been some wild tales about Hmyelnitzki's victory— but the fat knight didn't pay much attention to this peasant babbling. He knew from experience that word-of-mouth inflated all their stories to legendary dimensions, particularly among these avid, ignorant and superstitious people who liked to turn anything connected with the Cossacks into epics, miracles and magic. But there was no getting away from the awful truth among the howling, jubilant mobs gathered in Prohorovka. Zagloba felt as if his world had caved in all around him and, at first, he simply lost his head.

What, in the names of all the saints, was he to do now? He didn't doubt for a moment that Bohun was searching for him and that sooner or later he'd get on his tracks. True, he'd skipped and dodged this way and that like a hunted hare but he knew all about the relentless hound who was after him, and he also knew that this merciless pursuer would never give up the chase.

"Bohun's behind me," he muttered when nobody could hear him. "What's ahead is a sea of murder, arson, blood-mad mobs and Tartars, and there just doesn't seem to be an end to it. To keep on running will merely put off the inevitable, and not by much I'll bet, especially when you consider who I'm running with! It doesn't matter how I disguise that girl; she'll draw anybody's eyes no matter what kind of rags she's wearing . . . And that can only have one end."

But Pan Zagloba seldom lost his quick wits for long. Through all the chaos raging in his skull he could see quite clearly that he feared Bohun more than anything else under the sky, including the rebellion. The thought that he might find himself again in that raging Cossack's vengeful and unforgiving hands made him numb and blind to everything else around him.

"Will he have fun with me!" he muttered time and time again, wet with immediate sweat. "Any other death would be a real mercy . . ."

One way out of this terrible dilemma was to abandon Helen, let her shift for herself for as long as she might manage to keep herself alive in this appalling national convulsion that overwhelmed the entire country, and hope that God would let her die as quickly as Zagloba wanted for himself. But that was the one thing he knew he couldn't do.

"I don't know what it is, my girl," he whispered sadly, shaking his bald head in wonderment and despair. "You must've thrown some kind of spell on me, or fed me some potion to make me think about someone other than myself.

And the result will be that some murdering peasant is going to have a fine pair of Sunday boots stitched out of my hide."

But to abandon her was out of the question. The mumbling, desperate old knight didn't even let the thought take root in his troubled head.

' . . . So,' he searched his brains, *'what else is there for me to do in this situation?'*

"It's too late to go searching for the Prince," he explained to Helen. "Too late and too far. Alright, so there's a sea of rebellion boiling ahead of us. So why not dive right in? Let's become part of this mad ocean, like a couple of fish among other fishes, and get out of sight . . .! *'Dum spero, spiro,'* as the ancients said. While there's life, there's hope, and we can keep hoping as long as we're still able to breathe! And as long as we can keep ourselves alive we might be able to find some safe rock or quiet backwater somewhere."

And so he decided to risk everything on one desperate gamble, get across the Dnieper, and hide from Bohun where he'd least expect it: right in the heart of the rebellion!

But that was easier thought than done.

Pan Mikolai Pototzki had stripped the river of all boats, no matter how small, to transport the division he'd given to Kshetchovski, so that there was nothing all the way from Pereyaslav to Tchehryn that might float safely across the flooded Dnieper. There was only one broken-down rafting ferry rotting in the riverside mud in Prohorovka and thousands of fleeing peasants fought and jostled each other on the riverbank to be the first to use it.

Moreover, there was neither food nor shelter for these multitudes. Every hut, barn and pigsty in the village was jammed with would-be rebels, so that Pan Zagloba really had to earn his and Helen's bread with his songs and lyre. They waited a whole day and night on the riverbank because the leaky barge kept sinking and had to be repaired after every crossing and in the meantime scenes of unimaginable horror were playing out everywhere around them. The peasants caught and unmasked several disguised Ukrainian squires who hoped to find refuge from the Tartars in Prince Yeremi's country and murdered them in a particularly bestial fashion right under Helen's and Zagloba's eyes. Furthermore, there were two Jewish merchants living in Prohorovka and these, along with their terrified wives and a flock of children, were hurled into the Dnieper by the maddened mob which amused itself for hours by pushing them under the waves with long rafting poles.

The dreadful night went on amid crazed bursts of laughter, the screams of the victims, drunken howls and singing. A sharp, cold wind blew downriver and scattered the campfires so that the sky filled with sparks and flaming firewood that arced and fell hissing into the water. From time to time some hoarse, drunken voice yelled "*Ludy, spasayte! Yarema idut!*" and instant, mindless panic would seize the mobs at this announcement of the Prince's coming. They hurled themselves headlong down the riverbank, trampling and drowning everything before them, so that Zagloba— roaring and cursing as loud as everybody else—fought for his life and Helen's all night long with any sharp, hard object that fell into his hand.

Nothing in her life would have prepared Helen for anything like this, Zagloba was sure, but she fought as fiercely as he did himself, even though she was hardly able to stay on her feet. She was quite exhausted and close to collapse. The rough peasant boots scoured her feet and legs with seeping, open wounds. She looked as though she might drop at any moment with weariness and despair in spite of her determination to defy this brutal, savage and inhuman world, keep struggling against this incomprehensible fate, and to stay alive. Her suffering had changed her beyond recognition. Her face was coarse, cracked and darkened by the wind. Her eyes had dimmed and lost their brilliant luster, and all her inner strength drained out of her bruised and battered body with each passing minute. And, as Zagloba knew by his own rising terror, she'd also be tormented by that other fear that, at any moment, someone might find the woman under her disguise, or that the dark ranks of Bohun's Cossacks might rise like phantoms out of the relentless night and appear unexpectedly before her.

Yelling and cursing, whining and cajoling, the fat old knight managed to wrest a quart of vodka from some superstitious peasant whom he terrified with visions of hellfire, drank all he could and forced the rest on Helen. Otherwise, he was sure, she'd fall unconscious in the stifling press and die as so many others died that night under the trampling boots of the crazed, drunken mob.

"Drink," he hissed at her. "Don't think. Stay on your feet."

"And what if I can't?"

"You'll die. If you must think . . ." The fat knight cast about for something that might restore her strength and her will to live. "Think about . . . Skshetuski."

"Will this night never end?"

"It'll end. Drink. Look, the water's getting brighter already on the river. It'll be daylight soon."

"And then what?"

"Then . . . we'll see."

★ ★ ★

And eventually the terrible night did end. A grey, grim day boiled up from beyond the woods that blackened the horizon, and the pale light began to break whitely on the roiled Dnieper. The fat knight pushed and pulled Helen through the dense crowds that fought to reach the ferry.

"Room for the *staretz*! Room for the *staretz*!" he howled, holding Helen secure before him and kicking and elbowing his way through the senseless mob. "Make a little room for a poor old man, damn your pagan souls! Room for your *staretz*, all you good lads and kind Christian people, may the black plague strangle you and all your aunts and mothers! I'm blind, I can't see! I'll fall in the water . . . You'll drown an innocent boy too, and you'll roast in Hell! Step aside, dear children . . . may the fever shake your bones off their hinges! May you die like dogs . . . good people, gentle folks! Make room, the Devil take you!"

Yelling, pleading, cursing, begging and shoving the crowd aside with his great fists and shoulders, Zagloba managed to lift Helen onto the high-prowed ferry and then, having scrambled up on the deck behind her, began to shout in a different vein.

"Enough! That's enough for this load! What are you shoving for? You'll swamp the ferry! Get off! That's enough, I say. Wait your turn, and if you don't get one that's too bad for you!"

"Enough! Enough!" yelled all the others who had also climbed aboard. "Push off! Let's go!"

The oars and rafting poles splashed into the water and the ferry began to draw away from the crowded shore. The swift Spring current seized it at once and began to carry it down-

stream at a slant. But they had barely reached the middle of the
river when wild yells and shouts rose up behind them on the
eastern bank where the abandoned crowd seemed to be exploding in every direction. Some people ran in panic downstream
along the bank as if to keep up with the drifting ferry, others
leaped into the water as if trying to swim the swollen Dnieper,
yet others shouted to the ferrymen and waved their arms fran-
tically overhead or threw themselves down as if trying to burrow into the mud and gravel.

"What is it?" The anxious peasants on the ferryboat shouted
at each other, trying to understand the panic on the shore.
"What is happening there?"

"It's . . . Yarema!" a drunken voice shouted in such terror as if
the Hour of Judgment had come upon them all, and all the
other voices howled at once: "Yarema! Yarema! Hurry! Get to
the shore! Save yourselves!"

The oars began to drum on the water with a feverish beat and
the heavy, flat-bottomed ferry surged forward like a Cossack
skiff and, at that moment, galloping horsemen appeared beyond
the fragmenting fringes of the crowd.

"Yarema's army!" the panicked peasants shouted aboard the
ferry.

The horsemen reached the riverbank and began to mill
around among the huddled people, asking questions and pointing to the speeding ferryboat, and then began to wave their
arms and caps and to shout at the oarsmen on the river:

"*Stoy! Stoy!* Stop! Come back!"

"Who are they? *Lahy?* Cossacks?"

Zagloba took one look at the shouting horsemen and icy
sweat broke out all over him at once. It covered him like a
second skin from forehead to boot heels, and his mouth fell
open in his beard, but no sound came at first from his suddenly
parched and constricted throat. He recognized the scarlet caps
and coats of Bohun's Pereyaslav Cossacks.

"Holy Mother of God," he whispered after a long moment,
quite certain that his last hour was about to come. "Pray for the
innocent and punish the guilty . . ."

But there was this to be said about the fat, old noble: his
fertile mind was never without some ideas. He blinked. He
growled. He shook himself like a dog emerging from a stream
in Winter, shaded his eyes with his hand like a man whose
eyesight wasn't good enough for a quick assessment, and

started peering at the desperately waving horsemen on the dwindling shore. Then he leaped as if he'd been touched by fire, waved his arms with only partly simulated fear, and began to howl as if he were already being skinned alive:

"Children! That's Vishnovyetzki's Cossacks! I've seen them in Lubnie! Row faster, for God's sake! Forget about those others on the shore; poor devils, their time has come and we'll mourn them later . . .! Now row! Run for it! Get ashore! Tear up this old barge! Chop it up! Destroy it! Or it's a sure death for us all!"

"Faster! Faster! Wreck the boat!" cried all the other peasants on the ferryboat.

The pandemonium on the barge began to match the frenzy on the eastern bank as the flat-bottomed boat ran hard aground on the gravel of the western shore. Not even all the disembarking peasants managed to leap ashore before others started to tear down the tall sides of the grounded vessel, smash the oars, and to chop through the ship's bottom with their axes. The shouting horsemen merely added to the fear and panic; their waving arms seemed like shaken fists and, anyway, in all that noise and clatter it was impossible to hear anything shouted from the Prohorovka shore. Smashed boards and splinters sailed into the air as the wrecked barge began to turn into kindling wood. And in all this fearful clamor and frantic haste and chaos the booming roars of Pan Zagloba drowned out every other sound.

"Cut! Chop! Burn! Tear! Save yourselves! *Yarema idut!* Yarema is coming!" the fat knight howled as if he were either possessed or demented, and then he started winking at the astonished Helen with his one good eye.

★   ★   ★

Wheezing and muttering, Zagloba led the girl ashore and turned to view the scene on the river with certain satisfaction. They were across the Dnieper. They had eluded capture. Their pursuers milled about helplessly on the far side of the rushing water and their frantic shouts only hastened the destruction of the only barge that might have brought them over.

"Heh, heh, heh," the fat knight chuckled softly, and— thinking himself safe, at least for the moment—he started jeering at Anton's Cossacks whom he outwitted by such a narrow margin.

"So you thought you had Zagloba, did you? It would take

more than a pack of lame-brained mongrels to catch this old fox. Go hunt a one-legged chicken in a barnyard because that's all you're good for, not try to match your peasant wits with the likes of me. And when you see your crazy Ataman again give him my regards. Ask him how he liked the dressings I put on his head . . . I should've cut his throat when I had the chance, but I'm a noble, not a peasant, and murdering a helpless man is more your way than mine. Tell him to come after me himself next time he wants a chat, not send his dimwit lackeys."

His muttering was so soft that nobody heard it, anymore than he and the hard-working peasants on the barge could hear and understand the calls and cries of the Cossacks on the Prohorovka shore.

These, by this time, acquired a note of desperation as the rafting barge disintegrated under the peasant axes. But then another panicked howl burst out among the peasants who finished their destruction of the ferry and Pan Zagloba began to sweat again. "What's that? What are those devils up to now? Haven't they had enough?"

"*Skatchut v'vodu!*" the peasants cried in a fresh burst of terror. "They're jumping in the water! They're swimming over after us!"

Indeed, first the Cossack leader and then several dozen of his fierce young riders forced their horses into the flooded river and began to swim their animals across. It was an act of almost suicidal courage at that time of year since the raw Spring floods had turned the Dnieper into a raging cataract full of deep swift currents, swirling eddies, whirlpools and a savage undertow which seized the men and horses and began to carry them rapidly downstream.

"They won't make it!" the peasants shouted.

"They'll drown!"

"*Slava Bohu!* Oh! Oh! Look, there's one horse going under . . .!"

But Pan Zagloba wasn't quite so sure that the determined Cossacks would fail to reach the Ukrainian shore. He watched uneasily as the plunging horses swam one third of the way across the swollen flood although the current whirled them downstream faster than before. The swimming animals labored in the water; they seemed to be coming to the end of their strength and started to sink deeper, and soon their riders were sitting waist-deep in the swift, grey waves. But it seemed likely that most of them would manage to reach the west bank somewhere below the crossing.

Time seemed to be passing with a special slowness. The peasant mobs on both sides of the river watched this desperate struggle in numb, wide-eyed silence, while awed curiosity overcame their fear. New crowds of peasants, armed with guns and pitchforks, ran up to the crossing from the nearby settlement of Shelepukhy to see what the shouting was about, and now the mobs on each side of the river ran along the banks to witness the conclusion of the drama.

Zagloba ran with them.

Only the horses' heads were now showing darkly above the water while their riders sunk to their chests and shoulders but they had come halfway across the river and were drawing nearer. Then one horse and rider vanished. Then another. Then a third and a fourth . . . Then a fifth . . .

Zagloba breathed easier.

The numbers of the Cossacks dwindled rapidly. The sixth horse and rider disappeared. Then the tenth. The twentieth. But the remainder were across two thirds of the river and now the silent watchers around Pan Zagloba could hear the wheezing of the horses' breaths and the quick soft cries with which their riders were urging them along. It became clear that some of Bohun's Cossacks would get safely to shore.

And suddenly Zagloba's hoarse voice split the silent air. "Hey! Children! To your fowling pieces! To your guns and firelocks, whoever's got one here! Shoot down those hangmen of Yarema! Death to them! *Na Pohybel!*"

"*Na Pohybel!*"

Smoke boiled up at once along the riverbank and obscured the water; the ragged volleys thundered out one after another. What sounded like merely one, brief, hopeless cry lifted from the Cossacks in the river and echoed among the gunshots.

And then the smoke cleared.

The river was empty.

Far downstream in the whirling eddies a horse's belly turned over darkly and vanished behind a bend and a single scarlet Cossack cap gleamed briefly in the current.

Zagloba stared at Helen, a frightful grin split his shaggy beard, and he winked at her rapidly with his one good eye.

Part Four

Chapter Twenty-two

PRINCE YEREMI heard about the defeat of the Hetmans at Korsun several days before he came across the distraught Skshetuski among the ashes of Rozloghi, but the full extent of this unprecedented and irreparable disaster was still unknown to him. He supposed that the news was inflated by rumor and that a large part of the Hetmans' forces survived the defeat, and so he pushed on towards the Dnieper, summoning all his regiments to join him with all speed, so that he might avenge this insult to the Commonwealth and either drown the rebels in their blood or spill his own to erase the shame.

He thought that his eight thousand men reinforced by the survivors of the Hetmans' army stood a good chance against Hmyelnitzki's rebels if he could fall upon them before the war engulfed all of the Ukraine. But he no sooner arrived in Pereyaslav, sending men up and down the Dnieper in search of transport shipping, when unexpected news caused him to change his plans. Word came that several of his own Cossack companies mutinied in their outposts on the Tartar borders, either deserting into the Wild Lands or joining the rebellion, and that he'd need at least six weeks to build or gather enough boats to get his army across the river. In the meantime, as his patrols reported, the scattered remnants of the Hetmans' army could be counted in dozens rather than in thousands and Hmyelnitzki grew in power every day. Captured Cossacks gave his strength at two hundred thousand and this could double easily within days as word of the Hetmans' ruin spread throughout the country.

Bearing all that in mind, the Prince decided that a river

crossing would be suicidal on the middle Dnieper. A better plan suggested a long march north towards Tchernihov, which lay secure beyond its great forests, and then a crossing in the quiet region of Brahin which the war was unlikely to reach before his army got there. It would be a difficult and dangerous journey since, beyond Tchernihov, lay a thickly-wooded morass of swamplands and quagmires where even his foot soldiers would face heavy going, while the armored cavalry, artillery and their wagon-train would have to build their own roads as they went along. But before setting out on what he knew could be a journey of no return for him, the Prince wanted to show himself once more throughout his territories to discourage the rebellion there, gather the gentry, and leave a memory of terror among would-be rebels to protect the people who'd now be left without armed defenders. And since his wife and daughters were still in residence in Lubnie, along with all his court and a good part of his infantry, the Prince decided on a last farewell visit to his capital.

The army left Pereyaslav that same day. The countryside was still at peace even though gangs of marauders formed everywhere to loot the manors and pillage the peasants. These were crushed and scattered and their chiefs impaled as the army marched but the vast majority of the villagers sat quietly in their huts. Their minds may have been ablaze with hatred, and their carefully lowered eyes may have been dark with promises of bloodshed, but fear was still the master over their thirst for vengeance. The only sign of their real feelings was that even in those villages where the peasants hadn't run off to Hmyelnitzki, everyone fled at the approach of the Prince's army as if afraid that he'd be able to read in their faces what they were so careful to hide in their hearts, and that he'd inflict a terrible punishment on them in advance.

And they were right to fear him. Because just as he knew no limits in generosity and affection for those who served him and obeyed his orders, so he knew neither mercy nor restraint for those who opposed him.

It could be said that two vengeful apparitions were stalking both sides of the Dnieper in those days: Hmyelnitzki as the death and ruin of the gentry, and Prince Yeremi as the nemesis of the rebel peasants. The people whispered that when those two fell upon each other the sun would tumble from the sky and all the rivers would run red with blood. But that dreaded meeting was still far away because of yet another superstitious fear. Hmyelnitzki, who triumphed over everyone who ventured against him, who crushed the Hetmans and stood at the head of uncounted thousands of warriors and peasants, was simply terrified of this border lord who was preparing to seek him out in the Ukraine. The vast peasant mobs that poured into his camps fled at a whisper of Vishnovyetzki's name. He had perhaps fifty thousand Cossacks who could stand up to the Transdnieper soldiers and these, in his judgment, were poor odds against such a renowned and charismatic leader. And so he stayed in Korsun for weeks after his great victory, sorting his hordes of *tchernya* into regiments, appointing colonels and commanders over them from among the best Zaporohjan atamans and *esauls*, sending divisions to besiege the castles where the gentry were still holding out, and buying time with cunning and beguiling words which many of the Ruthenian border magnates were anxious to believe.

★ ★ ★

And so the day came when all the events noted in this narrative began to come together. The Prince's army crossed the Sleporod on its way to Lubnie, and the Prince took up his quarters in the nearby manor of his steward at Filipov, when word came that Hmyelnitzki sent emissaries with a letter. The Prince ordered them brought to him at once.

They entered the chamber where the Prince sat among his leading officers with something of a swagger: six Zaporohjans led by Ataman Suharuka, for whom his own fresh colonelcy and the memory of Korsun served as an antidote to fear. But they no sooner caught the Prince's eye when they were seized with such unreasoning terror that they threw themselves facedown before him and didn't dare to speak until the Prince ordered them to rise.

"Why are you here?" he demanded.

"A letter from the Hetman," Suharuka murmured, and the Prince fixed his cold eyes on the Cossack colonel as if the sight of these emissaries was abhorrent to him.

"From a thug, a robber and a rebel, not a Hetman," he said quietly but stressing each word.

The Zaporohjans became as pale as corpses and stood in

silence near the door while the Prince ordered the letter read aloud so that everyone might hear it.

The letter was so humble that the listening officers and Cossacks might have thought this was a vassal writing to his master instead of the undisputed ruler of territories and peoples whose size and numbers rivaled the German Empire. Hmyelnitzki blamed his enemy Tchaplinski for everything that happened; even the Hetmans' fate was due, he wrote, more to their own pride and cruelties against the Cossacks than to anything he wanted. He begged the Prince to forgive anything he might have done inadvertently to offend him, assured him of his continuing loyalty to the Commonwealth, and—to secure mercy for his emissaries—announced that he was releasing Skshetuski whom Tuhay-bey captured in the *Sietch*.

He went on to complain about Skshetuski's insulting behavior because he refused to carry this letter, and he attributed all the bloodshed and horrors of the Civil War to just such stiff-necked and relentless Polish arrogance and to the many humiliations which the Cossacks were forced to endure.

Listening to these assurances of loyalty and respect, the Cossack emissaries grew even more uneasy. They thought they'd hear harsh threats and a ringing challenge and they expected death in retribution. But this tearful listing of complaints seemed to seal their doom. If their victorious Hetman bowed and scraped like this before the terrible Yarema what chance did they have? They stared at him in fear, trying to read some sign of their fate in his cold, white face, but the Prince listened to the reading without a sign of feeling. Only his heavy eyelids drooped from time to time as if to mask the anger that boiled inside him.

The reading over, the Prince ordered little Pan Volodyovski to take the Cossacks out into the yard and place them under guard.

"See what a cunning enemy this is," he told his listening colonels. "Either he wants to fool me so that I'll drop my guard and let him fall on me in my sleep, or he's getting ready to go deep into the Commonwealth, wheedle his way into forgiveness by the King and the Diet, and trade his ambitions for his own security and safety. Because if I were to go on fighting him once he's made his peace with the Commonwealth then you and I would be the rebels, not he and his cut-throats."

"*O vulpes astuta!*" Pan Vurtzel cried out.

"Oh yes." The Prince smiled grimly. "He's a fox as well as a jackal. There's no doubt of that."

"That's how he's always been," said Pan Zachvilihovski. "As much a fox as a lion, as much a serpent as an eagle."

"What's your advice, then?" The Prince motioned to his assembled officers to come nearer and to be at ease. "Speak up, gentlemen. Say what's on your minds and then I'll tell you what I intend to do."

Old Pan Zachvilihovski, who left Tchehryn and joined up with the Prince while Skshetuski was still on his way to Kudak, was the first to speak.

"We'll carry out your wishes, Prince, no matter what they are. But if you'll permit advice from a man who's known Hmyelnitzki since he was a boy, then here it is. You've caught his intentions exactly. That's just what he's after. So I say that we should pay no attention to anything he writes but make sure that Her Highness and her court are taken to safety, and then cross the Dnieper and begin the war before Hmyelnitzki has time to strike some kind of bargain with the Diet in Warsaw. Beat him first, I say, and then offer him forgiveness and mercy. Or he'll heap such new horrors on the Commonwealth that none of us will be able to survive the shame."

Pan Aleksander Zamoyski, who held the title of King's Quartermaster and served as the chief of the Prince's military staff, struck his sheathed saber with his fist so that the metal rattled against his boots.

"*Senectus* and *sapientia* speak through you, sir," he told the old commissioner. "We should all admire your sagacity and wisdom. Let's pull the head off this monster before he grows so huge that he'll devour us all."

"Amen to that," Father Muhovyetzki said.

The other officers began to slap their sabers and to growl their unanimous approvals, and the thoughtful Vurtzel, who commanded the Prince's engineers and artillery, took a step forward to speak for them all.

"It's an insult to Your Highness's dignity and position that this rebel scum dares to write to you at all! The Chief Ataman of the Zaporohjans does have authority to speak for the Cossacks. He is commissioned by the King and the Senate as the Cossacks' leader so that even the *kujhen* atamans derive some sort of legality from him. But this self-styled 'Hetman' has no legal

standing whatsoever. He deserves no better treatment than any
other rebel!"

"That's my thinking too," the Prince said. "And since I can't
get my hands on him at this moment then let his emissaries
represent him for a little longer."

He nodded at the grim, red-haired Vyershul who commanded his own Tartar Light Horse, although the soldiers
serving in that regiment, as in the Valachian Light Horse of
Byhovietz, were neither Tartars nor Valachians but Ruthenian
gentry.

"Tell your Tartars to take the heads off those Cossacks'
necks," he ordered. "As for their leader, have them whittle a
stake for him at once."

Vyershul bowed his red head, saluted and stepped from the
room, while the kindly Father Muhovyetzki, who sometimes
managed to restrain the worst of Vishnovyetzki's ruthlessness
and anger, pressed his hands together in supplication and raised
his begging eyes to those of the Prince.

"No, Father," the Prince said firmly. "Not this time. This
must be done to avenge the cruelties they've allowed themselves
in the Ukraine, to add to the terror in which they hold my
name, and to serve as an example of what all rebels can expect
from us. We must show everyone in the country that there's still
someone left in this Commonwealth who's not afraid to treat
that upstart 'Hetman' like the cut-throat criminal he is. He may
play the fox with others as much as he likes but he isn't going to
get away with it with me."

"Prince," the priest begged. "Remember . . . He set
Skshetuski free . . ."

Anger appeared like a sudden storm cloud in Prince Yeremi's
face. "I thank you in Skshetuski's name that you hold him in the
same regard as common murderers," he said coldly, then turned
to the others.

"Enough of this. I see that all of you cast your votes for war.
That's my intention too. We'll march north to Tchernihov,
gathering all our loyal people as we go, and get across the
Dnieper in the shallows beyond the marshes. Then we'll turn
south and take the war to Hmyelnitzki's doorstep. And now
. . . perhaps for the last time . . . to Lubnie!"

"God grant success!" all the officers cried out in a strong, firm
chorus.

★ ★ ★

But in that instant the doors were flung wide so fiercely that whitewash and plaster trembled off the walls, and the tall, wiry Rostvorovski, who led another of the Prince's Valachian regiments, ran into the chamber.

"Highness!" he cried, out of breath. "The rebellion's spreading! Rozloghi is burned to the ground! The garrison in Vasilovka has been wiped out, cut down to the last man!"

"What? Where? When?" the other officers shouted, crowding around Rostvorovski who was sent out several days earlier on a scouting mission.

"Who did this?" the Prince demanded calmly.

"People say Bohun, Highness."

"Bohun?"

"That's right, Highness. About three days ago."

"You went after him? You caught up with him? You've confirmed all this from prisoners?"

"I tracked him as far as I could, Highness, but I didn't catch him," Rostvorovski said. "Three days gave him too much of a lead. But he rode like a madman, didn't seem to care who knew where he went, and I picked up good information about him all along the way. They were running back to Tchehryn and then they split up. Half of them turned downriver towards Tcherkassy and half went on to Zolotonosha and to Prohorovka."

Here young Kushel stepped up, snapped his fingers in anger and frustration and said: "That must have been the troop I met in that canyon near Prohorovka, as I've already reported to your Highness. They told me they were tracking runaways so I let them go."

"That was stupid of you," the Prince said, then shrugged. "But it's hard to know what to do when treason flares up underfoot at every step we take."

Then, suddenly, he seized his own head in both hands.

"God almighty!" he cried out. "Now I remember what Skshetuski told me about Bohun's fancy for the Kurtzevitch girl! That's why Rozloghi's burned down to ashes! Why else? Bohun must have seized her. Here, Volodyovski!"

"Highness!" The diminutive dragoon, whose reputation as a Steppe scout, tracker and light cavalry commander was unequaled in the Prince's service, and whose Ruthenian troopers were among the best-led and most loyal soldiers in the border army, stepped up for his orders.

"Take five hundred men at once back towards Tcherkassy! Byhovietz, you take five hundred Valachians towards Zolotonosha and the Prohorovka crossing! Ride like the wind! Whichever of you brings that girl to me will get the freehold and rents of my Yeremiovka property for life. Now go! Go!"

And to the other colonels and commanders, he said: "And the rest of us . . . to Rozloghi, and then on to Lubnie."

The officers ran out of the steward's manor, leaped on their waiting horses and galloped off to their regiments. The Prince's household staff, officials and courtiers also mounted and formed up behind the silvery dappled thoroughbred that Prince Yeremi rode on his campaigns, and with a swiftness that testified to their discipline, training and experience, the many brightly uniformed regiments, troops and companies spread out within minutes on the winding highway like a long multi-colored serpent gleaming with armored scales.

★   ★   ★

But if anyone who rode that day behind Vishnovyetzki's banners still harbored any doubts about the character and nature of this autocratic magnate—in whom cruelty, despotism, enlightenment and mercy seemed to illuminate each other like opposite images trapped in a single mirror—then the next few moments would have been revealing.

A bloody sight met the soldiers' eyes at the limits of the little village. Five Cossack heads regarded them blindly from mounds of brushwood piled at the roadside, while nearby, on a flowery green hillock a spear's length away, the impaled Ataman Suharuka still quivered in his agony on a sharpened stake. The rough-hewn point had passed halfway through his body but many hours of suffering were still ahead of him because as much as three days might go by before death brought merciful oblivion to an impaled man. Now the tormented Cossack was not only alive and conscious of every shard of pain but he was able to turn his head slowly from side to side and to follow the passing regiments with his frightful eyes as they rode below him.

Silent he may have been, but his eyes spoke clearly to anyone who dared to look into them and to read their message.

'*May God bring suffering on you all,*' they said as if in prayer.
'*May He send torments to you and your children and your children's
children through ten generations . . . for this blood, these wounds, this
torture . . . May you die like dogs, you and all your people! May all
misfortunes find you! May you be doomed to dying without end and
find neither the peace of death nor the ability to go on living in your
suffering . . .!*'

And although this was just a common Cossack who waited
for death on a rough stake under the open sky rather than in an
ornate castle hall, dressed in a split and threadbare *zhupan* rather
than cloth-of-gold and majestic purples, such was the gloomy
dignity of his silent torment, and Death which perched above
him in the golden air gave his red eyes such dreadful eloquence,
that everyone understood perfectly what he wished to tell them.

The glittering regiments rode past him in respectful silence
and he loomed over them in the bright beams of the noonday
sun like a burning torch of vengeance and hatred set up at the
roadside to light their way to Hell.

No one questioned the Prince's savage order. No one doubted
his right to make all decisions, whether for good or evil, but
this assenting silence was less the product of fear among men
who thought themselves fearless than the result of their iron
discipline, and the trust and affection won over many years.
Ruthlessness, courage and readiness to shoulder the most terrible responsibilities lived side by side in this strange single-
minded man, along with a fierce, overweening pride, impatience with anyone who failed to grasp his own lofty vision, and
a passionate devotion to his country and for what it stood.

He couldn't stand to have his word questioned or his motives
doubted. Once, when the Senate summoned him to Warsaw to
explain himself in a land dispute with another magnate, he
arrived at the head of four thousand horsemen whom he ordered to scatter the tribunal to the four winds if anyone there
cast doubt on his honor. On the other hand he provided homes
and lifelong care for four thousand orphans, built either a cathedral or a temple for every faith and sect in his territory, founded
five colleges in which the sons of his tenantry were educated at
no cost, and turned his capital in Lubnie into a haven for the
homeless and the dispossessed whom he provided with lands,
training, occupations and protection under his stern justice.

He rode past the dying Cossack without a second glance,

Father Muhovyetzki blessed the tortured man in passing with his crucifix, and almost all the iron ranks had clattered by him on the cobbled highway when a young serving lad wheeled his pony out of the rear ranks of the winged *husaria*, rode up to the sufferer, pressed a horse pistol against the victim's ear, and ended all his torments with one shot.

Everyone who saw this simple act of mercy shuddered and gave a gasp, thinking the boy was as good as lost. He had not only broken military discipline but contradicted Prince Yeremi's order and challenged his judgment. But the Prince said nothing. He rode on as calmly as if nothing unusual had occurred and it was only later, when the army halted for the night, that he had the boy brought to him in his quarters.

The boy went in, only half alive with fear and expecting terrible punishment, and stood before the Prince as if the earth were about to open under him.

"What do they call you?" the Prince asked.

"Zelenski," the boy whispered.

"You shot the Cossack?"

"Yes. I did."

"You understand the full extent of what you did?"

"I do."

"Then why did you do it?"

"I couldn't watch his pain," the boy confessed, expecting to see the instant lightnings and to hear the thunder of Prince Yeremi's anger.

But the Prince nodded quietly.

"You'll see worse than this when we come into their own country," he said in a voice which was both stern and gentle. "You'll see so much horror that all thought of mercy will fly away from you like angels from hellfire. But because you risked your life for the sake of your humanity I'll have the treasurer in Lubnie pay you ten gold ducats, and I'm taking you into my own service from this moment on."

Everyone wondered about this turn of events but, just at that moment, the patrols returned with news from Zolotonosha, and all thoughts turned elsewhere.

Chapter Twenty-three

LATE IN THE EVENING, with moonlight sifting through the cold, grey ashes, the vanguard of the Prince's army trotted into the ruins of Rozloghi where they found Skshetuski. The young knight was sunk in such profound despair that it took all of Father Muhovyetzki's admonitions to lift him out of it.

The night echoed with the shouts and calls of his many friends who ran to greet him and console him as best they could, and chief among them was the mournful giant, Longinus Podbipyenta, who was enlisted in Skshetuski's company since Spring. The gentle Lithuanian immediately vowed to the Virgin Mary that he'd fast each Tuesday if only She'd send some saving ray of hope to the young lieutenant and he got ready to add his own groans and tears to those of Skshetuski. But the grief-stricken young man seemed to have no tears left to shed.

In the meantime he was half-led and half-carried to the Prince's quarters in a peasant hut where Prince Yeremi welcomed him without a word. He merely opened his arms to him and waited until the young man stumbled into them and let his tears burst out of him at last, and then he pressed his favorite soldier to his chest, and stroked his head and hugged him as if he were his father, and the astonished officers who pushed into the huddled little *izba* saw tears in Vishnovyetzki's eyes.

It took some time before the Prince said anything. Then he began to speak in a low, gentle voice, while Skshetuski gave way to his pain and grief.

"I welcome you as if you were my son," Prince Yeremi said, "because I thought you lost to us, and that I'd never get to see you again, and here you are restored to us by God's great love and mercy which, I am sure, He wouldn't show if you weren't needed. Carry your cross and accept your burden just as Christ did his, and remember that you'll have thousands to share your suffering. Christ walked alone in his pain and sorrow but you'll have the company of an entire nation mourning lost wives and children and kinsmen and friends."

"God's will . . . be done," Skshetuski murmured through his tears and the Prince stroked his grey, worn face like a mother soothing an injured child.

"Think of your pain as just one drop in a sea of suffering," he said quietly but firmly. "Let your despair dissolve in that ocean of anguish that is about to drown our entire country. Listen to me. When our beloved Commonwealth faces such times as these, private tears become a selfish luxury. Anyone who wears a saber and calls himself a man will put aside his heartaches and run to save our Mother. And then he'll either find peace and forgetfulness in service and duty, or he'll die in a selfless cause, and that will earn him God's love and that eternal happiness that comes from a clear conscience."

"Amen!" said Father Muhovyetzki.

"Highness, I'd rather see her dead," the young soldier sobbed.

"Weep. Go on. Weep." The Prince nodded gently. "Don't try to hide your tears. A man would have to be an animal or a stone not to feel the kind of loss you've suffered, and we're all human here. We'll add our tears to yours because we're your brothers, not savages or Tartars, and your pain is ours. But tell yourself this, my son: '*Today is mine for sorrow over my own misfortunes, but tomorrow belongs to my Mother.*' Because tomorrow we begin her war and we will put aside all pity until it is over."

"I'll go with you, Highness, to the end of the world," the grieving young man murmured. "But . . . it's so hard for me to live without her that . . . I can't . . . I can't think . . . about what might be happening to her . . ."

And the despairing young soldier clawed at his unkempt beard and bit his calloused hands to muffle his groans because a storm of despair clutched at him again.

"You said: '*His will be done!*'" Father Muhovyetzki admonished quietly but sternly.

"Amen . . . amen!" Skshetuski murmured in a broken voice.

"I give myself over to His will . . . Let Him point my way. Only . . . only . . . I can't cope with this pain . . . this regret . . ."

Everyone in that cramped and smoky little room could see how hard he fought and struggled to overcome the images of Helen in Bohun's hands so that the quick, hot tears of their own pity for him shined in many eyes. The warm-hearted little Pan Volodyovski and the mournful giant, who were both easily moved to sentiment and affection, heaved huge sighs and let their tears run openly into their whiskers.

"Brother, dear brother . . ." The soulful Lithuanian twisted his powerful hands so desperately that the great, gnarled knuckles cracked like pistol shots. "Control yourself . . . I beg you!"

"Weep, weep!" cried the others.

"Listen," the Prince said suddenly. "I've a report that Bohun rode like a madman from here towards Lubnie. Something had driven him berserk or he'd never dare to attack my men in Vasilovka. So perhaps he didn't get his hands on your girl? Perhaps she escaped? Why else would he chase shadows on the Lubnie highway?"

"That could be!" the other officers cried at once, crowding around Skshetuski. "Don't despair, Yan! Be hopeful! God helps the innocent!"

Skshetuski stared at them with uncomprehending eyes as if he couldn't grasp what they were telling him and then their words took root; a wild hope gleamed in his eyes again and he threw himself headlong at the Prince's feet.

"Highness!" he cried. "You give me faith again . . . you restore my life . . . I'll give all my blood for this to be true!"

"See? See? Believe in the best!" cried the others. "You'll see her in Lubnie!"

Weakened by all his wounds, and drained by the shattered images of everything in which he believed before his journey to and from the *Sietch,* the worn-out young man slumped in exhaustion and couldn't say anything more just then. He grew so pale that Pan Longinus had to carry him to a bench and then seat him on it, but it was clear at once from the fevered light that spread across his face that he found new hope and seized onto it like a drowning man who clutches at a splinter.

★ ★ ★

Led to another peasant hut, where his friends went on celebrating his return till dawn, Skshetuski wavered all night between despair and hope until Byhovietz' troops returned from
Tcherkassy with word about Bohun. They brought back some
peasants who saw the rebel ataman only two days earlier, and
who reported that he seemed to be chasing someone, riding
every which way like a raving maniac, and questioning anyone
he saw about a fat, fleeing noble and a Cossack boy. They also
swore that they saw no young woman with him.

A new joy leaped up in Pan Yan at this news although none of
it made any sense to him. If Helen had got away from Bohun,
where could she have gone? Which way was she heading?
Bohun's wild ride towards Lubnie and then his sudden turn
towards Tchehryn, Tcherkassy and Zolotonosha suggested that
he didn't know any better than Skshetuski where to search for
her. Kushel swore that he'd have spotted her if she was with the
Cossacks he met in the canyon before Prohorovka, so that it
seemed that none of Bohun's men had tracked her down and
caught her.

"Tell me what to think," he begged his companions, "because
I can't make head or tail of any of this."

"You'll find her in Lubnie," Migurski assured him. "She's
sure to have gone there."

"Maybe that's where she was heading at the start," Pan
Zachvilihovski said. "But I don't think she got there or Bohun
wouldn't be searching for her in Tcherkassy and in Prohorovka.
If she was safe in Lubnie then Bohun would be running as fast as
he's able back to Tchehryn and then to Hmyelnitzki instead of
risking his neck in wild chases through the Prince's country.
No, no my friends, I'm sure that she's the object of all that
commotion."

"So what's all that business about a fat noble and a Cossack
lad he's asking about?"

"The Cossack?" The old commissioner pondered for a moment. "It wouldn't take much perception to assume that if she
was on the run she'd do it in disguise. So I would think this
Cossack lad is none other than she."

"That makes sense! It could be!" all the others cried.

"Then . . . what about that fat noble? Who is he?"

"That I wouldn't know," the commissioner said. "But we can
question some of the peasants here. They'll swear they know

nothing, like they always do, but they're sure to have witnessed everything that happened and seen everyone who was a part of it. Go get the man who lives in this hut, some of you, and we'll soon have answers."

The officers ran outside in a body and soon tracked down an old sharecropper who'd hidden in the byre and dragged him by the scruff of the neck back into the room.

"Listen to me, peasant!" Zachvilihovski turned on the quivering man. "Were you here when Bohun and his Cossacks burned down the manor house?"

As expected, the peasant swore by all the saints that he'd been nowhere near, that he saw nothing and didn't know anything about whoever might have been responsible, but the old commissioner wasn't to be fooled.

"Oh, of course you don't know anything," he said scornfully. "Of course I'll believe that you crawled under your bed and sat there quiet as a church-mouse while the rest of your people were looting the manor! Tell that to someone who doesn't know your kind. But take a look, here's a gold ducat on the table, see it? And there by the door is a lackey with a sword. Which would you rather have, the gold in your pocket or the sword laid across your neck? Take your pick and be quick about it! If you don't start talking we'll burn down the village and d'you know what'll happen then? The curses of your own kin will follow you to Hell and there's no sweeter music for the Devil's ears."

Thus encouraged, the peasant sang out the whole tale of the raid, including what he heard the next day about the young lady who got away with a nobleman who'd come to Rozloghi with Bohun.

"That's it! That's it!" Pan Zachvilihovski said. "Here is our answer, friends, and there's your gold-piece, peasant. And tell me, did you see that noble with your own eyes? Was it someone from these parts?"

"I seen 'im, lord. But he's not from here."

"And what did he look like?"

"Fat, lord, like a brick stove. With a white beard too, an' blind in one eye . . . An' he cursed like the devil, he did, an' drank like a Cossack . . ."

"Dear Lord!" Pan Longinus exclaimed, looking around in astonishment. "That sounds like Pan Zagloba!"

"Zagloba?" The old commissioner spoke the name as if it was

the last that would occur to him. "Hmm . . . Could it be? The description fits him . . . And wait my friends, wait . . . Now that you mentioned him I remember that he and Bohun got pretty close in Tchehryn in the last few weeks. They did a lot of drinking and gambling at Dopul's, thick as thieves they were . . . Yes, it could've been Zagloba, though it's hard for me to believe that he'd show such spirit."

Then he turned once more to the peasant. "And you say that it was this fat noble who carried off the lady?"

"Yes, lord. That's what people said."

"And you've seen Bohun too, have you? You know what he looks like?"

"Oy, master, he spent whole months here in the old days!"

"But maybe that fat noble took the lady somewhere with Bohun's consent?"

"How could that be, master?" Now that the peasant's story seemed to be something the knights wished to hear, the old sharecropper grew confident and bold. "He trussed Bohun like an ox for slaughter! Wrapped his head in his own coat, too, so he couldn't yell. And when he disappeared with the lady it was like the earth swallowed them up or something, nobody could find them. People say the ataman howled like a wolf when he found out about it. Right away he had a hammock and a featherbed slung between two horses and rode off to Lubnie as fast as a windstorm! He was back in two days, mad as the Devil and without the lady, and then he and his people rode off someplace else!"

"I still say she could've got to Lubnie!" Migurski exclaimed. "The fact that Bohun missed her on the highway and then looked for her somewhere else doesn't mean a thing!"

But by this time Skshetuski was already on his knees, praying his thanks to God.

"Hmmm . . ." The old commissioner went on wondering aloud and scratching his snow-white head, still not quite able to believe that the loudmouthed, roistering fat knight had it in him to show such unexpected courage. "I didn't think he'd dare to pick a quarrel with a man like Bohun. That just doesn't fit any image of him. Of course, he liked Skshetuski and praised him to high heavens for that vintage *Troyniak* our friend left with him, but he also drunk up a cellar or two on Bohun's money . . . Well, well, who'd have thought it of him? I know he's as quick and resourceful as a fox and knows how to look after his own skin. But I always thought him a coward and a braggart whose mouth was a lot bigger than his heart. It's hard to believe he'd show himself to be such a man!"

"Let him show himself as anything he likes," said little Pan Volodyovski, grinning from ear to ear. "It's enough for me that he got the Princess away from that demented Cossack. And since it's clear he knows how to use his head he'll make sure she's safe!"

"His own neck depends on that," Pan Migurski said, then cried out to Skshetuski: "Hey, my friend, it looks like we'll be standing up for you in church after all!"

"And drinking at your wedding!" all the others cried.

"And then at the christening!"

"And at all the other christenings too! *Vivat* the young couple! Long life to them both!"

"And long live Zagloba!"

And so they drank and cheered and embraced each other, not even thinking of the bloody years of war that stretched ahead of them, or of the death that waited for many among them, and raised their toasts to Helen and Skshetuski and to all their future children and descendants until the morning trumpets summoned them to duty.

★ ★ ★

The march resumed at daybreak. Because all these regiments were mounted on swift Steppe horses and riding without the infantry, baggage trains and cannon—not even stopping to rest and water their animals but hand-feeding them on the move in the Tartar fashion—they came within sight of the grey stone towers, gilded domes and spires of Prince Yeremi's capital by late afternoon.

Pan Yan wanted to ride in the vanguard with Byhovietz' Tartars, so as to be the first to reach the castle and to look for Helen, but he was still too weak for the hard riding of the Light Horse scouts. Besides, the Prince kept him at his side, wanting to hear an account of his mission to the *Sietch*, so the young lieutenant found himself relating and reliving his entire ordeal from the moment of his capture on Hortytza Island. The only thing he withheld and kept to himself was his argument with Hmyelnitzki so that the Prince wouldn't think him a boaster and braggart.

"But why didn't Pan Grodjitzki send to me for his shot and

powder?" the Prince demanded, visibly upset, when he heard that part of Skshetuski's story. "That fortress could have done a lot of damage to the rebels. I'd have been glad to supply him with everything he needed!"

"He probably thought it was the Grand Hetman's business to take care of that," Skshetuski suggested.

"And he'd be right," the Prince said abruptly and then grew silent for a bitter moment.

"The Hetman's an experienced soldier," he resumed after a long silence in a voice that held more regret and pity than that scathing anger that Pan Yan expected. "He's a famous warrior . . . But he was too full of his own great past, he had too much confidence in the power of his name and too much contempt for his enemies, and that's what destroyed him. He refused to take Hmyelnitzki seriously. And when I offered him my help he shrugged off the whole rebellion as a minor brushfire. He didn't want to share his glory with anyone and thought that I might get the credit for his victory."

"That's what I think too, Highness," Skshetuski said quietly.

"He thought he'd pacify the Zaporohjans with horsewhips and drive them back to obedience with a few kicks and curses, and now look what's happened! God punished his pride. It's through that same blinding, jealous and self-centered arrogance that the Commonwealth is dying, and there isn't one of us who's free of that sickness."

Then he was silent, letting his cold, embittered eyes sweep emptily through the broad Steppe that bordered the highway, as if remembering his own high-handed actions in that famous land quarrel with the Konyetzpolskis.

But in just that moment the tall, bright, copper-sheeted spire of St. Michael's Church appeared on the horizon among the clusters of Orthodox onion domes and gilded roofs of temples, and then the grey smudge of walls and towers began to rise out of the trembling mists, and they turned towards Lubnie.

* * *

It took the regiments until nightfall to enter the city. All the Transdnieper gentry seemed to have descended on that great, safe haven, and hundreds of new arrivals crowded through the gates along with their wives, children, servants and baggage wagons, armed lackeys and household retainers, burdened camel trains, cattle herds and horses. The violent spread of the rebellion across the Dnieper, and the seething discontent among their own peasants, drove all the officials of the principality to shelter behind the Prince's walls, and with them came all the merchants, traders, Armenians and Jews against whom the peasants' rage burned hotter than against anybody else.

It seemed to Skshetuski that some great, annual fair was in progress in the town's main square. The broad, cobbled space around the romanesque cathedral, as well as all the streets leading into it, were jammed with thousands of carts and wagons of every size and shape. Cossack *telegas* bumped and scraped the charabancs of the gentry among jostling crowds of soldiers and lackeys in bright uniforms and liveries, Jews in their foxfur hats and voluminous dark robes, Armenians in purple skullcaps, and even some Tartars from Astrakhan, and merchants from Moscow, who had been on their way to the Ukraine with their caravans of trade goods and stopped here because of the war beyond the Dnieper.

Skshetuski was among the first to reach the Prince's castle where all the important refugees and guests found hospitable refuge, but he found neither Helen nor Zagloba there. Once more disappointed, he locked himself in his quarters in the citadel, and tried to brush away his anxieties in much the same way that a wounded soldier abandoned on a battlefield struggles against the flocks of carrion birds that settle about him.

He fortified himself with the thought that the cunning and resourceful Zagloba would be shrewd enough to slip through all the dangers and, having heard about the destruction of the Hetmans' army, might head for Tchernihov which the Prince's army would reach within weeks.

He recalled the dimly noted and half forgotten image of the blind, naked beggar shivering in the reeds beside the Kahamlik with his deaf-mute lad, and his complaints about the 'Devil' who stripped him and robbed him only three days earlier, and he seized on the hope that this robber must have been Zagloba in search of disguises for himself and Helen.

"That's what it's got to be," he told himself over and over and felt some relief.

He prayed for hours.

Then, wanting to add greater value to his prayers, he sought out Father Muhovyetzki and asked to be confessed. The priest led him at once to the cathedral, heard him out, gave him absolution, soothed his anxieties and confirmed him in his faith while, at the same time, reading him a stern lesson in duty.

"No Christian can allow himself to doubt God's mercy and power," he said. "And no citizen may spill more tears over his own misfortunes than over the disasters that befall his nation. Pity for your own self rather than for others, and heartache over your own lost love rather than for the misery of your countrymen, brings just the sort of punishment from God which we are witnessing everywhere around us."

"I understand," the young lieutenant murmured.

His time among the Zaporohjans made him an eyewitness to unparalleled misery and shame; he'd seen examples of the selfishness, greed and preoccupation with private advancement over the public good that helped to bring about the fratricidal conflict. The priest's admonition was as clear to him as if he was guilty of all these sins that were beginning to destroy his country.

"Furthermore," the Prince's chaplain urged him. "You must rid yourself of that blinding and self-serving hatred for the Cossacks that I sense in you. By all means fight them as the enemies of your faith and country! Destroy them as the allies of the heathen Tartars whom they've brought among us! But you must forgive them every private pain that they may have caused you and give up any thought of personal revenge."

"I'll do that," Skshetuski said humbly.

"Do so and you'll find peace among all the horrors that we're about to witness and earn the love and happiness that God is sure to restore to you in time."

Then the priest blessed him, ordered him to do penance for his sin of hatred by prostrating himself until dawn on the stone floor before the altar, and left him to his thoughts.

The nave of the chapel was empty and dark, lighted by only two pale candles that flickered on the altar and illuminated the gentle alabaster face of Christ—so full, Skshetuski thought, of love and suffering and forgiveness—that looked down from his own cross at the silent soldier.

Skshetuski lay as still as if he was dead. But as the minutes passed, as they turned into hours, he started to feel as if all his bitterness, anxiety, anger and despair had begun to stir and uncoil within him, and then to slide and creep out of him, snaking along the cold stone floor to hide and vanish somewhere in the darkness.

He began to breathe easier, feeling a new strength take root in his body, while his mind acquired a fresh clarity and lightness.

Lying in silent, meditative prayer before that marble Christ and that softly and mysteriously illuminated altar, he found within himself all those uplifting and affirming qualities of goodness and virtue that a man of his times could discover in his own unquestioning and unviolated faith and in the simplicity of his absolutes and values.

His night passed in prayer. When he rose at dawn he felt as if he was born anew.

Chapter Twenty-four

THAT DAY AN ERA ended in the history of the Commonwealth and the Transdnieper Country, an irreversible process of territorial abridgement and decline from power had begun, and most of the men and women who rose with such a gloomy sense of foreboding from their beds in Lubnie on that grey Summer morning, and stared at the thickening clouds that boiled on the horizon, knew that nothing would be the same for them again.

From the first moments of daylight, even before the red streaks of sunrise shot above the dark rolling country hidden in the mists, the regimental officers were among their men, inspecting them and their horses and equipment and then marshaling them in the fields outside the city, while their Prince was listening to the last Mass he would ever hear in St. Michael's Cathedral. After the services he returned to the castle and gave a final audience to the Orthodox clergy of the region who would stay behind and to the mayors and representatives of his two chief cities.

He sat on a gilded throne in a chamber painted by Helm with allegorical murals, surrounded by his principal advisors and commanders, while the mayor of Lubnie addressed him in his own native Ruthenian in the name of all the townsmen of his territories.

"Don't leave us like a flock without its shepherd," Burgomaster Hruby begged him with arms extended and hands pressed together. "Don't abandon us . . . !"

And all the other gathered merchants and townsmen, taking

their cue from him, cried out at once: "Don't go away . . .!
Don't leave us!"

The Prince told them quietly that he had no choice. His duty
to the Commonwealth and their King was ordering him away.
Then they rushed forward in a noisy body and crowded about
him crying out and pleading. They knelt at his feet with loud
sobs and tears, either regretting the loss of a benevolent master
or pretending to do so since, as some people said, many of the
less successful townsmen favored the Cossacks and
Hmyelnitzki. But the pleas of the wealthy—all those who had
reason to fear the public riots, disorders and looting that were
sure to follow the departure of the Prince's army—carried the
ring of sincerity and truth.

Making his own impassioned farewell address, Prince Yeremi
urged the Ruthenian townsmen and their bearded priests to
remain loyal to the Commonwealth which, as he put it, had
been a sheltering and protecting mother just as he tried to be a
father rather than a master, and under whose care they came to
their wealth and possessions.

Then came the moment of leaving.

The last of the baggage train was loaded overnight and everything was ready. Prince Yeremi's proud and regal wife, the
Princess Grizelda, prepared the court for departure long before
her husband's return, and now she and the young women of her
household stepped into the courtyard. The girls wept and
fainted, or made a show of fainting if there were any young
officers close enough to throw a strong arm around them; the
servants howled and wailed in the castle corridors; and only the
Princess entered her coach with her head held high and without
a tear showing on her pale face. All the church bells in the city
rang in farewell and vast crowds of townsmen and country
people stood in a dense mass along the route between the castle
and the city gates where the Orthodox clergy gathered to bless
the long procession of coaches, carts and wagons.

Finally the Prince himself mounted his dappled horse. All the
regimental standards were lowered before him, the guns on the
city walls thundered their salutes, and the shouts and wailing of
the gathered thousands who came to see the end of the Vishnovyetzki rule in the Transdnieper Country became one with
the ringing of the bells, the thunder of the cannon, the harsh

cries of the war horns and military trumpets, and the booming of the kettledrums.

Then the march began.

First rode the two swift, darting Tartar Light Horse regiments under Vyershul and Rostvorovski, spreading their screen far and wide ahead of the army, then came Vurtzel's ponderous artillery and the superbly drilled infantry regiments of Oberst Mahnitzki. Behind them rolled the coaches of Princess Grizelda and her household, the court and the officials, and then the baggage train surrounded and watched over by the Valachian mounted archers of Byhovietz. Next came the main body of the Prince's army—the heavy armored regiments of steel-clad *pantzerni* and the winged *husaria*—and then the army's rearguard of dragoons armed with swords and muskets, and the remaining loyal Cossacks under Volodyovski. Behind the army trailed a procession of charabancs and wagons of every description, carrying all those tens of thousands of gentry and their families who didn't want to stay in the Transdnieper once the Prince was gone; and with them went all the landholders and officials and priests and scholars and magistrates, leaving the land they had enriched, nurtured and protected, and which sustained and enriched them in its turn.

The war horns played martial music among the regiments, the battle trumpets brayed and the pennons snapped and fluttered bravely in the breeze, but the hearts and throats of everyone in that exodus were constricted with a feeling of irrevocable loss as the white walls of Lubnie fell away behind them.

'*Dear home, dear country,*' each man among the iron riders whispered to himself, as their saddened eyes turned once more to the castle towers, the spires and the shining metaled roofs under which they spent so many of their years. '*Will I ever get to see you again?*'

Each of them knew what he was leaving behind and each man's memory was different. But everyone was bitterly aware that this vanishing treasury of vivid recollections would never be restored, that all the lighthearted pleasures of their youth were gone, and that the hopes of an entire lifetime were being taken from them. For many it was a farewell to their birthplace and the resting places of their ancestors who sprung from that rich, hard-won soil. It was as if each man and woman in that long procession was parting with a fragment of his or her soul, and no one in those slowly passing ranks could tell what waited ahead in that lowering grey distance where the wagon train crept across the horizon.

The city went on calling to them with its mournful bells as if pleading with them not to abandon it to an uncertain future and begging them to stay and to protect it along with everything else that was precious to them, and they stared back at its dwindling walls and mutely asked each other and themselves:

'*Is this the last time we'll ever set eyes on this country? Is it all truly over?*'

No one could tell with any certainty that morning, although a great many in that throng of thousands suspected it in their hearts and minds, but none of them, including Prince Yeremi, would ever again see that gleaming city or that vast open sweep of lush, untrammeled country through which they were passing.

★   ★   ★

The war horns played on as if in defiance of the day's grey shadows which deepened into afternoon and evening. The great cavalcade wound at a slow but steady pace under a clearing sky, and it soon seemed as if the receding city became misted over by the pale blue hues of distance and regret, and its roofs and spires appeared to flow together in a single mass and to shine and flicker as if they were glazed by the deep red glow of the setting sun.

Prince Yeremi spurred his horse ahead and rode out alone to the top of a rounded wayside mound marked by a stone cross and stood there in silence looking at his city.

He looked long and hard.

This town and castle gleaming in the sun, and all that blooming, cultivated land spread out before him as if for inspection, were the fruits of his forefathers' blood and labor and much of it had been his own work.

It was the Vishnovyetzkis who changed that former wilderness into inhabitable country and made it safe for human settlement, and he had done more of it than any of them. It was he who built those churches whose domes and spires gleamed in the bluing distance. It was his treasure that turned Lubnie from a primitive military outpost into a thriving city and linked it with roads and highways to the Ukraine and the rest of the Commonwealth beyond it.

It was his engineers, and the captives taken in his victorious wars, who cut through the dense primeval forests and drained the swamps for planting, and built the castles that protected the villages and plantations which he peopled with skilled new-comers from the west. It was his soldiers who pacified and disciplined the brigands of the wilderness and dispersed the Tartars who used to roam at will through those quiet spaces; and it was his laws and justice that encouraged the merchants and the traders of the Orient to venture west of Moscow, and opened the trails to new Asian commerce, so that, in effect, he breathed life itself into that land as surely as if he created it.

He knew that he was the heart and soul of whatever civiliza-tion the age permitted on this farthest, turbulent eastern frontier of Europe. The thought that he must abandon all of that was heartrending to him.

And it wasn't just the loss of his enormous fortune that saddened the Prince as he watched the sun setting over his capital. He had become accustomed to his work and loved it, and now he had no doubt that with his departure the labor of entire generations would prove as useless as if no one had done anything at all. The towns and villages would burn once more under scarlet skies. The Tartars would return to hunt people like game along the river crossings, and the forest would reclaim the cold and emptied ruins. And even if God granted his return from years of distant war it would all have to be begun anew.

But would his strength be there to serve him as before? Would he have enough time—enough life—left for the task of starting up again? He fought and struggled from his earliest manhood to build a nation in the endless emptiness of the unpeopled Step-pes; that was the fountainhead of his glory among men and of the merit he hoped to obtain in the afterlife. Now all that work and merit were vanishing like smoke in the wind, and so two cold tears rolled down his pale face and gleamed like jewels in the failing light. They were, he knew, the last tears he would ever shed; after this day his eyes would reflect only fire and project cold lightnings.

The tears dried.

He waited.

A sign was needed, something that might confirm him in his certainties and purpose as his gleaming city sunk into the shadows . . . sunk and dwindled . . . vanished.

His horse stretched out his neck just then, and raised his silvery, dappled head, and shook his great white mane and uttered a shrill neigh, and a hundred other horses answered him at once from the winged ranks of silent, armored riders who were passing the mound along the highway.

These harsh, animal voices broke through the Prince's heavy introspection, ended his reverie and lightened his spirits. Something was left to him, after all: six thousand loyal friends and faithful companions, six thousand sabers with which to carve new highways for himself and which the humbled Commonwealth awaited as its last salvation.

The Transdnieper idyll was over. But beyond those scarlet horizons in the west where cannon were roaring—where towns and villages burned like funeral pyres and the red nights filled with the howls of maddened mobs—a new destiny was calling out to him. Fresh fields of glory and merit waited in the plains where Tartar horseherds trampled the rich Ukrainian harvest among the desperate cries and pleadings of an enslaved nation.

He had to ask himself: '*Who else could attempt to reach for that fresh work and glory?*'

Who else in that wounded, disgraced and trampled Commonwealth could hope to become the savior of his dying country if not he, Yeremi Vishnovyetzki, and these regiments which shined and glittered in the last of the day's light below him?

The army's siege-train was passing the mound just then and at the sight of the Prince standing on its summit under the tall stone cross, with his gold *bulava* in his hand, a great single cry rose out of the ranks.

"Long live our Prince! Long live our Hetman and commander, Yeremi Vishnovyetzki!"

The Prince stirred then. He drew his saber and raised it towards the sky along with his eyes.

"I, Yeremi Vishnovyetzki," he began to speak. "The *Voyevode* of Ruthenia and Prince of Lubnie and Vishnovyetz, vow to You, our One Lord God in Your Holy Trinity, and to you, Christ's Holiest Mother, that as I draw this saber against those who are murdering my country, so I'll keep it drawn until I've crushed the rebels, brought peace to the Ukraine, washed away our nation's shame in the blood of all her enemies, and bent them to her will. And since I make this vow with no concern about my life nor any thought of gain or advancement among my countrymen, and since I freely offer up all of my own blood and treasure for this task, so I ask for God's help with a clear conscience . . . Amen."

He waited for a moment longer, looking up at the darkened sky. Then he spurred his horse off the mound and rode slowly towards his passing army.

★   ★   ★

That night the army reached the village of Basanye, owned by the widowed Pani Krynitzka, who met the Prince as if he was a savior, kneeling at her gate. His coming drove off a mob of her own peasants who were besieging her in her manor, and whom she managed to hold off with the help of a few loyal servants, but the providential arrival of the Prince's soldiers saved her and her nineteen children, fourteen of whom were young girls, from a brutal death.

The Prince ordered the marauders hunted down and hanged and sent his Household Cossacks under Ponyatovski on a long sweep towards Kaniov where they caught five Zaporohjans from the Vasyutinski *kujhen*. All of them fought at Korsun and when questioned over a coal fire gave the Prince a full account of what happened there. Cunning as much as courage decided that battle once again; Hetman Pototzki's Cossack regiments went over to the rebels just as Kshetchovski did before Yellow Waters. But a good part of the shattered army managed to fight its way out of the trap and, although it was now scattered to the four winds, managed to save itself.

The prisoners swore that Hmyelnitzki was still at Korsun while Tuhay-bey went back to Tchehryn with his Tartar corps, his mountains of loot, his slave train and the captured Hetmans, and that he planned to go home to the Crimea from there. Hmyelnitzki begged the Tartars not to abandon him and the Zaporohjans but the savage *murjah* wouldn't listen to him. He told Hmyelnitzki that with the Hetmans beaten the Cossacks could do well enough on their own. Besides, his *yassyr* was dying out in hundreds every day and he wanted to get it to the auction blocks while the captives lasted.

With their last, tortured breaths the Zaporohjans confirmed

Hmyelnitzki's strength at about a quarter of a million men but most of these were rabble who'd be no more reliable in a battle than stampeding cattle. Only fifty thousand were seasoned Zaporohjan warriors like themselves, or trained Cossack soldiers, who either mutinied against their Polish masters or deserted to the rebels after the Korsun victory.

By dawn the Prince's troops and convoy were on the move again. The prisoners' confessions heartened him even further. He expected that the fleeing Ukrainian gentry, some of the scattered household troops of the richer landlords, and whatever fugitives survived from the Hetmans' army, would come out of hiding and swell his ranks considerably once he crossed the Dnieper. But beyond Pereyaslav his men entered the vast virgin forests that stretched northward along the course of the Trubyezha River as far as the town of Kozyeltz and then ran northwest among broad swamps and quagmires almost to the outskirts of Tchernihov itself.

No army, not even the Tartars, ever penetrated that awesome natural barrier in which there were no roads or tracks of any kind, and where innumerable false trails led to morass and quicksand. Moreover, it was the end of May. The summer heatwave came early that year and a scorching swelter settled upon the forests like a burning lid. There wasn't enough air to breathe in that torrid stillness. The men and horses gasped at each step and began to falter. The cattle herds driven behind the wagons began to drop or, sniffing the dead, dry air for any trace of moisture, ran as if crazed into the swamps and mudpits, overturning carts and trampling down everything that stood in their way. The heavy cavalry, stifling in their armor, began to lose their horses.

Neither did their nights bring any relief. The air was thick with the cloying reek of pine-pitch dripping from the trees, and with clouds of insects.

Four days and nights passed like that and, on the fifth day, the heat became unnatural. The cattle and the horses filled that breathless air with harsh, rasping cries as if they could sense the approach of a terrible new danger that men were still unable to perceive.

"They smell blood!" nervous, frightened people began to mutter to each other among the wagons of the gentry that followed the army.

"The Cossacks are after us!" some half-crazed, heat-tormented carter bellowed out in terror and an immediate panic broke out among the crowds of the gentry's lackeys and house servants. "Run! Save yourselves! There's going to be a battle!"

The long lines of refugee carts and wagons burst apart at once, lurching past each other in a pell-mell race on the narrow trail, colliding, turning over, or driving off among the trees and deadfall where they snapped their axles, lost their wheels, tumbled and piled up among the roots and branches. It took the Prince's men most of the night to stop the panic and reform the column.

Meanwhile, light cavalry patrols rode out in every direction to see whether any enemy was near.

★   ★   ★

Skshetuski, who volunteered to lead a scout troop of Valachian Light Horse, was the first to return with news shortly before dawn and went at once to the Prince.

"Well? What's the story?" Prince Yeremi asked.

"The woods are burning, Highness," Skshetuski replied.

"Set on fire, were they?"

"Yes sir. I've caught some men who say Hmyelnitzki sent them to trail Your Highness and set the woods on fire if the wind was right."

"He'd like to burn us alive without a battle." Prince Yeremi nodded grimly. "Bring those prisoners here!"

Three wild *tchaban* horseherders were dragged up at once, babbling stupidly in terror and ready to admit that they'd been ordered to burn down the forests. They also said that a large Cossack army was trailing the Prince on the other side of the Trubyezha River, marching towards Tchernihov along another trail closer to the Dnieper.

"How big an army?"

But the *tchabany* couldn't say anything about that.

"Hang them," the Prince said and Rostvorovski's troopers hanged them at once on a nearby pine.

The other patrols began to return shortly after that and their commanders reported the same news: fires, set by hundreds of volunteers dispatched by Hmyelnitzki, were burning everywhere upwind of the army.

But Prince Yeremi didn't seem concerned.

"It's a primitive way to make war," he said and shrugged. "But it won't help them much. The fires won't get across all the swamps and tributaries that run into the river. They'll have to reset them after every crossing."

And that, as the events of the next days would prove, was just what did happen. The great fires that raged behind the army, filling the air with a thick, acrid cloud that choked the men and horses, couldn't leap across all those countless streams and rivulets that drained westward into the Trubyezha and formed wide swamps at their confluences. The arsonists had to start them up each night and the patrols caught these scorched, wild-eyed wretches by the dozens and dressed the wayside pines with their dangling corpses.

Day after day the army struggles through the thick, grey haze of smoke carried by the wind so that it seemed as if an endless fog settled throughout the country to obscure the sun. The fires spread widely east and west along the streams and rivers, turning the crimson night skies brighter than the day. The women among the refugees sang hymns all night, and animals fled from the burning thickets and ran behind the wagons, mixing with the fear-crazed cattle driven in the column.

Meanwhile, Vyershul's reconnoitering Tartars confirmed the presence of an enemy army making its way north on the other bank of the Trubyezha River.

★ ★ ★

And then another piece of dispiriting information reached the struggling army. One night during a rest halt, a man named Suhodolski, one of the Prince's old retired gentlemen-in-waiting who farmed some acres beyond the Desna River, rode into the bivouac. He too was fleeing from a peasant rising. Asked for news, he replied:

"Yes, I've news, and all of it's bad. I suppose you've heard about Korsun?"

"We've heard it," the Prince said.

"And the King's death, too?"

The Prince, who was sitting on a low stool in front of his tent, leaped to his feet.

"What's that? The King is dead?"

"That he is, Highness," Pan Suhodolski said. "His Most Merciful Majesty Vladyslav IV gave up the ghost in Metchet. Oh, a week before the Korsun disaster, it was."

"At least God spared him that terrible knowledge," the Prince said. "But—dear Lord!—could this have come at a worse time for the Commonwealth? Can you imagine an *interregnum* at this of all moments? All that political squabbling with the whole nation split into factions bickering with each other! All those interminable conventions and elections and that foreign bribing and manipulating at a time when we ought to be like one sword wielded by a single hand? God really must have turned his face away from us! What else could it be? He must really want to flog us for our sins! Even the Cossacks loved our King Vladyslav and followed his orders. No one else among us could even hope to persuade them back to their obedience. And besides, he was a warlike monarch. He might have managed to turn all this fury on the Turks and unite the country."

Skshetuski, Zachvilihovski, Vurtzel and a dozen other officers drew near at that moment and the Prince turned towards them.

"The King is dead, gentlemen!" he said.

All the hats and caps were swept to the ground at once. All faces grew somber. But it took some time for grief to break through their astonished silence.

"God rest his soul," Zachvilihovski murmured finally.

"God's light shine on him for ever," all the others chorused.

Soon afterwards Father Muhovyetzki intoned the '*Dies Irae.*' A thousand voices, thick with foreboding, picked up the mournful notes and sent them drifting like a warning of impending doom through the blue-grey haze.

A sad, depleting air of abandonment and loss spread through those burning woods that surrounded this last handful of the Commonwealth's defenders with a ring of flames. Grief and a nearly insupportable feeling of anxiety pressed down upon them out of the smoke that hovered in the treetops. It was as if they had suddenly become an army under siege, alone and unaided and able to depend on no one but their Prince, while a long-awaited force that might have come to help them was cruelly and capriciously turned away.

Drawn by an instinct that none of them could explain, the soldiers came in hundreds, and then in their thousands, to stand in silence among the trees around the Prince's bivouac. But there was nothing he could say to comfort them or set their minds at rest.

Later that night, as he walked among the picket lines and outposts of his armored riders, he said to Pan Zachvilihovski:

"We must elect a warrior king, nothing else will save us. So, if God allows us to live until the elections, we'll cast our votes for young Prince Charles who's much more of a soldier than his bookish brother."

"Prince Yan Casimir is a saintly and scholarly man," the old commissioner agreed, and sighed and went on sadly, "but what we need these days can't be found in hymnals or on parchment . . ."

"*Vivat Carolus Rex!*" cried the assembled officers.

"*Vivat!* Long live King Charles!" cried a thousand voices and the cry flew among the tree tops and echoed in wave after wave through the entire Vishnovyetzki army.

No one expected, the Prince least of all, that these hopeful but premature cries that hailed a new King among the burning forests of his Transdnieper Country, would fly as far as Warsaw, and that their echoes would resound in distant council chambers and help to knock the *bulava* of a Crown Grand Hetman out of his hands.

Chapter Twenty-five

AFTER NINE DAYS of that harrowing march through the burning forests, and then a three-day crossing of the swamps along the Desna River, the Prince's weary troops finally reached the town and castle of Tchernihov.

Skshetuski was the first to enter them. Yeremi Vishnovyetzki was the kind of leader who remembered his men's every need, and he sent Skshetuski ahead with the Valachian Light Horse to occupy the city and look as quickly as he could for Helen and Zagloba. But here, just as in Lubnie, no one had even heard of them. They seemed to have vanished without a trace, like stones cast into water, and the young lieutenant no longer knew what to think about their disappearance.

Where could they have got to?

Moscow . . . the Crimea . . . even the *Sietch* itself might offer greater safety than the raging sea of rebellion everywhere around them. Skshetuski thought they must have crossed the Dnieper into the Ukraine but that brought no comfort. The Ukraine flowed with blood like a butcher's block. It had become a charnel house full of drunken mobs, Zaporohjans, burning skies, and Tartars for whom Helen's disguise as a boy wouldn't make a difference. He even thought for one hair-raising moment that Zagloba might have taken her into the heart of the rebellion so that he could sell her to Tuhay-bey who'd pay more for her than even Bohun would be able to do.

Suspicions hissed within him like a nest of snakes and threatened to drive him mad until Pan Longinus set his mind at rest.

"Knock all such thoughts out of your head, dear brother. That's one thing that he'd never do!"

"How can you be so sure?"

"Think! If he wanted riches he could've taken a pack-train of them out of the Kurtzevitch manor. And he wouldn't have to risk his neck to get them. Bohun would gladly give up every treasure for your girl!"

"Yes, that's true," the troubled young man agreed. "But if that's so why did he head across the Dnieper rather than to Lubnie or here to Tchernihov?"

"Don't worry about it, my dear friend. I've known him long enough to know that he never does anything without a good reason."

"But can he be trusted? To hear Pan Zachvilihovski he's nothing more than a loudmouth, a braggart and a coward."

Pan Longinus shrugged, sighed, and turned his own child-like, trusting eyes on the troubled Skshetuski.

"I've drunk with him and lent him money that I know I'll never see again," he said. "He doesn't care about anybody's money. He'll drink up every penny of his own and then everything he can pawn or borrow, and the thought that he might have to give it back doesn't even occur to him. He has a lot of faults, I admit. But it wouldn't cross his mind to commit the kind of crime that you are suspecting."

"Hmm. Are you sure?"

"I'm sure, dear brother! Set your mind at peace."

But that was easier urged than done.

"Perhaps you're reading his motives as you would your own," Skshetuski insisted. "Perhaps you're just seeing him with your own decent, gentle and forgiving eyes . . ."

"Maybe so, sweet brother." The Lithuanian sighed with resignation as if his judgment could never be as sound as that of any other man. "But. . . I don't think so. I've known him a bit longer than you have, my friend."

"He's a weak man," Pan Yan went on worrying. "There's not much strength of character in him, from all that I hear."

"So perhaps he's weak in some respects . . . Is that such a sin? But he's also shrewd, sharp, quick-witted and clever enough to make a fool out of almost anyone, and to squeeze his way out of the tightest corners. Remember what Father Muhovyetzki told you and that's a saintly man who wouldn't lie about God's intentions. God will restore your girl to you because He always rewards a clean heart and an honest lover."

And here the gentle Pan Longinus, whose own anxious long-ings struggled against his vow more desperately than ever since Anusia Krasienska's bright little eyes did their work on him, began to heave huge sighs on his own behalf.

They went on searching through the town and questioning the gentry which had barricaded itself in the castle with their wives and children but no one could tell them anything. No one had seen Helen or Zagloba. Indeed, all of that upcountry gentry seemed strangely blinded to everything, including its own dan-ger. Prince Yeremi urged these confident local squires to aban-don Tchernihov and follow his soldiers, reminding them about the Cossacks who trailed him like a pack of wolves, but they refused to admit the possibility that any army could get through their forests.

"Mine did," the Prince said.

"Ah, well, Your Highness! That was you! That Cossack rab-ble is another matter! Those forests are too much for the likes of them!"

They stayed behind, watching from the walls as the Prince's army marched out the next morning. But neither those walls nor the forests saved them. The rebel army composed of new peasant regiments under Zaporohjan colonels reached the city not long afterwards, took and burned the town and besieged the castle. The gentry fought them off for three weeks which enraged the Zaporohjans to such an extent that when the castle fell they slaughtered everyone with a savagery not seen before during the rebellion. The captured men were skinned alive, gutted and dismembered and blinded with wood-drills. The women were raped, mutilated and roasted on hot coals. The children were torn apart like discarded dolls. Not one of the two thousand men, women and children in the captured castle sur-vived the massacre.

★ ★ ★

Meanwhile the Prince's army reached the Dnieper near the town of Lubetch where it pitched camp to rest and to complete its final campaign preparations, while Prince Yeremi crossed the river and took his wife and court to Brahin which lay secure beyond even thicker forests and deeper swamps. There the rested and refitted army joined him after a week-long crossing of the Dnieper and they marched on to Babitza, near the town of Mozyr, which they reached on the feast of Corpus Christi.

It was there that their exodus split in two with the court and the army each going its own way. Princess Grizelda and her household were to travel far north, into Lithuania, to stay at the court of her aunt who had been one of three Valachian beauties famous for their ambition in their time. Two of them married the most powerful border magnates of the Commonwealth. The eldest became the wife of Prince Yeremi's father only to die in childbirth. Her younger sister married Prince George Radzivill, the immensely rich and powerful *Voyevode* of Vilna and Grand Hetman of the Lithuanians. The third and youngest married her own uncle, the old Hospodar of Valachia, and sent her proud and beautiful daughter Grizelda to be the wife of her young cousin Yeremi in Lubnie. Turov, the semi-regal capital of a greater court than almost any found among the princes of the German Empire, would be the home of Prince Yeremi's wife while he took his army south into the Ukraine.

The Prince's soldiers loved her for her kindness to them, for her magnanimity and generosity and courage, and for the care which she gave to their families. Above all, they loved her because their Prince Yeremi adored her almost beyond reason. It seemed sometimes as if he and she were twin souls created for each other, both made in part of gold and in part of steel, but their farewell supper lacked the ease and gaiety common to their table. The young soldiers cast soulful glances at the girls of the Princess' household who, in turn, sniffed and squealed in their own dismay. Living as close together as they did at the far reaches of civilization, there was hardly a couple among them that hadn't come to some sort of understanding, so that when Prince Yeremi rose to say goodbye to his wife and court their sorrow broke all the restraining barriers of discipline and training.

The girls squeaked mournfully like abandoned kittens, one after another, and burst into tears. The knights, supposedly made of sterner stuff, leaped to their feet and roared: "We'll conquer and return!"

"God grant it soon," said Princess Grizelda.

The windows shook and rattled in the banquet hall, and the walls seemed to tremble as the assembled officers gave went to their feelings and bellowed in chorus: "Long live our gracious

Princess! Our mother and our benefactress! Long live! *Vivat! Vivat!*" and then each of those fierce young soldiers marched to her chair with his cup in hand, and knelt before her to pay his last homage, and she took each of them gently by the head and spoke a few kind words.

Finally it was Skshetuski's turn. He knelt before her while she smiled and took a small gold cross studded with green gems off her neck and clasped it around Skshetuski's.

"I think," she said, "it's likely that several of you gentlemen will leave here with some small reminder of a warmer moment. But since the lady from whose hands you'd most prefer to get some precious souvenir isn't with us just now, take this from me as if from a mother."

Prince Yeremi smiled, pleased to see such a high honor granted to his favorite whom he valued even more because he had refused to carry letters from Hmyelnitzki, and Princess Grizelda's young women immediately took her gesture for permission to give their own mementos. Ribbons, crosses, cameos, brooches and medallions appeared as if by magic in their hands and the young soldiers moved in a mass towards them, each heading for his own.

Only Anusia Krasienska, who had been loved at one time or another by every courtier and soldier in the room, now stood alone near the window with no one coming to her. Her beautiful little face was flushed with shame and anger. Her dark, lowered eyes shot anxious glances right and left, as if begging all her former cavaliers to save her from ridicule and disgrace, but only sly little Pan Volodyovski sidled up to her, moving his yellow mustache up and down.

"I too hoped to get some little token from you at one time, my lady," he whispered and grinned from ear to ear. "But I gave up the idea tonight."

"Why?" The girl struggled to conceal her shame and to pretend indifference. "Why tonight?"

"Because I was sure I'd never get through the crowd around you!"

Anusia's cheeks flushed even redder and she shot back at once: "I think you'd want your souvenir from other hands than mine! But if it's not too crowded for you there it's certainly too high for you to reach!"

The shot was painful and well placed. The sharp allusion to

Pan Michal's insignificant size was double-charged because the little knight had aimed the latest of his impossible affections at no lesser personage than Princess Barbara of Zbarajh, the younger daughter of the Prince himself. Hit a double blow where it hurt the most, especially since he thought his latest passion to be a deep secret, he couldn't think of anything to say. He started tugging at his little mustache and searched for some way to beat a dignified retreat or, at least, to walk away without looking more of a fool than he felt just then.

"Hmm . . . Ah . . . But it seems like I'm not the only one who's aiming high," he muttered at last, catching a glimpse of the Lithuanian giant who sat with cast-down eyes in the darkest corner of the room. "I can't think of a longer . . . or a taller target than . . . Pan Podbipyenta!"

"That's right, you can't," the proud young woman snapped right back at him. "That's because he's a bigger man than you in every respect! But thank you for reminding me about him. He'll do very well!"

And then she beckoned to Pan Longinus.

"Come closer, sir," she said. "Yes, you sir, you! I too want my own knight and I can't think of anyone whom I'd rather have remember me while he's away at war."

The astonished Lithuanian gaped at her as if unable to believe his ears and then hurled himself on his knees before her so violently that the timbers shook under the floor.

"Ah, my lady . . . Ah! Is this really true?"

Anusia took off her silk scarf and tied it around the Lithuanian's shoulder and then her small hands disappeared under his vast mustache.

"Listen to that smacking and muttering," the little knight hissed angrily to his friend Migurski. "You'd think a bear had got into the honey!"

Then he stamped off to the other end of the hall, feeling himself badly stung by jealousy and cursing his own sly malice, because he was one of the earliest and most enamored of Anusia's unsuccessful lovers.

But at that moment the Prince himself began to take his leave of Princess Grizelda and, an hour later, the coaches and wagons of the court rolled out towards Turov while the army turned southwest to the Pripet River.

★   ★   ★

Later that night at the river crossing, where the *husaria* watched over the engineers who were building rafts for the artillery and the army's wagons, Pan Longinus sidled up anxiously to Skshetuski.

"Ey, ey, dear brother," he murmured. "Ey, what a misfortune!"

"What happened now?" the young lieutenant asked.

"That news from the Ukraine!"

"What news?"

"What those five captured Zaporohjans said about the Tartars. That Tuhay-bey's gone back to the Crimea."

"So what's bad about that?"

"Well . . . you know . . . it's like you said," the heartsick giant muttered, twisting his great hands. "I mean that Cossack heads won't count towards my vow because they are Christians and like our own brothers in a civil war. So where am I going to get those pagans and foreigners I need? Where am I to look for them? And now I need my three heads more than ever before!"

Skshetuski smiled. "I can guess what this is all about since I saw how you were decorated after dinner."

"And that's the whole misfortune!" Pan Longinus cried. "I've fallen in love! There's no point in trying to hide it any longer!"

"Well, don't despair. It may not be as bad as you think. I don't believe that Tuhay-bey's gone home."

"You don't?"

"It wouldn't be like him."

"It wouldn't? And why not?"

"Because it's not like the Tartars to turn their backs on a helpless country that they can loot at will . . . No, no, my friend, they won't go home as long as there's one poor wretch left outside their slave pens. You can be sure you'll have as many Tartars around you in the Ukraine as these damned mosquitoes buzzing about our heads."

"Ah . . . ah! You think so? You think so?"

"I'll swear it if you like."

"God grant it!" the Lithuanian cried and turned a bright crimson. "Because . . . to tell you the truth . . . either my vow gets itself fulfilled right away or I'll burst like an overcharged cannon!"

★   ★   ★

The night was calm and clear and studded with stars but the insects swirled so thickly around the men and horses that at times they blotted out the moonlight. Once across the Pripet, the Vishnovyetzki army entered a land of swamps, sunken woods, sodden meadows gleaming under water and so many streams and rivers rushing across each other that all of them seemed like one. The awestruck soldiers who spent their lives on the high dry Steppes of the Transdnieper Country could find not one acre of dry land anywhere they looked. The whole country was a single, vast morass studded with dwarfed shrubs. There were no roads, no bridges. The few local inhabitants they glimpsed now and then moved past them in swift, silent skiffs and dugout canoes and vanished as quickly as they came. The woods and trees looked like skeletal black arms rising out of water. The thick, cloying mud sucked the boots off the soldiers' feet and gripped the legs of their horses, while dark streams of evil-smelling water bubbled out of the quaking ground under the wheels of the wagons and the cannon.

"How in God's name can anybody live here?" they wondered aloud. "And *does* anybody live here, in God's name?"

Vurtzel was in despair.

"What kind of march is this anyway?" he worried as his artillery pieces sunk into the mud. "Before Tchernihov we were smoked alive. Here we're being drowned."

There seemed to be no animals living in this strange, silent country where the rustling tree-crowns made the only natural and recognizable sounds, and where the earth offered no firm footing. Nothing in that apparently witch-ridden and enchanted land resembled anything that any of the Prince's soldiers ever saw before and they struggled with a ferocity that bordered on despair to escape from it.

It took the army four days just to cross the swamps that bordered both sides of the Pripet River. Then came weeks of rain and thick fog and mysterious mists, and new streams and rivers to bridge every day, and no dry island anywhere for a moment's rest or refuge from the endless mud and ever-present water.

But they wouldn't have been able to rest even if a miraculously dry patch of land was anywhere in sight. Prince Yeremi hurried them and drove them on in spite of their exhaustion, and they obeyed and worked until they dropped because he neither slept nor rested any more than they. He ordered entire woods cut down, crossings bridged and cleared, and corduroy roads laid out and built out of the fallen timbers. He seemed to be everywhere at once along the line of march, watching everything, so that his faltering men could see him riding up and down the trail on his dappled horse each time they raised their heads. No one dared to complain, seeing that he had no more mercy on himself than he showed the soldiers, and yet the hardships of this epic journey were almost past enduring.

The horses began to fall in dozens and then in tens of dozens. Their sodden hooves began to peel and fester in the mud. They sank down exhausted in their traces and drowned around the bogged-down cannon, so that Mahnitzki's infantry and little Pan Volodyovski's dismounted dragoons had to yoke themselves to the powder wagons and artillery pieces and haul them along by brute force. Even the elite senior regiments of heavy cavalry, such as the *husarias* of Skshetuski and Zachvilihovski— as well as the rich young lords who wore the leopard cloaks and gilded armor of the select *panzerni*—worked all day with axes side by side with camp servants and drovers.

Day after day this slow, exhausting journey went on among the swamps but it was a march that would make these soldiers famous in their time since no commander had ever brought an army through those lands before.

No enemy appeared in the steaming mists to oppose their passage. There were no ambushes, raids, night attacks or battles to hinder their progress. The Cossacks who trailed Prince Yeremi's army as far as Tchernihov lost his tracks beyond the Dnieper crossing, and Hmyelnitzki—who watched for his terrible enemy everywhere but there—never imagined that heavy cavalry and cannon could get across those swamplands to his north.

Nor were there any peasant risings or resistance in that silent country. The people of the marshlands were peaceful and uninvolved. The war was so far away from their hidden world that many of them hadn't even heard about the rebellion, and those that did know about it didn't want any part of it. They watched the armored ranks rising and flowing like a dream out of their fogs and forests and vanishing like the mist, but these were no more real to these water people than their own fairy-tales, and they did everything they were told to do as quietly and obediently as if they were deep in some strange sleep of their own.

The Prince, in turn, forbad any transgressions against them, and disciplined offenders, and when the word drifted to some sleepy village that it had been the terrible *Knaz* Yarema who had passed among them, the people murmured: "*Vre dobryi on, dobryi.* A good man, a good master."

Then, after twenty days that seemed to have neither a beginning nor an end to the struggling soldiers, the army stepped out of the swamps into rebel country.

"*Yarema idye! Yarema idye!*" the fearful cry flew from village to village throughout the Ukraine and sailed with the wind across the southern Steppes and the Wild Lands beyond them, and echoed grimly in the Tartar cities crouched at the mouth of the Dnieper along the Black Sea.

"Yarema is coming!"

Terror—as if this were a summons to Judgment Day— seemed to convulse the Ukraine at this cry.

The scythes and pitchforks and knives fell out of peasant hands. Harsh faces grew pale. Gangs of marauders slipped stealthily to the south like packs of wolves running before the sound of a hunter's horn, and the looting Tartars leaped out of their saddles and pressed their ears to the ground to listen for hoofbeats.

Church bells rang in all the forts and castles that still resisted the conquering Hmyelnitzki, and joyful voices sang "*Te Deum laudamus,*" while Prince Yeremi's army crouched like a pride of lions on the threshold of the rebels' country, and watched, and rested, and gathered its strength for what was to come.

Chapter Twenty-Six

SKSHETUSKI WAS RIGHT in supposing that the captured Zaporoh-jans lied about Tuhay-bey's departure from the Ukraine and Pan Longinus need not have worried about a scarcity of Tartar heads waiting across the Dnieper.

Not only did the fierce Crimean warlord remain with Hmyelnitzki, not even falling back to Tchehryn as rumors reported, but new Tartar *tchambuls* poured into the country like wolves drawn by the scent of blood. The two lesser Tartar khans of Azov and Astrakhan, who never came that far west before, joined Hmyelnitzki with four thousand fresh and hungry warriors. The petty khans of Belgorod, Nohai and the parched lands beyond Bessarabia—all of them once the sworn enemies of the Zaporohjans, but now their eager allies— brought another thirty thousand raiders impatient to share in the pillage, the bloodshed and the looting. And finally the Great Khan of the Crimean Tartars, the cunning old Devlet Girey himself, decided that the last hour must have come for the Commonwealth, and that the time was ripe to extend his empire into continental Europe, and arrived with twelve thousand picked and seasoned warriors of his Perekop Horde and all the chief beys and *murjahs* of his court.

All of the Ukraine seemed to groan and cry with a single voice under the yoke of these savage allies. More than a hundred thousand lives paid for the Tartars' new friendship with the Zaporohjans. And these were not merely the lives of the gentry and the Jews whom the peasants hated but also the Ruthenian inhabitants of the country who thought they had the most to gain from Hmyelnitzki's triumph. They threw their gates open to him and welcomed the Cossacks and now it was their villages and towns that turned into ashes. It was they who were robbed, looted and stripped of their possessions; and it was their bewildered men, wailing women and terrified children who were herded along the slave trails in their tens of thousands.

There was only one refuge for the Ruthenian peasant in those times of fire and bloodshed: to join Hmyelnitzki and become a murderer and looter rather than a victim. It was the only way for the tormented people to remain alive. Even the lesser gentry, seeing no other hope of salvation for themselves, fled to his camps, swore their loyalty to him, and joined the rebellion.

Meanwhile Hmyelnitzki, having stayed for several weeks in Korsun to whip and shape these fleeing masses into an ordered military force, moved his capital north to Byelotzerkyev, while his Zaporohjan atamans and colonels led his new armies all over the country to storm whatever castles still resisted him, and to season their men in battle for the great struggles that were still to come.

And so the Zaporohjan colonels Handja and Ostap went out to capture the town of Nesterwar with their regiments of *tchernya*, slaughtered its population of gentry and Jews so that not one escaped, and murdered the family of its Ruthenian master, the Prince Tchetvertynski, which ruled that country for two hundred years. The prince's own miller beheaded him across the castle threshold while Ostap turned the princess into his serving maid. Other peasant armies, led by experienced Cossack atamans, marched to other regions and triumphed everywhere because, as people said in those days throughout the Ukraine: *"the heart's gone out of the Lahy"* and *"their own fear and despair disarm them."* The Tartar hordes, now numbering more than seventy thousand warriors, established their vast camp and slave pens across the river from Hmyelnitzki's capital, and sent their raiding *tchambuls* across the entire Kiev palatinate, but the gloomy Zaporohjan Hetman, who had thrown his own country under their horses' hooves and led them all to victory, now seemed unable to decide what to do next.

He sat week after week in his littered chambers, stupefied with drink and immobilized by the terrifying specters of his own unexpected power, while witches and soothsayers cast spells and read his fortune in bones, entrails, fire and candle wax dripped on water.

His colonels raged at him, demanding that he lead them into the Commonwealth itself before that rich colossus shook itself free of the shock and fear that paralyzed its will and mobilized against him.

"What's the matter with you?" they shouted at him in their terrible impatience. "Why don't you march on Warsaw 'stead of lying about here, drunk like a hog and listening to the witches? You'll doom us all! You're giving the Poles time to come to their senses!"

Even the reeling, drunken mobs of Cossacks and *tchernya* howled at night around his quarters, demanding that he lead them at once west into Ruthenia. *"Lead us or we'll go alone and drag you with us on a rope!"* they threatened, and he shut his eyes and ears to them and ordered his witches to cast new spells and mutter stronger incantations.

He made the rebellion and infused it with his own rage and will, and he let loose all those smoldering forces that made it irresistible, but now he didn't know where this unharnessed power was about to take him. And so he sat night after night among his liquor kegs, either slumped in gloom or drunk and raving in his mindless rages, and stared blindly at his own clouded visions of an uncertain future.

"What do you want, then?" he asked his atamans in a voice dull with foreboding. "To go to Warsaw, eh? And what's going to happen here once we've gone?"

They stared like cowed dogs into his bloodshot eyes and trembled with terror as he raged at them: "*Knaz* Yarema will come down on your wives and children like a thunderbolt, he'll scorch the whole country so there'll be nothing left here except earth and water, and then he'll go after us to Warsaw with all the *Lahy* he'll gather on the way! And d'you know what that'll mean, eh? Have you thought about that? They'll have us between two fires, like cattle with no way to go except where they're driven! And if we don't find a quick death in the battles we'll be praying for it a long time on the stakes. Well? Speak up! Is that what you want?"

And when they muttered about their own successes and the strength of the Tartars camped across the river, he cursed them scornfully into a silence as gloomy as his own.

"Yes, they're with us today. But what about tomorrow? Let us get beaten just once and they'll turn on us like the wind, drive us all to the Crimea on a rope's end, or sell our heads to the *Lahy* for cold cash.

"Well? What else do you want?" he taunted. "Turn on Vishnovyetzki? That's just what he's after! He can hold us and the Tartars in check long enough for the Commonwealth to gather up its forces and then it'll be just the same as if we'd gone to Warsaw.

"Choose," he snarled at the humbled, worried atamans and colonels. "Which is it to be . . .? Well . . .? How come you're not saying anything anymore? Why have you suddenly shrunk down like rabbits in a hole? Where's all that yelling about a march on Ruthenia, Volhynia, Lvov and Warsaw?"

And when they sat humbled by his fury, mumbling their pleas for forgiveness and asking him to tell them what to do, he said with all the confidence that he didn't feel: "Leave it all to me. I'll find a way to save your heads along with my own. And I'll get justice for the Zaporohjans and satisfaction for all the other Cossacks."

★ ★ ★

The way that seemed to him the surest and the safest was through negotiations. He knew how far he could get in the Commonwealth by talking. He counted on the willingness of the *Seym*, or parliament, to seek accommodation rather than raise taxes, hire armies and opt for a dangerous and protracted war.

He knew there was a powerful party in Warsaw headed by the chancellor who wanted to put an end to the colossal fortunes of the border princelings and to the power of the Ukrainian magnates. The chancellor saw the Cossacks as a threatening sword that the King might hang over the heads of those proud, quarrelsome and disobedient autocrats of the Eastern Lands. He'd listen to any voice that suggested a lasting peace with the Zaporohjans whose vast new armies could be turned against fresh foreign threats like the newly wakened satrapy of Moscow. Under such circumstances Hmyelnitzki himself could hope for elevation to the highest ranks. He could become a royally appointed Hetman, with his status confirmed by the Senate and his power made permanent and legal by decree. His own dream was of peace, a pardon for himself and the Zaporohjans, a King's Commission, the terrible Vishnovyetzki forced to lay down his arms or, if he refused to obey the parliament, becoming the rebel whom he—Hmyelnitzki!—would crush with all the power of the Commonwealth behind him. And then the final hour would strike indeed for the Ukrainian princelings!

That's what he thought while drunk and bellowing in his murderous rages, or as he sat plunged in gloom and struggling against terrifying visions of disaster, while he groped for the one sure way to the power he wanted. That's why he stayed so long in Byelotzerkyev, no matter what he told his atamans and colonels, sending orders, appeals and manifestos all over the country; that's why he gathered those uncounted thousands, created new armies, seized the towns and castles and exterminated everyone who ventured against him, and why he did not move out of the Ukraine.

Great nations negotiated only with men and people more powerful than themselves, he knew; but was his own power great enough for that? Future historians would agree that news of King Vladyslav's death hadn't yet reached Hmyelnitzki at that time and so he wondered if the peace party in Warsaw was strong enough to force surrender on the eastern gentry.

Would they begin to negotiate with him before the war acquired its own dreadful life and spilled beyond control? And how long would the Senate and the *Seym* in Warsaw continue to turn a deaf ear to the cries of misery in the Ukraine? Would they be able to resist the pressures from magnates such as Vishnovyetzki whose own lives and fortunes were at stake in this tormented country?

He knew the temper of the people he was up against; he also knew the patience and the willingness of the King and his ministers to pardon most transgressions. But was this great Commonwealth so unnerved by fear that it would forgive him his alliance with Tartars?

And . . . finally . . . would he himself be able to halt the firestorm he unleashed? Alright, he thought, so he would make his peace. But would the swarms of peasants who'd tasted bloodshed, massacre, pillage and unbridled freedom go back meekly to their hated servitude and obedience? Or would they go on murdering and looting in his name? Right or wrong, he had inflamed their hopes of a better future; would they turn on him in their disappointment?

And what would happen then?

Doubts . . . superstition and uncertainty . . . shook him as if he were tormented by a fever.

Fear seized him by the hair as he tried to see into the future. Visions of failure—disgrace, death on the stake or repudiation, insignificance and anonymity—settled about him at night like vultures squawking their dark warnings. Whenever this happened he locked himself in his quarters and stupefied himself with vodka for days at a time, and the word would spread among his growling colonels and the seething masses: "*Hetman piyut!* The Hetman is drinking!" And then everyone would begin to drink as if their own nagging fears could be drowned in liquor.

The frail bonds of military discipline that he imposed so ruthlessly on those primitive, elemental people cracked and disappeared in an orgy of brutality and liquor, and the newly fashioned regiments turned once more into savage wolf-packs that fought each other over loot and women.

Prisoners were murdered by the hundreds.

Fires raged unchecked.

The local populations were pillaged and slaughtered and the country around Byelotzerkyev turned into a bloody anteroom of Hell ruled only by terror.

★   ★   ★

And then one day a prisoner named Vyhovski, captured at Korsun and turned into the Hetman's private secretary, pushed his way into Hmyelnitzki's room, seized the unconscious man by the neck and slapped him back to his senses.

"*Sh-sh-shtzo tam liho . . .?* Wha-what d'you want? What th' Devil's happening?" the drunken man muttered, struggling out of his alcoholic stupor.

"Get up, Hetman," Vyhovski answered roughly and shook him awake. "Get hold of yourself. There's a Polish emissary to see you."

Hmyelnitzki leaped to his feet as sober as if he'd been thrown into an icy river.

"Hey, boy!" he shouted to the Cossack serving lad who sat on the threshold. "Get my cloak and cap! Bring my *bulava!* Jump to it!" And then to Vyhovski: "Who is it? Who's he from?"

"It's a priest of your Orthodox Church. Father Patronius Lasko. He's been sent by the *Voyevode* of Bratzlav."

"By Pan Kisyel?" Hmyelnitzki cried, overjoyed, because this venerable Ruthenian senator was the foremost proponent of Cossack appeasement.

"That's right."

"God be praised!" Hmyelnitzki's face filled with sudden light as he made signs of the cross on his chest and shoulders.

His patience, as he thought of his long weeks of gloomy desperation, was being rewarded. All his hopes . . . indeed, his great dream itself . . . were justified and fulfilled and his fears about the future could be cast aside. The negotiations with the peace party were about to start.

★ ★ ★

But that same day he received news of another kind. Fear-crazed refugees from the north poured into his camp with word that Prince Yeremi, having rested his army after its march through the swamps and forests, had broken out into the rebel country with fire and sword.

"Say rather that he fell on us like a plague," the rebel fugitives wept before Hmyelnitzki. "He's killing everything that moves! He's murdering and burning!"

He or his raiding parties seemed to be everywhere. A picked cohort of two thousand Cossacks was surprised and slaughtered to the last man almost within sight of his own camp, Hmyelnitzki was told, and when he asked who did this he was told: "Skshetuski!"

Enraged, and wishing that he'd murdered the young Pole when he had the chance, he listened to the refugees' accounts of the storming of the town of Pohrebyshtchye, once a possession of the princes of Zbarajh, kinsmen by marriage to the Vish-novyetzkis, and now the lair of his best and fiercest Ruthenian marauders. "Yarema himself was there!" the fugitives reported. "He left nothing standing. It's all gone! There's nothing there now except earth and sky!"

"And the people?"

"Gone. Killed. Not a soul survived. He hanged seven hundred, impaled two hundred more. He told his men '*Kill them in such a way that they know they're dying*,' and that's what they did. They blinded people . . . burned them on slow fires . . ."

The rebellion died out at once in the entire region, Hmyelnitzki was told. The countryside was empty. All its inhabitants were either killed in the assaults or slaughtered like cattle after they surrendered, or they fled as far as their legs could take them, or they were meeting the terrible Prince on their knees, with bread and salt held out to him as a sign of fealty, and howling for mercy.

"And all my other troops over there?" Hmyelnitzki demanded.

"Gone. All dead. There's not one tree in the woods around Samhorod, Spitchin, Pleskov and Vahnovka that doesn't have a dead Cossack hanging on it. Save us! Avenge us!" the fugitives begged Hmyelnitzki.

"How?" he muttered, clawing at his mustache. "How?"

★   ★   ★

Seized by such fury that even the terrible Tcharnota hid under a wagon when he heard about it, Hmyelnitzki roared like a wounded auroch and ran out of his quarters. What was he to do? A peace envoy was waiting. If he moved against the Prince at once, as he had to do to save his rebellion, it would be just like saying he was choosing war. Yet if he didn't crush the terrible Yarema he'd have no convincing arguments of power for his negotiations.

His only hope lay in the Tartars if he could persuade them to march against Vishnovyetzki, so he leaped on his horse and galloped across the river to Tuhay-bey's encampment.

"I need your help, my friend!" he said as soon as the customary greetings and salaams were over. "Save me as you did at Yellow Waters and Korsun. Only you can do it."

"What do you want?" the Tartar gave him a long, narrow stare.

"I've got an envoy here from the *Voyevode* of Bratzlav. He's brought a letter in which the *Voyevode* promises he'll help me get everything I want if I stop making war on the Poles and start talking to them."

"So do it." The fierce *murjah* shrugged and turned away. "What's that to do with me?"

"That's right," Hmyelnitzki said and nodded and threw himself down on a pile of furs. "That's what I've got to do to show them my good will. But I can't at this time, don't you see? I've just got word that Vishnovyetzki is in our country and coming down on us from the north. He wiped my Pohrebyshtchye off the face of the earth! He murdered everybody there. He's killing my best lads, cutting them down like wheat stalks. He has their eyes put out! He roasts them alive! He stakes them out for crowbait along every highway!"

"So?" Unmoved, the Tartar started chewing a handful of dates.

"So, since I can't move against him because I need to talk peace to the other *Lahy*, I've come to ask you to do it with your Tartars. If you don't, he'll be burning down our own camps before long. And remember, he's your sworn enemy as much as he is mine."

The Tartar *murjah* sat silent and his slitted eyes narrowed even further as he watched Hmyelnitzki. He sat hunched over, spitting out the date pits and swaying back and forth on a pile of costly tapestries and carpets taken from the Hetmans' baggage at Korsun.

"Allah," he said finally. "I can't do that."

"Why not?"

"Because I've lost enough good men for you already. Why should I lose more? Yarema's a great warrior. I'll go against him when you go against him and that's my last word."

"But why can't you do me this one service?" Hmyelnitzki demanded. "I need your help, I tell you!"

"And I tell you that I won't do your fighting for you!" The Tartar's thick, protruding lips quivered with contempt. "Why should I? What good would it do me to go fight Yarema, and risk loosing even more of the Khan's best men than I did at Korsun and at Yellow Waters, when I can sit here sending my *tchambuls* after loot and *yassyr* at no cost at all?"

"But you know why I can't go after Yarema just now!"

"That's your lookout," Tuhay-bey said coldly. "What do your peace talks have to do with me? D'you think I'm a fool to risk everything in a single battle with a man like that? I've done enough for you unclean dogs! I won't go and neither will the Khan."

"But you've sworn to help me!" Hmyelnitzki cried out.

"That's right. But I swore to fight beside you, not in your place, you carrion. Now get out of here!"

"I've given you my own people for *yassyr*," Hmyelnitzki started pleading. "I've turned over my men's loot. And didn't I give you both the Hetmans for ransom?"

"That's right, dog. So you did." The Tartar grinned with

terrible contempt. "Because if you hadn't given them to me I'd have given *you* to *them!*"

"I'll go to the Khan!"

"Go to the Devil if you like, you foul piece of dogmeat," the *murjah* snarled thickly and his long, fanged teeth began to glitter dangerously between his twisted lips. "Now get out, I tell you."

* * *

Hmyelnitzki rose, biting back his anger, and went to beg an audience with the Khan, but Devlet Girey's *murjahs* gave him the same answer. Nothing that he was able to say could convince the Tartars that there was any profit in facing a commander as dangerous as Yeremi Vishnovyetzki.

Back in his quarters, he seized a demijohn of liquor to drown his despair, but Vyhovski ripped it from his hands.

"No drinking, Hetman!" he warned. "You've an envoy waiting."

"To Hell with the envoy!" Hmyelnitzki howled, enraged. "I'll have you *both* impaled!"

"Then you'll have to do it without getting drunk," Vyhovski said coldly and spat in disgust. "Tfui, Hetman! Aren't you ashamed to swill *gojhalka* like a common Cossack when fate has lifted you so high above ordinary people? This is no time for drinking! Rumors about the envoy are already running through the camp and both the army and the colonels want to know what's going to happen. You'd do better to seize the opportunity that Pan Kisyel gives you, send an embassy to Warsaw and beg the King's favor. Now's the time, sir, while the iron's hot, to get your peace along with everything else you're after. Let it all go too long and you might not be able to keep even your own head secure on your shoulders."

"You've a good head yourself," Hmyelnitzki muttered, calming down at once. "Alright, then. Go tell them outside to ring for a general assembly and send for the colonels."

Vyhovski left the room.

Alone and just as sober as if he never touched liquor in his life, the rebel Hetman underwent another of his transformations. His rage vanished. His bitterness disappeared. His calculating mind fixed on the needs of the moment while the great bell began to boom outside and the army of the Zaporohjans gathered for their council.

* * *

First to arrive was the grim, bandy-legged Krivoinos who acted as the right hand of the rebel Hetman. Next came the feared and respected Kshetchovski whom the Brotherhood had christened '*The Sword of the Cossacks,*' along with the old experienced Filon Djedjala, ataman of the Kropivnitzan *kujhen*, and the cruel Fedorenko of Kalnitze. Soon afterwards Fedor Loboda, longtime colonel of the Pereyaslav Regiment and Bohun's old commander, pushed his way inside. He came with the savage Pushkarenko of Poltava who led a corps of horseherding *tchabany*, Shumeyko of Nijhin, the wild, half-mad Tcharnota of Hadjatch, and Yakubovitch who commanded the Tchehryn division. Then came Nosatch who murdered the old Prince Tchetvertynski, along with Hladko, Adamovitch, Panitch, the legendary Burlay who was said to be protected by the Devil, one-eyed Glukh, the huge Pulyan who could wrestle bears, and the quarrelsome, sharp-tongued Zorko who was unique among them because he could read. Many others were away, leading expeditions, and some had already departed for the next world, sent there by Prince Yeremi. No Tartars were invited to this council but a swarm of Cossacks gathered in the square, arguing with each other and chasing away the mobs of curious *tchernya*.

Hmyelnitzki made his entrance dressed from head to foot in crimson and scarlet, wearing a sable *kolpak* on his head and carrying his *bulava*. The white-haired, dovelike Father Patronius Lasko flanked him on one side; Vyhovski, carrying papers, appeared on the other. Seated, he waited for the roar of excited voices to die down a little, then he took off his cap as a sign that the deliberations were about to start, and rose to his feet.

"Gentlemen, atamans, my good masters all," he began in the formal manner of the Cossack councils. "You all know how we were forced by cruelty and injustice to lift up our swords and demand our rights. You know how God blessed our claim to those old privileges and freedoms that treacherous tyrants stole from us against the King's wishes, how He let His terror fall on them and gave us our victories, and how, with the help of the illustrious Khan, we punished them for their disobedience to the King. But now that we've broken their pride it's time to think about an end to this shedding of good Christian blood which God and our Faith command us to do, just as long as all our liberties are restored to us and we're rewarded for our faithful service. All this can happen, as you'll hear in this letter from Pan Kisyel, the *Voyevode* of Bratzlav and a man of our own blood and faith, that he sends us through a priest of our own Holy Orthodox Church."

Some sharp cries and an excited muttering broke out among the atamans who saw no merit in interrupting a victorious war—with mad Tcharnota howling the loudest against any peace talks—but Hmyelnitzki didn't seem to notice. He sat in silence as if deep in thought but his hooded eyes took careful note of every man who opposed his wishes. Then, choosing his words in such a way that he seemed to be asking for his atamans' opinion while, in effect, giving them an order, he told them to listen to the letter, "put an end to bloodshed," and claim the Commonwealth's reward for their loyalty and service.

Meanwhile Vyhovski rose to read the letter while Zorko took a copy outside to the assembled army.

The *Voyevode* addressed Hmyelnitzki as a valued and respected friend in whose loyalty to the Commonwealth he believed '*no matter what some others may have said about it.*'

'*One reason why I think so,*' he wrote in his letter, '*is that while the Zaporohjan Army was always ready to defend its freedoms, it never failed to keep faith with the King and the Commonwealth. The second is our own Orthodox Religion which obliges us to be loyal and to obey the law even at the cost of our own lives. The third is that no matter what differences divide us in our Commonwealth, even if God wills that blood should flow now and then between us, this is our Motherland, and we are all her sons, and it is up to us to stand united in protecting her along with all those liberties which, sooner or later, she bestows on us.*'

Some of the atamans laughed, cursed and shouted, others demanded silence, and Hmyelnitzki snapped at Vyhovski to continue reading.

'*It's easier,*' Kisyel wrote, '*for us to make our grievances heard among our own brothers, sons of the same Mother, than to lose that freedom along with the Mother and then try finding justice among foreigners and strangers, because there is no country in the Christian world today and none among the heathen that might give us as much way in our own affairs.*'

"That's true!" old Loboda interrupted loudly. "*Pravdu kajhe.*"

"*Nepravdu!*" roared Tcharnota. "He's lying to us, the son of a bitch!"

"Shut your mouth!" yelled other atamans and colonels, leaping to their feet and shaking their fists under Tcharnota's nose. "Shut up! Listen! You're the son of a bitch here, you mad dog!"

"Traitors!" The furious Nosatch jumped up to back up Tcharnota. "*Na Pohybel!* Death to you all, you traitors!"

"Death to you! You're the traitor!"

"Silence! Keep quiet! Listen to the letter! Keep reading, Vyhovski! That's our own kinsman who's writing to us there! That's our own blood, our brother . . .!"

"A dog's blood and dogs' brother!" roared the huge pock-marked Hladko. "*Na pohybel!*"

The shouting died down as Vyhovski resumed the interrupted reading but the angry muttering went on in the council room while other wild outbursts erupted in the crowds outside. The *Voyevode's* letter assured the Zaporohjans that they could trust him because he shared their Ruthenian origins and Orthodox religion. It reminded them that he took no part in suppressing earlier Cossack risings, urged Hmyelnitzki to suspend the war and confirm his loyalty to the Commonwealth by entering the peace talks, and either send the Tartars back to the Crimea or turn his own army on them.

'*I promise you all,*' Pan Kisyel assured the Cossacks finally, '*as your brother in God's Holy Church and the son of an old Ruthenian family rooted in your soil, that I will do all I can for you in the Seym and Senate from which, as you know, all our freedoms and privileges flow.*'

The *Voyevode,* who was also one of the King's Privy Council, concluded by reminding the Cossacks of his powers. No war could be made by the Commonwealth without his approval in the Diet where all decisions had to be unanimous and a single vote cast in opposition ended all further discussion of the matter.

Joy gripped Hmyelnitzki who knew exactly how much this pious, well-meaning and conciliatory old man could do for him and the Cossacks. No taxes or war-levies could be voted without his consent. No armies could be raised. No war could be declared. And no new Grand Hetman of the Crown could be appointed by the King to mobilize the gentry against the rebellion.

★   ★   ★

But before he could reach out and grasp the opportunity that Kisyel's letter was suggesting to him, he had to master and pacify his colonels.

Most of them seemed to like the letter well enough, as did the massed Brotherhood outside. Others, led by Tcharnota, still shouted their protests. He knew he could inspire terror in them all with a single glance but some of them had become so full of their own successes that it was hard to say which way they'd choose to go. And what would happen if they went against him? Whom would they pick as their new war leader? Maksym Krivoinos? Kshetchovski . . .?

The mass outside swarmed like the population of a roiled beehive. Their loyalties were no more controllable than a storm at sea. The atamans, who respected only what they feared, were no more predictable than that human ocean that boiled in the *maydan*. They were all on their feet, brandishing the round, short-handled maces that were their symbols of authority, and spitting insults into each other's faces. He saw a blur of furious eyes and foaming mouths everywhere around him while Tcharnota, who howled threats of murder at anyone who argued against war, looked as if he'd gone completely over the edge into raving madness.

Watching him, Hmyelnitzki felt his own rage welling up inside. It would burst out at any moment, he knew, but before he could give vent to his fury and roar them all down into a trembling silence, Kshetchovski leaped up on a bench.

"This is a war council, you heathen cattle, not a *tchaban* orgy!" he shouted in a voice like thunder.

"Silence!" howled Tcharnota who, as Hmyelnitzki knew, might have expected this most famous war leader among them to harangue the meeting in favor of fighting. "Kshetchovski wants to speak!"

"Silence!" bellowed a dozen others. "Listen to Kshetchovski!"

★   ★   ★

Hmyelnitzki also listened, watching him uneasily. He knew that the Cossacks held this icy, calculating man in special esteem. They honored him for his great military skills and for the immense services he had rendered to them. But there was more to it than that. With their strange blend of love and hatred for the Polish gentry they admired Kshetchovski because he'd been ennobled. But Tcharnota was wrong to think that Kshetchovski would speak out for war. His icy reasoning, coupled with that insatiable ambition which Hmyelnitzki used so well before

Yellow Waters, led him to conclude that here was the moment he'd been waiting for: the time to reach out for those lands, positions and distinctions he craved all his life. He saw in a flash, as Hmyelnitzki realized himself, that he'd be the chancellor's first choice to bring the Cossackry to order once peace was restored, and to stamp out whatever smoldering embers of rebellion might be left among them.

Now, speaking to the atamans, he made himself sound like just another simple, rough-hewn Cossack so that everything he said would seem like something they might have thought out for themselves.

"My job's to fight, not talk," he told them. "But since we're here to make a decision then I'll tell you what I'd advise we do. It's simple. Why did we start the war? To get back our rights. The *Voyevode* of Bratzlav says that this must happen. If it happens, all's well and good, and we make the peace. If it doesn't happen then we go on fighting. But why keep spilling our good blood for nothing? Let them give us what we want and we'll whip the *tchernya* back into their byres and that'll be that! Our *Bat'ko* Hmyelnitzki thought it all out and fixed it very wisely so that we can stand on the King's side, punishing the princelings, and the King's got to give us a good reward for that. And if the princelings go on opposing us we'll play with them a little more, and with the King's blessing!"

"*Pravdu kajhe!*" old Loboda said.

"*Nepravdu!*" howled Tcharnota.

"There's only one thing I'd advise when it comes to Pan Kisyel's letter," Kshetchovski went on. "Let's keep the Tartars handy. Let them make camp in the Wild Lands until we know which way the wind is blowing. Then we can either call them in again or chase them back into their own country, whichever is best."

Hmyelnitzki smiled, relieved.

The great majority of the atamans began to call for an armistice, for an embassy to be sent to Warsaw with letters to the King, and for Hmyelnitzki to invite Pan Kisyel to come at once and start negotiations.

Tcharnota still shouted for war but Kshetchovski fixed him with an icy stare and said for all to hear: "You, Tcharnota! You're calling for war and bloodshed, but when the Light Horse of Pan Dmohovski went at you at Korsun you squealed like a stuck pig '*Braty ridniye, spasayte*! Spare me, brothers!' and you ran at the head of your whole regiment."

"You're a liar!" howled the furious Tcharnota. "The *Lahy* don't scare me, and you don't scare me either!"

Kshetchovski gripped his mace and leaped towards Tcharnota, and other atamans began to beat and kick him without mercy, while the deliberating Brotherhood outside erupted in wild roars of its own. Hmyelnitzki watched and waited.

Then he rose again.

★   ★   ★

"So, gentlemen," he began once more through the shouts and curses. "You've decided that we ought to send envoys to remind the King about our faithful service and ask him to reward it. But whoever wants to go on fighting is free to do that too! No, not against the King and the Commonwealth, because our war never was with *them*, but against the worst enemy that Cossacks ever had, that bloody-handed Yarema Vishnovyetzki! I sent him envoys asking him to stop his cruelties against us, but he murdered them and ignored my letter, by which he insulted you and the whole Zaporohjan army. And now he's come across the Dnieper, burning and slaughtering innocent people like he did last week in Pohrebyshtchye, and as he's just done at Nyemirov as well. And because the Tartars are afraid to go after him without us, he's coming here so puffed up and blinded by his pride that he's willing to rebel against the King's kindness to us, and he's ready to murder us all!"

The atamans became suddenly quiet and still. Hmyelnitzki took a breath.

"God gave us a great victory over the Hetmans," he resumed. "But that son of the Devil is worse than the Hetmans and all the other kinglets. I can't move against him or he'll cry through all his friends in Warsaw that we don't want peace, that we're the warmakers, and we can't let that happen! The King must keep on thinking that it's Vishnovyetzki who's making war on us! Besides, if I marched out who'd be here for the negotiations?

"So," he continued in the hushed, still chamber, while the atamans began to stir uneasily on their hard, deal benches, "what's to be done about that hellhound? Someone has to go after him and bring him down like we brought down the

Hetmans or he'll chip away at our power until we've nothing left! So I'm asking you now, my good friends and masters, to pull him down and crush him on your own, while I write the King that it was all done without me and that we did it only to defend ourselves against that warring devil's hatred for the Cossacks."

He paused and waited but not a single pair of eyes lifted to meet his own.

"Whichever of you takes up this work," he said, "will get everything he needs to crush Vishnovyetzki and, with God's blessing, win great glory for himself as well! I'll give him the pick of our finest lads, the best of the cannon . . ."

But not one of the atamans stepped forward or looked up from staring at their boots.

"I'll give sixty thousand of our best cavalry," Hmyelnitzki announced. His searching gaze moved back and forth among them but they sat in silence, averting their eyes, while a look of gleeful malice began to flicker on Vyhovski's face.

And yet Hmyelnitzki knew that these men were fearless. Their war-cries rang against the walls of Tsarogorod itself and terrified the Sultan; their fierce courage was the stuff of legends. It was perhaps the risk of losing fame, which was a Cossack leader's most precious possession, that made them think twice about volunteering to face Vishnovyetzki.

"I know one good lad who'd step forward now," Hmyelnitzki said and nodded sadly as if to himself. "But he's not with us just now . . ."

"Bohun," someone said.

"That's right. Bohun. He already wiped one of Yarema's regiments off the Lord's good earth! He'd go for the rest! But he got hurt in that fight in Vasilovka so now he's in Tcherkassy, struggling with Mother Death. And when *he's* not here then it looks like there's nobody here!"

Some of the atamans began to growl and hiss curses into their clenched fists, but still none of them rose or spoke up to protest the insult.

"So tell me, then," Hmyelnitzki went on coldly, prodding them to shame while stirring their ambition. "What's happened to our Cossack courage and our love of glory? Where's it gone . . .? Where are the old Steppe wolves who made the *Lahy* shake and run like rabbits in their time? Where are the Nalevaykos and Pavluks of our generation?"

And then a squat, hunched, thickset man with cat-green eyes, a wry mouth and a reddish mustache that twisted like a flame in his swollen face, rose from a bench and took a slow step forward.

"I'll go," he grunted.

"You Maksym?"

"Me," Krivoinos said.

Cries of "*Na Slavu!* Glory!" broke out at once as the other atamans rushed forward to embrace their champion and hide their relief while Krivoinos glared at them from under his thick red eyebrows and cocked his mace proudly at his hip.

"Don't you start thinkin', Hetman," he began in hoarse, broken phrases, "that I was afraid. Not me. I'd have stood up at once. Only I thought: '*There's better'n me here.*' But if that's not so, and if that's how it's got to be, I'll go. Why not? All you others, you've got heads to think with and hands to scratch the heads but all I've got is just my two good fists an' a saber in 'em. '*Raz maty rodila,*' like the saying goes, a man gets born just once and what's written is written, so why worry about what's going to happen? War's like a mother and sister to me anyways. But you, Hetman, you give me some good boys, you hear? Because *tchernya* rabble isn't any good for war with Yarema."

"You'll have the best we've got!" Hmyelnitzki assured him.

"Alright then, so I'll go," Krivoinos said grinning at the others. "I'll take the castles and the loot like I did before, and cut the throats, and beat the *pany* an' the *lytzari* an' hang 'em all in smoke! To hell with all them lily-handed *Lahy!*"

"An' I'll go with you, Maksym!" Pulyan cried, stepping into the middle of the floor to stand beside Krivoinos.

"And Tcharnota will go," Hmyelnitzki said quickly. "And Hladko and Nosatch!"

"We'll go," they chorused, heartened by the example of Maksym Krivoinos and because Hmyelnitzki left them no way out.

"*Na Yaremu! Na Yaremu!*" the atamans roared. "Death to Vishnovyetzki!"

"*Koli! Koli!*" howled the masses of the Cossackry outside, and shortly afterwards the council turned into a wild celebration that lasted long into the night as the picked regiments of the Zaporohjan army made ready to march out against Prince Yeremi. They drank *na umor*—to the death—because each chosen man was sure he would not return. "*Raz maty rodila,*" they shrugged and repeated after their commander and let all bonds of discipline burst and shatter into dust and the peasant rabble followed their example.

A hundred thousand voices roared out songs and ditties. Their drunken musketry stampeded the huge herd of remount horses through the camp, whipping up a dust storm and creating chaos, while the mobs chased after the animals with shouts and wild laughter. Masses of armed drunken peasants wandered about on the riverbank, shooting into the night and howling around Hmyelnitzki's own quarters until Yakubovitch had them driven off with sabers and whips.

Then a violent rainstorm burst out of the clouds that had been gathering through the evening and sent them all running for shelter into tents and under the wagons.

Lightning lit up the night. The storm raged in flashes of scarlet and white as if the skies themselves had become enraged, and it was by this fiery illumination that Krivoinos rode out of the camp, with sixty thousand picked Cossack and Zaporohjan warriors riding at his back and a mob of *tchernya* trailing at his heels.

Part Five

Chapter Twenty-seven

KRIVOINOS' ARMY MARCHED from Byelotzerkyev towards the Skvira River, and then to Pohrebyshtchye and Mahnovka, and all traces of human life disappeared wherever it passed. Whoever didn't join him died under the knife. Even woods, orchards and wheat fields were torched in his wake as if the Cossacks wanted to surpass Prince Yeremi's own program of destruction.

The Prince, meanwhile, after the massacre in Pohrebyshtchye and the bloody harvest that Pan Baranovski made in Nyemirov, crushed several dozen other rebel *vatahas*, each of several thousand men, and pitched his camp near Raygorod. A month had passed since his army broke into the Ukraine. It was a month in which his men hardly got off their horses and it was time to give them a rest. He even contemplated a temporary withdrawal into quieter country to fill up his depleted ranks and to buy new remounts for his cavalry because after a month of living on scorched and trampled grass the animals looked like skeletons.

But they were in camp barely a week when the patrols brought word of reinforcements. The Prince set out at once to meet them and discovered that this welcome addition to his tired army was led by Pan Yanush Tishkyevitch, the *Voyevode* or Palatine of Kiev, who brought his own household brigade of fifteen hundred seasoned eastern gentry, along with his cousin Kristof, the magistrate of Bratzlav, the young Pan Aksak, barely grown to manhood but leading his own well-founded *husaria* company, and many of the wealthier nobles of the region such as the two Sinyutov brothers, *Knaz* Polubinski with all his retainers, the Zhytinskis and the Yelovitzkis and all the men of the warlike Kyerdey family. Some of them led their own contingents of armed tenants while the lesser gentry came without followers, but altogether the new force exceeded two thousand fresh and well-armed men, not counting the drovers, carters, camp servants and retainers.

The Prince was delighted. He welcomed the Kiev *Voyevode* in the peasant cabin where he made his quarters, and where the new arrivals stared around in open-mouthed amazement; they couldn't reconcile their ideas about the rich and powerful Vishnovyetzki with the austerity around him. Pan Yanush, in particular, couldn't understand why the Prince allowed himself no luxuries during a campaign and insisted on sharing the privations of his poorest soldiers. His quarters were a one-room hut with such a narrow door that the corpulent *Voyevode* could barely squeeze through it, even with his lackeys shoving from behind. The crude peasant *izba* contained only a rough table and some plain deal benches, a camp bed covered with a single horsehide, and a straw pallet for an orderly.

Pan Yanush had seen the Prince in Warsaw at the Senate meetings, they were even distantly related, but he didn't know him very well and the astonishment in his eyes was clear to everyone. He was a rough-and-ready kind of man himself, the sort who slapped his fellow senators on the back and addressed even such lofty magnates as Prince Dominic Zaslavski as '*my dear fellow*,' but his bluff manner shriveled before the Prince. How such a soaring spirit could exist in such meager circumstances was clearly beyond him.

But the Prince greeted him with open arms.

"Thank God you've come with some fresh men," he said warmly. "Because I'm just about at the end of my strength and resources."

"Hmm. Yes." Pan Yanush stirred uneasily. "I've seen by the looks of your soldiers that they've worked hard, poor lads. Which worries me a little, I must say."

"Why does it worry you?"

"Because I've come here to ask for a bit of help."

"Is it something urgent?"

"*Periculum in mora*, Prince!" the portly *Voyevode* cried out dramatically and drew a deep breath. "*Periculum in mora*, we've no time to waste! There are several thousand of that rebel scum ravaging my regions, led by that devil Krivoinos who, as I hear

it, was sent after you! He thinks Your Highness is in Konstantinov so that's where he's heading and on the way he laid siege to
my Mahnovka and wreaked such havoc in the district that I've
no words to describe it."

"Then you're right, time's short indeed," Prince Yeremi said.
"I've heard about Krivoinos and I've been getting ready for him
here. But since we seem to have passed each other it looks as if I
have to go out looking for him. What kind of a garrison is there
in Mahnovka?"

"Two hundred German infantry. Good men, they'll hold out
quite a while. But the town's also full of local gentry and their
families which strains the supplies. What's worse, the earthworks aren't in the best of shape. Not even Germans can defend
them long."

"Time's pressing, then," the Prince repeated and nodded at
his orderly. "Zelenski! Get the colonels!"

The boy ran out at once and the fleshy *Voyevode* sank gratefully to a bench, breathed in satisfaction, and started sniffing for
some sign of supper. He'd ridden hard all day, he was tired, and
he was well known for his love of eating. Instead he heard the
heavy footsteps of armed men, watched Prince Yeremi's officers
file into the room, and his expectations of a well-laid table
turned to disappointment. He saw lean, bearded men with tired
eyes buried deep in their darkened sockets, and with the harsh
signs of innumerable hardships stamped into their faces. Their
hollow cheeks were blackened by the sun. Their faded uniforms
were bleached by Summer rainstorms and their dented armor
was scarred and scoured by the fierce Steppe winds. They
bowed in silence to the Prince and to his dumb-struck guests
and waited for orders.

"Are the horses fed?" Prince Yeremi asked.

"They are, Your Highness. Fed, saddled and ready."

"And your men?"

"Ready as always, Highness."

"Good. Get them mounted. We are marching against Krivoinos."

"Eh? Eh? What's that?" Pan Yanush stared with open disbelief
at his cousin Kristof. "Aren't we going to get anything to eat?"

But Prince Yeremi was busy issuing his orders.

"Vyershul and Ponyatovsky to set out at once. Then Baranovski and Volodyovski with all the dragoons, and then the

rest in usual marching order. I want even Vurtzel's cannon to be
on the road in under an hour."

The officers bowed and left the room and moments later
cavalry bugles sounded throughout the camp.

The hungry Palatine didn't expect such a swift response to his
plea for help; indeed he had quite different ideas about it,
hoping to rest a few days in the Prince's camp and still manage
to reach his besieged town in time. And now he was expected to
get back on his horse without sleep or supper!

"Highness," he tried with circumspection that was quite unusual for him and his kind. "But will your . . . ah . . . men
make it to Mahnovka? It's a long way and they seem terribly
fatigati, what?"

"Don't you worry about them, my friend," the Prince said
lightly. "They go to battle as if it was a wedding."

"Hmm. Yes. I see that. They're a hardy lot, there's no denying it. But . . . ah . . . my own people are a bit tired, you see."

"Didn't you say *periculum in mora?*"

"Yes. Yes, I did, Your Highness. But a night's rest won't
make much difference, will it? We've been riding all the way
from Hmelnik . . ."

"And we from Lubnie, sir. From across the Dnieper."

"We've been on the road all day!"

"And we the whole month," the Prince said and stepped out
of the hut to supervise the execution of his marching orders
while the unhappy Palatine slapped both his knees in anger and
stared at Pan Kristof.

"Well, I've got what I wanted!" he growled bitterly. "They'll
starve me to death here! What's the matter with them? Are their
heads on fire? I come to ask for help, to persuade them and
perhaps do a bit of bargaining . . . you know how it's done! But
what happens here? Slam, bang and they're off! I thought it
would take two or three days at least before they stirred themselves but they don't even let a man catch his breath in peace!
What's their hurry, I ask you? My leg's been rubbed raw by the
stirrup leather where that lout of a groom fastened it improperly
. . . my guts are twisted up in knots . . . Ah, the Devil take 'em!
There's time to think about Mahnovka and time to give some
thought to the belly too, isn't there? I'm an old soldier myself,
I've a few hard campaigns under my belt as well, but not like
this, I tell you. Don't they eat or sleep? All they do is fight! And

did you take a good look at those colonels, Kristof? They're more like *spectra* than human beings!"

"But they snap right to it, don't they," said Pan Kristof who admired soldiers. "Dear God, you know how much confusion there is in any other camp when it comes to marching out! All that rushing about, the packing, the wagons to be readied, the horses to be sent for from the pastures . . . And here—d'you hear?— there's the light cavalry going out already!"

"There you are, it's just as I said!" the gloomy *Voyevode* exclaimed. "It's enough to drive a good man to despair."

But the youthful Pan Aksak pressed his hands together and stared about with eyes full of worship. "Ah, what a leader," he sighed. "What a great commander!"

"What do you know about it, you young whipper-snapper?" the hungry *Voyevode* cried out in desperation. "Your nose is still wet from your mother's milk! The Roman *Cunctator* was also a great commander but he knew how to take his time, do you understand?"

"Mount up gentlemen, if you please," the Prince ordered briskly, entering the room. "We're leaving at once."

But the distraught *Voyevode* couldn't contain himself any longer. "God blast it, Prince!" he burst out. "I'm hungry! Let me eat something, will you? Send for some food, for God's sake!"

Prince Yeremi looked as startled as if the thought of hunger never occurred to him and then he laughed out loud and took the trembling and indignant old man in his arms.

"Forgive me, my dear friend, forgive me with all your great heart," he said and went on laughing. "But we tend to be a bit forgetful about such things in wartime. Of course I'll send for supper. There has to be something edible in this camp."

"What did I tell you?" the mollified Palatine turned to his friends. "Didn't I say that they don't eat here?"

★   ★   ★

The *Voyevode's* supper didn't take much time and within two hours even the pikemen and the musketeer infantry marched out of Raygorod. The army wound swiftly along the Hmelnik track to the small town of Vinnitza and then into Lityn, and near the settlement of Saverovka the Prince's Tartar Light Horse and dragoons under Vyershul and Volodyovski came across a real Tartar convoy. They freed several hundred slaves, most of them young girls and women whipped along the trail, and wiped out the escorting *tchambul* to a man.

Ruins and devastation, sure signs that Krivoinos also passed that way, appeared soon afterwards. The village of Stryzavka was burned to the ground and its population slaughtered. The inhabitants had shown some resistance and the merciless Krivoinos massacred them all. Their luckless master, Pan Stryzovski, hung naked from a tree at the entrance to his lifeless village with the severed heads of his wife and children strung across his chest in a grisly necklace. But an even more horrific sight met the Prince's men among the smoldering ruins where two long rows of corpses sagged against upright poles driven into the ground. Their arms were roped high above their heads and wrapped in pitch-soaked straw which had been set on fire from the top. Most of these mute, dead witnesses to the Cossacks' fury stood with only their hands or arms burned off since a sudden rain put out the flames before they consumed the rest of their bodies. But their contorted faces and the blackened stumps raised towards the sky seemed like a cry of horror none the less.

The stench of burned flesh and rotting offal lay thick among the ruins while vast flocks of carrion birds wheeled among the stakes, cawing and rising heavily as the riders neared them and moving on to settle on more distant corpses. A few grey timber wolves, gorged on the other dead who littered the wreckage, slunk softly out of the gutted village and watched the Prince's soldiers from the dark thickets beyond it.

The army marched in silence along this avenue of horror and the soldiers counted more than three hundred of these 'Cossack candles' before the scene gave way to open fields where a fresh, summer breeze blew away the rotted stench of death. But the signs of devastation spread many miles further.

This was the first half of July and the wheat fields were almost ready for an early harvest but now they looked as if a whirlwind had touched down among them. Whole acres were scorched and trampled under horses' hooves and trodden into the ground. Even the woods had been set on fire and now the seared dead trees, stripped of their leaves and bark, stood like black skeletons under a smoke-grey sky. Prince Yeremi's soldiers were familiar with the devastation that a Tartar raid inflicted on a prosperous countryside but this kind of savagery was new even in their experience.

Meanwhile the shocked Palatine of Kiev couldn't believe his eyes. Myedjakov, Zhar, Futory, Sloboda . . . one settlement and township followed another in this catalog of slaughter and destruction so that the whole country seemed like a single ruin. The men were all gone, swept up by Krivoinos; the women and children went into Tartar slavery. The earth was swept clean of life but the sky above it was dark with vultures, blackbirds, cawing crows and ravens which gathered from hundreds of miles around for this Cossack harvest.

"Ay, my poor Mahnovka," the shocked old Palatine murmured, staring numbly at this desolation. "My poor, poor Mahnovka . . . I see we won't be able to get there in time!"

"If we don't then we'll at least destroy the destroyers," Prince Yeremi said.

He hurried his army at a remorseless pace and soon they were passing fresher signs of the enemy's advance. The roadside was littered with brokendown carts and wagons, dead men and animals whose blood was still moist and whose bodies hadn't begun to rot, smashed pottery and abandoned skillets among the warm ashes of recent bivouac fires, sacks of rain-soaked flour, and ruins where flames still flickered among blackened timbers.

In Hmelnik trembling fugitives brought word that it wasn't old Maksym Krivoinos who left that dreadful trail but only his son Aleksei, detached with a corps of eighteen thousand men to besiege Mahnovka, who ravaged the whole district like a plague. The town, they told the Prince, had already fallen. The Cossacks butchered every Jew and every boy and man belonging to the gentry who took refuge there while the women were driven to the Zaporohjans' *tabor* where a much more dreadful and protracted fate was awaiting them. The small town citadel, commanded by Pan Lev, was still resisting the assaults that young Krivoinos hurled at it out of a nearby monastery but, short of men and powder, it wouldn't last the night.

"We'll split our forces," the Prince decided then. "The infantry, artillery and the wagon train will march to Bistrok at their own best pace along with the main body of the army while we take two thousand picked cavalry to Mahnovka as fast as we can."

"What? What?" The distraught Palatine objected. "Why split our forces when we've so few to start with?"

"Because it's speed and surprise that'll count from now on. Not numbers."

"It's too late, too late," the despairing *Voyevode* said over and over, losing his head at the news of this latest slaughter and all the destruction he saw on the march. "Mahnovka is gone! We'll be too late to help anyone there! We'd do better to fall back, fortify other places, and put strong garrisons in whatever towns may be left somewhere . . . If there *is* anything that's still worth defending in this unhappy country."

But Prince Yeremi wouldn't listen to him, and neither did Pan Kristof, young Pan Aksak, or the Prince's colonels. "Since we've come here to fight," they said. "Then let's go and do it."

And the picked cavalry regiments set off at a rapid canter.

★ ★ ★

They were within a half-mile of the besieged earthworks when a small group of wounded and disheveled horsemen galloped into their vanguard.

"That's Pan Lev!" the *Voyevode* cried out, recognizing the citadel commander and a few companions, and guessed at once what must have taken place. "The castle's taken!"

"That's right," Pan Lev said. He was bleeding from a dozen saber and gunshot wounds. But his companions shouted that there were still some gentry barricaded in the stone keep of the citadel and these could be saved if the rescuers would hurry.

They were still talking, gasping for breath and relating the horrors of the last assault, when Prince Yeremi ordered his two thousand horsemen forward at full gallop and a few moments later the town and castle rose before them with thick dark clouds of smoke boiling into the sky above them.

The night ebbed while they were on their way and now a vast red and purple dawn blazed so brightly in the eastern sky that the soldiers took it for the reflected glow of the burning town. They watched the ordered, singing ranks of Zaporohjans and masses of *tchernya* flowing downhill through the shattered gates of the little city that stood out stark and clear in that violent light. The Cossacks poured into the plain with beating kettle-drums and the blare of trumpets, forming up for battle all the more readily since no one in the town knew that Prince Yeremi was anywhere near. Indeed, having caught sight of the Palatine of Kiev, they raised a jeering cheer.

A fierce cry rose in reply from the Polish ranks and the Palatine had one more chance to admire the skills of the Prince's soldiers. They swung at once into perfect battle order, with the heavy cavalry in the center and the Light Horse galloping to the flanks, so that nothing more needed to be done before the battle started. The Prince, however, never left anything to chance. He galloped among the ranks with his gold mace in hand, bright as a flame in his burnished armor, inspecting everything and issuing his last orders. The red light of dawn blazed on his silver-plated helmet and cuirass so that he looked like a moving fire among the dark walls of his iron horsemen.

"What soldiers!" Pan Yanush cried out to Pan Kristof as they brought their own regiments into line. "With troops like that who needs a commander?"

No time at all seemed to pass while the three Polish battle lines were formed. The Palatine, Pan Kristof and young Pan Aksak led their three heavy regiments in the first line since Prince Yeremi wanted to conceal his own presence on the battlefield as long as he could. Baranovski's dragoons formed their supporting line. The huge, winged mass of the Prince's own gigantic *husaria* formed its grim ranks under Yan Skshetuski in the final line while the Tartar Light Horse, the Valachian archers and the Prince's own Household Cossack regiments under Vyershul, Kushel and Ponyatovski spread out like the open wings of a bird of prey on the flanks of the army and formed the points of the long crescent that curved towards the center.

The Palatine barely had the time to set his men in order when the Prince appeared before him and pointed his mace at the Cossack masses.

"For all you've lost, strike first," he said.

The *Voyevode* waved his own short-handled battle mace and his men moved forward. It became clear at once to the watching soldiers that for all his age and bulk and love of luxury and procrastinations the Palatine of Kiev was an experienced cavalry commander. He didn't hurl his men at once into an open charge but led them slowly forward, gathering speed and weight as they neared the enemy and saving their horses' strength until the final moment. He rode in the center of the first rank, clearly visible to all and armed only with his commander's mace, while

a young body servant carried his heavy broadsword close to
hand for when it was needed. The *tchernya* poured towards him
on foot, armed with scythes and flails, to take the first weight of
the attack and make the Zaporohjan's own charge easier in its
turn. Nearing him, some of the Mahnovka men who joined the
Zaporohjans recognized him by his size and girth and began to
jeer.

"Hey, mighty lord, illustrious *Voyevode!* Harvest time is coming! How come you're not sending your poor serfs into the
fields this year? Greetings, master, greetings! We've brought our
scythes to let the air out of that big belly of yours!"

A hail of musket balls rattled through the ranks of the *Voyevode's* soldiers but since they were already bent low in their
saddles and charging at full gallop it did little damage. The two
masses collided with the sound of a giant's hammer falling on an
anvil. Scythes and flails rang against the armor. The thunder of
the horses's hooves drowned the shouts and battlecries and the
howls of rage and the shrill, plaintive moaning of the wounded.
The lances of the armored riders tore a vast red gap in the
densely packed masses of the *tchernya* and the maddened horses
trampled everything that stood in their way.

It seemed to the watching soldiers of the second line as if this
was some kind of bloody harvest with rows of wheat stalks
falling before the grim ranks of advancing reapers whose flashing steel marked their line of passage. The splintered lances
were tossed aside and now the broadswords rose and fell, shattering the *tchernya*, and soon the howl of "*ludy, spasaytes*, save
yourselves" rose above the plain and the panicked masses broke
into headlong flight. The waiting Zaporohjans, concerned
about the good order of their own battle line, pointed a hedge of
spears at the fleeing rabble which scattered to the flanks, where
the Prince's light cavalry fell upon it, cut it down in hundreds,
and drove the rest back into the center.

Charging across the bodies of the *tchernya*, the Palatine's
horsemen now came face to face with the Zaporohjans who
charged them in an all-out gallop of their own so that the two
masses of armed men and horses came together like twin tidal
waves, forming a towering wall of flaying hooves and riders
locked in combat, with the white crest of sabers glittering above
them.

But it was one thing for the *Voyevode's* riders to crush and scatter panicked mobs of rabble and another to cross sabers with seasoned Zaporohjan soldiers. Here it was cavalry-fighting knee to knee, warrior against warrior and steel against steel.

Dead men fell thickly on both sides.

The two lines pressed against each other, bending and twisting but unable to break through, and the old Palatine thrust his mace into his sash, seized his battle-sword, and got to work as if he was just a common trooper, sweating and wheezing like a blacksmith's bellows. The Zaporohjans fought with equal fury, led by the burly Ivan Burdabut, an ataman of the Kalnitzki Regiment, who was all the more terrifying because he rode a killer stallion trained to attack like a mastiff with his teeth. The two Sinyutov brothers charged him first in their gilded armors but Burdabut's horse seized the younger Andrei by the face and crushed it in its jaws. The older, Rafal, slashed at the beast's head but his saber turned on a brass stud fixed to the monster's headgear while Burdabut thrust his own saber point through Pan Rafal's throat.

There was something unearthly about this murderous partnership between a horse and rider; something that called up superstitious terrors. Gunsmoke turned them both as black as midnight; both were splashed with blood and glaring with mad eyes so that they seemed like a single raging animal, half man and half beast, and some of the *Voyevode's* soldiers began to rein their mounts and back away in horror.

The wild ataman threw himself on young *Knaz* Polubinski, a lad of sixteen, and hacked off his sword-arm at the shoulder with one blow.

Pan Urbanski, wanting to avenge the death of a kinsman, fired a pistol point-blank into his face but missed and only shot off one of the Zaporohjan's ears while Burdabut slashed off his head with a single stroke.

The eighty-year-old Pan Zhytinski fell next, split in two, then two of the Niktchemny brothers, and others started to fall back and scatter, especially since two hundred bloody spears and sabers gleamed behind the Cossack.

Finally, the terrible ataman caught sight of the *Voyevode* himself and rode at him with a howl of joy, bowling over half a dozen riders who tried to bar his way.

Confident of his own great strength, the old Palatine snorted like a boar, lifted his broadsword and spurred his animal at the murderous pair. He would have been cut down like the others if his young body servant didn't throw himself on Burdabut and seized him around the waist. The lad died at once, sabered by the Cossack, but he distracted Burdabut long enough for some men of the Kyerdey family to bring help. Several dozen horsemen charged between Burdabut and the *Voyevode* and a new battle flared up around them.

The sun swept redly into the afternoon as the fighting raged up and down the field. Men and horses fell in dozens and then in tens of dozens and the weary Kievans began to give way under the swelling pressure of the Zaporohjans. The Polish line began to bend and buckle as if about to crack. Pan Kristof Tishkyevitch and the youthful Aksak brought up their men to help but young Krivoinos also sent fresh regiments charging down the slope and the carnage grew even fiercer than before.

Evening began to fall but the fires in the town spread to the suburbs and cast a lurid glow over the battlefield so that the Prince's soldiers in the plain below could see both sides of the battle line as clearly as if it were noon, and the shape of the day-long battle was starting to change. The widespread wings of light cavalry which had crushed the *tchernya* were pushing the Zaporohjans' flanks back towards the town while in the center the Cossack masses pressed the Polish horsemen downhill to where the Prince was waiting. Soon they were so near that the Vishnovyetzki troopers recognized individual fighters on both sides even though night had fallen. The whole town was burning by that time and the flames turned the battlefield into a crimson mirror of reflected fires.

Three new Cossack regiments galloped down the slope to break through the line but, at that moment, the Prince sent Baranovski's dragoons charging into the fight and then only the *husaria* remained in the plain behind him. Seen from a distance they were like a forest sprung out of the plain: a dark, silent thicket of iron men and horses, with the night breeze rustling softly through the lance pennons above them. They waited with confident patience for their turn to charge, knowing that it was their job to decide the battle. Skshetuski sat his horse quietly on their flank with his right sleeve rolled up to the elbow as a mark of rank and with his heavy battle sword grasped in his hard fist.

The Prince stood among the winged horsemen in his silver armor and shielded his eyes from the sharp glare of the fire as he watched the battle. The center of the Polish crescent slid slowly towards him as he watched and waited; he could see the flash of sabers glittering like lightning above the dense ranks of the struggling soldiers; he noted the dip and fall of every battle flag, the growing mounds of corpses, and the aimless gallop of riderless horses that burst out of that heaving mass in every direction.

But his eyes lifted higher.

They swept the brightly lit slope beyond the fighting and rested on the hillside where young Krivoinos waited with two picked *kujhenye* of Zaporohjan warriors to strike the final blow against the Polish center.

At last the Cossacks charged. Their last reserve was galloping downhill to the battle and Prince Yeremi nodded with satisfaction.

"Take them!" he shouted to Skshetuski and pointed with his mace.

Pan Yan raised his sword and spurred his horse forward and the iron riders thundered like an avalanche across the field behind him.

Chapter Twenty-eight

SKSHETUSKI'S MEN DIDN'T HAVE far to ride. The rear of the Polish battle line bulged heavily towards them under the pressure of the Cossack masses even before they reached their full speed and the crushing weight on which their charge depended. The hard-pressed dragoons parted instantly before them, springing aside like a crimson gate to expose the Cossacks, and the armored riders fell on the Zaporohjans like an iron wall.

"Yarema!" the winged *husaria* shouted, smashing everything before it.

"Yarema!" cried the army.

The dreaded name echoed through the ranks all across the plain, inspiring a joyous certainty of victory on one side and an unmanning hopelessness and fear on the other. It rang like an incantation that resurrected every superstitious legend that the Zaporohjans whispered to each other in their Winter quarters but for the embattled Polish knights it was a spell that poured new strength into their weary shoulders.

"Yarema! Yarema!" Even the *Voyevode's* soldiers took up the shout, pressing all the harder, and it was only then that the Cossacks realized whom they had been fighting.

They fell in hundreds before the iron onslaught. Whole companies disappeared under the horses' hooves as if a sudden hurricane swept them off the field. Entire regiments cracked and shattered like glass and trampled each other as they broke and ran. The name '*Yarema*' knocked the spears and sabers out of the Cossacks' hands as if it were magic but the *husaria* would have overwhelmed them no matter what they heard. The winged horsemen bowled them over as if they were helpless bystanders buried by a landslide. Their only refuge was to leap aside, let the steel avalanche sweep by and strike it from the flanks, but those open flanks were guarded by dragoons and light cavalry which drove-in the wings of the Cossack army.

Beaten, they fled.

And now the battle took yet another form. The Light Horse regiments of Vyershul, Kushel and Ponyatovski drove the Cossack flanks back upon their center, forming a kind of avenue through which the *husaria* charged down on the Zaporohjans and sent them howling back towards the burning town. If the light cavalry could have closed the circle around the fleeing Cossacks the slaughter would have been complete but the vast numbers of the fugitives made encirclement impossible and so the flanking troopers merely hemmed them in, cutting them down in dozens as they fled between them.

Seeing disaster, the young Krivoinos simply lost his head. His ruthless courage was never in doubt; like most Cossack leaders of his time he took great pride in a well-earned reputation for fearlessness and disregard of danger to himself. But now he ran for his life in front of all his men knowing that his military skills were no match for the terrible Yarema. He might have managed to rally his shattered regiments further up the hillside if the short-sighted Kushel hadn't spotted him in the jostling crowd and darted among the Cossacks from the side. Slashed in the face by Kushel's heavy saber, the young Cossack leader lost whatever confidence he had and let himself be carried from the field.

Kushel's own fate also hung briefly in the balance as Burdabut charged him at the head of his Kalnitzki *kujhen*. The raging ataman tried a suicidal stand against the *husaria* but his regiment was smashed and tossed aside like husks of wheat on a threshing floor and he finally decided to save what he could by breaking through the dragoons into the open plain. But before he and his maddened horse could tear their way through Kushel's crimson horsemen, the fleeing crowds overran his men and blocked all escape.

All sense of order left the battlefield after this last Cossack attempt to break out into the open. Even the *husaria* could no longer force its way through the dense, packed masses which fought with the hopeless ferocity of despair. The carnage was all the more terrible because it was pointless with the victory already decided beyond a doubt. Men went on hacking and slashing at each other until they were too exhausted to lift a sword or saber. They were too tightly packed for swordplay anyway and fought with knives and fists, using their iron sword hilts like hammers on each other's heads. The frightened horses, driven mad by the smell of blood and held fast in the thick tangle of dead animals and men piled under them, kicked and savaged each other and threw off their riders, until finally some Cossacks began to cry for mercy.

"*Pomyluyte, Lahy!*" The mournful howls began to rise throughout the battlefield. "*Pomyluyte, pany!*"

The plaintive voices spread and swelled until they over-shadowed the ringing clash of metal, the dull crack of iron falling on dead bone and the rattling coughs of dying men and horses, but there was no mercy to be found that night under that scarlet sky.

Only the blood-mad Burdabut who raged like an apparition from another world among the *husaria* refused to beg for pity. He and his killer horse were both red with blood, some of it their own. Foam stained their mouths under flared nostrils. Unable to swing his saber in the crowd around him he made room for himself with a Turkish dagger, ripping open the belly of the corpulent Pan Dzik who had time for only one desperate 'O Jezu!' before he fell under his horse's hooves.

Then, with some space around him, the terrible Zaporohjan sabered Pan Sokolski, a *husaria* trooper, splitting his head in two along with his helmet, and bowled over Pan Pryam and Pan Tzertovitch along with their horses while others started to back away from him.

Young Pan Zenobius Skalski stood up to him and slashed at his head but his saber turned in his sweating hand and struck the Cossack with only the flat of the blade. Burdabut, in turn, smashed him down with one backhand blow of his gigantic fist and looked for fresh victims.

"Witchcraft!" the armored troopers began to call out, giving way before him. "He's magic! A *charakternik!* Iron can't do him any harm!"

At last Burdabut saw Skshetuski, recognized him as an officer by his upturned sleeve, and charged down upon him.

The shouts of '*witchcraft*' didn't bother Pan Yan but he was so enraged by the devastation that Burdabut wreaked among his

best soldiers that he spurred his horse at the Zaporohjan with
fury of his own. They struck each with such force that their
horses staggered, thrown back on their haunches. Then steel
hissed through the air, metal clanged, and Burdabut's saber flew
apart, shattered to pieces by the blow of Skshetuski's broadsword.

The watching soldiers shouted out in triumph, knowing that
the next blow would hurl the Cossack to the ground, but
Burdabut leaned forward, slipped under the blade and caught
Skshetuski in his massive arms. Each was a powerfully-built
man, famous for his strength among his own people, so everyone else backed away to give them a clear space and to watch the
struggle. Their bodies locked together and the Zaporohjan's
curved Turkish dagger gleamed suddenly at Skshetuski's throat.
Pan Yan's broadsword was useless at such close quarters. He
dropped it, letting it dangle on its wrist-strap and caught the
Cossack's knife-hand in his own. The two thick, corded arms
lifted and began to strain against each other, trembling in the air
while Burdabut's men and Skshetuski's soldiers watched in
breathless silence, their own fight forgotten for the moment.
And then the Cossack gave one short, strangled howl, his
crushed fingers opened, and the knife fell out of them and spun
to the ground.

Skshetuski's troopers broke into a cheer as he let go of the
ataman's crushed fist, shifted his weight slightly in the saddle,
caught Burdabut by the neck and forced the huge unkempt
head down to the pommel of the Cossack's saddle. Then he
struck him twice, swift as a pair of lightnings, with the ridged
iron mace he pulled from his belt. Bone cracked, Burdabut's
breath rattled in his throat, he slid out of his saddle and fell
under his terrible horse's hooves. His men yelled, enraged, and
ran forward to avenge his death but the jubilant *husaria* charged
them at once and sabered them all.

★　★　★

Meanwhile the battle drew towards its end. The heavy cavalry moved forward in pursuit of those Zaporohjans who
looked for refuge near the town while Kushel's and
Ponyatovski's Light Horse surrounded the rest.

Expecting no more mercy than they gave, the Cossacks
fought to the death, buying time for others who fled across the

river in their wagon train. A sudden rainstorm extinguished the fires and the remaining Cossacks made good use of the darkness, so that when Vyershul and his Tartar troopers rode into the town only two hours later they found no sign of any Zaporohjans. An all-night chase failed to do much against the mobile fortress in which they escaped and which they defended with the tenacity that made Zaporohjans famous; their wagon train couldn't be taken without infantry and cannon.

Their escape, however, caused a serious breach between Prince Yeremi and the *Voyevode* who called off his men and ended the pursuit.

"Why did you do that?" the Prince demanded once all the troops returned and the chase was over. "You've let them get away!"

"What of it? They're beaten. What harm can they do us?"

"Baranovski already snatched forty wagons and two cannon from them! We'd have had them all if you hadn't pulled your men away. I thought you were a real lion in the field this morning but now you're losing all the glory you've won."

"My dear Prince," the *Voyevode* replied with some heat. "I don't know what kind of spirit drives you and your people, but I'm a man made of flesh and bone, not one of those curious mechanical *automata* made in foreign places, and I need rest after a day's work! And so do my men. I'll always fight an enemy in the field like I did today. But I'm not going to rattle around in darkness after fugitives."

"They should have been stamped out to the last man!" Prince Yeremi shouted.

"What good would that have done?" The *Voyevode's* full, high-colored face became maroon with anger. "We'll exterminate this lot and what will it mean? Another lot will come! We'll finish off young Krivoinos and the old one will come down here like the plague to settle the score. He will burn and loot and murder, like his son did in Stryzavka, and even more innocent people will go to feed the crows. And why, eh? Just because we couldn't let well enough alone?"

"I see that you too belong to the peace party!" the Prince said bitterly. "Along with the chancellor in Warsaw and all those other armchair generals who want to talk the rebellion to death rather than destroy it! But nothing will come of that, by God, and you can believe it! Not as long as I've a sword in my hand!"

But the old Palatine had been in politics too long to be impressed by the righteousness of anybody's anger, even Prince Yeremi's.

"I carry a lot more years on my back than hair on my head," he said quietly and shrugged with resignation. "My life is almost over so it's not some party to which I belong these days but to God himself who is going to sit in judgment on me soon enough. And if I don't want to be weighed down with blood when I stand before Him, especially blood spilled in a civil war, it shouldn't surprise anyone. As for you, Prince, perhaps you're disappointed that you weren't made one of those generalissimos you're so bitter about. And if that's so then I'll tell you this much: you should've been one for your heart and courage, but maybe it's just as well that they passed you over. Because you'd drown the whole country in its blood right alongside the rebels!"

Rage mounted to Vishnovyetzki's face. His dark brows drew together like a cloud, and his neck thickened with a rush of blood, so that the listening officers began to tremble in anticipation of some irrevocable tragedy. But Skshetuski stepped swiftly forward with fresh news that forced the Prince to control his anger. "There's word about the older Krivoinos, Your Highness," he said.

"What word?"

"People from Polonne."

"Get them in here!"

Four men, two of them Orthodox priests, were led into the room and threw themselves down on their knees at the foot of the Prince's chair.

"Save us, lord!" they begged in Ruthenian, stretching their arms towards him. "Save us! Our lives are in your hands!"

"Who are you, then?"

"We're from Polonne, Highness. Old Krivoinos is besieging our town and the castle and if you don't draw him away or destroy him he'll murder us all!"

But Vishnovyetzki watched the weeping emissaries with caution born of bitter experience.

"I know that many people took refuge in Polonne," he said thoughtfully. "But, as they tell me, most of you are Orthodox Ruthenians. It's to your credit that instead of joining the rebellion you're resisting it and standing by the Commonwealth.

But you could be laying a trap for me as your kind tried once already in Nyemirov."

The messengers began to swear by all they held holy that their town awaited the Prince as it would the Savior, and that no thought of treason could enter their minds, and the Prince nodded to show that he believed them. Like everyone else in the Ukraine he knew that the implacable Maksym Krivoinos swore death for all Ruthenians who refused to join the rebellion and opposed Hmyelnitzki. He mentioned Nyemirov, which Baranovski burned to the ground after its people tried to set a trap for the Prince's army, less for the benefit of the pleading envoys than for the listening *Voyevode.*

"Help us, Lord," they pleaded. "Have mercy! We'll be lost without you!"

"So be it, then."

He nodded his assent.

His main forces were still coming down from Bistrok so some time would pass before he was ready but he promised to challenge Krivoinos as soon as he could and sent off the overjoyed emissaries to find food and shelter. It said much for his generosity that he immediately turned to the *Voyevode* and admitted he was wrong in their heated exchange of a moment earlier.

"Forgive me," he said. "You were right, my friend. I see now that we've no time for chasing after the Little Krivoinos when we've the big one near. The whelp will have to wait a bit longer for his noose but his father needs our immediate attention. And I hope that I can still count on your help in this next enterprise."

"You know you can," the *Voyevode* said quickly. "That's quite a different matter."

Then the night's council ended and the relieved officers dispersed to their quarters.

★   ★   ★

The light regiments which were trailing the Zaporohjan *tabor* rode back to Mahnovka later in the day, and by next evening the remainder of Prince Yeremi's army marched in from Bistrok, but it was clear to everyone that they couldn't fight another major battle without rest.

However yet another envoy arrived in the camp that day, a

soft-spoken noble named Stahovitch, who brought a letter to the Prince from the *Voyevode* of Bratzlav, one of the twelve senators who formed the ruling regency of the Commonwealth since King Vladyslav's death, and who was the council's most fervent proponent of Cossack appeasement. Pan Kisyel wrote to assure the Prince of his personal friendship and devotion, calling him '*a second Marius and savior of his country,*' and congratulating him on his many victories. But the real reason for the letter came towards the end where the old senator announced the start of negotiations with Hmyelnitzki. He wrote that he and other peace commissioners were about to go to Byelotzerkyev where he hoped to offer satisfactory terms to the Zaporohjans and he begged the Prince to suspend all his warlike actions until further notice. Watching their Prince, the gathered officers and nobles were quite sure that if someone told him that his beloved Transdnieper was totally destroyed, and that all his towns and castles were turned into ruin, he could have looked no sadder than he did when he heard that letter.

"Dear God!" he burst out. "Let me die at last so that I won't have to witness more of these shameful and degrading humiliations!"

He covered his eyes with both hands and pressed his head back into his chair and the gathered officers stood in deathly silence.

"What sort of people are we?" he demanded. "Is there no end to the shame we have to endure? Here a foul rebel mob swamps the land with blood, brings in the Tartars against its own people, destroys the King's army and enslaves its Hetmans! It tramples the nation's glory in the mud and spits on its laws, burns churches, murders priests and slaughters the gentry! It sells its own women and children into slavery, and how does the Commonwealth reply to these horrors that all our ancestors would have died rather than endure? It comes hat-in-hand to negotiate with traitors. It promises to reward her tormentor and to offer him whatever he might want if he'd just stop butchering his own countrymen! Give us death, dear God! Relieve us of this burden of dishonor because this is no world for men like us to live in!"

The Palatine of Kiev said nothing, sitting in glum silence with his eyes averted. But his cousin Kristof, who was the chief civil magistrate of *Voyevode* Kisyel's Bratzlav palatinate and himself a high-ranking official of the Crown, said after a moment: "Pan Kisyel is not the entire Commonwealth, Your Highness."

"Don't tell me about Pan Kisyel," the Prince answered coldly, "because he's not alone in this. He has a whole party behind him, along with the primate and the chancellor and Prince Dominic Zaslavski, and many other great lords who now rule us in the *interregnum* and claim to represent the majesty of the Commonwealth. But I say they represent disgrace! They shame all of us with their conciliatory weakness before the whole of civilized mankind!"

"Strong words, Your Highness," the *Voyevode* murmured a troubled warning. "Perhaps too strong. Some people might think them self-serving and excessive."

"Perhaps they are. But it's better for a noble nation to die fighting for its dignity and honor than to treat with traitors, and then to live in shame with the contempt of the entire world."

Silent again, the Prince covered up his eyes as if unable to face his loyal soldiers who, as he knew, would sacrifice their own lives and honor if that's what he ordered. He didn't want to see their tears of pity; nor did he want them to see his own tears of shame. To men like the Palatine of Kiev who didn't know him well, his bitterness may have sounded like injured vanity and pride because he wasn't given command of the Crown armies in place of the captured Mikolai Pototzki. But for the officers who loved him and served him without question his words rang with the clarity and honesty of crystal. They knew how much he loved the Commonwealth; they understood everything that moved him and all that mattered to him, and they could feel his pain as deeply as their own.

"Well . . ." Old Pan Zachvilihovski found the temerity to break the long silence. "Let them do their fencing with their tongues, then, if that's what they want . . . And we, Your Highness, will just go on fighting with our swords."

"Even that's not as simple as it sounds," Prince Yeremi answered in a grim, low voice. "Even that promises nothing more than heartbreak. Because what more can we do that would make a difference?"

No one said anything. He let his eyes pass slowly over the gathered officers and gentry, reading their anger, worry and disappointment, and his gaze rested longest on the Palatine of

Kiev who looked as stricken as if he was standing before that Last Judgment he anticipated earlier.

"We've come here through burning forests," he murmured. "And swamps that no one ever crossed before. Because we heard that our Motherland was in pain and suffering in humiliation and despair. We've neither slept nor eaten," he went on remotely as if reciting a litany of futility and failure. "We've fought to the last measure of our strength to save this mother of ours from shame and destruction. Our arms fail us . . . our backs are breaking under all this work . . . our wounds have no time to heal . . . our bellies are empty . . . So what is it for?"

"Our glory," someone offered but the Prince ignored him.

"People . . ." And now he shook himself free of introspection and began to speak directly to his officers like a father instructing his children, or like a prosecutor reading an indictment. "People say I'm bitter . . . that I'm disappointed because I wasn't named one of the twelve regents or the three military commanders who are supposed to see to the safety of the country. Let the world judge between my merits and those who were chosen. But I call on God and all you gentlemen to witness that I don't serve our country for honors and rewards but out of pure love that's deeper and dearer to me than life, God's judgment or any hopes for my own salvation!"

"We know!" the officers cried out.

"Let God judge us all," the *Voyevode* murmured.

"But while we are here, you and I," the Prince resumed in a voice thick with disappointment. "Struggling with our last breath to defeat a terrible enemy, what are we told today? That Pan Kisyel and the gentlemen in Warsaw are thinking how they might reward that enemy, how to honor him and to confirm his power, and how to help him fulfill his every evil dream!"

"Kisyel's a traitor!" the impulsive Baranovski shouted and slapped his heavy saber, while Pan Stahovitch, who was known equally for his cool judgment and for his great courage, rose to protest this slander.

"I'm an envoy of the *Voyevode*," he said. "And I'm his friend as well. He too has grown grey with suffering and worry over the Commonwealth. He too is trying to serve her as best he can and as his conscience guides him. If his means are wrong then it's an honest error, coming from the same love of country as your own! I won't allow anybody here to call him a traitor."

Baranovski didn't dare to take this further in Prince Yeremi's presence. But he was a ruthless and unforgiving man, sometimes as savage as any Zaporohjan, so he fixed his cold grey stare on Pan Kisyel's envoy and placed his hand on his saber in a way that couldn't be mistaken.

In the meantime Vishnovyetzki sighed, shook his head, and spoke out again.

"There's only one choice, then, because it's the regents and commissioners who rule us in the *interregnum* between the death of one King and the election of another. Either we break our oath of obedience to them, with all that this means to us as soldiers, or we must do what they demand from us, turn our backs on everything that we've tried to do, and join in the dishonoring of our country."

"All of the Commonwealth's misfortunes stem from disobedience," the *Voyevode* of Kiev reminded the others.

"And if they tell us to hang ropes around our necks and go on our knees to Tuhay-bey and Hmyelnitzki are we to do that too in the name of orders and obedience?"

"*Veto!*" said Pan Kristof.

"*Veto!*" repeated the oldest of the Kyerdeys.

"Speak up, old friends," the Prince turned to his grimly silent officers. "Tell me where our real duty lies and what we should do."

"I'm seventy years old, Your Highness," Pan Zachvilihovski said quietly but firmly. "I'm an Orthodox Ruthenian, born and bred in the Ukraine and loving my country. I served as the Crown Commissioner to the Cossacks and Hmyelnitzki himself used to call me '*father*.' I should be among the first to call for peace, conciliation, and Cossack appeasement. But if I'm asked to choose between shame and war, then even as I step up for God's final judgment I'll be saying: 'war!'"

"War!" said Skshetuski.

"War!" cried Pan Kristof together with Baranovski.

"War! War!" repeated other voices while the *Voyevode* stared with resignation at the floor. "War!"

"So be it, then," Prince Yeremi said and struck Pan Kisyel's letter, which lay spread out on the table before him, with his golden mace.

Chapter Twenty-nine

THE NEXT DAY the Vishnovyetzki army halted near Rhilkov and the Prince summoned Pan Yan to his quarters.

"I need you to do something for me," he told him.

Skshetuski bowed and waited.

"We have to find some new men somewhere," the Prince said. "We are too few and too exhausted to handle Krivoinos who started out with sixty thousand men and grows stronger every day as new rebels join him. Neither can I count on the *Voyevode* of Kiev for very much longer. He's still with us but his heart's not in it; he's really more in sympathy with the appeasement party."

Pan Yan said nothing. He merely bowed again and waited for his orders. It was unusual for Yeremi Vishnovyetzki to share his thoughts quite as openly as this; to be admitted so frankly to his deepest worries was proof of his trust and Skshetuski was both flattered and grateful.

"I've heard," the Prince continued. "That there are two good, regular regiments quartered somewhere near Konstantinov under Colonels Osinski and Korytzki. I want you to go and get them for me if you can."

"But will they come, Highness?" Pan Yan asked. "If they're near Konstantinov they must be part of Prince Dominic's forces."

"And he," the Prince finished for him, "would rather see me dead than with another victory. I know it. But go anyway. You might have better luck with his officers than I've had with him. Take a hundred of Ponyatovski's Cossacks for an escort and tell those two colonels to join me here as soon as they can because in two more days I'm going to attack Krivoinos."

Pan Yan bowed and set out at nightfall, making use of darkness to avoid an ambush. The countryside was full of Zaporohjan raiders and roving bands of *tchernya* who attacked all travelers out of roadside thickets but he slipped past them all as quietly as a wolf.

He found the two colonels encamped at Vishovate Stavy, about a day's journey along the Konstantinov highway, and his heart leaped at the sight of their superbly drilled and equipped regiments. Osinski had the Royal Dragoon Guards under his command, trained and equipped according to the French order of battle, as well as an infantry regiment of Germans. Korytzki led another thousand veteran German musketeers, most of whom had served in the Thirty Years' War, and who moved with the cold precision of a single weapon at their colonel's command. It was a force worth twenty times its numbers if it were placed under a general as skilled as Prince Yeremi but the two colonels wouldn't hear of it. They were under strict orders from Prince Dominic Zaslavski to keep to themselves.

None of Skshetuski's arguments could shake their conviction that their first duty was to their master's wishes. Neither the country's need, nor the luster that service under Prince Yeremi would add to their own careers, could sway them from strict adherence to their orders. The only way, they said, in which they could justify marching their men to the Vishnovyetzki camp would be if they were attacked by overwhelming numbers or if they found themselves in danger of annihilation.

The loss of this splendid force would be a deep disappointment to Prince Yeremi, Pan Yan knew as he rode away, and even more so since such discipline, and such degree of training, were all too rare in the Polish service. Like every other officer in the Prince's army, Skshetuski knew just how exhausted and worn-out the Transdnieper soldiers had become; their endless marches, battles, raids and punitive expeditions turned them into shadows who no longer knew what it meant to relax their vigilance even for a moment, eat hot food, or sleep for more than two or three hours at a time. Under such circumstances they couldn't hope to face an enemy ten times their size in numbers.

It was clear to Pan Yan that the Prince would have to suspend his campaign, leave Krivoinos untouched and undisturbed in the Ukraine, and march his men into some peaceful province where they'd be able to rest, refit and refill their depleted ranks while the Zaporohjans ravaged the land at will. Adding more bad news to the many disappointments that beset his master wasn't a task that Skshetuski would enjoy.

★ ★ ★

It was with such gloomy thoughts that he rode back towards the Prince's camp with his Cossack troopers. It was a cautious march through a countryside teeming with rebel looters and huge bands of *tchernya* who terrorized the district and hunted for fugitives on every road and highway. If he had hurried, Skshetuski could have covered the distance in a day. But the young soldier was in no hurry to present Prince Yeremi with new disappointments.

There was no moon in the clear, starry sky under which he rode, but the night was dry and there was a soft, refreshing breeze rustling in the dead pine needles on the forest floor. His men walked their horses along a narrow path, guided by woodsmen who spent their lives among those giant trees and knew each turn and twist along every trail. The great, dark Forest of Myshnyetz was full of caves, dry stream beds and hidden ravines that closed around them as soon as they forded the swampy Baklay River, and now only the occasional snap of a dry twig under a horse's hoof broke the lulling silence.

But then a distant, murmuring sound began to intrude, and Pan Yan signaled to his Cossacks to keep still and listened to what seemed to be snatches of wild, faroff songs, a growling mutter, and strange baying laughter.

"What's that?" he asked quietly.

"Who knows, master?" his guide whispered in his turn. "Could be anything. These days the woods are full of people who've gone mad from all the awful things that've happened to them. There's one we seen, a gentlewoman by the looks of her, that goes around looking at the pinetrees and calling '*children, children . . .!*' Seems like the rabble murdered them or something. All the forests hereabouts are full of people like that."

Inured as he was to all the horrors of war, Pan Yan crossed himself and shuddered nonetheless.

"Could it be wolves?" he asked, listening to the sounds in the woods ahead. "It's hard to tell the difference from a distance."

"No way, master." The woodsman shook his head. "Not these days."

"Why not?"

The woodsman shrugged. "There's no wolves in the forests anymore. They've all gone to the villages."

"Why?"

"There's more to eat there."

"Dear God, what terrible times," the young knight murmured quietly. "Wolves go to live in villages and people wander howling in the woods . . ."

"That's how it is now, master."

They were silent then, listening to the soft hissing of the night-wind in the pinetops, and then the distant voices grew stronger and more distinct.

"Hey," the woodsman said. "Sounds to me like there might be quite a crowd out there. You'd better hold up a bit, Your Honor, or come up real slow, and me and my mates will go take a look."

"Go," Skshetuski said. "We'll wait for you here."

The woodsmen vanished in the darkness. They were gone so long that Pan Yan started to suspect a trap when one of them reappeared beside him as quietly as a ghost.

"They're there, master," he whispered.

"Who?"

"*Rezuny.* Marauders."

"How many?"

"A couple of hundred, master, maybe more. There's no way for us to get past them without being seen. They're camped out in a deep, dry riverbed that we've got to cross because it lies right across our trail and they've got fires going. You can't see the glow from here because the hole's so deep but there's no way for us to go around 'em."

"Good," Pan Yan said. "Do they have sentries posted?"

"We didn't see none, master. You can creep up to maybe bowshot range of 'em before you're in the light."

"Good," Skshetuski said again.

He beckoned to his *esauls* and gave them some quick orders while his experienced Cossacks dismounted without a sound.

★ ★ ★

Then they moved out. Not a single saber rattled against a stirrup iron as the troop crept softly through the quiet shadows; not one bridle chain jingled against another. Trained to silent marches, the horses neither neighed nor snorted in the cool night air.

Skshetuski divided his men into three detachments. One of them left their animals tethered among the trees and snaked quietly on their bellies until they lay hidden on the rim of the deep, dried-out riverbed, almost close enough to touch the unsuspecting rebels. Another waited where it was, out of sight but within one swift moment's gallop of the firelit entrance to the canyon. The third group, led by Pan Yan himself, began to work its way around the ravine to close the only exit at the other side.

Looking into the rough, steep-sided gorge, Pan Yan could see the whole of the marauders' encampment spread out as if for inspection at a distance of two dozen paces. Ten pale fires flickered there under iron kettles; their smoke and the thick smell of boiled meats drifted around his nostrils and blew into the faces of his hungry Cossacks. The armed peasants stood or sprawled around these smoldering campfires, drinking, talking quietly or muttering to each other, or leaned into the smoke on their homemade *spisy*, and each of those crude weapons bore its grisly trophy. The severed heads of men, the long-haired skulls of women and the pale faces of decapitated children stared blankly into the night with dead eyes in which the bivouac fires leaped and danced in ghastly reflections.

Some of the marauders lay snoring drunkenly against the far wall of the defile but several dozen others grouped around the biggest of the campfires where an old, thick-shouldered mendicant soothsayer sat with his back propped against a boulder and strummed on a lyre.

"Sing us a piece, father," some hoarse voices muttered. "Give us the one about the Shiftless Cossack."

"*Nyet, nyet!*" others cried. "The one about Marusia from Bohuslav! Sing about Marusia!"

"The Devil take Marusia!" shouted other voices. "Sing about the Master of Potok! About Pan Pototzki!"

The old man struck the lyre and began to sing. His voice was hoarse and dry; it crackled like the dry logs among the flames and the sparks that flew out of the fire. His song was one of those sad, heroic Ukrainian ballads full of love and longing and hope and betrayal in which the cruel history of those fierce, simple, and enduring people passed from one century to another through the generations.

He sang, sighing deeply, and something strange began to happen to Pan Yan. He knew that all his men were poised and

ready to attack but he delayed the signal. That soft July night
. . . those campfires . . . those dark, savage faces, and the
plaintive ditty about a fallen Hetman . . . all of it flowed together to fill him with pity, an inexplicable sorrow and a sense
of loss. He knew that in spite of all its cruelties something of
great value was disappearing before his eyes and ears, never to
return. Whole eras of heroic effort were about to vanish; a way
of life which no other generation would see or understand was
coming to an end. He felt like weeping for the vanished moments of the past, for the simplicity and directness of a lost
existence, and for his own abandoned happiness and hopes.

The broad-backed, white-bearded old singer went on with
his ballad, then paused and stared into the flames. The harsh
faces that loomed over him in the firelight became soft and
quiet. But in that instant a stone slipped off the rim of the ravine
where his Cossack troopers were crouching in ambush; it slipped and rolled, rattling down the steep wall of the gorge, and
the peaceful interval was shattered beyond recall.

The peasant *rezuny* shook themselves free of their own musing. Several dozen of them began to peer upward, shading their
eyes to see beyond the fires, and Pan Yan's brief reverie was
broken.

He leaped up and fired a pistol into the thick of the crowd.

"Kill! No quarter!" he shouted, and thirty troopers fired their
muskets right into the peasants' upturned, staring faces and
then, grasping sabers, leaped into the gorge.

"Kill!" cried the horsemen galloping into the mouth of the
dry riverbed.

"Kill!" cried the fierce voices of the troopers charging behind
Skshetuski.

"Yarema! Yarema!"

★   ★   ★

The attack was so sudden, and the terror that gripped the
peasants was so absolute, that the surprised marauders were
hardly able to defend themselves. Their long scythes and spears
were useless at close quarters and even those of them who found
room to swing them in that dense, jostling crowd were too
terrified to fight. The dreaded name of '*Yarema*' stripped them
of all hope. All of them knew that he had supernatural powers,
including Satan's own ability to be everywhere at once, and now

his terrifying shadow fell on them like a paralyzing curse and turned them to stone.

Herded against the far wall of the canyon, and then hacked, sabered, battered down and trampled underfoot, most of them merely raised mute, pleading hands as if to catch the whistling iron that fell on their heads, and died where they stood. A few tried to climb the steep walls of the ravine and tumbled down on the sabers that thrust at them from below. Some died in silence without any effort to defend themselves. Others howled for mercy, or covered their eyes so as not to see death reaching out for them, or threw themselves facedown on the ground as if to burrow into the rocky soil, while the triumphant cries of "*Yarema! Yarema!*" lifted the hair on their heads in superstitious terror.

Their one-eyed balladeer was howling in panic of his own as he fought for his life against half a dozen soldiers. He cracked one on the head with his brass-bound lyre, seized another by the sword-arm to prevent the saber from splitting his own skull and bellowed all the while like a maddened ox.

"Hold it! Let go! Get away! I'm on your side, Devil take your mothers!"

Other Cossack troopers caught sight of him and ran up with sabers raised and ready to hack him to pieces but Skshetuski spotted him just in time.

"Save him!" he shouted. "I want him alive!"

"Hold it!" the disheveled, white-bearded old man was howling. "I'm of the gentry! '*Loquor latine*,' d'you hear? Can't you tell it's Latin? I'm not a peasant, damn you! Hold it, I tell you, you misbegotten sons of a stray steppe bitch! Let go of me, you bowlegged, rickety spawn of a cross-eyed mare! Get away from me!"

And suddenly Pan Yan looked closely into his face and shouted so loudly that the canyon walls seemed to shake with echoes:

"Zagloba!"

"Ha? Hmm? What?"

Skshetuski threw himself like a madman on the struggling old man, seized him by the shoulders, and began to shake him so hard that his teeth rattled in his head. "Where's the Princess? Where's Helen?"

"She's alive! Safe! In good health!" the sweating old man

bellowed. "Let go of me, will you? Or you'll shake the living soul out of me!"

"Safe? Alive?"

"She couldn't be safer!"

And then the young knight whose courage, strength and force of character carried him safely through all his ordeals in the *Sietch*, who couldn't be defeated by the murderous Burdabut or by his own suffering or wounds, gave way before a sudden flood of happiness and joy.

His arms fell to his sides.

Sweat burst out on his forehead.

All strength drained out of his body. His eyelids closed on a sudden darkness and he slid down to his knees and pressed his face against the ravine wall.

★   ★   ★

Meanwhile the rest of the luckless peasants were either killed or captured. A few dozen lay trussed up in ropes, to be taken to the Prince for interrogation, and the remainder lay heaped and scattered about the canyon, slaughtered like cattle without a thought of mercy.

The fight was over.

Silence began to drift back to the peaceful forest. The worried Cossack troopers gathered around their kneeling young commander, wondering if he was wounded, but they could see no blood.

"What's wrong then, *bat'ku?*" one of the *esauls* asked, hurrying over. "Where're you hurt, Your Honor?"

But Pan Yan rose, unharmed. He turned calm and untroubled eyes on his anxious soldiers and his face seemed to shine with an unearthly peace as if the light of a profound revelation was glowing within him.

"Where is she, then?" he turned to Zagloba.

"In the fortress of Bar."

"Safe, you say?"

"It's a great castle. Nobody can take it. She's staying with the nuns, under the care of Pani Slavoshevska whose husband commands there."

"Thank God in all his mercy," the young knight whispered in a trembling voice and then stretched out his arms to embrace Zagloba. "Give me your hand, my friend. I have to thank you too with all my heart . . . with all of my soul. I'll be grateful to you as long as I live."

Then, turning to his soldiers, he asked: "How many prisoners do we have?"

"Seventeen, your honor, by quick count," the Cossack troopers chorused.

"Set them free."

". . . Sir?"

The soldiers stared dumbly at each other, unable to believe their ears. "You mean we're to let them go, lieutenant?" the senior Cossack *esaul* asked to make sure he understood the order.

"Yes," Pan Yan said. "Let them go. A great joy has been granted to me, you see."

"A joy, Your Honor?"

"God has allowed me to understand the meaning of mercy," Pan Yan said.

The Cossacks went away shaking their heads and muttering to each other that the end of the world couldn't be far away when a Vishnovyetzki officer showed mercy to cut-throats and rebels captured with weapons in their hands, but the chief *esaul* returned a few moments later.

"They won't go, Your Honor," he reported. "They don't dare. They don't believe they're free."

"Are their ropes cut?"

"Yes sir."

"Then mount up and leave them."

A half hour later the troop rode out of the quiet canyon while the released peasants knelt in a long, silent row among the stacks of their slaughtered comrades. They held their hands clasped behind their backs as if the rawhide thongs were still looped around their wrists and elbows. Their bare heads were bowed in patient submission as they waited for the stroke of a headsman's axe.

★　★　★

A large white moon had risen earlier and now it streaked the woodland clearings with a gentle light. The air was still and the soft, warm night seemed even more hushed and balmy than before. Riding beside each other on the narrow track Zagloba and Pan Yan talked about the old knight's adventures from the moment when he rescued Helen.

"So it was you who got her out of Bohun's hands?"

"Who else?" Pan Zagloba was so exhausted that he could hardly speak. "And I wrapped his coat around his head as a parting gesture so that he'd keep quiet . . ."

"But how did you get all the way to Bar?"

"That's a long story. Too long for now. Phew, what a night. I thought my last hour had come."

"Nothing can happen to you now, my friend," Pan Yan told him warmly. "You're as safe here with me as you'll be at Prince Yeremi's table."

"I can't say I won't be glad to get there," the tired old knight sighed and rubbed his forehead with a weary gesture. "I'm really worn-out. Not to mention that my throat's gone dry from all that singing that I've had to do."

"I've a little panikin of *gojhalka*," Pan Yan said and passed it to Zagloba who seized, lifted it to his mouth and started to gulp it down in long, breathless draughts.

"Hmm," he said. "Ah. Not bad. Is there any more?"

But Skshetuski couldn't wait until the fat knight finished. "Is she alright?" he asked. "Is she well?"

"Who?" Pan Zagloba was swaying in his saddle.

"Helen!"

"Why shouldn't she be well?" Feeling a little better with some liquor in him, the fat knight smacked his lips, wiped his mouth, sighed with satisfaction and peered into the emptied flask as if some stray drop might be hiding from him at the bottom. "In fact she's blooming like a rose!"

"Thank God for that! And how are they treating her in Bar?"

"She couldn't have it any better if she was in Heaven. Pani Slavoshevska couldn't be fonder of her if she was her own child. As for all the young men hopping around her like sparrows in a barnyard you wouldn't be able to count them on a rosary."

"Hmm. Young men, did you say?"

"I did. And why not? She's beautiful enough to turn a millstone into cottage cheese so why shouldn't she melt a few hearts? Eh? But she doesn't care any more about them than I do about this empty flask of yours, my friend, since you're the only man she ever thinks about."

"May God love her for it," Pan Yan murmured, sighing with happiness and joy. "So she thinks about me, does she?"

"Does she think about you? Hmm . . . Let me tell you, I couldn't understand where she gets the air for all that sighing

she does. I don't think there's anybody in the city, including the
nuns, who hasn't got infected by that love of hers. She even got
me to go searching for you, as you see, and that wasn't something I planned for myself."

"She sent you to look for me, you say?"

"Why else would I leave a comfortable place like Bar?" Worn-
out by his exertions, Pan Zagloba started to fall asleep, but the
gojhalka and the chance to hear himself talk about his own
adventures restored him for a moment. "I've earned some peace
and quiet, haven't I? Pan Slavoshevski provisioned the town and
castle well enough to hold out for a year and the cellars also have
a little something in them beside shot and powder . . . I thought
I'd sit out the rest of the war there, uplifting the next generation
by my good example. But it seems like there's no rest for me,
no matter how many miracles I accomplish. It looks like I've
just got to keep on shaking my old bones on the roads by
moonlight like a homeless dog."

"You'll have a home with me as long as you live," Pan Yan
assured him gratefully. Then he pressed on, impatient to hear
anything that had to do with Helen. "So it was she who sent
you out again?"

"Ah . . . hmmm." Pan Zagloba yawned hugely and rubbed
his good eye. "Who else? She tried to send messengers to find
out if you were still alive but nobody would risk it. Not
everyone is given my degree of courage. So I took pity on her
and set out to find you, which could've cost me my neck sure as
I'm sitting here on this tired old nag, if it hadn't been for my
wits and my disguise."

"God will reward you for it all," Pan Yan said.

"Yes. Well. I hope God let's a few terrestrial powers take a
hand in some of this rewarding. Which they should do if there's
still any justice left in our Commonwealth. Who else is more
deserving? But to tell you the truth it wasn't all that hard to
convince those flea-bitten peasants that I'm a country sage. They
take me for a real '*staretz*' wherever I go, partly because of my
natural modesty, partly through my sagacity, and partly because
I've such a fine singing voice."

"God bless you for it," Skshetuski said again.

★　★　★

Then they rode quietly for some time as the forest track
unfolded before them. The young lieutenant was too full of joy

to know what to say. His happiness seemed as boundless as an ocean in which all his former suffering dwindled to the insignificance of a single drop. All his memories of Helen rose up so vividly before him that he wasn't sure if he was still awake or asleep and dreaming. He saw her as she was in that cherry orchard in Rozloghi where he stopped to see her on his way to the *Sietch*; he listened to her voice and heard her happy laughter . . . and then a cuckoo was counting out the number of their future children . . .

It didn't matter to him where he was just then, or what was happening to him, nor could he tell if he should shout his joy to the moonlit forest or fall to his knees and thank God in prayer or to keep on questioning the sleepy Zagloba.

"So she's alive and well," he went on repeating.

"Alive and well," Pan Zagloba echoed him as if from a distance.

"And it was she who sent you?"

"She."

"And do you have a letter from her for me?"

"I have."

"Give it here!"

"Wait. Later. It's sewn into my coat. And how are you going to read it at night anyway?"

"I can't wait, as you see."

"I see it."

Pan Zagloba's answers became more and more laconic and, at last, he nodded once or twice, his heavy head sunk down onto his chest, and he began to snore.

Skshetuski saw that his questions would have to wait until a better time. There was no help for it, the old knight was just too exhausted to keep himself awake. He let his joyful thoughts carry him away, feeling alive and hopeful and at peace, until the rapid pounding of hooves on the track ahead brought him back to the dark reality of the war.

The new riders proved to be Ponyatovski with the rest of Prince Yeremi's Cossacks, whom the Prince sent out to reinforce Skshetuski in case he ran into trouble on the way.

Chapter Thirty

IT WASN'T DIFFICULT for Pan Yan to imagine how Prince Yeremi would receive the report of his unsuccessful mission. A lesser man would throw up his hands, believing that all further resistance was useless when his own countrymen did all they could to weaken and disarm him, but Prince Yeremi's pride wouldn't let him show how deeply wounded he was by this latest insult.

He found it almost impossible to believe that the personal ill-will of his peers could throw so many obstacles in his path so often. The King's death gave full rein to their preoccupation with their own affairs. It removed his last defender, gave power to his enemies, and pushed him outside the tight-knit circle of magnates grouped around Chancellor Ossolinski who made the country's political decisions. He did his best to hide his bitterness at his isolation but Pan Yan and the other officers who watched the angry struggle going on within him could tell that this new blow was a painful one; the silent questions that the Prince asked himself were clear to them all.

Why did he drain his fortune to maintain an army when no one else stirred to defend the country? Why should he keep throwing himself about like a netted lion, tearing off one arm of the rebellion after another, when all his efforts, unsupported by any other magnate, were doomed to failure in the end?

A time was coming, he was sure of it, when he'd have to admit his inability to affect events, look for some quiet refuge in a peaceful province, and become a mute and helpless witness to what was happening in the Ukraine and elsewhere in the country. And it wouldn't be the Cossacks' power that brought him down and turned him into yet another impotent observer. Having beaten the enemy every time he met him, he'd be defeated by the envy, jealousy and suspicion of his own unrelenting kind.

'*Why is that?*' he asked himself each day in the weeks that followed his victory at Mahnovka. '*Why should all this happen?*' Was there no other magnate in the borderlands who could see beyond the narrow boundaries of his private interests? Was he the only one who understood what was happening everywhere around them? Or was that too only some terrible, self-serving delusion?

The news which came daily to his camp was enough to dishearten the strongest. The flames of the rebellion leaped to the west and spread across the peaceful Ruthenian-Lithuanian provinces of Polesye and Volhynia which stood untouched by war for a hundred years. The shrewd Hmyelnitzki didn't stir from his main encampment near Byelotzerkyev. He kept writing his assurances of loyalty to the Commonwealth to every senator in Warsaw who was inclined to listen. But the ruthless and icily ambitious Kshetchovski, who wanted to seize some rich province for himself while there was still a war in which he could do it, took the rebellion north to the Ovrutch country where he unleashed a reign of terror on the tens of thousands of docile and contented people who refused to join him.

The Prince hoped to attack and smash Krivoinos with the help of those splendid regiments under Osinski and Korytzki, and then to march north into the Ovrutch territory where he and the armies of the Lithuanian Hetman could come together to destroy Kshetchovski. But all these plans, he knew as he listened to Pan Yan's account of his disappointing failure, foundered on the bitter enmity of Prince Dominic Zaslavski.

★ ★ ★

He heard Skshetuski's story in a stony silence. His worn face betrayed nothing, neither grief nor anger nor hopelessness nor disgust. But to the worried officers and gentry who gathered in his quarters this icy mask merely underscored his heart-wrenching struggle with himself.

Had he been wrong in May when he abandoned his undefended lands and took his men to this distant war? Was he a fool to expect the entire Commonwealth to rally to him once he struck the first victorious blows against the rebellion? Or was it just vanity that led him to believe that he'd be chosen to replace the Hetmans as the Commonwealth's instrument of pacification once he dammed the flood of Hmyelnitzki's victories?

It was all so clear to him and everyone around him while they were saying their farewells to the Transdnieper country. Not one of his men doubted that they were just the vanguard of an aroused and victorious Commonwealth, united by the King and led to triumph by Yeremi Vishnovyetzki.

Instead, the King had died.

His power passed into the hands of Prince Dominic and his fellow regents while Prince Yeremi was ostentatiously ignored as the first gesture of conciliation made towards Hmyelnitzki. But if the implacable Prince wanted to smother the rebellion with the corpses of the slaughtered rebels rather than bow to the humiliation of appeasement, it wasn't just because war could give him some new title, powers or distinction; it was because he couldn't bear the thought that the Commonwealth, which he loved with all the passion of his unrelenting nature, would humble itself before one upstart Cossack.

It was this abject lack of will, pride, dignity and determination among the leaders of the Commonwealth rather than any blow to his own pride of place that tore the Prince's soul apart as he listened to Skshetuski's story, and Pan Yan knew that it would take all of his submerged strength not to bow down before this fresh humiliation, not to abandon his faith in his country, and not to admit defeat when everything and everyone conspired against him.

★   ★   ★

His report given, Pan Yan stood in silence and fixed his eyes on Prince Yeremi's coldly shuttered face while all the other officers and gentry in the room stared numbly at the floor.

"So they won't come?" the Prince queried briefly.

"No, Highness. They must obey their orders."

"And you're sure it was Prince Dominic who sent them this order?" Prince Yeremi asked.

"Yes, Your Highness. They have it in writing. The only way they can place themselves under your command is if their men are threatened with destruction."

The Prince leaned forward, rested his elbows on the table and lowered his head into his hands.

"Yes," he said quietly after a long moment. "Yes . . . It does seem more than a man can bear."

His voice was soft, more questioning than complaining, as if he was truly puzzled by what seemed suddenly too difficult to understand.

"Am I the only one who is willing to do this bitter work? And with only fresh obstacles thrown under my feet in place of the help I need?"

His words were tinged with pity and heavy with bemusement.

"Couldn't I take myself off to some quiet corner in the west like so many others, and sit there in peace? Why didn't I do that? Because I love my country? But why should I be the only one who feels this terrible obligation to pay in blood and with everything I own for this love that never gives anything in return . . .?"

He was speaking calmly. His questions were aimed only at himself. But he was so full of pain and puzzlement that his officers stared at each other with tears in their eyes, wanting to comfort him but not knowing how to go about it. All of them saw that this one bitter Summer aged him beyond his years. His slight, youthful body was dangerously thin. His long black hair, once as lustrous as a raven's wing, was dull and edged with white. His eyes looked as dim as coals deadened under ashes as they peered at them out of deep dark rings pressed into his flesh by weariness and hardships, and the weight of the responsibility he shouldered every day bowed him towards the ground.

But when at long last he lifted his bowed head out of his hands and looked about the room they saw the glow of a deep inner peace rising into the open and spreading across his face as if he finally understood his own tragedy and accepted it.

"So be it, then," he said quietly. "We'll show this ungrateful Motherland of ours that we know how to die for her if she won't let us fight for her any longer."

He smiled a wry apology to the troubled colonels and shrugged his thin shoulders. "I'd have preferred to find my death in a better war than this peasant turmoil," he went on. "But if that's how it has to be then that's what I'll do."

"Don't talk about dying, Your Highness," the *Voyevode* of

Kiev broke in desperately. "True, no one knows his hour, it's all in God's hands. But you still have many useful years to give to our country! I'm full of admiration for your military genius and your great heart and spirit but I must give credit where I think it's due . . . I can't blame the chancellor and the regents for trying to end this civil war through negotiations. This is a war between brothers! The blood that flows on both sides is our own! And who'll profit most if we can't forgive each other and settle our differences in a peaceful way? Only some external enemy, that's certain."

"Show mercy to a defeated enemy and he'll accept it with gratitude and respect," the Prince told him quietly. "Offer it as tribute to a conqueror and he'll trample on it and on you as well."

"Our own kind is as much to blame for this rebellion as any of those misguided people," the *Voyevode* offered.

"I wish to God," the Prince cried out fiercely, "that no one ever injured these people and drove them to the madness of rebellion! But once that happened, once they turned against their own country, words lose all their meaning! Only the sword can provide an answer to the knife. Otherwise this will be the end for us all!"

"The end will come all the quicker if we keep fighting our own private war with no regard for the policies of our legal leaders," the *Voyevode* insisted.

"Does that mean, Palatine, that you're no longer with us?"

"As God's my witness, Prince!" the *Voyevode* cried out in his own distress. "I don't do this out of ill-will towards any of you! But how can I throw away the lives of my own people in a cause that I can't believe myself? Their blood is too important to the Commonwealth to be spilled for nothing!"

★ ★ ★

The Prince said nothing then. He let his pained eyes fall and turn aside and sat in deep silence. Then he turned once more to his silent colonels.

"But you, old friends?" he asked. "You won't leave me, will you?"

It seemed then as if a vast wind seized those armored men and swept them towards Prince Yeremi, shouting and in tears. Some fell on their knees before him and kissed the frayed ornamental edging of his robes. Others clasped his knees and pressed their heads against them. Yet others lifted their arms and eyes as if to swear an oath before God himself, crying out their loyalty and pledging allegiance.

"We're with you to the last breath!" they cried. "To the last drop of blood!"

"Lead us! Command us! We'll serve without pay!"

"Highness!" cried the young Pan Aksak, blushing like a girl. "If we must die . . . then let me die beside you!"

Eyes gleamed. Mouths and bodies trembled. Even the old *Voyevode's* stubborn and determined face changed color in a rush of feeling and his head slumped heavily towards his chest while the Prince began to walk among the cheering men, embracing them and giving them his thanks.

"I'll live or die beside you," he repeated to each of them in turn. "From now on all our fates are one."

"Lead us!" the officers and gentry shouted, laughing and weeping and shaking fists and sabers. "To Polonne! Let's have that Krivoinos! We'll march all the way to Hell behind you if that's where you take us! We don't need help from those who want to leave us! Let them go! We don't want to share either our deaths or our glory with anyone!"

The Prince let this enthusiasm run its course until it seemed that the walls would burst apart, and that all these drawn sabers and devoted eyes would outshine the stars, then he raised his hand for silence and issued his orders.

"This, then, is what we'll do. We'll march on Krivoinos. But first we'll pull back for a while into quieter country where we can rest our men and re-equip ourselves. It's close to three months since any of us spent a day out of the saddle. Our horses barely drag themselves along. Our infantry marches on bare feet. We need to fill up our ranks again. So we will go to my lands near Zbarajh where we can regain our health, find a few new soldiers if we can, and come back to the fight with fresh determination."

"When does Your Highness want us to march out?" Old Pan Zachvilihovski asked for all the colonels.

"At once, old comrade, at once!"

And then the Prince turned to the *Voyevode.* "And you, sir? Where d'you intend to go?"

"To Glinyany, Highness." The Palatine looked ill-at-ease and his voice took on a defensive tone. "I hear there are many gentry gathering over there . . ."

"Prince Dominic's new soldiers." The Prince nodded quietly. "We'll take you as close to them as we can so that no harm can come to you on the way."

The *Voyevode* said nothing. His mouth clamped shut and his full lips tightened as if he was being offered an insult rather than protection. He was a proud man, used to having his own way, and he could read the anger and contempt in all those fierce eyes that glared at him from all around the room. He understood those feelings. He was turning his back on Yeremi Vishnovyetzki when he was needed most, so what could he expect? And had there been a note of irony in the Prince's voice? He couldn't tell. Another man might sneer but not Vishnovyetzki, he'd learned that much about him in their weeks together. The one thing the old Kiev palatine could trust was what his own eyes told him, and what he saw in that prematurely aged, tired and disappointed face was genuine concern.

He bowed abruptly and walked out of the cottage with as much dignity as he was able to muster and, shortly afterwards, everyone else dispersed to their regiments.

★ ★ ★

Left alone with Skshetuski the Prince allowed his cheerful features to slump again into the grey, careworn lines of his disappointment.

"What kind of soldiers did they have in those regiments you saw?" he asked.

"The best, Highness. The dragoons are modeled on the western armies and the foot guards are all veterans of the German wars. I thought I was seeing Roman legionnaires when I looked them over."

"A good number, was there?"

"Two full-strength regiments of infantry. About three thousand men, counting the dragoons."

"Pity," the Prince murmured. "Pity . . . We could have done great things with that kind of help."

"The soldiers cheered, Your Highness, when they heard they might be serving under you," Pan Yan said.

"But the officers had to obey their orders," the Prince added curtly. "Pity . . . Still, discipline is what makes such men so valuable and rare."

A deep sadness settled like a cloud on Prince Yeremi's face and, after another darkly silent moment, he rose and began to wander slowly up and down the room.

"Pity," he said again and went on speaking in a tired, grey voice as if he forgot that he was not alone. "What a calamity it is that the Senate gave us such regents for these days of ruin . . . Firley would be alright if wars were won with rhetoric and Latin . . . Young Konyetzpolski has good blood in his veins, he may win a name for himself some day, but he's little more than an inexperienced boy. But Zaslavski . . . ah, he's the worst of them all. No heart. No mind at all. They'd have done better to leave him nodding over his cups and spitting on his belly than meddling with armies . . ."

He sighed, shook his head as if he was still lost in some oppressive nightmare, and fixed his stricken eyes blindly on Skshetuski.

"God . . ." His voice was dull with grief. "God, that such men should be set over us at this of all times . . . What will become of this poor Commonwealth of ours? What's left to us to even save our honor? I see nothing ahead but fresh ruin. New defeats, disasters . . . Ah, I tell you, I really long for death because I don't see how I can keep going much longer."

"Your Highness must take better care of yourself," Pan Yan begged urgently. "You're exhausted, sir! And the nation can't survive without you!"

But Prince Yeremi's moment of doubt and despair passed as quickly as it had fallen on him.

"The nation must think otherwise," he said, "since it didn't grant me a voice in its affairs. And now,"—he gestured with calm, matter-of-fact disdain—"its chosen leaders are doing the best they can to knock my sword out of my hand as well."

"God grant that young Prince Charles can change all this at the next election," Pan Yan said fervently. "He'll know who should be raised to power and whom he should punish. As for now, Your Highness, surely your place and position are high enough for you to go your own way?"

"Which is exactly what I'm going to do," Vishnovyetzki said.

It may not have occurred to him just then that he was doing

what the great magnates always did: making their own laws no matter what the nation needed nor what the policies of its leaders called for. But even if he recalled all the misfortunes that fell on the Commonwealth through such disobedience, he'd have followed his own vision anyway. He was a warrior, first and foremost, and he didn't know any other way to serve.

★ ★ ★

The drums, bugle calls and the shrill neighing of horses broke into their silence as the army formed outside for its march out of the Ukraine, and the Prince shuddered as if shaking off the last vestiges of doubt and looked at Pan Yan with sharp, questioning eyes.

"Did you have a quiet trip back?" he asked.

"I came across a good-sized crowd of rebels in the Myshynyetz forests. About two hundred men."

"You crushed them, of course?"

"I did, Your Highness."

"And you brought some prisoners for questioning? Because that's an important matter nowadays."

"I took some, Highness . . . but . . ."

"You've already dealt with them, is that right?"

"No, Your Highness," Skshetuski said quietly. "I let them go free."

Astonishment appeared in the Prince's face and then he flushed with anger. "You what? What are you telling me? Have you also joined the appeasers?"

"Your Highness, I've brought back a reliable informant because there was a disguised noble among the rebels and he survived unharmed. As for the others . . ."

"You let them go!"

"I did. God showed me great mercy and I had to show mercy in return."

"What mercy?" the Prince demanded fiercely, striding towards Skshetuski. "You know my standing orders!"

"That disguised noble was Pan Zagloba from Tchehryn, Your Highness. He brought me news about the Princess Helen."

The Prince stopped in mid-stride, staring at the trembling young soldier, and his anger vanished as swiftly as it had appeared. "Is she alive?" he asked quickly. "Is she well?"

"By God's mercy, yes!"

"Where is she, then?"

"In Bar!"

"She's safe then! That's a mighty fortress!" Laughing as if he'd never known a moment of worry, the Prince threw his arms around his young favorite. "Thank God. Thank God, my boy. No wonder you were moved to mercy!"

"I'm ready for any punishment you order, Highness," Skshetuski said simply. "The standing orders . . ."

"Never mind them now! But where's this shrewd fox of a noble? So he led her all the way from the Transdnieper, did he? That must be quite a man, this Pan Zagloba. Thank God we still have people like him in these dreadful times. Go and get him quickly so that I can add my thanks to yours."

★ ★ ★

Pan Yan stepped briskly towards the door but just then there was a violent drumming of horses' hooves outside, the door flew open before he could reach it, and Vyershul's tussled red head appeared in the opening.

"Your Highness!" he cried, out of breath. "Polonne has fallen! Krivoinos has massacred everyone in the town! Ten thousand men, women and children slaughtered without mercy!"

A crowd of officers and gentry pushed into the room behind him, questioning the exhausted light cavalryman and hardly able to believe his news because this act of Zaporohjan savagery surpassed all the others. Even the portly Palatine of Kiev came running, curious to see what the commotion was about.

"But that just can't be," he muttered once he understood what Vyershul's patrols discovered and reported. "There were only Ruthenians in that town, the Cossacks' own people . . .!"

"Not one human being got out of there alive," Vyershul said. "Everybody went under the knife."

"But why? Why?" Even Prince Yeremi looked surprised while the *Voyevode's* eyes bulged out and his mouth fell open. "The Cossacks' own people . . .?"

"Why should Krivoinos care about that?" the tired Vyershul snapped impatiently. "They resisted him. They didn't open their gates fast enough to please him."

"There's your answer, Palatine," Prince Yeremi said and nodded with a bitter smile. "Go and reason with a mob that murders its own kind."

"Oh, the Devil's sons!" The shocked *Voyevode* struggled to catch his breath. "Hmm. Hmm. So that's how they are, eh? So that's how it is? Ah . . . hmm, if that's so . . . if that's so . . . Ah, to Hell with everything! I'm going with you, Prince, and that's all there's to it!"

"Then you're my brother from now on," the Prince said and threw his arms around him.

"Long live the Palatine of Kiev!" cried Pan Zachvilihovski. "*Vivat!* Long live the *Voyevode!*"

"*Vivat!* Long live our unity!" the officers cheered. "*Vivat! Vivat!*"

But the Prince turned again to Vyershul. "Where will they go from Polonne? Is there any word?"

"The prisoners I've brought say they've been ordered to march on Konstantinov."

"Dear God!" the Prince cried. "Then those regiments out there are lost because the infantry will never get away in time! We have to forget their refusal to join us and go to their aid at once! To horse, gentlemen! To horse! There's not a moment to waste!"

The officers rushed out, crowding through the door, and the Prince stared after them with joy shining in his sunken eyes and the fire of excitement glowing again across his careworn face. Once more the road to glory was open before him. Once again he could scent and anticipate a battle and a victory.

Chapter Thirty-one

PRINCE YEREMI LED his army around Konstantinov and halted in the village of Rosolovtze, assuming that Osinski and Korytzki would retreat that way once they heard about the capture of Polonne. Then, if Krivoinos sent his own army in pursuit, he would stumble on the Prince's soldiers ready and waiting in prepared positions, and fall into a trap. But they were no sooner drawn up on the heights beyond the village, sending out strong patrols in every direction, when Vyershul's scouts sent word that a mass of infantry was nearing along the Konstantinov highway.

"Those will be our guests, I expect," the Prince said and went out to meet Prince Dominic's two colonels in the village street, surrounded by his officers and a few dozen of the serving gentry who ran up to see the new arrivals.

Meanwhile the newcomers halted outside the village and announced themselves with a blare of trumpets while their colonels hurried to the Prince's quarters to offer him the services they refused before. He met them in the yard of the cottage where he set up his quarters for the night. They came running up, out of breath and not quite sure how he would receive them, and then stood waiting to hear what he might have to say.

"Fortune is fickle," he said and nodded coldly while they swept their broad, plumed hats to the ground before him. "You chose not to come when we invited you but here you are anyway on your own."

"We'd have come, Highness," Osinski said at once, lifting his hard grey eyes at the grinning Vishnovyetzki soldiers. "We'd have come gladly, nothing would please us better than to fight under your command. But we had our orders."

448

"So I hear."

"Let the responsibility for them lie with the man who gave them." Osinski shrugged slightly, his tight lips twitched under his yellow mustache, and he drummed impatiently with his fingers on the hilt of his rapier. "Meanwhile we ask you to forgive us, Highness, even though our consciences are clear. Our job as soldiers is to do what we're told and not to question the will of our superiors."

"Did Prince Dominic cancel his orders, then?"

"Events canceled them, sir," the fiery Osinski said, while the dour and closemouthed Korytzki merely frowned and nodded. "We're here to serve Your Highness with all our hearts because that's the only way we can save our soldiers."

The Prince also nodded, accepting both the explanation and apology, and looked with frank curiosity at these two veteran commanders whom fate dropped into his hands when he needed them the most. He saw at once that Osinski's strong words, as well as his calm and confident military bearing, pleased and impressed everyone. The handsome colonel stood as tall and lean as a pike-shaft, reminding the Vishnovyetzki soldiers of one of those copperplate engravings popular in the broadsheets of the times, or an illustration from a western European military manual which all foreign armies copied from Gustaphus Adolphus, who conquered all of Germany in the Thirty Years' War. His long Swedish boots of untanned yellow leather, the wide hat with the brim pinned up to expose the left side of his face, and the long straight sword that hung from a crossbelt in an iron sheath, made him look as if he'd just stepped off one of those famous battlefields which turned the Swedes into the masters of Europe. Even his short, pointed beard was curled and clipped in the Swedish fashion, and he wore his mustache brushed upward and spread out at the ends like one of those German mercenary captains among whom he served in many foreign wars. Barely into his forties, he was a famous and experienced soldier, and Prince Yeremi's practiced eyes rested on him with pleasure.

Korytzki, who stood beside him, looked entirely different. A short, thickset, middle-aged man of Tartar origin, he stared about with cruel, slanted eyes in which a cold and suspicious fire flickered like a whip. He seemed uncomfortable and oddly out of place in his western-style uniform which didn't match his flat Asiatic features. But he was an acclaimed drillmaster, in great demand through all the European armies, known and respected as much for his own fierce dedication to his duty as for the ruthless discipline in which he held his German mercenaries.

"We await your orders, Highness," Osinski said proudly. "And we beg once more that you forgive our past refusal and take us into your service."

"Feel welcome," the Prince said. "I'd be the last man to blame anyone for obeying orders. In fact if I'd known that you were expressly forbidden to join me I wouldn't have sent for you in the first place. But what's past is past, what matters is our common future from now on, and I expect you'll find good reason to be pleased with your new service here."

"Just as long as Your Highness is pleased with us and our regiments," Osinski said and bowed.

"I expect to be. Now, tell me, how far behind you is the enemy?"

"His scouts are close but the main body can't get here before tomorrow morning."

"All the better then. We've time for an inspection. Order your regiments to march through the camp so that I may see what kind of men you've brought me and how much I might be able to accomplish with them."

The colonels bowed, saluted, and returned to their regiments at once, and in less time than it would take to say an evening prayer the heavy tread of several thousand massed military boots, striding in step on the hard-baked soil of the village street, brought a curious crowd of the Prince's own soldiers running to the square.

★   ★   ★

Nothing could have done more to restore the flagging strength of the Prince's tired and hungry soldiers than the imposing sight made by their new companions.

The King's Dragoons came first: tall, strong men recruited from the Prussian and Mazurian gentry, riding in ranks of six on large, well-fed Podolian horses whose well-brushed coats gleamed with health and grooming. The troopers looked confident and well-rested. In comparison with the threadbare ranks of the Prince's soldiers in their ragged, sunbleached coats and dented, rusted armor they looked like wedding guests who found themselves unexpectedly in a crowd of beggars. Armed with long, straight swords, holstered flintlock pistols and short-barreled carbines, they stared proudly from under heavy Swedish helmets with high steel combs curving across the crown, and their polished breastplates shined like silvered mirrors.

Watching them, the Prince's soldiers murmured with excitement. But they began to shout and cheer when the deep ranks of Osinski's and Korytzki's Germans appeared before them. They were large, broad-backed men, uniformed in open leather jerkins, who shouldered their heavy muskets as if they weighed no more than bird guns, and their measured tread made the parched soil tremble under them. They marched into the village in a battalion front, thirty men across, but to the milling crowd of the Prince's soldiers it must have seemed as if it was only one huge creature which was walking there; a thousand hobnailed boots struck the ground at each step as each regiment appeared, and beat out a rhythm like a clap of thunder.

Passing before the Prince, Osinski shouted "*Halt!*" and the regiment stood as still as if it were rooted in the soil.

"Salute!"

A thousand scarlet-coated arms slapped a thousand muskets, the company officers raised their reed canes and swept off their hats, and the standard bearer lifted the huge, square regimental banner and dipped it three times to the ground before the Prince.

"*Vorvarts!*" Osinski cried.

"*Vorvarts!*" the company officers repeated, and the deep, scarlet ranks stepped out again as one man.

Korytzki's regiment, uniformed in black under their yellow jerkins, made an even better showing, and the Prince's soldiers were wild with excitement. The Prince himself could hardly take his eyes off those perfectly dressed black-and-yellow lines, the gleaming muskets sloped precisely over every shoulder, and the harsh faces of experienced veterans turned as one towards him.

"That's it," he murmured, eyes gleaming, and started slapping one fist into another. "That's it! What did we lack the most?"

"Infantry," said Pan Zachvilihovski. "Ours is so spent it can hardly walk."

"That's right! And where could you find better infantry than this?"

"Not in this world, Highness."

The listening officers murmured in agreement.

"You can't fault the stubbornness of the Zaporohjan infantry," said Pan Sleshinski, one of Skshetuski's armored volunteers. "Particularly when they're fighting from their earthworks or out of their wagons. But they can't match these lads for discipline and training."

"Bah!" Pan Migurski cried. "This lot's much, much better!"

"Still," Vyershul said, "they seem like a heavy-footed crowd to me."

"So what? The heavier the steadier!"

"But not much good in a fast, mobile campaign in open country," the light cavalryman insisted. "I think my Tartars would have them worn down and running with their tongues hanging out in three days."

"Ha, ha! What are you saying, man? You'd never beat the Germans!"

At which point a soft, sing-song Lithuanian voice drew their attention to Pan Podbipyenta.

"Isn't it curious how God, in His kindness, gave all of us such different strengths and virtues?" he asked with childlike wonder and raised his gentle eyes towards the sky. "As I hear it said there's no cavalry in the world like ours. At the same time neither we nor the Hungarians can match our infantry with that of the Germans."

"That's because God is just," Zagloba said at once. "And you're the best example of how He compensates for one thing with another."

"How so, good friend, how so?"

"Because he gave you a great fortune, a long sword and a heavy hand, but shorted you on brains."

"There he goes again," Skshetuski said, laughing. "You're like a real horsefly! Always ready to sting."

Pan Longinus only sighed, lowered his head with a gentle and forgiving smile, and murmured: "And to you, dear friend, he gave a tongue that's maybe a bit too long?"

"If that's what you think," Zagloba fired back at once, "then you're bound for hellfire along with that unnatural chastity of yours because you're questioning God's design and that's a mortal sin."

"Is there anyone who could ever talk you into silence?" the Lithuanian asked.

"Never! And d'you know why?"

"I think you'll tell us anyway," Pan Yan said.

"That's right. I will. Because it's the duty of wise old heads to instruct the younger. And do you know why God put tongues in our heads and wits in our brains?"

"Probably because that seemed like the best place for them," Pan Sleshinski said.

"That's one reason of course. But there is another. He did it so we could tell the difference between dumb animals, which only bark or neigh, and people who think and talk. Which is the main difference between me and this Lithuanian beanpole."

"There's no stopping him," Pan Migurski said and shook his head in wonder.

"So if his puny wits can't tell you why the Germans have the best foot soldiers and we've the best horsemen, I'll explain what happened. God made a horse and took him out to show to the people because he wanted to hear some praise for his new creation. And there was this German standing in the crowd, the way they always push themselves into everything, and so God asks him: *'what's that look like to you?'* And the German says: *'Pferd!'*—which is their word for 'horse.' *'What?'* says the Creator. *'I show you one of my best creatures and you make a vulgar noise like this? Just for that you won't get to ride it, you leaky windbag, neither you nor any of your flea-bitten kind, and if you ever do then you'll do it badly!'* So He gave the horse to the Pole and that's why Polish horsemen are the best!"

"So how did He compensate the Germans?" Pan Sleshinski asked.

"The Germans? They ran so hard after the Almighty, begging His forgiveness and crying for another chance, that they turned into the world's best infantry."

"Hmm. I see that you have it all worked out very well," Pan Podbipyenta said.

"That's because every word of it is true," the fat knight said calmly. "And anyone who calls me a liar had better make his confession before tomorrow's battle because lack of faith is the worst sin of all."

★ ★ ★

But whatever else they might have wished to say had to be deferred because another group of the Prince's soldiers ran up with news that some other large body of troops was nearing the village. This couldn't be the Cossacks because they weren't coming down from Konstantinov but rode from the opposite direction where the River Zbrutch marked the western boundary of the Ukraine.

The new arrivals turned out to be an independent legion of six volunteer cohorts gathered in the wild Zbrutch country by Pan Samuel Lashtch, who was widely known as an arrogant and quarrelsome troublemaker, a cruel tyrant in whatever luckless neighborhood he happened to make himself at home, and a brutal egotist of the worst kind common on the borders. But he was well connected at the court in Warsaw and showed as little fear in battle as respect to his fellow gentry or to his superiors.

He led some eight hundred rootless men of the same lawless and violent stamp as himself, composed in part of landless petty gentry as savage as Tartars, and in part of mercenary Cossacks, all of whom would have been rotting in some gaol if this wasn't wartime. They entered the camp with such a thunderous roar of kettledrums and trumpets that every Zaporohjan within a dozen miles must have been alerted, and the angry Prince sent an orderly to quieten them down. Troops such as these were a doubtful blessing. But Prince Yeremi thought they'd soon come to order in his iron fist, while their ferocity in battle might make up for some of their shortcomings.

He felt himself especially blessed as the day ended and thought that his own lucky star must be shining with a special brightness in the clear night sky. Only the day before, threatened by the announced departure of the *Voyevode*, he decided to break off the war and go in search of rest and refuge in one of his peaceful provinces in the west; and now, little more than twenty hours later, he was standing at the head of a superb new army, almost twelve thousand strong and more than able to confront Krivoinos.

He locked himself that night in his quarters with Pan Lashtch, the *Voyevode*, the old experienced Pan Zachvilihovski, Colonel Osinski, and his own foreign-trained chief of staff, the *Oberst* Mahnitzki, to plan the new campaign and the next day's battle, while his soldiers sat quietly around their campfires and worked on their weapons and equipment.

★ ★ ★

The night was well advanced but no one in the camp even thought of sleeping.

The soldiers sat around their bivouac fires and talked, and sang songs as if nothing of any great importance was about to happen, although everyone guessed that one of the most important battles of the war would be fought tomorrow.

The officers and some of the more important gentry from the armored regiments gathered around the biggest of the campfires, chatting, telling stories and clinking their glasses. The warm, soothing beauty of the night, as well as the prospect of another victory, put them all in excellent humor and they looked forward to their morning's work with all the pleased anticipation of schoolboys heading for an outing.

"So tell us," they urged Pan Zagloba. "What happened next? What did you do once you crossed the Dnieper and how did you get across the Ukraine and Podolia all the way to Bar?"

"How did I do that? I'll tell you. It would take Homer to do it justice but a Polish noble can do just as well as long as his throat is moistened properly. I've a first-rate voice, particularly suited for recitation from the classics, but even the best-made wheel creaks until it's oiled."

The servants broached a new cask and refilled the goblets and Pan Zagloba prepared himself for his recitation, sighing with pleasure at the prospect of hearing his own voice.

The Summer's rains ended a few weeks earlier and the weather was as balmy as if made to order for life in the open. The sky was clear and glittering with a multitude of stars and a great white moon climbed slowly into the deep, domed Ukrainian night and made the thatched roofs of the village seem as if they were sheeted in silver and gold.

"'*Incipiam,*'" he said. "I'd need ten nights to tell you everything that happened, and we'd run out of mead long before the end, because an old throat has to be greased as often as a skinner's cart. So let me just say that I got as far as Korsun, into Hmyelnitzki's main camp, and that I got myself and the Princess out of that hellhole without any harm."

"You must be a magician!" said Pan Volodyovski.

"Well, yes, I did cast a spell or two," Pan Zagloba said with a modest smile. "I learned the black arts as a young man in Asia where, to keep it short, a certain witch fell in love with me because of my great beauty and taught me all the *arcana* of her hellish trade. But I couldn't do as much as I might have wanted because every measure has its countermeasure. There are more witches and fortune tellers in Hmyelnitzki's camp than fleas on a mongrel and they brought him so many devils for his private service that he's got them out in the fields, planting cabbages like peasants and plowing with their horns."

"The Devil you say," Volodyovski murmured.

"And may the Devil take me if I am a liar! He's got one to pull off his boots for him when he goes to sleep, and a half-dozen more to beat the dust out of his clothes with their tails, and when he gets drunk he belts one or another of them in the snout for being too lazy."

Pan Longinus crossed himself and raised his eyes piously to the stars. "If he has Hell on his side," he murmured, "then we must be the soldiers of Heaven, don't you think?"

"And that's exactly why Heaven protected me," Pan Zagloba said. "I was afraid Hmyelnitzki might see through my disguise because I ran into him at Dopul's in Tchehryn a couple of times last year. And there were a few atamans around who knew me too. But my belly had caved in, my beard was down to around my waist, and the clothes did the rest. So nobody saw through me."

"You mean you saw Hmyelnitzki himself?" the officers cried out. "And you talked with him?"

"Did I see Hmyelnitzki? Did I talk to him? Like I see you and maybe even better! He's the one who sent me across Podolia to spread his manifestos and incite the peasants! Gave me his personal medallion, too, to keep off the Tartars, so I traveled all the way from Korsun as safe as you please! I had every Cossack along the way jumping to bring me the best food and liquor so that my poor little princess quite recovered from all our earlier hardships. By the time I got her to Bar she looked even rosier than before. Pan Yan and Pan Longinus can tell you how beautiful she is, and all I'll say about it, gentlemen, is that you'd be pawing the ground yourselves if you could see her now, just like every young man in Bar is doing nowadays because the whole garrison is head-over-heels in love with her."

"I'm sure that's just how it would be," little Pan Volodyovski sighed.

"But why did you have to go all the way to Bar?" Pan

Migurski asked. "That's at the other end of Podolia. The end of the world, you might say."

"And that's exactly why I went there," Pan Zagloba said. "I saw enough smaller castles taken by the Cossacks. The farther the better, I told myself. And even if the rebellion should spread that far, which isn't very likely, then the rebels will break all their teeth trying to crack that nut. Does anyone see anything wrong with that? Or is somebody wondering if I was anxious to put some distance between me and the fighting?"

"Well, it does seem like you ran a little harder than you had to," Migurski suggested.

"It does, does it? And how could I be sure that Bohun wasn't chasing after me? You gentlemen don't know him but I do. He's nothing less than the Devil! He'd have nailed my hide to a barn door if he caught up with me and that's only if he was feeling charitable that day. God grant him a quick end, I say, because I'm not a vengeful man and don't wish him a slow death like he plans for me, but the quicker he meets that end the better because I won't feel safe on this earth until he's under it. Br-r-r . . . I tell you, gentlemen, my blood turns to ice when I think about him, which is why, as you see, I've taken to drinking a bit more than is normal for me."

"What are you saying, my dear friend?" Pan Longinus said in astonishment. "You drink like a fish."

"And you, sir, should never stare into a fishpond or you'll see a numbskull looking back at you. Anyway, let me tell you how we got to Bar . . ."

But the rest of Pan Zagloba's tale was interrupted by a sudden light rising in the east and spreading across the sky like a scarlet banner.

"Is that dawn already?" Pan Sleshinski asked.

"Too early," Skshetuski said. "Sunrise won't be for another hour."

"So what is it, then? It looks as if all the sky is burning above Konstantinov."

"That's what it is, then," Volodyovski said. "The town is on fire."

"You're right, by God! Konstantinov's burning!"

All the voices hushed and faces grew solemn as the assembled knights watched the conflagration which announced the approach of the enemy. "That must be Krivoinos coming from

Polonne . . . His advance guard must have fired the town or some of the villages around it . . ."

"That's him, alright . . ."

"And coming with everything he's got!"

"So soon?" Zagloba asked uneasily.

"What's the matter, father?" Pan Yan asked quietly. "I thought you were looking forward to paying the Cossacks back for some of your hardships."

"I am, I am . . .! But even the worst debts can keep. They don't spoil like a carp left out in the sun . . . The Devil take these Cossacks! Can't they wait? What's their hurry? A man barely gets away from them . . . barely has the time to draw a clean breath . . . and here they come again! Ah, may the plague take them all along with their mothers!"

The soft calls of muted trumpets began to sound throughout the camp and old Pan Zachvilihovski appeared suddenly at the fire where the officers were sitting.

"The patrols are in with news, gentlemen," he announced. "The enemy is in sight. To your posts, if you please, to your posts! We're moving out immediately!"

The group dispersed at once. The officers ran to their regimental lines as if the moon were a lantern hung to light their way, and the camp servants started to strike the tents, harness the wagons, and put out the campfires.

Chapter Thirty-two

THE DARKNESS DEEPENED above the Prince's army once all the campfires were put out, the tents struck and packed, and the lanterns extinguished. But out towards Konstantinov, where the glow of the burning town spread redder and wider, the stars began to dwindle, grow pale and disappear as the horizon lightened.

The soft calls of the muted trumpets drifted once more among the waiting ranks and the silent, unseen masses of men and animals stirred and began to move. The darkness filled with the sudden click and clatter of hoofbeats, the steady tread of marching infantry and finally with the deep rumbling of artillery and wagons.

There was something both ominous and baleful in this shrouded night-march, in the guarded voices that hissed their commands, in the rustling footfalls, in the occasional accidental clatter of spears and muskets, and in the blood-red glitter of the conflagration reflected in the weapons and the armor.

The regiments flowed across the fields towards the Konstantinov highway, turned towards the fires glowing in the sky barely a mile away, and wound through the fading darkness like a giant reptile, coiling and uncoiling.

The soft July night was ending.

The roosters stirred on their perches and began to cry out their challenges to each other on the village fences, summoning the sunrise, and a pale dawn spread behind the burning town. A fresh morning breeze lifted above the fields and rustled in the branches of the roadside trees and snapped among the banners.

The day came slowly, as if unwilling to look down on what

lay below it; it seeped in grey, grudging pools into the misted fields and crept into the woods as if in search of refuge in the disappearing shadows. It found the broad, white highway and the troops that marched steadily upon it, and then there was no way to deny that the new day had come. The shadows lifted. The forms of men and horses became distinct and clear in the sharpening light while the thick ranks of the marching infantry, beating out their relentless rhythm in the dust, created their own darkness.

Pan Zagloba rode beside Skshetuski with the long iron column of the *husaria* jingling and clattering behind him but he looked ill-at-ease at the prospect of the day's events, squirming in his saddle as if he couldn't find a comfortable spot on it for himself.

"Lieutenant?" He was whispering as if afraid that someone might hear him.

"Yes, my friend? What can I do for you?"

"Do? Nothing. But you can tell me something. Is the *husaria* going to charge first?"

"I thought you said you were an old soldier?" Pan Yan hid his smile from the uncomfortable fat knight who was peering about anxiously as he jogged up and down beside him. "Don't you know that the *husaria* is always held back to strike the deciding blow once the enemy has committed all of his reserves?"

"I know, I know," the fat knight murmured and mopped his sweating face. "I just wanted to remind myself. And to . . . ah . . . make sure that we see some action."

"You don't need to worry about that."

"Hmm. Hmm. Not to worry, eh?"

"We'll be in the middle of it all no matter what happens," Pan Yan said cheerfully. "The battle can't end without us, you can be sure of that."

They rode in silence for a little longer. Then Pan Zagloba started whispering again. "Is that Krivoinos over there? And is that his entire army?"

Pan Yan grinned. "It is."

"The Devil take him! And how many men does he have with him?"

"At least sixty thousand if you count the *tchernya*."

"The Devil you say! And why shouldn't I count them?

They're there, aren't they? And a pitchfork's just as sharp as a lance, isn't it? A scythe can whistle through the air as loud as a saber."

Pan Yan turned his head to conceal his smile and the worried fat knight went on whispering in an even lower and more nervous voice.

"Don't think that I'm feeling any kind of fear. Ho, ho, not a bit of it! It's just that I'm a little short of breath and I don't like crowds. It gets hot in a crowd and once I get over-heated it's all up with me. One against one . . . ah . . . that's alright, that's another matter. A man can use his wits, for one thing. He can see what's what and act accordingly. But a good head counts for nothing in a general free-for-all like this one . . . Then it's all in the fist and even Pan Podbipyenta is going to seem like Socrates. I don't mind telling you that I've two hundred gold ducats stuffed into my sash, a gift from His Highness, but I wish they were all somewhere else along with the sash and the belly that's shaking inside it. Tfui! Tfui! The plague take it all! I don't like these great battles, I tell you . . . May the Devil take them!"

"Nothing will happen to you, my good friend," Pan Yan assured Zagloba. "There's not much to it, believe me, so set your mind at rest."

"My mind's the least of it. It's my . . . ah . . . martial spirit that worries me, not my mind, because I'm so hotblooded my courage is likely to get the better of me and ignore all good sense once I've caught fire in a battle . . . I'm too eager for the fight, you see. Too impulsive . . . And I had a sort of premonition back there by the campfire. I saw two stars falling from the sky. Who knows if one of them wasn't mine?"

"God will reward your good deeds in Heaven and keep you from harm here on Earth."

"Just as long as He doesn't reward me too soon," Pan Zagloba muttered.

"But why didn't you stay with the wagons if you're worried about a premonition? Nobody would think any the less of you after all the great things you've already accomplished."

"Why didn't I? The Devil knows why. Maybe because I thought it would be safer in the ranks."

"And so it is. You'll see. We're so used to this kind of thing that we hardly give it another thought. '*Consuetudo altera natura*,' as the ancients said, and it's true enough that familiarity with danger breeds contempt. In our case fighting is such an every-day affair that nobody remembers anymore there's anything to fear. But look, there's the Sloyitch River ahead of us already, and the marshes of the Vishovaty Stav beyond it. We're almost there."

"The Devil you say . . . So soon?"

The army halted then along its entire line of march, the Prince's messengers galloped along the column, and the regiments began to move off the highway onto the narrow tongue of land that stretched eastward between the river and the broad swampy sheet of the freshwater lagoon.

"Is this the place?" The fat knight mopped his sweating head and peered uneasily into the near distance. "And when's it all . . . ah . . . going to begin?"

"Just as soon as His Highness has us all in order," Pan Yan said. "Be patient."

"Yes. Well. I'm quite willing to be patient for the rest of the day. Let some young pup who needs it go after the glory, I've had more than my share of it. Not that I'm nervous about anything, you understand. It's just that I don't like crowds."

"*Husaria* to the right flank!" cried an orderly officer galloping up to Skshetuski.

Pan Yan turned, barked an order, and the long ranks of his armored riders swung off the highway into the field behind him.

"I don't like crowds, I tell you," Pan Zagloba muttered desperately. "Phew, it's getting hot . . . Going to get a lot hotter too, if I know anything about it . . . Ah, tfui! The plague take it all. I just don't like crowds."

★ ★ ★

Daylight was all around them then. The last of the night was gone. The crimson afterglow of the burning town was blurring in the sunlight whose golden light brushed against the steel points of the lances and made it seem as if a thousand candles glowed above the army. With no further need for stealth and concealment, the regiments formed up in battle order at the foot of the long natural causeway that seemed to run all the way into the rising sun between the river and the deep, stagnant chain of marshy ponds and pools.

The army waited.

Waiting, they sung the morning prayer, "'*Open to us ye gates of salvation,*'" and their powerful chorus of twelve thousand voices echoed among the dark pines of the forest behind them and flew into the sky.

Singing, they watched as the far end of the grassy causeway began to darken with a mass of animals and men. The Cossack army stretched as far back into the sun as their eyes could see. One regiment followed another in an endless river of spears and lances, firelocks, scythes and flails. Beyond them, seen dimly as if through a mist, rolled the huge, dark square of the gigantic *tabor*, coming towards them like a moving city that filled the horizon. The great mobile camp of the Zaporohjans was still almost a mile away but the creak of its wagons and the neighing of its horses came to the ears of the Prince's soldiers as if multiplied by thousands.

The Cossacks came on in a thick, silent mass that filled the causeway between the river and the marshy pool and Pan Zagloba lost whatever composure he still had.

"*Jezu Chryste!*" he was muttering and grumbling at Skshetuski's side. "Why did you create so many of these scoundrels? This has to be Hmyelnitzki himself with every bit of his flea-bitten *tchernya* and all the devils he's got working for him. Look at them all, will you? Where did they all come from? This is too much, I tell you! They'll bury us with their caps! Ah, when I think how good life used to be in the Ukraine . . . and now this! Is there no end to them? May the devils roast them! May leprosy devour them!"

The Cossacks halted in the middle of the causeway and the two armies regarded each other quietly like wrestlers before a bout but that only drove the fat knight into a fresh eruption of frightful maledictions. "May you choke on your own blood, you vagabonds! May your windpipes freeze!"

"Don't curse so much," Pan Yan admonished quietly.

"Who's cursing? May fever strangle all these cut-throats. May they trip in their own guts on their way to Hell! May the Devil suck the marrow from their bones! What's wrong with wishing them a hot time in Beelzebub's kitchen?"

"Because today is Sunday."

"Ah, so it is. True, the Devil doesn't get a day off on the Lord's day, but it may be best to give some thought to the Almighty. '*Pater noster qui es in coelis . . .*' Nobody can expect any human feelings from that lot, that's certain. '*Sanctificetur nomen Tuum . . .*' We'll have Hell on earth here before very long. '*Adveniat regnum Tuum . . .*' Phew, it's hot. I'm out of breath already. '*Fiat voluntas Tua . . .*' May you die in agony, you murdering dogs! May you . . . ah! Ah! What's that? What's that? What's happening over there?"

A detachment of several hundred horsemen broke away from the mass of the Cossacks and rode into the open space between the two armies.

"Skirmishers," Pan Yan said. "What we call '*hartzovnitzy.*' They're coming out for a bit of single combat before the main battle. Our own people will go out to meet them in a moment."

"Ah, skirmishers . . ."

"An ancient custom," Pan Yan explained. "Comes to us from the East . . . Persia and the Mogul empire, and so on . . . where armies used to pick champions to decide the issue. And to read the omens for the battle to come."

"Ah. Ah. So now the battle is sure to begin?"

"As sure as David beat Goliath!"

"Ah to the Devil with it!"

And here all of Pan Zagloba's ill-humor, worry and rising irritations broke into open anger. "But for you all of this is no more than a spectacle on a feast day!" he bellowed at Pan Yan in exasperation. "As if your own skin wasn't at stake here as well!"

"I told you, we're used to it."

"And I suppose you're going out there too?"

"It's not the thing to do in the better regiments to go sword to sword with that kind of enemy. But some will, as you'll see. Not many people pay attention to dignity these days."

"There!" Zagloba cried, pointing to a crimson line of Volodyovski's dragoons who trotted towards the causeway. "There go our own men! And there go some others!"

Dozens of volunteers were spilling from the ranks of every regiment.

"There's Vyershul," Pan Yan said. "He loves this Tartar fighting. There's Kushel . . . Ponyatovski . . . the two Karvitch brothers . . ."

And then they both watched Pan Longinus Podbipyenta trotting into the plain on his Courland mare.

"You'll witness some extraordinary deeds today," Skshetuski told Zagloba as the distance between the two galloping detachments narrowed rapidly. "Pay special attention to Volodyovski and Pan Podbipyenta. They are rare fighters. Can you see them down there?"

"Yes."

"Then watch. You'll get an appetite for this kind of thing yourself."

"I wouldn't count on it," Pan Zagloba muttered but he strained his eyes towards the broad, grassy arena none the less.

★ ★ ★

The skirmishers, however, had another ancient ritual to observe, one that was perhaps made closer to home than Persia. Trotting up to within bowshot of their enemies they pulled up their horses and started hurling insults.

"Come closer!" cried the Prince's soldiers. "We need fresh carrion to feed to our dogs!"

"Yours aren't fit to feed hogs!" howled the Cossacks.

"You'll rot in that pond, you faithless scum!"

"Whoever's meant to rot is going to rot. But you're the likely ones to be feeding crayfish!"

"Back to the byres with your pitchforks, peasants!" the gentlemen-troopers cried in their own turn. "Shoveling manure fits you a lot better than carrying a saber!"

"We may be peasants!" the Cossacks yelled back. "But all our sons are going to be gentry 'cause they'll be born out of your wives and daughters!"

Some Cossack who must have come from Prince Yeremi's own Transdnieper Country, and who knew the depth of veneration in which the Prince's soldiers held their commander and his family, trotted out of the Zaporohjans' ranks to hurl the final blasphemy to infuriate them.

"Your *Knaz* has two daughters!" he bellowed in a voice loud enough to be heard by both the watching armies. "Tell him to send them to Krivoinos for the night!"

The Cossacks howled with laughter. The Prince's soldiers roared, enraged, and little Pan Volodyovski jerked in his saddle as if struck by a pistol ball and spurred his horse towards the blasphemer. Skshetuski saw him, recognized him, and pointed him out at once to Zagloba who was hurling his own terrible insults at the Cossacks.

"There goes Volodyovski! Watch him! Watch him!"

"I see him!" cried Zagloba, swept away by the general excitement in the ranks around him. "There he goes! He's got him! Once . . . twice . . . two strokes and it's over!"

The jeering Cossack threw up his hands at the second stroke of Volodyovski's saber and flew out of his saddle as if struck by lightning. He fell headfirst towards his own side as if to confirm an omen of disaster. Another Cossack, dressed in the crimson surcoat of some murdered noble, charged down on Volodyovski from the flank but his horse stumbled just as he struck his blow, his saber whistled harmlessly past the diminutive dragoon, and then the little colonel showed what he could do. His wrist flicked out and his arm barely seemed to move but the Zaporohjan's saber arced into the air and then his own hand clamped on the back of the Cossack's neck.

"He's got that one too!" the fat knight bellowed, shaking with such enthusiasm as if he never felt a qualm about the day's events. "Did you see how he husked that saber out of his hand! God love him! What a master!"

"Help me brothers!" the captive Cossack howled as Pan Volodyovski dragged him off the field, carrying him away in much the same way as a wolf drags off a helpless goat stolen from a farmyard. "*Braty ridniyeh, spasayte*! Help me, good brothers! Help!"

But he did nothing to help himself, knowing that any resistance on his part would mean instant death. Indeed, he dug his spurs into his horse's flanks and urged the animal to gallop all the faster while he bowed his neck without putting up any kind of struggle in Volodyovski's grip. A single great shout, mixing joy and rage, rose from all the skirmishers at this sight, and then, as if this were the signal for a general *melee*, both sides charged each other.

★   ★   ★

The grassy strip of land was too narrow to accommodate more than thirty or forty horsemen at one time so that only a few dozen riders collided with each other while the rest crowded up behind them, jostling for room to leap into the scrimmage. They galloped at each other singly and in pairs, horseman against horseman and saber against saber, so that their clash broke up at once into a series of scattered, individual duels, and the watching armies could have thought that they were witnessing a tournament or an exhibition. Only the riderless horses bursting out of the fight, and the occasional splash of a dead man tumbling into the water, suggested that this was something more deadly than a game. The new morning light was as bright as crystal, and the cool, fresh air was so clear and clean above the combatants that the spectators could recognize the faces of their champions and urged them on with cries of their own.

"Vyershul's been killed!" Skshetuski cried out suddenly. "He's down with his horse . . .! Wasn't he riding that white one over there?"

But the redhaired light cavalryman wasn't dead. They could see him crawling from under his fallen animal and limping away while the huge Cossack who had bowled him over charged another victim.

"Pulyan! Pulyan!" the Vishnovyetzki soldiers began to shout all along the line, recognizing the giant Zaporohjan who was once a trooper in Prince Yeremi's own Household Regiment, and who was now Krivoinos' second-in-command. So strong that he could crush two horseshoes in one hand, he had a reputation as invincible in man-to-man combat. Having knocked down Vyershul together with his horse, he charged another officer and killed him with one blow, splitting him from the head almost to the saddle. Everyone else backed away and scattered before him, and then Pan Longinus spotted him from across the causeway and turned his mare towards him.

"You'll die!" the Cossack shouted and drove his horse at the Lithuanian.

"If that's my fate," replied the gentle giant and raised his own saber.

He hadn't brought his terrible 'Cowlsnatcher,' saving it for confrontations more in keeping with his vow, but the first blow of his light Hungarian saber was enough to jar the Cossack's arm. Pulyan parried two more blows and then, either recognizing that he'd come up against a better swordsman, or fearing that the Lithuanian's heavy Courland mare would push his own lighter animal into the muddy swamp—or simply to show off his enormous strength to the watching armies—he forced his horse next to the Lithuanian's and caught him around the waist with both his huge arms.

Everyone else stopped his own duel to watch this silent struggle in which only the two horses walked around each other in a patient circle. Their riders seemed frozen into a single statue, locked together like bears fighting over a mate, or like two great trees which had grown entwined into a single trunk. Only the deepening color of their faces, the thick veins that stood out on their necks and foreheads, and the bowed arcs of their massive backs testified to the crushing force of this mute embrace.

Finally they both began to tremble.

The Lithuanian's face turned crimson but the Cossack's became blue with effort and his open lips became tinged with grey as the watching soldiers bit their own lips with worry and impatience.

"Let . . . go . . ." muttered Pulyan's strangled voice.

"No . . . little brother," said the Lithuanian.

And then something snapped and grated like a tree trunk cracking in deep Winter. A deep groan, like something bursting in the center of the earth, rose out of the struggling pair. A gush of black blood spurted from Pulyan's mouth and his head tilted sideways and flopped across his shoulder.

Pan Longinus sighed. He lifted the bearlike Cossack from his saddle as easily as if he were a child, tossed him across his own saddlebow like a sack of oats, and trotted off the field towards his own lines.

"*Vivat!*" shouted the Vishnovyetzki soldiers.

"*Na Pohybel!*" yelled the Zaporohjans and charged in a furious mass to avenge their leader.

The interrupted skirmish flamed anew. The dead and injured spilled across the grass as thick as leaves after an Autumn storm and it seemed certain that the Cossacks, whose swordsmanship seldom matched that of the warlike gentry, would die to a man in spite of all their ferocity and courage. But then the war horns sounded the signal for recall in the Zaporohjan *tabor* and the skirmishers withdrew.

The Prince's men stayed in the meadow for a little longer to show that they had won the field and then trotted back to their regiments.

The causeway emptied. Only the bodies of dead men and horses lay scattered on the trodden grass as if in prelude to what would happen later. A light breeze ruffled the still surface of the pond and hissed as if in pain among the lakeside willows.

★   ★   ★

Meanwhile the horns and kettledrums began to thunder in the Cossack *tabor* and the great, dark masses of Krivoinos' army rolled across the causeway. One regiment followed another in an endless column, packed so densely that not a single handful of earth could be seen under them, and their bobbing heads seemed to form a cobbled highway of their own. They came on in a deathly silence, without their usual wolflike howls and the savage yelling with which they were accustomed to whip up their courage, so that the watching Vishnovyetzki soldiers knew that this would be a merciless, no-quarter battle to the death.

First came the thick, formless masses of the rebel peasants, armed with whatever could be used for killing; then the deep, orderly ranks of the Zaporohjan infantry gleaming with muskets, pole-axes and spontoons; then the mounted cohorts under a forest of naked pikes and lances; then the auxiliary *tchambuls* of Tartar volunteers, and then the Cossack gunners hauling their heavy cannon.

On they came, crowding together without regard to order, as if to sweep across the Prince's waiting soldiers and overwhelm them by sheer weight of numbers. The fearless, half-mad and illiterate Krivoinos believed only in the saber and the fist; his understanding of the arts of war consisted of mass attacks, massacre and pillage, and he was ready to drown the Prince's army in his own men's blood if that was the only way in which he could beat him. His regiments pushed and drove each other forward like a human flood that engulfed everything it couldn't carry off and Prince Yeremi watched them with anger and contempt.

"They're coming at us like beaters at a boar hunt," he said to Mahnitzki. "Do they really think we're as easy to drive as all that?"

"Well, that's Krivoinos' idea of generalship, Your Highness," Mahnitzki shrugged and said. "He's mad, untutored, stubborn as an ox, overly ambitious, uncaring about his men's lives and driven by blind hatred. He's had a taste of power with his own command and he doesn't want to give it up. We've had word that Hmyelnitzki doesn't trust him to defeat Your Highness and that he's forbidden him to fight you until he himself gets here with the bulk of his forces. Which is exactly why Krivoinos moved against us when he did and why he's in such a hurry to beat us by himself."

"He won't do it this way," Prince Yeremi said.

From where he and his chief of staff sat their horses on the tall grassy riverbank, looking down at the vast mass of animals and men that pressed towards them along the narrow causeway, they could see the silent, ordered ranks of their own division. The Cossack cannon began firing then, and the iron balls splashed and skimmed the water of the pond or burst among the reeds, but the guns were still too far out of range to reach the Prince's army.

No one in those silent, steady ranks made a single movement. Only the regimental banners stirred in the light morning breeze and the red-and-gold pennons snapped and fluttered on the *husaria's* lances. The Prince's army waited in the classic Polish checkerboard formation of horsemen, musketeers and artillery at the mouth of the causeway as though the skirmishing would resume at any moment and as if they would continue to stand there as spectators.

Below them and before them the rebel tide pressed on. Not a single arrow flew towards it from the Prince's soldiers. Not one musket fired. No one spoke. Held on short reins, the horses were as still as the men who sat them. The Cossacks came halfway across the causeway, and the leading regiments began to halt and to mill around as if puzzled why they were allowed to come that far without opposition, but the dense masses pushing up behind them forced them to move again.

"Only a fool would attack on such a narrow front," one of the Prince's orderly officers said.

"Or a madman . . ."

The Prince nodded. "Krivoinos will throw away half his army before it comes near enough to harm one of us."

"So he'll lose thirty or forty thousand men," Mahnitzki said quietly. "Why should he care? He can get twice that many volunteers in a week if he can say he defeated Yeremi Vishnovyetzki. And think, Your Highness, what a coup it would be for him to bring your head to Hmyelnitzki as a gift."

"He'll find it hard to get," Prince Yeremi said.

"But he doesn't know it."

"Then we should make it seem even easier for him," the Prince said and signaled to his watching regimental officers with his gold *bulava*.

At once, as if they were waking from an enchanted sleep, the regiments wheeled about and marched off, clearing an area of about a quarter of a mile, then wheeled again with Korytzki's infantry parting to reveal the black, iron mouths of Vurtzel's cannon gaping at the causeway. The dragoons, light cavalry and Pan Lashtch's irregular volunteers massed on the flanks, the *husaria* formed its iron wedge behind the cannoneers, while the red coats and muskets of Osinski's Germans gleamed in the reeds that bordered the bend of the river.

Seeing what they took for a retreat of the Prince's army the dense mass of *tchernya* uttered a great, single roar of triumph and broke into a run.

"*Na Pohybel . . .!*"

"Kill 'em all! No prisoners!"

"Death to the *Lahy!*"

Yelling and trampling each other in their haste to get to close quarters with the Prince's soldiers, they spilled out of the narrow mouth of the causeway and crowded into the half-moon of cleared ground, and other Cossack regiments poured into the field behind them, and then Osinski's musketeers stepped out of the reeds and fired a thousand muskets straight into their flank. Prince Yeremi raised his baton in another signal and Vurtzel's cannon roared.

The earth seemed to shudder then.

Daylight disappeared.

Thick clouds of smoke shrouded the battlefield, the river, the marsh ponds and the causeway. From time to time an angry, crimson sunlight pierced this boiling cloud to flash off glittering armor and high-combed helmets bent forward in a charge. Muskets gleamed in measured scarlet volleys. Long streams of flame spurted from the cannon. Everything else was hidden and unknown.

Chapter Thirty-three

WHEN IT WAS TIME for the *husaria* to charge, Pan Zagloba stopped worrying about his shortness of breath and his dislike of crowds and galloped along with everybody else. Not that the armored knights gave him much choice about it; he knew that he risked being bowled over, trampled and crushed to death by the avalanche behind him if he didn't let his horse carry him into that terrifying smoke cloud.

He bounced in the saddle with his eyes shut tight and his head filled with desperate questions that crisscrossed like lightning.

'*How did I get into this?*' he asked himself. '*How can I get out?*' And then he gave up all hope of coming out of it alive. '*Only a damned fool wins in a thing like this!*'

Enraged by the injustice of it all, he hurled a string of maledictions at the war, the Cossacks, the *husaria* that was sweeping him along, and every living creature in the world.

He cursed and prayed trying to close his ears to the pounding hooves and the shouts around him. A hundred blacksmiths seemed to be hammering on a hundred anvils. A thousand wolves were howling. The air was whistling past his ears, robbing him of whatever breath he had, and then he felt that his horse had run into something that exerted pressure. He opened his eyes cautiously and saw swaying scythes, thrusting pikes and pitchforks, a whirling mass of axes, clubs and flails. A sea of glaring eyes and howling mouths roared in a single voice out of shaggy beards, all of them mad with rage and determined to kill him. Everything was blurred, unrecognizable, coming from who knew where and leaping like a fire.

Half-mad with terror of his own, Pan Zagloba found refuge

in a sudden, overwhelming hatred. He bellowed with the pure, white-hot rage of absolute despair at these detestable, obstinate enemies who didn't have the decency to run away and who were forcing him to take part in a battle. '*You wanted it? You've got it!*' he cursed his own foolhardiness and began to flail about with his saber, his eyes scrunched down so tight that he hardly saw anything around him.

"Take that!" he howled. "And this! May the Devil roast you over a slow fire! Holy Mother pray for us all! May your guts get twisted up in knots! Saints protect the innocent! To Hell with all this!"

Half the time his saber whistled through empty air. Now and then it connected with something hard that cracked and grated and gave way or became a sudden inexplicable weight on his dragging sword point. But at the same time he knew that time was passing and he was still alive and this realization filled him with fresh hope.

"Run, why don't you! Run!" he bellowed. "Ah, you sons of bitches!"

And at last the terrifying scene around him changed into something new. He could see through his watering, half-closed eyes that the furious faces were vanishing from the field. The swords and scythes and pitchforks also disappeared. In their place he glimpsed hundreds of bobbing, hunched-over backs and the canvas tops of greasy fur caps jammed down on lowered heads. The terror-stricken wails that hung in the smoke were so loud that he thought they'd deafen him for life, but they sounded like music in his ears.

'*Are they running yet?*' the question gleamed in his mind like a ray of sunlight in a thunderstorm. '*Are they? Are they? Yes, by God! They are!*'

All his valor reappeared at once, his confidence returned, and Pan Zagloba felt himself filling up with that joy of battle that bards sing about if they never heard a shot fired at them in anger.

"Oh you peasant pickpockets!" he roared, full of valiant rage. "Is that how you face the gentry?"

He kicked his horse forward into the heart of the fleeing mob, overtook a few hundred of the running peasants who fell to their knees before him and pleaded for mercy, and feeling much safer in the thick of this repentant crowd he began to work with greater awareness of what was going on around him. In the meantime, as he saw out of the corner of his eye, the *husaria* crushed and scattered all those Zaporohjans who managed to get off the causeway and drove them into the reeds and mudpits that bordered the river.

"Kill 'em! Slay 'em! Slaughter 'em!" he yelled galloping in the smoke and waving his saber at enemies who were no longer there. "Take that! And this! That'll show you! Ha!"

*   *   *

Charging about the field in pursuit of the fleeing Cossacks, Pan Zagloba didn't pay much attention to anyone else in the smoke around him. Seeing next to nothing he assumed that he didn't have anything to fear. But suddenly something hard and heavy landed on his shoulder, his horse groaned and staggered to a halt, while some kind of a blindfold whipped around his head. '*What is this? Am I captured?*' The thought filled him with such horror that he couldn't breathe. Nor could he see anything under that thick cloth.

"Help! Gentlemen! To the rescue! To the rescue here!" His muffled voice sounded so hopeless and so terrified that his meager hair rose up on his head. "Help! For God's sake! Help me!"

He tried to urge his horse forward with his heels but the winded animal only groaned again as if about to fall under the weight of its heavy rider and then it shuddered and its four stiff legs began to slide outward.

Pan Zagloba could hear the far-off, dwindling howls of the running *tchernya*, the shouts of the victorious soldiers who swept past him in pursuit, and the drumming of the horses' hooves receding in the distance. And then all sounds were gone and he was listening to a breathless silence while panicky speculations darted through his head.

'*What's happened, then?*' Sweat burst out on his forehead and poured into his eyes. '*What's that thing around me?*' Whoever caught him must have thrown a cloth over his head to blind him and to choke his cries just as he did to Bohun. That weight on his shoulder had to be the hand of some huge Zaporohjan, someone like the dreadful, bearlike Pulyan whom Pan Longinus captured in the skirmishing.

"God in Heaven, he's got me!" the fat knight howled. "Jesus and Mary, I'm a prisoner! Help me, someone! Help me anyone! Help! Longinus, help me!"

He knew that he'd gladly pledge himself to lifelong temperance from that moment on if he could just hear the gentle, chiding voice of Pan Podbipyenta but the suffocating cloth smothered all sound as well.

But then a new thought presented itself. Why was he standing still? Why was nothing happening? Why wasn't he being dragged off the field . . .? Or murdered?

"Let me go, peasant!" he appealed in his muffled voice and listened to the silence. "Let go, I say!"

The silence continued.

"Let me loose," he tried again, feeling some confidence returning. "Listen, let's come to an arrangement. I'll let you live if you let go of me! Understand? You leave me alone and I'll close my eyes while you scuttle back to your own kind. Eh? What do you say? What could be more fair?"

But no one answered him.

Pan Zagloba tried to kick his horse once more into motion but the exhausted, foundered animal merely uttered another helpless groan and stood where it was. The desperate captive reached stealthily for the dagger dangling on his belly. He drew it, slashed furiously at the empty air behind him, stabbed the air in front and to the sides, and then dropped the knife, reached up with both hands and tore the stifling blindfold off his head.

"What's all this, then?" he muttered, twisting around in his saddle and trying to see every which way at once. "What's going on here?"

To his amazement he found that he was quite alone. There was no one near him.

Far off in the smoke he could see the red coats of Volodyovski's dragoons bobbing above a dark mass of running men; a few furlongs down the field the *husaria's* glittering chain-mail caught the sun as the armored riders drove the last of the fugitives into the swamp and the river; and lying at Pan Zagloba's feet was a huge, crimson Zaporohjan regimental banner which a fleeing Cossack must have thrown at him in such a way that it landed with its heavy shaft on the fat knight's shoulder while the cloth wrapped itself around his head.

"Aha," Pan Zagloba told himself at once. "I've captured a banner! Well, didn't I? Who's to say I didn't . . .? If all *justitia* doesn't perish on this field along with what's left of reason and good sense, then I should be rewarded in some way for this act of valor. And why shouldn't I be? How many people get to seize a regimental standard . . .?"

Quite certain now that he had charged a Zaporohjan regiment single-handed to capture its banner, the fat knight looked fiercely around the empty battlefield.

"Ha, you damned rebel dogs!" he cried. "Thank all your saints that my horse failed me just when I started to get warmed up a bit! I'd have taken a lot more from you if that miserable beast hadn't run out of wind!"

Alone, out of danger, and with evidence of his unexpected bravery lying at his feet, Pan Zagloba observed himself with new eyes and liked what he saw.

"Ha! I had no idea I was such a hero. I thought I had to trust in quick wits and stratagems rather than my courage but I see that I'm far more than I thought I was. This military life isn't altogether without its good points. There may be more for me to do in this army than chewing on field rations!"

Delighted with his new image as a valiant warrior, he caught sight of something dark and threatening that galloped suddenly into his field of vision.

"Ah . . . ah! What's that now? Great God Almighty, here's some other cohort! Hasn't anybody told them they've lost the battle? Haven't I done enough? Don't come this way, you flea-bitten mongrels! Head some other way! May the wolves eat this useless horse . . .! Move you spavined nag, move! Ah . . . to Hell with it all!"

It seemed as if Pan Zagloba's short life as a military hero would end there and then. A mass of shattered Cossack cavalry was galloping towards him with the armored troopers of Pan Polanovski's *Pantzerni* riding hard behind them, and he had no means of getting away on his foundered horse. He'd have been ridden down for certain if Skshetuski's *husaria* didn't return just then from its own pursuit to drive these new fugitives into the pits and mudholes of the marsh pond. Others died on their knees, slaughtered without mercy, so that every man who managed to cross the causeway and fill the cavalry's killing-ground beyond it, found death in one way or another.

★ ★ ★

But the bloodiest massacre took place on the causeway where thousands of densely packed animals and men died under the avalanche of iron hurled at them by Vurtzel's cannoneers and by the measured salvos of Korytzki's and Osinski's German infantry. Unable to force their way through this deadly barrier, yet pushed on by the pressure of the fresh regiments crowding up behind them, they turned on each other trying to fight their way out of the trap and added to the carnage.

It seemed to the silent men around Prince Yeremi, who watched this terrible spectacle from the tall summit of a burial mound, as if Krivoinos had sworn to destroy his own followers who fought each other in a savage, fratricidal struggle in the middle of the bloody causeway. The decimated mobs which were trying to escape the firestorm behind them battled the fresh Zaporohjan regiments that Krivoinos kept driving onto the spit of land and died in their hundreds. One half of the causeway darkened under the panicked crowds that ran for their lives; the other half was thick with new regiments that pressed into the battle. Between them rose a hill of corpses on which they tore and trampled each other, adding their own bodies to the heaps of their slaughtered comrades underfoot.

Hundreds of them were pushed into the river or leaped in panic into the lagoon, trying to swim or wade to safety on each side of the causeway, and either sunk down into the dark tangle of mud and underwater roots or drowned in the current. The green basin of the Vishovaty Stav became so full of dead men and horses that its waters spilled across its banks. From time to time, when there were no more rebels left alive on the cavalry's killing-ground, Vurtzel's guns ceased firing. The musketeers took a breath and rested their weapons. Then the mouth of the causeway disgorged new mobs of *tchernya* and Zaporohjan warriors, hurling the Cossack regiments out into the field as if they were projectiles fired from a cannon. But when the mile-wide crescent filled up again so that the Prince's horsemen began a new slaughter, the guns and muskets threw out another flaming barrier, cut off the trapped rebels, and buried their reinforcements under an avalanche of metal. Hemmed in by the Prince's cavalry, sabered down in hundreds and trampled by the horses, the Cossack cohorts died under the sword or drowned in the lagoon, while the cold, pale sun marched steadily to the west and dipped towards evening.

Dressed in his silver armor, Prince Yeremi watched this day-long carnage off the round top of the burial mound. His face showed neither sadness nor elation. His eyes swept coldly over the spit of land that seemed to leap and tremble under the battering of Vurtzel's bombardment, the lagoon that had been bridged by corpses, the bloody battlefield and the reddened river, and lifted far beyond to where the vast Zaporohjan *tabor* lay wreathed in a blue-grey haze.

"We won't be able to take that today," he said at last to the portly *Voyevode* who sweated in his own gilded armorplate beside him.

"Good God, Highness!" the groggy Palatine exclaimed, staring at the slaughter in shock and despair. "Isn't this enough?"

But Prince Yeremi didn't seem to hear him. "It's getting late!" he said in disappointment. "Time's passing too quickly to do any more today. Look, Your Excellency, it's evening already."

The sun was almost gone. The light, high clouds which drifted in the sky like a flock of lambs grazing in the fields, began to redden and to scurry home beyond the horizon. The Cossack flood was ebbing from the causeway and those regiments which pushed on towards it were starting to turn about and flow back to their camp.

The battle was ending. Krivoinos, as Prince Yeremi knew, was staring at ruin. Ten thousand of his best Zaporohjan warriors, not counting at least twice that many *tchernya*, were dead on the battlefield or drowned beside the causeway. Some two thousand more were taken prisoner, which meant that they'd be dead by morning. He lost fourteen of his bravest atamans and colonels, nearly a hundred other *kujhen* leaders, and more than two hundred *esauls* and company commanders. His own deputy, the ferocious Pulyan, was taken alive even though all his ribs were crushed and he was near death. Infuriated mobs besieged him in his quarters, threatening his life if he didn't call off the battle for the night, and he swore to his desperate and despairing thousands that they would slaughter the Prince's army the next day.

Meanwhile forty captured Zaporohjan battle flags were carried to the Polish camp and piled at Prince Yeremi's feet. Each of the soldiers who captured one of these revered regimental ensigns paraded it before his commander and threw it down before him, and as the gathered officers and gentry counted these rare trophies they began to understand the full extent of their astounding victory; this was the Cossacks' greatest disaster in the war to date. Pan Zagloba, who took care to be the last in that parade of heroes, hurled his own banner to the ground with such force and clatter that the thick, gilded shaft snapped in two, and Prince Yeremi beckoned him to come closer.

"You took this with your own hands, my friend?" he asked with a cordial smile.

"I did," the fat knight said proudly.

"Then I see that you're not only our Ulysses but also our Achilles."

"I'm just a simple soldier," the fat knight replied with becoming modesty. "But I've the good fortune to be serving under Alexander of Macedon himself!"

"Since you're a volunteer, serving without pay, I'll have the treasurer find another two hundred ducats for you," the Prince nodded, smiling. "This kind of valor ought to be rewarded."

"Highness!" Zagloba cried, seizing the Prince by the knees and bowing before him as low as his girth allowed. "Your generosity is even greater than the virtues it rewards, though my natural *modestia* can do without any recognition!"

A small smile flitted across Skshetuski's face as he recalled Zagloba's anxious mutterings before the battle but whatever he knew he kept to himself. Meanwhile Pan Zagloba marched off with such a fierce look on his grimly righteous and forbidding features that soldiers from other regiments pointed him out to each other as the day's greatest hero.

★　★　★

Night came soon afterwards. Thousands of campfires glowed on both sides of the water and the columns of smoke rose into the sky as thickly as if they were saplings in a forest. The tired Vishnovyetzki soldiers sat around their fires, resting for tomorrow. Roast beef and mutton helped to restore their bodies; *gojhalka* raised their spirits, and so did the tales of this day's successes that they told each other. But loudest among them all was Pan Zagloba who related not only all the great deeds he actually accomplished on the battlefield but also everything he would have achieved if his horse hadn't failed him in his finest moment.

"I tell you, gentlemen," he addressed the Prince's officers and some of the Kievan gentry who came to share their suppers with the Vishnovyetzki men, "there's nothing new for me about a great battle, I've seen enough of them in Moldavia and in Turkey too, but I'm a peaceful man for whom bloodshed is always an unhappy business so I've let myself get a little out of practice.

"Which is why," he went on, throwing uneasy glances at Pan Yan, "I may have seemed a little . . . ah . . . nervous before we began. Not that I was afraid of those furrow-hoppers. Not at all! Because who'd need to worry about that peasant rabble? But I was anxious about my own hot-blooded nature which sometimes carries me away."

"Which it did," a respectful voice suggested.

"Which it did," agreed Pan Zagloba. "Ask Pan Skshetuski if you don't believe me! I wanted to charge right down into the thick of it as soon as I saw Pan Vyershul falling with his horse. But wiser heads prevailed."

"Yes, we did have to calm you down a little," Pan Yan agreed, smiling.

"But where is Vyershul, anyway?" Pan Korvitch asked.

"He's gone to reconnoiter Krivoinos' positions. That man doesn't know what it means to rest."

"Listen then, gentlemen, and I'll tell you how I came to seize that battle flag . . . ."

But Korvitch was more interested in Vyershul's condition. "He's not badly hurt, then?" he asked. "Not wounded?"

"It's not the first I've ever taken," the fat knight said loudly, annoyed by the interruption. "But I swear I never had to work this hard to get one before . . .! Or to tell about it afterwards!"

"Vyershul's fine," said Pan Azulevitch, one of that polonized Tartar gentry who settled in the Commonwealth many centuries earlier, and who served in regiments like Vyershul's. "He's bruised a bit, and he's had a bellyful of water because he went headfirst into the pond. Other than that there isn't a scratch on him."

"Then it's a wonder all the crayfish didn't turn bright red and die," the fat knight snapped angrily, irritated by lack of attention. "All the water must have boiled with such a flaming head of hair in it!"

"He's a fine soldier, nonetheless," Korvitch said. "A great cavalier."

But Pan Zagloba started to lose his temper.

"Not so great, it seems, that he captured many battle flags today! Tfui! What's the matter with you young men these days? Would you rather learn how to take banners from the enemy or boil carp for dinner? No wonder our poor Commonwealth is in such sad straits!"

However Pan Zagloba was to have no luck that night with his story-telling. Young Pan Aksak came up to the campfire, his boyish sense of wonder ringing in his voice, and said that he too had some important news.

"The nanny didn't wash his nappies," Pan Zagloba muttered in disgust. "The cat drank the milk and his puppy dog has fleas."

But the young man didn't take offense. "Pulyan is on the coals . . ." he began.

"So all the dogs in the camp will get a hot dinner tonight," Pan Zagloba snapped.

" . . . and singing like a bird. The negotiations have been broken off. Pan Kisyel is said to be going mad with disappointment and Hmyel is coming here with all his forces to rescue Krivoinos . . ."

"Who gives a damn about Hmyel?" Pan Zagloba burst out, angry to have his stories ignored as if they weren't the most important tales of the day. "Let him come, the hop-head! Beer is going to be a penny a barrel when we've sweated all the liquor out of him!"

"So that's Pulyan's story," young Pan Aksak finished. "He says that six thousand hand-picked cavalry have already got as near as Mahnovka. Bohun leads them."

"Who?" Zagloba asked in an altogether different voice. "Who?"

"Bohun."

"That can't be!"

"That's what Pulyan says."

"God help me," the fat knight groaned, all his heroic poses immediately forgotten. "And how soon can he get here?"

"Three days would be enough. But he wouldn't push too hard just before a battle, would he? I mean, he wouldn't want to wear out his horses . . ."

"But I'll wear out a few," Zagloba muttered, wet with sudden sweat. "God's angels, where are you when I need you most? I'll

gladly give back my battle flag if that demented devil twists his
neck somewhere along the way! Ah . . . ah . . . but surely we
won't be staying here much longer?"

"We might," Pan Yan said. "It depends on how much more
there is to do tomorrow."

★ ★ ★

But Pan Zagloba was suddenly anxious to be far away. He
caught Skshetuski by the sleeve and dragged him away from the
fire.

"What else is there to do?" he asked. "We've beaten Krivoinos! It's time to go somewhere for a rest. I'm a brave man,
I've proved it often enough, but something happens to me
when I hear that mad devil's name . . . Phew! Who'd have
believed he'd get back on his feet so soon? He must have heard
that I'm now with the army . . . Couldn't I have stayed comfortably in Bar? What obsessed me to come here instead?"

"Don't show your fear like that," Pan Yan said. "You'll bring
shame on yourself. Nothing's going to happen to you among us
anyway."

"You don't know this man!" Pan Zagloba glanced around
with a worried eye. "He could be creeping up on us somewhere
between the fires. And he wants you almost as badly as he wants
me!"

"Then I hope God grants me a quick meeting with him."

"If that's an act of God's mercy then I'll do without it! I'll be
glad to forgive all his trespasses against me, as a good Christian
is obliged to do, but only on condition that they hang him two
days before I forgive him! There's something infernal about that
man. He isn't like anybody else. I know how to handle gentry
and I know what to do when I'm with a peasant but he's neither
one nor the other, and half the time you wouldn't even believe
he's a human being. So what is he, then? I am not superstitious,
God help me, but he has to be some kind of evil spirit! You just
never know where you are with him. I did some dicey things in
his company, I admit it freely, but I'll never forget the look in his
eyes when I was wrapping up his head back there in Rozloghi
. . . I'll see those eyes burning up at me in my last hour on
earth."

"You've friends who'll stand by you here," Pan Skshetuski
said.

"And a lot of good they'll do me against a demon! I was lucky with him once by God's special mercy, but one good roll of the dice with a man like that is all anyone can count on. And I'll tell you something else, lieutenant, you're trifling with God's mercy yourself, and that's not likely to end well for you."

"*A quo modo?* What do you mean by that?"

"Hmm. Hmm." A new idea glimmered in Zagloba's brain and he was anxious to turn it into action. "Let's find a quiet corner somewhere and I'll explain it to you. Who knows, maybe I'm giving you another reason to be grateful to me. What it is, you see, it's your lack of feeling for our little Helen . . .!"

"What?" Pan Yan gaped at him, astonished.

"Yes, I know, you love her," the fat knight went on. "A blind man can see that. But where's this great love of yours when here you are, indulging yourself in all these warlike pastimes, and there *she* is, the poor girl, waiting for word from you and drowning herself in tears every day? If you really cared about her you'd have sent me back to her a long time ago!"

"So you were thinking of going back to Bar?"

"Today, if you like, I'm that sorry for her. But you don't seem to care!"

"Don't scratch open a wound that's barely healed, my friend," Skshetuski said. "It's not like you say. God knows there's hardly been a moment when I didn't think about her. But I didn't send you back with a letter to her because I wanted to go myself! I want to marry her at once and be done with this terrible separation!"

"So why didn't you go?"

"How could I, before the battle?"

"Yes, well . . . hmm . . . I can understand that," the fat knight was willing to be generous as long as he could vanish from the territory before Bohun got there. "I'm an old soldier and a noble too. But now the battle's over, am I right? So what's to stop us setting out today?"

Pan Yan sighed. "We still haven't finished with Krivoinos."

"What's left to be done?"

"Crush him," Pan Yan said. "Destroy his army. Protect the helpless and punish the guilty."

"That's more than I can understand," Zagloba complained. "You whipped the young Krivoinos and the old one came.

You'll beat him and then that other young devil will pop up, the
one whose name I'm not going to utter without God's daylight
to take the curse off it. You'll settle his hash and Hmyel will
arrive! If this goes on much longer you'd best make a pact like
Pan Podbipyenta! Then we'll have a double load of chastity
around here!"

And then the old knight lost his temper altogether, due as
much to his genuine affection for Helen as to concern about his
own safety.

"Come to your senses, will you?" he roared as loud as any
father whose daughter's happiness is in jeopardy. "Or I'll be the
first to urge my sweet Helen to show you the gate and fit you
out with a set of horns! There she is, by God, a girl like a peach,
and here you are prattling about battles! I'd understand it if you
were some piddling little snotnose who never smelled gunpowder and needs to make a reputation for himself. But you've
slopped up more blood then a pack of wolves! I hear you even
killed some kind of fire-breathing dragon at Mahnovka! I tell
you, as that moon is my witness, there's something wrong here!
Either you're trying to wriggle off the hook or you've become
so drunk on blood that you'd rather kill men than make love
with women!"

The young soldier's face grew so pale in the moon's cold light
that Pan Zagloba thought he was about to fall senseless at his
feet. But Skshetuski brought himself back under control.

"You're wrong," he said softly. "As God's my witness, I hate
all this bloodshed and I'm sick of killing. But I can't turn my
back on my friends, or the Commonwealth, and go off on some
private business of my own. The war will go on because the
rabble have got too high and mighty and it will take us a long
time to drive them back where they belong. But there'll be a
break in it when we've whipped Krivoinos. The Prince is a great
commander but he knows that we're too weak to handle
Hmyelnitzki. I know he plans to go west to Zbarajh, rest and
refit us there and gather new forces. It may be a month before
we can come back to the Ukraine and, in the meantime, I'll be
able to ask for leave with a clear conscience."

"Ah, that's more like it," the fat noble said. "One more day's
fighting won't make that much difference. So tomorrow's our
last day of work? And then the next day we can set out for Bar?"

"If that's how God wants it. And I'll tell you this much to set
your mind at ease: there's no way that Bohun can get here in

time for tomorrow's battle. It's a three day ride from Mahnovka even at a gallop."

"But what if he should? I tell you, you don't know this man. He has the Devil's luck! And he *has* to be some kind of a Devil himself!"

Pan Yan shrugged. "If he does get here then I trust his luck will end in the Prince's hands. Or in mine."

"Now that I'd like to see," Pan Zagloba said. "He's like a permanent hot wind blowing on my neck and I've a horror of air that smells of fire and brimstone. I told you I don't care for crowds but he's a mob all by himself as far as I'm concerned. No matter, though! Tomorrow we tan the peasants' hides and the day after we're off to Bar and Helen!"

Then the fat knight let himself be carried away by anticipation.

"Ha," he cried. "And will those pretty eyes start shining when they see you? Will that little face get pink with love and pleasure? I don't mind telling you my good friend, if you've not yet guessed it, that I've come to love her like my own flesh and blood. And why not? A man needs children to care for him in his old age. I've no sons I know of, at least not *legitime natos*, as they say, nor do I have a roof of my own anywhere . . . I had some great estates granted to me by a certain Pasha for services I rendered to him in his harem but they're far away, in a Turkish province, and I expect that my heathen bailiffs stole every goat by now. So here I am, wandering about the world like an orphan without kin or loved ones or a corner of my own. I expect I'll have to spend my old age with Pan Podbipyenta in those Lithuanian 'intestines' that he calls his home . . ."

"It won't be like that," Skshetuski assured him. "Don't worry about your future. After what you've done for Helen and me there's nothing that we wouldn't do for you."

"My little Helen already calls me 'Father'," the fat knight observed.

"And that's how we'll treat you."

★ ★ ★

A passing officer spotted them in the shadow of the trees just then and asked who they were.

"Ah, Vyershul!" Pan Yan recognized him. "Back from patrol already?"

"And from reporting to the Prince as well."

"So what's due for tomorrow?"

"Battle." Vyershul laughed. "It looks as if we may have taught Krivoinos a lesson in tactics. He has twenty thousand men carting earth to widen the causeway and he's building half a dozen bridges across both the waterways. You can hear the chopping and the hammering half a mile away."

"And what did the Prince have to say about that?"

Vyershul grinned. "The Prince said: '*Very well.*'"

"And that's all?"

"That's all." The light cavalryman laughed again. "Krivoinos seems desperate to get at us before Hmyel comes up and the Prince is more than willing to accommodate him."

"You've brought back some prisoners?"

"We snared seven. They confirm everything we knew about Hmyelnitzki but his main forces are still far away. In the meantime Krivoinos will be working all night on those crossings so I might as well go and get some sleep."

Then the lean Steppe raider sighed, glanced at the moonlit plain and sniffed the cool air. "What a night, eh?"

"Bright as dawn. And how d'you feel after your little tumble?"

"All my bones are aching. I'm on my way now to thank our Lithuanian Hercules for saving my hide from that human cannon that knocked me off my horse. And then to get my head down on a saddle-blanket because I'm worn out."

"Good night, then," Pan Yan said. "Sleep well."

"Sleep well yourself," Vyershul said.

"We might as well turn-in too," Skshetuski told Zagloba as they started back towards the main campfires. "If the Cossacks are widening their attack front we'll have some hard work tomorrow."

They made their way to the *husaria* bivouac, knelt to say their prayers, and stretched out by the fire. The night was cool and clear. The sky was full of stars. The great white moon made it seem almost as bright as day. The Zaporohjan campfires glittered across the river like a reflection of the spangled sky and the fires in Prince Yeremi's camp went out one by one.

It seemed as if they barely drifted into sleep when the bugles started calling reveille throughout the camp and a new sun began to climb into the cloudless sky.

Chapter Thirty-five

THE SECOND DAY of the battle proved an even worse disaster for Krivoinos than the first. The Zaporohjans lost all their field artillery, half their wagon train, and a great heap of battle flags which included those they captured at Yellow Waters and Korsun.

And yet at first it looked as if they might win. The Prince allowed most of their army to cross the widened causeway and the bridges they threw across the ponds without interference. In fact, to the astonishment of everyone who hadn't served under him before, he ordered a retreat all along the line when the Cossack masses drew up for battle in the open plain, and then, as soon as fighting began in earnest, he turned his horse and galloped off the field in what seemed like panic.

His army followed.

Pan Zagloba, who took the flight for genuine, bellowed in terror and rode like the wind.

The cheering Cossacks and the *tchernya* broke their formations and rushed pell-mell after them, to catch and surround these apparent fugitives and butcher them all, and then Prince Yeremi wheeled suddenly around and charged them with all his cavalry at once.

The blow was so frightful and so unexpected that the rebels were unable to stand up to it even for a moment. The Prince's horsemen drove them across a mile or more all the way back to their bridges and the grassy causeway and then chased them far beyond the crossings to the fortified wagon train itself. If Prince Yeremi's infantry and cannon could have kept up with the charging cavalry the whole huge mobile war camp of the Zaporohjans would have been taken at one blow.

But night had fallen by that time. The fleeing Cossacks put so many miles between themselves and the battlefield that the marching musketeers and gunners couldn't catch up with them. Two cavalry regiments under Zachvilihovski did break into that rolling fortress, and captured immense stores of food and ammunition, but the bulk of the Cossack wagon train escaped in the darkness and what was left of Krivoinos' wrecked army didn't stop running until it reached Mahnovka. Twice in the course of that night the maddened mobs seized their ruined leader to drag him as a peace-offering to the Prince and only his promise to lead them immediately to Hmyelnitzki's camp saved him from captivity and the hangman's rope.

He fled with the others, beaten and in despair, but if he hoped for any understanding or compassion from his furious Hetman he was disappointed. Enraged by the disaster, Hmyelnitzki had him chained by the neck to a cannon wheel as soon as all his own armies marched into Mahnovka, and the ill-starred Maksym Krivoinos prepared for a cruel death.

"Where is the flower of my army?" the raging Hetman howled at his luckless peasant general. "Where are all those beautiful young men I put into your keeping?"

"Drowned, slaughtered, hanged, impaled," muttered the assembled atamans and colonels, and Krivoinos knew that scores of other legendary Zaporohjan leaders were murdered for much lesser failures than his own.

"Dog!" his erstwhile friends shouted, demanding his death. "Traitor! *Na Pohybel!*"

He would have died too, torn apart by the mobs outside the council hall, if Hmyelnitzki didn't control his fury and remember how much he owed to this fallen Zaporohjan hero. It was Krivoinos who backed him in the *Sietch* when he was just a hunted fugitive among the *Nijhovtsy*; it was his iron fist that hammered down the opposition and turned Hmyelnitzki into a Hetman and ruler of millions. It was this same routed and disgraced Krivoinos who littered the vast spaces of Volhynia with the rotting corpses of slaughtered Jews and gentry, who stormed Polonne, and who was victorious everywhere until he came up against Yeremi Vishnovyetzki. And it was only after his first fury spent itself without instant bloodshed that

Hmyelnitzki allowed himself to think and to recall everything that this doomed man did for him since the rebellion started, and he had Krivoinos unchained, restored to command, and sent him off to carry the war to Podolia.

★ ★ ★

Meanwhile, Prince Yeremi finally announced the needed rest for his exhausted army.

Their victory over Krivoinos cost them heavily, especially at the storming of the wagon train which the Zaporohjans defended with their usual ferocity and skill. Some five hundred soldiers were killed in that savage fighting. Kushel, Polanovski, and the youthful Pan Aksak were among the wounded. Even Pan Zagloba, who forgot all about his dislike of crowds at the prospect of getting into the Cossack wagons, fought as bravely as the rest of Pan Skshetuski's troopers, and suffered a serious injury. Hit twice across the back with an iron flail he now lay like a corpse in Pan Yan's light-wheeled baggage cart.

So Pan Yan's wedding plans in Bar had to be put aside again, especially since the Prince sent him with several troops of light cavalry to stamp out a new peasant rising in the distant province of Zaslav. He went as ordered, without a word to the Prince about taking leave or going to Bar, and the injured fat knight who lay groaning and barely conscious in his bedding couldn't have told anyone about it even if he wished.

For five more days and nights the weary Skshetuski led his detachments on rapid forced marches across a hundred miles, burned rebel villages, ambushed and battled armed mobs of Cossackry and marauding *tchernya*, punished their butcheries and rescued hundreds of besieged loyalists and gentry at the eastern edge of Hmyelnitzki's empire, until his dog-tired men and animals were hardly able to move.

It was time, then, to call a halt to war. With the rebellion stamped out around Zaslav, and with the peasantry cowed into sullen and grudging obedience within a hundred-mile circle of the district, Pan Yan decided to rejoin the Prince near Tarnopol. He halted his troops in the village of Suhozhintze on the River Homor, knowing that without at least one night's rest few of them would be able to finish the journey. He felt that he had tapped and exhausted the last reservoirs of his own stamina and strength. He stumbled into a peasant hut as soon as all his men were safely quartered in the barns and orchards, threw himself down on a heap of straw, and sunk into sleep as suddenly as if he'd fallen into a dark, dry well.

It was a troubled sleep, full of fleeting but persistent images of the past, which continued their separate but determined existence all around him even when the cold light of dawn broke into his dream.

He woke and thought that he was still asleep and dreaming in his room in Lubnie. The images that crowded into his exhausted mind made it seem as if he'd never left on that dimly recalled journey to and from the *Sietch*; as if there was no war, nor any rebellion; and that he was at home and waking in his own quarters in the citadel of Prince Yeremi's capital, while Zjendjan went about his usual morning task of cleaning his master's equipment and laying out his clothes.

He struggled to free himself of this baffling vision, aware that he was still so befogged with weariness and sleep that he couldn't trust anything he saw around him, but the round, hunched figure of his servant lad didn't dissolve in the fog of his departing dreams; it remained seated by the window on a milking stool, bent over Pan Yan's armor with a scouring stone, and greasing the cracked leather straps which the Summer heat had shriveled into thongs.

Skshetuski closed his eyes, thinking that he must be in the grip of some strange hallucination, or that this had to be some kind of left-over fragment of his dreams, but when he opened his eyes again the boy was still there.

"Zjendjan!" Skshetuski called out at last. "Is that you? Or are you a ghost?"

"Oh my God!" The boy leaped to his feet, startled by the shout, and the dented breastplate clattered to the floor. "God almighty, master! Don't scare me like that! A ghost? Me? Why should I be a ghost when I'm alive and well?"

"And you're really here?"

"Well, master . . . you didn't chase me out, did you?" the lad cried out and burst into tears. "So why shouldn't I be here? I'm still in your service as far as I know."

"Come here then!" Skshetuski shouted, getting out of bed. "Let me hug you, lad."

The faithful lad threw his arms around Skshetuski's knees and the delighted soldier hugged him and went on repeating: "You're alive! You're living!"

"Ay, master, master," the boy gasped and sniffled, stammering in joy. "That I should be here . . . seeing you still in one piece and walking on this earth . . .! O God almighty! Only you yelled so loud, sir, that I dropped the armor. Those straps are in real bad shape, sir, by the way. Looks like you didn't have anybody looking after you while I was away . . . Ah, but thank God! Thank God that's all over! Now I can take proper care of things again. Ay, my good master . . .!"

"So when did you get here?" Pan Yan went on, astonished, but starting to believe that even this could happen on a morning which began with so many other strange dreams, memories and illusions.

"Last night," the boy said.

"Why didn't you wake me?"

"Wake you?" The boy stared at him as if he didn't understand the question. "Why should I wake you, sir, when you need your sleep? I just came over this morning to get your clothes ready . . . Didn't see no point in waking you when a blind man could see you were bone-tired and dead to the world."

"And where did you come from?"

"From Hushtcha," the lad said.

Pan Yan was puzzled. "But that's Pan Kisyel's country, isn't it . . .?"

"So it is, sir."

The boy spoke in such a casual manner as if it was the most natural thing for him to be visiting the chief town of the *Voyevode* of Bratzlav, the same Pan Kisyel who led the Cossack conciliation party, while a civil war was raging all around it.

"Only there's not much living in it now, I expect," he added, "since the Cossacks burned it."

"But how did you get there in the first place? And what were you doing there anyway? Speak up! Tell me everything that happened to you since I saw you last!"

"Seems like an awful lot to tell, sir," the boy said and shrugged, and then babbled out a bewildering and disjointed tale of how he had been in Hmyelnitzki's camp, how Pan Kisyel sent his chaplain, Father Patronius Lasko, with letters to Hmyelnitzki, how the kindly Greek Orthodox priest took him back to Hushtcha when his embassy was over, and then how the Cossacks came to loot and burn the properties of their greatest friend and murdered the priest.

"So that's how I lost another master," Zjendjan sniffed.

"Even though he wasn't my *real* master, sir, not like you. And that's what would've happened to Pan Kisyel too if he'd been there when the Cossacks came."

"I can't make head or tail of this!" Skshetuski shook his head. "Stop jumping from one thing to another. You mean you were in Hmyel's camp? In Byelotzerkiev? Living with the Cossacks?"

"Who else was there for me to live with in that hellhole, master? But here sir, get your clothes on, it's almost time for the morning muster. Oh my God, look at this shirt, will you? It's a wonder it holds together in your hand, never mind the wearing, it's nothing but rags!"

"Never mind the rags!" Pan Yan shouted, quite unable to make any sense out of the boy's story. "Tell me what happened! And for God's sake try to keep it all in some sort of order!"

Helping Pan Yan to dress and buckle on his armor, Zjendjan began to relate everything that happened to him from the moment Skshetuski sent him from Kudak to Helen and the old *Knahina*.

"Only I didn't get the letters to the lady," he confessed uneasily, peering up from under his tussled hair as if he expected punishment or a scolding, "because that thief Bohun took them from me in Tchehryn . . . But maybe you won't be too hard on me about it, master, 'cause I couldn't help it. I didn't give them up just because he asked me. He'd have taken my life too if that fat one-eyed noble hadn't got me away from him and hid me in a stable."

"I know all about that," Skshetuski interrupted. "That fat noble is in the Prince's camp. He told me what happened to you in Tchehryn. And also how he stole the Princess out of Bohun's clutches and got her safe to Bar."

"Ah, so our lady's safe, sir?" the boy cried out, delighted. "Thank God for that! I knew she got away from Bohun but I didn't know what happened to her after that. So I expect we'll be having the wedding soon, master?"

"Just as soon as I take my men back to Tarnopol and then go to Bar."

"Ha!" Zjendjan nodded wisely. "So it's all turning out like the witch foretold."

"What witch, for God's sake?"

"What witch? Why, Bohun's witch. What other witch was there? Bohun had her tell his fortune for him and she said he'd never get the Lady. Some '*Lah*' is to get her, she said, so that must be you, sir."

"And how do you know about that, for God's sake?"

"Bohun told me."

"You mean to say you were with him too?"

"Sure, master." The boy looked as if he couldn't understand why anyone would be puzzled or confused by his adventures or by the way in which he told his story. "How else could I've cured him and got him back on his feet if I wasn't with him? And it's thanks to him that I got to Hushtcha."

★ ★ ★

By this time Skshetuski was ready to give up. There was no way to hurry the unruffled boy no matter how exasperating he could be with his wide-eyed phlegmatic answers that made the most astonishing adventures sound as bland as a Sunday stroll. His round, red-cheeked face and bright button eyes made him look as naive and trusting as a child, but this childlike frankness hid a shrewd, calculating mind, a lot of common sense, and a great deal of stubbornness and courage. Nothing he did ever happened without a good reason and yet, as Pan Yan knew, his loyalties were so clear-cut and direct that he wouldn't think twice about risking his life for something he thought important.

"So what happened next?" Pan Yan asked.

"So there I was," Zjendjan said. "Where was I?"

"I don't know." Skshetuski ground his teeth. "In Tchehryn?"

"That's right, sir! In that stable . . ."

"Ah yes." Skshetuski sighed. "You were in a stable."

" . . . In Tchehryn, where the fat knight left me, flat on my back and hardly able to breathe after what that thief Bohun did to me . . . And then comes Hmyelnitzki with all the Zaporoh-jans . . ."

"I know about Hmyelnitzki."

"Yes sir. So you do, sir. Well sir, because earlier the Hetman laid into some of the Tchehryn people for being in sympathy with the rebels, and there were lots of beaten and cut-up folks lying about the town, the Cossacks took me for one of them and looked after me like I was their own. They dressed my wounds, kept me comfortable, and didn't let me get taken by the Tartars . . . which is a real wonder, sir, seeing as how they let those murdering heathens take whatever they fancy. And so I got my health back again and my head started working."

He paused and waited as if wondering what he should say next and Pan Yan sighed in exasperation. "Go on," he urged. "So your head is working."

"So then I'm thinking. '*What next? How do I get back to my master?*' And because I didn't know where to look for you, sir, I couldn't think of any place to go."

"But you thought of something," Pan Yan sighed, resigned to waiting but gnawing at his mustache.

"I did. I thought I might as well stay right where I was till things settled down a bit and I knew what was what. Meanwhile those robbers went off to Korsun and beat our own Hetmans, and then I really didn't know where to turn. Ay, master, what I saw in that place! What those people did! They've no shame and they thought I was one of them so they didn't hide anything from me. So I kept thinking, thinking . . ."

"About getting away from them?" Pan Yan prompted, shaking with impatience.

"That's right, master. That's just what I was thinking. It was hard to know, sir, what to do, but then they started hauling the loot from Korsun and I thought my eyes would pop out of my head! All that gold and silver! All that cloth-of-gold, and the brocades, and the jeweled trappings for the horses, and the silverware . . . Master, even you've never seen anything like it! Six silver spoons were going for a quart of vodka and a gold stud or an egret plume went for half a quart! So there I'm thinking, thinking . . ."

"I know what you were thinking," Pan Yan ground out between his teeth.

"That's right, master. '*Why shouldn't I get a bit of this?*' is what I was thinking. And why shouldn't I? Were those bloody-handed robbers to get it all? If God didn't mean me to have some of it, it wouldn't be there, would it? And then something else popped up for me to think about."

"God help me," sighed Skshetuski.

"He will, master. Like He helps everybody who bides his time and doesn't get impatient. So I thought that if God grants it someday I'll go back to Podlasye which is where my family has its holdings. Only there's not much left to hold seeing as we've been in this lawsuit with our neighbors, the Yavorskis, for the last fifty years, and all the money's just about run out. But I thought it's my duty to help out my parents and give them something so they can go on suing those Yavorskis!"

"Very worthy of you," Pan Skshetuski muttered.

"Thank you, master. So I bought and traded a few things and it got to be so much I had to get a couple of packhorses to carry it all. Which I saw as God's way to cheer me up in my misery, seeing that I was so sad from missing you so much, sir, and worrying about you."

"You'll never change, Zjendjan," Pan Yan sighed and shook his head in wonder. "You make a profit out of everything."

"And what's wrong with that, sir? Where's the harm in taking every blessing that God throws your way? I didn't steal all that booty, did I?"

The boy spoke with such total and transparent innocence that Pan Yan had to smile. And then, just as he thought that he could never be surprised again by anything that the lad might do, Zjendjan unbuckled his belt and took a small bag of coins from the money-pouch inside it and laid it on the table.

"What's that you've got there?"

"This is the purse you gave me, master, to take me to Rozloghi," Zjendjan said. "Every ducat's there. But since I never got to where you sent me, sir, I'd better give it back."

"You're probably richer by now than I am," Pan Yan said and hugged the boy again. "But go ahead and keep that purse as well."

"Thank you kindly, master! Well, God was good to me. My folks will be pleased, specially my old granddad who's more than ninety and who thought he'd never live to see the end of those Yavorskis. Now we can send them begging on the highways and he can die in peace. And my master will also get some peace out of my good fortune because I won't need to remind him about that new suit of clothes he promised me in Lubnie even though I took a real fancy to it."

"You won't need to remind him because you've just done it!" Pan Yan said and sighed, shaking his head in disbelief at the crafty lad. "I've no idea what happened to that suit but since I promised it to you I'll get you one like it."

"Thank you kindly, master," Zjendjan said and pressed his head once more against Skshetuski's knees in a gesture of gratitude, humility, loyalty and genuine affection.

★   ★   ★

But although it seemed to Skshetuski as if Zjendjan's story would never get told, he got to the end of it in his own good time. He told how he recovered in Tchehryn, how he learned the art of healing by watching the herbalists and leeches who patched up his bruises, how he found out that Bohun was lying wounded in Tcherkassy, and how he became Bohun's personal physician, confidant and friend.

"What bothered me the most all that time, master, was worrying about you and our lady," he went on. "I didn't know what happened to either one of you. So that's why I figured I'd better get close to that devil Bohun on whom, if God helps me, I'll get my vengeance someday for what he did to me."

"Was he ill a long time?" Skshetuski interrupted.

"Yes sir. A long time, sir. That's because he let his wounds go too long chasing about the country after our lady and that fat gentleman like he did. They got infected. He was in a fever. I had a dozen chances to cut his throat but, truth to tell sir, I just couldn't do it. I swore on my soul that I'd pay him for the way he treated me in Tchehryn but when it came down to it I got ashamed of stabbing him in his bed."

"That's to your credit," Pan Yan said. "A cold-blooded murder of a helpless man would dishonor you forever."

"That's what I thought too."

"You'd not only hang for it under the laws of the Commonwealth," Pan Yan added, "but you'd forfeit all your lands, holdings, titles and possessions."

"And that's something else I had to think about, sir. And then it came to my mind what my granddad told me when I was leaving home and that settled it."

"And what did he tell you?"

"First he blessed me, master. Then he said: 'Remember, you bonehead, that you're gentry too. Serve faithfully, keep your head high, and don't let anybody treat you like a dog.'"

"That was well said," Pan Yan said.

"Yes sir. He also told me that our good Lord Jesus weeps every time somebody from the gentry behaves like a brute."

"Then He must have done a lot of weeping in recent years," Pan Yan observed sadly, "because it's our own greed and bad faith and cruelties that helped to bring these tragedies on our country."

"Yes, master. So I didn't stick Bohun with a knife when I had the chance and he got to trust me more every day while he was getting cured. '*How am I to reward you?*' he'd say to me time and time again, and I'd say to him '*Any way you want.*' And, truth to tell sir, he's right generous and as open-handed as a real noble. And the other Cossacks also showered me with all kinds of goods 'cause there's nobody they love and honor more than him, even though he's harder on peasants than any gentry that I've ever seen."

Here Zjendjan began to scratch his head as if he remembered something he couldn't understand. "That's a strange man, master . . . Sure, he's just a Cossack, but half the time you'd swear you were with some great lord, the way he behaves. And as for our lady . . ."

"He still loves her, then?"

"Does he ever, master! '*Where are you, little bird?*' he'd say all the time. '*What's happened to you and where can I find you?*' And then he'd remember Pan Zagloba and grind his teeth and bite his bedding and tear off his dressings till I had to drug him to put him to sleep. Even then he'd cry out and mutter about her."

"You're right. He's a strange, contradictory man," Pan Skshetuski said. "Good and evil are so mixed up in him that it's hard not to feel some sympathy for him even though his crimes can never be forgiven."

"That's just how I see it, sir," the boy said.

"And you say he had spells cast? Fortunes told?"

"The witch Horpyna, who's a sister of their Colonel Donyetz, came to tell his fortunes all the time. '*The Lah stands near her, the Lah is near,*' she'd say, and he'd turn white as a sheet and twist his hands and beg our lady to forgive him for coming after her like a bandit, and he swore over and over that he'd never lay a hand on her again but serve her on his knees like a dog."

"A strange, unhappy man," Skshetuski said quietly.

And it was Bohun, Zjendjan said, who arranged for him to go to Hushtcha with Father Patronius after the ataman recovered from his wounds and illness.

"Why would he do that when you became such a friend of his?" Pan Yan asked.

"Who knows, sir? Maybe he thought I'd be safer there 'cause all my goods were too tempting for the other Cossacks. Sure, they left me alone, seeing I was with Bohun, but who could tell what they'd do from hour to hour?"

"You owe him something, then," Pan Skshetuski said.

A cold fire glowed suddenly in the boy's narrowed eyes. "That I do. I'll find him someday in the field where it's alright for gentry to kill a man. And then he'll be paid."

"You're that unforgiving, then?"

"Everybody's got his own nature, master," Zjendjan said and shrugged. "And mine is to pay with good for good and evil for evil. But that's for later and it's all in God's hands anyway. And now we'll be going to the wedding, sir? To Bar and to our lady?"

"As soon as I get leave from the Prince in Tarnopol."

"Glory be! And when will we set out for Tarnopol, master?"

"Right after breakfast," Pan Yan said. "Get something on the table for us and then we'll mount up."

Zjendjan's eyes shifted suddenly to the floor and then he peered upward at Skshetuski with a smile of such utter innocence that even Pan Yan was deceived for a moment. "So soon, eh? Hmm. Well, God be blessed, the sooner the better, only . . ."

"Only what?"

"It's just that my poor nags are so tired, sir . . . so worn out with all that hard riding I did to get here all the way from Hushtcha . . . that I don't know if I'll be able to keep up with you, sir."

"You really are a wonder, Zjendjan," Pan Yan said and laughed. "You never miss a chance to get something, do you. Alright, then. I'll give you one of my remounts for the trip and you can keep him later. Now jump to it lad, serve our breakfast and be quick about it because I'm really hungry."

"Yes sir, right away sir, and . . .thank you kindly, master."

Zjendjan busied himself at the hearth while Pan Yan shook his head again at the boy's uncanny knack to acquire possessions. Counting the purse of ducats, the promised suit of clothes and the remount horse, he'd added three new gifts to his hoard in less than an hour.

But Pan Yan no sooner dressed and ate and went into the church square where his troops were forming for the march to Tarnopol when a messenger from the Prince galloped into the village. The Prince was no longer in Tarnopol, he reported. He had withdrawn to Zbarajh where Skshetuski was to join him as quickly as he could.

Chapter Thirty-five

RIDING WEST TO ZBARAJH they trailed slowly through such devastated country that food and fodder for their horses were impossible to find. Nothing seemed to live in that new man-made wilderness. Everything was scorched, trampled, looted and destroyed. The few homeless people whom they tracked down in the thickets pleaded with them to kill them. Once in a while they came across some emaciated woman, with a dead infant cradled in her arms, who begged for death so that her suffering might be finally over. Even Tartar slavery seemed like salvation to these starving wretches because the slavers would at least feed them on the trail. And this was all the more heartbreaking for the weary soldiers because this used to be a land that 'flowed with milk and honey,' so rich in grain and cattle that it could nourish the entire Commonwealth, and where no external enemy had set foot for two hundred years.

It wasn't until Skshetuski's column rode into the neighborhood of Yampol that the land around them ceased to resemble a graveyard and a battlefield, and they could requisition some food for their cooking pots and oats for their horses, and their march became swifter and more cheerful.

Zbarajh itself, when they reached it, was packed with troops and gentry who flocked from all over the Commonwealth to enlist under the Prince's banners.

Everyone talked of war.

The ruling peace party in Warsaw still favored negotiations but some of its perceptions underwent a change. Even some of the men closest to the regents began to understand that treaties made better sense when backed by strong armies so that the

Diet met in an atmosphere of warlike preparations. Chancellor Ossolinski still believed in peace at any price but he acceded to the will of the Senate which summoned all the gentry of the Commonwealth to arms in the first 'General Levy' since the Teutonic Wars. Under that law every man between sixteen and seventy years of age, whose family was entitled to a coat-of-arms, was to come *'armed and with all retainers'* to serve at his own cost for as long as needed. The regular standing army, or *Kwarta* as these troops were called because they were paid on each quarter of the year, was called in from distant garrisons as far as the Baltic, while the great magnates competed with each other in hiring veteran foreign mercenaries and raising private armies.

'*War!*'

Every wind seemed to carry that cry from province to province. It flew among the rich crops that stood untouched and unharvested in the fields and echoed in the forests. It lay on everybody's lips in every town and village wherever the gentry gathered to drink or argue, and no one uttered it without an awed mention of Yeremi Vishnovyetzki. The Prince's victories fired all imaginations. He had become a symbol of courage, duty, patriotism and glory from the Baltic provinces of Courland and Prussia in the north to the dark woods and passes of the Carpathian Mountains in the south.

'*War . . . and Vishnovyetzki.*'

His name seemed to shine like a beacon in the dark night of terror in the Ukraine. It rang across Lithuania, Ruthenia, Podlasye and the Byelorusian forests and woke a lust for punishment and vengeance in the gentry. It flew like wildfire from the Steppes to the Mazovian Plain and inflamed all minds with a craving to avenge Korsun and Yellow Waters. It stirred the rich, commercial provinces of Great Poland in the west to a memory of their warlike past.

War could be read in strange signs glimpsed in the sky, and in the burning eyes and faces, hot with passion, everywhere that Skshetuski's horsemen passed on their way to Zbarajh. It glittered in the steel of the weapons forged day and night in the smithies. It could be heard in the mournful baying of the village dogs and in the shrill neighing of the horses which could smell the blood before it was spilled.

'*War!*'

And at that word, brought by galloping messengers to every sleepy village and provincial manor in the country, old men searched the attics for armor and swords, young men ran to saddle and equip their horses, and women knelt and prayed before chapel altars.

'*War!*'

. . . And Vishnovyetzki.

★   ★   ★

But if throughout the length and breadth of the Commonwealth all eyes turned to him, and all mouths cried his name as if he were the Roman Marius of his time, so discipline and order began to crack even among the newly-raised regulars of the Crown contingents.

The new army was to assemble around the royal city of Lvov in Eastern Malopolska, and then in Glinyany where Prince Dominic Zaslavski was named as its Generalissimo and principal commander, but one regiment after another refused to follow the orders of the regents and marched off to Zbarajh. All of the General Levies of Kiev, Bratzlav, and the palatinates of Lublin and Ruthenia swarmed into Prince Yeremi's city. Then came many of the 'Quarter Troops,' the foreign mercenaries, and the hard-fisted infantry of the *Furrow Soldiers*, so-called because they were enlisted from serfs supplied by their masters at a rate of one for each ten furrows plowed on their estates. Even some of the senior regiments of heavy cavalry, in which only the most soldierly of the gentry were allowed to serve, mutinied against the generalship of Prince Dominic Zaslavski and rode off to join Yeremi Vishnovyetzki.

His stature grew each day. It became gigantic. It cast its shadow over the chancellor, the regency and the Diet, so that the legal rulers of the country began to wonder whether they had another Hmyelnitzki on their hands. All of the gentry and the army waited at his bidding. They were his to do with as he pleased. Questions of war and peace paled beside his sudden might and the future of the Commonwealth fell into his hands.

" . . . *A Marius, yes,*" said the men around the chancellor in Warsaw, and then recalled his former high-handed acts of disobedience. "*But perhaps a Marcus Coriolanus or a Cataline as well?*"

They cited his boundless pride and ruthless ambition. They murmured about his disrespect for laws that weren't to his liking and his contempt for policies other than his own. "*Who can deny him anything after that historic march from the Transdnieper and all his successes in the Ukraine? What will happen to the Commonwealth when one citizen acquires such enormous power that he can trample on the will of the Senate and strip its legal appointees of their authority merely by his presence? Does he really want to be only a king-maker for the young Prince Charles? And how high will his ambition drive him after that?*"

Pushed aside by the regents and officially deprived of all influence, he was becoming the Grand Hetman and principal commander of the Commonwealth none the less, and this was happening by the will of the gentry and the common soldiers. But if he took any pleasure in this elevation, there was never anyone to see it.

Time and again some regiment of *Kwarta* or provincial levies would roll into Zbarajh, and he'd come out to the castle walls, assess its value with a single glance, and go back to his quarters without a single word of comment or welcome.

"Lead us!" the soldiers cried, running after him and falling on their knees before him. "We'll stand or fall beside you!"

But he would merely thank them for remembering the needs of their country, remind them that he had no legal right to decide their destinies, and lock himself alone in his rooms with no company other than his thoughts.

★ ★ ★

Days passed like that. Weeks followed.

The town seemed to bulge with new swarms of soldiers and provincial gentry which poured through its gates in a flood that seemed to have no end.

The provincials drank from morning to nightfall. They staggered about the streets and picked fights with the officers of the foreign regiments, creating riots and disorders. The regulars, sniffing the cracks in discipline, whiled their time away with flagons of liquor, heaped platters and dice.

Each day saw new guests clattering into the town square. Magnates in gilded coaches drawn by thoroughbreds. Matched pairs of horses dressed in ostrich plumes and leather traces stamped in gold and purple. Harsh cries. Imperious commands to scatter the crowds.

"Make way! Out of the way there for the *Voyevode* . . . for his

lordship the Senator . . .! For the Lord High Constable of the
Crown . . .! For His Excellency!"

The gaping mobs of rank-and-file gentry bellowed their '*Vivat! Vivat!*' at each new cavalcade of coachmen, postilions and
outriders in German or Hungarian costumes, liveried Household Cossacks and turbanned janissaries that trooped about the
gilded and enameled coaches. They cheered the companies of
armed lackeys dressed like Tartars with oriental splendor. They
pointed at the proud, haughty faces of the magnates that stared
at them with restrained disdain out of the curtained windows.
They hurled their caps into the air at the sight of the aristocratic
hands that fluttered at them from the carriages.

"*Vivat! Vivat!*"

"*Greetings, brothers . . . greetings.*"

All of it pulsed and throbbed in the din and commotion of
vast crowds, in a kaleidoscope of jarring sights and colors,
brilliant uniforms and cloaks, plumed caps and hats, ornamental Turkish chain-mail and helmets of every kind and era, weapons of every sort, and horses of every hue and size.

It seemed to Skshetuski and his men as if half the Commonwealth had come to some mammoth celebratory fair or to one
of those great lobbying convocations that so delighted the pleasure loving gentry. The tumultuous encampments spilled far
beyond the town walls and spread into the surrounding villages
for a dozen miles.

Each night brought a new banquet, ball or some other entertainment with the willing wives and daughters of the shopkeepers and merchants. Every house, tavern, inn and shed was
full of quartered gentry. Every street was jammed with bivouacking soldiers, their wagons and piles of stores. The smaller
alleys were so thickly littered with straw and bales of hay that
they no longer served as thoroughfares.

★　★　★

Riding into these huge, swirling crowds, Skshetuski's worn
and ragged men were dazzled by the glitter of the jewels, the
glow of multicolored satins and brocades, and the gleam of
armor untouched by either the fury of the elements or enemy
weapons. A sea of plumed hats, fur caps, hoods lined with silks
and sables and helmets scrawled with gold, parted before them
and closed immediately behind them. A roar of questions,

curses and demands drowned out the clatter of their horses' hooves on the littered cobblestones.

"*War! Bring on the Cossacks! Where's that damned Krivoinos? Where's Hmyelnitzki? How long are we to be kept waiting here for those peasants?*"

"They're coming," said the Vishnovyetzki soldiers in their tired voices. "They're on their way. Don't any of you worry about that."

"*Let's have them here at once! We'll chop them into mincemeat! We're ready for them all!*"

But were they ready to face warriors like the Zaporohjans, Pan Yan thought, looking at this army.

Here, as he watched, a cavalcade of wealthy volunteers whose silks and satins never felt the pressure of a breastplate, pushed through the crowd on their costly Anatolian horses with diamond studs and ruby clasps glittering at their throats and a cascade of lesser gems dripping from egret plumes that nodded at their caps.

"*Make way there! Make way!*"

The crowds of lesser gentry parted, bowing with respect in the presence of such imposing soldiers, each of whom carried enough gold and jewels on his well-fed body to hire a regiment of German musketeers.

And there, freshly stitched into a shining new military tabard and puffed up with pride on the porch of a noisy hostelry strutted the portly officer of some furrow-hopping provincial battalion, with a willow switch thrust under his arm like the cane of a veteran mercenary commander, and with a shopkeeper's nervous heart fluttering in his chest.

And everywhere, as far as the Vishnovyetzki men could see through the crowded alleys, swirled a mass of lackeys, messengers, gilded coaches and heavy baggage trains, and all of it was so splendid, so richly plumed and jeweled, that it made Prince Yeremi's soldiers look like beggars in comparison.

They rode in on gaunt nags that could hardly lift their shaggy heads or place one faltering hoof before another, and with hides that were so badly scabbed and blistered across their ribs that they seemed like rejects from a knacker's yard.

The soldiers' own coats gaped with holes. Their cloaks trailed in rags. Their once-brilliant uniforms were so patched and faded that they resembled shipwrecked mariners more than the

victorious troops of a great commander. Their armor was
scarred, pitted and brown with rust. Their dented helmets had
lost their plumes long ago, and their worn, bearded faces were
burned raw by the winds of their campaigns, scorched by the
sun of their legendary marches, and blackened with the gunpowder of their innumerable raids, ambushes and battles. But
all the jeweled hats were swept off before them as if they were
princes, and all the bared heads bowed low as they passed,
because this rust and misery were recognized everywhere as the
marks of heroes.

"*Vivat* the Vishnovyetzki men!" the crowds roared and
pressed around them, eager to touch that rust and those faded
colors as if they were relics. "Long live our conquering heroes!"

"*Vivat! Vivat!*"

"Make way for the victors! Saviors of the country!"

"Thank the Prince," the soldiers murmured. "Not us. We win
the battles only because he leads us."

"Long live the Prince, then! Our own Slavic Hercules! Caesar!
Scipio Africanus!"

As extravagant in all their sentiments as they were in dress,
the gentry viewed its leaders only in extremes. They offered
either boundless admiration or an equally unreasoning hatred
and contempt.

"We won't follow anybody else!" they bellowed, pressing
about the Vishnovyetzki soldiers. "Long live our Hetman! Our
own Alexander! To Hell with Prince Dominic and all the other
regents!"

"*Vivat Vishnovyetzki!*"

And the returning Vishnovyetzki soldiers creaked and clattered through those celebrating streets like bewildered specters
which had accidentally strayed from another world, hardly able
to understand what they saw around them, and even less able to
believe that days of rest were coming.

★   ★   ★

Pan Yan wanted to forget all the pains and stresses of his
deadly labors and to kick up his heels among his friends as
much as anyone. But what he wanted more than anything was
to go to Bar, find Helen again, and shed all his bitter anxieties
about her in her loving arms. This merciful, joyful end to his

tormenting visions would restore him better, he knew, than any amount of carefree celebrating.

He went to see the Prince as soon as Zjendjan found him some new clothes in the Armenian trading booths that sprung up like mushrooms outside the town walls, to give his report about the Zaslav expedition and to apply for leave.

He found Prince Yeremi changed beyond belief. He seemed aged by years, stooped like an old man under the weight of an insupportable burden, licking his parched lips and staring blankly out of caved-in eyes as if he were in the grip of some devouring internal disease.

In spite of all his own disciplined self-control, Pan Yan could only stare at him in horror. Nor could he hold back an involuntary shudder, sure that he was looking at a man drained to the limits of his strength and pushed far beyond all powers of endurance. He couldn't believe that this was the same indomitable leader whom he saw with lightnings flashing from his eyes at Mahnovka and at Konstantinov. The young lieutenant, whose own struggles between desire and duty streaked his beard and hair with a grizzled silver, simply couldn't recognize his energetic, ruthless and decisive master in this apparition. This was someone whom he'd never seen before . . . some tormented, nightmare-driven creature which had sunk into a morass of doubt like a fevered hermit wrestling with temptation.

Asked about his health, as the form and usage of the times demanded, the Prince snapped out a dry, abrupt reply that he was well enough and Pan Yan didn't dare to question him further. And it was only after his report, and after he asked whether he might have two months' leave so that he could go to Bar, marry Princess Helen, and then take her to his estates in Podlasye where she would be safe, that the Prince seemed to come alive again and to shake himself free of his oppressive thoughts like a man waking from a dream.

"Ah," he said warmly as his furrowed brows cleared and his eyes focused on his favorite soldier with something of their old brilliance and affection. "So that's the end of *your* suffering . . ."

"God was merciful, Highness," Pan Yan murmured.

"You must thank Him for it."

A spasm of pain twisted the Prince's features as if he'd long given up all hope of similar mercy for himself and Pan Yan felt his heart constricting with pity.

"Go, go then," the Prince went on and pressed the young soldier's head against his chest like a father sharing a son's joy. "And may God give you all His blessings because you've earned every one of them.

"Yes, I know,"—he nodded, looking into his own dark thoughts again—"I know that I should be going with you to your wedding . . . I owe at least that much to the Kurtzevitch girl as the daughter of *Knaz* Vasil who was my father's friend . . . And I owe it to you too, my dear loyal friend. But there can be no leave for me in these times . . . no, not in these days.

"So," he resumed after another moment. "When do you want to go?"

"I'd start out today if I could, Your Highness!" Skshetuski cried out.

"So take your leave from tomorrow morning, then."

Prince Yeremi nodded and smiled at Skshetuski and then a new deep line of worry creased his careworn face.

"But you can't go alone, not across that country," he snapped out in his old, decisive military manner. "I'll give you three hundred of Vyershul's best Tartars for an escort. They're my fastest horsemen and you might need them over there because, as I hear it, the rebellion has spread even as far as the territories around Bar. I'll get some letters written for you as well so that they'll hand the girl over to you without any trouble. But it'll be nightfall tomorrow, I should think, before all that is done and Vyershul's men are back from their own sweep. So get a night's rest, see your friends, pack and get ready for the trip and come back to see me tomorrow."

"Thank you, Your Highness!" Pan Yan bowed, kneeling before the Prince who once again pressed his head gently in his hands. "But, if I may ask for another favor . . ."

"What is it?"

"If Volodyovski and Podbipyenta could come with me . . ."

"Take them." Prince Yeremi nodded. "Come back and say goodbye to me before you set out. I'd like to find something for you to take along as a gift for your girl as well, because that's good, honest blood and ought to be honored. Go now. Be happy together. You deserve each other."

Once more, as if he were asking for a father's blessing, the young soldier pressed his forehead to the Prince's knees. "May God keep you," the Prince repeated quietly. "May He send you joy. Now leave me. Go and come back tomorrow."

But Pan Yan remained on his knees as if he had another request to make and, finally, after struggling with his own deep-seated sense of discipline and duty, he burst out: "Your Highness!"

"What else have you to tell me?" the Prince asked.

"Forgive the impertinence, sir, but . . . but . . . it's enough to break a man's heart, the way Your Highness looks. What's wrong with you, Highness? Are you ill? Or is it something else I would understand?"

"That's not for you to know about, my boy," Prince Yeremi said softly and placed his hand on the young man's head. "Go now. And be sure to come back tomorrow before you set out."

Pan Yan rose, bowed, and left with a dark wave of grief and pity flooding through his chest.

★ ★ ★

That night the young lieutenant had guests in his quarters. Old Pan Zachvilihovski came to welcome him back from his expedition and so did little Pan Volodyovski, Pan Longinus and Pan Zagloba as well. They sat down at the table even before the evening lamps were lit and, at once, Zjendjan brought in a tray of goblets and a keg of prime, vintage *Troyniak* sent over by the Prince's steward.

"In the name of the Father, the Son and the Holy Ghost!" Pan Zagloba cried out at the sight of Zjendjan. "I see we've had a resurrection here! So you're back from the dead, are you, my fine lad?"

Zjendjan grinned and embraced the fat knight's massive knees. "There was no resurrection because I never died," he said. "But the fact that I'm alive is all your doing, master, because I wouldn't be if you hadn't saved me."

"And then he joined up with Bohun himself," Skshetuski explained.

"He did, did he? Then he'll get a pension in Hell," Pan Zagloba said and added kindly to the grinning boy: "But since you couldn't have had much pleasure in that service, my lad, here is a silver thaler to make you feel better."

"Thank you kindly, master," Zjendjan said, bowing low and pocketing the coin.

"That one?" Skshetuski cried. "That's a fox if there ever was one! He bought up more loot among the Cossacks than you and I could find between us, even if you sold off all those Turkish possessions of yours."

"Is that so?" Pan Zagloba eyed the lad with new respect. "Keep that thaler then and grow, my little sapling, because even if you don't grow great enough to provide the timbers for a Holy Cross you might grow big enough to become a handy little gibbet."

And here the fat knight caught the boy by the ear and tugged it gently.

"I like quick wits," he went on. "And so I prophesy— which is an art I learned from a certain Magus when I was in service to the Sultan—that you'll get to be an important human being someday if you don't turn into an ox in the meanwhile. But how does Master Bohun remember your services, eh? With gratitude, I expect?"

"Oy master!" Zjendjan cried, flattered by Zagloba's interest. "I don't know how he remembers me but you should see him when he remembers *you*! He grinds his teeth so hard that sparks fly, I swear it!"

"Go to the Devil!" Pan Zagloba roared at once, losing his good humor. "What are you babbling about here, you damned little fool?"

Zjendjan bowed and left, somewhat puzzled by this sudden change in Pan Zagloba's humor, but glad to stow another piece of silver in his saddlebags.

They talked, then, about the next day's journey to Bar in Podolia and about the great happiness that waited for Skshetuski in that great eastern bastion of the Commonwealth. They let the wine flow freely, looking forward to better times, and the powerful vintage mead soon improved Pan Zagloba's humor. He teased Pan Yan about all the future christenings that he'd provide for their entertainment, and about the many good-looking young knights who flocked around Helen in Bar. He was particularly eloquent in his praises of the handsome young Pan Yendrei Pototzki, the youngest son of the captured Grand

Hetman of the Crown and the last surviving brother of the heroic Stephan who died at Yellow Waters.

"You'd think he was a stallion in the Steppe in Springtime," the fat knight related, "the way he snorts and paws the ground whenever she's around. Any day now he'll start neighing, I expect."

"A lot of good that'll do him once Skshetuski gets there," the old commissioner said.

"Well, one man's wedding is another's mourning." The fat knight tossed a sideways glance at the Lithuanian. "Particularly if he didn't make any vows of chastity, which is a pagan thing to do anyway and goes against the laws of nature as well as God's wishes."

Pan Longinus heaved a sigh, thinking about Anusia, and the little knight joined the Lithuanian giant with a few sighs of his own. Finally the talk turned to the coming resumption of the war and to their commander.

"What's wrong with him?" Skshetuski wished to know. "I tell you, that's a different man. I can't make head or tail of this change in him. I mean here he is, with one great victory after another behind him, and the entire Commonwealth knocking on his door. What difference does it make that they passed him over for the regency and the high command? All the gentry and half of the new army are marching to join him anyway. He'll be the Grand Hetman of the Commonwealth no matter what anybody says. But here he is like a man in the deepest mourning, or in some kind of fever . . . Does anybody know what it's all about?"

"Maybe he's got a chill in the bones," Pan Zagloba offered. "Sometimes when I get a twinge in my finger I'm out of sorts for three days or more."

"And I, sweet brothers, can tell you only this much about it," Pan Longinus murmured. "Mind you, I didn't hear it from Father Muhovyetzki himself . . . no, I can't say I did. But someone said—and I don't know who—that this is what the Father told him about the Prince's troubles . . ."

"Told him what?" Pan Zagloba said. "Said what? So far nobody here has said anything worth hearing."

"I'm not saying anything on my own part," the bashful giant stumbled on, twisting his great hands so that the knuckles cracked. "He's a great lord and a kindly master, I am sure, so

who am I to say anything about him? But if Father
Muhovyetzki said . . . or as I heard he said . . . ah, what do I
know anyway . . ."

"Not much, but that's no news to anybody!" Pan Zagloba
cried out at once, then turned to the others. "But will you just
listen to this Lithuanian? Didn't I tell you that they don't use a
human language up there in those forests? How am I to poke
fun at him when he can't dredge even one clear sentence out of
that beanpole head? What are you trying to tell us anyway,
Master Podbipyenta? You're running around in circles like a
blind jackrabbit that can't find the opening to his burrow."

"Seriously, though," Pan Yan said. "What did you hear? It
could be important."

"Ah well, if that's the case . . ." Red with embarrassment,
Pan Longinus struggled with his shyness. "Well, I don't want to
seem like I'm spreading gossip, but some people say that His
Highness has spilled too much blood, you see . . . He's a great
war leader, maybe the greatest that we'll ever see, but he has no
mercy in his punishments. So people are saying that now everything he sees turns red before his eyes. His days are red, they say,
his nights are all red . . . it's like there's a red fog around
everything he looks at . . ."

"Don't talk such rubbish!" old Pan Zachvilihovski exploded
in anger. "We've enough gossips among us as it is! There wasn't
a fairer lord in the Commonwealth in peacetime and if he has no
mercy on murderers and rebels, what of it? That's to his credit
rather than a sin. What kind of torture and what kind of punishment is too much for people who drown their own Motherland
in blood? Where else on earth will you find monsters who give
their own kind to the Tartar slavers? Who else ever committed
such atrocities on women and children? Where can you find
more frightful crimes than theirs? And you say that the stake
and the gibbet are too harsh for them? Tfui, tfui! You've an iron
fist, mister, but you've the heart of a woman! I heard you
groaning when they stretched that Pulyan over the coals after
Konstantinov. I heard you muttering that you wished you'd
killed him straight out instead of bringing him alive for interrogation. But the Prince isn't an old woman, he knows how to
reward and how to punish too! So don't sit here spinning fairy
tales!"

"But I said I didn't know anything about it at first hand," the distressed Pan Longinus tried to explain himself. "I said it was just something that people were saying . . ."

"If our people learned to use their tongues like millstones," Pan Zagloba said, "we'd grind enough flour in this Commonwealth to pave the world with pancakes."

But the old man wouldn't be appeased. "Red fog, indeed!" he grunted for a while longer, stroking his snow-white hair and quivering with rage. "I'll give them a red fog. Whoever thought up that one has a green fog in his head, not a red one!"

"So what do you think it is, father?" asked the little knight. "What's wrong with our Prince?"

"I don't know," the old commissioner muttered in reply. "Whatever it is he keeps it to himself. But it's some sort of a struggle with his own soul, I'd say. And the greater the soul, the harder the struggle."

Chapter Thirty-six

THE SENTRIES ON the castle walls were already calling out the '*All's Well*' of midnight but Yeremi Vishnovyetzki was still talking to his God and wrestling with his own ambition and his conscience.

He lay on the stone floor of his chamber, eyes fixed on the crucifix hanging on a wall, and fought the most terrible antagonist he ever faced. His mind and his spirit—that soaring pride and that overwhelming love of country that burned like twin beacons in his soul—struggled with his consciousness of his destiny and power as if they were bands of gladiators who fought each other in a duel to the death. It was a struggle which seemed to split his head with pain and to threaten reason. He felt as if his chest was crushed between a pair of millstones.

Here—against the will of the *interrex*, the Primate of his Church, and challenging the authority of the chancellor, the Senate, the regents and the government itself—all of the nation's armies were ranging behind him.

Here came the regular cavalry of the Crown and the other magnates; the foreign mercenaries who never before broke an oath of loyalty; all of the vast, unruly gentry in its many district and provincial levies; the disciplined, long-term veterans of the *Kwarta* and the *Furrow Soldiers*. The Commonwealth itself seemed to be running to him, looking for shelter under his outspread wings like a flock of fledglings, and pleading for protection.

"*Save us,*" it cried to him through the voices of its best and noblest sons. "*Only you can do it!*"

Another month, he thought, and a hundred thousand warriors will stand under these walls ready to follow him against the many-headed monster of the civil war.

And here the images of the future, bathed in some unearthly light of power and glory, began to pass before Vishnovyetzki's eyes.

Oh how they'll shudder, he thought about all those hostile, envious men in Warsaw who wanted to humble and humiliate him. How small they will become! How pitiful and contemptible and insignificant . . .!

And he, meanwhile, would seize these iron cohorts that flocked to him in thousands and lead them to such victories in the Ukraine that not even the recorded triumphs of imperial Rome would be able to match them.

And at this thought he felt a blast of superhuman power surging through his body. He felt as if huge wings were sprouting from his shoulders, as though he were being suddenly transformed into the Archangel Michael, the holy patron of his own family and House. He saw his own gigantic stature looming above the castle as if Zbarajh itself was too small to contain his spirit and casting his huge shadow across all the vastness of Ruthenia and the Eastern Lands. He knew beyond all doubts that he could crush Hmyelnitzki, trample the rebellion into dust and ashes, bring back a new and lasting peace and restore tranquility to his tormented country.

"I can do it!"

His cry, whether it was imaginary or real, flew along the stone walls of his chamber, echoed in the groined arches of the ceiling and seemed to burst through the walls onto the battlements and far into the night beyond them. His eyes filled with the sight of vast fields and a sea of warriors. He heard the roar of cannon thundering in his ears . . . Battle! A slaughter without precedent in history! A triumph beyond all triumphs known to any warriors anywhere! Thousands of corpses litter the landscape between the horizons. Thousands of fallen banners sheet the bloody Steppes. He saw himself trampling the carcass of the overthrown Hmyelnitzki, and he could hear the trumpets that cried out his victory, and then their brassy voices were proclaiming his triumph from sea to sea across the generations.

"I can do it! Only I can do it!"

Trembling as if in the grip of a mortal fever Yeremi Vishnovyetzki struggled to his feet, lifted his arms towards the

hanging Christ, and a terrible scarlet light seemed to burn in the
air around him.

"Chryste! Chryste!" he cried. "You know! You see that I can
do this! Tell me that I must!"

But the crucified image hung in deathly silence, the bloodless
face had fallen forward under its crown of thorns, and the
outspread arms gleamed whitely in the candleglow as if the Son
of Man had only just been nailed to his cross.

"It's for *Your* glory!" cried the Prince. "It's not for me or my
sake but only for *Yours!* It's for the Church . . . for all Christianity!"

In the red light which painted murderous shadows on the
grey stone walls his cry seemed to ring with the purity of crystal
but he heard it as the dull bronze booming of coronation bells.

"No, not for me!" he cried. "Not for me! *Non mihi! Non mihi!
Sed nomini Tuo da gloriam!*"

And then another vast, flowing image began to fill the burning
eyes of Yeremi Vishnovyetzki. The triumph over
Hmyelnitzki was only a beginning. The road lifted farther.
How far would it take him? Having crushed the rebellion and
swallowed its hordes like an avenging dragon, he'd add the
curbed, armed Cossack multitudes to his own, carry his fire and
sword into the Crimea, topple the minarets of Islam and, finally,
accomplish the goal of generations to nail Christ's Holy
Cross above the iron towers of the Khans where no bells had
ever called for a Christian prayer.

"For You," he whispered to the silent Christ. "Not for me.
For You."

But even that was only a beginning. He'd go into those
unknown eastern countries where only a few of his own ancestors
had ventured: the endless plains and rivers beyond the
Wild Lands and the Burning Deserts, that jeweled continent
which lay across the Mountains of the East; and he'd extend the
boundaries of his Commonwealth and of God's Church to the
farthest reaches of the earth!

"*Ad gloriam Tuam*," he whispered.

Where would this end? Where could it? When would he come
to the final limits of his might . . . his power . . . and his own
great glory?

"Never," he whispered.

There was no end to what he might achieve if he just reached out and seized the power that a desperate nation was thrusting upon him. If he did what his pride demanded of his genius. If he obeyed the call of his destiny.

The dead white light of the moon seeped through the transept windows into the cold stone chamber where the candles drowned in their own wax and guttered hours earlier. The tower clocks were striking the final hours of the night. Soon, he knew, the cocks would start crowing outside the town walls.

Daylight was almost here.

He listened to the silence, waiting for that bloodless, waxen face to lift on its cross, for those sad, knowing eyes to signal their compassion and their understanding, and for that one great voice which would raise him above all the men and peoples of his time.

"*Non mihi, Domine,*" he prayed. "*Non mihi . . .!*"

And then he was shuddering in the sudden grey chill of dawn. What will this new day bring to the sleeping, unsuspecting world other than a sunrise? Will another, earthly sun begin to shine in all its power and glory under that fiery brightness that God sent daily into the sky?

"*Chryste . . . Chryste . . .*"

And the terrible struggle went on, unabated.

★ ★ ★

He would have had to be a child, not a man, to think that there might be another way for him, or that he could turn his back on his destiny for whatever reason.

That's it, he thought. That's how it has to be. He was a man of his times, and a Prince-Palatine at that, and faith in the rightness of his causes was enough to make them both righteous and holy. Pride and ambition went hand-in-hand with duty, so what difference would it make if his own stature soared above all others as long as that elevation served and protected the Commonwealth as well?

"Your will be done," he whispered to the silent image of the crucified sufferer before him, sure that his own sudden sense of peace was the answer he was looking for, and that this answer came to him from God.

"*Fiat voluntas Tua.*"

He breathed easier then.

The roaring hurricane drifted from his mind, passed on,

disappeared. His thoughts calmed down, cleared and settled as gently as falling leaves into their natural and God-given order, and he could see and understand again all those essential matters that affected the Commonwealth at this decisive moment. The peace policy of the chancellor, the regents, and of *Voyevode* Kisyel was a bad one. Deadly for the country. He would tear it up. The road to a just and lasting peace had to be carved out with swords, not with pens on parchment. All of the *Zaporohje* had to be turned into a burial mound, the *Sietch* razed to the ground and the *Nizhovtsy* hammered into disciplined obedience. The murderous specter of unruly Cossack independence had to be exorcised, the Cossackry crushed and beaten down forever, its aspirations drowned in its own blood and its poison drawn.

'Then—and only then—grant to the conquered all they've ever wanted. End all excesses. Finish with oppression. Restore peace and tranquility to everyone who lives in the Commonwealth, not just to the gentry.'

"Instead of fear of death," he murmured. "Give them a new life."

In place of the expected *coup de grace*, he thought, extend the hand of brotherhood and friendship. Lift up the Cossacks to the equality they want. But do it as an act of grace, a gesture of nobility, forgiveness and mercy, not as surrender to their lawlessness and terror. It was all so clear to him that he could read his own thoughts as if they were written in letters of fire on the chamber walls.

'That's the only path worthy of this great and splendid Commonwealth. There isn't another. Perhaps in other times, long ago, there was a different road that all of us could travel together. We might have been able to talk to each other. Lords and magnates, the princes and the gentry, the Cossacks and the peasants, everyone. All faiths and conditions. But not now. Not now. No, not after all that treason, bloodshed and bad faith. Not when these armed thousands face each other in hatred, craving blood and vengeance. Peace on those terms? That's a dream for fools! An empty illusion! Giving way to terror will merely spin the war across generations. Such peacemaking will do nothing more than assure our children and grandchildren a sea of blood and tears.'

Let the Commonwealth take that other, nobler road, he thought. Let it destroy the monster, tear down its own edifices of injustice, and then build a splendid new reality from the blood and ruins. Let it do that and he'll be happy to sit quietly in his beloved Lubnie the rest of his life.

"That's all I want," he whispered.

But who was to lead the way? The Senate? The stormy Diets at which the gentry could agree on nothing? The chancellor? The primate and the regents?

Who other than himself could grasp and understand that great but simple truth of punishment before generosity and forgiveness? And who else had the means to transform this vision into a fact of history?

'*Find such a man and I'll follow him,*' he thought. But where is he? Who else in the Commonwealth has the ability as well as the power?

"No one," he whispered. "Other than myself."

It was to him that the gentry and the army were marching in their thousands, wasn't it? It was he who had turned himself into the sword and buckler of the Commonwealth. But where was his mandate? Who gave him the authority to decide on the life and death of these tens of thousands? This was no absolute monarchy such as existed everywhere else in Europe, he knew very well. Not Bourbon France or Stuart England where a monarch ruled by divine right, answerable to no authority but his own. The will of the nation ruled this Commonwealth even when there was a King on the throne in Warsaw, and how much more so now when there was no King?

"This is what gives us our power and our greatness," the Prince murmured proudly. "That's the '*lex suprema.*'"

That will expressed itself in more than parchment, argument, laws and manifestos. It had a life beyond the policies of chancellors, deputies and the Senate. Yes, they wrote the laws. But in whose name? Who gave them that power? This was a republic of the gentry, ruled by a King whom they elected to the throne only for the length of his own natural life, with no right of succession given to his heirs. The chancellor and the Senate governed in his name and by his appointment, provided that the Diets of Deputies, elected in every province and district of the Commonwealth by more than half a million of the voting gentry, gave their own unanimous approval to all resolutions.

So who were the real rulers of the country?

"We are," the Prince said, feeling the strength that comes

from certainty and conviction. "The knighthood . . . the *rytzerstvo* . . . the crested gentry . . . every man entitled by law to inherit lands and to wear a saber, and so obliged by that same law to serve and defend the Commonwealth."

And wasn't all the knighthood of the country coming here to Zbarajh in their tens of thousands to tell him that he was the commander of their choice? And was he to refuse this call to power and greatness? Why should he refuse it? What other nomination did he need? And from whom? From those whose timid policies threatened to destroy the Commonwealth and whose suspicions and ill-will humiliated him?

"And why do they do that to me anyway?" he muttered fiercely. "How did I deserve it? Is it because I was the only one among the magnates to strike at the Cossacks? Because I didn't give way to panic when the Hetmans went into captivity, the armies perished, the great lords hid themselves in their castles, and the Cossack put his knife to the throat of our Motherland? Because I wrenched that knife out of that bloody fist and lifted our Mother's head out of the mud, and breathed new life into her, and saved her from her shame?"

Pride soared before his anger like a crimson mist. Anger gave way to rage.

"Why didn't they see fit to sacrifice their fortunes and risk their lives for her?" he demanded. "Where were they when she was on her knees and begging them to save her? And now they dare to tell *me* what to do . . .?

"Show me someone who did more than I to earn this authority and power," he cried out. "And I'll give it to him. Gladly. Let him command here . . . rule . . . lead, if he knows the way. I'm tired. I've come to just about the end of all my strength. And I don't need the glory. I've won enough of it to reflect on all my children's children far beyond my grave. I'd just as soon ask God and the people to let me throw down this burden and go my own way. But where is this man? Who is he? Why doesn't he come forward?"

And if there is no such man, he thought, how can I turn a deaf ear to my country's pleading? And why should I do that anyway? By whose order?

He raised his head proudly once again, and his fevered eyes fell once more on the hanging Christ. The crucifix seemed to shimmer in a scarlet mist. The tortured head hung limp and lifeless above the wounded chest. The pale lips were parted in such agony as if another lancehead had just been thrust into Christ's bleeding side.

"Why?" the Prince asked aloud again. "Tell me why! Why should I?"

★ ★ ★

He pressed both his hands against his pounding temples. A voice . . . many voices . . . were calling to him through those blood-red visions of his future glory. He barely heard them through the rustling of those distant triumphs; they were so hard to catch across the urging of his own impatience and through the glittering awareness of his destiny and greatness and ambition.

'*Wait,*' they cried. '*Wait . . .*'

For what? And what was this new, gnawing pain that started to coil and uncoil in his chest as if a terrible serpent had awakened there?

Why was it that just when he was ready to cast all his doubts aside, and when he proved to himself beyond any question that it was his duty as well as his right to reach out for the powers of the supreme commander, something was whispering to him out of the deepest recesses of his conscience?

'*You are deluding yourself . . .*'

"How's that?" he demanded.

'*Your injured pride is leading you astray. The voices you heard were not those of reason.*'

"What voices were they, then?"

'*Satan is tempting you with visions of power, promising you a Crown . . .*'

And the terrible struggle broke out anew in Yeremi Vishnovyetzki. Again doubt seized him like a whirlwind and carried him off into uncertainty and terror. He asked himself: What was the country's gentry really doing when it came flocking to his camp rather than to the gathering place appointed by the regents? It trampled on the law, was the clear answer. What was the army doing? Disobeying orders. And was he—a loyal citizen, a patriot and a soldier—to place himself at the head of . . . lawlessness? Was he to give the dignity and authority of his name to public disobedience? What sort of example would that

be to the generations that must come behind him if this great
Commonwealth was to endure and prosper?

My God, he thought. My God . . .!

'*So Vishnovyetzki flouts the law today . . . so what magnate won't
feel free to do the same tomorrow? Who'll stop some future Pototzki,
Lubomirski, Firley or Zamoyski from tearing up the statutes any time
he pleases once the precedent of defiance has been set? And when each of
us does only what suits his own purpose, when he follows the dictates of
his own ambition rather than of conscience and serves his own needs
instead of the country, what kind of future can our poor Commonwealth
expect?*'

He shuddered. He slid back to his knees. His hands opened
and closed on empty air as if he were clutching and grasping at
something that must elude him for his own salvation and he
looked at them with disbelief and loathing.

'*Jezu . . . Jezu . . . What have I almost done?*'

Hmyelnitzki also justifies himself under the cover of a greater
good, Prince Yeremi thought, tugging at his hair. He also sees
himself as the only savior of his people while he turns on those
in authority over him, challenges the dignity of the State, and
defies the law.

'*Chryste . . .!*'

The Prince trembled from head to foot and crushed his pale
hands together in a paroxysm of disgust and terror. Blood filled
his mouth as he bit his lips.

"Am I to be a second Hmyelnitzki?" he cried out. "Tell me! Is
that what I'm doing?"

But the crucifix hung mute among its scarlet shadows as the
first rays of the sun began to seep into the greying chamber.

★   ★   ★

Hours passed like that. The struggle continued. The Prince
knew that if he seized the power of supreme command the
chancellor and regents would proclaim him a rebel and a traitor,
no better than Hmyelnitzki, and that a second civil war could
very well begin.

"Is that what you want?" he asked himself bitterly in a dull
voice heavy with self-contempt. "Is that where your pride has
led you?"

He knew that Hmyelnitzki wasn't the worst enemy who ever
threatened the life of this republic. Not in the past, and certainly

not now. There had been others . . . many, many others . . .
who brought invasions to these enduring lands and whose
bones were still littering the far-flung frontiers. How much
greater was the danger of absolute destruction when two hundred thousand armored Germans rode against the Poles and
Lithuanians of Vladyslav Yagiello on the field of *Grunwald* only
a little more than two hundred years ago! How much more
terrible the more recent moment when the hordes of Moscow
faced Stefan Batory in the plains of Pskov! And where were they
now? Only the wolves knew their resting places and the wind
whistled dirges through their scattered bones. So what would
one more Cossack hurricane mean in the context of such a
history? What could a single upstart Cossack and his Tartar
allies do against such an enduring and determined power?

No, the Commonwealth didn't need to fear foreign wars, he
knew. Germans, Russians, Hungarians, Turks and Tartars came
time and time again and crumbled before the iron walls of the
Commonwealth's defenders. It wouldn't be the clash of battle
that would ring the death-knell of that nation.

'*The seeds of our destruction are rooted in ourselves*,' he cried out
silently to himself.

And the most desperate and pernicious of these dangers, he
knew with bitterness and pain, lay in the pride and overwhelming personal ambitions of magnates like himself, each of whom
went his own way according to his fancy, choosing those laws
and policies that he would obey and those that he'd flout whenever he wanted, and setting an example of quarrelsome disobedience to the lesser gentry.

'*Anarchy instead of loyalty and obedience . . . Undisciplined armies
making their own decisions about who would lead them . . .*'

And what about that ungovernable population of eight hundred thousand bickering and squabbling nobles who questioned
and debated every law and order? What of the parliaments in
which nothing was decided because a single vote cast in opposition ended all discussion?

'*The rule of chaos, argument and disputes over private interests
which greed and envy always elevated above the common good. Inepti-
tude and indifference in the seats of power.*'

"That's what makes us helpless before one ambitious Cossack," he groaned in despair. "That's why callous neighbors
claw at our frontiers with impunity, why other nations laugh

and jeer at us, and why no one hears our voice or fears our anger."

A tree rots from the core, he thought. Any windstorm can topple a hollow forest giant. But cursed be he who'd help in the process! Damned be the man who set such an example to his children's children! An eternity of hellfire wouldn't be enough for such a matricide.

"So go now, you Prince-Palatine," he told himself in horror and contempt. "Go, you triumphant conqueror and commander, and take their lawful authority from the regents. Spit on the statutes, as you've done before. Trample on the law. Add to the disunity and disorder. Show future generations how to murder and disembowl their Mother."

Terror and desperation mirrored the sudden madness in the Prince's eyes. He cried out in a stricken voice, seized himself with both hands by the hair, and threw himself into the dust before the crucifix.

"Forgive me, Lord," he prayed. "Have mercy. Have mercy."

And he struck the stone floor with his forehead again and again.

★ ★ ★

Dawn had come some time earlier, painting the horizon in delicate shades of pink, and now the sun burst redly into Vishnovyetzki's chamber. The swallows that built their nests in the deep casements of the castle windows began to chatter, sparrows darted by, and he rose with a look of peace etched into his face, like a traveler who comes home from a difficult journey, and went to wake the young body-servant who slept outside his door.

"Wake up, lad," he murmured. "I've an errand for you."

The boy, that same Zelenski who risked his life in Lubnie by cutting short the torments of Hmyelnitzki's impaled emissary, leaped to his feet, rubbing the sleep out of his eyes, and stared at his master as if he were a dead man returning from his grave.

"H-H-Highness," he stammered, frightened by this drawn and pale apparition. "Y-y-your Highness . . . is . . . are you unwell? Are . . . is everything all right?"

"Run to the duty officer," Prince Yeremi said. "Tell him to send for all the colonels quartered in the town, the *Kwarta* as well as the provincials. Have them come to the Great Hall here in the castle as soon as they can."

The boy ran as if his shoes were burning and with excitement shining in his face because everyone expected Prince Yeremi to seize the powers offered by the gentry and the look in his eyes signaled a decision.

Within two hours the audience hall filled with Vishnovyetzki officers. Pan Yan and Pan Michal brought the fat knight and the Lithuanian giant who weren't troop commanders but who'd become so famous among the Prince's men that no one could remember the time when they didn't take part in their gatherings. The only absentee was Kushel who was off on reconnaissance in the direction that Skshetuski was to take later in the day because word had come that the rebellion was spreading in Podolia where Krivoinos was plundering the country near Bar.

"It looks as if we're going there just in time," little Pan Volodyovski murmured to Pan Yan, Zagloba and Podbipyenta, but Skshetuski was too happy to allow anything to darken his mood.

"It would take more than a mob of rebels to take a fortress like Bar," he said, shaking his head and smiling. "That's our strongest castle in the east next to Kamyenetz and Kudak."

"That's right," agreed the experienced Osinski. "You'd need Swedish infantry to storm walls like that."

"Or Germans," growled the dour Korytzki.

"And only after a regular, well-engineered siege," Osinski added. "Sapping, approaches, trenches, culverts and siege engines . . . mining the walls and gates . . . you know what I mean. The Zaporohjans are first rate defending their own earthworks but if they don't take a fortified position at one blow they tend to get discouraged and a siege takes time."

"At least six months for a place like Bar," Korytzki agreed.

"And we'll be there with Prince Yeremi long before that passes," said Volodyovski.

"God grant it soon!" cried the listening officers while Pan Zagloba let his enthusiasm sweep him away altogether.

"The sooner the better!" he shouted since the prospects of an actual battle were still somewhat distant. "This is what we've been waiting for! The Prince is going to send the regents packing, as I've advised him from the start. And why not? Who needs a mewling infant, a snoring pillow-thumper and a bleary-eyed spluttering old rhetor in charge of an army? Nobody ever captured any battle flags with diapers, featherbeds or Latin! Now we'll rub some paprika into those Zaporohjans.

Hmyelnitzki will be shaking in his boots when he hears about this!"

"God grant it!" all the others chorused.

★ ★ ★

Meanwhile the hall filled up.

It took some time for the leading nobles to arrive; the Prince's duty officers couldn't get some of the more important lords and regional officials who commanded the provincial levies to climb out of bed so early in the morning but, in due time, most of them came up to the castle. They grumbled and complained at having their rest disturbed but they were anxious to be part of a historic moment, while the lesser gentry poured out of the hostelries and taverns, shooting off their muskets and cheering Prince Yeremi as if he had already led them to triumph over the rebellion.

"*Vivat Yeremi! Vivat the Prince-Palatine, commander over all commanders and Hetman of all the Hetmans!*"

"Vivat Vishnovyetzki!"

The town merchants ran to bar their doors and board-up their windows thinking that some new insurrection must have broken out, but this only helped to inflame the celebrating gentry. Church bells began to ring as if to signal a fire in the city. A few Vishnovyetzki soldiers ran down from the castle to quieten the rioters and to caution them that their days of carefree carousing were about to end.

"You'll soon taste such discipline in the Prince's hands that every belly among you will shrivel and collapse," they warned.

But that only made the gentry bellow all the harder. "So be it! We'll obey and listen now that there's someone worth listening too! To Hell with the regents!"

"Down with Prince Dominic," they cried. "All he knows about battles is what he's seen embroidered on those fancy Dutch tapestries hanging around his bed."

"*Vivat Yeremi! Vivat our commander!*"

The castle windows shook and rattled to those cheers and volleys so that even the most serious-minded soldiers in the audience hall began to laugh, eyes shining with excitement, and to slap their sabers.

Still bleary-eyed and reeling from all their revels of the night before, the massed gentry milled at the castle gates, cheering the

Prince and jeering at the regents, and the less they knew about discipline and obedience, the louder they shouted. They mimicked the regents, mocked their weaknesses and failings, and ripped their public reputations into shreds. Pan Konyetzpolski escaped the worst of their malice since his only sin was youth and inexperience, and because his name was hallowed in the Commonwealth since his grandfather's victory over the Swedes at Kirkholm. But no one had any mercy on Prince Dominic Zaslavski.

"I hear Prince Dominic is getting a new family crest," Pan Zagloba said. "It's one half-closed eye and a motto that says *'What happened?'* "

"And how d'you get that idea, dear brother?" Pan Longinus asked.

"Because he mumbles Latin phrases all day, even in the council, and every night he sucks at a bottle and dribbles on his belly, and when anybody says anything to him he flips one eye half open and says, *'What happened?'* "

"In Latin, of course," said Zachvilihovski while all the other officers and gentry doubled up with laughter.

"Of course it's in Latin! With him everything is Latin! When he throws a bone to his dogs he asks them in Latin if they'd rather have oatmeal."

"What a tongue you've got!" cried the laughing nobles. "You must be a real *'vir incomparabilis'* if your sword is anywhere that quick."

"And who says I'm not? Ask Pan Skshetuski if you don't believe me. He knows who captured what at Konstantinov! Yes, yes, gentlemen, shout the name 'Zagloba' in any Cossack's ear and you'll find out something you didn't know before."

Mocking the regents and buttonholing castellans and *starostas*, Pan Zagloba couldn't have been happier. He was in his element among the laughing nobles just as he was with the revelers in the town. He had long recovered from the backache he earned at Konstantinov; and the hard-drinking, spendthrift gentry who followed him about in Zbarajh were like a gift from Heaven. It would take a Homer, he was sure, to describe how much he drank and ate at their expense and a Plutarch to match the heroic tales with which he regaled them.

He got ready to launch himself again into one of his tales of martyrdom among the Turks, the mythical estates that existed only in his imagination, all the exploits that preceded and followed his rescue of Helen, and the capture of the battle flag which, in his telling, decided the victory at Konstantinov. But just at that moment the doors were flung wide and Prince Yeremi came into the hall.

Years seemed to have fallen from his shoulders along with his burdens. Only his red-rimmed eyes showed that he had spent another sleepless night and only the deep hollows under them testified to the struggle he had waged.

"My lords and gentlemen," he said quietly but with such dignity and power shining through his words that everyone held his breath. "Last night I talked to God and to my own conscience to decide what I ought to do. And here is my decision. I'm telling you, and I ask you to announce it to all the *rytzerstvo*, that for the good of our country and for the sake of that unity we must have in these dangerous days, I place myself under the orders of Prince Dominic and the other regents."

Silence fell on the gathering with the weight and finality of a tombstone.

★   ★   ★

A few hours later, close to noon, three hundred of Vyershul's Tartar troopers prepared in the castle courtyard to ride to Bar with Skshetuski, while Prince Yeremi gave a banquet for his senior officers which, at the same time, was to serve as a bachelor dinner for the young lieutenant.

The Prince looked as young and carefree as if he were the intended bridegroom rather than Skshetuski. His eyes were warm and gentle and his face was as calm and sunny as the day outside. Pan Yan, as the real bridegroom, sat next to him at the head of the table. Pan Zagloba, as the hero who rescued the bride-to-be, flanked Prince Yeremi on the other side and raised so many toasts to the bridal pair that hardly anyone could keep up with him. But the Prince, as carefree and merry as if the bleak conflicts of the night had never taken place, matched him cup for cup and raised some toasts of his own.

"Gentlemen!" he cried. "May this third goblet go to the health of the coming generation! It's a fine clan, on both sides of the family, so let's expect that the little apples won't fall far from the tree. '*Hawk*' is the ancient totem of our young hero's clan, a hawk is the crest his ancestors painted on their shields, so let us hope that all the little hawks he's about to give us will fly as high as he does!"

"Long life to them! *Vivat!*" roared the officers and the distinguished guests while out in the hall the servants launched their own noisy celebration under the leadership of Zjendjan.

"And here's to you all, with my thanks!" cried the overjoyed Skshetuski, and drained a huge goblet of Malmsey while the cheering knights staggered to their feet.

"Long life!" they bellowed. "Long life!"

"*Crescite et multiplicamini!*"

"Go forth and multiply, as the Holy Book commands! And the sooner the better!"

"Ey, you ought to raise half a regiment at least," old Pan Zachvilihovski said, shaking with silent laughter.

"Him?" howled Zagloba. "He'll fill the whole army with little Skshetuskis!"

The gentry roared. They shouted, one across another. Wild bursts of laughter boomed like artillery salutes. Wine flowed by the barrel. Heads began to steam in the noonday heat. All the faces began to drip with sweat and flushed a deep crimson, and the walls and windows rang with the sound of their celebration.

"Ah, if that's so," Pan Yan gasped. "If that's so . . . then I'd better confess that the cuckoo counted out twelve boys for me."

"Great God Almighty!" Pan Zagloba shouted. "All the storks in the country will drop dead from overwork!"

The gentry replied with another huge bellow of laughter in which the Prince joined as loudly as all the others but then he noticed some grim, grey apparition on the threshold of the room and peered at it with narrowed eyes.

"Who's that?" he cried. "Ah, it's you, Kushel? Back from your sweep, are you?"

The dusty, travel-stained dragoon stood hesitating at the sight of the happy company as if he wished that he was anywhere but there. "Yes, Highness," he said.

"What's the news then?"

"Very bad, Your Highness," the young officer said in a strange, strained voice.

A sudden silence, dull and grey as lead, settled on the gathering as if an evil spell had fallen on the celebrating soldiers.

Raised cups and goblets hung suspended in midair halfway to the lips. All eyes fixed warily on Kushel in whose stricken face a sense of tragedy struggled with exhaustion.

"It would be better if you didn't bring me bad news while I'm in my cups," the Prince said, annoyed, and then sighed and shrugged with irritation. "But since you've started you might as well go on and finish it."

"Your Highness," Kushel murmured. "I'd rather be dead then to have to tell you . . . at this of all times . . ."

"But what, man? Speak up! What's happened!"

"Bar . . . has been taken by the Zaporohjans."

Part Six

Chapter Thirty-seven

ON A LATE SUMMER NIGHT along the right bank of the Valadynka River a group of a dozen or so horsemen rode slowly in the direction of the lower Dniester.

Their horses walked slowly, taking each step as carefully as if they were carrying something both fragile and precious, but even so, one of the two horsemen who rode several dozen paces in front of the rest turned now and then and cautioned greater care.

"Slowly, back there!" he cried. "Slowly!"

The cavalcade behind him moved at a snail's pace. It consisted of a dozen riders whose long bare lances without pennons identified them at a glance as Cossacks. Some of them led heavily burdened packhorses. Others, barely glimpsed in the shadowed darkness, rode in a loosely strung, uneven formation around a pair of animals which carried a cradle slung between their saddles. But once the group edged out from behind a concealing hillock and entered a stretch of moonlit open ground, the cold white light illumined the pale face and fallen eyelids of a still form carried as if lifeless in the cradle.

"Watch your pace!" their leader cried again. "Slowly, there!"

But if the two outriders seemed unconcerned about the country through which they were passing, talking in low voices to each other and paying no attention to the night around them, the Cossacks around the cradle seemed frozen with fear. They peered about as if expecting something terrible to leap out upon them from every clump of grass even though the gaunt, broken landscape seemed to be an unpeopled wilderness.

"Horpyna! Hey, Horpyna!" the leader spoke up then as if

waking from some deep dream of his own. "How much farther?"

"Not far."

His companion, whom the moon revealed to be a huge young
woman dressed in the coat and breeches of a Cossack, stared for
a moment at the starry sky.

"We'll be there by midnight," she went on. "There's a couple
of bad spots ahead . . . evil spots that you'd never get past
without me . . . and then it's a clear run all the way down to the
Devil's Gorge."

"Evil or not it's all one to me so long as nobody but you
knows the way," the Cossack leader said.

"Wouldn't do them much good if they did." The young
giantess shrugged and laughed shortly. "Nobody gets past there
after midnight. Not until cockcrow, anyways. I can do it, sure,
but nobody else."

"You're sure? I know that Satan is like a brother to you but
there's ways of dealing even with him."

"Don't worry," the young woman said. "You couldn't find a
better hiding place for your little princess if you searched the
whole wide world for it. Nobody comes here and lives to talk
about it unless I guide him through. There'll be neither Tartars
nor *Lahy* getting past this place. '*Tchortovyi Yar*' isn't called 'The
Devil's Gorge' for nothing. Nothing alive has ever set foot in
there. If anybody come to me for a spell or to see his future he
waits outside till I come out. It's a terrible place, you'll see for
yourself."

"So it's terrible." The tall, wind-burned rider shrugged in his
own turn. "But I'll come through any time I want."

"Just so you do it by daylight," she warned.

"Any time, I tell you! And if a horned devil bars the way I'll
twist his head off for him."

"Ey, Bohun, Bohun," she laughed.

"Ey, Dontzovna! Don't you worry about me. Let the Devil
take me if he wants to, it's all one to me. But you let something
evil happen to the Princess and not all your ghouls and devils
will tear you safe out of my hands."

She laughed and shrugged again.

"It's been tried. One time, when me and my brother was
living by the Don, they tied a millstone to my neck and threw
me in the river. Another time, over in Yampol it was, the

headsman was already shaving my head, ready for the axe, and that's why nothing more can happen to me. I'll watch her for you out of friendship, you mad dog, not because you threaten. The spirits won't take a hair off her head, you can believe that. As for men . . . ha! She's safe with me, I tell you. She won't get away from you now."

"Ah, you screech owl!" Bohun cried. "So why did you tell me back there in the Ukraine that the *Lah* would get her? '*The Lah is near her,*' you kept croaking in my ear. '*The Lah is near her.*' What was all that about?"

"That was the spirits talking, not me," the witch said and shrugged. "But maybe things have changed. I'll read your future tomorrow on the waterwheel. That's the best way there is. You can see everything so clear on running water that it feels like you can touch it, only you've got to be looking a long time. You'll see it for yourself. But you're a real wild dog, d'you know that? If you're shown something that's not to your liking you get mad and go for your knife right away . . .!

★ ★ ★

They rode quietly for a while then, saying nothing, and only the clicking of the horses' hooves on the wayside stones broke the moonlit silence. Then a strange rustling sound drifted towards them from out of the river, as if a cloud of locusts were stirring in the darkness, and the fearful, superstitious Cossacks drew closer together behind them.

But Bohun didn't give a sign of noticing anything out of the ordinary. He lifted his eyes to the moon, thought deeply in his own interior stillness, and then turned his wondering face to the young witch again.

"Horpyna!" he muttered at last.

"What now?"

"You're a witch . . ."

"So what if I am?"

"So you know about things like that . . . Isn't there some herb or root or something that, if you take it, you fall in love with someone? Mandrake, or something?"

"Mandrake's best." She nodded then grinned at the pale, wild-eyed young Cossack. "But it won't do for what's ailing you, Steppe hawk. If your little princess didn't love another . . . well that'd be different. A pinch of mandrake and some other things I know about and she'd be in your arms faster than it takes to say it. But the way things are, mandrake would just make her love that *Lah* all the more."

"To Hell with it, then, and you too!" Bohun shouted. "You know how to tell a man what he can never get but you can't help him find a way to get it."

"Maybe, maybe not," she said, still grinning. "There's another herb that grows around here."

"There is? What's it do?"

"You take it and you're out of this world for a day or more. Can't move hand or foot. Can't stir. I'll give some to your girl, and"—the witch laughed lewdly and made a vulgar gesture— "the rest'll be up to you."

The Cossack shuddered as if an iron fist had rocked him in his saddle and turned his glowing, yellow eyes on the laughing woman.

"What're you cackling about now?" he demanded.

"*Tay hodi!* Take her when you can!" the witch cried out and burst into a peal of laughter that sounded like the shrill neighing of a mare.

"Bitch!"

The woman's cackling bellow echoed like a grim foreboding of disaster among the ravines hidden in the darkness and Bohun shuddered again.

"Bitch!" he snarled, turning his face away, and the strange, mad light began to ebb slowly from his eyes.

"Cossacks take what they want, don't they?" She shrugged again, grinning. "You're a Cossack, aren't you? Though it does seem to me sometimes like you're a *Lah* inside."

"Oh God if I was!" Bohun cried out furiously, twisting his cap in his hands and grinding his teeth. "If only I was one! I'd give my soul for her, that sweet little bird. I'd throw the world down at her feet if she'd only love me. But I'm not going to lay a hand on her unless she says I can."

"She must have given you something, that's certain," the witch muttered. "It's just not natural for you to be carrying on like that about some *Lah* girl."

But Bohun went on speaking in a sick, desperate voice as if the huge young witch hadn't said a word.

"When we took Bar," he said sadly, looking up into the starry sky as if appealing to a silent witness. "I was the first at the convent just to keep her out of the hands of our people. I'd have strangled the first drunken swine that put his paw on her. And what did she do when she saw me there? She put a knife in her own side, that's what! She'd rather die than see me! And me . . . I'd rather it was me that died there at her feet than that she should have been hurt in any way. If I was as much as to come near her now she'd do it again, stab herself or jump in the river! So how can I keep her safe?"

"She must've put a spell on you," Horpyna said. "No question about it."

"Ah, maybe she did," he murmured as if in deep mourning and lost for any idea that might save him. "She must've . . . Ah, may the next stray bullet hit me! May I end up on a stake, if I know what to do about it! There's only this one girl I love in the whole wide world and she hates my sight."

"Idiot!" Horpyna howled at him, raging with impatience. "You've got her right here!"

"Shut your mouth, bitch!" the maddened Cossack shouted in his turn. "And what'll happen if she kills herself? I'll tear you apart with my own hands, that's what . . .! I'll smash my own head to pieces with a stone . . .! I'll bite people like a mad dog . . .! All I want is to live for her and to die beside her and she goes and stabs herself! And why? Because of me!"

"She'll be all right, don't worry," Horpyna said in a dry, cold voice. "She won't die."

"If she did I'd have you hammered to a door with horseshoe nails," he muttered. "I'd rather she had stabbed me than herself."

"God but she's stupid," the young witch went on as if she was unable to believe it. "Why can't she take to you of her own free will? Where will she find a better man than you?"

"Do that for me," he hissed. "Make her love me and I'll fill your cauldron with ducats and another one with pearls. We took a lot of loot in Bar and a lot more before."

"I know you're rich," she said. "Richer than Yarema, people say. And famous too. Bards sing about you. Every Cossack knows you. People say that even Krivoinos is afraid of you."

"What's that to me?" The Cossack made a quick, impatient gesture. "I'd give up everything I've got and throw in my good Cossack name as well if that would just make her feel better about me. What does it all matter when the heart is breaking?"

Horpyna shrugged again. Bohun sighed. They rode in silence
even longer than before. The riverbank grew steadily wilder
and the gaunt, rocky landscape became emptier and more mysterious in the moonlight which twisted the broken, jagged cliffs
and the skeletal trees into fantastic shapes. At last Horpyna
stirred, peered about and said:

"Here's '*Vrajhe Urok*,' what they call the 'Devil's Playground.'
We'd all better ride close together now."

"Why?"

"'Cause it's bad here."

"What happens here, then? Is this where the Devil comes to
play with you witches?"

She laughed shortly, teeth gleaming in the moonlight, and
licked her dry lips. "That's not for you to know. Hold up a little
and wait for the others."

They reined-in their horses and waited until the rest of their
troop caught up with them. The Cossack warriors who'd have
charged ten times their numbers without a second thought
peered about uneasily, making the sign of the cross across their
chests and shoulders and muttering prayers. They huddled together like a flock of geese which had caught sight of a fox
creeping through the grass.

Bohun rose in his stirrups and stared into the cradle.

"Still sleeping?" he asked.

"Sleeping, *bat'ku*," an old Cossack answered. "Soft like a
baby, *yakh detyna*, the little one."

"I gave her something for it," the witch said. "She'll sleep till
I wake her."

"*Ostorozno*! Take it slow with her," Bohun told the Cossacks.
"Don't wake her. Ay, look at the way the moon's peering into
her face. That's my heart it's seeing."

"Just looking won't wake her," a young Cossack whispered.

And they put their horses into a slow and careful walk again.

★ ★ ★

Soon afterwards they reached '*Vrajhe Urok*'—a low, treeless
hillock lying near the river like a round buckler thrown onto the
ground. The harsh, pale light of the moon bathed the whole
escarpment, bringing the scattered piles of white stones and
boulders into sharp relief. Some of them looked like gnawed
skulls, thrown about the whole breadth of the hillock. Others

seemed like the heaped rubble of gutted towers and churches as if there had been life here at some bygone time, perhaps in the days of the Yagellonians who had united Poland and Lithuania three hundred years earlier and civilized the country. Here and there great stone slabs leaned against the darkness like crumbling tombstones in an abandoned graveyard and the whole mound had the air of ghostly, unpopulated ruins.

But something stirred there. Something hissed and whispered among the piled stones when the cavalcade had ridden halfway up the mound. The light night breeze swelled suddenly into a howling gale which swept across the rubble, and the trembling Cossacks were sure they could hear other threatening sounds rising from the ruins. It seemed to them that they were hearing sighs, as deep and despairing as if they'd been pressed out of chests crushed under a millstone. They heard mournful groans, sobs, bursts of dreadful laughter . . . the plaintive twittering of children.

The entire hillock appeared to come alive and to call out in a variety of voices. Gaunt, dark shapes seemed to stand behind the graveyard slabs, peering at the riders, and strangely twisted shadows began to creep towards them among the piled boulders. On the dark, outer edges of the mound gleamed pairs of yellow eyes, blinking and glowing like funeral candles, and then a deep, throaty howl rose from the largest of the stone heaps and other voices bayed in reply out of the distant darkness.

"Wolves?" whispered a young Cossack.

"Vampires," the old *esaul* answered even lower.

"*Hospody pomyluy!*" the warriors cried out, tearing their bright caps off their heads and making swift signs of the cross. "God help us! God have mercy!"

The horses began to press their ears back on their heads like dogs and to utter harsh, snoring sounds while Horpyna, who rode at the head of the terrified procession, muttered a string of strange, dark words that no one understood. But then the mound was behind them, gleaming like a white, moonlit pool in the sheltering darkness, and she sighed, shook herself and said: "It's all right now. It's all over. I had to hold them back with spells because they're real hungry. But you're quite safe now."

A great sigh of relief burst out of the men. Bohun and Horpyna trotted ahead once more and the Cossack troopers began to tell each other stories of their own adventures with vampires and spirits.

"We'd never have got by here without Horpyna," one said.

"A strong witch," said another.

"But that ataman of ours, did you see him? Paid no mind to anything. He don't fear nothing, not even the Devil. All he had eyes for was his girl."

"If he'd ever gone through what happened to me one time he'd feel a lot less safe," the old *esaul* said.

"And what was that, Father Ovsivoy?" the young Cossacks chorused.

"I'll tell you. I'm riding one night from Reimentarovka to Hulaypol and I go by some burial mounds. Then I see something jump off a mound and land on the back of my saddle. What the devil, I say to myself, a wildcat cub or what? So I look around and there's a baby, all pale and blue. Seemed like maybe the Tartars were driving its mother down the Slave Trail and it died on the way without baptism. So there it sits, squealing like a cat, and its little eyes are glowing like hot coals, and then it jumps off the saddle and bites me behind the ear."

"*O Hospody*, a vampire!" a young Cossack cried.

"That's just what I said that night. But I served a lot of years in Valachia where there's more vampires than people, so I knew the way with them."

"There's a way, then, Father?"

"Sure. The little squealer bites me and I jump off my horse, drive my knife into the ground and cry: '*Get lost! Disappear!*' And right away it groans, catches hold of the knife and slides along the edge into the ground. I cut a cross into the spot and rode on."

"So there's a lot of vampires in Valachia, Father?"

"Sure there is. Every other Valachian turns into a vampire after his death. And theirs are the worst. They call them *bruholaki* over there."

"But who's stronger, Father? *Dit'ko* the Devil or a vampire?"

"*Dit'ko* is stronger, you can bet on that, but a vampire's harder to get rid of once he smells a victim. Old *Dit'ko* will serve you if you know how to turn him the right way but all a vampire wants is to suck your blood. Still, even so, *Dit'ko* is their ataman."

"And Horpyna is like a Hetman over all the *dit'ki*, right Father?"

"Sure she is. She'll have them jumping at her orders as long as she lives. Ho, d'you think our ataman would've given her his little sweetheart to keep safe for him if she didn't have no power over all them spirits? A *bruholak* wants a virgin's blood more than anything."

"But I hear tell they can't do nothing to an innocent soul?"

"Sure. The soul's safe enough from them but the body isn't."

"Ey, but it'd be a waste of such a *krasavitza*," a young Cossack murmured. "D'you know what I mean? So pretty. It's like she's made out of blood and cream. Our *bat'ko* knew what to take in Bar."

Old *Esaul* Ovsivoy grinned and smacked his lips. "You're right there, son," he said. "She's a golden one, there's no doubt about it."

"Ay, but I'm sorry for her, Father," the young Cossack said. "You know, when we was putting her down in the cradle, she pressed her little white hands together and begged us to kill her. '*Ubiy, kazhe. Ne huby.* Spare me the shame,' she said."

"She won't have it bad."

Just then Horpyna rode back to the Cossacks to set their minds at rest about the next trysting place of demons that they were approaching.

"That's *Tatarskiy Rozlog* right ahead," she said. "It's the worst place there is. Used to be a Tartar camp one time in the past so there's thousands buried there without a priest's blessing. But don't you worry now, it's bad there only one night in the year and that's not due till the next full moon."

"*Hospody pomyluy . . .!*"

"It's all right, I tell you. And then it's just a short ride from there down to the Devil's Gorge and my own homestead. Nothing can happen to you there, lads, unless I want it to."

They smiled at her humbly, baring their heads before her in respect and fear and bowing all the way down to their saddle horns. They heard hounds baying in the near distance as the wilderness fell away before them and they began to enter a deep and forbidding canyon that seemed to lead them down into the center of the earth.

★ ★ ★

The ravine was so narrow that only four horsemen at a time could enter it if they rode abreast. It ran at a sharply angled slant towards the Valadynka, a deep rocky defile bordered with blackened cliffs, as if it had been an ancient tributary gouged by time itself into the dark soil. A swift, rustling stream coiled along its bottom, glittering in the moonlight like a prehistoric serpent, and seeped into the river. But as the cavalcade crept into the chasm the landscape began to change. The steep, jagged walls began to draw away, and the floor started to tilt upward and to broaden out, so that the riders found themselves suddenly on the bottom of a fair-sized valley locked on all three sides by a towering escarpment.

No wind blew there and the cool night air was unnaturally still. The ground along the canyon walls was studded with tall trees that cast long shadows into the moonlit glen where a litter of strange white objects—some small and round and some elongated—gleamed with an eerie light.

"What's that there?" one of the young Cossacks whispered.

"Skulls and bones," hissed another, crossing himself in superstitious fear.

"Men's or animals'?"

"Human."

They rode on, peering about with dread, until suddenly a small yellow light blinked among the trees in front of them and, at the same time, two huge black wolfhounds with shining crimson eyes came bounding and baying towards the men and horses. Horpyna's order silenced them at once but they went on running around the riders with deep, throaty snarls and glaring at them with their blood-red eyes.

"What kind of dogs are those?" a young Cossack whispered. "Are they real or what?"

"Not on this earth, they're not," said another.

"So what are they, then?"

"Them's not dogs, whatever they are," old *Esaul* Ovsivoy said and nodded with conviction. "You can be sure of that."

"*Hospody pomyluy . . .*"

In the meantime they rode up close to the tall, thick trees huddled in a dark grove against the canyon wall at the far end of the rising slope, and saw a large rough-hewn timber cabin that looked big enough for half a dozen chambers, a wide low-roofed stable beyond it, and another long, dark building rising beyond that.

"This is my place," Horpyna said to Bohun. "And that's the mill behind it. We grind our own cornmeal here and I use the wheel to see into the future. I'll read yours too in the millrace tomorrow, when there's light to see by. The girl can live in the main room of the house but if you want to dress up the walls a little then we've got to shift her somewhere else for now. And now stop, all of you, and get off your horses!"

The troop halted and the Cossacks leaped out of their saddles as if a Grand Hetman had give them an order while Horpyna began to call out:

"Tcheremiss! Hey, Tcheremiss! Come on out!"

A dark shape, dwarfed and twisted like a shrunken troll, appeared in the doorway of the cabin, holding a sheaf of burning pine twigs overhead and peering silently at the new arrivals. At the sight of this monstrously disfigured old man even the Cossack veterans stepped back and began to mutter.

"What kind of a devil are you, then?" Bohun asked, staring down at the flat, square face, fanged teeth and eyes as narrow as slivers.

"He can't tell you," the huge young witch said and laughed. "His tongue's been torn out."

"Come closer then," Bohun told the dwarf. "Let me look at you. I've never seen anything as ugly as you before."

But Horpyna called him back to their business.

"Listen," she said. "Maybe we'd better take the girl to the mill? If the lads are going to be dressing up the cabin, hammering nails into the walls and putting up the hangings, the noise might wake her. Well, what do you think?"

Bohun nodded.

The Cossacks untied the cradle and lowered it gently to the ground.

"Easy now. Be careful."

Bohun himself lifted the head of the cradle when they began to carry it to the mill. The dwarf, trotting ahead in a strange rolling gait, lit up the scene with his crude torch of resinous pine branches which cast a flickering red glow on Helen's pale face, bathed her in warmth and color, and made the drugged, sleeping girl seem excited and glowing with life.

"Easy. Careful with that torch."

But the sputtering red light didn't wake her. Only her smooth white eyelids quivered now and then. Perhaps she dreamed that she was somewhere else, with someone she loved, because a gentle smile drifted across her parted lips as the slow procession wound carefully step by step like a funeral cortege through the gloomy darkness, while Bohun stared down at her with as much despair as if his heart were about to break out through his ribs and burst from his body.

"*Mylenka moya, zazula moya,*" he whispered hoarse endearments which, in that scarlet torchlight, sounded as grim and savage as a threat. But his dark, finely chiseled features were soft and gentle with longing and affection.

"She'll be all right when she wakes," Horpyna said beside him. "The wound will heal quickly. She'll live."

"*Slava Bohu!*" he whispered. "*Slava Bohu!*"

Meanwhile the Cossacks at the cabin began to unload the huge, heavy bales off the six packhorses and to unwrap the carpets, tapestries, wall-hangings and other precious ornaments and objects that Bohun picked as his share of the loot in Bar. A bright, cheerful fire was soon leaping redly in the hearth of the main room of Horpyna's lair, and as the men staggered in with one heaped bundle of costly decorations after another, and as they nailed them to the whitewashed timber walls, the room began to acquire the rich shapes and textures of some great lady's sleeping chamber. Bohun not only made sure of an inaccessible and secure hiding-place for his captive princess but tried to think of everything that might make this cage seem as homelike and familiar to his '*little bird*' as if he'd never murdered her family and burned down her Rozloghi.

He came back from the mill a short time later to supervise the work himself. The looted treasures were piled in great heaps at his feet and he ordered them arranged and hung just like he remembered the costly draperies in the Kurtzevitch manor. Moonlight ebbed gradually off the towering rim of the surrounding cliffs, a blue-grey dawn crept into the patch of sky that gleamed like a polished lid over this stone cauldron, and the night in the cabin passed wearily to the muted thudding of the hammers which transformed this rough-hewn peasant homestead into princely quarters.

At last, when all the walls and floor and ceiling disappeared under gold-stitched tapestries and silk and satin hangings, and when the warm glow of the fire began to shine in the polished surfaces of a dozen gold and silver mirrors, the princess was carried back from the mill, still sleeping, and lowered as gently as a feather onto the glittering brocades and the embroidered quilts piled on the bed.

Then silence began to return to the greying canyon. The hammers were hushed. No bird song broke through the stillness of the air. Only the stables echoed for a while with bursts of wild laughter as the young witch rolled about in the straw, playing with the Cossacks.

Chapter Thirty-eight

THE SUN WAS already high when Helen awoke and opened her eyes and began to look around the dim-lit chamber in which she found herself.

Where was she? What she saw was distantly familiar, like a room through which she may have passed on some forgotten childhood visit to one or another of her father's friends. The golden stars and moons threaded into the silk canopy that hung above her head reminded her of something she should have remembered. From Bar, perhaps? From a place of refuge? Yet it was all disquieting, unknown to her, and never seen before.

Her eyes remained fixed on the ceiling for a while longer and then began to wander uneasily about the room, darting from one rich object to another as full consciousness returned. Her face, glimpsed in a silver mirror, showed astonishment and the start of fear.

"Where am I?" she asked herself again. "And how did I get here?" And then the most pressing questions of them all: "*Who brought me here? In whose hands am I now?*"

She wasn't sure if she was wide-awake or still asleep and dreaming. What should she think about this almost regal opulence around her? Did it mean that she was rescued? Safe? What has been happening to her up to this moment of awakening in a strange, dark chamber, rich and silent as a treasure house, when her last clear memory was one of terror and despair?

She closed her eyes and shuddered. She saw at once the bloody scenes of carnage that followed the storming of Bar by the Zaporohjans which would be imprinted on her memory as long as she lived. Her ears still rang with the screaming of the

546

murdered thousands as if they were being slaughtered once again right before her eyes.

"Oh God," she prayed, hoping against all hope that she was only remembering a nightmare. "Oh God . . . Did all that really happen? God help me, God help me!"

She saw the flames. There was smoke and fire everywhere. Blood. So much blood. Such huge heaps of corpses. The howls and screams drowned-out the roar of cannon. Memory rushed at her like a wall of fire destroying a city. Masses of blood-mad *tchernya* were storming the walls and slaughtering the defenders until blood ran in the gutters like the aftermath of some scarlet rainstorm. That was no nightmare. That had really happened. In spite of every horror she saw since the rebellion started she knew she wouldn't be able to imagine anything that dreadful.

Then, somehow, not even knowing how she managed it, she was remembering all of it at once. Every scene and moment stood stark and clear before her as if they were one: the three-day siege that ended as unexpectedly as it began; the day-long massacre of more than twenty thousand people; the wholesale slaughter of gentry, merchants, priests and nuns and children butchered in their hundreds. The bestial faces of the murderers, black with smoke and streaming with fresh blood, appeared once more before her on the convent stairs. She saw the thick necks and ungainly bodies red from head to foot with the blood of their victims. She heard the drunken howls. The terrible mad laughter. A merciless Judgment Day had fallen on a city that turned into a charnel house for its population which was quite literally trampled into the cobblestones.

And then the staring white mask of Bohun's face was burning like a cold fire before her eyes. She saw and felt again the knife she had seized. "*Dear God, where am I?*" she whispered, numb with fear. "*And who brought me here?*"

She remembered how she set the point of the dagger against her ribs, how her hands trembled on the iron hilt, and how she threw herself down on the marble floor to drive the knife deep into her body, and an icy sweat burst out on her forehead once again.

"I'm alive," she whispered, sick with disappointment. "The blade must have slipped."

She felt the fresh wound burning like a red-hot iron all along her side and she clenched her teeth so that no accidental cry would give her away until she knew where she was and why she was there. In spite of all her longing to be dead rather than a captive of some kind, she felt both her courage and her strength returning. She recalled at last a carrying-cradle slung between two plodding horses and a long, rocking journey into the unknown.

But where? What was this place? Some great royal fortress far from the rebellion? Or some safe castle of a border lord? Did someone rescue her from the Cossacks and bring her here to safety?

Her eyes swept nervously back and forth along the chamber walls. The windows were small and square as in a peasant hut but she could see nothing through them of the world outside. The pale, opaque sheeting of pressed and untanned leather that stretched across these meager little openings in place of leaded glass, admitted only a grudging and uncertain light. But how could this be a peasant hut? Above her head hung thick folds of purple silk studded with stars and moons. The walls were low but covered with priceless tapestries threaded in gold and silver. Silk carpets, embroidered with flowers, seemed to turn the floor into a living meadow. A glowing Persian drapery concealed the chimney-piece above the open hearth where a cheerful fire burned and warmed the room. And everywhere she looked she saw thick, golden cords, tassels, jeweled draperies and hangings, cloth-of-gold, brocades . . .

Daylight seeped into this barbaric splendor through the little windows and sunk into those soft, glowing violets and purples, creating a kind of amaranthine twilight filled with rainbow colors.

She stared in amazement.

A dream? Could she still be dreaming? Was it some kind of beneficent magic? Or was she really safe, torn from the Cossacks' hands by Prince Yeremi's army and brought here to one of his many castles?

She pressed her hands together.

"O Holy Mother, immaculate and pure," she prayed in a whisper. "Grant that the first face I see in this doorway should be the face of a defender and a friend . . ."

She closed her eyes as if to will that vision to come to her at once and then she heard the soft strumming of a *teorban* played outside the windows and a clear young voice singing a familiar love song.

> *"Oy, tze lubosti . . .*
> *Hirshe od slabosti . . .*
> *Slabost' perebudu . . ."*

The words were gentle, sad and full of longing. The song was one that she knew from childhood and she thought that she had heard that strong, lilting voice singing it before. But where? When? And why was she suddenly trembling and growing cold with fear?

> *"Zdorovshe ya budu . . .*
> *Vimoho kohanya . . .*
> *Po vik ne zabudu."*

She rose on her pillows to listen to this old Ruthenian ballad and to place that voice, and she saw her own eyes looking back at her from the mirrors and stretching wide with horror, and then, without warning, she cried out and fell back on her bedding as if she were dead.

The voice, she knew, was that of Bohun.

★   ★   ★

She prayed. But there was no hope in her prayer. She had cried out in anger as well as in fear and disappointment but the strongest feelings that swept over her and remained within her were disgust and horror. The riches which surrounded her seemed suddenly obscene. She didn't think her cry was strong enough to be heard outside but it must have been loud and sharp enough to pierce the thick log walls because, almost at once, the hangings that masked the door were thrust aside and the young ataman himself appeared on the threshold. Helen hid her eyes behind trembling hands while her bleached lips repeated *"Jezus Maria . . . Jezus Maria"* as if she were burning.

And yet the sight which numbed her with disgust and fear would have made almost any young girl's heart beat a little faster. The dark, intense beauty of this young man's face seemed to glow with passion. His dress was dazzling. The diamond studs of his long, silver 'zhupan' undercoat glittered like stars stolen from the sky; the sheath and pommel of his Turkish dagger and of his short, curved saber were a mass of jewels. His scarlet 'kontush'— the long, flared satin coat of a Polish noble with the sleeves split open to the shoulders and pinned back behind him like the wings of a splendid bird of prey—revealed a low-collared shirt of snowy Persian silk cuffed at the neck and wrists with clusters of emeralds and rubies. Tall, slim as a sapling, dark-browed and poised as proudly as a prince, he could have found no rival among all the young Cossack warriors of the Ukraine, she knew. But this did nothing to lessen her feeling of revulsion.

"Jezus Maria," she continued whispering.

"You cried out," he said softly. "Are you ill? Can I get you something?"

His great, luminous eyes were alive with anxiety as he looked down at her from the open doorway.

"Don't be afraid, Princess," he said in a low, sad voice as if he was ashamed to be standing there. "How can you be afraid of me? How could I ever hurt you?"

"Where am I? Where am I?" she cried feverishly, her face still hidden in her hands.

"Safe. Far from the war."

"But where?"

"In a safe place, I tell you. You've nothing to be afraid of here. I brought you to this quiet, hidden refuge far from wars and people so's no harm of any kind would come to you again. Not from the fighting, not from Cossacks, Tartars, soldiers . . . not from anybody. You're safe and well here. Nobody else got out of Bar alive."

"And why are you here, then?"

"I came with you."

"Why? Why do you haunt me like a nightmare? Why do you persecute me so?"

"I? Persecute you?" Pale with sudden pain, he spread his arms in a helpless gesture like a man confronted by a terrible injustice. "How could I persecute you?"

Unthinking, he took a step towards her and she cried out at once and crouched against her pillows like an animal at bay. Nodding his head in a sad acknowledgement of her hatred for him, Bohun backed away and then his arms fell limply to his sides and hung there as if they were broken.

"You are my soul," he muttered. "The blood of my own heart . . . There's no way I could harm you."

"I can't stand to look at you!" she cried out.

"But why? And why are you always so afraid of me? I'm your dog, your servant! Look, I won't move from this door if that's what you order. I'll just sit here on the threshold and stare into your eyes and what I read in them that's what's going to happen."

His voice was low, troubled and unhappy.

"Why do you hate me so much, Princess Helen? I've never wanted to do anything but look after you, take care of you, defend you . . . Why do you look at me like I was your enemy? Hey, dear God almighty! You took a knife to yourself when you saw me coming through that door in Bar even though you knew me from childhood and so you must've known I came to protect you!"

She shuddered, as if the memory was unbearable for her, and he stepped back against the wall and shielded his eyes with a troubled hand.

"Harm you!" he cried out sadly and shook his head as if the thought defied his understanding. "Harm you? I'm not some man you've never seen before, not some stranger that you've got to fear! I've been near you and watching over you since you were a tot in swaddling clothes. You know that. And still you go and stab yourself like this!"

A sudden rush of blood stained Helen's pale face.

"I'd rather be dead than . . . dishonored," she said with such conviction that the Cossack ataman shuddered in his turn. "D'you know what I'm saying? And I swear to you that if you as much as touch me I'll find a way to kill myself even if I'm to burn in Hell for it afterwards."

Anger, contempt and determination were blazing in her eyes. Bohun looked down at her, nodding, saying nothing, and she stared back into his gloomy face. He'd know—he had to know!— that if he drove her to it she'd do just what she said she would. And next time she'd hold the dagger steadier and place the point better.

"I swear it," she said.

He nodded again and took two slow steps towards the nearest window and sat down heavily on a bench covered with gold brocade and let his head drop down towards his chest.

"Don't worry," he muttered through tight, whitened lips. "As long as I'm sober . . . as long as vodka doesn't set fire to my head . . . you're like an icon to me."

Helen said nothing then.

"I haven't had a taste of liquor in my mouth since I found you among those nuns in Bar," he went on quietly. "Not once. Before that . . . sure . . . I drank. I drank a lot. And why not? How else was I to drown my misery? But now I never touch spirits. Never. Neither sweet wine, nor mead, nor homebrewed 'palanka.' Nothing."

Helen's silence continued and Bohun sighed, shrugged and went on in his low, sad voice: "So I'll just sit here for a bit, look at you a little, make my eyes happy for a while, and then I'll go my way."

"Set me free," she said.

"And what are you, a prisoner in this place?" His eyes were clouded over with bitterness and pain. "You're the lady of the manor here. Where would you go if I set you loose? All your Kurtzevitches are gone. The fire's eaten up all the villages and castles as far as you can ride in a week and more. Yarema's not in his Lubnie anymore, he's marching on Hmyelnitzki and Hmyelnitzki's going after him. There's war all around, blood flows like water everywhere you look. The country's full of Cossacks and Tartars and all kinds of soldiers burning and looting and killing each other. Who'll respect you out there? Who'll take pity on you and look after you if I am not with you?"

She raised her eyes towards the silken, starry ceiling because she knew that there was such a man out there in the war-torn country—a strong young man who'd press her to his heart and care for her and defend her if defense were needed, and with whom she'd always feel safe and protected—but she didn't want to name him so as not to drive the Cossack into fury.

But anxiety about him gripped her nonetheless.

Where was he now? And was he still alive? She knew while she was in the sanctuary of the nuns in Bar that Yan Skshetuski was still among the living because his name was prominently mentioned in all the tales of the Prince's victories. But so many days and nights passed since then, she thought. There could have been a dozen battles in which he'd have fought and each of them would bring death to thousands . . . Now any news of him could come to her only through Bohun whom she neither wanted to ask about Skshetuski nor dared to do so.

Her eyes dropped and her head fell back on the pillows. "So I'm to be your captive here, then?" she asked.

He shrugged, looked away. "If that's what you'd call it."

"What did I ever do to you," she demanded, desperate and near to tears, "that you follow me about like a curse?"

"What did you do to me?" The Cossack lifted his own proud, puzzled face and began to speak so softly that she had to strain all her attention. "I don't know what you've done. But I know this much, that if I've been any kind of curse to you then you're my bad luck and my misfortune too. Hey, girl! Hey . . .! If I didn't love you I'd be as free as the Steppe wind! Free in my heart and soul and caring about nothing except my Cossack glory! But what do I care now about everything that made my life worth living? Where's that love of freedom that was like a sweet, clear breath of air to me? What happened to that Cossack pride I rode on where and when I pleased as if it was just another wild horse I broke to my will . . .?"

He grew silent then, plunged into such bewilderment and grief that even Helen's horror of him abated for a moment.

"What did I care about women before you grew into one?" he resumed bitterly. "Hey, listen, one time in the Black Sea, I remember, I took a Turkish galley full of the most beautiful young girls a man would want to see. Picked for the Sultan's harem from all over the world they were, and not one of them sparked anything in my heart. Not one! So what happened then? So my good brother Cossacks had themselves some fun and then I had a stone tied to the neck of each of these beauties and tossed them overboard! What did they mean to me? I didn't care about anybody in those days! Didn't fear anything alive between the earth and the sky! I made war on the Tartars, took my loot where it came, and lived in the Steppe like a prince in his castle . . . I was free! I did what I wanted! And what's the story today? Eh? Will you tell me that? Here I sit like a slave, like a dog . . . a beggar waiting for one kind word from you. But I never hear it. Like I didn't hear it in those other days when your own people were planning to marry you to me. Why is that? Why can't you ever say it?

"Ay, my sweet girl," he went on like a man bewildered by a life that he never wanted. "If only you'd been good to me, if you had been different, nothing that's happened would've taken place. I'd never have cut down your kin or burned your Rozloghi. I wouldn't have taken up with the peasants or joined the rebellion. You could've led me anywhere you wanted. I'd have spilled my own blood for you and been glad to do it. I'd have given my soul to the Devil if that's what you wished . . .

"Now,"—he shrugged and stared into his open hands like a man whose life had lost its meaning—"I'm covered like a butcher with the blood of gentry. But in those other days, when you could have loved me, the only people I killed in the Steppe were Tartars. Or Turks in the galleys . . .

"And the loot," he said. "The goods I took from them and brought home to Rozloghi. It wasn't for me. None of it was. What would I want with silks and satins and yellow gold and jewels in those days? What does a free Cossack care about bags of treasure? It was for you! I brought it all for you because you were my heart and my soul and because I loved you. I killed a hundred men, burned a dozen palaces in the Crimea and took a score of caravans so that you'd be able to walk about shining in gold and jewels like one of God's angels . . . Ay, girl, ay . . . Why couldn't you have loved me then?"

His thick, droning voice dropped into a whisper and the short, broken phrases followed each other like stones thrown into water.

"It's hard to take that. Hard to understand it. Seems like there's no way for me to live with you now but neither can I live without you. Neither now nor back then when you could've loved me . . . Ah, the heart breaks, the soul cries . . ."

He paused, breathing deeply, and then his low, sing-song voice sharpened with sullen anger.

"It's your beauty, girl, that's been my undoing," he growled bitterly. "That's been *my* curse, that's *my* misfortune, Princess. It's that fear I always see hiding in your eyes that drove me off my head. That's why I came for you like a Cossack that time in Rozloghi . . . came with a sword in my hand and fire in my heart . . . and with my poor, sick wits drowning in *gojhalka* and with anger at your traitor kin . . ."

He sighed again. He passed his long, trembling hand across his eyes as if to wipe away a stain and perhaps to change reality as well.

"So maybe you'd better forgive me for what I did that day,"

he said sadly, hunched over like a brooding animal and nodding dully to himself. "A Cossack is what he is and does what he does. You look at him kindly and he'll love you like nobody else God put on this earth. You spit on him . . . you treat him like a dog . . . and he'll kill you for it. Ay, but it could've been different."

"I'll forgive you everything you've done to me and my family," Helen said urgently, pressing her palms together. "I'll do it gladly, with all my heart, and I'll bless you and think of you as a friend if you let me go."

"Let you go," he murmured. "Lose you." He shook his head and shrugged. "Ah . . . what's done is done. Forgiveness won't raise the dead, anyway, nor will it change things from the way they are . . .

"Hey,"—and his great dark eyes were full of bitter fire when he raised them from his empty hands and turned them towards her—"hey, my sweet girl, d'you know what I did the last time that you got away from me? I howled like a mad dog. I hurt so bad I clawed my wounds open just so there'd be another kind of pain to take my mind off you. I wouldn't eat. Meat turned to sour ashes in my mouth. I begged Death to take me and be done with it, but she's a cruel mother, hard on her poor sons, and she let me suffer. And now you want me to give you up and lose you all over again? How can I do that? That'd be like tearing the heart out of my chest a second time and throwing it away!"

His hoarse, cracked voice thickened and turned into a heavy groan deep inside his throat, and Helen felt blood rushing hotly into her face.

"God help me" she whispered.

The deeper the passion that she heard pouring out of Bohun, she knew in despair, the hotter this dreadful love for her burned in that bitter soul, and that dark, awful pit that had opened up so terribly before her became more abysmal, so that she felt as if she was staring up at him out of the bowels of the earth without hope of rescue or escape.

'*God save me,*' she prayed silently.

But it seemed unlikely that her prayers could be heard in the bottomless cavern into which she'd fallen, or that they would be answered.

★ ★ ★

Meanwhile the Cossack drew a long, shuddering breath, shook himself like a dog climbing out of water, and brought himself under control again.

"Ask for anything you want," he said heavily, then nodded at the richly decorated walls. "Here, look around you. That's all mine. That's my loot from Bar. It took six horses to carry it here and there's a lot more. You want gold? Shining jewels? People at your feet? Slaves? Servants? Peasants in your fields? Speak up and it's yours. I'm a rich man and if I need more I know where to get it. Hmyelnitzki will give up his own treasure for me if that's what I want. Krivoinos will give even more. You'll live better with me than Vishnovyetzki's wife ever did with Yarema."

His dark, slanted eyes were shining with that strange yellow glow, and she felt all her anger welling up in her at his presumption that she could be bought.

"You want a country of your own to rule? I'll take and give you all the castles you want. I'll give you half the Ukraine and more if that's not enough. I may be just a Cossack, not a noble, but I'm a Zaporohjan Army ataman for all that, with a horsetail standard carried over me and ten thousand good men riding at my back and jumping at my orders. That's more than your Yarema Vishnovyetzki ever had and I can have ten thousand more anytime I want."

Nodding, as if to confirm his power to himself, the Cossack hero stared at her with the quiet humility and hunger of a begging child.

"So ask for anything," he said. "D'you want a kingdom? It's as good as yours. You're my queen. I'm your dog and warrior. Just tell me what to do, what to get you. Just so long as you don't run from me anymore. Just so you'll stay with me, and just so you'll love me."

She rose up on her pillows, feeling as if her anger and disdain would burst into flame in that rainbow twilight and burn up the air. Her own bloodless face stared at her coldly out of all those gold and silver mirrors with such strength and power, and with such pride and such indomitable will, that she seemed more like an avenging angel or a legendary fury than the mild and gentle icons to which he compared her.

She shuddered then with the force of the anger that leaped in her breast.

She was a woman living in a time when few of her sex could decide their lives, direct their courses, or design the content of their fates. An orphan, thrown on the mercy of ruthless relatives, she'd never had much say in what might happen to her. But she was a Ruthenian princess none the less, in her veins ran the hot, proud blood of Kurtzevitch warriors who traced their lineage back to the dawn of history, and she knew her own worth and value.

The Cossack waited. He'd dealt in death all his life, she knew. Her life was sacred to him only as long as he thought that he might win her over—win her and possess her—and she stared at him with a depth of loathing that startled even herself.

"Speak up, then," he said, blind to everything except his own need and longing. "Tell me what you think."

"I have before," she said, cold as ice. "But if you need it said again, here it is. You've the power to keep me here until God takes mercy on me and death sets me free. Whatever happens to me at your hands is His will, not mine. But I give my love where and when I choose! That's *my* will! That's *my* power! And I swear to you that I'll never love you. Never. So let me go, and build your dream castles with some other woman. If you keep me here I'll never look at you with anything but contempt and hatred!"

Bohun leaped to his feet, his dark face twisted in a spasm of rage. Foam bubbled out between his grinding teeth. He hissed as he fought for air. His chest heaved in fury. The struggle between his strange twin natures seemed like the clash of two huge prehistoric creatures risen from a swamp.

★   ★   ★

She watched, without hope, as he glared at her with blazing, bloodshot eyes, mouthed broken phrases and clutched at his dagger. Love, hatred, passion, jealousy and pride flashed in swift, sudden spasms across his twisted face but the great silent battle inside him would go on until one side triumphed. But which would it be? She waited until his fury passed and he could speak again.

"Don't . . . tell me . . . things like that," he croaked in a shaking voice.

"And don't you tell me about your love," she cried. "Do you hear? I am shamed by it."

"Shamed . . ."

"Yes! It's an insult to me!"

"Ah . . . insult, you say . . ."

"I'm not for you. Can't you understand that?"

"Ah . . .!" and now his dark, grim voice was bubbling in his throat and his wet, white teeth glinted under his mustache like those of a wolf. "Ah . . . and whose are you then, you Kurtzevitch princess? And whose would you've been in Bar if I wasn't there to beat back those peasants?"

"He who saves my life to shame me and to jail me is an enemy, not a friend!"

"Shame . . .?" The dark voice thickened. "Life? D'you think that drunken rabble would've killed you? You'd have wished a hundred times you were dead before they finished with you and tossed you on a pile of corpses."

"My knife would have killed me!" she cried out. "If you hadn't torn it from my hands."

"But it didn't, did it," he ground out softly through his teeth. "And it won't. I've got you and I'll have you and that's all there's to it."

"I'll find a way to die."

"No you won't," he snarled. "You'll be mine. You've got to."

"Never."

"Ay," he said hoarsely. His head was nodding up and down as if keeping time to the pulsing fury that thundered in his brain, and he twisted his powerful fists until the knuckles cracked.

"Ey, my little bird. If you weren't hurt so bad . . . and after what you've just said to me, too . . . You know what I'd do? I'd send a troop to Rashkov to drag a monk here by his neck before this day was over and tomorrow morning I'd be your husband in every way there is . . .! You'd love me then. Oh yes, you would love me. You'd be a good wife then, a dutiful wife like the Holy Writ commands. Or you'd be damned to hellfire."

"God have mercy on me," she whispered.

"Oh yes," Bohun raged. "So a Cossack's love is an insult to the highborn lady? So she's angered by it? And who are you now, you noble Princess Helena Vasilyevna Kurtzevitchovna, that I'm such a lowborn peasant to you? Where're your lands and castles and gentlemen and armies? You're my loot! You're war booty! I took you in battle . . .!"

And suddenly he was laughing, looming over her, and smacking one fist into the palm of the other.

"Hey, if only I *was* a crude, dull-witted animal like you think I am! If I was a peasant! I'd teach you your duty and obedience in the peasant way! I'd write my noble pedigree on your silk white back with a rawhide whip! I'd have you here right now without any thought of priests, monks or marriages, you hear me? That's if I was a peasant, you noble highborn lady. Not a knight and soldier!"

She prayed, eyes closed, all hope gone. But whatever her bloodless lips were whispering was quite lost in the thunder of his rage. His fury, whipped up by her unresponsive silence, boiled up beyond even his control and spilled over her like a hurricane.

"I know," he hissed out through clenched teeth, "for whom you're saving your little maiden treasures. But he'll never have them! I swear it on my life, on my Cossack honor . . .!

"Ah . . ."—and the hatred spilled out of him like a river dammed by Winter ice and breaking free in Summer—"That petty little noble! That strutting lieutenant! That traitor *Lah* with his pretty phrases, taking what's been promised to another! Death to him! *Na Pohybel!* One look, that's all it took him with you. One quick look and one turn around the dance floor and he's got you, heart and soul, and what's left for me? What's left for the poor, faithful Cossack dog except to hammer his sick head against a wall, eat his own heart and choke on his misery?

"But I'll find him," the thick, snarling voice went on. "And then I'll have him peeled out of his skin and stuff him with hobnails. Hmyelnitzki's marching on the *Lahy* any day now and I'm riding with him, and I'll find your little lover boy if I've got to dig him up from under a mountain, and when I come back here I'll throw his bloody head right under your feet!"

But Helen no longer heard anything he said.

Her sense of hopeless and irremediable entrapment, her anger, the white-hot pain in her side where the wound broke open and drenched her with blood, the icy grip of her own terror and her fear for Skshetuski, and— finally—the toll taken on her by all her spent emotions, drained away the last of her strength.

Her eyes dimmed. A terrible lassitude seeped through her limbs and body. Her thoughts fluttered weakly in a spreading darkness and she drifted, gently as a leaf, into a void of silence and oblivion.

The grim ataman stood over her for a while longer. His bloodless face, contorted in his rage, gleamed like a skull in her shrinking memory. He wiped the foam of fury off his mustache and bit his own hands.

Then he let out a groan. He saw her trailing arms and her lifeless face tilted towards the ceiling. He saw the blood spreading across her bedding and an inhuman howl broke out of his chest.

"*Vhje po nyey!* She's gone! Horpyna! Horpyna!"

The giant witch ran into the room.

"What's wrong? *Shtcho s'toboyu?*"

"Save her! Save me!" Bohun howled. "I killed her! I killed my heart . . . my soul! *Svitlo moye* . . . my light . . .!"

"*Shtcho tih, zduriv?* Have you gone mad, or what?"

"I killed her . . . killed her," the Cossack moaned and twisted his hands above his head as if to trap and strangle his own escaping soul.

But the young witch bent over the girl, peered closely into her half-closed eyes, grinned and shook her head. "She's not dead. Just gone off in a faint, a deep one. She'll be alright. Get out of here now and I'll soon have her awake again."

Clutching his bowed head in both his hands, Bohun ran into the cold night air.

Chapter Thirty-nine

TWO MORNINGS LATER Bohun and Horpyna sat under a willow near the millrace and stared down into the roiled waters flowing across the wheel.

"You'll guard her, right?" Bohun pressed. "You'll keep her safe, you've got that? You're not to take your eyes off her, understand? She's never to go outside the canyon."

"She won't," the young witch said. "The mouth of the gorge is as narrow as a dried-out gourd but here inside there's plenty of room to live in. Have your men block the entrance with a rockslide as you're going out, eh? That way nobody'll get in and we'll sit here as snug as three ears of corn in the bottom of a pot."

"You'd bury yourself here along with her?"

"Me?" The witch laughed shortly. "I've ways of getting out if you pulled the whole canyon down on me."

"What do you live on here?"

"Tcheremiss plants corn next to the cliff, and tends the grapevines and sets traps for birds. With what you've packed in she won't lack a thing. Don't worry, she won't go outside and nobody's going to find out she's here unless your own men flap their mouths about this."

"They won't," Bohun said. "They've sworn it. They're a good, loyal lot and they'd keep their mouths shut if they were being skinned alive. But you said yourself that people come here now and then to have their futures told."

"Yes they do. From Rashkov and God knows where else if they've heard about me. But they wait by the river till I come out to them. Nobody comes in here. They're too scared. The ones that tried it . . . well, you've seen their bones in the neck of the ravine."

"Who murdered them? You?"

"Maybe I don't need to." The witch shrugged and grinned. "Who's to say? Anyway, if anybody comes to hear his future told he waits outside and I go to the waterwheel. If I see something in the water I come out and tell it. I'll take a look for you too in a while only sometimes it doesn't show too well."

"Just as long as you don't see something bad," Bohun muttered.

"If there's something bad waiting for you in the world then you can stay here. Listen, it'd be better for you not to go back to the war anyway."

"I've got to. Hmyelnitzki sent me word in Bar to get back to him as fast as I can. So did Krivoinos. The *Lahy* are coming at us in great strength so we've all got to band together too."

"When will you be back?"

"*Ne znayu.*" Bohun shrugged and spat into the water. "When it's all over, I guess. There'll be a great battle, the biggest there's ever been, and it'll be life or death for us or the *Lahy* once and for all. If they beat us I'll come and hide in here, if we beat them I'll come riding back for my little bird and take her to Kiev. The archmandrite himself will marry us there."

"And if you get killed?"

"That's for you to warn me about, isn't it? You're the witch."

"But," she persisted, pressing for an answer. "What if they do kill you?"

He shrugged again. "Then I'll be dead. One life is enough."

"That's easy for you to say," Horpyna snapped at him. "But what am I to do with the girl if you don't come back? Eh? Twist her neck or what?"

"You lay a finger on her and I'll have you threaded on a stake like a rusty needle," he threatened, then sat staring gloomily into the water. "All right, if they kill me, you tell her to forgive me, you hear? I don't want her hating me after I'm dead."

"Ey, she's a stupid, ungrateful little bitch that she doesn't love you for all that loving she gets out of you," Horpyna said and shot Bohun a sly, sideways grin. "Now, if it was me, I'd let you have what you want without any fuss, ha ha!"

"You . . ."

"Sure," she elbowed him playfully in the ribs and showed all her teeth. "Why not?"

"Go to Hell!"

"I will, sooner or later, that's for sure." She laughed again. "All right, I know you're not for me but there's no harm trying."

But Bohun was staring into the water which leaped and foamed in the sluice below them.

"Horpyna?" he murmured after a long moment.

"What now?"

"After I go, will she miss me?"

"Why should she?" The young witch glanced at him with something like pity. "You're not leaving her much to remember, are you? Now, if you'd take her the hard way, like a real Cossack, then she'd have something to think about when you're gone. But this way? Forget it."

"I can't do that, I tell you," he snarled. "Not with her."

She shrugged. "So maybe it's just as well you're going away."

"She'd die if I forced her."

"So go, go!" Her strong young face twisted in a flash of anger. "As long as you're here she won't even look at you. But once you're gone, who knows? A month or two of sitting here with nobody but Tcheremiss and me and maybe she'll change her mind about you."

"If only she wasn't sick!" he cried out, cracking his great knuckles. "I'd know what to do. I'd get a priest from Rashkov, have him marry us, and that'd be that! But I don't dare do that while she's so weak. One good fright and she'll give up the ghost. You saw it yourself."

"Oh give it up yourself, will you?" the huge young witch snapped at the gloomy Cossack with impatience. "What do you want with priests and marriages anyway? There's times you don't seem like a Cossack at all, you know that?"

He sighed and turned his face away.

"Listen," she went on, quietly now but with sharp insistence. "I don't want any priests coming around here, specially not from Rashkov. There's Dobrudjan Tartars camped out that way. All you'd need is for some of them to follow you down here and that's the last you'd see of your little princess."

Bohun clenched his fist. "They'd never take her from me," he said coldly.

"Sure, sure," the witch grinned and nodded. "I know. You'd take on a whole *tchambul* of them with a dozen lads, you've done that before. But what about after you've gone, eh? Who'll be here to fight them off then?"

"Your devils," he said. "Your dark ones. Whoever does your killing."

"Even they know better than to tangle with Dobrudjan Tartars," Horpyna said and laughed.

"I don't care about Tartars any more than I do about all your devils, vampires and dark spirits," he spat out with contempt. "I'm just saying what I'd do if my little bird wasn't so close to dying."

It was Horpyna's turn to shrug and shake her head again because the darkly handsome, glowering ataman was suddenly a creature she never saw before.

"Hey Bohun, Bohun . . . what's come over you?" She was looking at him as if his strange, tortured passion was a sign of weakness. "Where's your hard Cossack head, my lad? Where's your dash and fire? You'd better go to your war as quick as you can, I'm thinking . . . Maybe those *Lah* cannon will knock some sense into you again."

"I'll go," the Cossack muttered. "Don't you worry about that. And now you start looking into that water and tell me what you see. And no lies, mind you. Tell the truth, you hear? Even if your devils show you my rotting corpse."

★ ★ ★

Horpyna climbed the hillside to the waterwheel, raised the crude wooden sluice-gate above the rocky channel, and soon the dammed spring stream poured with double force across the weir and into the pool below it. The heavy oak wheel creaked and rattled as it gathered speed. A thick white mist boiled up above it while the dark water in the pool started to foam and bubble as if brought to a sudden boil. As still as if she was carved out of the limestone walls around her, the young witch fixed her deep black eyes on the swirling whiteness, grasped the long black braids plaited behind her ears, and began to call: "Hoo-koo, hoo-koo! Show yourself. On the oak wheel, in the white foam, in the bright mist . . . Come! Come! For good or for evil, show yourself!"

Bohun lowered himself to the ground beside her. His face felt hot and feverish with anxiety and his hands were trembling with impatience.

"Well? D'you see anything? Well?"

"I see it!" she cried out.

"What? What?"

"My brother's death! Two yoked bulls are dragging poor Donyetz on a stake! Ay, my poor brother . . .!"

"To Hell with your brother," he snarled, wanting to hear about something altogether different. "What else is in there?"

Eyes wide, she stared into the foam. The waterwheel whirled under the mist, roaring as if maddened. "Poor Donyetz," she cried. "His head's all bloody . . . a raven's tearing at it, pecking at his eyes . . ."

"And what else?"

"Nothing . . . That's all for now." She began again. "Hoo-koo, hoo-koo! On the oak wheel, in the white foam . . . show yourself! Ah, I see it!"

"What?"

"A great battle!" she cried.

"Where? When?" Bohun's wild black eyes were burning with impatience as he stared into the foaming water. He chewed his lips and snapped his powerful white fingers with anxiety as if to help the witch in summoning her visions. "Who's winning?"

"Wait . . . Ah, I see it. The *Lahy* are running from our lads!"

"Ha!" he cried and clenched his fists together. "And I'm chasing them?"

"I see you too." Sweat beaded her smooth white forehead with the effort. "You're fighting with someone . . . A boy? No, it's not a boy, it's a real small knight! Ah, ah . . . there's a black cloud over you, there's a shadow falling. You watch out for that little man, you hear? You be careful with him!"

"And what about the Princess?"

"She's not there. I see you again. And there's somebody with you . . . a good mate you trusted . . . some false friend who's going to betray you . . ."

Bohun fixed his own feverish stare on the foam as if to summon up a fresh clear glimpse of his destiny. "What false friend is that?"

" . . . Can't see," she muttered. "Can't tell if he's young or old."

"Old!" he cried out and ground his teeth in fury. "He's sure to be old."

"Maybe. I can't tell."

"I know who he is." Bohun's strange, glowing eyes were ablaze with hatred. "He's already done it to me once, the damned thieving traitor! Look again! A fat old noble with a big grey beard and one blind, white eye. That's him, right?"

" . . . Can't tell."

"That's him! Bound to be. To Hell with him, the old hog!" But the Cossack's rage cooled almost at once and his contorted face grew thoughtful as he reconsidered. "Wait though. He's no mate of mine, no not any more. He's my mortal enemy. Look again, Horpyna. It's got to be somebody else you're seeing in there."

"Maybe it is." The witch's face and hands were glistening with her sweat. "But he's dark with hate for you, he's like a shadow at your back, so I can't see too clear . . . Ah, wait now! There's something else! I see your little princess, she's in a long white dress and she's got a wreath of Spring flowers in her hair."

"A wedding!" he cried.

"Sure, that's what it looks like. A wedding. And there's a hawk hovering over her."

"That's me," he said.

"Maybe it is. A hawk . . . or is it a falcon? It would be you for sure if it was a falcon. No, it's a hawk, alright."

"It's got to be me."

"Could be . . . could be . . . Ah, wait. It's gone now."

"Keep looking!" the Cossack shouted, twisting and wringing his hands with impatience.

"Hoo-koo, hoo-koo . . ." Horpyna stretched her broad, sweat-stained hands above the furious water, calling to her spirits, and Bohun clawed at his face and mustache as if they were burning, having caught fire from the mad light glowing in his eyes.

" . . . In the white foam, on the dark oak wheel," the witch chanted. "Ah, ah ha!"

"What is it?"

The young witch gasped, wide-eyed, and shook her head

with wonder. "I see such an army, so many of our lads . . . Ay, they're like trees in a forest or bright thistles nodding in the Steppe. There's no counting them in their tens of thousands . . . And I see you standing high over all of them and they're carrying three horsetail standards over you! You're the chief of them all! You're the Hetman!"

"Is Helen with me?"

"No. She's not there."

"So where is she? With whom?"

There was another long silence as the young witch stared intently into the boiling foam. The waterwheel spun so swiftly now that it vanished from sight altogether in the swirling mist and its booming roar was so loud that it made the old wooden mill shake on its foundations.

"Hey, how much blood there is . . .," the witch murmured softly and shook her head again as if unable to believe her vision. "How many dead and dying . . . There's nothing but still, white corpses like a carpet stretched between the horizons, and there're grey wolves crouching over them, and crows and ravens falling down on them out of the black sky . . . Ah, I see plagues rising from the ruins . . . death spreading everywhere . . . the whole world dying out . . . blood . . . so much blood . . ."

Then, covering her eyes, she said: "That's all. That's enough."

A sudden gust of wind blew the mist off the spinning waterwheel and the misshapen Tcheremiss appeared on the slope above the mill with a bundle of firewood strapped across his shoulders.

"Shut the sluice, Tcheremiss," the witch called out and went to wash her sweat-streaked hands and face in the cold stream running above the channel.

★ ★ ★

Left alone, Bohun sat slumped in thought above the waterwheel which creaked and turned slowly over the trickling stream that flowed under it across the dammed weir. The witch and her visions were gone. The monstrous dwarf had vanished. The cold, dark walls of the canyon rose high into the blue sky everywhere around him.

Three horsetail standards carried over me, he thought. A sea of blood. A carpet of corpses. Tens of thousands riding at his orders. Helen in white, a wreath of wedding flowers twisted in her hair . . .

Ah, but that hawk, he thought. That hawk! The one the witch saw hovering above Helen. Could that be him or was it Skshetuski? '*A falcon, that'd be me. There'd be no question about it if it was a falcon.*' That's what people called him across the length and breadth of the Ukraine, he knew. That's what the blind folk-singers celebrated all along the Dnieper, down past the cataracts and throughout the Wild Lands. He was their '*Falcon of the Steppes,*' their '*Prince of the Nijhovtzy,*' the fabled exemplar of Cossack pride and freedom, fearlessness and glory who rode the Khan's own horses, slept in the Sultan's bedding, and whose name rang like a cry of terror in all the Tartar Summer palaces and cities on both sides of the sea.

'*If I had a noble's coat-of-arms that swift, dark swooping bird of prey would be on it,*' he thought.

Ah, but he didn't have a coat-of-arms, he knew, and he stared into his empty hands with bitterness and anger.

Rage welled up in him again. Rage and a helpless fury. He clenched his fists and pressed them to his icy face while hatred—for himself, and for everything that made him what he was—swept through him once more like fire, the kind that bursts out in the Steppe after a bolt of lightning sets the dry Autumn grasses alight and starts a conflagration.

"If I had a name, a coat of arms," he muttered. "If I'd been born a noble . . . I wouldn't be here."

He'd be with them, the gentry. The *Lahy* who cheated and betrayed him but whom he'd have embraced like brothers for the sake of Helen. He'd be a terror to the Zaporohjans as he'd been to Tartars. Not a rebel ataman but a King's commander as great or even greater than the Vishnovyetzkis . . .

"And Helen wouldn't hate me, she wouldn't run from me or stab herself at the sight of me. There'd be no blood between us and she'd be looking at me with soft and gentle eyes . . ."

Ah . . . but he wasn't a noble, he knew bitterly, no matter how famous he'd become. His ancestors, lands and titles weren't enshrined in parchment. And was that all it took in this huge, rich Commonwealth of the Gentry, to decide on a man's true merit, happiness and worth?

The dark, still water of the millpond stared up at him as if it was the eye of some tormented spirit trapped in the soil and longing to be free. Hmyelnitzki and Kshetchovski had their patents of nobility. They could own lands. They could lead royal armies and elect a King. But he, for all the glorious ballads that were sung about him, was just another Cossack . . . a peasant to the gentry . . . and at this thought his hatred blazed up in him as wildly as his vast, doomed passion for the Kurtzevitch princess.

"Why is this so?" he asked himself in fury, and then went on with a bitter sadness: "In what way am I worse than all those crested nobles? I've spilled more Tartar blood than any thousand of them! I've won more battles . . . took more loot and booty . . ."

But his blood wasn't noble and that was what mattered. He never knew his parents. He didn't know who named him, or where he was christened, and his solitary Cossack name didn't count for anything among the Polish, Ruthenian and Lithuanian gentry despite all its glory. He didn't know where he was born or where he came from to the Vishnovyetzkis' country or how it happened that he grew to manhood in the Kurtzevitch manor. Helen's burned home and murdered family were the only kin he had ever known.

"But even there," he muttered, pale and drawn with hatred. "Even there I was just a Cossack."

And now there was this bird hovering over Helen. He knew, because such things were known to everyone in those times, that there was some kind of bird of prey in the Skshetuskis' crest. A hawk or a falcon?

"No," he said fiercely, staring up into the empty sky. "No. I'm the falcon. It's got to be me."

★   ★   ★

He heard the sound of footsteps and loose stones clattering on the hillside behind him, looked up and saw the witch coming back.

"So," he said, waking from his thoughts. "Is it all over, then? Or are you going to look some more into the water?"

"No more," she said wearily. "It's over. There's no more to see."

"And you're sure you didn't see any more than what you said you did?"

"I saw what was there."

"And that was all? You're not lying, are you?"

"What's there to lie about?" She sighed, stretched her arms and rubbed her tired eyes. "I can't see what doesn't show itself on the wheel. You heard it all. I'll swear to that by my brother's head, if that's what you want. He'll die on the stake, like I said. I saw a team of oxen dragging him by the legs right on the point of a sharpened log."

"*Raz maty rodila,*" Bohun said.

"Ay, I'm right sorry for him," Horpyna sighed. "Right sorry . . . but the waterwheel doesn't lie and he's not the only one that's got death written on his head these days. I tell you, the water never showed so many dead before. There'll be a great war in the world."

"And her . . . the Princess . . . you saw her with a hawk over her head?"

"That's right."

"And she was in a wreath?"

"In a wreath. And in a long white dress."

"And how d'you know this hawk is me?" Bohun pressed her. "I told you about that young *Lah* noble, the one that got to her. Maybe it's him?"

"A *Lah*?" She narrowed her dark, thick brows, thought deeply for a moment, and shook her head slowly from side to side. "No," she said. "*Budiv Lah, budiv orel.* If it'd been a *Lah* he'd have shown up in the water as an eagle. That's their sign. A white eagle. This was a dark hawk."

"*Slava Bohu, slava Bohu,*" he breathed in relief. "Well, I'll go down to the stables now and tell the lads to get the horses ready to ride out at sundown. We'll be on our way tonight."

"Ah," she said. "You're sure, then, that you've got to go?"

"Hmyel ordered it," he said. "Krivoinos ordered it. You saw it right about a great war because that's what I read myself in the letters that I got in Bar."

The young ataman flushed as he told his lie and glared fiercely at the giant witch as if daring her to laugh or challenge his ability to read. But she knew better than to risk his anger.

"Well then go," she said, staring down into her open hands. "Go if you must though you're welcome here as long as you want. Poor Donyetz is going to die on a stake but you've good things coming to you in the war. You'll become a Hetman. I saw those three horsetails waving over you as clear as I see these fingers on my hand!"

"Yes. I'll be a Hetman." He nodded proudly, believing in his destiny and sure of his power, yet a bitter note of regret continued in his voice. "That's what I'm meant to be no matter where I've come from. That's what's written for me. And I'll take the Princess for my wife like that's meant to be, because it's not right for my kind to marry a peasant."

"You'd sing a different tune with a peasant girl," she said and sighed. "I know. I know you. But you're ashamed to have your way with this one . . . Ah, you should've been a *Lah* yourself, Bohun, not a Cossack."

"That's not what fate ordered."

He sighed, rose and went down the slope towards the stable where his warriors lay about in the straw among their saddled horses while Horpyna made her way slowly to the hut to see to their suppers.

★ ★ ★

Night fell swiftly in the deep, shaded canyon. The Cossacks sat quietly on their horses, waiting for their leader from the moment when the sun first began to slip behind the canyon wall, but he couldn't bring himself to leave his captive and return to the war.

He sat in the main room of the house on a pile of precious eastern carpets, with a mute unstrung *teorban* in his hands, and stared silently at Helen.

She was beginning to recover. Still pale, still looking ill but clearly no longer in any serious danger, she had got up and dressed and sat in the farthest corner of the room, paying as little attention to Bohun as if he wasn't there. He, as if to underscore the vast differences between them, sat with his eyes fixed on her like a pilgrim to a holy shrine where she was the miraculous painting that might cure his own gnawing illness and soothe every pain.

All of the afternoon and evening passed like that between them. Her lips were barely moving in a prayer. The beads of her rosary slipped quietly through her fingers. He watched her every movement. His ears caught every whisper and rustle of her robes. But even though he opened his mouth a dozen times to start speaking to her, his words died in his throat. A cold, monastic graveness lay on her pale lips and her drawn, dark brows and robbed him of courage to break the grim silence; it was a look that Bohun never saw on her before.

He watched. Against all his will, he remembered other evenings of this kind. Not all that long ago. In Rozloghi. The
young Kurtzevitch princes sitting around the great oak table in
the dining hall, throwing dice out of a leather cup and laughing.
The old *Knahina* husking sunflowers and cracking seeds over by
the hearth. The fire crackling. Shadows leaping among the
ornaments and hangings on the walls. And he himself, staring at
the beautiful young princess just as he did now.

What struck him dumb, what seemed to rob him of the
power of speech was the look she was wearing now, as if her life
was over. As if he was seeing her in a convent cell or from
beyond a grave. He had been happy in those other times that
leaped so suddenly into his memory. He'd been full of stories
about his expeditions into the Tartar lands. She'd be listening
then; and now and then her deep, dark eyes would rest on him
quietly; and her lips would part, and he'd be lifted to some
unknown heights of poetry when he knew he had her full
attention. She both looked at him and listened when he sang
and played his *teorban* on such evenings and his heart would feel
as if it was melting in his chest.

Now she didn't throw a single glance his way and he knew
that she had stepped far beyond his reach; she was gone from
him, withdrawn into the cold, still silences of her own mind and
thoughts where he couldn't follow.

How was that, then? He didn't understand how he could have
lost her so completely. He was her master here. She was his
captive, his slave if he wanted her that way. He'd taken her like
loot. Like the rich carpets on which he was sprawling. He could
order her to do anything he liked. And yet, in those other times,
he felt closer to her and more like her equal.

What was this anyway? Witchcraft? Some evil spell, or what?

Here he was, a future Hetman of the Zaporohjans, greater
than Hmyelnitzki! She was his to do with whatever he wanted,
and yet there she sat—an aloof, unapproachable lady, regal and
remote in that vast, cold distance etched into her face—and he
couldn't even find his tongue in her presence and felt as poor,
dull-witted, insignificant and humbled as a churchyard beggar.

Anger stirred in him again. Rage leaped up and vanished,
bitten back before it could spill out. He'd show her quick
enough what it cost to humiliate a Cossack if he didn't love her!
Oh yes, he'd show her! But each time his anger seized him by

the throat some kind of invisible hand seemed to reach out and catch him by the hair while a threatening voice thundered in his ear and ordered him to hold himself in check.

He let himself explode once already and what good did it do him? None. Worse than that, he had almost killed her. Rage was useless here. Yes, he could frighten her. Terrorize her. Fill her with shame and horror. But the terror merely flooded back into his own chest, turned to a howling shame and pity for himself, and forced him to beat his head bloody against the wall outside.

'*Ay, if she'd just smile once,*' he thought. '*If she'd just say one word.*'

He'd go then. He'd fall at her feet, beg forgiveness and then ride to the Devil or anywhere else that the Steppe would take him. Go to the war, the new battles that were waiting for him, where he'd be able to drown all this misery and anger and pity for himself in blood . . .

"Ay, if she was only some other *Lah* woman I took from some noble's manor that I burned and looted," he muttered silently through his teeth. "If only I didn't love her or know who she was . . . I'd know how to treat her."

But this was Helen, that Kurtzevitch princess who was like a sister until she grew into her teens, the woman for whose hand he bowed to her old aunt and step-brothers and for whom he was ready to give up Rozloghi and everything he owned.

"Ey, if she was just some other girl I took as spoils of war," he growled into the fists that clenched and opened before his face like talons. "I'd treat her like a Cossack. I'd be a Cossack with her if I can't be the kind of man she wants."

Instead, he kept still. He watched and listened to her whispered prayers. He didn't dare to do anything that might remind her of his origins and the gulf between them.

The hours fell like stones. The quiet murmurs of his mounted followers came to him from outside where the Cossacks waited, ready to ride wherever he led them. The firelight gleamed in reflected brilliance on his rich *kontush*, his silent *teorban*, and his jeweled weapons. One look, he thought. Just one warm look would do . . . one friendly word said in farewell . . .

But she said nothing. She had dismissed him from her consciousness as if she were able to turn him into air by an act of will. He didn't want to leave her with that bitterness and anger roaring in his brain. He wanted warmth, a feeling of acceptance,

and felt instead like a fool—a wordless, dumb-struck peasant—
and he gnawed his hands at this new humiliation.

Then a horse neighed outside.

The ataman shook himself free of his heavy musing. He
cleared his dry throat. "Princess," he muttered. "It's time for me
to go."

Helen said nothing.

"Won't you say '*Go with God*' to me?"

"Go with God," she said.

His heart leaped up, then tightened. She said what he wanted
but not how he wanted; it might have been a whisper coming
from a grave.

"Yes. Well. I know you're angry with me," he said. "I know
that you hate me. But you'd be worse off with anybody else, I'll
say that much to you."

She remained silent and he nodded slowly, like a man accepting a verdict he didn't deserve, and went on talking as if to
himself.

"I brought you here because that's the only thing that was left
for me. How else could I get you? But what harm did I do?
Didn't I treat you well? Didn't I show you the respect you
wanted? A royal princess couldn't have it better, you can see that
much for yourself, can't you? And yet here you are, in my
hands, and God only knows what any other man would've
done to you."

"I'm in God's hands," she reminded him with the same grave
quietness as before. "But I'm grateful for the restraint you've
shown me."

"Well," he said. "Well. If that's the warmest word you can
find for me . . . if that's the best you can do . . . I'll go with that
much. Maybe you'll feel more kindly towards me later on.
Maybe you'll think about me now and then."

Helen said nothing.

He sighed. He rose to his feet.

"It's too bad I've got to leave you cold like this," he told her.
"It's hard to go without a kind word to take away. Without
some sign, like maybe a little cross to wear for luck and a
keepsake. Ay, girl, what do I have to do to win you over?"

"Set me free,"—her soft, gentle voice rang like a bell in his
fevered head—"and God will forgive you everything you've
done."

"God, yes," he said. "He'd do that. He knows what's in my heart. But what about you?"

"I'd bless you and remember you always as a friend."

"Well, if that's all," he said. "If that's all you want . . . maybe it could happen." He was ashamed to lie to her like this but it was all he had with which to buy that moment of farewell illusion. "Who knows. And if that's possible maybe you'll feel better about me now and feel sorry later that you were so hard on me . . ."

He kept his eyes down, and his face averted, and listened to his own voice as if it were a stranger's. He wanted that warm moment at any price and a half-promise that he'd never keep was as good as any. His reward came at once. Hope shined in Helen's eyes, her hands came together, and the cold, distant frown vanished from her face.

"Do you mean that?" she asked. Her voice was soft and trembling and he felt his own heart hammering in his chest.

"Hmm. Well. *Ne znayu*," he muttered deep down in his throat. "Maybe. I don't know. I can't do it now, it's too dangerous . . . All the Tartar Hordes are camped in the Wild Lands, their *tchambuls* go where they please all over the country. The Dobrudjans are heading this way from Rashkov and they're the worst of the lot of them. It'd be sure death for you . . . But maybe when I come back. Maybe then, eh? I'm like a child beside you. Warm clay in your hands. You can make me do anything you want. So maybe then, eh? *Ne znaju*, I don't know . . ."

"May God show you the light!" she cried, and her warm, crystal voice rang with gratitude and hope. "May our Holy Mother lead you into mercy. Go with God!"

" . . . And come back to you?"

"Yes." She nodded. She stretched out her hand. "Come back unharmed, as a friend."

The Cossack threw himself down on his knees before her, seized her hand with a savage hunger and fixed his lips on it as if to devour it; but then he glanced up, caught the cold, distant look returning to her eyes, and dropped her hand as if it had burned him.

"I will," he muttered, bowing from the waist in the Cossack manner, and backed away from her, his cap in his hand, all the way to the hangings that shielded the door. "I'll be back. When the war's over. Then . . . we'll see."

She watched the rich embroideries fall into place behind him and pressed her hands together to offer her thanks to God. Still hardly able to believe it, she thought that she was witnessing an act of God's mercy. From outside came the quick, lively sounds of questions and orders, a brief laugh, the rattle of weapons and the stamping of the horses' hooves, and soon afterwards she heard a Cossack riding song sung in many voices.

". . . *Budejh slava slavna*
Pomejh Kozakami..
Pomejh druhami . . .
Do kintza, vikha . . ."

The voices dwindled and the hoofbeats faded down the canyon but their echoes still drifted behind them among the granite walls, and she listened to them as if they were the voices of her own new hope.

". . . *There'll be fame to spare*
Among Brother Cossacks . . .
Among faithful friends . . .
Not just for the year . . .
But until time's end . . ."

And then the song, its echoes and the hoofbeats died down altogether. And then there was silence.

Chapter Forty

IT HAPPENED AT ABOUT that time that Skshetuski's three friends—the fat knight, Pan Longinus and little Pan Michal—sat in his quarters in the great encampment of Tcholhanski Kamyen where the warriors of the Commonwealth were gathering for the coming battle, and nodded sadly over a jug of wine, and worried about him and his missing Helen.

"Our Good Lord already granted her one miraculous rescue," Pan Zagloba offered. "Let's hope that He'll show her another act of mercy. Ah, if we only knew that she was still alive somewhere!"

"How can she be?" Pan Michal shook his head and sighed. "Nobody survived the storming of Bar. The rabble murdered everyone."

But Pan Zagloba seized on a thread of hope and started to develop his own thought without attention to anybody else. "Is that so? Hmm. Well. Maybe. Maybe. But something is whispering in my ear that Bohun's got her in his paws again. We know that after Pan Longinus captured that halfwit Pulyan, Bohun became Krivoinos' second-in-command. His right hand so to speak, may the Devil chew it off at the shoulder! And if that's so then he was there when Bar fell to the Zaporohjans."

"True, true," the Lithuanian murmured, clasped his hands, and raised his eyes hopefully to the ceiling.

"He could've missed her among all those victims," Pan Michal suggested. "There were more than twenty thousand people killed in the streets after the assault."

"You think so?" Zagloba shook his head. "Then you don't

know that man. I'll swear he knew that Helen was in Bar. And if he knew it then he'd have got to her in time and saved her from the massacre."

"That's not much consolation for Skshetuski," the little knight said. "If I was Yan I think I'd rather see her dead than in those hands again."

"Ay, it's a shame even to think about it," sighed the mournful giant.

"Shame? I think it's a lot more than just a shame," the little knight sniffed away a tear. "It's enough to drive anybody mad."

"Sheer desperation!" cried the Lithuanian, tugging at his huge, dangling mustache. "Is there nothing anyone can do?"

"There's got to be something."

"Yes, but what?"

Pan Zagloba began to twist his own beard and mustache, trying to think of some miracle that might have saved Helen, and he was as desperate about that as if she were his own natural daughter. But all his best ideas foundered on uncertainty about her survival.

"It can't be," he muttered. "It can't be that I saved her that last time just so she'd die in Bar. It can't be, I tell you."

"And even if she did die," Pan Michal sniffed in chorus with the Lithuanian. "She'd have died dishonored."

"Oh the shame of it!" Pan Longinus cried again, smearing his own tears across his face with his enormous fists.

Finally the fat knight himself started to lose hope and looked for relief in cursing the rebels. "Oh those flea-bitten dogs!" he roared out. "May the Jews grind their bones into flour and fry them for pancakes! May the Tartars twist all their guts into bow strings! God created all men, I admit, but there's no way He had anything to do with those hellish people. The Devil made them, that's who! May all their women turn into fallow mares!"

"I never met that sweet lady," little Pan Michal said and nodded sadly while a tear curved down his cheek and hung suspended on the point of his yellow mustache. "But . . . I tell you . . . I'd rather have misfortune falling on my head for the rest of my life than that she'd suffer what she must have suffered."

"I only saw her once," the Lithuanian murmured. "But when I think of her now . . . ah . . . ah, it's hard to go on living."

"You say that?" howled Zagloba, now totally beside himself

with grief. "You who hardly knew her? And what am I to say about it . . . I, who loved her as if she was my own only daughter? Who saved her once already? And for what? Eh? What about my feelings?"

"And what about Skshetuski?" asked Volodyovski.

They sat in a gloomy silence but Pan Zagloba simply wouldn't let himself believe that everything was lost. "Can it really be that we can't think of something?" he asked.

"If we can't, then it's our duty to avenge her," Volodyovski said, moving his whiskers fiercely up and down.

"God grant that this next great battle takes place soon," Pan Longinus murmured. "They say the Tartars are already gathered in the Wild Lands."

But Pan Zagloba's thoughts darted off on a different course. "I can't believe that the three of us would leave that poor, helpless girl to her fate," he said. "I've rattled my old bones enough around the world, and I'd just as soon spend the rest of my days in peace behind some baker's oven, but I tell you that I'll go to Istanbul after her if I have to. Even if I've got to get dressed up again in those bug-infested rags and spend the rest of my life playing that damned lyre that I can't think about without getting hoarse."

"If anybody can think of something," Pan Longinus said. "It's sure to be you."

"Hmm. Yes. Well. I've thought of lots of things," the fat knight said. "If Prince Dominic had half as many ideas in his head we'd have Hmyelnitzki stuffed and dangling upside down tomorrow. I've tried to share some of these ideas with Skshetuski but there's no way to talk to him about anything these days. He's all chewed up with pain. You'd better keep a sharp eye on him, gentlemen, or he might lose his reason altogether."

"Ah, ah! You think so?" Pan Longinus worried.

"I know so. If you let suffering ferment in the brain it sours the mind. Even the best wine turns to vinegar if you leave it in the cask too long."

"True, true," Pan Podbipyenta murmured. "It's been known to happen."

But the restless little knight was stirring with impatience. "So what did you think of?"

"What did I think of? Well, first we've got to make sure that she's still alive, may the angels guard her! And there are two ways to do that. We'll find some good, loyal men among the Prince's Cossacks who'll pretend to desert to the rebels, join Bohun's people, and find out what those cut-throats know about all this . . ."

"I've just the men for that!" Pan Michal interrupted. "Ruthenian dragoons! Leave that part to me."

"Yes, yes, but wait a bit," the fat knight went on. "The other thing is to get our hands on a few of those butchers who sacked Bar. If Bohun was there, and I'll swear he was, they'd know everything he did. You wouldn't believe how they revere that Devil. He's their sun and moon and all the stars together and he can't lift a finger without one of them making a song about it. If he stole our poor girl from that convent you can be sure that all those witless dogs were howling about it the next day."

"We can do both, can't we?" Pan Longinus asked. "Send the disguised dragoons and try to capture a few prisoners as well."

"That's it exactly!" Pan Zagloba cried. "And then, once we know she is still alive, we can all get dressed up as peasants and go searching for her! In fact the more I think about it the better it looks to me. Whom can we trust more than ourselves? Hmm. Yes. Why bother sending others when we can do it all? Eh? What do you say? Let's send out right now for some homespun shirts and set out tomorrow!"

"That just can't happen," Volodyovski said.

"And why not? Hmm? What's to stop us?"

"Discipline," said the little colonel but Pan Zagloba wasn't quite as familiar with that word as a Vishnovyetzki soldier.

"What's that got to do with anything?"

"Duty, that's what. Orders. There isn't a soldier in the Prince's service who'd ask for leave on the eve of battle. Not if his father and mother were both on their deathbeds! Don't you know what it means when the gentry is ordered to report for war '*nemine excepto?*' I thought you've seen a few campaigns in your time."

"Eh? What? Have I seen campaigning?" the fat knight cleared his throat and assumed his most grim and martial expression. "Of course I have! More than you, I'd wager. Of course I know about duty coming first and '*nemine excepto.*' No exceptions means just what it says! I just forgot it for a moment, that's all . . . Still, I think His Highness might listen to us if we were to ask him . . ."

"Don't even dream of it," Pan Volodyovski said. "There couldn't be a greater dishonor for a soldier. Once the battle's fought and the enemy is scattered that's a different story. Then we can ask for leave. But never before."

"But the Prince cares about Skshetuski," the fat knight tried again. "And since what we're doing is for him . . ."

"He'd just tell us to follow Skshetuski's example," the little knight broke in, and then went on to explain to the fidgeting Zagloba. "Don't you think Yan would be the first to go searching for his girl if it was possible for anyone to go? He'd fly if he had wings! He'd let himself be torn apart by wild horses to save her . . .!"

"Well, then . . ." the fat knight started to put up an argument but the indomitable little soldier wouldn't let him finish.

"Look," he said. "Skshetuski's reputation is made in this army. Nobody would even think of questioning his courage if he went off somewhere before a great battle. And yes, it's true, the Prince loves him as he would a son. But Yan knows his duty. He wouldn't breathe one word about his own concerns while he is under orders. The one thing is service to the country, you see, and the other is just private business, no matter how distressing or important. Skshetuski would gnaw his own heart into pulp before he put his private needs above his country's service."

"Hmm. Yes, I know he's got the soul of a Roman," Pan Zagloba muttered. "And . . . ah . . . I can see that it wouldn't do to ask for leave while the army's gathering for an important battle. But if someone was to whisper in the Prince's ear . . . remind him, so to speak, about Skshetuski's suffering and tell him about Helen . . . maybe he'd give us permission to go anyway. Without the need for anybody asking . . ."

"It wouldn't even occur to him," Pan Michal shook his head. "D'you think he'd take the time to worry about some private tragedy when the fate of the whole Commonwealth is resting on his shoulders? But even if the impossible could happen, and if His Highness did decide to send his best officers on leave when he's about to fight the most decisive battle of the war, not one of us would take it! We too know our duty."

"Of course, of course . . ." The fat knight sighed, resigned.

"I wouldn't go either, that goes without saying. Service is . . . ah . . . service, and duty is duty . . . I only mentioned this possibility because it happened to pop up in my head. But popping up is one thing and staying is another . . .

"And anyway," he went on, just as quick to give up an unpopular idea as he was to seize one. "We probably wouldn't get far among the rebels while their whole might and power is still untouched and they've control of all that country out there. Once they're beaten . . . scattering and all that . . . it'll be easier to make our way among them. Safer too, I'd say. And they'll be more willing to tell us what we need to know if they're worried about their own necks."

"That makes good sense," Pan Longinus said.

"And in the meantime there are those two other plans of yours that we could try," Volodyovski added. "The Prince would be glad to approve that kind of a mission."

"So be it then," Pan Zagloba muttered, sighed, and started peering around for another flagon of Skshetuski's *Troyniak*. "It's just so hard to sit here, doing nothing, while the army is still in the process of assembling. I tell you, if our own Prince was the commander here we'd have been on our way a long time ago but Prince Dominic doesn't seem to be in a hurry to lead us anywhere. Or even to get here, come to think of it."

"They say he's expected in three days," Pan Michal said.

"The sooner the better."

★ ★ ★

Just then the door creaked open and Skshetuski came into the room. He was as cold and remote as if his three friends were total strangers to him; looking at him Pan Zagloba thought that he had never seen such a stony grimness chiseled into a living face.

'*Could he be that indifferent?*' he wondered. '*That unfeeling?* '

No sign of life sparkled in the young man's eyes. His face was rigid. He moved, yes, but other than that he seemed like a statue carved from ice and granite, as if the warm glow of a smile had never crossed those features. His thick, black beard hung down to the middle of his chest and showed some new silver threads that aged him by years but his friends could only guess at the depth of his suffering. Ever since the news of the fall of Bar struck him like a thunderbolt, he showed so little interest in anything other than his military duties, and he was so wholly and implacably turned to the grim business of the war, that the fat knight felt a sudden rage at the thought that he might have turned his back on Helen and forgotten her.

"We were just talking about your misfortune," he said to Skshetuski. "It's our own tragedy as well, God knows, since we can't think of anything that might help. But these would be only empty phrases if we weren't ready to spill our blood for her as well, along with our tears. We'll do all we can to find her and restore her to you if—as God must grant it in His mercy!— she is still alive."

"Thank you." Skshetuski nodded.

"We'll go with you right into Hmyelnitzki's camp if that's what it takes," Pan Michal added with a worried glance at his friend's cold face.

"Thank you." Skshetuski turned away.

"We know,"—Zagloba felt anger rising along with uneasiness—"that you've sworn to search for her, alive or dead, so we're also ready . . . even if we're to start today . . ."

But the urgency went out of his voice before the cold, withdrawn emptiness in Skshetuski's face. The young man sat down heavily on a bench, fixed his blank eyes on the floor as if he was bored, and Pan Zagloba dwindled into silence. He told himself that his suspicions about the young lieutenant just couldn't be true. He remembered the joy with which Skshetuski embraced him in the little canyon where his masquerade as a peasant *staretz* had come to its end. He recalled every eager question that the young man asked him. If he said nothing now . . . if he seemed to have abandoned every hope and feeling . . . it was— it had to be!—only because he'd gone beyond the last barriers of his own endurance, and his icy surface was just the cold foreshadowing of that death for which he was longing.

There was no sound then in the small, whitewashed room of the peasant hut in which Zjendjan set up his master's quarters just outside the camp. No one stirred. No one seemed to have anything more to say. The dim and meager candlelight threw their twisted shadows high onto the ceiling and only the deep, occasional sighs of Pan Longinus broke the heavy silence.

★   ★   ★

Finally the little knight moved over to sit beside his friend
Skshetuski and to nudge him gently on the shoulder.

"Where have you been?" he asked

"To the Prince."

"Is there any news?"

"Just orders."

"Anything important?"

"I'm taking out a reconnaissance tonight."

"A big one?"

"One regiment of Cossacks and one of Valachians. Five hundred men altogether."

"Hey, that's not a recon party!" Volodyovski laughed, brightening for a moment. "That's an expedition! Are you going far?"

Skshetuski shrugged. "As far as Yarmolinsk if the road is
clear."

"Yarmolinsk?" The little knight glanced quickly at Zagloba.
"That's out towards Bar, isn't it?"

"About halfway there."

"Hmm. Is that so?" Pan Zagloba caught Volodyovski's eye,
signaled a question and read his quick agreement. "We . . .
ah . . . might just come along to keep you company if that's all
right with you . . ."

"It's fine with me," Skshetuski said. "If the Prince agrees. I'll
go and ask him for you."

Then, turning to the little knight, he added: "You'd better
come and see if he doesn't have something else for you to do in
the time that we'd be away."

"Good." Pan Michal grinned and cocked his eyebrow mutely
at Zagloba. "Then we'll go together. I've something else to ask
him anyway."

"And we'll go with you," Pan Zagloba said and winked
rapidly at Pan Podbipyenta whose mouth flew open as if he was
about to speak.

★ ★ ★

Two hours later, even as the last red traces of the day sunk in
the west behind them, the four friends rode out of the encampment.

They rode southeast, then turned due south towards Bokh
and Medvedovka. Prince Yeremi not only allowed Pan Michal
and Pan Longinus to join Skshetuski's party—indeed he was

glad to add two experienced officers to this important mission—but he was quick to approve Volodyovski's private plea
for a few dozen disguised Ruthenian dragoons who might be
left as spies among the Zaporohjans.

"I'd gladly let you go to search for Skshetuski's girl," he told
Volodyovski out of Pan Yan's hearing. "But that'll have to wait.
How is he, by the way? I worry about him. Has he said
anything to you about her?"

"Not much, Highness. His first thought was to rush in
among the Cossacks, come what may. Then he remembered
that we're here *nemine excepto* and that our duty must come first.
That's why he never breathed a word about this to Your Highness. But God only knows what's going on inside him."

The Prince nodded. "I can't tell you how I pity him. Look
after him well because I see that you're a good friend of his."

They rode swiftly, without taking any special precautions so
near to the camp, and the bright, warm night soothed even Pan
Zagloba's anxiety and impatience. Although September already
turned the leaves into their Autumn colors, the night seemed
like one that belonged to Summer. But then the whole year was
like that, Zagloba reflected. There'd hardly been a Winter worth
talking about, and Spring breathed an early life into everything
that bloomed on the Steppes normally only in the Summer, and
the Autumn nights were warm and pale with moonlight.

"Look how the moon shines on that hillock over there," he
whispered to the little knight and the Lithuanian. "You'd swear
it was daytime."

The three friends trotted side by side, their companies riding
quietly in column behind them. They spoke in low voices.
Skshetuski and several dozen of the Prince's Cossacks were
scouting the road ahead.

"They say that bright nights like this come only in wartime,"
the fat knight went on. "So that the souls of the dead don't lose
their way to Heaven in the darkness or crack their skulls on
some low-hanging branch like sparrows in a stable. What's
more this is Friday, when evil spirits can't get too close to a man
and the earth keeps a tight lid on all the evil that spews out of
Hell. I'm starting to feel better. I feel new hope rising up inside
me. I've this sudden feeling that something useful is going to
come out of this little trip of ours."

"The main thing is that we're on the road," Pan Michal

agreed. "There's nothing worse than sitting around and worrying and doing nothing."

"Right," the fat knight said. "Once you start bumping up and down on a horse all of your desperations slide down your spine until they reach the place where they can shake themselves right out of you. It's always like that."

"Still," the small knight murmured, nodding towards the moonlit road ahead where Skshetuski rode. "I don't believe you can shake your deepest longings out like that. Love, for example, which bites into your heart like a tick and hangs on no matter what you do."

"Oh yes, oh yes," Pan Longinus sighed. "You can wrestle with it like a bear but it'll get you down anyway if it's the honest kind . . ."

He heaved another sigh thinking about Anusia, his Courland mare followed his example, and the sentimental little soldier raised his eyes soulfully to the pale stars. They were as distant and unreachable as the new object of his own affections. Now that the Prince's older daughter, Anna, announced her engagement to one of the Pototzkis, he transferred his unrequited passions to the younger Barbara. The horses began to snort and toss their heads among the regiments that rode behind them, and the troopers answered with their traditional '*Zdrov! Zdrov!* Keep healthy!' and then a lone, soft voice in the rear ranks began a plaintive song.

> '. . . *Goin' to war, my lad*
> *Goin' to the fight . . .*
> *Your days will be cold, my lad . . .*
> *An' you'll weep at night . . .*'

★ ★ ★

Some hours passed as the horsemen rode into the rolling plains which lay as wide and open under the full, white moon as if they were a carpet embroidered with darkly muted colors, and which spread out before them like the rich offering of an oriental trader. The track was soft and silvery with dust. The column moved swiftly. They rode southeast across this peaceful northern corner of the Ukraine that was still practically untouched by the war and they could marvel at the beauty of the land around them which lifted their spirits.

"Old soldiers say that it's a good sign when the horses snort at the start of an expedition," the little knight observed. "It means they're sure of coming home again, which is what my own father, may he rest in peace, used to tell me when I was a boy."

"I've got a good feeling myself about this jaunt of ours," Pan Zagloba said.

"God grant that Pan Yan also finds some ease," Pan Longinus murmured.

"Yes, yes," Zagloba said and squirmed in his saddle like a man who can't quite shake off an oppressive worry. "But I've something altogether different rattling in my head. I don't know . . . maybe I see it wrong . . . but it seems to me that he's less concerned about that poor girl than any of us."

"You couldn't be more wrong!" Volodyovski answered.

"Well, that's what it looks like."

"You just don't know him well enough," the small knight explained. "He's a very private sort of man who doesn't spill his own anxieties all over everybody else. He keeps it all bottled up inside him which is why we're all so worried about him now. Believe me, I've know him for years, and he's always been like that."

"Hmm. Well. That may be. But remember how he was when we tried to offer him a little hope? '*Thank you*,' he said as if it didn't matter one way or another. He couldn't have been more offhand about it if he tried. And God knows it would be the blackest ingratitude on his part if he forgot about her. You can't imagine how she cared for him. I watched it for months with my own eyes."

"No, no." Volodyovski shook his head. "That simply couldn't happen. Not with him."

But Pan Zagloba was difficult to convince once an idea took root and sprouted in his head. "It's hard to believe that any man can have such iron self-control," he said.

"You should've seen him when Bohun seized the girl the first time," said Volodyovski. "We thought he'd go mad. But if God helped him find some sort of peace in this terrible situation, and if Yan found a way to live with his pain, then that's all the better! As his true friends we should be glad of it rather than criticizing something we don't understand."

Annoyed, the little knight spurred his horse and galloped ahead to join Skshetuski while Pan Zagloba and Pan Podbipyenta rode in silence for a while longer.

"Ah," Zagloba sighed at last. "It seems to me that the world would be a lot happier without all this loving. Nothing but grief comes out of it. Thank God that's all behind me."

"No one can avoid what's meant for him," the Lithuanian said.

"And you, my Lithuanian hop-pole, always miss the point! What does fate have to do with anything I'm saying? Eh? Look at Troy. Why did it fall? Even the ancients weren't smart enough to avoid squabbling over a flighty woman. And what about this war of ours? Hmm? So Hmyelnitzki had an eye for Pani Tchaplinska, or maybe Tchaplinski wanted a piece of Pani Hmyelnitzka, the Devil take them both, and look at the mess the rest of us are in!"

"That's because it was an unclean kind of love," the gentle giant murmured and heaved a sigh as heavy as a bellows. "But there's the other kind that brings happiness to people and adds to God's glory."

"Now you're a little closer to the truth of it," Pan Zagloba muttered. "And how soon d'you plan to start working in that little vineyard? I heard about that silk scarf you got as a keepsake."

"Ey, ey, good brother," the Lithuanian murmured, turned as crimson as a boiled beetroot, and lowered his head.

"It's that bad, is it?" Pan Zagloba smiled. "But those three missing heads are still in the way?"

"Ah! Ah! That's just it!"

"Hmm. Well I'll tell you what to do about it. Take one good swipe at Hmyelnitzki, Bohun and the Khan and we'll all go home to dance at your wedding."

"Ah . . .! If only they'd line up and hold still!" cried the desperate Lithuanian and clasped his hands as if about to pray.

*   *   *

Meanwhile the little knight caught up with Skshetuski and rode beside him with nothing much to say. Pan Yan was silent and withdrawn. Pan Michal shot a number of quick glances at him, peering up from under the rim of his helmet at his friend's lifeless face, and finally he nudged Pan Yan's stirrup with his own.

"Listen Yan," he said gently. "It's bad to plunge like that into heavy thinking. It's not good to dwell so much on your own pain."

"I'm not thinking about anything," Skshetuski said quietly. "I'm praying."

"Yes, well that's a holy and worthy thing to do, I know, but you're not a monk to live on your prayers."

Pan Yan turned his worn, harrowed face towards Volodyovski and the little knight shuddered under the impact of those tortured eyes. "What else is left for me, Michal?" Skshetuski asked in a dull, leaden voice, as full of resignation as if his life was over.

"What do you mean '*what's left?*' "

"If not a monk's habit?"

"What's left is your duty to save her," Pan Michal insisted. "To search for her and find her wherever she is, that's what."

"And that's just what I'll do while there's still any breath left in me," the young soldier whispered. "But won't it be too late? I can search for her . . . even find her, yes . . . But save her? God keep me from these thoughts . . . God save me from these visions! I can think about anything except her suffering!"

"Have you no hope left?"

"I've nothing left except the wish to tear her out of those cursed hands," the low, broken voice went on as if each word was a separate particle of pain. "I'll look for her. I'll find her if she is still alive. But . . . after that . . . let her turn to the kind of forgetfulness and peace that I'll be seeking for myself as well."

"Where, Yan, where?" the little knight cried out. "In a monk's cell?"

"Where else? What else is there, Michal?" Skshetuski asked so softly that Volodyovski could barely hear him although he strained to listen. "Tell me, what else is left for either her or me after what has happened? God's will just wasn't with us . . . It wasn't meant to be. So let me alone, my dear friend. Leave me to my prayers. And don't stir up the horrors in my mind."

Volodyovski felt as if his own chest was gripped in an iron vise. He wanted to say something else . . . anything . . . and he groped for consoling words that might show his grief and pity and affection, and perhaps stir the ashes of Skshetuski's hope to some new form of life. But he was never very good with words, and when he did stumble on some that he wanted, they refused to squeeze out of his dry throat. He rode in helpless silence beside Skshetuski whose dry lips moved swiftly in a soundless prayer; and he stared with a terrible premonition at that gaunt, drained face of a monk resigned from the cares of the world, or of a bearded hermit, alone in a wilderness, who had abandoned all hope of life among his fellow men. In that still night, and in that silver moonlight, it seemed like a face glimpsed in an open grave.

And suddenly that lone, sad voice in the rear ranks was singing again:

> ' . . . *When you come home, my lad*
> *When you come home again . . .*
> *You'll find an empty bed . . .*
> *And a heart full of pain.*'

Chapter Forty-one

SKSHETUSKI LED HIS RAIDERS into rebel country as swiftly and as cunningly as if they were a pack of timber wolves running among hunters. They moved only at night. By daylight they lay low in the woods and thickets, hidden without campfires or any other sign of life in the deep, overgrown ravines which dotted that region, and they crept out into the open, as silent as shadows, only after nightfall.

Nearing some village, Pan Yan would throw a tight cordon around it so that no fugitive could break out and run with a warning, and then his men charged in from all directions at the same time. He had the terrified inhabitants pulled out of their beds and driven into the village square; he requisitioned food for his men and fodder for the horses; he rounded up and questioned the village elders and left the frightened peasants unharmed unless they resisted. And then he and his men would vanish in the night as suddenly and unexpectedly as they came.

Once out of sight of the panicked villagers, his column took a sudden turn, changed the direction of its march, and disappeared in the forests long before the sunrise so that the Zaporohjans were never able to discover which way it had gone. The point of his expedition, as he told his officers, was to ascertain if Krivoinos and his forty thousand Podolian insurgents were still besieging the stronghold of Kamyenetz or whether they were coming back into the Ukraine to augment Hmyelnitzki.

"We're also to track down the Dobrudjan and Belgorodian Tartars," he told his three companions as they jogged one night along a moonlit country track. "The Prince must know at once if they're already across the Dniester and joined up with Krivoinos, or if he plans to give up the siege and march north to reinforce Hmyelnitzki."

"You'd think the regents would've seen to all that a long time ago," the little knight observed. "Their best chance is to attack Hmyelnitzki right now, before he gets too strong."

"Well, you know the regents."

"When's Prince Dominic expected at the camp?" Pan Longinus asked.

"When he fills up his belly at those banquets he's been giving every day on his way from Warsaw," Pan Zagloba said. This was about a week after Skshetuski's raiders left the army's camp on their expedition. "And judging by the size of his belly that might take some time."

"At this rate," said the little knight, "even the Khan will have time to come up with his Perekop, Nohay and Azovian hordes, not to mention Krivoinos and the other Tartars. And we are outnumbered five to one as it is."

"We faced greater odds at Konstantinov," Pan Longinus murmured.

"Yes," Pan Yan said quietly. "But it was Prince Yeremi who commanded there."

★   ★   ★

They rode in silence after that, each thinking of all the other lost chances to defeat Hmyelnitzki, but for Pan Yan the mission acquired an additional importance.

It didn't take a soldier of his wide experience to see that two hundred thousand Tartar warriors, added to the hundred thousand Cossacks whom Hmyelnitzki had already gathered for his final confrontation with the Commonwealth, were a deadly danger. Defeat, he knew, would allow Hmyelnitzki to invade the heart of the country, with nothing left to bar his way before the great regional capitals of Krakow and Lvov, and leaving the road open all the way to the gates of Warsaw. Under these circumstances Krivoinos was all the more dangerous because he could march due north from Kamyenetz, return to the devastated country around Konstantinov, and cut off the regents' last line of retreat if they should move deeper into the Ukraine.

If nothing else, he thought, that savage old marauder with his mobs of *tchernya* had to be kept pinned down in his Kamyenetz trenches.

"What we'll do, then," Pan Yan said to his three companions, "is not only find Krivoinos and discover what he plans to do but we'll try to keep him in Podolia."

"How?" Pan Zagloba was immediately alarmed. "Fight his thousands with our five hundred men? Doesn't that seem . . . ah . . . more than even we could manage?"

"That's one way of putting it," Pan Michal said and grinned at the worried fat knight and winked at Skshetuski. "That way we'll hold them up for about an hour."

"If that long," Skshetuski agreed. "No. There's a better way. We'll convince him that Prince Yeremi himself is marching down on him again."

"But won't that stir him to come looking for us?" The night was balmy—in fact a brisk, pleasant breeze gave the expedition the quality of a country outing—but Pan Zagloba felt sweat trickling suddenly into his coat collar. "Not that I'm worried about it, you understand. Of course I'm not worried! But I've been feeling a little out of breath in the last few days . . ."

"No," Pan Yan said. "I doubt he'll move if he thinks that we're the vanguard of the Prince's army. His own men won't let him face the Prince in another battle."

"We might even panic him into running east," Pan Michal suggested.

"We might."

"So let's do it."

So first they told their own soldiers that they were only an advance guard for the Prince's entire division, and then they started spreading rumors among the local peasants that the regents had already fought and defeated Hmyelnitzki and that Prince Yeremi was on his way to Podolia to settle with Krivoinos once and for all.

The news spread like wildfire, as they knew it would. It ran through every river settlement and village all the way to the banks of the Dniester. It emptied the rebel countryside all along the Zbrutch and Smotrytcha rivers as if it were an announcement of the plague. It flowed like a threatening, poisonous mist down the quick waters of the Studyenitza, Ushka and Kalusik, and the wind itself seemed to carry it southeast to Kamyenetz and the wilderness of the Yahorlik beyond it.

And once more the terrifying cry rang among the rebels: "*Yarema is coming!*"

* * *

Krivoinos himself heard it and believed it because this was what he expected all along. What else made better sense for the Commonwealth commanders? The regents would march on Hmyelnitzki, and the terrible Prince would fall on him again, and at first the canny old marauder didn't know what to do. March his own army to meet Yarema in the field? He did it once already and lost half his *tchernya*. His own colonels threatened to murder him at Konstantinov if he tried to lead them once more against Vishnovyetzki. He knew that his *moloytzy*, as young Cossack warriors were known in those days, would fight like wild dogs against any other soldiers of the Commonwealth, but they'd scatter like a flock of geese before an eagle if Yarema came near them again. To crouch under the walls and cannon of Kamyenetz until Vishnovyetzki trapped him in his trenches promised an even greater certainty of disaster.

So what should he do? Neither fortune-tellers nor buckets of *gojhalka* offered inspiration. Sitting still and waiting meant death and destruction for his men. Marching to meet and fight Yarema in the open field meant sure death for him even before he found the terrible Vishnovyetzki; either his own atamans would kill him or the *tchernya* would tear him into pieces. And he had all too many rivals among his own colonels who would be glad to pull him down, drag him to Hmyelnitzki, and have him chained like a dog to another cannon.

He'd march, yes, he decided finally, but not towards Yarema; he'd ride as far east as he could, maybe as far as Bratzlav, then circle around to the west and run to join the Tartars and Hmyelnitzki. He knew that if he dodged about like that he'd probably miss the great battle that would decide the fate of the rebellion but at least he'd hear about the outcome in good time and think of some way to save his own skin if the regents triumphed.

And then came the rumors that Hmyelnitzki was already beaten. Could that be true? Fugitives from the north confirmed it every day. Some claimed to have heard it from the advance guard of Yarema's army which passed through their villages or those of their neighbors; others didn't know how they'd heard about it except that the wind itself seemed to be hissing the news throughout the whole country.

"Hmyel's beaten!" the refugees howled throughout his camp. "The Tartars are beaten!"

"*Yarema is coming!*"

And at the first echo of this news twenty thousand of Krivoinos' Cossacks broke camp and galloped pell-mell to the east as if to look for shelter among the Dobrudjans camped beyond the Wild Lands.

★ ★ ★

Krivoinos chewed his callused hands, beat his shaved head on the earthen floor of his tent and tore at his scalp-lock, but no ideas came. Yarema wouldn't have left the regents until the great battle was over one way or another, he knew; if the terrible Prince was really marching down on him then Hmyel must be finished, there was nowhere left for him to run and he was as good as dying on a stake!

But before the fierce old ataman could order a general retreat into the Steppe he had to make sure from which direction his enemy was coming. But which of his colonels could he send to find out? None would volunteer. It had to be a man, he knew, who had no fear of death and who wouldn't break under torture and reveal the planned flight into the Steppes if he was defeated and captured by Yarema's soldiers.

And then one night he sent for Bohun.

"Listen, Yuri," he said. "Yarema's coming down on us. Looks like we're lost."

"I heard he's coming, *bat'ku,*" Bohun said. "We talked about it before, you and me, remember? But why does it mean we're lost?"

"*Ne zderjhymo,* that's why. We can't hold out against him. Anybody else we can take, and the more of 'em the better, but not that bloodthirsty devil Yarema. He's an evil spirit, not a man. The *moloytzy* are afraid of him."

"I'm not afraid of him." The young ataman shrugged and smiled coldly in contempt. "I've already wiped out one of his regiments right under his nose back in Vasilovka."

"I know, my good friend, I know," the cunning old man muttered, sighed and nodded. "You're not afraid of anything, you're our hawk . . . our falcon. That's why I love you, lad. Like you was my own son."

"And you, Maksym Krivoinos, you've been like a father to me," the young Cossack murmured.

"Yes, yes I have," the old ataman went on, peering up at Bohun out of hooded eyes like a sleepy raptor. "You're as good a man as Yarema any day . . . Your bright Cossack fame is as great as his princely one, maybe even better . . . But I can't give him battle, you know that, 'cause the *moloytzy* won't follow me against him!"

He paused and gnawed his own bloody hand, as if ashamed of all his young warriors, and then he let a plaintive note creep into his voice.

"Hey, son, d'you remember how the atamans threatened me in council? Eh? How they went for their knives and sabers and shook them in my face and howled for my blood?"

Bohun nodded. "I remember, father."

"I want to fight Yarema," the old Cossack's hoarse voice trembled with self-pity. "You know I do. But the lads say I just want to drive them like cattle to slaughter. They say I'm throwing good Cossacks on a butcher's block. So how can I fight him? And now I hear he's coming down here after me . . ."

"So let's leave this cursed place, father," Bohun said simply. "Why not? We aren't doing much good here anyway against that *Lah* castle. Let's go and join up with Hmyel and fight in the open where there's new blood to spill and fresh loot waiting for us."

"Ah, but people are saying he got beat already . . ."

"That I don't believe, Father Maksym." Bohun shook his head. "Hmyel's a fox. He's cunning. He wouldn't take on the *Lahy* without the Tartars right there beside him, every last one of them. And anyway, if he could beat the Hetmans he can beat those regents."

"That's what I think too," Krivoinos said quickly. "But we've got to know, son. Right?"

"If you say so, father."

"That's right. And I say so. We could go around that devil Vishnovyetzki and join up with Hmyel, but we've got to know for sure what Yarema's doing."

"So let's find out, Father Maksym," Bohun said.

"Aye, son, but how?" A sad, hopeless tone crept into the

canny old Zaporohjan's voice. "Who'd offer to go find his trail? The atamans don't want to go anywhere near him, the young *moloytzy* are afraid of him . . . Ey, if I had just one good man who wasn't scared of that evil spirit, who could track him down like a wolf in his lair and bring back a few prisoners we could question, I'd fill his cap with gold, I would . . . But where can I find such a man?"

"I'll go, Father Maksym," Bohun said.

"You?"

"Why not?" Bohun burst out laughing. "Hey, if I could run rings around the Tartars in the old days, if I had the Khan himself tearing at his beard and peering into shadows, what's a few *Lah* soldiers? And it won't be for the gold either that I'll be going, father. I'll go just for the glory of it, for my good Cossack name."

"You'd go yourself, Yuri?" Krivoinos pretended vast astonishment and then an even greater joy. "You, my son? You're the second ataman here after me, you're an important man, and you want to go on a thing like this?"

"Why not?" Bohun shrugged again. "Yarema's no different than any other man. He'll bleed if you cut him."

"Sure he will." Krivoinos shrugged his own thick shoulders, looked sideways at Bohun out of his slanted, cruel little eyes and nodded his huge head. "Sure he would . . . But it takes a real man to know that. It takes the heart of a Hetman to see it that way . . . Ey, Yuri lad, you'll be the first ataman over all the Cossacks someday, and d'you know why? Because you're just like me. You're not afraid of Yarema either."

"Yarema or the Devil," Bohun said, unsmiling. "It's all one to me."

"So fly then, you falcon!" A cold, hard gleam flickered briefly in the cunning eyes. "Go and snap at Yarema' heels, find out where he's heading, and you can ask for anything you want after you've come back! Ay, I tell you lad, I'd have gone myself if I was free to do it. Why not? A man can never have too much glory, eh? But how could I go and leave the camp when I'm the first ataman in this army?"

"That's right, father." The young ataman nodded seriously. "If you were to go the *tchernya* would panic. They'd run for their lives. The *moloytzy* would start crying out that you were running out on them, abandoning the army, and they'd scatter to the four winds themselves. But when they see me go it'll just put a new heart in them all."

"So go, go! How many men d'you want?"

"The fewer the better, father, on this kind of party. A small detachment moves faster and it's harder to spot. Five hundred men will do."

"Against Yarema's soldiers?"

Bohun laughed and bent down to embrace the old ataman as if this was, indeed, the father he never knew. "Don't worry, Father Maksym. I'll be back. I'll bring you all the prisoners you want, and they'll be gentry who can tell you everything that you need to know, not some rear rank spear-carriers."

"So go right away, son," Krivoinos said hoarsely. "As soon as you're ready. Those *Lahy* here in Kamyenetz are shooting off their cannon every day to celebrate their victory and all my *tchernya's* melting away like snow in the Spring."

★ ★ ★

Bohun left at once to make his preparations. The half cohort of his best *moloytzy* whom he detailed for the expedition did what Cossacks always did at a time like this: they rolled huge vats of liquor into the *maydan*, stove-in the lids and started drinking themselves into a mindless frenzy as if trying to drown all their fears in *gojhalka*.

"*Na slavu!*" they bellowed. "*Na pohybel Lahom!*"

They drank *na umor*, until all their senses sunk into oblivion, crying out that they wanted to forget all about life and living even before '*Mother Death takes us to her breast!*' Their young ataman drank vodka by the bucketful right along with them until he seemed to be spitting raw spirits with every breath he blew out of his heaving chest. He howled and leaped around the campfires with the best of them, and they pressed eagerly around him to touch him for luck because they knew that he was invincible and that neither Death nor the Devil could get near him. Then he ordered a barrel of pitch rolled out into the camp square and plunged into it in all his costly garments.

"I'm black now as Mother Night!" he howled while his *moloytzy* reeled about bellowing with laughter. "The *Lah* eyes won't see me!"

"Death to them!" they shouted. "Glory to us!"

He dipped his head in the pitch time and time again so that it covered him in a thick, black coat from scalp-lock to boot heels and then he jumped out and rolled himself like a dog on a pile of captured tapestries and carpets.

"Now I'm as black as Mother Death herself!" he shouted while his Cossacks cheered.

"Death to the *Lahy!* Death to them! Luck and life to us!"

Then he leaped onto his horse and galloped out of the camp while his faithful troopers clattered after him into the falling twilight. "*Na slavu! Na sh'tchastye!*" howled the crowds that gathered along all the Cossack siege works to see them riding out of camp against Yarema. "Luck and glory to you!"

But because they were riding to look for Vishnovyetzki nobody thought they'd ever see them alive again.

Left alone in his tent, Maksym Krivoinos watched their departure with savage satisfaction. Vishnovyetzki hadn't robbed him of all his luck, he thought; it was all turning out better than he hoped. If Bohun came back alive he'd bring the information that the cunning old marauder needed to make his next move; and if the young ataman fell into the Prince's hands he'd be rid of a dangerous young rival.

★ ★ ★

Meanwhile Skshetuski's raiders reached Yarmolinsk, gave the rebellious inhabitants a night of blood and fire, and allowed a panicked mass of fugitives to run south in terror to spread the word of Yarema's coming. Then, having posted an announcement that the Prince would sit in judgment on all the people of the region the next day, Skshetuski rested his men and horses for the night.

"God gave us luck so far," he told his companions around their supper table. "But I think we'd better do something to improve it."

"Such as what?" asked Volodyovski.

"I judge by the terror that's seizing the locals everywhere we go that they're convinced the Prince isn't far behind us. But how long will that last? We must think of something to make sure they don't catch on to our deception."

"They're sure to put two and two together sometime," the

little knight agreed. "Especially when they realize that it's the same detachment that's showing up everywhere in turn."

"And how much longer are we going to be wandering about like that?" Pan Zagloba asked.

"As long as there's any doubt about which way Krivoinos plans to move," Pan Yan said.

"Is that so? Then we might not make it back to the camp in time for the big battle?"

"Even that could happen."

"What? No more battles?" the fat knight cried out, rolling his good eye fiercely around the company. "That's not to my taste at all, my good friends! No, that's not to my liking!"

"It's up to Krivoinos."

"I can't say I'm a bit happy about that!" the old knight complained. "No, not a bit of it! I've whetted my appetite a bit at Konstantinov, the old right hand regained a few of its skills, and the fingers itch for another battle flag or two . . ."

"You might see more fighting here than you think, my friend," Pan Yan told him quietly.

"Oh? And how's that?" the fat knight asked and stirred uneasily on the hard oak bench beside their supper table. "*A quo modo?*"

"Because every day brings us closer to Krivoinos' army," the little knight explained. "We're liable to come face to face with a regular Zaporohjan cohort at almost any moment."

"The Devil you say," Pan Zagloba muttered. "Any moment, eh?"

"In fact I'm surprised they haven't sent out anyone to track us down already and check on all these rumors we've been starting," Pan Skshetuski said. "But to get back to the point I'm making, we have to start covering more ground to make our story sound a little better."

"More ground, eh?" Pan Zagloba moved uneasily on his bench. "Seems to me we're covering enough as it is."

"We have to make it seem as if there was a much greater number of detachments screening the Prince's army, not just our own party. I think we ought to split our forces so that we can start showing up in several places all at the same time, spread the panic over a wider area, and terrify the country."

"That's my thinking too," Pan Michal agreed. "That way we'll convince Krivoinos that there's a real army coming down on him. The word will spread faster. And rumor will swell our numbers into thousands."

"Yes, that makes sense," Pan Longinus said. "So how shall we do that, lieutenant?"

"Split our command in four," Pan Yan said. "I'll take half a regiment to Zinkov and fan out northeast towards Solodkovtze and beyond. Pan Podbipyenta will go straight south towards the old Tartar camping grounds along the Dniester. You, Michal, creep up as close as you can to Kupin and stir up that country, and Pan Zagloba will take the word as far as the Zbrutch River near Satanov."

"Me?" the old knight sat up, eyes bulging, and his mouth fell open. "Me?"

"Yes you," Skshetuski said. "Why not? You're a smart, clever man, you should have little trouble."

"Trouble, eh?" Pan Zagloba muttered. "Well, I don't know about that . . ."

"I thought you'd like a chance for a little independent action," Pan Yan said, then shrugged. "But if you'd rather not take on the job we'll give the last detachment to old Sergeant Kozma. He'll know what to do."

"He will!" Pan Zagloba cried out recklessly, dazzled by the sudden vision of himself as a military leader. "But . . . under my orders!"

"Good. That's settled then."

"Only . . . are you sure you've enough experience in this kind of thing?" Pan Michal asked Zagloba.

"Do I have experience?" the fat knight roared and slammed his fist so hard on the table that the platters jumped. "Me? I was leading greater expeditions than this one, my small friend, before any storks thought of making your parents a present out of you!"

"Hmm. Is that so," the little knight murmured, not quite as sure about Pan Zagloba as the fat knight would have liked to see.

"I'll have you know I spent half my long life in the service," the old knight went on. "And I'd still be leading my old regiment if it wasn't for some spoiled biscuits that I ate one time. They were stuck in my belly for three years, which is why I had to take leave and travel to Galata for a certain famous purgative that the Turks invented for the Sultan . . .! But you'll have to

wait for that story until some other time because right now I'm
in a hurry to get on my way!"

"Good," Skshetuski said. "Let's get started, then. Be sure to
move fast, spread terror and panic, let everyone think that
Hmyelnitzki's army is beaten and that the Prince has passed
through Ploskirov already. Don't bother taking just any prisoners, gentlemen, but if you run into a detachment from Kamyenetz try to cut out a few Cossacks who'd know about
Krivoinos' intentions. The few we've taken so far are mostly
peasants who tell contradictory stories."

"I hope I come across Krivoinos himself!" the fat knight
roared, pounding on the table. "Hey, if he'd only stick his nose
out of his encampment, I'd give him something to remember!
Ho, ho! Don't you worry gentlemen, I'll teach those birds how
to sing a tune that we want to hear . . . and how to dance it
too!"

"Good," Pan Yan said again. "Let's meet back here again in
three days. And now let's mount up and go."

"In three days back in Yarmolinsk," repeated Pan Longinus,
Pan Michal and Pan Zagloba.

"And spare the men," Skshetuski reminded. "We've none too
many as it is for a job like this one."

The four officers gathered their cloaks and weapons, stepped
outside, called for their horses and rode to their commands. A
few moments later the four detachments wheeled out of the
column and each trotted off in a direction of its own.

Chapter Forty-two

FINDING HIMSELF suddenly alone at the head of his own detachment, Pan Zagloba became somewhat ill-at-ease, if not downright frightened.

"Here's a fine pot of stew I've cooked for myself," he muttered in gloom. "What the devil am I supposed to do now? May a rooster mistake me for a hen and chase me around a barnyard if I ever got myself carried away by a worse idea."

Those sudden dreams of glory which fired his imagination at the thought of actually becoming a military commander, something that he claimed to have been in all sorts of great moments in history, evaporated quickly. The sun had barely broken out above the horizon and the new morning still carried the chill of dawn, but he found himself mopping his sweating forehead as if it were noon.

"One man alone and thinking only about his own neck can come up with something now and then to keep his skin intact," he grumbled to himself and glanced uneasily at the soldiers clattering behind him. "But what am I supposed to do with a hundred men?"

His confidence dwindled with each fresh mile that separated him from Pan Michal, Pan Longinus and Skshetuski. He found himself irritatingly short of breath and he began to lose the rest of it along with his temper.

"Who needs those soldiers? What good are they to me? There's not enough of them to hold off somebody like Bohun, Devil take him, but they're far too many to watch me shaking in my boots at the thought that I might come across that bloodthirsty demon."

603

He knew that he would gladly give all those mythical estates among the Turks just to have Skshetuski, Pan Michal and Pan Longinus somewhere close at hand. No matter how he blustered and postured in their company, quite aware that they only half believed the tales he told them, and no matter how cruelly he teased the gentle Lithuanian, he was full of profound respect and admiration for them all. He was willing to place his faith, blindly and without a question, in their military skill, judgment, experience and courage, and he was quite sure that he never felt safer with anybody else. So now he plodded along the dusty track with a gloomy scowl on his florid face, squirming in his saddle and peering around suspiciously for every imaginable danger, and grumbling curses under his breath mile after mile.

"It'd be a lot more cheerful if one of them was here to keep me company," he muttered. "I'm a peaceful man, as God is my witness, and they were made for this kind of thing. God designs every creature according to its function, and those three should have been buzzing around as horseflies because bloodletting comes as easy to them as ringing to a church bell."

Feeling more lonely than ever, Pan Zagloba became quite miserable and that made him angry.

"They're as much at home with fighting as another man is with a jug of wine," he muttered. "Or like a fish is in a water bucket. They take to wars like bread goes with goose-grease. Their bellies may be too lean to be considered dignified, but they're a hardheaded young lot, handy with a saber, and though they're no match for me behind a tavern table they more than earn their keep on the back of a horse.

"That Pan Skshetuski, now," he mused half aloud. "He's really something with a sword in hand! He cracks a skull as easily as a monk rattles off his prayers, and he has a pretty sound head on his shoulders too. But this idea of splitting up his troops wasn't such a great one."

Wishing with all his heart that his three friends would suddenly materialize around him, the fat knight glared bitterly into the roadside shadows which, he was certain, were full of bloodthirsty enemies gathering in ambush, and he felt his thin hair stirring on his head.

"That Lithuanian beanpole is another one. He ought to be looking for four heads instead of three because he could use a good one screwed into his own shoulders, but he's no slouch either with that long roasting-spit of his. I'd give a lot to see him here right now, along with his virtue. I don't know much about that little fellow but judging by what Skshetuski says about him, and by what I saw myself at Konstantinov, he's also got to be some kind of a hornet.

"Ha!" And suddenly a gleam of hope appeared in Pan Zagloba's gloom. "It's a good thing he's not too far away. I think I'd best join up with him and let him do the leading . . . Because if I know what to do in this situation then may I get trampled by a herd of wild ducks in a millpond!"

The world had never seemed colder and less friendly to him, and he was seized by a sudden flood of pity for himself, and a tear trickled slowly into his white beard.

"Yes, yes," he murmured sadly. "That's the way it is in this ungrateful world. Everyone has someone to look after him. Even an egg has a shell around it and the scurviest mongrel has his fleas for company! But what do I have? Nobody! And nothing! No father . . . no mother . . . not even a good companion to while away a moment . . ."

He heaved a sigh of such misery that his plodding mare groaned under him as if in sympathy. "Ah!" he cried out suddenly in a fit of anger. "I'm a real, honest-to-God orphan, that's what I am! Without a soul to care about me on this whole wide earth!"

Old Sergeant-major Kozma picked this gloomy and ill-chosen moment to trot up to Pan Zagloba and ask for instructions. "Where are we going, commandant?" he asked. "If you don't mind my asking."

"Where? Where?" Pan Zagloba blinked rapidly, twisted about in his saddle, and suddenly remembered every military commander he had ever seen. "Where, you say?"

"If you don't mind saying . . ."

"I don't mind at all!" Pan Zagloba roared and twisted the ends of his mustache straight up in the air, as he saw Pan Michal do on numerous occasions. "We'll go all the way to Kamyenetz if that's what I fancy! Is that clear, sergeant? Any other questions?"

The old sergeant-major bowed in puzzled silence and drew back into the ranks where the soldiers started whispering to each other about their commander's sudden show of rage. Pan

Zagloba hurled another dozen fierce glances at the silent shadows and returned to his own gloomy muttering and grumbling.

★ ★ ★

But it wasn't long before the old sergeant was back beside the fat knight.

"Excuse me, commander," he murmured with respect. "But there are riders of some kind coming this way."

"Riders? What riders, Devil take them? Where?"

"Over behind that hill up ahead, commander. I've seen what looks like banners."

"Troops?"

"Could be troops, sir."

"That's all I need," the fat knight groaned, all his anxieties confirmed. But then he remembered the sergeant who was staring at him and waiting for his orders.

"How many are there?" he snapped. "Do you know?"

"It's too far to tell, your honor." The old sergeant peered around and pointed towards a rockpile that rose beside the road, providing a deep shadow. "We could take up positions over by these rocks here and hit 'em from ambush. If there's too many of 'em, Pan Volodyovski isn't far. He'll hear the firing and come up to help."

"Ha!" roared Pan Zagloba. "So that's what you think?"

It may have been a fit of desperation, or perhaps a hope that the fierce little knight might appear at any moment to rescue him from trouble, but a wave of courage mounted as suddenly as aged vintage wine to Pan Zagloba's head. He flashed his saber, rolled his eyes in a terrifying manner and bellowed at his soldiers.

"Get behind the rocks! We'll hit them from ambush! Ah, the sons of bitches . . . we'll show them . . . we'll show them!"

The well-trained Vishnovyetzki soldiers wheeled at once into the roadside shadows and the fat knight took his place beside them.

"What if it's Bohun?" he muttered to himself. "What if it's Krivoinos?"

Sweat poured into his eyes, his knees were knocking against his pistol holsters, and terrifying visions of capture by the Zaporohjans galloped through his head. But the hardbitten Vishnovyetzki troopers looked as calm and matter-of-fact as if nothing out of the ordinary was about to happen, so he stifled his panic under savage curses. And then he heard the hum of many voices nearing in the distance, the echo of happy and light-hearted singing, the squealing of a fiddle, the wail of a bagpipe and the rattling of a tambourine.

"Them's not troops, sir," the sergeant-major whispered to Zagloba.

"Not troops?" Hope reappeared so suddenly that Pan Zagloba lost his bearings for a moment. "What do you mean *'not troops?'* "

"Sound like a wedding party."

"A wedding?" Dizzy with relief, Pan Zagloba could hardly believe his ears, and then a true warrior's rage lifted the sparse hair on his skull. "A wedding, you say? I'll give them a wedding! I'll play them a tune to dance to!"

He spurred his horse into the road, the soldiers followed, and the ranks reformed at once in the open and spread across the highway.

"Follow me!" the fat knight roared fiercely and kicked his mare forward.

"At a trot . . . forward!" cried the sergeant-major.

The ranks advanced at a trot, broke into a gallop, and appeared seemingly out of nowhere before a large crowd of unsuspecting people in carts and on horseback who backed away with loud cries of terror.

"Stop! Stop! Hold it!" startled voices called out on both sides.

"Forward!" cried Zagloba, all the more fiercely because he couldn't see a weapon anywhere before him.

"Now what's he up to," Sergeant Kozma muttered, then shrugged and spurred forward.

"Charge!" cried Pan Zagloba.

★　★　★

It was, indeed, a peasant wedding party, as Pan Zagloba could see immediately, but for some reason this enraged him even more.

First to catch his eye as he charged down upon them was a mounted piper, a *teorban* player, a fiddler and two drummers, all of them already four sheets to the wind and playing jittery little *kolomiyka* dances. Behind them rode the bride, a rosy young girl in a cherry-colored *zhupan* and with her unbound hair flowing

about her shoulders. Her mounted bridesmaids who sat astride
their horses like men but who wore field flowers and ribbons
streaming from their hair, surrounded her with wreaths of
cornflowers and poppies looped around their arms. The bridegroom and his lads rode in a column behind the singing
women, with more wreaths and streamers fluttering on long
poles above their heads so that, seen from a distance, the whole
cavalcade did have the look of a brightly dressed regiment of
Cossacks. The parents of the bridal pair and a large gathering of
older wedding guests rode behind the young people, while the
light, straw-filled carts that bumped and rattled at the end of the
procession proved to be carrying kegs of beer, casks of mead
and flagons of *gojhalka*.

"Halt! Stop! Wait!" the shouts came from all sides, and then
the wedding party scattered in confusion. The girls squealed
and screamed, pushing to the rear, while the lads, the bridegroom and whatever older men were still sober among the
wedding guests, kicked their horses forward to bar the way and
to protect the women with their own unarmed bodies.

Howling and bellowing like a one-man *tchambul* of Dobrudjan Tartars, Pan Zagloba pulled up his mare to a rearing halt in
front of the terrified young peasants, and shaking his saber
fiercely overhead, began to yell and curse.

"Ha, you rascals! Scoundrels! Cut-throat rebels! So you feel
like joining the rebellion, do you? So you're on your way to sign
up with Krivoinos, are you? Off on a little spying mission, are
we, eh? Speak up! Admit it! I've caught you redhanded! So
you'd raise your blasphemous peasant paws against the gentry,
would you? I'll show you what we do with rebels in Prince
Yeremi's army! I'll show you!"

Pale as death, the bridegroom and his friends stared in such
terror as if their last hour had come down upon them. The girls
and women wailed prayers and pleaded for God's mercy. But
the fat knight was completely swept away by his own performance.

"I'll have you hammered into the stocks!" he bellowed. "I'll
have you impaled! Oh you dogs! You heathen! You'll pay for all
your crimes, I promise you!"

At last an old, silver-haired member of the wedding party
jumped off his horse, neared the frightening noble, clutched at

his stirrup, and started bowing to the ground as if his life depended on a show of abject subservience.

"Have mercy, kind master," he pleaded. "Don't hurt the innocent. As God's our witness, we've not done any harm! We aren't on our way to join any rebels, no sir! We're coming home from the church over in Husyatin, where we just joined our kinsman here, young Dmitri the blacksmith, in holy bonds with Ksenya Bondarovna . . . We're here with a wedding . . ."

"These are harmless people, sir," the sergeant-major whispered.

"Harmless? I know what they are!" roared Pan Zagloba. "They're cut-throats! They've come to this wedding from Krivoinos' army!"

"*Kolyb yeho trastya mordovala!*" shouted the old man, beating his chest in terror. "May the plague stifle 'im! We never even set eyes on 'im, the dog . . .! We're simple folk! Have mercy, lord, have mercy! Let us go. We know our duty and our place and we don't harm nobody . . .!"

"You'll all go to Yarmolinsk on the end of a rope!" Pan Zagloba bellowed. "And then we'll see just how innocent you are!"

"We'll go!" whined the old man. "Yes we'll go, master, if that's what you order! It's your business to give orders and ours to obey! But show us mercy, lord knight! Tell them soldiers not to harm nobody and do us the honor of sipping a little something . . ."

"Sipping?" Somewhat mollified, Pan Zagloba glared at the old man none the less. "You'd ask a noble to drink with a peasant?"

"Yes, yes, we know it's a great honor, master," the sly old peasant had begun to grin. "We know it's a lot for poor folks like us to ask of your lordship . . . But we beg you humbly, on our knees, to drink a mug or two to the health of the happy pair . . .! Do us the honor, kind lord, noble sir . . . make simple folks happy . . . Have a drink with us in good will and friendship like God and the Holy Gospels tell us all to do."

"Hmm. All right, then. All right," Pan Zagloba muttered. "Maybe I'll do it just this once to bring luck to the newlyweds . . . Only don't think I'll let you off the hook!" he added fiercely.

"Never, master!" the old man cried out, overjoyed and grinning like a fox. "We won't think nothing! Who thinks at a wedding? Hey lads, ha ha!"—and he ran towards the terrified musicians — "Play something for the good knight, because the good knight's a kind man and he'll show us mercy! And you other lads, run and get some fine mead for the good, kind knight! He's got a heart of gold! He'll spare us! He won't harm us! Jump to it now!"

The young lads leaped off their horses and ran to the barrels, the drums began to thump and rattle, the fiddle squeaked again, the piper blew out his cheeks and started squeezing the goatskin bag under his arm, and the bridegroom's friends shook the wedding wreaths on their long, spearlike poles.

"U-u-ha!" someone cried.

Pan Zagloba was still not quite sure what he ought to do but his soldiers, as he noted quickly, started to edge up closer to the girls, who grinned and giggled at them from behind the lads, and all their former fears seemed to drift away in the warm morning air. But the fat knight's face remained glum and stormy even after a quart mug of dark, sweet vintage mead was placed in his hands.

"Ah, the rogues, the rascals," he muttered as his long whiskers dipped under the surface.

Eyes narrowed, beard lifted to the sky, he smacked his lips and tasted the liquor, and then a shadow of surprise and outrage passed across his face.

"Ah, what times we live in!" he groaned in disgust and anger. "When peasants get to drink this kind of mead . . .! Dear Lord . . . You see this and You're not tossing lightning bolts at such a blasphemy?"

Then he sighed, shook his head sadly at this clear sign that all sense of natural order and propriety was vanishing from the world, and drained the quart mug to the bottom in a single swallow.

*   *   *

Meanwhile the whole wedding party began to crowd around him, pressing fresh tankards into his hands and begging him to let them go unharmed. The bride herself came forward—a beautiful, dark-browed girl with tears in her eyes and the flush

of all her hopes and fears glowing in her face—and Pan Zagloba
felt a thaw stirring in his sentimental heart.

"Spare us, master," she begged in a soft, trembling voice.
"*Pomyluyte, pa'ne . . .*"

He looked down at the tall, slim girl, thought at once of
Helen, and his ferocious military air dissolved like frost beside a
glowing fire. Loosening his broad, leather belt, he began to
rummage in the pouches that were sewn inside it, fished out the
last few ducats left from the purse which Prince Yeremi gave
him after Skshetuski brought him to the Vishnovyetzki camp,
and pressed them into the young woman's hands.

"Here," he said in a gentler voice. "Here's a little something
to help you get started. And may God bless you, as He does all
that's innocent."

His heart, he felt, was melting like a ball of wax although he
did his best to look as frightening as his role demanded but he
knew that he was no longer fooling anybody.

'*Where is she now?*' he asked himself, thinking about Helen.
'*Where is that poor, sweet girl? What is happening with her? And
are there any good angels near to guard her in her pain and fear?*'

And at this thought the fat knight's face flushed even redder,
his chest heaved with sighs, and a tear rolled down into his
beard and mustache. But his generosity and his show of feeling
dispelled the last vestiges of fear in the wedding party. The
country folk ran to thank him and to press about him, singing
and crying out their blessings and kissing the edges of his coat
as if he were their savior. The sweating fiddler sawed away as if
he'd gone mad. The piper's eyes threatened to pop out of his
head and his face turned purple, and the drummers pounded
their leather kettles until their hands grew numb.

"*Dobryi on!*" the crowd repeated over and over. "He's a good
man, a golden *Lah*. He don't hurt nobody! He gives out his
money! *Na slavu! Na sh'chastye!*"

The bride's father, who kept carefully out of sight behind the
wedding guests, now pushed forward with his wife and the
bridegroom's mother to bow to the ground and to beg Pan
Zagloba to join the celebration. A guest like that would bring
good luck to the newlyweds. It would be an honor that the
happy couple would remember the rest of their lives.

"So what's the harm in it, master?" he cajoled.

The grinning, relieved bridegroom bowed beside him. The
Bondar homestead wasn't far, they said, it wouldn't be much
out of the great lord's way, and the old man was a rich peasant
with a good store of aged vintage mead.

"Better than this?" Pan Zagloba asked and held out his quart
mug to be filled again.

"Much better, sir! Much better!"

"Hmm. Well. In that case . . . let me think about it."

But it was the shy, young bride who helped Pan Zagloba to
make his decision. She stepped up, raised her long, dark lashes,
and smiled softly at the old knight who felt all his artificial
fierceness turning into sentimental pity. She bent to kiss his
hand. She may have been only a simple peasant girl but she
guessed at once that her pleas would have a quicker effect on the
ferocious noble than all the rest of the pleading and cajoling, and
she went down on her knees before him, and hugged his yellow
boot, and begged him with tears still shining in her eyes to
honor her wedding.

"What better omen could I ask for, master . . .?"

"Well . . . Hmmm . . . If that's the case . . ."

Pan Zagloba hesitated only a moment longer. He glanced at
his soldiers. The old sergeant-major was looking fondly at the
casks and barrels, moving his huge grey whiskers up and down
like a rabbit in a cabbage-patch. The soldiers were whispering
with the girls and grinning at the prospect of vodka and dancing. None of them dared to ask to go to the wedding but a short
break in their mission couldn't do much harm.

"All right, then," Pan Zagloba said. "I'll come."

"God be praised!" cried the peasants and the soldiers cheered.

And a few moments later Pan Zagloba rode as if in triumph in
the place of honor at the head of the singing procession. His
soldiers and the wedding party followed side by side in perfect
amity behind him as if the only reason for their expedition was a
peasant wedding.

★   ★   ★

The bride's home lay quite near. The peasants hadn't lied
about that, Pan Zagloba was pleased to observe. Nor had they
lied about the quality of the mead. Ksenya's father proved to be
a wealthy independent farmer, the mead was plentiful and

strong, and in a short time the entire party was well refreshed and liquored.

Tankards foamed, casks bubbled, the musicians played until the rafters trembled, and Pan Zagloba was soon in a first rate humor. '*Hmm,*' he thought. '*If this is what campaigning is about then I'm going to turn out a top-notch commander!*' And because he knew that a good officer leads his men by personal example he was quick to put himself at the forefront of everything that happened.

Meanwhile the ritual of a peasant wedding went on all around him.

First the old crones of the village gathered around the bride and led her solemnly into the *komora*, an inner chamber that doubled as a bedroom, where they locked themselves with her for some time. Then they emerged, wreathed in toothless smiles, to announce that she was, indeed, '*pure as a dove and white as a lily,*' and then the celebration soared to a higher pitch. All the married women nudged and grinned slyly at each other and cried out that they never had a doubt about the girl's virtue, her mother breathed a vast sigh of relief and burst into tears, the old men clapped their hands and plunged their heads into the liquor barrels, and the young men stamped their hobnailed boots on the wooden floor. As the commotion grew, each of the bridegroom's friends danced, one by one, with a quart of *go-jhalka* in his hands which he drained at a gulp, for good luck, on the threshold of the bridal chamber.

"*Na slavu! Na sh'chastye!*"

"U-u-u-ha!"

Pan Zagloba also danced his turn, pouring with sweat but kicking up his legs as high as any Cossack, with only one departure from this peasant custom to mark the difference between himself and everyone else. His dignity and stature as a noble, he was sure, demanded that he drank to the health and good luck of the newlyweds out of a half-gallon copper kettle instead of a tin quart mug. Then, while the whole company sang the wedding song, the bride's parents and the bridegroom's mother led the flushed young man to his waiting wife, and because the young blacksmith didn't have a father, Pan Zagloba was asked to play that role and gladly consented.

But the celebration reached its highest pitch once the fat

knight and the parents returned to the main room. The old
farmer started to hug and kiss the mother of his new son-in-law
while she wept, laughed and giggled at the same time, making a
show of fighting off an ardent young lover. The other women
screamed with laughter and crowded around the bride's mother
to congratulate her on keeping her daughter's virtue intact until
her wedding; all the young men broke into frenzied dances; and
the soldiers who were staggering among the barrels in the yard
outside fired their pistols and shouted Tartar war cries.

" . . . U-u-u-ha! U-u-u-ha!"

"*Na slavu!* Luck and fortune to them . . .!"

And the day passed, unnoticed in its going, and the night
began.

★   ★   ★

Blinded with his own sweat, and carrying at least a cask of
vintage mead inside him, Pan Zagloba was no longer quite sure
where he was or what he was doing. He was at a wedding, he
knew. But whose? Helen's and Skshetuski's? Acting in the role
of the bridegroom's father, he danced like a dervish with the
mother of the bride, hopping about and leaping and stamping
his boots until splinters flew from the wooden floorboards, but
everything else was becoming hazy.

He was outside, he knew, in the moonlit yard, where most of
the wedding party had spilled out of the crowded house. But
what house could it be?

He could see faces, as red and sweated as his own, and he kept
staggering into people who, in turn, leaped and danced and
staggered into others, but he had no idea who all these people
were. The thought that he was at the wedding of Helen and
Skshetuski seemed the most likely one. It became fixed in his
head like a fresh nail gleaming in a horseshoe and filled him
with an overwhelming sentimental joy.

"*Vivant!* Long life to them!" he howled like a madman, draining his copper kettle time and time again.

"To your good health, my lords and brothers!" he addressed
the drunken peasants and staggering soldiers as if they were
gentry. "Let us all love each other! Long life to our beloved
Prince! May all be well with us . . .!"

Grief seized him at this point and he began to weep for the
threatened Commonwealth. "May this paroxysm come finally

to an end . . .! May peace and good times come back to our beloved country!"

He tripped over someone on his way to the liquor barrels, and then he tripped again and again because the ground was littered with sprawled, snoring bodies as if in aftermath of some great Steppe battle, and that reminded him of all the terrible disasters of the war.

"God, God . . . Are there no more manly virtues left in this Commonwealth of ours?" he mourned and raised his eyes to the starry sky. "Is there only one man left among the gentry who knows how to drink? Yes, yes, there's only Zagloba. He's the only one. As for the rest . . . ah, dear God, what has happened to us? How can the country live and prosper with such weak heads to run it? What will happen in the years to come?"

And then he noticed that the stars themselves appeared to have lost their dignity along with their position in the firmament and their sense of place. Some hopped up and down. Some danced in pairs opposite each other like Cossacks at a wedding. Some spun in great circles like dogs chasing their own tails and others looked like golden snails squirming from their shells.

"Am I the only creature in the universe who's still sober?" he asked himself in astonishment. "Is the whole world drunk?"

But suddenly the earth itself spun and shuddered under him, the ground opened into a giant whirlpool, and he fell headlong into the dust as if he'd been hit on the head with a battle hammer.

And then he dreamed.

A frightful nightmare came upon him, an unknown terror seized him, but he couldn't shake himself awake no matter what he tried. He felt as if some terrifying monster squatted on his chest, pressing the air out of him and crushing him against the cold, dry soil. It seemed as if his arms and legs were being roped together, as if he'd died and fallen into the hands of demons. His ears were full of frightful howls, screams and yells of fear.

He thought he could hear the rattle of gunshots while a bright red light glowed and flickered just beyond the eyelids that he couldn't open.

And then his body rose into the air as if he'd been lifted by his hands and feet. He felt his head hanging down, swaying in space and bumping on the ground. Some vague fear that he couldn't quite identify settled on him like a flock of vultures as he struggled in vain towards a distant consciousness. He didn't know why he should be afraid but he was sure that whatever this dream was all about it was the worst nightmare that he ever had.

He felt ill . . . unhappy . . . lost and terribly alone. He couldn't remember the last time that life seemed so dreadful. Half conscious but beginning to feel alive again, he couldn't understand why he was unable to move any part of his frozen body. He had no strength at all. Some kind of vise gripped his arms and legs. His head seemed fixed to the top of a strange, metallic spine, and the ground under him was suddenly as hard as a board.

Fighting his way out of this awful nightmare he finally managed to get some light between his parted eyelids only to find another pair of eyes—hot as coals, hungry and glowing with a terrifying joy—that stared down into his own. He read so much hatred, such dark malevolence, and such a cold anticipation of vengeance in that unmoving gaze that, at first, he thought it was the Devil who was looking at him.

"*Ave Satanas,*" he muttered, gripped by sudden terror, but there was no way for him to lift his hand for the sign of the cross that might dispel this awful apparition.

He closed his eyes quickly, blinked them and opened them again, but the nightmare vision hadn't gone away. Those hungry eyes kept staring. The dark face behind them seemed terribly familiar.

And suddenly Pan Zagloba shuddered from head to foot. He was immediately wide awake and sober, bathed in an icy sweat and feeling as if a thousands ants were running along his spine.

He recognized Bohun.

Chapter Forty-three

PAN ZAGLOBA LAY on the cold, hard floorboards of the peasant *izba* in which the wedding had been taking place, roped like a hunter's trophy to his own sheathed saber, while the terrible young ataman sat above him astride a milking stool and feasted his eyes on his victim's terror.

"Good evening to you," Bohun said at last, seeing that the fat knight's eyes had finally blinked open.

Pan Zagloba didn't say a word. He was suddenly as sober as if he'd never tasted a drop of liquor in his entire life. But those ants that were galloping down his spine now turned about at his heels and marched back up to the top of his skull while the marrow in his bones turned as cold as a frozen stream.

He knew the saying about a drowning man who experiences a moment of absolute clarity in which he sees his entire past in a single flash; just such a moment of total recollection gripped the old knight, and the brightest thought that gleamed in all that chaos was a single, silent sentence which echoed in his head as loud as a cry.

'*Am I going to get it now . . .!*'

Meanwhile the young ataman said again with a dreadful softness: "Good evening to you."

Pan Zagloba shuddered. He'd have liked it a lot better if the Zaporohjan had gone mad with rage; then the whole thing would be over quickly.

"Don't you recognize me, Mister Nobleman?" the young Cossack murmured.

"Hmm . . . Yes . . . I do." Made even more uneasy by the ataman's contrived politeness, Pan Zagloba thought that he might as well go along with it. "How have you been, then? All right? How's your health?"

"Not bad. Not bad at all. As for yours, let that be my worry."

"Hmm. Hmm. I didn't ask God for your kind of doctoring and I've some doubts if I'll be able to digest your medicine but if that's His will, so be it."

"Well, you know how it is," Bohun said with a terrifying calmness. "You looked after me, that time in Rozloghi, now it's my turn to take care of you. We're old friends, you and me, remember?"

Bohun's eyes began to fill with that wolflike glow that always made Zagloba think of dark, subterranean powers while the thin black line of the Cossack's mustache stretched in a dreadful grin.

"I remember that I could've cut your throat," Pan Zagloba said.

"And did I cut yours?" Bohun went on grinning. "Of course not. I wouldn't think of it . . . No, no, you're my old drinking partner, my faithful companion . . . You an' me, we were like two sides of the same bad coin, weren't we. Oh, I'll take better care of you than you'd get from your own brother, if you had one."

"You will, eh?"

"You can bet on it."

"I always said you were a decent fellow."

The fat knight shuddered once more. He thought that he might as well pretend to take Bohun's friendly words at face value but in his racing mind, where he was leaping from one unworkable and impossible idea to another, a single bright image burned as hot as a branding iron. His death, he knew, wouldn't be a quick one.

"Yes. A decent fellow," he said again. "A good cavalier, that's what I always said."

Bohun smiled.

"Is that what you said? Well, then you said it right. You're also a decent fellow, a good cavalier. So here we are, two good, decent fellows, together again like we're supposed to be. You wouldn't believe how I missed you! How I looked for you!"

"Is that right?"

"That's right! And you missed me too, didn't you. I can see by the way you're sweating that you really missed me."

"Hmm. Yes. Well, to tell the truth, I didn't really miss you all that much, you know. But thanks for the kind words anyway."

"Oh, you'll thank me a lot louder before you're much older. And I'll thank you too. I've a lot to be grateful to you for, you see."

"Think nothing of it," Pan Zagloba murmured.

"Oh, but I do! I do! You brought the girl all the way to Bar for me, didn't you. Sure! And that's where I found her. I'd ask you to the wedding, like the good friend you are, but that can't happen for a while yet. That's got to wait till the war's over, right? And you're an old man, aren't you, you might not live that long."

Despite the terrifying situation in which he found himself Zagloba cocked an ear at this information.

"A wedding?" he muttered.

"Sure!" the Cossack snarled. "What do you think I am, some kind of a peasant to take her without a priest? You think I can't afford to get married in the Kiev cathedral with fifty nuns singing in the choir and a hundred deacons standing behind the best beeswax candles? It's not for some stinking clodhopper that you brought my sweet girl all the way to Bar but for an ataman! A Hetman!"

"I'm glad to hear it," Pan Zagloba said.

"And I'm also glad. And I'll be glad to make you even gladder, just you wait and see."

"No hurry about that, is there?" Pan Zagloba sighed.

"That's right." Bohun's dark, cruel face was suddenly alight with anticipation. "There's no hurry at all. Fact is, the longer it takes to show you how I've missed you the better I'll like it."

"So why don't you have me untied for a while?"

"Because I worry about you." Bohun smiled. "You've a long trip ahead of you so get a little rest down there on the floor. You're an old man and you ought to get your strength up before you start a journey."

"A journey, eh? And where am I going?"

"Well, you're my friend, aren't you?" Bohun grinned and nodded. "Sure you are. My good loyal brother and faithful companion who was so good to me back there in Rozloghi. So now I'll take you to meet another friend of mine, my good friend Krivoinos. He and me, we'll take good care of you, you can bet your hide on that. We'll think of some real special way to make you feel welcome, don't you worry, like you've never been welcomed anywhere before."

"Phew." The old noble licked at a bead of sweat dripping from his mustache. "You think so?"

"Take my word for it."

"Phew . . . It's getting hot here."

"Sure," Bohun said. "And it'll get hotter."

Life never seemed more precious to Pan Zagloba than now when he could count on so little of it, but a quick death, inflicted in a fit of fury, would be a lot better than a patient, slow one. And once again he felt as if a regiment of ants was marching and counter-marching up and down his spine.

"I know you think you've a bone to pick with me," he began. "But why, eh? Why? God knows I don't deserve it. We got on alright together in Tchehryn, you and I. We emptied a few flagons between us, didn't we? I even felt kind of like a father to you because I really liked your spirit . . . And d'you know why? Because there are few real knights in the Ukraine who have as much heart and fire as you, and that's a fact, my lad. So how did I get in your way? Eh? What harm did I do you? If I hadn't gone with you that time to Rozloghi we'd be living like brothers to this day."

Bohun said nothing.

"And why did I go with you if it wasn't out of caring for you?" the fat knight went on. "I thought you'd need me, and if you hadn't gone stark raving mad and murdered all those people you'd have nothing to complain about where I'm concerned, God's my witness to that! What did I ever care about other people's business? I mind my own. I'd just as soon have seen that girl with you as with anybody else! But what choice did you give me? You must've learned your courting from the Tartars."

"And that's not all I learned from them," Bohun hissed. "As you'll see."

"I dare say I will. But there it was, I couldn't just stand by while you slaughtered all those poor, unfortunate people, could I? That wasn't just some *tchaban* homestead in the Steppe somewhere, those people were gentry! My conscience woke in me, and that's all that happened. You'd do the same if you were in my boots . . .

"Fact is," he went on, "I could've sent you packing straight to

Hell, which would've saved me a lot of trouble right now, but I let you live. And why? Because I'm a noble and I was ashamed to act like a peasant. So why don't you try to do the same? Find some shame in yourself, show a sign of breeding, and act like a knight. Murdering helpless people is work for the rabble."

Bohun's dark, wolflike eyes seemed to be on fire, and his breath hissed out of him as if he were a reptile, and Pan Zagloba took a deep breath of his own.

"What do you want from me anyway?" he asked. "The girl is in your hands no matter what happened, you've got what you were after. And didn't I look out for her like she was my own? Who saved her from all those murdering mobs? Who kept her from the Tartars . . .? Listen, the fact that you've acted decently towards her proves that you've both a conscience and a sense of honor! But how are you going to reach out towards her if your hands are dripping with my blood? Hmm? Eh? How will you tell her that you threw her savior to the torturers?"

Bohun's livid face had begun to twitch and his hands clawed at the dagger hanging from his belt, and Pan Zagloba knew that if he couldn't hope any longer for his life and freedom then he'd at least provoke the violent, infuriated Cossack into a quick murder.

"So think again," he said. "Look into your conscience and let me go free. What's in it for you, anyway? It's not much of a victory. It's just my bad luck that you caught me off my guard, my lad. There's no more glory for you in roping a lot of drunks who're sleeping off a wedding than in spearing a carp in a bucket . . .

"Listen,"—and his voice rose in a last appeal to reason which, he knew, wouldn't help at all—"you're still a young man. You've no idea what's ahead for you, anything might happen . . . And God's vengeance will find you, no matter where you hide, even if you've a dozen devils jumping at your orders. Yes, it will! You can't escape His justice. And d'you know how He'll punish you? He'll pay you for my murder by taking from you what you want the most! You'll lose the girl, Skshetuski will get her, and it'll be your fault."

Bohun leaped off his stool. He was white with rage. His eyes were wide with madness and flecks of foam bubbled out at the corners of his twisted mouth.

"You filthy hog!" he howled, and clawed at his victim. "I'll have your stinking hide peeled off you in strips . . .! I'll hammer you full of hobnails like a human horseshoe . . .! I'll have your fat carcass dripping out your juices like a spitted ox over a slow fire . . .!"

His curved, naked knife gleamed for a moment before Zagloba's eyes and the fat knight closed them to shut out the sight and resigned himself to dying.

"*Ave Maria,*" he began to murmur. "*Gratia plena . . .*"

But the enraged Cossack managed to get himself under control again, sheathed his trembling weapon, and gnawed his clenched fists.

"Moloytzy!" he shouted.

Six Zaporohjans ran into the room.

"Take this foul piece of *Lah* carrion out of here and throw him in the pigsty!" he snarled. "And watch him! Don't let him get away! Or you'll take his place on the coals, you understand?"

"Aye, *bat'ku*. We hear you."

Two Cossacks seized Zagloba by the legs and two by the elbows and dragged him out of the hut while another held his dangling head by the hair out of the farmyard refuse. They carried him across the entire yard to a small, barnlike structure, heaved him headlong into a pile of soiled, reeking straw and manure, and then he heard them slam and bar the heavy doors behind him.

He lay in darkness, facedown in the muck, and hardly able to breathe. When he rolled over on his back, trussed to his sheathed saber like a slaughtered goat made ready for roasting, he saw pale streaks of moonlight seeping between the logs of the byre around him and glinting through the knotholes of the feed-loft overhead.

"I'm lost," he muttered. "I really did it this time, and no mistake about it. Well, that's what happens when you play the fool . . . Sooner or later the joke's on you, and that's all there's to it."

But what bothered him more than anything just then was the shamed thought that he had failed so terribly at his first try as a military commander.

' . . . *What will they think of me?*' he thought about Pan Yan, Pan Michal and Pan Longinus as if he expected them to sit in judgment on him any moment and to condemn him with as much contempt as he deserved. '*How will I ever be able to look them in the eye . . .?*'

He sighed.

It didn't occur to him that he'd be quite unable to look at them anyway because they'd never see him alive again but once his eyes became accustomed to the murky twilight he could look around. He saw that he was alone in a squat, log cabin that must have seen some service as a pigsty to judge by its stenches but there were neither hogs nor Cossacks anywhere near him. He could hear the sentries talking to each other all around the structure, their voices came to him clearly through all the four walls, so he knew that he was guarded just as closely as Bohun had ordered. But if some way of escaping didn't present itself to him immediately at least he was alive. And that, he thought, promised a far better chance of finding some way out than if he was dead.

"A live man thinks," he muttered to himself. "A thinking man ought to be able to come up with something, oughtn't he? I still have my head on my shoulders, for what that's been worth so far on this expedition . . . But no man's lost altogether as long as he can keep his wits well oiled and turning."

And although he was quite unable to imagine just then how he might save himself this time from his desperate danger, he drew a deep, grateful breath in any event, feeling a lot better about his situation no matter how grim and unpromising it appeared to be.

★ ★ ★

An hour passed like that, maybe more.

Whatever fate had in store for him it wouldn't happen right away, he knew, no matter how eagerly the savage young ataman wanted to savor his unimaginable vengeance on the man who made a fool of him, stole his girl and robbed him of so much of his precious Cossack pride. He had a little time, he thought; a few days at least if Bohun wanted to take him to Krivoinos. And that might mean a chance to slip off somewhere along the way if he just managed to keep himself alive and to fool his guards.

"They're not a bad bunch of lads when they're sitting quietly at their master's heel," he assured himself. "But dumb like all dogs. An old fox ought to be able to fool a hound or two."

That was the good side. The bad side lay in what would happen to him once he was handed over to the torturers and his interrogation started at the Zaporohjans' leisure, and the anticipation of his dreadful torments sent the imaginary ants scampering along his spine again.

"They'll dress my hide for glove leather before they're done with me," he muttered. "There's no doubt about it. Dear God, what have I done to deserve this rotten turn of luck? If there's one man in the whole world I wanted to avoid it's that handsome cut-throat and here I am, in his hands, roped like a hog and ready for stuffing, and I can't think of one thing I can do about it. Solomon himself would be stuck for a good idea in this situation."

The ropes and rawhide thongs that bound him tightly to his own sheathed saber were cutting off the circulation in his knees and elbows and he began to squirm in the straw to ease them a little, rocking back and forth on his spine and moving an inch at a time towards the nearest wall. Once there, he squirmed the other way, rocking from side to side instead of head to heel. The Zaporohjans trussed him knees-to-elbows, in the traditional Tartar fashion, with his own sheathed saber thrust under the knees, and at each rocking motion the end of the iron sheath knocked against the wall while the weapon began to slide out on the other side.

"That's it," he muttered, out of breath and listening for any sound of footsteps. "That's it. Ah . . . ah . . . that's got it!"

The saber slipped halfway out from behind his body as he rocked and tapped and Pan Zagloba's heart began to beat as loud in his chest as a blacksmith's hammer.

"Easy now, easy," he whispered to himself.

He paused and listened.

Had anybody heard him?

But the Cossack guards on the other side of the thick log walls were too busy gossiping with each other, and speculating about where they were likely to go next, to notice the soft knocking from inside the byre.

"Good. Good," the fat knight muttered, rocking all the harder. "Keep talking. You'll have something else to talk about in a little while. Ah . . . ah . . . A little more. Ah, that's it . . . The Devil take this work. Any more of it and I'll drown in my own sweat like a boiled carp. Tfui, I must stink worse than the pigs who live here, wherever they've gone to . . . But I'll take a vow of chastity, I swear it, like that mournful Lithuanian beanpole, if I can get this blade knocked out altogether."

★   ★   ★

Tapping the rounded end of his saber sheath against the wall only when the talk outside was loud enough to cover-up the sound, Pan Zagloba worked and sweated harder than he'd done while dancing at the wedding and, finally, he reached the point where the end of the sheath lay in line with his knee and elbow. That was as far as he could knock it out but the bulk of the heavy saber, together with its grip and crosspiece, extended on the other side of his sweated body.

"Hmm. Yes. That's it. Here we go again."

This time he rocked his arced, trussed-up trunk so as to turn himself feet-first to the wooden wall. Having accomplished even that gymnastic feat, he started walking his boot heels quietly across the coarse, uneven logs, swaying and heaving the rest of his body through the piles of straw and refuse on the littered floor so that the hilt and hooked crosspiece of the protruding saber scraped along the ground.

"Come on now," he addressed the weapon. "Catch on something, will you? Why do you think our forefathers designed you with an open guard? Isn't there enough muck and stuff down here to let you snag on something?"

Finally the crosspiece at the hand-grip did hook into some solid substance on the ground. Pan Zagloba closed his eyes and rested for a moment, drew a deep breath and gathered all his strength, and then he heaved his body sideways one more time and breathed a stifled prayer as the saber slid out altogether along with its sheath.

"Huh," he muttered, blinded with sweat but grinning from ear to ear. "Hmm. Ah, you rebel scoundrels! So you thought you had old Zagloba where you wanted him, did you, eh . . .? Well, not quite, my hearties. Not quite by a long shot."

Whispering a quick prayer of thanksgiving, Pan Zagloba set about freeing himself from his remaining bonds. It took some time before he could work his roped wrists down across his boot heels and up onto his belly, seize the saber hilt with both hands, and holding the sheath firmly between his knees draw the long, sharp blade. To cut the rawhide thongs at his ankles took a single stroke. The wrists took heavier work. He had to fix the hilt of the weapon firmly in the muck between his boots, set the point upward with the curved blade laid across his

shoulder, and then he sawed his roped wrists up and down the
edge until the strands parted.

"Come on, now," he urged. "Come on, get on with it. We
haven't got all night . . ."

And then the rope burst open. He was free. He grinned. He
breathed in relief and peered about in the silent darkness as if
expecting murmurs of applause.

"Well," he addressed the walls. "What did I tell you? Eh?
Catching Zagloba by a dirty trick, after he let his natural
goodness get the better of him and show his kindness to a pretty
bride, is one thing. Anyone could do that. Holding onto him is
something else again. Now those rebel halfwits will see who
and what they are up against."

When he rose to his feet he was not only free of his bonds but
armed.

★   ★   ★

But to cut himself loose was one thing, he knew; to escape
out of Bohun's hands entirely was something altogether
different.

"So what do I do now?" he asked himself and failed to find an
answer. The byre was sealed as tight as a drum with sentries all
around. '*There must be at least a hundred of them sitting along the
walls,*' Pan Zagloba thought, listening to their murmurs; a
mouse wouldn't be able to squeeze through without being
spotted, he was sure.

"Seems like all my ideas are running around in circles nowadays," he muttered in disgust. "My brains are just about good
enough for boot-grease, although I've bought better saddle soap
at a country fair. If God doesn't send me some good new idea
I'll end up as a roast for the crows, that's as clear as day."

A loud exchange between the Cossacks on the other side of
the nearest wall drew his attention and he bent his ear to a chink
between the dry, pine logs.

"So where will we go from here, Father Ovsivoy," asked a
soft, young voice.

"Dunno," said another, older voice. "Back to Kamyenetz, I
reckon."

"How? The horses can hardly drag one leg after another,
they're so worn."

"That's why we're still here. They'll be rested up well enough by morning."

"So the raid's all over?"

"Looks like it, son. We got us the prisoners we wanted and that's what we come for."

"And the ataman's got himself that fat *Lah* he wanted so bad . . ."

"God works things out in strange ways."

"Seems to me, though, Father Ovsivoy," the younger voice resumed after a pause, "like the ataman might want to go to that place out there beyond Yampol as soon as he can."

Zagloba held his breath.

"Keep your idiot mouth shut!" the older Cossack snarled. "If you want to keep breathing!"

"I didn't mean nothin . . ."

"Not a word about that place! Never! Not even in your sleep, understand?"

"I know . . . I know, father. I was just thinkin' out loud, that's all. I wouldn't talk about it."

Curious, because he was suddenly quite certain that this had something to do with Helen, Zagloba waited to hear more. But the two Cossacks had nothing more to say. The low muttering voices he heard after this exchange came to him only from beyond the other three walls.

"They're everywhere," Pan Zagloba sighed.

He moved to another wall.

This time he heard the soft crackling of animals chewing on their fodder and the quiet voices of the young *moloytzy* sprawled among their horses.

"Hey," one said. "Here we are, come all this way without sleep, without eating. And for what? Just so's we can end up on Yarema's stakes."

"So it's sure he's coming?"

"The Yarmolinsk people seen 'im as clear as I see you. Scares you just to listen to them. He's big as a pine tree, they say. His eyes are like torches. And his horse breathes fire like a dragon."

"*Hospody pomyluy!*"

"What we ought to do is take this fat *Lah* and his soldiers and run back to Kamyenetz as fast as we can . . ."

"On what? The nags are half dead."

"Ay, it's bad. Bad. If I was the ataman, I tell you, I'd cut that *Lah's* throat and get back to our own people if I was to walk."

"We'll take the *Lah* with us, seems to me. Our atamans will play a few games with him at Kamyenetz."

"First the Devil will play a few games with you," Pan Zagloba murmured.

In spite of all his terror of Bohun, or perhaps just because of it, he swore that the Cossacks wouldn't take him out of the byre alive. '*If they cut me into pieces, so be it,*' he thought. But he'd elude the torments.

★   ★   ★

Meanwhile various unlikely means of escape or rescue, each more fantastic than the one before, darted through Pan Zagloba's head like a flock of sparrows.

'*If I could just break through that wall,*' he thought, and then went on muttering: "I'd get on one of those nags and that's as much as they'd see of me, the scum! It's hard enough to track a man along all those canyons and ravines in daylight, let alone in the darkness . . ."

But he'd have to have Pan Podbipyenta's strength to break through those thick oak logs, he knew.

"And if I burrowed under them those scurvy dogs would hear me and grab me by the neck as soon as I poked my head out of the hole. Ay, ay, it's starting to look like the end of the road for me. Can this really be the end of Zagloba?"

He shook his head and sighed.

Thoughts whirled through his head so thickly that he couldn't seize on anything practical among them. He shrugged, turned, walked back and forth like a caged bear, and marched off to listen at yet another wall. But suddenly he walked head-first into something hard. He reached out, felt around in the darkness and recognized the rungs of a ladder. The byre had obviously housed buffalo or cattle sometime in its history and the ladder led into a little hayloft that stretched for half its length above it.

Pan Zagloba climbed into the loft without another thought. Then he sat down in the dusty straw, drew a deep, hot breath and began to pull up the ladder after him.

"Hmm. So I've a little fortress here," he muttered, pleased and feeling his hopes starting to stir again. "Not bad! Not bad at all. Even if they find another ladder it'll take them a good while to climb up here after me . . . And, in the meantime, if I don't split the first head that pokes up through this hole I'll let them turn me into a smoked ham!"

That phrase, however, brought another worry.

"They can do more than smoke me out, the scoundrels," he growled. "They can fry me like a Christmas goose and boil me down to cooking fat and boot-grease if they set this dry old tinderbox on fire . . . Ah to Hell with it, damn their murdering souls! Let them roast me if they want. I don't care if the crows eat me cooked or raw. The main thing is not to let them take me out of here alive for that devil Bohun to play with at his leisure . . ."

But the old knight never strayed too far into despair. Indeed, armed and sitting in the hayloft, he started to feel as confident as if he was safe among his friends in Prince Yeremi's camp.

"Hmm. Yes. I've time, if nothing more. Something's sure to turn up. I might still be able to think of something useful"

He got to his feet with some difficulty under the low thatched ceiling and began to rummage quietly among the bundles of weathered old thatching to make a small lookout opening for himself. Once that was done he poked his head outside and started to peer around. The night, as he could see, was ending. The sky was greying in the east and the pale light showed the entire yard filled with nodding horses. Long ranks of Cossacks lay bundled up in blankets and sleeping beside the homestead. Beyond them, on the other side of the well and closer to the gates of the broad enclosure, lay other still ranks of sleeping men guarded by Cossacks with drawn sabers.

'*Those must be my men,*' Pan Zagloba thought. '*Roped and trussed like geese at the market . . .*'

And then he cursed himself for his own stupidity, carelessness and folly.

"If only they *were* mine!" he groaned. "But they aren't mine at all, they are Prince Yeremi's . . ." And here remorse clutched him by the hair. "A fine commander I turned out to be. I've fed them like cold noodles into a dog's throat . . .! If God ever shows me a way out of here it's going to be hard to face anybody . . . It's all the fault of wine and women, like everything else that's evil in this world. What do all these marriages and romances have to do with me? I'd no more business at this peasant wedding than I'd have at a dog's . . . Damn that green, rotten mead that gets into the legs rather than the head. Bohun would never have got his paws on me if I had been sober."

Here the fat knight's glance fell once more on the peasant homestead where Bohun was sleeping.

"Sleep, you damned horsethief," he muttered. "Sleep! I hope you dream the Devil is skinning you alive, which is what's going to happen to you anyway once you've gone to Hell. Try to get up here after me and we'll soon see what your hide is made of! Ah, if only I could think of some way to get away . . . But how?"

There was, he realized, no way to get through the roof unnoticed. The yard between the buildings, the fences and the gate was so tightly packed with animals and Cossacks that someone would be sure to spot him before he took half a dozen steps. And even if he did manage to untether and mount a horse he'd never get as far as the gaping gates and the road beyond them. And yet he felt that he accomplished the most difficult part of his bid for freedom. He was out of his ropes. He was armed. He was sitting comfortably in that hayloft as safe for the moment as if it were the keep of a castle.

"What the Devil," he growled and glared fiercely at the sleeping Cossacks. "Did I get out of those ropes just so's I can hang myself on them? There has to be some way to slip out of here. There just has to."

And again a swarm of wildly optimistic plans and impossible ideas darted through his brain. But there were so many of them, and they whirled so swiftly, that he couldn't get a good tight grip on one for a closer study.

Chapter Forty-four

MEANWHILE THE MORNING gave the air a soft, silvery glow, a pale light crept into the shadows around the peasant homestead, and the thatched roofs began to look as if they were sheeted with copper and lead. Peering out of the hole in his roof Pan Zagloba could see groups of Bohun's sentries huddled in the yard; he was also able to distinguish the red coats of his own men stretched out beyond the well from the furs and sheepskins of the sleeping Cossacks.

He saw a figure rising from among the sleepers and then watched as the man yawned and stretched and started pacing slowly across the enclosure. Pan Zagloba thought at first that this might be Bohun and wished he had a musket to put a lead ball in his head. The man was obviously an officer of some kind. He stopped near the pickets, spoke briefly to the sentries who guarded the trussed-up prisoners, and began to near Pan Zagloba's byre. Then the dim, silvery light passed across his face and the fat knight recognized him as *Setnik* Holody, an old company commander of Pereyaslav Cossacks, whom he remembered from the roistering days when he and Bohun went about together in Tchehryn.

"Hey there, lads," he heard Holody speaking below his perch. "You keeping awake?"

"Sure, *bat'ku*. Though it's hard to keep the eyes open. It's time we was relieved."

"You'll be relieved soon enough. And that *Lah* son of a bitch didn't get away?"

"No way he could, *bat'ku*. Maybe his spirit's flown out of his body somewheres, scared as he's got to be. But his carcass never left the barn. There's been no sound out of him all night."

"No sound, eh? Hmm. He's a cunning old dog. Go in there, one or two of you, and take a look at him, will you lads? He could've turned into thin air, for all you'd ever know. He's got a smart head on his shoulders, that one."

"Right away, *bat'ku!*" A group of Cossacks turned towards the doors of the byre.

"And get some hay out of the loft while you're at it. Get the horses rubbed down. We're riding at sunrise."

"Right away."

Pan Zagloba quickly abandoned his perch under the roof and crawled to the opening in the hayloft floor. He waited, hardly daring to breathe. He muttered a soft prayer. He heard the screech of the wooden bar drawn out of the door and then the soft rustling of straw under the Cossacks' boots, and his heart started hammering so hard in his chest that he was sure the young *moloytzy* would hear it down below. He clutched the hilt of his saber in a sweating hand and renewed his vows not to let the Cossacks take him alive again. Then he scrunched down his eyes in anticipation of the raging howls he'd hear from the searchers once they found him gone.

But he was wrong. Minutes passed in silence. Nobody yelled out in alarm. The old knight could hear the Cossacks stumbling about below him, kicking the soiled straw, and searching for him with a rising urgency, but they seemed more puzzled and annoyed than frightened and angry.

"Hey, what the Hell's all this anyways?" one said. "I can't feel him around anywhere . . . . We threw him down right here, didn't we?"

"Seems about right."

"So where the Hell is he? Is he a magician, or something? Hey Vasil, strike a light, will you? It's dark here like in the middle of a forest."

A brief silence followed while one of the *moloytsy* began to search his pockets for flintstone and tinder and then another called out softly: "Hey, Mister Noble, where are you? Say something!"

"Kiss a dog's ear," Pan Zagloba muttered.

Then the fat knight heard the sharp, clicking sound of a horseshoe nail scraping a piece of flint, and saw a sudden shower of sparks scattering below him, and then the hunched, dark silhouettes of hooded heads as the *moloytzy* moved about, kicking through the straw.

"You see him, Yuri?"

"Not a sign of him."

"So where'd he get to, then?"

When the brief bright glare died down and darkness returned to the byre below, the silent old knight was sure that it was even blacker than before.

"He's not here! He's gone!" feverish voices cried out in the byre. "Hey, *bat'ku* Holody!"

"What's up, then?" the old captain snapped, appearing in the doorway.

"The *Lah's* not here!"

"What do you mean '*not here!*'"

"He's gone! It's like the earth swallowed him up or something! *Oh hospody pomyluy!* We struck a light but there's no sign of 'im!"

"Christ," hissed Holody. "The ataman will tear you limb from limb! How did he get away? Did you fall asleep on guard or what, you damn fools?"

"Not us, *bat'ku*! We kept a good watch. He didn't leave the byre."

"Quiet, for Chrissake! Don't wake the ataman . . .! If the *Lah* didn't get out of the byre then he's in here somewhere. Keep looking! Get a good light going! Did you kick through the straw everywhere?"

"Sure did, *bat'ku*!"

"How about up there in the loft?"

"No. What for?"

"What d'you mean '*what for*,' you damn fool?"

"Well, *bat'ku* . . . how's he going to climb up into the loft when he's all tied up?"

"How d'you think, idiot? If he hadn't got himself out of the ropes he'd still be here, wouldn't he? Look upstairs! Get that light, I said!"

The sparks flew again. Word about the prisoner's disappearance spread swiftly among all the guards outside and they began to crowd into the byre, cursing, asking worried questions and offering advice.

"Let's get up into that hayloft, then!"

"Search outside!"

"Don't wake the ataman, whatever you do, or he'll have our heads!"

"Get the ladder. Where's the goddamn ladder?"

"It's gone! The son of a bitch must've pulled it up after him."

"So get another. Go see if you can find one by the house."

"Oh, that goddamn *Lah*!"

"Get up on the roof, somebody, and then on down through the thatch inside . . ."

"Can't do that without a ladder. The overhang's too wide. And the damn thatch is laid over solid boards."

"So go get some lances. You get a half-dozen lances angled right in that hole overhead and you can crawl up them like it was a ladder . . ."

"Get your lances, then!" Holody ordered. "Jump to it lads! Move it!"

A group of Cossacks bolted out of the barn doors through which, in the meantime, daylight began to flood into the byre, showing the upturned Cossack faces staring into the opening overhead.

"Hey," a soft, friendly voice called out from below. "Why don't you be a good man, Mister Noble, and let down that ladder? Why don't you come down? There's no way you can get away so why cause us trouble? Come on down!"

The fat knight said nothing.

"Come on down!" the Cossacks urged. "Be a good fellow, now. There's no point getting everybody in an uproar, is there? Get your carcass down here!"

But Pan Zagloba only clamped his teeth, blinked his good eye, and took a better grip on his ready saber.

"Listen, you're a smart man," Holody tried in a conciliatory tone. "If it was to help you in some way, it would make sense for you to sit up there, I know. But how can it help you? We can get you down soft and easy or we can get you down rough and hard but either way we'll get you and you damn well know it. So come on down on your own like the good man you are and save everybody a lot of grief and trouble."

The fat knight crouched in silence, out of sight, and lifted his saber.

"Come down, then!" Holody roared at last, having lost his patience. "Or we'll tear the skin off your bald skull and pitch you headfirst through that hole!"

Deaf to threats as he was to all the futile attempts to cajole him out of his defenses, Pan Zagloba sat as still as an embattled badger trapped in his hole by a pack of terriers, holding a tight grip on his saber and breathing a bit deeper as he whispered a few odds and ends of prayers and prepared to fight for his life. Meanwhile other *moloytsy* came running with their slim, ten-foot lances and fastened them with rawhide into a crude tripod-like contraption that they propped under the hayloft opening and prepared to climb. Peering through a crack in his floor, the fat knight saw that the whole byre below him had now filled up with Cossacks who jostled each other for room on the makeshift scaling implement.

"I'll go!" they shouted. "Hey, let me! I'll give it a try!"

"Wait for a proper ladder," Holody advised.

"What for, *bat'ku*? Won't do no harm to try it this way first. What d'you say?"

"Let Vasil try it," cried several voices. "He climbs like a cat!"

"Try it, then," said Holody. "But be careful, hear?"

"Hey, Vasil," joked another young voice. "You watch out, you hear? He's got a saber up there! He might trim the hair on your neck!"

"Or he'll grab you by the ears and pull you up there and then he'll stuff you good and proper, like a bear!"

But the grinning Vasil only shrugged and spat into his hands for a better grip.

"The *Lah* knows," he said in warning to the silent and invisible Zagloba, "that the ataman will feed him piece by piece to the Devil if he touches a hair on my head! And he knows what you'll do to him too, brothers. He's a smart one, right? So he won't do a thing."

But the other Cossacks fell suddenly into that childlike humor common to simple soldiers, turning the whole affair into a huge joke at Vasil's expense, and started poking fun at their grinning comrade.

"He won't care, Vasil, how we'll pay him for your head."

"Hell, no. And it's not worth much, anyways."

"There'll be one less blockhead walking about the earth in a minute, that's for sure."

"That's for sure, ha ha! He's a magician, Vasil, remember? Devil knows what he's changed himself into up there, you'd better believe it. You don't know what you'll find waiting for you up in that dark hole."

"What's that?" The young Cossack had started to climb the rickety scaling ladder but now he jumped down. "I'll go up against a *Lah* anytime," he said and spat three times to avert black magic. "But I'm not climbing up there if that's some kind of Devil."

Holody cursed, muttered a thick threat and took his place on the creaking lance shafts.

"Look here, Mister Nobleman," he called up as he started climbing slowly towards the dark opening. "The joke's over, get it? You want to sit up there, that's your business. But don't you put up any kind of fight! We'll get you down no matter what happens, understand? Even if we was to tear this whole damn sty apart board by board!"

Zagloba still said nothing.

"You be a smart fellow, now," Holody said and stuck his head cautiously into the loft opening. "Be good. Don't cause trouble."

But the old Cossack captain had no sooner started peering into that silent darkness, his head and shoulders hidden from the *moloytzy* who crowded up behind him, when a sudden hiss of a saber sweeping through the air whistled through the shadows, there was the dull thud of iron striking bone, and he screamed once as if struck by lightning and tumbled back down onto the heads of his yelling followers, with his shaved skull split in two all the way to his shoulder blades.

"*Koli! Koli!*" the enraged Cossacks howled in the byre below. "Kill 'im! Kill!"

And then a pandemonium of yells and curses spilled into the *maydan* where the morning sun had finally burst over the horizon.

★   ★   ★

Yelling and sweating so that he could hardly see, Pan Zagloba flayed about with his saber, cutting down the Cossacks who swarmed up the ladder several at a time, until Bohun himself ran into the byre, clutching a drawn saber.

"Over the roof, you useless dogs!" he shouted. "I want him alive."

"Come here yourself, you peasant clown!" Pan Zagloba bellowed. "I'll save your neck for the hangman because that's his property but I'll have your nose and ears for a keepsake!"

Bohun glared up at him, pale with fury and dressed only in his boots, shirt and breeches, and the fat knight hurled down such curses at him and his men that the fierce *moloytzy* might have been amazed if they hadn't gone mad with rage themselves.

"Come up here you footpads, cannibals, scurvy whelps, sweepings from the gutter . . .! Here, you gelded hogs! I'll stamp you all into the ground, I will! I'll show you what it means to lock a noble in a pigsty or tangle with a knight! Try it, dogs! Come here all you mangy, flea-bitten mongrels, and the more the better! But leave your ugly snouts behind you in the muck or I'll send you back down without them!"

And then he turned on Bohun:

"What's that? Lost all your guts, have you? Dumbfounded, are you now, you boot-licking lackey? Throw a rope around that scoundrel's neck, you others, and I'll show you mercy! What have you to say now, you hangman's delight? The Devil got your tongue, you dumb piece of carrion? Come on up here yourself so I can make *you* welcome for a change! Come on! I'll serve you a breakfast that'll remind you of your Devil father and your harlot mother!"

Meanwhile the wooden braces of the roof started to creak under the boots of the men swarming over it, and a thick, choking dust drifted down into the loft as the Cossacks began tearing at the thatch. Fear lifted the hair on Pan Zagloba's head but he was too intoxicated with rage and excitement to give it more than a passing thought.

"So be it," he muttered. "It had to happen one way or another. I'll put my back against a wall and die there on my feet . . ."

But at that moment a storm of gunshots crackled in the *maydan* and a dozen Cossacks ran into the byre. "*Bat'ku!*" they screamed and crowded around Bohun as if Hell itself had opened up behind them. "Come on out! Come quickly!" And in another moment Pan Zagloba found himself peering down into an empty byre.

"What's this?" he called out, alarmed and astonished. The roof, he noted, had also stopped creaking. "What's going on out there?"

Then it occurred to him that the Cossacks might be shooting pistols into the dry thatch to set it on fire.

"Very well, you butchers. Try to smoke me out and to the Devil with you. Whether boiled or broiled, you're not getting me out of here alive."

But the yells outside seemed to be composed at least as much of fear and despair as fury and vengeance, Pan Zagloba noted. The shouts and pistol shots were only part of a much greater sound, and then the fat knight heard the clash of sabers.

"My God, that's a battle!" he cried and leaped towards his lookout.

What he saw struck him with a rush of such overwhelming joy that his knees buckled under him. The battle, or rather the disaster that overwhelmed Bohun's surprised and unprepared Cossacks, raged throughout the *maydan*. The scarlet ranks of Prince Yeremi's soldiers pressed on them from all sides, firing their pistols right into their faces and sabering them remorselessly a dozen at a time. Without a chance to form ranks, reach their weapons or to mount their horses, the terrified *moloytsy* milled about in hopeless confusion or died where they stood. Only a few scattered, desperate groups managed to make a stand and defend themselves in the angles of the barns and buildings; the rest ran through the smoke and chaos to throw a saddle on a maddened pony, cinch a strap, and die before they could set one foot in a stirrup, or to clamber over the fences and crawl through the ditches before their redcoated pursuers caught up with them and killed them.

It must have seemed to these trapped and massacred hundreds in the *maydan* that Prince Yeremi himself had fallen on them magically out of the morning sky, Pan Zagloba thought. Shots and the dreadful howling of their slaughtered comrades, the furious cries of triumph and the whistling sound of sabers falling on their necks, followed them like a storm everywhere they fled without a chance to catch and draw one chaotic breath or come to their senses.

"*Ludy, spasayte!*" the calls for headlong flight into the Steppe sounded from all sides.

"Kill!" replied the victors.

And finally Pan Zagloba caught sight of Pan Michal himself standing in the gateway at the head of a large group of soldiers, calling out orders, and pointing with his colonel's *bulava* to where he wanted his reserves to strike. Once in a while he spurred his bay gelding into the fight, made one or two swift movements with his saber, and trotted back leaving a corpse on the ground behind him, until the fat knight started to clap and cheer.

Oh, what a soldier this was, he thought in admiration. That's the way to be a real commander! Not for a moment did he lose control of the fight that raged among all the buildings of the *maydan*. The little colonel seemed to watch and direct everything at once. Every so often he'd move in to correct some error or to save some soldier, and go back to his position to keep an eye on the entire field, so that Pan Zagloba was reminded of a royal 'kapelmeister' directing musicians. Once in a while he'd play a phrase or two himself, sometimes he'd watch and listen and signal a new pitch for this or that player, but his ears were tuned to the entire work and his attention was always focused on the whole performance.

"Bravo!" the fat knight bellowed. "Kill them all! Cut them down! Chop them into mincemeat! That's Bohun! Those are Bohun's men! Don't let one of 'em get away! Tan their mangy hides!"

He leaped about, clapped and stamped his boots until dust billowed up into his bloodshot eyes, but when it settled and he could see again he caught sight of Bohun, coatless and hatless and with his shirt-tails flying in the wind, galloping into the fields at the head of several dozen riders, with the remorseless little knight and his soldiers at his heels.

"Get him! That's Bohun!" Pan Zagloba roared but they were too far to hear him.

The fugitives and pursuers scattered in the plain, and Pan Zagloba's eyes bulged with the effort to see them long after they were out of sight. He ripped out more thatching and climbed out on the roof. The excitement robbed him of breath as he caught a glimpse of the principal actors of this sudden drama. There . . . like a greyhound about to catch a hare . . . rides the little knight. There, like a panicked boar scuttling before a wolfhound, gallops the desperate Bohun. The distance narrows. The young ataman turns and thrusts out his saber . . .

"They've closed!" the fat knight was howling in delirium. "They're fighting!"

A moment more and Bohun fell, together with his horse, and the little knight rode right over him and vanished in the distance in pursuit of others.

"He's down!" Zagloba shouted. "Down and finished!"

But Bohun was still alive, he saw at once; alive and running towards an outcropping of rocks nearby, seeking shelter, while the red coats of the Prince's soldiers dwindled in the distance.

"No! No!" the fat knight yelled, leaping about like a madman on his rooftop. "That's Bohun over there! Get him! Get him! Don't let him get away!"

And then another mass of fleeing Cossacks swept into the field, reached Bohun, lifted him up and vanished in the mouth of a ravine with a troop of soldiers galloping behind them.

Then they were all gone.

The smoke began to lift in the silent *maydan*. Nothing stirred anywhere the fat knight could see. There wasn't a living man in sight because even Pan Zagloba's soldiers, cut loose from their ropes, had seized the weapons of the slaughtered Cossacks and leaped on their ponies to join in the pursuit.

Only the dead littered the trodden ground.

★ ★ ★

Pan Zagloba lowered his ladder into the byre, climbed down from the loft, and stepped into the open.

"I'm free," he said with some surprise.

He started walking slowly among the corpses, peering carefully at each of them as if searching for a fallen friend, and then he stooped and knelt beside a dead soldier. He reached out, groped under the body, found a tin canteen and shook it near his ear. It sounded full. He drank deeply until the flask was empty.

"And not bad either," he muttered. Then he looked around the littered yard, found nothing that was likely to contradict him, and said once more: "I am free!"

Then he walked slowly to the broad, thatched homestead where the wedding took place just the day before and where he opened his bleary eyes only a few hours earlier to see Bohun's yellow stare fixed on him with a terrifying joy. He stepped across the body of the old householder whom the Cossacks murdered and left on the threshold, and disappeared in the shadows of the wooden cabin. When he came out again he wore Bohun's broad, gold-embroidered sash knotted around his belly, and behind the sash gleamed a richly jeweled Turkish dagger with a great ruby shining in its hilt.

"So God rewards a hero," he said with satisfaction. "Particularly since the purse is also nice and full. But I hope that damned cut-throat doesn't get away! It'd be a shame to have to give him another beating . . ."

Pan Zagloba had apparently forgotten who had captured whom in that silent *maydan*, or perhaps it merely seemed to him that a different story would sound better in a later telling. At any rate he started to prepare his own version of what happened here, more in keeping with his reputation.

"A snappy little hornet," he wagged his head in admiration of Volodyovski. "I'll have to take a closer look at him. I could see right away, of course, that he was a good fellow. But to ride on Bohun's neck like that . . . Phew! That takes some doing. Imagine so much fire in such a little body! Bohun can carry him in his coat-tail pockets like a whittling knife but he chased that bloody-handed Devil as if he was a turkey in a barnyard . . ."

The reek of gunpowder still lay thickly in the air and Pan Zagloba sniffed and rubbed his nose.

"Phew, what a stink," he shook his head in wonder. "I've been in some tight spots in my time, but to get out of this one in one piece . . . Hmm. Hmm. God be praised. That's really something the younger generation ought to hear about. That little ferret may also have had a bit to do with it, God love him. I'd better keep an eye on him because it's clear that he has a future."

Musing in that manner, Pan Zagloba found a comfortable place to sit on the threshold of the byre and waited for Pan Volodyovski's soldiers to reappear.

★　★　★

Meanwhile Volodyovski's squadron appeared in the Steppe far beyond the highway, riding back from their pursuit of Bohun's scattered Cossacks, with the little knight trotting at their head. Seeing Zagloba sitting in the farmyard Pan Michal spurred his horse rapidly towards him.

"Is that really you?" the small soldier cried jumping off his gelding and running towards him. "I didn't think I'd see you alive again."

"Oh, it's me alright," Pan Zagloba stated, very much at ease. "In the flesh."

"Thank the good Lord, then, that I got here in time," cried the little knight, pumping Zagloba's hand with every sign of pleasure.

"Yes, indeed, God bless you. But how did you find out about the little spot of trouble I was having here?"

"The peasants brought word."

"What peasants?"

"The ones who got away from here. From the wedding party."

"So they told you, eh? And I thought it was they who had betrayed me."

"No way, those were decent people. The boy and the girl barely got away with their lives. As for the rest of the wedding party they don't know what happened to any of them."

"Well, if they weren't traitors then the Cossacks killed them. The householder is over there by the house. But no matter, no matter . . . Tell me, did Bohun get away?"

"Bohun? This was Bohun?"

"Himself! The one without a hat or coat whom you cut down together with his horse!"

"I cut him in the arm, that's all . . . Damn, I wish I'd recognized him!" Then the small soldier glared at Pan Zagloba. "But you, my dear Zagloba, what the Devil did you think you were doing here?"

"What was I doing?" the fat knight repeated. "You want to know what I was doing, eh? Come with me, Master Michal and I'll show you just what I was doing!"

So saying, the fat knight caught Pan Michal by the arm and led him into the byre. "Look and learn," he said.

The little soldier couldn't see anything for some time, having stepped into the darkness of the byre out of the bright noon sunlight, but when his eyes grew accustomed to the murky shadows he saw a heap of Cossack corpses sprawled in the soiled straw.

"And who did all that?" he asked.

"I did," Pan Zagloba said with a lofty stare. "You asked what I've been doing so I'm showing you."

"Well!" The young officer began to twist his head in surprise and wonder. "And how did you do it?"

"I was up there, in the hayloft," Pan Zagloba pointed overhead. "Holding the fort, so to speak, and they were attacking me from down below. I don't know how long I had to fight them all alone because a man loses track of time in the heat of battle, but it was Bohun himself I was holding off here, along with his best men! Oh, he'll have good reason to remember me as well as you, my friend! He won't forget this dent in his glory! I'll tell you some other time how I happened to fall into his hands and what humiliations I've had to endure . . . Right now I'm so *fatigatus* with all this gory work that I can hardly keep myself upright in my boots."

"Well, well . . ." The little knight nodded with approval. "You certainly put up a good fight, there's no denying that. But it seems you're a better swordsman, my dear friend, than a troop commander."

"Hmm. Is that so? We'll see about that when it comes to counting casualties," Pan Zagloba said, knowing that Bohun had been more concerned with taking prisoners than killing his soldiers. "This isn't the time to debate such matters. We'd do better to thank God for the great victory that he sent to both of us here, and the glory that we'll be sharing for a long time to come."

The little knight looked even more astonished because this 'great victory' didn't seem much more to him than a minor skirmish which, as he recalled it, he won without much help from Zagloba. But the fat knight was staring at him with such unshakable assurance, and with such a fierce and martial air of challenge and conviction, that he only shrugged and scratched his head again.

"So be it then," he said.

An hour later, with Pan Zagloba's soldiers rearmed and re-mounted, both their troops formed up behind them on the country track and set off to Yarmolinsk together.

Chapter Forty-five

IT SEEMED as if all of his famous luck deserted Bohun in that expedition. Surprised and beaten by Volodyovski despite his own great courage and military experience, and certain that the whole Vishnovyetzki army was marching on Krivoinos since that was what Zagloba's captured soldiers told him, he could do nothing more than gather whatever men were still close enough to find and get back to Kamyenetz as quickly as he could.

But even that wasn't as simple as it sounded. It took him three days after his defeat to collect about two hundred of his scattered and demoralized *moloytsy* who panicked and ran at the first suspicion that an enemy might be somewhere near. The rest of his command was either dead, or wounded and in chains, or hiding in the deep sump-holes and ravines that dotted that inhospitable landscape, or wandering lost and dazed in the wild, broken land for miles around, not knowing where to turn or how to save themselves. None of them realized how small Pan Michal's detachment really was; caught while asleep and totally unprepared, and then slaughtered without the means to offer any organized resistance, they were convinced, as Bohun was himself, that they were overwhelmed by enormous forces led by the Devil-Prince Yarema in person.

Bohun himself went almost mad with rage. Slashed in the arm, trampled by a horse and, once again stricken by a fever, he raved at every thought of the disaster which robbed him at one stroke of his glory, his best men, and his most hated enemy as well.

He knew that those veteran Cossack raiders whom he picked from ten thousand of the finest warriors in the *Sietch*, and who

only a few days earlier would have followed him to the gates of
Hell if that's what he ordered, now lost all faith in him and in
themselves and that their only common thought was how to
save their necks.

And yet, he knew, he had done everything that a skilled
Steppe soldier could have done.

He'd forgotten nothing.

He rode from Kamyenetz at such lightning speed that no
news of his coming warned the enemy. He sent listening posts
and pickets into the Steppe and posted alert sentries all around
the homestead, and he passed the night at the site of his attack
only because his horses were too exhausted to go any farther.
But Pan Volodyovski, who spent his adolescence hunting Tartars and ambushing marauders in the same cheerful, light-
hearted way in which a young man of another country might
have hunted quail, crept up on him like a wolf, seized his guards
and pickets before they could make any sound of warning, and
struck him with such sudden and unexpected violence that he
could save himself only by wild flight. He escaped in his shirt-
sleeves, riding without a saddle like a fleeing peasant, with his
command and his precious reputation equally destroyed.

How could that happen? It seemed to him—when he could
bring himself to even think about it—that his life was finished,
and a despairing rage tore at his spirit like a rabid dog. He
gnawed his hands in fury until they were bleeding. How could
he—Bohun, the legendary Falcon of the Steppes—survive this
disaster? How was it possible for him who stormed Turkish
galleys almost singlehanded, who used to chase shattered Tartar
tchambuls all the way to the Black Sea and fill the Khan himself
with fury and fear, and who massacred one of Prince Yeremi's
own regiments right under his eyes, to be on the run . . .
surprised like a beginner and wandering in the Steppe like a
coatless beggar . . . having lost even his saber in his brief clash
with the little knight?

"So much for your fame, and glory," he raged when no one
could see him. "So much for the witch's prophecy of a Hetman's
horsetails!"

And when such howling rages seized him in the brief moments when he halted his shattered remnants for a rest, he drank
himself blind and clawed at his hair, and then he threw himself
on his horse and shouted at his men to follow him against the

Prince himself so that he could die in one last all-out battle and be gone for ever.

He may have wanted that but they didn't.

"*Ubiy, bat'ku,*" they muttered. "Kill us if you want. But we aren't going."

They weren't afraid of dying. No Cossack ever was. But they lost their faith in his luck and legend and he was now a symbol of their doom.

But even that wasn't disastrous enough for his reputation. Riding east rather than straight south towards Kamyenetz where any likely pursuit would be sure to follow, he ran into the detachment of Pan Podbipyenta but the watchful Lithuanian didn't let himself be caught by surprise; he ambushed Bohun's column, smashed it again all the more readily since the *moloytsy* lost their will to fight, and drove it straight into the half-regiment led by Pan Skshetuski. Pan Yan completed their destruction with such thoroughness that barely a dozen Cossacks survived the disaster.

Days later, after a long time of wandering and hiding in the Steppe, the ruined ataman appeared before Krivoinos with only a handful of ragged men around him. But the savage Krivoinos who showed no mercy to subordinates who failed in a mission forgave him at once. He knew from his own experience what it meant to confront Yeremi Vishnovyetzki. He soothed the wretched young ataman, consoled him like a father, and tried to reassure him as best as he could. And when Bohun became seriously ill again he had him watched over as carefully as if he really was his own favorite son.

★ ★ ★

Meanwhile the four knights filled the rebel countryside with rumor and fear and reassembled in Yarmolinsk to rest their men and horses for a day or two and to tell each other what they had accomplished.

But once they were seated around a jug of mead in Skshetuski's quarters they found that Pan Zagloba had more to say than all of them together.

"True," he said. "I was captured. But so what? The wheel of fortune isn't round for nothing. Bohun was fortune's child all his life, he's never known a setback, but now we've beaten him so thoroughly that he must be howling somewhere like a wounded dog and it'll be a long time before he dares to stick his snout into open air again."

"We, dear brother?" asked Pan Podbipyenta. "We beat him? It seems to me you were just telling us how he captured you."

"Well, that's war for you." Pan Zagloba shrugged. "One day you're knocking somebody about and the next day he is belting you. Anyway, God punished Bohun for sneaking up on my people in their sleep, when they were resting after honest labor, but even that turned out to be a disaster for him because he babbled out a lot of things he didn't want anyone to know. Ho ho! He thought he could put the fear of God in me with his blaspheming tongue! Well, let me tell you, I soon put him in his place *and* got some really important information for us in the bargain."

"Was that before or after he locked you in a pigsty?"

"Eh? What? Well, it's a good thing he did! If he hadn't done it then Pan Michal wouldn't have a reason to attack him, right? And the two of us together wouldn't have given him the beating that we did, and that in turn would've meant that you, my short-witted Lithuanian beanpole, wouldn't have your crack at him and, finally, that Pan Yan couldn't have demolished him altogether! And if that's not enough for you then consider this! If we hadn't crushed him, he'd have beaten us! And since every good oak begins with an acorn maybe you'd like to tell me who planted the seed of our success?"

"So it's you, then, who's responsible for defeating Bohun?"

"And who else?"

"Ay, you're amazing, sweet brother," Pan Longinus murmured, shaking his head in wonder. "You're as slick as a fox when you get to talking. You flick your tail this way, you dart off somewhere else, and you're always off and running no matter how hot the hounds are on your trail."

"And why not? It's a stupid animal that chases his own tail," Pan Zagloba said. "*Primo*, because he'll never catch it. *Secundo*, because he's unlikely to smell anything pleasant while he's doing it, and finally because he'll soon run out of wind for nothing! So just tell me this much, my fine friend, how many men did you lose?"

"About a dozen," Pan Longinus said. "And a few wounded. The Cossacks didn't have the heart to fight us very hard."

"And you, Master Michal?"

"Thirty all told, because we hit them unexpectedly and gave them no chance to get themselves together."

"And you, lieutenant?"

"About as many as Pan Longinus," Pan Yan said.

"And I lost two," Pan Zagloba said.

"So?" Pan Longinus asked.

"So who's the best commander? Furthermore, why did we come here in the first place? To get news about Krivoinos, am I right? Well I not only got *that* out of Bohun, and I know that Krivoinos is sitting tight at Kamyenetz, keeping his ears down and not sure which way to jump, but I also got him to tell me something else! And that, my good friends, is something that'll have you jumping through hoops out of sheer joy!"

"For God's sake," cried Volodyovski. "What is it, then? Something to do with our poor, lost girl?"

"That's right, God bless her. And the reason I haven't mentioned it before is that I wanted all of you to hear it together. Besides, all this rattling about in the saddle and that Tartar-style roping back there in that byre quite knocked the wind out of me."

"Speak up then, for God's sake!"

"Yes. Tell us," begged the Lithuanian.

But Pan Yan said nothing. He rose and straightened up with such a painful slowness, supporting himself against the table with trembling hands and arms, that it seemed as if all his strength had suddenly drained away, and then he stared at the fat knight as if he'd seen a ghost. Then he fell heavily back to his bench again, still unable to speak. The others also waited in such breathless silence that the thin whining of a fly trapped between the windows seemed as loud as trumpets.

* * *

"She's alive," Pan Zagloba said once he knew he was the focus of all their attention. "Bohun's got her. I know this for certain. Yes, I know those are dreadful hands to be in but God's been watching over her. She hasn't been harmed or shamed in any way. Bohun himself boasted to me about that and he'd be more likely to boast about something else if he could."

"How can that be?" Pan Yan murmured as if in a fever. "How could that be?"

"Listen, if I'm lying then may lightning set my head on fire,"

Pan Zagloba swore. "I know I sometimes touch up the truth a little but this is God's business and I don't fool with that."

"But how do you know all this? How?"

"From Bohun himself. This is what that damned scoundrel said to me, wanting to amuse himself at my expense before I set him back on his heels. '*What did you think,*' he says to me, '*that I'm some kind of peasant to take her by force? That I can't afford a proper wedding in a church in Kiev? I'll have bells and music,*' he says. '*I'll have three hundred candles burning on the altar,*' he says to me, the dog, '*as befits an ataman and a Hetman!*' And all that time he's stamping about and waving his knife at me, thinking that he'd scare me. Ha! Ha! I told him straight off to go scare the crows."

Skshetuski managed to get a grip on his long-suppressed and suddenly released feelings, but his grim monklike features began to quiver under the impact of new hope, fear, doubt, uncertainty and joy.

"Where is she, then?" he said anxiously. "Where? If you've discovered that as well then you're a gift from Heaven!"

"That he didn't tell me," Pan Zagloba said. "But a wise ear doesn't need more than a word or two. Listen then to what he said before I taught him not to take liberties with his betters. '*First,*' he says, '*I'll take you to Krivoinos, and then I'd invite you to the wedding, but that won't be for a while yet because of the war.*' You note that '*for a while?*' That means we've a bit of time, we don't have to rush. And then again, '*first to Krivoinos and then to the wedding.*' Which means she's not in Krivoinos' camp. And if he doesn't have her there then he's hidden her somewhere far away from danger."

"You are pure gold, you are!" Pan Volodyovski cried.

"Yes, that's occurred to me too now and then," Pan Zagloba said, enjoying the awed admiration in Pan Michal's eyes. "So where could she be? First I thought he might have sent her off to Kiev to wait for him there. But then why would he say that he'd *take* her there if that's where she was? Besides, he's far too smart for that. He knows that if Hmyelnitzki marches west into Ruthenia the Lithuanian Hetmans can come down on Kiev and take it back again."

"That's true!" Pan Longinus cried out and pressed his hands piously together. "As God's my witness, many great statesmen could afford to change their brains for yours!"

"I wouldn't doubt that for a moment," Pan Zagloba said. "Only I'd be careful who I changed them with, particularly if I was near any Lithuanians."

"There he goes again," Longinus said sadly.

"So let me finish quickly. So where is she, eh? If she's neither in Kiev nor with Krivoinos?"

"That's the hard part," Pan Longinus murmured.

"Listen!" cried Skshetuski. "If you've any thoughts or ideas about that, speak up for God's sake! I feel as if I'm going to burn up!"

"Oh I've more than just a thought," Pan Zagloba said and rolled his good eye around the others in a glance of triumph. "I know she's somewhere beyond Yampol."

"And how do you know that?" pressed Volodyovski.

"How do I know? I'll tell you. I was sitting in that pigsty where that scoundrel tossed me—may hogs get to chew on him for it if there's any justice—and there were Cossacks talking all around me. So one says: '*So now maybe the ataman will head back beyond Yampol, eh?*' And another snaps back at him: '*Keep your mouth shut about that place if you want your head to stay on your shoulders!*' I'll bet my own neck that she's somewhere in one of those out-of-the way canyons on the other side of Yampol."

"As God's in His Heaven!" Volodyovski cried. "That's got to be right!"

"So then there's hope again," Pan Yan whispered.

"Yes. There's hope." Pan Zagloba nodded. "He'd hardly take her all the way into the Wild Lands, that's asking for trouble at the best of times. So the way I see it he must've hidden her somewhere between Yampol and Yahorlik which, as you know, is just about the end of civilization anyway. I spent a little time out that way a few years back because that's where the Khan's negotiators and the King's commissioners meet to settle disputes about stolen horseherds. Anyway, that whole Dniester region is full of secret hideouts, canyons, caves and undiscovered gorges where you've all kinds of queer folk living in hidden homesteads. It's a real, honest-to-God wilderness out there. He could have hidden her with somebody he knows in some out of the way place like that."

"He could have," agreed Pan Longinus. "But how can we get there with Krivoinos stretched out across our way? And Yampol itself, as I've heard it, is a real thieves' and cut-throats' lair."

"I'd risk my head ten times over to find her," Pan Yan cried. "I'll go in disguise. And if God wills it, I'll get to rescue her."

"And I'll go with you, Yan!" cried the little knight.

"And so will I," Pan Zagloba said. "Only this time I'll take bagpipes rather than a lyre. I may get short of breath once in a while but I've had enough of strumming on those cat guts to last me a lifetime."

"And maybe I can make myself useful too, in some way?" Pan Longinus wondered.

"Of course you can," Pan Zagloba said. "If we have to wade the Dniester you can carry us across like St. Christopher carried the infant Jesus. Or we can stretch you out from one bank to the other, use you for a plank, and keep our boots dry."

"I'm a lucky man to have friends like you," Pan Yan said gratefully. "With your help and God's blessing . . . well . . . I can hope again."

"And why not?" The fat knight grinned around the table. "The good Lord is always on the side of unity and friendship. Mmm. Mmm. I'll get drunk at this wedding like I've never been drunk at one before. Ah, I can already taste the fruits of our labors."

"Well then," Pan Yan took a deep, shuddering breath and resumed after a short silence. "If that's how it is . . . if that's what we're doing . . . then all that's left is to take the regiments back to Prince Yeremi and set out!"

"Any time!" the little knight cried out.

"Yes." Serious again, Skshetuski nodded thinking about their duty. "Hmyelnitzki is sure to be crushed by now, or he will be by the time we get to His Highness, so it'll be alright to take a month's leave."

"That's right." The little knight grinned and moved his pointed whiskers up and down like a hungry rabbit. "We'll search all along the Dniester between Yampol and Yahorlik . . ."

"I suppose the troops will go back to the Ukraine to stamp out the last of the rebellion," Skshetuski observed. "But that's just pursuit. We won't be needed there."

"Ah, ah, but wait!" Volodyovski slapped his small hand on the tabletop. "If they've finished with Hmyelnitzki then it will be Krivoinos' turn. And if that's so we can go to Yampol with the army."

"No," Pan Zagloba said. "We've got to find Helen before that devil Bohun runs for cover there. So let's get those regiments back to the Prince, get his permission and take it from there. I expect His Highness will be pleased with us, don't you think?"

"Especially with you, my dear, dear friend" Pan Skshetuski said.

"Hmm. And why not? I'm bringing him the best possible news. I don't mind saying that I expect a little something in reward."

"So, are we ready then?"

"Dear God, no," said Pan Michal. "If we don't rest our horses at least overnight we'll lose every nag we have."

"So we'll start tomorrow."

★   ★   ★

They set out next morning. According to Prince Yeremi's orders they were to go back to Zbarajh and wait for new instructions there. They took the trail to Kuzmin, then turned towards Felshtyn and Hlebanovka which lay at the head of the old Zbarajh highway, but it was a hard and depressing journey. Heavy rains fell unseasonably early, there were many large bands of marauders to fight along the way, and by the time they reached the sleepy little town of Volotchysko they were all glad to find dry quarters for a short night's rest. But they were no sooner wrapped in their sodden blankets when the pickets rode in with the news that some unknown horsemen were galloping towards the town. Then came word that identified the new-comers as a troop of Prince Yeremi's Tartars and soon a muddy and bedraggled Light Horse officer staggered into Skshetuski's room where the four friends waited.

Pan Yan could hardly recognize him. "Vyershul!" he cried out, astonished.

"Yes . . ." The haggard, redheaded officer was struggling for breath. "Yes . . . it's me."

"What happened to you?"

"Ah . . .! What didn't happen?"

"Are you coming from the Prince?"

"Yes . . . Christ, let me catch my breath!"

"So, is it all over with Hmyelnitzki?"

"It's . . . all over . . . with the Commonwealth!"

"What? Are you mad, for God's sake? What are you saying, man? Another disaster?"

"Panic . . . shame . . . without a battle . . . ah . . ."

"What? What?" the four knights shouted across each other's questions. "That's impossible! What happened? What about the regents?"

"Fled . . ."

"And the Prince?"

"Escaping . . . alone, without troops . . . I'm here from him with orders . . . You're to go at once to Lvov . . . At once! They're right on my heels . . .!"

"Who, for God's sake? Calm down! Get a hold of yourself. Who's on your heels?"

"Cossacks . . . Tartars . . ."

"In the name of the Father, the Son and the Holy Ghost!" Pan Zagloba cried. "Is this the end of the world, then? Or what?"

But Skshetuski understood at once what had to be done. "Questions for later!" he ordered. "Now mount up and ride!"

"Ride! Ride!" the others cried and ran from the house into the street outside where the hooves of Vyershul's horses were already rattling on the cobblestones. The townsmen, wakened by the precipitous arrival of fresh soldiers, began to come out of their houses with lanterns and torches, and then the news flashed through the town like a streak of lightning. The church bells began to sound the alarm. The little town, so peaceful only a moment earlier, exploded into shouts of panic, the drumming of the horses' hooves, and the pleading wails of the terrified Jews who knew what waited for them at the hands of the Cossacks.

Everyone wanted to leave along with the soldiers. The burghers loaded their wives and children and featherbeds and boxes into open wagons. They harnessed teams of horses. The town mayor came to beg Skshetuski to escort the exodus at least as far as Tarnopol, but Skshetuski had to refuse no matter how terrible the results of that refusal would be. His orders directed him to ride with all speed to the old royal city of Lvov and the troops set out at once in that direction.

★ ★ ★

It was only then, with the miles falling away behind them, that Vyershul could begin to tell his story.

"As long as the Commonwealth has existed," he said, "there's never been a catastrophe like this one. Korsun and Yellow Waters were nothing in comparison."

"It can't be! It can't be!" the others went on in utter disbelief.

"It can't but it was."

"The mind just won't grasp it," Pan Yan said. "Where was the Prince while all that was going on?"

"Pushed aside. Ignored. They wouldn't let him command even his own division."

"So who commanded, then?"

"Everyone and no one. I've spent my life in the service but I tell you I've never seen that kind of army or leaders like those regents."

Zagloba, who didn't know much about Vyershul but who didn't like him, began to twist his head and smack his lips in pretended wonder.

"My dear sir," he said at last. "Could it be that you have things mixed up a little bit? Maybe you've taken a minor setback for a general disaster."

"I wish I had," Vyershul said and sighed. "I'd gladly give my own head if that would prove me wrong."

"Hmm. Then tell me. How is it that you're the first to get to Volotchysko after this defeat? I'd hate to think that you were the first to turn tail. Where are those shattered troops you're telling us about? Which way are they running? What happened to them all? Why haven't we seen either hide or hair of anyone until you showed up?"

Vyershul wouldn't have let anyone speak to him like that at any other time but now all he could think about was the disaster that stripped the Commonwealth of its last defenses so he merely shrugged, sighed again, and said:

"I'm first in Volotchysko because everyone else is running the other way and because the Prince sent me here to find you. He wanted you warned so that you'd be on your guard. You may not believe it, but your five hundred troopers are a strong force for him nowadays. The rest of his army is either dead or scattered."

"Strange times, I must say," Pan Zagloba muttered.

"God's final judgment, that's what it has to be," the little knight despaired. "The country's lost, disgrace everywhere, such a great army thrown away for nothing . . .!"

"A man would be hard-pressed to find even a clean, honest death these days if that's what he wanted," Pan Longinus sighed.

"Don't interrupt him," Skshetuski reminded. "Let him tell his story."

★   ★   ★

But Vyershul could say nothing more for a long time. He rode in silence as if gathering his strength. The rain kept falling and the only sound was the splashing of the horses' hooves in the puddled ruts. The night seemed especially dark and threatening under the low clouds, and Vyershul's words, when he did finally begin to speak again, seemed laden with a sense of evil in that drizzling darkness.

"If I didn't expect to die in battle anyway," he said, "I think I'd go mad. You talked about Judgment Day. I think you're right about Armageddon coming soon. Everything's falling apart. Evil wins over virtue. The Antichrist is already walking among the people. You weren't there to see what happened but if even hearing about it is more than you can stand then what about me who witnessed the disaster and the overwhelming disgrace of it all . . . ?"

He shuddered, as if unable to go on, but then he clenched his fists and forced himself to continue.

"God gave us a good beginning. Our Prince made peace with Prince Dominic for the sake of the country and we were all happy to see them united. He led another expedition to Konstantinov, stormed and took the town, and then we took the road to Pilavtse although His Highness advised against going there. But right from the start we found ourself in the middle of intrigues against him. Ill-will. Jealousy. Envy. Call it what you want. No one in council listened to what he had to say. Prince Dominic's backers worked from the beginning to split up our division so that he wouldn't have it all under his control, and he let them do it. If he opposed them, you see, they'd have been able to accuse him of pride and rebellion, so he said nothing . . . took it all in silence . . .

"Ah," he went on after another pause. "How he suffered under these indignities and humiliations! As God's my witness, half of us would have raised a riot if we were in his place. But he swallowed all his bitterness. He humbled himself. To look at him then you'd think he had turned to stone. He let the regents do what they wanted to him. They ordered him to leave his light troops at Konstantinov, along with Vurtzel's guns and Mahnitzki's people. They detached Osinski's and Korytzki's infantry. All that the Prince had left under his command was the *husaria* under Zachvilihovski, two dragoon regiments, and some of my Light Horse companies . . . no more than two thousand men, that's all. A mere handful. No one paid any attention to him after that. I heard Prince Dominic's supporters boasting that they'd drawn his teeth. *'People won't say now that it was Vishnovyetzki who won the great victory,'* they assured each other. They want Prince Yan Casimir elected King, you see, and they were afraid that if our Prince won too much glory in this war he'd be able to force the election of Prince Charles instead . . ."

"So they've even politicized the army?" the little knight burst out.

"Army?" Vyershul said bitterly. "It wasn't any army. It was all meetings and discussions. Talks, speeches. Delegates sent this way and that. Nobody thought about the battle. You'd think the enemy had been crushed already! You'd swear we had gathered for some kind of political convention! If I began to tell you about those feasts . . . about all those banquets . . . about that opulence and the display of riches, you wouldn't believe me. Not even the legendary hosts of Pyrrhus could've dripped with so much gold, with such quantities of jewels. They must've plucked every ostrich in the world to get all those plumes . . . I tell you, we had two hundred thousand lackeys, valets and servants trailing behind that army! You wouldn't be able to count all the baggage wagons. The horses were falling under the weight of all those silk pavilions, the carts were breaking down under all that gold-plate . . . You'd think we were out to conquer the whole world, or better yet, to dazzle it with treasures!"

★ ★ ★

Again a gloomy silence settled on the riders. The rain had thickened. A cold, grey curtain seemed to hang before them; water dripped off their faces as thick as mourners' tears; and the light of a running moon glinted in their beards.

"And so it went," Vyershul resumed hoarsely. "The gentry

from the General Levy went about all day cracking their bull-whips and boasting that they'd '*settle the peasants' hash without a need for sabers.*' The few real soldiers among us could see right off that this would end badly. The different factions argued all over the camp. Then they started fighting each other. Guns, pistols, sabers . . . every day there was some kind of riot. Nobody enforced discipline. There weren't any camp wardens or provosts appointed to keep order. Every night the drunken partisans of one party battled with another. Nobody exercised command or gave any orders. Everybody did whatever he wanted, went where he pleased, formed up wherever and whenever he felt like doing it, and the camp-servants took the cue from their masters and started their own riots. Dear God, you've never seen a campaign like that one. This was no army! It was just one vast self-centered mob at a country outing, a drunken orgy at which they boozed and ate and danced and argued away the last hope of the country!"

"Not while we're still alive!" Volodyovski said.

"And not while there's still a God over us," said Skshetuski.

"Maybe it's true about Judgment Day," the stricken Light Horse leader ground out between his teeth. "But if that's so then we'll be swept completely off the face of the earth unless God grants a miracle, shows us the mercy that we don't deserve, and stops flogging us so terribly for our sins. Sometimes even I can't believe what I saw. Could it have been a nightmare?"

But Pan Zagloba who knew better than almost anyone about the rowdiness of the undisciplined, quarrelsome and self-centered gentry shook his head in silence.

"It wasn't," he said at last. "But go on. What happened after you got to Pilavtse?"

"Nothing. We just sat there. I don't know what the regents deliberated about in that place; they'll answer for it before God's tribunal, that's certain. But that's all they did. As God's my witness, if they'd attacked Hmyelnitzki as soon as they got there he'd have been crushed even by the kind of army that we brought against him. There was already panic among the *tchernya* who wanted to trade him and his top commanders for their own forgiveness. Our Prince rode from one tent to another, pleading and tearing the hair out of his head. '*Let's strike them now,*' he urged anyone who'd listen. '*Before the Tartars join them,*' he warned. '*Give battle now!*' he begged. But they just looked at each other and shrugged and went on with their feasting and their politicking . . .

"Word came that the Khan was on his way with two hundred thousand warriors . . . the pick of all Asia . . . and the regents just went on with their deliberations. The Prince closed himself like a hermit in his tent because they wouldn't even let him talk to them anymore. Rumors started all over the camp that Chancellor Ossolinski had forbidden Prince Dominic to fight, that there were new negotiations under way, and the riots and disorder got worse than ever before . . .."

"And then the Tartars came?" Pan Zagloba prompted.

"Some of them. Yes. Tuhay-bey and his corps. And things went well the first day. Our Prince led the cavalry and even the provincials put up a good fight. So did Osinski and a few other experienced commanders. We broke the Horde, chased it off the field, and then . . . and then . . ."

And here Vyershul stopped, unable to go on.

"And then?" asked Zagloba.

"Then . . . came the night. Dreadful. Terrifying. Beyond understanding. I was down by the river with my men, on watch where our Prince had us posted. And then I heard gun salutes fired in the Cossack camp. I heard shouts and cheering. '*What the devil's that,*' I wondered. Then I remembered that the Tartars we'd already fought were just the ones who came with Tuhay-bey and so I realized that now the Khan himself must have come up with the bulk of his army. '*Well, it's too late now for anything but dying,*' I remember thinking. I was just about to send word back to His Highness when I heard what seemed like a wild panic breaking out in our own camp behind me. I ran there with a few of my men. '*What's going on?*' I asked. '*The regents have run off,*' they tell me. '*What are you saying?*' I tell you, I couldn't believe my ears. '*Gone!*' everybody's shouting. '*Fled! Escaped! Abandoned the army!*'"

"Great God almighty," Pan Zagloba murmured.

"So,"—Vyershul took a breath, went on—"I ran to Prince Dominic's quarters . . . Gone! To old Chamberlain Firley's encampment . . . Empty! To young Konyetzpolski's tents . . . Nobody in sight! Gone, all of them, vanished like the wind, and not even a sign left behind that they'd ever been there!"

"It . . . can't be," whispered Volodyovski.

"It can't?" the bitterness in Vyershul's voice threatened to spill over any moment into rage and madness. "You mean that I dreamed it after all? And did I also dream up those crowds running every which way through the camp . . . that bedlam of yells, howls, questions, panicked answers? I tell you I can still see that mob, I still hear its terror. Some of them want to know where the regents went to. Others are yelling '*Mount up! Ride! Save yourselves!*' Others howl '*Treason! Treason! We've been sold out, betrayed!*' Everywhere you look there are mad, shouting faces full of wild fear, crazed bulging eyes, hands raised to the skies, shaking fists . . . Ah, my good friends, you can't imagine what it was like that night. All those tens of thousands stampeding like cattle, knocking over the tents and scattering the campfires . . . Some jumped on their horses and galloped off God only knows where. Others fled on foot, pushing and shoving and trampling each other . . . throwing away their weapons, helmets, armor, everything . . ."

"And the Prince?" asked Skshetuski. "What about the Prince?"

"The Prince. Yes. He comes riding up in his silver armor. *Husaria* behind him. Six torches burning all around him so the mob would see him and know who he was. '*I didn't leave you!*' he cries and stands up in his stirrups. '*Look, I'm still here!*' he tells them. '*Join me!*' he pleads with them. '*Stay with me!*' Ah, he might as well not have been there at all . . ."

"Nobody rallied to him, then?"

"I don't think anybody even saw him." Vyershul's voice broke in mid-word and he had to struggle to stifle his shame. "If they did, they were too far gone to care about anything. The mob just ran right over him, pushed through the *husaria*, bowled over the men and horses and went on! We barely managed to drag the Prince himself from under their boots."

"And then?"

"And then this whole huge army breaks . . . tramples the camp, abandons all its guns and throws down all its weapons and runs out into the darkness, and runs . . . runs . . . disappears . . . saves itself in flight without a shot fired behind it by the enemy . . . escapes . . ."

Cracked in two, the soldier's voice fell to a stricken whisper.

"There's no more army. No leaders. No one to command.

Life's over as we know it. The Commonwealth is gone. Now all we've left is only endless shame and a Cossack boot standing on our necks."

★ ★ ★

And here Pan Vyershul moaned as if he'd been mortally wounded by what he had to say, and he began to pluck and claw at the reins of his frightened horse, and this sudden bout of hopelessness and despair infected the others as if it was the plague. They rode in silence, staring blindly into the wet darkness and tearing at their beards. Finally Pan Zagloba found refuge in curses.

"Oh the dogs! The scoundrels! Do you remember how they puffed themselves up in Zbarajh? How they boasted they'd eat Hmyel without salt and pepper? And now they run off without a fight!"

"On the contrary!" Vyershul cried. "They ran off after they *won* a battle! That's the point! A battle against the *tchernya* and the Tartars in which even the General Levy fought like a pride of lions!"

"There's God's finger to be seen in that," said Skshetuski. "But there's also some mystery about this that has to come to light sooner or later."

"A sudden panic, troops running off, that's happened before," Volodyovski said. "But here it's the commanders who were the first to run, as if they wanted to hand the victory to the enemy and to destroy the army."

"That's it! That's it!" Vyershul said. "People were saying that this was done on purpose."

"On purpose! How can that be, God help us?"

"Then how else could it have happened? How?"

"May they be crushed to dust by their own crumbling tombstones!" Pan Zagloba swore. "May they and all their kin vanish from the earth! May their names remain in human memory only as a curse!"

"Amen," said Skshetuski.

"Amen!" said Pan Michal.

"Amen," murmured the gentle Lithuanian.

"There's only one man now who can save the country," the fat knight said fiercely. "That's if they'll give him the Hetman's *bulava* and whatever forces the Commonwealth can still find somewhere. Only that one man! Because from now on neither the regular army nor any of the gentry will ever want to hear about anybody else as leader or commander!"

"The Prince!" said Skshetuski.

"That's right," Volodyovski said.

"We'll stand behind him for good or for evil, and we'll die beside him if we have to!" shouted Pan Zagloba. "Long live Yeremi Vishnovyetzki!"

"Long live!" cried the knights.

"Long live . . .!" replied a few uncertain voices on the road behind them. But the cry died down at once and dissipated in a gloomy silence because in this time of darkness and disaster, cheers and salutes seemed to them all like an obscenity and a curse.

Meanwhile, the rain had stopped. The sun began to rise. The white walls of Tarnopol appeared in the distance.

Part Seven

Chapter Forty-six

THE EARLIEST FUGITIVES from the disaster of Pilavtse reached Lvov at dawn, on the twenty-sixth of September, and the calamitous news flew through the city as soon as the gates opened in the morning.

At first nobody could believe it. The catastrophe was so incredible and so unprecedented in the nation's history that people simply refused to trust their ears. But then as more and more mud-spattered, hungry and bedraggled soldiers stumbled through the gates, each with his own tale of Tartars closing in just over the horizon, this scornful rejection of the truth turned into an appalled and withering panic of its own. Some of the townsfolk threw themselves into a frenzy of packing. Others resolved to fight and resist. By the time that Skshetuski and his horsemen reached Lvov two days later the entire city was packed from wall to wall with soldiers, gentry and armed merchants, most of whom appeared anxious to defend the town, but since nobody knew who was in command, nor how the defense was to be conducted, the ferment and the wild rumors and sudden alarms kept the whole population poised on the edge of uncertainty and chaos.

The Tartars were expected any hour. Crowds jammed the streets. Masses of wagons packed with women, children, bedding and belongings collided with each other in the city gates as some of the burghers tried to get away; others who thought they might find safety inside the town walls were crowding in from the suburbs and the outlying districts; and every so often a panicked cry of "*They're coming! They're coming!*" sent them all running in every direction until the new arrivals were identified as yet another shattered troop of fugitives.

Pan Yan and his men worked their way slowly through these barricades of wagons, animals and people, making their difficult progress from the Halitch Gate towards the city center, until a troop of the familiar redcoated dragoons showed in the street ahead to beat back the crowds of refugees and locals.

"Kushel!" Skshetuski cried to their officer. "So you've survived too, have you?"

"As you see. What times, eh? What times . . .!"

"Where's the Prince? Is he in the city?"

"He's quartered at the Bernardines. Thank God you've finally got here, Yan; he's been worried sick about you and your men! Come on to the church, he'll be glad to see you. They're all sitting in council there right now."

"They're holding a war council in a church?"

"That's right. The word is that they're going to offer the hetmancy to His Highness over there today because all the soldiers declared that they won't defend the city under anybody else!"

"So they're still making their own rules, are they?" Pan Yan asked.

"Ah, Yan my friend," Kushel said and shook his head sadly. "Nothing would surprise you any more if you had been with us at Pilavtse."

The combined detachments moved off. On the way Pan Yan questioned the young dragoon if the town really meant to defend itself.

"That's what they're deliberating about in the church," Kushel said and shook his head in wonder. "Mayor Grossvayer and his merchant guilds want to make a stand. Our nobles don't know what to do, they'd go either way."

"The townsmen want to fight?"

"Look for yourself."

Kushel pointed. They were passing a company of stolid, grim-faced burghers dressed in makeshift armor and with a chaotic assortment of spears, halberds, pole-axes and pikes waving against the sky.

"Makes you think, eh?" He laughed without humor. "The knighthood hoofs it from the field like jack rabbits in heat and the bean-counters want to stand and fight!"

"And the regents?" Pan Yan pressed. "What's happened with the regents?"

"Ah, to the Devil with the regents," Kushel said.

"But are they in the city? And are they likely to get in the Prince's way?"

"If only *he'd* stop getting in the way of his own promotion!" Kushel cried. "Of course there was a lot better time to give him the *bulava*. It's too late for that now. What's left for him to command even if he took it? Just rabble and wreckage. As for the regents, they're careful to keep out of sight. Prince Dominic barely set foot overnight at the archbishop's palace and left the next morning. And a good thing too or he'd have been torn to pieces by the mob. You wouldn't believe how everybody hates him!"

"And the other two?"

Kushel shrugged.

"Old Firley's here. In fact he was the first to get here, way ahead of everybody else, and still wagging his tongue against our Prince. But now he's keeping quiet, worried about his own neck, and weeping like a woman every time somebody brings up Pilavtse. You should thank God you weren't there, my friend. The fact that the rest of us are still sane is a miracle in itself."

"And what about the rest of our division?"

"Gone. There're only remnants left. Vurtzel, Mahnitzki, old Zachvilihovski . . . God only knows where they are and what happened to them. Neither Vurtzel nor Mahnitzki were with us at Pilavtse. That lisping Beelzebub Dominic left them at Konstantinov to strip the Prince of soldiers and undermine his standing and nobody knows if the Zaporohjans swept them up or not. As for Zachvilihovski, nobody has any idea where he might have got to."

"How about the rest of the regents' army?"

"Oh, there's enough of it here. But what use are they? Only His Highness might be able to do something with them because they won't take orders from anybody else."

"Well, I can't fault them there," Pan Zagloba said. "Can you?"

"Maybe not. But all they're trying to do is cover their own shame. They complain to anyone who'll listen about how they were betrayed, and argue about who was the first to turn tail and run, and they blame everybody but themselves.

"Some soldiers!" he went on with contempt. "Believe me Yan, the Prince was really anxious about your regiments because they're just about the only battle-worthy units he has left. Ah,"—and he laughed abruptly—"we were all getting ready to hold a wake for you and go into mourning."

Pan Yan sighed. "That's the only kind of man who can still find a reason to be happy these days."

"What kind's that?"

"The kind who is mourned."

★   ★   ★

They rode in silence for a time, looking at the unkempt, milling crowds of loud, mud-splattered gentry and bedraggled soldiers who strutted about in such splendid colors only a few weeks earlier; they watched the artisans of the city guilds formed up with pikes and muskets under their own banners; and they pushed through mobs of townsfolk who pressed about them anxiously, crying out for news. Tens of thousands of avid spectators darkened all the windows, roofs and church spires; all the bells were ringing as if the city was in flames already; and the shrill, wailing voices of women and children spilled out of every place of worship that they passed.

Bells. Shouts.

Yells of rage and fear.

"*The Tartars are coming!*"

On one street corner they passed a grim reminder of the city's volatile fury: some hapless man torn into pieces by the mob which had accused him of being a spy.

"How soon will the Tartars get here anyway?" Pan Zagloba asked.

"The Devil knows." Kushel shrugged. "Today's as good a time for them as any. This town won't be able to hold out for long anyhow."

"Why not? The burghers seem determined."

"So's Hmyelnitzki. And he's coming with two hundred thousand men as well as all the Tartars."

"That's that, then," the fat knight muttered and passed the edge of his hand across his throat. "We'd have done better to go on somewhere else. Ah, why the Devil did we bother to win all those victories?"

"What victories?" Kushel asked.

"What do you mean '*what victories?*'" the old knight exploded. "D'you think everybody runs without a fight? Victories, that's all!"

"Over whom?"

"Bohun!" The fat knight started waving his arms about. "Krivoinos! The Devil knows who!"

"Ah, that reminds me . . ." The young dragoon nodded, turned to Skshetuski and lowered his voice. "Did anything . . . ah . . . happen to comfort you, Yan? Did you find what you were after? Any sign of your lady, my poor friend?"

"There's no time to think about that now!" Skshetuski said coldly.

"True," Kushel murmured. "True . . "

"Ah, it's all vanity, I tell you!" Pan Yan snapped. "Vanity and illusion! And it all ends in death and darkness everywhere you look no matter what hope might shine somewhere now and then."

"That's how it seems to me too," Kushel said and shrugged. "The end of the world can't be far away."

★ ★ ★

Meanwhile they made their way to the Church of the Bernardines which, like so many of the brick and limestone buildings in that wealthy city, seemed to crouch, as wide as it was tall, under rounded arches, copper-sheeted cupolas, and ornamental rooftop balustrades and urns. It was ablaze with multicolored lights that poured out of its stained-glass windows and through the great, arched doors. Lvov was an ancient city, the capital of Ruthenia, founded several centuries before there was a Commonwealth. It lay astride Europe's main trade-routes to the East and its population consisted of as many different peoples as could be found between the Rhine and the plains of Persia. Huge crowds, as loud and restless as a stormy ocean, surged in the square outside that famous church, pushing against a hard-pressed cordon of halberdiers who parted only for the arriving dignitaries and senior officers.

Forcing his own way through the crowd, and catching the imploring glance of the halberdiers' commander, Skshetuski added his own soldiers to that living barrier and jumped off his horse.

"Let's go inside," said Kushel.

Skshetuski nodded. "We've some important information for the Prince."

"He's in there. God grant that next time he comes out he will be our Hetman. Either way it's a historic moment."

"We've seen and heard a few of those before," Pan Zagloba muttered.

"Not like this one." Kushel's strong, young voice rang with reassurance. "They're finally going to place the Hetman's *bulava* in the only hands that are fit to hold it. They'll have to or the army will tear them limb from limb. I tell you, it'll be worth seeing."

"If we can push our way in," Pan Yan said.

"Who'd stop a Vishnovyetski officer on this of all days?" The young dragoon laughed harshly. "I think you'll find half the Commonwealth in there anyway."

They entered the church.

Kushel hadn't exaggerated the size of the gathering by much, as they saw at once. Everyone who was anyone in the city and among the soldiers had come to this council at which the fate of the city and of the Commonwealth itself was to be decided. The broad nave and transepts were jammed with palatines, castellans, district and Crown dignitaries, senators and colonels. Mustached cavalry commanders jostled for elbow-room with plumed officers of foreign mercenaries. Priests, deacons, monks and abbots, who were pressed together with as little regard for their calling as if they were humble penitents, shoved and muttered curses at the lesser gentry and whatever junior officers managed to squeeze inside. The Burgomaster, who had mobilized and armed the guilds of the city, stood at the altar rail in his robes of office along with some of his more warlike aldermen.

Candles blazed everywhere, glittering on the weapons and the jewels, and somber icons peered darkly through the smoke, while the growl and mutter of excited voices echoed against the groined ceiling as if it were a drum. One speaker after another mounted to the pulpit to plead with the conferring dignitaries to defend the city, while the swell of voices and the clash of hands that slapped impatiently against sheathed swords and sabers drowned their impassioned rhetoric and interrupted their ornate Latin phrases.

"We've the walls! We've the men! We've the swords and cannon!" cried the gathered thousands. "We've the heart and the spirit! All we need is a leader and commander!"

And then all eyes turned to the hunched, whispering dignitaries who sat in gilded, tall-backed chairs before the high altar. These were the Prince, the white-haired, grey-faced Firley who was the highest ranking Crown official there as well as the only member of the regents' council who still dared to show himself in public, the *Voyevode* of Kiev and the *Starosta* of Stobnitze, the Seneshal of Lithuania, and the two famed foreign-trained generals, Wessel and Artishevski, who had spent years abroad in the Spanish wars and helped the Hollanders create their overseas empire.

"Don't give up the city!" the speakers appealed to the huddled leaders, one after another. "Hold up the enemy here until the Commonwealth can gather some new strength! Let's wash the shame of Pilavtze off our hands with our own blood, if that's what it takes! Let's shield our country with our bodies right here on our walls!"

Waves of emotion swept through the church at such words, tears of exaltation ran down a hundred faces, a thousand drawn sabers glittered in the candlelight, and the high, vaulted ceiling echoed with new shouting.

"We'll die here if we have to, we'll die gladly! We'll save the country yet! We'll restore its honor!"

And others shouted: "Who's to lead us, then?"

"The Prince! Prince Yeremi! Give him the *bulava*! Make him our commander! Long live Vishnovyetzki!"

And again the naked steel of drawn swords and sabers glittered among the candles.

Prince Yeremi rose as slowly as if a heavy weight rested on his shoulders. He stood in silence, deep in thought, and then he raised his darkly troubled eyes and let them fall upon the gathering, and an instant hush settled on the crowd as everyone strained to hear him.

"When the barbarians threatened the Roman republic," he said quietly. "No one wanted to be named Consul until Marius took the power and responsibility. But Marius had a right to take it because there were no other leaders appointed by the Senate. I can't do as he did because we have such leaders. To take supreme power, against the wishes of the Senate, would undermine the authority of the Commonwealth itself. Here,"— and he pointed to the seated Firley—"is one to whom the Commonwealth gave the power to lead us . . ."

But that was as far as the Prince could get because he no

sooner mentioned the discredited old generalissimo when a
frightful massed howl of rage and protest burst out of every
throat throughout the church.

"No! No! *Veto!* Never!"

Fists shook. Sabers rattled. The crowd swayed like a forest
struck by a sudden wind. Its roar was as vast as if all the pent-up
shame and passion and despair burst out of these infuriated
thousands in a single flash like a powder keg touched off by a
spark.

"Away with him!" shouted furious voices. "Get rid of the
traitor!"

And then, cutting through the chaos like the voice of doom,
came the dreaded phrase with which condemned felons were
sent to the gallows: "*Pereat!*"

"*Pereat!*" the shouts swelled into a single roar and spread
throughout the church until they seemed to fill all the open
spaces between the massive columns. "*Pereat!* Let him perish!"

The shaken old man staggered to his feet, eyes staring wildly
and thick drops of sweat forming on his forehead, while threatening figures leaped up and pushed against the altar rails. Hands
reached out for him. Drawn weapons gleamed. Everyone knew
that in just one moment more the crowd would seize him,
ignore the sanctity of the walls around them, and either drag
him to his death outside or murder him right there under the
pained eyes of that other victim whose crucified white image
gleamed in the light of candles above the high altar.

"No," Skshetuski whispered.

But he knew that nothing would stop that crowd under these
circumstances, and that neither he nor a hundred like him
would be able to save the Commonwealth from this ultimate
dishonor and disgrace.

★ ★ ★

Then Prince Yeremi rose again. He lifted his arm for silence
and such was the natural power of his authority over everyone
that the frenzied crowd stood as quiet and still as if it never
stirred and never made a sound.

They waited. His slight, worn body appeared to swell and to
grow before them until he dwarfed the candlelit statuary behind
him, turning them all into silent statues too. But he said
nothing more. He only wanted to prevent the blasphemy of

bloodshed in the church, Pan Skshetuski knew; but once the most threatening moment had gone by, and the huge, angry crowd remained as quiet and still as if each man there had turned into stone, he dropped back into his chair and leaned back with his face hidden behind his hand.

Two chairs down from him, and separated only by the portly *Voyevode* of Kiev from the silent Prince, the weeping old Firley sat with downcast eyes, arms hanging as if broken, and with his silvery hair trailing across his shoulders.

"Lord . . .! For my sins," he sobbed and murmured through his tears. "I accept this cross . . ."

His age and helplessness might have moved the most hardened conscience at any other time but an impassioned mob seldom has time for mercy even if it can be cowed and diverted for a moment.

"Down with him!" the cries of rage and hatred and despair began to echo once more in the church, swelling and gathering fresh volume and power as they filled the nave and rang among the rafters. "Down with him! *Na Pohybel!* Give up your *bulava!*"

"Quiet!" others shouted. "Don't interrupt the council! Let's have order here!"

But the frenzied gathering would have none of that. A thousand sabers were shaking in the air again, eyes shined with a mad light, the yells and curses boomed among the arches, and now the crowds of impatient citizens outside burst through the cordons and poured into the church as well.

"No more talk! No more arguing! Long live Prince Yeremi! He's our only Hetman! Give him the *bulava!*" And then to the silent Prince: "Accept! Accept! Lead us! Save us!"

Then the Palatine of Kiev, whom these desperate masses knew as a war companion of Yeremi Vishnovyetzki, and one who had shared in some of his victories, got to his feet and signaled that he wished to speak. Knowing this proud and stubborn man's concern for the rule of law, his respect for the authority of the chancellor, the regents and the Senate—and also his bitter hatred of bloodshed in a fratricidal war—the Prince's officers didn't expect much from him. But the *Voyevode* turned towards the Prince himself.

"Accept!" he pleaded. "Let the procedures of law be put aside when the Commonwealth is dying. Let it be saved by the man who is best qualified to do so rather than one who was named to do it but who may lack the necessary strength, endurance and skill! So take the symbols of authority that we're offering to you! Take them and save us! Save this town and this Commonwealth as well!"

Shaken by the passion that rang in his own voice, the Palatine raised his arms and hands towards the ceiling as if calling upon God to witness his appeal, and his voice filled with tears.

"All of our country's citizens are calling out to you through my lips right now!" he cried. "All the different kinds and conditions of people who inhabit this great Commonwealth of ours! All of us—the great lords and nobles and the lesser gentry as well as the commons—are begging you to take us in your hands and carry us to safety! All your brothers and sisters are on their knees before you, crying: '*Save us! Save us!*' Accept the *bulava!*"

And then there took place one of those strange, providential events that seize the imagination, inflame a nation's will, and turn the hardest-held convictions into other channels. A woman dressed in mourning pushed through the crowds to the altar rail, and pouring out her jewels at the Prince's feet, threw herself on her knees before him.

"Take all we have!" she wept. "We place our lives in your hands! Save us, or we'll perish!"

A huge cry echoed through the church until the windows trembled. "Save us!" roared the assembled thousands. "Save us!" came the echoes from the crowds massed in the square outside.

The cry went on and on amid sobs and tears so that it seemed like a single pleading exclamation coming from the torn heart and racked conscience of a nation. Everyone wept. Senators and castellans wiped their dripping faces. Palatines were on their knees with upraised arms, bellowing like children. Tears flowed down the harsh, cruel faces of the soldiers and glittered in their beards.

"*Salve Respublicam!*"

"Save the Commonwealth!"

"Save us! Save us!"

The Prince lowered his head and put his hands across his face, and when he lifted it up again and stared at the pleading masses on their knees before him, his eyes were wet with tears. What could he do? What would happen to the dignity and authority of the Commonwealth if he accepted the powers he was being offered? How would he differ from any other rebel, and how would he be better than the malevolent Hmyelnitzki, if he reached out for that golden symbol of a supreme commander and took it out of old Firley's trembling hands against the will of the Senate which had placed it there . . . ?

He had wrestled with such thoughts before. He had subdued his own soaring pride. He humbled his vision of himself and turned his back on his own destiny. He had emptied himself of anger and ambition.

"*Domine, non sum dignus,*" he whispered through pale lips and stared at the floor.

He had sworn to himself in Zbarajh to uphold the authority of the regents no matter how unworthy they might prove to be because they represented the will of the Senate and spoke with the voice of the Commonwealth. So he sat unmoving, his half-closed eyes fixed on the marble flagstones while the huge crowds pleaded, until the old, discredited generalissimo struggled to his feet. All color had drained out of that grey and harrowed face. The old man started speaking but at first nobody could hear him. He stood as if condemned, the gold *bulava* clutched against his chest in thin, birdlike fingers, and his cracked, frail voice was quite lost in all the pleading and shouting that echoed around him.

"I'm . . . an old man," he murmured as softly as if he wished to hide his terrible humiliation under all those voices. "Old and unlucky. Worn out and broken under this awful load. Too weak for the burden placed upon my shoulders. I've the right to lay it down. To find stronger shoulders. To place it in younger, stronger hands . . ."

The crowd began to quieten just enough to hear him but not enough to show him either respect or forgiveness.

"So," the quavering voice gathered strength and firmness as Firley turned towards Yeremi Vishnovyetzki. "In the sight of Christ and all the knighthood gathered in this place . . . and in the name of the authority vested in me by the Senate and the Commonwealth . . . I hand it to you."

The crowd roared again.

"Accept!" cried all the other dignitaries seated at the altar while the old man shuffled towards the Prince and held out the gold baton of authority.

"Take it," the old man said.

There was then such a hushed and breathless stillness in the crowded church, and among the masses of the people who waited in the square outside, that the gathering could hear the whine of insects darting among the flames and the hiss of candles guttering in the wax. Then the Prince spoke, still seated and staring at the cold, stone floor as if he were watching a dark and forbidding chasm opening at his feet.

"As penance for my own sins," he said. "I accept."

Madness seemed to seize the crowd at these pained, quiet words. The huge mass of people surged towards the altar, hurling jewels and money and vowing obedience. They threw themselves on the flagstones before their new Hetman. They pressed about the pale, silent Prince, clutching at his knees and kissing the edges of his coat. Bells started clanging in the belfry overhead. The church rang with cheers. The news flashed like lightning into the streets and the tens of thousands of gathered citizens and soldiers went mad with joy all over the city.

The soldiers howled for battle . . . at once! Immediately! Let the Cossacks and the Tartars come! "*Lead us! Lead us!*" The townsmen swore to defend their walls against the Sultan himself if he should appear, and those who had already left the city and now got the word from the messengers who galloped out into the countryside, turned their wagons around and drove back to take part in the defense.

The Armenian merchants started dragging coffers full of gold and silver to the city treasury long before the town council and the aldermen could vote the necessary taxes, and the Jews who gathered in their temples raised a thankful wail.

Night fell at last but the celebration went on uninterrupted.

The cannon on the city walls thundered with salutes. The singing, cheering masses in the streets fired guns and pistols, and the cries of "*Vivat!*" and "*Long live Prince Yeremi!*" lasted until dawn.

A stranger who didn't know about the dangers that were about to descend on that merrymaking city, might have thought that he had walked in on a celebration of an accomplished triumph, or some kind of feast-day of joyful thanksgiving. And yet an army of three hundred thousand warriors, greater than all the armies of the Holy Roman Emperor and more savage than the hosts of Tamerlane himself, was pouring towards those gates and walls just beyond the burning red horizon. A terrible siege could start at any moment.

Chapter Forty-seven

DURING THE NEXT ten days Prince Yeremi reorganized the Pilavtse fugitives into another military force, armed the determined citizens of Lvov and equipped them to defend their city, strengthened and garrisoned the powerful fortress of Zamost further to the north, and led as many of his regiments as he could spare to Warsaw.

At first the citizens of Lvov felt themselves abandoned and the word 'betrayal' was whispered here and there among them. But General Artishevski soon explained to the city fathers that if Vishnovyetzki locked himself and all his soldiers within their walls, where hunger would eventually force them to surrender, the Commonwealth's last hope would vanish beyond recall. Instead, the twin bastions of Lvov and Zamost—the first defended by Burgomaster Grossvayer and himself and the other by the experienced Pan Veyher, the *Starosta* of Valitch—would hold up the enemy long enough for fresh forces to be raised elsewhere in the country. A large new field army, led by Prince Yeremi, was a better guarantee of their safety than if he were besieged in their town along with themselves. Hmyelnitzki, as both the burgomaster and the general explained, would never allow a Vishnovyetzki army to operate at his back while he tried to take both Zamost and their city; on the contrary, he'd go after Prince Yeremi, wherever he was, knowing that the Prince would always represent the deadliest threat to the Zaporohjans.

Meanwhile the Prince took the road to Warsaw. He traveled in good spirits, knowing that he had done everything possible for the moment to check and divert the Tartar and Cossack invasion, and entertaining high hopes that the Diet would vote him the necessary means to raise and equip the new forces he had to create.

He was also anxious to take an active part in the royal elections announced for October. The two leading candidates were both Polish-born although several French, German and Hungarian princes were also bidding for the Polish-Lithuanian crown. It seemed likely, however, that the new King would be Polish, and that presented a problem of its own.

The competition was the sharpest between the two younger brothers of the late King Vladyslav Vasa, a descendant of the Roman Catholic Royal House of Sweden which lost its Scandinavian throne during the Reformation. The younger Prince Charles seemed more determined to pursue the war, which would mean an all-out struggle against Hmyelnitzki and the Tartars if he were elected, with Prince Yeremi confirmed as the new Grand Hetman. The older, Prince Yan Casimir, would be more inclined towards negotiations, Cossack conciliation, and the peace party of Chancellor Ossolinski although he was also well-known for his generosity, fortitude and courage.

The strength of both the brothers was just about even at this point, Prince Yeremi knew, since the powerful and influential magnates appeared to be evenly divided between war and peace and no one could predict which way this critical election would go. Of course, the chancellor and his supporters feared that Prince Yeremi's fame, and the admiration in which the knighthood held him, could sway the vast masses of the voting gentry to Prince Charles' side, and—for the first time in his life—the Prince could agree with something that the chancellor believed.

The election, in the Prince's view, had to be decided in his favor, less for how it would affect his own destiny and fortunes than for the effect it would have on the Commonwealth itself. The question was more than merely choosing between total war and negotiations; this election, more than any other, could change the nature of the government.

Left to themselves, his fellow magnates might bring about the election of Yan Casimir simply to check the rising power of the Vishnovyetzkis, which Prince Yeremi was willing to ignore, but he was looking far beyond the war. He could admire Chancellor Ossolinski's energy and learning. He could sympathize with his vision of a powerful Commonwealth ruled by a strong central government. But this same strengthening of the King's authority would undermine the power of the gentry, threaten the semi-regal *latifundia* of the eastern magnates, and strip them of their rights to rule their principalities like independent kingdoms.

True, Prince Yeremi knew, such unbridled freedom led to many of the cruelties, abuses and high-handed acts of civic disobedience that brought about the present tragedy; it was a system doomed to fall eventually because of its own injustices, anarchy and corruption. But Ossolinski's long-range policies were also aimed at the creation of western-style royal absolutism in the Commonwealth, including an end to the elective monarchy and the *liberum veto* power of the gentry, which the proud and fiercely independent Yeremi Vishnovyetzki would never permit. The election of Prince Charles would mean a decline in the influence and power of Chancellor Ossolinski, and Prince Yeremi was anxious to do all he could to see the crown placed on young Prince Charles' head.

★ ★ ★

In the meantime, he thought that he had every reason to be optimistic. He left Skshetuski and Pan Longinus in Zamost with *Starosta* Veyher and he was certain that this great fortress city, founded and owned by the powerful Zamoyskis, would check Hmyelnitzki and the Khan for as long as needed; it would bar their way to Warsaw, Krakow and the heart of the Commonwealth itself. Lvov was as good as saved by the same means; the enemy would hardly waste much time in besieging such a well-armed city with the threat of Zamost hanging over their necks.

Such thoughts affirmed his purpose, dispelled some of his anxieties, and restored his hopes for the eventual salvation of the country. He could breathe easier for the first time since the war began. He believed that no matter who won the election the war would continue until the rebellion drowned in its own blood. He expected that the Commonwealth would reach once again into its great resources of brave men and treasure and give him that new army that it had to have, because—as he saw it—even if there were to be new negotiations they had to be conducted from a position of strength.

Relaxed in his carriage by such speculations, Prince Yeremi

traveled towards the national capital under the escort of several of his newly refurbished regiments and with Pan Zagloba and Pan Michal in attendance. The little knight was there as commander of the Prince's lifeguards while the fat knight, who had no military functions to perform, amused His Highness with the frightful oaths he swore that he'd bring about Prince Charles' election singlehanded.

"First," he said. "I know how to talk to the gentry and how to win them over, which is something that many of our great lords have forgotten, seeing themselves so high above the rest of us."

"A good point," Prince Yeremi nodded. "And one that the chancellor may not remember either."

"And second," the fat knight continued. "I know how to drink with them, which the chancellor, being a religious person, might not be willing to do."

"Ey, there you're off the mark," the Prince murmured sadly. "Some of the best ideas of Bishop Ossolinski's supporters have come from a bottle."

"Sacramental wine is one thing but good mead is another," Pan Zagloba cracked boldly to the Prince, shocking Volodyovski. "Particularly the kind of vintage *Troyniak* that Your Highness' stewards hoard in the baggage carts."

"Well, then we'll have to have a jug or two given to you for practice," the Prince answered, laughing. "Since even the best sabers rust unless they're exercised."

"And that's the third thing, Highness," Zagloba shot back. "Because all those whom I fail to persuade with my tongue will have to argue with Pan Michal's saber."

"Well, well." Amused, the Prince allowed himself a moment of relaxation. "I see that you've the election all decided. Pray God that the polls agree."

"I'll let myself be skinned and turned into a gourd if I'm not the first to kneel before His Majesty King Charles!" Pan Zagloba bellowed, carried away by his own enthusiasm. "Or worse yet, I'll let his reverence the chancellor appoint me a generalissimo over his quill sharpeners."

Then, seeing a dark cloud of anxiety returning to the Prince's face, he changed the subject to an account of his own youthful exploits in some distant wars which no one within hearing could possibly remember.

★ ★ ★

So they traveled as far as Minsk in Mazovia where a pleasant though unplanned surprise awaited the Prince. His column ran into a string of coaches in which his wife, the Princess Grizelda, was traveling from Brest Litovsk to Warsaw, in part for greater safety deeper in the country and in part because she expected that he would also go there for the great electoral convention.

Their coming together after such a long and bitter separation was emotional enough to move the most hardened soldier in the Prince's escort. The Princess had a reputation for icy dignity. Her pride and lofty self-control were proverbial among the knights at Lubnie. But now her cries and tears astonished even Pan Zagloba who had never been in her company before. It seemed like hours before she could tear herself out of her husband's arms and every time she did so she'd burst into fresh weeping. How many times she must have doubted whether she'd ever see him again! How often did his dangers rob her of her sleep? Joy and pity shared the deep, dark spaces of her eyes when she looked into his thin and harrowed face, into those red-rimmed, fevered eyes whose weariness all the others learned to take for granted, and at that lined, worn brow.

She could read all his sleepless nights and all of his exertions and anxieties in those ruined features, and her own pride in his new fame and his accomplishments only added to her pity and her pain. Her young ladies, many of whom looked in vain for some knight who courted them in Lubnie, echoed her tears with loud wails of their own.

Finally the princely couple found shelter in a large local parish hall where questions could be asked and answered.

"Where is Yan Skshetuski?" she wanted to know.

Prince Yeremi set his wife's mind at rest about her favorite soldier. He'd left him in Zamost, he told her, so that the young man could drown his grief in the turmoil of warfare rather than suffer reminders of his loss in the gaiety of Warsaw.

Then he introduced Pan Zagloba, whom he described as a '*vir incomparabilis*'—a man beyond comparing.

"It was he who tore the little Kurtzevitchovna out of Bohun's hands and then led her to safety in Podolia through all the rebels and Tartars," he said. "And then he won such new glory for himself at Konstantinov that few of us would ever be able to match it."

Hearing this, the Princess added her thanks to her husband's praises, giving Pan Zagloba her hand to kiss repeatedly and promising richer rewards in due time. Lost for words for the first time in his life, the '*vir incomparabilis*' bowed, mumbled modest phrases, and puffed himself up like a peacock as he shot quick glances at the pretty girls who trooped around the Princess.

"Old I may be," he muttered to Pan Michal. "And there's not much I can promise myself from the distaff side of the company any more. But it's still pleasant to know that these twittering little birds heard all this praise of my accomplishments."

And there were other tears. Time and again Princess Grizelda's questions brought a cold, dry answer: "Killed . . . dead in battle . . . missing . . ." And then the girls wept anew, hearing a name that was dear to one or another of them.

★ ★ ★

So joy and mourning went hand-in-hand to mark this unexpected reunion. But little Pan Michal, whose hopeless passion for the Prince's daughter made him something of a joke even to himself, appeared to be the saddest and most uneasy of them all. No matter how he squirmed and peered about he couldn't see the young Princess Barbara anywhere. His passions weren't anywhere as constant as they were sudden, he knew very well, and he had managed to forget this latest impossible attachment under the pressures of his months of warfare; but it would have been pleasant to heave a few sighs again, he thought, particularly when this gathering reminded him so powerfully of the lost, courtly life of Lubnie.

Brought to mind again, all his old romantic involvements started to torment him as if they were new, and he stood as glum in that gathering as if someone had thrown a bucket of rainwater over him. His head hung low; his pointed little whiskers, which normally curled up like a beetle's alongside his nose, drooped sadly; the uptilted button nose seemed to lengthen and acquire new inches of gloom; and his normal cheerful and untroubled air ebbed out of his face even when Prince Yeremi began to praise his heroism and to laud all his extraordinary achievements. Because, as he told himself, what did praises matter when *She*—whichever 'she' it might have been at that moment—wasn't there to hear them?

Finally Anusia Krasienska took pity on him.

"And a good morning to you," she murmured, sidling up to him. "It's been a long time since we've seen each other."

"Ay, Miss Anusia." He heaved a melancholy sigh. "A lot of time has gone by, and hard time at that. And we're not all here either, as it seems."

"That's right," she sighed in turn. "So many knights have fallen. And we here at the court aren't in the same numbers as before. Senyutovna—do you remember her?—got married . . . And Princess Barbara stayed behind in Vilno."

"And she's also planning to get married, I expect?"

"No, she hasn't been thinking much about that," the girl said, grinning, and then teased the small knight. "But why are you so curious about things like that?"

"Why? Ah . . . out of friendship for the family," Pan Michal muttered. "Why else?"

"And so you should," she went on and giggled. "Because you've a great friend in Princess Barbara."

"I do?"

"Certainly. She often asks about you."

"She does?"

"I've heard her myself. *'Where's that small knight who won the swordsmanship tournament at Lubnie?'* she asks all the time. *'What's happening with him, and does he still think about any of us?'* She remembers you very well, you see."

"You don't say . . ." Pan Michal looked up with gratitude at the girl.

"I just have," she said.

"But . . . just to tease, eh?"

Delighted at her words, although he was too much of a realist to believe them, the little knight also managed to note how pretty she'd become since he last saw her on the road from Lubnie.

"The way you always tease anyone in breeches?" he reminded her.

"That's not fair! I don't! And why should I tease you any-way?"

The girl shot a sly glance at him, remembering how they had teased each other in the past, and turned to hide her own delighted grin.

"She does speak about you!" she insisted. "She even remembers the time you jumped your horse across the castle moat to show off before her!"

"Ah, that time," he muttered.

"Yes! The time you fell in!"

"Hmm . . . Ah . . . Yes. And where's the Princess now?"

"With her aunt, of course. They were with us at Brest. A week ago they set out for Byelsk. But they're both planning to join the court in Warsaw to help with the election."

Pan Michal shot the girl another grateful glance and then burst out suddenly: "But you . . . I've got to say it, right or wrong, my lady . . . you've become so pretty that it hurts the eyes just to look at you."

"You think so?" The girl smiled with pleasure and hid behind her fan. "Well, thank you . . . But you're just saying that to flatter me, I think. And to win me over."

"Hmm. I might have done that at one time." The little knight grinned and nodded in his turn. "In fact I did try to get a little closer to you, as you might remember. But now I just wish the best of luck and happiness to Pan Podbipyenta, because it's hard to think of a more loyal and deserving cavalier."

"Ah . . ." and the girl's eyes fell, and her voice dropped to a softer whisper. "And where might he be now?"

"In Zamost with Skshetuski. They've both been promoted and Pan Longinus serves now as Yan's first lieutenant." Then the small knight grinned again and winked at Anusia. "But if he'd been able to guess what he'd find waiting for him on the road to Warsaw he'd have killed a dozen horses to catch up with us, duty or no duty."

"And . . . did anything in particular happen to him in the war?" The girl looked down into her hands. "I mean . . . he wasn't hurt or anything, was he?"

"Ey!" Pan Volodyovski laughed. "It seems to me that you're wondering less about his health than those three heads of his!"

"Why should I wonder about that?" she asked and turned a bright crimson. Then she sniffed and tossed her head as if she really didn't care one way or another. "I can't believe he'd be all that serious about those heads anyway. I mean . . . how could he be?"

"Oh, he's deadly serious!" Pan Volodyovski nodded, just as serious as the subject of the Lithuanian's singular and forbidding vow was to Pan Longinus. "Believe me, I know him well enough by now, and I tell you that nothing's going to happen until he keeps that promise he made to himself. I know it's hard to believe, even in our times, but that's how he is. It isn't possible for that man not to keep his word."

"But that . . . might take years," the girl murmured. Her eyes moistened and she looked down at the floor.

"Maybe. Maybe not." Then the little knight took pity on the dismayed Anusia. "Take my word for it, though; he really looks hard for every opportunity. I've seen some scenes of slaughter in my time but nothing like the places where he has been fighting. I tell you, my dear, when he wraps that scarf of yours around his helmet it's unbelievable what he does in battle. Oh, he'll find his three heads soon enough, you can be sure of that."

"Let everyone find what he needs to find," the girl sighed and whispered.

And Pan Michal heaved a deep sigh of his own.

$$\star \quad \star \quad \star$$

Then, lifting his troubled eyes into the far corner of the room, Pan Michal caught sight of a furious face he'd never seen before: a glowering visage that peered at him from behind an enormous nose and a huge pair of whiskers that dangled like two lengths of hemp on the stranger's chest and moved fiercely up and down in a grip of passion. It was a sight to alarm almost anyone but all it did to the little knight was merely surprise him.

"Who's that?" he asked Anusia.

"Who's what?" the girl spun around to peer about the room.

"That strange long-nosed creature there in the corner, the one that's glaring at me as if it wanted to swallow me at one gulp."

"Oh, that one?" The girl laughed.

"Yes. The one whose whiskers twitch like those of an old tomcat at a mousehole."

Anusia giggled, showing her small white teeth, with all her tears forgotten. "That's Pan Kharlamp."

"What sort of a heathen monstrosity is he, then? He looks like one of those African '*monstra*' that carry a horn instead of a nose."

"He's no heathen monster. He's a captain in the Light Horse regiment of the *Voyevode* of Vilna and commands our escort. I wouldn't get in his way if I were you, Master Michal. He's a real fire-eater."

"Hmm. Is he now? But if he's such a fire-eater why isn't he sharpening his teeth on some of these other fiery cavaliers around here? Why's he glaring at me?"

"Well . . ." and the girl shrugged and giggled again.

"Well what?"

"Well . . . because he's panting after me. He told me himself that he'd chop anybody who comes near me into little pieces. He'd be right here beside us, looking for a quarrel, if it wasn't for His Highness being here as well."

"Well I'll be damned!" Pan Volodyovski broke into open laughter. "So that's how things are going again, is it? Ay, I see we didn't serenade you for nothing in Lubnie! '*Like a Tartar's darts, you pierce all men's hearts!*' D'you remember? Eh? How is it that you can hardly move without some poor wretch falling in love with you?"

"That's just my misfortune," the girl murmured, sighed, and lowered her eyes, but not before she shot another quick, side-long glance at the glaring Kharlamp.

"Huh, what a heartbreaking little tease you are!" Pan Michal went on laughing. "And what's Pan Longinus going to say about all this, eh?"

"And is it my fault that this Pan Kharlamp is after me like that?" Anusia protested. "All I did was smile at him. And only that one time. Because he's a stranger at our court and I wanted to cheer him up a little."

"Yes, that would do it," Pan Michal said grinning and shaking his head. "But you take care, my girl, that somebody's blood doesn't get spilled because of your little tricks. Pan Podbipyenta is a saint in a lot of ways . . . we'd all make a fortune if we could find a way to bottle his goodness and peddle it to the surgeons for a balm . . . but there's no joking with him in matters of the heart."

"Let him trim that man's ears, for all that I care!" Anusia cried, embarrassed. Then she spun on her toes like a startled bird and flew across the room where she began an animated conversation with the Prince's elderly Italian physician who looked as dumbstruck and bug-eyed as if the gates of Heaven had opened before him.

★ ★ ★

Meanwhile Pan Zagloba appeared near the little knight and started winking at him with his one good eye.

"Ho ho," he said. "And who was that pretty little dish? Something you're planning to sample a little later? My congratulations!"

"Shame on you!" Pan Michal cried, all the more vehement because just that idea had glimmered for a fraction of a moment in his head. "That's Pan Podbipyenta's fiancee, or as good as one."

"Good God! That little thing? He'll be able to carry her behind his collar, like a flea! And what about that chastity of his anyway? Ha, I'm beginning to understand our Lithuanian beanpole a lot better now! No wonder all his wits are down in his saddle! Let's just hope she doesn't fit him out with a pair of antlers, which is what I'd be the first to help her with, given half a chance."

"Many have tried it," Pan Michal said, smiling a little at some of his own Lubnie memories. "Yan and me once fought a duel over her."

"Good God!" Pan Zagloba cried. "And you're both still alive to talk about it?"

"Well . . ." the little knight grinned, shrugged and twisted his pointed little whiskers past his nose again. "We weren't all that serious about it, to tell you the truth. But she's a good girl, for all of her flirting."

"Hmm. You say that because you're a decent sort yourself," Pan Zagloba said. "But I wouldn't want to be in our virtuous Lithuanian's boots anyway you see it. She's a flighty bird."

"Only because she's young and pretty," the little knight was always quick to defend Anusia. "But she'll settle down, you'll see. She'll make our friend happy. Hercules was also a mighty man but a woman cooked his goose for him, didn't she?"

"I think that was Samson."

"I know her, I tell you. She can't help it if she draws men like flies to molasses. Look at that long-nosed captain in the corner, for example. He's supposed to be head over heels over her."

"Huh!" the fat knight nodded. "He'd better hang a lantern on that nose of his or he'll have hens nesting on it. And what about that skinny-legged stork that she's talking to? What kind of foreign freak is that?"

"That's Carboni, the Prince's Italian physician."

"Look at that moon-eyed stare on his face," Pan Zagloba noted in displeasure. "And d'you see the way he's rolling his eyes? You'd think he was in some kind of a delirium, the half-wit. Ey, I tell you Michal, our poor Longinus is in for a lot of trouble! I've some experience in such things, having been a hot-blooded lad myself in my younger years, which I'll be glad to tell you about sometime. Or now, if you're interested."

And here the fat knight bent over Pan Michal's ear and started whispering into it and blinking even harder than he'd done before.

★   ★   ★

Soon afterwards it was time to resume the journey. So many tens of thousands were on their way to Warsaw that it seemed as if the entire country was on its way to the election, and not just from the nearby counties but from the far reaches of Lithuania and Ruthenia where the approach of war may have done more to awaken people to their civic duties than any workings of patriotism or conscience.

Crowds jammed the highway. Every so often the dust blew apart to reveal columns of gilded coaches surrounded by out-riders and lackeys in oriental costume, household troops of German and Hungarian lifeguards, turbanned janissaries, com-panies of Cossacks and, occasionally, entire regiments of the matchless Polish heavy cavalry accompanying the court of some district potentate or magnate. Everyone who was anyone tried to appear as richly and as powerfully equipped as their means allowed. The lesser households of regional and county digni-taries crowded against these cavalcades of the magnates and, at each patient step, some individual squire's charabanc, padded with black leather and pulled by pairs of horses, rattled out of the dust and jostled for room among the carriages and coaches. Armed to the teeth, with a musket barrel protruding on one side of the seat and a saber on the other, its single occupant crouched above the reins with a traveling crucifix or an icon dangling around his neck on a silken scarf. Packs of hunting dogs trotted beside the wheels while further back grooms led remount horses with their rich saddles covered against the dust. Then came the creaking baggage carts with tents and supplies for the swarms of servants and their impatient masters.

Whenever a breeze blew aside the dust cloud that hung like a lid above the crowded highway, the whole procession turned into a living many-colored serpent or a silk ribbon stitched with gold and jewels. The vast sound that boiled out of this slowly flowing river of the gentry was like a cloud of yet another kind. Calls and cries to give way, to clear the road. Questions and demands. Shouts and quarrels about precedence and about who should give way to whom. Musicians dressed in Tartar and Valachian style squealed on their fifes and thumped and pounded on their kettledrums at the head of the regular regiments of Polish and Lithuanian cavalry which were obliged to ride in the trains of the greater magnates.

Every so often some mounted soldier, courtier or a servant would gallop up to the Vishnovyetzki column, demanding the right of way for his master or asking who it was who was traveling there.

But at the words '*the Prince-Palatine of Ruthenia*' they fell back and informed their masters who ordered their own men and wagons off the road at once. Then there'd be cheers and excited comments shouted from the roadside as the Prince's regiments and coaches passed the curious crowds for whom they seemed like something out of legend.

Prince Yeremi looked sadly through the windows of his coach at these teeming masses of soldiers and armed gentry, and at these ostentatious displays of private wealth and power, and asked himself how many armies could be raised for the Commonwealth with just a fraction of these men and riches. Why was it that this powerful, populous and wealthy land, filled with a hardy knighthood and flowing with treasure, was unable to cope with a single Cossack rebel and his savage Tartars? Each of Hmyelnitzki's cohorts could be answered with a greater, better armed, and far more warlike host if only all that soldiery and that numerous gentry—and all those powerful magnates with their private regiments and armies— wanted to serve the public cause as eagerly as they served their own.

'*We've lost our ancient virtues,*' the Prince thought bitterly as he waved and smiled at the men who cheered him. '*The heart has gone out of the Commonwealth. Our blood has turned to water, our spirit is dying. And now even the great body has begun to rot.*'

But he knew even as such gloomy thoughts descended upon him that he was looking at the shortcomings of the Commonwealth only through the eyes of a warlord and a military commander who wanted to turn his whole nation into a single weapon, wielded by one strong and determined hand, against the enemy.

"It's good times and an easy life at a magnate's table that our gentry's after these days," he murmured. "Not sacrifice and hardships."

But at the same time he suspected that greed, selfishness, love of luxury, or simple lack of courage and devotion to the common good weren't the whole problem. The Commonwealth needed something more, something that would always continue to elude him because he couldn't grasp the breadth and scope of its real nature with the sharply delineated mind of a fighting soldier. His enemy—the great chancellor whom he admired as profoundly as he hated—might have a deeper understanding of what needed to be done.

★   ★   ★

Meanwhile the pointed spires of Warsaw began to gleam in the haze ahead and the Prince's musing turned to simpler matters. He called an orderly officer to his side and issued crisp orders. The officer saluted, wheeled his mount and galloped back along the column until he found the escort commander. Pan Volodyovski, who was riding alongside the coach that carried Anusia, chatting and joking with her to pass the time and to remind himself of those bygone, light-hearted years of their life in Lubnie, trotted back to his regiments to set them in order for the entry into the capital.

But he no sooner spurred his horse away from Anusia when he heard the pounding of other hooves behind him. It was, he saw, Pan Kharlamp, the long-nosed captain of Lithuanian Light Horse who glared at him so fiercely the night before.

"Ho ho," he murmured, grinning in anticipation and twirling his pointed little whiskers. "Looks like something's going to happen after all."

He slowed his horse. Despite Anusia's friendly chatter he found the journey boring and he was anxious to relieve the tedium with some entertainment. But the Lithuanian captain didn't seem to know how to start a quarrel. He caught up with the little soldier, bared and ground his teeth, and started moving his huge mustache up and down as if he was chewing on a mouthful of insults he couldn't quite spit out.

Then he growled out roughly: "'Morning, Mister Dragoon."

"'Morning, Mister Lightfoot," Pan Michal shot back.

"Whom are you calling a Lightfoot, you mounted foot soldier?" The huge nose pointed like a spear at the little knight. "I'm a regular officer and a member of the serving gentry! Can't you tell the difference?"

Pan Michal grimaced at the silver cord which the furious captain wore looped at his shoulder in the Lithuanian fashion and grinned into the sky.

"Hard to tell what you fellows are," he said amiably. "One little hangman's noose looks like another to me."

"That's our rank insignia!" Pan Kharlamp's teeth started clattering in rage. "The heavy regiments of Lithuanian Horse wear a gold one, we of the Light Horse wear a silver one! Don't you know even that much, you ignorant dragoon?"

Pan Michal, who knew these rank insignia very well, grinned again and started tossing his short battle-hammer high into the air, concentrating on catching it by the handle each time it whirled down.

"You're insulting the entire Lithuanian Army!" growled the furious Kharlamp. "Seems like I'd better teach you some respect!"

"You can try." Pan Michal's unconcern only served to goad the Lithuanian into greater fury. "Could it be, my good fellow, that you're looking for a fight with me?"

"And maybe I am!"—and here Pan Kharlamp leaned closer to Volodyovski's ear so that he could whisper—"And I might just clip your ears for you if you keep getting in my way with Mistress Anusia."

Pan Volodyovski turned his whole attention to tossing his battle-hammer into the air, as if he had nothing more important on his mind, and answered in a mild, conciliatory tone.

"Ey, my good sir, let me live a little longer, will you? Let me off this time."

"No way!" Kharlamp bellowed and caught the small soldier by the sleeve. "You're not going to get away with this, not now and not ever!"

"But I'm not trying to get away." Pan Michal did his best to sound reasonable and humble. "Only I'm on duty just now, as you see. I've got His Highness' orders to carry out. So let go of my sleeve, I beg you, or I just don't know what I'll have to do

. . . Like maybe crack you on the head with this mace of mine and knock you off your horse?"

Here Pan Volodyovski's humility and patience took on such a deadly, hissing quality that Pan Kharlamp stared at him in surprise.

"It won't make any difference in the long run!" he growled after a moment. "You and I will meet me in Warsaw, I'll make sure of that!"

"Gladly, gladly,"—and the little knight grinned at the furious Lithuanian in his most innocent and engaging manner— "only how are we to fight there? I'm just a simple soldier, I've never been to Warsaw, but I've heard about summary courts-martial that punish people with a headsman's axe for drawing a saber anywhere near the King or the *interrex*. So how are we to do this fighting, if you'd tell me kindly?"

"Hmm." The long-nosed Lithuanian glared at the little soldier with contempt. "It's easy to see you're a provincial boor and that you've never been anywhere important if courts-martial scare you! Don't you know that it's an ecclesiastic court that judges capital offenses when the throne is vacant? They're a lot more lenient. And anyway, I hardly think they'd want my head for cutting off your ears."

"Thank you kindly, sir, for instructing me," the little colonel murmured. "Thank you very kindly. I can see that you're a widely traveled and educated man who knows his way around. As for me . . . well, I barely managed to get through my Latin grammar and get my *adjectivum* to agree with my *substantivo*, if you know what I mean. And if, God forbid, I wanted to call you a dimwit or a damn fool I'd know just enough to say you were '*stultus*,' rather than '*stulta*' or '*stultum*.' "

Here Pan Volodyovski began to toss his battle hammer again while Pan Kharlamp stared at him with bulging eyes, not quite sure if he had been insulted by the little fellow.

But then he realized that Volodyovski had made a fool of him and was laughing at him. A sudden rush of blood turned his long, sallow face the color of a boiled beetroot, and he clutched the hilt of his saber and hauled it from its scabbard. Pan Michal instantly flashed his own in the Lithuanian's eyes and they sat side by side on their horses glaring at each other like two snorting boars, until Pan Kharlamp recalled that he'd have to answer to the Prince himself if he was to attack one of his officers while he was on duty.

"I'll find you, you whelp!" he snarled. "You can be sure I will!"

"And I'll help you do it," Pan Michal said and shrugged and slipped his saber back into its sheath.

They parted then; one to return to the cavalcade of coaches and the other to the half dozen regiments which trailed at some distance behind the carriages since this was peaceful country, untouched by the rebellion, and the soldiers were there only to demonstrate Prince Yeremi's power and not to protect him from any actual danger. Pan Michal soon had the cavalry trotting in close order and the infantry marching in an even step and set himself at their head for the entry into the capital.

Pan Zagloba joined him soon after.

"What did that long-nosed freak want from you anyway?" he asked.

"Pan Kharlamp? Nothing much. He wants me to fight him."

"Now there's a fine stew!" the fat knight observed. "If you don't watch out he'll run you through with that proboscis like one of those spearfish that travelers talk about. That must be the biggest nose in the Commonwealth! You'd better make sure you don't slice it off or they'll have to dig a separate grave for it. Ha, the *Voyevode* of Vilna is a lucky man! Other commanders have to send patrols to sniff out the enemy but this fellow can do it for him from a distance! But why does he want to fight you?"

"Because I rode beside Anusia's carriage."

"You should've told him to visit Pan Longinus if he's that anxious to have his whiskers trimmed. Now that would be a fight worth seeing! The beanpole against the beak! But it looks to me like that fellow's luck is running a lot shorter than his snout."

"I didn't mention Pan Longinus in case this feisty fellow gave up on me and I lost out on a bit of fun," Volodyovski said. "In fact I'll make it a point to court Anusia with real fervor from now on! After all, what else will we have for amusement in Warsaw?"

"Plenty, my friend, plenty!" Pan Zagloba said, winking and grinning broadly in his beard. "Way back in my youth, when I was a provisioning officer for my regiment, I covered quite a bit of country here and there. But I've never come across better times than I had in Warsaw."

"Could it be that much different from what we had in Lubnie?"

"Heaven and earth, my dear fellow. No comparison."

"Hmm. It might not be so bad then," Pan Michal said. "But I'll trim that nosy fellow's whiskers anyway."

"Why bother?"

"Because they're too long."

Chapter Forty-eight

SOME WEEKS PASSED. Warsaw's population swelled to ten times its usual size as the gentry poured in ever-growing numbers into the great walled city on the Vistula which, even in ordinary years, housed more artisans and merchants than London and Paris. Thousands of merchant caravans came from as far as Persia, and fleets of traders sailed from all the countries of the West to pitch their tents and set up their booths in the plains and suburbs that surrounded Warsaw.

Eight hundred thousand persons jostled each other in the crowded capital; hundreds of thousands more of the voting gentry bivouacked in huge tent-cities spread around the walls; and although the election was still many weeks away, there were so many feasts and banquets given every day that newcomers like Pan Volodyovski, for whom Prince Yeremi's distant capital of Lubnie seemed like a cosmopolitan metropolis, walked about with eyes as big as saucers.

The Senate deliberated in a great wooden amphitheater built for that purpose in the fields of Vola but it was still too soon to tell which of the two leading candidates would emerge the winner. Both sides worked day and night to promote their man; both the royal brothers issued stacks of broadsheets singing their own praises and pointing out the shortcomings of the other. Both had numerous and powerful supporters.

Prince Charles Ferdinand, the young Bishop of Plotzk, had the backing of the Vishnovyetzkis, which was all the more dangerous for the opposition because it seemed likely that the famous and admired warrior would pull the great masses of the voting gentry to his candidate. But Yan Casimir had the advantage of being the elder and therefore more seasoned in his judgments. He could command the influence of the chancellor; the primate seemed ready to throw the support of the Church behind him; and he could count on the vast majority of the magnates, each of whom was richer and more powerful than any prince in Europe, and who could tip the scales in his favor with the sheer weight of wealth, patronage and numerous connections.

Even so, the supporters of Yan Casimir had some bitter moments. The politicking gentry who turned out for this election in greater numbers than ever before, favored the young Prince Charles, drawn by the magic of Prince Yeremi's name and by the candidate's thoughtful generosity. Charles Ferdinand was known not only for his public works but also for the shrewd management of his own estates so that he could afford to raise and equip many new regiments which were to serve under Vishnovyetzki. Yan Casimir might have done the same but he was so open-handed in his giving, and so willing to believe anyone who came to him for help, that his treasury was almost always empty.

Messengers galloped every day between the two courts. Yan Casimir begged his brother to step down in the name of his rights as the elder; the young bishop declined, pointing out that the laws of primogeniture, by which the oldest brother inherited estates everywhere else in Europe, didn't apply in Poland.

★   ★   ★

Meanwhile time passed. October soon ended. Three quarters of a million gentry camped, feasted, argued, quarreled and fought each other in and around the city. The six-week limit for the electoral convention was almost upon them, and along with that came the news of fresh Cossack terror. As Prince Yeremi had foreseen in Lvov, Hmyelnitzki soon abandoned the siege of that city, contenting himself with a face-saving ransom, and massed all his forces under the walls of Zamost, storming that last bastion of the Commonwealth day and night.

Pan Zagloba was particularly worried about that.

"What if they take it?" he muttered time and time again, peering uneasily towards the horizon. "The new army's barely getting itself together. There'd be nothing to stop Hmyel between Zamost and here."

"Don't worry." Pan Michal's cheerful grin helped to set the fat knight's mind at rest. "The Prince didn't leave his best regiments in Zamost for nothing. The Cossacks will break their teeth on those walls and that'll be that."

"May the Devil take them! People say there's a lot of them right here, posing as eastern gentry and sniffing out whatever they can."

"That could be."

"No way to tell them from the rest of us," the fat old knight complained. "By God, what times we live in when a gentleman can't even tell who he's drinking with! Some of those Zaporohjans are gentry themselves. They even know Latin. You could be sitting right next to one in a tavern and never know you're clinking tankards with a rebel."

"That's right." The little knight didn't seem concerned. "Come to think of it, Latin's not all that common even among the gentry in our part of the country. Look at the Kurtzevitch princes, for example, may they rest in peace. Fine ancient blood, a lineage that goes back to Rurik and the Kievan boyars, but not a speck of learning between the lot of them. Some of the young atamans, who've been rubbing shoulders with us at the court in Lubnie, would do a better job of passing as gentry."

"Such as who?"

"Such as Bohun. Why not? That man's got to have some great lord's blood somewhere in his veins."

"It's a Devil of a thing none the less!" Pan Zagloba railed bitterly. "They say that Hmyel himself is sending an embassy to Warsaw to cast his vote for Yan Casimir. To which he's entitled as a Polish noble! Can you imagine such a thing happening in any other country?"

"Well, let's just hope Prince Charles gets the votes." The little knight neither knew nor cared much about politics and what he knew of the law could've been written on his saber blade. "Then we'll give Hmyelnitzki everything he's earned."

★　★　★

But speculation about disguised Zaporohjan leaders lurking around Warsaw, along with rumors of Hmyelnitzki's continuing successes, inflamed the volatile gentry in and about the city. Some swore that they had seen Cossack and Tartar patrols as far west as the lower Vistula. It was enough for someone to be accused, no matter how unjustly, of being a Zaporohjan for a raging mob to cut him into pieces. Many innocent men died that way and the seriousness of the deliberations was interrupted time and time again by outbursts of violence, especially since sobriety was never one of the gentry's virtues. The magistrates who were charged with keeping public order couldn't cope with the constant tumults and eruptions in which tipsy men fought and sabered each other at the slightest pretext.

But if the serious-minded men who feared for the Commonwealth in this time of danger deplored this constant rioting, drunkenness and duels, it also seemed like a providential opportunity for all kinds of wastrels, scoundrels, drifters, bullies and brawlers. It went without saying that Pan Zagloba felt right at home in that kind of company, assured of a place at any tavern table not only by his vast reputation as a Vishnovyetzki warrior but also by his monumental thirst and his willingness to drink with everyone anywhere and at anyone's expense.

The only time when he lost his swagger and aplomb and gave way to doubt and self-recrimination was when he fell victim to what he called his bouts of '*melancolia*.' When these came upon him, he barricaded himself in his room and refused to talk to anyone, and if he emerged at such times out of whatever lair he found for himself, he was irritable, quick to pick a quarrel and looking for trouble. On one such day he cut up Pan Duntchevski, a gentleman from Ravyan, simply because the unfortunate man tripped on Pan Zagloba's saber while passing him in a crowd.

The little knight was the only man whose company he tolerated during his melancholy moments. "It's because I miss Skshetuski," he complained. "And that poor, lost girl. That's why I get like this."

"We'll see Yan soon enough," Pan Michal assured him. "Just wait 'til the election is over and the fighting heats up for us again. Our Prince won't even wait for the coronation before he gets back to the army and the war."

"And what about my sweet little songbird? Eh? What about my Helen? What's happening with her?"

"It's all Christ's will." Pan Michal sighed. "All we can do is pray for her and hope for the best."

"And is it Christ's will for us to abandon her? To leave her helpless in those Godless hands? What kind of Judas trick is that? And don't tell me about that military '*nemine excepto*' of yours either. I've heard quite enough about that, thank you very much! We've turned our backs on her, that's what we've done! We've abandoned that poor child! We've sold her out, that's what!"

It didn't help for Pan Michal to point out that they were helpless to go in search of Helen after the disaster of Pilavtze when all of Hmyelnitzki's swollen hordes lay across their path. The fat knight refused to be consoled. His rage merely deepened, fueled by shame, anxiety and guilt. And his attacks of remorse drove him to even greater excesses than before.

★   ★   ★

But these mournful moments never lasted long. Climbing out of gloom as quickly as he plunged into it, Pan Zagloba partied, drank with the most notable guzzlers in the capital, and paid such ardent court to so many ladies of questionable virtue that he more than made up for the time he lost in remorse and sadness.

Little Pan Michal was delighted to join him in all that carousing. He knew himself to be a good soldier and his reputation as a first-rate officer was second to none. But he was also honest enough to know that he didn't have a penny's worth of that dignity, seriousness and maturity which Skshetuski's suffering and misfortunes had stamped into his soul. He understood his duty to the Commonwealth as a simple matter of fighting anyone he was told to fight; everything else, including political opinions, was an unfathomable mystery to him and he didn't bother his young head about it. He was always ready to shed tears of grief over the Commonwealth's military disasters but it didn't occur to him that the spendthrift debaucheries, willful disobedience and profligate self-indulgence of his fellow gentry could be just as harmful to the country as any number of defeats in battle. He was, in short, a young man eager for any new excitement and experience, and the fast and noisy turbulence of a great city's seamier side of life drew him as naturally as a humming beehive might attract a curious little bear.

He attached himself happily to Pan Zagloba—indeed, he clung to him with the persistence of a bug clamped to an old dog's tail—and treated the roistering fat knight as his guide and tutor in that newly discovered underworld of big city pleasures and carousals. They went everywhere, buzzing about like flies around a stew pot, until soon everybody knew them and competed in inviting them to their celebrations. They drank with everyone. They didn't miss a single feast, banquet, ball or drinking bout anywhere near the city; they attended every supper given by the magnates. They were soon as much at home at the hospitable courts of both the royal princes, where thousands of visiting gentry stuffed themselves and guzzled every day at the candidates' expense, as they were in every inn, wineshop and tavern of the town, and the more often they showed up among the carousers the more they were welcomed.

"That's the life, eh?" Pan Zagloba sighed with pleasure every day as they set out in search of good company and excitement.

"It is," the little knight agreed.

"Didn't I tell you there's no place anywhere as lively as Warsaw?" The old noble seemed created for the wine cask and the banquet table. He treated the endless round of roistering as if it were one of his inventions. "And you thought you'd be bored here, didn't you."

"I did. And you were right. I'm not."

"Hah! Well, now at least you know I'm not a liar."

"Hmm." Pan Volodyovski may have turned himself into the fat knight's pupil in carousing, but that didn't mean that he dispensed with all his intelligence and judgment. "I wouldn't go quite as far as that."

"Ah . . . ah! You mean the tales I spin? The stories that I tell them?"

"To listen to you a man would think that nothing important ever happened anywhere in history without you having a finger in the pie."

"And who's to say I didn't? What if I do bend the truth a little if it's in a good cause? '*Pro publico bono*,' my dear Michal, that's the key to a useful and successful life . . . Hah! Do you think I like to waste my breath on every guzzler that we come across? You know that I'm a temperate and abstemious man and that I like to treat good mead with respect. But every time I clink a cup or two with our brother gentry I win votes for Prince Charles, and if he doesn't reward me for all that hard work with at least a stewardship of a province then there's neither gratitude nor decency left in this Commonwealth of ours and it deserves to perish."

"Hmm. You're right about the votes you're getting for Prince

Charles," the little knight was forced to admit. "And it is thirsty work. But I don't think we'll save the Commonwealth by drinking it dry."

"And why not? Isn't that better than looting it bare? Stick with me, my good little friend, and you'll soon learn how to become honored and respected and rise to great heights. You can't help being pint-sized, and as skimpily constructed as a tick on a hound's ear, since that's how God made you. But you can still get to be a man to whom the world listens with proper attention."

Pan Michal matched the fat knight cup for cup as long as he was able, listened to his tales and harangues along with the rest of the fascinated gentry and, when needed, backed him up with his saber if the arguments got heated. He was a restless, spirited young man used to living in the Steppe a day at a time and doing it on horseback. Such heady stuff as public affairs, or thinking about what might reform the country, was totally beyond him, and the right or wrong of anything never troubled his conscience. He was more than eager to show everyone that the Ukrainian gentry were better than that of any other region, and that the Vishnovyetzki soldiers were more to be feared and respected than all the other warriors of the Commonwealth, and so he trailed behind Zagloba through the taverns in search of the most ferocious swashbucklers— particularly among the partisans of Prince Dominic Zaslavski—and they usually set up the procedures for their quarrels in advance.

"You start things off with your tongue," Pan Michal would say. "And then I'll step in."

"What? What? And I'm to miss all the fun?" The fat knight, a fair hand with a saber in his own right, didn't always agree to step aside for the little swordsman.

But often, especially when they found themselves among the eastern and northeastern gentry who had well-earned reputations as the best sword-masters in the Commonwealth, Pan Zagloba confined himself to his infuriating witticisms and hair-raising insults and then, when the offended noble reached howling for his saber, he stepped back and nodded at his small companion.

"My dear sir," he'd say with a superior smile. "I'd have to have no conscience to take you on myself. That would be sheer murder. So why don't you have a go instead at my young son

and pupil over here? He'll give you some idea of what to expect
from me because I taught him everything he knows."

At which point Pan Michal slid from behind the old knight's
massive back, moving his pointed little whiskers up and down
like a questing beetle, and looking about as bright and dangerous as a country sparrow. And then, because he really was a
swordsman without an equal, he soon stretched out his unfortunate victim in half a dozen strokes.

"If that's what the pupil's like," the awed gentry told each
other in and around the city, "how great must the teacher be?"

So they amused themselves through the long Autumn days.
And so their fame and reputations grew, particularly the aura of
invincibility that settled on Zagloba. The only famous saber
rattler whom they failed to track down and provoke into a fight
was the long-nosed, long-whiskered Pan Kharlamp for whom
Pan Michal looked with special eagerness.

"I really did think those whiskers needed trimming," he
complained.

"Not to mention that cannon he's got sticking out between
his eyes," Pan Zagloba noted. "Well. Well. We'll keep looking."

But the ferocious Lithuanian captain seemed to have disappeared so that, in time, the disappointed little knight began to
think that he must have been sent back to Vilna on some
mission for the Lithuanian Hetman.

* * *

The six weeks of the electoral convention passed like a
blurred dream of a vast faceless crowd, of a booming roar that
could be heard for miles around Warsaw, of feasts and broached
casks of liquor and wine flowing as free as water in the Vistula,
and of the bitter pressurings and maneuverings for political
advantage with which the two royal brothers struggled for the
crown. Then, suddenly, the great matters of public importance
were finally resolved. Prince Charles withdrew without warning in favor of his brother. A new King, Yan Casimir of the
House of Vasa, would be crowned in Krakow and, by an odd
turn of fate, it was Hmyelnitzki's vote that appeared to count
more than any other because it was generally expected that the
powerful rebel would be more likely to submit to the monarch
of his choice.

The gentry started packing up and drifting off to their manors and estates. The vast encampments emptied. And just as before the disaster of Pilavtze the cry of 'War' echoed among the fields and forests throughout the whole country so now, with Yan Casimir named as the new monarch, 'Peace' was the word that lay on the lips of the dispersing, joyful and war-weary gentry.

But for Prince Yeremi—who had turned himself into a sort of Cato, insisting that the Zaporohjan 'Carthage' be razed to the ground and warning that only the utter destruction of the Cossacks would bring peace to the Ukraine—this disappointment was yet another blow, and one he took to heart. New negotiations with the Cossacks were now a foregone conclusion. The peace party of the chancellor and *Voyevode* Kisyel had captured control of the country; Cossack conciliation won the day; and a hasty armistice would put an end to the fighting even if it was unlikely to lead to lasting peace. The angry and embittered Prince was sure that giving Hmyelnitzki everything he wanted would merely result in yet another war and that the fresh conflict would be all the more terrible because the Zaporohjans now held all the wealth and people of the Ukraine in their grasp. Having been legalized by the Senate as the Grand Hetman of the Ukraine, the rebel Hmyelnitzki was immeasurably stronger while the Commonwealth became even weaker.

And who would lead the new Crown armies against Hmyelnitzki once the armistice was broken? It wouldn't be himself, Prince Yeremi knew. As the most ardent of Charles Ferdinand's supporters, he could harbor no further illusions about seeing the Grand Hetman's *bulava* placed in his own hands.

True, he could tell himself, Yan Casimir was known for his magnanimity. He pledged to treat his brother's backers as he would his own. But he was also sworn to the policies of the chancellor who was Vishnovyetzki's most implacable opponent.

"So it'll be some other hands that'll lift the burden," the Prince announced to his gloomy officers soon after his candidate's withdrawal had dashed all his hopes.

"Who, Highness?" they cried, hardly able to believe how quickly and how utterly their own high hopes were shattered and destroyed. "Who but you can do it? Who else among us will be able to lead the Commonwealth against an enemy as powerful and confident as the new Hmyelnitzki?"

The Prince couldn't tell them.

"Won't there be fresh calamities?" the gathered gentry and officers insisted. "More defeats, humiliations and disasters? And how long will it be before the last strength of the Commonwealth is spent?"

And at this thought a double spasm of pain contorted the Prince's pale, harrowed face. One, as all of his men knew, was fear for the country; it was a fear they shared and understood. The other, which the Prince kept hidden in himself, was the embittering, gnawing disappointment of a man who had given everything he owned to a cause in which he believed; who spent all his treasure, abandoned his lands, and sacrificed his own past and future; and who now saw his merits dismissed and ignored. His just rewards would elude him once again and other heads would rise above his own.

His pride gnawed at him. He could hardly stand this new humiliation. He wouldn't have been the man he was if he weren't also a vastly proud and willful magnate who was always conscious of his own destiny and greatness, of his role in history, and of his soaring vision of himself.

He had the strength, he knew, for the dreadful tasks that waited for him just beyond the temporarily pacified horizon. He had earned the power. And he had lost it all on the whim of one young royal prince who was unable to resist the pressures of Vishnovyetzki's enemies and who passed an almost certain crown to his older brother.

Chapter Forty-nine

THERE WAS SOME TALK among the officers in Warsaw that Prince Yeremi was so humiliated by Yan Casimir's election that he would leave the capital at once and retire from public affairs somewhere in the country. But he was too great a man, moved by too great a spirit, to allow private disappointments to gnaw at him for long. Yan Casimir, in turn, received him graciously when he called on him, and Vishnovyetzki settled down in the city for a lengthy stay. As always, he was absorbed by military matters, which called for heavy lobbying in the Diet for an army budget. Moreover, Prince Charles continued raising fresh regiments of infantry and dragoons which had to be organized and trained so that Vishnovyetzki's experienced officers were in great demand. Kushel and Vyershul were both sent to new commands and, finally, it was the turn of Pan Volodyovski.

"You'll go to Zaborov," the Prince said to the little soldier. "I want you to look over the horseherds gathered there, pick out the best and buy them for the cavalry. Here's a chit for the treasurer. Take the money and leave as soon as you can."

Pan Michal got to work at once, loaded the bags of gold on a heavy cart, picked a platoon of dragoons for an escort, and he and the fat knight were on the road the same day. They took the quickest route, the highway that ran through Babitze and Lipkov, but it was slow going anyway; the road and all of the countryside in that direction were so densely packed with dispersing gentry, along with their servants, horses, baggage carts and wagons, that even the local peasant huts were jammed with guests and boarders.

They were about to take a break at a country inn near

Babitze, where several dozen gentry were mounting up to leave, when one of the departing riders threw a sharp look at the little knight and spurred his horse towards him.

"Got you!" he shouted. "You hid yourself somewhere but I've found you, fellow! You won't get away from me now! Not this time! Hey,"—and he turned to his surprised companions— "hold up a minute, will you, gentlemen? I've got a few sharp words for this little man and I want you to witness what I've got to say!"

Pan Volodyovski grinned happily recognizing Kharlamp.

"God knows I wasn't hiding," he said. "In fact I looked for you all over Warsaw to ask if you're still angry at me. But what could I do? We simply missed each other."

"Michal," Zagloba warned softly. "You're on duty."

"I know it," Volodyovski said.

"Pick your spot right now!" Kharlamp howled, bouncing up and down in his saddle as if he'd gone mad. "Hey,"—he shouted to his friends—"I promised this little pipsqueak that I'd trim his ears and that's what I'll do as my name is Kharlamp! So all of you act as witnesses that it's all fair and square. And you, you barefaced little pest, pick your spot and go for your saber!"

"God knows I'd like to," Pan Michal sighed. "But I can't. You'll have to give me a few more days, my ferocious friend."

"Days you want? Days? What's the matter, got cold feet all of a sudden, have you? Take your place at once or I'll paddle you with the flat of my saber so hard your own grandparents won't know you! Oh, you little horsefly! Oh, you poisonous little reptile! You know how to pester people, you're great at getting in their way, you're fine when it comes to stinging with your tongue! But where are you when it comes to sabers?"

Here Pan Zagloba took a turn.

"Seems to me," he told Kharlamp, "that you're about to bite off more than you can chew yourself. What the Devil, can't you see this officer's on duty? Take a look at those money bags we're escorting and try to get it into your thick head that this man's time is not his own just now! Duty must come first and whoever can't see that is a dolt, not a soldier! We serve under the *Voyevode* of Ruthenia, and we've tangled with better men then you, but today's not the day for dancing. So step back, be patient, and let us go our way. A little waiting never spoiled a dinner."

"Seems like that's right enough," one of Kharlamp's companions pointed out to the furious Lithuanian captain. "If they're escorting money they can't do anything to oblige you now."

"What the Devil do I care about their money!" Kharlamp howled. "Let him fight me like a man or I'll start on him with a horsewhip!"

But Pan Michal had enough of this posturing and howling.

"I won't fight you now," he said, "but I'll give you my word that I'll meet you in three or four days, wherever you want, as soon as I've finished with the job at hand. And if that's not good enough for you and your friends then I'll have my men take care of you with muskets because it'll look to me like I'm dealing with bandits not with soldiers. Make your choice then, Devil take you, because I've no more time to waste!"

Hearing this, the escort dragoons immediately turned their musket barrels on the Lithuanian's party and Kharlamp's friends began to calm him down and pull him back by the sleeves of his coat.

"Take it easier will you?" they urged. "You're a serving officer yourself, you know the regulations. He'll meet you. He looks like a pretty scrappy little fellow, like all that lot in Vishnovyetzki's army. So get a hold of yourself and calm down while we're still in the mood to ask."

Pan Kharlamp yelled and ranted for a while longer but it didn't take him long to realize that he would either earn his own companions' anger and contempt or force them into a risky clash with the well-armed and disciplined dragoons.

"Hurry up and choose!" snapped the little knight.

"So I've your word?" Pan Kharlamp asked Volodyovski. "You'll show up?"

"I'll search you out myself just because you think you've got to ask me about a thing like that."

"When?"

"Four days ought to be enough to finish what I have to do. Today's Wednesday, right? So let's make it Saturday afternoon, about two o'clock. Where do you want to meet?"

"Hmm. There's a lot of people staying here in Babitze," the Lithuanian said. "Might get in our way. Make it nearby, in Lipkov. It's quieter there and easy to get to."

"And will there be as many of you there as here, gentlemen?" asked the prudent old knight.

"No need for great numbers," Kharlamp said. "I'll be there with two kinsmen, the Syeletzki brothers. And you two will also come without your dragoons, I expect?"

"Maybe it's the fashion where you come from to bring a military escort to a duel," Pan Michal said coldly. "We've some different customs."

"All right then," Kharlamp said. "So it's to be in four days, at two in the afternoon on Saturday, in Lipkov? You'll find us waiting in front of the inn there."

"We'll be there. And now go with God."

"Go with God," chorused Kharlamp's party.

★ ★ ★

The two groups parted. Each rode its own way. The little knight was delighted by the turn of events, promising himself some good entertainment out of what was coming and planning to make a present of Kharlamp's whiskers to Pan Podbipyenta. He was so pleased about it all that he finished his assignment in two days, picked out and bought a fine herd of horses, reported back to the Prince in Warsaw, and waited at the Lipkov tavern an hour ahead of time along with Zagloba and Pan Kushel whom he asked to be his second witness.

They went into the public rooms to wet their throats with a little mead and to kill the hour.

"Hey, Jew," Pan Zagloba turned to the innkeeper. "Is the local master home at the manor?"

"The master's in Warsaw," the Jew said.

"And is there a lot of gentry staying here in Lipkov?"

"What's a lot?" The Jew shrugged his shoulders. "All I've got staying here is one. But he's a rich lord. Lots of men and horses. He's sitting in the private parlor if you want to know."

"So if he's such a rich lord why's he staying with you? How come he didn't put up at the manor?"

"Who knows about great lords? But maybe he doesn't know our local landowner. And anyway the manor's been closed up for a month and more."

"Maybe that's Kharlamp?" Zagloba asked the others.

"I wouldn't think so," said Volodyovski.

"Well I've got an idea it's him. I'll go take a look. Listen, Jew, how long's this lord of yours been here?"

"He's just come today. It's hardly been two hours."

"And where did he come from?"

"He didn't say." The Jew shrugged again, hurrying with the flagon and the pewter mugs. "But it looks to me like he must've come from far away. His horses are worn like they've been ridden hard and his people said that they've come from way beyond the Vistula."

Pan Zagloba didn't really care about the unknown visitor but he was bored, the mead wasn't up to his expectations, and he looked forward to hearing the sound of his voice with a fresher audience.

"So why didn't he go a little farther and find rooms in Warsaw?"

"I should know?" the Jew asked. "I should question him? I'm just glad he's spending his gold in my place. I don't get a rich lord like that staying here that often."

"Think I'll have a look anyway," Pan Zagloba said, yawned, and got to his feet. "It could be somebody we know if he's from the East . . ." And then, knocking on the closed parlor door with the hilt of his saber, he called out pleasantly: "Ho! I say, in there! Can I come in for a moment?"

"Who are you?" a muffled voice asked from beyond the door.

"A friend," Zagloba said, put on his best smile, and pushed the door ajar. "I hope I'm not intruding at an awkward time?"

He stuck his head into the narrow opening and suddenly leaped back as if he'd seen a ghost, slammed the door shut and turned to the others with utter terror and absolute amazement spread across his face. His mouth fell open. He flapped his arms and gasped for breath as if he was drowning. Both his eyes bulged out at Kushel and Volodyovski as if they were about to pop out of his head.

"Hey," Pan Volodyovski said, alarmed. "What's wrong with you? What's the matter?"

"Quiet!" hissed Zagloba. "In the name of Christ's sweet wounds . . . be quiet, you hear? That's . . . that's Bohun in there!"

"Who?" The two young dragoons looked no less astonished than the thunderstruck Zagloba, then jumped to their feet. "Have you lost your wits?"

"That's . . . Bohun, I tell you! Bohun . . . As I live and breathe!"

"But how can that be?"

"How do I know how it can be?" cried out the terrified and bewildered fat knight, forgetting his own admonition about keeping quiet. "But I swear by God and all His saints that that's who it is!"

"So why are you so upset about it?" Pan Volodyovski asked. "We've met him before."

But this time the fat knight was really out of breath. He stood shaking and sweating by the parlor door while his wide, blood-shot eyes swept the room as if he'd forgotten where to find the exit.

"Don't be so worried, old friend," Pan Michal said softly. "Relax. If that's really Bohun then God's given him into our hands and that's all there's to it. Calm down, now. Calm down. Don't get so excited. Are you quite sure there's no mistake? It's really Bohun that you saw in there?"

"I'd rather see the Devil himself," Zagloba groaned at last, mopping his head and clutching at his chest as if to keep his heart from leaping out of it. "But that's whom I saw. It's Bohun all right. He's in there, changing clothes."

"And did he see you?" Volodyovski's eyes were glittering now as if he smelled the blood before it was spilled.

"I don't know. I doubt it."

"Good enough. Listen, Jew,"—the little knight turned to the anxious tavern keeper—"is there another door to that parlor?"

"No sir. Just this one from the public rooms. But . . . but . . . but . . . you aren't going to cause any trouble in here, Your Worship? Are you, master? Eh?"

"Kushel! Get under his window," Volodyovski hissed. "Huh, looks like we've got him now!"

Kushel ran out of the room without a word. The Jew sat down heavily on a bench and started swaying back and forth, his hands about his ears, and a despairing moan bubbled out of his wispy beard as he contemplated the ruin of his property and livelihood which was sure to follow any kind of brawl in his little taproom. Pan Zagloba still gasped, struggling for his breath, and rolled his good eye blindly about the room as if his shocked senses couldn't come to terms with what he had seen.

"Get hold of yourself, my friend," Volodyovski urged him. "What do you have to be nervous about here? It's not your neck that's in trouble now but Bohun's. What can he do to you? Not a thing. He's in your hands this time, not the other way around."

"Eh? Eh?" Still quivering and gasping, Pan Zagloba started to think that he was giving quite the wrong impression of his vaunted valor. "Hmm? It's . . . ah . . . the astonishment of it all, don't you know . . . That's what's got me shaking. Nervous . . .? Me? Ha Ha! It's Bohun who should be shaking in his breeches, what with you and me both after him again!"

"That's it," said the little knight, rubbing his hands in anticipation. "And this time we've got him."

"Ha!" Pan Zagloba was beginning to feel a great deal better. "That's right! There's the two of us here, after all, and each of us has already given him something to remember!"

And then, with a quick, thankful glance at the quiet little swordsman, as if he wanted to make absolutely sure that the small knight was there, he donned his own most terrifying expression and clutched at his saber.

"He won't escape us now!"

"No way he can." Pan Michal nodded calmly. "Only . . . you're quite sure that was him? I can't imagine what he'd be doing here."

"He's Hmyelnitzki's spy, that's what he's doing here. And that's a hanging matter. Huh! He'll be dancing on a rope before the day's over! Well, well, the Devil's waited a long time for that handsome puppet to give to his children but now the waiting's over! And not a minute too soon, the way that I see it."

"Pity, though," said Pan Michal.

"Pity?" Pan Zagloba stared at his little friend in utter amazement. "What do you mean by '*pity*?' What's wrong with Bohun dangling before morning?"

"It's a shame to think of such a famous soldier dying on a gibbet. I'd rather see him go down with his sword in hand."

"Listen here," the fat knight said in utmost seriousness, wagging his great bald head and tugging his beard. "Any way he goes is good enough for me. But . . . hold on a minute . . . I've just thought of something. What if we seize him and give him a choice? Either he gives us Helen, or at least tells us where to find her, or we'll turn him over to the public hangman!"

"You'd let him go, then?"

"Ah, ah . . .!"—a terrible struggle was clearly taking place in Pan Zagloba, where his desperate fear and hatred of Bohun fought against his love and concern for Helen—"It's an awful thing to do, I know, but isn't our sweet girl worth it, hmm?

Isn't that what we should do for our friend Skshetuski, if not for ourselves?"

"Suits me." Pan Michal shrugged. "I don't care what happens to Bohun once he's given up Skshetuski's princess. Let him go to the Devil if that's where his road takes him." Then he heaved a sad little sigh of his own. "Although I wouldn't mind seeing if he's as good a man with a saber as all those story tellers say he is . . ."

"He is. Take my word for it."

Once more visibly ill-at-ease, Pan Zagloba stared anxiously at the parlor door. "But . . . are there enough of us to take him? You and me and Kushel for a third . . . He'll fight like a madman, and he's sure to have a good two dozen men out in the stables, that's certain."

"Kharlamp with his seconds will get here soon." The little knight shrugged, unconcerned. "There'll be six of us. That's enough for any Cossack, no matter how famous."

But at that moment the parlor door swung open and Bohun stepped into the room.

★   ★   ★

He must not have noticed Pan Zagloba earlier when the fat knight peered into the parlor, because now, catching sight of his most hated enemy, his whole body quivered, his face blazed with hatred as if a sudden crimson light had swept violently across it, and his hand fell with lightning speed to the handle of his ornate saber. But all of this lasted for only a fragment of a moment. The wild fire died out of his eyes and a terrible, graven pallor spread across his features.

Zagloba stared at him in his own turn, saying nothing, while the young ataman stood as still as if he'd turned to stone so that their silence seemed as heavy as a boulder. Neither man appeared to breathe. Their silence was total. If Pan Volodyovski didn't know how closely these two men's fates were intertwined and tangled he might have thought that they didn't even know each other. It seemed to him that hours went by before Bohun spoke.

"You there, Jew," he said. "How far is it to Zaborov?"

"Not far," the Jew said anxiously. "Your lordship's leaving right away?"

"Yes," Bohun said and turned towards the door.

"A moment!" cried Zagloba.

The ataman stood as still as if his booted feet were rooted to the floor. "What is it?" he asked abruptly, spun around and fixed his cold, dark eyes on the fat knight like a forest adder coiled to strike its prey.

"Ey," the fat knight said softly, enjoying the moment. "Ey, don't we know each other? Seems to me like we've met before. Didn't we see each other at a peasant wedding a while back in the Ukraine? Or was it Podolia?"

"That is so," the ataman said coldly and touched his saber hilt again.

"Hmm. Ah. And how's your health been since then?" the fat knight queried with grim irony. "Because you left in such a hurry that I didn't even have a chance to wish you God speed and a happy journey."

"And that bothered you?"

"Of course it bothered me. We'd have had a little more amusement because the company got a little larger." And here Pan Zagloba grinned with savage pleasure and pointed to little Pan Volodyovski. "That's the cavalier who joined us there so unexpectedly . . . I'm sure he'd like to get to know you better."

"Some other time," said Bohun and turned to the door.

But Pan Michal had enough of this private game of cat and mouse. "Stand where you are, traitor!" he shouted, leaping from his chair. "You're under arrest!"

"By what right?" the ataman demanded, raising his head proudly.

"Because you're a rebel, an enemy of the Commonwealth and a spy!"

"And who are you?"

"I don't have to introduce myself to the likes of you!" the small knight snapped. "I've got you where I want you, and that's that."

"We'll see about that!" The Cossack's eyes gleamed with that familiar yellow light that terrified Zagloba and his thin lips tightened under his long mustache. "I wouldn't even bother talking to you if you'd called me out, like a soldier, to fight you outside. You'd have found out on your own skin who and what I am! But since you come at me like a process server, threatening me with arrest, then I'll tell you who you're dealing with. I'm an envoy. I've got letters from the Hetman of the Zaporohjans to Prince Yan Casimir, and I'm to meet him in Zaborov which is where I'm going. So how are you going to arrest me now?"

Bohun looked down at the little knight with such disdain in his glowing eyes that Pan Michal didn't know what to say. He felt like a greyhound who had lost the scent of a running hare and turned an uncertain, questioning glance at Zagloba.

"An envoy?" the fat knight asked.

Bohun nodded and a long, heavy silence settled on the room.

"Ha! If that's so . . . if that's so,"—Pan Zagloba also looked suddenly nonplused and stood there blinking in worry and confusion,—"then you're safe from us . . . We can't touch you if you're an envoy, that's certain. But don't talk to that cavalier about fighting him because you already ran from him once! And you ran so hard that you lost your saber."

Blood mounted suddenly into Bohun's face. He recognized the small knight, remembered his bareback escape, and all his hurt pride and his damaged glory blazed up in him at once. The shame of that moment must have burned in the proud young Cossack like a fire, Pan Zagloba knew, and a new idea leaped up in his head.

"Oh yes," he taunted. "You ran so hard it's a miracle you didn't loose your breeches! *Tfui*, ataman, aren't you ashamed? You've a face as pretty as a woman's and it looks like you've got a woman's heart as well! You were brave enough with the old *Knahina* and a baby princeling, but when it comes to a real knight you skedaddle like a jackrabbit in a cabbage patch! You'd better stick to running errands, carrying other people's letters and abducting girls who can't defend themselves, not going to war. I tell you, fellow, I almost fell off that barn roof laughing at the way your drawers were drooping! You'd have lost them for sure if this cavalier hadn't felt sorry for a miserable, skulking wretch like you and let you get away! *Tfui, tfui* I say. And even now you talk about fighting when you're carrying letters! How are we to fight you when you hide behind a piece of paper? It's all hot air, my little Cossack warrior. You're not fooling us. You're about as much of a real man as a gust of wind. I admit that Hmyel's a good soldier when he's sober and Krivoinos is something to reckon with as well. But you? Ha! What a joke! There are just too many worthless fakes among you Cossacks, that's certain!"

Bohun's grim face flushed with rage and he took a violent step towards Zagloba who jumped with equal swiftness behind Volodyovski so that the two young men stood face to face, confronting each other.

"I didn't run from you out of fear," Bohun hissed down at the little knight. "But to save my people."

"Who cares why you ran?" Pan Michal shrugged, sensing which way Pan Zagloba's strategy was heading. "You ran, that's enough for anybody."

"I'll fight you anywhere," Bohun ground out between his teeth. "Anytime. Here and now, if you want."

"But you've those letters to deliver," Pan Zagloba prodded.

"That's my business. Somebody else can deliver them if that's what I want."

"Are you calling me out, then?" Pan Michal asked softly.

"You took my fame from me!" the Cossack snarled with a mad white light gleaming in his eyes. "You've shamed me before my own people! I want your blood for that!"

"Suit yourself." Volodyovski shrugged. "I'll fight you right now if that's what you want."

"'*Volenti non fit iniuria,*'" Pan Zagloba quoted from the statutes and grinned from ear to ear. "If an envoy wants to lay aside his privileges of immunity and challenges another man to fight a duel that ought to be his business. But who'll deliver that letter to Prince Yan Casimir?"

"Let me worry about that," Bohun said.

"Well, fight then, if that's how it has to be," Pan Zagloba said and laughed happily. "And if your luck holds good with this gentleman, Master Ataman, then I'll face you next! And now, Michal, step outside for a minute, will you? I've something important to talk to you about."

★ ★ ★

The two friends went outside, called Kushel from his post under Bohun's window, and then Pan Zagloba confided what still troubled him.

"Here's the thing. We've some real problems. I think he really is carrying letters to the King-elect so if we kill him it's a hanging matter. Remember that the edict against duels is good for two miles around the polling booths or the monarch's person and he's an envoy too. So we'll either have to hide somewhere afterwards, or Prince Yeremi will have to take us under his protection, or it'll be our necks. On the other hand how can we let him go? Seems to me this is our best chance to rescue our poor girl; she'll be easier to look for once that Devil is under the ground where he belongs. It's almost as if God himself is stepping in to help her and Skshetuski. But let's give some thought to how we're to do this without joining Bohun on a gibbet as a tidbit for the crows."

"Can't you think of something?" Kushel asked.

"I've already got him to toss out a challenge, haven't I? But we need witnesses, somebody impartial. My thought is to wait for Kharlamp. I'm sure he'll agree to wait his turn and, if necessary, to testify that Bohun challenged us and that we just had to defend ourselves. We'd better also find out where Bohun hid the girl. If he's to die then he shouldn't care one way or another what happens to her so maybe he'll tell us under some kind of oath. We've got to figure it all out very carefully because there's a lot at stake."

"Who's to fight him, then?" Kushel asked.

"Michal goes first and I'm second," Pan Zagloba said.

"So I'll be third."

"No way," Pan Michal said. "I'll do the fighting and that'll be that. If he cuts me down that's his good luck. Let him go in peace."

"Hmm. I already told him I'm going to fight him," Pan Zagloba muttered, recalling suddenly that Bohun was one of the best swordsmen among the Cossacks, cursing his own quick tongue and regretting his misguided impulse. "But if you gentlemen think that's the thing to do then I'll withdraw my offer."

"That's up to Bohun," said the little knight. "But you and me are the only people he'll have to face today."

"So be it then," Kushel said. "Let's go back inside."

"So be it."

★ ★ ★

They found Bohun sipping a glass of mead in the main room of the tavern. The young ataman had regained control over himself and returned to a cold, indifferent calmness.

"Listen to me a minute," Zagloba began. "These are serious matters. You called out this cavalier so you can have your duel but you're also an envoy and nobody can fight you unless you announce before witnesses that you challenged us out of your own free will. There'll be a few gentry coming here soon with whom we were to have another such meeting so you can make your declarations before them. We on our part will give you our word that if things go well for you with Pan Volodyovski you'll go free and nobody will get in your way unless you also want to try your hand with me."

"Agreed," Bohun said and shrugged. "I'll say what must be said in front of that gentry. I'll also tell my own people to deliver Hmyel's letters if I'm killed and to pass the word to Hmyelnitzki that it was me who called you out so he'll have no complaints. But if God lets me repair my Cossack fame with this here cavalier then I'll ask *you*, my old drinking partner, to dance a little dance with me as well."

He looked up and stared so hard into Pan Zagloba's eyes that the fat knight lost his composure for a moment, coughed, and covered his confusion by spitting on the floor.

"Agreed," he replied. "When you've tried your hand with my pupil here then you'll know what kind of work you'll have with me. But no matter. There's another item, and a more important one, in which we're appealing to your conscience as if you were a gentleman yourself. You're only a Cossack, we know that, but we're ready to treat you like one of ourselves."

"Kind of you," the ataman grunted with contempt.

"Well, here's the thing. You carried off the Princess Helen Kurtzevitchovna, the fiancee of a friend of ours, and you have her hidden somewhere in the Wild Lands. That's '*raptus puellae*' by the statutes, a capital crime, and you'd hang for it no matter what kind of an ambassador Hmyelnitzki made out of you. But we're going to fight you, not accuse you, and you might give some thought to what'll happen to her if you should get killed. You claim to love her. Well and good. So prove it. D'you want to deprive her of all care and protection? D'you want to doom her to shame and misfortune even when you're gone? Are you going to be her oppressor even in your grave?"

Here Pan Zagloba's voice rose to a tone of such quiet dignity and judgment that it surprised everyone and Bohun was suddenly pale with a deep and thoughtful contemplation of his own.

"What do you want from me, then?" he asked finally.

"Tell us where you hid her so that if you're killed we can find her and take her to her future husband. God will have mercy on your soul if that's what you do."

The young ataman rested his pale forehead in his palms, his elbows on the table, and plunged into thought while the three companions watched the sudden changes that flashed across his face. There was so much sadness in those softened features, and such a depth of feeling in those dimmed, dark eyes as if neither cruelty, savagery nor fury had ever twisted that handsome mask with hatred. No one spoke, as if afraid to break that spell of unexpected humanity, and the long silence went on until Zagloba's shaking voice creaked through it in a painful worry of his own.

"But if you've already shamed her," he went on, resigned, "then at least let that poor girl find shelter in some Holy House . . ."

Bohun looked up then. His eyes were wet with tears and dark with pain and longing.

"Shame her?" he asked in a soft sing-song voice. "Me? Ey, I don't know how it is with you gentry. I don't know how you do your loving, all you *Pany* and lords and cavaliers. Me, I'm just a Cossack, like you said, but I kept her from both death and shame in Bar and then I hid her in the wilderness where she could be safe. I've watched over her like she was my own heart, my own soul . . . never lifted my hand to her . . . never shook a finger in her face! She never heard one harsh word from me! I went down on my knees before her like she was an icon . . . did what she wanted from me. '*Go!*' she told me, so I went, and that's all I saw of her because Mother War called me soon after and wouldn't let me go . . ."

"God will take that into account when it's time to judge you," Zagloba said, relieved. "But is she safe there? What about Krivoinos and the Tartars?"

"Krivoinos is still down around Kamyenetz. He sent me to Hmyelnitzki to ask if he's to go for Kudak next, and chances are he's already gone there. And that place where she's at, there's neither Cossacks nor Tartars anywhere there, nor any *Lahy* either. She couldn't be safer."

"Where is this place, then?"

"Alright then, I'll tell you. And I'll send word that she's to be given to you if it goes bad for me here. But you, in your turn, you've got to give me your own solemn word that if I live through this then you'll stop looking for her. You swear for yourselves and for Pan Skshetuski too and I'll tell you what you want to know."

The three friends stared at each other for a long, uncomfortable moment.

"We can't do that," Zagloba said at last.

"And why can't you do that?"

"Because Pan Skshetuski isn't here, that's why, and we can't make promises on his behalf. And anyway, there's no way any of us would ever give up searching for her even if you've hidden her under the earth!"

"That's right! There's no way we'll ever stop looking for her!" Volodyovski and Kushel cried out together.

"Is that so?" Bohun's dark brows drew angrily together and his eyes glittered with fury and contempt. "So that's the kind of trade you offer, is it? You, Cossack, tear out your heart and soul, throw away your life, and we'll give you the edge of the knife? You'll never see the day! What do you think anyway, that my Cossack saber isn't made of steel and that I'm dead already that you hop around me like a flock of vultures? Why should I be the one that dies here, and not you? You want my blood, do you? Well, I need some of yours! We'll see who gets his fill!"

"So you won't tell?

"Why should I tell you anything?" Bohun snarled. "To Hell with you all!"

"And to Hell with you! You deserve to be turned into carrion like a dog!"

"Try it!" the ataman said and rose to his full height while Kushel and Volodyovski leaped to their feet as well.

★   ★   ★

Fierce glances locked and chests heaved with anger and the scheduled duel might have turned into a taproom brawl if Pan Zagloba hadn't glanced out of the window and caught sight of new riders trotting into the yard.

"Kharlamp!" he cried. "Along with his witnesses! And in the nick of time!"

And a moment later the Lithuanian Light Horse officer and his two companions walked into the room.

Pan Zagloba took them aside to explain what had happened

and to ask for a short delay on the little knight's behalf while he fought the Cossack but at first the stubborn Kharlamp wouldn't hear of it.

"If this Cossack's as bad as you paint him we ought to chop him into mincemeat right now, all of us together, and then Volodyovski can fight me as arranged! Why stand on ceremony with a rebel and a peasant at that?"

The fat knight had to explain all over again why all the decencies had to be observed. The two Syeletzki brothers helped his arguments, being both reasonable and mature men, and finally the stubborn Lithuanian gave way.

"Have your delay, then," he told Volodyovski. "But make sure I'm next!"

Bohun, meanwhile, went to his own men and came back with *Esaul* Elyashenko, whom he told how he'd challenged the two Polish nobles, and that he was fighting them of his own free will, and then he made the same declaration before the irritated Kharlamp and the two Syeletzkis.

"We on our part," said Pan Volodyovski, "declare that if you win your fight with me it'll be up to you if you fight Pan Zagloba too. But nobody else is going to challenge you after us, nor will there be any mass attack upon you, and you'll be free to ride off wherever you want. That we swear to you, I and Pan Zagloba, and we ask everybody else here to give the same promise."

"We swear it," chorused Kharlamp and the two Syeletzkis.

Bohun then handed Hmyelnitzki's letters to *Esaul* Elyashenko with instructions for their delivery to the Polish King-elect in Zaborov.

"And if I fall here, old comrade, you're to tell both Hmyel and the *Lah* prince that it was by my doing, understand?" he went on in Ruthenian. "You're to say it was me that called out these two nobles, and that it wasn't by any treachery that they killed me. That's clear to you, is it?"

Elyashenko nodded, his dark face indifferent. But Pan Zagloba, who started watching these proceedings with rising anxiety, noted that the old Zaporohjan captain didn't seem at all worried about his ataman.

"Hmm. Could he be right?" he muttered to himself. "Is Pan Michal really the better swordsman here?"

All the songs and tales about Bohun's fame seemed to be

ringing in the fat knight's head all at the same time but the young Cossack ataman gave only a calm, cold nod to his subordinate and turned haughtily to the waiting gentry.

"Alright, then," he said. "It's time to see who's to die here today. We can start whenever you're ready."

"Yes, yes, it's time," all the others chorused. "Let's get on with it."

They tucked the long tails of their *kontush* coats into their broad sashes, slipped their curved *karabela* sabers under their arms, and trooped out of the tavern into the yard outside.

Chapter Fifty

THEN THEY WERE WALKING to the river that flowed through a thicket of gooseberries, brambles, wild roses, ferns and pine. November had already stripped the shrubs of leaves but the lower vegetation was so dense and dark that it seemed like a mourning veil thrown across the broad, empty fields to the woods beyond. The day was pale but calm with that Autumn sadness that suggests the end of things, the death of a season. The ebbing sun barely warmed the afternoon but it gilded the gaunt, bare branches and whitened the low yellow sand dunes that stretched on the right bank of the stream.

That's where they stopped and turned.

"This is the place for it," Pan Zagloba said. "Don't you think?"

"Agreed," said both the Cossack and the little knight.

Zagloba grew more fretful and uneasy with each step. At last he edged closer to Volodyovski and whispered: "Listen, Michal . . ."

But the small knight seemed preoccupied. "What is it now?"

"For God's sake, dear friend, do your best, will you? It's all in your hands."

"What is?"

"Skshetuski's fate. Helen's freedom. Your life and my own as well. Because, if God forbid, things don't go well for you then I won't be able to manage with that monster."

"So why did you offer to fight him?"

"Why? Why?" The fat knight threw up his arms, shrugged and cursed into his beard. "The Devil knows why! The words just popped out and there they were. I trust in you but I'm getting old, I'm short of breath and I get winded easily, while that young animal can leap about all day as if he had steel springs in his boot heels. That's a tough nut to crack, my friend."

"I'll do what I can," said the little knight.

"God guide you! Don't lose heart!"

"Eh . . .!" Pan Michal shrugged. "Don't worry too much about it."

One of the Syeletzki brothers came up to them then.

"That's a proud, stiff-necked beast, that Cossack of yours," he whispered in open admiration. "Do you see how he looks at us all? He's as nonchalant and haughty about all this as if he was our equal or even our superior. Ha! What mettle he's got! Seems to me like his mother must've looked too fondly at some noble."

"It's more likely some great lord got too fond of his mother," Pan Zagloba muttered.

"I think so too," Volodyovski said, and then the sand of the riverbank was crunching underfoot.

"This will do!" Bohun cried out suddenly.

"Alright. Let's take our places."

They halted in the dunes. The watching gentry formed a loose half-circle, giving the duelists room to dodge and leap and to swing their sabers, and Bohun and Volodyovski took their places face to face with some half a dozen yards of open ground between them.

A groan escaped Zagloba.

Volodyovski sighed.

He tapped the sandy soil with his foot to test how firm it was. He glanced carefully around to note all the rough, uneven spots which might trip a swordsman or cause him to stumble. It was easy to see that he wasn't leaving anything to chance. He was about to fight with the most famous warrior of the Ukraine, a man whose name was whispered with fear and rage in the Crimea itself, and one who inspired more of his People's folklore than any other man living in his time. Pan Michal, who thought of himself as just an ordinary, unimportant officer of dragoons, promised himself a great deal out of this duel. Either he'd die in a way that would be remembered far and wide as part of Bohun's legend, or he'd win undying renown for himself and perhaps become a legend of his own. Such things were vastly

important in his times, he knew, because they represented the
first steps in the gentry's progress towards advancement, lands,
offices, titles and position.

He took great pains to assess and memorize the various
features of the small arena in which the fight was going to take
place. He tested the direction of the wind and noted how the
riverside breeze shifted the soft, powdery sand along the dunes.
He sniffed and tasted the quality of the air.

"He's nervous," Pan Zagloba murmured to himself, misread-
ing Pan Michal's seriousness, and began to sweat. "He's lost his
confidence. It's all up with him and that means that it's all up
with me too . . .!"

Meanwhile Volodyovski began to unbutton his coat.

"It's cool out here," he observed. "But we'll get warmed up
soon."

Bohun nodded and followed his example. They threw off
their heavy outer garments and remained dressed in their boots,
shirts and breeches, and then each of them began to roll up his
right sleeve, baring his forearm to the elbow. Oh but how slight
and puny the little knight appeared beside the tall, broad shouldered ataman! He was, Pan Zagloba thought, so frail and under-
sized in comparison that he seemed hardly visible at all! The
witnesses looked uneasily at the Zaporohjan hero's deep chest
and at the thickly knotted muscles of his forearms, and the
image which leaped up unbidden in Pan Zagloba's anxious
mind was one of a stunted little rooster standing up to a giant
raptor.

Bohun's nostrils flared as if he could already smell the acrid
stench of spilled blood drifting in the air. His face appeared to
shorten as he ducked his forehead so that his thick black mane
fell across his brows. The saber quivered slightly in his iron grip
as he fixed his predatory eyes on his enemy and waited,
breathing evenly, for the command to start.

Pan Volodyovski peered once more at the edge of his saber,
holding it up against the light, and took up his stance.

"This is going to be simple murder," Kharlamp shrugged and
muttered to one of the Syeletzkis.

Then Pan Zagloba spoke out in a trembling voice: "In God's
name . . . begin!"

★   ★   ★

The sabers whistled through the air. The blades clanged together and, at once, the action shifted closer to the dunes. Bohun attacked so fiercely that Pan Volodyovski had to leap several paces backwards and the witnesses also stumbled back to keep their positions. The strokes of Bohun's saber fell as thick as hail. They seemed as swift as a blur of crisscrossing lightnings so that the observers' frightened eyes couldn't follow them; each watcher could have sworn that Pan Michal stood surrounded by a hissing, mobile wall of steel, and that God himself would be unable to protect him in that whirlwind of glittering thunder-bolts. The slashing blows created one continuous whirring in the heated air and a sudden wind warmed the observers' faces. The fury of the ataman's attack gave way to a wild, berserk rage as he drove Volodyovski into the dunes like chaff before a storm.

"It's hopeless," muttered Kharlamp.

"Hopeless," echoed one of the Syeletzki brothers. "He's as good as gone."

And '*Hopeless*,' thought the terrified Zagloba, peering at the mismatched fighters out of one half-closed eye and already seeing himself taking his own turn under Bohun's saber, while the little knight kept giving way before that attack.

Back and back he went. All the fury lay in Bohun's powerful assault while the small soldier merely defended himself. His outstretched right arm hardly seemed to move; only the hand turned and twisted in small, endless circles, and each of these timid, barely noticeable movements came so quickly one after another that they outstripped the watchers' ability to tell what was happening. His saber had the look of a fragile, moving shield which somehow managed to deflect the Zaporohjan's hurricane of blows but he offered no riposte of his own. He kept on retreating, his eyes fixed on the Cossack's, and as unruffled as the still waters in the center of a sea storm, but two vivid splotches appeared in his cheeks to betray the extent of his effort and his concentration.

Unable to watch this unequal contest, Zagloba closed his eyes. He could hear one stroke after another. He winced each time the sabers came together and metal slid and grated. He dreaded the expected, inevitable silence.

'*Ah* . . .,' he thought listening to the clang and clatter of the sabers and to the dull pounding of blood in his ears. '*So he's still fighting . . . still defending himself . . . But for how much longer?*'

"It can't be long now," whispered Kharlamp and the two Syeletzkis.

"He has his back against the dune already," Kushel murmured quietly.

Zagloba raised an eyelid and peered fearfully through the glittering lightnings of the Cossack's saber. Volodyovski was still on his feet. He had been backed all the way to a sand dune but he didn't appear to be wounded, not yet anyway. His flushed face seemed redder, that was all. A few beads of sweat were shining on his forehead, and the fat knight's heart leaped with a sudden hope.

'... *Ah*,' he thought, remembering all the other duels the little knight had fought. '*But Michal's also no mean player at this game ... And that other fellow's sure to get tired soon ...*'

Bohun's face was now seamed with oily, white lines and ridges. Sweat gleamed in his hair. But his small opponent's continuing resistance merely inflamed his fury. His long, white teeth flashed like a wolf's fangs under his sweated mustache and a snarling growl boiled up from his chest.

"You'll die," he grunted.

"You'll die," Volodyovski echoed in a lifeless tone.

He didn't take his eyes off Bohun for a moment. Then, feeling the sand dune brushing against his back, he twisted as if wounded so that the observers were certain he'd been hit at last; he stooped, crouched down and seemed to shrink into himself as if to gather the last of his strength, and then launched himself like a projectile from a catapult into the Cossack's chest.

"He's attacking!" Pan Zagloba shouted.

"He's attacking!" repeated the others.

It was now the Cossack ataman's turn to start a slow retreat while the little knight's lightning saber strokes seemed to shine and glitter everywhere around him. Having gauged and tested all of his opponent's skill and imagination, the small soldier was attacking with such unexpected vigor of his own that the observers watched with bulging eyes, hardly able to breathe with the excitement and surprise.

Pan Zagloba felt as if he'd suffocate with the sudden onrush of hope and relief. His heart seemed to climb into his throat. Volodyovski's little eyes, he noted, began to shine and twinkle. He seemed like a dancer. He leaped, dodged, crouched and twisted, never letting his cold, watchful gaze stray from his opponent. He changed his stance and position faster than the eye could follow, threatening the furious ataman from all sides at once and forcing him to turn in place like a raging but bewildered ox beset by a wolfpack.

"Ah, what a master!" Pan Zagloba cried.

"You'll die," Bohun grated out again.

"You'll die," Pan Michal echoed as before.

Suddenly Bohun did something that only the finest and most experienced swordsmen could attempt in combat; moving so swiftly that the watchers missed the blur of the flying metal, he hurled his saber into his own left hand and struck a terrible, slanting blow at his opponent's undefended side while Pan Michal fell to the ground as if struck by lightning.

"*Jezus Maria!*" Pan Zagloba shouted.

But the small soldier had thrown himself to the ground on purpose so that Bohun's saber whistled harmlessly through the empty air while he leaped up again, nimble as a wildcat, and brought the full length of his own saber blade crashing into the Cossack's open and unguarded chest.

Bohun staggered. He took one more stumbling step towards Volodyovski and struck out again, but Pan Michal knocked the blow aside like brushing away a fly. Then he stepped closer to the reeling Cossack and brought two more smashing blows across his bowed head. Bohun's saber slid out of his hand while the ataman toppled facedown into the sand which immediately started to turn scarlet with his blood.

Elyashenko, who was watching the fight along with the gentry, threw himself on the body of his ataman with a wail of mourning.

★ ★ ★

No one among the watching gentry could speak for some time. Pan Michal himself couldn't find either a word to say or the breath with which to say it. He stood with bowed head, leaning on his saber with both hands, and breathing heavily like a man who had run a long and difficult course, or a swimmer who had come safely to the shore of a great lake he'd crossed.

At last Pan Zagloba shook himself free of his dumbstruck wonder and broke the long silence.

"God bless you, lad," he murmured, shaking with emotion, and threw both his arms around the small soldier. "God take care of you!"

The others pressed forward then, each with his own expressions of praise and relief.

"What a fight!" cried the Syeletzki brothers. "And what a fighter you are, Devil take you! I've never seen anything like it, and neither has anybody else I know!"

"Talk about quiet waters," Kharlamp said. "Well . . . listen, I'll go up against you like we agreed, just so that people won't be able to say that I lost my nerve. But even if you slice me up the same way I've got to congratulate you now and wish you the best."

"Why don't the two of you forget about your fight?" Zagloba suggested. "Because, come to think of it, you don't have anything to bump heads about anyway, you know."

"No, no!" cried the Light Horse officer. "This is a matter of my reputation and that's a lot more important to me than my neck."

"I've no use for your neck, to tell you the truth," the small soldier said. "Why don't we just forget this quarrel of ours? I wasn't really trying to knock you out of the ring with Anusia, my friend. There's a lot better man than I who's likely to do that. I've nothing against you."

"You mean that?"

"You've my word on it."

"Alright," Kharlamp said and threw open both his arms so that the two knights could embrace like brothers. "Let it go then. I tell you, I'm full of admiration for you anyway. To do a job like this on a giant like that! And he was damn good with a saber in his own right!"

"He was a lot better than I expected," Pan Michal agreed. "That left-hand shift, that's rare. Where could he have learned it?"

Here all attention focussed on the fallen ataman whom Elyashenko now turned over on his back. The old *esaul's* bitter, weathered face was wet with tears as he searched his young commander for a sign of life. Bohun's own face was unrecognizable under the thick streams of blood that flowed from the two great wounds carved across his head which were already clotting in the chilly air. His slashed shirt-front was also red with blood. But he was still breathing. His legs jerked and twitched as if he was in the grip of his death-throes and his crooked fingers clawed at the sand like talons.

Zagloba gave him one quick glance and shrugged his great shoulders. "He's done for," he said.

"That's right," said one of the Syeletzkis looking at the body. "That's a corpse already."

"With wounds like that, there's no hope for him," the other agreed.

"Pity," Pan Michal murmured.

"Pity? You have pity for him?"

"He was a great knight in his own way," the small soldier said.

"Hmm. Yes." Pan Zagloba muttered. "I ought to know a little about that . . ."

★ ★ ★

Meanwhile the weeping Elyashenko tried to lift and carry the huge, bloody body, but he couldn't do it. He was a slight, thin, narrow-shouldered man and long past his prime while the young ataman had been practically a giant. The tavern stood a good half mile away and the broken, sandy soil of the riverbank made walking difficult even for a young man.

"*Pany, pomojhite!*" he begged in Ruthenian, pressing his hands together as if he were praying. "Give us a hand, masters! By God and his Mother, don't let him die here in the sand like a dog! I'm an old man, I can't make it by myself, and my people are a ways off . . . *Na Spasa, na Svyatuyu* . . . Help me!"

The gentry looked at each other for a moment but all their bitterness and hatred for the Cossack had ebbed long before.

"It just isn't fitting for us to leave him here like a dead dog," Pan Zagloba muttered. "If he was good enough for us to fight him then we have to treat him like a soldier, not a rebel peasant. Am I right on that?"

"As Gospel!" said Kharlamp and the two Syeletzkis. "That's the least we can do."

"Yes." Pan Zagloba nodded. "Let him breathe his last decently in a bed like a human being. Who'll help me carry him, gentlemen?"

"I will," Volodyovski said.

"So will I," said Kushel.

"Use my coat for a stretcher," Kharlamp offered.

A moment later Bohun lay on the long, outspread *kontush* coat of the Lithuanian captain with Zagloba, Volodyovski,

Kushel and Elyashenko grasping the four corners, and the whole group began its slow return to the tavern.

"Look at the way that hard, stubborn soul is hanging on," Pan Zagloba said nodding down at Bohun. "He's still breathing, still trying to move. My God, if anyone had told me I'd ever become his nursemaid I'd say he was trying to make a fool out of me. Ah, I'm too soft-hearted, that's always been my trouble. But what can I do? I'll even dress his wounds for him when we get there. I've good reason to hope that he and I won't cross paths in this world again so let him think kindly of me in the next one."

"So you think there's no way for him to recover?" Pan Kharlamp asked.

"Him? Look at him! I wouldn't give an old dishrag for his chances. That life's finished. Well, well, that's the way it must've been written for him . . . that's the way it was supposed to be. Because even if he managed to get through Pan Volodyovski he'd have to go up against me and that would've been his end and no mistake. But I'm glad I didn't have to kill him because there's enough gossip about me as it is. People say I've no mercy. That I'm too hot-blooded and too quick to fight. But what am I to do if somebody gets in my way? Tell me, what?"

"Not much," Kharlamp agreed. "That's how it is with all of us gentry, I expect. If somebody treads on our coat-tails we fight him and that's all there's to it."

"Hmm. Well. I wish that's all there *was* to it. I've had to pay five hundred ducats in compensation to Pan Duntchevski," Zagloba complained. "And our Ruthenian lands don't bring much income nowadays, you know."

"That's right," Pan Kharlamp nodded solemnly. "They really plundered you fellows over there, didn't they."

"Genghis Khan could've taken lessons from them!" the fat knight exclaimed. "There hasn't been any looting like that anywhere on earth since the Greeks took Troy! I hope the new Diet will think of some relief for us or we'll all lose our bellies before a lot longer . . ."

Then he wheezed, snorted, sniffed and took a deep breath as his attention shifted to the dying Bohun.

"Phew! That's a heavy carcass, and no mistake. I've quite lost my wind. Hah, look! He's bleeding again! Why won't he just give up and die and be done with it? And why don't you go ahead, Mister Kharlamp, and tell the Jew to knead some bread and cobwebs so I can glue all those wounds together? It won't resurrect the corpse, at least I hope it doesn't, but it's a Christian thing to do and maybe he'll die a little easier."

Pan Kharlamp strode out briskly ahead and when, at long last, they carried Bohun into the Jew's tavern, the rough field dressing of mixed cobwebs and thick, moist black bread was ready for Zagloba. The fat knight got to work at once with the skill of long practice and experience. He dammed the blood-flow, plastered the yeasty mixture to the open wounds where it would start its mysterious healing process in a day or two, drawing out the poisons and cooling the fever. Bohun was too far gone too recover, he was sure, but he found a strange consolation in trying to help him.

Then he turned to the grief-stricken Elyashenko.

"Nobody needs you here," he said. "Your ataman is as good as dead. So get on your way to Zaborov, beg to see our new King-elect, give him Hmyel's letters and tell him everything you saw and heard here. Understand?"

The old Cossack nodded but he didn't move.

"And if you lie about any of it, I'll know it!" Pan Zagloba threatened. "Because I'm a close friend and confidant of his Royal Highness and he tells me everything! You say one word out of line to anyone and I'll have your head for a trophy and your carcass stuffed with straw to use for a scarecrow, you hear me?"

"I'll tell it like it was," the old Zaporohjan muttered, wiping away his tears.

"See that you do. Then, when you're done with your mission and back with Hmyelnitzki, give him my regards because he and I go back a long way together and he loves me like a brother. Is that clear too? Hmm?"

And then because the old *esaul* seemed unable to tear himself away from his commander's body, the fat knight went on in a kinder tone.

"Look," he said. "It's all over here with your ataman. He's done for. There's nothing more you can do for him. We'll give him a decent burial so his black soul won't have to wander around at night scaring decent people. You just make sure you do what he told you. Don't waste time, don't hang around anywhere too long, and don't get in anybody's way or you'll get chopped up into chicken feed before you can explain what you're all about. Now get out of here and take care of yourself until you've done your job. Go, will you? Go!"

"Can't I stay with him till the body's cold, at least?" the old Cossack begged.

"On your way, I tell you!" roared Zagloba. "Or I'll have the peasants drag you to Zaborov on a rope!"

Elyashenko sighed, bowed to the waist and left, and the fat knight turned to Kharlamp and the two Syeletzkis.

"Well, that's that," he said. "I've sent off that Cossack because the sooner he gets to His Royal Highness the better. Someone is sure to spot him for a Zaporohjan and turn him into mincemeat before very long and we'll get blamed for it. All the boot-lickers and pen-pushers who hang around Prince Dominic Zaslavski and the chancellor would howl to high heaven that Vishnovyetzki's men murdered an entire Cossack embassy. That's all our Prince would need! But a wise head can stop a wagging tongue before it gets going."

"And yours," said Kushel with immense respect, "is one of the wisest."

"You think so, eh? I agree. God knows which barrel to fill with oil and which with dishwater. And you, gentlemen, also keep yourselves ready to testify that he challenged us."

"We'll be ready," chorused Kharlamp and the two Syeletzkis.

"All that's left now is Bohun's funeral," Pan Zagloba said. "I'll have a word with the local elders over in the village. They'd have no way of knowing who he really was. They'll think he was a noble and plant him decently enough, I expect. Meanwhile, Michal, you and I and Kushel had better get our story to Prince Yeremi first-hand before some envious little tongues start wagging with gossip."

Here Bohun's weak, rattling breath broke into Pan Zagloba's monologue.

"Aha!" the fat knight said softly, nodding to the others. "Here's another soul asking the way to the next world, do you hear? Eh?"

"God give it rest," Volodyovski said.

"Hmm." The fat knight shivered. "It's getting dark outside already. Cold too. That poor, doomed spirit will have to grope his way along like a blind beggar on a country highway. But since the fellow didn't hurt or dishonor our poor girl then may he find his way, and may God give him eternal rest and show mercy to his soul. I forgive him all his sins against me. Gladly. From the heart . . . Although,"—and here Pan Zagloba's voice took on a somewhat shamed and troubled tone—"to tell the whole truth, I caused him a lot more trouble than he ever did me. But that's all over now. So . . . God be with him."

"Amen," the others chorused.

"And now, gentlemen, let's all be on our way."

The six nobles quickly gathered their coats and sabers, went outside, mounted their horses and rode off into the falling darkness.

Chapter Fifty-one

PRINCE YEREMI took the news of the duel with comparative indifference especially when he heard there were impartial witnesses ready to swear that it was Bohun who issued the challenge. If the affair took place before the election, while the political infighting was still going on, his enemies would have turned it into a weapon against the Vishnovyetzkis; the chancellor and Prince Dominic would have seen to that. But after Charles Ferdinand's withdrawal from the race everyone's thoughts turned to other matters and the incident was unlikely to cause serious trouble. True, Hmyelnitzki could complain. He'd be sure to use the sabering of his ambassador as an example of the gentry's high-handed mistreatment of Ukrainian people. But if the King-elect explained what happened in his reply to Hmyelnitzki's letter, the cunning Hetman of the Zaporohjans wouldn't make much of a fuss about it.

Moreover, the report of Bohun's death had a pleasing aspect for the Prince; he was sad to see the end of such a famous soldier but it would make the search for Skshetuski's girl much less dangerous and her recovery more certain. If she was found, her freedom could be won either with the sword or by simple ransom, something that would have been impossible while Bohun was alive. And the Prince would gladly spend whatever was needed to bring some happiness again into the grim and bitter life of his favorite soldier.

Going to see the Prince, Pan Michal had no way of knowing that his terrifying master stood ready to reward him or, at least, to dismiss the dueling infraction as a trivial matter. He feared few people—indeed, the little knight didn't really understand the meaning of fear—but a single frown on Vishnovyetzki's forehead was likely to make his knees shake as badly as an erring schoolboy's. So he was open-mouthed with surprised relief when the Prince-Palatine heard his report, pondered its implications for a moment, and then pulled a costly ring off his finger and dropped it into Volodyovski's palm.

"You did well not to kill him out of hand," he said. "There'd have been a lot of harmful squabbling in the Diet about it. But if this helps Skshetuski to find and free his princess then you've earned my gratitude as well as his."

"It was a fair duel, Highness," Pan Zagloba stated.

"I don't doubt it if you had a hand in it." Prince Yeremi smiled at the fat knight, then nodded slyly at the little one. "I'm told that just as some people find it hard to keep a still tongue in their heads so you've a problem in keeping your sword in its scabbard. But since this time you drew it on a friend's behalf, and since you've upheld the reputation of our Transdnieper gentry against such a warrior, take this ring to remind you of this day. I knew you were a fine soldier and a first-rate swordsman, but now it's clear that you're a real master."

"Him?" Pan Zagloba cried. "He'd cut the horns off the Devil in three strokes! If Your Highness ever orders me beheaded I'll ask that you tell him to do it. That way, at least, I'll get to the next world in one jump! He split Bohun's chest just about in two and then, for good measure, sliced him across the brain a couple of times as well."

The Prince smiled again.

"Have you ever found anyone as good as you?"

"With a saber, H-h-ighness?" The little knight was stammering with pleasure at this unexpected kindness.

"Saber, straight-sword, rapier, anything."

"Skshetuski put a notch in me one time, and I did the same to him that day Your Highness had us locked up in the guard-house, if you deign to remember . . . Pan Podbipyenta would probably hold his own against me, being such a strongman . . . and Kushel would do well enough if he had better eyes."

"Don't you believe him, Highness," Zagloba broke in. "Nobody can stand up against him!"

"Was Bohun hard to beat?"

"He forced me to do my best," Pan Michal said. "He even knew how to change hands for the left-hand stroke."

Feeling left out of the conversation, Pan Zagloba dared to intrude again. "Bohun told me himself that he used to fight all day for practice with the Kurtzevitch princes. And I watched him do it in Tchehryn with my own eyes."

"Listen, Volodyovski," the Prince said with mock solemnity. "Why don't you go to Zamost and challenge Hmyelnitzki? You'd free the Commonwealth from all her pains and troubles with one blow."

"Gladly, Highness." Pleased beyond measure, the little knight grinned from ear to ear. "If only Hmyelnitzki would take up my challenge."

But the warm, easy smile began to ebb from Prince Yeremi's face and the weight of his burdens settled again on his frail shoulders. "Ay, here we're making jokes and the world is dying. But you'll have to go to Zamost anyway. I've word from the Cossack camp that Hmyelnitzki will drop his siege of Zamost and pull back to the east just as soon as Prince Yan Casimir is proclaimed as King. He's losing too many men against those defenses and here's a good, face-saving chance to show his supposed loyalty to the new sovereign and the Commonwealth."

"Hmyel's loyalty is to Hmyel," Pan Zagloba said. "It's never been anything else with him."

"Tell that to the chancellor," the Prince said and shrugged. "Anyway, an armistice is now certain. We'll have to stand down so that Pan Kisyel can resume his talking. But this spell of peace will give Skshetuski a chance to search for his girl. So go to Zamost, tell him what happened here and give him my permission to pick whatever men he needs from the troops I left with *Starosta* Veyher. I'll give you a letter for him, granting him leave to go. If no other good comes from all that shameful pleading with murderers and looters perhaps Skshetuski will be able to find joy in his life again."

Moved, Volodyovski fell to his knees. "Your Highness is a father to us all," he cried. "And that's why we'll all serve you to our dying breath."

"I don't know how well you'll be eating in that service soon, my friend," Prince Yeremi said with a bitter smile. "There will be some lean and hungry days when my Transdnieper fortune is gone altogether. But while there's still something left in my coffers you're all welcome to it."

★ ★ ★

Pan Michal and Zagloba made their way out into the avenue as soon as their audience with the Prince was over.

"Well, we've wormed our way out of that spot of trouble!" The fat knight grinned and threw his arm across the small knight's shoulder. "You can be sure of promotion and advancement from now on, Master Michal, I'll bet my last pair of boots on that. Let's take a look at that ring. By God, that's worth at least a hundred and fifty gold ducats if I'm any judge. That stone's a real beauty. Let's go to the bazaar and ask the Armenians how much they'll give us for it."

Shocked as if Zagloba had just blasphemed God and all the saints, Pan Michal stared at him in horror. "That's Prince Yeremi's ring!"

"Well it's not mine, that's certain!" Pan Zagloba smiled. "But it'll help to fill my grumbling belly as well as yours if you've any sense. Remember the soldier's maxim, my young friend: '*Today's barracks are tomorrow's coffins.*' Or if you'd like to hear it said another way: '*Yesterday's medal is tomorrow's cross.*' Either way it means that a smart man lives one day at a time and lets his tomorrows take care of themselves. Life's short, my good Michal! But what counts is that from now on the Prince is going to keep an eye on your future."

"He will?" The little knight was still unable to believe that he had finally won the great *Voyevode's* favor. And then the bright, distant image of the Princess Barbara glowed for a moment in his dazzled mind.

"He'd give ten times the value of that ring to make Skshetuski happy," Pan Zagloba said and peered slyly at his small companion. "And you did the job for him at one stroke, didn't you. So what's one little ring in those circumstances? Not too much, I'd say. No, not much at all."

"It's a great honor," Volodyovski said and looked at the ring as reverently as if it were an icon, while Pan Zagloba threw him a quick sideways glance and chuckled softly inside his own beard.

"You can expect greater rewards than that," he said. "Believe me. Hasn't the Prince leased half a hundred freehold villages to

his various courtiers? Hasn't he given a dozen good estates in
outright grants to others? That ring is nothing compared to
what might come your way. Why,"—and here the fat knight let
his eyelid drop innocently over his good eye—"he might even
see his way to marrying you to some kinswoman of his."

Hit unexpectedly right where he was most vulnerable, the
little knight gulped, gasped and tripped on the cobblestones. He
would have tumbled nose-first into the gutter if the grinning
old noble hadn't caught him by the collar, lifted him in the air
like a struggling cat, and set him down on his feet again.

"How did you guess . . .!" the redfaced little knight began
and then bit down on his mustache.

"Hmm? How did I guess what?" Pan Zagloba asked.

"Nothing! Nothing!"

"There seems to be a great deal of humming and hawing over
nothing, then."

"All I meant," Pan Michal hurried to correct himself. "That is
to say I just meant to ask where you could get such a wild idea?
Me? Married to his kinswoman? How could something like that
happen, anyway?"

"What's so unusual about it?"

The fat knight grasped his small friend by the arm and started
to steer him firmly in the direction of the Armenian quarter.

"Aren't we all equals?" he went on. "And doesn't just about
every *magnatus* have a whole flock of blood-relatives among the
lesser gentry whom he marries off to his more deserving courtiers? I've heard that Suftchinski, the freeholder of Syentcha, is
married to some distant cousin of the Vishnovyetzkis so why
couldn't something like that happen to you as well?"

"Because I'm not high enough for that threshold!" the desperate small knight burst out.

"Yes. Hmm. There I agree. You are a little hard to see
sometimes, particularly in a crowd. But if you can't be *seen*
without a lot of eye-strain, you can make yourself *heard* about
and that's what matters in the long run. See, we're all blood-
brothers in the gentry, Michal, all of us great or small, because
we're all descended from the high-born Japhteh just as peasants
and other lesser people come to us from Hem. The only difference between you and me and the *magnateria* lies in their
wealth and offices and positions and that's something any one of
us can reach by hard work and merit."

"Yes, but a marriage . . . Me? To the Vishnovyetzkis . . .?"

"Why not? I hear there are different grades and categories of nobles in other countries," Zagloba held forth, catching fire from his own exposition but careful to steer it just where he wanted it to go. "Just as they've different kinds of dogs in a royal kennel. Greyhounds for chasing wild hares and foxes and other kind of vermin. Yapping poodles that snap at the ankles. Mastiffs for chasing off the Jews who come for their money and pit bulls for bear-baiting. Terriers, ratters, sniffing bloodhounds and God knows what else. They even have lapdogs, I am told."

"So what?"

"So this! It all makes sense in France, Spain, England and among the Germans, which is why their nobility is such a flea-bitten lot of mongrels ready to snatch at any bone a King might toss their way. But here, thank God, we don't have differences in scale and degree, one nobleman isn't any more noble than another, and every one of us can become a King if he is elected."

"Yes, yes, I see all that," Pan Michal said, somewhat mystified by this booming flood of rhetoric, and feeling that he was being drawn into a trap that he couldn't see. "But the Vishnovyetzkis . . . that's almost royal blood!"

"And you, my dear Michal, couldn't you be elected to the throne? Hmm? I'd be the first to vote for you if that's what I felt like. Just like Pan Zygmunt Skarjhevski who swears he'll vote only for himself if he can just stay sober and keep away from the dice long enough to do it. I tell you, everything is '*in liberis suffragiis*' with us in this Commonwealth, we all have an equal say about everything that matters, and the only reason why you wouldn't be elected is that your pockets are full of holes and those of our King-elect rattle with gold ducats."

"Well, there you are." Pan Michal heaved a sigh. "We may all be equal under the law but some of us sit higher along the table than the rest."

"That's true."

Pan Zagloba nodded and hung his head in gloom but his sharp eye glittered sideways nonetheless.

"It all comes down to money, wealth, lands, influence and position. I'd take a well-stocked larder and a decent cellar any day but even that's out of a poor man's reach. And is it our fault that we have empty pockets? Haven't we been robbed, looted and plundered of everything we owned, all the while shielding the whole Commonwealth with our naked bodies? Ah, it's enough to make a man desperate enough to join up with Hmyelnitzki! I tell you, we'll be in sad straits if the Diet doesn't come up soon with some kind of pension!"

"Well, poverty isn't yet a hanging offense," the little knight observed.

"Maybe not but it's never been a cause for a celebration," Pan Zagloba said and played his final card. "It's a good thing we have that ring of yours. It'll at least let us drown our misery in a little wine if you peddle it."

★   ★   ★

Talking like that they came to the Old City and stepped into a wineshop in front of which a few dozen serving lads held the coats and cloaks of their masters who were drinking their morning cups inside. They found a quiet corner near the tiled stove, ordered a demijohn, and sat down at a secluded table to decide what they should do as a result of Bohun's death in Lipkov.

"If it really happens that Hmyelnitzki pulls back from Zamost and there's peace again then Helen's as good as ours," Pan Zagloba said.

"We ought to get back to Skshetuski as soon as we can. Then we'll stick to him like thistles to a dog's tail until we've found the girl and that'll be that."

"Of course we'll stick with him. That goes without saying. Only it's going to be hard to get to Zamost for a while longer."

"That doesn't matter. We'll get there. What counts is that God should help us in our search afterwards."

Pan Zagloba emptied his glass and refilled it. "He will, he will!" he said. Then he closed his eyes and smiled with satisfaction.

"You know something, Michal?" he asked after a while.

"What's that?"

"Bohun's dead."

Volodyovski stared at him in amazement. "Who should know that better than I?" he asked.

"I know, I know." Zagloba looked at the little soldier with genuine affection. "God gave you a miraculous hand, my lad, even though He skimped on the rest of your body. I watched you cutting down that monster, and I see you now, and I've got to say it to myself over and over because it seems no more believable to me now than it did then. Bohun's dead! How much suffering is gone all at once! What a terrible knot of worry you've severed at a blow!"

"God's will," said the little knight but Pan Zagloba couldn't be restrained.

"I'm quite lost for words," he confessed. "I don't know how to tell you what this means to me and to the rest of us. Ah, what's the harm in being sentimental? Come here my dear boy, let me give you another good hug! I can't believe that when I first caught sight of you I thought you were a paltry little whippet. Dear God, some whippet, that could chew up a Bohun! Ah, ah, he's gone, it's all over with him! There is no more Bohun! He is dead and buried for all time, for ever and for ever, amen!"

Here Pan Zagloba began to hug Volodyovski, while the little knight whose sentimental heart was easily moved to tears after a jug of wine, sniffed and snuffled into the old noble's collar.

Finally he freed himself from his friend's embrace and reminded the overjoyed old knight that they weren't there when Bohun breathed his last. "He's a tough, husky fellow, you know. What if he recovers?"

"For God's sake, what are you saying, man?" Pan Zagloba cried. "I'm ready to gallop to Lipkov tomorrow and pay for the finest funeral anyone's ever seen if only that should send him faster on his way!"

"What would you go there for? If he's dead, he's dead. If he's still alive there won't be anything you can do about it. You can't finish off a wounded man like common cut-throat."

"I sometimes wish I hadn't been born a noble!" the fat knight exclaimed. "Life would've been a lot simpler if I'd been whelped in some peasant hut without a sense of what is right and proper. But do you think it's possible that he's still alive?"

"You can never tell with a saber wound," the little knight observed. "If you don't die straight away there's a good chance you might lick your way back to health someday. A sword cut isn't like a bullet in the head."

"No, no, that couldn't happen in this case!" Pan Zagloba struggled to reassure himself. "I heard the death-rattle starting up when we were riding off. He's got to have died! I dressed his wounds myself and I never saw anything more deadly. His chest was split wide open, ribs and all, like a tavern door on market day."

"He was a pretty rugged fellow, you know," Pan Michal said again.

"Don't I know it? But rugged or not, you split that brute like a pig for stuffing, he's gone and there's no point talking anymore about him. What we've got to do is get to Skshetuski as quickly as we can, tell him the good news and help him find his Helen. If we don't, he might die himself out of sheer grief."

"Or worse," Pan Michal offered, sniffing tearfully into his mug of wine. "He might become a monk."

"Ay, and why wouldn't he? I'd do the same in his place, I expect. I don't know a better man, I tell you, but I've never known one with greater misfortunes. God gave him a heavy cross to bear, and that's no mistake."

"Enough, my friend, enough!" wept the little soldier. "I can't stand to think any more about it."

"And do you think I can?"

And here the fat knight bellowed with his own sentimental tears.

"Such a decent fellow," he sniffed. "Such a faithful soldier . . . and she's . . . ah, you don't know her my dear friend . . . such a dear little flower, she is . . . such a sweetheart!"

His low basso hooted in counterpoint to Volodyovski's thin, sentimental snuffling because he really loved Helen as if she was his own only child. They sipped their wine mixed with the salty tears that ran down their whiskers, and then they had to drink another flagon to wash away the taste of the tears, and then they sat in bleary-eyed, alcoholic gloom with their heads drooping down on their chests.

Then Pan Zagloba looked up and slammed his fist on the table until the glasses jumped.

"Why are we crying?" he asked.

"I don't know," said Volodyovski.

"Bohun's dead."

"Hey, that's right," Volodyovski said.

"We should be laughing, dancing, jumping up and down! This is a cause for a celebration! We'll be a couple of dim-wits if we can't find our sweet girl after this!"

"Let's go, then!" Pan Michal said and staggered to his feet.

"First thing tomorrow!" corrected Pan Zagloba. "Let's have another demijohn to drink to Pan Yan and my little sweetheart! God will see to it that we'll dance at their wedding and then we'll stand as godfathers to their children. And do you know why?"

"Why?" asked Volodyovski.

"It'll be all because we've sent that monster Bohun into the next world."

"And a good thing too," Volodyovski said, not noticing that Pan Zagloba already managed to give himself a share of credit in the death of Bohun.

Chapter Fifty-two

THEN AT LAST the '*Te Deum Laudamus*' echoed in the choir of St. John's Cathedral, a new King was proclaimed, bells rang, the cannons shook the walls, and hope began to enter the hearts of the people.

The unsettled times of the interregnum were over. The regency had ended. The stormy days of public distress and disorder, all the more worrisome because they had come in the midst of a general catastrophe, were as good as gone. Those who had grown sick at heart at the thought of the dangers that threatened the country could draw a thankful breath of relief; it seemed for many as if the terrors of the Civil War had passed into history and that all the new monarch needed to do now was to sit in judgment and punish the guilty, and Hmyelnitzki himself fed this universal hope. The vast masses of his Zaporohjans proclaimed their loyalties to King Yan Casimir and the Commonwealth even as they stormed the walls of Zamost and went on pillaging the country, while their shrewd leader sent the King fervent letters of submission along with humble pleas for mercy for himself and his followers. Everyone knew that the King would follow Chancellor Ossolinski's policy of conciliation, and everyone hoped that after so many terrible calamities the Commonwealth would breathe freely once again and find the time to heal all her wounds.

Then, in quick succession, came the news of Pan Smyarovski's mission to the Cossacks which was to prepare the ground for negotiations, the new King sent Hmyelnitzki a letter promising him justice, and soon afterwards came word that the

Cossacks turned their backs on Zamost and started their long retreat into the Ukraine. They were to wait quietly in their own new country for the Diet's orders and for a royal commission which was to look into their grievances. It seemed to many as if a glorious, multicolored rainbow rose above the country, as if the dreadful storm had finally blown away, and as if the healing sunshine of peace was about to follow.

True, there were some threatening prophecies and signs here and there. But the visible new reality seemed so promising that few people paid attention to warnings and omens. The freshly chosen sovereign of eight million Poles, Lithuanians and Ruthenians took the road to Yasna Gora, to thank God's Mother at her greatest shrine for his elevation, then he began his stately royal progress to the ancient capital of Krakow where he was to be crowned. The lords and dignitaries followed him. The lesser gentry scattered. Warsaw became as still and silent as if a plague had swept it clean of people, and soon the only wanderers in its quiet, grey streets were the homeless exiles from the East who either didn't dare to go home to their ruined country or who had nothing left to which to return.

Prince Yeremi, as a senator of the Commonwealth, had to follow the King. Volodyovski and Zagloba, leading a well-manned and equipped new regiment of dragoons, set out by rapid marches towards Zamost, in a hurry to bring Skshetuski the news of Bohun's death and then to help him in his search for Helen.

★ ★ ★

Pan Zagloba left Warsaw with highly mixed feelings. On the one hand he felt right at home in the noise and bustle of the vast electoral gathering of the gentry; he knew he'd miss the good times, the feasts and the carousings, and some of the turmoil and excitement that he and Volodyovski helped to create for their own amusement. On the other hand he consoled himself with the thought that he was returning to life in the field, to new adventures in the search for Helen, and to a fresh exercise of his shrewd instincts and imagination. As to the dangers that might be waiting for him in the east, he thought them far less threatening than some of the temptations he experienced in the capital, and he was quick to tell Pan Michal all about it.

"It's true," he said, "that we accomplished great things in Warsaw, you and I. No one can deny it. But if we'd stayed there any longer I wouldn't have been able to guarantee our safety."

"And why's that?" the little knight asked sleepily.

The day was warm. The air was soft with Autumn. The rapid march wearied both the men and the horses and the small soldier was peering about for a place to rest.

"We'd have become soft," the fat knight announced. "We would have lost the rest of our virtue like that famous Carthaginian who turned into wax in Capua and whose manhood melted away altogether in the hands of women. Women, my friend, are the worst danger that a man can face. There's nothing more treacherous. They'll lure the strongest of us to destruction. I'm getting on a bit in years and ought to know better but they still exercise their fascination on me."

"Ey, don't you think you're a little past that kind of thing?" The little knight had quite a different idea about women; and Princess Barbara never seemed more desirable nor farther beyond his reach. "Why don't you give it a bit of a rest?"

"Yes, I've thought of that." Pan Zagloba nodded. "I've thought of it often. It's time to settle down. Age calls for a certain dignity, don't you know, and I ought to pay greater attention to my status as an elder statesman. But I've a particularly hot kind of blood bubbling in my veins and that's my whole problem. It's easy for you because you're a bit of a cold fish in such matters, little as you are, while I am full of fire. But no matter. All that's over now. Bohun's as dead as a rusty nail and we're off to a new life again."

"Have you missed campaigning?"

"Have I ever! I've got to admit that even though I'm a peaceful and quiet man by nature, as you know, I've been longing for hard days in the field."

"There're still rebel bands looting and pillaging the country around Zamost," said Volodyovski. "Armistice or not, you may find all the hard days you want."

"You think so, eh?" Not quite sure how to take this piece of information Pan Zagloba thought it over for a while. "Good. I won't get out of practice, then. We'll have some fun with them on our way to Helen. But d'you know what I've missed the most?"

"No. But I'm sure you'll tell me."

"Of course I will. Why not? I've missed our Skshetuski. And call me a liar if you like but I also miss that Lithuanian beanpole, that long drink of water, that skinny giant with his pious chastity and those three elusive heads of his. It'll be good to see him again."

"You miss him," the little knight observed. "But when you're with him you pester and harass him like a horsefly."

"That's because every time he opens his mouth it's as if his Courland mare was flicking her tail," Pan Zagloba said. "And it's as hard for him to recognize the obvious as if his eyes were crossed behind his nose. All his wits are in his arms and shoulders, his head's full of that dreamy Lithuanian air, and there isn't an infant in the Commonwealth that couldn't melt his heart with some cock-and-bull sob-story that nobody in his right mind could believe. Who ever heard of such a wealthy man who had so little practical common sense?"

"Is he really so rich?" Poor as a church mouse, the little knight didn't really understand the meaning of riches. "Or is that just another of your stories?"

"Is he rich? When I first met him he had a money belt so stuffed with gold that he couldn't bend it or wrap it around his waist. He carried it under his arm like a smoked veal sausage. You could chase dogs with it or use it for a fencepost. I can't remember all the villages he owns, it's at least half a county, and every one of them has a name that has something to do with some kind of entrails. Myshikishke . . . Psyekishke . . . who can remember all those heathen *kishkes*? The Podbipyentas are a great family among the Lithuanians."

"You're sure you aren't stretching it a bit?"

"Not in the slightest. I'm only telling you what he told me himself and that man hasn't uttered a lie in his entire life. His wits are too dull for even that much."

"Well!" Pan Michal grinned. "So it looks as if Anusia is going to be a really great lady! Good for her. But all that stuff about how dull-witted he is that's just your own hot air. He's a quiet, thoughtful and generous man. You couldn't ask for gentler or more understanding help whenever you need it. As for his supposed lack of wits . . . well, not everyone can have a tongue as sharp as yours. He's a great knight and the kindest man alive and the best proof of that is your own affection for him, no matter how you try to hide it."

"He's God's trial on my patience," Pan Zagloba muttered. "Yes, I've missed him. Yes, I am looking forward to seeing him again. But the best part of it will be the pins I'll be able to stick in him about Miss Anusia."

"That,"—Pan Michal became suddenly serious and alert—"I wouldn't advise. He's a sweet, patient man but some things are holy as far as he's concerned. You prod him where it matters and you're likely to bring the sky falling on your head."

"So what?" Still full of his Warsaw triumphs, and already quite convinced that it was he who had conquered Bohun, the fat knight let himself be carried away by his own imaginary prowess as a duelist.

"I'll trim his ears," he said. "That's what I'll do. Just like I did with Pan Duntchikovski."

"I wouldn't wish my worst enemy a duel with Longinus Podbipyenta," said the little knight.

"Well we'll see, won't we," Pan Zagloba said. "We'll just have to see."

★   ★   ★

Zagloba's wish to see Pan Longinus came true sooner than he expected. Volodyovski ordered a halt to rest the men and horses near the small provincial town of Konskovola and the two knights hurried to the inn where they hoped to find some of that famed mulled ale for which that part of the country was known throughout the Commonwealth. But the first man they saw when they marched into the taproom was Pan Podbipyenta.

"Hey, hey! How are you! It's been a long time!" Pan Zagloba shouted. "So how is it that the Cossacks didn't manage to get you in Zamost? Did they run out of siege towers to reach your head? Couldn't they find a scaling ladder that was long enough? Or did they think that you were just the *Starosta's* flagpole?"

Pan Longinus seized them in his arms, one after another, and hugged and squeezed them until their ribs began to ache and they gasped for air.

"What luck! How wonderful to see you!" the overjoyed giant cried out over and over and threw his huge arms around them both again.

"So where are you off to?" Volodyovski asked, slipping out of the dangerous embrace.

"To the Prince in Warsaw."

"The Prince isn't there. He's gone to Krakow with His Majesty. He's to carry the orb at the coronation."

"And here I've got letters for him from Pan Veyher," said the troubled giant. "The *Starosta* wants to know where to dispatch the Prince's regiments now that he doesn't need them in Zamost anymore."

"We've got the orders with us," said the little knight. "You can spare yourself the journey."

Pan Longinus slumped down on his bench as if he'd just been told the saddest story he had ever heard and Pan Zagloba began to wink rapidly at Volodyovski.

"No need for you to go at all," Pan Michal repeated.

"No need . . . ?" The Lithuanian began to groan and heave his great sighs and the two knights grinned at each other, guessing what and who was really drawing Pan Longinus so urgently to the Prince's court.

"None at all," said the cruel Zagloba. "You can go on with us back to Zamost. True, Princess Grizelda and all her little chickens are with His Highness for the coronation but that would hardly interest you, I expect."

"Ah . . . but, hmm . . . the *Starosta's* letters," the anxious giant murmured while his long face turned the color of a boiled crayfish. "I think I'd better go on anyway."

"Suit yourself." Pan Zagloba shrugged and winked at Pan Michal. "Meanwhile what about something to wet the tongue? We've lots to talk about and the mulled ale is supposed to be rare in these parts."

★　★　★

The old noble ordered three quart tankards of the thick brown ale with which to cut the dust of travel in their throats and the three knights, as unlike each other as if each belonged to a different species, sat down to catch up on their news. Pan Longinus told the story of the siege of Zamost which began with massed charges by the Zaporohjans in which thousands died; of how their friend Skshetuski distinguished himself in the defense, finding some relief from his private anguish in selfless attention to duty and service; and of Hmyelnitzki's treachery in trying to bribe Pan Veyher into a surrender.

"He must've thought that Pan Veyher was a foreigner who might be for sale," the Lithuanian said. "He obviously never heard of the Pomeranian Veyhers who've been palatines and senators for two hundred years. Anyway, it all came to nothing. Pan Veyher soon put a bee in his ear. In fact it was I who carried his letter to Hmyelnitzki's camp. Which is where I met Bohun, by the way."

"Who?" the fat knight and the little one shouted out together.

"Bohun," the giant said mildly. "Surely, dear brothers, you remember Bohun . . ."

"Remember him? We just killed him!" Pan Zagloba cried and launched himself into the tale of how he and Volodyovski killed Bohun in a duel.

"Dear brothers!" cried the Lithuanian. "Have I heard you right? Is that possible? Is it really true?"

"As you see us here."

"And both of you killed him?"

"That is so," Pan Zagloba said with his fiercest gesture as if daring the astonished giant to call him a liar. "He came with letters from Hmyelnitzki to the King-elect. And he called us out. And so we . . . ah . . . killed him."

"What news! God be thanked!" The Lithuanian clapped his huge hands in delight. "But . . . both of you cut him down, you say?"

"Both." Pan Zagloba nodded, dismissing the topic.

"But how could that be?" The peculiarities of Pan Zagloba's reality and logic, by which things were seldom quite what they seemed to others, puzzled the honest Lithuanian knight for whom truth was truth without shades of meaning. "What do you mean . . . both?"

"I mean both!" Pan Zagloba growled in a threatening voice. "First I provoked him into fighting us, is that clear to you? And then Pan Michal took the first turn with him and sliced him up like an Easter roast. Now d'you understand?"

But Pan Longinus failed to follow Zagloba's fanciful adjustment of events by which he could take the credit for the famous ataman's demise.

"Wait, dear brother, wait." Pan Longinus started to count off the various points of Zagloba's story on his massive fingers. "Pan Michal fought him first, you say?"

"That's correct."

"And Bohun died?"

"That's right! I heard his death rattle as we rode away."

"So you didn't actually fight with him yourself?"

"Listen to him, will you?" Out of patience, the fat knight sought support from Volodyovski. "It's enough to drive a good man to despair!" And then to the puzzled, questioning Lithuanian: "What's the matter, did a leech bleed you recently so that your weak brains lost whatever powers of reasoning they once had? Can't you put such a simple thing together? How was I to fight a corpse, or a near-corpse who was breathing out his last?"

"But . . . sweet brother," the mild-mannered giant defended himself. "You said that you and Pan Volodyovski killed him both together . . ."

"And we did! God give me patience with this man!" Pan Zagloba raised his eyes to the ceiling and shook both his fists. "Tell him, Michal! Didn't Bohun call out both of us?"

"He did," Volodyovski said.

"Well, there you have it," Pan Zagloba said. "Is it all clear to you now? Do you get it?"

"No. No, I don't. But never mind," Pan Longinus said. "The main thing is he's dead. It'll be a great weight off Pan Skshetuski's mind which, as God knows, is just about cracking under all his worries."

"Which is exactly why we killed that man!" Pan Zagloba said.

★ ★ ★

Pan Zagloba went off in a huff to calm himself alone over another tankard of heated brown beer and the gentle giant told the little knight how he met Bohun in Hmyelnitzki's camp before the ataman's fateful trip to Warsaw.

"Hmyelnitzki was drunk and in a rage over the *Starosta's* letter. He howled and ranted and threatened me with his *bulava* so that I started thinking that my time had come, consigned my soul to God, and got ready to crush Hmyel's skull with my fist as soon as he touched me. There's been so much bloodshed, I know, but what else was I to do, dear brother? Tell me, was it wrong of me to think like that?"

"You couldn't have done anything else," Pan Michal assured him.

"But some of his colonels tried to hold him back, especially one young one who didn't show any fear of him but caught him by the waist and pulled him away. '*You're drunk, bat'ku*,' he said.

'Leave the Lah alone. You don't know what you're doing so just cool down and behave yourself.'

"I took a good look at this man who was trying to save my life with so little regard for his own and it was Bohun. We'd seen each other in Rozloghi and he recognized me. *'That's a good friend of mine,'* he says to Hmyelnitzki. *'Ah,'* Hmyelnitzki says, *'if he's your friend, my son, then give him fifty thalers and let him go free. Any friend of yours is holy among us.'* And so I walked out of Hmyelnitzki's tent alive."

"Bohun saved Hmyelnitzki as much as he saved you," the little soldier pointed out. "And he probably knew it."

"Perhaps he did. But I no sooner stepped out of that tent when Bohun came over. *'We saw each other in Rozloghi,'* he says. *'That's right,'* I told him. *'Only I never thought I'd see you in this camp.'* He shrugged, looking as grief-stricken as a mourner, and said: *'I hoped for something else but bad luck pointed me another way. Misfortune drove me here.'* He asked about Pan Yan and when he heard that he was in Zamost he said that maybe they'd meet some day in combat because there was no room for both of them under the same sun. He saw me safely past their picket lines and that's the last I saw of him. Hmyelnitzki must have sent him to Warsaw soon after."

"That's how it must have been," Volodyovski said.

"A strange man," said the Lithuanian. "You'd think he was a great lord sometimes, not just a simple Cossack. What a shame it is that the Commonwealth lost such a son."

"I think so too," Pan Volodyovski said.

★ ★ ★

Pan Zagloba rejoined them shortly afterwards still muttering darkly about Lithuanian bean poles but ready to forgive the soft-hearted giant whom he loved and admired far deeper than he would admit even to himself. Asked about Skshetuski, Pan Podbipyenta said he was no longer to be found in Zamost.

"But you can hear about him anywhere you go. He's out with a brigade, crushing rebel bands wherever he can find them, and freeing the captives. He smashed the Cossack Colonels Burlay and Kalina a few days ago and then he beat and scattered two Tartar *tchambuls* and freed their *yassyr*. He's sent several thousand rescued people back to the fortress already and he frees more each day. I've never seen a man who works so hard, with so little care about himself, and who gives so much and asks for so little."

And here the gentle Lithuanian sighed, nodded and raised his mild, childlike eyes to the others.

"I can't help thinking that God in His mercy will let him have some joy before very long," he said. "Because I've never known a finer and more decent man. Anyone else in these selfish times would think about his own happiness first and foremost. The Prince would have let him go searching for his lady a long time ago. But he has no thought for himself and he suppresses his own suffering in a way that's quite past believing."

"He's got the soul of a Roman, there's no doubt about that," Pan Zagloba nodded. "I've said it before but I don't mind saying it again."

"He's an example to all of us, dear brother."

"And especially you, Master Podbipyenta," the fat knight thundered suddenly like a voice of conscience. "Because you're less concerned with service to your country than with finding your three heads!"

"God sees into my soul," the Lithuanian whispered and raised his mournful eyes to the tavern ceiling. "Let him judge my motives."

"God's already given Pan Yan one reward in removing Bohun from this earth," Pan Zagloba said. "This moment of tranquility for the Commonwealth is another blessing. He'll have the time now to go looking for what's dearest to him. He can't ask for anymore than that."

"And you'll go with him, brothers?"

"Of course! Aren't you going with us?"

"I'd go . . . with all my heart," cried the Lithuanian while a look of desperate longing passed across his face. "But what about those letters? I've one from the *Starosta* to the Prince . . . one to His Majesty the King . . . and one from Skshetuski asking His Highness for leave so he can go looking for his lady at long last . . ."

"We've got his leave right here," Pan Volodyovski said.

"That's right," said Zagloba.

"Ah . . . ah!" It was quite clear to both the knights that poor Pan Longinus was totally consumed by his unexpected passion

and all the secret longings which burst open in his heart after so
many loveless and resigned years of abstinence. "But . . . what
about the other letters I am carrying?"

"Your letters?" Pan Zagloba smiled, scratched his head as if
pondering the matter deeply for a moment, and then took
mercy on the tortured giant. "I think you'd better take them
where they're supposed to go. You've no choice about that.
Your superior gave you the assignment so it's your simple
duty."

"You think so? You think so?"

"I'd be glad to have a pair of fists like yours when we go
searching for our little Helen," Zagloba went on. "But the rest
of you wouldn't be much help. We'll have to go disguised as
peasants, as likely as not, and there's never been a peasant like
you since God made the world. Besides, you don't speak
Ruthenian so you'd just give the game away. No, no. You'd
better go to Krakow. We'll manage without you."

"I think so too," grinned Volodyovski.

"You're sure, sweet brothers?" Hope and gratitude glowed in
the pale blue eyes; the anxious smile was that of a delighted
child. "You're quite sure about that?"

"Go! Go!" Then Pan Zagloba grinned and winked at Pan
Michal. "And give my best regards to Pan Kharlamp when you
get to Krakow."

"Pan Kharlamp? And who might he be?"

"Oh, he's a certain Lithuanian gentleman of great charm and
beauty over whom all the women of Princess Grizelda's household have quite lost their heads."

Pan Longinus shuddered in such utter terror that the oak
bench quivered under him and all the glasses jumped and rattled
on the table.

"Sweet brother!" he cried. "Are you joking?"

"I wish I was," the fat knight said, sighed, shrugged, hid his
grin behind his tankard, and winked at Pan Michal. "Have a
pleasant journey."

Chapter Fifty-three

THE DISTRAUGHT PAN LONGINUS took the road to Krakow while the cruel Pan Zagloba and Volodyovski rode to Zamost where they spent no more than a day. Pan Veyher hadn't heard from Skshetuski for some time and didn't know where they should look for him. He thought that the four regiments that Pan Yan led on his expedition would, most likely, go to reinforce the garrison of Zbarajh to protect those lands from the looting rabble. This was all the more probable since Zbarajh was a possession of the Vishnovyetzkis and, as such, particularly tempting to Hmyelnitzki's Cossacks.

The road that opened before Volodyovski and Zagloba in this uncertain fashion was a long and hard one. But since they had to go eastward sooner or later anyway in their search for Helen it made no difference to them when they set out in that general direction. They left at once, riding as quickly as they could to catch up with Skshetuski, and breaking their pace only long enough to rest their men and animals when fatigue brought them to a halt, or to fight the bands of robbers, small Tartar *tchambuls* and loose detachments of marauding Cossacks that still swarmed through the lands between Zamost and the borders of western Ruthenia.

They rode through such utter devastation that they seldom caught sight of a living creature; days passed sometimes before some starving wretch appeared in the rubble. The towns lay in ruins. The villages were lifeless and burned to the ground. The people were dead, scattered or driven off by Tartars. All that they passed along the way were rotting corpses, gutted homes and homesteads, the gaunt, burned skeletons of churches, the smoldering debris of wayside villages, and packs of homeless dogs howling among the ashes. Whoever managed to survive the receding Tartar-Cossack tide lay hidden in the forests, half-starved and freezing in the cold November nights, but not yet ready to believe that the time of terror had passed for the moment.

It took well-trained and experienced soldiers to survive in such a man-made wilderness. Pan Volodyovski fed his horses on bark peeled off the roadside birches and on the scorched, fermenting wheat and oats that his men dug out of the shells of former barns and byres. But they rode swiftly nonetheless, supplying themselves mainly from the stores and rations recaptured from the robber bands they trapped and destroyed. The little knight was right in promising new hardships, Pan Zagloba thought.

Meanwhile November was coming to an end.

Every sign on earth and in the sky suggested that a fierce Winter was coming that year. If the previous one was so unusually mild that the Steppe burst into life long before its time, so this new Winter promised a severity without parallel. The soil was already as unyielding as a slab of stone under the horses' hooves. The horseshoes clicked and rattled on the country tracks as if they were striking city cobblestones. The long, dark fields lay in the grip of such deep early frost that the soil in the furrows was as hard and flinty as Carpathian granite. Snow lay in broad sheets on the mounds and hillocks, and the banks of the streams and rivers that they forded were stiff and grey with a covering of ice.

The nights were freezing.

The days were dry and pale.

The sun barely warmed the air at noon. At dawn and in the first hours of the evening twilight the sky burned with a crimson fire that was the surest herald of an early and severe Winter. And yet the few survivors they came across in the fields and ruins said that they looked forward to the killing snows because a bitter Winter meant the end of war. They might die of the cold. They might starve to death before the snows melted. But, as they said whenever they were questioned, snow and ice brought peace.

★ ★ ★

Pan Volodyovski, who knew the Steppes and the Ukraine through and through, was certain that the expedition in search of Helen would succeed because, if nothing else, they wouldn't have to fight their way into that vast wilderness in which she was hidden.

"I don't believe in Hmyelnitzki's protestations of loyalty," he said as they rode. "Why should he want peace? War's given him everything he's got and who knows how high his ambition is likely to take him? He's not retreating into the Ukraine out of any love for our new King or the Commonwealth."

"It's a surprise to me that he's doing it at all," Pan Zagloba said.

"He's a fox. He knows that Cossacks don't fight well in the field if they can't entrench themselves as well. They'll go to Winter quarters and send their horseherds into the southern Steppe where there's always some kind of fodder to be found. The Tartars also need a few quiet months to get their captives safely to the markets. If this Winter is as hard as it promises to be we might have peace until the new grass comes up in the Spring."

"Maybe even longer." Pan Zagloba nodded. "God willing, we'll be dancing at Skshetuski's wedding before Lent."

"I just hope we don't pass him somewhere along the way without knowing it. It isn't hard to lose even a whole army in this kind of country."

"Well, somebody ought to have heard something about him. They're sure to know in Zbarajh."

But news of Skshetuski was hard to find. The few peasants whom they found now and then foraging in the ruins did hear about some battles fought by Polish horsemen with bands of pillagers and looters. But there were other Commonwealth cavalry commanders crisscrossing that country and the peasants had no way of knowing whose horsemen they were.

★ ★ ★

There was, however, another kind of news that flew like a breath of Spring across that wintry landscape: the tide of the rebellion turned against the Cossacks further to the north where the Lithuanian Army of the Commonwealth was avenging the disasters suffered by its Polish comrades. There were some rumors of a Cossack setback floating about Warsaw even before

the two knights left on their ride to Zamost but they were just
too difficult to believe. Now couriers, refugees and Cossack
fugitives confirmed the reports in every detail.

Prince Yanush Radzivill, the Grand Hetman of the Lithuanians and Palatine of Vilna, had trapped and crushed
Kshetchovski in the Pripet marshes and paid the rebels for
Korsun, Yellow Waters and Pilavtze in one dreadful blow. Two
great Cossack leaders, 'Half-moon' and Nebaba, were dead
along with all their followers. Twenty thousand Cossacks
drowned in the swamps as they tried to escape after this disaster
and Kshetchovski himself was dead on a stake. A strange twist
of fate threw him into the hands of Radzivill's German mercenaries, as if some vengeful forest deity demanded payment for
the German blood he spilled into the Dnieper. Even though
he'd been shot and severely wounded before he was captured,
the Germans impaled him at once and he died in agony after a
full day and a night of agonizing torment.

News of his death spread terror throughout the Ukraine
because no Cossack ataman, not even Hmyelnitzki, enjoyed as
much authority among the Zaporohjans as this ennobled former Pereyaslav colonel. Every hut and village and lone Steppe
homestead and canyon and ravine filled with the frightened
whispers of shaken marauders for whom this ambitious, calculating chieftain had been like a beacon or a star to follow. If
the best and most experienced of their leaders could end on a
stake, what could their futures be? Every knoll seemed to echo
with the fearful doubt that paralyzed the most bloodthirsty
rebels. They thought this great Steppe commander was invincible. His fame brought tens of thousands of their kind into the
rebellion and to that independent Cossack principality he
planned for himself. A brilliant destiny had beckoned to him
even before Hmyelnitzki's cunning inflamed his ambition and
now old men started to recall other Cossack risings which
promised freedom and ended in death.

Hmyelnitzki himself hid in his tent and howled in drunken
rage when he heard about the death of his most talented and
irreplaceable companion.

"Kshetchovski?" he muttered. "Kshetchovski?"

The gloomy Hetman of the Zaporohjans knew that he stood
at the height of his power and renown. He triumphed everywhere. No one could resist him. He was the absolute ruler of

more people than all the kings and princes of Germany, France and England. He had turned a horde into a People and created a nation while four hundred thousand warriors trembled at his word and fought at his bidding. But Kshetchovski's fall and death seemed like twin icy fingers of a dreadful prophecy pointed at himself. Once again, as before the battle of Korsun, he summoned soothsayers and witches to look into his future. Once more the hags gathered to tell him about great new wars and victories. But none of them, no matter how he threatened, could tell him what his own fate would be.

Nor was this all. The Lithuanians' destruction of Kshetchovski had yet another effect. It made every Cossack think twice about his own chances. Even more than the advent of a savage Winter, it brought an assurance of a lengthy peace.

The country began to heal its wounds again.

Life started to return to the abandoned villages and townships. The people crept out of the forests and began to plant Winter seed in the scorched, black plains.

Hope took root and grew.

★ ★ ★

This same sense of high anticipation carried Pan Zagloba and Volodyovski through their long, hard journey. The cold days seemed merely brisk and refreshing to them. The ice on the rivers was a thing of beauty. The stray blades of grass for which their horses snuffled in the snow were cause for excitement as if the country were renewing itself right before their eyes. They rode through the gates of Zbarajh feeling as if all the agonies of the Commonwealth were ending along with their journey and they were anxious to find their friend Skshetuski and to begin the search.

Pan Yan, however, was nowhere to be found. Vyershul, who acted as town commandant in his place, said only that Skshetuski had ridden away. He hadn't told anyone why he was leaving or where he was going; he merely left a request that if anyone came looking for him in Zbarajh he or they were to wait for him there until his return.

"How long ago was that?" Pan Zagloba asked.

"Ten days."

"And he just went away? Without leave?"

"It's quiet around here these days." Vyershul shrugged and

bobbed his red head. "He turned the command over to me and went to scout out the country. There's nothing unusual about that."

Zagloba and Volodyovski glanced quickly at each other. Ten days ago Bohun was still alive and they were in Warsaw. The news of the Lithuanian victories was still a mere rumor and the Cossacks had barely started on their retreat from Zamost. The two knights had a dozen questions to ask and Vyershul looked as if he had a few dozen of his own but none of them would say much with servants in the room.

"Hmm, hmm." Pan Zagloba muttered at long last and turned to Volodyovski. "Why don't we ask Pan Vyershul to give us a bite to eat? The head doesn't work all that well on an empty belly. We've a lot to talk about, a lot to decide. Let's talk while we're eating."

"By all means!" Vyershul cried and ordered a meal served in the commandant's quarters. "I was about to sit down to supper myself. Anyway, since Pan Volodyovski's commission is older than mine then he's the commanding officer here, not I. I'm at your service, gentlemen!"

"Keep your command, my friend," Pan Volodyovski said. "You're older than I am. And I'll be leaving soon anyway, I expect."

Supper was served at once. The night was cold. A harsh wind came out of the eastern plains and rattled the windows. A melancholy light fell from the burning torches in the small stone chamber and threw twisted shadows across their bearded faces. They ate in silence until Pan Zagloba satisfied his first pangs of hunger with two large bowls of '*polevka*' soup, a platter of sausage, and a huge tankard of hot buttered beer, after which he sighed with satisfaction, wiped his mustache and turned to Pan Vyershul.

"Ah . . .," he said. "That's better. I can feel ideas stirring in my head. There is nothing like a good, thick *polevka* to fuel the brain and good hot beer to carry it there. Now, my good sir, do you have any thoughts of your own as to where Pan Skshetuski might have gone? It isn't like him to go off like that, without a word."

"Not like him at all," Vyershul said. "Yes, I've thought about it. Secrecy was important to him for some reason so that's why I didn't want to say anything in front of the servants. But it seems to me that he took advantage of these quiet new times, which are sure to last at least until Spring, to search for his lady whom Bohun holds somewhere."

"Bohun's dead," Pan Zagloba said.

"How's that?"

"Dead, *finis*, and done with."

And Pan Zagloba launched once more into the tale of the duel in Lipkov which he told with a great deal of pleasure and with more conviction of his role every time anyone gave him the opportunity to tell it.

"Well, that'll make things a lot easier for Skshetuski," Vyershul said.

"It will. If he finds her. But that's just the thing. She can be hidden anywhere in that wilderness, anywhere at all. And that's more ground for one man to cover than if he was searching through the rest of Europe."

"Did he take any troops?" Pan Michal wished to know.

"No. He went alone."

"What?" The little knight sat up as suddenly as if a coiled spring snapped open in his spine and looked at Vyershul with wide, staring eyes. "He didn't even take Zjendjan?"

"Zjendjan?" Vyershul laughed and shook his head in wonder. "We'd better think of him as *Pan* Zjendjan from now on! Skshetuski gave him leave of his own to go home with all the loot he's gathered. That shrewd little pack rat had half a dozen wagons with him when he left! No, Pan Yan just took a young Ruthenian lad and an extra horse."

"Well, that was wise of him," Pan Zagloba nodded. "A lot of men wouldn't be any good for a thing like that and a single man can do a great deal better. You might get through as far as Kamyenetz with troops at your back but beyond that, in the Ushitza and Mohilev country, you're sure to get among a swarm of wintering Cossacks. And Yampol's like a breeding ground for them . . . No, no, if you were heading into that hornets' nest you'd have to bring either a whole division or slip through alone."

"But how do you know that Skshetuski would go towards Yampol?"

"Because Bohun hid the girl somewhere in that country and Skshetuski knows it. But that's like knowing that she's still somewhere on earth."

★ ★ ★

They sat at the table late into the night wondering where Skshetuski might be at that moment, whether it was likely that he'd find Helen's hiding place, and what they should do to help him on their own.

"I've been out that way," Pan Zagloba said. "And I tell you it's like the end of the world. Nothing but rocks, cliffs, dried-out riverbeds, canyons so deep that the sun never touches the bottom, and holes in the ground where you could hide an entire army. You could ride for two days in that country without ever seeing anything alive. At least, nothing human. And what you might see after sundown is best not talked about."

"Yan's an experienced man," Volodyovski offered.

"But he's alone there. He'd have a hard time finding the place in that country even if he knew exactly where to go. Wandering about that wilderness without any clear idea where to look would call for a miracle. There isn't even anybody he could ask! You can bet your lives Bohun made sure that nobody knew where he hid that poor, sad child . . ."

"So you don't think he'll find her?" Vyershul asked.

"I don't know, I don't know." Pan Zagloba buried his head in his hands and tugged at his beard. "If we were with him I might be able to think of something. But this way? I doubt it. I doubt it. Hmm. Hmm. The Devil himself wouldn't know what to do about this . . . Should we go after him, Michal, or what?"

"I'll let you decide that for both of us," the little knight said.

"Hmm. Ten days . . . it'll be hard to catch up with him wherever he's gone. And which way did he go anyway? We don't know that either! He could have taken the old highway for Ploskirov and Bar. Or he could've cut straight down through Podolia to Kamyenetz . . . I'll be damned if I know what to suggest. Moreover, he left word for us to wait for him here."

"And don't forget that we're just supposing he went after his girl," Vyershul added.

"There you are," Pan Zagloba muttered. "That's another problem. He could've just gone off on a reconnaissance, to sniff around a little and ask a few questions, and plans to be right back! He knew that we were supposed to go all together and he must've expected us to join him here because now is the best time to go! It's hard to decide what to do."

"I'd advise waiting another ten days or so," Vyershul said.

"What would ten days give us? Except the need to make another decision? The thing to do is either go at once or not go at all."

"And I'd say we should start out tomorrow," the little knight offered. "What do we lose by going right away? Either we catch up with Skshetuski or we don't and we aren't searching for him anyway, are we? So if Yan doesn't find his poor lost girl wherever he's looking, maybe God will let us do it for him somewhere else."

"Hmm. Yes. That sounds good as far as it goes," Pan Zagloba muttered. "But there're a few other things to bear in mind. You're a young fellow, Michal, you're thirsty for another adventure, and that's as it should be. But there's a danger that if too many of us start poking around in that country we'll stir up suspicions. They're a shrewd, tricky lot, the Cossacks out that way, and God only knows what they're up to on their own these days. They might be plotting some new deviltry with the Turkish pasha down around Khotim. Or making plans with the Tartars about next year's campaign. They'll all be keeping an eye out for any strangers wandering in those parts, especially strangers who ask for directions. Believe me, I know them. It's easy to fall under suspicion over there. And once that happens God help everyone!"

"All the more reason to go!" Pan Michal insisted. "What if Skshetuski gets in some kind of trouble? He might need our help!"

"Hmm. That's also true."

Pan Zagloba began to think so hard that the veins started to bulge and swell in his temples and the top of his bald skull turned as purple as a plum.

Stray moments from his past—a past he never talked about, and people and events that he never mentioned—began to flicker behind his lowered eyelids. Yampol . . . Yahorlik . . . the great horsemarkets where no one asked questions about ownership or brands . . . The vast, gaunt wilderness where a nimble man could hide forever from the tribunals if he couldn't talk his way out of trouble . . . A land of a thousand secrets, most of them never thought about, where no one questioned birth or antecedents and where a sharp young man could call himself a noble even if he himself wasn't sure who or what he was . . .

It was a dream. Old, jumbled memories which had been a nightmare all too often . . . One that he avoided as often as he could.

Waking out of it, Zagloba peered suspiciously at the others as if they might have read his thoughts.

"Well," he said. "Well. Considering everything . . . it looks as if we ought to go."

Volodyovski breathed a sigh of relief. "When?" he asked.

"Let's rest a couple of days. Get body and soul together, so to speak. Get the right disguises. What would you say to starting in three days?"

"It couldn't be better," Pan Volodyovski said.

★ ★ ★

The two friends began their preparations the next day when Skshetuski's young Cossack lad arrived with news and letters for Vyershul. Getting word of this, Zagloba and Volodyovski hurried to the commandant's quarters where Vyershul tossed them Skshetuski's letter without another word.

"*'I am in Kamyenetz, to which the highway is quite safe as far as Satanov,'*" Zagloba read aloud.

"Good! Good!" Volodyovski cried. "Now we know which way to go to join him!"

"Wait," Pan Zagloba said. "Listen to this: '*I'm going to Yahorlik with a caravan of Armenian traders whom Pan Bukovski, who commands the fortress, recommends as honest. They've passes from the Cossacks and the Tartars as far as the Aral Sea. We're heading for Ushitze, Mohilev and Yampol, stopping wherever there might be someone to trade with, and I pray God that we might hear something of what I am seeking.'*"

"He will, he will!" Pan Michal interrupted. "But does he suggest anything we might do for him?"

"Wait," Pan Zagloba waved the crumpled sheet of paper in the air and settled down to read once again. "You might find out if you'd stop interrupting. Here, listen to this.

"'. . .If, as I expect, my two good comrades Zagloba and Volodyovski show up in Zbarajh, tell them, my dear Kristof, to wait for me there unless there's something better for them to do because the road I'm taking is too dangerous for more than one of us. The Cossacks who are wintering in great numbers around Yampol, and who have pastured* *their herds from the lower Dniester as far as Yahorlik, are jumpy and suspicious . . .'*

"Ah," the fat knight cried out, forgetting his own injunctions against interrupting. "And what did I tell you? But listen to this part:

"'. . . *I doubt if the three of us would accomplish more than I can do alone and I can pass for an Armenian much better than they.'*

"That's true!" he exclaimed. "He's as dark-skinned and black-haired as a Valachian. He'd pass for an Armenian even among Armenians. But you, Michal, you'd stick out among them with your pale little mustache like a yellow-jacket among bumblebees!"

"So what else does he say?"

"'. . . *Thank them as warmly as you can for their good intentions for which I'll be grateful to them as long as I live but I just couldn't wait for them any longer. Each day was a torment, as I'm sure they know, and I had no way of knowing when they might be free to join me. Now is the best time to travel throughout the East when all the merchants' caravans are crisscrossing the country so I couldn't miss the opportunity.'*"

"He's right about that," Pan Michal sighed. "It's a pity, though. I was really anxious to give him a hand."

"Well we couldn't get here any sooner, could we?" Pan Zagloba said. "And we've already helped him more than he knows by taking care of Bohun. But let me finish, will you? There isn't much more.

"'. . . *I'm sending my lad home because I won't have much use for him from now on and I'm afraid he might give the game away. He's a good, faithful boy but he's still a child and he might babble out something at a wrong time. Don't be concerned about me. Pan Bukovski vouches for the good faith of these Armenians and I agree with him. They are sharp traders but they're honest people. I also place my trust in God who, if He so wishes, may show us all His great love and mercy and relieve everyone's suffering and pain.'*"

"Amen," Vyershul said.

Pan Zagloba finished, passed the letter back to Vyershul, and stared in silence at his two companions.

"I knew that's what he was up to," Vyershul said.

"So what should we do now?" asked Volodyovski.

"What can we do?" Pan Zagloba shrugged and spread his

hands. "We've nothing to go for. He has the best possible cover
with those traders. Even I couldn't think of anything better. He
can poke around in every hut and lair without anybody cocking
an eyebrow at him because everybody out that way has something to trade. Good God, why shouldn't they? They've looted
half the Commonwealth, haven't they? And he's right, he can
pass for an Armenian without any trouble while you and I,
Michal, would have a hard time getting near Yampol in any
disguise."

"I don't know," the little knight muttered. "I'd still like to do
something for him."

"What?" Disappointed but seeing the wisdom of Skshetuski's
way, Pan Zagloba showed some irritation. "Go galloping off to
join him just so that you can draw attention to him and give him
away? No, no. There's nothing useful we can do out there.
Absolutely nothing! Ah . . . I so wanted to have a hand in
rescuing our sweet girl or, better yet, freeing her myself! But if
it can't be, it can't be, and that's all there's to it. Let's just pray
that God grants him everything he needs and leave it at that."

Pan Volodyovski went on grumbling for a while longer but
he knew there really wasn't anything the two friends could do
for Pan Yan at this time. He too was disappointed. The expedition promised fine excitement and many new adventures, and
what faced the little knight instead was a long and boring
Winter within the walls of Zbarajh.

"Maybe we should go to Kamyenetz anyway?" Pan Michal
suggested.

"To do what? What difference does it make which set of walls
we sit on and twiddle our thumbs? A journey like the one that
Skshetuski's making is likely to take months."

And here the old noble let his head droop glumly to his chest.

"A man stays young as long as he keeps moving," he muttered. "Old age comes quickly when you're just snoring by the
fire with your hands clasped on your belly with nothing to do.
But if that's how it has to be . . . Well, that's God's will too.
We'll pay for a Mass tomorrow so that Pan Yan can have the
Lord's blessing. Ah, at least we've killed Bohun for him, and
that's a big help."

"And that's it?" Pan Michal asked. "That's all we're going to
do?"

"That's all. You might as well tell them to unpack our saddlebags and stable the horses, Michal. We will wait."

★　★　★

Next morning there began long days of waiting, each of them drifting by in exactly the same dull and boring way as the day before, and each seeming as interminable as Winter itself. Neither their games of dice nor their drinking bouts helped to kill time in a useful or memorable manner. Pan Michal wandered about the town, looking for challenges and adventures, while Pan Zagloba grew glum and irritable, claiming that he was getting old.

Meanwhile the fierce Winter which everyone expected fell upon the country. Deep snows covered the walls and battlements of the Zbarajh castle and all the land around it. Wild birds and animals drew nearer to human habitations.

December passed like that. January ended. February came and went. The cold white days went on and on and there was no word of any kind from Skshetuski.

Part Eight

Chapter Fifty-four

THE PEACE COMMISSIONERS sent by the King and the Senate to offer a treaty to Hmyelnitzki, managed to reach the small provincial town of Novosyel only after a difficult and dangerous journey across the Ukraine. They halted there for the night, waiting to hear from the victorious Zaporohjan Hetman where he would receive them since he refused to let them enter his temporary capital in Tchehryn.

Each mile along their journey was marked by danger and humiliation; each threatened to be the last. They sat hour after hour in the little town, waiting in gloom bordering on despair, while their escort fought a pitched battle with vast mobs of *tchernya* who besieged them in their quarters and howled for their blood. Pillage and murder stripped these frenzied thousands of the last vestiges of civilization. Lawlessness and bloodshed were as natural to them after a year of savage civil war as if they were wolves, and even the former town dwellers among them were now as merciless as the innumerable bands of cutthroats and marauders, obedient to no one, who trailed the peace commission night and day.

Hmyelnitzki himself sent Donyets, one of the fiercest of Bohun's young colonels, to reinforce the commissioners' embattled dragoons with five hundred of his best *moloytzy*. But even this force could barely hold its own against the mobs which swelled by the hour and grew more threatening at each step of the way. The envoys were like a handful of travelers battered by a sea storm; whoever stepped away from the sleighs, or strayed accidentally from the watchful eyes of Pan Bryshovski's overworked dragoons, was swept up at once and

771

vanished without a trace. Each hour in those weeks of travel was an unexpected miracle of survival, but on the evening when they came to Novosyel all of them were sure that the next day's sunrise would find none of the commissioners alive. The dragoons and Donyets' Cossacks were fighting a formal battle for their lives since nightfall, while the peace envoys knelt in prayer in a small, requisitioned dwelling, and offered their souls to God. The Carmelite Father Lenkovski heard their confessions and gave them absolution.

Meanwhile the windows shook and rattled to mad howls, pistol shots, volleys of musket fire, screams and hellish laughter, the ringing clash of scythes, and cries demanding the blood of the envoys and the head of *Voyevode* Kisyel.

"*Ora pro nobis, Domine,*" prayed the Carmelite Lenkovski.

"*Na Pohybel!* Death! Death! Give us Kisyel's head!" roared the mobs outside.

' . . . *Why am I here?*' the worn old man asked himself in silence. '*What am I trying to accomplish?*' And then his hopeless and despairing thoughts appeared to shrink and crumble, and the remnants of his shaken faith formed into the most depleting question of them all: '*Have I lived for nothing?*'

The howls of the mob and the rattle of musketry were his only answer.

★ ★ ★

The long Winter night seemed to have no end.

Voyevode Kisyel sat with his eyes closed and his head cast down as the hours passed. His forehead lay buried in the palms of his hands while the voice of hatred hammered against the windows. It was a matter of indifference to him whether he lived or died. Sleepless, worn out and exhausted as he was, he thought that death would be a welcome relief, putting an end to an existence that had lost its meaning. But a profound despair gripped his mind and soul, a torment of doubt robbed him of all his strength, and the gloom of self-contempt denied the possibility of peace even beyond the grave.

It was he, as a native-born Ruthenian, who championed Hmyelnitzki in the Senate from the start. His voice had been the first to cry for Cossack conciliation and appeasement; he was the principal peacemaker in this unparalleled civil war which killed more people in its first ten months than all the victims of murder, pillage, looting and starvation that marked the horrors of the Thirty Years' War in the rest of Europe. As an ardent supporter of the chancellor and the primate, and as the architect of their policy of concessions and reform, he was the most implacable opponent of that other great Ruthenian magnate, Yeremi Vishnovyetzki. But now a dreadful doubt seeped into his soul and undermined his strongest convictions.

He had believed with all his heart that only a just settlement of Cossack grievances could bring about a lasting peace, restore a shattered unity, curb the unruly gentry, discipline the magnates, and save the Commonwealth and the Ruthenian people before the growing power of Moscow became great enough to overwhelm them both.

Just as the ruthless and single-minded Yeremi Vishnovyetzki gave everything he had to winning the war, so this frail, white-haired Palatine of Bratzlav ruined himself in the cause of peace. And now, even as he was bringing to Hmyelnitzki the trappings and *bulava* of a Hetman of the Ukraine, along with privileges and concessions beyond the Cossacks' most unbridled dreams, he could see the fruitlessness of all his best efforts and tasted bitter failure.

And where had he failed? Was he so wrong to think that a power as mighty as the Commonwealth might find room under its outspread wings for yet another nation? He shared the genius of Hmyelnitzki's vision; he was among the first to see the populous Ukraine as a separate people; and he spent his life in trying to expand that voluntary union of Polish, Lithuanian and Ruthenian nobles to include the new nation of the Ukrainians.

'*And have I so misread and misunderstood the nature of my own countrymen?*' he asked himself in torment. '*Did I let myself be blinded by my wishful thinking?*'

It seemed to him that a journey of a lifetime was ending in disaster at just the point where all his hopes should be converging on success. The insignia of rank that the King and Senate were sending to Hmyelnitzki were more than mere baubles; the new title of '*Hetman of the Ukraine*' was not just the elevation of a Zaporohjan rebel to the rank and power of the Radzivills and the Vishnovyetzkis; they denoted recognition for the Ukrainian people as equal members of the Commonwealth with all the rights and privileges they had ever wanted.

But what he wanted for them, and what the Commonwealth

herself was finally perceiving, lay far beyond the understanding of the mobs outside. Listening to them he felt as if his whole life was a bitter mockery. Each of the painful and humiliating steps he took towards their liberation seemed rooted in illusion. His vision of a brave new future for a reformed, revived and strengthened Commonwealth had merely brought him to the edge of a cataclysmic precipice from which there was no possibility of returning. It was as if the earth had suddenly split right under his feet and he found himself staring bleakly into a mocking void.

'*Could I have been so wrong?*' he asked and tasted the bitterness of his own despair. '*Do they really want nothing more than blood and loot and pillage and murder?*'

The mobs outside were howling for his head. They craved his blood and the corpses of all his companions. But the words that echoed with even greater horror in his ears were those that welled up from his own constricted chest: '*Is this the only freedom that they really want? The freedom to burn and pillage? Have they no other consciousness beyond one of murder?*'

The mob's reply thundered hour after hour through the windswept Winter night outside:

"*Holovu Kisyelovu!*"

"*Give us Kisyel's head! Death to him! Na Pohybel!*"

The worn-out and exhausted old man thought he'd gladly give them that tired, troubled head if that would mark the last bloodshed of this terrible, fratricidal war. But he knew that his murder and the massacre of all his companions wouldn't satisfy their appetite even for that one night.

How could they be saved, he asked himself over and over as the night continued. Who could transform their savage, primitive fury into a social conscience and save them from themselves? They'd been deprived so long! They needed so much more than any other people! Someone must teach them what it meant to be a civilized human being and to demand such things as decency and humanity and justice rather than blood and vengeance. And at this thought a pale ray of hope glimmered in the darkness of the *Voyevode's* despair. He told himself that this was, after all, only a mob of *tchernya* and savage *tchabany*. This wasn't Hmyelnitzki and his atamans with whom the real negotiations could begin.

But doubt returned at once. Because how could a negotiated

peace have any lasting value as long as half a million lawless serfs, who had tasted the wild intoxication of murder and unbridled vengeance, stood armed to the teeth and waiting only for the war and the massacres to resume?

'. . . *Wouldn't such peace melt with the first warm breath of Spring just like that ice and snow which grips the countryside and the Steppe beyond it?*'

And at this gnawing thought the old man heard once more the words of the implacable Vishnovyetzki: "*Mercy can be given only to the conquered . . .*" And the darkness of his own despair reached out for him again.

★ ★ ★

Meanwhile midnight passed. The shouts and gunshots began to die down a little in the streets outside. The chilled and tired mobs started to drift off to their camps and homesteads and the besieged commissioners began to feel a touch of resurrected hope.

Pan Voyt Myaskovski, the Chamberlain of Lvov, rose from his bench, listened for a moment at the snow-covered window, and said: "It seems that by God's grace we'll be alive at least until tomorrow."

Pan Zyelenski, the High Steward of Bratzlav, showed a bitter smile. "Who'd ever think that we were *peace* commissioners?" he asked.

"I've been an envoy to the Tartars more than once," said the venerable old Constable of Novgorod. "But this kind of embassy is something new to me. The Commonwealth is suffering more humiliation through us and through what we are doing than it ever did at Korsun and Pilavtze! I tell you, gentlemen, let's turn back. Let's forget about this. There is no point in even thinking of negotiations here."

"Let's turn back," echoed Pan Brozovski, the Castellan of Kiev. "If they don't want our peace then let them have their war."

Kisyel sighed. He lifted his washed-out red-rimmed eyes with such pain and effort as if they were coins laid on the eyelids of a corpse, and fixed his glassy stare on the castellan. War had only one meaning for this blindly dedicated man and now he searched for the words that might convey it to his dispirited companions.

"Yellow Waters," he said at last in a toneless voice. "Another Korsun? Pilavtze . . .?"

Then he was silent and so were the others, listening to the dull roaring of the wind outside and to the hiss of snow through the cracks in the windows. Only the quiet voice of Pan Kultchynski, the Treasurer of Kiev, broke through the stillness with the murmur of the rosary, while Pan Kretovski, the King's Master of the Hunt, seized his head in both hands and said what all the other commissioners were thinking:

"What times these are! God help us! God have mercy on us all."

*   *   *

The doors creaked open then and Captain Bryshovski stepped wearily into the room. "Your Excellency," he turned to Kisyel. "There's some Cossack outside who wishes to see you."

"Very well," Kisyel said. "Has the *tchernya* dispersed?"

Bryshovski nodded. "They threatened to be back tomorrow."

"Did they press you hard?"

"They couldn't have tried harder. Donyetz' Cossacks killed several dozen of them. But tomorrow, they say, they'll burn us out into the open and that'll be the end."

"Very well." Kisyel merely nodded. "Bring in that Cossack, will you?"

The doors opened again and a tall, dark-bearded figure appeared on the threshold.

"Who are you?" Kisyel asked.

"Yan Skshetuski, *husaria* commander of the Prince Palatine of Ruthenia."

Castellan Brozovski, Pan Kultchynski and Pan Kretovski leaped to their feet and stared in amazement. All of them served the year before with Prince Yeremi at Mahnovka and Konstantinov and knew Pan Yan very well. Kretovski even claimed to be his distant kinsman.

"My God, that's true! It's true!" they repeated, crowding around the tall, broad-shouldered figure in its worn quilted coat and cracked peasant boots. "That *is* Pan Skshetuski!"

"What are you doing here?" Pan Kretovski cried, taking the gaunt dark apparition in his arms. "How did you get through to us?"

"In Cossack clothes, as you see," Pan Yan said.

"My lord!" Castellan Brozovski turned to the *Voyevode*. "This is the greatest knight in all of Vishnovyetzki's army! Everybody knows him!"

"Welcome," Kisyel murmured. The name of Vishnovyetzki filled his mouth with the taste of ashes, but he was a great magnate in his own right and he had been a famous soldier in his youth, and he could still appreciate courage and determination.

"You must be a hard man to stop," he said, "if you managed to get through to us. What can we do for you, then?"

"Let me go with you, sir," Pan Skshetuski said.

"You want to join us in the dragon's throat?" the old peacemaker asked bitterly and sadly. "Are you sure that you understand what this means?"

Skshetuski bowed in silence and Pan Kisyel was struck by the depth of suffering etched into Skshetuski's face.

"Well, I can't stop you, I suppose." The quiet dignity and pain stamped into those young features struck a responsive chord in the agonizing Kisyel. "But why would you want to go into that Hell? What possible reason could you have to place yourself where no sane man would venture of his own free will? It must be something more important to you than your life."

"It is."

"What is it, then?"

"A misfortune, sir," Skshetuski said quietly and the old man nodded.

"I might have known."

The snowy head bowed down towards the frail, birdlike chest as if all of mankind's suffering and grief were locked in his heart.

"Yes, yes . . . What else do these times offer?" he murmured as if to himself. "What else is there? You must have lost someone dear to you, is that right? And you want to look for him over there?"

"Yes sir."

"God help you, then . . ." The gentleness and caring in Pan Kisyel's voice came from his own convictions, the sadness came from his sense of failure. "But when did it happen? Recently, I expect?"

"Last Spring."

"What?" Disbelief appeared briefly in the worn eyes of the old Ruthenian. "That's almost a year! Why did it take you that long to get around to searching? What were you doing all this time?"

"Serving with Prince Yeremi."

The name of the *Voyevode's* most bitter enemy, who would stop at nothing to frustrate his efforts, struck an instant spark of suspicion in Pan Kisyel's mind and he let a note of irony and scorn creep into his voice.

"Do you mean to tell me that such a generous master, who is so well know for the affection he has for his people, wouldn't give you leave?"

"I didn't ask for one," Skshetuski said simply.

Kisyel stared. He let his eyes rest longer on the silent soldier as if to read the secrets of his own commitments repeated in that harrowed face. The brief glow of suspicion died down in the presence of that transparent honesty and grief. Pan Kisyel wouldn't put an attempt on Hmyelnitzki's life past the Transdnieper warlord, but this wouldn't be the man Vishnovyetzki would dispatch to do it, and the old statesman who was so familiar with the machinations of powerful politicians found himself puzzled by this simple soldier. What kind of man is this, he had to ask himself. What selfless impulse keeps him chained to duty? Where does such dedication come from in these selfish and self-centered times?

But the young knight had nothing more to say.

The silence in the room seemed as if it would stretch forever until the Castellan of Kiev stepped forward with an explanation.

"All of us who served with Prince Yeremi know this young man's troubles," he told the *Voyevode*. "We've all shared his grief. We've even shared his tears. But if he chose to serve his country when it needed him rather than taking care of his private business then—surely!—it's all the more to his credit in this rotten era of greed and corruption."

"I see." Kisyel nodded and turned to Pan Yan. "If my words have any value to Hmyelnitzki you can be sure that I'll do my best for you, young man."

Skshetuski bowed once more.

"Now go and get some rest," the *Voyevode* said kindly. "You look worn out. As, indeed, we all seem to be, having had no rest since our journey started."

"I'll take him with me to my quarters," Pan Kretovski said.

"Yes. Yes. Let's all try to get some sleep," said Castellan Brozovski. "Who knows if we'll manage to find time for any rest tomorrow?"

"The rest that we do find might be an eternal one," said the *Voyevode*.

★　★　★

The commissioners scattered, each to his own quarters, and Pan Kretovski led his kinsman to a nearby house where he had taken a room for the night. A lad trudged through the snow before them carrying a lantern.

"Ey, my dear Yan, what we've lived through today," the King's official said. "I tell you, it was Judgment Day. We already said our goodbyes to each other. I was convinced that our last hour had come."

"I was moving about among the *tchernya*," Skshetuski replied, "listening to their talk. They've sent word about you to a powerful band of marauders which is nearby and they expect a full cohort of them by nightfall tomorrow."

"Will we be able to hold them off, you think?"

"We'll have to be long gone by then," the young soldier said, then added in a softer but more pressing tone: "It's Kiev you're going to, isn't it?"

"Yes, if Hmyelnitzki agrees to meet us there. We've sent word ahead but so far there's been no reply. But here's my hut. Come in and rest a bit. I've ordered some hot wine so perhaps we'll sleep a bit better for a change."

They pushed their way into the peasant *izba* where a huge fire crackled on the hearth and the steaming wine stood waiting on the table. Skshetuski seized his glass and drained it at one gulp.

"I haven't drunk or eaten in a day," he whispered in shame-faced explanation.

"And quite a few other days beside that, I'd say," Pan Kretovski murmured, a look of pity in his tired eyes. "You're worn to the bone. But tell me about yourself! Where have you been? What have you been doing? Are you hoping to find your lost princess in Kiev?"

Skshetuski nodded.

"But how d'you know she's there? Or that she might be there?

"Because I've already looked for her everywhere else that she might have been."

"Like where, for example?"

"All along the Dniester. Yampol . . . Ushitza . . . as far as Yahorlik itself. There's not a door in that whole country that I haven't knocked on. I was traveling with some Armenian traders and we stopped at every hut, homestead, village and Cossack *hutor* in the wilderness."

"And now Kiev? Why?"

"I heard that that's where Bohun was supposed to take her."

"Ah!"—and suddenly the King's huntsman slapped his forehead with his open palm—"but I haven't told you the most important news that you couldn't have heard about being away so long! Bohun is dead!"

Skshetuski turned as pale as the snow that covered the narrow windows and then the blood rushed back like a wave of fire into his face.

"How? When?" he stammered. "Who told you about this?"

"That old friend of yours!" Pan Kretovski laughed, sure that he was giving his kinsman good news. "That fat, one-eyed noble who already rescued your girl once before and then performed all those wonders at Konstantinov!"

"Pan Zagloba? But how did he know?"

"Well, listen, that's the best part of it!" Pan Kretovski cried. "I met him—oh, it must've been the last week of autumn — on his way to Zamost. We passed each other on the highway. I just had time to call out '*Hey, how are you,*' and ask him what was new, and he says, fast as a pistol shot: '*Bohun's dead.*' I asked who killed him because that was, after all, a famous soldier and the man who killed him would have to be some kind of a giant, and Pan Zagloba snapped back: '*I did!*' And then we parted and each of us went his own way."

The light of sudden hope that started to glow so brightly in Skshetuski's eyes went out at once, the rush of blood into his cheeks receded, and his face greyed again.

"That noble," he said bitterly. "Talks through his hat as often as not. You can't believe anything he says. There is no way in which he could have killed Bohun or anyone like Bohun. That's just another of his lies."

"But didn't you talk to him yourself? Because, as I recall, he also said something about being on his way to see you in Zamost . . ."

"I left before he got there. God only knows if anything he ever said was true, including what he supposedly overheard about Helen's hiding place when Bohun held him briefly as a prisoner at the end of Summer."

"And what was that?"

"Ah,"—pain, weariness and disillusion settled like a shroud on the young soldier's face—"it was all a fool's dream anyway . . . Bohun was supposed to have hidden Helen somewhere beyond Yampol, according to Zagloba. And then, again according to Zagloba, he was planning on taking her to Kiev . . . But,"—and he lifted his shoulders in a tired shrug, as if waking once more to a reality of loss and disappointment—"it was probably just a pack of lies from start to finish."

"So why are you going there, then?"

Skshetuski said nothing.

★ ★ ★

They sat in silence for a time, listening to the hiss and crackle of the flames in the hearth, to the crunch of snow under the boots of the dragoon pickets outside the commissioner's window, and to the mournful baying of the wind.

"Have you thought," the older man resumed, "that if Bohun is still alive you might fall into his hands out here? And especially in a place like Kiev?"

Skshetuski shrugged again. "You asked why I am going there. That is why. Let there finally be God's judgment between us."

"But good God, man! He won't fight with you! He'll just have you roped like an ox for slaughter or sell you to the Tartars!"

"I'm traveling with the peace commissioners."

"And what does that mean? We're just as likely to go under the knife ourselves!"

"A bitter life makes for easy dying," Skshetuski quoted from an ancient proverb.

"Good God, Yan!" the commissioner cried out. "It's not a question of a simple death because that's something none of us can avoid eventually and all of us are ready for in wartime. I'm talking about the living death of years as a slave on the Turkish galleys!"

"Do you think that would be worse than the life I am living now?"

"You talk like a man who's lost his faith in God!"

"You're wrong there," said Skshetuski. "If I say that I am sick of living that's because it's a life without joy or promise but I've made my peace with God's will a long time ago. I'm not complaining. I don't curse my fate. I don't pound my head against a wall. I only want to do my part as best I can while there's still some strength left in me to do it."

"But your pain is gnawing at you like a poison."

"God gives the pain to test our faith. He'll send down the cure when He chooses."

"Well," the troubled peace commissioner stared into the fire. "I can't argue with you about that. Everything is in God's hands nowadays. He's our only hope, our only salvation . . . yours, mine, and the entire Commonwealth's as well. The King has gone to pray at Yasna Gora and maybe the Holy Mother will take mercy on him. Otherwise everyone is lost."

Again there was a long silence in the room and only the slow, drawn out 'Who goes there' of the dragoons outside echoed in the wind.

"Yes, yes," Pan Kretovski murmured. "We're all closer to death than to life these days. People have forgotten how to laugh in this Commonwealth of ours. I also thought that better times could come with greater understanding. But now I see that it was just another foolish hope, that it was all for nothing. God has turned His back upon the Commonwealth and there is nothing for us in the years ahead except war, famine, slaughter, tears and mourning. Nothing else."

Skshetuski sat in silence. Only the flames that leaped up suddenly in the hearth sent dancing crimson lights across his gaunt, grey face.

"Yes. It's all vanity," he agreed at last. "An empty illusion. It'll pass with all material things. And there'll be nothing to show for it after it has vanished."

"You speak like a monk," Pan Kretovski said.

Skshetuski said nothing. The wind went on sighing and moaning in the chimney.

Chapter Fifty-five

THEY LEFT THE TOWN of Novosyel early the next morning,
starting a journey that seemed like the penitent Stations of the
Cross to the heartsick Kisyel. It was a journey in which passage
through every shabby little town carried a threat of death while
the jibes and vulgarities that rained on the envoys along the way
were all the more unbearable because these men bore the dignity
of the Commonwealth in their hands.

Pan Kisyel became so ill under the strain that he had to be
carried out of his sleigh each time the convoy halted for the
night. The senator from Lvov raged and clawed his beard at the
brutality and contempt he had to endure, both in his own right
and as a representative of the King and senate. Captain
Bryshovski collapsed from exhaustion. Lack of sleep, anxiety
and the need for constant vigilance finally snapped his spirit so
that Skshetuski took his place as escort commander and led this
grim parade through the press of cursing, threatening and insulting mobs like a cortege of beggars.

"How long, dear Lord, how long," murmured the helpless,
grief-stricken *Voyevode* as he watched his dreams crumbling all
around him. Death, he thought, would be a mercy. "Peace,
amity, justice, love . . . respect among all men," he whispered
staring all around with tear-filled desolate old eyes and saw
clenched fists shaking in return.

He heard the snarling curses and asked himself again how he
could have been so wrong about his own people. In Byelgorod
the commissioners were sure that their last hour was about to
strike, and this time for good. The mob threw itself on them in
the street, battered the ill Bryshovski, dragged Pan

Gnyazdovski off his horse and trampled him to death. Only the unannounced arrival of the Orthodox Metropolitan who was on his way to Tchehryn for a conference with Hmyelnitzki staved off the general massacre that was being readied.

Kiev with its golden cupolas and castle and cannon, and with its famous Latin Academy and its seats of learning, seemed like the only refuge for the battered envoys; they longed for it as a haven of civilization in a storm of savagery and madness.

But Kiev barred its gates to them.

They were left to wander about in the open country where the mobs grew bolder every day. And then, as if to undermine the strongest among them, the venerable *Knaz* Tchetvertynski, who traveled to Hmyelnitzki earlier in the journey to fix the commissioners' agenda, returned from Tchehryn in mid-February with no idea of what Hmyelnitzki intended.

"He wouldn't even see me," the old Ruthenian prince reported to the *Voyevode*.

"*He* wouldn't see *you*?"

"Ah, he's a great lord now."

The peace commissioners didn't know where to turn, what to do, or even how to keep themselves alive. Should they go on? Should they confess failure and turn back? The roads to the west were blocked by wintering regiments of Cossacks who waited only for the truce to end so that they could slaughter every one of them, while the frenzied mobs of peasants pressed them ever harder, clawing at the reins of the dragoons' horses, and hurling shards of ice, stones and lumps of frozen earth into the *Voyevode's* sleigh.

"Don't they want peace, then?" the heavy-hearted *Voyevode* kept asking himself. "What is it they want?"

"Blood!" howled the mobs. "Death!"

"*Na Pohybel!*"

"Give us Kisyel's head!"

★   ★   ★

But if their days passed like a journey into purgatory, their nights were like traveling through Hell. Skshetuski and Donyetz had to fight a pitched battle near Gvozdovo, scattering several hundred peasants and marauders, and Pan Smyarovski and the Constable of Novgorod set out once more to persuade Hmyelnitzki to receive the envoys.

"Beg him," Kisyel told them. "Beg him, if you must, to meet with us in Kiev."

"Beg him?"

"Yes, beg him," the *Voyevode* pleaded but he didn't even hope they'd get through alive.

Meanwhile, in the town of Hvastov, the representatives of the Commonwealth had to watch in silence while the mobs murdered several hundred captives. Men and women of every age from childhood to senility were drowned in iceholes chopped in the frozen river, tossed about on pitchforks, stripped naked and doused with water buckets in the killing frost, or skinned alive with gelding knives and shears.

Eighteen days of terror, helplessness and despair passed like that before Hmyelnitzki sent word that he didn't feel like traveling to Kiev but that he'd wait for the envoys in Pereyaslav lower down the Dnieper. It seemed then to the wretched emissaries as if, at last, the cold Winter sun was breaking through the dark malevolence around them. Their hearts and minds felt lighter as if a huge millstone rolled off each of them and as if they had already brought about that just and honorable peace that they came to offer. They could breathe again; their torments, they assured each other, were as good as over. They had themselves ferried across the Dnieper near Terepol and reached the old Orthodox monastery of Verenkov by nightfall.

From there it was only six miles to Pereyaslav beyond the bend of the river. They could hear bells ringing in that town as they fell asleep.

★   ★   ★

The bells still rang and twenty cannon roared in the city as the *Voyevode's* sleigh-train made its way towards Pereyaslav the next morning. The old man had spent a restless night; the nightmare visions of his journey gnawed at him until dawn. He sat wrapped in furs in his open sleigh, shivering with fever, as the town gates before him darkened with a mass of horsemen, banners and musicians.

"Ah," Pan Kisyel sighed, clutching at every hope. "At least they're coming out to greet us."

The Zaporohjan Hetman met the envoys half a mile outside the city walls, as if to show some grudging respect for the Commonwealth, but Kisyel hardly recognized this new Bohdan

Hmyelnitzki. He knew him in the days when this rising young member of local Ukrainian gentry was quarrelling with Tchaplinski; indeed, he was among the first to give him a hearing. But the proud, ducal figure who rode out to meet him under flags and banners was like nobody he ever saw before.

Hmyelnitzki rode surrounded by a dense suite of atamans and colonels, with mounted musicians playing shrill military music, and with a half-dozen horsetail standards carried on foot before him. The great crimson banner of the Archangel Michael snapped and rattled in the wind above his head. Egret plumes nodded at his sable cap. Rich furs were gleaming and gold badges glinted in the cold morning light, and his billowing scarlet cloak and snow-white Arab stallion merely underlined his new princely image.

" *Quantum mutatus ab illo!*" the old Palatine murmured to himself. "How the man has changed."

"He comes like a monarch," whispered Prince Tchetvertynski. "I remember him when he could barely manage to bribe the court bailiffs to get him a hearing."

"And perhaps we should have listened to him then."

The envoys' convoy halted. The commissioners waited in the snow in a vain hope that the Zaporohjan Hetman would make some gesture of submission to the authority that they represented. It would be a good sign if he dismounted and made his way to the Commonwealth's representatives on foot. But that didn't happen. Instead Hmyelnitzki trotted up to the leading sleigh, stared down for a long, silent moment at the frail Kisyel and touched his fur cap in a careless gesture.

"Greetings to you, *Voyevode,*" he ground out hoarsely. "And to you, *pany komisary.*"

His huge claret-colored face swayed above them like an angry moon. His voice was thick with pride and crackling with power. Framed in its long black mustache, his full red mouth was twisted with contempt and a terrible amusement.

"So you've come to beg me for peace, have you?" he growled in dialect before the *Voyevode* could catch his breath and speak. "Ey, you'd have done better to talk to me when I was weak and asking you for justice. That was the time to talk, Kisyel, before I knew my own strength. Now I don't have to talk to any of you. I don't even have to find the time to see you. Still, since the King sent you all this way to see me I might as well hear what you've got to say. So . . . welcome to my country!"

"Greetings to you, Hetman." Kisyel spoke as firmly as he could but the quavering old voice betrayed his despair. "His Majesty the King sent us here to offer you his mercy . . . and to show you justice."

"He did, eh?"

Hmyelnitzki leaned over in his saddle and the reek of his thick, sweated body, raw spirits and *gojhalka* swept over the fainting *Voyevode* like an exhalation from a byre.

"Well,"—Hmyelnitzki's mouth stretched in a broad red grin but his bloodshot eyes remained cold and watchful—"Why not? I can always use a little mercy. Might need some for you! As for justice, I already got that for myself!"

His quick, barking laugh brought a loud response from his massed atamans and colonels who burst into fierce laughter of their own.

"This,"—and he slapped his saber with his fist while his harsh voice tightened into a snarl of fury—"that's what I used to carve my own justice out of your bloody hides! And I'll do more such carving if you don't bend those stiff *Lah* necks of yours and give me what I want!"

"That's a harsh way to greet the King's envoys, Hetman," Pan Kisyel protested but Hmyelnitzki merely shrugged and spat into the snow.

"Ah, it's too cold to stand out here talking in this weather," he grunted. "We'll do our talking later. In a house. Like gentry."

"I'm glad to hear it, Hetman."

Watching him and listening and remembering who this man had been, Pan Kisyel wondered at Hmyelnitzki's sense of theatre and the ease with which he could transform himself into anything that the situation called for. His voice was thick, abrasive and abrupt, like that of a freebooting Steppe Cossack who never bent his back to anyone; hoarse with liquor, he was as coarse and rough-hewn as the men over whom he exercised his uneasy power but there was something unreal in this sudden vulgarity and crudeness. His loutish mannerisms, ill-bred words, and his choppy gestures were as primitive as if he'd never spent a moment among cultivated people and yet, Pan Kisyel knew, this had been a consummate courtier in his time.

"Move over, Kisyel," he growled. "Make room for me in that sleigh of yours."

His voice was slurred with drink and heavy with impatience. That may have been part of a contrived performance but the sharp, angry gestures were alive with power. And then the great thick body clambered off its horse which a groom caught at once by the reins and led to the rear.

"I want to show you honor, Kisyel, you and your commission, by riding into my town beside you."

"Gladly, Hetman."

The *Voyevode* edged over to the right side of the seat, leaving a space for Hmyelnitzki on his left, and prayed that the Hetman would show him at least that much respect.

"You give me the right-hand side!" Hmyelnitzki roared, suddenly enraged. "Who do you think you are to put me on your left?"

"I'm a senator of the Commonwealth!" Pan Kisyel struggled to contain both his despair and anger.

"And what's that to me? Pan Pototzki is the first senator among you, isn't he? And a Grand Hetman too! But I've got him trotting on the end of a rope like a dancing bear! And I'll have him twitching on a stake if that's what I feel like!"

Blood mounted into Kisyel's pale face. "I represent the King's person here!"

"And what's he to me?"

Pan Kisyel knew that both his mission and his life could end here and now, but Hmyelnitzki started calming down at once. Perhaps he still didn't trust his own might and power as much as he claimed. Perhaps Kshetchovski's death loomed darkly in his thoughts and reminded him of the Commonwealth's continuing resources and of the fates of other Cossack rebels. Or perhaps he simply wasn't drunk enough for murder. He stared at the old man with his bulging, calculating eyes and his fist relaxed on the hilt of his saber. Then he shrugged, glanced away and spat into the snow again.

"Well, let him rule in Warsaw, then," he muttered and climbed into the left side of the sleigh. "Like I'm the ruler here." And then he shook a clenched fist in Pan Kisyel's face. "But I see I need to crack a few more of your stiff *Lah* necks!"

Pan Kisyel couldn't trust himself to say another word. He fixed his fevered eyes on the looming snow clouds and began to pray. He knew that the violence and indignities and humiliations were not over yet; the dangers weren't finished along with the journey. If that painful progress across the Ukraine was like the tear-strewn path to Golgotha, he thought, then being an ambassador in Hmyelnitzki's capital will be like the torment of the cross itself.

★ ★ ★

Meanwhile the horses lurched forward, the iron runners hissed across the snow, and the long stream of sleighs, horsemen, cheering atamans and Zaporohjan colonels, Cossack standard bearers, musicians squealing on their Tartar fifes and pounding on kettledrums, Donyetz' *moloytzy* who shouted out Steppe songs and battle cries, and Pan Yan's dragoons, wound towards the town where every bell was ringing and every gun flashed and roared salutes on the walls.

"Don't think that this is just for you," Hmyelnitzki said coldly to the *Voyevode*. "That's how I receive all my foreign envoys."

And he spoke the truth, as Pan Kisyel knew. Only a year earlier he was a felon hunted in the Steppe by the lackeys of a vengeful provincial *starosta*; now he played host to a dozen foreign embassies like an independent prince.

But how did that change him? While he was still pulling back from Zamost, under the spell of Yan Casimir's election and the Lithuanian victories, he may have doubted his power and importance. But when ancient Kiev, the capital of Old Ruthenia which was so much greater than the upstart Moscow, welcomed him with church banners and ten thousand torches, when the famed philosophers and theologians of the Kiev Academy greeted him in Latin as '*another Moses— the servant, savior and liberator of the people,*' when the Archmandrite of the Eastern Church addressed him as '*Bohdan, given to us by God,*' and when—to cap it all—foreign rulers wrote to him as '*illustrissimus princeps,*' or most illustrious prince, then he could doubt no longer. How could he? In the parlance of his day 'the beast arose within him'; he realized who he really was and how much he commanded, and what solid footing he had among his people. A crown wouldn't be too much for him now.

And why not, the wretched Kisyel had to ask himself. Who could deny his power? The foreign embassies which hurried to his capital were an acknowledgement of his independence. The friendship of the Tartars, bought with the bulk of the pillaged booty and with the tens of thousands of Ukrainian captives whom this 'liberator of the people' gave to the Muslim slavers, assured him of the Khan's help against any enemy.

So what more would he need? He may have been willing to acknowledge the new King while he was fretting under the walls of Zamost, the *Voyevode* knew; his protestations of loyalty to the Commonwealth could have been genuine when the peace commissioners started on their journey. But now? Filled with pride, and convinced of the helplessness of the Commonwealth before him, he'd raise his hand against the King himself!

So what could he be offered in negotiations?

The dreams that gnawed at that gloomy, unforgiving spirit had nothing more to do with Cossack freedoms. He had gone far beyond demanding restoration of ancient privileges to the Zaporohjans. As for his professed defense of the old Ruthenian Church, a thousand burned and looted Orthodox monasteries and churches stood as mute witnesses to his lack of interest in faith and religion.

'He wouldn't even care about his own old grievances,' thought the *Voyevode*.

He'd dream now of a kingdom. Of a crown and scepter.

★ ★ ★

The Commonwealth peace commissioners entered Pereyaslav with their heads hung low like condemned men going to their executions. And who could say they weren't?

Meanwhile, sprawled in the sleigh beside the *Voyevode*, Hmyelnitzki brooded about his past and future. He was the undisputed master of the Ukraine. Every Zaporohjan stood behind him to a man, he knew. Never before, and never under any other leader, did those ruthless warriors enjoy so much loot. They never spilled so much blood, beat such powerful enemies, pillaged so many towns, monasteries and manors, nor won so much glory. Now they lay at his heels like faithful, panting wolfhounds, ready to leap at anyone he pointed out to them; they'd follow him through Hell as long as he continued to lead them to victories. The Tartars also had what they wanted most. This year's price of a prime captive on the Bridge of Sighs was only ten arrows, Tuhay-bey had told him; there were so many Polish and Ruthenian slaves offered for sale along the Black Sea coast since he let the Tartars into the Ukraine that three men or half a dozen women went for the price of one fire-hardened bow. Towns, townships and villages disappeared across the length and breadth of the country to pay the cost of that terrible alliance. The rich and fertile soil turned into a scorched and emptied wilderness to feed his ambition. It was a wound that centuries wouldn't heal.

And what about the people?

The great masses of the common people flocked to him because he offered what they craved the most: life without a master. But how would they fit into his great design? There were no peasants like them anywhere in Europe, Hmyelnitzki was certain; no, nor anywhere else on earth where the wretched peasantry bowed without a murmur under the burdens of serfdom and oppression. But the Ukrainians were a different breed. They breathed a different air. Why should they crawl behind some noble's plow when the horizons promised them a masterless existence everywhere they looked? The open Steppe beckoned to them every day. The tall grasses whispered. The wilderness filled their minds and souls with such insatiable hunger to be free, and with such abundant sense of space and of their own unfettered possibilities, that they clung to their liberty even more ferociously than to life itself.

The *Sietch* called out to them from beyond the cataracts; every sunrise whispered '*Damn your masters! Come and get your freedom!*' And who could hold them back? The Tartar raiders taught them war from childhood. The savagery of life in the borderlands inured them to the cruelties of survival, accustomed their hands to weapons and their eyes to bloodshed. Hey, they asked themselves, wouldn't we have it better slitting throats with Hmyel and pillaging our masters than bowing to some bailiff? And so they ran to him in their tens of thousands, and Hmyelnitzki knew that they would keep on coming as long as they lived, because those who refused went into the slave pens of his Tartar allies and vanished in that endless river of misery and tears that flowed to the auction blocks beyond the Black Sea.

"They called me a Moses in Kiev," he remembered. "Leader and liberator. God's gift to his people."

But there was also that bitter new ballad about him that the *tchernya* had begun to sing even as they ran for refuge to his armies, and marched to his orders, and burned down their own country at one word from him.

" . . . *Ay, may the first bullet*
Not pass by that Hmyel,

> *May he live to rue it*
> *For ever in Hell . . ."*

Having risen against their Polish masters, Hmyelnitzki asked
himself, would they let him turn them into serfs again if he
made his peace with the Commonwealth? Free of the crushing
weight of their Polish landlords, would they return humbly to
the soil and bow before the whip of a new Cossack master?

Never, he thought.

So be it.

Let the blood keep flowing. Let the horizons burn down to
the ground. Let the people drown in their own tears as long as
all this served that greater purpose which now appeared before
him.

' . . . *Princeps*,' he thought. "*Illustrissimus . . .*"

Barely a year ago they almost hanged him on the
Omelnitchek, he smiled as he remembered. Now he was leading an embassy from the King and senate into the gates of one
of his cities—riding in a sleigh with a *Voyevode* who would
shortly plead with him for peace—while his guns flashed and
thundered on his walls and all the bells were pealing in his
churches, and all his people gathered in his streets to see the
homage of a conqueror that he would receive.

Like the true master of the Ukraine, he thought. A *Hospodar*.
A King.

★   ★   ★

The peals and roars of the bells and cannon barely pierced the
cold indifference in Skshetuski's mind. His eyes moved back and
forth among the faces of Hmyelnitzki's colonels oblivious of
everything else around him. His search along the Dniester
proved fruitless. He was resigned to the loss of Helen. But now
he searched for Bohun so that he might kill him or be killed
himself.

He knew there was a chance that the Zaporohjan might have
him murdered out of hand or seize him like any other captive
and sell him to the Tartars; there were always such risks when
dealing with the Cossacks. But he also knew something of
Bohun's soaring pride in his reputation, his strangely knight-
like vision of the code of manhood and his boundless courage,
and he could hope that this Cossack hero would accept his
challenge.

He no longer wanted anything for himself. He didn't think that Bohun would tell him where he'd hidden Helen even on his deathbed. He expected that the ataman might demand his promise to give up his search if he won their duel and he was willing to bind himself to even that kind of sacrifice if it would free her from shame and degradation.

'*Let her find her peace among the nuns after that*, he thought. '*Let God soothe her pain.*'

As for himself, he would seek death in war or, if God refused to grant him that eternal rest, he'd look for some form of peace in the oblivion of a monastery.

But he didn't see Bohun anywhere among the atamans and colonels who rode around Hmyelnitzki. Zagloba's words about Bohun's wedding plans ground in his memory like shards of broken glass and he started thinking that he ought to go to Kiev after all. And then he caught sight of some Cossack atamans he knew before the war. He spotted old Filon Djedjala whom he used to see often in Tchehryn, and Yashevski who'd been an envoy to Prince Yeremi from the *Sietch*, and Yarosh who was once a troop leader among the Prince's Cossacks, and Hrusha who used to wrestle bears in the Lubnie courtyard and who could bite through horseshoes with his teeth, and the half-mad Naokolopaletz.

Perhaps they'd know where he might look for Bohun, Pan Yan thought.

He edged his horse towards Yashevski, touched his cap and nodded.

"We know each other," he said.

"Sure." The Cossack colonel nodded in his turn. "I seen you in Lubnie, you're Yarema's *lytzar*."

"Ah, you remember."

"Why shouldn't I remember? We drank a bit together, you and me, last time I came to Lubnie. Had a good time together. And how's your *Knaz* doing?"

"He's well."

"He won't be feeling so well come Spring." The Zaporohjan's teeth gleamed in a yellow smile. "He and Hmyel never got to lock horns this past Summer but that's bound to happen when we go west again. Stands to reason, don't it? And when they come head-on against each other one of them's sure to go down into the ground."

"Whoever God picks," Pan Yan said.

"That's right. And God's been real kind to our *bat'ko* Hmyel. That Yarema of yours won't get to see his Transdnieper lands again. He and your kind are all done with that and your day is over. Hmyelnitzki has all the *moloytzy* he can use and more, and what's your *Knaz* got? Empty pockets, that's what, and a handful of people that don't have no other place to go. And what about you? You still riding for him?"

"Right now I'm with the envoys," Pan Yan said.

"Well, I'm glad to see you anyway," Yashevski said and grinned. "We're old drinking comrades, you'n me."

"Then maybe you can do me a small service, eh?"

"And what would that be?"

"Tell me where I can find Bohun," Pan Yan said. "You know who I mean, don't you? That famous ataman from the Pereyaslav Regiment. He's got to be pretty high up with you people now."

"Silence!" snarled Yashevski. "Not another word, you hear? You're lucky we're old acquaintances, you and me, and that I drank with you, or you'd be dead right here and now!"

Skshetuski stared at the Cossack as if he had suddenly gone mad. "Have you lost your mind?"

"My mind's alright and I don't want to threaten you either, but Hmyel's given orders that if any of you ask about anything they're to be killed at once."

"But I'm asking about a private matter, nothing military."

"It doesn't matter what you ask about. Hmyel made it clear to all us colonels and we passed the word. '*If they so much as ask about firewood or a bowl of soup,*' he said. '*They're to be cut down without another thought.*' So tell that to the rest of your people."

"Thanks for the warning," Pan Yan said.

"You're the only one I'd warn," the Zaporohjan grunted. "If you was any other *Lah* you'd be in Hell right now, dead as a horseshoe and chewing on the coals."

Then they rode on without another word.

The road leading to the gate and both sides of the street beyond it were packed with a dense mass of *tchernya* and Cossacks who watched the passing of the envoys in a glowering silence of their own. Hmyelnitzki's presence in the *Voyevode's* sleigh restrained them from spitting out their curses and from hurling the stones and fist-sized lumps of ice they clutched along with their knives and sabers, but their dour, unforgiving hatred was clear enough without that.

Pan Yan dressed his dragoons' ranks, raised his head high, and rode behind the long line of sleighs as if he was impervious to those threatening glances. But he felt each of them like a knife pointed at his chest. He remembered the admonition of Father Muhovyetzki in the church in Lubnie, and knew that he would have to cling to all his faith, and hold tight to all his charity and patience, to accomplish what he set out to do without allowing himself to sink into that bitter sea of unrelenting hatred.

Chapter Fifty-six

TWO MORNINGS LATER Hmyelnitzki waited for the envoys in front of his quarters, surrounded by his colonels and other Zaporohjan elders, and by a vast assembly of rank and file Cossacks. Masses of *tchernya* were also brought into the town because he wanted all his people to see for themselves how high he had risen, how mighty he'd become, and just how much the King himself valued and esteemed him.

All the church bells in the town were ringing as if for alarm, summoning the people. The cannon boomed with salutes since the first light of dawn. But the day came slowly. The sky looked as if it were molded out of lead. It hung like a dull, listless canopy sagging with black clouds that promised a new storm gathering below the horizon. The sun was cold and pale from the start. It seemed to drag itself out of the morning mists as if angry to be disturbed for nothing; then it slipped furtively into the clouds like an unwilling witness to that act of reconciliation which few people in Pereyaslav believed anyway. But as far as Hmyelnitzki was concerned this grey threatening day was the most important moment of his life.

He sat on a wooden dais under a mulberry banner and his horsetail *buntchuk*, the traditional insignia of an eastern warlord borrowed four centuries earlier from Mongol invaders. He was dressed in scarlet ceremonial robes lined and edged with sables, and with the ambassadors of Moscow, Novgorod and other neighboring principalities and tsardoms grouped near him to add to his stature with the crowd. He rested his booted feet on a velvet cushion with gold knots and tassels, his great red fists were clenched tightly on his hips, and he waited for the Commonwealth's peace commissioners with a dark frown of impatience on his florid face.

"Where are they?" he muttered to the shadowy Vyhovski at his elbow. "How come they're so late?"

Vyhovski shrugged. "They're arguing," he said.

"About what?"

"Whether to give you the King's gifts right away or to wait for some sign of your humility and contrition."

"Contrition?" Hmyelnitzki's bloodshot eyes began to bulge with rage. "I'll show them contrition!"

"Don't worry. They're coming. They think they'll get to you with a show of humanity and compassion. A demonstration of the King's mercy and their own good faith."

"I'll give them compassion!"

A vast, sleeping anger lay hidden in the folds of that heavy face and it was easy to see how an entire people could be cowed by that dreaming fury and why the masses bowed down before him like a forest beaten to the ground by a hurricane.

The campaigns of the year before made him look far older than his early fifties but they didn't crush him; he'd merely thickened, aging like a mountain. His massive arms still looked powerful enough to overthrow empires and to create new kingdoms. His huge, lowering face, stained a choleric crimson by his bouts of drinking, expressed an irresistible and unbending will, an overwhelming pride in his own achievements, and an unshakable confidence in himself. He sat in brooding stillness like a living storm cloud. Power and terror had always been one and the same to the masses of his exploited people and they valued nothing that they didn't fear. Nothing spoke to them louder or more clearly than an iron will, a ruthless ambition accountable to no one, and the ability to kill and destroy like lightning out of a clear sky; and they stared at him in fear and admiration as those seething furies began to wake and stir.

Impatience glittered in his red-rimmed eyes. His clenched teeth glittered like fangs under his drooping mustache, and his breath seeped out in two twin wisps of steam from his flared nostrils so that he seemed like a fire-breathing dragon to the awestruck, superstitious peasants, or like the dreaded image of Lucifer himself. Proud, gloomy, grim as death and glowering with anger, he sprawled in his thronelike chair among his savage generals and colonels, surrounded by whispering ambassadors and envoys, and a deep murmur of joy and worshipful admiration rose time and again out of that other unbridled elemental force: the vast human ocean of his people.

This was their chief, their champion. The conqueror of Hetmans. The destroyer of those dukes and princes and Ukrainian kinglets whose power had seemed unlimited and eternal. The whip of God which lashed the gentry and cowed the *Lahy* who always passed for invincible until Hmyelnitzki's coming.

"Hmyel . . .! Hmyel . . .!" The deep, admiring mutter swept through the dense, swaying crowds like a wind across a restless sea. *Na slavu! Na pohybel lahom!* Glory to us and death to the Poles!"

And then the procession of the Polish envoys appeared at the end of the crowded street.

★   ★   ★

First came the Cossack drummers pounding a slow, dirgelike beat on their kettledrums. Then came the trumpeters with long brass horns at their bulging lips, throwing deep, mournful notes into the frosted air as if in requiem for the dignity and glory of the Commonwealth. Then came Pan Kretovski carrying a jeweled gold *bulava* on a velvet cushion while Pan Kultchynski lifted a huge red banner with an inscription and the symbol of a great crowned eagle embroidered on it in silver and gold.

The *Voyevode* walked behind them, as solitary as if he was repudiated and abandoned by all of his own kind, with deep lines of suffering etched into his pale, aristocratic face, and with his long, white beard hanging limply down his frail chest. The rest of the envoys straggled after him, followed by their escorting dragoons under Pan Skshetuski.

Kisyel walked as slowly as if each of his dragging steps brought a separate agony. Despair threatened to overwhelm his thinking. He could see with a sudden and unforgiving clarity that all his years of work were a terrible mistake, that he had lived a lie, and that a wholly different truth was peering at him out of the shredded remnants of his hopes.

He'd managed to convince himself up to this final moment that he came to offer royal clemency and mercy to a loyal but misguided people but now another image rose up to mock him in his own dulled mind. Naked and ugly as a jeering hag, the

awful truth cried out to him so loudly that even the deaf could
hear it and the blind could see it.

'. . . *You're not here to offer mercy! You're here to beg for it! To buy
it with that flag, these parchments, and that golden baton . . .*'

His mind reeled under the shock. He had refused to see
anything but his own vision of events even after the rebellion
shattered his other illusions, and now remorseless voices jeered
at him, accused him, went on hissing their mockeries in his
head.

'. . . *Look at yourself, Kisyel! See that palatine and senator of the
Commonwealth coming on foot in the name of his King and nation
. . . coming to surrender all your dignity and the majesty of the people
whom you represent . . . humbling yourself like a penitent before the
rabble and its upstart leader . . .*'

It seemed then to this proud and deeply learned lord of
Brusilov that his soul had dwindled into dust; that he was no
more than a crawling insect; and his ears filled with the remembered thunder of Yeremi Vishnovyetzki crying in the senate: '*It
would be better for us not to live at all than to live as the slaves of
peasants and pagans . . .!*'

How would history judge the two of them? How would he—
Kisyel the appeaser—appear beside that single-minded, ruthless
Knaz of Lubnie who never showed himself to rebels as anything
but a wrathful Zeus with fire striking from his hands and
lightnings in his eyes? How would future generations assess him
beside that warlike image which he had done his best to weaken
and destroy?

His mind seemed to crack under the weight of his self-
contempt; his heart sagged and faltered. He felt that he would
much rather drop dead like a homeless dog than take one more
step on this degrading journey to his complete humiliation. But
he went on, propelled step by step by his entire past, by all his
work and efforts, and by the remorseless and inevitable logic of
everything he had ever done.

Meanwhile, Hmyelnitzki waited for him like a conqueror:
frowning, contemptuous, and impatient.

★ ★ ★

At last the procession halted before the dais. Kisyel stepped
forward. The drummers let their padded drumsticks rest on the

copper kettles, the trumpeters ceased blowing their strident, brassy calls. Even the avid crowds grew quiet and strained forward in a breathless silence, and the only sound came from the great red banner carried by Pan Kultchynski which flapped in the icy air as if its outspread eagle wished to tear itself free and fly from this scene.

And then a single voice—sharp and dry and ringing with the sort of strength that comes only from utter desperation— cut into the silence: "Dragoons, about turn! Follow me!"

The *Voyevode* spun around and shuddered. The voice had been Skshetuski's. Pale as death and uncaring about any consequences either to the envoys or himself, the young lieutenant was standing in his stirrups, his sword in his hand.

"Follow me!" he repeated and the order was as loud as a thunderclap in that sudden silence.

The trained dragoons turned their horses in place with parade precision. The freshly swept cobblestones clicked under the hooves. Skshetuski's hot, angry eyes seemed to be dripping fire but the commissioners turned as white as linen and the *Voyevode* felt as if he had just seen death's bony claw reaching out for them.

"What's going on? What's happening?"

The volatile crowd swayed like the dark surface of a lake struck by a sudden wind. It rustled with questions. Eyes peered, hoarse voices started shouting, men began to climb up on each other's shoulders, and even Hmyelnitzki shifted slightly in his chair to see what was happening.

"At a walk," Skshetuski ordered harshly and signaled with his saber. "Forward!"

The dragoons rode away, heading back towards Pan Kisyel's quarters at the far end of town. Doubt and astonishment spread across every face ranged behind Hmyelnitzki because there was something so extraordinary in the young soldier's bitter voice and eyes that no one could be quite sure what it meant. Only Kisyel knew that the sudden departure of the escort had nothing to do with the ceremony. He grasped at once what Pan Yan was doing and he also understood that the lives of the envoys as well as the escort were suddenly hanging by a single thread so he stepped up to the dais and began to speak.

But he barely started reading the formula of a royal pardon

for Hmyelnitzki and the Zaporohjans when another distracting incident took place, the mob's attention shifted, and Pan Kisyel could sigh in relief. The veteran Djedjala, standing next to Hmyelnitzki's chair, lurched forward, shook his short, bone-handled mace under the *Voyevode's* nose, and started cursing him and shouting.

"Hey, you, Kisyel!" He was swaying like a drunken bear at the edge of the dais. "What are you babbling about here? The King, that's one thing! But your kinglets an' your gentry are something else again! You've given us enough trouble an' you'll pay for it! As for you, you whining old windbag, you're nothing but a traitor! You're our own blood an' bone . . . you're one of our kind . . . but you broke away from us, you son of a bitch! You stick with the Poles! We've had enough of your fancy talk, you hear? We don't need it no more! 'Cause we'll get what we want with our swords anyway!"

And now it was the *Voyevode's* turn to stare at Hmyelnitzki with disgusted eyes. "Is this the discipline you've taught your colonels, Hetman?" he demanded.

"Shut your mouth, Djedjala!" Hmyelnitzki roared out, shamed and dark-faced with sudden rage.

"Shut up! Keep quiet!" the other colonels bellowed. "Look at 'im, will you? It's hardly daylight an' he's soused already! Get out of here, you drunken hog, or we'll toss you out!"

Djedjala threw himself about for a moment longer but half a dozen rough hands seized him by the neck and heaved him out of the circle into the crowd behind.

The *Voyevode* resumed his address.

He pointed out with smooth and soothing words how great was the King's magnanimity and how important were his gifts to Hmyelnitzki. The Zaporohjan Hetman was now vested with legal authority over the Cossack armies rather than the unlawful power he'd seized for himself.

"His Majesty could punish," he went on. "Instead he forgives you because of the good will and respect you showed when you pulled back from Zamost. And because everything that's happened, terrible though it was, took place before his ascension to the throne."

So it was only right, he continued softly, for Hmyelnitzki to show his gratitude for this unparalleled act of clemency and grace by putting an end to bloodshed, leading the peasants back to their obedience, and entering into treaty negotiations with the royal envoys.

But Hmyelnitzki didn't say a word. He accepted the *bulava* and the royal standard which he ordered unfurled above himself at once and the *tchernya* broke out into such joyful howls at this triumphant sight that it became impossible for anyone to hear anything. He waited while the mob howled and danced, and his colonels cheered, and a certain cold, disdainful pleasure spread across his face.

Then he nodded. He raised his golden mace and there was instant silence.

"Well," he began quietly in a brooding tone, nodding his great head slowly up and down as if each of his words was weighed with meditation. "I'm grateful to His Majesty—we're all grateful to him—for this authority he's given me over the Zaporohjan army, and for his forgiveness of all my past sins. Of course the authority is mine anyway, because it was given to me by the Zaporohjan army, but it's good to know that the King is with us. I always said that he was on my side, didn't I? It's the King himself who's against you princelings and here's the proof of it! Here's my reward for cutting you down to size! And I'll keep chopping you off at the neck like he wants me to, unless you obey me and him in everything, you hear me?"

His voice rose and hardened as he spoke so that the final question was an angry shout and the crowd howled with joy and admiration. Here was their Hetman! Here was their commander humbling the envoys and everything that they represented! The Cossack colonels and the Zaporohjan elders shouted as wildly as the mob and shook their furious fists at the commissioners who looked as ill and stricken as if all the blood had drained from their bodies.

"The King wants you to stop the bloodshed, my lord Hetman," Kisyel tried again. "And to start working with us on a treaty . . ."

But the new Royal Hetman of the Ukraine waved him into silence.

"Bloodshed?" he roared. "It's not me that's spilling blood these days, it's the Lithuanians! I've just got word that Radzivill has taken my Mozyr and my Turov! And that he's sent every living soul into the next world! If that turns out to be true then you'll see blood flowing right before your eyes! I'll have four hundred prisoners' throats cut while you're watching, you hear me? I've enough of your kind in chains to build a mountain out of their skulls so don't you talk to me about ending bloodshed!"

Then he shrugged. His bloodshot eyes narrowed, blinked and turned away. His huge, dark face grew careless with indifference.

"As for treaties and the like, that'll keep 'til later. There's only a handful of my colonels with me, the rest are away in Winter quarters, so I can't decide anything right now if I wanted to. Besides we've talked enough for now. You've done what you came to do. You've given me what you were sent to give and the whole world's seen how I'm now a Hetman with the King's own authority behind him! So come on in out of the weather and have a drink with me because I'm hungry and it's time to eat!"

He rose, turned his back on the envoys and strode into the town governor's house where he made his quarters. The colonels, ambassadors and commissioners followed in his wake, Kisyel last of all.

★ ★ ★

Inside—in the steamy, low-ceilinged, whitewashed *izba* which formed the main room of the house—the long trestle table looked as if it were about to collapse under the weight of looted silverplate among which, had he been less distracted and distressed, the wretched Kisyel would have recognized his own, pillaged the year before from his estates in Hushtcha.

Whole carcasses of roast pig, sides of smoked beef and steaming slabs of mutton, lay piled in pools of grease the length of the table, along with crystal bowls and ornamental platters heaped with Tartar pilaf, while the sour, biting smell of home-brewed millet liquor and the raw, acrid reek of *gojhalka* wafted from dozens of carved silver beakers.

Hmyelnitzki took his place at mid-table, seated Pan Kisyel on his right, and beckoned to Castellan Brozovski to sit on his left.

"They say in Warsaw that I drink *Lah* blood," he said. He gave a sharp, abrupt bark of laughter, grinned at his silent

guests, and winked broadly at his colonels who were clambering across the rough-hewn benches on both sides of the table.
"But that's a lie. And d'you know why I don't?"

"No, Hetman." The pale Kisyel felt beads of sweat gathering
on his forehead.

"Because I'd rather drink corn liquor any day," Hmyelnitzki
roared out. "The dogs can have the other."

The colonels howled with laughter. The sound was so vast in
that low-ceilinged room, and it burst out so suddenly, that it
drowned out the thunder of the cannon that still boomed outside. The walls seemed to shake in that greasy air, while the
peace commissioners bit down on their lips and fixed their eyes
mutely on the table. To provoke Hmyelnitzki's rage meant
death to each of them, and all of them knew it. Only the
castellan's proud, aristocratic face turned a violent crimson
while Kisyel's forehead gleamed with nervous sweat.

"Eat! Eat! Enough of this talking!"

The Cossack colonels tore at the meats with their bare hands
and began to feed. Hmyelnitzki himself ripped great chunks of
crackling flesh off the roasts and piled them on the envoys'
platters.

"Eat! Eat! *Na zdorovye! Na slavu!* To your health and glory!"

No one had much to say until they sated the first pangs of
hunger. The only sounds came from the gnawed crackling
bones, smacking lips, the slurp of sucked marrow, and the
gurgling of drained vodka flagons. Words fell here and there,
snapped and bitten off like the bones and passing without reply,
until Hmyelnitzki sighed, wiped his greasy mouth with the
back of his fist and pushed away a little from the table.

"Who led your escort?" he turned suddenly to the *Voyevode.*

Anxiety flashed across Pan Kisyel's face. "His name's
Skshetuski," he said. "A good man . . ."

Hmyelnitzki nodded. "*Ya yeho znayu,*" he said in Ruthenian.
"I know him. How come he didn't want to be there when you
honored me?"

"Because he had no part in the ceremony. His job was security on the road and there was no more need of that. Those
were his orders."

"Orders, eh?" Hmyelnitzki stared sideways at the pale Kisyel.
"And who gave those orders?"

"I did," Kisyel said and added as swiftly and persuasively as he could: "I didn't think it fitting to have dragoons standing over our necks while we were handing you His Majesty's gifts, Hetman. That would've been . . . unseemly."

"Hmmm." Hmyelnitzki's red-rimmed eyes clouded with suspicion. "And I thought something different. Because I know that young man has a stiff neck of his own."

Here Yashevski leaned across the table and broke into their conversation.

"We got no cause to be worried about your dragoons," he said to Pan Kisyel. "No, not any more! You *Lahy* were strong once. Oh yes, you were something to fear at one time! But we found out at Pilavtse that you're a different people now . . .!"

"That's right!" Hmyelnitzki interrupted. "You're dogs now, not lions! Puking infants dressed in iron swaddling! You just about wet yourselves with fear at the sight of us, and you ran like rabbits, even though there were hardly three thousand Tartars with us at Pilavtse!"

The peace commissioners said nothing. They sat bowed over their food in shamed and stony silence as if the meat and drink were suddenly as bitter as wormwood and gall.

"Hey, hey!" Hmyelnitzki turned to them with a mocking smile. His hoarse, breathy voice was thick with an ironic imitation of hospitality. "How come you're not eating? Eh? What's the matter? Can't you get our simple Cossack fare down your lordly throats?"

"If their throats are too tight we can slit 'em for them!" Djedjala shouted further down the table.

The Cossack colonels, starting to feel their liquor, filled the room with laughter but their Hetman threw them one sharp, warning glance and they quietened down at once. Kisyel, who had been ill for days, looked as white as a winding-sheet. Brozovski was so flushed with fury and humiliation that his face looked ready to burst with blood.

"What is this!" he exploded, unable to hold back his anger any longer. "Did we come here to eat or to be insulted?"

"You came to make a treaty," Hmyelnitzki said coldly. "And in the meantime the Lithuanian armies are murdering our brothers and burning down our homes. If it's true what I hear about the sack of Mozyr and Turov, where Radzivill is said to have cut down every living soul, then you'll see another kind of meat piled in front of you first thing in the morning!"

Brozovski bit his lips. The lives of thousands of war prisoners still in Cossack hands were hanging by a hair and the envoys knew it. A single frown on that dark, lowering mask which changed so swiftly from mockery to fury could send them all to slaughter. They had to bear all the indignities and humiliations without a word of protest and soothe this new, omnipotent Ukrainian Hetman as best as they could.

"God grant that this news from Lithuania turns out to be an exaggeration," said Father Lenkovski."

But he'd hardly spoken when Fedor Visnyak, the murderous, epileptic successor of old Barabas as ataman of the Tcherkassy Cossacks, swung his iron mace at the nape of the priest's frail neck. "*Movtchy, po'peh!*" he roared.

He couldn't quite reach his intended victim because four other broad-backed atamans sat hunched over their meat and vodka between them at the table but he cursed and bellowed at the terrified Carmelite none the less: "You shut your mouth, priest! Speak when you're spoken to when you're with your betters! Now get out of here, you hear? Out with you! Or I'll teach you how to show respect for Zaporohjan colonels!"

Others leaped up to calm the infuriated Cossack but he had worked himself into a rage beyond control. Foam boiled out on his mustache. He kicked and struggled, howling threats of murder, until his comrades dragged him to the door and threw him into the snow outside.

Meanwhile the liquor flowed by the flagon and then by the bucket and the feast continued. The mobs still milled about outside in the freezing air. The air in the overheated *izba* turned so thick and foul with the reek of unwashed clothes and bodies dripping sweat, the exhalations of drunken men who snored with their arms and heads pillowed on the platters, and the stench of spilled spirits and congealing greases, that even the powerfully built Castellan Brozovski began to choke on it, while the frail Kisyel felt as if he was about to faint.

"When, Hetman,"— he tried again, to give a reasonable turn to the mindless bellowing around him—"would you want the treaty talks to start?"

But Hmyelnitzki was no longer sober.

"What're you bothering me for with all this talk about treaties?" he roared. "How come you won't let me eat an' drink in peace? Can't you see I can't talk now? I'm drunk, can't you see it? Leave me th' hell alone!"

"The peace . . .," the *Voyevode* began.

"To Hell with your peace!"

And here Hmyelnitzki slammed his huge fist on the table so hard that all the dishes jumped up in the air, the flagons toppled and splashed *gojhalka* all over the feasters, and the gnawed bones and meats tumbled to the floor.

"I want war not peace! I'll turn your whole world upside down in the next four Sundays! I'll trample you all into the ground and I'll sell what's left of you to the Turkish Sultan! That's what you'll get from me, understand?"

"The King expected . . .," Kisyel began again but the drunken Hetman slid away into his own gloomy introspection.

"The King . . . well, all right, let there be a King so he can hang the gentry and the dukes and princelings . . . Cut their necks if they cross me. Like I'll cut Cossack necks if they don't do everything I tell 'em . . . You threaten me with Swedes, do you? I'll settle the Swedes after I'm done with you! Tuhay-bey's nearby in the Steppe . . . He's like my second soul, like my brother ready to do anything I want . . .!"

And at the thought of his Tartar ally the drunken Hetman passed from howling rage to sentimental tears.

"He's the only true falcon left in the Steppe," he sobbed. "And you want me to turn my sword on him and on his father, the Great Khan? You want me to lead the Cossacks against the Turks in Spring? Nothing'll come of that! I'll ride you down instead, me an' my good Tartar brothers. I've sent out word already to the regiments so the *moloytzy* feed their horses well on Winter grain and hold themselves ready for the road . . ."

But thought of war changed his mood again. He jerked erect as if rage seized him by the hair, his red eyes rolled madly in his head and his voice gasped with fury.

"That's right . . .! We'll go without wagons, without cannon too!" he howled, beating on the table. "We'll find all that among the *Lahy* like we've done before! I'll cut the throat of any Cossack that takes a cart along, an' that goes for me too! All I'll need is saddlebags for rations and sacks for the loot!"

Kisyel closed his eyes while his mind fogged over. He longed for oblivion. But the terrible ranting voice went on pounding in his ears none the less.

"I'll go all the way to your Vistula that way!" Hmyelnitzki was shouting. "An' when I get there I'll call out: '*Hey, you Lahy! You sit still, right where you are, an' keep your mouths shut or I'll shut* '*em for you!*' An' any of you make a sound, it'll be your last one! I've had it with your gentry rule . . . with your lords and masters! With your damned dragoons! An' I'm done talking to you too, you cursed reptiles that live on lies an' trickery!"

Here he struggled up to his feet, kicked over the bench, tore at his hair with both fists and stamped his boots in rage until dust billowed and splinters flew up from the floor.

"War!" he bellowed. "War! Right now! Right away! I got my blessing for it from the King, didn't I? He made me his Hetman! I got his blessing an' his absolution too! So who needs your commissioners an' commissions? Who needs to talk treaties? I won't even let an armistice begin!"

Then, suddenly, seeing the utter terror that gripped the commissioners, and remembering that Cossacks seldom did well in a Winter war when the frozen ground was too hard for digging entrenchments, he staggered back to the table and slumped heavily on another bench.

He sat in silence. His huge head drooped down towards his heaving chest. His voice made strangled, snoring noises in the back of his throat.

Chapter Fifty-seven

BUT THE TORMENTS of that degrading and humiliating day weren't over yet for the stricken envoys. Hmyelnitzki shook himself awake and seized another flagon of *gojhalka*.

"To the King's long life!" he shouted.

"*Na slavu! Na zdorovye!*" roared the drunken colonels. "To his health and glory!"

"Here you, Kisyel," the Hetman turned again to the exhausted and drained *Voyevode*. "Don't you get so gloomy. Don't take it all to heart. I'm drunk now an' I don't remember half of what I'm saying. The *vorojhykhi*, the witches, told me there's going to be a war so there's got to be one. But I'll hold off until the new grass. Then we can call a commission to look at a treaty an' I might even let the prisoners go free. People tell me that you're an ill man, that you're sinking fast, so here's to your health as well!"

"I thank you, Hetman," the fainting Kisyel murmured.

"You're my guest." Hmyelnitzki shrugged and nodded his huge head and a quick wave of sentimentality engulfed him again. "I don't forget about things like that."

He seized the *Voyevode* by the shoulders with both his great hands and pushed his red, sweating face close to the gaunt grey cheeks of his despairing guest. "I got to look after you," he told him. "You're one of us. You're like my little treasure. What'll people say if you drop dead right here at my table? They'll say I'm a peasant, not a Hetman, an' that I don't know how to behave in good company. So drink up, Kisyel! Keep healthy!"

The atamans at once took their cue from their grinning Hetman. They came staggering up to the envoys to squeeze their hands, throw their arms around them, and slap them familiarly on the shoulders.

"Here's to the new grass," they raised their cups with good-natured, easy-going gruffness, repeating the phrase after Hmyelnitzki, while the haughty Commonwealth commissioners had to hold still and permit themselves to be mauled and pulled about by the drunken, sentimental peasants. The thick, foul breaths beat against their faces, the red, sweaty hands grasped and shook their own, and greasy whiskers rubbed against their cheeks with coarse familiarity. The stench of raw spirits, rancid sweat and tallow choked them, turned their stomachs and filled their nostrils to the point of suffocation, but they had to put up with it all and smile as they did so. Nor were they spared the jibes and crude vulgarities that passed for humor in this gathering.

"We're after Polack blood," some of the atamans shouted into the *Voyevode's* face. "It's their necks we want. But you're our man, you're one of us, we got nothing against you!"

Pan Kisyel felt as if he was about to lose both his consciousness and his mind. His hands were shaking. His entire body quivered in a paroxysm of fever and the sweltering room was spinning before his eyes. The world as he knew it seemed to lose the last of its sense and all the faith and logic of his life became a mocking and degrading nightmare. Grotesque, grinning masks, more animal than human, were leering down at him wherever he looked and thick, grimy claws clutched at his hands and shoulders. He saw himself caught in a vortex of his own creation and watched as irreversible forces sucked him down into a dark pit that he had dug unknowing with his own hands; and cringed as yet another hamlike fist thumped his back with a terrible familiarity, and another hoarse, hot voice breathed its sour fumes into his dulled ear.

"*My Lahov kh'shtchomo rizaty* . . . It's Polack throats we want to slit, Kisyel. Not yours. You're one of our kind!"

"No," he whispered. "No . . ."

"*Na pohybel Lahom!*"

"Hey, you gentry," cried some of the others. "Used to be you'd kick us around anytime you wanted! And now you're on your knees and begging us to let you breathe a little bit longer, eh? Well, to Hell with you, you lily-fingered lordlings! *Na pohybel* with you! It's our turn to do the kicking now!"

Ataman Vovko, at one time a miller of the Tchetvertynskis who murdered the younger prince when the rebellion started, now shouted out the details of his accomplishment into the face of his victim's father.

"Lucky for you you wasn't there, eh? But don't you worry none, old man! You'll get to see your boy again come Spring, ha ha ha! You'll join him in Hell! An' maybe I'll do for you quicker than I did for him!"

"Give us Yarema," yelled the drunken, staggering Yashevski. "Send us his head an' maybe we'll let you go home with your own heads still fixed on your shoulders."

"Ha ha ha! U-u-ha!"

They reeled about, staggering into the envoys, into each other, and into the fouled, littered table, sliding and falling in spilled liquor and trampling the cold, scattered meats and marrow bones. And then the doors flew open and the witches among whom Hmyelnitzki passed his nights, drinking and listening to their spells and visions, pushed into the room.

Some were old and gnarled as dead trees. Some looked like stooped skeletons barely covered with dry, leathery skin and grinning with gapped teeth. Others were young, bursting with health and beauty and showing all their white teeth in invitation to the younger atamans who crowded around them.

"Ah! The *vorojhykhi*! Now we'll hear what's going to happen when the new grass comes!"

But Kisyel couldn't bear the evening any longer. "We thank you, Hetman, for the banquet," he said in a weak voice. "And we'll leave you now."

"Going so soon, are you?"

"It's . . . late."

"And getting later, eh? Well, well, there's not much heart in any of you, that's clear enough. Like I said before, your blood has turned to water. But no matter. I'll come and eat with you tomorrow, Kisyel, so be ready for me. Donyetz is waiting outside with his *moloytzy* to see that you get to your quarters without any trouble from the mob. Now get out of here."

The envoys bowed and left. "God . . . God . . . God . . ." Pan Kisyel whispered in a broken voice, his face in his hands, but no one else among the peace commissioners had anything to say.

* * *

Exhausted to the point of collapse, Pan Kisyel went to bed at once, unable to see anyone else that day. He lay in a torment of fever and despair until midmorning on the following day when he summoned Skshetuski.

"What did you do, Mister?" he began. "What did you think you were doing? You exposed all our lives to the greatest danger, including your own."

"*Mea culpa*, Excellency," Skshetuski said quietly.

"How could you do such a thing?"

"I'd have preferred to die a hundred times than to watch such a shameful humiliation."

"And do you think you're the only one?" Grief and regret replaced the anger and anxiety in the *Voyevode's* voice. "Hmyelnitzki caught on in spite of everything I could say to smooth things over and explain. But he's supposed to come here today and he's sure to ask about it when he sees you. So make sure you tell him that I ordered you to lead your men away."

"Bryshovski is taking over his command again, Excellency," Pan Yan said. "He's back on his feet."

"Feeling better, is he? Good! Your neck is too stiff for these times, young man. Yes, I know, you think you had good cause to do what you did, but you have to learn to be a lot more careful. It's easy to see that you've still to learn how to cope with suffering."

"I'm used to suffering, Excellency," the young soldier said. "It's been my daily bread for more than a year. It was the humiliation of our country that I couldn't watch."

Kisyel gasped softly, in much the way that a wounded man might hiss under a surgeon's knife. Then he showed a sad, resigned smile and turned his face away.

"I used to weep bitter tears over words like those," he murmured. "Now they're *my* daily fare. And the tears are all used up as well."

Pity touched the young soldier at the sight of this worn old man with the face of a tortured martyr, whose last days were passing in the double agony of a broken body and a tormented soul.

"As God's my witness, sir, all I meant was the deed itself, not your motives," he tried to console. "I blame these times in which we are living. But what's happened to us, my lord? Why do our noblest minds have to stoop to murderers whose best reward is the point of a stake?"

"May God bless you," the old man murmured. "You're an honest young man, I know you meant well. But what you're saying is being said today by your Prince, by the entire army, by all the gentry and the Diets, and by half the Commonwealth as well. And the whole weight of their contempt and hatred comes down on my head."

"Everyone serves his country as he knows best," Pan Yan said quietly. "Let God judge the intentions of each of us, sir. As for Prince Yeremi, he's given up his whole life in that service along with everything else he had."

"And he's loved for it," the *Voyevode* said. "And he walks in his glory like the sun. But what do I have to light my way in this dreadful darkness? Ah, lad, you said it well: '*let God judge our intentions.*' And let Him give me the peace of a quiet grave at last."

Skshetuski said nothing. Kisyel lifted his eyes to the ceiling in a silent prayer and then began to speak again in a broken voice.

"I'm a Ruthenian, blood and bone. I loved this holy country and all of its people. I saw the evil done to it by both sides . . . the wild lawlessness of the Zaporohjans as well as the unbearable tyranny inflicted by those who want to turn this brave and freedom-loving people into serfs and peasants. So what else was there for me to do . . .?"

Skshetuski bowed his head in silence and the silvery-haired old man went on in a whisper, as if speaking only to himself. "I, a Ruthenian, and at the same time a loyal son and a senator of this Commonwealth, what choice did I have? I joined those who said '*Pax vobiscum*' and who wanted justice for both sides. I worked for peace and brotherhood among all our people, as did our late King and the primate and the chancellor and so many others . . .! And do you know why?"

Skshetuski said nothing because there really wasn't anything to say.

"Because that's what my own Ruthenian blood ordered me to do," the old man confessed. "That's what my heart told me. Because I could see that hatred among brothers meant doom to us all. I wanted to spend my life working for love and unity among us. What could have been better? And when the bloodshed started I told myself: '*I'll be the voice of reason . . . of conciliation . . . of mending, not destroying . . .*'"

Silent once more, the weary old man struggled with his visions.

"So I went the way of peace," the thin, soft voice continued. "I worked for unity and I'm still working for it. In pain. In torment. In disgrace. And among doubts that are more terrible than the rest of it together . . .!"

Skshetuski felt the crushing weight of the other's pain and bowed silently before it.

"Dear God," the old man whispered in despair. "It's all become so blurred for me. I can hardly see the right and wrong of anything anymore. All the good and evil has flowed into one. I can no longer tell if your Prince came too soon with his sword or if I came too late with my olive branch! All I know is that my whole life's work has been all for nothing, that I'm no longer strong enough to finish what I started, that I'm beating my head against the wall to no useful purpose, and that now . . . even as I go down to my grave . . . I see only darkness ahead of me. Calamity, perdition and darkness for us all."

"God will send help," the young soldier whispered.

"Oh, let Him send us just a single ray of hope," cried the *Voyevode*, "so that I'll be able to die without despair . . .! If I could just believe that some shred of goodness and mercy is still alive somewhere I'd be able to thank Him for that cross I've carried all these years, for the *tchernya* that howls for my head and for all the cries of '*Traitor!*' I've heard in the senate . . . I'd be grateful for all my lost possessions and for that contempt in which I've spent my days. I'd even thank Him for that bitter hatred with which I've been paid by both sides."

Overwrought, the old man lifted his thin, dry arms towards the dark storm clouds that passed beyond the windows while two grey tears rolled down his parchment cheeks.

Skshetuski could no longer fight off his own sense of pity, shame and understanding. These could well be the sick old man's last tears, he thought, and he knew that he was far beyond any tears of his own. He knelt beside the *Voyevode* and grasped his frail hand in both of his.

"I'm a soldier, like my Prince," he said in a voice shaken by compassion. "I chose a different way. But I can pay respect to suffering and merit."

And then this fierce young soldier of the Vishnovyetzkis, who only a few months earlier joined everyone else he knew in calling this great Ruthenian lord '*a coward, an appeaser and a traitor*' pressed his lips to that brittle old hand.

Kisyel sighed. He freed his hand from Skshetuski's grasp and placed both his palms on Pan Yan's bowed head.

"May God also grant you some consolation, son," he said quietly.

⋆ ⋆ ⋆

The peace talks, if that's what one could call them, began that same day. Hmyelnitzki came to supper with the *Voyevode* as he said he would, but he arrived late and in the worst humor possible. His first act was to revoke every promise he made and every concession he might have suggested during that drunken feast that followed his investiture as Hetman.

"I was drunk!" he raged. "You took advantage of me! Forget about any armistice or peace talks in Spring! And I'm not going to release my prisoners either!"

Pan Kisyel did his best to soothe him, calm his fury and bring him back to reason, but—as the Chamberlain of Lvov wrote about it later—it was all *'surdo tyranno fabula dicta,'* or a tale whistled into a windstorm. The Zaporohjan Hetman fell into such foul temper, and acted with such premeditated malice, that the peace commissioners longed for the crude, vulgar, drunk and sentimental Hmyelnitzki of the night before. He cursed Pan Kisyel to his face, hurled insults at the others, and threatened to have all the Commonwealth ambassadors thrown to the mercy of the mob outside if they tried to pull the wool over his eyes again.

All of the *Voyevode's* patient reasoning and pleading fell on stone-deaf ears. Hmyelnitzki wasn't disposed to listen to logic, although—as the wary Kisyel could perceive quite clearly— there was at least as much cold calculation as spontaneity in his capricious rage. He yelled and shouted and stamped his boots, and spat in the envoys' faces, and he cracked old Pan Pozovski's head with his new *bulava* simply because the unlucky noble, having fallen ill, came late to the meeting.

Only after he swilled down a quart of *gojhalka*, and sampled the *Voyevode's* vintage Hushtcha mead, did he start to settle down to something like civilized behavior. But even then he refused to talk anything important. "If we're drinking, let's drink!" he ordered. "Tomorrow's time enough for talking."

"That's what you told us yesterday, Hetman," Pan Kisyel protested.

"And that's what I'll tell you every day if that's what I feel like! And if you don't like it then I'll leave right now and that's the last you'll ever see of me!"

By three o'clock in the morning Hmyelnitzki insisted on going into the *Voyevode's* bedroom, which Kisyel resisted with all the diplomacy left at his disposal because that was where he hid Skshetuski, and he feared that the sight of the young soldier might remind Hmyelnitzki of yesterday's insult. But the Hetman pushed past him into the sleeping room and the *Voyevode* was obliged to follow.

"Hey!" Hmyelnitzki cried, on seeing Skshetuski. "What are you doing here?"

The *Voyevode* took a step between them, searching for some phrase that might avert the storm that he expected for the Vishnovyetzki soldier, but Hmyelnitzki pushed him roughly to the side and advanced on Pan Yan with a hand thrust out before him in a friendly greeting.

"How come you're not drinking with us?" Hmyelnitzki demanded.

"Because I'm not well," Pan Yan bowed and said.

"You didn't feel all that well yesterday either, did you," Hmyelnitzki said with an ironic smile. "Taking yourself off like that, you an' your dragoons. None of that ceremony meant anything to me after I saw you leaving."

"Those were his orders," Pan Kisyel said quickly.

"Don't you tell me about those orders, *Voyevode*," the Hetman snapped back. "*Znayu ya yoho!* I know he didn't want to watch the homage you paid me and that's why he rode off. Ey, I tell you, nobody else would've got away with that! But he's safe with me! Not a hair's going to fall off his head among us 'cause he's my good friend and I love him like he was my own brother."

Kisyel stared in amazement at the grinning Hetman and Hmyelnitzki turned once more to the silent soldier.

"And d'you know why I love you, eh? You think it's because of that rope that you cut me loose from by the Omelnitchek? That time when I was nothing, even less than nothing, and people were hunting me like an animal in the Steppe? But you're wrong. It's not for that at all. And anyway, I paid you for that by buying you from Tuhay-bey and giving you your freedom."

He started laughing, stepped up to Skshetuski and embraced him warmly while Pan Kisyel stared.

"Hey," the Hetman cried out and hugged the grim young soldier. "I gave you a ring that time, one that had dust from Christ's tomb locked under the stone, didn't I! But you're a proud young devil, aren't you, eh? You hid that ring from me when I had you in my hands later in the *Sietch*. You didn't show it to me to remind me that you'd saved my life. Well, I remembered anyway. I let you go free and then we were quits. No, no, it's something else you did for me that made you my brother."

He laughed again, patted Pan Yan's shoulder, and tugged his beard fondly. "D'you have any idea what that was?"

It was Skshetuski's turn to look astonished.

"No idea, eh?" Hugely pleased, the Hetman grinned at Pan Yan and Kisyel. "So let me remind you what people told me in Tchehryn when me and Tuhay-bey got there after Yellow Waters. I turned that town upside down looking for my enemy Tchaplinski but he'd flown the coop and then people started telling me what you did to him after our first meeting. How you picked him up by the neck and the seat of his breeches and broke a tavern door open with his head. Hey, hey, that was good to hear! You remember now?"

"That's true," Skshetuski said, recalling the moment. "I did do that to him."

"Well, that was well done, my good friend!" Hmyelnitzki laughed and threw his arms once more around the young soldier. "That's something I owe you. Oh, I'll find that mangy dog somewhere, you can be sure of that. There won't be any peace talks until that debt is settled and paid up in full! But you gave him something on account for me in the meantime, and that's why I love you."

★   ★   ★

Watching this laughing, jovial man, the *Voyevode* could hardly believe that this was the same brutal and violent Hmyelnitzki who only moments earlier cracked an old man's skull, threatened death to all the peace commissioners and demanded war. His whole nature seemed to turn around. His face glowed with friendship. A swift and genuine affection replaced his murderous fury, and kindness lit up the eyes that had been icy with cruelty and malice.

"By the scruff of the neck, he caught him!" he shouted and burst into such laughter that it silenced all the whispering commissioners in the other room. "Lifted him up like a pup-dog! Broke his head! Threw him out into the street like garbage!"

Laughing, the Hetman turned to Kisyel and demanded mead so that he could drink Skshetuski's health, and when the serving lads ran in with the goblets he drained his so swiftly that sweat burst out on his forehead and began to steam in the overheated room.

"Ask me for anything you want!" he cried out and then immediately corrected himself. "Anything, that's to say, that doesn't have something to do with Kisyel and his business."

Drunk or sober, as the *Voyevode* noted, he was still Hmyelnitzki.

Blood rose to the young soldier's face but he couldn't bring himself to ask for anything. Pride . . . duty . . . hatred of the rebels and loathing for this huge, murderous, unpredictable yet childlike destroyer of his country, struggled against each other in those harrowed features. He'd sooner die than be in Hmyelnitzki's debt, Pan Kisyel could tell, and he wondered how many times Skshetuski must have cursed himself for saving that life.

"Speak up, then!" the Zaporohjan Hetman was nodding his huge head in encouragement. "My word isn't smoke, it doesn't blow away with the wind. If there's something I can do for you it's yours. Just ask and it's done."

"Justice," Skshetuski said at last. "You can give me justice."

"What justice? Against whom?"

"One of your atamans did me an injury," the young soldier whispered.

"I'll have his head on a pike at once!"

"That's not what I want. Order him to fight me, man to man. To accept my challenge."

"You want to kill him? Go ahead and kill him!" the Hetman shouted. "Who is he? Which one is it?"

"Bohun."

"Ah . . ." Hmyelnitzki paused, plunged into sudden thought, and his eyes blinked slowly like a sleepy vulture's, and then he slapped his forehead with his palm as if remembering something.

"Bohun's dead," he grunted. "Killed in a duel in Warsaw."

And then a note of pride crept into his voice. "The King himself wrote to me about it."

" . . . Bohun killed?"

Skshetuski was less astonished by this confirmation of Pan Kretovski's story than by the thought that Zagloba might have told the truth.

"So the King wrote me." Hmyelnitzki's heavy shoulders lifted in a shrug and the red, bulging eyes glinted with curiosity. "What did Bohun do to you, anyway?"

Skshetuski said nothing. His flush deepened further and Pan Kisyel thought that he would never mention his lost girl to the drunken Hetman in case he heard some coarse jibe that would shatter his iron self-control.

"It's a serious matter," he said to Hmyelnitzki. "Bohun carried off this young officer's fiancee and hid her somewhere."

"So go look for her," Hmyelnitzki told Pan Yan.

"I already have."

"Where?"

"All along the Dniester. He was supposed to have hidden her in the wilderness. But I didn't find her."

"Hmm. The wilderness." The great head lifted. The sleepy eyes fixed themselves on Skshetuski as if to judge and measure his determination. "That's a big place to look. It'd take a year and an army to comb it out and even then you'd miss half of it."

"There's a chance that Bohun might have hidden her in Kiev," Skshetuski said slowly.

"Kiev, eh? None of you people are allowed in there."

"Kiev," Skshetuski said again. "I heard there were some gentlewomen hiding in the convents, which I'm sure you know very well yourself. If you'd give me the right to search for her in Kiev, Hetman . . ."

"So?" Curiosity replaced all other feelings in Hmyelnitzki's face. "And what if I do?"

Skshetuski's next words came with difficulty, as if strained out of the young man only after an enormous struggle. "I'd . . . be grateful to you."

"You're my good *druh*, my brother . . ." The late hour and the vast amounts of liquor he had drunk were having their effect on the Zaporohjan Hetman. "You smashed up Tchaplinski . . . I'll not only let you go to Kiev but I'll give you a safe-conduct to look for her anywhere you want."

Skshetuski bowed. "Thank you."

"Yes. Broke his head for him, he did . . ."

The dulled red eyes turned to the *Voyevode* as if he hadn't told the story just a moment earlier.

" . . . Tossed him out into the street like a bucketful of slops . . . That's something. That needs to be paid for. An' I'll give an order for whoever holds her,"—he turned his restless, gloomy eyes once more on Skshetuski—"to give her up to you on demand."

The huge, shaved head began to sag down towards the massive chest. The harsh breathing thickened. The sleepy eyes blinked around the room and fixed themselves uneasily on the dark corners of the *Voyevode's* chamber.

"Who's there?" he muttered. Startled, he sat up again and stared at Skshetuski. "Ah. It's you. My good friend. That was a good thing you did with Tchaplinski . . . I'll have a letter written for the Metropolitan in Kiev so's you can look for your girl in all the convents there . . . My word isn't smoke!"

It was already close to dawn. The windows were still dark, the day was still to come, but a blue-grey edge was already showing along the rooftops to the east, and the candlelight in the room was growing pale and dim.

Hmyelnitzki roused himself long enough to bellow for Vyhovski to write the letter to the Kiev Metropolitan and the blanket order for Helen's release. The grumbling Tcharnota had to run for the Hetman's seal. Djedjala was pulled out of his bedding to find a 'pyernatch,' a safe-conduct medallion that every Cossack and Tartar leader would recognize at once; and the weary Donyetz, who slept no more than Skshetuski on the envoys' long journey to the Zaporohjan Hetman, was ordered to mount an escort of two hundred Cossacks. They were to take Pan Yan to Kiev and then as far west as the first outposts of the Polish army.

That morning, shortly after daybreak, Pan Yan left Pereyaslav on a Dnieper galley and sailed for Kiev.

Chapter Fifty-eight

IF PAN ZAGLOBA believed that he would die of boredom in Zbarajh—convinced that mushrooms would start to grow on him as if he were an old abandoned ruin or a toppled tree trunk—the little knight complained that he'd go mad.

He needed action. War. Great campaigns. Adventure. Instead, the only enemy he could find was time and nothing with which to turn it into entertainment.

Winter, the harshest in men's memories, dragged on. There seemed to be no end to the snows and ice and the bitter winds that turned all of the country for miles around into a frozen wasteland as desolate as prison. True, once in a while a regiment or two would ride out to fight bandits and marauding looters on the nearby western border of the Ukraine along the Zbrutch River. But this was only a petty war of raids and ambushes and exhausting marches, all the more brutal because of the cold, that cost a great deal of effort and brought neither glory nor any notable triumphs over the enemy, so that the restless little soldier pestered Zagloba night and day to set out on a private expedition in search of Skshetuski, from whom there'd been no news since the end of Autumn.

"All sorts of things might have happened to him," Pan Michal insisted. "He might even be lying dead somewhere for all that we know. We ought to go after him at once."

"What for, if he's dead?" Pan Zagloba muttered lazily, as indolent in those Winter months as a hibernating bear. "And how are we going to find him if he isn't? Here, at least, we've a warm fire at our feet and a roof over our heads and the mead isn't all that bad either in these parts."

"It'd be better to die out there with him, if we have to, than rot behind these walls with nothing to do," Volodyovski grumbled.

"Speak for yourself," Pan Zagloba answered whenever their conversations took this turn. "I'd rather not rush in anywhere where I'm not invited, particularly a place like the next world from which it's hard to get back if it doesn't suit you. Pan Yan is a brave man but he's not a fool. He knows what he's doing. He told us to sit still and wait so let's do it for a few more days until we hear something. He'd call for us if he needed us, wouldn't he?"

"Yes," Pan Michal was obliged to agree. "If he could."

"There you are, then."

Pan Zagloba admitted to himself that he'd gladly go almost anywhere—the boredom of the small town and the little fortress was, as he insisted, driving him to drink—but he wasn't quite so desperately sick of his inactive life that he'd court death in the Winter gales.

"What's the point of going off God knows where?" he reasoned. "Blundering about in the snows and probably freezing in the process? If Skshetuski's doing well without us then all that effort and hardship would be for nothing. And what if he really did need us and sent for us and we weren't here?"

Pan Volodyovski saw the logic of such arguments and did his best to arm himself with patience but time seemed to weigh more heavily on his hands each day. By the year's end even the occasional forays after bandits were given up because of the snow storms. Ice gripped the country with such a bitter chill that nothing stirred anywhere for miles around, and the only distraction came from news and rumors that reached the white walls of Zbarajh now and then.

That Winter people gossiped about the coronation. They argued about the peace party's new campaign for Cossack conciliation which divided the Senate and the Diet. They speculated on whether Yan Casimir would confirm Prince Yeremi as the new Grand Hetman which, in the minds of most of the soldiers and the minor gentry, he deserved better than any other warrior. There were violent quarrels about appeasing the brooding and uncommunicative Hmyelnitzki which would pave the road of Kisyel's elevation more than that of anybody else.

Everyone had opinions on everything but no means to affect

matters one way or another. Volodyovski fought several unnecessary duels, and Pan Zagloba roared and argued his way through so many drinking bouts that his admirers made bets against the survival of his liver until Spring. This seemed all the more unlikely because he not only drank with the officers and gentry but took care to attend every wedding, christening and Saint's Day celebration in the neighborhood. The little knight was particularly incensed about that, chastising his fat friend for undermining respect for the gentry by hobnobbing with the lower orders. But Pan Zagloba blamed the statutes which—as he put it—*'let the shopkeepers grow too many feathers,'* and to indulge in comforts that should have been the prerogative of nobles.

He prophesied that such relaxing of mankind's natural barriers, which couldn't have reflected what God had in mind when He created different social classes, would not do humanity much good in the long run. But what Zagloba said was one thing; what he did was quite another matter. He drank more than ever anywhere he could, and few people had the heart to blame him in those cold, gloomy, Winter days of uncertainty and waiting.

Meanwhile more and more of Prince Yeremi's soldiers arrived in Zbarajh, raising lively speculations about the outbreak of a new war in Spring. Pan Podbipyenta, who was now Skshetuski's deputy commander of the Prince's elite *husaria*, brought in his regiment among the many others. He also brought the latest news from the King's court in Krakow where Prince Yeremi was pushed into the background and had little to say about public matters. His friend, the Palatine of Kiev, had died and Kisyel was seen as the most likely candidate for that vacant office. The Prince himself told Pan Longinus that a new war was inevitable because Kisyel's peace commission was ordered to give Hmyelnitzki whatever he wanted. This meant that the Zaporohjans would become so inflated with their own importance, and that they would make such impossible demands, that the talks would collapse under their own weight.

Pan Zagloba was especially loud in denouncing *Voyevode* Kisyel's mission, claiming that all of his good work at Konstantinov was being undermined, and swearing to start up a rebellion of his own.

★　★　★

February went by in this frustrating and irritating manner, and March was half over, and there was still no news from or about Skshetuski, so that Pan Michal became truly anxious.

"Look now," he told Zagloba. "It's no longer a question of going after him just because we've nothing better to do, or setting out to find Skshetuski's princess because we're sorry for him. It's now a matter of finding the man himself!"

But, by the end of March, Pan Zagloba was proved right in putting off the journey. An old Cossack named Zakhar came from Kiev with a letter to Pan Michal written by Skshetuski. The little knight immediately called Zagloba; they found a quiet corner in a tavern right outside the castle where they could huddle with the messenger out of sight and hearing of all the other bored and curious soldiers, and Volodyovski broke the seals with anxious, trembling fingers.

"Well? Well? What does he say?" Pan Zagloba had quite lost his breath but the excitement sobered him at once. "Did he find my Helen?"

"No," Pan Michal said, and started reading the letter aloud. "Not yet, he hasn't. But listen."

"I'm listening! I'm listening!"

"*'I found no sign of her anywhere along the Dniester,'*" Pan Michal read out. "*'But, supposing that Bohun might have taken her to Kiev, I joined up with the peace commissioners and went with them as far as Pereyaslav . . .'*"

"He must've looked like an eagle in a flock of geese!" Zagloba broke in. "But why didn't the Cossacks spot him for what he is?"

"You might find out if you don't interrupt."

"Hmm. Another sparrow twittering in a barnyard," Pan Zagloba muttered. "But go on, go on . . . I didn't run all the way here just to be subjected to a young whipper-snapper's disrespect."

"Here it is, then," said the little knight. "*'From there, getting unexpected permission from Hmyelnitzki, I went to Kiev where I've been searching everywhere. The Orthodox Metropolitan himself is helping all he can. There are many of our people here, hidden among the merchants and in the monasteries and convents, but they're so terrified of the mob that they don't breathe a word of their own whereabouts, so it's hard to track them down and find out anything they might know about anyone else . . .'*"

"And who'd blame them?" Pan Zagloba broke in again, unable to sit still in his excitement or to keep quiet longer than a moment. "Even the meanest jackrabbit knows how to keep his ears down *in perriculo*. If the hounds can't sniff you out they can't run you down."

"Nor can a letter be read out with windy interruptions," Pan Michal said. "'. . . *But God has led me this far and even moved Hmyelnitzki to some friendship for me so I'm full of hope that He might continue to show me His mercy.*' Thank God for that!"

"Now who's interrupting?"

"He ends by asking us to speak to Father Muhovyetzki about a votive Mass that he'd like to offer for his intentions," Pan Michal concluded. "And then he signs his name."

"But there's a *postscriptum*," Pan Zagloba said, peering across Volodyovski's shoulder.

"True! Listen to this, then. '*The man who brings you this letter is a former esaul in the Mirhorod regiment who looked after me when I was a prisoner in the Sietch and who's been helping me here in Kiev. He risked his life to do me this service, Michal, so protect him and look after him as if he was one of us.*'"

"Thank God there's at least one decent man still left among you Cossacks!" Pan Zagloba said and thrust out his hand towards the old *esaul* who grasped it firmly and shook it without any sign of deference or inferiority.

"And you can count on some reward from us," added the small soldier.

"*On sokol!*" The old Cossack shrugged. "He's a real falcon. I looked out for him that time in the *Sietch*, and watched him eating out his heart when we beat the Hetmans, and I was sorry for him like he was my own son. I came here out of my own good heart, not because of anybody's money."

"Good for you! That's a spirit that a lot of nobles could use nowadays," Pan Zagloba said. "Hmm. Seems like not all of you people have turned into wild beasts over there, that's certain! But no matter, no matter . . . So Pan Skshetuski is in Kiev, then?"

"That he is."

"Is he safe, though? Because I hear the *tchernya* is on a real rampage out that way."

"They think they've got a country of their own now, the scum." The old Cossack shrugged and spat with a Zaporohjan's contempt for the peasants. "So they're celebrating. But he's safe enough. Everybody knows him as '*Hmyel's Lah.*' Lives in Donyetz' house. Hmyelnitzki told Donyetz he'd have his head if his Polish brother lost one hair off his head, so Donyetz is watching over him like a hawk."

"That's almost past belief," the fat knight observed and shook his head in wonder. "Who'd think Hmyelnitzki would show so much affection for a Polish soldier? And an officer of Prince Yeremi Vishnovyetzki at that?"

"Oh, he's loved that one a long time," the old Cossack said.

"Hmm . . . He's a real puzzle, that Hmyel of yours," Pan Zagloba muttered. "Just when a man's ready to believe that there isn't a drop of decent blood in his entire body he comes up with something that shows him to be a human being after all. Holds his mead quite well too, I am told, and that's always a sign of a worthwhile nature so perhaps God will let him off a few centuries of hellfire. But the Devil's going to be chewing on his bones for a lot longer than that."

★ ★ ★

They read the letter again, talked a little longer, and Zakhar told them about the *tchernya's* murdering rampages that he witnessed in Kiev with Skshetuski. Every few days the mob would go hunting for refugee gentry and drown them in the Dnieper along with those who had been hiding them.

"Monks and nuns too," he said. "It don't matter to them."

Pan Zagloba started to fidget on his bench, worried about Helen, but the little knight insisted that Bohun's name, and his feelings for the captive princess, were her best protection wherever she was.

"I've really become convinced that there was noble blood in that man's veins," he said. "If Kiev is where he hid her, he'd make sure she was somewhere safe."

"Hmm . . . You think so? And what about you, Zakhar? Do you think she's still alive somewhere?"

Zakhar shrugged. "*Ne znayu.*"

"Skshetuski seems optimistic, anyway. So maybe he knows something. God gave him a hard row to hoe but maybe things will go easier for him now."

Then he called for a flagon of good mead and a platter of smoked meats and sausage and they sat down to supper. Zakhar wolfed down his food as if he hadn't had a solid meal for longer than he cared to remember. Then he dipped his long mustache in the rich, dark liquid, drank deeply, sighed and smacked his lips with satisfaction.

"Good mead," he said.

"Better than all that blood you people drink over there in the Ukraine," Pan Zagloba offered. "But it seems to me that since you're a decent man yourself and since you love Skshetuski you won't go back to the rebels now. Why not stay with us? You could do a lot worse, you know."

Zakhar lifted his head, pondered for a moment, then dismissed the notion. "No, I'll go back. I'm a Cossack. I may like one or another of you but it's not for me to look for brothers among the *Lahy*. Those days are long over."

"And you'll fight against us again?"

"Sure I will. I'm a *Sietch* Cossack, not a manor lapdog. We picked Hmyel for our Hetman and we're sticking with him. And specially now when the King himself sent him the *bulava* and the banner and gave him the lordship over all our people."

"There you have it, Michal," the fat knight turned angrily to Volodyovski. "Didn't I say that all my hard work at Konstantinov would go for nothing with all this appeasement? Maybe it's not too late to kick up a fuss about it even now. I know half the gentry would follow me because of all my achievements in the past and my great merits on the battlefield and in the council chamber, and the army would follow you because of your saber. It wouldn't take much to get a tumult going. We could chase old Kisyel to the Devil, and give the Grand Hetman's *bulava* to the Prince, and that'd be the end of Hmyel and the whole rebellion."

"And you'll always be an old undisciplined troublemaker no matter how long you serve with real soldiers," Volodyovski snapped and turned to the Cossack.

"You ride with Donyetz now, Zakhar?" he asked. "What happened to your own Mirhorod *kujhen*?"

"Pan Tcharnyetzki's *usari* wiped it out at Yellow Waters. What's left of us is with Donyetz now. Hey, that Pan Tcharnyetzki, that's a real soldier! But he's a prisoner with us now, along with all the other *pa'ny* and *hetmany*."

"We've a few of yours too," Pan Zagloba muttered.

"And that's how it should be." The old Cossack nodded,

shrugged and drank again. "People say you've got the most famous of all the *moloytzy*, though some say he's dead."

"And who might that be?"

"Bohun," Zakhar said.

"Bohun's dead," the fat knight said. "Cut down in a duel."

"He is, eh? And who could do that to a man like him?"

"That gentleman," Pan Zagloba said, pointing at Pan Michal.

Zakhar, who at that moment was guzzling another quart of mead, gasped and began to choke. His eyes bulged out with disbelief, his face turned a deep crimson as if he were strangling, and then he burst out laughing.

"Him . . .?" he spluttered. "That . . . little knight . . . killed Bohun?"

"What the devil is this?" Volodyovski shouted, red with sudden anger. "A messenger can get away with a lot, I know, but this one's taking things too far!"

"Easy, easy!" Pan Zagloba soothed him. "This is a decent, simple man, he doesn't think you're funny. He laughs because he doesn't know any better. He's a Cossack, isn't he? On the other hand it's to your credit that you managed to achieve so much with so little, Michal. God may not have given you much of a *corpus*, my small friend, but there's a great soul in it."

"Yes, but . . . but . . ." It was Pan Michal's turn to choke and splutter with a crimson face.

"Yes but what? I was there, remember? But even I found it difficult to believe my eyes. That such a little fellow could cut down such a giant . . . In times to come this will be counted as one of the wonders of the world!"

"Enough, enough," Volodyovski muttered but the garrulous old knight could always find something more to say.

"Don't blame me for your insignificant appearance." He waved a thick finger under the little soldier's nose. "I am not your father. But I don't mind saying I'd be proud to have a son like you. I'll adopt you if you like and make you my heir, because it's no shame to be a great man inside a small body. Our own Prince isn't much taller than you but he could give lessons in greatness to Alexander of Macedon himself."

Mollified, the little knight settled back on his bench again but he was careful not to look at the grinning Zakhar.

"What makes me angry, though," he grumbled, "is that there's really nothing good in Skshetuski's letter. It's a sheer miracle he didn't die himself in the wilderness but he hasn't found his girl and there's no guarantee he will."

"That's true."

Pan Zagloba sighed, saddened by the thought of Helen in captivity, but it wasn't in his nature to give way to gloom for long.

"Yes," he said. "It's true that Skshetuski's troubles aren't over yet. But if God has seen fit to free him of Bohun through our hands, if He's led him safely through all those other dangers— and if He's gone so far as to breathe this strange affection for him into Hmyelnitzki's heart—it wasn't just so he'd dry up like bacon from all his sufferings and torments. If you can't see the hand of Providence in all this, my friend, then your wits need sharpening a lot more than your saber. Which, by the way, is only right and proper because no one should have all the virtues, as we can see in our Lithuanian giant who has a great heart and a heavy hand but whose wits are lighter than a feather."

Pan Michal sighed as well. His little whiskers moved sadly up and down. "All I can see is that there's nothing useful for us to do out there," he grumbled. "And that we've got to keep on sitting here 'til we rot."

"If we do then I'll rot before you, because I am older. But let's keep hoping. Let's thank God for at least a promise of good things ahead. I've chewed my heart out over my little Helen—a lot more than you, that's certain, and maybe as much even as Skshetuski—but you wouldn't catch me in this good frame of mind if I wasn't sure her misery will end soon."

"If there was at least something with which to keep busy," the little knight complained. "But we can't even be sure of a war in Spring! Ah, may the Devil carry off that damn traitor Kisyel and all his commissioners and treaties! Pan Podbipyenta, who spent some time in Krakow at the Prince's court, says they'll make peace as sure as two and two make four!"

"Pan Podbipyenta knows as much about politics and statecraft as a goat knows about fancy cooking," the fat knight snorted in contempt. "He spent more time at that court sniffing after that flighty little bird of his then paying any mind to public affairs. I don't deny that Kisyel is a traitor, the whole Commonwealth knows that. But making treaties is one thing, keeping them is another."

Then, turning to the old Cossack, Pan Zagloba asked what

the Zaporohjans thought about the possibilities of peace.

Zakhar shrugged. "Nothing'll happen 'til the new grass comes. Then it'll be *na pohybel* either for us or you."

"There, you see? Take heart, Michal. You'll have all the war you want once Winter is over. Everybody knows that the peasants are arming themselves everywhere."

"Aye," Zakhar said. "There's goin' to be a war like no one's seen before. People say the Turkish Sultan is coming this time, and the Khan with all the Tartar armies. Our good *druh* Tuhaybey is wintering in the Steppe this year and never went home at all."

"There you are, then," Zagloba said again. "There's even a prophecy that King Yan Casimir will have no peace throughout his whole reign. Either way, it looks like a long time before any of us gets to hang his saber on the wall. We'll get worn down like old brooms before the Commonwealth's troubles are all swept away . . ."

Nodding and drinking and muttering to himself, the fat knight took refuge in his memories, or perhaps his rich imagination, and started talking about other wars.

"Stay close to me when it comes to fighting," he told the small soldier, "and you'll get to see some wonderful things! You'll see how we used to fight in the old days! Ha, those were real wars! My God, how people have changed in these miserable times! Even you can't match those old heroes, Michal, although you're a great soldier in your own right . . . Even you, my friend, though you carved Bohun like a Sunday roast."

"You've got that right, sir," old Zakhar said and nodded slowly up and down. "We don't have men like we used to see walking on God's good earth, neither us nor you." Then he shook his head at Pan Volodyovski. "But that a little fellow like that could beat Bohun . . . well, well . . . that's hard to believe."

Chapter Fifty-nine

OLD ZAKHAR went back to Kiev after a few days' rest and, in the meantime, the peace commissioners returned from the Ukraine. All that Hmyelnitzki gave them was a promise of an armistice until early May; formal peace talks were to take place later. But since the Cossacks were demanding virtual independence, with Hmyelnitzki setting himself up as a hereditary ruler, a new war was certain. Both sides began to arm. Hmyelnitzki sent one envoy after another to the Khan, begging him to come to his aid with all the Tartar armies. He also sent an embassy to the Turkish sultan. The gentry expected the King's call for a General Levy any day.

Among the other news that reached Zbarajh in the first few days of Spring was the appointment of three war commanders who weren't much more experienced than the hated regents. These were Pan Lantzkoronski, the son of a distinguished family and a promising cavalry commander; Prince Ostrorog, an eastern magnate known for his caution and delays; and old Pan Firley, the Castellan of Beltz, who had already shown his mettle at Pilavtse. Prince Yeremi was pushed aside, ignored and completely shut out from military matters although no one could stop him from raising whatever regiments he could on his own.

"How can this be?" Pan Zagloba bellowed to anyone who'd listen. "Are they all blind? Stupid? Drunk? Have they lost their reason? Even if their cajoling of Hmyelnitzki justified this kind of thing while they were hoping for a real treaty, how can they do it when the war is certain?"

Nor was he alone in his indignation. The army and the eastern gentry were close to rebellion. Even the clients and

supporters of the former regents were in despair about this un-
forgivable blunder. Everyone in the country knew that Yeremi
Vishnovyetzki was the only military leader able to face and
defeat Hmyelnitzki; everyone, it seemed, except the Diet and
the King's advisors.

The Prince himself came to Zbarajh in April to gather his
troops and to crouch like a watchdog on the threshold of the
border country. Raids, pursuits and formal pitched battles went
on everywhere; the armistice was observed only to the extent
that the King and Hmyelnitzki didn't take to the field themselves; and the first warm rays of the new Spring sun fell as
before on burning villages and towns, scorched castles, slaughter and human misery.

Volodyovski found himself in his element again. Pan Zagloba
was right in supposing that he'd find all the war he wanted no
matter what Pan Kisyel's supporters were saying. But for all his
rage against the new generalissimos, and the bloodthirsty oaths
he swore against the Zaporohjans, the old knight resisted all of
his small friend's urgings to join him on his raids and expeditions.

"No, no, my dear Michal," he explained. "My belly's too big
for all that shaking and tossing about on horseback. It's bad for
my liver. And, anyway, each of us is created for something
different when it comes to war. My specialty is to charge with
the *husaria* on a clear day, storm a Zaporohjan wagon train and
take a battle flag or two. That's what God made me for and
disposed me towards. But beating the bushes at night after cut-
throats is more in your line than mine because you're as quick
and nimble as a fox, and as little as a ferret, and you can squeeze
in anywhere. I'm a knight in the old style and I'd rather charge
like a lion than sniff like a bloodhound. And anyway I need a
night's rest after a day's work."

★ ★ ★

So the little knight went raiding without his boon companion
until one day near the end of April, when he returned from a
particularly successful expedition looking as sad and troubled
and depressed as if he'd suffered a crushing defeat and thrown
away the lives of his men for nothing.

His friends came running up with questions as soon as he
dismissed his men in the castle courtyard but he refused to tell

anyone what happened. He went at once for a long talk with Prince Yeremi, along with two grim young knights whom no one saw in Zbarajh before, and then hurried with them to Pan Zagloba's quarters.

The fat knight looked with some surprise at the two tall, broad-shouldered young newcomers whom he didn't know but whose dark good looks seemed disturbingly familiar, and who, to judge by the gold loops dangling from their shoulders, served in the Lithuanian army of the Commonwealth.

"Have the door closed and keep everyone out of here," Volodyovski said as soon as they entered. "We have grave news and serious matters to discuss."

Zagloba ordered the doors barred and then began to peer uneasily at his unknown guests whose troubled faces promised nothing good.

"These," Volodyovski said at last, pointing to the grim-faced young men, "are the two surviving Kurtzevitch princes, Yur and Andrei."

"Helen's adopted brothers!" Pan Zagloba cried.

The two young princes bowed. "God rest her soul," they said in unison.

"What? What? What's that?"

All color drained out of Pan Zagloba's crimson face. It turned a sickly blue. He started flapping his arms and gasping as if he'd been shot. His eyes bulged. He couldn't catch his breath.

"What d-did you say?" he stammered out at last.

"There's news that the Princess was murdered in the Convent of the Good Mikolai in Kiev," Pan Michal said sadly.

"The *tchernya* suffocated twelve young women and several nuns with smoke in one of the cells there," *Knaz* Yur added. "Our sister was among them."

This time Zagloba didn't make a sound. His livid face became suffused with such a sudden rush of blood that Pan Michal feared he would have a stroke; his eyelids slipped down over his lifeless and uncomprehending eyes; he buried his face in both his hands and then a single moan seeped out between his fingers.

" . . .God!"

And then he neither moved nor made another sound while the two young princes and Volodyovski began to grieve out loud and to cry out in mourning.

"Here we are, your brothers and your friends," the little

knight sighed as he addressed the spirit of the murdered victim. "Gathering to go to your rescue . . . But we've come too late. You've left us for a better world and a better life in the household of a greater Queen . . ."

"Sister!" cried the tall, thick-shouldered Yur, tearing at his hair. "Forgive us all our sins! We'll spill a river of blood for every drop of yours!"

"So help us God!" *Knaz* Andrei added.

Both the young men lifted their knotted arms and fists towards the ceiling, calling on God to witness their determination, while Pan Zagloba rose slowly from his bench, took a few stumbling steps towards his cot, reeled like a drunken man and fell on his knees before a small icon. The noon bell began to ring the hour in the castle tower but the sound seemed more like a summons to a funeral.

"She's gone," lamented Pan Volodyovski. "Gone . . . the angels took her, leaving us only sighs and tears . . ."

And then vast sobs began to shake Zagloba's heavy body while the others sighed, cried out and lamented and the bell kept ringing.

★ ★ ★

Hours seemed to pass before he finally stopped shaking but he stayed on his knees—his face hidden in his hands and his upper body slumped across his cot—so that Volodyovski thought that he'd fallen asleep, exhausted by his tears. But he stirred at last, lifted himself heavily off the floor, and slumped on his bedding without another word. He looked like no one Pan Michal saw before. Both his eyes were as red as if they were bleeding, his head hung down on his chest as if his neck was broken, and his lower lip quivered and gaped vacantly like that of an idiot. A blank, numb helplessness settled on his crumpled face along with a strange look of decrepitude, so that it seemed as if the jovial, irrepressible Zagloba, who was always so full of life, quips, witticisms, stratagems and fire, had really died on his knees beside that cot and that some broken old man had risen in his place.

Pan Longinus pushed into the room just then despite the protests of Zagloba's servant and then the lamentation started up all over again. The Lithuanian recalled his day in Rozloghi, his first glimpse of the murdered girl along with all the images of her youth and beauty and, at last, he reminded his fellow mourners that there was someone else, namely Pan Skshetuski, who had more reason for grief than all of them together.

"Where is he and how is he?" he asked the small soldier.

"He's in Koretz, at the home of Prince Koretzki, which is as far as he got on his way home from Kiev," Volodyovski said. "His health finally failed him, his body just broke down out of sheer exhaustion, and what is happening in his mind is beyond anything in my experience. He collapsed and hardly knows which world he is in."

"Then shouldn't we go to him at once?"

"What for? He probably wouldn't even know we're there. Prince Koretzki's doctor swears that he'll pull through if he's left alone to rest and to forget all that he's been through. Pan Suhodolski who commands a regiment under Prince Dominic, but who loves Skshetuski like a brother, is also there to take care of him. So's our old friend Zachvilihovski. Yan doesn't lack for anything in their hands."

"But surely there is also something we could do," the gentle giant insisted.

"Such as what? Bring to mind his pain? Remind him of his loss? It's better for him to forget us all for a while and to lose touch with reality for now."

"Aye, aye . . . but the heart breaks to think of him like that," the Lithuanian murmured. "Did you get to see him for yourself?"

"I saw him. But if they hadn't told me who he was I wouldn't have known him."

"And did he see you?"

"He must have. He smiled. He nodded. But he didn't say a single word to me and I couldn't bear to stay there any longer seeing him like that. *Knaz* Koretzki plans to march here to Zbarajh with his regiments, old Zachvilihovski is already packing, and Pan Suhodolski also swears he'll join us even if Prince Dominic forbids it. They'll bring Skshetuski with them if his pain doesn't eat him up in the meantime."

"But where did you get the news of Princess Helen's murder?" Pan Longinus asked and nodded towards the two Kurtzevitch princes. "From these gentlemen?"

"No." Volodyovski sighed and shook his head. "They heard about it in Koretz at the same time I did. They brought a few reinforcements from the *Voyevode* of Vilna and then came here with me because they also had some letters to deliver to our Prince. But the news came from Pan Zachvilihovski."

"And how did he know?"

"Yan told him. He got permission from Hmyelnitzki to search the Kiev convents where the last of our people were hiding from the mob and the Metropolitan himself was helping him with that. They both knew about the twelve young women murdered at the Good Mikolai but they were optimistic anyway. Neither of them believed that the *tchernya* would dare to kill a girl that Bohun planned to marry . . ."

"But they did?" Pan Longinus murmured, interrupting. "You're sure she was there? At the Convent of the Good Mikolai, I mean?"

"Skshetuski is sure and he ought to know. He tracked down Pan Yoahim Yerlitch who was also hiding in one of the convents and Yerlitch told him what happened at the Good Mikolai. Kurtzevitchovna was supposed to have been there too. No one remembered the names of all those murdered girls but the surviving nuns recognized Yan's princess from his description of her. That's when he fell ill and left Kiev."

"It's a wonder that he's still alive, then," sighed the mournful giant.

"I know."

Pan Michal turned his face. He was so badly shaken by his friend's collapse that he couldn't think about it without tears.

"He'd have died for sure," he resumed after a long moment, "if it weren't for an old Cossack he'd known in the *Sietch* whom he sent here with a letter to us and who then went back to help him in Kiev. This man brought him to Koretz and handed him over to Zachvilihovski. And that's the whole story."

"May God have pity on him," Pan Longinus murmured. "Because there's no other way for him to find any consolation now."

Volodyovski only sighed and nodded and no one else could think of anything to say. The two young princes who showed a certain family resemblance to the dark-browed Helen in that grey Winter light, sat with their heads lowered into their hands, their elbows on the table, and with their strong, handsome faces twisted by pain and contorted with visions of vengeance. Pan

Podbipyenta raised his eyes sadly to the ceiling, while Zagloba fixed a glassy stare on the opposite wall as if he'd fallen into the deepest trance imaginable.

"Wake up, my friend," Volodyovski said to him at last and shook him by the shoulder. "What are you thinking about so hard? There's nothing to think about anymore, no new rescue ideas to come up with, and all your plots, plans and stratagems are for nothing now."

"I know," Zagloba muttered in a broken voice. "It . . . just occurred to me that I'm an old man . . . And that there's nothing left for me to do in this world."

★ ★ ★

A few days later the worried Volodyovski came to see Pan Longinus about their old friend who seemed to have aged by twenty years in less than an hour, and who'd turned into a shadow of what he used to be.

"I can't believe it's the same man," Pan Michal confided. "You know how he was. So full of talk, bombast, witticisms, quips, bragging and boasting. Always with something to say about everything and as stuffed with stratagems and ideas as Ulysses himself. Now he sits half asleep and dozing all day long, hardly says a word except to complain about old age, and mumbles to himself as if he was dreaming. I knew he loved that girl but I didn't realize how much."

"What's so surprising about that?" The Lithuanian raised his eyes thoughtfully to the ceiling and clasped his palms together. "She deserves anyone's loving and affection. And he'd be all the more devoted to her, don't you see, because he pulled her out of Bohun's hands, saved her at least a dozen other times, and lived through so many dangers getting her to safety."

"Yes, but to give up everything like this . . . to talk about dying . . ."

"Why not, my good friend? Why not? While there was still some hope of finding the Princess he kept his mind working. That's what kept him going. But what's left for him now? He's all alone now, without anything he really cares about or anyone to whom he might attach himself, and no one to think about anymore. Believe me, I know, the world is really empty unless you have someone you can love."

Pan Michal shook his head in bewilderment and lifted his thin shoulders. "I even tried to drink with him hoping that would get him back to his old form."

"And nothing happened?" Amazement spread on the Lithuanian's gentle face. "Good God! This is worse than I thought! Mead was like his lifeblood!"

"Oh, he drinks alright," Pan Michal sighed again. "He drinks. But does he say anything? Does he boast? Tell his fantastic lies? Poke fun at anyone? Bellow about something? All he does is sniff a little, lets his tears run, and then he hangs his head down on his belly and begins to snore. I don't know if Skshetuski himself has fallen into deeper desperation than this poor old man."

"Aye, it's a shame . . . a shame," Pan Longinus murmured. "Because he was a great man in his own way, you know. Why don't we go to see him? He used to like poking fun at me; maybe he'll feel like doing it again?"

"Let's go, then," Volodyovski said. "Maybe that's worth a try. God knows I can't think of anything else to snap him out of it."

"Ay,"—the gaunt giant nodded his head sadly—"how people can change . . . What a pity! What a merry, happy-go-lucky fellow that man used to be. But are you sure it's not too late to see him? He might be asleep."

"Evenings are the worst for him," Volodyovski said. "He snoozes all day, you see, on and off, and then it's hard for him to fall asleep at night."

★ ★ ★

They found the old knight seated by an open window in his room with his bowed head propped up in his hand. It was late. Night had already fallen. The castle had quietened down, all of its many sounds died down hours earlier, and only the sentries on the walls called out their '*All's well*' in drawn out, sing-song voices. But in the cool green groves that separated the castle from the town a swarm of nightingales started their trills and warbles. The warm night air seeped into the room along with the white beams of a full, silver moon that gleamed on the top of Zagloba's bowed bald head and illuminated his grey, lifeless features.

"Good evening," the two knights said, walking in.

"Good evening," said Zagloba.

"Not interrupting anything, are we?" Pan Michal asked and elbowed the Lithuanian giant in the hip.

"No-o-o," the old knight quavered in a tired, thin voice and peered up at his two friends as if he wasn't quite sure who they were.

"Maybe you'd like to go to sleep, though?" Pan Longinus asked.

"Sle-e-ep? No . . . I'm thinking . . ."

"What about?" Volodyovski asked, knowing that nothing used to bring the fat knight to life quicker than a chance to spin some of his reminiscences.

"It's a year now . . . yes, it's about a year . . . since she and I were running from Bohun across the Kahamlik . . . and the same little birds were twittering for us then . . . And where is she now?"

"God's will," Pan Michal murmured.

"His will is my sadness, Michal . . . There'll never be any other feeling for me."

Then they were quiet, staring at the floor. But the Spring night outside never seemed more alive then it did just then. It burst into fresh joy with each passing moment, and the calls and whistles of the nightingales seemed to fill the whole sky as richly as the stars.

"Just like on the Kahamlik," the sad old man whispered, listening to the songs and warblings of the birds. "That's just how it was."

Pan Longinus sniffed and squeezed a tear out of his pale mustache while the little knight sighed, cleared his throat and said after a moment: "Ey, d'you know what? Sadness is sadness, my dear old friend, and there isn't much anybody can do about it when it comes. But why don't you drink a little mead with us? There's nothing better for a bitter moment, you've said that yourself."

"Hmm. Did I?"

"Often," Pan Longinus said.

"We'll drink and talk about better times," Pan Volodyovski added.

"Better times . . .?"

"Yes. And you can tell us about all the great things you've done."

"Alright." The old knight nodded as if resigned to everything and finding joy in nothing. "I'll drink a little with you."

Pan Michal shouted for Zagloba's servant to run for more lights, a straw-wrapped demijohn of old, vintage *Troyniak*, and tall, two-handled cups, and when all these were ranged on the table before him he urged Zagloba to tell them once again how he rescued Helen from Rozloghi and brought her to Bar.

"It was a year ago, you said?"

"In May. It was in May," Pan Zagloba muttered. "We crossed the Kahamlik to go to Zolotonosha. Ey, it's a bitter life that we're living these days . . ."

"And she was in disguise?"

"Yes. As a Cossack lad. I had to cut off her hair with my saber, the poor thing . . . I know the place where I buried it, along with my saber . . ."

"We'll all go there and get it back for you someday, old friend," Pan Volodyovski offered but Pan Zagloba turned his dull, red-rimmed eyes on him as if he didn't understand what the small knight said, nor what it was that he was promising to get back for him.

"She was a sweet lady," Pan Podbipyenta murmured with another sigh.

"I tell you . . ." The old knight's head started shaking on his neck and his eyes began to fill with tears. "I loved her from the first moment I caught sight of her as if I'd brought her up from a baby. Some people even said that she looked like me . . . but no matter. No matter. I'd have loved her even without that. And all that time we were on the road, and in all that trouble, she'd just press her little hands together . . . and thank me . . . for the care and rescue . . ."

Here two great tears started rolling down the old man's stubbled cheeks and Pan Volodyovski hurried to fill Zagloba's cup again.

"Drink, and it'll ease the sadness," he said.

Zagloba tossed down the aged vintage mead with as little pleasure as if it was water.

"Ah, sadness . . .!" he cried. "I wish I'd never lived to see this day! I wish they had killed me!"

"To better times, my friend," Pan Michal said quickly. "Let's drink to better times."

"Ah . . . I thought I'd live to see a peaceful old age beside those two good and decent young people," Pan Zagloba murmured, and the three friends sipped and drank their mead watered with their tears. "But now . . ."

And then his hands dropped to his sides and hung limp and empty and his head began to droop down towards his belly.

"No help anywhere," he murmured, drifting into sleep. "No life. No hope . . . Nothing to look forward to except a quick grave . . ."

Pan Michal looked helplessly at Pan Podbipyenta and then both friends raised their eyes sadly to the ceiling because each of them knew that their attempt had failed and that only a real miracle could cure the old knight.

Chapter Sixty

PAN ZAGLOBA SAT slumped in gloom, the tears streaming unnoticed down his crumpled face, and the two knights didn't know if they should stay or leave. There wasn't anything they could do to restore his spirits but to walk out on the wretched old man, especially when they recalled so vividly how he used to be, was impossible for them.

Volodyovski sighed and stared into his hands, Pan Podbipyenta prayed and heaved his own soulful sighs towards the smoky ceiling, and then a sound intruded—loud, argumentative, insistent—as if someone was trying to break in on their solitude and scuffling with Zagloba's servant just outside the door. The fat knight gave no sign of noticing the disturbance but Pan Michal thought that he knew that stubborn, confident young voice, and he called out to the servant to let the newcomer into the room.

The door creaked ajar. A round, red-cheeked face peered around the doorjamb with Pan Zagloba's own borrowed serving lad hovering anxiously behind it.

"Praised be the Lord Jesus Christ," the newcomer said, glanced quickly at everyone, bowed from the waist and stepped into the room.

"Zjendjan?" The little knight sat up. "Is that you? And where did you spring from?"

"It's me alright, sir," the lad said and grinned. "And happy to see you all again like I always am!" Then, tossing more quick glances all around the chamber, clearly expecting to find Skshetuski sitting with his friends, he asked for his master.

"Your master's in Koretz," Volodyovski said.

842

"Ah, ah . . ." The shining red face, bursting with confidence and curiosity like an intelligent ripe apple, turned from one of the seated knights to another. "And what's he doing there, then?"

"He's ill," Volodyovski said.

"Lord help me!" the boy exclaimed, his round little eyes growing even rounder. "What are you saying, master? He's not badly ill, God forbid?"

"He was but he's getting better. The doctor says he'll be all right quite soon."

"Hmm . . . That's good! God be praised for it! But,"—and the pudgy young face which turned solemn with anxiety broke into another wide, self-assured grin—"I'd better go on to Koretz, then, to see him . . . I've got some news for him about our young lady."

The little knight began to nod slowly in a melancholy manner.

"You needn't hurry," he said. "He already knows about her death and we're sitting here, as you see, weeping over her."

Zjendjan's mouth fell open and his wide, staring eyes seemed ready to pop out of his head. "Holy Mother of God!" he burst out. "What is this I hear? Our young lady has gone sick and died?"

"She didn't die, not exactly, not by getting sick," Pan Michal explained, bowing his head again under a sudden onrush of pity for Skshetuski. "They murdered her in Kiev."

"What Kiev?" the boy cried, looking as if he'd never understand anything again. "What are you saying, sir?"

"What do you mean, '*what Kiev?*'" the little soldier shouted in return. "You know Kiev, you halfwit! What's the matter with you?"

"But . . . but . . . but . . ." the boy began to stammer, turning a bright crimson and switching his astonished, wide-eyed stare from one of the three knights to another. "How could she be in Kiev when she's hidden in a canyon by the Valadynka, a day's ride from Rashkov?"

"What? What?" Pan Michal and Pan Longinus both leaped to their feet, seized Zjendjan by the shoulders and started to shake him. "What was that, you fool?"

"I mean . . . I mean," the bewildered lad blinked like a startled owl at his master's friends. "The witch had orders not to stir out of that place until Bohun came for the young lady or sent someone for her! So what's all this about Kiev? Am I crazy or am I hearing things? Are you joking, master?"

But both the knights had now let him go and stepped away from him, staring at the trembling, uncomprehending lad as if he was a strange and unknown creature that had just fallen among them from another planet.

"What witch!" Volodyovski shouted. "What are you talking about?"

"Horpyna, that's who!" the boy howled. "Donyetz' sister! For God's sake master, I know that witch better than I know myself!"

And then all three of them stood in slack-jawed silence, glaring at each other in complete confusion, and suddenly Pan Zagloba stirred, looked up, and began to rise slowly to his feet with what was left of his meager hair standing up on his head as if he'd seen a ghost.

" . . . What?" he murmured. "What . . .?"

★ ★ ★

He looked like a man who had been sucked down into a lake and now made one last attempt to save himself from drowning. His arms whirled like the sails of a windmill as if he were clawing his way towards open air. His mouth hissed with effort. His bulging eyes, fixed in a staring paroxysm of resurrected hope, looked as if they were about to burst with blood. His sudden bellow was so terrifying that Zjendjan jumped back while his own servant hid behind the door.

"For God's sake! Be silent, all of you! By Christ's wounds, let me question him!"

Pan Zagloba was now so pale, and there was such a flood of sweat pouring down his forehead, that he seemed ready to drop dead of a heart attack. Instead, he made one great soaring leap across the bench, seized the terrified Zjendjan by the shoulders, and yelled into his face: "Who told you that she's hidden near Rashkov?"

"Who else?" the boy wailed. "Bohun!"

"Have you gone mad, you yokel?" Pan Zagloba roared, shaking the boy as furiously as if he were a pear tree. "What Bohun? How could it be Bohun?"

"Help! Help! Let go of me, master!" Zjendjan bleated. "What

are you shaking me for like that? Let me think a little! What other Bohun could it be? There's just the one you know sir, isn't there?"

"Talk or I'll slit your guts!" The pale, wild-eyed Zagloba howled as if he'd gone completely off his head and pulled a knife out of his sash. "Where did you see Bohun?"

"In Vlodava . . . ! Hey,"—and the terror-stricken lad turned his pleading eyes on Pan Michal and the Lithuanian as if to beg for help—"what have I done? What am I, a rebel? Hey my good masters, what d'you want from me?"

Pan Zagloba gasped, fell back and clutched his chest. It seemed as if he'd finally come to the last of his strength and, at the same time, to have lost the last of his senses. His mouth hung open. His eyes were loose and rolling in his head as if he'd been hit on the head with a battle hammer. He let go of Zjendjan and dropped heavily back to the bench again and Pan Michal stepped forward to take up the interrogation.

"When did you speak to Bohun?" he asked the wailing Zjendjan. "Speak up boy. Don't be afraid. We simply have to know."

"Three weeks ago, master!"

"So he's alive, then?"

"Alive?" The lad sniffed, blew his nose, and took a deep breath. "Why shouldn't he be alive? He told me himself how you carved him up, sir . . . But he licked himself back to health again."

"And it was he who told you the lady is near Rashkov?"

"Who else would've known?"

"Listen, Zjendjan," the small knight ground out between his teeth, speaking as softly and as reasonably as he could but with such threatening firmness that the boy leaped to attention like a terrified recruit and fixed his wide-eyed stare on the end of Volodyovski's nose. "This is important, boy. This can decide whether your master lives or dies and it can also decide the life of your lady. Did Bohun tell you himself that he never took her to a monastery in Kiev?"

"Sir," Zjendjan said, as self-assured as ever. "How could she be in Kiev when he hid her with Horpyna near Rashkov, and told the witch to keep her there until he sent for her? And now he's given me this *pyernatch* and this ring that must be worth at least a hundred ducats, and told me to go there with fresh orders from him because he's laid up in Vlodava, and his wounds have opened up all over again, and he can't stir hand or foot for God knows how long . . . Our lady's not in Kiev, sir. She's never been anywhere near there. How could she be, when she's with Horpyna?"

Anything else that Zjendjan might have said was interrupted by an overjoyed Zagloba who leaped up from his bench, grasped the last of his hair in both hands, and began to roar, bellow and howl like a madman until the rafters quivered.

"She's alive! My little daughter is alive! It wasn't her they murdered in Kiev! She's alive! Alive! My own dear sweet girl!"

The old man sobbed, wept, laughed, jumped up and down, stamped his boots and danced about the room and finally clutched Zjendjan by the head, pressed it against his chest, and began to kiss and embrace the struggling and protesting boy until the lad broke free so that he could breathe.

" . . . For God's sake, master! For God's sake . . . do you want to kill me? Of course she's alive . . . We'll all go for her together, if that's what God wills . . .! Hey, master! Master! Let go or I'll strangle!"

"Ha!" Pan Zagloba shouted and seized the boy again. "Ha Ha! And didn't I tell you? Didn't I tell you all not to lose hope? Didn't I warn you against giving way to despair? How could God permit the slaughter of a sweet lamb like that? Of course He wouldn't! Any fool would know it! Next time you'll know better than to doubt God's mercy . . .!"

"It's a miracle," Pan Volodyovski said. "God's mercy be praised."

"A miracle," Pan Longinus whispered looking fondly at the restored Zagloba while two warm tears of gratitude and joy trickled down his nose and dripped into his whiskers.

★   ★   ★

Volodyovski finally managed to calm everybody down and prevailed on Zjendjan to tell his story from the start so that the three knights could grasp and understand everything that happened. But no matter how they urged, threatened or cajoled him he couldn't be hurried.

"Well, you remember how it was, good masters, don't you? I mean after the rebels took Bar? When we thought it was all over with the lady? Well, that's when I went back to Zjendjany, which is the property where my folks still live along with my old gran'daddy who's ninety years old, God bless him. Ah, ah . . .! But what am I saying? He's ninety-one now."

"May he be nine hundred and one," Pan Zagloba grated out. "Will you get on with it?"

"Thank you master! Thanks for the good wishes! May God give him as many years as He can. Well, that's where I went with all the goods I got among the Cossacks. Because, though you may not remember, I spent a lot of time with those rebels after they took me in Tchehryn last year. That's when I nursed Bohun back to health and got to be real close to him so that he and all the rest of them took me for one of their own. And so I bought up a lot of their loot. Silver, jewels . . ."

"We know." Volodyovski tried to hurry him along. "We remember."

But the flushed, happy lad was taking his time. Being the center of attention, heard eagerly by the greatest knights in the Commonwealth, and allowed to sit at the same table with his master's friends was too great an opportunity to miss.

"Yes," he said, savoring his moment. "Well. My parents couldn't believe their eyes when they saw everything I brought them. I had to swear to my gran'daddy that I came honestly by it all! You should've seen how happy they were then because, you see, we have this court case with our neighbors, the Yavorskis, about this pear tree that stands between our properties with half its branches on their side and half on ours. So what happens when the Yavorskis shake the tree is that they knock down our pears along with their own and they even claim the fruit that falls along the property line . . ."

"Don't drive me to an act of desperation!" Pan Zagloba groaned. "Stick to the point and don't babble about things we don't want to hear!"

"Yes, yes, sweet brother," Pan Longinus murmured. "Tell us about Bohun not your pear tree."

"Ah, Bohun. Well, alright, let it be about Bohun, then. So Bohun thinks he doesn't have a better friend than me, and that's in spite of how bad he hurt me that time in Tchehryn. I lied to him then about how I'm through with serving Polish masters because it pays better to stick with the Cossacks, and he swallowed it all like it was the Gospel. And why shouldn't he when I patched him up and looked after him?"

"Go on," Volodyovski hissed. "Go on. Never mind the Gospel."

"Yes, well . . . He'd have no way to guess that I swore vengeance on him for what he did to me and the only reason I didn't stick him with a knife that time he was sick was because it's not fitting for a gentleman to slit the throat of a helpless enemy as if he was a pig."

"It's tempting, though," Pan Zagloba grated out, glaring at the lad.

Pleased with this support, the boy turned grateful eyes on the grim-faced old knight who was shaking with barely controlled impatience.

"Yes, sir. It surely is. Well, kind masters, so once we squeezed the Yavorskis to the wall—and you've got to know that this court case has been going on for fifty years now, so it's no small thing—well, then I told myself: *'It's time to look for Bohun and settle my account with him as well.'* So I told my secret to the family, and my old gran'daddy said that if I'd sworn vengeance I had to keep my word. *'Because if you don't keep your word,'* he said, *'and if you don't pay your debts, evil along with good, then you'll be a capon, not a man.'* So I went off again, thinking that when I found Bohun I'd be able to get something about the lady out of him before I took a shot at him, and that my master would be happy to know where to find her and that he'd maybe give me a little something for my trouble . . ."

"He'll cover you with gold," Pan Michal assured him. "And you're sure to get something from each of us as well if you'll just get on with it and finish your story."

"You already have a horse and gear coming from me," Pan Longinus said.

"Thank you kindly, masters!" the lad cried out. "Thank you kindly! It's only right, isn't it, that good news ought to be rewarded!"

"I'm going to strangle this long-winded whelp, so help me," Pan Zagloba muttered.

"So," Volodyovski prompted. "You left home. And then what?"

"Well, then I thought: *'where should I go?'* I thought that Zbarajh would be as good a place as any, seeing it's close to Bohun's country and I might be able to hear where he is, so I headed this way. I took the road through Byala and Vlodava because it's the shortest, and in Vlodava I thought I'd better get some rest 'cause my horses were getting real worn. But it was market day, and the town was full of gentry buying their Spring corn, and every inn was full. And then this Jewish innkeeper says to me, '*I had one room left but a wounded noble took it just this morning.*' So I said, '*Maybe I can help 'cause I know how to dress a wound and your local leech is probably too busy, what with all the arguing and quarreling that goes with market day.*' So he says, '*Why not? The quicker he's cured and out of here the quicker I can get that room rented out again.*' So I go in and whom do I see on the bed?"

"Bohun?" Pan Longinus prompted with his mild, patient eyes fixed on the ceiling and his huge fists clenched so tightly that the knuckles whitened.

"Bohun," said the lad.

"At last!" cried Zagloba.

"That's just what I said to myself, kind master. '*At last!*' And Bohun was real pleased to see me too because his wounds had got infected and he didn't think he'd pull through without help. '*God sent you to me,*' he says, the murdering dog. And I thought to myself, '*Oh you'll pull through, alright. I'll see you fixed up right and proper if I've got to drag you by the scalp-lock all the way to Hell!*' And then he told me what happened to him when he went to Warsaw."

"Did he have any kind words to say about me?" asked the little soldier.

"As to that, master, I've got to give him credit." The stubborn, unforgiving boy shook his head in grudging concession. "'*I thought I was dealing with some no-account little runt,*' he told me, '*and he turned out to be a real whirlwind.*' It's only when he mentioned Pan Zagloba as the one that got him into all that trouble that he ground his teeth and said things I wouldn't like to say out loud to anyone."

"To Hell with him!" Pan Zagloba snapped. "I'm not afraid of him any more. Not after everything that's happened."

★ ★ ★

It was well past midnight, and the night was far along towards dawn and sunrise when Zjendjan finally reached the point of his story. The sentries huddling in their cloaks against the morning chill ceased to call out the hours a long time before, and the nightingales stopped their trills and warbles so long before that, that they were quite forgotten.

"We soon came back to our old familiarity with each other,"

the boy related about himself and Bohun. "He told me he was making for Volhynia and then on to Kiev where he'd be able to nurse himself back to health among his own kind, and he'd have made it too if his wagon hadn't overturned near Partchev and if his wounds hadn't broken open in the fall. As it was, he said, he was lucky to get to Vlodava without the local gentry finding out who he really was."

"He was right about that," Pan Volodyovski nodded in agreement. "If anybody along the way got an inkling that he was a Cossack they'd chop him into fishbait."

"That's just what he said to me, master," the boy said. '*Going the other way I had Hmyelnitzki's letters,*' he told me. '*I was an envoy and nobody could touch me. But now I've got nothing to show anybody and the first Polish commandant I came across would hang me out of hand . . .*' "

"Which might still happen if there's any justice left in the world," Zagloba broke in. "But go on . . . go on!"

"So," the boy went on. "He had to lie low. And then he asked me to do him another service. '*Why me?*' I asked him. '*Because you're the only friend I'd trust with this,*' he says and right away I knew he'd tell me something my master would be pleased to hear about. '*I'm sick,*' he says. '*I can't go all the way to the Dniester country on my own just now.*' And then he begged me to go in his place. '*I'll cover you with jewels,*' he says. '*I'll bury you in gold . . .*' if I'd just do that one service for him."

"And I'll bury you in something else if you don't get this story told!" Pan Zagloba shouted. "God, is there any way to hurry this snail along? You're dragging that tongue around as if you were grinding corn with it!"

"That's as may be, master. But it's all getting told and my master's going to be real pleased with me and that's all that matters. I asked Bohun exactly where he wanted me to go, 'cause that's a big, wild country around there, and he says: '*Near Rashkov, because that's where she's hidden with Horpyna, that witch sister of Donyetz that you met when you were with me in Tchehryn last year. The one that took such a fancy to you.* I asked him who it was he'd hidden with the witch, and he says: '*the Princess.*' "

"God be praised! God be praised!" cried out Pan Zagloba. "That's what he really said?"

"They're his own words, master. '*That's where I hid her,*' he told me. '*It's a terrible place and nobody goes near it, but she's as well-off there as Yarema's wife in her husband's castle, and she walks on silk carpets and sleeps on cloth-of-gold.*'"

"For the sake of God!" Pan Zagloba pleaded. "Can't you tell it faster?"

"What's stitched in haste comes apart even quicker," the calm, unhurried boy said and shrugged and grinned while the fat knight glared and ground his teeth at him. "That's what my master always says and a good servant pays heed to his master. It's what my old gran'daddy taught me too. '*Take your time and you'll get to where you want to go,*' is the way he put it. '*Run and you'll break a leg.*' And what would be the good of that, master? Trying to get somewhere with a broken leg?"

"None," the fat knight sighed.

"That's right," Zjendjan nodded. "None at all. So anyway, when Bohun told me where he'd hidden our lady I asked how he knew that she was still down there. And he swore that Horpyna is his faithful bitch and that she'd hold the lady there the rest of her life 'til he told her different. It's a place, he said, where nobody would ever dare to come,—'*neither Cossacks nor Tartars nor the Lahy,*' was the way he said—and the lady doesn't even have the Devil to fear with that witch watching over her."

"So that's it, then," Volodyovski murmured and sighed in relief. "She's alive and safe, thank God."

"She's down near Rashkov, then?" Pan Longinus wanted to make sure.

"In a canyon just off the Valadynka," Zjendjan said.

★ ★ ★

While he was talking, or rather while his story was pulled out of him a piece at a time, Pan Zagloba squirmed like an eel on a hook, the little knight nodded as if keeping time, and Pan Longinus whispered thankful prayers. Now they sat back and grinned at each other like hounds scenting prey.

But the boy had more to say. His moment of glory was too precious to give up so soon. "The best proof that she's there is that he's sent me to her," he said.

"That's right," Pan Michal said. "But you didn't give yourself away, did you? Bohun's no fool, even if he was fool enough to trust in your friendship."

"What do you think I am, sir?" The boy looked indignant. "Sure, I kind of hung back at first, so's he wouldn't see how eager I was to get all this information for my master, but that's only being smart about it. '*Why do I have to go?*' I asked him. '*I mean why just now?*' And he said he wanted her taken to Kiev, to the convent of the Holy Immaculates, and that I was to help Horpyna get the Lady there."

"To the Holy Immaculates, eh?" the fat knight cried out. "Not to the Good Mikolai, then?"

"No sir. To the Immaculates. That's the biggest one, as I'm sure you know sir, and that's where Bohun wants to have his wedding."

"He can marry the Devil for all that I care," Pan Zagloba was back in form and grinning as if he'd never shed a tear. "They'd make a good couple! So she was never at the Good Mikolai at all, was she?"

"How could she be?" Zjendjan's grin was wider than those of all the knights together. "Horpyna still hasn't got the word to take her anywhere!"

"Ha!" Pan Zagloba shouted. "Ha! And what did I tell you? Pan Yerlitch is a liar, too busy filling his breeches at one end of his *corpus* to think straight with the other! Didn't I say from the start that she couldn't have been at the Good Mikolai? Well, didn't I?"

Pan Michal and Pan Longinus remembered something altogether different but they were so pleased to see the old knight restored to all his bombastic omniscience that they were happy to go along with him.

"Yes, it's to be the Holy Immaculates," Zjendjan said uneasily. His moment in the center of affairs was coming to an end and he was anxious to prolong it as much as he could. "Ah . . . ah . . . but don't you gentlemen want to hear about the recognition signs he gave me? And about how to get there?"

"Of course, my little bird," Pan Zagloba crooned. "Of course, my little pickle. Tell us all about it. Take your time. Only a fool runs pell-mell towards wisdom, a wise man knows that patience is the brightest of all the virtues. Tell it to us exactly as he told it, in his own words if you can."

"Right sir!" Pleased, Zjendjan put on his fiercest expression and deepened his voice to sound so much like Bohun that Pan

Zagloba jumped back as if he'd brushed against a fire and Pan Michal instinctively dropped his hand to the hilt of his saber. "This, then, is what he said and that's how he said it:

'I'll give you a ring, a pyernatch *and a knife, and Horpyna will know what they mean because that's what we agreed. God's been specially kind to send you to me because she knows you and she also knows that you're my good* druh. *So take the Princess to Kiev, the both of you together, and don't be afraid of the Cossacks or the* tchernya. *Show the* pyernatch *to any Cossack who asks you your business, and the whip to any peasants that get in your way, and they'll let you through. Only keep clear of Tartars because they pay no mind to any safe-conducts.'"*

"That's good advice for all of us," Pan Michal observed. "You've done really well, my lad."

"Thank you kindly, master. But don't you want to hear the rest that he said?"

"Go on, then. Go on." Pan Michal nodded. Pan Longinus smiled. Pan Zagloba sat back grinning and humming happily to himself. "Tell us the rest of it, then."

"Yes sir," the boy said and switched again to Ruthenian and his Cossack cadence: *'There's money and jewels buried in the canyon so take all you need. Only you've got to swear you'll go there for me. Who else can I ask here in enemy country? Who else can I trust?'"*

"So you swore you'd go," Volodyovski prompted.

"That I did, sir, begging your pardon kindly. That I did. And to myself I said: *'Oh, I'll go alright. I'll go with my master.'* And Bohun was so pleased about that, and he was so grateful, he gave me all the money and jewels he had with him. And he gave me all the signs we'll need for Horpyna."

Here Zjendjan showed a richly studded Turkish *yataghan* with a turquoise like a plover's egg set into the hilt, a ring with a pale blue diamond as large as his thumbnail, and the short bone-handled cherrywood baton that was known as a *'pyernatch'* among the Zaporohjans when used as a safe-conduct.

"Then he told me which canyon it was by the Valadynka, and every twist and turn that'll take us there, and I've got it all pictured in my head so clear that I'd get there with a blindfold tied around my eyes. Which you gentlemen will see for yourselves, I expect, because it seems like we'll be going there together. Am I right?"

"First thing in the morning!" Volodyovski cried.

"It's morning now!" Pan Zagloba shouted. "We'll go in an hour!"

★　★　★

A great joy seized them all, and the only sounds that the passing sentries heard outside their windows were loud cries of thanksgiving, the clink of demijohns and glasses, the clapping of hands, and new questions tossed at the hero of the hour which the pleased, grinning boy answered with his usual blend of wide-eyed innocence and unhurried shrewdness.

"Well, I must say!" Pan Zagloba shouted. "You must've been born with a hood on your head like a hunting falcon. Does Skshetuski know what a treasure he has in you, my lad?"

"I expect he does, sir," the boy answered smugly.

"He'll cover you with gold from head to foot!"

"That's what I think too," the boy sighed with pleased anticipation. "Even though I serve him out of loyalty, not for some reward, and because he treats me like a friend more'n just a servant. But those Yavorskis won't give up, you know, and we'll need all the treasure I can get to beggar them once and for all and to send them packing. Fifty years, that court case has been dragging on . . . fifty years! I'd like my old gran'daddy to see the end of it so he'll rest easy when it's his time to go."

But Pan Zagloba's fertile mind was already seething with new plans and projects.

"There's no time to waste, gentlemen," he said. "God has chosen to give us an unparalleled opportunity through this bright, young lad and it would be blasphemy to waste it. We've got to leave as soon as we can. The Prince is away, but when he knows about all this later on, he'll forgive us for going without leave. God knows what might happen if we waited for him to return. So here's how we'll do it. It'll be Pan Volodyovski, me and Zjendjan that'll go on this rescue mission while our long Lithuanian friend stays here to explain our absence if the Prince returns before we've made it back ourselves."

"No, no, sweet brother!" Pan Podbipyenta protested. "I am going too!"

"It's for Helen's safety that I'm asking you to stay behind," Pan Zagloba said. "Your size and your good nature would give us away. Nobody who set eyes on you would ever forget you and you were strangling Pulyan in plain sight right in front of half the Zaporohjan Army. True, we've Bohun's *pyernatch* but even that won't get you past the first rebel outpost. If the Cossacks had such a walking beanpole in their ranks they'd know all about him."

"Even so," Pan Longinus persisted, twisting his huge hands. "Even so . . ."

"Even nothing!" Pan Zagloba stated, already taking charge of the expedition. "You won't find those three heads you're after on this trip and your own wouldn't help us much. You'll be a lot more useful if you sit here and wait."

"Aye," the Lithuanian sighed. "I see that. But . . . still . . . it's a pity."

"Pity or not that's how it has to be. When we go to pick crows' nests out of the trees we'll take you along. But not this time."

"There he goes again," the Lithuanian whispered with a gentle smile.

"Give me a hug, old friend, only take care you don't crush my bones," Pan Zagloba cried and threw his arms around the Lithuanian. "We'll make it up to you in some other way."

Then he grew stern, his voice dropped and hardened and he fixed his good eye coldly on the others.

"But there's one more thing!" he warned. "Not a word to anyone about this. I don't want this story spreading among the soldiers and then passing through them to any local peasants. It's most important that this be a secret!"

"Even from His Highness?" the small soldier asked.

"His Highness is away."

"Even from Skshetuski if he should get here before we come back?"

"Especially from Skshetuski!" Pan Zagloba warned. "He'd want to go after us at once and he's in no shape to do it. You said yourself, Michal, that he's hardly aware of the world around him. Besides—if, God forbid, we fail—the fresh disappointment would do him in for certain. No, no, my friends, this stays between ourselves. Give me your words of honor, all of you, that you won't breathe one word about this to a living soul."

"You've mine," said Podbipyenta.

"And mine," Volodyovski said.

"And mine too," Zjendjan said. "I may be just a servant but I'm gentry like the rest of you gentlemen. And I know better than most how to keep faith once I've given it."

"And now let's give our thanks to God and pray for His help with what we are about to do," Pan Zagloba said.

He knelt at the table and all the others followed and they prayed with all sincerity and devotion until the sun broke into the sky and the new day came.

Part Nine

Chapter Sixty-one

PRINCE YEREMI HAD indeed gone to Zamost a few days before young Zjendjan's arrival, to inspect the ravages of Hmyelnitzki's siege and confer with Pan Veyher, so the three friends and the lad could make their preparations without the need to explain or inform anyone. The knights were too well known to ride out of Zbarajh without causing comment, but since everyone in the castle knew about Helen's murder by that time, even Vyershul assumed that their departure had something to do with Skshetuski's illness and asked no further questions. Pan Longinus, who pressed a well-stuffed moneybelt on Zagloba to help with equipping the secret expedition, didn't breathe a word about it even in his prayers.

In Hlebanovka, where they made their first halt, Pan Zagloba bought five strong Podolian horses which were the favorite mounts of Polish cavalry and the richer Cossacks. The breed was known everywhere in the Steppelands for its stamina and endurance especially in a long-distance chase. A horse of this kind could run all day after a Tartar pony; it was swifter than even the light, highly-prized Anatolian mares of the Turkish sultans; and it was far superior in resistance to changes in the weather, cold nights and rainy days. Zagloba also bought some plain but sturdy Cossack coats and cloaks of the kind favored by Zaporohjan gentry, intending them as disguises for himself, his companions and the girl whom they hoped to rescue, while Zjendjan took care of the packhorse and supplies. Dressed in their Cossack finery they were easily taken for rich atamans, while Pan Zagloba, with his huge belly and his fierce, blind eye, could pass for a *koshovy*, or Chief Ataman, or at least a *kujhen* commander, so that Commonwealth garrisons and patrols scattered throughout that country all the way to Kamyenetz stopped them and questioned them closely every time they met them.

They rode for several days through safe and settled country occupied since the armistice by troops of Pan George Lantzkoronski, the head of one of the noblest and most famous families in the Commonwealth and one of the King's three new principal commanders. These regiments were converging slowly on the territory around Bar where large masses of Cossacks also began to gather. The Pereyaslav armistice was due to end in the first days of May and the unofficial war of ambushes and raids was heating up to a general conflagration which everyone expected almost anytime.

Meanwhile it was a time of promise in the reawakening Steppe. Spring moved across it like the touch of a loving hand. The trampled grasses sprung up again among a sea of flowers, and the wounded soil, torn and crushed by the hooves of last year's warring armies, healed itself with a luxurious new abundance made all the richer by the bones and bodies of the fallen warriors who lay under it. The air was sweet and clean. The endless, open sky was unmarred by smoke. The soft night horizons didn't glare with the red glow of burning villages and cities. Young birds filled the waterways with song; newborn cubs and animals gamboled in the clearings; the widespread surfaces of the lakes and rivers glistened with silvery, gently moving waters stirred by the touch of warm, evening breezes; and the whole vast landscape seemed to cry out: '*Spring . . .! Life . . .! Joy . . .!*' with a rich chorus of bird and animal voices.

It seemed to both Pan Michal and Zagloba that nature herself wished to close the country's wounds, soothe its agonies and bury its graves under banks of flowers. The sky had never seemed so bright nor the soil as fruitful, and everything around them was fresh, airy and trembling with new hope. Seen from the occasional roadside mounds where they stopped to rest and to fill their eyes with this breathtaking beauty, the sunlit Steppe glowed like cloth-of-gold. It shimmered like a jeweled, newly-woven tapestry in which skilled weavers blended all the hues and half-tones of the rainbow.

★ ★ ★

Riding within this humming, whispering kaleidoscope of color, and warmed by the broad winds that played among the grasses, the two knights and the lad never even thought about the possibility of failure.

Pan Michal sang songs all day long. Zjendjan grinned. Pan Zagloba stretched and warmed his bones while bobbing up and down on horseback, purring and muttering as if he'd suddenly become an enormous cat, and letting the sun stroke his back whenever he could.

"I feel . . . blessed. Yes, blessed," he said to Pan Michal sighing with huge and blissful satisfaction. "There are only two substances better than the sun for getting the marrow moving in old bones and that's an aged *Troyniak* or a Hungarian brandy which God invented to bring some joy to mankind on cold Winter nights."

"It's not just old bones that the sun is good for," Pan Michal observed, pointing to the various animals they passed in the Steppe. "Notice how even the young *'animalia'* like to sun themselves."

"Which also proves that the *genus humanus* is fashioned in the image of its Maker," Pan Zagloba added, "since He didn't forget about us in the colder seasons. It's lucky that we're going for our little sweetheart at this time of year. It'd be a lot harder running with her in this open country if the frost was cracking in our bones."

"Let's just get our hands on her," Pan Michal said lazily, grinning at the sun. "And I'll let a tinker use me to plug holes in a leaky pot if anyone gets her away from us again."

"It'd have to be an awfully small pot," the fat knight remarked, unable to resist the opportunity. "A tailor would have better use for you as a darning needle, I should think. But there's one thing that does bother me, I admit, and that's the idea of Tartars. If war breaks out in earnest before we've finished with our business, those devils are likely to start moving this way from the east. I'm not concerned that much about the Cossacks; with Bohun laid up and out of the way we'll manage the others. The *tchernya* also shouldn't be much of a problem for us; you notice how the peasants take us for Cossack atamans everywhere we go. But the Tartars are another story. They wouldn't care if we were Hmyelnitzki and Krivoinos, especially with our rescued girl riding with us."

"I know how to handle Tartars," said the little soldier. "Our whole lives in Prince Yeremi's country were spent in keeping them in line."

"I know them too," Pan Zagloba said. "I spent a lot of years among them and I could've risen to great heights in the Khan's court only I didn't want to become a Muslim. So, instead, they martyred me, as you can see by this eye of mine, because I converted their chief shaman to Christianity."

"But didn't you say that happened in Galata?" Pan Michal said, grinning. "And that it was the Turks that did it to you? Or was it Valachians?"

"Galata was one thing and the Crimea was another," the fat knight replied, unperturbed. "If you think that the world ends at Galata then you don't know much. There are a lot more pagans than good Christians on this earth."

★   ★   ★

But here Zjendjan broke into their conversation. "Ey, master. There's something else we ought to be worried about," he said.

"Such as what?" Feeling lazily relaxed and content in the balmy sunshine Pan Zagloba didn't want to hear about any worries. "The nurse didn't wash out enough diapers for you? The milk has turned sour?"

"Evil spirits, master," Zjendjan said.

"What evil spirits?"

"The ones up ahead. They're the one thing I didn't get around to when I told my story. There are all kinds of unclean things guarding that canyon, or so Bohun told me. The witch that watches over our young lady is a powerful necromancer, I've seen her at work, and she's got a whole slew of devils jumping at her orders. Could be they'd warn her to watch out for us. I've got a silver bullet loaded in my pistol, one that I cast myself over grain kernels washed with holy water, so that should take care of the witch, I expect. But all those vampires and ghouls and such, begging your pardon kindly, let that be your business. You've got to keep those things off my back or how will I live to see that reward my master's bound to give me after we get back?"

"Ha! You grasping little pissant," Pan Zagloba glowered with artificial gruffness. "As if we had nothing better to think about than your expectations! The Devil isn't going to twist your neck for you this time, though it wouldn't make much difference if he did because it's bound to happen in the end. You're sure to wind up in Hell because of your greed! So she's a great witch, is she? Ha! Good enough! I'm a mighty wizard myself, I'll have you know. I learned all the black arts in Persia, and there's none blacker than that . . . .! So she's got a devil or two working for her, does she? I could plow my fields with a whole herd of devils as if they were oxen, only I don't want to risk my soul's salvation by meddling with unclean powers."

"That's good to know, master," the awed Zjendjan murmured. "That's good. Salvation's important. Only could you use your powers just this once? It's always better to cut down the risks when you're dealing with devils."

"As for me, I've more faith in the rightness of our good cause and in God's protection," Volodyovski said, smiling mildly at the sun and sky. "Let Bohun and Horpyna have their devil helpers. We'll stick with God's angels and their field commander, the Archangel Michael, who's just as invincible in Heaven as our own Prince Yeremi is on Earth . . . To which intention I'll offer seven wax candles when we're back among Godfearing people."

"I'll pay towards another one myself," Zjendjan muttered, sniffing. "Just so's Pan Zagloba don't scare me no more with all that talk about greed and going to Hell. Greed is greed, and that's a deadly sin, but prudence is a holy virtue. And it's a prudent man who looks to his future."

"I'll be the first to send you to damnation if it turns out you don't know the way to that witch's canyon," the little knight threatened.

"I shouldn't know the way?" The plump, rosy cheeks of the cunning lad flushed with indignation. "Once we get to the Valadynka I can find it with my eyes blindfolded. Here's the way Bohun told it: '*You go downriver along the Valadynka to where it joins the Dniester. Then you turn sharp right, climb a ridge, and enter broken ground. You'll know the canyon by the great slab of rock that blocks the entrance so at first sight it looks like there's no way in. But there's a cut in the rock wide enough for two horsemen abreast, and that's the only way in or out because the cliffs around it are so high that even a hawk can't fly over them once he's down inside.*'"

"And that's it?" Pan Volodyovski queried.

"That's it, master. Just about. The witch murders anybody who gets in there without her permission so there's a lot of bones lying around the entrance. But Bohun said not to worry on that score. He said to ride right on in and start shouting '*Bohun! Bohun!*' and she'll come out to greet us."

"And she's alone in there, is she?" Pan Michal asked and grinned slyly at the lad. "Other than those devils?"

"No. There's Tcheremiss. He's not much to look at, Bohun says, but he's a dead shot with a musket. We've got to kill them both."

"That Tcheremiss . . . hmm. I don't see why not," the little knight agreed. "But surely it'll be enough to bind the woman with a good strong rope and leave her behind."

"Bind her!" Zjendjan burst out into such loud and disbelieving laughter that a cloud of grouse scurried out of the grass and flew off towards the setting sun with a rush of wings. "I'd like to see anybody bind her. She's so strong she rips armor in half with her bare hands. She crushes horseshoes in her fingers as if they were eggshells. Maybe Pan Podbipyenta could manage her, master, but not us!"

"Yes, but to kill a woman . . . That's something that a decent man shouldn't be able to do."

"Enough, master, enough," Zjendjan begged. "I didn't melt good silver into a bullet for the fun of it. Let the Devil finally take her to Hell, where she belongs. Otherwise she'll come flying after us, and howl for the Cossacks, and we'll not only lose the lady again but our own necks as well."

★ ★ ★

This kind of talk made the time pass quicker on the trail. They hurried past small towns, homesteads, old burial mounds and scattered country dwellings. Their track was taking them towards Yarmolinsk, and Bar beyond that, where they expected to slant off into the wilderness, heading in the direction of Yampol and the Dniester. They were now in the country where Pan Volodyovski surprised and defeated Bohun and rescued Zagloba after that peasant wedding. They even found the lone, abandoned homestead where this had taken place and spent one night there, but most of the time they bivouacked in the Steppe under the open sky, where Pan Zagloba filled their evening hours with so many stories of his past adventures that their own journey began to seem like a Homeric legend. Most of their talk, however, dealt with Skshetuski's princess and with her coming rescue.

At last they left the country held in uneasy submission by Lantzkoronski's soldiers and entered territories controlled by the Cossacks where no Jews or gentry remained alive, not even in hiding. Those who hadn't saved themselves by flight to the West were rooted out and exterminated with fire, sword, butcher knife, hangman's noose and pitchfork, and even their graves were trampled down and scattered. Such was the Ukrainian peasants' hatred for their past oppressors and exploiters that they drove herds of cattle and horses across their graves to erase the last traces of their presence in the country.

Then May drew to its end. Summer was almost there. The air grew heavier with the heat but the distances kept unrolling endlessly towards the horizons. They had covered only one third of their journey by that time, and the miles became more difficult to cross every day as their trails disappeared in the open Steppe but at least they were in no danger from the Cossacks. The huge, marauding bands of armed peasants didn't bother them, taking them for important Zaporohjan elders, while the more disciplined *Nijh* and *Sietch* patrols they encountered paid due respect to Bohun's safe-conduct. Once in a while some drunken chieftain of a band of *tchernya* barred their way, demanding to know who they were and where they were going, and Pan Zagloba, who seemed to know these people very well, had a simple answer. He'd kick the man in the chest without even getting off his horse, knock him on his back and ride over him, while the rest stepped back, bowing to the ground.

"Them's our own people," they'd mutter with awe and admiration. "And important, too. Got to be, or they wouldn't kick us. Hey . . . maybe it's Hmyel himself? Or Krivoinos? Or Burlay?"

But their greatest ally was Bohun himself. His name opened every door. His fame was so widespread, and the curiosity about him was so deep, that Pan Zagloba started to complain because all the questions about him and his whereabouts that they had to answer robbed them of precious time and slowed down their journey.

"Who'd think that devil could be loved so much?" he muttered to Volodyovski when no one could hear him. "I know there's no one like him—dear Lord, do I ever!—but you'd think he was God himself the way people revere him in these parts!"

The news of Bohun's death had flown with the wind as far as Yahorlik and the Dnieper cataracts. It was already part of the folklore and the peoples' legends. And when the travelers said that, on the contrary, he was alive and well, and that they were his emissaries going on his business, every heart and home opened to them—along with every larder, smokehouse, stable, liquor barrel, purse and moneybag—of which Skshetuski's cunning young servant made good use.

★ ★ ★

In Yampol they were received by Burlay himself. That famous old ataman, who was second only to Krivoinos in ferocity, was the third most powerful and important Zaporohjan leader now that Kshetchovski was dead on a stake. He had been Bohun's patron and tutor many years earlier, teaching him the arts of war, looting the Tartar settlements on the Black Sea coast, and going with him on raids across the sea. He loved Bohun as if he were his father so he greeted the young hero's friends as gladly as if they were his own kin.

"What do you need?" he asked. "Men? Horses? Money? You can have anything you want. Nothing's too good for Bohun's good brothers. Just ask and it's yours."

"We've no need for men, ataman," Zagloba said quickly. "We're traveling among our own kind and we don't need an escort. But we could use some horses, and the faster the better."

"And money," Zjendjan added, even quicker. "Our ataman didn't give us much 'cause he was a bit short himself, and a quart of oats costs a thaler the other side of Bratzlav."

Burlay had no reason to suspect them, especially since he had seen Zjendjan at Bohun's side in Tchehryn last year, and hearing that Bohun was alive and heading for Volhynia he gave a banquet that night in celebration. Pan Zagloba worried that the boy might get tipsy and babble out something dangerous but the shrewd lad handled himself very well. In fact he proved himself so adroit that the fat knight watched him with amazement.

'. . .Hmm. *That little fellow isn't going to die of old age, nor by his own choice,*' he mused in admiration. '*And even then he'll probably cheat the Devil of his passage money . . .*'

Zjendjan, meanwhile, played the role of a bluff young Cossack to perfection. He sounded as if he'd never told a lie in his entire life. His voice rang with sincerity. His face was as open as the Steppe itself and without a shadow of guile in his bright blue eyes, and he was clever enough to speak the truth as often as he could so that old Burlay took everything he heard as if it were Gospel.

"Ay, we heard about that duel of Bohun's," he said. "We worried about it. Who was the man that cut him down, then? Do you know?"

"Man by the name of Volodyovski," Zjendjan said in a calm, matter of fact tone while Pan Zagloba shuddered. "One of Yarema's officers."

"Ey, if I could just get my hands on him," Burlay growled and clenched his fists as if he was strangling someone in the empty air. "I'd pay him for our falcon. I'd have his hide peeled off in strips and stitched back to his body with redhot hobnails."

Pan Michal moved his little oat-colored whiskers up and down, looking at Burlay like a mastiff whose chain isn't long enough to let him reach his prey, and Zjendjan stared back at the Zaporohjan with total innocence.

"That's why I'm telling you the name, ataman," he said. "So you'll know him when you find him."

"Good lad," Burlay growled. "I'll keep him in mind."

"But there's another *Lah* that's even worse than him," the boy said, nodding at Zagloba as if about to call him as a witness. "That Volodyovski's not that much to blame. Our ataman called him out with no idea what a swordsman he was picking on so he had to fight him. But there was this other noble there, Bohun's worst enemy. The one who stole the ataman's girl from him once before and hid her in Bar. He's the one that stirred up all the trouble."

"And who's that?" Burlay roared.

"Ah, a worthless old guzzler who hung around our ataman in Tchehryn, pretending to be his good friend and brother," the boy said and shrugged with terrifying candor, while Pan Zagloba felt icy sweat breaking out across his bald head.

"He'll hang too!" Burlay roared.

"And so he should," the boy said. "I just hope I am there to see it."

Pan Zagloba hid his face in a quart of mead, swearing silently to himself that he'd cut off Zjendjan's ears the first chance he got, but the brash lad wasn't done with his master's friends.

"Aye, aye . . . They carved up Bohun so bad we didn't think he'd pull through alive. We thought the crows would sure get at him this time . . ."

"But he's all right now, you say?" Burlay interrupted.

"He's got a 'horned soul' in him, as the saying goes, and he recovered well enough to drag himself as far as Vlodava where we took good care of him and sent him on to our own people in Volhynia. So then he asked us to get his girl and bring her to Kiev where they're going to get married before the war starts up again."

"Women will be the death of him," Burlay muttered. "I warned him about that. Many times."

"Ah, well, you know our ataman," Zjendjan shrugged.

"I know him. Sometimes he doesn't seem like any kind of Cossack, you know what I mean? Couldn't he have his fun with the girl and then tie a millstone round her neck and toss her in the river? Like we used to do on the Black Sea? Wouldn't that be better?"

Pan Michal, whose sentimental soul thrived on his attachments to revered and unattainable women, barely managed to restrain himself. But Pan Zagloba burst into hoarse, coarse laughter.

"Sure it would," he cried.

"Aye, I can see you're real good brothers to him," Burlay said and nodded. "You didn't turn your backs on him when he needed you . . . And you, you little one,"—and here the half-drunk ataman turned his maudlin, sentimental eyes on the grinning Zjendjan—"you're the best of all. I seen you that time in Tchehryn how you took care of our falcon Bohun. Well, I'm your brother too. You just tell me what you want and I'll get it for you. You sure you don't need some good *moloytzy* to ride along with you?"

"No need for the *moloytzy*, ataman," Zagloba reminded. "But we could use those horses."

"And as much money as you've got to spare," Zjendjan added quickly.

"So come on in the back room with me, then," the old Cossack said.

Zjendjan followed the ataman into an inner room while Pan Zagloba looked after him in wonder and the little knight sat at the table shaking his head in his own amazement. Both of them had seen some bold, brassy fellows in their time, but neither saw anything like the boy's performance, and they took care not to catch each other's eye until they could do so unobserved. But they could see when the boy reappeared in the banquet room that his round, pink face glowed with a vast new satisfaction and that the thick moneybelt wrapped around his waist sagged considerably lower.

"So. Go with God," the old Zaporohjan said, hugging and kissing each of them in turn. "And if you're passing this way with the girl stop in and see me, hear? I'd like to take a look at this wonder that's got our falcon into all this trouble."

"Oh, that can't be, ataman," Zjendjan said calmly while Pan Zagloba felt the sweat bursting out on his head again and pouring down into his collar.

"And why not?" Burlay's eyes narrowed in sudden suspicion.

"'Cause she's scared of Cossacks," Zjendjan said and guffawed like a simple-minded fool. "She's already stabbed herself once, who knows what she'll try again? Let our ataman handle her himself and the quicker the better."

"So a Cossack stinks in her nostrils, does he?" old Burlay muttered and spat in contempt. "What's Bohun want with one of them *Lah* lily-whites, anyway? Aren't our young women good enough for him?"

"Well, you know those *Lah* women, ataman," Zjendjan said and shrugged again. "You know what they're like."

"I know them. And pretty soon they'll know me again."

They bowed and followed Burlay outside where two Cossack grooms handed them the reins of two black, glistening stallions which looked like the swiftest and most costly racers that even Pan Zagloba could claim to have seen.

"Ride with God," Burlay cried out to them.

"Stay with God," they answered. Then the rough, stony streets of Yampol clattered under them and they trotted out again into open country.

Chapter Sixty-two

IT WASN'T FAR from Yampol to the Valadynka, a mere dozen miles across the roadless wilderness, but the gaunt, broken country made their progress more difficult and slow. They took a westerly direction out of Yampol, leaving the broad waters of the Dniester flowing far behind them, and then, guided by the stars and the shrill chatter of the nightbirds crying in the reeds, followed the course of the narrow Valadynka northwest towards Rashkov.

At first they rode in silence. The night was cold but clear and a great, white moon hung above the boulders and escarpments through which they guided their snorting, nervous horses which seemed to sense dangers that their riders could neither see nor hear. But then the sky above them began to lighten, the moon lost its luster, and the first blue-grey streaks of dawn appeared in the water.

Pan Zagloba drew a long, careful breath, released it, and sat back in his saddle. He was pleased. Burlay's feast went on late into the night and now he calculated that they had at least a full day's ride before they found the gorge. But that, he thought, was all to the good. He wanted to find the canyon as close to nightfall as possible so that they'd have darkness to cover their traces and hinder whatever pursuit there might be when they fled with Helen. Meanwhile he had every reason to feel optimistic. Their luck served them well throughout the whole journey and now it looked as if it would hold for a while longer.

"Notice how these Cossacks, who live in brotherhood among themselves, help and support each other at all times," he remarked. "I'm not talking about the way they treat the peasants, whom they despise to the point of hatred and for whom they'll be even harder taskmasters than we were. But when it comes to dealing with another Cossack they'd jump through fire for him. It's a far cry to our own gentry each of whom thinks only of himself."

"No way, master," Zjendjan said at once. "I spent a long time among them and I saw how they tear and claw at each other. If Hmyelnitzki didn't hold them together by cunning and terror they'd eat each other alive like a pack of wolves. But that Burlay's a great man among them and Hmyel himself treats him with respect."

"Which you don't share now that he let you make a fool of him," Pan Zagloba said. "Ey, Zjendjan, my lad, take care. Somebody will twist your neck for you some day, you mark my words. You're too cocky for your own good."

"If that's what's written for me, master, then that's what'll happen," the boy shrugged, not caring. "But what's the harm in pulling the wool over an enemy's eyes? I'd think God would be pleased to see it."

"Yes, that's to your credit," Pan Zagloba said. "No question about it. But your avarice is another matter. That's a peasant sentiment, unworthy of gentry, and that's why you'll end up in Hell."

"I'm not so fond of money that I won't buy a candle to light in a church," Zjendjan offered quickly. "That way God will also get something out of my good luck and keep on sending me His blessings. As for helping out my family as much as I can, is that a sin, master?"

"What a glib and quick-witted little weasel this is!" Pan Zagloba turned to Volodyovski. "I thought that all my own sharpness would go to the grave with me but now I see that here we have an even bigger rascal than I ever was! Imagine! It's thanks to his sharp wits that we're going to rescue Helen out of Bohun's clutches, and we are doing it with Bohun's own per- mission, on Burlay's horses and with Burlay's money! Have you ever seen such a thing? But at first sight you'd hardly give three farthings for this fellow!"

As fond of praise as he was of money, Zjendjan smiled, content. "It could be worse, master, couldn't it?" he said.

"I like you," the fat knight said. "Yes, indeed. I like you. And if you weren't such a rapacious little fox I'd take you into my own service so that you could learn a few noble virtues and grow up into a decent human being. Ha, but since you skinned Burlay like you did I'll forgive you for calling me a worthless old guzzler."

"It wasn't me that called you that, master," Zjendjan said at once. "It was Bohun."

"Yes," Pan Zagloba said sternly and wagged a warning finger. "And look how God punished him for it."

★ ★ ★

The morning passed in this kind of half-serious and half-jocular talk about important matters, something that Pan Zagloba knew would ease his nervousness and help to convince him that they had nothing more to worry about. But when the sun climbed higher into the sky, hanging like a great yellow eye in the cloudless blue canopy overhead, they found themselves saying less and less, and in quieter tones, until their light-hearted banter dwindled into silence.

The Dniester and the Valadynka both vanished during the night but they would reappear in due time, Zjendjan assured the others. In a few more hours they'd pass the confluence of these two rivers and begin the last stage of the search. Their long and dangerous journey was almost at its goal and now each of them began to show his own variety of tension.

Was Helen still alive? And if she was, would they find her in that witch's cauldron? Horpyna, Pan Zagloba knew, could have carried her off somewhere else, Bohun or no Bohun. Or she might hide her in some dark corner of the canyon where a stranger would never think to look. All the obstacles weren't overcome; there were sure to be many other problems still ahead; and all the dangers weren't safely behind them. True, they had the ring, the knife and the *pyernatch* by which Horpyna should be able to tell that they were Bohun's messengers carrying out his orders. But what if her devils had warned her about them?

Zjendjan worried the most about evil spirits but even Pan Zagloba who claimed to be a skillful necromancer was nervous about them. Because if she'd been warned they'd either find the canyon empty or—and this was the most likely possibility—full of Cossacks summoned from Rashkov by the witch and waiting in ambush. Their hearts beat faster as the morning passed, and their glances sharpened, and by the time they finally climbed to the top of a high ridge and saw a broad, bright ribbon of water gleaming in the distance, Zjendjan was pasty-faced with fear.

"That's it," he said so quietly that they hardly heard him. "That's the Valadynka."

"Ah . . . so soon, then," Pan Zagloba grunted.

"May God protect us now! Master . . .? Hey, master . . .? D'you think you can start up your incantations now? 'Cause I'm awful scared . . ."

But if the fat knight really knew how to deal with devils he seemed to have forgotten how to go about it. "Forget the incantations," he muttered, shrugged and mopped his sweating forehead. "Let's just make the sign of the cross over the river and all these caves around here. That'll work much better."

Pan Volodyovski seemed the least affected by superstition but even he was silent and concerned. He drew the loads out of his holstered pistols then reloaded them carefully with fresh ball and powder and tested the priming, and then he checked to see if his saber slid easily from its sheath.

"Well," Zjendjan whispered. "Well . . ."

Then he followed the small knight's example with one of his own handguns whose bright silver bullet gleamed in the harsh, high sun like a blind, white eye.

"In the name of the Father, the Son and the Holy Ghost," he said. "Let's get started."

"Let's go," said Zagloba.

"Forward!" Pan Michal ordered and they kicked their reluctant horses into a slow walk.

Another hour brought them to the riverbank where they turned downstream. The quick, white water hissed and bubbled on their left. The grimly littered wilderness extended on their right with its caves and ridges. The broad, dark loops of the lower Dniester lay somewhere ahead.

And here Pan Volodyovski halted for a moment.

"Let Zjendjan take the *pyernatch* and ride out ahead," he said. "The witch knows him so let him be the first to talk to her or she might panic and hide the Princess in some hole where we'd never find her."

"Good idea," Pan Zagloba said.

"No it's not," said Zjendjan.

"What do you mean it's not, you poisonous little beetle? Ride

out like you've been told to do or I'll cut off your ears right here
and now!" the fat knight roared, glancing nervously around.

"No way," Zjendjan mumbled, sniffling. "Do what you like,
master, but I'm not going to be the first to go into that canyon."

"Then be the last!" Volodyovski snapped and spurred his
horse forward.

Pan Zagloba followed.

Zjendjan trailed after them, with the remount horses plodding behind him on long reins, and peered around with the
greatest agitation that he'd shown so far. The horses' hooves
clipped and clattered on the stones and shale, an occasional
bridle chain rattled and saddle leather creaked, but these were
the only sounds they made. The deep oppressive silence of the
wilderness settled around them as the sun slid down into the
afternoon and now the swarms of locusts hidden among the
rocks began to stir and rustle.

At last the horsemen came to a flattened hillock that looked
like a giant's buckler tossed into the wasteland, with crumbling
cliffs looming up around it like scorched, mysterious towers
and battered walls, or like the gaunt ruins of desecrated
churches. The dry desert wind hissed and moaned among these
piles of stone as if they were the rubble of a city stormed and
pulled down only yesterday.

Zjendjan, who had been drawing closer to Zagloba as they
rode, took one quick look around and nudged the fat knight's
shoulder.

"That's '*Vrajhe Urotchysko*,'" he said. "The 'Devil's Playground,' as Bohun described it. Nobody can get past this place
alive after sundown."

"Then it's a good thing we're here in bright daylight," Pan
Zagloba snapped, hiding his own nervousness under irritation.
"Tfui! What a cursed, Godforsaken country this is! No wonder
people pay more attention to evil and malignant powers around
here than to love and mercy. But at least we're heading the right
way."

"It's not much further now," Zjendjan said.

"And how far is that?"

"Maybe another hour . . ."

"Thank God."

A strange, elusive feeling passed through Pan Zagloba as he
rode along those savage banks of the Valadynka. It was impossi-

ble for him to believe in the midst of that grim and inhospitable wilderness that Helen was so near at last, that this girl for whom he'd struggled through so many dangers, and whom he'd come to love with a degree of passion and commitment he'd never understand, would be crying out with joy and weeping in his comforting old arms in just another moment. She came to mean so much to him in a single year that his life lost all its purpose when he heard that she was murdered in that Kiev convent; he saw no point in living or even thinking about what to do with his remaining years; and a lonely and embittered old age, full of loveless hours that would seem like years, became a burden that came near to breaking him altogether.

Oh yes, a man could make his peace with even the most devastating calamity, he knew; he could find a kind of numb, despairing solace in acceptance, as the tormented Skshetuski had done, and drown his sorrow in service and duty, but that was an option for the young. Zagloba had nothing to sustain him because he didn't really have anything in which to believe except his own survival. He'd lived so long with the idea that Helen had been carried off by Bohun, that she was far away, and that years of war might pass before any trace of her emerged from the murk of time and the pain of all his disappointments, that he didn't dare to think of any other ending to his search.

And now, could it really be that all those fears and all that loneliness and longing were about to end? That the search was over? That a new era of calm prosperity and untroubled peace lay only a hand's reach away?

And then another mass of questions pushed into his head. What will she say and do when she sees him? This rescue, after such a long and terrible captivity, will fall on her like a bolt of lightning, he was sure. Will she be able to believe it and survive it without going mad?

'God has His ways,' he thought, drifting off on a reflective tangent. The paths of providence unfolded in their own mysterious fashion, and who was he to question miracles? God saw to it that Bohun, who almost murdered Zjendjan, became his trusting friend, Pan Zagloba mused. God saw to it that war drew the dangerous ataman away from this wilderness where he hid his prey like a wolf in a secret lair. God placed him in Volodyovski's hands and then, again, in Zjendjan's . . .

It didn't occur to the musing knight, moved by the realization of God's just and watchful presence in everything that happened, that he too was a crucial link in this chain of planned and ordained events. All he knew and dared to think about in that telling moment was that while Helen waited only a few yards away, perhaps giving up the last hope of rescue, her rescuers were at hand.

"It's time to end your tears, my sweet little girl," the old knight whispered within his own reflections. "It won't be long before you are restored to everything you've prayed for . . ."

And here the girl's remembered image rose before his eyes so sharply that it seemed as if she were actually there. He could see her at last as more than just a fragment of his memory and imagination, and the old noble let his grateful tears flow and drip into his beard.

Then, with no warning, Zjendjan was tugging and pulling at his sleeve.

"Master! Hey, master!"

"What now?"

"Did you see? A wolf just ran past up ahead."

"So what?"

"But what if it wasn't just a wolf?"

"Then run after it, shake it by the tail and ask it to introduce itself to you properly!"

★ ★ ★

Annoyed to have his warm, sentimental musing interrupted with such abrupt insistence for such a foolish reason, the fat knight fell into a sudden rage in which he recognized more than a touch of fear. But at that moment Pan Volodyovski pulled up his horse and glanced back at Zjendjan and Zagloba with his own puzzled irritation.

"Did we get off the track somewhere?" he asked. "Seems to me that we've been riding this way far too long."

"No sir," Zjendjan said. "It's just as Bohun told it. I wish it *was* all over and done with, master, if you don't mind me saying, rather than still ahead . . ."

"It will be soon if you haven't got us heading in a wrong direction."

"No sir, it's been just like Bohun said, so far. But I've one more thing to beg of you, good masters, if you'd be so kind . . .

And that's to keep an eye on that Tcheremiss when I'm talking to the witch. He's as ugly as sin, people say, but he's a crack shot and fast as a viper."

"Don't worry about him," Pan Volodyovski said. "Alright, let's get going."

But the horses took barely a dozen paces when they began to balk. They tried to stand rooted in the shale under them, made harsh snorting sounds, pressed their ears back along their heads, and rolled their eyes in fear.

" . . . O *Jezu*." Zjendjan seemed to shrink. "O holy Mother of God . . .!"

If he was expecting to hear the howl of a vampire from under the rockfall, or if he thought that some monstrous shape would come bounding down the hillside to leap on his back, he was disappointed, and the fetid stench of a wolf's lair in a nearby cave explained the horses' terror.

Zjendjan took a breath. The silence everywhere around them seemed even thicker than before, the shadows of late afternoon began to creep out from under the boulders, and the dry, overheated air seemed particularly still. Zjendjan scrawled a quick sign of the cross and calmed down at once. But suddenly Volodyovski reined his horse again and pointed to a deep declivity that opened up among the piled boulders and tall, brown walls of limestone and jagged flint beside him.

"I see a steep ravine with a slab of rock wedged into the entrance," he called back. "And there's a passage gouged into the rock."

"In the name of the Father, the Son and the Holy Ghost," Zjendjan said again. "That has to be it."

"Follow me," Pan Michal ordered quietly and turned his horse into the narrow opening.

★   ★   ★

One after the other, the fat knight and the boy followed Volodyovski through this tall, vaulted natural gateway into a deep ravine which fell steeply to the dark floor of a widening canyon. They heard the soft rustling of a stream and saw, unfolding as far as their eyes could reach, a broad half-moon clearing overgrown with stunted trees and strangely twisted bushes that crept up the sheer cliffs, singly and in clusters, towards the darkening sky.

Zjendjan began to call out as loudly as he could: "Bo-hoon! Bo-hoon! Come here, you witch! Come on down! Bo-hoon!"

They halted at the bottom of the gorge and waited quietly for several minutes and then the boy started crying out again but all they heard in reply were the distant howls and baying of great hounds.

"Bohun! Bohun . . .!"

"Could she have gone away?" Pan Zagloba worried. "Could we be too late?"

"No. Look up there," said the little knight, pointing up the cliffside where a large, dim form appeared almost at the top of the escarpment.

The witch, if that's who it was, stood in the red and yellow glare of the setting sun, a dark, broad-backed creature peering down from among the thick knotted brambles and stands of dwarfed wild plum, and the boy nodded with a strangely calm and chilling satisfaction.

"That's her," he said. "That's Horpyna!" And then making a trumpet out of his folded hands he cried out again: "Bo-hoon!"

The tall, dark woman began to descend the cliffside, leaning back for balance, while some kind of twisted little shape seemed to roll and bounce along in her wake. Bushes cracked and splintered under her heavy feet. Huge boulders broke loose and crashed to the bottom of the chasm with a noise like thunder. Bathed in the crimson light on the canyon floor, she really did seem like something from another world while the rolling little shape behind her proved to be a small hunch-backed man who carried a long Turkish musket.

"Who're you?" she demanded in a booming voice.

"So how are you, you old bass fiddle?" Zjendjan called out calmly. He may have been ready to drop dead of terror at the thought of spirits, Pan Zagloba noted, but he had no fear of any human being, no matter how gigantic or grotesque.

"You?" The huge young woman grinned, showing an even row of bright, white teeth. She took a step forward. "Bohun's boy? Hey, little one, I know you! I remember you! But who are these others?"

"Bohun's friends."

"Hmm. A goodlooking witch, I must say," Pan Michal muttered and moved his little whiskers quicker than before.

"And what'd you come here for, then?" she wanted to know.

"Here," Zjendjan said and reached into his coat. "Take a look. Here's Bohun's *pyernatch*. Here's his knife. And here is his ring. D'you know what they mean?"

The young giantess took the objects in one hand and examined them closely in the failing light.

"They're the same." She nodded. "You here for the girl?"

"That's right. How's she doing?"

"She's in good health." The huge young woman shrugged, not caring about her prisoner one way or another. "But how come Bohun didn't come himself?"

"He's sick. He's been wounded," Zjendjan said.

"Wounded eh?" She didn't seem surprised. Then she shrugged again. "Yes . . . I saw it in the millrace."

"If you saw it,"—Zjendjan laughed straight into her face—"then why were you asking? Hey, you're a liar, you old mattress cover! What've you been drinking?"

The young witch bared all her white teeth in a wolflike smile, closed a huge fist and punched the boy lightly in the side. "Gimme a kiss," she said.

"Get out of here!" he shouted.

"Hey, come on, little one. Hey! Hey!"

"Don't you get enough from all your devils?" The boy pushed the huge young woman's shoulder but he might as well have been shoving against the cliffside. "Leave me alone, you hear?"

She laughed again, a wild shrill sound like a neighing mare, and stepped back. "When are you taking the girl, then?" she asked.

"Right away. Just as soon as we've rested the horses."

"Good. Take her, then. Is it Kiev you're going to?"

"Yes. To Kiev."

"Good. Then I'll go with you."

"You? What for?"

"To see my brother Donyetz one more time. His death's been written, I've seen it on the waterwheel. The *Lahy* are going to kill him on the stake."

"Hmm. Is that so."

While they were talking Zjendjan bowed forward in the saddle as if to make their conversation easier and let his hand drop lightly to his holstered pistol.

"Hey, Tcheremiss, Tcheremiss!" he called out, wanting to draw his companions' attention to the dark, squat shape with its Turkish musket.

"What are you calling him for?" the witch asked. "He can't talk. His tongue's been cut out."

"I don't want to talk to him," Zjendjan said and grinned. "I just want to look at him again, he's such a rare beauty. But you're not going to leave him here, are you? No, you're not. How could you? He's your man."

"He's my dog," she said.

"And there's just the two of you in the canyon?"

"Just us. And the princess."

"That's good. But you won't leave your Tcheremiss here alone, I'll tell you that much."

"I'm going with you like I said."

"And I say you won't."

There was something so cold and dangerous in the lad's soft voice, something so suggestive and insidious, that the huge woman stepped up and peered at him closely while a sudden spasm of suspicion flashed across her face.

"*Sch'tcho tih?*" she hissed out. "What's the matter with you?"

"What's the matter? This!" Zjendjan answered, pulling out his pistol with one hand and cocking it at the same moment with the other. Then, with what seemed like the continuation of the same swift movement, he plunged the barrel between her breasts and pulled on the trigger.

Horpyna staggered back out of the black cloud of smoke with her arms flying apart like wings. Her eyes bulged out with disbelief and fury. A strange, sharp animal cry boiled out of her shattered chest and then she toppled over on her back. In that same instant Pan Zagloba hauled out his saber and slashed Tcheremiss with so much weight behind it that the misshapen skull split and grated under the blow.

The dwarf made no sound. He merely curled up like an insect on the canyon floor, twisting and quivering like a snake which had been cut in half by a scythe in a harvest field. His hands, opening and closing as if they had their own lives separate from the body, clawed at the earth like talons for a moment, and then he lay still. Zagloba wiped his saber on the tail of his coat while Zjendjan leaped off his horse, lifted a massive boulder and threw it down on Horpyna's chest. Then he started searching for something in his shirt.

The witch was still alive. Her huge body trembled in an effort to raise itself again. A red spasm of rage convulsed her twisted features, foam boiled out of her mouth in a rush of blood and her throat uttered a deep, booming growl.

"My God," Zagloba said. "How can she be still alive with a wound like that?"

"She's a witch," Zjendjan said and shrugged.

He found a piece of chalk inside his shirt, fished it out, and scrawled a large white cross on the boulder he'd thrown down on Horpyna's chest.

"But she'll stay put now," he said and leaped back on his horse.

"Now, ride!" Volodyovski ordered.

★　★　★

They spurred their horses. They galloped like the wind alongside the fresh, cold spring that bubbled down the middle of the valley floor, passing great toppled oaks tossed about like kindling, and then their eyes fixed on a large squat homestead crouched among tall trees. Beyond it stood a mill whose glistening waterwheel shined like a crimson star in the glare of the setting sun. Two huge black dogs, chained to the base timbers of the hut, hurled themselves towards them as far as they could, howling in the fury of frustration.

Volodyovski was the first to get to the cabin. He jumped off his horse, kicked open the door and ran into the front room with his saber in his hand. Through an open door to his right he saw a large, smoke-filled room, obviously a kitchen, with kindling and wood shavings piled in the corners and a cooking-fire laid in the middle of the earthen floor. The door to his left was shut.

'*That's where she must be,*' he thought.

One more leap took him to that door. He threw it open, stepped across the threshold, and that was as far as he could move because it seemed as if his boots had sprouted sudden roots. Standing as far back as she could in that glowing, richly jeweled chamber was the most beautiful woman he had ever seen. White as a sheet, with loose coal-black hair flowing down across her back and shoulders, the Kurtzevitch princess leaned for support on one of the tall, carved pillars of her bed, and her terror-stricken eyes numbed him with her questions.

'*Who are you?*' she seemed to be asking without a sound, never having seen the little knight before. '*What do you want here?*'

He stood as dumbstruck and bewildered as if he had lost the ability to move. He was astonished by her beauty, fixed in place by her terror, and as dazzled by the unexpected opulence of the chamber as if he'd fallen, by some witch's spell, into a realm of magic and illusions.

"Don't be afraid, my lady," he muttered at last. "We're friends of Skshetuski."

"Then save me!" she cried and went down on her knees before him.

But in that moment Pan Zagloba—redfaced and shaking with emotion and gasping for breath—burst into the room.

"Sweetheart!" he cried. "It's us! With help!"

Hearing those words and seeing that familiar face, the young woman bowed like a cut flower, her arms fell to her sides, her eyes closed, and she fell unconscious to the floor.

Chapter Sixty-three

THEY BARELY TOOK the time to feed and water the horses and then they fled into the Steppe, riding so swiftly that they were far beyond the Valadynka before the new moon rolled into the sky. Volodyovski scouted the way ahead. Zagloba rode with Helen a little behind him. Zjendjan closed off the cavalcade with the remount horses and two fresh pack animals he hadn't forgotten to take from Horpyna's stable.

Zagloba's mouth hardly closed throughout the night as he told the girl everything that happened since she was cut off from contact with the world.

"Dear God," she said, lifting her pale face to the moon in wonder. "So Pan Skshetuski went all the way beyond the Dnieper after me?"

"To Pereyaslav, like I told you. To Hmyel himself and then to Kiev and back." Careful not to mention Skshetuski's collapse so as not to add to her anxiety, he said that Pan Yan was away on duty. "He'd have come with us if we had time to send for him. But we were in a hurry to get here as soon as we could so we left without him. He doesn't even know that you are still alive, dear girl, and he prays every day for the peace of your soul, but don't feel too sorry for him about that. He can afford to worry for a little longer seeing what a reward he's about to get."

"And I'd begun to think that everyone had forgotten me," Helen said. "And all I prayed for was a quick death."

"Not only did we never forget you," Pan Zagloba said. "But all we talked about for a year or more was how to find you and get you out of Bohun's hands. It's really quite amazing, when you think about it! I mean it's no surprise that I'd rack my head

883

about you, or that Skshetuski would just about dry up with
worry, but that this little knight ahead there, who'd never even
met you, should work as hard as he did to save you is a bit of a
wonder nowadays."

"God bless him for it," Helen said.

"He will, if there's any justice." Zagloba smiled and sighed
with pleasure, then went on shaking his head in amazement.
"You've something special about you, you and Skshetuski both,
that makes people as fond of you as if you were their own kin.
Even so, you do owe a great debt to Pan Volodyovski because,
like I said, he and I carved up Bohun between us like a Sunday
roast and all this would have been quite impossible if he was on
his feet."

"Yan used to talk about Pan Michal in Rozloghi," Helen said.
"He said he never had a better friend."

"And he was right to say that. There's a real giant's soul in that
little body. Now he's kind of dumbstruck by your beauty, and
looks rather like a bug-eyed schoolboy on a country picnic, but
wait until he gets used to you and finds his voice again. Hey, but
we did some wonderful things in Warsaw at election time!"

"So there's a new King?"

"Even that's news to you, my poor child?" Zagloba went on
shaking his head with amazement and clicking his teeth. Then
he started babbling about everything at once.

"Yes, we've a new King. Yan Casimir Vasa, elected last fall,
and now in the eighth month of his reign. We're going to have a
great war with the rebels almost any day and I just hope it'll end
successfully because the chancellor and his cronies pushed our
Prince Yeremi right out of it all and picked some new commanders that are about as fit for that job as I am for marriage."

"I suppose Yan will go to war again . . ."

"He's a great soldier." Pan Zagloba nodded. "I don't think
even you could manage to keep him at home. But then we're
both like that, he and I! One sniff of gunpowder and we're on
our way!"

"Dear God," Helen sighed. "When will it all end?"

"When? Hmm. I don't know. When it's all over, I suppose,
and that's up to the Cossacks as much as to us. Ey, but you
should've seen us last year, Skshetuski and me! We really gave it
to those cursed rebels, good and proper. The whole night
wouldn't be enough to tell you about it."

"So I am to find him at last," she said quietly and sadly. "Only to lose him to another war?"

But Pan Zagloba was following his own trend of thought and didn't hear her troubled tone or note her new anxiety.

"Yes, we'll go," he said. "But it'll be with a lighter heart this time. Lighter by a mountain! Because we've found you again, my dear, and that's worth a whole new life to every one of us."

★ ★ ★

Then they rode without speaking for some time. The flat, dry Steppe unfolded quickly under them. The night was cool and clear. The moon rose higher by the hour into the starlit sky, shrinking and growing whiter as the dawn drew nearer, and the only sounds other than the drumming of the horses' hooves were the quick, sharp snorts with which the animals seemed to be signaling good omens for their journey.

"*Zdrov! Zdrov!*" the riders echoed them mechanically, in keeping with the custom of the Steppe. "Stay healthy!"

But the animals began to run more slowly as the night grew brighter, their breathing became heavier, and soon the riders themselves began to nod and sway sleepily in their saddles.

Volodyovski was the first to slow his horse into a trot so that the others could catch up with him.

"Time to stop," he said to Pan Zagloba. "Don't you think? Dawn's not far off."

"Hmm. Yes. It's time," the tired old knight murmured, yawned, and tried to rub the sleepiness out of his face. "Ooof," he gasped and groaned. "I wouldn't mind stretching my bones a bit and resting my eyes . . . Ay, I'm starting to see things in this tricky moonlight. It looks to me like my animal has two heads nodding on his neck."

"Let's stop, then," Volodyovski said. "A few hours' rest will help us make better time after sunrise."

"Rest, yes. Hmm. And perhaps a bit of shut-eye? I don't think I've slept soundly for a single night since we left Zbarajh."

But before they stretched out to rest around a small campfire they did what all Steppe travelers always did; they saddled fresh horses so as to be able to ride off without a moment's pause if some unexpected danger appeared in the night, rubbed down and tethered all the other animals and let them loose to graze while Zjendjan set about preparing their supper. He made sure that their small fire was well screened from sight and then unloaded the saddlebags he had filled in Yampol out of Burlay's stores. There was a round flat wheel of hard-baked cornbread, cold smoked meats, some sugared Tartar *bakalya* in honey and syrup, and two large leather gourds of Valachian wine. At the sight of these bulging, gurgling sacks, Pan Zagloba forgot all about sleeping and sighed with pleased anticipation.

"I'll say this to the end of my days," he announced after he'd drunk and eaten. "There's no accounting for God's mysterious ways. Here you are, my sweet girl, free as a bird in the Steppe, and here we are beside you, at ease '*sub Jove*' as the ancient Romans described their country outings, pleased with a good day's work and sipping Burlay's wine. I won't say that a jug of good Hungarian '*Vengjhyn*' wouldn't have been better, particularly since this Valachian grape smells a bit of the leather, but it's certainly good enough for a trip like this one."

"There's only one thing that puzzles me," Helen said. "And that's how Horpyna would let me go so easily."

"How she let you go?" Here Pan Zagloba began to squirm a little as if the hard Steppe soil was suddenly too uncomfortable to sit on, and threw a couple of quick pleading glances at Zjendjan and Volodyovski who, however, couldn't do anything to help him. They kept their eyes down, staring at the fire, and the fat knight was left to find the explanation on his own.

"Well," he said. He cleared his throat. "She . . . ah . . . let you go because she couldn't do anything about it."

"Why not?" Helen asked.

"We had all those signs that Bohun gave Zjendjan, as I've told you."

But, unaccountably, this partial truth troubled the fat knight who never worried about stretching a fact into a better story. He sighed, grimaced and shook his head with a helpless and resigned expression on his face.

"Besides, why hide it?" He shrugged and sighed again. "Hmm. We . . . ah . . . took care of her and that Tcheremiss both."

"What do you mean '*took care*'?"

"We killed them," the fat knight said and looked despairingly at Zjendjan and Volodyovski but they kept their eyes averted from him and Helen. "Didn't you hear the shooting?"

"I thought that was Tcheremiss . . ."

"Well, it wasn't." Ashamed for reasons he didn't understand, Pan Zagloba took refuge in gruffness. "It was this boy here who shot a hole right through that damned witch. I agree that he has his own demon sitting inside him too but this time there was no other way. Either the witch knew something and didn't quite believe us, or she was just determined to have her own way, but she insisted on going along with us and she'd soon have seen that we weren't taking you to Kiev. So, anyway, to cut it all short, he shot her and I cut down Tcheremiss, or whatever that monstrosity called itself. I've never seen an uglier looking creature and I'm sure that all the devils in Hell are sick to the stomach now that he's among them. I don't see how God could hold that against me . . . But, *incipiam*, or to get back to the point, I went out ahead before we set out and pulled the bodies aside so you wouldn't be upset at the sight or read some bad omens in all that."

"I've seen too many people whom I loved murdered before my eyes to be frightened by the sight of corpses," the pale girl said quietly. "But I wish we weren't leaving spilled blood behind us. There's been so much of it in my life, you see, that I don't want to add to any more of it. And it can only bring new misfortune to us."

"It certainly wasn't something that a knight would do," Pan Michal said abruptly.

Pan Zagloba sighed.

"Ey . . . what's there to talk about?" Zjendjan broke in uneasily. "There just wasn't any other way to rescue you, my lady, and that's all there's to it! Maybe if we'd done that to some decent person . . . well, then it'd be different, I wouldn't deny it. We'd have cause to think badly of ourselves. But those two were enemies of God, weren't they? So what's wrong with sending them to Hell? I've seen that witch myself hobnobbing with her devils! No, no, that's not what I feel so bad about."

"What is it then?" Helen asked.

"Well . . . you see, my lady,"—and here the boy's voice rang with the grief of real tragedy—"there's all this treasure buried by that mill . . .! Bohun himself told me where to dig but the masters hurried me so much I didn't have the time to go after it! And my heart's also breaking over all those goods we had to leave behind in that chamber where your ladyship was staying . . ."

"Now you see what kind of a servant you are going to have," Zagloba told Helen, throwing up his hands and shaking his head in wonder. "He'd skin Lucifer himself if he thought he could stitch himself a fur collar out of that hairy hide and slice the horns into new coat buttons. Though I'll be the first to say you won't find fault with his loyalty to his master."

"If God sees us through to safety," Helen told the boy, "you won't find me ungrateful. Perhaps even enough to make up for what you didn't bring out of the canyon."

"I thank you kindly, my lady," Zjendjan said, still mourning for the treasures that had slipped from his grasp but mollified by the promise of a fresh reward. He kissed Helen's hand with the devotion of a loyal servant and bowed to the ground before his future mistress.

★ ★ ★

All this time little Pan Volodyovski sat without saying a word to anyone, sipping wine out of a gourd and frowning to himself, until his unusual introspective silence attracted the fat knight's curiosity and drew his attention.

"Hmm. How is it that you're sitting there as if someone had let all the air out of you?" he asked, knowing very well the effect that beautiful young women had on the warm-hearted little soldier, then grinned and turned to Helen: "Didn't I tell you that he's been struck dumb by your beauty? Hey, hey, my dear Michal, you'd feel a lot livelier if you turned your thoughts to some of those little birds we trailed in Warsaw."

"And you'd do a lot better to get some sleep before daylight," Pan Michal mumbled, feeling like a fool, while the points of his little mustache twitched up and down exactly like a field hare when it wants to make itself appear both dangerous and attractive.

But the old noble had hit the nail on the head. The glowing richness of this girl's extraordinary beauty, and the promises she made of banked fires that were ready to burst into flame at a touch of a loving hand, seemed to have cast some sort of spell on the little soldier.

He felt dull, witless, clumsy as a schoolboy and—above all—'*little*'.

He knew that he was staring at her like a gaping fool and kept asking himself if he was really seeing what he thought he saw. Was it possible that a human being could be that stirring and exciting? What kind of creature, and coming from what planet, could project such a breathtaking combination of unapproachable stateliness, dignity and assurance with such an earthy, genuine and unaffected honesty? And how could a man come close to that kind of flame without turning either into ashes or a pile of scorched and smoldering rubble?

He had seen many beautiful women, he knew. Perhaps too often for his own good. The two Vishnovyetzki princesses, Anna and Barbara of Zbarajh, could dazzle and dumbfound even the most successful and experienced lover; he'd seen for himself how the pert and flirtatious Anusia Krasienska turned the smoothest courtiers into mumbling idiots, and the less said about her effect on the loving and susceptible Longinus Podbipyenta the better, he was sure. He had been happy enough to forage among the many other Polish, Valachian, and Lithuanian beauties of Princess Grizelda's household who made him feel sometimes as if he'd stepped into a garden of animated roses, but none of them came anywhere near this darkly glowing Steppe flower, he was sure.

With the others . . . '*ho, ha, ho,*' he thought, scrambling desperately for something to sustain his confidence and make him feel less like a dumbstruck yokel . . . '*Ho, with the others . . .*' There weren't many problems with any of the others! He'd been full of talk, jokes, witticisms, sly comment, teasing and the rest of that innocent back-and-forth of courtly flirtations. And sometimes it wasn't necessary to be all that innocent! But now, when he caught himself looking into those luminous, calm eyes so laden with promise, at that mass of scattered blue-black hair that fell like a gleaming waterfall down her back and shoulders, at that poised, slim, arrow-straight back and the womanly roundness of her breasts lifting with each breath . . . and when he felt the warmth of the fire smoldering just under that cool, smooth, alabaster skin . . . he thought that he'd leap right out of his own puny little hide!

But where would such a leap take him? And how was he to go about making himself interesting to her? And, above all, why would he want to do it in the first place? What good would it do him?

He felt foolish, stupid, tongueless and so small and puny as to have gone beyond mere insignificance into some kind of cruel comedy.

'*That's a Queen,*' he thought bitterly. '*A real princess in every meaning of the word. And I'm a clumsy oaf.*'

With such thoughts and feelings weighing on Pan Michal's mind, Zagloba's mild jibes and good-natured needling came close to throwing him into a towering rage. He longed desperately for the sudden appearance of some legendary monster . . . some kind of giant or ogre or fire-breathing dragon that populated the myths and imaginations of his time . . . so that he'd be able to show this regal young woman just how large and important he himself could be!

But the wide, silent Steppe whispered to him only with the cool breezes of the early morning. There were no dragons for the little knight to slay, not here anyway, and all those other dangers from which he could rescue her better than any man alive seemed so distant as to be unreal for everybody but himself. She sat by the dimming fire, bathed in its flickering shadows and the glow of moonlight, and the small soldier shrunk into himself and dwindled even more.

★   ★   ★

Out in the Steppe in the morning, when he and Zagloba found themselves riding side-by-side for a moment, the old knight was full of pride in 'his little daughter' and babbled about her beauty as if he'd had something to do with it.

"You'll admit, my friend, there isn't another girl like her anywhere in the Commonwealth. Show me one and I'll let you call me a windbag and use me for a bellows."

"That I won't deny," said the little soldier. "I've seen nothing like her, not even among those marble goddesses we saw in the Kazanovski Palace gardens during the elections. I can understand now why two such knights as Bohun and Skshetuski were ready to tear off each other's heads over her."

"Aha? Aha?" the fat knight bubbled proudly. "God help me if I know when she's prettier, at night or in the morning? I told you once that I used to be an unusually handsome specimen myself, but even then I would have had to step back before her poise and beauty. Even though there's some talk that she looks as much as I did in my youth as if we were a pair of matched drinking cups."

"Ah, drop it will you?" shouted the small soldier. "Can't you find something else to babble about?"

"Don't get angry, Michal. Don't get all upset. You're doing enough growling and frowning as it is. You gape at her like a goat at a head of lettuce, and you lick your chops like a mongrel at the sight of a smoked pork sausage, but that little dish is for another's table."

"Tfui!" Volodyovski spat into the wind. "How can an old man like you say such stupid things?"

"Stupid, are they? Let's hope they are stupid. But if they are then why are you walking about with thunderheads wrapped around your noggin?"

"Because you act as if all the danger was over, and as if nothing more could happen to us from now on, while the truth is that we've barely scratched the surface of our difficulties! We still have weeks ahead of us, and every step of the way is as dangerous and threatening as everything we've faced up to this moment, because the part of the country where we're heading now is sure to be on fire already."

"Hmm." Brought to earth in such an abrupt fashion, Pan Zagloba started peering around him in alarm. "You think so? So soon?"

"No question about it. Burlay was ready to march at a moment's notice. He was just waiting for the Bessarabian Tartars to come in from the Wild Lands. There's already been some heavy fighting around Bar and every Cossack we've seen on our way has been drinking *na umor*. The war will be raging everywhere around us long before we bring Helen to where she'll be safe."

"Hmm. Hmm. Somehow with her so near I'd forgotten all about the war. You may be right. Still, it was a lot worse when I stole her from Bohun in Rozloghi. He was boiling with rage and chasing after us, the whole rebellion lay ahead of us, and yet I got her safely across the Ukraine like one of those Eastern holy men that walk across fire. It's all a matter of quick wits and imagination. That's why we carry heads on our necks, isn't it? If things come to the worst, Kamyenetz isn't all that far away."

"And neither are the Turks and the Tartars."

"Turks!" Pan Zagloba snorted. "What kind of new poppycock is that? Don't we have enough trouble with the Cossacks and the Tartars? What do we want with Turks under our feet?"

"I wish it was poppycock," the little solder said. "But those are the Sultan's treaty lands, down below Kamyenetz. That's where the Turks and Tartars graze their herds in Winter. And if they're all going to be a part of Hmyelnitzki's new war, as every rumor has it, then that's the last place in the world for us to think about."

"Damnation!" the fat knight burst out. "Is there no end to these monsters that are tearing at us? You cut off one head and they grow a hundred new ones in its place! Why don't they eat each other if they're so hungry? I was counting on Kamyenetz as a sure refuge if the war overtook us before we reached real civilization."

"And I say we should bypass Kamyenetz," Volodyovski said. "The road past Bar is a lot better for us. The Zaporohjans respect their safe-conducts, and we'll manage the *tchernya* one way or another, but if one Tartar catches sight of us then it's all over with us, especially for Helen. I've trailed and tracked them for years, and I can run before a *tchambul* along with the wolves, but if we should come face to face with one of their sweeps then even I won't be able to lead us out to safety."

"So let's head for Bar," Pan Zagloba said. "Let the plague take all those Podolian Turks, Tartars, half-breeds and Tcheremiss monstrosities!"

But as the miles passed, and as the swift, galloping Steppe mustangs and Podolian pacers took them towards another glowing sunset, his spirits took a fresh turn for the better.

"What you don't know my friend, is that Zjendjan weaseled another *pyernatch* from Burlay himself, and that's a real Godsend because if what you say about the war is true then Burlay is now the ruler of this whole territory. With his safe-conduct, and looking like real Zaporohjan *starshyzna*, we can trot around any Cossacks like sheepdogs around a flock of lambs. The worst of the wilderness is behind us now, we'll soon be coming into settled country, and we should also give some thought to finding some quiet homesteads for our stops at night rather than bivouacking in the open country. Some unassuming, out of the way hut would be a lot more comfortable for a girl than sleeping on a horse-blanket in the grass. A woman needs a few private moments now and then."

"Agreed," Pan Michal said.

"I thought that you would."

Then Pan Zagloba grinned again, winked at the gloomy little knight and peered about with much greater confidence than before.

"Seems to me," he resumed, "that you take a rather dark view of our chances. I think better of them. What the Devil, if three good men like us—and, not to be too flattering to either myself or to you and Zjendjan, first rate men at that—if, as I said, we can't manage a few days in the Steppe then there's something wrong! My wisdom and experience, Zjendjan's sharp wits and cunning, and your superb saber are an unbeatable combination. If the King had three such men as his personal advisors we'd be eating tonight's dinner in the Sultan's palace while Hmyel shined our boots and Burlay held our horses. So let's push on, and the harder the better. Once we're past Bar we'll be among Lantzkoronski's regulars and that'll be that. So 'hayda,' my good friend. 'Hayda, tally-ho!' We've no time to waste!"

And they spurred their horses.

Chapter Sixty-four

THEY RODE AS swiftly as their horses could take them, galloping north and northwest across the Steppe for hours at a time, until it seemed that the animals could carry them no longer. But the Podolian runners and Burlay's thoroughbreds kept going none the less.

Nearing Mohilev, they began to enter more populated regions, so that, at nightfall, they were sure to find shelter at one or another of the many scattered Steppe settlements or homesteads. But each new dawn found them already on horseback and deep in open country.

The last few days of May passed without anything remarkable to either worry them or please them. June brought dry, hot days but there was always a cool wind rustling through the grasses so that the journey was not as exhausting as it would have been later in the Summer. The nights were cool and moist with dew, so that when the morning sun rose above that rolling sea of grass, the Steppe looked as silvery and liquid as if it were a real restless ocean. But the wind and sun dried the widespread waters left by the Spring thaws throughout that whole country; the streams and rivers sunk deep into their channels and the fugitives forded them without much trouble.

Running north along the Lozova River for some time they stopped for a longer rest at Shergorod in which one of Burlay's Cossack regiments was quartered, and there they found several of his messengers who had come to mobilize the country for the coming war. Among them was a Zaporohjan *setnik* named Kuna whom they had seen in Yampol at Burlay's celebration. He was surprised to see them so far to the north and west but shrugged off his suspicions when Pan Zagloba explained that they were taking a round-about way to avoid the Tartars who were already moving west from beyond the Dnieper.

Kuna, in turn, told them that Burlay was also on his way to Shergorod, along with all the Yampol men and the Bessarabian Horde, and that they would then march north and west at once. Word had come from Hmyelnitzki that the war was starting up again, and Burlay was to sweep into Volhynia as soon as the Tartars joined him, even though the old Cossack general had been making plans to march on Bar instead.

"And why's that?" Pan Zagloba queried.

"Because there's bad news for us from that part of the country."

"Our luck's turning then?" Zagloba questioned, still in his role as a rebel and comrade of Bohun.

"So they say," Kuna said and shrugged. What happened, he explained, was that Pan Lantzkoronski crushed several powerful *vatahas* assembled in that region, recaptured the town of Bar and garrisoned the castle.

"Many thousands of good Cossacks went down in those fields," Kuna mourned. "Old Burlay wants vengeance. He'd have gone to Bar a long time ago only Hmyel's orders about Volhynia were getting in his way."

"So we won't be besieging Bar right away, then? Volhynia comes first?"

"I s'pose it does." Kuna shrugged. "Unless the Tartars get real hot about getting into Bar again."

★ ★ ★

"What did I tell you?" Zagloba asked Pan Michal the next day as they were galloping once more through the open country. "Bar lies straight ahead. It's in our hands again and I could hide our girl there as I did before. But to the Devil with Bar and every other fortress! I've quite lost my taste for fortifications. Only a fool would place any trust in walls when peasants have more artillery than the Commonwealth commanders. What worries me, though, is that things are getting a little stormy around us."

"It's not just getting stormy," the little soldier said. "The storm is real and it's blowing right there at our backs. Burlay and the Tartars are coming up behind us and neither is much to joke about."

"So who's joking? Do you hear me laughing? I could make a jackass out of a fool like Kuna about why we're here but Burlay wouldn't believe me for a moment. He knows the road to Kiev. And he'd show us quite another road, namely the one to the next world, if he ever caught up with us."

"Just pray it's Burlay not the Tartars," Volodyovski said.

"That's a choice?"

"Not for us. It's death either way if we're caught and the quicker the better. But what about the girl? She could maybe find a spark of mercy in a Cossack, as she did in Bohun. But what could she expect among the Dobrudjans or the Turks or on the auction block out in Asia somewhere?"

"May the Devil take them all!" Pan Zagloba ranted. "Why is there so much of that flea-bitten vermin in the world? I hate to say this but things don't look quite as good as they did before. Listen, let's agree on one thing. When it comes to dealing with Cossacks and the rabble I'll pull the strings for all of us. I can run rings around any of them. But if it's ever a matter of dealing with the Tartars, my good friend, then let it all be in your hands."

"Seems like you're giving me the hard part," Volodyovski said and smiled without amusement. "The mobs and the Cossacks take us for their own so there's all kinds of room for maneuver among them. But it doesn't matter how clever you are when it comes to Tartars. There's only one piece of advice that makes any sense with them."

"And what's that?"

"Avoid them at all cost. Slip away while there's time and if they do catch sight of you then ride as hard as you can and for as long as your horse can stay on his legs. Which means that we have to keep buying horses wherever we can so's to save wear and tear on the few good animals we have because we might need them."

"There's enough for a herd of horses in Pan Longinus' purse," the fat knight said, patting his well-stuffed sash. "And if we do run a little short we'll take Burlay's money bags away from young Zjendjan. But for now let's stop wasting breath! Let's ride! Let's keep going!"

And they spurred their horses even harder, galloping on and

on until sheets of foam began to form on the animals' heaving flanks and to spatter the Steppe in their tracks like a drift of snowflakes.

★ ★ ★

Days passed like that, days and nights that began to flow together and to seem like weeks. There was little rest. Miles flew past them one after another, and the Steppe drifted and unfolded under them and stretched out behind them. Creeks and streams splashed by. Rivers fell away.

They crossed the low, slow and sandy Derla and swam their horses across the swifter and deeper Ladava and, at the horse fair in the market town of Barek, Volodyovski bought half a dozen strong, young Tartar ponies without trading or discarding the worn animals they had. Burlay's thoroughbreds, he knew, would recover quickly if they were allowed to run for a few days without a load; they had to be kept fresh for a time when only speed might save Helen from the Tartars. He didn't mention to Zagloba that there were only two of these enduring, indefatigable racers for all four of the fugitives, but the fat knight probably knew it anyway.

In the meantime the little Steppe raider drove them without mercy. Their halts for rest became shorter every day. Their stops at night turned into two or three hours of deep, exhausted sleep at most. They were in the saddle and galloping long before the sunrise and for hours past sunset. But their strength, as Volodyovski noted, seemed to grow greater with the daily hardships. Helen, in particular, seemed to bloom in the open air. She had lived a shuttered, cloistered life in Horpyna's canyon, hardly even leaving the silk-lined jeweled cage that Bohun fashioned for her, so as to avoid seeing the crude young witch and listening to her hot whispers and her vulgar urgings. But now the clean Steppe air sent the blood surging through her body and lifted new color into her pale cheeks. The sun and wind were darkening her complexion and filled her eyes with a new eagerness and brightness, and when the swift, warm air threw her hair into a tumble of disordered coils she seemed to turn into an embodiment of pagan joy and freedom.

"A Gypsy princess," Pan Zagloba muttered then in wonder. "A witch in her own right, wouldn't you say? Eh?"

"That she is."

"You'd think she drew strength out of the Steppe itself! Well, why not? She's as much a part of this country as that open sky! No wonder she blooms here like a wild rose!"

The little knight agreed, saying nothing, but thinking of old legends in which ancient tribal queens rode across the Steppe with flowers strewn before them and knights galloping behind them.

"She goes to the head, like wine," he muttered to himself when the fat knight wasn't near to hear him. "There's no doubt about it. But I won't let myself get drunk on that sweet vintage because it isn't for me."

And then the little soldier spurred his horse ahead and vanished in the tall grass like a diver plunging into the sea, where the instincts born of long years spent in the raids and ambushes of the borderlands, turned all his attention to the job at hand. Was the road safe? Were they heading in the right direction? Was there any sign in the sky or among the grasses that might suggest some danger? And then he'd rise up in his stirrups, lift his little yellow mustache above the dark, abundant, windswept waves of the rolling grassland, and sniff the air like a Tartar scouting in the Wild Lands.

Pan Zagloba was also in fine health and fettle.

"This run is a lot easier than what Helen and I went through that time on the Kahamlik," he said with satisfaction. "At least we've horses to ride instead of trotting on foot like a pair of mongrels. I thought that long walk would dry out my tongue for shoe-leather. But here we are now, God be thanked for it, well mounted and in good company, and there's even something in the gourds to wet the throat now and then."

"And do you remember how you used to carry me across the rivers in your arms?" Helen asked.

"How could I forget? But you'll have something to carry in your arms yourself soon enough, I think. Unless Skshetuski's not the man that I take him for."

"Hoo-hoo-hoo," Zjendjan laughed.

And then it would be Helen's turn to spur her horse and gallop on ahead.

★ ★ ★

At last, several days past Barek and Yeltushkov, they came to a torn and ravaged country that showed the raw wounds and fresh scars of the fighting which hadn't ceased in that region even during the uneasy armistice of the Winter. These were lands newly scorched by bands of armed marauders as well as Lantzkoronski but the Commonwealth forces were no longer there. All the *Lahy*, as the fugitives were told everywhere, were pulling back towards Zbarajh because their soldiers were refusing to serve under any general other than Vishnovyetzki and the King's generalissimos had no choice but to follow their men.

Hmyelnitzki and the Tartar Khan were also on the move with all their massed armies, and everyone speculated about the final battle—the one that would decide who in the Ukraine would live and who'd be wiped off the face of the earth forever—that would take place when their *Bat'ko* Hmyel and the dreaded Yarema locked horns at long last.

It seemed to the hurrying travelers that every living creature in those territories had seized a weapon and headed north to join Hmyelnitzki. From deep in the south, from below the headwaters of the Dniester in the wilderness, came Burlay with all his masses of *Nijhovtsy* and Podolian Cossacks, the *tchernya*, the Zaporohjans, and both the Dobrudjan and Bessarabian Tartars. Krivoinos and his thousands marched out of the Podolia. And everywhere along their lines of march the wintering Cossack regiments and garrisons rose up and fell into their columns, and pastures emptied as if swept by plague, and the villages lost their entire populations.

Regiments, brigades and free companies of horsemen, and the incomparable Zaporohjan infantry and cannon, crowded every highway, and along with them flowed the vast, formless mobs of peasants armed with flails, pitchforks, axes, knives and scythes fashioned into halberds.

"*Na Lahiv! Na pohybel Lahom!*" the war cries sounded in every settlement and hamlet, and the clustered little villages of the Ruthenian Steppe turned into ghostly and abandoned silence.

"Death to the Poles! *Na Lahiv!* Death, once and for ever!"

And at this cry that flew like wildfire across the whole country, men reached for weapons, women cursed and wailed, boys who had barely entered adolescence and gnarled old men hardly able to drag themselves along grasped any tool or farmyard implement that could be used to kill and flooded every track.

"*. . . Na Lahiv! Na Lahiv! Na pohybel Lahom!*"

No one ignored the call. Everyone had learned what it meant to oppose Hmyelnitzki. The herdsmen and the wild *tchabany* left their lairs and pastures, the shepherds butchered their flocks and loaded them on wagons, the lone grazers of the Steppes abandoned their homesteads, the savage fishermen of the creeks and the swampy bayous rose up in their reed huts buried deep in the banks of the rivers, and the hunters poured out of the forests. At times it seemed to the galloping fugitives as if the huge ancient oaks themselves had pulled up their roots and were now rolling north in the dust clouds to make war on the Commonwealth and on their own hated kind.

Towns emptied.

Villages stood silent.

Fields lay abandoned throughout the Ukraine as in these three palatinates of Ruthenia through which the two knights, Helen and Zjendjan were hurrying to the west. The darkened huts where they knocked for a few hours of shelter in the night were empty except for bent, toothless crones and frightened infants mewling in their cribs because even the young girls and women had armed themselves and followed their men to war. And, at the same time—as everyone on the roads could tell them— Hmyelnitzki and the Khan were coming from the east with multitudes of warriors beyond reckoning, roaring through the country like a firestorm, crushing whatever towns, castles or fortified Polish manors might stand in their way, and slaughtering the survivors of last year's war along with everyone else who didn't run to join them.

" . . .*Na Lahiv! Na pohybel . . .!*"

"Ey!" Pan Zagloba worried. "This is getting to be a bit too tight for my liking. D'you think we'll slip through ahead of the storm?"

"As long as we avoid the Tartars," Pan Michal replied.

"Damn them! Damn them all to Hell!" Pan Zagloba ranted. "Why can't those Mongol dogs stay in their own *yurts* and villas, chewing their dates and palm seeds and minding their own business? Who asked them to come here bothering Christian people who don't need heathen help in settling their own quarrels?"

"Hmyelnitzki did," the little knight replied. "That's who asked them."

And then they were silent.

Once more the night skies were lurid with a scarlet light, and fires glowed redly on every horizon, and the morning sun peered like a malevolent crimson eye through dark clouds of smoke.

★ ★ ★

With the grey walls of Bar, which were so full of terrible images and memories for Helen, left far to the southeast behind them, the four fugitives reached the old Royal Highway that was the main overland eastern trade route of the Commonwealth and Europe, and which led west to Latitchev and Ploskirev and Tarnopol, and then ran as far as the great commercial capital of Lvov. Here they encountered orderly Cossack wagon trains, marching infantry and cannon, regular and harshly disciplined regiments of horsemen and large *vatahas* of armed peasants and marauders led by iron-fisted Zaporohjan colonels, as well as vast herds of cattle driven to the main camps of the Cossack and Tartar armies. Here too the road acquired new dangers. Pickets and patrols challenged every traveler. When questioned by Cossacks Pan Zagloba showed Burlay's *pyernatch* and explained that they were his men taking Bohun's bride to her lover who was raiding the *Lah* camps near Zbarajh. No one who knew the fiery young ataman found reason to doubt them. But it was far more difficult to get past the brutal, drunken and illiterate troops of horseherders and peasants who had no notion of safe-conducts and military passes and who didn't much care whose bride Helen was supposed to be.

So sometimes Pan Zagloba argued and showed their passes and sometimes Pan Michal flashed his saber and showed his teeth, and corpses began to mark their trail more often; and then the journey which started out so well on the Valadynka turned into a daily odyssey of dangers, uncertainty and fear. It was often only the speed of Burlay's matchless racers that saved them from disaster.

"If we just get across these human ant heaps,"—the fat knight comforted the worn and weary Helen—"If we just manage to get close to Zbarajh before Hmyelnitzki and the Tartars flood the countryside everywhere around us, we'll be able to draw a safe breath."

"Is that where we're going, then?" she asked. "To Zbarajh?"

Brave, strong and determined as she was, the young woman

was starting to show the crushing weight of sleeplessness and
the constant dangers. Indeed, the fat knight thought, she now
looked very much like what they said she was: a captive bride
dragged against her will to her captor's tent.

"Yes," he said. "To Zbarajh. That's where the King's commanders seem to be assembling with all of their forces, from
what people tell us. That's where Prince Yeremi should be
coming too with his whole division, especially since many of
his regiments are already there."

"So Pan Skshetuski should be there as well?"

"He is sure to be."

"To Zbarajh, then!" Helen said. "How much farther is it?"

"Not far," Zagloba lied each day. "Not far."

★ ★ ★

And then, at last, the end of their journey seemed to be in
sight. They came close to Ploskirev and the dense human
masses on the roads began to thin out because the country held
by the Crown forces began a scant ten miles away. The Cossacks halted on the threshold of this no-man's land, waiting for
Burlay's and Hmyelnitzki's armies to converge behind them
before moving further, and the worst of the dangers that threatened the fugitives appeared to be over.

"Only ten miles!" Pan Zagloba cried, rubbing his hands
together in anticipation. "Just ten miles more! If we'd just get to
the first Polish pickets, to the nearest Crown regiment, we'd be
safe all the way to Zbarajh."

But the experienced little Pan Volodyovski wouldn't leave
anything to chance.

"We need to buy fresh horses," he said.

"What for?" Despite his own experience in survival the fat
knight sometimes let himself be dazzled by his own successes.
"We're almost there!"

"That's not quite the same as being there, is it," Volodyovski
said. "We need new horses because the string I bought in Barek
is as good as dead. The Podolians are used up and won't run a
mile. And Burlay's animals have to be saved for an emergency."

"But it's just ten more miles," Zagloba persisted, thinking
that a night's rest, over a jug of wine, would suit him much
better than rattling around Ploskirev in search of horse traders.

"And Hmyelnitzki is already in Konstantinov," the little soldier reminded him of the news they picked up the night before. "And the Khan's in Pilavtse with the entire Horde and heading this way. And it only takes one false step for a worn out animal to stumble and fall."

"Hmm. So it does. I think we need fresh horses," Pan Zagloba said.

Meanwhile they rode up to an abandoned, empty manor house not far from the town, and Pan Volodyovski pulled up his animal at the gaping gateway and turned to Zagloba.

"It's best if no one catches sight of the princess in the market place," he said. "We'll let her rest here for a bit and do what we can with the nags we've got, and you go on into the town and see if there's anyone around who'll sell us a good new string of remounts. It's close to sundown but we'd better not waste any time."

"And then we'll rest a bit, eh?"

"No. We'll ride hard all night."

"So be it, then. I'll be back soon," Pan Zagloba said and spurred into the swiftly falling darkness.

Volodyovski told Zjendjan to loosen the saddle girths on their panting horses and led the girl into the dark, cold house where she could lie down for an hour or so and restore her strength with a little wine. "It's hard, I know," he said. "I know you are tired. But I'd like to get across those last ten miles before dawn."

"Don't worry about me," the young woman whispered. "I am far stronger than you think."

"Yes you are." The young man's voice was full of admiration, affection and pity. "Just one more night of riding, my lady, that's all that we need. Then we'll all be able to rest as much as we want to."

But he no sooner brought in the wine gourds and the provision satchels when hooves rattled in a driven, desperate hurry outside the manor windows, and he caught sight of Pan Zagloba leaping off his horse with an agility he wouldn't have believed.

"Our friend is back," he turned to the young woman. "It doesn't seem as if he's found us any remounts."

"Is that bad?" she asked, too tired to think.

"No . . ." he began. "No . . ."

But before Pan Michal could think of a noncommittal answer

that wouldn't frighten or depress the exhausted young woman even more than she appeared to be, the fat knight himself was standing in the room before them—pale as a corpse and with livid spots stamped into his grey, stubbled cheeks as if he'd been branded— running with sweat like water and gasping out of breath.

"No horses?" Volodyovski asked.

"Mount up!" Zagloba croaked. "Mount and ride, for God's sake!"

The young dragoon had far too much experience in night raids and ambushes to waste time on questions. He didn't even waste it on the gourds and satchels which, however, Pan Zagloba snatched up on the run. Instead he led Helen outside, swung her into the saddle, checked the girth on her horse's belly with one quick glance, and shouted his own order.

"Ride!"

"Ride!" Pan Zagloba bellowed and leaped into his saddle as if he were no older or heavier than Zjendjan.

The hooves drummed out their own sudden desperate beat on the parched earth highway and, in another moment, the horses and their riders vanished in the darkness.

★ ★ ★

They rode a long time at a break-neck gallop, saying nothing until at least a mile lay between them and the town, and until the moonless night spread so thickly and darkly around them that no pursuit would have been possible.

Then Pan Volodyovski caught up with Zagloba and asked: "What's this all about?"

"Wait . . ." Still out of breath, the fat knight was wheezing as hard as his horse. "Wait . . . It's the shock, you know . . . I thought I wouldn't make it back at all . . . Ooof, what a hellish night!"

"Yes, but what happened? What was it?"

"The Devil in person, nothing else," Zagloba gasped and babbled. "The Devil, I tell you . . . You cut off his head and he grows another, just like that! There's no way that could be an ordinary man!"

"Calm down, will you?" Pan Michal had to know what to expect in order to prepare a defense against it. "Make some sense, will you?"

The fat knight took a deep breath and expelled it in a tight, hoarse whisper. "Who . . . do you think I saw in the market place?"

"Well? Who?"

"Bohun."

"Bohun?"

"Bohun!"

"Are you delirious?"

"I wish I was! But I saw him even better than I see you now. There he was, looking as fit as if nothing had ever happened to him. Five, maybe six men around him, holding torches. I thought I'd drop dead. What is it with that Hell's spawn, Michal? Eh? What is it? Is he immortal or what? You slice him up like a capon, Zjendjan sees him at death's door, he's trapped and hiding among people who'd kill him at a whisper . . . But no, that's not enough for him! Here he is again, alive, free and getting in our way! Ooof! Dear God! I tell you, I'd rather see a gibbering *spectrum* in a graveyard than that hellish fellow! What do we need to put him down for good, will you tell me that? Holy water? One of Zjendjan's silver bullets? A stake through the heart? Or what?"

"It's a lucky thing you saw him first," Pan Volodyovski murmured.

"Lucky, is it? Why is it that it's always my luck to run across him? The dogs should chew such luck! Aren't there enough other people in the world to cross his path? But no, no . . . it's always Zagloba . . . I tell you, I've quite lost my taste for this whole enterprise of ours. The Devil himself's out to stop us, that's certain. It can't be anything else."

"But did he see you?"

"Listen, if he'd seen me then you wouldn't be looking at me now. Seen me . . .! That's all I need!"

"It would be good to know if he's found out about us and is after us or if he's still unaware of what happened in that canyon on the Valadynka and is merely on his own way there."

"If he's alive and here, he knows everything," Pan Zagloba muttered in despair. "Or he'd be in Kiev."

"Maybe."

Always the calmest in moments of the greatest danger, the little knight began to calculate their possibilities.

"And maybe not. He could've found out and now he may be

hoping to catch us somewhere between here and the Valadynka. He'd hardly know how far we have come."

"Oh . . .!" Hope reappeared in Pan Zagloba's desperate, rolling eye. "D'you think so?"

"Yes. It's possible. Either way I don't think he's chasing us. Not yet, anyway. I think he's heading for the Valadynka."

"You think so?" Hope turned to wild joy in Pan Zagloba's voice. "Thank God for that! You've poured a healing balm all over me, my friend!"

"Yes . . . That's how it has to be," Volodyovski nodded. "And now there's more than just a mile or two between us. In another hour there'll be even more. Before he finds out about us from the patrols we talked to on the road and turns around to come after us we'll be way past Zbarajh."

"You say so? Thank God," Pan Zagloba said, mopping his forehead and calming down again. "Thank God. I feel hope returning. Not that I really lost it, you understand. That's hardly my nature. It's just that this man has the most terrible effect on me, which is one more proof that he's some kind of unearthly demon from the underworld, because I have no fear of anything else as you don't need telling. But not a word about this to Helen. Let's not worry the poor girl any more than she must be worried. Are we agreed on that?"

"Agreed."

Chapter Sixty-five

THEN THEY WERE traveling at a slower pace to give at least that much rest to their tired horses. The moon rose in the meantime and hung like a white, gleaming lantern nailed among the stars. The mists that shrouded the countryside at nightfall had fallen away and the night became almost as luminous and clear as a clouded day. Volodyovski sunk into deep thought while Pan Zagloba groaned, sighed, muttered and gnawed on the last remnants of his terror for a while longer.

"Hmm," he said at last. "I'm not the only one on whom Bohun would love to get his paws just now. Just think what he'd do to Zjendjan if he ever got hold of him again."

"Why don't you tell him what you saw in Ploskirev?" The little soldier yawned and looked wearily at the road ahead. "It will do him good to know what it feels like to be scared. Meanwhile I'll ride with our lady for a while."

"Good idea." Pan Zagloba thought that he would feel much better about his blind, superstitious fear of Bohun if he could share it with the self-possessed, nonchalant and unflappable young man. "Hey, Zjendjan!" he called.

"What's up then, master?" The lad pulled up his horse and waited while Zagloba and Volodyovski caught up with him and Helen, but the fat knight said nothing until the small soldier and the girl had ridden ahead.

"Ha!" he said then, peering at the boy. "Do you know what's happened?"

"About what?"

"About Bohun."

"He's dead, I expect." The boy shrugged, indifferent. "If he

907

didn't die of his wounds back there in Vlodava then the local gentry caught onto him and hanged him. Ah, it's a real shame I didn't get to kill him like I swore I would an' my grandpappy's not going to be too pleased about that."

"So why didn't you kill him when you had the chance? You'd have rid the world of some real nastiness and evil and earned yourself some merit in Heaven."

"How could I when he was flat on his back again?" The boy looked offended by Zagloba's question. "I couldn't stick him with a knife, could I? Like a peasant? Ay, master, it's just my hard luck that every time I get close enough to kill him he's all cut up by somebody else and I end up curing him instead."

"Why not just let him die, then?"

"If I did," the boy shot back, indignant. "Then how could I kill him?"

"Hmm. Yes. Well. I suppose there's some kind of logic in that," Pan Zagloba mused, then hissed out in a voice he tried to make as frightening as he could. "But Bohun didn't give up the ghost in Vlodava, my lad.

"He didn't?"

"No. I saw him in Ploskirev."

"In Ploskirev?" Zjendjan stared at Pan Zagloba with enormous eyes. "Just now, a while back?"

"That's right." The fat knight peered closely at the staring lad, searching for the tell-tale signs of expected terror. "Well? Aren't you scared? Aren't you falling off your horse yet?"

Zjendjan tilted his round, pudgy face into the cold white moonlight but Pan Zagloba searched it in vain for some sign of fear. Instead he saw the same harsh, relentless stubbornness he glimpsed in Zjendjan's eyes when this seemingly unperturbable and simple-minded boy—so comically determined in his avarice and cunning—was murdering Horpyna.

"Why should I be falling off my horse?" The boy sniffed. He scratched his head. He shrugged. "If he didn't die then he's still mine to kill, and I'm glad to hear it. I swore it and I'll do it and that's all there's to it. He not only wounded me back there in Tchehryn but he shamed me too and there is no way I'm going to let him get away with that."

"You're that set against him, are you?" Pan Zagloba asked and wondered how so much hatred could find room in such a slight body.

Zjendjan shrugged again. "If it wasn't that we're here to take the lady to a safe place somewhere, I'd go after him right now. What's mine is mine, that's the way I see it, and that goes for settling all my scores as well."

A sudden cold breeze passed across the old knight's sweated back and Pan Zagloba shuddered. He muttered a soft curse under his breath and swore to himself that he'd take good care never to get in that boy's bad books. Or even hurt his feelings.

"So that's how it is with you, is it?"

"That's right," Zjendjan said. His matter of fact simplicity, as if what he was saying was the most natural thing under the sun, seemed even more chilling than the wind. "How else could it be?"

Pan Zagloba had nothing more to say. He kicked his horse into a trot and joined Volodyovski and the girl and then they rode in silence.

★ ★ ★

An hour later they splashed across the Medvedovka which cut through the hard-packed dirt road at this point and plunged into a dark expanse of woods that spread northwest from the riverbank as far as the horizon. Pan Zagloba knew that country well.

"These woods will end ahead of us in a while," he said to the others. "Then there'll be about a quarter of a mile of open heath with the highway from Tchornyi Ostrov running right across it, and then more forest, even darker and deeper than this one, all the way to Matchin. With God's help and mercy we might find a few Polish regiments there."

"It's high time we found some kind of sanctuary," Volodyovski muttered. Then they were silent for a while longer, riding quietly along the bright, moonlit trail between the parallel dark walls of trees.

"Two wolves just ran across our path!" Helen said suddenly.

"I see them." Volodyovski nodded. A large grey shadow flitted across the pale patch of moonlight some hundred paces ahead of the horses. "Ah . . . and there's another!"

"And there's a fourth!" Helen called out.

"No, that's a doe. Look, my lady, there are two more. No, three!"

"What the devil!" Pan Zagloba snapped, alarmed as always by

anything he didn't understand, and more so now than ever after his scare with Bohun. "Since when have the deer taken to chasing after wolves? Is the whole world turning upside down or what?"

"Let's ride a little faster," Pan Michal said quietly. "Zjendjan! Come up here at the double! Gallop ahead with the lady. Move it, now!"

They spurred their horses into another gallop but Pan Zagloba turned to Volodyovski anyway.

"Hey, hey, my friend," he murmured. "What's all this about? What's happening?"

"Nothing good," Volodyovski snapped. "Animals running from their lairs at night . . . you saw it yourself."

"Yes, but what does it mean?"

"It means they're being driven."

"By whom?"

"Troops, most likely."

"Troops, eh? Well that's a good sign, isn't it?"

"I doubt it. They're coming at us from somewhere on our right."

"The devil you say! But couldn't it be our soldiers just as well?"

"I don't see how. The animals are running out of the northeast, from the direction of Tchornyi Ostrov. So it's most likely Tartars sweeping down from Pilavtse on a broad front."

"My God, let's run, my friend!" Pan Zagloba felt his last remaining hairs rising on his head. "Let's run while we can!"

"That's just what we're doing. Hey,"—and the little knight heaved a regretful sigh—"if it wasn't for Skshetuski's princess, we'd be able to dart right up to the *tchambuls* and take a bite out of one or two of them! But with her here . . . ah, I tell you, it isn't going to be much fun if they catch sight of us."

"God forbid, Michal!" Pan Zagloba cried. "Don't even think such things! Should we turn off into the woods like those wolves, or what?"

"That wouldn't do at all. Because even if they missed us for the moment they'd flood the entire countryside ahead and then how would we get through?"

"May lightning strike the lot of them!" Pan Zagloba cursed. "That's all that we needed! But listen, Michal, maybe you're wrong about those wolves? I mean, don't they usually trail behind an army?"

"Yes, those that might have been on the flanks gather behind the Tartars, along with every other predator for miles around. But those that are right in their line of march break out ahead. Look now, over there to the right among the trees! The sky's red with fires."

"Jesus of Nazareth, King of the Jews!" Pan Zagloba prayed.

"Quiet now. You'd best save your breath. How much more is there of this forest?"

"Not much . . ."

"And then an open field?"

"That's right. Oh, Jesus . . .!"

"Save your breath, I said. And then there's another belt of woods spreading beyond those fields?"

"All the way to Matchin . . ."

"That's good then. If they don't run us down in that open space we'll be as good as home. Let's keep together now and ride like the wind! It's a good thing the princess and Zjendjan are on Burlay's horses."

★   ★   ★

Then they were galloping all together again, bunched in a tight group across the width of the forest track, and Helen asked about the dark red glow that was now blooming behind them in the eastern sky.

"There's not much point in trying to keep this from you, my lady," said Volodyovski. "Those could be the Tartars."

"*Jezus Maria!*" she cried out.

"Don't worry," he tried to put her mind at ease. "I'll bet my neck that we'll get away from them. And there are sure to be a few of our own regiments in Matchin."

Then they were silent once more and flying like grey ghosts along the moonlit highway. The walls of trees beside them began to thin out. The forest was ending. But the red glow in the sky behind them began to spread as well.

Suddenly Helen turned to Volodyovski.

"Swear to me that they won't take me alive," she said.

"They won't," he said harshly.

And then they were out of the protecting forest and into the fields, or rather into a spur of the Steppe that cut between the two sheltering belts of woods. The next dark smudge of trees was already looming in the distance but the open space before them was silvery with moonlight and seemed as bright as day.

"That's the worst part of the way," Volodyovski murmured to Zagloba. "Because if they were in camp near Tchornyi Ostrov then they'll be coming down this way, southwest between the forests."

But Pan Zagloba had nothing more to say to him or any of the others. He was kicking the flanks of his horse as hard as he could and murmuring nervous prayers.

They were perhaps halfway across the fields, and the next belt of woods was getting closer every moment, when the little knight thrust out his arm suddenly to the right.

"Look over there!" he said to Zagloba. "Do you see them?"

"Eh? Hmm? What?"

"Over there. Look!"

"Shrubs? Some other woods?" The fat knight saw only what he wished to see. "A dense mass of bushes? Some kind of undergrowth?"

"That mass is moving! Ride like you've never ridden before because they'll spot us now for sure!"

"Oh dear God . . .! Oh, the devils . . ."

The wind was whistling in their ears. Their weary horses plunged ahead with their breath rattling in their chests and their hooves pounding with the last of their strength. Salvation seemed no farther than the nearest trees but now a low growling murmur, like that of a surging tidal wave, rose out of the great grey mass which grew ever closer and more distinct on the right periphery of the fields, and then a single vast triumphant howl burst out across the intervening air.

"*Allah! Allah!*"

"They see us!" wailed Zagloba. "Oh the dogs! The scum! The devils . . .! Cut-throat wolves . . .!"

The forest was now so near that the fugitives could feel its chilly breath brushing across their faces but, at the same time, the swarm of Tartars became quite clear and distinct, and several thin, elongated arms began to reach out of that looming dark mass like the grasping tentacles of some gigantic monster and to approach them with alarming speed.

An old familiar chill settled about Pan Volodyovski. His experienced ears could now pick out the individual shouts of '*Allah il-Akbar . . .! Allah!*' in the protracted, ululating howl of the approaching Tartars.

"My horse tripped!" wailed Zagloba.

"Forget it!" Pan Volodyovski answered.

But a lightning thought flashed across his mind and formed a dreadful question: *'what'll happen if the horses fail and give out? What if one of them should fall'*? They were riding on swift Tartar mustangs bred to an almost iron stamina and endurance, and Helen and the boy were mounted on even swifter horses, but the animals were running at a dead gallop all the way from Ploskirev, with next to no rest after that early, mad dash from the abandoned manor house to the first belt of woods, and none of them could keep galloping much longer.

His heart was hammering wildly in his chest—not in anxiety about his own survival because he'd never given a thought to it in his entire life—but in fear for Helen whom he had come to treasure as a sister, knowing that there was no other way in which he could love her. He also knew that once the Tartars picked up a chase they never turned away.

". . . Let them come on, then," he hissed softly to himself and clenched his teeth in anticipation. *"But they won't get that girl."*

"My horse tripped!" Zagloba howled again.

"Forget it!" he answered.

★ ★ ★

Meanwhile they plunged into the new belt of woods. Darkness engulfed them like a sheltering cloak but the nearest Tartars were a scant two or three hundred paces behind them and closing at great speed.

However the little knight knew what he had to do. "Zjend-jan!" he cried. "Turn with the lady into the first track you come to off the highway!"

"Very good, master," the boy answered calmly, and Pan Michal turned to the terrified Zagloba.

"Pistols in hand!" he shouted and, in that same moment, he seized the reins of Zagloba's horse and began to pull back on them to break the animal's stride.

"What are you doing?" howled the frightened noble.

"Forget it! Halt your horse."

The distance between them and Zjendjan who was galloping away with Helen stretched out even more. Then they came suddenly to a spot where the highway made a rapid westward turn, heading towards Matchin and Zbarajh, while a narrow dirt track opened up straight ahead under a thick canopy of leaves and low, concealing branches. Zjendjan and Helen fell into that overgrown dark gap and disappeared from sight while Volodyovski brought his horse and Zagloba's to a halt.

"In God's sweet name!" the fat old knight was shouting in utter bewilderment and terror. "What do you think you're doing?"

"We'll slow the pursuit," the little knight answered. "That's the only way."

"We'll die!"

"So we'll die but Helen will get away. Here, take your stand at the side of the highway." And the small soldier positioned the protesting old man in the shadows of a roadside tree and then backed into his own patch of shadows on the other side. "Right here! Here! That's fine."

They crouched down, waiting in their ambush, while the violent beat of approaching hooves filled the darkness around them like a thunderstorm.

"Ah . . . Ah . . . So it has come to pass," Pan Zagloba said with resignation and raised the heavy wineskin to his mouth. "So be it, then."

His head tilted back and the wineskin gurgled. He drank on and on. Then he shuddered. "In the name of the Father, the Son and the Holy Ghost," he said and took a deep breath. "I'm . . . ready."

"Here they come," Volodyovski murmured, peering down the highway. "Three of them up ahead of the rest. That's just what I wanted."

Moonlight revealed the three riders as clearly as if they were galloping under a noonday sun, with several dozen others riding some two or three hundred paces behind them, and a dense mass of warriors following beyond. When the three leaders reached the line of ambush two pistol shots crashed out, the two flanking riders toppled from their saddles, and then Volodyovski leaped into the middle of the highway. A saber glittered whitely in the moonlight and the third Tartar fell as if struck by lightning.

"Ride!" the small soldier shouted.

Pan Zagloba didn't need any further urging and they fled like two wolves chased by a pack of hounds. Meanwhile their pursuers reached the three corpses, realized that their quarry could bite as well as run, and slowed down their own mounts until more of them could catch up.

"There, you see?" Pan Volodyovski turned to the fat knight. "I knew they'd hold up!"

But though the fugitives gained a few hundred paces the pause in the chase was merely a brief one and the Tartars came on in a tighter pack with no one forging out ahead of the rest. In the meantime it became quite clear that the two knights' horses, particularly the one that carried the bulky Pan Zagloba, couldn't run much farther. The animal tripped again, broke its pace and staggered, and the old knight who apparently wasn't quite as ready to die as he said he was, felt his thin hair rising on his head again at the thought of falling.

"Michal, my dearest friend!" he bellowed in desperation. "Don't abandon me!"

"Don't even think about it," Pan Volodyovski said.

"Ay, damn that lazy, good for nothing brute!" The fat knight cursed his gasping horse. "May the wolves have him for breakfast tomorrow . . .!"

But he barely started a new string of curses when the first Tartar arrow hissed beside his ear. Another passed so close to the old knight's head that it brushed his stubbled cheek with its feathers. Volodyovski turned and fired his pistols twice more at the dark mass behind them and then Zagloba's horse tripped again and staggered so heavily that it almost buried its nostrils in the ground.

"God help me, my nag's falling!" Pan Zagloba howled in a voice of utter terror and despair.

"Dismount and run into the woods!" Volodyovski shouted, reined-in his own mount and jumped out of the saddle.

The two knights vanished in the darkness among the trees but this maneuver wouldn't have escaped the Tartars' slanted eyes, Volodyovski knew. He heard their shrill calls, the clatter of their mustangs' hooves sliding to a halt on the graveled highway, and then the snap and crackle of the undergrowth trampled behind him by several dozen hunters.

Beside him as he ran he could hear the wheezing breath and the despairing curses of the galloping Zagloba who hurdled fallen tree trunks and leaped across the bushes as if he'd lost thirty years off his age along with his horse. A low-hanging branch had whipped off his cap, other twigs and branches slapped his face, clawed at his coat and clutched at his arms, but the cursing old noble put on a burst of speed that left the nimble little soldier far behind.

★ ★ ★

Pan Zagloba couldn't remember the last time he had moved that quickly. He vaulted across fallen trees that had been blown down by the winds, soared over piles of deadfall, ran like a deer through undergrowth and branches, tripped and fell headfirst over roots, leaped up and ran even faster than he had before, all the while wheezing like a blacksmith's bellows. At last he tumbled headlong into a deep, dark crevice in the forest floor where he lay gasping and unable to move.

"Where are you?" he heard Volodyovski whispering somewhere near.

"Here, in the pit." The fat knight knew that he'd be unable to run another step. "Save yourself, Michal. It's all up with me."

But Pan Michal jumped down into the hole without another word and clamped his hand across Zagloba's mouth.

"Keep quiet," he hissed urgently into the fat knight's ear. "They might miss us in here. And if not . . . well, we'll defend ourselves."

Meanwhile the Tartars had come running up. Several dozen of them spread out beyond the pit, beating the bushes wide into the forest, but others crouched nearby, groping among the tree trunks and peering into shadows.

The two knights held their breaths.

' . . . *Ah, it'd be just like one of those clumsy heathen dogs to trip and fall in here,*' Pan Zagloba thought, dull with resignation. '*And then it'll be my turn to shake hands with the Devil.*'

But at that moment sparks began to shower all around them. The Tartars were striking fire to light torches. Peering out, the fat knight could see flat, savage faces with high cheekbones bent over glowing tinder, and swollen lips blowing on the sparks.

' . . . *Keep blowing,*' he cursed them to perdition. '*May you burst your bellies . . .*'

The squat, bowlegged figures he saw all around him seemed to have no relation to anything human. They were, he thought, more like nightmare animals of the imagination. Or vengeful forest spirits wandering about in search of a victim that came ever closer.

He closed his eyes. He didn't want them to be the last sight he was to see on earth. He didn't want to listen to their guttural mutterings and questioning exclamations. But suddenly another sound started to intrude from somewhere at the edge of his desperate awareness. He thought he heard a strange rumbling from beyond the trees, some kind of dim and uninterpretable clatter coming from the highway, along with a swelling murmur that he recognized as shouting diminished by distance. The Tartars dropped their flints and tinder and stood as still and poised towards these new sounds as if they'd been turned by magic into twisted statues and Volodyovski dug his fingers with fierce urgency into Zagloba's shoulder.

And then the sounds acquired a sudden new identity that made the fat knight dizzy with relief and hope; they became loud shouts, strident calls. Sharp yells and battle cries! A bright red light flared in a single violent glow beyond the trees and a salvo of musketry shattered both the darkness and the silence of the woods.

"Muskets!" shouted Pan Volodyovski, pounding the fat knight's back in excitement. "Tartars don't use muskets!"

The muskets crashed out once more in a measured volley, then fired again, and then came new shouts, fierce cries, Tartar howls for Allah, a quick spatter of pistol shots, the clash of swords and sabers, the scream of wounded horses and pounding of hooves.

"What is it? What is it?" Pan Zagloba gasped, and then he knew the meaning of all these separate sounds: there was a battle raging on the highway.

"Those are our people!" Volodyovski shouted.

"Kill! Slaughter! Show no mercy! Cut them down!" bellowed Pan Zagloba.

A moment more and a loose crowd of panicked Tartars ran past the rim of the pit back towards the highway. Volodyovski jumped out and vanished, sword in hand, behind them.

★ ★ ★

Relieved but quickly finding something else to worry about in the rustling darkness, Pan Zagloba sat alone at the bottom of the crevice, wondering if it was now safe to crawl out into the bushes, and listening to the sounds of the battle that dwindled in the distance.

He made a half-hearted effort to clamber out of the deep, steep-sided pit but that proved quite beyond his strength. He was drained and exhausted by all his sudden mental leaps between hope and terror. Every bone in his body seemed to be aching with a separate pain and his legs were no more capable of carrying his bulky trunk than his foundered horse had been able to do it earlier on the highway.

"Ha, you pagan cut-throats," he cried out into the empty darkness largely to hear the welcome sound of his own voice. "So you've hauled tail, have you? Pity! I'd have liked some company in this hole. And I feel like teaching at least one of you a lesson you'll remember . . .."

He listened carefully for a moment, just in case some stray Tartar had stayed nearby, but all he heard was the reassuring roar of the running battle on the road.

"Oh you heathen dogs!" he shouted more fiercely. "So you'd hunt decent people like boars in the forest, would you? Well, now you're being hunted, and it couldn't happen to more deserving creatures! Oh, they'll slice you up out there on the highway like mutton for the stewpot. My God, what a noise those pagans are making. Keep howling! Keep howling! The wolves will be howling in a while over what's left of you!"

But the shouts and gunfire began to recede and Pan Zagloba was left to contemplate his own isolation.

"Hmm . . . hmm," he muttered. "Who'd have thought Michal would leave me all alone out here? Where's his sense of duty? But I suppose I'd better be charitable about this. He's young, excitable and hungry for adventure. That's normal enough before a man acquires maturity and reason. So I'll just have to forgive him this small lapse in manners . . .

"And anyway,"—the old knight reasoned, feeling all his confidence returning—"after what we've been through together, he and I, I'd go with him all the way to Hell because he's not the kind of friend who abandons you when you need him most. However, what I could use even more than his company right now is that wineskin . . . But what's the use of wishing? I suppose that's gone along with my horse."

The sounds of the battle had now drifted far towards the east, in the direction of the open fields and that original belt of woods beyond them, and Pan Zagloba listened to that ebbing clamor with a blend of loneliness, self-pity, and quiet satisfaction.

"Aha!" He tried again to climb out of the pit, failed and settled down comfortably on the bottom. "They're chasing the pagans, are they? Good for them! The heathen dogs couldn't hold our men for long, thank God! That's the way to do it . . . but this damn hole is more than I can manage without help."

And then another worry presented itself. "Ah, ah . . . What kind of a pit is this anyway? A wolf's lair, or what? Let's just hope that none of the residents come home tonight for dinner. All I'd need now is to get eaten up by wolves or stung by a viper . . . My God, is there no end to what I've got to endure? First Bohun, then the Tartars, and now wolves . . .!"

Then he called out: "Michal! Michal? Hey, hey, where are you my friend?"

But his only answer was the cool, soothing rustle of the forest and a spreading silence.

"What am I to do here, then?" he demanded. "Go to sleep or what? Ah, to the Devil with it all! Are there to be no limits to these impositions on my good nature and my Christian patience?"

But Pan Zagloba's patience was to be sorely taxed that night. The sky was already turning grey between the tall branches overhead before he heard, once more, the beat of many hooves rattling on the highway, and saw the red gleam of torches moving among the trees.

"I'm here!" he shouted, and then he saw his small friend standing on the rim of the pit above him, with a burning bundle of pine fronds and pitch twisted about the long pole he grasped in one hand.

"So why don't you come out?" Helping to pull the fat knight out of the dark crevice, Pan Michal looked as pleased with himself as a young greyhound that had run down a hare. "Or have you found yourself a home in that ditch?"

"If I was as little as a flea," Pan Zagloba answered testily. "Or like some other insignificant creatures of no girth and stature that I know but wouldn't like to mention, I'd jump out of here readily enough! But what happened to all those Tartars anyway?"

"We rode on their necks all the way through the other woods," Pan Michal said grinning.

"Thank God for that." For once in his life the fat knight had no barbed comments to offer. "Who was it that came to our rescue, then?"

"Kushel and Roztvorovski with two thousand men. My own dragoons are with them."

"And was there a lot of that Tartar vermin?"

"Ah . . ." The little knight waved a careless hand. "A few thousand. It was a fair-sized *tchambul*. But they won't be coming back this way for a little while."

"They won't, eh?" Safe again among his friends, Pan Zagloba could turn to more important matters. "Then there's time for dinner! For God's sake give me something with which to wet my throat or I'll dry up into a piece of tinder."

★ ★ ★

Two hours later, with even his remarkable thirst quenched and his hunger sated, Pan Zagloba sat in a comfortable saddle among Volodyovski's troopers while the little knight tried to set his mind at rest about the missing Helen.

"Don't fret that we're returning to Zbarajh without her," he urged the worried and disappointed noble. "At least we know she escaped the Tartars."

"But maybe Zjendjan will turn back towards Zbarajh after all?" Zagloba insisted.

"He won't." Pan Volodyovski shook his head. "He's too smart for that. All the roads to Zbarajh will be cut before this day is over. That *tchambul* that we chased away will be on our heels again in no time at all. Burlay himself will be camped all around Zbarajh before Zjendjan has time to circle back. And both Hmyelnitzki and the Khan are marching down on us from the Konstantinov side."

"Dear God!" the fat knight cried, appalled by the picture that the little soldier was painting for him. "So Helen and that boy are riding right into the jaws of a trap! Hmyel's army on one side and the Tartar *tchambuls* on the other! How will they get through?"

"Zjendjan's own head depends on slipping through in time before Hmyel and the Tartars close the gap," Pan Michal assured him. "And I believe that tricky little fox can do that better than anyone we know. You've enough shrewd ideas in your head, my friend, to lead the Devil himself into holy water but that boy's an even greater wonder. Look how we racked our brains about rescuing that girl and he made it all happen as if it were nothing! He'll be as slippery as a snake, believe me, especially since his own hide is at stake. And anyway, remember what you told me yourself in Zbarajh last fall. God protects the innocent. He'll look after that girl."

"Ah . . . ah, that's true." Pan Zagloba nodded, some of his fears relieved, but a new doubt appeared at once and began to gnaw at him hungrily.

"Ah . . ." he turned again to the little soldier. "Did you happen to ask Kushel about Skshetuski?"

"He's in Zbarajh. In good health, too, by all accounts. He came in from Koretz a few days ago with Pan Zachvilihovski."

"That's good to hear. We'll all be together again and I must say I've missed him and our Lithuanian beanpole. But . . . what are we going to tell him about this adventure?"

"Hmm." The little knight lost some of his good humor. "That's a problem, isn't it."

"My advice is to say nothing," Pan Zagloba said. "Not to Kushel, not to Pan Yan, not to anybody. I trust along with you that Zjendjan will see our Helen through to safety. God does protect her innocence, we have to believe that. But these are terrible times. There's more misfortune in this world than there are honest people. And if—God forbid!—she should fall again into evil hands it would be like tearing open Skshetuski's wounds all over again."

"Zjendjan will save her!" cried the little knight. "I'll bet my life on it!"

"I'd bet mine too if that did any good. But let's leave it all in God's hands, place our trust in Zjendjan, and keep our mouths shut tight."

"So be it then," Pan Volodyovski said. "But wouldn't Pan Longinus tell Skshetuski where we'd gone and why?"

"You know him better than that!" Pan Zagloba said. "He gave his word and that's a holy thing for that Lithuanian just like all his vows. No, no, he wouldn't breathe a word about it to anyone."

Then Kushel trotted up to them and they rode on together the rest of the way, warmed by the first light of a bright new day, talking about public matters and the war.

The King's three generalissimos had assembled in Zbarajh with all of their forces, Prince Yeremi and the rest of his division were expected any day, and the final battle for the Commonwealth—that long awaited clash between Vishnovyetzki and Hmyelnitzki—was about to take place at last.

Part Ten

Chapter Sixty-six

COMING INTO ZBARAJH, or rather into the fortified tent city that had sprung up before the town, Zagloba and Volodyovski found all the regular Polish forces of the Commonwealth gathered and waiting for the enemy.

The King's three commanders—Crown Councillor Ostrorog, old Pan Firley, and the courageous Lantzkoronski, Castellan of Kamyenetz—wanted to fight Hmyelnitzki further to the east, making their stand among the lakes and forests of Konstantinov and Mahnovka until the King assembled all the gentry of the Commonwealth, but their soldiers refused to follow anyone but Yeremi Vishnovyetzki. When they heard that Prince Yeremi was urging their generals to make their stand in Zbarajh, even the elite heavy cavalry and the disciplined foreign mercenaries threatened to march off to Zbarajh on their own.

No amount of pleading or cajoling could make them change their minds. Not even the authority of the golden batons could force them to obedience. Faced with this desertion of their entire army, the royal generals had no choice but to bring their ten thousand regulars to the Prince's city where General Pshiyemski, an engineer skilled in siegework and the defense of cities, entrenched a strong walled camp.

Zbarajh itself was a small walled town huddled at the foot of a Vishnovyetzki castle on the gentle slopes of the meandering little Gnyezna River and two swampy lakes. Pshiyemski's earthworks crouched in the half-circle formed by the Gnyezna and the lakes, with their rear protected by the town and castle so that they could be assaulted only from the front, and it was here that all the standing forces of the Polish Crown waited throughout June for the Cossack storm.

But the war leader whom they came to follow had not yet arrived and in the meantime the small Crown army seemed to rot and crumble in the hands of the King's commanders. Sick of inept generals and their private quarrels, and anguished by the unprecedented disasters that Hmyelnitzki heaped upon the Commonwealth, the soldiers refused to listen to anyone but the Prince. Discipline cracked at once and began to crumble. The King's generals bickered with each other and gave contradictory orders which their men ignored or obeyed with ill-will and grumbling. It was already widely known that Hmyelnitzki was on his way with a greater army than anything seen since the days of Tamerlane. Rumors flew through the camp like carrion birds, spreading doubt and undermining courage, so that some men saw the specter of a new Pilavtze that would scatter this last handful of the Commonwealth's defenders and leave the country open to invasion.

★ ★ ★

It didn't take Pan Zagloba and Volodyovski long to see what everyone else in Zbarajh knew since their own arrival: that it was only Prince Yeremi who could avert a new catastrophe that hung over the camp, the army and the future of the Commonwealth itself. Riding into the camp with Kushel's regiments, they found themselves at once in the center of an eager, swirling mass of soldiers who bombarded them with questions and demanded news, while the sight of Tartar prisoners brought hundreds of other men running into the *maydan*.

"They've nipped the Tartars!" some men cried, anxious for anything that might give them hope or which might be taken for a lucky omen. "God's given a victory!"

"To arms, gentlemen!" others shouted, crying out for the immediate execution of the captured Tartars, while exaggerated rumors of Kushel's success flew about the camp and grew in the telling. "To the walls!"

Still others, to whom the sight of the dark, slant-eyed warriors brought instant memories of fierce, no quarter battles to the death, and of burning towns and enslaved populations, ran to the ramparts to see if Burlay and the Tartars were at hand.

Kushel ignored them all and hurried off to give his report to the ailing Firley, while Pan Zagloba and Volodyovski went in search of Skshetuski whom they eventually tracked down in

Pan Zachvilihovski's quarters. The young knight grew a little pale when he saw them because they resurrected too many painful memories, but he greeted them with as much joy as he was able to show. Thinking his Helen dead, he would no longer hope for anything, Pan Zagloba knew. He'd have nothing more to wish for or want out of life, nor would he expect any kind of happiness again. Having come to terms with the grim reality of his loss, he'd have no suspicion that their long absence might have something to do with him or Helen. He sat at the old commissioner's table with Pan Longinus and two local priests and showed no special interest in where his two friends had been.

They, in turn, didn't breathe one word about their expedition even though Pan Longinus kept peering anxiously from one of them to the other, cracking his huge knuckles and squirming in his seat, as he tried to read some sign of success or failure in their words and faces.

But they were both too preoccupied with Skshetuski to give the poor Lithuanian giant as much as a wink. Pan Michal, in particular, kept taking his old friend in his arms, feeling as if his sentimental heart would break at the sight of those worn, gaunt features that seemed already far removed from all worldly matters and brought to mind the stillness of a grave.

"Here we are again, then," he assured Skshetuski as best as he could. "Old friends gathering once more and what could be better?"

Then, seeing a tremor of pain pass across Skshetuski's face, he hurried on: "You'll be all right here with us, you'll see! There's going to be a war such as the world hasn't seen before, enough to warm the heart of any good soldier . . . Ah, Yan, believe me, as soon as God gives you back your strength you'll be leading your *husaria* for a long time to come!"

"He has already restored me to health," Skshetuski said quietly.

"He has, eh?" Doubt trembled in the voice of the little soldier. "And you've . . . ah . . . made your peace with everything else, have you?"

"All I want now is to keep on serving as long as I'm needed," Pan Yan said.

Youth, stamina, and strength had conquered his illness, as his friends could see. Pain had gnawed through all his emotions but couldn't quite consume his powerful body, even though it scorched and seared his spirit and left him as hollow as an urn filled with funeral ashes. He'd grown as thin and bony as the mournful Lithuanian giant, Pan Zagloba noted. His skin had greyed under a yellow sheen so that he seemed like an image molded from candle wax. All of his former thoughtful gravity was intact, and his grim preoccupations were carved as deeply as ever into his stony face, but his eyes had acquired the cold, unfeeling detachment of the dead.

Watching him and wishing that he could burst out with the news that Helen was alive—that she'd been torn out of Bohun's hands and was now riding somewhere to safety with the faithful Zjendjan—the old knight could hardly keep his tongue clamped behind his teeth. He could see new silver threads twisted thickly in the young man's heavy beard and mustache. He knew that he admired Skshetuski more than any other young man he ever met. All too aware of his own shortcomings, he was awed by that iron will, that ability to suppress pain and master the deepest and most fervent longings, that rare sense of duty and of service to a cause greater than any man alone, and that unswerving dedication to his country.

He thought of everything he'd heard about this young soldier who seemed so much like every other proud, careless, hot-blooded young noble when the old knight met him in Tchehryn. Quick to fight, quick to drink, lighthearted and cheerful in good company, he was just as careless about the needs of others as any other wealthy, well-born soldier of his time; and just as indifferent to anything that didn't affect either himself or the lives of his friends until he met Helen.

But now he was changed beyond recognition. His journey to and from the *Sietch*; the ruin and humiliation of his country which he witnessed daily; the war and his loss of Helen—not just once but twice!—made him a different man. The torments that he suffered stripped him of emotion and rendered him incapable of showing what he felt.

But—and here Pan Zagloba grew morose with worry— did that mean that he had lost his capacity for feeling? Was he changed forever? Or was he still the man who could make Helen happy? He had acquired a reputation for taking pleasure in the company of priests from whom he could hear about the peace and oblivion of monastic life which—as rumor had it— was what he wanted for himself as soon as the war ended.

Meanwhile he did his duty. He spared no energy when it was a matter of doing something connected with the war and the coming siege. And it was in that single-minded iron dedication to service and duty, Pan Zagloba thought, that his continuing salvation might be found.

★ ★ ★

Their talk soon turned to war because that was the only subject that anyone cared about in the camp, the castle and the town. Old Pan Zachvilihovski was particularly curious to hear about the great Burlay whom he knew quite well in the past.

"I doubt if there's a better general among all the Cossacks," he said, reminiscing. "Aye, it's a real shame that he'd rise up against his Motherland along with the others . . . We were together at Khotim, you know, when Hetman Zolkievski beat back the Turks and kept them out of Europe for a generation. Burlay was just a young fellow then but he already showed uncommon promise . . ."

"He's from across the Dnieper, isn't he?" Pan Yan asked. He addressed the old commissioner as '*Father*,' which was the way young soldiers paid homage to age and experience in those days.

"Yes he is," Zachvilihovski nodded.

"And isn't he leading our Transdnieper people? How is it then that he's marching up from the deep south? Out of the wilderness in Lower Podolia instead of his own country?"

"Looks like Hmyelnitzki assigned him Winter quarters away from the Dnieper because that's where Tuhay-bey had gone into camp. There's no love lost between those two, you know . . . Tuhay-bey hates Burlay worse than any man alive."

"And why's that, father?"

"Because no other soldier in the Commonwealth had ever driven the Tartars so close to despair. My God, how he tormented them!"

"And now they're his comrades!"

"Such are the times." Pan Zachvilihovski shrugged his shoulders and went on: "But Hmyelnitzki will keep them both in line once they get to Zbarajh. He'll see to it that they claw at us and not at each other."

"And when do you expect Hmyelnitzki to get here, father?" Volodyovski asked.

"Any time. He could be here tomorrow. But who can tell for

certain? Our generalissimos should be sending scouting expeditions in every direction but that seems like the last thing they have on their minds! It took me days to get them to send Kushel to the south and another sweep towards Tcholhansky Kamyen! I wanted to go myself but all we get here is talk and deliberations. God grant that our Prince gets here before it's too late or we'll see a disaster that'll make Pilavtze look like a Roman triumph."

Pan Zagloba who had sat quietly far longer than he liked broke in with a disparaging comment of his own.

"I saw some of these soldiers in the *maydan*," he said. "They look more like squabbling ribbon clerks than fit companions for men like ourselves who value fame and glory more than our own lives!"

"Nonsense!" the white-haired old commissioner snapped back. "I don't deny your courage, my good sir, although I held a somewhat different view of it at one time, but these are the finest soldiers the Commonwealth ever had! All they need is a commander they trust and respect! Lantzkoronski is a great knight. No one questions his gallantry or courage. Give him a long-range cavalry raid to lead and you won't find anyone who could do it better, but he's no commander for an army. Pan Firley is an honest and dedicated man but he's so old he can barely get out of a chair far less mount a horse. And as for Ostrorog, he won his reputation with Prince Dominic at Pilavtze. So why should anyone want to take their orders? We've had enough disasters! Our people are always ready to fight to the death if they know that their lives aren't being thrown away for nothing. But who can blame them for refusing to be led to slaughter again and again by incompetents and fools? Even now, when Hmyelnitzki is breathing in our faces, our generals are squabbling about points of precedence at a conference table rather than provisioning the army."

"Ah, ah . . ." Pan Zagloba stirred in some alarm. "But we aren't short of rations, are we?"

"We could use better stores." The old man shrugged again. "But it's even worse with fodder for the horses. If the siege lasts longer than a month we'll have to feed our animals on gravel and woodchips."

"There's still time to take care of that," Volodyovski said. "One good sweep into the countryside . . ."

"Then go and tell it to our generals!" the old man cried out bitterly. "I repeat, God send our Prince, and the sooner the better."

"And we're not the only ones who are anxious to see him here," Pan Longinus murmured and looked sadly out of the chamber window to the *maydan* and the walls outside.

"That's right." The old commissioner nodded and turned to Volodyovski and Zagloba. "Take a look out there, gentlemen. Take a look. Everybody's sitting on the walls and staring out towards the Old Zbarajh road. Others are climbing up on roofs and church spires and hanging out of windows. And if some joker cries out '*He's coming*' the whole camp goes absolutely mad with joy. A thirsty deer doesn't long for water more desperately than we do for him . . .! God help us all if he doesn't reach us before Hmyelnitzki gets here."

"That's something for which all of us pray every day," said one of the priests.

★ ★ ★

And it seemed as if these prayers were to be granted soon although the next day, the first Thursday in July, brought even greater consternation and some new misgivings.

A terrifying rain and thunderstorm burst over the town and the new earthworks surrounding the camp. The downpour fell in torrents. It washed away a part of the fortifications. The Gnyezna and the two small lakes spilled out of their banks and flooded the countryside for a mile around. At nightfall lightning struck the banner of Firley's household infantry, killed several men and turned the flag itself into burned rags and kindling wood. This was taken at once for the worst possible omen—a sure sign of God's displeasure with the army—especially since Pan Firley was a Calvinist, and Zagloba urged that a deputation be sent to the old man demanding his conversion to Catholicism.

"How can God bless an army whose leader persists in gross errors that cause disgust in Heaven?" he demanded, and many of the distraught gentry wanted to run at once with a petition. Only the dignity of the castellan's position and the respect due to his *bulava* held back the deputation but the dismay and confusion in the camp became even greater.

Meanwhile the storm raged on without a pause.

The earthen ramparts were piled on a stone foundation, and reinforced with a hardwood palisade and bundles of willow tied into fascines, but they turned into soggy mounds of mud none the less. The cannon sunk up to the axles in the quaking slime so that thick oak planks had to be levered under the grenade throwers, heavy carronades and mortars, while the deep defensive ditches before the entrenchments turned into rushing streams.

The night brought no respite.

A howling gale blew out of the east as if it were Winter. It piled new masses of layered black clouds above the camp and town and whipped them into a boiling, booming cauldron that spilled out all of their stored rain, thunderbolts and lightning and hurled them at Zbarajh. Only the camp servants remained huddled under canvas in the regimental bivouacs throughout that long night. Everyone else—the private soldiers, the gentlemen-troopers, the senior officers, and all the commanders except Lantzkoronski—sought shelter in the town. If Hmyelnitzki had come under the cover of the storm he could have taken the camp without a shot fired in its defense.

Next morning was a little better although the rain kept on falling through the day. It was only at about five o'clock in the afternoon that the wind finally blew the clouds away, a clear blue sky spread above the camp, and—in the direction of Old Zbarajh, which lay about a day's ride to the north and west—a magnificent, seven-colored rainbow rose glimmering in the air. One of its shining, widespread arms reached far beyond Prince Yeremi's other city, and the other seemed to dip for moisture into the dark woods of Tcharny Las that bordered the highway, and the whole great arch gleamed and glittered with its many colors like a triumphant gateway.

Hope, confidence and good spirits returned to the army. The mass of knights and soldiers straggled back into the camp and climbed up on the sodden ramparts to watch that glowing spectacle and to speculate on what this good sign could mean, when Volodyovski, who stood with a crowd of others at the edge of the moat, shaded his sharp eyes and shouted:

"There are troops coming out from under the rainbow!"

The quietly chatting mass of men who were trying to find some reassurance after that night of violence, and who'd begun to draw a measure of peace from the glowing splendor painted in the sky, stirred as suddenly as if a new windstorm had whirled in among them.

Heads craned.

A murmur rose and spread.

The words '*there's an army coming*' flew like an arrow from one end of the entrenchments to the other and the soldiers started to crowd excitedly together, to push and to peer, uneasily poised between uncertainty and hope. All hands flew up as if on command and rested above the eyes. All eyes fixed themselves on that gleaming distance, straining for the first sight of that announced arrival, and everyone held his breath and every heart had begun to hammer.

And then something else began to shine and glitter under that soaring arch. A dream? An illusion? A result of all this longing and all that wishful thinking? But no, this was something real that appeared at the edge of distance and started to emerge and darken as it came. It grew and swelled and took form and acquired texture; and soon this faintly luminous new mass began to break down into the familiar, recognizable images of pennants and banners and horsetail standards, and what seemed like a forest of spears and lances that flowed into the plain.

And then one huge cry of irrepressible joy welled out of every chest: "*Yeremi! Yeremi! Yeremi!*"

Even the oldest and most respected soldiers seemed to go mad in that moment of joy and exaltation. Some leaped off the walls, splashed across the moat and ran across the flooded plain towards the approaching regiments. Others ran to their horses and then galloped out to meet the new arrivals. Yet others simply wept, laughed, raised their arms towards the sky and shouted: "*He's coming! He's here . . .!*"

And the heartfelt cries of gratitude that burst skyward from those muddy earthwalls seemed like a single great thanksgiving prayer.

"*Our Father!*" cried the soldiers. "*Our deliverer . . .! Our salvation!*"

Their joy was so wild and so beyond control that it looked and sounded as if the coming siege was already over and Hmyelnitzki's hordes repulsed in defeat. In the meantime the Prince's regiments approached even closer. It seemed to the watchers on the walls that the sunlit, winged *husaria* in polished steel cuirasses, and the *panzerni* gleaming in gilded chainmail, were already bathed in the scarlet aura of triumph and victory. The slanting beams of the disappearing sun splintered on their armor and on the points of their tall, upright lances and turned them into a thousand glittering prisms, so that they rode as if surrounded by their own firmament full of stars. There were only three thousand men marching under Yeremi Vish-novyetzki's banner at this juncture of his means and fortunes but they seemed like thirty times that number to the cheering soldiers who ran out to meet them. The King's three generals also climbed up on the walls, along with every senior Polish and foreign officer in the city, and their joy was no less heartfelt and sincere than that of the soldiers.

Days of doubt, confusion and disorder were as good as over and even Skshetuski's sallow cheeks acquired a touch of color.

Pan Zagloba threw him a quick, sideways glance, noted a bright new light beginning to shine again in his stony eyes, and drew a slow, grateful breath. So he *could* still feel something! So he wasn't totally beyond the reach of that warmth, excitement, fire and affection that the old knight wanted so desperately for Helen!

The young soldier seemed to find new life in the sight of those familiar ranks and lances and banners. His whole body trembled. His thin lips found the shadow of a smile. He recognized his own regiment which he left in Zamost all those months before and he began to breathe as steadily and deeply as if a great weight had shifted on his chest or as if a boulder had rolled off his shoulders. He knew along with every man crowded on those walls that grim days of work and danger were marching towards them along with these warriors. They would be days in which all private grief would dwindle, personal suffering would be driven deep into some hidden recess of the soul, and the most depleting nightmares would crumble under the burdens of constant vigilance and labor.

"There!" Lantzkoronski cried, extending his *bulava* in the direction from which the Prince was coming. "There's our true commander! And I'll be the first to report to him and ask for his orders."

"*Vivat! Vivat! Vivat Vishnovyetzki!*" shouted the whole army, and then the Prince's regiments began to enter the walled half-circle of earthworks and fortifications through the three bridged gates carved in the defenses.

* * *

The sun was already low on the horizon before the Prince himself rode into the camp. The cheering soldiers lit every kind of torch, cresset, link, flambeau and lantern to greet him. They waved burning firebrands and pine-staves dipped in pitch. They pressed around him in such a dense, agitated mass that his nervous stallion was unable to move, held as fast in this throng as if he'd stepped into a living quagmire.

Fierce, bearded men wept like children crowding around this frail mounted figure for whom they waited with as much anxiety as if he was their promised Savior or Messiah. They clutched at the reins and bridle of his horse, so that they might keep him with them in the *maydan* for a moment longer; and they clung to his stirrups and kissed the edges of his coat. Their enthusiasm reached such a pitch of fervor that even the foreign mercenary regiments declared that they would serve through the quarter without pay, and he sat quietly among them on his spirited white horse, nodding his thanks and smiling at them like a shepherd at his milling flocks, while the cries and cheers echoed without ending.

The rest of the night was calm and the sky was brilliant with starlight after the day's storm.

Thousands of stars glittered in the cloudless sky and suddenly one of them—the largest and the brightest—broke from the firmament and began to fall towards Konstantinov, trailing a long stream of fire behind it.

"That's Hmyelnitzki's star!" the cheering mass of soldiers began to shout, even as Lantzkoronski took a step towards Prince Yeremi to hand him his *bulava*. "It's a miracle! It's a sign from God!"

"*Vivat Vishnovyetzki!*"

Ten thousand hoarse, ecstatic voices repeated the cry, a thousand muskets fired in salute, and Lantzkoronski stepped up to the Prince.

"Yes!" he cried out. "Hmyelnitzki's star is falling and ours is ascending! *Vivat* Vishnovyetzki! The King gave me this *bulava*," he went on loudly enough for everyone to hear him. "But let me be the first to place it in your hands and surrender my authority to a greater soldier. From now on, Highness, I obey your orders."

"And so do we," the other two royal generals said, and the three golden symbols of command extended towards the Prince. "Take these insignia and lead us to victory!"

"They're not yours to give, gentlemen," the Prince said quietly. "Only the King can give them."

"Then you be a living fourth *bulava* over the three of them," Castellan Firley said.

The massed soldiers cheered again and went on cheering through all the long minutes in which none of the generals' prepared speeches could be heard. All their doubts were gone. All their fears vanished at one stroke as if the specter of defeat had never stirred among them.

Their eyes were shining with courage and devotion. They shouted pledges of loyalty and obedience no matter what would happen, calling on God to witness their oaths and to strike down anyone who'd break his solemn vow, and swore to fight to the death beside Prince Yeremi and the other generals. "So help us God . . .!"

And at that moment the Prince's stallion lifted its great white head, shook out its curled, purple-stained mane and uttered a shrill neigh while every other horse in the camp neighed powerfully in reply.

"An omen!" roared ten thousand voices. "A sign of God's blessing!"

"*Vivat* Yeremi, victor! Long live Vishnovyetzki!"

Men laughed and wept.

They fell to their knees and prayed in fervent gratitude. They ran to the walls and shook their fists at the dark horizon from which the enemy was coming.

"Come up, come up, you sons of bitches!" they shouted as they laughed, wept, cheered and prayed. "You'll find us ready for you . . .!"

No one slept that night throughout the camp. The cheers echoed long into the sunrise and the torches burned and waved until the first light of dawn.

Chapter Sixty-seven

THE NEXT DAY passed in preparations for defense. The Prince issued orders which were obeyed at once. Discipline was restored. The soldiers worked readily and swiftly so that it seemed as if a wholly new army had entered the camp, not just a new spirit, and by midday everything was in order. Every man had his assigned position. Everyone knew where to fight and how to assist everybody else. Pickets were posted in the countryside. Patrols brought in news of the enemy all day long and foragers went out to requisition whatever food and fodder could be found in nearby villages. The night passed quietly. The soldiers dozed among their fires ready to man the walls at one trumpet call as if the assault was to come at any moment.

At dawn on the following day the horizon darkened in the direction of Vishnovyetz, the town from which the Prince's ancestors took their name. It was as if a wide, low cloud crept out of the sunrise. All the bells in the town began to ring, signaling alarm, and the mournful cries of the war horns alerted the camp. The foot regiments stood to arms all along the ramparts, the horsemen formed up in the intervals ready to charge out at a single order, and the thin blue smoke of lighted fuses rose skyward from beside every cannon on the walls.

"They're coming!" the hushed, tense murmur swept the walls. "They're here!"

The Prince appeared among his soldiers bareheaded but dressed in his silver armor and riding his white horse. Not a single line of worry marred his quiet features. On the contrary, his face and eyes glowed with pleasure and amusement.

"We've guests, gentlemen!" he called out, riding along the

walls. "Our guests are arriving! Let's be sure to give them a proper welcome!"

"*Vivat!*" cried the soldiers.

Then there was silence, broken only by the crack and rattle of battle flags and banners snapping in the breeze.

In the meantime the enemy drew near enough to be seen clearly with the naked eye. This was the first wave of the approaching masses, not Hmyelnitzki and the Khan but a picked corps of thirty thousand Tartars armed with horn-bows, firelocks and sabers. Having swept up some fifteen hundred camp servants sent out for provisions the day before, they rode on a broad front from Vishnovyetz and then, spreading out into their classic crescent, started to reach out towards Old Zbarajh, the highway that connected the two towns, and the woods beyond them.

Prince Yeremi, seeing that this was only a mounted force without supporting infantry and cannon gave orders for the cavalry to move out against it.

Orderlies galloped at once among the ranks of horsemen. Orders began to snap. The regiments stirred and started to spill out of the earthworks like bees from a hive. The plain began to fill with mounted men and horses. The watchers on the ramparts could see the captains galloping among their companies with their short, ridged iron maces in their hands, dressing the lines for battle. The horses pranced and snorted with nervous, tossing heads and, from time to time, a long, shrill neighing swept along the entire battle line. Then two regiments of Prince Yeremi's Tartar Light Horse and his Household Cossacks broke away from this assembled mass and began to trot quietly towards the enemy. Their cased bows bounced on their backs, their caps gleamed in bright reds and yellows, and at their head rode Vyershul on a restless stallion that reared up and pawed the air as if he wanted to leap all the sooner into the spreading dark mass ahead. Not a single cloud marred the bright, blue mirror suspended above them. The men and horses trotting in the plain were as sharply etched as if each was a perfect, intricately carved miniature held in the palm of the hand.

But at that moment something else appeared at the edge of vision. The Prince's small campaign wagon train hadn't managed to reach the town the night before with the rest of his army and now it hurried down the highway to get under the protection of the guns. But the sharp-eyed Tartar warriors caught sight of it, their exultant yell came clearly to the infantry on the rim of the earthworks, and the long dark crescent turned at once towards the wagons with the curved points thrusting forward like the lowered horns of a charging bull. The air filled with the familiar warbling Tartar battle cry and Vyershul's regiments galloped to the rescue.

The crescent was the first to reach the wagon train which, in the meantime, formed into a rolling hollow square that bristled with light artillery and muskets, while several thousand Tartar warriors turned towards Vyershul's men and charged them with a drawn-out howl. And here the discipline, training and experience of the Prince's soldiers brought cries of admiration echoing from the ramparts. Seeing the horns of the crescent sweeping around their flanks, they split into three groups and leaped to the sides to outflank the flankers; then they divided themselves into four and then split once more; and each time the Tartars had to check their charge, reform and swing their entire front, because there was only empty air in front of them while the Prince's men were tearing at their flanks.

At the fourth turn the two bodies of horsemen finally came together but Vyershul brought his whole strength charging down into the weakest point of the Tartar line, broke through at once and swept on like a storm towards the surrounded and embattled wagons.

"Will you just look? Will you see this? Only the Prince's captains can lead like that!" cried the veteran Crown soldiers watching from the walls.

In the meantime Vyershul drove his wedge into the swarm of Tartars who ringed the wagon train, cut through them like an arrow piercing a soldier's body, and brought his troops inside the rolling little fortress. A single battle blazed out in the plain in place of the two separate encounters but it was all the fiercer for being concentrated in a smaller space. Its core was the ring of wagons, spewing fire and smoke; around it swirled the howling mass of Tartars like a dark whirlpool spinning in wide circles; and beyond this smoke-filled circular arena full of yells and screams and the rattling of firelocks and muskets galloped a growing herd of riderless horses.

★   ★   ★

It must have seemed to the watchers in the earthworks as if a boar beset by a pack of mastiffs was scurrying towards the safety of a thicket and fighting for his life each step of the way. The fierce hounds leaped and snapped at him, baying all around him, and he ran doggedly, turning and flashing his sharp white tusks at them, and ripping the most persistent. The little wagon train defended itself just as savagely, pushing towards the earthworks, while the watchers speculated on when the Prince would send some really meaningful and decisive help to rescue the defenders.

"It's time," some of the older soldiers started muttering. "The odds are just too heavy over there . . ."

But they'd barely spoken when the Prince signaled with his *bulava* and the plain reddened with the scarlet coats of Kushel's and Volodyovski's dragoons as if a sudden burst of poppies bloomed across the plain. The dragoons struck and vanished in the mass of Tartars like a swirl of autumn leaves swept by the wind into a dark and agitated forest, or like divers disappearing under a stormy sea. Only a fresh cluster of panicked horses carrying empty saddles burst out of this churning mass of animals and men to show where they had been.

"Why is the Prince feeding his reinforcements piecemeal into that cauldron?" some of the newer Crown soldiers asked each other. "Why is he sending his men in there a few regiments at a time? Why not hit the Tartars with everything at once?"

But the older practitioners grinned and nodded, guessing his intentions. "That's to show you snotnosed, virgin warriors what kind of help he's brought you."

But they could hear the crack and rattle of musketry weakening among the wagons where the defenders no longer had the time to load their overheated weapons while a sharp note of triumph began to sound through the Tartar baying.

"Ay, that's getting close," they started to mutter. "Too close. They won't last much longer."

Then the Prince snapped an order to his aides, pointed with his *bulava*, and three *husaria* regiments—his own under Skshetuski, that of Pan Marek Sobieski, the *Starosta* of Krasnostav, and the King's own led by Pan Piglovski—rode out of the camp and started their slow, massive run towards the battle. They gathered weight and speed at each step of the gallop until they were rolling like an avalanche across the open plain. They reached the Tartars, struck them like a wall, broke and scattered them at once and drove them towards the woods.

Sweeping them up like chaff, they squeezed them once more into a dense mob that they crushed and trampled and scattered again, and then they chased them off the field for a quarter of a league or more while the wagon train rolled into the camp among shouts of joy and the booming of saluting cannon.

The day's fighting, however, wasn't over yet. The Tartars didn't vanish from sight altogether knowing that Hmyelnitzki and the Khan were close at their heels. They were soon galloping around the camp and circling the town, cutting all the roads and occupying every neighboring settlement and village where thick clouds of smoke began to rise at once into the hot dry air. Several hundred of their better warriors, looking to win some individual distinction for themselves, rode up to the earthworks to challenge the defenders and a similar crowd of 'Kwarta' men and Vishnovyetzki soldiers spilled out of the entrenchments to meet them. They rode at each other in small groups, seized prisoners and fought single duels, littering the glacis with dead men and horses until the day ended.

Vyershul, who never missed these deadly preliminary games, wasn't there this time. Slashed six times across the head in the defense of the little wagon train he lay close to death in his tent but Pan Volodyovski avenged him a dozen times over.

★ ★ ★

The night darkened slowly but the sky stayed bright with a lurid glow as a dozen villages began to burn one after another. The whole countryside seemed on fire as far as the eye could have seen in daylight. The smoke climbed redly into the pale, night sky; the stars seemed like a bloody pink froth through those crimson coils; and clouds of birds rose screaming off the lakes and out of the woods and thickets, and whirled through that crimson air, while the cattle in the camp, terrified by this unusual sight, began to bellow mournfully.

"It can't be that those few thousand Tartars could've done all that," the more experienced soldiers told each other on the walls. "It must be Hmyelnitzki himself."

"And the Khan with all his Hordes."

These, as all the men knew very well, weren't just idle guesses. The patrols had reported the main force of the enemy not far behind the dispersed Tartar screen and every soldier in the camp was up on the walls. All the townsfolk and refugee local peasants climbed into church towers and clung to the rooftops while women wept and wailed in the churches. The waiting, which seemed like the heaviest burden of all, hung above the camp, the town and the castle like a leaden cloud, but it was quickly over. The night was still not altogether dark, and the sun was still burning redly below the horizon, when the first ranks of the vast Cossack and Tartar army appeared in the plain. On they came, in hundreds and in thousands and then in tens of thousands, bringing to mind the uneasy image of a marching forest as if every tree and shrub in the Commonwealth had pulled its roots out of the soil and swept towards Zbarajh.

It seemed as if there was no end to those dense dark ranks that flowed on and on out of the red horizon; they dwindled far beyond the range of the human eye. They spread across the landscape like a growling cloud or like a rustling coverlet of locusts that would devour all of the habitable spaces under them. The threatening mutter of their coming drifted before them like a wind blowing through the dry tops of old trees. Having filled the countryside all around the camp they started to settle themselves for the night and light their bivouac fires and then it seemed as if the sky itself had fallen into the plain scattering all its stars.

"Do you see all those campfires?" the watching soldiers whispered to each other. "They stretch farther than a horse could gallop in a day . . ."

"Jezus Maria!" Pan Zagloba muttered to Skshetuski. "Is there no end to this vermin? There's a lion in me, as you know, and I don't understand the meaning of fear, but I'd be glad if lightning would strike that human ant-heap before dawn. As God's my witness, there's just too many of them! Jehosophat's valley won't get a better crowd on Judgment Day, I'll bet. And will you just tell me what these scoundrels want? Wouldn't every mother's son among them be better off at home? What's wrong with working on their masters' acres, anyway? Is it our fault that God created us as gentry and them as our peasants?"

Skshetuski said nothing, watching the vast spread of the enemy's bivouac fires and estimating their numbers, and the fat knight broke into a sudden rage.

"Tfui!" he spat into the glowing night. "I'm going to get carried away with anger unless I really watch it! I'm a sweet, gentle man by nature. A surgeon could use me for a balm to plaster a wound! But they're going to drive me into a real passion! They've had it too easy with us, that's what was the matter. They've been fed too well so they've been breeding like mice in a grain-loft and now they think they can go after the cats. Just you wait, you vermin! There's one cat here whose name is Yarema and another who is called Zagloba! They'll chew your tails for you!"

But the bellowing and bluster didn't help to set his mind at peace and Pan Zagloba turned to different speculations.

"What do you think, though, will they try a few negotiations? Eh? Wouldn't that make sense? We could offer them their lives if they'd just show some humility and go back where they came from, don't you think? Not that they worry me, of course! The more the better is what I always say! But I'm just wondering if there're enough provisions in the camp . . . Ah . . .! But will you just take a look over there? There are more fires starting up in the distance. And more beyond that! May the Black Death itself come calling on every one of them!"

"Why should they negotiate anything?" Skshetuski asked quietly. "They must be sure they have us exactly where they want us."

"But they don't, do they?" the fat knight asked quickly.

"That's up to God. Whatever happens won't be easy for them, not with our Prince here."

"Thanks for the comfort," Pan Zagloba muttered. "I'd rather hear that they won't manage it at all!"

"It's no small thing for a soldier to know that he's not going to give his life for nothing," Pan Skshetuski said.

"Certainly, certainly . . . But may the Devil take it all along with this talk of dying! I'd rather think I'm not going to give up anything!"

★ ★ ★

But at that moment they were joined by the little knight and Pan Podbipyenta.

"Good news, gentlemen," the Lithuanian said. "The waiting is over! They say there's half a million Cossacks and Tartars out there."

"May your tongue turn into a roasting spit!" Pan Zagloba cried, driven at last into a towering rage. "You call that good news?"

"They won't seem like so many when they're storming the walls," Pan Longinus hurried to comfort the quivering fat knight. "They can climb the scaling ladders only so many at a time, you see . . ."

"And since our Prince and Hmyelnitzki are finally confronting each other, I don't expect any more talk of negotiations," Pan Michal broke in and grinned and then began to rub both his hands together. "It's going to be the end once and for all either for us or for the rebels and there aren't going to be any two ways about it."

"Ah . . . to the Devil with it all," Pan Zagloba muttered, no longer caring what anybody thought.

He could see Prince Yeremi further along the earthwall looking across the plain at the Tartar and Zaporohjan masses that were beyond counting. He could imagine Hmyelnitzki staring up at the Polish camp and saying to himself: '*There's my most terrible enemy, my greatest danger, and my most implacable opponent. Who will be able to resist me and deny me whatever I want after I've wiped him off the face of the earth?*' In this terrible civil war which had already lasted far too long, these two larger than life heroes of their people never yet faced each other in a battle. One was the destroyer of Hetmans, royal generals and regents; the other was the Nemesis of the Zaporohjans who crushed powerful Cossack atamans as if they were wheat stalks. Each was a conqueror trailed by victories and exercising an almost superstitious hold over his followers and each had become the terror of his enemies. But now, at last, they were standing face to face. Which would prove the greater? It was easy to guess that the struggle between them would be fought to the last drop of blood but which of them had more of it to spare?

This lone Ruthenian *Knaz* stood at the head of fifteen thousand men, Pan Zagloba knew, and that included the camp laborers and servants, while the grim peasant chieftain was followed by entire nations, leading innumerable peoples who lived in the vast spaces from the Don River and the Azov Sea in the east to the mouth of the Danube in the west. Riding beside him was the Khan of all the Crimean, Belgorodian, Nohay and Dobrudjan Tartars. Marching behind him were all the freebooters who swarmed along the tributaries of the Dniester and the Dnieper, all the *Nijhovtzy* and the uncountable hordes of *tchernya* that poured out of the Steppe and from every village, settlement, town, and forest in the eastern lands. He commanded every Cossack who had served in the destroyed Crown army of Hetman Pototzki and in the private companies of all the Ukrainian magistrates and magnates. He led Circassians from the Caucasus, Valachian mercenaries, Silistrian and Rumelian Turks, and even hordes of Serbs and Bulgars sent by the Turkish Sultan.

It almost seemed as if this was a second great migration of barbarian tribes which had abandoned their distant eastern grasslands and flowed to the west to seize new lands and create new countries.

These, then were the proportions between the two sides, Pan Zagloba knew: a handful against hosts. An islet against an ocean. "There's not much chance of coming out of here alive," he muttered unhappily to himself. The entire Commonwealth, he knew, looked at these puny earthworks, surrounded by an ocean of the world's fiercest warriors, as if it was already a burial mound of doomed knights and their legendary leader.

* * *

Hmyelnitzki must have had the same idea because just as soon as his campfires glittered across the plain a Cossack emissary started waving a white flag before the entrenchments, blowing a trumpet and shouting at the sentries not to shoot. The pickets went out and seized him at once and brought him to the Prince.

No sign of worry showed in Vishnovyetzki's face. He was still on horseback, still touring the trenches, and his face was as clear and untroubled as a Summer sky. The red glare of the Cossack campfires was shining in his eyes and tinted his delicate, pale features with a ruddy glow.

"Who are you?" he asked the trembling Cossack.

"I'm . . . Sokol. Leader of a Hundred. From the Hetman, lord . . ."

"And what do you bring me?"

The old Steppe warrior began to bow as low as if he were an oriental slave salaaming a sultan. "Forgive me, lord," he begged. "Have mercy. I'll say what I've been told to say but it's not my doing . . ."

"Speak up, then," Prince Yeremi said quietly with a pale smile. "Nothing is going to happen to you here."

"The Hetman said to tell you that he's come to visit . . ."

"Tell him I'm ready for him," the Prince interrupted.

" . . . Yes lord. He also said to tell you that tomorrow night he's going to be dining in your castle . . ."

"Tell him that I'm giving the banquet tonight, not tomorrow," the Prince said, nodded pleasantly, turned his horse and rode away along the ramparts down into the camp.

The Cossack left, hardly able to believe that he was still alive, and an hour later the Zbarajh cannon began to thunder with salutes, the earthworks echoed with cries of joy and pleasure, and a thousand candles gleamed like fireflies in all the castle windows.

★ ★ ★

Encamped at some distance beyond the bivouac fires of his army, Khan Devlet Giray, hereditary ruler of the Crimean Tartars and overlord of all the Tartar clans in Asia and Europe, also heard these cries and trumpets and kettle-drums and artillery salutes, and stepped out of his tent.

He was a man in his middle years with small black eyes, shaped like gleaming almonds, which hid the coldest and most calculating mind of his two-hundred-year Giray dynasty. His plump, hairless face and soft, fleshy body belied the ruthlessness and cunning with which he ruled his satraps, kept his proud and jealous *murjahs* in humble subjection, and played the powerful *beys* of the four great Tartar clans one against the other. He paid nominal homage to the Ottoman Turkish *Porte* as the sultan's hereditary *padishah*, or principal underlord on the borderlands of Europe, but his control over all the Turkic tribes and nations between Astrakhan and the Moldavian plains was as independent as it was absolute. He traced his lineage to the *ulans* of the Golden Horde and, through his great-great-grandfather Haci Giray, the first Crimean Khan and founder of the Giray dynasty, to the horsehair yurts of Genghis Khan himself.

His dignity as well as Tartar custom obliged him to conceal surprise but the sounds of celebration in Zbarajh disturbed his meditation.

He stood outside his carpeted silk pavilion with his brother, the 'Nurradin Khan,' or heir-designate and chosen successor, and with the Sultan Galga, Tuhay-bey, and a crowd of other *ulan* knights and *murjahs*, and sent for Hmyelnitzki.

The Cossack Hetman was already somewhat the worse for

liquor but he arrived at once, bowing to the ground in the oriental manner and placing the fingers of his right hand on his forehead, mouth and heart as he waited for the Khan's command, but long minutes passed before the Khan showed that he noticed his ally's arrival. He stared in silence at the gleaming castle, which shined in the distance like a great stone lantern, and nodded his head thoughtfully up and down, and stroked the two thin wisps of hair that straggled to his chest from the bottom of his chin.

Then he thrust out a soft finger towards the strange illumination where only terror and trepidation should have been evident that night.

"What does that mean?" he asked.

"Mighty ruler," Hmyelnitzki replied. "That's *Knaz* Yarema feasting."

Astonishment crept out on the Khan's cold face. "He's feasting?"

"He's giving a banquet for tomorrow's corpses."

A new artillery salvo boomed in salute on the distant walls, trumpets blared a fanfare, and protracted cheers reached the Tartars' ears.

"There's but one God," the Khan murmured, hiding his amazement. "There is a lion living in the heart of that unbeliever . . ." Then, after another long and thoughtful silence, he added with a cold, expressionless glance at the Zaporohjan Hetman: "I'd rather stand with him than with you."

Hmyelnitzki shuddered.

Drinking himself into oblivion every night was less a matter of habit for the Zaporohjan Hetman than a way to escape his terrifying doubts and bouts of despair.

He knew the price he paid for the Tartars' unreliable friendship which could dissolve or turn against him at a whim. Devlet Giray brought his Crimean Khanate to the peak of its historic power less by war and victories than by skillful manipulation of alliances, switching his loyalties back and forth between Muscovy and the Commonwealth so that neither could have the upper hand for long or overwhelm the other. Hmyelnitzki also knew that while the Khan rode with him for the sake of the rich Ukrainian booty, for the gifts of treasure he received from the Cossack Hetman, and for the unfortunate captives who nourished his slave trade, he was secretly ashamed of his alliance with the Zaporohjans. Knowing himself to be a monarch by the will of Allah, and one whose right to rule was rooted in Islamic law, he hated the idea of supporting rebels against a lawful King. Given an even choice between a 'Hmyel' and a Vishnovyetzki, he would turn against the Cossacks without a second thought.

But the serpent was never far from the lion in Bohdan Hmyelnitzki.

"Great monarch!" he addressed the Khan. "Yarema is your deadliest enemy. It was he who took the Transdnieper from the Tartars. It was he who hanged captured *murjahs* along his borders to serve as a warning, as if they were of no more account than dead wolves. It was he who wanted to bring his fire and sword into the Crimea . . ."

"And didn't your people do the same?"

"I'm your slave," the Hetman murmured humbly.

The livid lips of Tuhay-bey began to quiver, he noted out of a corner of a watchful eye. The Tartar's yellow fangs gleamed under his wispy mustache. Hmyelnitzki knew that this proud and powerful bey had a mortal enemy among the Cossacks, one who exterminated his entire clan and almost captured Tuhay-bey himself, and now that hated name began to gurgle in the Tartar's throat.

"Burlay . . . Burlay . . ."

"Tuhay-bey!" Hmyelnitzki said at once. "You and Burlay poured water on your swords last year, remember? The Great Khan himself ordered that you become brothers!"

Tuhay-bey's twisted lips sprung open but before he could break into a string of curses a new salvo of salutes thundered in Vishnovyetzki's earthworks and the dangerous moment passed without an explosion. The Khan thrust out his hand, drew it slowly along the line of the entrenchments, the castle and the town, and then turned his narrowed eyes coldly on Hmyelnitzki.

"That will be mine tomorrow?"

"Tomorrow they'll be dead," Hmyelnitzki said firmly. Then, thinking the conversation finished, he started making his salaams again, touching his forehead, mouth and chest with his outspread fingers.

The Khan sighed. He nodded. A tremor passed across his sallow face and he wrapped himself more closely in his fur-lined kaftan. The warm, July night was coming to an end and the air turned chilly before dawn.

"It's late," he murmured and turned thoughtfully towards his pavilions.

All the Tartar lords, princes, minor khans and sultans of his suite began to sway gently, rustling with respectful murmurs like a wheatfield stroked by a sudden breeze, and he walked slowly into his great tent.

" . . . God is one," he murmured.

Hmyelnitzki rode off towards his own quarters.

"You can have the castle," he muttered savagely as he came to the Zaporohjan lines. "I'll give you the town and all the loot and every man and woman alive in the ruins . . . But Yarema will be mine, not yours, even if I've got to pay for him with my throat!"

He sat for a long time in his tent, stifling his rage at his humiliation and looking out into the night as the campfires began to die out one by one.

A deep, quiet stillness replaced the murmur of several hundred thousand voices in the plain. Tartar fifes still squealed and shrilled here and there, the voices of the Nohai horseherders still called out in the near distance as they drove their herds of mustangs and shaggy-haired ponies to pasture and water. Then even these last sounds dwindled into silence and sleep fell on all the Tartars and the Cossacks.

Only the castle went on booming with gun salutes and ringing with cheers long into the night as if a wedding was in progress there.

Chapter Sixty-eight

THE DAWN CAME slowly, creeping like a spy across the horizon. The night's shadows backed away into their hiding places as the reluctant sun rose out of the mists, turning a quick deep crimson in a lowering sky as if offended by the need to look down on the carnage that everyone in the camp expected.

No one in the Crown camp doubted that the assault was coming. Mobs of *tchernya*, Tartars, Cossacks and all the other different kinds of people who'd come together behind the Zaporohjan Hetman began to stir in their bivouacs long before first light, while every soldier in the camp stood to arms behind their parapets.

Day came at last. The angry sun glowed like a bed of coals and a hot red light flooded the strip of plain that lay between the earthworks and the Cossack lines; it piled a deep shadow in front of the huge, outspread wings of the Zaporohjan *tabor* and in the teeming roosts and lairs of the enemy's encampment. Numbed by the sight of this vast assembly, whose threatening growl drifted towards them like an approaching storm, the defenders felt the blood draining from their faces. They tried in vain to tally all the campfires that glittered in the dark plain during the night before; and now this colossal human ant hill was spilling out all of its angry contents. Then tongues of fire licked out from the Cossack revetments, cannon started booming, and the great mass heaved itself into the open ground and began to roll towards them and their parapets like a black cloud falling upon the head of a mountain.

Pan Zagloba closed his eyes when the assault began.

"They'll smother us with their caps," he groaned squirming

on his horse. "Great God almighty, why did you have to make so many of these vermin? Aren't there enough rag pickers in the world?"

"Don't worry," Pan Yan calmed him. "This isn't the real assault."

"It isn't? It looks real enough to me," the fat knight muttered, mopping his flushed face. "How much more real does it have to get?"

"This will be just a probe. You'll see. They'll hit hard here and there but they won't really press the attack anywhere to drive it home. They just want to test the strength of the defenses. And to feel out where our men fight with less determination."

"What?" Pan Zagloba bellowed, much encouraged. "They dare to doubt our manhood? Oh, the scum! Probe us, would they? Poke at us as if we were a pack of mangy dogs? I'll show them a probing!"

The dark mass poured across the plain like a roiled sea bristling with weapons and glowing with infuriated faces but the attack proved to be exactly what Skshetuski said it was. Just as a tidal wave driven by the wind might foam and thunder against a rocky shore, piling up upon itself and then ebbing back into the depths behind them, so the attackers struck powerfully here and there and withdrew to gather new strength and strike somewhere else. It was as if they wanted to sap the defenders' spirit with their awesome numbers before getting down to the serious business of shattering their bodies.

In the meantime a religious procession appeared on the walls. Father Muhovyetzki carried a gilded monstrance shaped like a little sun and containing the Holy Sacrament which he raised high overhead to put new heart into the shaken soldiers. He walked with eyes half closed as if in a trance. His drawn, ascetic face was set in lines of infinite peace and calmness, while two other priests marched beside him and supported him firmly by the elbows. One was the Reverend Yaskolski, chaplain of the Crown *husaria* and a famous former military commander; the other, also an ex-soldier, was a gigantic Bernardine named Zabkovski who was second only to Pan Longinus in physical strength and almost equaled Pan Zagloba's prowess at the dinner table. They paced along the ramparts under a canopy carried by a nervous and uneasy Pan Zagloba and three other nobles, followed by all the senior officers of the army, while a dozen sweet-faced young girls dressed all in white and wearing wreaths of flowers in their hair scattered blooms and petals before them.

The sight of the Sacrament, as well as the calmness of the priests and the chanting children, put fresh heart into the soldiers, dispelled their doubts and reaffirmed their courage and determination. The fresh morning wind spread the scent of myrrh burning in the censers. Every few paces Father Muhovyetzki halted, raised the monstrance and chanted an invocation which the stentorian voices of Yaskolski and Zabkovski picked up at once while the entire army sang out the responses. The deep bass voices of the cannon seemed to boom with a rhythmic incantation of their own.

Sometimes a cannon ball rumbled close to the canopy, or struck the parapet next to the procession, or buried itself in the earthwall under it and spattered the priests and acolytes with dirt, while Pan Zagloba tried to shrink and make himself as thin as the pole of the baldachin he carried. He was particularly terrified whenever the procession stood still for the chanting of a lengthy litany or for silent prayer. The passage of the solid iron shot, which whirred overhead like the beating of great wings, was especially loud and frightening at such moments, and the old noble flushed a deeper crimson while Father Yaskolski squinted in disgust. As an old soldier, he couldn't stand to see such inept gunnery and such a waste of projectiles and powder.

"Blast their eyes!" he'd mutter when a particularly ragged salvo flew high over the walls and rattled down into the camp or splashed into the river. "They ought to be planting turnips, not fooling with cannon."

At last the procession reached the east end of the ramparts and the Tartars and the Cossacks began to pull back. They had tried a dozen mass attacks, especially on the uncompleted redoubt by the western lake, to see if they could create a panic among the defenders. But when they were beaten back all along the line they retreated behind their own cannon and stayed there for the rest of the day.

★　★　★

Then came the memorable Tuesday of July 13 which passed in feverish preparations on both sides.

The grand assault was now certain beyond anybody's doubt. The trumpets, kettledrums and war horns in all the Cossack camps and *tchernya* encampments filled the air with their raucous blaring from the day's first light, while the great holy drum of the Tartars, known as the '*Bhalt*,' boomed like thunder well into the sunset.

The evening began on a gentle note. The church bells in the town tolled the Angelus and the army knelt in prayer on the walls as the sun hurried off the western sky. A light breeze cooled the heated plain and a mild mist rose out of the two lakes and the little river. And then the first of the night's stars gleamed in the darkening sky and sixty Zaporohjan cannon bellowed with one great voice. Three hundred thousand human throats roared out a reply with one huge, hoarse cry, uncountable ranks threw themselves into a headlong charge towards the walls, and the assault began.

The thunder of their coming deafened every ear. The ground seemed to leap and quiver under their pounding boots so that the soldiers who crouched behind their barricades and loopholes felt the tremors under their own feet while the vast booming roar made their vision shake. It drowned out the war horns and the drums and overwhelmed even the bellowing of the cannon. The oldest and most experienced men among the defenders couldn't remember hearing anything like it in their lives.

"Great God Almighty!" Pan Zagloba's eyes bulged out and his mouth hung open. "What's that coming at us?"

He sat on horseback beside Skshetuski in one of the sally intervals cut into the earthwall where the cavalry was waiting, and he couldn't understand what he saw because it seemed as if a sea of bellowing, wild-eyed animals was pouring across the plain.

"Those aren't human beings!" he spluttered at last.

"You're quite right," Skshetuski said calmly. "The enemy is driving herds of cattle before them so that we'll empty our guns into the animals."

" . . . Cattle?" The old knight's eyes bulged out even further. "They are driving cattle?"

Skshetuski shrugged. "As you see."

But at this Pan Zagloba turned as crimson as a boiled beet, his disbelieving eyes grew red in indignation, and he spat out the one word that contained all his rage, terror, hopelessness and fervent desire to be somewhere else.

" . . . Scoundrels!"

Lashed with rawhide whips by wild, half-naked *tchabany*, and scorched from behind with flaming torches by Tartar horseherders, the fear-crazed cattle ran for the walls with a gloomy bellowing until Vurtzel's gunners began to mow them down with fire and iron.

Then thick black smoke seemed to darken the earth and to obscure the planet.

The sky blazed red with fire, flashing with the reflected glare of the flames that spewed from the cannon. Half of the terror-stricken animals were hurled to the ground, hundreds more scattered as if seared by lightning, and the advancing human tide swept forward across the torn carcasses of the rest.

First came a mass of captives and local peasants from the countryside who hadn't managed to reach the shelter of Zbarajh before they were swept up by the Tartars and invading Cossacks. Hundreds of men, women, small children, old crones and young people ran in tears and with such heartrending wails that they moved the most hardened consciences among the defenders. They prayed and pleaded, crying out for mercy and staggering under the sacks of sand and gravel with which they were to fill the moats dug before the walls. The soldiers' hair rose under their helmets in horror at this sight. But they closed their ears to these pitiful appeals and aimed their guns and muskets at the luckless captives, thinking less about these wretched, driven masses than about the dangerous loads they carried. In other times, they might have acted differently. But all mankind lost the quality of mercy in those days and even the gentlest men had become immune to other people's suffering.

"*Fire!*"

The cannon boomed salvo after salvo.

"*Fire!*"

The muskets flamed and crackled all along the line of parapets and breastworks.

Stabbed and goaded by the knives and spears behind them, and torn by the shot and shell that gouged long scarlet furrows in their wailing masses, the captives ran and fell and got up again and staggered on through pools of their own blood. Driving them on was a flood of Cossacks who, in turn, were pushed forward by a sea of Turks, Tartars, renegade Serbs and Valachians who had accepted Islam, Bulgars and warriors of unknown origin and allegiance except to loot and slaughter.

The moats filled up quickly with their corpses and the sand they'd brought. And then the great tidal wave of the enemy swept across their bodies with a howl of triumph.

★ ★ ★

Night fell soon after and darkened the far edges of the plain but the walls and the forefront of the ramparts were as bright as day.

Broad sheets of fire flared out of the cannon and illuminated the massed regiments that pushed against the earthworks. One regiment climbed across another. The scarlet light showed the Cossack colonels driving fresh ranks across the bodies of those who'd gone before them, and their best regiments threw themselves at the bastions held by Vishnovyetzki because there, as Hmyelnitzki knew, the fierce resistance would be the most stubborn.

First in these charging waves came the disciplined *kujhenye* of the *Sietch*, and then the awesome Pereyaslav Cossacks led by the veteran Loboda. Vorontchenko followed with the Tcherkassy Regiment and behind them came Kulak with the Karviv Cossacks. After them pressed the dense ranks of the great Bratzlav Regiment under the ruthless Netchay, and the Khumin Cossacks under Stempka, and then the powerful Korsun regiments led by the Polish renegade Mrozovyetzki.

Then came the wild Kalnyitch Cossacks, both on foot and horseback, and the picked Byelotzerkiev Regiment mustering fifteen thousand men with Hmyelnitzki himself riding in their ranks. Scarlet as Satan in the lurid glare, and with his shirt thrown carelessly open across his wide chest as if he were immune to the death of ordinary men and impervious to arrows and bullets, he seemed to be everywhere at once in that fiery chaos. With his huge red face, fearless as a lion's, and his sharp darting glances that noted everything around him, he loomed through the smoke and fire like a creature out of ancient legends that could see everything at the same time out of a hundred eyes.

Behind the regular *moloytzy* pushed the fierce hordes of independent Cossacks who owed no allegiance to anyone, the primitive dwellers of the remote and barely settled lands along the River Don, and the savage tribes of Circassians who fought with long knives. And behind them, like a pack of wolfhounds that herded them forward, rode the picked warriors of the Khan.

Tuhay-bey himself led the merciless *Nohajtzy* who had brought fire and sword to the borderlands for three generations; Subaghazi, the Khan's favorite nephew, commanded the Belgorodian Tartars; and Khan Kurdluk, the lord or '*Agha*' of all the lands along the Sea of Azov, led the sallow-skinned warriors of Astrakhan who fought with eight-foot horn and iron bows and arrows that were almost as long as javelins. They trod so closely on each other's heels that the hot breaths of the rear ranks flooded the necks and shoulders of those who pressed on ahead of them.

No one would ever know how many thousands of them died before they reached those ditches bridged with the corpses of the slaughtered captives. But they got there, crossed the bloody moats, and started to claw their way up the steep glacis to the parapets above. The cannon, which couldn't be depressed enough to harm the near ranks, went on hurling their fire and iron at the deep ranks that followed. Rockets and grenades curled down from the sky with a whistling sound that resembled the shrill laughter of the mad and gave the night a sort of hellish daylight in which the German musketeers, the regular Polish infantry, and Prince Yeremi's dismounted dragoons, poured their lead and fire straight into the faces of the storming Cossacks.

Their near ranks may have wanted to pull back but shoved forward remorselessly from the rear they stood and died instead. Blood splashed the ranks that trod upon their bodies, and gurgled in deep dark pools that formed at their successors' feet, and soon the walls became so slippery that they no longer offered any grip or foothold. But the charging waves pressed on and climbed and slid or tumbled back on the pikes and spears of the men behind them, and were immediately replaced by new swarms of climbers.

Scorched and black with gunpowder and sheeted in smoke, they fell in dozens under the thrusts and blows of spears, halberds, sabers and pole-axes that swept them off the ramparts, but they went on clawing their way up the walls. No one on either side cared about his wounds. Everyone on both sides became oblivious to any feeling other than hatred for their enemies and contempt for death.

Here and there along the blood-soaked wall the swarming masses managed to sweep across the breastworks, and there smoke-blackened men grappled with each other like demented bears, locked in hand-to-hand combat and fighting with knives and fists across a thick carpet of the dead and dying.

No one gave orders any longer because there was no one who could still hear or understand commands. The total fury of the sounds around them overwhelmed their senses with one vast, formless roar that swallowed everything; and all the shouts, the cries, the screaming of the wounded, the dry rattling of musketry and the whir and hiss of mortar bombs and grenades, became a single unidentifiable sound that drowned out even the red blasts of the cannon.

★ ★ ★

Hours passed like that but the merciless struggle went on without a pause. A new wall, built with the bodies of the dead attackers, began to rise between the Polish earthworks and the plain, creating yet another barrier against the assaults.

The storming *Sitchovtzy* were shot, cut, and beaten down almost to a man. The Pereyaslav Cossacks littered the glacis and the palisade with their trampled dead. The Karviv, Bratzlav and Khumin regiments were decimated, with ten men in every hundred killed and other dozens wounded, but the survivors pressed on, pushed forward by the Hetman's Byelotzerkiev guards, the Rumelian Turks and the mounted Tartars. Running with blood and sweat, and with acrid gunsmoke burning in their lungs, the defenders fought as if they'd been driven half-mad by the carnage. A berserk fury seized them by the hair and they threw themselves at the enemy with the ferocity of wolves just when Hmyelnitzki launched his final waves of Byelotzerkiev guardsmen, Circassians, Turks and Tartars.

But by that time the character of the battle had begun to change. Unnoticed in the hours of uninterrupted slaughter, the bright scarlet glare ebbed out of the sky. The cannon were now silent. Their iron barrels were too hot to load. The grenades ceased to illuminate the battleground and even the musketry sputtered out in the sudden darkness. Only the clash and grating of cold steel resounded through the smoke that lay in a thick low cloud along the whole length of the western wall.

No one could tell any longer what was happening under that

pall of gunsmoke. There was merely a sense of something vast and dangerous convulsing in the half-light like a mythical beast thrashing in its death throes while shouts no longer signified either despair or triumph.

From time to time these scattered, indistinguishable cries died down. There'd be a sudden and unexpected moment of weighted and maleficent silence. And then there'd come something like a groan . . . a great single shudder . . . lifting as it seemed out of the earth itself. It would rise and hang suspended in the air as if even the souls of the slaughtered were unable to break away from this killing ground and drift towards the quietness of their final peace.

But such pauses in the sound of the battle were both brief and rare. The shouts and screaming boiled out with even greater fierceness after every break, and each time that they rose again above the bloodied ramparts they became hoarser, more grating and less human.

The crash of musketry rattled out again as Oberst Mahnitzki brought the last reserve of the Prince's German musketeers running to the walls, and finally, at long last, the horns and bugles in the rear ranks of the attacking Cossacks sounded the retreat.

★   ★   ★

There was then a brief interval, almost miraculous in itself, in which to rest exhausted minds and bodies, to draw a breath, and to still the uncontrollable shaking of arms and hands. The Cossack regiments fell back into their own lines and took shelter in the shadow of their guns, but within half an hour Hmyelnitzki launched them forward in a new assault.

But this time Prince Yeremi himself appeared on the parapet in his silver armor. He was easy to see on his milky stallion, with his own banner and a Hetman's horsetail standard carried over him, and with pine-pitch torches blazing all around him. The Cossack gunners took aim at him at once but the shot carried far beyond him, falling into the Gnyezna, while he stood as calm and silent as a statue and watched the new storm gathering at his feet.

The advancing Cossacks broke their rhythmic pace when they caught sight of him. They faltered and slowed down as if mesmerized and started to peer uncertainly at each other, while a deep murmur, laden with foreboding, swept along their ranks like the sighing of a cold wind among forest branches.

" . . . *Yarema! Yarema!*"

Stained crimson by the glow of fire on his silver armor, he must have seemed like a threatening giant sprung out of their superstitious folklore, and so a shudder ran through their weary bodies while their hands rose to make quick signs of the cross.

"Did you see?" they muttered to each other. "The cannon can't touch him . . ."

"*Div! Div!* Magic! Witchcraft!"

"He's some kind of Devil!"

He sat, unmoving, while they rolled heavily into the littered forefield before the entrenchments. Then he gave one short signal with his gold *bulava* and—immediately—the walls erupted with the crash of mortars and whine of grenades. The whole dark sky seemed to fill with the hiss and humming of these feared projectiles which arced down and fell, exploding among the stunned ranks of advancing Cossacks, so that they broke apart, collided with each other, and twisted like a reptile struck a mortal blow.

A yell of rage and terror swept the stricken masses and then came the fresh urgent shouts of their atamans and colonels:

"At a run . . . forward!"

The entire Zaporohjan army surged forward, charging headlong towards the shelter of the walls where they'd be safe from the grenades and rockets which the Cossacks never encountered anywhere before. But they barely managed to cross half the field when the Prince turned slightly to the west, and gave another signal, and long lines of horsemen started to emerge from the gap between the western lake and the unfinished bastion.

Out they came, trotting in tight military fours as if for review, and swung immediately with the cold skill of their long experience into a darkly glittering battle line that faced the flank of the attacking Cossacks. The bursting rockets and grenades illuminated the huge armored troopers of Skshetuski's and Zachvilihovski's *husarias*, the poppy-red and crimson dragoons of Kushel and Volodyovski, and the Prince's Tartar Light Horse under Rostvorovski. Trotting out behind them came the new brigades of Prince Yeremi's Household Cossacks and Valachian archers led by Ponyatovski and Byhovietz.

Not merely Hmyelnitzki but the least experienced recruit among the Zaporohjans could tell at once that the incalculable Prince was about to hurl the full weight of his entire cavalry into their open flank.

Cries of fear and warning rose in their milling ranks. The Cossack bugles began to sound retreat.

"Turn to face cavalry!" came the frantic orders.

Hmyelnitzki knew at one glance what was about to happen, and tried to reform his battle front and shield his infantry with horsemen of his own, but he had neither the time nor the drilled men for such a difficult maneuver. Before he could do more than shout the necessary orders the Prince's riders were in full gallop and hurtling down on his jostling and disoriented masses. And here again the unpredictable Prince Yeremi did something that neither Hmyelnitzki nor anyone else expected: he reversed a century of tradition and sent the armored mass of his *husaria* charging first like the iron head of a battering ram into the densely packed ranks of the Zaporohjans. They hurtled upon the Cossacks like a falling mountain. They seemed to fly across that bloody plain as if the wings that curved upward from their shoulders were real, and not man-made devices designed to goad their horses into greater fury and to protect the riders from the Tartar lariats.

"*Bij! Zabij!*"

Their rhythmic battle cry promised death to anyone who heard it.

The wind cracked and rattled through their wings as if they were eagles hurtling at their prey. Their lance pennons whirred and hissed like a pit full of serpents preparing to strike and their chainmail and armorplate ground and grated with a harsh metallic sound.

"Strike!" they cried. "Kill!"

Their long, wooden lances ripped open a yawning gateway in the dark human wall that turned to dust before them, and they crashed through that sudden void into a frenzied mass of men who barely had the time to clutch their heads before they were hurled down, thrown onto the spears of their own panicked comrades and trampled into the ground.

No one—not even the most feared and iron-willed commander—could have held those stricken foot regiments in place after that. They reeled, staggered and burst apart like a stone shattered with an iron bar.

A mindless panic seized the picked men of Hmyelnitzki's Byelotzerkvian guard. These were Yarema's Devils who were killing them! The Zaporohjans threw down their firelocks, spears, scythes, javelins and sabers and ran, with their fists clamped in their own hair and uttering a protracted wail of superstitious terror straight at the massed ranks of Tartars who waited behind them.

The Tartars, anxious to protect their own massed formations, met them with a shower of arrows, so they swerved desperately aside and fled along the whole curving length of their own vast wagon train, under the volleys of the infantry in the earthworks and the chain-shot hurled at them by Vurtzel's cannoneers. They ran in utter panic, abandoning all hope of surviving this cataract of fire, and fell so thickly under that hail of iron that it was seldom that one slain man didn't drop on the body of another.

★ ★ ★

Meanwhile, watching the disaster that overwhelmed the assaulting Zaporohjan masses, the fierce Tuhay-bey joined the hordes of Subaghazi and Urum-bey to his own and charged the *husaria*.

He entertained no hopes of turning this iron avalanche; that was beyond the means of his lightly armed and mounted Tartar horsemen. Nor did he care about the fate of the slaughtered Cossacks whom he had hated all his life. He merely wanted to hold up that crushing landslide of armored men and horses long enough for the Sultan's janissaries to form their battle square and for the fleeing Byelotzerkvians to recover from their pell-mell panic.

He charged like a man possessed by *djins* and devils, sabering and killing men with his own hand like a common Tartar, oblivious of his rank and ignoring danger. The short, crooked sabers of his warriors rang on the steel breastplates and cuirasses, their drawn-out wolflike baying overwhelmed every other sound on the battlefield, but they couldn't stop that glittering steel tide.

Thrown back on their horses' haunches, hacked and pierced by the long swords and crushed by the remorseless weight of the iron horsemen whom they weren't used to meeting head-on in the open, they toppled from their saddles like chaff before the wind. Beaten down and ground into the soil as if they were no more than a swarm of vermin, they fought with such single-minded fury that they managed to slow down the irresistible pressure of the armored riders, but each of them knew that it was only a matter of moments before they too would have to turn and run or be totally destroyed.

Tuhay-bey raged among them like one of those mysterious firestorms that spring out of the desert sands of Asia, devouring everything that stands in their path. Foam bubbled out of his twisted lips. His eyes blazed with madness. He pressed on, killing as he went, and his fierce warriors galloped beside him like a pack of young wolves running beside their mother, driven into a killing-frenzy by the reek of blood. That combined Turkish battle cry and prayer of 'Allah il-Akbar!' was already thundering in the field behind him, announcing that the janissaries had formed their ranks for battle and that the Tartar charge bought them the time they needed, when a powerful young *husaria* officer charged up to the maddened Tuhay-bey and brought his broadsword whistling down on the Tartar's head.

But either Pan Skshetuski hadn't yet recovered all his strength, or the Tartar's tall, high-pointed helmet forged out of the best Damascus steel, deflected the blow. Whatever happened, the long sword twisted on the foot-long spike of the Tartar helmet, struck the Bey's temple with the flat of the blade, and shattered like glass.

None the less, Tuhay-bey's eyes and ears filled with sudden blood. Darkness embraced him. He fell back into the arms of his howling warriors who finally broke and scattered, carrying him away.

★　★　★

All of the Prince's cavalry was now face to face with the Silistrian and Rumelian Turks, the Sultan's janissaries, and the regiments of renegade Serbian converts who had accepted Islam under Turkish rule. These were the most feared warriors of their time, the conquerors of all of Asia Minor, Syrian Arabia, North Africa and half of Mediterranean Europe from the ancient walls of Constantinople to the Lower Danube. They were formed out of the children of captured Christian slaves raised to manhood in the Sultan's military schools and didn't know any life other than that of iron discipline, obedience and war.

Now they formed a solid square, grim as a moving fortress.

Their steel caps and chainmail glinted coldly above their uniform white kaftans. They bristled like some strange, spiked prehistoric creature with twelve-foot pikes and halberds whose cutting blades were a yard across, grasping their scimitars and long-barreled ornamented muskets, as they made their slow retreat towards the wagon train.

The Prince's horsemen flew towards them as if carried by a hurricane and leading them, with a deep booming sound like a roll of thunder, galloped the *husaria* under Pan Skshetuski.

The young knight himself was riding in the front rank, as cold as ice and watching everything around him; and beside him, leaping in huge bounds on his Courland mare, rode Pan Longinus with his murderous Cowlsnatcher lifted overhead.

The great, white, steel-topped square halted and turned to receive them. Pikes and lances glinted. The long silvered barrels of Turkish muskets lifted towards them like a thousand darkly gleaming eyes. The hiss of the wind and the drumming of their horses' hooves deafened Pan Yan to his mens' battle cries, and his vision blurred as the open plain between him and the janissaries shrunk at a dizzying speed. Soon, he thought, the dark gap between him and that wall of spears would become measurable in heartbeats. And suddenly that wall was flaming from one end to the other with a red belt of fire. A swarm of musket balls whistled in his ears. Men cried out and groaned, saddles emptied, horses screamed and stumbled and cartwheeled to the ground. The charging lines shuddered and recoiled along their whole length but the mass of animals and men galloped on. The last few yards were narrowing into nothing. Skshetuski could see cruel faces, staring eyes. A sea of white turbans topped with steel. A hedge of spearpoints was glittering coldly in his own wide eyes and each of these, he knew, represented death. He also knew that no one would be able to stop or turn the maddened animals that carried him and his soldiers into that wall of spears.

But then, glimpsed suddenly out of the corner of an eye, a huge apparition rose above the spearpoints. A giant soared above the wall of pikes. The hooves of a great black mare flailed for a moment in the reddened air and then the animal and its rider plunged like a thunderbolt into the dense white ranks, smashing the deadly hedge into kindling wood, splintering the spears and trampling and destroying everything before them. It was as if a huge silvery bird of prey had fallen upon a huddled flock of snow-white herons in their winter plumage, tearing them apart with his beak and talons.

Pressed shoulder-to-shoulder, the janissaries couldn't fling themselves aside. Nor was there any way for them to stop Pan Longinus or to shield themselves from the havoc he wrought among them with his terrifying sword. He raged in that tightly-packed mass like a typhoon ripping through a forest. Kislar-Bak, a gigantic *Agha,* charged him desperately and fell, split in two. Whoever reached out towards him or tried to bar his way died as if struck by lightning. The stiff white ranks buckled, trying to escape from that unearthly giant, and grim warriors backed away in terror.

"*Div! Div!* A *djin!*" cried terrified voices.

And then the avalanche of winged iron riders swept in behind Skshetuski through the portals carved in those living ramparts by the Lithuanian knight, the four sides of the square burst outward like the walls of a collapsing building, and the massed janissaries spilled out in all directions, running for their lives.

Nor was that all. The Tartars, running like wolves towards the scent of blood, were galloping back into the battle under Subaghazi, while Hmyelnitzki—who managed to halt and reassemble his Byelotzerkiev guardsmen before they scattered among the wagons of the Zaporohjan *tabor*—was leading them back into the field to help the janissaries. But now all these masses crashed into each other, collided, lost all sense of order, and became yet another jumbled and confused mob of panicked fugitives.

Someone shouted that everything was lost. Someone cried out: "Treason!"

"*Tuhay-bey zabit!*" howled some fear-crazed Cossack. "Tuhay -bey's dead . . . Hmyel's taken! The atamans are running!"

"*Ludy! Spasayte!*" roared the panicked thousands. "Run for it, people! Save yourselves!"

And then all the frenzied Cossacks, Tartars, Turks and janissaries broke into headlong flight towards their fortified wagons and encampments, offering no resistance to the Prince's horsemen who cut them down like rows of harvest wheat. All of Hmyelnitzki's choice militia—the splendid Zaporohjan infantry and horsemen— and all the regiments and *tchambuls* of Turks, janissaries and Tartars, turned into a single shapeless crowd, blind and mad with terror, that trampled its leaders, overturned their cannon, and ran in mindless panic. They tossed away their weapons, banners, caps and even coats to run all the faster. The white cloaks of the janissaries sheeted the field like snow.

The armored riders had done their work in shattering resistance. Now it was the turn of the light cavalry to complete the rout. The chase was so savage that the leading ranks of Kushel's and Volodyovski's dragoons overtook the rearmost masses of the fleeing mob. Whoever managed to escape the sabers of Pan Michal's troopers in the first half-mile of the chase died during the second. The soldiers slashed and hacked at the bobbing heads around them until their arms grew too numb to lift a sword and the unarmed, helpless crowds didn't stop running until they reached the shelter of their wagons and Prince Yeremi's trumpeters called off the pursuit.

So ended the first meeting between Hmyelnitzki and the terrible 'Yarema.' The soldiers rode back singing and shouting out with joy, pointing with bloody sabers to the piled corpses of the enemy that littered the field, and trying to count as many as they could. But this was quite beyond anybody's means. Thousands had fallen there. The stacks of bodies piled along the earthworks reached higher than a man. The tired soldiers, dazed by the reek of carnage, reeled in their saddles as if they were drunk until a quick, light breeze sprung out of the lakes and blew these violent stenches towards the enemy.

Chapter Sixty-nine

THE BATTLE IN THE PLAIN was over for the night but the fighting at the far end of the earthworks was still raging fiercely when Prince Yeremi's victorious cavalry returned to the camp. What happened, as a mounted messenger galloped to inform Skshetuski, was that while the Prince was repelling the assaults aimed at the right flank of the entrenchments, Burlay almost made himself the master of the eastern end. Circling the castle and the town under the cover of the general assault, the canny old Steppe wolf brought his Transdnieper warriors quietly into the gap between the eastern lake and the ramparts manned by Pan Firley's soldiers. The castellan's redoubt was undermined by flooding during Thursday's storm, a part of the palisade had toppled and washed away, and the Hungarian infantry who were quartered there broke under Burlay's charge.

"Their standard-bearer was the first to run," the Prince's messenger reported. "And the rest of the regiment wasn't far behind him."

"And Burlay?

"Burlay got across the walls and into the camp. He came close to taking it, too! If it hadn't been for General Pshiyemski coming up with a few hundred Germans he'd have captured the castellan himself."

The Transdnieper warriors overran some Crown cavalry, took several cannon, and got as far as Pan Firley's quarters when Pan Pshiyemski came running up with a dozen companies of German mercenaries. He killed the panicked standard-bearer, seized the Hungarians' banner, and charged Burlay's horsemen while the Germans grappled with the Cossacks in his wake.

It was, as the messenger related, a battle to the death between Burlay's fierce and fearless *moloytzy* who savaged their enemy with all the fire and ferocity of their kind, and the hardbitten German veterans of the Thirty-Years' War whose stock in trade was iron discipline and courage. Burlay himself fought with the blind fury of a wounded boar. His men fought like demons. But neither their overwhelming numbers nor their contempt for death could stop the Germans who crushed them like a merciless machine. Thrown out of the camp and pressed against the earthworks, the Transdnieper warriors were decimated in an hour's fighting and pushed beyond the walls.

"Are they still there, then?" asked Pan Yan.

"They're still there, a couple of thousand of them. Still fighting in the angle of the lake, the river and the earthworks. Pan Konyetzpolski is bringing his *husaria* out against them."

"And what are my orders?"

"Join up with Konyetzpolski!" the messenger shouted, galloping way.

Skshetuski nodded. He dressed the ranks of his armored riders. Flashes of gunfire, the dim sounds of shouting, and the crackle of musketry in the near distance, showed him where to lead them.

*   *   *

Out in the bright-lit fields along the lake, Burlay knew that he was in a terrible position. His only avenue of escape to the Zaporohjan lines was the way he came. But since all sounds of battle had now ceased on the other flank, which meant that Vishnovyetzki must have beaten the right wing of Hmyelnitzki's army, his whole cavalry division would bar the road and cut off Burlay's regiments from their only refuge, so that the old Cossack general knew that his end was near.

Some help reached him in the form of Mrozovyetzki's horsemen a few minutes later, but in that moment young Pan Konyetzpolski's *husaria* appeared in the field along with Vishnovyetzki's own. These blocked his retreat, charged him, overwhelmed his Cossacks, and launched a massacre of a kind not yet seen that night.

Caught in that iron vise, Burlay's men had nowhere to go except to their deaths. Few of them bothered to beg for their lives. Thrown into disorder and then compressed by an iron ring that they couldn't break, they fought with grim disdain, contemptuous of dying, defending themselves either singly or in small, desperate groups. The battle turned into hundreds of individual duels and pursuits, brief savage clashes between little clusters of victims and killers, and deadly encounters in the pits and ditches and dark folds of land where some of the fugitives had crawled to hide themselves.

Subaghazi's Tartars galloped up to help but Pan Marek Sobieski, the brave young Starosta of Krasnostav, rode them down with his own *husaria*, and then Burlay knew that his life was over. Others might run, slipping through the darkness or trying to crawl to safety between the hooves of their killers' horses, but the fierce old warrior would have none of that. His Cossack fame was dearer to him than anything that life could bring him from that moment on. He'd sell his life dearly. He turned alone against his galloping tormentors, charging them like a lion and wreaking his own slaughter, and then searched the field for fresh enemies to kill. He caught Pan Dabek, a wealthy landowner serving in the Crown *husaria* of Pan Konyetzpolski, and cut him down with one stroke of his saber. He killed Pan Rositzki. He ran across Pan Aksak, the same brave young lad who covered himself with glory at Konstantinov, and killed him with one blow. He sabered Pan Savitzki and then two more winged and armored knights so that others began to back away from him with cries of amazement.

And then he caught sight of some fat, broad-shouldered knight, who was galloping alone across the battlefield bellowing like a bull, and charged after him.

★ ★ ★

Pan Zagloba, who had clung as close to Skshetuski as he could throughout the night's fighting, but who lost sight of him in the wild confusion of this new free-for-all, bellowed all the harder.

The last of his hair rose up in terror on his head as he turned his horse away from the charging Cossack. He may have been terrified out of his wits but he remained as clearheaded as a man could be in his circumstances. Ideas flashed and zigzagged through his mind like lightning, although none of them promised to do him a great deal of good. Great, flaming barrels of pitch were hurtling through the air, catapulted from the earthworks to illuminate the killing ground, and he kicked his horse as hard as he could towards them, praying that someone might see his plight and come to his aid.

"For God's sake, gentlemen!" he howled, catching sight of a larger group of Polish riders in the distance. "Help me if you care about your own salvation . . .!"

But nobody heard him. Burlay, meanwhile, was coming at him like an arrow fired from the darkness. Pan Zagloba scrunched down his eyes, groaned like an ox being led to slaughter, and realized that this time nothing and nobody could help him.

'*This is the end!*' he thought. '*I've had it . . . And so have all my fleas!*'

No one was hurrying to his aid, he could see. He wouldn't get away. He heard the hoarse, snorting breath of the Tartar horse on which the Cossack was coming up behind him, and longed for one of those tireless mustangs for himself. His own animal was grunting with exhaustion and ready to drop. Another step or two, he was certain, and it would all be over.

But in that moment which, he knew, contained the final seconds of his extraordinary life, all of his fear and despair turned suddenly into a savage rage. He became blind with fury at the thought that his sharp wits were useless. Useless? They were worse than useless! They were an impediment to that mindless action that alone could save him! Sweat burst out on his forehead. He bellowed frightful curses. Was his whole life to be exposed in its final moment as a cruel joke? Would his remaining seconds prove him a fake and a liar for the whole world to see?

"Never!" he roared, spun his horse around, clamped his eyes shut and charged his pursuer. "You're chasing Zagloba!" he shouted, blind with fear and rage, and slashed the air wildly with his saber, just as a new load of pitch-barrels flamed across the sky like a shower of comets and burst in the field.

The night around him was suddenly as bright as day and Burlay stared, astonished. Zagloba's desperate roar meant nothing to him. He never heard that name anywhere before. But he recognized the fat one-eyed man whom he knew as Bohun's faithful friend and whom he both enriched and entertained in Yampol only a few weeks earlier. Surprised, he hesitated. That flash of indecision doomed the old Steppe warrior. Before he could come to terms with what he was seeing, Pan Zagloba's blindly flailing saber slashed him across the temple and knocked him off his horse.

The yells of triumph that came from the armored soldiers at this sight were answered by the stricken wails of Cossack despair. The death of their famous leader, whom they revered as the best among them, sapped their strength and will. Those who were still alive no longer bothered to defend themselves. Those whom Subaghazi couldn't rescue were killed to a man because no one took prisoners that night.

Finally Subaghazi himself fled towards the distant wagon train, chased by Pan Sobieski and all the light cavalry in the camp. The assault was now beaten off along the whole line and the only sounds of fighting came from the Zaporohjan *tabor* where the pursuing Light Horse cut down the survivors.

★   ★   ★

A shout of joy and triumph swept across the entire besieged encampment and soared towards the sky. The bloodstained, weary soldiers, streaked with sweat and powder, stood on the walls leaning on their weapons and gasping for breath. Their smoke-blackened brows were still furrowed in the terrible concentration of hand-to-hand combat. Their eyes were still burning with the madness of the battle. But they looked ready to spring up again to fight if they had to.

Below them in the littered, corpse-strewn plain the cavalry was coming back from its own bloody harvest at the Cossack *tabor* and then the Prince himself rode out into the battlefield along with the three Crown generals, young Pan Konyetzpolski, Pan Sobieski and General Pshiyemski. The whole cavalcade rode slowly along the whole length of the entrenchments, inspecting the damage done to the fortifications, while the soldiers on the walls cheered their commander.

"*Long live Yeremi! Long life to our Father!*"

The Prince bowed his bare head to all of them in turn and saluted them with his gold *bulava*. "Thank you, gentlemen," he repeated in his clear, bright voice. "Thank you with all my heart."

Then, turning to General Pshiyemski, he said: "These entrenchments are too wide for us. Make them tighter. We must be able to come to each other's aid much quicker than we're doing."

Pan Pshiyemski inclined his head in agreement.

Meanwhile, a few dozen yards behind the generals' procession, a crowd of cheering soldiers hoisted Pan Zagloba to their shoulders and carried him into the camp as the day's greatest and most triumphant warrior. Ten pairs of arms lifted him high into the air while he flapped his own arms wildly to keep his lofty balance, a hundred voices hailed him as the army's champion, and his happy bellow echoed like a new cannonade among the crowded embrasures.

"Ha! I really gave it to him, didn't I! Easy . . . easy there, don't drop me for God's sake! We won't be seeing any more Burlaying in these parts, eh? Hey, watch out! Take care! I faked escape at first to draw him after me but then I gave him something to remember if he's got the time for memories in Hell! Hmm. Ha. Watch it now! I had to show a good example to some of our young people, after all . . ."

Redfaced, sweating and out of breath, Pan Zagloba knew that he was never happier nor more deserving of the cheers that thundered in his ears.

"Hey, careful there!" he urged. "Hold on tight, will you? Keep a good grip if you've got to hold me up at all and watch where you're going! Don't drop me, for God's sake!"

"*Vivat!*" cried the gentry.

"Phew . . . ." the old knight wheezed. "I don't mind saying that he put up a hell of a fight! One of the better ones I remember . . . Ah, but what pestilent times these are when any old cut-throat thinks he can cross swords with a noble . . . Tfui! But we taught those scoundrels something, didn't we? Careful, for God's sake! Put me down!"

"*Vivat! Vivat!* Long life!" cried the cheering gentry.

"To the Prince with him!"

"*Vivat! Vivat!*"

★   ★   ★

Quite another kind of shouting rang at the far end of the battlefield where Hmyelnitzki had run into his tent, tearing his clothes in fury, clawing at his face, and howling like a wounded animal.

Those of his colonels who had survived the night stood around him in grim and gloomy silence. None of them had anything to say that could make them feel better about the disaster. He, in the meantime, ripped the hair out of his head, bit his lips until they foamed with blood, and raged as if he'd been driven beyond the last bounds of sanity and reason.

"Where are my good regiments?" he went on shouting to himself. "Where are all my fine *moloytzy*? What will the Khan think about all this? What will Tuhay-bey have to say about it? Give me up to Yarema right now, why don't you? Go on, do it! Do it! Let him stick my head on a lance or nail it to a gibbet and be done with it . . .!"

The atamans kept their silence.

"Why did the witches tell me I'd win out?" the Hetman kept raging. "How come they were lying? Go get them! Slit their throats at once, the dog-loving bitches! Why did they promise me Yarema's head . . .?"

Normally, whenever he fell into one of his murderous rages, his colonels took care not to draw his attention to themselves. But now he'd been beaten. His luck seemed to be abandoning him. He had been trampled and humiliated.

"You won't take Yarema," Stempko muttered. "He's too much for you."

"You'll lose your neck and ours along with it," Mrozovyetzki growled.

"And who gave you Korsun?" The Hetman leaped at them like an infuriated tiger. "Who brought about Yellow Waters? Who won at Pilavtze?"

"You did," Vorontchenko barked into his face. "But Vishnovyetzki wasn't there!"

Hmyelnitzki seized himself again by the hair and stared around blindly like a drunken man. "I promised the Khan he'd sleep in the castle tonight," he wailed in despair.

"What you promised the Khan is your own hard luck," Kulak said. "You watch out for your own neck with him. But don't you push us into any more assaults! Don't you waste our people! You get their walls ringed with some of our own, put up our own batteries and earthworks, and you start up a real siege! Or it's going to be the end for you!"

"You watch your step!" other grim voices muttered.

"You watch yours!" snarled Hmyelnitzki.

Then he reeled wildly like a pole-axed steer and threw himself down on a pile of sheepskins covered with sleeping-robes and carpets in the corner of his tent. The atamans stood around him in a gloomy circle.

"Vodka!" he ground out hoarsely.

"You're not getting any!" Vyhovski snapped back. "Not tonight, you're not. The Khan will send for you any minute now. You've got to stay sober."

★　★　★

The night moved on. Warm, silent and fanned with a silken breeze, it seemed like a time removed by centuries from the battlefield, distant by a mile and veiled by darkness, so that not even the far-off murmur of the cannon had troubled the Khan. He sat at peace in that balmy stillness, surrounded by his *beys* and *aghas* and religious *mullahs*, and chewing honeyed dates piled on a silver tray beside him, while he waited for the news of victory. Every so often he glanced up at the starry firmament. It was, he thought, as endless as the love of Allah for his faithful children. His cushions, prayer-rugs and carpets were spread outside his pavilion under the open sky so that he might breathe the quiet, fragrant air until he could savor the new triumph that was promised to him.

"Allah is great," he murmured.

He was untroubled by the slightest doubt. Logic and faith permitted only thoughts of death for the unbelievers and victory for himself.

Then he heard urgent hoofbeats. He looked up. He saw Subaghazi leaping from his saddle. Love flooded him at the sight of his favorite nephew who was the shining example of an Islamic warrior: brave, faithful, true to Allah's will, unable to speak anything but the truth. If the unbelievers had their Roland to sing about, Subaghazi was the exemplar of the Faithful.

But this time Subaghazi's gilded chainmail and helmet were scarred and dented and streaked with dust and blood. His eyes were veiled with grief. His chest heaved as if each breath brought him a new shard of pain as he bowed and waited for permission to intrude on his master's silence.

"Speak," the Khan said.

"Great Khan," the young general salaamed, beginning the formula without which the Khan of all the Tartars couldn't be addressed. "Most mighty ruler of all the Hordes. Grandson of the Prophet. Lord of all wisdom. Lord of happiness and fortune. Lord of the Tree of Knowledge known in the West as it is in the East. Lord of the Flowering Tree . . ."

The Khan gestured briefly, stopped the flow. He felt a sudden fleeting touch of doubt, perhaps even fear, and needed time in which to compose himself. He spat out the handful of dates he was eating and passed them to one of the respectful *mullahs* who began to chew them with every sign of pleasure. Meanwhile, Devlet Giray's sharp, hooded eyes studied the pain and grief and despair in Subaghazi's face. The dark blood that streaked it and clotted on his armor seemed suddenly like a terrible insult to Allah and himself.

"Speak quickly, Subaghazi," the Khan said. "And speak well. Is the camp of the unbelievers in our hands?"

"God did not grant it, Lord!"

"The *Lahy*?"

"Victorious . . ."

"Hmyelnitzki?"

"Defeated."

"Tuhay-bey?"

"Wounded, Great Lord!"

"Allah's will," the Khan said and, after a moment, asked softly: "How many of the Faithful have gone to Paradise this night?"

Subaghazi raised his stricken eyes and pointed at the glittering night sky. "As many as there are stars glowing under the feet of Allah."

The Khan's fleshy face became suffused with blood. A terrifying anger seized him and shook him like a desert lion tearing at his prey. His slitted dark eyes narrowed even further.

"Where is this dog," he snarled between his teeth. "The one that promised I would sleep this night in Yarema's castle . . .? Where is this hissing serpent whom God will trample with my foot . . .? Let him come here and account for his lying tongue!"

A dozen *murjahs* left at once to fetch Hmyelnitzki while the Khan brought himself gradually back under control. Anger, like joy, might be taken as a comment on the will of Allah which every follower of Islam accepted without question and as naturally as breathing. It could also be taken as a sign of weakness. An inscrutable serenity, the Khan knew, had always been his most successful weapon.

"God is one," he murmured softly, bowing in submission. "His will is the Law."

Then, noting again the blood that caked Subaghazi's lean and handsome features, he gestured to him to rise from his knees and to step towards him. It was a sign of great favor and kindness.

"Whose blood is that, Subaghazi?" he asked. "Yours or theirs?"

"It's the blood of the unbelievers, Lord," Subaghazi said.

"Tell us how you spilled it and please our ears with the exploits of the Faithful," the Khan ordered.

Here Subaghazi gave a full but concise account of the entire battle, praising the heroism of Tuhay-bey, the Khan's cousin Galga and the *Nurraddin*. Nor did he pass over Hmyelnitzki's generalship and courage. On the contrary, he praised the Cossack Hetman along with all the Tartar heroes, ascribing the night's catastrophe to the will of Allah and the unprecedented fierceness of the unbelievers.

One aspect of the tale, however, struck the Khan with particular significance. "You say, then, that at first the unbelievers didn't harm our people?"

"They did not, Lord. They fired only at the Cossacks. Their horsemen struck the Faithful only after we barred their way."

"Allah . . ." the Khan murmured. "They didn't want war with me, it would seem."

"It seems not, Great Lord."

"But now it's too late . . ."

"Why is it too late, Lord?"

"The blood of the Faithful lies between us now, Subaghazi," the Khan said, nodding quietly and lowering his eyes so that no one might read them, or guess the thought of changing sides which occurred to him again.

★ ★ ★

He sat deep in contemplation, and wondering if it were indeed too late to make his peace with the Commonwealth and turn against Hmyelnitzki, when the Cossack Hetman himself appeared before him. Hmyelnitzki's raging agony was long over by then. He approached the Khan with his head held high, staring straight into the Tartar's eyes, and with a calm, untroubled mask of confidence spread across his face.

"Come closer, traitor," the Khan hissed, feeling his rage boiling up again.

"I see no traitors here," Hmyelnitzki said firmly. "I see only your faithful ally, Mighty Khan. One to whom you promised your help in the face of every kind of fortune, not just when it smiled."

"Go sleep in the castle like you promised!" the Khan ground out between his teeth. "Go pull the *Lahy* from their burrows by the neck, like you swore you would!"

"Great Khan of all the Hordes," Hmyelnitzki addressed him in a strong, calm voice. "You are the greatest and most powerful ruler on earth, second only to the Sultan of the Turks! You are wise and cunning! But can you send an arrow to the stars or measure the depth of oceans?"

The Khan showed a flicker of astonishment, quickly veiled.

"No, you can't," Hmyelnitzki spoke with even greater calmness and assurance. "That lies beyond even your great powers. In just that same way I couldn't measure the full extent of Yarema's pride or his contempt for you."

" . . . Contempt?"

The Khan's astonishment was giving way to anger. No one had ever used that word in reference to himself.

"Contempt," Hmyelnitzki pressed. "Disrespect. Lack of that abject fear and submission which is your natural due by the will of God! Who could have expected that he'd fail to fear you? That he wouldn't humble himself before your greatness and beg for your mercy? How could I guess that he would dare to raise his arm against you, spill the blood of your finest warriors and jeer at you, Great Monarch, as if you were the least of your *murjahs*? If such a thought ever occurred to me then you'd be right to call me a traitor."

"*Bismillah!*" the Khan exclaimed, even more astonished. He stared at Hmyelnitzki with curiosity and perhaps even a measure of respect.

"And this too I must say," Hmyelnitzki went on with new power and assurance in his voice and posture. "You are great and mighty. All the Kings and peoples of the East and West bow down before you and call you a lion. Only Yarema refuses to fall on his face when you come before him."

"God will punish him," the Khan murmured, eying the Cossack Hetman as if he never truly noticed him before. "If that is His will . . ."

"It is!" Hmyelnitzki said. "It must be!"

"And why must it be?"

"Because if God doesn't grasp that *Lah* princeling by the neck with your mighty hand and throw him to the ground, and if you don't use his bowed back for a stepping stone when you mount your horse, all your great power will be as good as nothing! All your fame and glory will fly off with the wind! The world will say that if one *Lah* lordling can show such disrespect to the Crimean Khan and escape unpunished, then there can't be very much to fear from the Tartars! And what will happen to the sources of your power after that? Who'll tremble at your frown or throw himself on his face at your coming? Who, Mighty Ruler, will pay you tribute in exchange for peace? Who'll still be able to fear you?"

The Khan did not reply.

The silence spread until Hmyelnitzki thought that he'd be unable to stand it much longer. He had staked everything on one desperate gambit. He thought he knew his Tartars but no one could ever be certain what they'd think or do, and none of them would utter a word until the Khan had spoken.

The silent *murjah* lords, the *mullahs* who interpreted the Koran, and the *beys* and *aghas* who led the Khan's armies, stared at their master's face as if it was the sun, watching for any cloud that might pass across it. They hardly dared to breathe without his permission but Hmyelnitzki knew that they'd throw themselves on him like famished wolves at a single sign of the Khan's displeasure. He, in turn, sat with closed eyes, his face as smooth as soapstone, revealing nothing behind his mask of serene indifference. The night, Hmyelnitzki thought, was as still and chilling as if it was Winter.

"I hear your words," the Khan said at last.

"I wait to hear yours, Mighty Lord," Hmyelnitzki said calmly.

"Hear this, then." The Khan nodded quietly. "I will bend Yarema's neck. I will use his back to mount my horse. I will break his pride and grind him into dust so that no one, either in the East or in the West, will be able to say that one dog of an unbeliever had dared to oppose me."

"God is great!" all the Tartar lords cried out in one voice.

"That is the will of Allah," the Khan said.

Joy passed like lightning across Hmyelnitzki's face. He knew that the incalculable Tartars depended at least as much on the fear they could evoke in their enemies as they did on their *tchambuls*, hordes and armies. But, even so, the risk he'd taken was like nothing he ever tried before.

He expelled a long and careful breath, averting his eyes from the watchful *murjahs*. At one bold stroke, as dangerous as it had been brilliant, he turned away the sword that hung over his head and changed a doubtful and uncertain ally into a faithful one.

"That lion knows how to turn into a serpent," the Khan murmured softly as he watched him mount his horse and ride away back to his own encampment.

★   ★   ★

No one slept in either camp that night. A deep droning murmur came all night long from the Polish earthworks as from the Cossack lines outside. But in the battlefield between them there spread the stillness and the silence of the dead.

Moonlight crept whitely among those fallen warriors whose sleep was for ever. It sought out its reflection in the broad pools of drying blood; it found new mounds of slain animals and men as it wandered about the battlefield and drew them for a moment out of darkness; it looked into the blindly staring eyes and brushed the livid faces, and its own soft light paled even more as if terrified by what it encountered.

The battlefield was silent but it wasn't altogether lifeless. Its stillness was deceptive. Dark shadows moved about it, singly and in groups, like evil spirits who feast on the fallen. These were the camp servants and lackeys who'd come to rob the dead in just the way that jackals might trail lions to their kill. But even they didn't scurry through those fields for long. Some superstitious fear drove them away from these heaps of pierced and emptied bodies which, only hours earlier, had been among the living.

There was something gripping and mysterious in that peaceful stillness of enemies who had no more harm to do to one another, and in that quiet harmony, beyond either love or hatred, with which these silent Poles and Turks and Tartars and Cossacks lay next to each other or clasped each other in a last embrace. The wind rustled now and then in the thickets around the battlefield; and the soldiers on watch in the earthworks thought they could see the dead men's souls wheeling above their bodies; and when the church bells in the town tolled the midnight hour, it seemed as if vast flocks of birds had lifted suddenly from the entire plain that crouched between the walls of Zbarajh and the Zaporohjan *tabor*, and rushed into the sky.

The sentries huddled behind their parapets, listening to strange, tearful voices moaning in the air; they heard a profound subterranean groaning; and sweat burst out on their foreheads as they made hasty signs of the cross and whispered quick prayers. Those who expected to die in the coming battles, and who thought that their ears were better tuned to the calling of unearthly voices, swore that they heard the souls of the dead Poles offering themselves for judgment to God, while the spirits of the slaughtered Cossacks moaned '*Chryste, pomyluy*' as they circled upward.

The watchers whispered that since these men had fallen in a fratricidal conflict their souls couldn't fly straight to the eternal light but were doomed to wander through dark voids, and to fly with the wind above scenes of pain and desolation, and to weep with rain, until God forgave their sins against each other and granted them the peace of mutual understanding.

But at this time, they knew, human hearts could grow only more embittered, and they listened in vain for some angel of harmony and forgiveness flying above the field.

Chapter Seventy

EARLY NEXT MORNING, even before the sun climbed into the sky, there were new walls ringing the Polish camp. The entire army had worked with picks and shovels through the night, officers and the senior regiments of *husaria* along with the rest, and it was only shortly before dawn that they could throw themselves down to sleep.

The living slept as heavily as the dead. Only the sentries peered towards the enemy who had worked just as hard, and slept just as deeply, taking a long time to stir after their disaster.

Skshetuski, Pan Longinus and Zagloba sat in a tent over a tureen of steaming ale soup thick with aged, yellow squares of floating farmers' cheese, and talked about the successes of the night before.

"It's been my custom to end my day at sunset and start it at sunrise," Pan Zagloba said. "Which is the way the heroes of antiquity used to live. But it's hard to keep that up in wartime. You sleep when you can and you wake when they blow a trumpet in your ear. I'm not complaining, mind you, but what makes me angry is that we've got to turn our lives inside out because of a lot of worthless, disobedient peasants. There's just no more respect for age, virtue and merit nowadays! Still, we paid them well last night for the inconvenience, didn't we? Eh? What? A few more paydays of that kind and they'll learn to let us sleep in peace."

"Does anyone know how many of our people fell in last night's battle?" Pan Longinus asked.

"Ah, it wouldn't be many." Full of hot ale and his own fresh stature as the army's champion, Pan Zagloba was in his new element as an expert warrior. "It's well known that it's the attackers who suffer the greater losses in a siege. You may not know as much about it as I do, because you haven't seen as many wars as I have, but old campaigners like me and Pan Skshetuski don't have to count corpses to see how things stand."

"Maybe I'll learn a bit about it with such friends as the two of you," Pan Longinus murmured.

"You would if your wits were as sharp as your sword," the fat knight said at once. "But the way they are I doubt if even you could lift them off the ground."

"Stop teasing the man," Skshetuski threw in quietly. "This isn't the first time that Pan Podbipyenta had a whiff of gunsmoke. And God grant the finest knights a chance to do as well as he did yesterday."

"One does what one can," the Lithuanian sighed. "Maybe not as much as one would like, but still . . ."

"Yes. Well. I don't deny that you put up a fairly decent show last night," the fat knight remarked loftily and combed the ends of his mustache upward with his fingers. "It's not your fault if some others made you seem somewhat puny in comparison."

The Lithuanian sighed again and stared at the ground. Perhaps he was thinking about his ancestor Stoveyko and the three elusive heads. Perhaps his thoughts had turned to warmer memories of Krakow and Anusia. But at that moment the tent flap lifted and Pan Michal stepped under the canvas, as pleased with himself as a lark on a sunny morning.

"Well, now we're all together again!" Pan Zagloba cried, brightening up even more at seeing his small friend. "Give him some beer! And I'll take a little more myself to keep him company."

The Little Knight pressed his friends' hands warmly and squeezed in beside them at the small camp table.

"You've never seen as many cannonballs as there are lying outside on the parade ground," he said with pleased excitement. "A man can't take a step without tripping on one."

"Yes, I know. I know. I took a stroll myself around the camp this morning," Pan Zagloba said. "It'd take two years for all the hens in Lvov province to lay that many eggs. If only those were eggs, eh? Wouldn't we have an omelet? I'll take a bowl of scrambled eggs and fatback over anything, as long as it's a big one! That's my soldier's nature. That's also why I'm fonder of a good fight than some of these young snot-noses we've got in the army nowadays who'll grab their guts and groan the moment they've eaten something a little bit greasy."

"Speaking of fighting, though," Pan Michal broke in. "I must say that you showed me a side of yourself yesterday that I never expected to see! To cut down Burlay like that! That man was famous all across the Ukraine! And in the Turkish world as well!"

"Eh? What? Not bad, hmm?" Pan Zagloba was always pleased to hear himself praised and this praise was all the sweeter coming from a swordsman like Volodyovski. "That really was something, wasn't it? But it's not the first time, my dear Michal; no, not by a long shot! I've had a few good moments of that kind before! Still, I've got to say that we're a matched set, the four of us, aren't we? There can't be another quartet like us in the whole of the Commonwealth. By God, with the three of you at my side and with the Prince to lead us I'd take on the Sultan himself!"

★   ★   ★

Loud exclamations coming from outside the tent interrupted further conversation so the four knights stepped out to see what was happening there. Day had already come, the sun was rising steadily into a clear sky, and a thick crowd of soldiers was standing all along the earthwall looking out curiously into the countryside.

The broad vistas of the plain had changed through the night and went on changing even as they watched. The Cossacks hadn't been idle since their last assault. They raised high bastions of their own, hauled up heavy cannon of such range that there was nothing like them in the Polish camp, and dug concealed traverses and approaches which zigzagged towards the Polish earthworks like enormous molehills.

The whole landscape seemed to have erupted with these excavations. Black, new-turned soil marred the grassy meadows across all the space between the distant Cossack wagon train and the Polish earthworks, and swarms of men were working everywhere that the knights could see. The bright caps of the *moloytzy* were already gleaming along the parapets of their nearest walls.

Prince Yeremi was standing on his own new redoubt with Pan Sobieski and General Pshiyemski, while slightly below them, on the forward slope of the Polish glacis, Pan Firley trained a long looking-glass at the Cossack diggings.

"I see the enemy's starting a regular siege," he said to Pan Ostrorog beside him. "It looks to me like we should give up our camp and move into the castle."

"God keep us from anything like that!" the Prince called down to him cheerfully from above. "We'd be trapped and starved there in no time at all! No, no, gentlemen! This is the place for us, right here on these walls!"

"That's what I think too," broke in Pan Zagloba. "Even if I've got to kill a Burlay every day! I protest in the name of the entire army against the opinions of the castellan!"

"That's none of your affair, Mister!" the Prince snapped at once.

"Keep quiet," Volodyovski hissed and tugged at the fat knight's sleeve. "What's the matter with you?"

But the old noble was feeling too full of himself for any words of caution. "We'll smoke them out of those holes of theirs like badgers!" he went on. "And I'll beg Your Highness to let me lead the first sally against them. They already have good reason to know me, the scoundrels, so let them get to know me even better!"

"A sally?" The Prince narrowed his brows in thought. "Hmm. Wait a minute. The evenings get dark quickly this time of the year . . ." Then, turning to the three Crown generals and to Pan Pshiyemski, he said: "Please join me for a consultation, gentlemen."

He made his way off the earthworks, and the senior officers followed him down into the camp, while Pan Volodyovski turned his shocked eyes on the pleased Zagloba.

"What in God's name do you think you're doing, breaking in like that while generals are talking? Haven't you heard about military discipline? His Highness is a kind and forgiving master but don't you dare to fool with him in wartime!"

"Ah, what the devil!" The fat noble shrugged, grinning from ear to ear. "He's not the first great commander I've advised and none of them were any the worse for it. I know how to talk to high-ranking people. And anyway, did you see how pensive he became when I suggested rushing those Cossack molehills? If

God gives us a good success with a sally who'll be responsible for it, eh? You?"

At that moment they were joined by Pan Zachvilihovski who stared for a long moment at the Cossack trenches, bastions, revetments and approaches.

"There they go, rooting about in the ground again like a pack of hogs. Earthworks have always been their specialty, you know. Few people do it better."

"If they were hogs we'd have nothing to complain about," Pan Zagloba said immediately. "Because we'd have pork sausage for a groat a yard! As it is, their carcasses aren't fit for even dogs to chew on. Pan Firley's men had to dig new wells today over by their lines because the East Lake is so full of corpses that you can't see the water. Come Friday, we won't be able to eat the fish because they'll be stuffed with Cossack meat. Father Zabkovski is particularly worried about that. He says that our supply situation isn't all that good and he's got a belly like a silo."

"Hmm. That's true enough," the old commissioner said, nodding in quiet wonder. "I'm an old soldier but I haven't seen such a slaughter since the Turkish War when the janissaries stormed our camp at Khotim."

"You'll see even more," Zagloba said grandly. "I'll guarantee you that!"

"Yes. Well. I expect I will. But I think they'll try us again today at nightfall if I know anything about them. Or even sooner than that."

Zagloba shook his head. "And I'm telling you that they'll leave us alone until at least tomorrow."

But he no sooner spoke when long plumes of smoke bloomed in the Cossack bastions and a flock of fire bombs hissed across the wall and burst in the camp.

"Well, what do you expect from a pack of peasants?" the fat knight muttered, irritated to be proved wrong so quickly. "How would the likes of them know anything about the arts of war?"

★ ★ ★

Pan Zachvilihovski's judgment proved even more correct before the day was over. It became clear to everyone in the Polish camp that Hmyelnitzki was settling down to a regular siege. He cut all the roads and trails leading to the town, blocked all avenues of ingress and exit, stopped the supplies of food and fodder from entering the earthworks, built bastions, batteries, entrenchments and redans and sapped towards the Commonwealth defenses with covered approaches, but the assaults went on as before. Even Pan Zagloba was forced to concede that the Cossack Hetman had set out to wear down the defenders with unrelenting pressure all along their line, and to keep them sleepless, anxious and on edge with uncertainty and fear, until they were too weary to fight any longer.

A new massed assault went in against Prince Yeremi's bastion just as the old commissioner predicted. The Cossacks charged as soon as the sun began to set but with no better results than before. They were beaten back with even greater losses because the *moloytzy* didn't attack as fiercely, nor were they as eager to reach the Polish walls, and so they stayed longer under the hurricane of fire hurled at them by the infantry and Vurtzel's cannoneers.

The next day passed in an unending Cossack cannonade. Their covered underground approaches snaked so close to the Polish earthworks that even musket fire could reach the defenders, and the innumerable dugouts that dotted the plain all around the walls smoked from dawn to sunset like miniature volcanoes. There was no open battle that day in the sense of a face to face encounter between the two armies; instead there was an uninterrupted firefight that lasted ten hours. Once in a while a few troops of the defenders rushed the nearest of the Cossack molehills and then there'd be a flurry of sabers, flails, scythes and spear-fighting. But they no sooner crushed one cluster of Cossack sharpshooters when a new crew of marksmen occupied the trenches. There wasn't a moment of rest for the soldiers in the Polish earthworks throughout the whole day. And when the sunset finally brought some hope of a respite, another mass of Cossacks, *tchernya* and Tartar volunteers stormed the walls.

At nightfall on July 16 the two fierce Zaporohjan colonels Hladko and Nebaba attacked the Prince's bastion once again and once more they were beaten back with a heavy loss. Three thousand of the best and bravest Cossacks were killed along the ramparts; the rest, pursued by Pan Sobieski, fled in utter panic as far as their *tabor,* abondoning all their weapons and precious powder-horns which the defenders recovered to replenish their own shrinking stocks.

No better luck crowned the efforts of the shrewd and savage Ataman Fedorenko who used the cover of a dense fog at dawn to break into the town itself. Pan Korf repelled his *moloytzy* with a charge of Germans, while the *Starosta* of Krasnostav and young Pan Konyetzpolski slaughtered all but a few of the survivors during their pursuit.

★   ★   ★

But all of this paled beside the terrible firestorm, both earthly and celestial, that raged above the Polish earthworks on July 19.

During the night before, the Cossacks raised a tall rampart in front of Prince Yeremi's lines where they emplaced a battery of heavy cannon that rained its shot on the Vishnovyetzki men all day. Then, as soon as the first stars glittered in the sky, tens of thousands of them gathered for attack. At the same time several dozen siege towers appeared in the distance and began to roll heavily towards the entrenchments. On they came, like enormous windmills, with bridges raised like crooked wings at their sides, and with light swivel guns and firelocks blazing from their tops. Red with the glare of gunfire and then, in turn, vanishing in their smoke, these frightening apparitions seemed like gigantic colonels marching before the vast crowds that flowed after them.

"That's what the Cossacks call 'hulay-horodyny,'" the soldiers told each other on the parapets. "It's us that Hmyel's going to be grinding in those mills."

"Look how they roll," others whispered. "Listen to them, will you? They're as loud as thunder."

"Turn the cannon on them!"

Vurtzel's gunners began to send grenades and iron shot at those grim machines but since they were clearly visible only when the muzzle blasts tore apart the darkness they were almost impossible to hit. Meanwhile the dense mass of Cossacks flowed ever closer, like a dark tide rolling in from an invisible horizon.

"Phew," Pan Zagloba found time to complain. "I've never been this hot and sweaty in my life. Not after sundown anyway! The air's so close and stifling that there isn't a dry thread left on me anywhere."

He was sitting on his horse beside Skshetuski, and the rest of the cavalry who were formed up in the intervals, while sweat poured down his face as if he'd just stepped out of a Turkish steam-bath.

"The Devil gave them those cursed machines, that's certain," he grumbled. "I wish God would split the ground ahead of them and let Hell swallow all of them! I've had my fill of those scoundrels, and amen to that! There's neither time to sleep nor anything worth eating in this place. Stray dogs live better than we do! Phew . . . what heat . . . Have you ever known such a steamy night?"

The night air was, indeed, heavy with moisture and thick with the stench of the unburied dead whom Hmyelnitzki ordered left to rot in the fields all around the earthworks to add to the defenders' discomfort and aid the spread of sickness. Low clouds hung darkly in the sky, promising a storm. The soldiers sweated in their heavy armor and gasped for breath as if they were drowning but at that moment drums began to rattle in the darkness.

"They'll be charging now," Skshetuski said quietly. "Do you hear the drumming?"

"I hear it, may the Devil pound their flea-bitten hides! It's enough to drive a good man to despair!"

"*Koli! Koli* . . .!" the vast mobs roared, throwing themselves into a headlong charge against the entrenchments.

The battle flared along the whole length of the Polish line. The Cossacks struck the walls held by Vishnovyetzki, Lantzkoronski, Firley and Ostrorog all at the same time so that none of them could go to another's aid. Inflamed with *gojhalka*, which Hmyelnitzki ordered them to drink by the bucket before the assault, the howling masses charged even more fiercely than before, but that merely added to the defenders' obstinate resistance. The fearless spirit of their indomitable leader imbued the soldiers to such an extent that they sought out the most desperate positions and the deadliest dangers. The dour, hard-handed 'Kwarta' infantry, formed for the most part out of Mazurian peasants, fought with the ferocity of the boars and wildcats that infested their distant, lakeland forests; they tore at the Cossacks with their teeth, clawed and strangled them with their bare hands, and clubbed them with their muskets, until both they and the Cossacks turned into a single, heaving mass in which no one could tell a friend from an enemy.

Several hundred of the best Zaporohjan infantry fell under the blows of the enraged Mazurians, but fresh mobs came pouring in at once to cover them completely. The fighting reached such a degree of savagery along the whole entrenchment, and the attackers were so tightly locked with the defenders, that all of them— both the Poles and Cossacks—seemed like a herd of monstrous, prehistoric reptiles entwined in a deadly struggle at the dawn of time.

The heat of red-hot musket barrels scorched the hands of the reeling soldiers. They gasped for air, strangling in the smoke and the press of bodies. The officers lost their voices. Skshetuski's and Sobieski's cavalry galloped time and time again into the Cossacks' flanks, trampling entire regiments in their deadly charges, but the battle went on, unremitting, hour after hour because Hmyelnitzki threw one fresh, charging mass of men after another to fill the great red gaps torn in the Cossacks' ranks. The Tartars helped by sending clouds of arrows arcing down on the defenders and by driving new masses of *tchernya* forward with their rawhide whips.

And suddenly the earth heaved and shuddered under the warriors' boots. The entire sky blazed with a lurid glare as if God himself could no longer bear to look down at the horrors wreaked by men below. The clouds exploded with a sheet of fire, lightning streamed down as thickly as if it were hail, and the huge sound of thunder drowned out all the human shouts, musketry and cannon.

It seemed to the dazed masses of struggling men as if the sky had burst along with the storm clouds and that it was hurtling down upon their heads. The air itself appeared to be burning; it blazed around them like one vast, living flame and then everything in sight disappeared in impenetrable darkness only to be revealed once more by the glare of lightning. A hot wind roared across the battlefield whipping away tens of thousands of caps, battle flags and banners and hurling them out of sight; the thunderbolts crashed down as fast and furious as a madman's drumming; and all the sounds and sights of that bloody night vanished in the chaos of fire, thunder, darkness and the wind as if the Heavens themselves became as crazed with violence as the men below them.

A storm of such intensity and power that not even the oldest men ever saw before, raged above the town, the castle, the camp and the Zaporohjan wagons. The battle bogged down at once and then dissolved in water, as the clouds split open and rain flooded down with such a blinding force that no one could see beyond a hand's reach into the darkness. All the dead and wounded heaped in the moats and ditches were swept away in that roaring torrent; the Cossack regiments broke off their assault and ran for the distant shelter of their camps; and all their cannon, powder carts and wagons were swamped and sucked down by the flood which rushed across the open plain behind them as if in pursuit.

The sudden cataracts washed away most of the Zaporohjan earthworks and revetments, rushed along their trenches and flooded the covered demilunes and dugouts, even though each of these had been roofed with logs and thick slabs of turf and ringed with moats and ditches of their own.

$$\star \quad \star \quad \star$$

The storm raged on, doing what all the Cossack cannonading and attacks failed to achieve before: it drove the defenders off the walls and sent them running for shelter to their tents which the howling gale seized, shredded and carried off at once. Only the glistening steel ranks of Skshetuski's and Sobieski's armored knights, who were forgotten in that headlong rush and never received their orders to withdraw, sat on their horses in that roaring downpour hour after hour.

They stood like that as if in the middle of a lake while the maddened elements around them began to return gradually to normal. The storm, driven by its gale, flew towards the west. The rain turned into a thin, cold drizzle which dwindled out altogether shortly after midnight, and stars began to glitter here and there among the passing clouds. Within another hour the level of the muddy water in which they were standing started to drop, the flooded countryside before them began to drain and dry, and then, seemingly out of nowhere and with no warning of his coming, Prince Yeremi himself appeared before Skshetuski.

"Is your powder dry?" the Prince asked.

"Yes, Highness," Pan Yan said saluting.

"Very good. Dismount your men, wade out to those mobile siege towers, pack your charges in them and set them on fire. Pan Sobieski will go with you. Just make sure you're quiet about it!"

"Yes sir," Skshetuski said.

Then the Prince caught sight of the sodden, shivering Zagloba. "You wanted a sally, didn't you? Now you have what you wished for. So be off with you too!"

"That's all I needed," Pan Zagloba muttered. But, fortunately for him, the Prince had already ridden too far away to hear his grumbling and complaints.

★ ★ ★

Half an hour later the five hundred knights shed their wings and armor and ran sword in hand and waist-deep in water towards the silent *'hulay-horodyny'* which were bogged down in the mud a quarter of a mile from the walls. Pan Yan led one troop of them. Pan Marek Sobieski led another. He was known as 'the bravest of the brave' in the Polish army; he'd find a hero's death in another Cossack war just a few years later; and his younger brother would become King John III Sobieski, the conqueror of the Turks and savior of Christendom at Vienna; but that was all a long time ahead. Now he ran with the dismounted horsemen through the Zbarajh mud like a simple soldier. Camp servants carried tubs of pitch, dry torches and kegs of gun-powder behind them as they swooped down on the Cossack dugouts like wolves on a sheepfold.

Pan Volodyovski, who loved such expeditions more than anything, attached himself to Skshetuski's squadron. Next to him marched Pan Longinus with the naked Cowlsnatcher in his fist and looming over everyone else around him. Between them, and vainly trying to match his step to the trotting of the little knight and the long strides of the Lithuanian, ran the wheezing, muttering and complaining Zagloba.

"*'So you wanted a sally, did you?'*" he mocked Vishnovyetzki's words. "'*Off with you, then.*' And off with all this bloody-minded nonsense. A mad dog wouldn't go to a wedding on a night like this. May I never get to drink anything but water if this is the kind of sally that I had in mind! I'm not a duck and my belly's not a river barge! I've always hated the taste of this stuff, even without peasant carcasses rotting in it everywhere you look, but this is more than even my forgiving nature can stand without complaint."

"Keep quiet," hissed Pan Michal.

"You keep quiet! You're not much bigger than a trout and you swim like one too, so it's easy enough for you! But it's a different matter with someone like me. I'll even say that it's a mean-hearted thing for the Prince to do, sending me out like this. Wasn't the killing of Burlay enough of a service? What else does Zagloba have to do to earn a little peace and quiet for himself? You'll all be in fine shape when you've worn him out, mark my words. And, for God's sake, make sure you pull me out if I fall into some hole, will you? If I'm to drown let it be in a barrel of good mead, not this stinking water!"

"Keep quiet, father," Skshetuski ordered gently. "There are Cossacks sitting in those dugouts over there. They'll hear you."

"What Cossacks? Where? What are you talking about? I don't see any Cossacks!"

"Over there, under those mounds of turf."

"Cossacks?" The fat noble groaned. "My God, didn't they run for cover with the rest of them? Don't they know any better than to stay out in a storm? May lightning strike the lot of them! Now I've really come to the end of my rope!"

Pan Michal put an end to the fat knight's complaints by clamping his hand across Zagloba's mouth because the low mounds of earth were now barely a scant fifty paces away. They crept towards them as softly as they could. The water splashed with each step, and the mud sucked greedily at their boots, but the rain started to fall again and its rustling covered up whatever sound they made. No one could have expected a sally after such a storm, and on the heels of an assault as violent as the one they repelled that night, so there were no sentries posted around the dugouts. Pan Michal and Pan Longinus were the first to reach the line of artificial hillocks where the little knight began to call out softly in Ruthenian.

"Hey, people! Hey!"

"What do you want?" rumbled the voices of the Cossacks under the turf lids.

"Orders from the *tabor.*"

"What about our relief?"

"It's coming in a minute."

"*Slava Bohu,*" the sleepy voices answered. "God be praised for that."

"So how about letting me in there?"

"What's the matter, don't you know the way?"

"I know it now," said Volodyovski, groping for the trapdoor over the entry hole.

He found it, threw it open and jumped in. Pan Longinus and

half a dozen others jumped in after him and the mound erupted with a howl of terror. The raiders gave one loud, threatening cry of their own and charged into all the other dugouts, and the rainy darkness filled with sudden shouts, pistol shots, cries of pain and fear and the clash of steel.

Dim forms leaped out of the greater darkness. Some ran. Others fell facedown into the water. The Cossacks, caught for the most part in their sleep and cut down before they could reach for a weapon, hardly bothered to defend themselves. It was all over in less than a quarter of an hour.

"To the towers!" shouted the *Starosta*.

"Burn them from the inside!" Skshetuski ordered. "The wood's too wet outside!"

But the order wasn't easy to carry out. The huge siege towers, built out of thick, solid trunks of untrimmed pine and sheeted with wet oxhides, had neither doors nor any other openings. Cossack sharpshooters and scaling parties climbed into them on ladders while their light cannon were hauled up into the roof gallery on ropes. The knights milled around them aimlessly, hacking at them with sabers and tugging at the joists without much effect until the camp servants came running with the powder charges, pitch barrels, torches, sledge hammers and axes.

But before the hacked, wet tree trunks could be set on fire Pan Longinus bent down and lifted an enormous boulder that the Cossacks unearthed from the foundations of a dugout.

Four of the strongest men in the kingdom could hardly have managed to shift that huge slab of granite. But he raised it high above his head, swayed with it back and forth for a moment while the veins bulged out with effort on his forehead, and hurled it at the nearest tower. The boulder hissed like a thunderbolt through the air while the awed knights scattered and ducked their heads. Struck dead-center where they'd been joined together, the timbers cracked wide open, the wall of tree trunks parted like a shattered door, and the siege tower crashed down to the ground.

"A Hercules, by God!" cried the cheering knights.

In moments, the toppled timbers were doused with pitch, set alight and burning. Within a half hour some sixty giant torches of that kind were blazing in the rain. Stempka, Kulak and Mrozovyetzki came running with several thousand *moloytzy* to save their siege engines but the flames had bitten through to the dry core of the timbers and the huge *hulay-horodyny* burned beyond control.

Showers of sparks shot high into the sky. Columns of fire rose like scarlet pillars under the thick, black thatch of smoke and cast a blood-red glow all across the plain. Their leaping flames reflected in a thousand pools that seemed to turn the countryside into a burning lake.

★ ★ ★

Meanwhile the dismounted knights were marching back to the Polish earthworks where a crowd of soldiers had climbed up on the parapets and cheered them from a distance.

Pan Yan was tired. He'd had next to no sleep in the week of fighting and the strain was showing on him as much as on everybody else. Images from the past flickered before his eyes. Helen's pale face glowed dimly in his memory and vanished in darkness. Bohun's bitter stare blazed suddenly before him like twin yellow torches. Scenes of carnage . . . the tens of thousands of slaughtered men that littered all the battlefields on which he had fought, the scorched countryside and the massacred populations that cried out for vengeance . . . pressed in upon him and made his vision shake.

He had stifled all of his own anger. He suppressed his bitterness and buried his despair. He turned himself into a stone so that he'd neither think, love, care or remember. But now, among the glad cries of his victorious men and the cheers of the soldiers massed on the walls ahead, he felt as stricken with regret and pity as if a new calamity had fallen upon him. A year and a half of a merciless civil war had gone by. God only knew how many more would follow. And what would be left of the country in the end?

Nothing but ruins. Provinces torn away. The tears of thousands. Mourning for tens of thousands. Unforgiving hatred passed onto unborn generations in the form of legends.

"Peace," he whispered thinking of a monastic cell. Forgetfulness. Oblivion.

He was marching in the rear of the returning column to make sure than no exhausted soldier fell out to be left behind. Pan Zagloba was wheezing happily beside him—splashing and snorting like a buffalo through the ebbing water—and too glad

to be getting back to the safety of the camp to pretend that he
hadn't had enough danger for one night. That, Pan Yan knew,
would come later over a keg of ale with Pan Longinus and
Volodyovski. But Skshetuski couldn't see his other two friends
anywhere. The burning towers made the night as clear as day all
the way to the crowded walls ahead but Pan Longinus and
Volodyovski were nowhere in sight.

"Halt!" he cried out, suddenly cold as ice.

"What's wrong?" cried Zagloba.

"Michal and Pan Longinus aren't with us!"

"What? What? Are you sure? Where are they, then? What's
happened to them?"

"I don't know. Perhaps they went after some Cossacks hiding
in some hole. Perhaps they just got carried away and didn't hear
the order to withdraw. Whatever happened we can't go back
without them."

"I should say not!" Pan Zagloba cried.

Pan Sobieski came running back from the head of the column
to ask what was happening, but in that moment both the
missing knights appeared in the plain about halfway between
the burning towers and the halted column. Pan Longinus
stalked with long cranelike strides through the crimson water,
his gleaming Cowlsnatcher in his fist, while the little knight was
galloping at full speed beside him. Both held their heads turned
towards a swarm of shouting Cossacks who were running in a
thick mass after them.

"They'll die!" the fat knight howled as if the worst thing that
he could imagine was about to happen. "For God's sake, let's
run back! Let's help them!"

The red glare of the fires showed the flight and pursuit as
clearly as if the scene was painted upon canvas, and suddenly
Pan Yan knew that he hadn't been stripped of everything that
was precious to him; that he still had something valuable to lose;
and that as long as he had friends that he cared about there was
something else in his life that could be taken from him.

"They won't die!" he said quietly and ordered his men back
into the field.

"For God's sake, hurry! Hurry!" Pan Zagloba howled.
"Those damned dogs will bring them down with muskets!
They'll shoot them full of arrows!"

And mindless of the odds ahead, or that a new battle could

begin in the next few moments, the fat knight charged out into
the field with his saber raised high overhead. He tripped, fell
into pools and mudholes, scrambled up again, limped and
stumbled, cursed, bellowed, gasped for breath, and ran as if all
those enraged *moloytsy* and *tchernya* were at his heels instead of
before him. Pan Yan, Pan Marek Sobieski and the other knights
hurried at his side.

But the *moloytzy* didn't use either bows or firelocks to bring
down their quarry. Their bowstrings must have softened in the
downpour and the rain had soaked the priming in their fire-
arms. Instead they pressed ever closer after the two retreating
knights with swords, scythes and spears. Several dozen of them
ran out ahead of the rest, and they were almost within reach of
the trotting pair, when the two knights stopped and turned on
them like a pair of boars pursued by hounds and hunters. Their
raised weapons flashed in the scarlet light and the Cossacks
stopped to wait for the rest of their running pack. Pan Longinus, who towered over his small companion like an upright
bear over a cub, must have seemed particularly awesome with
his gigantic sword.

They made their way across the field, running and turning
now and then with a threatening shout, and each time their
pursuers halted to wait for greater numbers. Only once did one
of the Cossacks run at them with a scythe but Pan Michal leaped
towards him, nimble as a lynx, and killed him with one blow.

The Cossacks came on but the ranks of Skshetuski's soldiers
were also drawing closer with the bellowing Pan Zagloba
charging far ahead.

Then, suddenly, the bastions behind them erupted with fire.
Grenades and rockets arced into the air and plunged down on
the pursuing Cossacks, trailing streams of fire. A cry of terror
rose among the *tchernya*. The high-pitched warbling sound
made by the grenades as they spun and tumbled in their flight
drove the bravest of them into mindless panic unless they were
drunk because they saw them as yet another proof of 'Yarema's
witchcraft.'

"*Spasaytes, spasaytes!*" fearful voices began to shout among
them. "Christ have mercy!"

Their ranks recoiled. They broke and scattered whenever the
rockets hissed down and exploded among them. And then the
running masses halted and began to ebb.

★   ★   ★

Meanwhile Pan Longinus and the little knight reached the cheering ranks of Skshetuski's soldiers where Pan Zagloba threw himself on them as if he'd gone mad with joy. He clutched at one of them after the other, embracing them and cursing them in turn, so as not to show how worried he had been about them nor how moved he was by their escape.

"Damn your souls!" he shouted. "What kind of soldiers are you, anyway, to lag that far behind? Didn't you hear the orders to withdraw? I'll be the first to turn you in for punishment to the Prince! He ought to have you tied to a horse's tail and dragged through the camp by the heels!"

"It wasn't all that bad out there," the Lithuanian giant said with his gentle smile. "They weren't coming really close to us, except for a few. And the grenades frightened them off anyway."

"And what about the fright you gave the rest of us?"

"Don't tell me you were worried about us?" Pan Michal grinned at the fat knight.

"Worried? Of course I wasn't worried. Why should I be worried? Who'd care about a couple of fools who can't tell when the job is done and it's time to go home to sleep? I thought for sure that we'd be singing a requiem for you two in the morning, that's all . . ."

"But you ran to help them harder then all the rest of us," Skshetuski remarked.

"What if I did? I'd rather fight than do nothing while people I know are getting their throats cut, even if I don't care about them one way or the other . . . But I suppose all's well that ends well, so let's thank God that we're all back in one piece and can get our throats wet in celebration! I'm just angry that those grenades chased off all those Cossacks before I could get at them."

Then the returning soldiers marched into the camp while the army cheered. Hmyelnitzki's 'hulay-horodyny' burned for the rest of the night in the plain behind them.

Chapter Seventy-one

THE STORM WREAKED its havoc in the Polish earthworks just as it did among the Cossack trenches, and the walls had to be torn down and rebuilt even closer to the center of the camp, retreating grimly into a tighter circle. Once again there was no rest for the weary soldiers. Their losses during the last assault whittled down their numbers so that even the new entrenchments of the night before were too spacious for them.

But the besiegers worked just as hard as the besieged. Having crept up quietly in the night of Tuesday, July 20, they ringed the entire Polish camp with a second earthwall, much taller than those of the defenders, and unleashed a hurricane of gunfire that lasted without a break for four days and nights. From time to time huge crowds of Cossacks and *tchernya* leaped up as if to attack but they drew back short of the Polish walls. The point of these sudden surges and withdrawals was to wear down the defenders, keep them constantly on the alert and force them to expend their precious ammunition. Hmyelnitzki who had a quarter of a million men under his command could change his fighting units every hour. But there was no relief for the soldiers in the Polish camp. The same men worked the guns, raised new barricades and shored the defenses, crouched with their muskets behind whatever cover they could find on their riddled walls, leaped up to face assaults, dug new wells and buried the dead.

Exhausted men threw themselves down behind their parapets in a dazed half-sleep and dozed on and off in a waking nightmare among the dead and dying. The musket balls rained on them so thickly that, in the morning, the camp servants would sweep the lead out of the camp with brooms.

For four nights and days no one in the camp had time for warm food. Their damp, sweated rags dried on their bodies, scorching them in the hot Summer sun and chilling them at nightfall. They gnawed hardtack and chewed on dried meat but their mainstay was the harsh, homebrewed *gojhalka* which they laced with gunpowder to give it more bite.

They were, as Prince Yeremi knew, ready for anything, wanting nothing more than to know that they were giving up their lives for something of value. They abandoned all concepts of mercy, even for themselves. They seemed to find a wild, derisive joy in everything and accepted horror with as little caring as if each of them had fallen in love with danger, wounds and killing. Even the great landed nobles serving in their ranks took a savage pleasure in their own hunger, sleeplessness, disease and exhaustion as if any form of comfort insulted their manhood.

The terrible cannonade went on day after day but this rain of lead and iron merely inflamed their will to fight. The various regiments competed with each other in the ferocity of their contempt for death, indifference to hunger, endurance under fire and the back-breaking labor of rebuilding their battered defenses.

They were so ignited with a lust for battle, and they acquired such a thirst for blood, that their commanders couldn't keep them on the walls after an attack; once they had beaten off an enemy assault they'd charge out in their own turn and claw their way up the Cossack ramparts like starved wolves tearing at a cattle pen.

And everywhere, in every regiment of whatever kind, there was a dark, contemptuous sort of humor underlying every feat of courage as if it were a point of honor to despise the heroism which had become as common and unremarkable as killing and dying.

★ ★ ★

One evening, as he was making his inspection rounds along the walls, Prince Yeremi heard the musketry slackening in the bastion held by the Leshtchynski Regiment.

"So why aren't you shooting?" he asked the soldiers there.

"We're running out of powder, Highness!" they cried out. "We've sent to the castle for some more."

"The Cossacks' powder barrels are a lot closer," he said.

He barely finished speaking when the entire regiment leaped off the wall, charged across the killing ground between the entrenchments, and stormed the Cossack cannon. They clubbed down the *moloytzy* with their muskets and whatever weapons they grabbed on the run, spiked four guns, and half an hour later their decimated companies were back in their own trenches with a sizable supply of gunpowder in kegs and hunting horns.

After that, whenever the cry of *"Powder! Ammunition!"* echoed along the line, the regiments would leap up and charge the Cossack cannon. Any commander who sent for ammunition to the castle was jeered off the wall.

★　★　★

A week passed like that. Another week began. The Cossack tunnels and covered dugouts crept ever closer to the Polish earthworks. Soon they were sapping under the walls while their sharpshooters were firing from such close range that they were killing ten men in each company every day, not counting those who fell in repelling new Zaporohjan charges.

The priests could no longer comfort all the dying with the Sacraments; there were just too many of them to reach in time even though the walls were shrinking every day. The living crouched behind overturned carts from sunrise to sunset and masked their positions with skin and canvas screens but that hailstorm of bullets found them none the less. The dead were buried after dark wherever they'd fallen and their comrades fought all the harder on their graves.

The commanders showed no more mercy for themselves than the men they led. Prince Yeremi slept on the bare earth at the foot of the walls, drank *gojhalka* and ate salted horsemeat like the most deprived of his 'Furrow Soldiers,' sharing their privations as if he'd been doing it all his life.

Young Pan Konyetzpolski, who was one of the greatest and richest magnates in the Commonwealth, and Pan Marek Sobieski, the powerful and wealthy *Starosta* of Krasnostav, went out on night raids as if they were no better than the poorest of their common soldiers, charged the enemy in the first rank of their men, and stood on the walls without armor in the thickest of the fighting to set an example during the assaults. Even such inexperienced leaders as Ostrorog, whom the soldiers wouldn't trust before, seemed to become new men under Prince Yeremi's eyes. Old Firley and Pan Lantzkoronski fought and slept in the trenches beside their men, while General Pshiyemski spent his days working at the cannon and his nights in sapping under the Cossacks' approaches, tunneling under their mines with mines of his own, blowing up their dugouts, and opening up those secret access routes through which the soldiers carried death and terror to the sleeping Cossacks.

Hmyelnitzki poured out his people's blood as if there'd never be an end to it but every new attempt to overwhelm those stubborn defenders brought him only fresh and greater losses. He counted on time to drain the strength, endurance and the will to resist out of this handful of besieged soldiers, noblemen and gentry but time passed and they merely fought him all the harder.

Finally, he tried negotiations.

On a late afternoon in the last week of July, during one of the fiercest firefights since the siege began, the Cossacks in the burrows closest to the wall began to cry out to the soldiers to stop shooting.

"Hold your fire, *pa'ny! Ne strilat!*"

"Why should we?" cried the soldiers.

"Our Hmyel wants to talk!"

"So let him go talk to the Devil if he wants to," Pan Zagloba shouted, safe behind the angle of the wall, but the shooting started to die down none the less.

"It's bound to be a trick," Pan Marek Sobieski said to Skshetuski. "Don't you think?"

"I don't doubt it for a moment. But even one hour's ceasefire would be a welcome break. Let's use it to get some hot food for the men."

"And to repair the damage."

Prince Yeremi must have had the same thought in mind because shortly afterwards all the trumpets in the Polish camp began to sound the long, wailing call for cease fire. The Cossack siegeworks bloomed like a Spring meadow with the brightly colored caps of the *moloytzy*, their own cannon were no longer firing, and a Zaporohjan officer rode up under a white flag to invite old Pan Zachvilihovski for a talk with the Cossack Hetman. Men staggered to their feet along the parapets like the dead returning from the grave, stretching their numbed backs and shoulders, and rubbing the harsh residue of burned gunpowder from their eyes. The thick black clouds of smoke began to drift away and a deep, breathless silence crept back into the battlefield. But after all those days of endless gunfire, musketry, cries, curses and explosions, the sudden stillness seemed as loud as thunder.

Unbelievable as this may sound to anyone who didn't live through those nights and days of fire, it seemed to everyone as if the war was over and peace had returned. The smoke drifted off the battlements. A blue, untroubled sky reappeared above them. After a short consultation with the King's commanders, the Prince allowed Pan Zachvilihovski to meet with Hmyelnitzki, and the soldiers gathered on the earthwall could see the Zaporohjans bowing to him as he rode into their lines. In his short time as a Commonwealth commissioner for the Ukraine he had won the affection and respect of the savage brotherhood and even Hmyelnitzki honored him for his integrity. But to the weary gentry on the walls it seemed as if the old order, shattered forever by that year of war, had been suddenly restored.

In the meantime the gunfire ceased all along the line. Both sides kept a sharp eye on the other, neither would trust the other ever again, but each had won new respect in those weeks of fighting and now a series of cautious meetings took place all along the littered no-man's land. The Cossacks came sidling up to the walls along their covered trenches, the knights came down the slope of the glacis towards them, and they began to talk to each other as naturally and calmly as if a sea of spilled blood didn't lie between them.

None of this surprised anyone who understood the strange blend of admiration and contempt, and of love and hatred, which lay under the centuries-old relationship between the free-booting Cossacks of the Steppes and the warrior gentry. No matter how the nobles pretended to despise the Cossacks they always treated them with more respect than they showed to the common *tchernya*; now, recognizing their courage and stubbornness in battle, they talked to them as equals. The Cossacks, in their turn, looked with admiration and curiosity at that lions' lair which barred their way so stubbornly along with all the might of the Tartar Khan. So they stood chatting like old neighbors, complaining about all the Christian blood that was being spilled, and sharing each other's *gojhalka* and tobacco.

"Ey, *pa'ny lytzari*," the older Zaporohjans said, nodding with admiration. "If you'd always put up that kind of a fight there'd never have been a Yellow Waters, Korsun or Pilavtze . . . You must be devils, not just men. We haven't seen anything like you in all our born days."

"Come back tomorrow and the day after and you'll find us just the same," the knights answered.

"We'll come back, you can count on that. And we'll find what we'll find . . . Meanwhile God be praised for a little breather."

"So thank him if you need it."

"Maybe we need it, maybe not. There's a lot of good Christian blood flowing here for nothing and God only knows if it's in a good cause. But hunger's going to get you down in the end, that's for sure."

"The King will be here before we get hungry," the soldiers said and hoped that this was true. "Our camp's well provisioned. We've plenty to eat."

"And if we run short of food we'll come looking for it in your wagon train," Pan Zagloba added.

"Well, let's hope old *bat'ko* Zachvilihovski gets something worked out with our Hetman. 'Cause if he don't, we'll be storming you again at nightfall."

"We're looking forward to it," the knights said in turn. "You'll find a hot welcome, as usual."

"The Khan swore he'd feed all your corpses to his dogs."

"Our Prince swore that he'll tie the Khan by the beard to the tail of his horse."

"He's got strong magic, there's no denying it, but it won't be strong enough in the end."

"You think so? You'd do better to go with our Prince and us against the heathen," the knights said. "Instead of raising your hands against authority."

"With your *Knaz*, eh? Hmm . . . That might'n have been so bad . . ."

"So why are you rebelling? The King's on his way here. You'd do well to be afraid of him. And *Knaz* Yarema himself was like a father to you . . ."

"Him? Ha ha! He was a father like death is a mother! The plague didn't kill as many good *moloytzy* as he's done!"

"He can do even worse. You don't know him yet."

"And we don't want to know him either . . . Old men say

among us that once a Cossack sets his eyes on him then he's sure to die."

"They've got that right. And that's how it's going to be with Hmyelnitzki too."

"*Boh znayet sh'tcho budet.* God knows what's to happen. It's for sure that the world's too small for both of them to walk on it together. Our *bat'ko* Hmyel says that if you'd just bring him Yarema's head he'd let you all go free and bow to the King along with all of us."

But at this point the soldiers started to snarl, frown fiercely and slap their sheathed sabers.

"Silence! Or we'll draw on you!"

"Ey, *serdyte Lahy*," the Cossacks said, nodding in quiet understanding. "There's no fooling with *Lahy* like you . . . But you'll all go for dog meat none the less."

★   ★   ★

And so they talked through the quiet, warm evening as if time had rolled back for them all beyond the origins of hatred and suspicion. Sometimes their words were friendly. Sometimes a threatening note rumbled in them like thunder. The night passed peacefully although every man in the camp worked with picks and shovels to shore up the defenses wherever the Cossack cannon had done the most damage and the work continued after the morning muster on the walls.

Pan Zachvilihovski came back after noon. The negotiations were broken off before they could properly begin. Hmyelnitzki, drunk and raving, demanded the heads of Prince Yeremi and Pan Konyetzpolski before he'd give any thought to an armistice. Then he launched into a long list of Cossack grievances and started pressuring the old knight to stay with him and join the rebellion. That was enough for Pan Zachvilihovski who leaped to his feet and left in disgust. He barely had the time to reach the Polish walls when the war horns sounded in the Cossack lines and another all-out grand assault roared towards the earthworks and raged for two hours before it was bloodily repulsed. This time the defenders not only drove the Cossacks away from the walls but charged them in their own fortifications, capturing their foremost siegeworks, tearing down their covered loopholes and blowing up the dugouts, and setting fourteen more siege towers on fire. Hmyelnitzki swore before the Khan that night that he wouldn't lift the siege as long as a single man remained alive in Zbarajh.

★ ★ ★

Dawn brought another day-long cannonade, tunneling and mining and then a fierce, twelve-hour hand-to-hand battle with sabers, clubs, scythes, iron flails, stones, lumps of earth, wagon poles, fists, teeth and nails. The friendly feelings expressed the day before gave way to an even more implacable savagery and hatred. Great nobles, gentlemen-troopers, foreign mercenaries and peasant foot-soldiers swore to fight to the last man and never to surrender even though the grim specter of famine made its first appearance among them.

Rain drizzled on and off all that day and the soldiers were issued with half rations for the first time since the siege began. Pan Zagloba ranted half the night about that but, for the most part, empty bellies merely drove the knights to a greater fury. The Cossacks attacked dressed as Turks to give the impression that a great new Turkish army had come to support them but they fared no better than before. Then, until dawn, and setting the pattern for every night thereafter, the battle broke down into a series of individual challenges and duels fought out in the no-man's land between the two armies. The musketry and cannon fire boomed and rattled through the night without a moment's pause. The combatants fought each other singly and in troops of several dozen horsemen under the glare of exploding shrapnel-bombs and rockets. No one would fight Pan Longinus, whose awesome reputation in both armies had come to match his size, but the little knight, whose puny stature misled the foolhardy, attracted many challengers who didn't live long enough to regret their error.

Pan Zagloba also went out every night but only to duel with his tongue because, as he explained, after killing a man of Burlay's stature he couldn't cheapen himself by fighting unimportant people. But when it came to exchanging jibes, taunts, threats and insults from a distance, he didn't find an equal among the infuriated Cossacks.

"Sit here at Zbarajh, you peasant scum!" he'd bellow out of some hole in the ground, well covered with turf, so that his deep, booming voice sounded as if it came out of the bowels of the earth. "Sit here with us while the Lithuanian army's marching down the Dnieper! They're paying their respects to your wives and daughters right now, and you know it! Come Spring, you'll find a lot of little Lithuanian cabbage-heads growing in your houses. That's if you find the houses!"

This would enrage the Cossacks all the more because it was true. While Hmyelnitzki drove his armies west into the Commonwealth, stripping Byelorusia, Volhynia and the Ukraine of all their defenders, the Lithuanian army of Prince Radzivill was on its way out of the north, sweeping down the whole course of the Dnieper, burning and slaughtering everything they found in their path.

Driven to desperation by Zagloba's taunts, the Cossacks answered him with a hail of bullets but he kept his head well down behind cover and bellowed all the stronger.

"You missed, dog-souls! But I don't miss, ask Burlay when you shake hands with him in Hell! Come here, you flea-bitten mongrels! Try your teeth on me! Shoot while you can because next Spring you'll be washing diapers for little Lithuanians or digging out the sewers for the Khan! Come on then, what's holding you? I'm waiting! Spit in your Hmyel's face for me, you hear? Tell him it's from Zagloba! Well, what do you say to that, you turd-shovelers? Aren't there enough of your carcasses rotting in these fields? You stink like dead dogs which is only right because your mothers were bitches, every one of them, and only the Devil knows about your fathers! Get back to your plows and pitchforks, you jumped-up peasant cut-throats! Back to the galley-sweeps with you! That's what God made you for, you mangy clodhoppers, not to make nuisances of yourselves and annoy your betters!"

The Cossacks hurled back their own taunts about *'great lords who rush out three at a time after one crust of bread,'* and they asked, jeering, why the masters weren't coming around this year for their rents and tithes, but sooner or later Pan Zagloba bellowed them into a raging silence among wild bursts of laughter, curses, and the unending crash and rattle of cannon and muskets.

★   ★   ★

By this time the siege acquired its own natural order; it became a deadly everyday routine of massed assaults at nightfall, sniping at dawn, day-long artillery bombardments, counterattacks and sallies between firefights with cannon, mortars, rockets, muskets and handguns of all kinds, desperate cavalry charges from behind the walls, and bloodshed without precedent in history.

Pan Yanitzki, who had been the late King's envoy to the Khan and spoke the Tartar language as well as his own, rode out several times under a flag of truce to start negotiations but the Khan merely repeated his promises to Hmyelnitzki. "You'll all be *kensim*," he threatened. "You will all be corpses."

"You've been promising us that from the start!" the envoy finally retorted, having lost his patience. "And nothing's happened to us yet! He who comes to get our heads also brings his own!"

The Khan did propose a meeting in the open field between his Grand Vizier and Prince Yeremi but that turned out to be a trap which was uncovered in good time and put an end to all further parleys. A strange sort of exaltation seized those gaunt, bedraggled soldiers in their tattered uniforms and rusted armor who stood on the walls of Zbarajh night and day, in any kind of weather, with broken weapons in their hands and a mad, glaring light in their red-rimmed eyes.

No one looked for surgeons if they were hit and wounded. No one left the trenches. The wounded man would merely wrap a dirty rag around his bloody head and go on fighting along with everybody else, and if anyone dared to say the word 'surrender' he was hacked and torn into living pieces on the spot.

Nothing surprised these soldiers. Nothing daunted them. None of them gave a thought to the future, knowing that only one of two eventualities could end their days in Zbarajh: relief and rescue by the King's assembling new army or death, whichever came first; and the more unlikely their survival seemed, the less they cared about giving up their lives. They went to battle as if to a wedding, driven by such contemptuous indifference for their lives and such a lust for danger that odds of a hundred to one seemed barely sufficient. Troops of a few dozen men fought off attacks by hundreds and each day witnessed a score of times when they charged out of their entrenchments and attacked ten times their own numbers. They became so inured to the constant roar of guns and explosions that those of them who were called down from the parapets for an hour's rest slept without noticing a sound.

★ ★ ★

In the meantime Hmyelnitzki watched and listened. He never doubted the military genius of Yeremi Vishnovyetzki, nor his ability to inspire other men and win their devotion, but now even he had moments when he wondered if he was fighting some supernatural being.

At nightfall, when it seemed to him that wounds, hunger, illness and exhaustion would have disarmed the strongest men alive, and as he gathered up his own seething masses for another murderous assault, he would hear singing among the explosions in the Polish earthworks.

"They're singing," he'd mutter, staring blindly at his gloomy colonels. "How can they be singing?"

"Yarema," they shrugged in reply.

He could believe then that the Transdnieper prince was truly a magician whose occult powers dwarfed the skills of all the witches, prophets, soothsayers and enchanters he dragged along in his own wagon trains.

Night after night he howled like a mad dog. He clawed at the furs and carpets in his tent. He drowned his fearful visions in buckets of *gojhalka* and tore the hair out of his head and mustache. He flew into a wild rage, all the more impotent because he saw his own star dimming beside that of the hated Vishnovyetzki, and then he'd send his tens of thousands charging to their deaths.

The Cossacks sang about this *Knaz* Yarema as if he was a hero of their own. Songs full of awe and fear and hate and admiration. Their campfire tales whispered about him as an apparition from another world.

"That's not a man," the grizzled old Zaporohjan warriors murmured while the young Cossacks stared.

"Not a man, father? Not even a magician?"

"He's an evil spirit."

"*Hospody pomyluy!* God have mercy on us!"

"He comes at night, out of nowhere. You look, and there is nothing . . . nothing. There is only darkness. And then you see him. On his horse. On the wall. Shining like silver and growing right in front of your eyes until his head is higher than the castle towers . . ."

"*Hospody pomyluy!*" the young *moloytzy* whispered. "And then what do you see?"

"His eyes are like two red moons. The sword in his hand is like that bloody star that God sends into the sky as a sign of doom . . ."

"A comet?"

"God knows what to call it. But when you see it you know that you're not much longer for this world. Aye, and when he cries out . . . when you hear his voice . . . do you know what happens?"

"No, father. No. What happens?"

"All the dead *lytzari* rise up from the field and take their places in the ranks along with the living."

"*Div! Div!* God help us! The dead rise up, you say?"

" . . . I seen 'em myself. I heard the way their armor creaks and rustles in the night wind . . . the way it shines bloody red in the moonlight . . ."

"*Hospody pomyluy!* How can we fight him, then, if he calls up the dead?"

"Nobody can fight a spirit."

Ballads sung in fear. Tales told in wonder. And in that telling, under all that hatred and superstitious terror, there was a strange, primitive devotion and a sense of boundless admiration with which these proud Steppe warriors worshiped their destroyer.

The Cossacks loved their terrible Yarema even as they hated everything he stood for and Hmyelnitzki knew it. He saw himself shrinking beside Yarema's legend. As Vishnovyetzki's reputation soared so his own stature dwindled not only in the eyes of the Khan and the Tartars but in his own people's eyes as well.

He knew that he had to take Zbarajh at all costs. He had to bring down that legendary rival or his own name would lose all its magic for the Zaporohjans and if that happened he'd be swept away like the awesome shades of a stormy night before the glow of sunrise.

Meanwhile, the Vishnovyetzki legend grew and swelled each day. The terror and the carnage seemed to nourish the spirits of the defenders while the *tchernya* and the Cossacks were starting to lose heart. They began to murmur doubts about their Hetman's wisdom in bringing them there. They started wondering if he was as invincible as they thought he was.

Hmyelnitzki raged at them but he knew that he couldn't blame them.

They too were suffering in the smoke and fire and the stench of the unburied dead. They too faced death every day in the assaults and in the hail of bullets. The heat of the burning July days and the chill of night tormented them no less than it did Vishnovyetzki's soldiers. But Hmyelnitzki also knew that death, privations and discomfort weren't the reasons why they were losing their will to fight. War was the Cossacks' natural element. Storms, bloodshed and a proud, fierce courage were the staples of their way of life. His brave *moloytzy* had no fear of death but they feared Yarema.

Part Eleven

Chapter Seventy-two

MANY SIMPLE SOLDIERS would cover themselves with glory in those Zbarajh earthworks. Their names would pass into the country's folklore to be murmured with reverence on cold Winter nights. They would become the stuff of poetry and legends from which future generations drew sustenance and strength in their own times of trouble. But no one earned greater fame than Pan Longinus Podbipyenta whose feats of courage found their match only in his gentleness, humility, and love for his friends.

Weeks passed.

July ended as bloodily as it had begun. Another ten days of bombardments and assaults went by.

And then there came a night of such unnatural stillness as if the besiegers were finally beaten to their knees by their own attempts to wear down the defenders. None of the usual jeers and calls and curses came from the Cossack trenches which had crept up to within thirty paces of the Polish earthworks. A thick, dull rain hissed softly to the ground.

Prince Yeremi's armored regiments were on dismounted duty in the camp that night. The soldiers dozed behind the parapets, leaning on their weapons. From where they stood on the wall, listening to the whisper of rain in the moat and peering out into the moonless night, Skshetuski, Pan Longinus, Zagloba and Volodyovski heard only the soft notes of a Cossack ballad strummed in a nearby dugout, the far-off neighing of the Tartar horseherds in their pastures, and the tired calls of the sentries further along their own battlements.

"There's something strange about this quiet," Pan Yan observed. "My ears have become so used to gunshots and shouting that the silence is ringing in them like a bell . . . Let's just hope that there isn't some kind of trickery under it."

"Ever since I've been on half rations it's all one to me," Pan Zagloba grumbled. "My spirits need three things to function like they ought to: a wet throat, a full belly and a good night's sleep. Even the best strap will dry up and crack unless it's well greased and what if it's also getting soaked night after night like hemp in a washtub?"

His three friends smiled mildly at each other, irritating the fat knight even more, and his complaints soared to an angrier pitch.

"This rain gets right into the bones!" he muttered and squeezed the water out of his beard and mustache. "Those Cossacks have us gasping like fish in a bucket. So who's to wonder that the stuffing's coming right out of us these days?"

"A soldier's life has never been a picnic," Pan Michal offered and winked at Skshetuski.

"Picnic? Who's talking about picnics?" Pan Zagloba roared. "I'm talking about keeping body and soul together! A half-loaf of bread already costs a florin in the town and a quart of vodka goes for five! A dog wouldn't dip his tail in our drinking water because every well stinks of rotting corpses and I'm so thirsty that even my boots are gaping open like a couple of mouths."

"At least they're not too fussy about the water," Pan Michal said with another grin.

"And you, Master Michal, you'd do better to leave well enough alone!" Exasperated by his thirst and hunger, the fat knight fell into a rage. "You're as little as a Junebug so you can fill your belly with a grain of corn and drink out of a thimble! But I—thank God!—I'm shaped like a human being, not like something that a hen scratched out of the sand, and that's why I need to eat and drink like a man! And since I've had nothing except spittle in my mouth since noon I find nothing to laugh about in your attempts at humor!"

★　★　★

Here Pan Zagloba began to huff and snort, grumbling about the indignities he had to endure, while the little knight grinned at him, reached under his coat, and swung a large, round canteen forward on his hip.

"Hmm . . . I've this little panikin that I wrestled off a Cossack in last night's assault," he murmured and tossed it up and down as if wondering what to do with it. "Smells like good corn liquor . . ."

"Ah . . .!" Pan Zagloba sighed, brightening up at once. "Corn liquor, you said? There's nothing better to warm the marrow in the bones than a good corn liquor."

"That's what it seems to be." The little knight shot another sly grin at Pan Yan. "But since I'm just something that a hen scratched out of the sand . . . since I'm such a worthless, insignificant creature . . . well, I expect Pan Zagloba would refuse a drink from someone like me."

"Eh? What's that?" The fat knight looked at the panikin with anxiety and longing. "I . . . ah . . . wouldn't take it quite like that, my dear friend! A few unguarded words . . . a moment of anger . . . It's hardly something that could threaten a friendship like ours, is it now?"

"So here's to your good health, my friend," the grinning little soldier murmured, turning to Skshetuski.

"And to yours," Pan Yan said, amused. "Pass it over. It'll cut the chill."

"And you pass it to Pan Longinus when you're done with it."

Meanwhile the fat knight had put on his most ingratiating smile. "Ha! Ha! You're a real tease, my dear Michal. What a sense of humor!" As desperate for a drink as if his salvation was hanging in the balance, the fat knight had begun to sweat. "But you know what I think of you! You're one in a million! And one of the great things about you is that you share your blessings which means that God will bless you even more! Ah, if there really were any hens that could scratch up soldiers as fine as you, the Pope would have canonized them long ago! And it wasn't you that I had in mind when I was making my comparisons."

"Is that so? Well, in that case you'd better help yourself after Pan Longinus," said the grinning knight. "I wouldn't want to add to your miseries."

"I will!" Pan Zagloba cried. Then he started peering at the drinking Lithuanian with alarm. "Hey! What are you doing? Leave some for me, will you? Don't tilt your head that far back! May you get stuck like that, curse your thirst! Your guts are too long, that's the trouble with you. Look at him, will you? He's pouring it down as if he was watering a dead pine!"

"But I've barely had a taste, dear brother," Pan Longinus

murmured with his gentle and forgiving smile and passed the
canteen to the anxious noble.

Pan Zagloba seized it, lifted it to his mouth, pointed the
bottom of the panikin at the clouded sky and gulped it dry, then
blew out his breath in satisfaction.

"Ah," he gasped. "That's better! The one good thing about
these privations is that we'll really appreciate eating when
they're over. Father Zabkovski knows how to put away a meal
but I'll make him look like a fasting dervish. And Father
Muhovyetzki was saying much the same thing this morning
although he had the soul in mind rather than the belly."

"And what else did Father Muhovyetzki have to say?" Pan
Longinus asked in his gentle, unassuming murmur. "That's a
saintly man and always worth hearing . . ."

"Hold it a minute," Skshetuski ordered suddenly.

"Why? What's the matter?"

"Someone's coming from the camp."

★ ★ ★

They were quiet at once, alert and watching as a dark,
cloaked figure came towards them along the wall, and the three
soldiers came to attention as they recognized the Prince.

"Are you managing to stay awake?" he asked.

"We are," said Skshetuski.

"Good. Keep alert. I don't like this quiet."

"Yes, Highness," they chorused.

Prince Yeremi nodded to them and went on. His pale, drawn
face was preoccupied and distant. But his dark, probing eyes
seemed to see and note everything around him so that even Pan
Zagloba had scrambled to his feet, while Pan Longinus heaved a
huge sigh, raised his eyes to the dark sky, and pressed his hands
together as if in prayer.

"What a leader!" he whispered softly, sighing with emotion.
"What a great commander!"

"He gets even less rest than we do," Pan Skshetuski said. "He
walks the entire wall like that every night."

"God bless him for it, then!"

"Amen."

★ ★ ★

Then they were staring quietly into the darkness of the Cossack trenches. The Zaporohjan batteries and revetments showed

no sign of life. Even the stray, pale flickers of lantern light that seeped earlier from some of the nearest dugouts had now died away.

"Hmm. They're all asleep. We could go down there and pick them out of their holes like crayfish from a mudhole," the Little Knight murmured.

"Maybe. Who knows?" Pan Yan said.

"What I'd like to know is when we'll be allowed to get a little sleep," Pan Zagloba muttered and yawned until his jaws appeared ready to come off their hinges. "Any more of this watching and my eyes will pop right out of my skull! You'd think that we'd be able to get our heads down for a bit since nobody's doing any shooting, what? But no! Not in this army! Any damn fool dog knows better than to stand shaking in the rain but here we are, under arms even when it's quiet, and swaying from fatigue like a lot of rabbis on a Friday night."

"Well, that's the service for you," Pan Michal observed and yawned in his own turn.

"A dog's service! That's what it is! I can't tell if it's your *gojhalka*, Michal, that's knocking me off my feet, or if it's the memory of that insult that Father Zabkovski and I had to suffer this morning at the castle."

"Ah, and what was that all about?" Pan Longinus asked, as curious as a child. "You started telling us, good brother, but we were interrupted . . ."

"So I'll tell you now. Maybe it'll help us to keep our eyes open. Well, what happened was that Father Zabkovski and I went to the castle to see if we could sniff out a bite in the kitchens. We looked everywhere. We must've walked a mile up and down those stairs. But no luck! Their larders are as empty as our bellies. So we were on our way back, if you get the picture, mad as hornets and fed up with it all, when we ran across a Calvinist minister near the lazaret. Seems like Captain Schenberg, the one from Pan Firley's household regiment, was dying of his wounds and this preacher fellow had been getting him ready for his journey into the next world."

"That's a good soldier, this Schenberg," Pan Yan interrupted.

"Maybe he is. For a heretic." Awed as he always was by the quiet, thoughtful knight, Pan Zagloba couldn't stand to have anyone breaking into his monologues. "They're all a walking blasphemy, every one of them, as far as I'm concerned!"

"Sorry," Pan Yan said. "Please go on."

"I will! I caught hold of that long-nosed bible thumper and told him to hoof it. *'Get out of here, you damned weasel,'* I said. *'D'you want to turn God against us and lose us His blessings?'* And he, probably feeling safe under the castellan's protection, says to me: *'My faith's as good as yours. Maybe even better!'* I thought Father Zabkovski would turn to stone when he heard that!"

"The preacher said that?" The gentle Lithuanian looked as shocked as if he'd been struck by lightning.

"He did!"

"Ah . . . ah! And what did you do then?"

"Nothing."

"Nothing, sweet brother?" The Lithuanian's mouth fell open in amazement and his wide, childlike stare fixed on the fat knight in utter disbelief. "How could you do nothing? I mean to say, dear brother, I mean to say . . . why didn't you show him the error of his ways? Couldn't you cite the proper arguments?"

"Of course I could have!" Pan Zagloba shouted, almost as angry to have his story interrupted as he was by the doubt cast on his erudition. "Didn't I tell you once that I was brought up to enter the Church? I'd have done well, too, because I had a true vocation and because I'm a naturally studious and pious man, as you ought to know! And just because I'm not overly fond of fasting that wouldn't have stopped me from becoming at least an archdeacon or even a bishop!"

"Why didn't you speak up, then?"

"Why didn't I speak up?" Pan Zagloba turned his bulging eyes on Pan Yan and Volodyovski. "Will you listen to that Lithuanian beanpole? Father Zabkovski was there, wasn't he? Would you want me to take the bread out of a priest's mouth by doing his work? Let him debate theology, I told myself. That's his field of action. Like mine is to soldier. And he did a very nice job of it too, I must say."

"Ah . . . Ah! So there was a debate after all, was there?" Pan Longinus asked, pressing his hands together. "And what arguments did the good Father cite?"

"What arguments? Well, I think I'd call the first one a left hook to the jaw. The second looked like a straight right to the ribs. Anyway, that long-nosed heretic blasphemer didn't stop rolling until he hit the wall."

" . . . Dear God in heaven!"

The gentle giant stared, appalled, while the fat knight finished off his story.

"You'd think that would be enough to merit some reward in Heaven, eh? But who should come walking up just then but the Prince and Father Muhovyetzki? They really gave it to us for brawling and dissension! So all right, so maybe this isn't a time for theological discussions. But I still say that those heretic ministers of Pan Firley's are going to bring down some misfortune on our heads."

"And this Captain Schenberg, did he recant in time?" Pan Michal asked.

"No way! He died in mortal sin just the way he lived."

"Imagine that," the Lithuanian murmured. "You'd think a man would take some care about his salvation. But there's no accounting for human stubbornness, I expect . . ."

★ ★ ★

Anything else they might have said just then was interrupted by Volodyovski who seized Skshetuski's arm and hissed urgently for silence.

"What's the matter?" the fat knight asked, annoyed.

"Quiet! Listen!"

And the little knight leaned across the rim of the parapet, straining his sharp eyes and ears in the rustling darkness.

"Listen to what? I don't hear a thing," Pan Zagloba grumbled.

"The rain distorts the sounds," Skshetuski said quietly. "What do you hear, Michal?"

Pan Michal waved them into silence, listened a moment longer, then jumped off the parapet and turned to his companions with an excited grin spreading across his face.

"They're coming," he said.

"Who? What? Where?" Pan Zagloba cried, and then groaned: "Again?"

"Look at it as a sign of God's favor, sweet brother," Pan Longinus murmured. "The more we can serve Him here on earth the greater will be our rewards in Heaven."

"Run and tell the Prince," Skshetuski said to Pan Volodyovski. "I think he's gone towards Ostrorog's quarters. Meanwhile we'll alert the troops."

★ ★ ★

The word spread with the speed of lightning among the soldiers who crouched along the wall. It flew in whispers throughout the makeshift shelters in the *maydan*, alerting the camp, and the entire army stood to arms without a single trumpet call or one roll of drums. The rain had thickened, masking the slurred, muddy trampling of their boots and the creak of their armor and equipment as they took their places in the line, in just the same way that it concealed the approaching enemy.

In less than a quarter of an hour Prince Yeremi himself stood among his soldiers, mounted on his milk-white stallion and dressed in his familiar silver armor, and issuing quiet orders to the officers. Because the enemy was clearly trying to surprise the camp, believing that everyone had been lulled to sleep by the silence and the stillness of the gloomy night, the Prince ordered his men to continue the deception. The soldiers were to let the enemy climb right up on the walls before throwing themselves upon them at the sound of a cannon fired from the castle.

It must have seemed to the approaching enemy masses beyond the walls as if they were about to enter a graveyard, drained of life and movement and veiled in a dismal shroud of rain. No stray beam of moonlight broke out of the clouds to betray the defenders with a glint of armor or the brassy gleam of a musket barrel. Meanwhile three thousand primed and loaded flintlocks fell into place with a soft, hushed whisper unheard through the rainfall, and four thousand sabers slid out of their scabbards.

Skshetuski, Pan Longinus and Pan Volodyovski knelt side by side behind the parapet. The little knight was quivering with excitement, hardly able to wait for the enemy to appear, as the muttering fat knight could see with annoyance. Pan Yan, in contrast, had grown as still as an effigy carved above a tomb, deep in his own interior battle-ground where his grim longing for peace and oblivion struggled against his iron sense of duty. He had the cold, unfeeling look of someone who was already dead, but the white knuckles clenched around the grip of his broadsword betrayed his dark tension.

Pan Longinus, in yet another contrast, waited with a gentle smile as though he was kneeling at an altar rail.

His huge hands were clasped on the pommel of his enormous sword. He had bowed his head. He looked as thankful, trusting and untroubled as a man who was kneeling at the altar with a new bride beside him, and with a wedding hymn ringing in his ears.

His lips were moving in a silent prayer.

★ ★ ★

Pan Zagloba found himself a spot a little behind the three knights so that the first shock of the attack might splinter on their swords before it got to him. His knees were shaking under him in the mud and his heart was pounding like a kettledrum. His quick, sharp mind seemed as slow and sluggish as if a sudden freeze had gripped him by the temples. He searched for some excuse that would let him go down into the camp without betraying his nervous discomfort but he couldn't think of anything that anyone would believe.

"All right," he groaned under his breath. "Here we go again . . . There's to be no peace for poor Zagloba in this world, that's certain, and I'm in no hurry to see what's waiting in the next one . . ."

But he decided not to look for shelter in the camp after all. Experience told him that more cannonballs and bullets were likely to rain down among the tents and wagons than here on the wall.

" . . . Besides," he muttered to himself. "Where else can I find such sabers as those three? Nowhere! If they can't keep the Cossacks off my neck then my goose is cooked anyway you see it and there's no point in worrying about it any more."

In the meantime he tried to catch what Pan Michal and Pan Yan were whispering to each other.

"Can you hear them now?" the little soldier hissed in Skshetuski's ear.

"Yes. Barely. You've good ears, Michal."

The little knight shrugged and Pan Zagloba heard a soft, sad sigh. "God didn't give me much else with which to impress anyone."

"But he was generous to you with everything a Steppe soldier needs."

"That's why I'm not complaining. Let's hope each of us is granted whatever means the most to him."

"No knight could ask for more," sighed the Lithuanian.

Then they were quiet. The rain had thickened and now it was splashing so loudly in the moat that even their whispers were difficult to hear, but then a dull murmur began to drift towards them from the darkness in the plain as if a distant tide were surging across a sea towards them.

"Ah . . . I hear them now," Pan Yan murmured suddenly and Pan Longinus cocked his own ear at the darkness and nodded his head slowly. "They're keeping in step."

"That means they're neither Tartars nor *tchernya*," the Little Knight whispered, rubbing his hands together in anticipation.

"Zaporohjan infantry, do you think?"

"Or the janissaries. They also march like that. Ey, we'd be able to cut down a lot more of them from horseback than on foot . . ."

"It's too dark for cavalry tonight," Pan Yan whispered.

"Ha . . . Listen to them coming . . ."

The whole hushed camp seemed to have become a single listening ear, Pan Zagloba thought, but for some moments longer the only clear sounds he could distinguish were the splash and hissing of the rain. Then another, deeper rustling began to seep through the spattering drizzle. It was all the easier to catch because it pulsed with a steady, measured beat as if a subterranean tremor had begun to roll in the near distance. Its cadence quickened, nearing with every pace, and suddenly a dark, elongated mass burst out of the lighter darkness of the rainy night and stood, as if poised to leap, at the edge of the moat.

"*His will be done,*" Pan Zagloba muttered helplessly, numb and blind with fear which no amount of bluster and experience ever dispelled for him before an action started. "*His will be done on Earth as it is in Heaven . . .*"

The soldiers held their breaths. Even Pan Zagloba clamped a hand across his wheezing mouth while Pan Michal kept pinching Yan Skshetuski's arm as if to share his own pleasure and excitement.

★　★　★

Pan Longinus knelt just a little closer to the parapet than the other knights so he knew that he would be the first to strike the enemy when they began to rise above the wall.

He should have been at peace, untroubled. His conscience was clear. He lived as cleanly and as simply as the conditions of his service allowed anyone but he sensed the accusing, disapproving stares of all his ancestors everywhere he looked.

He knew that he had done his best and given all he could. He fought like all the Podbipyentas who had gone before him, trying to model himself in all things on the hardworking and uncomplaining Skshetuski, and he knew that he'd done nothing of which anyone would need to feel ashamed. But even when he closed his eyes in sleep or in prayer he always saw the disapproving stare of his ancestor Stoveyko. The capture of the savage Pulyan . . . the breaking of the janissaries' square and a dozen other feats of strength and courage which would have had any other soldier walking about in glory like the sun . . . left the poor, soulful Lithuanian giant empty, dissatisfied and disgusted with himself. No matter what he did his oath remained unfulfilled, the three heads continued to elude him, and his shamed sense of failure filled him with resignation.

He sighed.

He was the last of his line. His family's name would vanish when he died and what would all the spirits of his forefathers have to say to him when he appeared among them? How would he be able to account to them for his stewardship of all their traditions? Even the precious memory of the bright-eyed, heart-stirring Anusia failed to lift his spirits; on the contrary, her unnerving image merely underscored his own lack of real worth and value.

If he had failed, he thought in misery, it must have been because he wasn't good enough to succeed.

In the meantime, the dark, still mass halted beyond the wall was starting to stir. Ladders appeared among them. They started climbing down into the moat and then up the muddy slope of the embankment to the parapets. No one moved there. Nothing seemed to breathe. Only the soft, cautious creaking of the ladders drifted through the silence.

Pan Longinus sighed again.

He took a deep breath.

He shifted and tightened his grip on the long, iron handle of his terrible Cowlsnatcher, gathered up the strength of his hunched, wide shoulders, and tried to clear and sharpen his vision as the tops of three scaling ladders thudded into the wall below him. Pan Michal also ceased to hiss and squirm beside him, as he could see out of the corner of an eye. Pan Zagloba seemed to have stopped breathing at his back. And then, as he peered into the night ahead, three pairs of hands grasped the edge of the parapet in front of him and three sharp, spiked helmets began to rise slowly above the wall.

'Turks,' Pan Longinus thought.

And suddenly a cannon boomed, the sky seemed to turn into

a sheet of fire overhead as three thousand muskets crashed out in one flaming volley, and the night became as bright as day. In that white, flaring moment Pan Longinus swung his sword with such force that the air howled as the blade cut through it, three bodies plunged into the moat below, and three heads, encased in spiked helmets, rolled against his knees.

Then, even though Hell erupted on earth everywhere around him, the sky seemed to open above Pan Longinus. He felt as if great wings had sprouted from his shoulders. He thought that he could hear choirs of angels singing in his ears as they gathered to lift him up to Heaven. He fought for the rest of the night as if in a dream and each stroke of his sword was like the flame of a votive candle lighted in gratitude and joy.

He had fulfilled his vow.

He knew with all the certainty of his childlike faith that his forefathers were gathered in the clouds above him—every last one of them, including the great Ancestor Stoveyko—and that they were pleased with the last of the Podbipyentas.

Chapter Seventy-three

THIS ASSAULT, which was made mostly by Rumelian and Silistrian Turks and the Khan's own janissary guards, was beaten back with particular ferocity and brought down a storm of rage on Hmyelnitzki's head.

He had assured the Khan that the Commonwealth commanders wouldn't fight as hard against the Turkish mercenaries, trying to keep up the fiction that their war was only with the Cossacks, and that he'd take the camp if he was allowed to use them. Now he was forced to soothe the Khan and the infuriated *murjahs* with gifts of gold, paying ten thousand ducats to Devlet Giray and two thousand each to Tuhay-bey, the *Nurradin* and three other warlords.

Meanwhile the Crown soldiers rested until morning, guessing that no more assaults would be thrown at them that night, while the camp servants worked to clear the moat of the slaughtered Turks who had been massacred almost to a man.

The army slept. Only the duty regiments stood to arms on the walls until after sunrise. The only other man who kept a night-long vigil was Pan Podbipyenta. He had prostrated himself in the castle chapel, lying in prayer on his sword, to thank God for allowing him to fulfill his vow. At one stroke, as miraculous as it was unexpected, he freed himself of his tormenting loneliness and saved his family from extinction; he was at last at liberty to reach out for happiness with Anusia; and he had covered himself with such glory that his name rang on everybody's lips in the camp and the town.

Next morning the Prince himself called him to the castle while the soldiers came in crowds to congratulate him and to look with awe and envy at the three heads which the servants lined up before his tent.

"You're a real *sartor*, and no mistake," the visiting gentry told him. "Everybody knew that you're a man to be reckoned with, but a blow like that is something that even the heroes of antiquity would envy. The King's own executioner couldn't do a cleaner job of work."

"They're sliced off as neatly as if you'd snipped them off with scissors," others said, shaking their heads in wonder. "Steel caps, chainmail and all!"

"The wind couldn't have lifted them any better if they'd been cloth caps," said others, crowding around the gaunt Lithuanian giant to shake his hand, pound his back and slap him on the shoulders.

He, in the meantime, stood among them with his eyes fixed on the toes of his boots, red with embarrassment and mumbling like a schoolboy.

" . . . They just lined up properly, that's all."

Everyone wanted to try his hand with the huge sword as well but since this was one of those two-handed weapons that disappeared with the Middle Ages no one could even lift it off the ground. Even Father Zabkovski, who could snap horseshoes with his fingers, managed no more than a few clumsy strokes with those two yards of steel.

Zagloba, Skshetuski and Volodyovski played the role of hosts, having nothing to offer to their guests other than a handshake and eyewitness accounts of their friend's achievement. The army was living on dried bread. Meat was available only when a horse was killed. Hunger was stalking openly through the camp and famine wasn't far away.

★ ★ ★

Pan Marek Sobieski arrived when most of the visitors had started to drift away. "I hear you've reason for a celebration," he said to Pan Longinus, squeezing his hands warmly.

"We do indeed!" Pan Zagloba cried. "Because our friend here has fulfilled a vow!"

"Would that mean that we'll be hearing wedding bells in the near future?" the *Starosta* grinned. "Is there someone our friend has in mind?"

Pan Longinus turned as red as a boiled crayfish and lost whatever poise he had. "I . . . ah . . . eh . . . thank your lordship . . ."

"But is there a lady? Hm?"

"There is!" Zagloba said. "And a friskier little bird never hatched an egg! If God lets us carry our own heads out of this hungry pest-hole we'll be dancing at the wedding in no time at all! And I guarantee a christening soon after!"

"All the better!" The *Starosta* laughed and hugged the stammering Lithuanian. "All the better then! It's your holy duty, my good friend, to make sure that a line like yours doesn't die out on us. I only wish that every stone in the Commonwealth could breed such soldiers as you four."

"That, my lord, couldn't happen," the fat knight said at once.

"And why not?"

"Because stones are pledged to a stone-cold chastity. It's an unnatural habit they got from Lithuania."

Redder than ever, even though he was now laughing at the jibe, Pan Longinus raised his eyes to the canvas ceiling while the others laughed along with him.

"Ah, it's . . . a shame to listen," he sighed out of habit.

But Pan Zagloba had found his stride again and couldn't be turned back. "Yes, yes," he went on. "You can strike them together all night long and all you'll get is dust! But it works the other way in Lithuania, I am told, where men live like monks but little cabbage-heads pop up in every gravel pit anyway!"

Pan Longinus stuck his fingers in his ears. Pan Sobieski laughed until tears ran down along his nose.

"I wish I could ask you all to dinner over in my tents," he said, pressing their hands in turn. "Valor and wit both deserve a real celebration. But it's been since noon yesterday that I've had anything to eat myself, and that was just a crust of dry bread and a marrow bone."

"Let's pray that the King comes to relieve us soon," Pan Zagloba said. "The gentry of the General Levy always travel with all kinds of rare foods and liquors in their wagons and I'll be the first to lead a sally into them. I tell you, gentlemen, if they cared half as much about the Commonwealth as they do about their own guts and bellies Hmyelnitzki would never have got into the Ukraine, far less out of it! I'd rather eat with them than fight beside them, that's certain, but perhaps they won't do too badly this time, eh? What with the King himself keeping his eye on them . . ."

"Yes. Hmm." The *Starosta* grew serious and started nodding thoughtfully. "His Majesty can't come too soon, that's certain. But you all know how long it takes the General Levy to gather for military service. I wouldn't say this to anybody else because we wouldn't want to start any kind of panic but we have to be ready for the worst. Our provisions are almost at an end. The wells stink of corpses. And what's worst is that we're running out of powder. Another few days and we'll have nothing left to fight with but our fists and sabers. We all swore to fight to the last man and that seems the most likely prospect for us every day."

"If that's what has to happen we'll be ready for it," Skshetuski said quietly and Volodyovski nodded.

"But surely, my lord," Zagloba said in a worried tone. "Surely the King wouldn't abandon us here? The flower of the nation is locked within these walls!"

"The King is a great-hearted man," the *Starosta* said. "I'm sure he'd waste no time in coming to help us if he knew what straits we are in these days. Even if all his new forces aren't ready yet, and if the assembling gentry is dragging its heels, his own presence here would shake the rebellion. But how is he to know that our days are numbered? Hmyelnitzki's seen to it that a mouse wouldn't be able to slip out of these trenches to get our news to the outside world."

Pan Longinus sat quietly through all this, too diffident to speak before the *Starosta*, and certain that anything he said wouldn't be worth hearing. He kept his wide, gentle eyes cast down. His whiskers drooped sadly. His broad, gentle forehead was furrowed in deep thought. Meanwhile the others talked in calm, measured voices about the unavoidable conclusion to their weeks of fighting.

"If there was someone who'd undertake to get word to the King he'd win immortal glory for himself and save both the army and the country," the heroic young *Starosta* said at last and shrugged, and shook his head as if the idea wasn't worth any further comment. "But who'd try something as desperate as that? With every road and bolt-hole blocked by the Horde and by Hmyelnitzki's pickets it would be certain death."

"Not one chance in a million of getting through alive," Volodyovski murmured.

"But what chance do we have without it?" Pan Skshetuski asked, plunged into deep thought of his own. "Sometimes that one chance in a million is the only one left."

"What if we bribed a Cossack?" Zagloba suggested. "We take a handful of prisoners every day, don't we? Let's pay one to pretend that he escaped from us and then send him looking for the King."

"Hmm. That might do,"—the *Starosta* nodded—"but it's a risky business putting so much trust in a man who'd betray his own kind for money. He might take our bribe and go straight to Hmyelnitzki with our own account of our true situation here. Whatever happens we mustn't let the enemy know how close we've come to the end of all our resources."

Then Pan Longinus raised his head, turned his clear, childlike eyes on the troubled gathering, and smiled his gentle smile. "I'd like to try it," he said softly.

"You?" Pan Zagloba stared at him with bulging eyes and his mouth hung open. "Try what? Suicide?"

"Get through the Cossacks, sweet brother," said the gentle giant. "Get word to the King."

★ ★ ★

The three knights and Pan Sobieski reacted to this offer in quite different ways. Pan Zagloba looked as dumbstruck as if a thunderbolt had struck him out of a clear sky and turned him into stone. Skshetuski seemed to shrink into himself and his sallow face lost a little color. Volodyovski's pointed little whiskers moved up and down as if he were a beetle testing dangerous air while the *Starosta* slapped his own thigh and jumped to his feet.

"You'd make the attempt?" he cried out.

"Have you considered what you're saying, my dear friend?" Skshetuski asked quietly.

"I've thought it all out a long time ago," the Lithuanian said in his bashful, unassertive manner, as if expecting that anything he said would be dismissed out of hand as beneath anybody's notice. "You know what everybody's been saying for weeks. I mean that someone ought to tell the King about the way that things are here in Zbarajh . . . So I've been thinking, you see, that I'd go if the good Lord let me fulfill my vow . . ."

"Have you gone mad?" Pan Zagloba recovered from his shock, leaped up before the startled Lithuanian, and started shaking both his fists in Pan Podbipyenta's face. "You call this thinking? That Courland mare of yours has better ideas!"

"It's really the only thing to do," Pan Longinus murmured, looking at the enraged fat knight with an apologetic smile. "I'm just an ordinary man, I don't amount to all that much, so even if the Cossacks do cut me down along the way it wouldn't be a loss to anyone. And if they don't . . . well, then I'd be of some service."

"But there are no *ifs* about this!" Pan Zagloba cried. "It's certain death, don't you understand? Weren't you listening to what the *Starosta* was saying?"

"So what, good brother?" the Lithuanian murmured with his humble smile. "If the good Lord wants me to get through He will lead me through. If He doesn't then He'll reward me in the next world. It's all in His hands, isn't it?"

"Yes, but first you'll be in the Cossacks' hands! They won't let you die easily, don't you know that much? Man alive, have you lost whatever puny wits you've ever had?" Quite certain that Pan Longinus was throwing his life away the fat knight turned for help to Pan Yan and Volodyovski. "Listen to that beanpole! Have you ever heard a more harebrained idea?"

"Even so." The Lithuanian turned his own shy smile on his friends as if anxious to avoid adding to their burdens of anxiety, but determined to do what he thought was right. "Even so, good brothers, I'm going."

"A bird wouldn't be able to get past!" Pan Zagloba bellowed, beside himself with fury and impatience. "They've got us trenched around like badgers in a hole!"

"So they have." The soft, gentle note remained undisturbed in the Lithuanian's voice. "But I'll go anyway, my dear brother."

"Will you listen to him?" Pan Zagloba yelled. "Have you ever seen anyone more stubborn? It's worse than trying to pound reason into an ox! Why don't you just have your head cut off and fired out of a cannon at the Cossack *tabor*? That way you'll save yourself and them a lot of trouble and the result will be just the same!"

But Pan Longinus had made up his mind. "I owe it to God, you see, for letting me fulfill my vow," he said and smiled around with a childlike innocence and sweetness, and pressed his hands together as if begging for an unearned and undeserved favor.

"Well, then you won't go alone," Pan Yan said. "Because I'll go with you."

"And so will I," Volodyovski said.

But at this point Pan Zagloba lost whatever control he possessed. "May God curse you all!" he howled and clutched at his head. "May the Devil take you with your '*me too, me too*' and your damned courage and determination! Do you need more bloodshed? Hasn't there been enough death and dying everywhere around you? Do you want to make sure that you won't leave this place alive? To Hell with you then! Go to the Devil, the lot of you, and leave me alone!"

Then he began to run around the tent, flapping his arms and turning in aimless circles as if trying to find a way out of a trap that didn't have an exit.

"Ah, it's all my own fault," he mumbled in utter desperation. "That's God's judgment on me! Why couldn't I look for sensible company among reasonable people instead of throwing in my lot with these mindless hotheads? Serves me right . . .! Ah, it serves me right . . .! And is this what all my years are to amount to in the end?"

And then he stopped before Skshetuski, clasped his hands behind his back and stared angrily into the young lieutenant's face. "What have I done to you that you torment me so?" he demanded, with his red, swollen face quivering in despair.

"You? Us? Torment? God forbid!" Pan Yan said. "What are you saying, father?"

"I'm not surprised to hear such a witless scheme out of Pan Podbipyenta," the fat noble grumbled. "He always had his brains in his fists and now that he's beheaded the three biggest idiots in the Turkish army he's become the champion fool of all mankind!"

"Here he goes again," the Lithuanian murmured, shaking his head with his patient smile.

"And I'm not surprised at him either!" Pan Zagloba shouted, pointing at Pan Michal. "He'll hop into some Cossack's boot or attach himself to his breeches like a burr and squeeze his way through faster than the lot of us. The Holy Ghost missed them both when He came down from Heaven to enlighten men..! But you, Yan? An officer whom the Prince himself takes seriously and treats with respect? I can't believe that you'd encourage them instead of shoveling some sense into their empty heads. And that you'd offer to go yourself! That you'd expose all four of us to certain death and torture! That's . . . just too much! That I can't forgive! That's . . . the living end."

"What do you mean '*all four of us*?'" asked the astonished Skshetuski. "D'you want to go too, then? Is that what you're saying?"

"Want?" howled the fat knight. "Who said anything about *wanting*? But what choice are you giving me? If you're all going then I *have* to go! It's either all of us or none of us, don't you understand that? Ah, may my innocent blood be on your heads!"

"God love you!" cried Skshetuski, laughing in amazement while Pan Michal and Pan Longinus crowded around the disconsolate Zagloba, taking him in their arms and embracing him until he gasped for breath. But this time he was really angry, not merely pretending, and wouldn't be appeased.

"Go to the Devil, the lot of you," he growled. "I don't need your Judas embraces. Let this be a lesson to me about the kind of company I'm keeping."

★ ★ ★

Just then cannon and musketry began to boom and rattle on the walls again and the fat knight jerked his head towards the sound.

"There!" he cried. "There! Go through all that, will you?"

"That's just the normal morning cannonade," Pan Skshetuski said.

"'*A normal cannonade*'!" the fat knight mocked. "Listen to him, will you? Half the army's melted away in those normal cannonades and these fellows are sneering as if it was nothing!"

"Be of good heart, dear brother," Pan Longinus tried to soothe the agitated noble. "Don't be so upset. It'll all turn out for the best, you'll see."

"And you'd do best to keep your silly mouth shut!" Pan Zagloba roared. "You're the guiltiest of the lot of them! This whole mad enterprise is your idea and if it isn't the brainchild of an idiot then I'm a damn fool myself!"

"Even so, I'm going," the Lithuanian said, as undismayed and stubborn as before.

"Oh you'll go! You'll go!" The fat knight had flown into another rage. "And I know why! You've fulfilled your vow and now you're itching to get rid of that damned chastity of yours, so you're anxious to get it out of these trenches into open country! You're the worst, not the best of us! You're like a slut with her virtue for sale! Tfui, I say. Shame! Shame! It's not the King you want to get to! On no! You want to gallop about in the fields for a bit, neighing like a stallion through the villages and making up for lost time, you scoundrel! Look at him will you? Some knight he is, with his honor and his innocence up for grabs! It's a disgrace to us all, that's what it is!"

"Ay, it's a shame to listen!" the Lithuanian cried with his fingers firmly in his ears.

"Come on now, let's stop all this bickering, shall we?" Pan Yan said seriously. "We'd do better to give some thought to how we're going to go about this mission."

Pan Marek Sobieski, who watched and listened to all this as if he had never come across anything like it in his life, now slapped his thigh again and helped to restore a sense of gravity to the moment.

"These are vitally important matters," he reminded firmly. "It's nothing to argue about nor can we make such decisions on our own. You're all under orders, gentlemen, and subject to military discipline. We must see His Highness. It'll be up to him to decide who goes and who doesn't or whether anyone may go at all."

"And if I know anything about him he'll say just what I did," Pan Zagloba said, brightening up at once. "And that'll be the end of all this silly nonsense."

★ ★ ★

They all got up and trooped out into the open where the shot from the Cossack cannon was already falling. All the Polish soldiers were now at the walls which, glimpsed from the *maydan*, had the tumbled and ramshackle look of sleazy market stalls heaped on an embankment. There were so many old clothes, raw sheepskin coats and torn tents draped about the parapets and loopholes, and so many wrecked wagons, boards and broken timbers piled along the ramparts, that the earthworks looked less like a battle line than the debris of a looted and dilapidated village. All of this was supposed to serve as shelter from the lead and iron that rained on these frail defenses night and day for weeks at a time. And now, even as the knights were passing this crackling heap of rubble, a thick cloud of gunsmoke bloomed out and spread above it, as the long lines of soldiers dressed in tattered red and yellow surcoats, who lay behind their muskets in that devastation, fired their volleys at the Cossack bastions and approaches.

The open *maydan* itself had long ceased to resemble a military parade ground. The flat grassy space, ripped up with grave-diggers' shovels and trampled by horses, had turned a rusty grey. Heaps of sandy soil, gouged by exploding bombs and attacked every day by well-diggers and the burial parties, littered the whole area among the smoldering wreckage of burned wagons, smashed artillery pieces, burst barrels and piles of gnawed bones. A dead or wounded horse wasn't to be seen anywhere in the camp because every injured animal or carcass was immediately turned into soldiers' rations. But every glance revealed stacks of spent Cossack cannonballs, already turning red with rust.

Hunger and privations glared at every step. The knights passed whole companies of soldiers carrying dead and wounded comrades, or hurrying to replace the fallen on the walls. They stared into fierce red-rimmed eyes that peered at them in turn out of deep, dark holes. They saw torn, faded uniforms, broken weapons, and heads wrapped in filthy, bloodstained rags in place of hats or helmets. And each of these gaunt faces, scoured raw by the wind and sun and scorched with gunpowder, told them the same unavoidable truth: another week or two and it would all be over.

"Look, gentlemen," Pan Sobieski said. "Do you see . . .? It's time . . . it's really high time to let the King know what is happening here."

"Yes," said the little knight. "We're as good as finished without some help soon. My men are so worn-out and so whittled down that I can get barely a company together for a counter-attack during the assaults."

"And what'll happen when we've eaten the last of the horses?" Pan Skshetuski asked.

★   ★   ★

Talking like this, they reached Prince Yeremi's tents which stood in a small cluster in an angle of the western wall. Several mounted orderlies, whose job was to carry messages and orders through the camp, waited in front of them; but because their animals were fed with the only food or fodder available in the besieged entrenchments, namely smoked horsemeat cured with birdshot, they couldn't stand still for a moment and threw themselves about in wild leaps as if gnawed by fire. This was true of all the cavalry in the camp which charged the enemy nowadays in great chaotic bounds as if the knights were riding on unbroken mustangs or legendary griffins.

"Is His Highness in?" the *Starosta* asked one of the duty riders.

"Yes sir," the trooper answered. "He's in the main tent with General Pshiyemski."

Pan Marek Sobieski, enjoying the privilege of his rank and station, went inside without an announcement while the four knights waited outside. But they didn't wait long. Pan Pshiyemski peered out almost at once and called them inside.

Pan Zagloba entered in good spirits, sure that Prince Yeremi wouldn't send his best soldiers to a certain death, but he barely managed to make his salutes when the Prince shocked him with fresh disappointment.

"The *Starosta* told me that you're ready to go out of the camp," he said. "I accept your offer. There's no such thing as excessive sacrifice when the good of the country is at stake."

"We've merely come to ask your permission, Highness," Skshetuski replied. "Since it is up to you to decide how we can be most useful."

"So it's all four of you that want to go?"

"Highness!" Pan Zagloba stepped forward and bowed while beads of sweat glistened on his pate. "They want to go. Not I. God is my witness that I didn't come here to boast about the services I've rendered and if I mention them now it's just to make sure that no one accuses me of lacking the necessary courage. These men are great soldiers and fine knights but so was Burlay who, in my view, was worth a Bohun, a Burdabut and any amount of janissary heads! But courage is one thing while madness is another. We don't have wings to fly with and there's no way for anyone to get through on foot."

"So you're not going, then?" the Prince asked.

"I said I didn't want to go. I didn't say that I wasn't going. Since God has seen fit to burden me with such friends I don't have any choice but to stick with them to the end. Zagloba's saber might prove useful even in a lost cause like this one. I just don't know what good it'll do for the four of us to die for nothing and I trust that Your Highness will avert this useless sacrifice by refusing your permission for such an act of folly."

"You're a good, decent man," the Prince said and nodded. "It's to your credit that you don't abandon your friends in moments of danger. But your trust in me is misplaced because I'll not only let you go but I applaud your offer."

'So that's that,' Pan Zagloba sighed under his breath and his shoulders slumped in resignation.

But Pan Firley limped into the tent just then and a new hope glimmered dimly in Zagloba's mind because this learned and thoughtful old man was known for his caution.

"Highness," the castellan reported. "My people caught a Cossack who says that they're getting ready for another full assault tonight."

"I've heard that too," Prince Yeremi said and turned to Pshiyemski. "Are the new walls ready?"

"They'll be done by nightfall."

"Good." The Prince nodded. Then he turned to the four knights. "If it's a dark night then the best time to go out will be after the assault."

"Are you getting ready for a sally, Highness?" the castellan asked.

"A sally after the attack is one thing," the Prince said and nodded. "And I'll lead it myself. But now we're discussing something else. These four gentlemen have offered to go through the Cossack lines and get to the King with word about our situation."

The castellan stared, astonished, at each of the four knights in turn while the Prince smiled quietly. It was a point of vanity and pride with this Ruthenian magnate that he liked to hear his soldiers admired and praised.

"Dear God!" the castellan cried out, destroying Pan Zagloba's last hope of a voice of reason. "So there are still such great-hearted people left in this selfish world! What a noble gesture! I'd be the last to turn you gentlemen away from such an attempt, no matter what the danger."

The fat knight quivered, crimson with disappointment, but said nothing more. He only grunted like an angry bear while the Prince thought deeply for a moment.

"But Pan Zagloba makes one good point," he said. "I don't want to risk all your lives for nothing so I won't allow the four of you to go out together. One of you will go first. If the Cossacks kill him they'll make sure we know it, as they've done before with all our men they've captured. Then a second man can try it. Then, if necessary, the third and the fourth in turn. But it's just possible that the first man will succeed in which case there'll be no need to send out the others."

"Your Highness . . ." Skshetuski broke in but the Prince silenced him with a glance.

"Such is my will and that is my order," he said. "But to make sure that there's no quarreling among you I want the first man who made the offer to be the first to go."

"That would be me!" Pan Longinus said with a glowing smile.

"You'll go tonight, then, after the attack," Prince Yeremi said. "I won't give you any letters to carry in case they fall into Cossack hands, but you can tell His Majesty what you know and what you've seen here and that should suffice. I will, however, give you my signet ring as a sign that you're coming from me."

Pan Longinus accepted the ring and bowed deeply before the Prince who seized his lowered head in both his hands and pressed it to his chest.

"You're as close to me as a brother," he said at last in a voice heavy with emotion. "May God and the Queen of Angels see you safely through."

"Amen!" cried the *Starosta*, the castellan and General Pshiyemski.

"Amen," said Pan Yan and Pan Volodyovski.

Prince Yeremi's dark and troubled eyes were shining with tears and so were those of everybody else, while Pan Podbipyenta shuddered throughout the length of his gaunt, bowed body with joy and enthusiasm. He felt as if molten fire was running through his bones and happiness glowed in his grateful eyes.

"History will write about you!" the castellan cried out.

"'*Non nobis, non nobis,*'" the Prince quoted then. "'*Sed nomini*

Tuo, Domine, da gloriam.' May God's be the glory."

The four knights bowed and left.

★ ★ ★

Gunfire crackled all around them as they walked back towards their own part of the camp which the servants were tearing down in preparation to that night's retreat into new and still tighter walls closer to the castle.

"Ey, something's got me by the throat," Pan Zagloba murmured. "My mouth tastes as bitter as if I'd been taking ashes for a purge. Listen to those Cossack devils working at their cannon, may lightning strike them all! It's a hard world to live in these days and no mistake . . ."

Then he turned his sad eyes on the Lithuanian. "Longinus, my dear friend, are you sure you have to go tonight? It's not too late to change your mind, believe me! No? No, I suppose not . . . Well, that's that, then . . . May the angels watch over you . . . And may the plague strangle all that peasant scum!"

"I have to leave you now, my friends," Pan Longinus said.

"Leave us? What for? Why?" Pan Zagloba was immediately alarmed. "Where are you going already?"

"To Father Muhovyetzki, dear brother," the Lithuanian said. "To make my confession. I can't go out on a thing like that with sins on my soul."

He hurried off towards the castle and the others made their way towards the new earthworks. Pan Yan and the little knight walked as gloomily and with such bitter faces as if they'd been poisoned but Pan Zagloba couldn't stand a moment of silence, particularly if that silence was his own.

"What would that sweet, innocent man have to confess?" he wondered. "He doesn't even know the meaning of sin. Ah, I tell you, I didn't expect to be so shaken by this business but that's the best and kindest and most decent being in the world! Let someone say he isn't and I'll cut his ears off!"

Mumbling and muttering and sighing and cursing, the fat knight stumbled upon a stack of rusty cannonballs to sit on and mopped his wet eyes.

"Dear God," he groaned. "Here I thought the castellan would pour some cold water on this lunatic idea but he only tossed new coals on the fire. *'History,'* he says, *'will write about you.'* Let history write about him but not on Pan Longinus' skin! Why didn't he offer to go himself if he's so concerned about history? He's got six toes on each foot like all those Calvinists so it'd be easier for him to walk, the damned heretic. I tell you, my friends, this earth is getting to be a bad place to live on. Father Zabkovski may be right when he says that the end of the world isn't far away."

Neither Skshetuski nor the little knight said anything in reply and Pan Zagloba soon lapsed into a gloomy silence.

"Well . . . let's sit here by these walls for a while," he muttered. "And then let's go up to the castle for a bit. I'd like to spend as much time with our dear good friend as I can, while he is still with us."

★　★　★

But Pan Longinus spent the whole afternoon in prayer and they didn't see him until he returned for that night's assault, which proved to be the most dangerous since the siege began because the Cossacks struck at the exact moment when the Polish troops, artillery and wagons started to leave their earthworks and to move to their new line of bastions and entrenchments closer to the river. It looked for a time as if the shrunken Polish forces might be overwhelmed. The Cossack charge broke across the old wall and stormed into the camp where their vast swarms became so tightly locked and entangled with the retreating Commonwealth brigades that no one could tell an enemy from a friend.

Beaten back, they charged again and then for a third time. Hmyelnitzki threw everything he had into this assault since both the Khan and his own Zaporohjan colonels had served him notice that this attack was to be the last. Thereafter the besieged were to be starved to death or submission but there were to be no more attempts to storm their walls.

It took three hours of bitter hand-to-hand fighting to break and drive away this onslaught by the combined Tartar and Zaporohjan forces in which, according to later historians, one hundred thousand men took part and forty thousand were wounded or killed. This much, however, was certain at the time: captured Cossack battle flags and banners were thrown down before Prince Yeremi in hundreds that night. The shrunken Polish regiments dug in on their new walls and saw no more massed attacks thereafter. Cannon, musketry and famine would be their enemy from then on.

It took another hour for all the fighting to stop after this assault because the inexhaustible Prince Yeremi sallied out in pursuit with his weary soldiers.

They were so worn and drained that they could hardly move. They ran forward as if they were blind. They staggered with exhaustion, shooting and stabbing at shadows they could barely see. But they drove the Cossack masses all the way to the Zaporohjan *tabor* none the less, and made their way back to their own entrenchments where each of them collapsed wherever he happened to be standing.

Only then did silence come slipping back to the Polish earthworks and the Cossack wagons and the quieter secret drama of the night could start to unfold.

Chapter Seventy-four

IT WAS WELL PAST midnight when four shadowy figures appeared on the earthwall.

The night was warm. It was thick with clouds. There was no moonlight to brighten the dark gloom of the heavy silence. The deep sleep of exhausted men that settled on the camp and the invisible Zaporohjan dugouts had the gravelike stillness of the dead. Thick with the stench of slaughter and the exhalations of the recent carnage, the night seemed further laden with anxiety, grief and premonition for the three knights who crept with Pan Longinus to the east end of the wall.

They made no sound. They would have seemed like ghosts sprung out of the freshly dug and bloodied soil if anyone had seen them. But they were moving so quietly and so carefully that not even the most alert of the exhausted sentries spotted their black shadows and called out a challenge.

Nervousness, however, drove them to break their tense and worried silence.

"Be sure you wrap your pistols well," Pan Yan said. "Keep your priming dry. I'll hold two regiments mounted and ready until dawn. Just fire your two shots and we'll come riding out to help."

"My God it's dark," whispered Pan Zagloba. His cracked, old voice quavered with fear and worry. "Can't see a foot ahead, curse it all . . ."

"All the better, brother," murmured Pan Longinus.

"I still think this is a dam'fool, hopeless thing to do . . . Listen, you could still change your mind. No one would think any the worse of you . . ."

"Quiet now," Pan Michal held up his hand in warning.

They heard a harsh, gasping sound, halfway between a snarl and a breathless groaning.

"What is it?"

"Nothing. Just a death rattle out there in the moat. Somebody's dying, that's all."

"Just a death rattle . . ." Pan Zagloba sighed and shook his head as if to free himself from his bewilderment and anxiety. "That we should come to this . . ."

"If you make it as far as the oak grove, out there between the Cossack *tabor* and the Tartar *kosh*," Skshetuski instructed. "Then you'll stand a chance. But for God's sake, Longinus, watch yourself. Take no unnecessary risks. You've three hours until dawn."

"Dear God," Pan Zagloba whispered, shaking as if in the grip of fever. "Oh dear sweet God . . ."

Then they were quiet, crouched at the edge of the wall, and peering into the dark night around them.

"Well, it's time to go," Pan Longinus said after a moment.

"Yes. Time. It's time," Pan Yan repeated, biting back the emotion that welled into his throat. "Go with God, good friend."

"God keep you and guide you," the little knight whispered while Pan Zagloba began to shake with sobs he could no longer stifle.

"Be well, brothers," the Lithuanian murmured.

"And you too be well. Watch yourself . . ."

"And forgive me if I've done any wrong to any of you . . . I've never meant to harm anybody."

"Wrong? Harm? You? Dear God!" Pan Zagloba cried out and threw his arms around the Lithuanian.

Then it was Skshetuski's and Volodyovski's turn to embrace the quiet, gently smiling giant. There was a moment when all three knights fought back their sobs and wiped away their tears. Pan Podbipyenta was the only one among them who had no tears to shed. He was moved by their love for him, each one of them could see that. But his long, mild face seemed to be glowing with an inner joy that went beyond the warmth and caring of simple human friendships as he waited calmly for their emotions to subside.

"Be well," he said again. "God keep you."

" . . . And you! And you!"

Then he slipped gently out of their arms, edged across the wall and slid into the moat.

They saw him a few moments later as a long, black shadow rising beyond the ditch. He stood there long enough for half a dozen heartbeats. Then he waved to them once more and vanished in the darkness.

★ ★ ★

Between the country track that wound towards Zalost and the old highway to Vishnovyetz which had been built by Prince Yeremi's ancestors a hundred years earlier, spread several miles of woodland, mostly ancient oak groves broken by intermittent, narrow strips of pasture, which ran all the way to the broad primeval forests that stretched westward in a dense, unbroken mass beyond the horizon.

This was the path that Pan Podbipyenta had picked for himself. It was a dangerous route because he had to pass through the entire depth of the Zaporohjan *tabor* to reach the shelter of the trees. But that was one of the reasons he chose to go that way. The closer he could come to that huge arc of wagons, shacks and campfires, the more people would be moving about in that hostile darkness, and the less attention the Cossack pickets and patrols were likely to pay them.

Besides, as he reasoned, every other road, track, path, ravine and fold of land that led from the earthworks had been thickly studded with roadblocks and guardposts which the *esauls*, troop leaders, and regimental colonels inspected all the time. Hmyelnitzki himself was known to appear every night among these barricades and every Cossack found dozing at his post was hanged out of hand. The only other possible avenue, across the low meadows along the Gnyezna River, didn't even enter Pan Podbipyenta's head. The Tartar pickets and crowds of fierce horseherders who watched over their grazing stock in those fields and clearings from sunset to sunrise made sure that a wolf wouldn't be able to slink past their eyes.

The night was so black that even tree trunks were invisible ten paces away. This, Pan Longinus thought, was just what he needed, although it also meant he had to move with extraordinary care, feeling his way through the darkness a step at a time. Every square yard of the battlefield was gouged and pitted with ditches and dugouts which had been battered down with cannon and littered with corpses and which opened up before him without any warning.

Creeping along like that he reached the second Polish wall, the one which the army abandoned earlier in the evening. He crossed the moat which had been bridged by the Cossacks with fascines and corpses and turned towards the Zaporohjan gun posts and approaches.

He stopped and listened time and time again but the Cossack ramparts were silent and empty. Prince Yeremi's sally had either killed or driven out the *moloytzy* who were fighting there; those who weren't lying dead on the slopes and summits of their fortifications had fled to the wagons, although now and then a soft moan or a sigh suggested that a few of the thickly scattered bodies still contained some life.

Beyond these ghostly ramparts stretched a broad, dark plain that ran all the way to the original Polish walls, the ones built by the Crown generals before Prince Yeremi's arrival. This wide and silent space was the site of the first Polish camp and it was an even greater ruin than the defenses through which Pan Longinus had already passed. The old parade ground was ripped and furrowed by deep, caved-in ditches, sunken tunnels and exploded mines, and the entire area was thick with shallow graves and unburied corpses over which Pan Longinus tripped at every step.

He stopped again, hunched over in the darkness, and began a prayer for the souls of the dead.

Nothing moved in that black, moonless night. He could see no sign of life anywhere around him. There was no glimmer of a campfire anywhere ahead. He couldn't hear a sound other than the soft hissing of his breath. Even the deep droning murmur of the Polish camp which followed him all the way to the second wall had dwindled and fallen away behind him. He took his bearings as best he could without a star to guide him. He glanced for the last time towards the dark earthworks from which he had come as if in hopes that some continuing thread of warmth and affection would have marked his trail. But there was almost nothing left to see. There were no fires burning in the camp. Only a dim, pale light gleamed high in a window of the castle tower which the low-hanging clouds covered and revealed like the flickering of a firefly.

'*Dear brothers,*' Pan Longinus thought. '*Will I ever see any of you again?*'

And suddenly he longed for the company of his friends. His own loneliness settled on him with the weight of a boulder that bowed him to the ground.

'*There, near that pale light, is life,*' he thought. '*Warm hearts. Men who care about me.*'

. . . Prince Yeremi, Skshetuski, Volodyovski, Zagloba, Father Muhovyetzki . . . Their images rose clearly in his mind, glowed with concern and anxiety about him, then dimmed and began to vanish.

'. . . *There,*' he thought, '*is home, devotion, love and trust and friendship . . .*'

And here? What was here around him?

'*Night,*' he thought.

Darkness. Emptiness. Dead men underfoot. Dead souls lifting coldly and flowing in the mists.

And in the distance, not yet in sight but drawing nearer with each step he took, a vast encampment of bloodthirsty enemies sworn to his destruction, men for whom such words as mercy simply had no meaning.

★ ★ ★

That camp he left behind him, those mounds of rubble where starving men huddled under a daily avalanche of iron, seemed to him like the safest haven in the world just then. A sense of loss and longing crept to him from the dark.

Anxiety whispered to him:

'*You won't get through. Go back. There's still time. Fire your pistols now and a whole brigade will charge to your rescue . . .*'

No one would think badly of him, Pan Zagloba said. He could just say that the thing was beyond anybody's doing. No one would question that since everybody knew it. No one else would try it. They'd just wait for God's will and the King's mercy to manifest themselves.

. . . But what if Skshetuski went out anyway? And died in his place?

"In the name of the Father, the Son and the Holy Ghost," Pan Longinus shuddered. "That is Satan's whispering. That's just the Devil tempting a weak soul. It's just an illusion fed by the emptiness, the darkness, the silence and the dead. Satan will use anything to confuse a man."

Was he to cover himself with shame, lose his good name and his hopes of salvation at one stroke, and fail to save the army? Were his friends to die because he was too weak-willed to make sure they were rescued?

"Never!" he whispered. "Never!"

If he was to die he was ready for it. Nothing worse could happen. He crossed himself and went on, stretching his arms in front of him in the darkness.

He heard a sudden sound, something between a mutter and a whisper, but not from the receding Polish camp behind him. No. This grim sound drifted through the darkness from the other side. There was a deep, threatening note in that muted growl as if a killer bear had wakened in the black depths of a primeval forest. But Pan Longinus' brief moment of anxiety and doubt was already past him. His sense of loss changed into a gentle memory of people whom he loved and wanted to protect. His soul felt lighter and his heart had lifted.

"I'll go on anyway," he told himself, as if replying to that threatening murmur that floated to him from the invisible Zaporohjan wagons. "No matter what happens."

After a time he found himself on that battlefield where the Prince's cavalry overwhelmed the Cossacks and shattered the Turkish janissaries on the first day of the siege. Here the way was easier. There were fewer holes, ditches, and dugouts to fall into, and hardly any corpses to trip over, because the Cossacks shoveled away most of the litter of those earlier battles.

It was also lighter. The night was greying. It was easier to see what lay ahead because the flat plain offered no intruding objects that might block his vision. The land dipped steeply towards the south at this point but Pan Longinus turned at a sharp angle away from the thin, blue-grey line that had begun to edge the eastern horizon, wanting to pass between the *tabor* and the western lake.

★   ★   ★

He had his bearings now and he strode out ahead at a rapid pace, bypassing swiftly whatever lay across his path, when a new set of sounds intruded from the Cossack camp.

He stopped at once. He listened. In less than a quarter of an hour he heard the dull thudding of hooves on the damp ground, the soft rustling of parting grass, and the quick snorting of approaching horses.

'*A guard patrol*,' he thought.

Then he heard human voices.

He threw himself at once to the side, found a long, coffin-like declivity of some kind and stretched himself in it like a corpse, with a cocked pistol in one hand and his Cowlsnatcher in the other.

The riders drew near and began to pass him. It was too dark for him to count them but there must have been at least a forty-man platoon to judge by the amount of sound they made, and he listened to their talk, their curses and their muttering as they rode along the edge of the ditch in which he'd found shelter.

"Ey, they might be having a hard time of it over there," some sleepy young voice complained. "But it's no paradise for us either, lads. No, not by a long shot . . ."

"And how many good *moloytzy* bit the earth right here, eh? Who could count that many?"

"*Hospody*," said another. "People say the King's not far away . . . ey, what'll happen to us when he gets here?"

"The Khan's mad at our Hmyel too . . . an' the Tartars threaten they'll take us for *yassyr* if they don't get the *Lah* slaves they've come for . . ."

"Aye, it's hard. Getting harder, too. Our people and the Tartars are already fighting with each other in the grazing grounds. It's as good as death to take a horse to pasture nowadays. And if one of us goes into the *kosh* alone it's all up with him! He don't come out alive!"

"Aye . . . It's worse for us now than it used to be before, my lads, you know that? A lot worse."

"The King is near. An' all the *Lah* power with him, people say. That's the worst thing yet."

"Hey, wouldn't it be something to be back in the *Sietch* right now? Sleeping in your own warm bedding . . . A good dram of vodka bubbling in your head and meat in your belly . . . And here we are instead, dragging our tails through the night like homeless old wolves."

"Aye . . . An' there's got to be real wolves around here somewhere. You see how the horses shie?"

"So maybe there's a corpse lying somewhere near . . ."

The voices faded. The hoofbeats drifted away in the darkness. Silence returned. Pan Longinus rose, crossed himself again, and went on.

Then rain started falling—a soft, thin drizzle, no thicker than the morning mist—and the night around him became even darker.

★ ★ ★

Now, seen about a mile past Pan Longinus' left shoulder, a pale pink light had begun to flicker as he walked, and then he saw another and another, and then a dozen more.

It was the Cossack *tabor*, he was sure. Its fires were few and small which suggested that most of the *moloytzy* were asleep and that only a few hardy souls had stayed up here and there to drink or to cook hot food for the morning.

'. . . *Thank God*,' Pan Longinus thought, without considering how hard he himself had fought through half the night nor how tired he was. '*They must be as worn out right now as our own people. Cannon wouldn't wake them . . .*'

But he no sooner comforted himself with this thought when he heard another patter of approaching hooves. Another roving cavalry patrol was coming his way. He threw himself down once more and this time the horsemen passed so close that they almost rode right over him. He thanked God that the horses were used to passing near dead men and failed to alert their riders with any nervous rearing.

He went on. Twice more along a distance of a thousand paces he had to hide from passing horsemen who patrolled the darkness. It was clear that the entire forefront of the wagon train was guarded just as closely as everyone in Zbarajh supposed it might be, but he was pleased that he'd managed to avoid the sentry posts and pickets that were sure to be scattered all along the ground. Getting around those, even assuming he spotted them in time, would be far more difficult.

His pleasure, however, proved to be short-lived. He barely went another hundred yards or so when something dark rose out of the ground before him in the greater darkness and stood, swaying dangerously towards him, no farther than a scant ten paces away.

Pan Longinus didn't know what it meant to be afraid. His

gentle, trusting nature gave him a childlike faith in the triumph of goodness over evil and right over wrong, but now an icy shiver ran along his spine. It was too late to drop back and go around, he knew. Too late to stoop and hide. The wavering dark figure took a step towards him. Apparently he'd been spotted by a sentry or a foot patrol.

And then a hushed, hoarse voice floated towards him out of the intervening darkness. "Vasil . . . is that you?"

"It's me," Pan Longinus murmured.

"Did you get the vodka?"

"I got it."

"Give it here, then."

Pan Longinus took a few steps forward. "Hey," the frightened voice snapped out. "How come you're so big?"

It seemed to Pan Longinus then that he had stepped out of his own body, that what he saw and heard didn't have anything to do with what he was doing, and that he was merely a detached observer witnessing a murder.

Something heaved and thrashed for a moment in the stifling darkness. A short, half-strangled cry burst out of the sentry. And then there was a dry, snapping sound as if a fistful of reeds had been crushed and broken, a thick gurgle rattled into his ear, and a heavy body slid softly to the ground.

★   ★   ★

Pan Longinus stepped across the corpse but this time he didn't follow the line of march he had chosen earlier.

He moved a few paces closer to the wagon train so as to slip between the pickets and the mass of wagons he could imagine in the darkness on his left. That way he'd be cutting down his risk if there wasn't a second chain of guardposts on this line, he thought; all that he might come across would be the reliefs sent out to the pickets now and then. And, what was even more important, none of the ubiquitous horse patrols would have any reason to be riding here.

After a few minutes it became clear that the *tabor* was protected by just that one arc of lookouts that he'd put behind him. He sighed with relief. But the dark mass of Cossack tents and wagons was now a mere two bow-shots away and looming ever closer no matter how carefully he tried to keep his distance. It also became clear that not everyone was asleep in that vast encampment. Groups of black figures huddled around the dim little campfires scattered through the darkness and he could see other black silhouettes moving before the glow. One of these fires, larger then the rest, leaped and crackled so high that its glare threatened to pick him out of his protecting darkness and Pan Longinus had to drop back towards the picket line again to hide from the light. He could see slaughtered oxen hanging by the dozen on thick crosslike structures near those yellow flames, and swarms of butchers working on them with their skinning knives, and groups of spectators clustered idly about. He heard the thin piping of their little reed flutes and the growl of their bored, sleepy voices.

The more remote rows of wagons blended with the darkness and vanished in a distance that made him feel as if it would go on for ever. But the wall of the *tabor*, thrown into black relief by the pale fires flickering beyond it, was looming closer once again, and he stopped, confused.

Had he lost his bearings? At first the silent wall seemed to have been creeping along beside him on his left. Then it was on his right. Now it appeared in front of him as well. He stood still, trying to reorient himself and choose a new direction. He knew that he had to find another route and chart a fresh course and that he had no time to waste because his sheltering darkness wouldn't last much longer. He had three hours left before daylight when he set out from Zbarajh and at least two hours must have passed already.

But at first he couldn't think where to turn among all the dangers that threatened him everywhere he looked. He was quite surrounded. In front of him lay the vast Cossack wagon train and bivouac with its human masses, the wide-flung crescent of the Tartar *Kosh* and the sprawling, ramshackle shacks and shelters of the *tchernya* which ringed Zbarajh for a thickness of more than a mile. Inside that ring lay the concentric lines of the pickets and patrols he had already passed. He could try to break out of this trap by creeping through the rows of wagons that stretched for several miles to both sides, or find some empty passage between the separate Tartar and Cossack encampments. Otherwise he'd be doomed to wander along this circle until dawn.

Nor was there a safe way back to Zbarajh any longer even if he could consider giving up his mission and tried to return. The blue-grey light around him was becoming brighter. Dawn was almost there. The pickets and the horse patrols would be on him before he was halfway across that silent battlefield where he had broken the janissaries' square . . .

He had to go on. But how? It seemed unlikely that the massed Zaporohjan wagons would stand so close together that he'd be unable to find some kind of gap between them, no matter how narrow. The broken ground that he was encountering as he groped along would make that kind of tight formation impossible here. Besides, he reasoned, there had to be a few passages left for the movement of large bodies of troops, and as corridors for cavalry and communications.

Pan Longinus crossed himself once more.

He took a deep breath.

He decided to search for one of those communications lanes. That meant drawing even closer to those dangerous wagons which could erupt with murderous crowds at a moment's notice. But there was no way he could see to avoid that risk. He knew that the campfires could catch him in their light and that any of those wandering shadows might see him and challenge his right to be there, but the dull red glow would also serve to outline the dense mass of wagons and any possible intervals between them.

Luck seemed to be with him, or perhaps his whispered prayers had been heard and answered, because within a quarter of an hour he found what he was searching for. He recognized the passage by its long stretch of thick, uninterrupted darkness. No cook fires glowed there. Nor would there be any men camping along that strip if it were used as a corridor for cavalry, he thought.

He flopped down on his belly and crept into that narrow void like a snake crawling into a pit.

It occurred to him that the fate of Zbarajh and everyone for whom he cared within its walls depended on whether he succeeded in worming his way through that lifeless corridor which made him feel as if he'd slid into the gaping jaws of some prehistoric beast.

Nothing stirred around him. No men moved. No horse neighed or snorted. Not even a dog came bounding out to bark an alarm. He prayed not only for himself, committing his soul and body to the will of Heaven, but also for those dear and precious friends who, at that very moment, would be praying for his safety on the walls of Zbarajh.

★   ★   ★

Minutes passed. Minutes that seemed like hours. He crept on, praying without a sound.

And then, miraculously, he was through the gap. The dim greying light ahead revealed shrubs and bushes beyond which he glimpsed the tall crowns of an oak grove.

It took him a moment to believe what he was seeing and his relief was almost overwhelming. Beyond those trees would be the next belt of woods, he knew, and then the next one and the next . . . Then there'd be the deep primeval forest stretching all the way to Toporov. And what beyond the forest?

' . . . *The King, salvation, glory, fame among men and merit in Heaven . . .*'

His feat of cutting off three Turkish heads at one blow would be like nothing in comparison with this accomplishment, he knew, but he didn't feel a single twinge of pride, vainglory or self-congratulation. Instead his simple, childlike heart welled over with gratitude and with a sense of his own unworthiness and humility.

He prayed.

He felt immensely privileged and grateful.

Then he got to his feet and went on. There'd be no need for guardposts on the far side of the mass of wagons. And if he did come across one, the sentries would be less watchful and easier to avoid, he knew. Rain started falling, drowning his footsteps with its heavy rustle, and Pan Longinus strode out, covering the distance of five normal paces with each of his own. The dark mass of wagons receded behind him.

The oaks drew near. Black shadows thickened under their outspread branches, darker than the night, although the pastures were already greying. The wind had freshened. It murmured in the tree crowns so that they too appeared to be praying. Sweat blinded him and the air among the trees became close and still as if a storm was brewing somewhere in the thickets. But he didn't have a thought to spare for any storms. He felt as if angelic choirs had burst into a hymn inside him. He pressed on with his gigantic strides, no longer caring whether anybody heard him, because there'd hardly be anyone here to hear anything at all! Shrubs crackled underfoot. Bushes parted. The trees around him started to thin out.

'Ah, that'll be the first of the pastures,' he thought and stepped into the open space.

' . . . *Wait*,' the trees seemed to whisper then. '*Stay in our shelter. Wait . . .*'

But the hurrying knight had no time to waste. One huge old oak stood in the middle of that broad, grey meadow and Pan Longinus headed straight towards it.

He was within a few dozen paces of the gnarled old tree when its shadows erupted with dark, leaping figures. Ten . . . or maybe twenty . . . he had no time to count them. They came on like a pack of wolves, baying as they bounded. He saw their pointed hoods, caught a glimpse of their bulky sheepskins, and heard a burst of questions in a language he didn't understand.

"*Hto tih? Hto tih?*"

These were Tartar horseherders, he knew at a glance. They'd have been hiding from the rain under the oak's broad branches.

"*Hto tih?*"

And suddenly thunder crashed out all around him. A red sheet of fire spread across the sky. It stripped the meadow and the oak of all their shadows and made them bright as day. The Tartars saw him, recognized him for what he was, howled and threw themselves upon him like wolves at a stag, and a savage battle broke out at once.

Twenty thick, corded arms wound around his body. A dozen hands clawed at him and fixed themselves to his arms like talons.

He shrugged them off.

He tossed the Tartars to the ground like ripe fruit scattering at the foot of a shaken tree and then the Cowlsnatcher grated in its iron scabbard, the air hissed in wide circle all around his head, the wild howls of rage turned into screams of pain and moans and yells of terror, and the trees echoed the frenzied calls for help and cries of amazement.

"*Div! Div!* A giant!"

And then the quiet meadow filled with every kind of sound that mankind could make.

★   ★   ★

But the savage howling didn't pass without an echo. Within a half hour the meadow filled with running crowds and horsemen— Cossacks, Tartars, *tchernya*—who came swarming at him with their scythes and axes and bunches of burning reeds which they used as torches, while even more boiled out of the woods behind them to see what all the shouting was about.

"What is it?" Feverish questions flew through the milling mob. "Who's that? What's going on here?"

"A wonder," the horseherders explained. "*Div*! A *Lah* giant! It's death to come near him."

"Kill him!" cried some of the new arrivals.

"No! Take him alive!"

Pan Longinus fired his pistols but he knew that no one in the Polish earthworks would be able to hear them. He backed up to the tree and waited, sword in hand, under the cool green canopy like a grim forest giant sprung out of ancient legends. He watched the mob coldly.

The crowd flowed towards him in a dense half-circle. It seemed to crouch at his feet, like a pack of wolfhounds ready to leap at a mired bison while he towered above them, and then a commanding voice shouted: "Take him!"

The mob surged forward as if it were a single living organism, one many-headed creature driven by one will. All the shouts died down and dwindled into a grating silence. Those of the attackers who couldn't push their way within reach of their quarry held the torches that illuminated the field for the others. A dark, human whirlpool seemed to boil and swirl at the roots of the tree, scattering bodies as if they were the debris of a massive shipwreck, and then a howl of rage, fear and despair thundered among the branches.

The mob burst apart, fell back.

Pan Longinus stood alone in front of the oak, a wall of corpses piled before his knees.

"Ropes! Bring ropes!" some Cossack voice commanded.

The horsemen galloped off at once and were back in moments with coils of cable that several dozen heavy-shouldered peasants grasped at each end and wound about the giant and the tree. But Pan Longinus freed himself with one slashing blow of his sword and the peasants tumbled to the ground. Then Tartars tried to take him with their whirling lariats and fared no better than the howling *tchernya*.

Seeing that the throng was merely getting in its own way and accomplishing nothing, a dozen Tartar warriors made room for themselves with their whips and sabers and charged the giant wanting to take him alive at all cost. But Pan Longinus cut them down as fiercely as a forest bear might rip and crush a pack of snapping mongrels. The massive oak, formed of twinned trunks that had grown together, fashioned a curved shield at his back and whoever came within the reach of his sword in front died without a chance to utter a sound.

His strength seemed to grow rather than diminish with each passing minute and, at last, the enraged Tartars chased the Cossacks and the *tchernya* off the field and called for bows and bowmen.

"*Ukhi!*" they cried. "*Ukh! Ukh!*"

Pan Longinus didn't understand the word but when he saw the short, curved horn-bows massing in front of him, and the bundles of long-feathered arrows spilled out of their cases at the archers' feet, he knew that the hour of his death wasn't far away and he began to recite the litany to the Holy Mother.

It was quiet then. The curious crowd had surged into the field once more behind the rows of archers but it made no sound.

The first arrow hissed into the oak as Pan Longinus murmured: "Mother of the Savior."

It brushed past his temple.

The second pierced his shoulder as he said: "Most glorious Virgin."

The third and fourth and fifth struck him as he recited the beatitudes, and then the hiss and thudding of the arrows became intertwined so closely with the words of the prayer that they seemed as natural as mere punctuation.

By the time that Pan Longinus murmured "Light of Dawn and Star of the Morning" the grey goose feathers were protruding from both his arms and shoulders, from his flanks, and from his thighs and knees.

Blood flowed down into his eyes from his wounded forehead and obscured his vision. He felt his great strength ebbing like a warm, red tide but he no longer felt or heard the flight and arrival of the arrows. He could see the Tartars and the meadow dimly . . . as if through a mist.

Finally, his legs buckled. He slid to his knees.

His head tilted forward and brushed the bloodied grey feathers that sprouted from his chest. The last flight of arrows struck him as he murmured: "Queen of the Angels" and those were the final words he uttered on earth.

Chapter Seventy-five

UNABLE TO SLEEP that night, Pan Zagloba and Volodyovski found themselves on the walls early the next morning. They stood in a crowd of other soldiers peering towards the Cossack encampments where a vast mob of *tchernya* spilled out of their bivouacs and poured towards the earthworks with an unusual degree of energy for that time of day.

"I've a bad feeling about that." Pan Zagloba nodded towards the flowing masses. "They're probably getting ready to attack again, and I can't think of anybody here whose arms aren't ready to drop off from exhaustion."

"An attack in broad daylight?" the little knight shook his head. "I doubt it. All they'll do is occupy our old walls and start tunneling into this one. And then they'll get down to their usual shooting."

"Look at them." Worried about Pan Longinus, the fat knight was hard to reassure. "They swarm like ants, don't they? Why did God have to make so much of that rabble? And why don't our cannoneers give them a taste of grapeshot?"

Pan Michal shrugged, looked around to see if anyone was close enough to hear him, and dropped his voice to a cautious murmur.

"The gunpowder's almost finished. I hear that we'll be out of it completely in six days if we keep up our normal rate of fire. Vurtzel is probably saving ammunition."

"Let's hope the King gets here before it's all gone."

Restless, depressed and irritable, Pan Zagloba couldn't find a comfortable spot for himself on the wall and the little soldier was in no better spirits. "He'd better," he muttered.

"Ah . . . I tell you . . . I no longer care what happens to me. Let fate take its course. I just want our poor Pan Longinus to get through all right! I couldn't close my eyes all night thinking about that good, dear man, and every time I'd doze off a little I'd see him in trouble. I must've sweated buckets worrying about him. That just has to be the best and finest human being you'd find in the Commonwealth if you searched it from end to end for three years' worth of Sundays!"

"So why were you always poking fun at him?"

"Because I'm cursed with a stupid mouth," Pan Zagloba muttered. "But don't remind me, Michal! Don't remind me! I wish I'd died ten times for every time I jeered at that sweet man. And if—God forbid—something happens to him I won't forgive myself until my dying day."

"Ey now . . ." the little knight patted Pan Zagloba's arm, trying to keep down his own anxiety. "Don't take on like that. He never felt anything but affection for you no matter what you'd say. He often said that you had a brass mouth but a golden heart. I heard him myself."

"He said that? God bless him for a true and decent friend! He never could put two coherent sentences together but he more than made up for that with all his other virtues. What do you think, Michal? Did he get through alright?"

"He could have . . . The night was pitch-black and the rabble must've been worn out after the beating we handed them in that last attack. My God, our own sentries were falling off their feet so how could theirs have done any better?"

"Thank God, then!" Soothed for the moment, Pan Zagloba tried another subject. "I urged him last night to ask about our poor Helen wherever he went. Seems to me Zjendjan would've tried to get her to the King, wouldn't he? Where else would she be safer? I doubt if Pan Longinus would take time to rest once he got there. He'd hurry back here along with the King's army so we might have some good news about her soon."

"I trust Zjendjan's wits, especially if his own neck's at stake," Pan Michal agreed, but worries weren't put aside that easily. "I'd have no peace for the rest of my time if something evil happened to that girl. I didn't know her long but I came to care of her as if she was my sister."

"And to me she's like my dearest daughter," Pan Zagloba sighed, plunged into new gloom. "My beard's going to turn completely white with all this anxiety. I can't take a lot more of it, I must say. To Hell with these times! You no sooner get to love someone these days and they're gone! And all you've left for yourself is grief, worry, bitter thoughts, an empty belly and holes in your hat so that every bit of rain drips on your bald head . . . Dogs have it better than gentry in this Commonwealth and the four of us have it worse than anybody . . .! It's getting to be time to leave this world, I'm thinking, and try for a happier life in the next!"

They sat in gloomy silence for a time, staring at the huge masses of armed peasants, *tchernya* and captive laborers pouring towards them from the Cossack *tabor*. Skshetuski was away just then, in council with the Prince, but their worrying related to him as well.

"You know, I've been thinking," Pan Michal murmured and scratched his close-cropped head. "Shouldn't we tell Yan that we rescued Helen? I mean, the way things are, none of us might leave this place alive. All of us could use something to feel good about, so why not help him find a little ease?"

"You mean you want to sweeten his last moments?" Pan Zagloba sighed.

"Do I? Perhaps I do. The only thing that held me back from telling him is that he never mentions her himself. It's as if his mind can't bear a fresh image of her but I know that he thinks about her all the time."

"So why bring it up?" Pan Zagloba's red, tired eyes filled with some unbearable images of his own. "If this dreadful war managed to cauterize the worst of his wounds then it's an act of God's mercy, pure and simple. Why rip those scars open again? Why feed him new hope when some damned Tartar slaver could be dragging our sweet girl across the sea right at this minute? I go blind with grief when I think about it, so what would he do? Ah, I tell you, it's time for me to die. There's nothing but pain and suffering left for decent people in this world. I'd gladly shrug off my old, useless life if only God would lead our Pan Longinus safely past those dangers . . ."

"He will." Pan Michal sighed and patted Pan Zagloba's shoulder once again. "Our friend must have better connections in Heaven than most other people because he's an innocent and virtuous man . . ." Quiet for a moment, the little knight, threw another glance at the enemy work parties. "But take a look now, will you? What are those people doing out there by the old wall?"

Pan Zagloba shaded his eyes against the sun and stared into the plain. Then he shook his head. "It's too bright out there. I can't see a thing."

"Looks like they're digging through our old entrenchments."

"I told you they'd attack. Why don't we get off this wall for a while and go back to camp?"

"It doesn't need to be an attack just now." Pan Michal shook his head again. "They have to tear down our old walls to have an avenue of retreat for later. And to bring in their siege towers and artillery. Ey, look at them work! You can almost hear the shovels whirring in the air!"

"Let them dig their way all the way to Hell," Pan Zagloba muttered.

"Hmm . . . Look . . . They've cut a breach for a good forty paces already . . ."

"May they all drown in their own sweat!" Pan Zagloba cursed but without his usual inventiveness and conviction. "May the plague smother the lot of them! May their wives and daughters give birth to nothing but sway-backed dogs for the next hundred years . . .! Ah, I see them now."

★ ★ ★

The distraught fat knight peered with real hatred at the mass of *tchernya* pouring through the long breach they had cut through the abandoned walls. He watched them spilling across the whole wide space between the old Polish earthworks and the new. Some of them starting shooting firelocks and muskets at the soldiers. Others attacked the soil with shovels and picks, digging trenches and planting a new chain of dugouts, ramparts and revetments to enclose the Commonwealth defenders in a third and final ring.

"Oho!" Volodyovski cried. "Didn't I tell you? Look, they're wheeling in the towers now!"

"Then it's got to be an attack, doesn't it?" The fat knight stirred uneasily and started to fan himself with his cap as if the air was suddenly too uncomfortably hot. "Phew! What a stifling morning! It's getting hard to breathe. Let's look for some shade in the camp for a while, what?"

"No," Pan Michal shook his head, peering at the rolling

towers with his sharp little eyes. "Those aren't scaling towers. They look more like some kind of mobile sniper posts."

The lean wooden structures which began to creep out through the breach were, indeed, of a different kind than the heavy-timbered assault machines to which the defenders had become accustomed. Lighter and taller, they were pieced together out of interlocking ladders, and covered with oxhides to shield the marksmen who crouched in their upper halves all the way to the open top.

"Let's go down into the camp, eh?" Pan Zagloba urged. "You may know they aren't going to attack but I don't think they know it."

"Wait," Pan Michal said and began to count the towering gun platforms as they rolled one by one from behind the old Polish wall. "Two . . . three . . . they must have a good supply of them . . .four . . . five . . . six . . . Ah, they're getting bigger! Seven . . . eight . . ."

"Phew," Pan Zagloba muttered and mopped his red face. "It's really getting hot again. Why don't we look for a bit of shade somewhere, eh?"

"Now there're some really big ones," Pan Michal exclaimed. "They'll pot every stray dog in the *maydan* out of those huge things because they've got to have their best marksmen up there."

"This sun's awfully bright," the fat knight complained. "It's right in my eyes too. I can't see a thing."

"Nine, ten," the little knight kept counting. "They'll make life on this wall really difficult for us. There's no doubt about it. Eleven . . ."

Then he paused. He stared. "What's that?" he asked in a strained, thin voice.

"What's what? Where?"

"There!" the little soldier pointed. "On that tallest one . . . Isn't that a man hanging from the top?"

Zagloba strained his weary, bloodshot eyes against the sun's bright glare and saw a long white shape swaying on a rope near the top of the loftiest tower. It seemed to be the naked body of a hanged man. The corpse turned slowly with the motion of the rolling structure, swinging back and forth like a monstrous pendulum as the machine edged out through the breach and lurched into the open.

"Hmm," the fat knight murmured and turned uneasily to Volodyovski. "Yes. I see it now. What do you suppose that's all about, then?"

But suddenly Pan Michal's pointed little face turned as white as that bleached long body twisting on its rope. "Dear God Almighty! That is Podbipyenta!"

A swift, harsh murmur flew among the watching soldiers on the wall as if a sudden wind had passed through a forest of dry trees.

" . . . W-w-what?" the fat knight stammered in a strangled whisper. "W-what did you say . . .?"

"That is Pan Longinus!"

Zagloba's body jerked spasmodically as if he'd been struck by an epileptic seizure. His head snapped back as if a musket ball struck him between the eyes. All color drained at once out of his florid face. His hands clutched at his hair and his grey lips whispered '*Jezus Maria . . .! Jezus Maria . . .!*' in a voice of utter and complete despair.

★ ★ ★

But now that shocked and threatening growl that flew the length of the Polish wall turned into a roar. Fierce shouts. Foul curses. Fresh men ran up with questions no one bothered to answer. Grief choked everyone. Rage began to lift the hair on the soldiers' heads. Whole regiments pressed together on the wall, climbed the breastworks, and stood exposed to enemy fire on the parapets oblivious of danger. Each man among them knew that a great and noble spirit had been torn from them, that an unblemished life was being brutalized and shamed before their eyes, and that it wasn't just some evil, obscene apparition that dangled on that degrading rope but a good and loyal friend, one who had shared all their miseries, and who gave up his life in an attempt to save them.

At last, Zagloba tore his hands away from his face. His ghastly features were transformed with fury. Spittle turned into foam on his mouth and dripped into his beard. His eyes bulged outward, red as bursting plums, while an onrush of blood suffused his deathly pallor with an apoplectic stain.

"Give me blood!" he howled and leaped into the moat.

The whole army followed.

No power on earth could have reined them in. Not even

Prince Yeremi's orders could stifle that eruption of uncontrollable fury. The knights and soldiers swept off the wall into the freshly-dug dry moat like a roaring tide. They clawed their way out of the ditch across each other's bodies. They used each other's backs and shoulders as if they were stepping-stones and ladders, oblivious of anyone trampled underfoot. Once out, they threw themselves blindly at the enemy without caring if anybody followed. The gun towers became wreathed in smoke and shuddered with their own fiery eruptions but no one among the charging knights paid attention to that hurricane of lead that burst out around them. Zagloba bounded far ahead of everyone else, a saber raised above his head and murder in his eyes, looking less like a human being than a maddened stallion.

The Cossacks ran out to meet them with scythes and flails and the two waves collided with a crash like two stone walls falling on each other.

But not even the fiercest wolfhounds can withstand a pack of blood-mad, hungry wolves. Hurled back, slashed with sabers, crushed, beaten down and trampled underfoot, the Cossacks gave way at once, then turned and fled towards the breach they'd leveled in the wall behind them.

Meanwhile Pan Zagloba seemed to have gone mad. He threw away all caution as if he'd never had a thought about his own safety. He hurled himself into the thickest crowds, roaring like a lioness which had lost her cubs, and the sounds that welled out of his throat had nothing human in them. Men fell around him as if struck by lightning, or as if they'd been seized and swept away by a roaring tempest, and he raged like a demon of destruction among them, creating a void wherever he appeared. He slaughtered everything that stepped in his way—biting, tearing, stabbing and trampling the fallen—and the grim little Pan Volodyovski ran beside him like another deadly spirit of murder and vengeance.

All the marksmen crouched inside the towers were pulled down, dragged out and butchered without mercy, and the rest of the fleeing *tchernya* was chased far into the plain beyond the next wall. After which the soldiers climbed the tallest of the siege machines, lifted Pan Longinus' martyred, naked body off its makeshift scaffold and lowered it gently to the ground.

Zagloba threw himself on the corpse like a grieving mother keening over the body of a murdered child, blind to everything around him and covering his dead friend with tears.

Volodyovski was also on his knees and weeping and so were half the soldiers who crowded around them.

It was easy to guess how the Lithuanian knight had died; his entire body was spotted with the livid scars left by Tartar arrows. Only his drained, parchment face remained unmarked except for one long cut high above the temple where an arrowhead grazed it in passing, and a few dark drops of blood that dried on his cheek. His eyes were closed. His lips were set in a quiet, shy smile. If it wasn't for the bluish pallor of his face and body he'd have seemed to be peacefully asleep. His comrades picked him up at last and carried him back inside the walls and then to the castle chapel.

★ ★ ★

By nightfall the dead giant's coffin had been knocked together. The funeral took place at the Zbarajh cemetery rather than the *maydan* where every other soldier was buried when he fell. All the clergy of the town and castle were present at the graveside. So was Prince Yeremi who handed over his command to Pan Sobieski for the length of the ceremony, the three Crown generalissimos, Pan Pshiyemski and Pan Konyetzpolski, along with the inconsolable Pan Zagloba, Pan Yan and Pan Michal. All of the gentry of the regiment in which Pan Longinus served stood behind the coffin as did every officer in the entire army who didn't have to be with his soldiers on the walls that night.

The night air was warm and soft, untouched by a breeze. The sky was bright with stars. The torches burned in even rows, undisturbed by any straying gust of wind; they cast their light on the yellow planks of the rough-hewn coffin that rested on a trestle by the open grave, on the slight, stooped figure of Father Muhovyetzki, and on the harsh bowed faces of the knights and generals and soldiers and commanders who were sunk in deep meditations of their own. No one spoke. The sweet smoke of incense drifted upward in unruffled spirals as if to underline the ancient nature of the sacrifice that this death represented, and only Pan Zagloba's unrestrained and despairing sobbing, the deep sighs of the gathered men, and the dull thunder of the cannonade on the walls behind them, broke the grieving silence.

Then Father Muhovyetzki signaled the start of the ceremony, lifted his eyes slowly to the starry sky and began his funeral oration.

"' . . . *What is that knocking that I hear this night on the gates of heaven?*'" he called out, as if playing the role of Christ's venerable gatekeeper disturbed in his sleep. "'*Who's out there? And by what right does he come to this place?*'"

He paused and cocked his ear like a sentry listening for a password and then supplied his own answer in a gentler, supplicatory voice: "'*Let me in, good Saint Peter. It's I, Podbipyenta . . .*'

"But what achievements qualify you to ask for admission?" he called out again. "What rank and honors bring you to these doors which don't open even for a King without special merit?"

He paused again. He stared out over a profound and unbroken silence. This was a priest of an almost saintly reputation, so honored for his gentleness and wisdom that even Prince Yeremi sometimes stayed his unforgiving hand at his entreaties and extended mercy instead of ruthless punishment. But now his gentle eyes seemed like an admonition.

"The road which leads to those portals isn't a broad, paved highway that one travels in a coach drawn by six white horses," he went on, as if in challenge to all those listening knights and generals. "You don't come to *this* Diet with lackeys standing on the footstep, a suite at your back, and outriders galloping before you . . . Neither birth nor bloodlines, even if they are as ancient and distinguished as those of our departed friend, can buy admission to the House of God . . .

"Oh yes," he argued like a traveler stopped by a porter at a gate. "We know that neither senatorial rank nor the power of Crown offices and positions can guarantee a welcome to that great assembly of martyrs, saints and heroes . . . We know it, kind Saint Peter. We know it. And so did our friend."

He waited as if listening for an answer from the sky to which he was speaking, then nodded quietly and continued in his own soft voice.

"We know that the only path which lifts mankind to that sublime place you guard is a steep and thorny one, Great Peter! Like Christ's own road to Golgotha, it's full of suffering endured with humility and patience. We know that only goodness, kindliness, honesty, generosity and sacrifice for the sake of others can pave the way, that only virtue is the price of entry, and that is why we ask you, Holy Gatekeeper, to let our friend Longinus Podbipyenta come in through your doors because it's exactly that hard path of kindness, honor, gentleness, self-denial, innocence and love for his brothers that he took to get there . . ."

His voice soared and trembled as if it were a soul flying up for judgment and the assembled soldiers beat their breasts and their bloodstained armor with callused fists that had long forgotten the gentling touch of mercy.

"Let him in, Peter!" cried the priest while a great sigh swept across the gathering and remorse gripped all those hardened warriors. "He comes to you like a sacrificial lamb, pure and undefiled. His soul flutters down to your hand like a dove worn out after a stormy flight! He comes as naked as Lazarus . . . as torn by pagan arrows as the martyred Saint Sebastian . . . as poor as Job . . . and as free of blemish as a pascal offering whose blood was poured out joyfully in the service of his mother country . . .

"So let him in!" the priest cried.

"Let him in!" murmured the assembly.

"Open your gates to this lamb of Christ," the priest called out, swept up by his own passion. "Let him graze a little in God's pastures! He's hungry, you see . . . he comes to you from Zbarajh . . .!"

"Have mercy!" cried the soldiers.

" . . . Because," the priest went on. "If you bar your gates to that unblemished soul, with the blood of his sacrifice still warm upon the ground, what man alive in these Godless times can hope to be admitted? Whom *can* you let into paradise if you keep *him* out . . .?"

★ ★ ★

He spoke on and on and his simple eloquence soared into the skies like a sacrificial offering of its own.

The gentry gloried in such things. These may have been Christendom's fiercest fighters, for whom bloodshed, war and death were as unremarkable as breathing, but each of them, no matter how poor or unimportant, was brought up on Greek and Roman classics. Each of them spoke Latin as their '*lingua franca.*' Each quoted Virgil, Cicero and Cato as easily as they cursed, drank, fought and quarreled, taking vast pride in their erudition, and that's how Prince Yeremi's confessor began his funeral oration. He went on to paint Pan Longinus' life in such glowing bursts of oratory that everyone, no matter how powerful or important, thought himself worthless in comparison. Even Prince Yeremi beat his breast and questioned his conscience.

These were excessive times, when people loved and hated to the limits of their passion, as everyone there knew by his own experience. Polite conventions hadn't yet corrupted the honesty of feeling. No one felt shamed by tears. Everyone was weeping. Their clenched fists thundered on their armored breasts and their huge bowed shoulders shook in paroxysms of sobbing as they absorbed the great loss to them and to their country this death represented. Their time was passing. A storm of changes was sweeping through their world. The qualities of knighthood would soon have no meaning. And many of them knew as they mourned Longinus Podbipyenta that they were also weeping for their nation and themselves.

The priest himself burst into tears as he related the events of Pan Longinus' blameless life, his gentle habits and his heroic death.

"Goodbye to you, then, our dear friend and brother!" he cried over the corpse and sobbed as brokenly as the inconsolable Zagloba. "You didn't reach our earthly King, that's true, but you brought our tears and hunger and misery and word of our suffering to the King of Heaven! That's a much more certain source of our succor and rescue! But you, yourself, won't be coming back to us again. And that's why we weep over your body . . . why we bathe your coffin with our tears . . . because we loved you with all of our hearts!"

Everyone—the Prince, the generals, the assembled army, and Pan Longinus' three friends more than anyone—wept openly along with the priest. Every face shined with tears.

But when he intoned the final '*Requiem eternam ei, Domine*' their grief broke through all restraints anyone might have had. Death was a constant in their lives, they knew. They were inured to slaughter by a daily practice and regarded even the worst bloodshed with comparative indifference. But at these final words of farewell each of them lifted his arms to Heaven and cried like a child.

It proved almost impossible to tear Zagloba away from the coffin. He clung to it as desperately as if the man inside it were his son or brother but Skshetuski and Volodyovski finally managed to drag him to the side. Prince Yeremi stepped up and took a handful of earth from the excavated pile, the priest began the recitation of the 'Anima eius,' and the casket rattled down into its hole on the lowering ropes.

The Prince threw in the first few handfuls of dry soil. After him came every other officer and soldier in the army, from senators and dignitaries of the Crown to the simplest trooper, who filled the grave with their hands and helmets. They went on piling the cold, dark earth above Pan Longinus' body long after the grave had turned into a tomb, and soon a tall burial mound of the kind that men built in ancient times for great Kings and heroes marked his resting place, while a late white moon appeared among the stars and painted it with silver.

★ ★ ★

After the funeral the three knights made their way from the town to the camp in silence. The night was bathed in moonlight and as bright as if a thousand votive candles were flickering in the sky but neither Volodyovski nor Skshetuski seemed to have anything to say. None of them, especially the overwrought Zagloba, wanted to break the introspective hush that linked them to their buried friend.

But other clusters of knights praised Pan Longinus as they passed them, heading for the earthworks where the sky leaped and trembled redly under new explosions.

"He had a funeral like none I've ever seen," said some officer, pushing past Skshetuski.

"He earned it," said another. "Who else would've undertaken a mission like that?"

"I heard that there were several volunteers among the Vishnovyetzki people," said another. "But I suppose that after this terrible example they'll have changed their minds."

"And why shouldn't they? A snake wouldn't be able to slip through those siege lines."

"You're right about that, friend. It'd be pure madness to try it again."

They passed. The silence returned. Then suddenly Pan Volodyovski murmured: "Did you hear them, Yan?"

"I heard," Skshetuski said.

"The man's right, you know."

"Perhaps he is. But it's my turn tonight."

"Yan, my dear friend . . ." The little knight's young and normally carefree face was suddenly aged and grave. "We've known each other for years, haven't we?"

"We have. And they've been great years, Michal. I'd hardly be able to ask for any better."

"Yes. Well . . . Then you know that I seldom pull back from any dicey business. But risks and danger are a fair gamble, my good friend . . . A clear-cut case of suicide is something quite different."

"And is it really you, Michal, who's saying this to me?" Pan Skshetuski smiled quietly.

"It is. Because I'm your friend."

"Just as I am yours," Pan Skshetuski said. "So give me your word of honor that you won't try to go if I'm killed in my own attempt."

"Oh that can't be!" Volodyovski cried. "That's out of the question!"

"There, you see?" Pan Yan smiled fondly at the little soldier. "How can you ask me to do something you wouldn't do yourself? Look, let's just allow God's will to be done in this matter as in everything else and leave it at that."

"So let me go with you, then," Pan Michal urged.

But Pan Yan shook his head.

"I can't think of anybody I'd rather have with me in a thing like that," he said. "But the Prince forbids it. And you're a soldier, Michal. You must obey orders."

Pan Michal was, indeed, a soldier first and foremost, so he said nothing more, only his pointed little whiskers started twitching agitatedly up and down which, as Pan Yan knew, was what always happened whenever he was so deeply moved or stirred that he was lost for words.

"It's awfully bright tonight," he muttered at last.

"Yes, it is." Pan Yan nodded quietly. "I'd rather wait for a darker night, given any choice, but there's no time for waiting. We're in for good weather and clear nights for several more weeks before the autumn rains."

"Another day or two . . ." Pan Michal began but Pan Yan cut him short.

"We're almost out of ammunition and food is so scarce that I've seen starving soldiers digging for roots. Others have jaw-rot from all the filth they're eating. If I don't go tonight there'll be no point in going."

"You've seen the Prince? He agrees?"

"I've already said goodbye to him."

"Well. That's it then. I don't suppose there's much point in arguing with a man who is sick of living," Pan Volodyovski said with one last sly and appealing glance at his determined friend.

"God bless you, Michal." Skshetuski smiled sadly in the moonlight at the little soldier. "Of course I can't claim to be ecstatic about my life these days but I'm not going to look for death of my own free will. To start with, that's a sin. And in the second place the point of going is to find the King and save all our people. Not to throw away an unendurable life and get killed for nothing."

"Well . . ."

The little knight felt an overwhelming urge to tell Pan Yan about Helen's rescue, just to make sure he'd want to go on living and so, perhaps, think twice about his attempt, but he knew Skshetuski. Nothing would change his mind or turn him from the course of service and duty, so he clamped his mouth shut and bit down on his tongue.

'What if the news drives him wild?' he thought. 'He might get careless. They'll catch him all the sooner . . .'

Instead, he asked: "Which way will you go?"

"I told the Prince I'd try it through the lake and then along the river where it cuts between the Cossack *tabor* and the Tartar *kosh*. It's the long way around, I know, but the Prince agrees it's probably the best one."

"Well, then that's that," Pan Volodyovski said, nodding in resignation. Then he sighed and shrugged. "Everyone has to die in some way sooner or later, and in our kind of life it might as well be in the field. At least this can be of some use to others . . . What more can I say? God guide you, Yan! God watch over you! If we don't see each other again in this world then we'll get together in the next, I know. Meanwhile my heart goes with you."

"And mine stays with you. God bless you for all the friendship that you've given me. But there's one more service I'd like to ask of you."

"It's yours, you know that. What is it?"

"Well . . . if I should die . . . the Cossacks might not show it off as they did with poor Pan Longinus. The lesson we gave them for that was a frightful one. But they'll make sure that you find out about it in some way, just to undermine your confidence and rob you of hope, so see to it that old Zachvilihovski goes to see Hmyelnitzki and gets my body back for a decent burial. I don't want some dogs dragging my bones all over their encampments."

"Rest your mind on that score," Volodyovski said and then they were silent.

Pan Zagloba, who listened to them from the start without really grasping anything they said—hearing them through a dull, mindless haze of grief in which neither words nor anything he saw had any real meaning—suddenly understood what was going on. But his heart was gone out of him; he could find no more strength to argue. All he could manage was a pitiful, broken, old man's groan.

"That one last night," he whispered, trembling along the length and breadth of his entire body. "And this one today . . . God! God! God . . . !"

"Have some faith," Pan Volodyovski urged him. "Believe in the best."

"Yan, my dear friend," Zagloba began but that was as much as he was able to say.

All he could do then was to press his white, troubled head against the young man's chest and to cling to him like a frightened and abandoned child.

An hour later Skshetuski slipped into the waters of the western lake.

Chapter Seventy-six

THE NIGHT WAS SO CLEAR and so brightly lit that the center of the lake looked like a polished silver shield but Pan Yan disappeared at once in the darkly tangled mass of the lakeshore reeds.

The muddy banks of that broad sheet of water were overgrown so lavishly with tall, slender stalks, nodding rushes and thick lily pads that spread all the way out to the middle of the lake that wading through that knotted snarl of intertwined and twisted vegetation was much like the hopeless struggle of an insect in a spider's web. The whole dense jumble of sharp, pointed leaves, slippery stalks, and grasping sunken roots clung to Skshetuski at each step. But at least it hid him from the eyes of the Cossack sentries who, he knew, would be posted all the way around.

To swim across the bright pool of open water in the center was out of the question; any dark object moving across that glassy mirror would be spotted at once. He'd have to inch along through the slimy edges of the waterway.

Pan Yan decided to circle through the rushes to the narrow swamp that festered around the mouth of the little river which drained into the lake. Time, he knew, was precious. That open channel that snaked into the swamp would be well-guarded, he was sure; he could expect Tartar pickets on one side of it and Cossack lookouts posted on the other. But a whole thicket of snarled reed-like cane crowded in a dense, concealing mass along either bank and spread well into the middle of the river with only a few bordering strips and patches carved out of it to make roofing for the *tchernya's* shelters. Once he was in that swamp he'd be able to slip through among the reeds and rushes even in the daytime, he believed, unless the quagmire underfoot proved to be too deep.

But even this slower and safer way he chose, sliding at a snail's pace through the slimy webwork of rotting vegetation, had a variety of hazards. Under the dark, still water lay thick pools of mud a yard or more in depth, and a whole carpet of gassy air bubbled out to the surface at each cautious step. This bubbling seemed as loud to his nervous ears as goose grease spluttering in a frying pan. The still, dark air magnified each sound. Moreover, no matter how carefully he moved, a broad, bright wake rippled out behind him and spread beyond the reeds into the open water where the cold white light of the moon broke on it like a glittering swarm of fireflies.

Within an hour he was wet with sweat.

Had it been raining, Skshetuski could have swum the lake in half that time, he knew. But there wasn't a sign of a rain cloud anywhere in the sky. Streams of greenish light fell on the lake, turning the lily pads into silver platters and the feathery heads of the reeds into nodding plumes. The air seemed breathless, still as death. There wasn't even a suggestion of a breeze to create a concealing rustle in the rushes. By an ironic stroke of good fortune, the dry rattle of musketry in the Polish earthworks and Cossack revetments covered up the popping hiss of the air bubbles, and Pan Yan took care to hold absolutely still until the firing crackled out behind him at a faster rate.

Yet this was not the end of his fears and torments. A thick cloud of flying leeches and mosquitoes rose out of the reeds in the dry, warm air and settled on his face, stinging and whining and swarming about his eyes and ears.

He harbored no illusions in choosing this route that it would be easier than going by land but he failed to anticipate everything he was likely to encounter. He'd forgotten about the cold, dank fear that comes from the unknown. Just how deep was that mud anyway? And what lay waiting in it? Imagination joined with superstition to fill his mind with horror and revulsion. He knew that any stretch of water, even the most familiar, had its own mysterious and unnerving quality, especially at night and in the dark. But those Zbarajh lakes were simply terrifying. Their depths seemed heavier and more oily than ordinary water. They exuded a thick, greasy stench of decomposing corpses. Hundreds of drowned Cossacks and Tartars were rotting in that mud, he knew. Both sides fished out as many of them as they could each day, less out of any sense of respect for the dead than to avert the outbreak of the plague, but how many more were lurking among the reeds? How many would be hiding in the underwater tangle of sunken roots and branches and in the knotted webs of rotting cane stalks matted on the bottom?

Skshetuski's lower body was chilled by the water but his forehead was dripping with an icy sweat.

'*What,*' he thought, '*will happen if some slimy arms reach for me from behind?*'

. . . And what if he should see a pair of green gloating eyes shining at him out of that ghostly darkness?

Roots snagged his ankles. The long, soft ropes of floating lily stalks coiled about his legs and clutched at his body. The damp, furry heads of the reed cane brushed against his neck like thick, stroking fingers and he felt the hair rising on his head at the thought that these could be the hands and arms of some foul drowned creature sliding up to grasp him and pull him down into the slime for ever.

"*Jezus Maria, Jezus Maria,*" he whispered over and over as he waded forward in that bubbling darkness.

Every so often he stopped and looked up into the sky as if some sort of calmness could be drawn from the sight of moonlight and the stars.

"There *is* a God," he told himself just loud enough so that he could hear his own words, but not so loud that the sound could carry beyond his own breath.

The shore, glimpsed through occasional breaches carved into the canebrake, beckoned to him with a nearly irresistible hypnotizing power. It seemed to him whenever he caught sight of that broad, grassy plain that he was a lost soul peering at this familiar, God-created landscape out of some cursed extraterrestrial world of mud, black pits drowned in a ghostly moonlight, dead men, doomed spirits and eternal night, and he was seized by such a desperate longing to break out of this malevolent morass that it took all his courage and willpower and faith and awareness to stifle his cries and keep him where he was.

★ ★ ★

He crept on through that world of imaginary terrors until the shooting on the earthworks slipped far beyond the range of his hearing.

He saw then, on that familiar shore for which he'd been longing, a lone mounted Tartar who stood a few dozen paces from the water's edge.

The man seemed asleep. He swayed softly, hunched in his tall wooden saddle, his reins slack and his horse nibbling at the grass. His dark, hooded head bobbed up and down as if he were nodding amiably to the hidden knight and Pan Yan held his breath as he fixed his eyes on this real danger.

That calmed him. He could breathe easier then. This tangible and recognizable reason for tense nerves, calling for a cool head and a disciplined reaction, dispelled all his imagined horrors and brought him back to earth. Instinct, experience and years of training offered instant help. '*Is he sound asleep?*' he asked himself at once. '*Or just dozing off a bit? Should I wait a while? Or should I keep on going none the less?*' He was betting his life on a sentry's carelessness and boredom but he had nothing better on which he could depend.

He took no chances. He edged past the sleeping picket with even greater caution than he'd shown before.

★   ★   ★

Time passed at a rate that defied all his calculations. Minutes seemed like hours.

He may have gone halfway around the lake to the swamp and the mouth of the river when the first of the sharp night breezes rustled through the rushes.

He could grin then, worn out as he was. That crisp, dry sighing of the wind filled him with delight. It muffled whatever accidental sounds he might have been making despite all the painstaking care he took with every step and he whispered his fervent thanks to God for this timely help. He could move out more boldly under this providential cover, his slurred, dripping footfalls masked by the loud creaks and whispers of the cane all around the lakeshore, and even the low fetid water near the banks, stirred into gentle ripples by that moving air, began a rhythmic slap and gurgle against the oozing mud.

But something else seemed to have come awake as well. A new terror leaped out of the imagination as a dark hunched shape appeared suddenly in the reeds before him. Its arms were lifted, hands dangling at the wrists. It swayed toward him, sagging among the reeds as if getting ready to spring at him out of the mud, and Skshetuski almost cried out in horror and revulsion. His mouth flew open and a wail of terror gathered in his chest but that same sudden onrush of superstitious fear silenced him better than a gag. It choked the air out of his throat like a cold hand clamped around his neck. He gasped. His shout died without a sound. A foul cloying stench drifted from the corpse that had been trapped upright by the cane and swayed there, moved by the lakeshore ripples, so that it looked alive. It made his stomach heave, wrenched him back into reality and filled his eyes with water.

Sickened, he took a tighter grip on his imagination. "Old wives' tales," he muttered in disgust. The thought that this drowned cadaver had been getting ready to leap on him drained out of his mind and he pushed on, swallowing his revulsion. The soft hiss and clatter of the reeds and rushes went on all around him. He parted them with great care before he slipped through them, listening and watching after every step, and he caught sight of two other Tartar pickets standing just beyond them.

He passed them as quietly as if he were a ghost. He edged past a fourth one.

"I must've circled half the lake already," he whispered to himself. "That's the *kosh* back there . . ."

The swamp and the river would be the dividing line between the two main enemy encampments, he knew by experience; not even Hmyelnitzki could keep these ill-matched, temporary allies from leaping at each other's throats at every chance they got.

He rose a little higher in the reeds so that he could peer around and see where he'd come to.

Something nudged his knees.

He looked down, saw a white face staring at him from below the water.

'*Another one*,' he thought.

But this time he could ignore the corpse. It was lying flat on its back, still as a sunken log. Its stench made him dizzy but there was nothing about this cadaver that made it seem alive.

He moved out with a greater urgency so as to clear his head but the going was becoming harder at each step. The farther he went, the more the cane thickened, but this was yet another kind of blessing. The dense reeds gave him better cover although their dark, crackling walls impeded his progress and slowed him even further.

A half hour passed in that silent struggle. Maybe more. He

lost all track of time. The hours dragged by and he pushed on, determined to keep going even though a dreadful, depleting lassitude settled about him like a suffocating cloak, and a dull stone-like weariness pressed down on his shoulders.

" . . . Keep on," he whispered. "One step at a time . . . That's the way. Now another. Keep going."

But even this slow, dogged progress taxed him to the limit. The black muddy water was so shallow near the bank that it barely reached the tops of his jackboots while in other places he sunk up to his waist in the bubbling ooze that sucked at his legs so greedily and clung to him so tightly that he was hardly able to break free. Sweat blinded him. It seemed as cold as ice. And, at the same time, his whole body began to burn with fever.

" . . . What is this?" he asked himself. "Delirium? That swamp . . . where is it? Did I miss it?"

The thought that he might not recognize the mouth of the river and go on, circling the lake all night until he ended where he started from or—worse yet—until he blundered in exhaustion into a Cossack outpost, caused another swift lurch of panic in his chest.

' . . . I've picked a bad route,' he thought, feeling his spirits sag. 'These lakes are impenetrable. This is hopeless. I'll go back . . . rest a bit . . . and try it tomorrow the way Pan Longinus did it . . .'

He suppressed his doubts or at least beat them back for a little while. They'd be back, he knew. But he went on because he realized that he was merely lying to himself by thinking that he might turn back and then start out again the next day after a few hours rest. He was aware as soon as he thought of turning back that once he was among his friends again . . . once their familiar, loving warmth had been restored to him . . . no power in Heaven or on Earth would be able to send him out again.

Then it occurred to him that the bog and the mouth of the little river could be still ahead; moving as slowly as he had, and stopping as often as he did, he might not have reached them . . .! But the thought of resting was almost irresistible none the less.

' . . . Here. Just for a moment. To lie down a bit. A few minutes on this clump of rushes . . . Sleep. Close the eyes for a moment . . . Rest here. In this mud . . .'

He went on, struggling against himself just as bitterly as he did against the real and imagined difficulties and fears and dangers.

He prayed.

The sight of the occasional Tartar outpost brought him to his senses. But hot white lights were flashing behind his eyes, his vision was blurring, the fever shook him like a dog worrying a bone, and he knew that he was so utterly exhausted that just the mere act of pulling his legs out of the mud took a heroic effort.

* * *

Another half hour went by and the mouth of the river remained as elusive as it had been all night. But the floating corpses were now everywhere around him. The drowned bodies, the hissing of the reeds, the weight of the darkness, the strain of watchfulness, the hardship of the journey and the lack of sleep began to confuse him. His perceptions tilted. He began to see things that weren't there.

. . . Helen waits in Kudak and he is on his way to her, sailing with Zjendjan on a Dnieper galley. Hey, there's a song in the air . . . the Steppe wind murmurs its melancholy ditties in the reeds and rushes, and Father Muhovyetzki steps forward to start the nuptial mass . . .

But where had he been all this time?

Why is he so late? And why is the grim old one-eyed Pan Grodjitzki going to give the bride away?

'*Ah, of course. Of course,*' he told himself with the logic of a deranged or hallucinating mind. '*Her brothers are away. Gone to the horse fair at Zolotonosha . . .*'

No matter. No matter.

"*Hey master,*" Zjendjan says, tugging at his sleeve. "*The Lady is waiting.*"

Waiting. Stretching out her arms. Watching from the walls. Any minute now she'll be clapping her hands together and crying out: "*I see him. He's here!*"

. . . And now Zjendjan is pulling at the buttons on his coat, helping him to dress . . .

"*Hurry master, hurry!*"

Skshetuski's eyes snapped open. He shook himself awake and the vision vanished. A clump of reeds had barred his way, that's all, pushing against his chest and clutching at his arms. He splashed cold water on his face. His dreamscape disappeared. He pushed on, feeling a little stronger, driven by his fever.

'. . . *Ah, ah . . . Is this the swamp already?*'

But the reeds around him were the same as ever. He might as well have been standing still for all the difference he could see in the surrounding darkness. If he had come to the rivermouth there would have been a break in the cane, wouldn't there? Yes. Had to be. Of course. So the swamp must be still ahead, he thought.

He went on. But his mind seemed to be going its own way no matter what he did to keep himself fixed in some sort of tangible reality. His thoughts flew far away.

. . . And he is once more on the Dnieper, sailing with the current. He sees skiffs and galleys. Kudak and the Sietch seemed to have flown together along with all the faces that drift before his eyes . . .

Helen smiled at him, her eyes alight with joy, and stretching out her arms.

So did the Prince beside her.

So did Hmyelnitzki and the old Grand Ataman of the *Sietch* whose name he'd forgotten, and the gently smiling Pan Longinus, and grinning Pan Zagloba and the glum, bitter Bohun, and the lively, loving little Pan Volodyovski. Vyershul, Kushel, Byhovietz whose place he'd taken to go on his mission to the Zaporohjans, old Pan Zachvilihovski . . . everyone he had ever known was crowding around him dressed in their richest clothes.

. . . But why are they waiting? What's been going on? Ah, of course. Of course. The wedding. But where is this wedding to take place?

And where was he right now anyway?

This was neither Lubnie nor Rozloghi nor Kudak nor the Zaporohjan *Sietch* . . . This water . . . full of mud and reeds . . . floating corpses . . .

Skshetuski woke again. Or rather he was pulled out of his dream by a loud new rustling coming from up ahead, and he stopped, held himself quite still, crouched down and listened. He heard a splash. And then another. And another. The dull thump of oars rattling in the rowlocks.

'*. . . Ah,*' he thought, thick and dull with his own exhaustion. '*A guard boat.*'

He saw it then: a flat-bottomed Cossack skiff creeping through the reeds. Two *moloytzy* in it. One rowing. The other standing in the bows and poking among the rushes with a long birch rod that looked from the distance like a silver ceremonial staff.

Skshetuski sunk down into the water until only his head showed above the tangled, rotting vegetation.

'*Is this just an ordinary guard patrol?*' he wondered. '*Or are they on to me? Are they looking for me? Do they know I'm here?*'

But the *moloytzy* were too calm, too careless in their movements, and too bored to be part of a searching sweep beating the reeds after a fugitive that they knew was there. The surface of the lake had to be full of boats, he assured himself. River Cossacks never went far without them, just like Steppe Cossacks were never without their horses. If they were looking for him they'd have gathered dozens of boats and a crowd of people.

Meanwhile the skiff slid past him.

The hiss and crackling of the reeds drowned the Zaporohjans' voices and the hidden knight caught only a few harsh, grumbling words.

" . . . to Hell with them anyways, I say! Sending good men out at night to guard this stinking water . . ."

And then the skiff crept out of sight among the reeds and rushes. Only the tall, glum Cossack in the bows, who slapped at the water with his staff as if he wanted to scare the fish and drive them into a waiting net, stood out above the grassy plumes for a while longer.

Skshetuski went on.

He caught sight of another mounted Tartar picket watching by the lakeshore. The moonlight slanted right into the man's squat, sharply angled face and made it seem like the lean and bony muzzle of a wild Steppe dog.

Chapter Seventy-seven

TIME SEEMED TO BE standing still although Skshetuski knew that it was passing much too quickly. He was still far away from the swamp and the mouth of the river which he had to reach before daylight trapped him in the open water; and the Tartar pickets he spotted on the lakeshore were becoming more frequent.

But Pan Yan was less worried now about these outposts than by the fear that he might lose consciousness out of sheer exhaustion. He was quite literally falling off his feet. He harnessed all his willpower in an effort to stay awake, and to remain aware of his time and place and where he was going, but that grim struggle only added to his weakness, weariness and lassitude.

His eyes blurred. Things, whether real or imagined, acquired double images. Sometimes they came in threes. The flat, open center of the lake took on the appearance of the trampled *maydan* of the camp he'd left far behind, and the clumps of reeds became his regimental tents. He had a nearly irresistible urge to call out to Volodyovski, urging his small friend to join him and give him a hand in this back-breaking struggle, but managed to cling to his ebbing sense of reality just long enough to stop himself in time.

"Don't shout! Don't shout!" he whispered to himself. "That'd be the end."

But winning in that inner battle was becoming harder with each step.

He left Zbarajh tormented by hunger and worn down by that dreadful sleeplessness which was beginning to kill dozens of soldiers every day. This night march through terror had just about brought him to his knees. Whatever strength he summoned until now out of his starved and tormented body was quite spent and drained away by the wet chill and the return of fever. The foul graveyard stenches of the water, the hopeless stumbling through the mud, and that remorseless wrestling with the sunken roots threatened to undermine him altogether. The flying leeches had cut his face to ribbons.

Worn out, covered with blood and shaken by the terrors of his imagination, he felt that only one of two things would happen at any moment if he didn't get to the swamp and river right away. He'd either climb out to the shore so that he might speed up the inevitable process of his dying or he'd fall senseless into the mud and drown. That rivermouth, where a wholly new set of hardships and dangers would begin for him, had become his beacon of salvation.

He went on, half out of his senses and racked by his fever. He knew that he was becoming careless but there didn't seem to be anything he could do about it. Luckily for him the reeds and the rushes hissed and whispered at him even louder than they had before, masking the sounds of his stumbling passage through the cane. Those creaks and rustlings seemed like human voices discussing his chances of coming through alive. The dead were making room for him in the mud, he thought. They were watching. Waiting. Whispering the odds.

' . . . *Would he get to the marshy rivermouth or not? Will he climb out at the next sentry post? He will. He will not . . .*'

Even the thick cloud of insects swarming about his face seemed to be humming with eager speculation.

The water was becoming deeper, he noted, only half aware of what this might mean. The thick, muddy ooze was now bubbling about his chest. But it seemed colder. Perhaps even fresher. He thought he might try swimming in a moment. Perhaps he'd have to swim if the water became any deeper. But he was so spent, and the rotting cane was so thick around him, that he was sure he'd sink down among the reeds and drown anyway.

Once more he felt that overwhelming urge to call out to Volodyovski. He had already lifted his hands to his bloody face and framed them about his lips, and the words '*Michal! Michal!*' were about to spill out of his throat and ring through the darkness, when some wet, swaying plume of swamp vegetation struck him across the mouth.

He shook himself back into consciousness. He looked around, shaken and confused, knowing that he'd been saved by a miracle and his sweat felt like a sheet of ice laid across his forehead. His knees sagged in terror. He saw a pale light shining ahead and slightly to the right and he turned towards it, hardly conscious of what he was doing, and pushed on doggedly for some time.

But the cane seemed to be thinning out. Yes, he told himself. It was. He could see blue-grey light through the black lattice-work of the nodding reed stalks. The water slapped and rippled against his chest, tapping his shoulders with cold, moving fingers. Something new was tugging at his legs and body. He could feel a current of colder water seeping through the ooze. And could he let himself believe that the air was freshening? Was that wood smoke that he could smell hanging in the mist? And were those cooking fires up ahead?

And then he saw a stretch of clear, open water laid across his path like a strip of moonlight and he stood still, breathing deeply, and hardly able to believe that what he saw was actually there to see.

'. . . *That's it, then,*' he thought, weak with relief and trying to reorient himself. '*That's fresh river water. That's the end of my wandering around this lake* . . .'

Hope threatened to unhinge him as suddenly as his sense of hopelessness did just a little earlier.

'. . . *Who knows* . . . *I might get past the tabor before daylight* . . .'

Ahead of him and slightly to his right lay the mouth of the river edged by tufts of swamp grass and deep stands of mangrove.

★ ★ ★

The mouth of the river and the broad, moonlit path that spread out behind it seemed like a wedge of brightness driven into the night, and he moved into it, slipping through the mangrove and buoyed by his feverish expectations for a little longer. But he was too exhausted, he knew, for mere hope to carry him all the way to safety.

His legs bent under him as if he were a boulder supported by reeds. His whole body shuddered. A thick black cloud seemed to be hanging in front of his eyes out of which he peered with the greatest difficulty, seeing almost nothing.

" . . . Got to rest," he murmured. "Get up on the shore. Crawl out. Lie down and sleep a bit. Can't help it. Can't go on."

Then he tripped.

He fell headlong into what he was certain would be muddy water and felt, instead, a thick, dry clump of tangled, matted roots and reeds overgrown by moss; a little island had appeared as if by magic under his groping hands. He crawled out into the middle of this sudden refuge, sat up and starting brushing the blood and the dried mud off his face.

He took deep, painful breaths.

"Rest," he murmured. "Sleep . . ."

But the air was sharp with resin. The smell of wood smoke was suddenly acrid in his nostrils. Peering out towards the shore he saw a large, bright campfire burning a hundred paces off beyond the riverbank. He saw a dozen dark forms hunched and huddled around it.

The breeze freshened then. A sudden gust of wind pushed the sheltering reeds aside for a moment and he could see everything around the fire as clearly as if he were sitting beside it himself. One quick glance sufficed to show him a group of Tartar herdsmen. They were eating something.

Food . . . the thought of eating . . . awoke a savage hunger. He hadn't eaten anything since the day before and that was just a scrap of horseflesh that wouldn't have satisfied a month-old pup. He started pulling up the stalks of water lilies growing near his island and gnawing on them and sucking out their bitter, pulpy marrow. At the same time he didn't take his eyes off the campfire which seemed to fade and dwindle as if he were looking at it through a cloud, while the men around it shrunk and diminished in an imaginary distance.

'Sleep's getting to me,' Pan Yan thought. '*Consciousness is going . . . I'm going to go under right here on this clump of turf.*'

His head slumped, dull as lead. Another moment and he'd be unconscious, he was sure. But the men around the campfire began to stir, to call out, and to mount their ponies. He heard their shrill whistles and the crack of their rawhide whips. He couldn't understand why they began to scatter in the pastureland among the herds of horses they were guarding there, and then he saw that the nodding plumes of cane around his island had started to change color.

Black turned to grey. The blue-grey fronds were becoming silver. The water seemed to shine more brightly than it did in moonlight and a soft white mist was hanging now above the greening marshland.

He looked up. He saw a greying sky. The night was over and a new day had come. It had taken him the whole night to circle the lake to the rivermouth. Still ahead lay the dangerous daylight journey past the Cossack *tabor*.

★   ★   ★

But there was something else he had to do first; if he didn't do it, he knew that he would lose the last of his senses and his journey would be over before it properly began.

He slid off his island and crept closer to the shore, trembling so violently that he was hardly able to stay on his feet, and using up the last of his strength to keep himself from screaming out with hunger. Hunger was blinding him but he peered feverishly out of the reeds anyway, barely able to remember that urgent need for caution and concealment. He saw another mounted Tartar picket about five hundred paces up the river but the rest of the broad meadow was deserted as far as his eyes could reach. Only the abandoned fire glowed in the near distance and Pan Yan crawled towards it through the grass on his empty and constricting belly.

Once there, he searched the embers for remnants of the horseherders' meal. He found a few freshly-chewed mutton bones still bearing some fat and gristle. He dug some half-burned turnips out of the ashes and tore at them with the savagery of a starving dog until he noticed that the mounted pickets he had passed earlier in the night were coming back to their camp along the shore and would be on him in another minute. He crawled back to the reeds, crept out on his hidden little island without a sound, and gnawed at the mutton bones he brought from the campfire. He cracked them in his powerful jaws, sucked out their marrow, stripped them of their last shreds of meat, fat and gristle, and finally chewed and swallowed the pulped bonemeal as if he were a wolf. It had been a long time, he thought, since he'd enjoyed that kind of feast in Zbarajh.

He felt stronger then.

Daylight . . . the end of his blind wandering among imagined horrors . . . was doing as much to restore him as the meal, he thought. He breathed a thankful prayer.

The dawn spread as he watched. The wet, morning mist would be another torment, he was sure, unable to keep his teeth from rattling in the sudden chill. But he knew that the rising sun would soon dry and warm his cold and aching body. He looked around. His round, mossy clump of matted reeds and swamp grass was wide enough for two men to stretch out on it, and the surrounding reeds were as thick and tall as if they were a wall hiding him from any eyes that might be glancing his way from along the bank.

'They won't find me here,' he thought. 'Unless they come through after fish . . .'

But there were no more fish in those Zbarajh lakes, he remembered then. They had all died a long time before, poisoned by the foul water and the rotting corpses.

" . . . So what now?" he muttered. "What do I do next?"

He didn't really have any choice about it. He had to go on. Passing the Cossack *tabor* in broad daylight where any one of two hundred thousand men could catch sight of him and raise the alarm didn't offer him many reasonable chances. But he believed he'd have at least one piece of luck to help him if the fresh morning breeze kept on gusting among the creaking reeds along the overgrown shore.

" . . . Thank God I've got this far anyway," he whispered.

He raised his eyes gratefully to the reddened sky and then his thoughts flew off on a journey of their own. He could see the distant castle quite clearly from where he was lying, especially since its metaled copper roofs were now gilded by the rising sun and flashed their own signals of encouragement and secret recognition. Perhaps some anxious watcher in the tower had turned a spy-glass on the lakes and river, he thought, longing for the illusion of that connecting nearness.

"I'm here," he whispered to that distant sentry. "I'm still alive. I'm here."

All his friends seemed to be calling out to him through that cold, enervating mist. Praying. Urging Godspeed and caution. Zagloba and Volodyovski were sure to be standing on the walls, he knew; they'd spend the whole day there, peering out towards the enemy revetments and wondering if they'd see his body dangling from some piece of Cossack siege machinery.

'*Well . . . they won't see it,*' he thought, carried away by the anticipation of survival. '*They won't. Not today.*'

He didn't really come very far in the night, he knew. He'd covered less than half the distance needed to get beyond the vast enemy encampments. But without that first half safely behind him now there'd be no way to attempt the second.

"God brought me this far," he whispered. "He'll help with the rest."

And then the eyes of his imagination lifted beyond the Cossack *tabor* and the Tartar *kosh*. He saw himself marching through the deep woods and the ancient forests beyond which the new royal forces were gathering all Summer. He stood among the massed regiments . . . the armed warlike gentry summoned from all over the entire country . . . the iron *husaria* . . . the guns and cannon and infantry and foreign mercenaries in their plumes and laces . . .

'*The earth itself will moan under their weight,*' he thought, dazed with hope, rejoicing and fulfillment, and then he saw some strange prophetic battleground sheeted with clouds of gunsmoke, a broken Cossack wagon train sinking in a swamp, and the Prince flying like an avenging God across stacks of corpses at the head of all the cavalry . . .

But the vision darkened. His swollen, aching eyes were starting to dim. The mirage began to ebb away. His head bowed and sunk down to his chest, unable to support the chaotic weight of his hopes and dreaming. A soft, warm cloak of gratitude and contentment enveloped him as if he were a child laid down in his cradle and he stretched out and slept.

★   ★   ★

When he awoke it seemed as if he hadn't slept at all. The sky had darkened. The red glow of sunset was still hanging in the west and the black canopy overhead glittered with new stars. The reeds were rustling even louder than before and he was listening to the shrill screams of horses biting each other in the invisible pasture beyond the riverbank and to the hoots and yells of the wild horseherders who were trying to quieten their mustangs with their whips.

He realized that he had slept through the entire day. But he felt neither rested nor stronger. On the contrary, every bone and muscle in his body seemed to twitch with pain.

"It'll get better when I start moving again," he told himself and lowered his legs into the dark water. "I'll get stronger as I go along."

This time he slipped through open water, keeping close to the inner edge of the reeds, so that the crackling of his passage through the cane wouldn't be heard by the Tartars on the shore.

The sun set quickly.

The last of its red glow seeped out of the sky but the moon was still low on the horizon and the chilly darkness settled all around him. The water here was so deep that Skshetuski lost contact with the river bottom time and time again and had to start swimming. His clothing hampered him but he didn't dare to shed any of it in case it floated out behind him and caught some Tartar's sharp, suspicious eye. The slow, sluggish current of the river also created a slight problem for him; it kept pushing him back towards the lake. But at least, he thought, no one, no matter how watchful, would be able to spot a low, dark object as small as his head moving against the darker wall of the reeds behind it.

He moved quite boldly, then, swimming or wading up to his armpits in the chilly water, until he reached a bend where he saw tens of thousands of red and yellow fires glowing on both sides of the river, while his ears filled with the humming roar of half a million voices.

'*That's the tabor and the kosh,*' he thought and prayed for God's special care and guidance.

On the left bank of the river, across the open water through which he was moving, lay the huge Cossack wagon train with its thousands of heavy carts, tumbrels, campfires and tents; on the right bank, beyond the reeds he brushed with his shoulder, stretched the horsehide *yurts*, cane shacks and silk pavilions of the Tartars.

He stopped then.

He was chilled to the bone by the night and water but he began to sweat. A sense of evil and of a dense, dark power that dwarfed him and undermined his courage, flowed to him out of these vast encampments.

He listened to the savage Tartar and Zaporohjan voices. He couldn't stop shuddering, chilled even further by the fierce beating of their drums and the squeal of their primitive reed flutes and whistles. The lowing of enormous cattle herds, the shrill coughing grunts of camels, the neighing of tens of thousands of horses and ponies, and the wild shouts and calls of all those savage warriors created an unbreachable and impenetrable mass of their own.

He moved a few dozen paces and stopped again as if a dark, cold fist was pushing against his chest. He thought that he had never felt weaker or more alone. He was suddenly quite certain that all that savage energy and all that fierce, inimical attention were focusing on him and rendering him helpless.

'No one will get through all this,' he thought. 'It just can't be done.'

But he went on, driven now by a terrible curiosity. No one he knew had ever come this close to such a vast assembly of the world's fiercest warriors and lived to tell about it.

*   *   *

The river was wider at this point, almost as if another lake was spilling out across the marshy banks, and it occurred to him that the stream might have been widened on purpose to serve as a better barrier between the two armies; the mutual hatred between the Cossacks and their Tartar allies ran too deep for any kind of trust.

And there was something else he suddenly encountered, another obstacle that brought him to a halt: the dense wall of reeds beside which he was creeping ended as abruptly as if it was sliced off with a knife. In its place lay a long stretch of open water, glowing as red as blood with the reflections of the fires on each side of the river, and two of those watch fires were burning just ahead. They threw broad circles of light that met in midstream. A Tartar horseman stood as motionless as a statue beside the tall pile of burning logs that Skshetuski would have to pass along the open shore, while the dark silhouette of a Cossack sentry leaned on a pike beside the other fire. They didn't take their eyes off the water or each other. Beyond them, Skshetuski could see other such pairs of guardposts watching each other by fires of their own. The flames cast bright bridges of light across the river for half a mile or more. Between them he could see dark rows of flat-bottomed skiffs, like the one that passed him in the lake, moored along each bank.

" . . . Impossible," he muttered.

And suddenly despair gripped him by the throat. He couldn't go forward. There was no way for him to return; he knew that he had no strength left for another night like the one before. A whole day went by since he began his struggling in that quagmire, breathing that stinking air and freezing in the water! And for what? Only to learn, once he reached those camps through which he undertook to pass to the King, that he couldn't do it!

'. . . *Nor can I go back,*' he thought, sick with the knowledge that he might have found enough determination to drag himself forward in some way, but that he'd never find the sheer physical stamina to get back to Zbarajh.

Rage flooded him, along with that despair.

'. . . *I'll come out,*' he thought. '*I'll strangle that sentry and then charge the rest. At least it'll be a quick, clean death . . . an end to this misery . . .*'

But suddenly the thin sound of the Zbarajh church bells came drifting to him from across the lake, brought by the rustling breeze. Skshetuski bowed his head.

He prayed.

His weak, clenched fist tapped against his chest.

". . . Shame," he whispered. "Shame."

There, in that embattled camp and town, were all his friends who'd die if he failed them. There—calling out to him with the cracked iron voices of the bells—was the Prince and his heroic soldiers. And here he was, thinking about a quick death for himself while damning them to the slow agonies of torture and starvation!

'. . . *That just can't happen, God. That's out of the question . . .!*'

He prayed with all the urgency and zeal of a believing man who knew that God could save him in any circumstances, even though he was at the point of drowning in despair, but there was no answer to his prayers just then. Instead the *kosh* and the *tabor* boomed with their malevolent rumbling. Dark figures, stained with scarlet light, drifted among the fires like herds of demons wandering through Hell. The sentries stood as still as if they'd been poured out of molten metal and the river between them ran as red as blood.

'*Maybe they'll douse the fires later in the night,*' Skshetuski told himself. '*I'll wait.*'

And he waited.

★　★　★

Hours passed. The night deepened. The dull, booming roar of the encampments began to ebb into a muttering silence and the many campfires started to go out one by one. But the two watch fires by the riverbanks burned brighter than ever and Pan Yan saw the guards changed at each of them.

"Looks like they'll be on watch until dawn," he noted, grim with disappointment.

He toyed with the idea of slipping through in daylight when the sentries would have been withdrawn but he abandoned the thought as soon as it appeared. The river would be full of men during the day, as he knew by his own campaign experience.

'. . . *They'll come for water. They'll bathe and wash their clothes. They'll be watering their horses and their livestock . . .*'

And then his worn, aching eyes drifted once more to the rows of skiffs moored along the shores. There may have been a hundred at each bank and on the Tartar side they spread all the way to where the reeds had been cut away.

'. . . *Perhaps,*' he thought. '*Perhaps.*'

He lowered himself deep into the water, sinking up to his mouth and nostrils, and began to creep cautiously towards the boats while keeping his eyes fixed on the Tartar sentry.

In half an hour he reached the first moored skiff in the line of more than a hundred. His plan was straightforward. The raised squared-off sterns of the shallow dugouts formed a sort of small, dark roof under which a man's head could pass without too much trouble. If all the boats were moored side-by-side without any gaps, the Tartar guards wouldn't be able to see him under those upraised sterns. The Cossack sentry on the other side was far more likely to spot him sliding under the Tartar boats but there was just a chance that he would ignore him particularly since the bright glow of his watch fire didn't quite reach into all those dark recesses.

It was a chance. Besides, he thought, there was no other way. He slid under the stern of the first skiff and began to crawl on his belly in the shallow water. He was so close to the mounted Tartar that he could hear his pony's snorting breath. He lay as still as a corpse and held his own breath and listened between each slow movement of his creeping body. But luck was with him. The boats were pressed fairly close together and the glow of the Tartar's fire merely deepened the murk under their stern platforms. Skshetuski's eyes were now fixed on the Cossack sentry, whom he could see as clearly as if he stood beside him, but the Zaporohjan was peering far across the boats towards the Tartar camp.

Pan Yan had crept under perhaps fifteen boats in turn when, suddenly, he heard booted feet crunching through the gravel on the shore. Then he heard the harsh, guttural clatter of Asiatic voices. In his travels to the Crimea he'd learned enough of the Tartar language to understand some of the phrases he was hearing then and his blood seemed to turn to ice when he heard the order: "Get in and row!"

Immersed as he was in cold water, Pan Yan felt himself burst into an icy sweat. If the Tartars got into the boat under which he crouched then he was finished. Lost. As good as dead even if they caught him still alive. The same was true if they used one of the skiffs that lay ahead of him because they'd be leaving a lighted, open space which he would be unable to cross without being seen. Every passing second seemed to him like an hour until he heard the boots thudding into one of the boats he had left behind him and then the Tartars pushed off from the shore and started rowing downriver towards the lake.

Weak with relief, Pan Yan barely stopped himself from whispering a thanksgiving prayer. He hardly dared to breathe. The activity on the Tartar shore attracted the attention of the Cossack sentry and Skshetuski didn't stir for another hour. Only when the guards were changed again did he put himself once more into motion.

Creeping, halting, listening and watching for minutes at a time, and then sliding forward under the boats again, he reached the end of the anchorage, slipped into a new mass of dark vegetation and crawled into another sheltering, dense thicket of reeds that rose once more between him and the shore.

Once in that whispering cave of reeds and rushes, he rose to his knees and bowed his face into his hands. Worn out and out of breath, he rested and prayed.

★ ★ ★

After that he could move a little more boldly. He pressed on, taking advantage of every gust of wind which set the cane to rustling and rippled the water. Every so often he stopped and looked back and listened.

"Keep going," he told himself over and over. "Don't stop for anything. Keep moving."

The watch fires between which he was passing began to dim

and to appear weaker as he peered at them. They grew more pale and uncertain as if they were marching away from him in the spreading distance and it took him a long time to realize that this wasn't just another tormenting delusion.

The fires were burning further away from the river's edge, opening up a broader avenue of darkness around the widening stream. The belts of reeds were also growing darker and thicker as he went along because the banks of the river were flatter now, and the ground beyond them was even more marshy, and the sentries had to stand at a greater distance from the shore.

He went on.

He crawled.

He swam. Several times he thought that he would drown, sucked down by the mud, and it took all the strength he had left in his weary body to struggle out again into the open water.

He had no idea at that point what force kept him going. Faith, he supposed. Anger. Blind determination. His love for his waiting friends whom he had to save.

He clawed his way through the reeds, stumbled across tufted clumps of swamp grass, sunk in the mudpits, fell and clambered out again. The sounds of the encampments were falling away behind him with each step but he still didn't dare to crawl out on dry land.

He had no way of telling how much time had passed or how much distance he'd been able to cover before the moon began to slide out of the sky. All he could see around him was a thickening darkness. The watch fires behind him dwindled into pale pinpoints of flickering light and then, suddenly, vanished altogether. The air, he noted painfully, became even colder.

'*What's this, now?*' he thought. Was there some new lake that he hadn't been told about?

The wind seemed to be sighing with a deeper note. And then the stench of mud gave way to something new. He smelled the sweet perfume of pines, sap and pitch. He sniffed the breeze, hardly able to understand the fresh new taste and texture of the air. He stared across the reeds. He was no longer sure what he was able to actually see and hear, and what was merely the imagined product of his immense exhaustion, but he almost cried out with joy anyway. A tall black wall, darker than the night, was rising beyond the reeds on each bank of the river.

"Trees," he whispered. "Trees . . ."

He crawled out of the water and lay, breathing deeply, on the dry, piney soil of the forest floor.

"I am saved," he whispered.

His journey, he knew, was far from finished. Nor was he past all the hardships and dangers. But when he thought that he had managed to escape from Zbarajh, that he'd crept past all the outposts and patrols and that he'd come through alive despite all those hundreds of thousands of savage enemies sworn to his destruction, the rest of the road seemed to him like nothing more than a simple outing in the country.

He went on.

He was wet, weak with hunger and shivering with the cold. He was smeared with the black, stinking mud of the swamp and river, with the red soil of the forest on which he'd been lying, and with his own dark blood.

Where was the King? Where was he to find those powerful new armies?

He had no idea.

All he knew was that his friends in Zbarajh wouldn't be left to wait for rescue in vain, and then the sound of the forest whispering in his ears seemed like distant music.

He'd be back, he knew. With the King. With the royal armies. The dense pine forest through which he was walking seemed as wide and welcoming as an open highway. The trees beckoned to him and opened before him and drew him into their deep, sheltering darkness.

Chapter Seventy-eight

THREE MEN SAT that night in the drawing room of Toporov Castle conferring behind locked doors.

The light of several candles cast its reddish glow on a table littered with charts and papers, on a tall-crowned hat with a black ostrich plume, on a jeweled court sword and a lace handkerchief thrown across the weapon, and on a pair of soft elkskin gauntlets tossed down beside a short field telescope.

It was late.

The men sat in silence.

The flickering candle glow helped to underline the gloom on their faces. It played along the gilded back of a tall armchair, added a touch of animation to the slightly built, dark-eyed man who sat in thought behind the table, and brushed some color into his sallow skin. It sunk without a trace into the black velvet of his western-style clothing and whitened the stiff Spanish ruff that circled his neck. It glittered on the gold chain that hung on his chest.

This was Yan Casimir Vasa, a cardinal before his election to his dead brother's throne, whose worn, yellowed face showed the pride, stubbornness and courage that characterized him. A long, black Swedish wig spread across his shoulders in a mass of curls, a thin black mustache twisted upward on the edges of his upper lip, while the full lower lip pouted out above a stubborn chin, giving his features the look of a sullen lion.

It was a striking face rather than a handsome one. It combined an aloof, recessed sensuality with a kind of dry renunciation that brought to mind the chill of a monastic crypt. He lay back in his chair with the resigned, bleak indifference of an effigy, struggling between a sense of helplessness and boredom. Pride and ambition led him to renounce his vows, reach out for a crown, and marry a French princess for whom the limitations of a Polish monarch were beyond endurance. But the weight of that regality, and the intrigues that attended his political marriage, were proving harder to bear for this generous but uncertain man than a crown of thorns.

Now he sat lost in thought. His two companions glanced at him now and then but they could read next to nothing in his half-closed, inward-gazing eyes; whatever he was feeling lay buried deep beneath a mask of weary resignation, as lifeless as if it were molded out of wax. Each of them knew that this closed, darkly brooding face could blaze with joy or anger without any warning. Or it could come alive with kindness and compassion.

Next to him, and a little deeper in the shadows, sat Hyeronim Radeyovski, the devious and ambitious *Starosta* of Lomza who had maneuvered his way into the highest councils and played the role of the King's confidant and friend. He was a squat, fleshy man in his early fifties, with the flushed, arrogant face of a successful courtier and so fat as to be repulsive. But court rumor already marked him as the new Queen's lover.

Silent now, and watchful, he kept his small, calculating eyes on the third man there and so did the King.

But that third man said nothing.

He leaned on his elbow above the maps and parchments spread out on the table, occasionally glancing up at the King with piercing, sky-blue eyes that seemed unable to perceive anything he didn't wish to see. His thin yellow finger traced aimless paths among the charted cities, mountains, provinces and forests as if it were an ivory stylus or a pointer.

Yan Casimir watched him, waiting.

But not even the whisper of a breath seemed to come from that handsome, grim-faced man who had designed and guided the policies of this tottering kingdom and called up the demons of rebellion in the name of progress. George Ossolinski, the Grand Chancellor of the Crown and a prince of the Holy Roman Empire, was an orator and statesman admired throughout Europe, the King knew well enough. He was one of the great ministers of his time, as brilliant and determined as those who served the rulers of France and Spain. But he seemed to have no words of advice to offer him now.

"Well?" the King asked finally. "What are we to do in this situation? What course do you propose?"

"I propose that we wait, Your Majesty," Ossolinski murmured.

"For what?"

"Information, Sire." The Chancellor's thoughtful shrug was so slight as to be almost imperceptible. "There is too much at stake for any rash, impulsive action when Your Majesty's own person might be placed at risk."

"It seems to me, Chancellor, that there has been too much at stake for some time," the King observed coldly. "And not enough strong, decisive action."

The Chancellor inclined his head in a brief bow. Not a flicker of expression showed on his stern, unyielding face while Radeyovski grinned broadly in the shadows. Neither man said anything for a weighted moment in which the silence seemed to ring like an accusing cry.

The King sighed. He shook out his black wig and stirred with impatience. Then he tilted his head back across the top of his gilded chair and stared at the ceiling.

"How much more patience do we have to show?" he burst out at last. "Are we to sit here, doing nothing, while Vishnovyetzki is dying in Zbarajh?"

"And winning undying glory for himself in the process," grunted Radeyovski.

"Which is his due!" the King snapped out, showing a flash of anger. "And which is a lot more than we are doing either for our country or ourselves! So how much longer is this shameful procrastination to go on?"

"Until the situation clarifies itself, Majesty," Ossolinski offered.

"Clarifies? How is it to clarify itself? By Vishnovyetzki's death? Is that why you're waiting?"

"We must know more about the enemy," Ossolinski reasoned, bowing before the thrust. "Our forces are still gathering, we are not yet ready. To move now against Hmyelnitzki and possibly even the Khan himself, without knowing what we might be facing, would expose Your Majesty to dangers that the Commonwealth simply can't afford."

"And could it afford Pilavtze? Korsun? Yellow Waters? Can it afford the same catastrophe in Zbarajh?"

"We can lose battles, Majesty." The Chancellor's grave, uncompromising eyes fixed on the King without a flutter of doubt or quiver of uneasiness. "We can bear humiliations. We can continue to exercise forbearance and patience. But we can't allow your person, Sire, to fall into the hands of rebels. Or those of the Khan."

"That's if the Khan is there." The King frowned darkly at the sputtering candles and began to drum on the tabletop with agitated fingers. "It could be just Tuhay-bey's *tchambuls* with Hmyelnitzki, as before, not the Khan himself."

"That's just the point, Majesty," Ossolinski began to explain. "We've a mere twenty-five thousand men at hand and few of them are experienced soldiers. Yes, it is possible that we could do something against Hmyelnitzki if he is there alone, without the Khan. Your presence, Sire, will put some backbone into our inexperienced gentry of the General Levy and the Cossacks may not fight as fiercely against you as they would against any of your generals. We must remember that they still revere Your Majesty and see themselves as your loyal subjects. But if the Khan himself is at Zbarajh with his entire army then we've no chance at all."

"So what do you advise?"

"Reason, majesty."

"Reason? What do you mean by reason?"

"Patience, Majesty." The long, dry finger scrawled a number of small, cautious circles around the little castle that represented Zbarajh on the illuminated parchment. "Statesmanship. Logic. Calm thought rather than impulsive and unconsidered action, no matter how appealing it may seem for whatever reason. Sooner or later the situation will clarify itself. Once all the facts are spread out before us we will know exactly what we'll have to do."

"And in the meantime what about Vishnovyetzki and those ten thousand men in those wretched trenches?"

"They'll last," the fat *Starosta* drawled carelessly, shrugged and leaned back in his comfortable chair with elaborate indifference. "They'll keep a little longer."

"If that's your best advice then you might as well not give any at all!" the King snapped out. "Isn't there some way to get information? Can't you seize a few high ranking Cossacks who would know if the Khan is there? Haven't we been sending raiders towards Zbarajh?"

"All they bring in are peasants from the neighborhood and

they can't tell one kind of Tartar from another."

"What about Pan Pelk?" Yan Casimir was as obstinate in his way as Ossolinski was in his. "Isn't he supposed to be a famous raider? When is he expected back from his latest sweep?"

"Pan Pelk isn't expected back at all." A soft, dry chuckle came from Radeyovski. "Pan Pelk is dead."

The gloomy silence returned to the room.

★   ★   ★

The Chancellor's reasoned gravity seemed almost majestic. But he'd know, as Yan Casimir knew, that Vishnovyetzki's death would rid him of the only man who could challenge him in the eyes of a restless and embittered nation and ruin his life's work.

Ossolinski's stern, unbending features betrayed nothing of the disappointments that gnawed at his soul. He held himself as still as if he was carved out of pale marble. His eyes were cold, confident and contemptuous of any ideas but his own. But the King knew how deeply hurt he was by the universal hatred that was heaped upon him.

' . . . *He sees himself as the savior of his country*,' Yan Casimir thought. '*The nation looks at him as the creator of its tragedies.*'

And now some of that national bitterness was spilling over on the chancellor's master, the King knew.

His own cold, brooding eyes turned on this architect of disasters. Perhaps it wasn't too late to replace him? To change course? To pull this foundering Ship of State off the reefs where it had run aground, driven by Ossolinski's blind, single-minded purpose, before it was battered beyond reconstruction?

But who'd take that tiller? Vishnovyetzki? Radeyovski? And what sort of vision would they impose on the shattered Commonwealth? Where would they steer his kingdom?

Right or wrong, Ossolinski's course was the only one that might have taken this vast, disjointed assembly of different cultures, religions and peoples into a new future, Yan Casimir knew.

Ossolinski's talents had been spotted under other rulers in that remarkable age of able Kings and brilliant chancellors who trained and raised him to the highest state positions at an early age. Hardworking, thoughtful, committed to a vision of a disciplined and governable modern state and making his plans for many years ahead, he could have guided any country but this Commonwealth to strength, peace and prosperity at home and decades of power and influence abroad.

Yes, the King thought sadly. He could have done all that. But only if he'd been the omnipotent minister of a monarch like Louis of France, and Carlos of Spain, or the English Stuarts who ruled by divine right. He needed a king who was responsible to no one and whose will was the law.

Raised in the courts and chancelleries of Western European princes, Ossolinski was fascinated by western examples of government and statecraft. In spite of his brilliance and years of experience he never grasped the central fact of the Commonwealth's existence. He couldn't come to terms with rule by consent. Republics appalled him unless they were modeled on late Roman lines, complete with a compliant Senate, a disciplined populace and an obedient knighthood. Himself a noble, he grew to hate the gentry for whom a strong central government was anathema. They were the rock that shattered all his plans and drowned all his efforts until, at last, he unleashed the Cossack storm upon it.

But he'd miscalculated.

Hmyelnitzki was a weapon that turned in his hand. The violent passions of the Commonwealth refused to fit themselves into the classic pattern of rule by dividing. Hmyelnitzki rose in the Ukraine, brought in the Tartars and became a giant who didn't merely curb the magnates and humiliate the gentry as the chancellor had planned, but who created a nation of his own. The rebellion overwhelmed its own original idea, inflicting one calamity after another on the Commonwealth, and now it threatened the existence of the state itself.

Watching him now with a detached blend of pity, disillusion, regret and understanding, Yan Casimir felt a fresh wave of resignation creeping up around him.

The conference had gone on too long.

He was depressed and tired.

His natural inclination was a fatalistic one. He knew that his chancellor was looking out upon a vision of catastrophe and ruin. There was nothing else left for him to see out of that glorious and enduring Commonwealth he planned.

But the King still admired him. Not having a firm policy or vision of his own he had to believe in that of Ossolinski. He longed to see it taking root and blooming into a new beginning for all the peoples of the Commonwealth even though his own perception of reality told him that this would never happen in his lifetime.

He also knew that the nation would blame their King, not his minister, if Zbarajh became the burial mound of its finest soldiers.

★   ★   ★

He tried again.

"The crux of the problem, then, is whether the Khan is there?"

Ossolinski nodded.

"Then find out!"

"Your Majesty could send someone with letters to Hmyelnitzki," the *Starosta* offered. "Pretend that we want to start new negotiations, eh? Why not? It's been done before. A good man would sniff out quick enough if Devlet Giray is there in person. When he returns he'd tell us."

"Out of the question!" Impatient, Yan Casimir was becoming angry. "Now that we've declared Hmyelnitzki a rebel and an outlaw, and placed a price on his head, and given the Zaporohjan hetmancy to Zabuski, we've nothing more to discuss with him! How would it look? I'd just as soon negotiate with highwaymen and bandits!"

"Then why not write to the Khan? That'd be a straightforward embassy, one monarch to another. If he's there he'd have to take the letter."

The King turned questioning eyes on the Chancellor who thought for a moment and then shook his head.

"Hmm . . . It's a good thought," he mused. "But not workable. Hmyelnitzki is sure to see through that deception. He'd detain the envoy. He would never let him get back to us alive."

"So much for your ideas, then!" The King made a quick, dismissive gesture. "Now listen to mine! I'll have them sound assembly and march the army to Zbarajh at once! I'm tired of all this talk. Let God's will be done. We'll find out for ourselves if the Khan is there!"

Ossolinski knew the Vasa impulsiveness, stubbornness and courage; in this respect Yan Casimir was much like his dead warrior brother, who had been one of the most decisive kings since the end of the Yagiellonian dynasty which brought Poland

and Lithuania together two hundred years earlier and laid the
foundations of the Commonwealth. He was ready to do exactly
as he said and neither the Chancellor nor Radeyovski had any
doubts about it. The shrewd, experienced chancellor also knew
that once this King made up his mind he refused to listen to any
arguments. So he suppressed his surge of opposition. He
praised the idea. He merely cautioned against undue haste.

"Tomorrow . . . or even the day after . . . might be a better
time."

"Why?"

"It's a question of making sure that nothing has been left to
chance. Every day will add to the rebels' losses and their disillu-
sionment with Hmyelnitzki. They must be sick of their defeats
at Zbarajh. The longer we give them to lose heart and suffer,
Majesty, the less likely they'll be to want another battle. We
must let the news of Your Majesty's coming spread gradually
among them, start them talking among themselves, stir their
doubts, provide a focus for their discontent, set them to fearful
speculations and undermine their will to fight even further."

"Time is on our side," Radeyovski added in a way that could
be taken as both a statement and a question. But his wry,
knowing grin acknowledged all his cynical amusement at Ossolinski's efforts.

"Let them be dazzled by the thought of Your Majesty's imminent arrival,"—the Chancellor took up a rhetor's stance and
reached into his store of poetic imagery as if the beauty of his
words could fill them with meaning—"let them begin to feel
the warmth of a regal presence, Sire. The rebellion might melt
away like snow in the sun . . ."

The Chancellor spoke on while Radeyovski hid his artful
smile. The King's impatience, as both of them were very well
aware, quickly gave way to weariness and boredom. A terrible
lassitude was spreading through his tired body and Ossolinski's
measured eloquence drained him even more.

" . . . Each passing day will strengthen your army. The
gentry has been slow to respond to the mobilization order but
more and more of them straggle into the camp practically every
hour. However, every moment will help to dishearten the Cossacks . . .

"Your Majesty carries in himself the fate of the entire Commonwealth," the Chancellor went on. "You are responsible for

the life and happiness of future generations and that's too much
to expose to unnecessary risks! Your person, Sire, is our only
hope! And should your expedition meet with an unforeseen
misfortune the defenders of Zbarajh would be lost in any
event."

Tired out by the rhetoric, the late hour, and his own sense of
hopeless disappointment, Yan Casimir slumped into sullen apa-
thy again.

"Do what you like, then," he muttered testily, raising his face
again to the shadowed ceiling. "Just make sure we have some
news tomorrow."

★   ★   ★

And again there was a long moment of silence. A great white
moon appeared in the window but the room darkened as the
candles guttered.

"What time is it?" asked the King.

"Near midnight," Radeyovski said.

"I won't sleep tonight," Yan Casimir muttered. "I want to
ride through the camp and you will come with me. Where are
Generals Ubald and Artishevski, do you know?"

"In the camp," the *Starosta* said and rose. "I'll go and have the
horses brought over from the stables."

But he had barely taken a step towards the door when a flurry
of activity broke out in the hall. They heard quick footsteps,
rapid questions and agitated voices, and then the doors flew
open and Tyzenhaus, one of the King's gentlemen-in-waiting,
ran into the room.

"Majesty!" he called out. "A Zbarajh soldier is here!"

The King leaped out of his chair, the Chancellor also rose,
and the same sharp, astonished cry broke out of them both:
"That can't be true!"

"It is, Sire! He's waiting in the outer hall!"

"Bring him here!" the King shouted and clapped his hands
together. "Let him dispel our worries! By Our Lady, get him
here at once!"

Tyzenhaus vanished and a moment later some tall, strange
shadow stood swaying in the doorway.

"Come closer, sir!" Yan Casimir beckoned. "Closer! We are
pleased to see you!"

The soldier stepped slowly into the dim circle of light near the conference table, and the King, the Chancellor and the *Starosta* stared at him with new astonishment.

"Dear God," the King whispered.

He didn't know what he thought he'd see—perhaps a polished, shining officer like those of his Lifeguards—but he never expected what he saw instead. The man's foul, shredded rags barely covered a skeletal body. His face was blue with cold, caved-in from starvation, and smeared with blood and mire. His eyes burned with fever. A tangled black beard straggled across his chest, and a thick, corpse-like stench spread from him like a graveyard fog. His legs shook so badly under him that he had to grasp the edges of the table to stay on his feet.

The King and the two officials stared at him in amazement, unable to imagine what kind of news such a messenger was bringing, while a swarm of officers and civil dignitaries crowded into the room behind them. All of them peered at the apparition as if it were a specter, not a human being, while the King asked: "Who are you?"

But the man couldn't say a word. Some kind of spasm locked his jaws together. His mouth fell open. His beard began to jerk. At last he managed a strangled, broken whisper:

"From . . . Zbarajh."

"Get him some wine!" someone cried.

A filled cup was brought to him at once. He drank with an effort. Meanwhile the Chancellor covered him with his own furlined cloak.

"Can you speak now?" the King asked after a time.

"I can," the man said in a firmer voice.

"Who are you, then?"

"Yan Skshetuski . . . *husaria* commander . . ."

"In whose service?"

"The *Voyevode* of Ruthenia."

An excited murmur spread through the room and the King's own voice acquired a feverish quality as he asked: "How are things with you people over there?"

"Misery," the young knight said. "Starvation . . . It's a living grave . . ."

"Oh Jesus," the King whispered, covering his eyes with both hands. "Oh dear sweet Jesus."

Then, after a moment, he asked again: "Can you hold out much longer?"

"Can't say, Sire. The powder's run short. The enemy is inside the walls."

"How strong are they?"

"Hmyelnitzki . . . The Khan with all the Hordes . . ."

"The Khan is there himself?"

"Yes . . ."

A dull, apprehensive silence hung throughout the room. The gathered dignitaries and commanders stared at each other with uncertain eyes, reading doubt and fear in each other's faces.

"How did you manage to hold them off?" the Chancellor questioned. "If, as you say, the Khan himself is there?"

Skshetuski stirred at the suspicion he heard in that voice. He sighed. A tremor ran through his body. His head jerked up as if a current of new strength and courage flooded into him out of the memory of those embattled ruins.

"Twenty assaults beaten off," he said proudly. "Sixteen pitched battles won in the open field. Seventy-five counter-raids and sallies . . ."

And again there was a dull, uncomprehending silence.

★   ★   ★

Then the King drew himself erect. He shook his curled wig as though it were the mane of a lion. A flush of anger rose into his sallow face and his eyes shined with determination and impatience.

"By God's breath!" he cried. "I've had enough of this talking, this waiting and all these delays! I don't care if the Khan is there or whether we're ready! It's enough, by God! We are going to Zbarajh today!"

"To Zbarajh!" a dozen strong voices cried out after him. "To Zbarajh!"

Skshetuski's worn face quivered with emotion. His dim eyes showed the light of joy. He whispered his thanks. Yan Casimir seized him in his arms, not caring about his stinking rags or the blood and filth that clung in layers to his body, and pressed him to his chest.

"We're all in your debt," he said. "By Our Lady, many others have become *Starostas* for less than you've done. No, don't deny it! Don't minimize your merit! And you can be sure that we'll think of something to show our gratitude. I won't forget about you no matter what happens in Zbarajh or anywhere else."

Praise, questions and congratulations fell on the bedraggled and exhausted soldier as all the court dignitaries hurried to follow the King's lead.

"There never was a more deserving knight!" the lords and nobles and commanders cried out to each other, crowding about Pan Yan. "He's the best among us. Not even Zbarajh could have any better!"

"You've won immortal glory for yourself, young man," said Pan Vitovski, the Castellan of Sandomir, whom Pan Yan remembered from his own days of service in Zamost.

"How did you do it?" Others pressed about him. "How did you get through the Tartars and the Cossacks?"

He did his best to answer but his words were becoming incomprehensible even to himself. "I hid in the reeds . . . in the mud. I went through the woods . . ."

"And you were the only one to undertake such a desperate mission?"

"Another man tried before me," Pan Yan whispered. "A great knight . . . a great soldier. But he lost his life . . ."

"That makes your merit all the greater! Your career is made, young man. You've done the impossible! Oh, you'll have nothing to worry about now!"

The King ordered that food be brought for him. Skshetuski tried to eat but he was too weak to lift the silver implements to his mouth. His head began to spin. In the meantime the King's confessor came into the chamber, a famous Jesuit whose influence over Yan Casimir was even greater than that of Ossolinski. Told about the new arrival he looked at him curiously and then asked his name. "Skshetuski, did you say?"

"That's right. Yan Skshetuski."

"The one who commands Prince Yeremi's *husaria?*"

"The same."

The priest sighed softly, smiled with a strange, appreciative awareness of something no one else would know, lifted his face towards the ceiling in a brief, silent prayer and murmured quietly as if to himself: "Let's thank God for His mercy. His ways are surely beyond our understanding. But our Heavenly Father grants peace and happiness to the deserving in His own good time and in His own manner."

"If anyone deserves happiness . . .," someone began to list Skshetuski's achievements, but the Jesuit merely nodded, smiled again and said: "Yes. I know all about him."

Then, turning to Yan Casimir, he asked if the King's decision to march to the relief of Zbarajh was an irrevocable one.

"It is," the King said. "I know that it's a desperate gamble. The risks are enormous. But we simply can't allow Vishnovyetzki to perish in those wretched earthworks along with such brave men as this. I commend our country, the army and myself to your prayers, Father. Let God's will be done!"

"He'll grant a victory!" a dozen voices shouted.

"Amen," said the priest.

"Amen!" cried all the others.

A great peace spread across Yan Casimir face. The last traces of his doubt, hesitation and uncertainty disappeared in a single flash and a strong, determined light glowed in his clear, black-eyes. Only the Chancellor murmured a few words of caution, asking when the King wanted to set out.

"It's a cool, clear night," Yan Casimir said glancing through the window at the moonlit landscape. "The horses won't get overheated and tired too badly. Gentlemen, return to your troops! Rouse your regiments! I want the trumpets sounding in an hour!"

The Chancellor murmured that not everyone would be ready to set out that quickly. "The baggage train alone, Majesty, would hardly be able to move before dawn . . ."

But the King made an abrupt gesture of angry dismissal.

"Whoever's more concerned about his baggage than about his country can stay behind!" he snapped angrily. "The talking is over!"

The dignitaries, generals and commanders saluted and started to leave the room.

★ ★ ★

Left alone with the King, the chancellor, the priest and Tyzenhaus, Pan Yan began to sink into a waking dream. Reality ebbed for him. Consciousness started to slip away. He heard the others talking as if through a fog but he didn't really understand what anyone was saying. The priest was asking whether he might take Pan Yan to his quarters so that he could rest. The King agreed, telling Tyzenhaus to help him since it didn't look as if the exhausted young soldier would manage on his own, and to make sure that a horse, new accouterments and clothing were given to him after he'd had some sleep.

"Go. Go, my dear friend," he heard the King saying. "No

one has earned his rest better than you have. You couldn't be dearer to me than if you were my brother. And remember that I am your debtor."

Then the scene changed and he was outside, on his way somewhere, supported by the courtier and another noble, with the priest walking on ahead and a lad with a lantern running to light the way. The lad and his lamp weren't really necessary. The night was quiet and clear. A great golden moon sailed through the sky like a stately galleon and cast a bright, warm light over Toporov. The deep murmur of many voices, creaking carts, and trumpets playing reveille and assembly came from the encampment. Crowds of foot soldiers and horsemen were already forming ranks in the street in front of the church, and the soft autumn air filled with the neighing of horses and the rumbling of innumerable wagon wheels and cannon.

"They're starting out already," the priest said.

"To Zbarajh," Pan Yan whispered.

"Yes. To Zbarajh."

Joy, gratitude, relief and exhaustion combined to drain him of the last remnants of his strength and he collapsed in the arms of the courtiers who were leading him.

They were heading towards the parish house, pushing through a great, milling crowd of soldiers who were gathering in the church square and all the streets that led into it. Pan Yan recognized their uniforms and colors as belonging to Sapyeha's Lithuanian corps and to Artishevski's foreign infantry but even that was just a dim impression that didn't really register in his tired brain. They were still in the process of forming their ranks, jostling in disorder, and Skshetuski's escorts found their way blocked time and time again.

"Make way there! Let us pass!" the priest called out but the King's troopers weren't eager to oblige at first.

"And who wants to pass?" they challenged.

"A soldier from Zbarajh."

"Good luck to him, then!" many voices shouted. "Welcome to him! Welcome! God bless him! Hey, give way there, will you? Let him pass!"

And they gave way at once as if to a superior, but others pressed forward even harder, eager to catch a glimpse of the Zbarajh hero. They pointed him out to each other, stared open-mouthed at his rags and at his gaunt grey face that seemed like a bloodless deathmask in the moonlight, and a hushed whisper rustled among them like an autumn wind.

" . . . *From Zbarajh . . . from Zbarajh . . .!*"

It took the greatest effort for the King's confessor to get Skshetuski to the manse of the local pastor where he was bathed and put to bed in the priest's own room.

He was only half-conscious by that time. Fever kept him restless and awake but he no longer knew where he was or how he had got there. He heard only the humming roar of an advancing army, the clatter of hooves and jingling of bridle-chains, the deep measured tread of marching infantry, the shouts of command and the calls of the assembling soldiers. Adrift on this warm, familiar sea of military sounds, he heard the drums and trumpets and the heavy rumble of rolling carts and cannon as a single booming resonance, which swallowed and consumed all the individual impressions and blurred their identities into one.

"There's an army on the march somewhere," he muttered to himself but he couldn't remember any longer what army it was nor where it was going.

Meanwhile, that deep humming roar began to abate. It dwindled to a whisper like an ebbing tide and drifted away in a spreading distance.

A moonlit silence settled on the town.

It seemed to Skshetuski that he and his bed—along with whatever house and town or village contained them in that moment— began to fall into some dark, warm pit that sunk deep into the center of the earth.

Chapter Seventy-nine

HE SLEPT THROUGH several days. When he awoke he went on drifting in a fever that kept its grip on him for several days longer.

He thought he was in Zbarajh. He talked to Pan Michal and Zagloba. He shouted '*No! Not this way! Go back! Go back!*' to Pan Podbipyenta, and engaged in long, rambling monologues with an imaginary Prince Yeremi.

He didn't recognize anyone who came to see him and babbled mindlessly about every subject except Helen, as if she alone of everyone who peopled his chaotic dreams failed to appear in his hallucinations. It was clear that he had driven every thought of his lost love so deep below all his levels of awareness that he could lock her out of memory even when he was unconscious.

But one persistent image haunted him no matter where he floated in his fevered dreams. He thought that he could see the round, pudgy face of Zjendjan bobbing worriedly above him each time his eyelids twitched ajar and he managed to focus his eyes for a moment. He looked up and there it was time and time again, like a pink, bug-eyed little moon hanging in the shadows, just as it had been that time near the Homor River when Prince Yeremi sent him to stamp out the bands of Krivoinos' marauders who'd scattered through the country after Konstantinov, and the lad showed up after his pretended desertion to the Cossacks. No matter what other images rose out of his memory and imagination, and no matter how he struggled to push them aside, that small, intrusive face remained suspended over him so that he started thinking himself returned magically to another time.

'*Yes,*' the thought formed itself wordlessly in his head. '*That's what it must be . . . Time has turned about and is running backwards and I'm back on the banks of the Homor, waking in that hut, and all those things that happened since that morning have been erased as if they never existed at all . . .*'

Or perhaps they were just a terrible nightmare from which he was waking? Had he imagined Zbarajh, the royal elections, Pilavtse and his search for Helen? He thought that he must have. It was all a dream. He'd wake in just another moment . . . order the lad to see to the horses . . . take his brigade back to Tarnopol . . .

'*That's it. That's what must be happening. Krivoinos is beaten and running to Hmyelnitzki. Zjendjan has come back. Helen is safe in Bar and, in a day or two, I'll ask the Prince for leave . . .*'

He wanted to cry out to Zjendjan to bring him his clothes, pack up his gear and saddle the horses but he couldn't do it. His voice seemed to have dried up and no matter how he searched his confused and unsteady mind he couldn't find the words he needed to call out the orders.

'*But no,*' he thought after a while. '*Wait a minute . . . It can't have been like that . . . Bar has been taken, hasn't it? I know it was taken! And Bohun has hidden Helen somewhere else . . .*'

Grief fell on him again like a wall, and buried him under a crushing avalanche of pain and disappointment, and he plunged once more into the refuge of mindless oblivion. But even as he burrowed desperately for shelter in that sudden darkness he knew that it had no more substance than any of his other shimmering illusions. Because there *had* been Zbarajh after all. The siege and the hunger. The heroism and the slaughter on those bloody earthworks couldn't be denied. They rose up in his memory with such appalling vividness that he couldn't refute them no matter how he tried.

"Twenty assaults repelled," he muttered as if he were still reporting to the King. "Sixteen pitched battles won. Seventy-five sallies."

Where did that fit in time if time had indeed turned back in its course and was now flowing upstream to its own beginnings?

'. . . *That happened. It wasn't just a dream. The siege was real. It wasn't an illusion. And if that's so then everything else must have taken place as well . . .*'

He could feel himself drifting slowly out of that sheltering darkness in which his mind took refuge from his memories, lifting as helplessly towards consciousness and that bright, unwelcome morning light, as if he were a drowned swollen body rising to the surface of a lake, and although he wished that he could remain suspended for ever in that comforting oblivion where he was free of his tormenting thoughts, he knew that his brief withdrawal from reality was over once again.

'*So I'm not waking near the Homor,*' he thought. '*I am somewhere else.*'

But where? Still in Zbarajh?

'*. . . No. Zjendjan is real, isn't he? And he was never there . . .*'

He couldn't understand why the concerned, moonlike face of his imagined servant wouldn't disappear along with all the other visions created by his fever.

'*It can't be Zbarajh if Zjendjan is real . . .*'

Daylight poured into the room through the heart-shaped openings carved into the shutters. It destroyed the shadows. It lit up those caring and familiar features that hung over him like a child's lantern cut out of a pumpkin, or a clown's mask in a Passion Play that was supposed to represent anxiety and fear. No matter where *he* happened to be at this moment, Pan Yan knew the boy was really there.

"Zjendjan!" he cried out.

"Oh my God! Oh master!" the boy shouted, throwing his arms around Skshetuski's body and pressing his own forehead to his master's knees. "I thought you'd never wake! I thought you was gone for good, this time! Oh my God!"

★ ★ ★

Then there was another long silence, charged with intense emotion and interrupted only by the boy's heartfelt and joyful sobbing. The faithful lad grinned through his dripping tears, smearing them all across his face.

"Ey, master, master," he went on repeating. "I just didn't think I'd see you alive again."

"Where am I?" Pan Yan asked.

"In Toporov, master. You came here to the King from Zbarajh. Ah, thank God you're awake again! Thank God! Though it's easy to see you didn't have anybody to look after you, the way you looked when they brought you here."

"And the King? Where is he?"

"Gone with the army to rescue the Prince."

"Thank God."

"Thank God indeed, master," the boy said.

Then he rose and threw open the shutters and the windows. Bright daylight and crisp morning air poured into the room and blew away the last of the shadows.

"So I did manage to get here after all," Pan Yan whispered.

"That you did, master! That you did! It's only because of you that the King's gone to rescue the Prince, and everybody's saying there'll be great rewards coming your way soon. You're the biggest hero in the country, master. Every great lord's been here to pay his respects, and as for the goods and gifts they brought you . . . phew! You wouldn't believe it! A good trader, one that knows what's what, could buy a fair-sized village for just half of it! Nobody else could've done what you did, master, nobody! And the whole army is talking about it."

"Pan Podbipyenta tried it before me," Pan Yan said. "God rest his great soul."

"You mean he's dead, sir?"

"Yes. They caught him and killed him."

"They did?" Zjendjan's mouth fell open in astonishment. "Ey, what a shame! Such a kind, good-hearted man he was, and so generous too . . . '*Here's a gold-piece for you*,' he'd say all the time. '*And here is another.*' But how could they get him down, master? A strong man like that?"

"They shot him."

"Hmm. Yes. They'd have to, I expect. And Pan Zagloba and Pan Volodyovski? Are they all right, master?"

"They were when I last saw them."

"Thank God for that too. They're real great friends of yours, master. Ey, if you only knew! But the King's chaplain told me to keep my mouth shut about that whole business . . ."

Skshetuski sighed. He nodded.

"I know they're my friends."

"Hmm. You do, do you sir?" Zjendjan grew quiet then, clearly doing some heavy thinking of his own. His plump, round face grew scarlet with the effort. "Maybe so, master. And then again, maybe not . . . Ey, if only I was free to tell you! But that priest said he'd skin me alive if I breathed a word . . . "

Pan Yan closed his eyes again, feeling fatigue stealing over him once more, and Zjendjan sat down at the foot of his bed and stared at the floor.

"Master?" he began as if uncertain how to find something new to talk about.

"What, lad?"

"And what'll happen to Pan Podbipyenta's fortune now that he's gone? D'you happen to know? People say he had more goods and villages than a man could count up in a week . . . Did he maybe leave something to his friends? I mean, since he didn't have no kin of his own . . ."

Skshetuski didn't answer. It was clear that the question wasn't to his taste and Zjendjan sighed, shrugged, sniffed and blew his nose.

"Well," he resumed. "The main thing is that both Pan Zagloba and Pan Volodyovski are alive and well. I thought the Tartars would've got them for sure. We went through a lot together, them and me. I'd tell you all about it, master, if the Reverend didn't say I was to keep my mouth shut and not breathe one word . . . But that one time—Phew!—I thought the Tartars would nail us for certain!"

"So you were with Pan Zagloba and Pan Volodyovski?" Pan Skshetuski asked. "When was that? They didn't mention anything about it."

"They didn't, eh?" Zjendjan began to fidget. "Hmm. Well. I expect they weren't sure if I got out alive . . . Didn't want to worry you about it . . ."

"And where did you run into those Tartars, then?"

"Where? Well, it was beyond Ploskirov, on our way to Zbarajh . . . Because we'd been off on a trip for a while, master, see? We'd gone way to the other side of Yampol . . ." And then the boy clamped his hand across his mouth. "Ey, master, ey! If only the King's chaplain hadn't told me not to talk about it . . ."

Skshetuski nodded. His face had greyed and hardened once more with remembered grief.

"God will repay your good intentions," he said quietly. "I know why you went there."

"You do, sir?"

"Yes . . . I'd been out there myself."

"You were, master, were you?" Zjendjan seemed hardly able to breathe with suppressed excitement but Skshetuski didn't notice it. Memory passed like a dark shadow across his harrowed face and he closed his eyes as if to shut it out along with the sharp morning light.

"Yes." His shrug of resignation was as bitter as a spasm of pain. "But it was all for nothing."

"For nothing? Hmm. Maybe it was, master. And maybe it wasn't . . . Ey, if only the Reverend hadn't made me swear . . . But he said to me: '*Listen, clown,*'—that's the way he put it, although I'm not anybody's clown, as my master knows—'*I've got to go with the King and the army, and you stay here and watch over your master.*' Which nobody needed to tell me anyway . . .! And then he says: '*Don't you dare tell him anything that's happened or the shock might drive his soul right out of his body* . . .' So what can I do?"

But Skshetuski had discarded all hope so many months before that even these strange, halting words failed to ignite any spark of curiosity within him.

★ ★ ★

He lay still for several silent minutes. The warm midmorning air soothed him and revived him and set his troubled mind more or less at rest and he felt his old strength beginning to return. Fully awake and conscious of everything around him he started questioning the uneasy Zjendjan.

"How do you happen to be here with the King?"

"Well master." The boy took a deep breath and launched into his story. "I was in Zamost, see? With Pani Vitovska, the wife of the Castellan of Sandomir. And she sent me here to let her husband know she'd join him in Toporov. That's a real brave lady, master, and she's right anxious to be with the army. So I got here a day before you did. Pani Vitovska ought to be along any time now, I expect. I did like she told me. But what's the use? Her husband's gone off with the King so it looks like they aren't going to meet . . ."

"Hold on a minute," Pan Yan interrupted. "Not so fast! What were you doing in Zamost when you'd gone to Yampol with Pan Zagloba and Pan Volodyovski? Why didn't you come to Zbarajh along with them?"

"Well, master,"—and now Skshetuski finally took notice of Zjendjan's frantic fidgeting—"when those Tartars got onto us, that time that I mentioned, we . . . uh . . . had to separate. So the two masters turned to hold them up, and me and . . . ah . . . and me . . . I had to get going. They told me to. And I didn't stop running till I got to Zamost."

"Thank God they got through that alive," Skshetuski said

and murmured a quick prayer and then turned angrily on his troubled servant. "But I thought better of you, boy! How could you leave them at a time like that?"

"Ey, master, ey . . ." The boy's anxious squirming was becoming desperate. "If it was just the three of us out there, I'd have stayed with them. I surely would've. I felt real bad about leaving them behind. But there was . . . ah . . . the four of us, you see. So they turned on the Tartars to buy us some time, and me . . . well, they said I was to get to a safe place as fast as I could . . ."

"There were four of you?" Pan Yan began to stare carefully at the sweating lad and a great chill tightened in his chest like an icy fist. "Four, did you say?"

"Ey, master . . . If only I could be sure the joy wouldn't kill you . . . Because, you see, we found . . . way there in the wilderness on the far side of Yampol . . . But the chaplain said I wasn't to tell you . . ."

Skshetuski began to blink slowly like a man struggling out of a terrifying nightmare. He lost whatever color there'd been in his face and now he became even whiter than the sheets on which he was lying. His blind stare sharpened as if a veil was lifting in his mind, and then some great inner structure seemed to crack and give way within him as if a huge dark dam had burst, and shattered all his carefully constructed defenses, and flooded him with all the memories and feelings he had suppressed for so many months.

He sat up, as wild-eyed as a madman, as if he was about to throw himself on the startled boy and tear him to pieces. "Who was with you?" he whispered.

"Ey, master!" Zjendjan cried, frightened by the violent change in Skshetuski's face. "Ey, be careful, sir!"

"Who was with you?" Skshetuski shouted, shaking as desperately as if he was still in the grip of fever, and then he reached out, caught the boy in his iron fists and began to shake him madly in his turn.

"Alright! Alright! So I'll tell you!" Zjendjan howled. "Let the chaplain do what he wants with me! The Lady was with us. And now she's with Pani Vitovska!"

Skshetuski grew suddenly as stiff as if he'd suffered a paralytic seizure and lost his ability to breathe. He closed his eyes and fell back on his pillows, bloodless as a corpse.

"Oh my God!" Zjendjan wailed. "Oh great God almighty!

I've killed him! The chaplain was right. I should've kept my dam'fool mouth shut like he told me to . . . Master, hey, master! Wake up, will you? Say something!"

"I'm alright," Skshetuski said at last.

"You sure, master? You sure?"

" . . . Yes. I'm fine . . ."

Then the young soldier turned his quiet, dark eyes on the trembling lad. "Where is she now?"

"Thank God you've come back from the dead again, sir!" Frightened out of his wits, Zjendjan had fallen on his knees once more beside Skshetuski's body and now he started sniveling in earnest. "Ey, maybe I ought to keep my mouth shut, master, after all? What if you was to die on me again?"

"I'm alright. Don't worry." A great, soothing calmness settled on Skshetuski like the stillness that falls on an ocean after a great storm.

"You're sure about that, master?"

"Yes. Just answer my question."

"Well, alright sir, since I already told it anyway . . . Only don't die again, will you?" Still terrified, Zjendjan had to make a choice between the wrath of the King's confessor and his master's orders. "She's with Pani Vitovska, like I said, and ought to be here soon . . ."

He babbled on but Skshetuski was no longer listening. He lay as still as if all his need for self-control was now put away. He felt as if an icy barrier was melting inside him, and the rigidity of all his terrible restraints was ebbing from his powerful young body, but his eyes were open and staring at the ceiling as if he was still unable to believe anything he saw. His worn face had the grave look of a man who witnessed a real miracle, and felt the touch of God's hand on his forehead, and whose faith thereafter would be beyond all question because it was rooted in his own undeniable experience.

"Get me some clothes," he ordered quietly, sitting up. "And then go and order the stablemen to saddle our horses."

"Clothes? Horses?" Zjendjan stared, astonished. "And where d'you have a mind to go, sir? The way you look, master, you ought to spend another week in bed."

"Get me some clothes, I said!" Now on his feet, Pan Yan was swaying like a naked apparition risen from a grave, but his eyes were calm, at peace and shining with new life and a restored faith. "And be quick about it!"

★ ★ ★

Zjendjan set about laying out his master's clothing and ordered the rectory servants to prepare a hot, nourishing broth thickly laced with wine, to which Skshetuski sat down with the sudden appetite of a starving wolf. The King and all the nobles had sent such a rich supply of coats, undercoats, sashes, plumed caps, cloaks, ornaments and jeweled weapons as gifts for the hero that Zjendjan had a difficult time in choosing what Pan Yan ought to wear on this special day.

"There's even three fine horses in the stables," he reported. "Ey, if only somebody would give me one like that . . ."

"Take any one you like."

"Thank you, master! But wouldn't it be better if you'd take it easy for a few days more?"

"I'm fine. I can ride. For God's sake, lad, will you stop babbling and do what you're told?"

While Pan Yan dressed and ate, Zjendjan told him about the rescue expedition to the Valadynka.

"The worst of it all was in those woods where the Tartars spotted us," he said. "I don't know how Pan Michal and Pan Zagloba got out of that alive, God be thanked for it! Me and the lady turned off towards Konstantinov, thinking to squeeze through between Hmyelnitzki and those Tartars. See, master, I was sure they'd go on down to Zbarajh after they got done with Pan Zagloba and the Little Master . . ."

"They didn't," Skshetuski interrupted. "Pan Kushel got there just in time. But go on, go on!"

"Ah, if I'd only known! But I didn't, did I? And maybe that's a good thing, the way things turned out. I mean, our lady got spared the hardships of the siege, didn't she? Anyway, we got through alright, the lady and me, running between the Cossacks and the Tartars like we was in some kind of canyon between two forest fires. The country was empty all around us. Everybody had run off because of the Tartars. But I sweated buckets anyway thinking we might be swept up by some raiding party . . . Which is just what happened in the end."

"What?" Skshetuski stopped dressing and stared anxiously at Zjendjan. "You got caught? How? What happened?"

"Donyetz happened, master." The boy shrugged, unperturbed, as if oblivious of Skshetuski's anguish and impatience. "And you know what happened with Donyetz, I expect . . ."

"No, Devil take you, I don't know what happened with Donyetz and I don't care what's going to happen! Get on with your story!"

"Well, master, nothing more's going to happen to him because he is dead." Nothing could hurry the phlegmatic Zjendjan in his storytelling, Pan Yan knew, and he ground his teeth in helpless rage.

"Go on, for God's sake!"

"Yes master. Well, Donyetz was one of Bohun's colonels, as I expect you know, and Horpyna's brother. And Horpyna was the witch who kept the lady in that canyon by the Valadynka. Ah, but you'd know all about Horpyna, master, wouldn't you? I mean having been in Hmyelnitzki's camp and all and seen all his soothsayers and witches . . ."

"No, God blast you, I don't know Horpyna," Skshetuski ground out. "Will you get on with it?"

"Yes master. Well, me and Donyetz knew each other well enough from that time when I was with Bohun. And since he was a friend of Bohun's he knew all about his sister watching over our lady. So he believed me when I told him I was taking the lady to Bohun in Vlodava. I thought he'd let us go, and maybe even give us a few goods and horses like Burlay had done. Because I had to spend a lot of my own money on the way, you see, and I thought it would be good to get a little back . . ."

"I'll give you ten times what you spent," Skshetuski hissed. "Go on!"

"Thank you kindly, master! Anyway, Donyetz had a lot different idea. '*Don't go to Vlodava*,' he says to me. '*That's where the Poles' General Levy is assembling. What if they should catch you? You'd be better off going with me to Hmyelnitzki's army. Hmyel will guard the girl like she was his own once he knows she's Bohun's.*' Which he would have done, master, sure enough."

"So what did you do?"

"I argued with him as best I could. '*Bohun's waiting for us in Vlodava*,' I told him. '*He'll get mad if I don't carry out his orders just the way he wanted.*' But nothing I said worked on that stubborn Cossack. '*Never mind your orders*,' he tells me. '*I'll send word to Bohun that I've got you and the girl over at the main camp and that'll be that.*' He was a smart man and what he said made a lot of sense if I'd been Bohun's man like I said I was . . ."

Pan Yan groaned.

"Oh, it was a bad time for us, master," the boy went on, unhurried. "I felt like groaning myself. Many times. We got to arguing, that Cossack and me, and then he got suspicious. '*How come you're so all-fired eager to go into Lah country*' he asks me. '*How come you're scared to go back among Cossacks? Maybe you've turned traitor?*' I tell you, master, I thought it was all up with me and the lady then."

Dressed now and ready to go, Pan Yan started gnawing his nails with impatience. "For God's sake, will you get to the end of this story?"

"And that's just what I thought it was, master," the calm, slow-spoken lad went on. "The end for us both! I didn't know what to do. Honest to God I didn't. Donyetz started watching me like a hawk. I figured the only thing to do was to creep out some dark night and run God knows where and I started getting things ready to make a quick bolt. But that would've been touch-and-go, master, the way Donyetz watched us . . . And he'd have gone after us too, you know, and maybe he'd have caught us, and then everything would've been for nothing."

"God help me," Pan Yan murmured. "God help me."

"That's what I said too, master! And God sent the help. Pan Pelk, that famous raider, came up in the night, wiped out the Cossacks, took Donyetz, and set us free. It's been a week now since they impaled Donyetz, just like his sister Horpyna always said they would . . . Ay, but then some new troubles started with Pan Pelk . . ."

"What troubles, for God's sake?" Skshetuski held his breath.

"Well, master, that Pan Pelk was a great soldier. Maybe even as good at raiding as Pan Volodyovski. I say *was* because he got killed a few weeks back, I hear. But he was also a real devil with the women."

"I know that," Pan Yan grated out between his teeth. "He was famous for it."

"So he almost jumped out of his skin when he saw the lady. I had a devil of a time with him, God rest his troubled soul. It looked for a while like our lady was going to come to harm from our own kind, having been spared by Bohun and the Cossacks."

"Yes, yes. I see," Pan Yan muttered, tearing at his beard. "That . . . wouldn't surprise me."

"The good thing about Pan Pelk was that he loved our Prince," Zjendjan said. "Every time he mentioned him he took off his cap and swore he'd take service with us as soon as he could. So that's what saved us."

"What do you mean, that saved you?"

"Well, master, as soon as I picked up on how Pan Pelk felt about His Highness I told him that our lady was the Prince's ward, and a blood relative at that. And right away he started treating her like she was an icon! Gave us an escort all the way to Zamost where the King was staying at the time. And once we got there I could hand over the lady to Pani Vitovska."

Skshetuski sighed, weary with relief. Then he took the boy in his arms and hugged him as if he were his brother.

"God bless you, lad," he murmured. "You'll never be just a servant to me again! So Helen is with Pani Vitovska, is she?"

"Yes she is."

"And when was Pani Vitovska supposed to get here?"

"A week after me and it's been ten days already. Eight since you got here, master. She's got to be somewhere close, I expect."

"Let's go, let's go then," Pan Yan said again. "Let's ride out to meet them. Hurry! Or I'll go mad with joy."

⋆ ⋆ ⋆

But Pan Yan barely turned to go when the cobbled courtyard echoed with the sudden clatter of iron-shod hooves and the bright windows darkened with the moving shadows of animals and riders.

"We've guests, sir!" Zjendjan cried and, looking out, Skshetuski caught sight of the King's confessor clambering out of a four-wheeled *kolaska*; and then he saw the gaunt faces of Zagloba, Volodyovski, Kushel and many of his other Zbarajh friends bobbing in a crowd of Prince Yeremi's redcoated dragoons. But they caught sight of him as well through the open window, a great joyful shout boomed out in the yard, and then a swarm of cheering knights pushed into the room.

"The war's over!" the old priest called out, hurrying in behind them. "A treaty's been signed at Zborov! It's not the best kind of treaty, and few of us think it will hold for long, but at least all this bloodshed will stop for a few years."

But Skshetuski already guessed as much. If Zbarajh hadn't

been relieved his friends wouldn't be here. Now they were crowding around him, hugging him with undisguised affection, and Pan Michal and Pan Zagloba were literally tearing him out of each other's arms.

"They told us you're alive!" Pan Zagloba bellowed, shaking with emotion. "But hearing about it is one thing, seeing you up on your feet, and so well so soon, is something else again! We got here as fast as those worn out nags of ours could take us. Oh, but Yan, you've no idea what fame and glory you've won for yourself! Nor what a reward you're about to get!"

"His Majesty is going to reward you in one way," the old priest said, smiling quietly. "But the King of Kings has something even better in mind for you, young man."

"I know," Pan Yan said. "And may God bless you for it, my dear friends. Zjendjan has already told me what you've done."

"What? And your joy didn't strangle you? So much the better!" Pan Zagloba shouted. "*Vivat* Skshetuski! Long live Princess Helen! Listen Yan, we couldn't tell you about it before because we didn't know if she got through alive, but that lad of yours pulled it off in fine style! What a fox he is, eh?"

"I know, I know," Pan Yan murmured. "I just don't know how to thank you all."

"Oh *vulpes astuta!*" Pan Zagloba turned to Zjendjan who stood grinning broadly across Skshetuski's shoulder, but who kept his eyes fixed anxiously on the King's confessor. "Oh you sly, cunning little fellow! So you did it, eh? I knew that you'd make it! Pan Michal and me charged a whole *tchambul* behind you, can you imagine that? I was the first to throw myself on those howling heathen and Pan Michal didn't do so badly either! You should've seen how they ran from us and how they tried hiding from us in holes in the ground! But nothing helped them against old Zagloba!"

Then he threw his arms around Pan Yan again.

"We went all the way to the Yahorlik after my little girl and we found her for you! Imagine, I had to kill some kind of a monster that was guarding her! And now the Prince is waiting to give the bride away!"

"God give you joy, Yan," the little knight murmured over and over. "God give you joy. You've earned the gratitude of the entire country."

"But how am I ever going to show my gratitude to you?" Pan

Yan asked, as moved as all the others. "I don't even know how to start thanking you for all you've done for me. My whole life won't be long enough to repay you."

But Pan Zagloba still had more to say.

"Hey, hey!" he shouted. "Won't there be some wedding? Hmm? The last time I danced at a wedding that devil Bohun showed up uninvited and I had to teach him a lesson in manners. But he won't bother anyone again, which is something else I'll tell you about later on when we've some time for idle gossip and chatter. Let me just say this much for now, Yan my lad, those twelve sons of yours have been dodging you and Helen long enough! It's high time you caught up with them and a few more besides! Hey, hey! Listen everybody! Listen! I'm going to be a grandfather! I'll have grandchildren to pester me in my old age! And now where's my daughter? Eh? Where's my little girl?"

"I was just about to ride out to meet her," Pan Yan said.

"And we'll go with you!" Pan Zagloba shouted. "Just like a wedding party! So mount up, gentlemen! Mount up! Let's be on our way! And the sooner the better!"

But Skshetuski was already outside and leaping into his saddle as lightly as if he'd never known a moment of pain or illness or exhaustion in his life.

Chapter Eighty

THEY FLEW along the old bricked highway that led northward out of Toporov, looking in their new red and yellow caps and their bright scarlet coats like so many autumn leaves carried by the wind, until they came to a turn in the road where they saw a long line of carts and coaches surrounded by several dozen armed lackeys and liveried outriders. A few of these, catching sight of the horsemen bearing down upon them, spurred forward to challenge them and ask who they were.

"King's soldiers!" Pan Zagloba cried out. "From the Royal Army! And who's that up ahead?"

"The Lady of Sandomir!"

"That's it, then. That's it!"

"Your moment's here, Yan," Pan Michal murmured.

Skshetuski was so swept away by feeling that he didn't know what to do. He had to ask himself again: was this really happening? Or had his illusions and hallucinations turned into a habit? He reined his horse, slid out of his saddle, and stood cap-in-hand like a beggar at the side of the highway. Sweat burst out on his temples, his legs bent under him and his whole body started trembling in anticipation of that long deferred, miraculous reunion. Pan Michal jumped to the ground to help hold him up. The rest of the officers, gentry and dragoons followed their example and so the entire group stood bareheaded at the side of the road while the line of coaches and baggage carts creaked by them in the dust.

At last there came a larger and richer traveling carriage in whose window they saw the grave features of an older woman and, peering out beside her, the beautiful and gentle face of the Kurtzevitch princess.

"My little daughter!" howled Zagloba, hurling himself blindly at the carriage. "My sweetheart! Skshetuski is with us!"

The carriage horses began to stamp and rear in panic. Dust billowed out. The coachmen and escort riders shouted for everyone to stand still, thrown into sudden panic by the troop that milled around the carriage.

"Stop! Halt! Help! What is this?"

Meanwhile Volodyovski and Kushel led the weakened Pan Yan to the carriage door where he slid to his knees on the mounting steps but a moment later Helen's strong and gentle arms were holding up his head.

Seeing the astonishment on the face of the older woman, Zagloba cried out: "That's Skshetuski, the hero of Zbarajh! He's the one who made his way through the whole enemy horde to get word to the King! It's he who saved Zbarajh, the army, the Prince and the entire Commonwealth as well! Long life to him and to my little sweetheart! May God bless them both!"

"Long life!" cheered the assembled gentry. "*Vivant! Vivant!*"

"Long life!" the dragoons roared in their turn, and the deep, booming echoes of their cry rolled like thunder far across the fields and woods of Toporov.

But Pan Zagloba's bellowing drowned every other sound. "To Tarnopol! To the Prince! To the wedding! Hey, hey, my sweet girl, and what do you say to that? Your suffering is over! There is only joy and happiness in store for you from now on. And for Bohun there's only the headsman and the axe . . .!"

★   ★   ★

They seated Skshetuski in the carriage next to Helen and the procession moved forward once again. The day was bright and clear and soft with warm breezes. The fields and woods through which they were passing were bathed in gleaming sunlight, and the frail, silvery threads of autumn cobwebs drifted in the air like the snow that would cover that entire landscape just a few weeks later. There was peace and silence everywhere they looked.

"I tell you, my friend," Pan Zagloba sighed and nudged Pan Michal's stirrup with his own. "Something's got me by the throat like that time when Pan Podbipyenta, God rest his saintly soul, was slipping out of Zbarajh . . ."

They were riding side-by-side near the carriage windows

through which they could see Skshetuski and the beautiful young woman they both loved, each in his own fashion, looking at each other with joy in their eyes. The little knight sighed and nodded, and twitched his pale whiskers up and down, delighted for his friend but wishing that he too might find such happiness some day.

"Yes," the fat knight went on. "It's got me and it won't let go. But when I think how these two have finally got together . . . after all their troubles . . . then my whole heart rolls over like an old dog sleeping in the sunlight. Yes, yes, my friend, everyone gets to meet his or her destiny according to God's plan and finds the kind of ending he or she is supposed to have. And if some kind of marital adventure doesn't sweep you up as well we'll spend our old age, you and I, helping to raise their children . . ."

Pan Michal sighed again but the fat knight was too full of his own musing speculations to note the sudden longing in his small friend's face.

"Each of us is born to a different task," he went on. "Each has his own role to play on God's earth . . . And ours, my dear Michal, seems to have more to do with war and service than with wedding bells."

The little knight said nothing in reply. Only his pointed whiskers moved up and down even more swiftly than before. They rode back to Toporov and then to Tarnopol where they were to rejoin Prince Yeremi's army and go on with it to Lvov and then to the wedding. As they rode, Zagloba entertained old Pani Vitovska with an account of everything that happened in the time since she had left Zamost, and Skshetuski listened to this avidly because it was all news to him as well.

So Pan Zagloba told about the murderous but inconclusive battle of Zborov, and about the new treaty with the Khan which assured some respite for a year or two. The treaty confirmed Hmyelnitzki as the Zaporohjan Hetman and allowed him to pick a regular army of forty thousand men out of the huge swarms of *tchernya* he commanded. In exchange, he swore allegiance to the Diet and the King.

"It's not much of a peace," Pan Zagloba offered. "And it's sure to lead to another war before we're much older. But if our Prince gets the Hetman's *bulava* that he's earned so well then things will be a lot different the next time . . ."

"But you're not telling Yan the most important thing of all," the little knight murmured.

"I'm not? That's right, I'm not!" Pleased to have a new subject for his peroration, the fat knight leaned through the carriage window towards Pan Yan and Helen. "I should've started out with this piece of news, my dears, only it's taken me all this time just to catch my breath . . .! You've no idea, Yan, what happened after you left Zbarajh. So you can't have heard that Bohun's been captured! Our Prince has him chained and locked up in Tarnopol."

The news was so astonishing that the two young people stared at Zagloba and each other as if they couldn't understand what the fat knight had said. Bohun had cast such a pervasive shadow on their lives, and his role in their destinies was so devastating, that he had started to acquire the supernatural qualities of an evil myth; it sometimes seemed to both of them that the sound of his name was enough to chill the air around them.

But there was more than that to that tragic figure as everyone was aware. Fierce and untamed as the Steppe itself, wild as the wind and as savage as the times that bred him, Bohun was more like the passing spirit of their own cruel and heroic era than just another man. And so now, hearing about his fall, Pan Yan and Helen showed several mixed and opposite reactions. Fear and relief struggled in their faces against awe and wonder. Hatred gave way to sorrow at the thought of all that wasted talent, and tragically misused power, and disappearing glory; and whatever bitterness each of them might have been remembering began to crumble before regret and pity.

Time passed in silence. Neither of them could say a single word. It was as if a damned, doomed soul appeared at the roadside before them, crying for love so that it might be saved, and bringing death to everyone who'd reach out towards it.

Helen lifted and opened her hands as if acknowledging her own unwilling role in that tragedy and accepting God's will without further question.

Pan Yan shook his head.

Both of them knew that they, along with Bohun, were innocent participants in a cruel drama that mirrored the immemorial struggle between love and hatred, and all of them knew that this was the disease that gnawed at the soul of their entire country.

"How did it happen?" Pan Yan asked in sadness and regret.

"It was the damnedest thing!" Pan Zagloba said. "The treaty was already signed, you see. The fighting was over. We were on our way out of that stinking heap of corpses that people call Zbarajh, and the Prince took all the cavalry out on the left flank just in case the Tartars pulled one of their tricks. You know how they are about breaking treaties . . ."

"Yes." Skshetuski nodded. "We all know their ways. And what happened then?"

"What happened? A troop of about three hundred Cossacks came out of nowhere and charged our whole army!"

"Only Bohun would have dared something as mad as that," Pan Yan nodded quietly.

"That's just who it was! He'd been away somewhere during the siege, licking himself back to health after our Warsaw duel, I expect. We'd have known it if he was with Hmyelnitzki. But anyway, there he was again, charging all of us with three hundred madmen just as desperate to die as he was himself! Pan Michal soon surrounded them and cut them to ribbons, and Bohun himself, wounded twice more by our little friend, went into the bag . . .! I tell you, he just doesn't have any luck with Michal. No, he doesn't! This was the third time that they locked horns in combat and it looks to be the last for that miserable young devil."

"It turned out," Volodyovski added, "that he'd been burning up the miles all the way from the Valadynka . . ."

"That's right," Zagloba nodded. "We know what he discovered there. We can imagine what it did to him. He must've ridden like a crazy man to get to the fighting before it was over."

"But it's a long, hard road," the little knight threw in, nodding quietly in his own turn. "So he didn't get to Zbarajh before the peace was signed. The Cossacks say that when he heard about it he just went off his head with rage and disappointment. And that he didn't care what happened to him after that."

"Yes. Well. He'd do that, wouldn't he." A strange blend of fear, relief, admiration and regret flitted across Pan Zagloba's face. "What else was left for him? What more could he want? And how was he to get it?"

Then he sighed and shrugged. He nodded his head slowly up and down, like a man for whom life held neither secrets nor any new discoveries, and who had a few too many unsettling memories of his own.

"A man who rides the whirlwind dies out with the storm," he observed uneasily. "It's a law of nature. Anyway, we almost had a new war over Bohun's outbreak! Our Prince was the first to cry out that he broke the treaty and Hmyelnitzki was all set to go to Bohun's rescue. It was a real touch-and-go situation for a couple of hours and God only knows how it would've ended! But the Khan insisted that Bohun be condemned. Because—as he said it— it was *his* word that Bohun broke, and *his* heathen honor that he shamed, not his own. So the Khan ordered Hmyel to mind his ways and stop howling about Bohun or he'd let loose all his armies on him! And he sent word to Prince Yeremi that Bohun should be treated with no mercy, like any bandit or marauder."

★　★　★

Then, seeing the surprise on Skshetuski's face, the fat knight shrugged again and made a wry gesture.

"Yes, yes, I know," he said. "It all sounds a little strange if you know the Tartars. A lot of people wondered at all this punctilio. I think it's likely that Devlet Giray was less concerned about points of honor than with getting all his slave caravans away before anybody asked too many questions. People say the Tartars have so many captives penned up in the Ukraine that a good peasant won't be worth more than a couple of horseshoe nails in the Turkish markets for a year or more."

"And what did Prince Yeremi do with Bohun?" Skshetuski asked uneasily.

"The Prince? Well, the first thing he ordered for him was a sharpened stake. But then he changed his mind. '*I'll give him to Skshetuski*,' he said. '*Let him do what he wants with that Cossack firebrand. He's earned the right to exercise his own justice on the fellow for all the misery that this hothead caused him.*' And so that's how things stand. The wretched fellow is rattling his chains in the cellar of Tarnopol Castle while the local leeches are patching up his head, although I'm sure he'd much rather give up the ghost for good. So it's up to you, Yan, to decide what's to happen to him."

And here Pan Zagloba began to shake his head with wonder.

"Amazing, isn't it?" he mused. "Just think how many times

that man should've died. No wolf alive ever had his skin flayed as often as we've tanned his hide. Pan Michal himself cut him up three times! But that's one stubborn soul . . ."

"It's hard not to feel some pity for him," Pan Michal observed quietly. "He was a great soldier."

"A devil rather than a man!" Pan Zagloba cried. "But I must say I've long forgiven him for all his sins against me even though I didn't merit one of them! I mean, didn't I go drinking with him? Didn't I let him spend his money on me as if he was my equal? I could've knifed him back there in Rozloghi but I let him live. He should've been grateful instead of going after me as hard as he did . . ."

Then the fat knight shrugged once more, sighed, and nodded into the glowing, sunlit distance where the towers of Tarnopol rose above the trees.

"We might've gone on like that for ever if he hadn't raised his bloody hand against you, sweetheart," he said fondly to the grave young Princess who sat in deep thought of her own. "But that's the way things go . . . Fate rolls the dice and few men remember the good that's done to them if they've a chance to dwell on something evil . . ."

Then he turned to Skshetuski.

"But what about you, Yan? What do you plan to do with that wretched soul? The soldiers are betting that you'll turn him into a stable hand because he's good with horses. Or maybe a footman because he's a handsome, strapping devil who'd look good in livery. But it's hard for me to believe that you'd treat him like just another serf."

"You can be sure I won't," Skshetuski said quietly. "There is more of a knight in that unhappy man than in many of the lords and nobles we've met in the last two years. And just because he lost everything he cared for that's no reason to humiliate him further."

But it was not really up to Skshetuski to judge Bohun, and to decide his fate, and all of them knew it. No one said anything but every eye turned with curiosity on the Kurtzevitch princess who'd lost and suffered more at that doomed Cossack's hands than anyone else.

She sat in silence. Suffering had brought a new gravity to her pale face, but it had done nothing to mar her quiet beauty, break her pride or undermine her courage. A deep, inner strength stirred and glowed just below the delicate surface of her golden skin and her large, luminous eyes were dark with new maturity and knowledge.

"May God forgive him everything he's done and may he find his own peace as best he can," she said.

"That's what we'll do, then," Pan Yan said and looked with pride at his wife-to-be.

"And amen to that," added Pan Zagloba.

★   ★   ★

They were quiet then, thinking about the different ways in which God's will could manifest itself and men's lives and fortunes changed in unsettled times, until they came to the ruins of Grabova where they stopped to rest.

They found the burned township full of soldiers going home from Zborov. Pan Vitovski, the Castellan of Sandomir, was there with his regiment, having made a forced march to meet his wife's party. So were the heroic *Starosta* of Krasnostav and General Pshiyemski. So was a large and lively gathering of demobilized warrior-gentry whose road to their country manors happened to lie that way. The manor house of Grabova had been burned and looted by Cossack foragers and Tartar slave raiders, as were all other buildings in the countryside, but no one bothered to look for shelter anyway. The day was so calm, warm and sunny, and the nearby oak and birch groves were so soothing and inviting, that the whole bivouac turned into a carefree country outing under the clear sky.

Because the gentry of the General Levy were always well supplied with hampers of food and liquor, the servants set about at once preparing an open-air supper, while the castellan had several dozen tents put up in the grove for the ladies and the various dignitaries.

These soon became the focus of everybody's curiosity and interest. A crowd of knights and gentry gathered before them to catch a quick glimpse of Skshetuski and the Kurtzevitch princess, whose story was now part of the country's folklore, all the more popular because of its promise of a happy ending. Others told war stories, argued politics and discussed the likelihood of a lasting peace. Those who hadn't been at Zbarajh, but who had fought only in the Zborov battle, questioned the Vishnovyetzki soldiers about the details of that famous siege, clustering with special eagerness around Pan Zagloba who had more to say about everything than everybody else, and whose voice soon drowned out every other sound. His account of how he killed the legendary Burlay became such an epic in its thousandth telling that some of the listeners wondered why anyone else was needed to defeat the Tartars and Hmyelnitzki.

★ ★ ★

Meanwhile the servants who were laying out the banquet on the grass had their own hero in Zjendjan. But the boy appeared restless and uneasy. Nothing seemed to please him. His shrewd little eyes had scrunched down into bitter slits. Something gnawed at him. Not even the rare delicacies that he stole and sampled with the other servants came anywhere near to satisfying his deep, inner hunger.

He went on snapping, grumbling and fidgeting about until he found a convenient moment when he could draw Skshetuski to a quieter corner of the grove.

"Master," he pleaded humbly, bowing to his knees. "Can I ask for something?"

"It'd be hard for me to refuse you anything," Pan Yan said, lifting the boy to his feet and speaking to him as if they were equals. "How could I, seeing that it's your doing first and foremost that we're all here together?"

"That's what I thought too," the lad sniffed uneasily. "It seemed only right that you'd think of some reward for me, sir . . ."

"Just tell me what you want."

Zjendjan's pink, pudgy face darkened with sudden hatred and a fierce, determined light gleamed coldly in his narrowed eyes. "There's only one thing I'd ask for, master. Nothing else."

"Ask me for anything you wish," Pan Yan said. "I meant it when I said that you'd be more like a brother than a servant to me. So what can I give you?"

"Just Bohun. That's all I want. Give me Bohun, master."

"And what would you do with him?"

"Oh . . . I'll think of something."

The hunger in the boy's round, moonlike face was so fierce and cruel that Pan Yan stepped back a pace, suddenly aware that he never really knew his young servant at all.

"Oh yes, I'll think of something, master, to pay him for what he did to me in Tchehryn," Zjendjan ground out coldly. "And with interest, too . . .! I expect you'll have him killed off anyway. Everybody says so. So let me be the first to have a go at him."

But Skshetuski shook his head.

"I can't do that," he said.

"Oh God!" Zjendjan wailed suddenly like a heartbroken child and burst into tears. "Is that what I've lived for then? So people can say I'll swallow injuries and insults without paying them off in kind? Honest to God, sir, I wish I'd been killed . . .!"

"Ask me for anything else and it's yours," Pan Yan said evenly. "Lands, money, horses . . . anything! I'll gladly give you everything I own. But don't ask for Bohun."

"But I swore vengeance on him!" Zjendjan sobbed. "I took an oath! What will my grandpappy say if I don't keep my word?"

"Ask him if keeping such a promise wouldn't be a greater sin than breaking it," Skshetuski said quietly. "Try simple forgiveness. God has already punished that tragic man. Don't add your own hand to that of providence or you'll bring new misfortunes on yourself. You're a fine, loyal lad and I owe you more than I'll ever be able to repay but you ought to be ashamed to ask for such a favor."

"One thing's a shame and so's the other," sobbed the boy. "Ai . . . what am I to do?"

"Just think, lad. Think. Look into yourself. What is it you're asking? The only mercy that this man begs from God is death anyway. He has nothing left to live for. He's lost everything. And he's wounded and in chains on top of all that! Do you want to be a common hangman for him? Will that satisfy your injured pride and add to your honor? Are you going to torment a helpless, shackled prisoner, or murder a man who is sick and wounded and can't defend himself? Have you turned into a Tartar or a Cossack cut-throat to think of such a thing? No, lad. No . . . I won't allow that as long as I live so never even mention it to me again."

There was so much strength and power in Pan Yan's quiet voice that the disappointed boy lost all hope at once.

"Ai . . .ai," he mumbled tearfully. "Where's the justice, then? When he's well and healthy he's too much for two like me. And when he's ill and weak then it's a shame to touch him. How am I going to pay him, then, for what he did to me?"

"Leave retributions to God," Pan Skshetuski said.

★ ★ ★

Zjendjan stared at his master in bewilderment but Pan Yan turned about and left him.

He made his way slowly to the large square tents spread out in the sunlit meadow where a numerous and lively company had gathered in the open air. Pani Vitovska sat in the center of the group with Helen beside her, while all the knights, soldiers, officers and gentry sat or stood in a broad arc around them. Before them stood Pan Zagloba, bareheaded and perspiring in the warm afternoon sun, telling the story of the Siege of Zbarajh.

Never before did he have such an attentive audience. Everyone listened, holding their breaths as the tale unfolded, and only their faces showed the play of feeling that swept through them all. Those who had been there sighed, nodded solemnly, wiped an occasional tear and stared off into the distance, as if to catch some recessed glimpse of precious memory that lay buried in the rubble of those silent earthworks. Those who weren't there wished that they had been able to share in the glory.

Pan Yan sat down beside Helen, pressed her hand to his lips, and then they leaned against each other, sitting close together, and listened as quietly as the rest.

The sun had started to slip out of the sky, evening was on its way. Skshetuski's thoughts drifted as he listened. The shadowed images passed like regiments in review; remembered moments rolled by in a vivid cavalcade of color and emotion; and he saw them all as something that would never leave him no matter how deep and far into the future it would go.

The words rose and soared like firebombs and rockets. They hissed like hot lead and thundered through the air like whirling stone and iron. Pan Zagloba mopped his glistening pate and stroked his wispy hair. His voice had deepened, hardened and acquired new resonance and power as he described those days and nights of courage, sacrifice, heroism and selfless devotion, and the listeners saw either in their memories or imaginations a passage of events that had already taken them marching into history.

They saw once more the smoking ramparts surrounded by howling human tide. They felt the booming surge of the fie[ ]assaults pulsing in their blood. They heard the shouts[ ]screams and the roar of cannon and the rattle of firelock[ ] muskets. They could see Prince Yeremi in his silver armor standing unmoved amid the hail of iron.

They felt the thirst and hunger. The cold clutch of famine. They breathed the desperate air of those crimson nights in which death hung above the pitted earthwalls like a fearsome raptor circling above its prey on black, silent wings.

They watched Pan Podbipyenta slipping into the night and walking towards his own martyrdom and glory. They crept with Yan Skshetuski through the hissing reeds.

They listened without a sound, totally enthralled, merely lifting their hot eyes to the darkening sky or clutching the cold, sweated hilts of their swords and sabers, while Pan Zagloba brought his story to its end.

"It is all one vast burial mound today," he said, and it wasn't clear if he meant just the silent, empty earthworks of Zbarajh, or if he was mourning more than that. "It is just a grave. And the only reason why the glory of our nation isn't buried there with the flower of our knighthood, and with the Prince Palatine and me and all of us whom the Cossacks themselves call 'The Lions of Zbarajh,' is that this man saved us."

And here he pointed to Pan Yan Skshetuski.

"That's true!" cried Pan Marek Sobieski.

"As God's our witness!" Pan Pshiyemski added.

"Glory to him then!" shouted a hundred voices. "Glory! And gratitude! And all honor! *Vivat* Skshetuski! Long life to the newlyweds! Long life to the hero!"

A great surge of feeling swept through the gathered gentry. Some wept. Some cheered and shouted. Others ran to fetch ιps and goblets so that they might drink the health of their ιic savior and his future bride. Yet others tossed their caps ιe evening air.

ιatching soldiers shouted battle cries and rattled their ιbers and soon one vast cheer was echoing through ιve.

ιy! *Vivat!*"

ιned to these cries with his head bowed upon ιhis eyes cast down, because only he knew the ιain and hardships that led to fame and ιfaith in God and love for his country

ιet, shook out her braided hair and

stared proudly at the men around her. A rush of blood glowed redly in her pale cheeks. Her shining eyes seemed to scatter fire. This was her man whom they were honoring—she'd be his wife before the week was over—and a man's glory falls upon his wife in just the same way that the rays of the sun warm and enrich the soil from which new life comes.

★ ★ ★

It was long after sunset when the gathering finally broke up and everyone went his way. The Vitovskis, the *Starosta* and General Pshiyemski rode off with their regiments towards Toporov. Skshetuski and Helen made their way towards Tarnopol, escorted by their friends and Volodyovski's dragoons who started singing as they rode along.

The night was just as calm and clear as the day had been. The starlit sky was glittering like a jewel box and a great white moon rose out of the east to cast its silver light across the misted fields.

On just such a night Skshetuski left Rozloghi to ride to the *Sietch*. On just another like it he crept out of Zbarajh. Now he could feel Helen's heart beating against his own.